12 ✓ P9-CMF-621

20—

MR. JONATHAN OLDBUCK, OF MONKBARNS.

THE ANTIQUARY.

By SIR WALTER SCOTT, BART.

A. L. BURT COMPANY, PUBLISHERS,
52-58 DUANE STREET, NEW YORK.

INTRODUCTION TO THE ANTIQUARY.

THE present Work completes a series of fictitious narratives intended to illustrate the manners of Scotland at three different periods. *Waverley* embraced the age of our fathers, *Guy Mannering* that of our own youth, and the *Antiquary* refers to the last ten years of the eighteenth century. I have, in the two last narratives especially, sought my principal personages in the class of society who are the last to feel the influence of that general polish which assimilates to each other the manners of different nations. Among the same class I have placed some of the scenes in which I have endeavoured to illustrate the operation of the higher and more violent passions; both because the lower orders are less restrained by the habit of suppressing their feelings, and because I agree with my friend Wordsworth that they seldom fail to express them in the strongest and most powerful language. This is, I think, peculiarly the case with the peasantry of my own country, a class with whom I have long been familiar. The antique force and simplicity of their language, often tinctured with the Oriental eloquence of Scripture, in the mouths of those of an elevated understanding, give pathos to their grief and dignity to their resentment.

I have been more solicitous to describe manners minutely than to arrange in any case an artificial and combined narrative, and have but to regret that I felt myself unable to unite these two requisites of a good Novel.

The knavery of the Adept in the following sheets may appear forced and improbable; but we have had very late instances of the force of superstitious credulity to a much greater extent, and the reader may be assured that this part of the narrative is founded on a fact of actual occurrence.

I have now only to express my gratitude to the public for the distinguished reception which they have given to works that have little more than some truth of colouring to recommend them, and to take my respectful leave, as one who is not likely again to solicit their favour.

To the above advertisement, which was prefixed to the first edition of the *Antiquary*, it is necessary in the present edition to add a few words, transferred from the Introduction to the *Chronicles of the Canongate*, respecting the character of Jonathan Oldbuck.

"I may here state generally that, although I have deemed historical personages free subjects of delineation, I have never on any occasion violated the respect due to private life. It was indeed impossible that traits proper to persons, both living and dead, with whom I have had intercourse in society should not have risen to my pen in such works as *Waverley* and those which followed it. But I have always studied to generalise the portraits, so that they should still seem, on the whole, the productions of fancy, though possessing some resemblance to real individuals. Yet I must own my attempts have not in this last particular been uniformly successful. There are men whose characters are so peculiarly marked that the delineation of some leading and principal feature inevitably places the whole person before you in his individuality. Thus the character of Jonathan Oldbuck in the *Antiquary* was partly founded on that of an old friend of my youth, to whom I am indebted for introducing me to Shakspeare and other invaluable favours; but I thought I had so completely disguised the likeness that it could not be recognised by any one now alive. I was mistaken, however, and indeed had endangered what I desired should be considered as a secret; for I afterwards learned that a highly respectable gentleman, one of the few surviving friends of my father, and an acute critic, had said, upon the appearance of the work, that he was now convinced who was the author of it, as he recognised in the *Antiquary* traces of the character of a very intimate friend [1] of my father's family."

I have only farther to request the reader not to suppose that my late respected friend resembled Mr. Oldbuck either in his pedigree or the history imputed to the ideal personage. There is not a single incident in the Novel which is borrowed from his real circumstances, excepting the fact that he resided in an old house near a flourishing seaport, and that the Author chanced to witness a scene betwixt him and the female proprietor of a stage-coach very similar to that which commences the history of the *Antiquary*. An excellent temper, with a slight degree of subacid humour; learning, wit, and drollery the more piquant that they were a little marked by the peculiarities of an old bachelor; a soundness of thought, rendered more forcible by an occasional quaintness of expression, were, the Author conceives, the only qualities in which the creature of his imagination resembled his benevolent and excellent old friend.

The prominent part performed by the Beggar in the following narrative induces the Author to prefix a few remarks on that character, as it formerly existed in Scotland, though it is now scarcely to be traced.

Many of the old Scottish mendicants were by no means to be confounded with the utterly degraded class of beings who now practise that wandering trade. Such of them as were in the habit of travelling through a particular district were usually well received both in the farmer's ha' and in the kitchens of the country gentleman. Martin, author of the *Reliquiæ Divi Sancti Andreæ*, written in 1683, gives the following account of one class of this order of men in the seventeenth century, in terms which would induce an antiquary like Mr. Oldbuck to regret its extinction. He conceives them to be descended from the ancient bards, and proceeds: "They are called by others and by themselves Jockies, who go about begging, and use still to recite the Sloggorne (gathering-words or war-cries) of most of the true ancient surnames of Scotland, from old

[1] George Constable of Wallace Craigie, near Dundee (*Laing*).

experience and observation.　Some of them I have discoursed, and found to have reason and discretion.　One of them told me there were not now above twelve of them in the whole isle; but he remembered when they abounded, so as at one time he was one of five that usually met at St. Andrews."

The race of Jockies (of the above description) has, I suppose, been long extinct in Scotland; but the old remembered beggar, even in my own time, like the Baccach, or travelling cripple of Ireland, was expected to merit his quarters by something beyond an exposition of his distresses.　He was often a talkative, facetious fellow, prompt at repartee, and not withheld from exercising his powers that way by any respect of persons, his patched cloak giving him the privilege of the ancient jester.　To be a "gude crack," that is, to possess talents for conversation, was essential to the trade of a "puir body" of the more esteemed class; and Burns, who delighted in the amusement their discourse afforded, seems to have looked forward with gloomy firmness to the possibility of himself becoming one day or other a member of their itinerant society. In his poetical works it is alluded to so often as perhaps to indicate that he considered the consummation as not utterly impossible.　Thus, in the fine dedication of his works to Gavin Hamilton, he says:

> And when I downa yoke a naig,
> Then, Lord be thankit, I can beg.

Again, in his Epistle to Davie, a brother poet, he states, that in their closing career—

> The last o't, the warst o't,
> Is only just to beg.

And after having remarked that

> To lie in kilns and barns at e'en,
> When banes are crazed and blude is thin,
> Is doubtless great distress;

the bard reckons up, with true poetical spirit, the free enjoyment of the beauties of nature, which might counterbalance the hardship and uncertainty of the life even of a mendicant, nance was of the true Scottish cast, strongly marked, and rather harsh in features, with a shrewd and penetrating eye, and a countenance in which habitual gravity was enlivened by a cast of ironical humour. His dress was uniform, and of a colour becoming his age and gravity; a wig, well dressed and powdered, surmounted by a slouched hat, had something of a professional air. He might be a clergyman, yet his appearance was more that of a man of the world than usually belongs to the Kirk of Scotland, and his first ejaculation put the matter beyond question.

He arrived with a hurried pace, and, casting an alarmed glance towards the dial-plate of the church, then looking at the place where the coach should have been, exclaimed: "Deil's in it, I am too late after all!"

The young man relieved his anxiety by telling him the coach had not yet appeared. The old gentleman, apparently conscious of his own want of punctuality, did not at first feel courageous enough to censure that of the coachman. He took a parcel, containing apparently a large folio, from a little boy who followed him, and, patting him on the head, bid him go back and tell Mr. B—— that, if he had known he was to have had so much time, he would have put another word or two to their bargain; then told the boy to mind his business, and he would be as thriving a lad as ever dusted a duodecimo. The boy lingered, perhaps in hopes of a penny to buy marbles; but none was forthcoming. Our senior leaned his little bundle upon one of the posts at the head of the staircase, and, facing the traveller who had first arrived, waited in silence for about five minutes the arrival of the expected diligence.

At length, after one or two impatient glances at the progress of the minute-hand of the clock, having compared it with his own watch, a huge and antique gold repeater, and having twitched about his features to give due emphasis to one or two peevish pshaws, he hailed the old lady of the cavern.

"Good woman—what the d—l is her name?—Mrs. Macleuchar!"

Mrs. Macleuchar, aware that she had a defensive part to

sustain in the encounter which was to follow, was in no hurry to hasten the discussion by returning a ready answer.

"Mrs. Macleuchar—good woman" (with an elevated voice)—then apart, "Old doited hag, she's as deaf as a post. I say, Mrs. Macleuchar!"

"I am just serving a customer. Indeed, hinny, it will no be a bodle chaper than I tell ye."

"Woman," reiterated the traveller, "do you think we can stand here all day till you have cheated that poor servant wench out of her half-year's fee and bountith?"

"Cheated!" retorted Mrs. Macleuchar, eager to take up the quarrel upon a defensible ground; "I scorn your words, sir; you are an uncivil person, and I desire you will not stand there to slander me at my ain stairhead."

"The woman," said the senior, looking with an arch glance at his destined travelling companion, "does not understand the words of action. Woman," again turning to the vault, "I arraign not thy character, but I desire to know what is become of thy coach?"

"What's your wull?" answered Mrs. Macleuchar, relapsing into deafness.

"We have taken places, ma'am," said the younger stranger, "in your diligence for Queensferry." "Which should have been half-way on the road before now," continued the elder and more impatient traveller, rising in wrath as he spoke; "and now in all likelihood we shall miss the tide, and I have business of importance on the other side; and your cursed coach——"

"The coach! Gude guide us, gentlemen, is it no on the stand yet?" answered the old lady, her shrill tone of expostulation sinking into a kind of apologetic whine. "Is it the coach ye hae been waiting for?"

"What else could have kept us broiling in the sun by the side of the gutter here, you—you faithless woman? eh?"

Mrs. Macleuchar now ascended her trap stair (for such it might be called, though constructed of stone), until her nose came upon a level with the pavement; then, after wiping her spectacles to look for that which she well knew was not to be found, she exclaimed, with well-feigned astonishment: "Gude guide us, saw ever ony body the like o' that!"

"Yes, you abominable woman," vociferated the traveller, "many have seen the like of it, and all will see the like of it that have anything to do with your trolloping sex"; then, pacing with great indignation before the door of the shop, still as he passed and repassed, like a vessel who gives her broadside as she comes abreast of a hostile fortress, he shot down complaints, threats, and reproaches on the embarrassed Mrs. Macleuchar. He would take a post-chaise—he would call a hackney-coach—he would take four horses—he must—he would be on the north side to-day—and all the expense of his journey, besides damages, direct and consequential, arising from delay, should be accumulated on the devoted head of Mrs. Macleuchar.

There was something so comic in his pettish resentment that the younger traveller, who was in no such pressing hurry to depart, could not help being amused with it, especially as it was obvious that every now and then the old gentleman, though very angry, could not help laughing at his own vehemence. But when Mrs. Macleuchar began also to join in the laughter, he quickly put a stop to her ill-timed merriment.

"Woman," said he, "is that advertisement thine?" showing a bit of crumpled printed paper. "Does it not set forth that, God willing, as you hypocritically express it, the Hawes fly, or Queensferry diligence, would set forth to-day at twelve o'clock; and is it not, thou falsest of creatures, now a quarter past twelve, and no such fly or diligence to be seen? Dost thou know the consequence of seducing the lieges by false reports? Dost thou know it might be brought under the statute of leasing-making? Answer—and for once in thy long, useless, and evil life let it be in the words of truth and sincerity —has thou such a coach? Is it *in rerum natura?* or is this base annunciation a mere swindle on the incautious, to beguile them of their time, their patience, and three shillings of sterling money of this realm! Hast thou, I say, such a coach? ay or no?"

"Oh dear, yes, sir; the neighbours ken the diligence weel—

green picked out wi' red, three yellow wheels and a black ane."

"Woman, thy special description will not serve; it may be only a lie with a circumstance."

"Oh, man, man!" said the overwhelmed Mrs. Macleuchar, totally exhausted by having been so long the butt of his rhetoric, "take back your three shillings and mak me quit o' ye."

"Not so fast, not so fast, woman. Will three shillings transport me to Queensferry, agreeably to thy treacherous program? or will it requite the damage I may sustain by leaving my business undone, or repay the expenses which I must disburse if I am obliged to tarry a day at the South Ferry for lack of tide? Will it hire, I say, a pinnace, for which alone the regular price is five shillings?"

Here his argument was cut short by a lumbering noise, which proved to be the advance of the expected vehicle, pressing forward with all the despatch to which the broken-winded jades that drew it could possibly be urged. With ineffable pleasure Mrs. Macleuchar saw her tormentor deposited in the leathern convenience; but still, as it was driving off, his head thrust out of the window reminded her, in words drowned amid the rumbling of the wheels, that, if the diligence did not attain the ferry in time to save the flood-tide, she, Mrs. Macleuchar, should be held responsible for all the consequences that might ensue.

The coach had continued in motion for a mile or two before the stranger had completely repossessed himself of his equanimity, as was manifested by the doleful ejaculations which he made from time to time on the too great probability, or even certainty, of their missing the flood-tide. By degrees, however, his wrath subsided; he wiped his brows, relaxed his frown, and, undoing the parcel in his hand, produced his folio, on which he gazed from time to time with the knowing look of an amateur, admiring its height and condition, and ascertaining, by a minute and individual inspection of each leaf, that the volume was uninjured and entire from title-page to colophon. His fellow-traveller took the liberty of inquiring the subject of his studies. He lifted up his eyes with something of a

ence between the mode of entrenching *castra stativa* and *castra æstiva*, things confounded by too many of our historians. Lack-a-day, if they had ta'en the pains to satisfy their own eyes, instead of following each other's blind guidance! Well! we shall be pretty comfortable at the Hawes; and besides, after all, we must have dined somewhere, and it will be pleasanter sailing with the tide of ebb and the evening breeze."

In this Christian temper of making the best of all occurrences our travellers alighted at the Hawes.

CHAPTER II.

Sir, they do scandal me upon the road here!
A poor quotidian rack of mutton roasted
Dry to be grated! and that driven down
With beer and buttermilk, mingled together.
It is against my freehold, my inheritance.
WINE is the word that glads the heart of man,
And mine's the house of wine. *Sack*, says my bush,
Be merry and drink sherry, that's my posie.
BEN JONSON'S *New*

As the senior traveller descended the crazy steps of the gence at the inn, he was greeted by the fat, gouty, pursy land lord with that mixture of familiarity and respect which the Scotch innkeepers of the old school used to assume towards their more valued customers.

"Have a care o' us, Monkbarns (distinguishing him by his territorial epithet, always most agreeable to the ear of a Scottish proprietor), is this you? I little thought to have seen your honour here till the summer session was ower."

"Ye donnard auld deevil," answered his guest, his Scottish accent predominating when in anger, though otherwise not particularly remarkable—"ye donnard auld crippled idiot, what have I to do with the session, or the geese that flock to it, or the hawks that pick their pinions for them?"

"Troth, and that's true," said mine host, who, in fact, only spoke upon a very general recollection of the stranger's original education, yet would have been sorry not to have been supposed accurate as to the station and profession of him or any other occasional guest—"that's very true; but I thought ye had some law affair of your ain to look after. I have ane mysell—a ganging plea that my father left me, and his father afore left to him. It's about our back-yard. Ye'll maybe hae heard of it in the Parliament House, Hutchinson against Mackitchinson: it's a weel-kenn'd plea; it's been four times in afore the Fifteen, and deil ony thing the wisest o' them could make o't, but just to send it out again to the Outer House. Oh, it's a beautiful thing to see how lang and how carefully justice is considered in this country!"

"Hold your tongue, you fool," said the traveller, but in great good-humour, "and tell us what you can give this young gentleman and me for dinner."

"Ou, there's fish nae doubt—that's sea-trout and caller haddocks," said Mackitchinson, twisting his napkin; "and ⬛ be for a mutton-chop, and there's cranberry tarts very ⬛ reserved, and—and there's just ony thing else ye like."

⬛ hich is to say, there is nothing else whatever? Well, ⬛ he fish and the chop and the tarts will do very well. ⬛ n't imitate the cautious delay that you praise in the ⬛ of justice. Let there be no remits from the inner to the ⬛ house, hear ye me?"

"Na, na," said Mackitchinson, whose long and heedful perusal of volumes of printed session papers had made him acquainted with some law phrases—"the denner shall be served *quamprimum*, and that *peremptorie*." And with the flattering laugh of a promising host, he left them in his sanded parlour, hung with prints of the Four Seasons.

As, notwithstanding his pledge to the contrary, the glorious delays of the law were not without their parallel in the kitchen of the inn, our younger traveller had an opportunity to step out and make some inquiry of the people of the house concerning the rank and station of his companion. The information which he received was of a general and less authentic nature, but quite sufficient to make him acquainted with the name, history, and circumstances of the gentleman, whom we shall endeavour in a few words to introduce more accurately to our readers.

Jonathan Oldenbuck, or Oldinbuck, by popular contraction Oldbuck, of Monkbarns, was the second son of a gentleman possessed of a small property in the neighbourhood of a thriving seaport town on the northeastern coast of Scotland, which, for various reasons, we shall denominate Fairport. They had been established for several generations as landholders in the county, and in most shires of England would have been accounted a family of some standing. But the shire of —— was filled with gentlemen of more ancient descent and larger fortune. In the last generation also the neighbouring gentry had been almost uniformly Jacobites, while the proprietors of Monkbarns, like the burghers of the town near which they were settled, were steady assertors of the Protestant succession. The latter had, however, a pedigree of their own, on which they prided themselves as much as those who despised them valued their respective Saxon, Norman, or Celtic genealogies. The first Oldenbuck, who had settled in their family mansion shortly after the Reformation, was, they asserted, descended from one of the original printers of Germany, and had left his country in consequence of the persecutions directed against the professor of the Reformed religion. He had found a refuge in the town near which his posterity dwelt, the more readily that he was a sufferer in the Protestant cause, and certainly not the less so that he brought with him money enough to purchase the small estate of Monkbarns, then sold by a dissipated laird to whose father it had been gifted, with other church lands, on the dissolution of the great and wealthy monastery to which it had belonged. The Oldenbucks were therefore loyal subjects on all occasions of insurrection; and, as they kept up a good intelligence with the borough, it chanced that the Laird of Monkbarns who flourished in 1745 was provost of the town during that ill-fated year, and had exerted himself with much spirit in favour of King George, and even been put to expenses on that score, which, according to the liberal conduct of the existing government towards their friends, had never been repaid him.

By dint of solicitation, however, and borough interest, he contrived to gain a place in the customs, and, being a frugal, careful man, had found himself enabled to add considerably to his paternal fortune. He had only two sons, of whom, as we have hinted, the present laird was the younger, and two daughters, one of whom still flourished in single blessedness, and the other, who was greatly more juvenile, made a love-match with a captain in the "Forty-twa," who had no other fortune but his commission and a Highland pedigree. Poverty disturbed a union which love would otherwise have made happy, and Captain M'Intyre, in justice to his wife and two children, a boy and girl, had found himself obliged to seek his fortune in the East Indies. Being ordered upon an expedition against Hyder Ally, the detachment to which he belonged was cut off, and no news ever reached his unfortunate wife whether he fell in battle, or was murdered in prison, or survived in what the habits of the Indian tyrant rendered a hopeless captivity. She sunk under the accumulated load of grief and uncertainty, and left a son and daughter to the charge of her brother, the existing laird of Monkbarns.

The history of that proprietor himself is soon told. Being, as we have said, a second son, his father destined him to a share in a substantial mercantile concern carried on by some of his maternal relations. From this Jonathan's mind revolted in the most irreconcilable manner. He was then put apprentice to the profession of a writer or attorney, in which he profited so far that he made himself master of the whole forms of feudal investitures, and showed such pleasure in reconciling their incongruities and tracing their origin that his master had great hope he would one day be an able conveyancer. But he halted upon the threshold, and, though he acquired some knowledge of the origin and system of the law of his country, he could never be persuaded to apply it to lucrative and practical purposes. It was not from any inconsiderate neglect of the advantages attending the possession of money that he thus deceived the hopes of his master. "Were he thoughtless or light-headed, or *rei suæ prodigus*," said his instructor, "I would know what to make of him. But he never pays away a shilling without looking anxiously after the change, makes his sixpence go farther than another lad's half-crown, and will ponder over an old black-letter copy of the Acts of Parliament for days, rather than go to the golf or the change-house; and yet he will not bestow one of these days on a little business of routine that would put twenty shillings in his pocket—a strange mixture of frugality and industry and negligent indolence; I don't know what to make of him."

But in process of time his pupil gained the means of making what he pleased of himself; for, his father having died, was not long survived by his eldest son, an arrant fisher and fowler, who departed this life in consequence of a cold caught in his vocation, while shooting ducks in the swamp called Kittlefitting Moss, notwithstanding his having drunk a bottle of brandy that very night to keep the cold out of his stomach. Jonathan, therefore, succeeded to the estate, and with it to the means of susbsiting without the hated drudgery of the law. His wishes were very moderate; and, as the rent of his small property rose with the improvement of the country, it soon greatly exceeded his wants and expenditure; and, though too indolent to make money, he was by no means insensible to the pleasure of beholding it accumulate. The burghers of the town near which he lived regarded him with a sort of envy, as one who affected to divide himself from their rank in society, and whose studies and pleasures seemed to them alike incomprehensible. Still, however, a sort of hereditary respect for the Laird of Monkbarns, augmented by the knowledge of his being a ready-money man, kept up his consequence with this class of his neighbours. The country gentlemen were generally above him in fortune and beneath him in intellect, and, excepting one with whom he lived in habits of intimacy, had little intercourse with Mr. Oldbuck of Monkbarns. He had, however, the usual resources, the company of the clergyman and of the doctor, when he chose to request it, and also his own pursuits and pleasures, being in correspondence with most of the *virtuosi* of his time, who, like himself, measured decayed entrenchments, made plans of ruined castles, read illegible inscriptions, and wrote essays on medals in the proportion of twelve pages to each letter of the legend. Some habits of hasty irritation he had contracted, partly, it was said in the borough of Fairport, from an early disappointment in love, in virtue of which he had commenced misogynist, as he called it, but yet more by the obsequious attention paid to him by his maiden sister and his orphan niece, whom he had trained to consider him as the greatest man upon earth, and whom he used to boast of as the only women he had ever seen who were well broke in and bitted to obedience; though, it must be owned, Miss Grizie Oldbuck was sometimes apt to jibb when he pulled the reins too tight. The rest of his character must be gathered from the story, and we dismiss with pleasure the tiresome task of recapitulation.

During the time of dinner Mr. Oldbuck, actuated by the same curiosity which his fellow-traveller had entertained on his account, made some advances, which his age and station entitled him to do in a more direct manner, towards ascertaining the name, destination, and quality of his young companion.

His name, the young gentleman said, was Lovel.

"What! the cat, the rat, and Lovel our dog? Was he descended from King Richard's favourite?"

"He had no pretensions," he said, "to call himself a whelp of that litter; his father was a North of England gentleman. He was at present travelling to Fairport (the town near to which Monkbarns was situated), and, if he found the place agreeable, might perhaps remain there for some weeks."

"Was Mr. Lovel's excursion solely for pleasure?"

"Not entirely."

"Perhaps on business with some of the commercial people of Fairport?"

"It was partly on business, but had no reference to commerce."

Here he paused; and Mr. Oldbuck, having pushed his inquiries as far as good manners permitted, was obliged to change the conversation. The Antiquary, though by no means an enemy to good cheer, was a determined foe to all unnecessary expense on a journey; and, upon his companion giving a hint concerning a bottle of port wine, he drew a direful picture of the mixture which, he said, was usually sold under that denomination, and, affirming that a little punch was more genuine and better suited for the season, he laid his hand upon the bell to order the materials. But Mackitchinson had, in his own mind, settled their beverage otherwise, and appeared bearing in his hand an immense double quart bottle, or magnum, as it is called in Scotland, covered with sawdust and cobwebs, the warrants of its antiquity.

"Punch!" said he, catching that generous sound as he entered the parlour, "the deil a drap punch ye'se get here the day, Monkbarns, and that ye may lay your account wi.'"

"What do you mean, you impudent rascal?"

"Ay, ay, it's nae matter for that; but do you mind the trick ye served me the last time ye were here?"

"I trick you!"

"Ay, just yoursell, Monkbarns. The Laird o' Tamlowrie, and Sir Gilbert Grizzlecleugh, and Auld Rossballoh, and the Bailie were just setting in to make an afternoon o't, and you, wi' some o' your auld warld stories, that the mind o' man canna resist, whirl'd them to the back o' beyont to look at the auld Roman camp—ah, sir!" turning to Lovel, "he wad wile the bird aff the tree wi' the tales he tells about folk lang syne—and did not I lose the drinking o' sax pints o' gude claret, for the deil ane wad hae stirred till he had seen that out at the least!"

"D'ye hear the impudent scoundrel!" said Monkbarns, but laughing at the same time; for the worthy landlord, as he used to boast, knew the measure of a guest's foot as well as e'er a souter on this side Solway; "well, well, you may send us in a bottle of port."

"Port! na, na! ye maun leave port and punch to the like o' us, it's claret that's fit for you lairds; and I dare say nane of the folk ye speak so much o' ever drank either of the twa."

"Do you hear how absolute the knave is? Well, my young friend, we must for once prefer the Falernian to the *vile Sabinum*."

The ready landlord had the cork instantly extracted, decanted the wine into a vessel of suitable capaciousness, and, declaring it "parfumed" the very room, left his guests to make the most of it.

Mackitchinson's wine was really good, and had its effect upon the spirits of the elder guest, who told some good stories, cut some sly jokes, and at length entered into a learned discussion concerning the ancient dramatists; a ground on which he found his new acquaintance so strong that at length he began to suspect he had made them his professional study. "A traveller partly for business and partly for pleasure? Why, the stage partakes of both; it is a labour to the performers, and affords, or is meant to afford, pleasure to the spectators. He seems in manner and rank above the class of young men who take that turn; but I remember hearing them say that the little theatre at Fairport was to open with the performance of a young gentleman, being his first appearance on any stage. If this should be thee, Lovel? Lovel! Yes, Lovel or Belville are just the names which youngsters are apt to assume on such occasions. On my life, I am sorry for the lad."

Mr. Oldbuck was habitually parsimonious, but in no respects mean; his first thought was to save his fellow-traveller any part of the expense of the entertainment, which he supposed must be in his situation more or less inconvenient. He therefore took an opportunity of settling privately with Mr. Mackitchinson. The young traveller remonstrated against his liberality, and only acquiesced in deference to his years and respectability.

The mutual satisfaction which they found in each other's society induced Mr. Oldbuck to propose, and Lovel willingly to accept, a scheme for travelling together to the end of their journey. Mr. Oldbuck intimated a wish to pay two-thirds of the hire of a post-chaise, saying, that a proportional quantity of room was necessary to his accommodation; but this Mr. Lovel resolutely declined. Their expense then was mutual, unless when Lovel occasionally slipt a shilling into the hand of a growling postilion; for Oldbuck, tenacious of ancient customs, never extended his guerdon beyond eighteenpence a stage. In this manner they travelled, until they arrived at Fairport about two o'clock on the following day.

Lovel probably expected that his travelling companion would have invited him to dinner on his arrival; but his consciousness of a want of ready preparation for unexpected guests, and perhaps some other reasons, prevented Oldbuck from paying him that attention. He only begged to see him as early as he could make it convenient to call in a forenoon, recommended him to a widow who had apartments to let, and to a person who kept a decent ordinary; cautioning both of them apart that he only knew Mr. Lovel as a pleasant companion in a post-chaise, and did not mean to guarantee any bills which he might contract while residing at Fairport. The young gentleman's figure and manners, not to mention a well-furnished trunk which soon arrived by sea to his address at Fairport, probably went as far in his favour as the limited recommendation of his fellow-traveller.

CHAPTER III.

He had a routh o' auld nick-nackets,
Rusty airn caps, and jinglin-jackets,
Would held the Loudons three in tackets
    A towmond gude ;
And parritch-pats, and auld saut-backets,
    Afore the flude.

BURNS.

AFTER he had settled himself in his new apartments at Fairport, Mr. Lovel bethought him of paying the requested visit to his fellow-traveller. He did not make it earlier because, with all the old gentleman's good-humour and information, there had sometimes glanced forth in his language and manner towards him an air of superiority which his companion considered as being fully beyond what the difference of age warranted. He therefore waited the arrival of his baggage from Edinburgh, that he might arrange his dress according to

3

the fashion of the day, and make his exterior corresponding to the rank in society which he supposed or felt himself entitled to hold.

It was the fifth day after his arrival that, having made the necessary inquiries concerning the road, he went forth to pay his respects at Monkbarns. A footpath leading over a heathy hill and through two or three meadows conducted him to this mansion, which stood on the opposite side of the hill aforesaid, and commanded a fine prospect of the bay and shipping. Secluded from the town by the rising ground, which also screened it from the northwest wind, the house had a solitary and sheltered appearance. The exterior had little to recommend it. It was an irregular old-fashioned building, some part of which had belonged to a grange or solitary farm-house, inhabited by the bailiff or steward of the monastery when the place was in possession of the monks. It was here that the community stored up the grain which they received as ground-rent from their vassals; for, with the prudence belonging to their order, all their conventional revenues were made payable in kind, hence, as the present proprietor loved to tell, came the name of Monkbarns. To the remains of the bailiff's house the succeeding lay inhabitants had made various additions in proportion to the accommodation required by their families; and, as this was done with an equal contempt of convenience within and architectural regularity without, the whole bore the appearance of a hamlet which had suddenly stood still when in the act of leading down one of Amphion's or Orpheus's country-dances. It was surrounded by tall clipped hedges of yew and holly, some of which still exhibited the skill of the "topiarian" artist, and presented curious arm-chairs, towers, and the figures of Saint George and the dragon. The taste of Mr. Oldbuck did not disturb these monuments of an art now unknown, and he was the less tempted so to do as it must necessarily have broken the heart of the old gardener. One tall embowering holly was, however, sacred from the shears; and on a garden seat beneath its shade Lovel beheld his old friend, with spectacles on nose and pouch on side, busily employed in perusing the *London Chronicle*, soothed by the summer breeze through the rustling leaves and the distant dash of the waves as they rippled upon the sand.

Mr. Oldbuck immediately rose and advanced to greet his travelling acquaintance with a hearty shake of the hand. "By my faith," said he, "I began to think you had changed your mind, and found the stupid people of Fairport so tiresome that you judged them unworthy of your talents, and had taken French leave, as my old friend and brother antiquary Mac-Cribb did, when he went off with one of my Syrian medals."

"I hope, my good sir, I should have fallen under no such imputation."

"Quite as bad, let me tell you, if you had stolen yourself away without giving me the pleasure of seeing you again. I had rather you had taken my copper Otho himself. But come, let me show you the way into my *sanctum sanctorum*, my cell I may call it, for, except two idle hussies of womankind (by this contemptuous phrase, borrowed from his brother antiquary the cynic Anthony a' Wood, Mr. Oldbuck was used to denote the fair sex in general, and his sister and niece in particular), that, on some idle pretext of relationship, have established themselves in my premises, I live here as much a cænobite as my predecessor John o' the Girnell, whose grave I will show you by and by."

Thus speaking, the old gentleman led the way through a low door; but, before entrance, suddenly stopped short to point out some vestiges of what he called an inscription, and, shaking his head as he pronounced it totally illegible: "Ah! if you but knew, Mr. Lovel, the time and trouble that these mouldering traces of letters have cost me! No mother ever travailed so for a child, and all to no purpose; although I am almost positive that these two last marks imply the figures or letters LV, and may give us a good guess at the real date of the building, since we know, *aliunde*, that it was founded by Abbot Waldimir about the middle of the fourteenth century. And, I profess, I think that centre ornament might be made out by better eyes than mine."

"I think," answered Lovel, willing to humour the old man, "it has something the appearance of a mitre."

"I protest you are right! you are right! it never struck me before. See what it is to have younger eyes. A mitre—a mitre! it corresponds in every respect."

The resemblance was not much nearer than that of Polonius's cloud to a whale or an owzel; it was sufficient, however, to set the Antiquary's brains to work. "A mitre, my dear sir," continued he, as he led the way through a labyrinth of inconvenient and dark passages, and accompanied his disquisition with certain necessary cautions to his guest—"a mitre, my dear sir, will suit our abbot as well as a bishop; he was a mitred abbot, and at the very top of the roll—take care of these three steps—I know Mac-Cribb denies this, but it is as certain as that he took away my Antigonus, no leave asked. You'll see the name of the Abbot of Trotcosey, *Abbas Trotto-cosiensis*, at the head of the rolls of parliament in the fourteenth and fifteenth centuries—there is very little light here, and these cursed womankind always leave their tubs in the passage. Now take care of the corner; ascend twelve steps and ye are safe!"

Mr. Oldbuck had by this time attained the top of the winding stair which led to his own apartment, and, opening a door and pushing aside a piece of tapestry with which it was covered, his first exclamation was, "What are you about here, you sluts?" A dirty barefooted chambermaid threw down her duster, detected in the heinous fact of arranging the *sanctum sanctorum*, and fled out of an opposite door from the face of her incensed master. A genteel-looking young woman, who was superintending the operation, stood her ground, but with some timidity.

"Indeed, uncle, your room was not fit to be seen, and I just came to see that Jenny laid everything down where she took it up."

"And how dare you, or Jenny either, presume to meddle with my private matters? (Mr. Oldbuck hated "putting to rights" as much as Dr. Orkborne or any other professed student.) Go sew your sampler, you monkey, and do not let me find you here again, as you value your ears. I assure you, Mr. Lovel, that the last inroad of these pretended friends to cleanliness was almost as fatal to my collection as Hudibras's visit to that of Sidrophel; and I have ever since missed

> My copperplate, with almanacks
> Engraved upon't, and other knacks;
> My moon-dial, with Napier's bones,
> And several constellation stones;
> My flea, my morpion, and punaise,
> I purchased for my proper ease.

And so forth, as old Butler has it."

The young lady, after courtesying to Lovel, had taken the opportunity to make her escape during this enumeration of losses. "You'll be poisoned here with the volumes of dust they have raised," continued the Antiquary; "but I assure you the dust was very ancient, peaceful, quiet dust about an hour ago, and would have remained so for a hundred years had not these gipsies disturbed it, as they do everything else in the world."

It was, indeed, some time before Lovel could, through the thick atmosphere, perceive in what sort of den his friend had constructed his retreat. It was a lofty room of middling size, obscurely lighted by high narrow latticed windows. One end was entirely occupied by book-shelves, greatly too limited in space for the number of volumes placed upon them, which were, therefore, drawn up in ranks of two or three files deep, while numberless others littered the floor and the tables, amid a chaos of maps, engravings, scraps of parchment, bundles of papers, pieces of old armour, swords, dirks, helmets, and Highland targets. Behind Mr. Oldbuck's seat (which was an ancient leathern-covered easy-chair, worn smooth by constant use) was a huge oaken cabinet, decorated at each corner with Dutch cherubs, having their little duck-wings displayed and great jolter-headed visages placed between them. The top of this cabinet was covered with busts and Roman lamps and pateræ, intermingled with one or two bronze figures. The walls of the apartment were partly clothed with grim old tapestry, representing the memorable story of Sir Gawaine's wedding, in which full justice was done to the ugliness of the Lothely Lady; although, to judge from his own looks, the gentle knight had less reason to be disgusted with the match on account of disparity of outward favour than the romancer has given us to understand. The rest of the room was panelled or wainscotted with black oak, against which hung two or three portraits in armour, being characters in Scottish history, favourites of Mr. Oldbuck, and as many in tie-wigs and laced coats, staring representatives of his own ancestors. A large old-fashioned oaken table was covered with a profusion of papers, parchments, books, and nondescript trinkets and gewgaws, which seemed to have little to recommend them besides rust and the antiquity which it indicates. In the midst of this wreck of ancient books and utensils, with a gravity equal to Marius among the ruins of Carthage, sat a large black cat, which to a superstitious eye might have presented the *genius loci*, the tutelar demon of the apartment. The floor, as well as the table and chairs, was overflowed by the same *mare magnum* of miscellaneous trumpery, where it would have been as impossible to find any individual article wanted as to put it to any use when discovered.

Amid this medley it was no easy matter to find one's way to a chair without stumbling over a prostrate folio, or the still more awkward mischance of overturning some piece of Roman or ancient British pottery. And when the chair was attained, it had to be disencumbered with a careful hand of engravings which might have received damage, and of antique spurs and buckles which would certainly have occasioned it to any sudden occupant. Of this the Antiquary made Lovel particularly aware, adding, that his friend, the Rev. Doctor Heavysterne from the Low Countries, had sustained much injury by sitting down suddenly and incautiously on three ancient calthrops or "craw-taes" which had been lately dug up in the bog near Bannockburn, and which, dispersed by Robert Bruce to lacerate the feet of the English chargers, came thus in process of time to endamage the sitting part of a learned professor of Utrecht.

Having at length fairly settled himself, and being nothing loth to make inquiry concerning the strange objects around him, which his host was equally ready, as far as possible, to explain, Lovel was introduced to a large club or bludgeon, with an iron spike at the end of it, which, it seems, had been lately found in a field on the Monkbarns property, adjacent to an old burying-ground. It had mightily the air of such a stick as the Highland reapers use to walk with on their annual peregrinations from their mountains; but Mr. Oldbuck was strongly tempted to believe that, as its shape was singular, it might have been one of the clubs with which the monks armed their peasants in lieu of more martial weapons, whence, he observed, the villains were called "Colve-carles," or "Kolb-kerls," that is, *clavigeri*, or club-bearers. For the truth of this custom he quoted the *Chronicle* of Antwerp and that of St. Martin; against which authorities Lovel had nothing to oppose, having never heard of them till that moment.

Mr. Oldbuck next exhibited thumb-screws, which had given the Covenanters of former days the cramp in their joints, and a collar with the name of a fellow convicted of theft, whose services, as the inscription bore, had been adjudged to a neighbouring baron in lieu of the modern Scottish punishment, which, as Oldbuck said, sends such culprits to enrich England by their labour and themselves by their dexterity. Many and various were the other curiosities which he showed; but it was chiefly upon his books that he prided himself, repeating with a complacent air, as he led the way to the crowded and dusty shelves, the verses of old Chaucer:

> " For he would rather have at his bed-head,
> A twenty books, clothed in black or red,
> Of Aristotle, or his philosophy,
> Than robes rich, rebeck, or saltery."

This pithy motto he delivered, shaking his head, and giving each guttural the true Anglo-Saxon enunciation, which is now forgotten in the southern parts of this realm.

The collection was, indeed, a curious one, and might well be envied by an amateur. Yet it was not collected at the enormous prices of modern times, which are sufficient to have appalled the most determined, as well as earliest, bibliomaniac upon record, whom we take to have been none else than the

renowned Don Quixote de la Mancha, as, among other slight
indications of an infirm understanding, he is stated by his
veracious historian Cid Hamet Benengeli to have exchanged
fields and farms for folios and quartos of chivalry. In this
species of exploit the good knight-errant has been imitated by
lords, knights, and squires of our own day, though we have
not yet heard of any that has mistaken an inn for a castle, or
laid his lance in rest against a windmill. Mr. Oldbuck did
not follow these collectors in such excess of expenditure; but,
taking a pleasure in the personal labour of forming his library,
saved his purse at the expense of his time and toil. He was
no encourager of that ingenious race of peripatetic middlemen,
who, trafficking between the obscure keeper of a stall and the
eager amateur, make their profit at once of the ignorance of
the former and the dear-bought skill and taste of the latter.
When such were mentioned in his hearing, he seldom failed
to point out how necessary it was to arrest the object of your
curiosity in its first transit, and to tell his favourite story of
Snuffy Davie and Caxton's *Game at Chess.* " Davie Wilson,"
he said, "commonly called Snuffy Davie, from his inveterate
addiction to black rappee, was the very prince of scouts for
searching blind alleys, cellars, and stalls for rare volumes.
He had the scent of a slow-hound, sir, and the snap of a bull-
dog. He would detect you an old black-letter ballad among
the leaves of a law-paper, and find an *editio princeps* under
the mask of a school Corderius. Snuffy Davie bought the
Game of Chess, 1474, the first book ever printed in England,
from a stall in Holland for about two groschen, or twopence
of our money. He sold it to Osborne for twenty pounds and
as many books as came to twenty pounds more. Osborne re-
sold this inimitable windfall to Dr. Askew for sixty guineas.
At Dr. Askew's sale," continued the old gentleman, kindling
as he spoke, "this inestimable treasure blazed forth in its full
value, and was purchased by Royalty itself for one hundred
and seventy pounds! Could a copy now occur, Lord only
knows," he ejaculated, with a deep sigh and lifted-up hands—
" Lord only knows what would be its ransom; and yet it was
originally secured, by skill and research, for the easy equiva-

lent of twopence sterling.[1] Happy, thrice happy, Snuffy Davie! and blessed were the times when thy industry could be so rewarded! Even I, sir," he went on, "though far inferior in industry and discernment and presence of mind to that great man, can show you a few, a very few things, which I have collected, not by force of money, as any wealthy man might, although, as my friend Lucian says, he might chance to throw away his coin only to illustrate his ignorance, but gained in a manner that shows I know something of the matter. See this bundle of ballads, not one of them later than 1700, and some of them an hundred years older. I wheedled an old woman out of these, who loved them better than her psalm-book. Tobacco, sir, snuff, and the *Complete Syren* were the equivalent! For that mutilated copy of the *Complaynt of Scotland* I sat out the drinking of two dozen bottles of strong ale with the late learned proprietor, who, in gratitude, bequeathed it to me by his last will. These little Elzevirs are the memoranda and trophies of many a walk by night and morning through the Cowgate, the Canongate, the Bow, Saint Mary's Wynd—wherever, in fine, there were to be found brokers and trokers, those miscellaneous dealers in things rare and curious. How often have I stood haggling upon a halfpenny, lest, by a too ready acquiescence in the dealer's first price, he should be led to suspect the value I set upon the article! How have I trembled lest some passing stranger should chop in between me and the prize, and regarded each poor student of divinity that stopped to turn over the books at the stall as a rival amateur or prowling bookseller in disguise! And then, Mr. Lovel, the sly satisfaction with which one pays the consideration and pockets the article, affecting a cold indifference while the hand is trembling with pleasure! Then to dazzle the eyes of our wealthier and emulous rivals by showing them such a treasure as this (displaying a little black smoked book about the size of a primer), to enjoy their surprise and envy, shrouding meanwhile under a veil of

[1] This bibliomaniacal anecdote is literally true; and David Wilson, the author need not tell his brethren of the Roxburghe and Bannatyne Clubs, was a real personage.

mysterious consciousness our own superior knowledge and dexterity—these, my young friend, these are the white moments of life, that repay the toil and pains and sedulous attention which our profession, above all others, so peculiarly demands!"

Lovel was not a little amused at hearing the old gentleman run on in this manner, and, however incapable of entering into the full merits of what he beheld, he admired, as much as could have been expected, the various treasures which Oldbuck exhibited. Here were editions esteemed as being the first, and there stood those scarcely less regarded as being the last and best; here was a book valued because it had the author's final improvements, and there another which (strange to tell!) was in request because it had them not. One was precious because it was a folio, another because it was a duodecimo; some because they were tall, some because they were short; the merit of this lay in the title-page, of that in the arrangement of the letters in the word "Finis." There was, it seemed, no peculiar distinction, however trifling or minute, which might not give value to a volume, providing the indispensable quality of scarcity or rare occurrence was attached to it.

Not the least fascinating was the original broadside—the Dying Speech, Bloody Murder, or Wonderful Wonder of Wonders—in its primary tattered guise, as it was hawked through the streets and sold for the cheap and easy price of one penny, though now worth the weight of that penny in gold. On these the Antiquary dilated with transport, and read with a rapturous voice the elaborate titles, which bore the same proportion to the contents that the painted signs without a showman's booth do to the animals within. Mr. Oldbuck, for example, piqued himself especially in possessing an unique broadside, entitled and called "Strange and Wonderful News from Chipping-Norton, in the County of Oxon. Of certain dreadful Apparitions which were seen in the Air on the 28th of July [1610], which began about Half an Hour after Nine of the Clock at Night, and continued till near Eleven, in which Time was seen the Appearances of several

Flaming Swords, strange Motions of the superior Orbs, with the unusual Sparkling of the Stars, with their dreadful Continuations. With the Account of the Opening of the Heavens, and strange Appearances therein disclosing themselves, with several other prodigious Circumstances not heard of in any Age, to the great Amazement of the Beholders, as it was communicated in a Letter to one Mr. Tho. Colley, living in West Smithfield, and attested by Tho. Brown, Eliz. Greenaway, and Ann Gutheridge, who were Spectators of the dreadful Apparitions. And if any Person would be further satisfied of the Truth of this Relation, let them repair to Mr. Nightingal's, at the Bear Inn, in West Smithfield, and they may be satisfied." [1]

"You laugh at this," said the proprietor of the collection, "and I forgive you. I do acknowledge that the charms on which we doat are not so obvious to the eyes of youth as those of a fair lady; but you will grow wiser, and see more justly, when you come to wear spectacles. Yet stay, I have one piece of antiquity which you, perhaps, will prize more highly."

So saying, Mr. Oldbuck unlocked a drawer and took out a bundle of keys, then pulled aside a piece of the tapestry which concealed the door of a small closet, into which he descended by four stone steps, and, after some tinkling among bottles and cans, produced two long-stalked wine-glasses with bell mouths, such as are seen in Teniers's pieces, and a small bottle of what he called rich racy canary, with a little bit of diet-cake, on a small silver server of exquisite old workmanship. "I will say nothing of the server," he remarked, "though it is said to have been wrought by the old mad Florentine Benvenuto Cellini. But, Mr. Lovel, our ancestors drunk sack; you, who admire the drama, know where that's to be found. Here's success to your exertions at Fairport, sir!"

"And to you, sir, and an ample increase to your treasure, with no more trouble on your part than is just necessary to make the acquisitions valuable."

[1] Of this thrice and four times rare broadside the author possesses an exemplar.

After a libation so suitable to the amusement in which they had been engaged, Lovel rose to take his leave, and Mr. Oldbuck prepared to give him his company a part of the way, and show him something worthy of his curiosity on his return to Fairport.

CHAPTER IV.

The pawky auld carle cam ower the lea,
Wi' mony good-e'ens and good-morrows to me,
Saying, Kind sir, for your courtesy,
Will ye lodge a silly poor man ?
The Gaberlunzie Man.

OUR two friends moved through a little orchard, where the aged apple-trees, well loaded with fruit, showed, as is usual in the neighbourhood of monastic buildings, that the days of the monks had not always been spent in indolence, but often dedicated to horticulture and gardening. Mr. Oldbuck failed not to make Lovel remark that the planters of those days were possessed of the modern secret of preventing the roots of the fruit-trees from penetrating the till, and compelling them to spread in a lateral direction, by placing paving-stones beneath the trees when first planted, so as to interpose between their fibres and the subsoil. "This old fellow," he said, "which was blown down last summer, and still, though half reclined on the ground, is covered with fruit, has been, as you may see, accommodated with such a barrier between his roots and the unkindly till. That other tree has a story: the fruit is called the Abbot's Apple. The lady of a neighbouring baron was so fond of it that she would often pay a visit to Monk-barns to have the pleasure of gathering it from the tree. The husband, a jealous man belike, suspected that a taste so nearly resembling that of Mother Eve prognosticated a similar fall. As the honour of a noble family is concerned, I will say no more on the subject, only that the lands of Lochard and Cringlecut still pay a fine of six bolls of barley annually to atone the guilt of their audacious owner, who intruded himself and his worldly suspicions upon the seclusion of the abbot and his penitent. Admire the little belfry rising above the ivy-mantled porch; there was here a *hospitium, hospitale*, or *hospitamentum* (for it is written all these various ways in the old writings and evidents), in which the monks received pilgrims. I know our minister has said, in the *Statistical Account*, that the *hospitium* was situated either on the lands of Haltweary or upon those of Half-starvet; but he is incorrect, Mr. Lovel: that is the gate called still the Palmer's Port, and my gardener found many hewn stones when he was trenching the ground for winter celery, several of which I have sent as specimens to my learned friends, and to the various antiquarian societies of which I am an unworthy member. But I will say no more at present; I reserve something for another visit, and we have an object of real curiosity before us."

While he was thus speaking he led the way briskly through one or two rich pasture meadows to an open heath or common, and so to the top of a gentle eminence. "Here," he said, "Mr. Lovel, is a truly remarkable spot."

"It commands a fine view," said his companion, looking around him.

"True; but it is not for the prospect I brought you hither. Do you see nothing else remarkable? nothing on the surface of the ground?"

"Why, yes; I do see something like a ditch, indistinctly marked."

"Indistinctly! pardon me, sir, but the indistinctness must be in your powers of vision: nothing can be more plainly traced—a proper *agger* or *vallum*, with its corresponding ditch or *fossa*. Indistinctly! why, Heaven help you, the lassie, my niece, as light-headed a goose as womankind affords, saw the traces of the ditch at once. Indistinct! why, the great station at Ardoch, or that at Burnswark in Annandale, may be clearer, doubtless, because they are stative forts, whereas this was only an occasional encampment. Indistinct! why, you must suppose that fools, boors, and idiots have ploughed up the land, and, like beasts and ignorant savages, have thereby obliterated two sides of the square, and greatly injured the third; but you see yourself the fourth side is quite entire!"

Lovel endeavoured to apologise, and to explain away his ill-timed phrase, and pleaded his inexperience. But he was not at once quite successful. His first expression had come too frankly and naturally not to alarm the Antiquary, and he could not easily get over the shock it had given him.

"My dear sir," continued the senior, "your eyes are not inexperienced; you know a ditch from level ground, I presume, when you see them? Indistinct! why, the very common people, the very least boy that can herd a cow, calls it the Kaim of Kinprunes; and if that does not imply an ancient camp, I am ignorant what does."

Lovel having again acquiesced, and at length lulled to sleep the irritated and suspicious vanity of the Antiquary, he proceeded in his task of cicerone. "You must know," he said, "our Scottish antiquaries have been greatly divided about the local situation of the final conflict between Agricola and the Caledonians: some contend for Ardoch in Strathallan, some for Innerpeffray, some for the Redykes in the Mearns, and some are for carrying the scene of action as far north as Blair in Athole. Now, after all this discussion," continued the old gentleman, with one of his slyest and most complacent looks, "what would you think, Mr. Lovel—I say, what would you think, if the memorable scene of conflict should happen to be on the very spot called the Kaim of Kinprunes, the property of the obscure and humble individual who now speaks to you?" Then, having paused a little to suffer his guest to digest a communication so important, he resumed his disquisition in a higher tone. "Yes, my good friend, I am indeed greatly deceived if this place does not correspond with all the marks of that celebrated place of action. It was near to the Grampian Mountains; lo! yonder they are, mixing and contending with the sky on the skirts of the horizon! It was *in conspectu classis*—in sight of the Roman fleet; and would any admiral, Roman or British, wish a fairer bay to ride in than that on your right hand? It is astonishing how blind we professed antiquaries sometimes are; Sir Robert Sibbald, Saunders Gordon, General Roy, Doctor Stukeley, why, it escaped all of them. I was unwilling to say a word about it till I had secured the ground, for it belonged to auld Johnnie Howie, a bonnet-laird hard by, and many a communing we had before he and I could agree. At length—I am almost ashamed to say it—but I even brought my mind to give acre for acre of my good corn-land for this barren spot. But then it was a national concern; and when the scene of so celebrated an event became my own I was overpaid. Whose patriotism would not grow warmer, as old Johnson says, on the plains of Marathon? I began to trench the ground, to see what might be discovered; and the third day, sir, we found a stone, which I have transported to Monkbarns, in order to have the sculpture taken off with plaster of Paris; it bears a sacrificing vessel, and the letters A.D.L.L., which may stand, without much violence, for *Agricola Dicavit Libens Lubens.*"

"Certainly, sir; for the Dutch antiquaries claim Caligula as the founder of a lighthouse on the sole authority of the letters C.C.P.F., which they interpret *Caius Caligula Pharum Fecit.*"

"True, and it has ever been recorded as a sound exposition. I see we shall make something of you even before you wear spectacles, notwithstanding you thought the traces of this beautiful camp indistinct when you first observed them."

"In time, sir, and by good instruction——"

"—You will become more apt? I doubt it not. You shall peruse, upon your next visit to Monkbarns, my trivial *Essay upon Castrametation, with some Particular Remarks upon the Vestiges of Ancient Fortifications lately discovered by the Author at the Kaim of Kinprunes.* I think I have pointed out the infallible touchstone of supposed antiquity. I premise a few general rules on that point, on the nature, namely, of the evidence to be received in such cases. Meanwhile be pleased to observe, for example, that I could press into my service Claudian's famous line,

Ille Caledoniis posuit qui castra pruinis.

For *pruinis*, though interpreted to mean "hoar frosts," to which I own we are somewhat subject in this northeastern sea-coast, may also signify a locality, namely, Prunes; the *castra Pruinis posita* would therefore be the Kaim of Kin-prunes. But I waive this, for I am sensible it might be laid hold of by cavillers as carrying down my *castra* to the time of Theodosius, sent by Valentinian into Britain as late as the year 367 or thereabout. No, my good friend, I appeal to people's eye-sight—is not here the decuman gate? and there, but for the ravage of the horrid plough, as a learned friend calls it, would be the prætorian gate. On the left hand you may see some slight vestiges of the *porta sinistra*, and on the right one side of the *porta dextra* wellnigh entire. Here, then, let us take our stand, on this tumulus, exhibiting the foundation of ruined buildings—the central point, the *prætorium*, doubtless, of the camp. From this place, now scarce to be distinguished but by its slight elevation and its greener turf from the rest of the fortification, we may suppose Agricola to have looked forth on the immense army of Caledonians, occupying the declivities of yon opposite hill, the infantry rising rank over rank as the form of ground displayed their array to its utmost advantage, the cavalry and *covinarii*, by which I understand the charioteers—another guise of folks from your Bond Street four-in-hand men, I trow—scouring the more level space below—

> See, then, Lovel, see—
> See that huge battle moving from the mountains,
> Their gilt coats shine like dragon scales, their march
> Like a rough tumbling storm. See them, and view them,
> And then see Rome no more!

Yes, my dear friend, from this stance it is probable—nay, it is nearly certain—that Julius Agricola beheld what our Beaumont has so admirably described! From this very *prætorium*——"

A voice from behind interrupted his ecstatic description: "Prætorian here, prætorian there, I mind the bigging o't." [1]

Both at once turned round, Lovel with surprise and Old-buck with mingled surprise and indignation, at so uncivil an interruption. An auditor had stolen upon them, unseen and unheard, amid the energy of the Antiquary's enthusiastic

[1] See Prætorium. Note 1.

declamation and the attentive civility of Lovel. He had the exterior appearance of a mendicant. A slouched hat of huge dimensions; a long white beard, which mingled with his grizzled hair; an aged, but strongly marked and expressive countenance, hardened by climate and exposure to a right brick-dust complexion; a long blue gown, with a pewter badge on the right arm; two or three wallets or bags slung across his shoulder, for holding the different kinds of meal when he received his charity in kind from those who were but a degree richer than himself—all these marked at once a beggar by profession and one of that privileged class which are called in Scotland the King's Bedesmen, or, vulgarly, Blue-Gowns.

"What is that you say, Edie?" said Oldbuck, hoping, perhaps, that his ears had betrayed their duty; "what were you speaking about?"

"About this bit bourock, your honour," answered the undaunted Edie; "I mind the bigging o't."

"The devil you do! Why, you old fool, it was here before you were born, and will be after you are hanged, man!"

"Hanged or drowned, here or awa, dead or alive, I mind the bigging o't."

"You—you—you," said the Antiquary, stammering between confusion and anger—"you strolling old vagabond, what the devil do you know about it?"

"Ou, I ken this about it, Monkbarns—and what profit have I for telling ye a lie?—I just ken this about it, that about twenty years syne I and a wheen hallenshakers like mysell, and the mason-lads that built the lang dyke that gaes down the loaning, and twa or three herds maybe, just set to wark and built this bit thing here that ye ca' the—the—prætorian, and a' just for a bield at auld Aiken Drum's bridal, and a bit blythe gae-down we had in't some sair rainy weather. Mair by token, Monkbarns, if ye howk up the bourock, as ye seem to have begun, ye'll find, if ye hae not fund it already, a stane that ane o' the mason-callants cut a ladle on to have a bourd at the bridegroom, and he put four letters on't, that's A.D.L.L.—Aiken Drum's Lang Ladle; for Aiken was ane o' the kale-suppers o' Fife."

4

"This," thought Lovel to himself, "is a famous counterpart to the story of 'Keep on this side.'" He then ventured to steal a glance at our Antiquary, but quickly withdrew it in sheer compassion. For, gentle reader, if thou hast ever beheld the visage of a damsel of sixteen whose romance of true love has been blown up by an untimely discovery, or of a child of ten years whose castle of cards has been blown down by a malicious companion, I can safely aver to you that Jonathan Oldbuck of Monkbarns looked neither more wise nor less disconcerted.

"There is some mistake about this," he said, abruptly turning away from the mendicant.

"Deil a bit on my side o' the wa'," answered the sturdy beggar; "I never deal in mistakes, they aye bring mischances. Now, Monkbarns, that young gentleman that's wi' your honour thinks little of a carle like me; and yet I'll wager I'll tell him whar he was yestreen at the gloaming, only he maybe wadna like to hae't spoken o' in company."

Lovel's soul rushed to his cheeks with the vivid blush of two-and-twenty.

"Never mind the old rogue," said Mr. Oldbuck. "Don't suppose I think the worse of you for your profession; they are only prejudiced fools and coxcombs that do so. You remember what old Tully says in his oration *Pro Archia poeta* concerning one of your confraternity: *Quis nostrum tam animo agresti ac duro fuit—ut—ut—*I forget the Latin; the meaning is, which of us was so rude and barbarous as to remain unmoved at the death of the great Roscius, whose advanced age was so far from preparing us for his death that we rather hoped one so graceful, so excellent in his art, ought to be exempted from the common lot of mortality? So the Prince of Orators spoke of the stage and its professors."

The words of the old man fell upon Lovel's ears, but without conveying any precise idea to his mind, which was then occupied in thinking by what means the old beggar, who still continued to regard him with a countenance provokingly sly and intelligent, had contrived to thrust himself into any knowledge of his affairs. He put his hand in his pocket as the readiest mode of intimating his desire of secrecy and securing the concurrence of the person whom he addressed; and while he bestowed him an alms, the amount of which rather bore proportion to his fears than to his charity, looked at him with a marked expression, which the mendicant, a physiognomist by profession, seemed perfectly to understand. —Never mind me, sir, I am no tale-pyet; but there are mair een in the warld than mine," answered he as he pocketed Lovel's bounty, but in a tone to be heard by him alone, and with an expression which amply filled up what was left unspoken. Then turning to Oldbuck: "I am awa to the manse, your honour. Has your honour ony word there, or to Sir Arthur, for I'll come in by Knockwinnock Castle again e'en?"

Oldbuck started as from a dream; and in a hurried tone, where vexation strove with a wish to conceal it, paying at the same time a tribute to Edie's smooth, greasy, unlined hat, he said: "Go down, go down to Monkbarns; let them give you some dinner. Or stay; if you do go to the manse, or to Knockwinnock, ye need say nothing about that foolish story of yours."

"Who, I?" said the mendicant. "Lord bless your honour, naebody sall ken a word about it frae me, mair than if the bit bourock had been there since Noah's flood. But, Lord, they tell me your honour has gien Johnnie Howie acre for acre of the laigh crofts for this heathery knowe! Now, if he has really imposed the bourock on ye for an ancient wark, it's my real opinion the bargain will never haud gude, if you would just bring down your heart to try it at the law, and say that he beguiled ye."

"Provoking scoundrel," muttered the indignant Antiquary between his teeth; "I'll have the hangman's lash and his back acquainted for this!" And then in a louder tone, "Never mind, Edie; it is all a mistake."

"Troth, I am thinking sae," continued his tormentor, who seemed to have pleasure in rubbing the galled wound— "troth, I aye thought sae; and it's no sae lang since I said to Luckie Gemmells, 'Never think you, luckie,' said I, 'that his honour, Monkbarns, would hae done sic a daft-like thing as to gie grund weel worth fifty shillings an acre for a mailing that would be dear o' a pund Scots. Na, na,' quo' I, 'depend upon't the Laird's been imposed upon wi' that wily do-little deevil, Johnnie Howie.' 'But Lord haud a care o' us, sirs, how can that be,' quo' she again, 'when the Laird's sae book-learned there's no the like o' him in the country-side, and Johnnie Howie has hardly sense eneugh to ca' the cows out o' his kale-yard?' 'Aweel, aweel,' quo' I, 'but ye'll hear he's circumvented him with some of his auld-warld stories,'—for ye ken, Laird, yon other time about the bodle that ye thought was an auld coin——"

"Go to the devil!" said Oldbuck; and then in a more mild tone, as one that was conscious his reputation lay at the mercy of his antagonist, he added: "Away with you down to Monkbarns, and when I come back I'll send ye a bottle of ale to the kitchen."

"Heaven reward your honour!" This was uttered with the true mendicant whine, as, setting his pike-staff before him, he began to move in the direction of Monkbarns. "But did your honour," turning round, "ever get back the siller ye gae to the travelling packman for the bodle?"

"Curse thee, go about thy business!"

"Aweel, aweel, sir, God bless your honour! I hope ye'll ding Johnnie Howie yet, and that I'll live to see it." And so saying, the old beggar moved off, relieving Mr. Oldbuck of recollections which were anything rather than agreeable.

"Who is this familiar old gentleman?" said Lovel, when the mendicant was out of hearing.

"Oh, one of the plagues of the country. I have been always against poor's-rates and a workhouse; I think I'll vote for them now, to have that scoundrel shut up. Oh, your old-remembered guest of a beggar becomes as well acquainted with you as he is with his dish, as intimate as one of the beasts familiar to man which signify love, and with which his own trade is especially conversant. Who is he? why, he has gone the vole—has been soldier, ballad-singer, travelling tinker, and is now a beggar. He is spoiled by our foolish gentry, who laugh at his jokes and rehearse Edie Ochiltree's good things as regularly as Joe Miller's."

"Why, he uses freedom apparently, which is the soul of wit," answered Lovel.

"Oh ay, freedom enough," said the Antiquary; "he generally invents some damned improbable lie or another to provoke you, like that nonsense he talked just now; not that I'll publish my tract till I have examined the thing to the bottom."

"In England," said Lovel, "such a mendicant would get a speedy check."

"Yes, your churchwardens and dog-whips would make slender allowance for his vein of humour! But here, curse him, he is a sort of privileged nuisance—one of the last specimens of the old-fashioned Scottish mendicant, who kept his rounds within a particular space, and was the news-carrier, the minstrel, and sometimes the historian of the district. That rascal, now, knows more old ballads and traditions than any other man in this and the four next parishes. And after all," he continued, softening as he went on describing Edie's good gifts, "the dog has some good-humour. He has borne his hard fate with unbroken spirits, and it's cruel to deny him the comfort of a laugh at his betters. The pleasure of having quizzed me, as you gay folk would call it, will be meat and drink to him for a day or two. But I must go back and look after him, or he will spread his d—d nonsensical story over half the country."

So saying, our heroes parted, Mr. Oldbuck to return to his *hospitium* at Monkbarns, and Lovel to pursue his way to Fairport, where he arrived without farther adventure.

CHAPTER V.

Launcelot Gobbo. Mark me now: now will I raise the waters.
                                                    Merchant of Venice.

THE theatre at Fairport had opened, but no Mr. Lovel appeared on the boards, nor was there anything in the habits or deportment of the young gentleman so named which authorised

Mr. Oldbuck's conjecture that his fellow-traveller was a candidate for the public favour. Regular were the Antiquary's inquiries at an old-fashioned barber who dressed the only three wigs in the parish, which, in defiance of taxes and times, were still subjected to the operation of powdering and frizzling, and who for that purpose divided his time among the three employers whom fashion had yet left him—regular, I say, were Mr. Oldbuck's inquiries at this personage concerning the news of the little theatre at Fairport, expecting every day to hear of Mr. Lovel's appearance, on which occasion the old gentleman had determined to put himself to charges in honour of his young friend, and not only to go to the play himself, but to carry his womankind along with him. But old Jacob Caxon conveyed no information which warranted his taking so decisive a step as that of securing a box.

He brought information, on the contrary, that there was a young man residing at Fairport of whom the town (by which he meant all the gossips, who, having no business of their own, fill up their leisure moments by attending to that of other people) could make nothing. He sought no society, but rather avoided that which the apparent gentleness of his manners, and some degree of curiosity, induced many to offer him. Nothing could be more regular, or less resembling an adventurer, than his mode of living, which was simple, but so completely well arranged that all who had any transactions with him were loud in their approbation.

"These are not the virtues of a stage-struck hero," thought Oldbuck to himself; and, however habitually pertinacious in his opinions, he must have been compelled to abandon that which he had formed in the present instance but for a part of Caxon's communication. "The young gentleman," he said, "was sometimes heard speaking to himsell, and rampauging about in his room, just as if he was ane o' the player folk."

Nothing, however, excepting this single circumstance, occurred to confirm Mr. Oldbuck's supposition, and it remained a high and doubtful question what a well-informed young man, without friends, connexions, or employment of any kind, could have to do as a resident at Fairport. Neither port wine nor whist had apparently any charms for him. He declined dining with the mess of the volunteer cohort, which had been lately embodied, and shunned joining the convivialities of either of the two parties which then divided Fairport, as they did more important places. He was too little of an aristocrat to join the club of Royal True Blues, and too little of a democrat to fraternise with an affiliated society of the *soi-disant* Friends of the People, which the borough had also the happiness of possessing. A coffee-room was his detestation; and, I grieve to say it, he had as few sympathies with the tea-table. In short, since the name was fashionable in novel-writing, and that is a great while agone, there was never a Master Lovel of whom so little positive was known, and who was so universally described by negatives.

One negative, however, was important: nobody knew any harm of Lovel. Indeed, had such existed, it would have been speedily made public; for the natural desire of speaking evil of our neighbour could in his case have been checked by no feelings of sympathy for a being so unsocial. On one account alone he fell somewhat under suspicion. As he made free use of his pencil in his solitary walks, and had drawn several views of the harbour, in which the signal-tower, and even the four-gun battery, were introduced, some zealous friends of the public sent abroad a whisper that this mysterious stranger must certainly be a French spy. The sheriff paid his respects to Mr. Lovel accordingly, but in the interview which followed it would seem that he had entirely removed that magistrate's suspicions, since he not only suffered him to remain undisturbed in his retirement, but, it was credibly reported, sent him two invitations to dinner parties, both which were civilly declined. But what the nature of the explanation was, the magistrate kept a profound secret, not only from the public at large, but from his substitute, his clerk, his wife, and his two daughters, who formed his privy council on all questions of official duty.

All these particulars being faithfully reported by Mr. Caxon to his patron at Monkbarns, tended much to raise Lovel in the opinion of his former fellow-traveller. "A decent sensible lad," said he to himself, "who scorns to enter the fooleries and nonsense of these idiot people at Fairport. I must do something for him—I must give him a dinner; and I will write Sir Arthur to come to Monkbarns to meet him. I must consult my womankind."

Accordingly, such consultation having been previously held, a special messenger, being no other than Caxon himself, was ordered to prepare for a walk to Knockwinnock Castle with a letter, "For the honoured Sir Arthur Wardour of Knockwinnock, Bart." The contents ran thus:

"DEAR SIR ARTHUR:

"On Tuesday the 17th curt. *stilo novo*, I hold a cænobitical symposion at Monkbarns, and pray you to assist thereat, at four o'clock precisely. If my fair enemy Miss Isabel can and will honour us by accompanying you, my womankind will be but too proud to have the aid of such an auxiliary in the cause of resistance to lawful rule and right supremacy. If not, I will send the womankind to the manse for the day. I have a young acquaintance to make known to you, who is touched with some strain of a better spirit than belongs to these giddy-paced times—reveres his elders, and has a pretty notion of the classics—and, as such a youth must have a natural contempt for the people about Fairport, I wish to show him some rational as well as worshipful society.—I am, dear Sir Arthur," etc., etc., etc.

"Fly with this letter, Caxon," said the senior, holding out his missive, *signatum atque sigillatum*—"fly to Knockwinnock and bring me back an answer. Go as fast as if the town-council were met, and waiting for the provost, and the provost was waiting for his new-powdered wig."

"Ah! sir," answered the messenger, with a deep sigh, "thae days hae lang gang by. Deil a wig has a provost of Fairport worn sin' auld Provost Jervie's time; and he had a quean of a servant-lass that dressed it hersell, wi' the doup o' a candle and a drudging-box. But I hae seen the day, Monkbarns, when the town-council of Fairport wad hae as soon wanted their town-clerk, or their gill of brandy ower-head after the haddies, as they wad hae wanted ilk ane a weel-favoured, sonsy, decent periwig on his pow. Hegh, sirs! nae wonder the commons will be discontent and rise against the law, when they see magistrates and bailies and deacons, and the provost himsell, wi' heads as bald and as bare as ane o' my blocks!"

"And as well furnished within, Caxon. But away with you; you have an excellent view of public affairs, and, I dare say, have touched the cause of our popular discontent as closely as the provost could have done himself. But away with you, Caxon."

And off went Caxon upon his walk of three miles:

> He hobbled, but his heart was good;
> Could he go faster than he could?

While he is engaged in his journey and return, it may not be impertinent to inform the reader to whose mansion he was bearing his embassy.

We have said that Mr. Oldbuck kept little company with the surrounding gentlemen, excepting with one person only. This was Sir Arthur Wardour, a baronet of ancient descent, and of a large but embarrassed fortune. His father, Sir Anthony, had been a Jacobite, and had displayed all the enthusiasm of that party while it could be served with words only. No man squeezed the orange with more significant gesture; no one could more dexterously intimate a dangerous health without coming under the penal statutes; and, above all, none drank success to the cause more deeply and devoutly. But, on the approach of the Highland army in 1745, it would appear that the worthy baronet's zeal became a little more moderate just when its warmth was of most consequence. He talked much, indeed, of taking the field for the rights of Scotland and Charles Stuart; but his demi-pique saddle would suit only one of his horses, and that horse could by no means be brought to stand fire. Perhaps the worshipful owner sympathised in the scruples of this sagacious quadruped, and began to think that what was so much dreaded by the horse could not be very wholesome for the rider. At any rate, while Sir Anthony Wardour talked and drank and hesitated, the sturdy provost of Fairport (who, as we before noticed, was the father of our Antiquary) sallied from his ancient burgh, heading a body of Whig burghers, and seized at once, in the name of George II., upon the Castle of Knockwinnock and on the four carriage-horses and person of the proprietor. Sir Anthony was shortly after sent off to the Tower of London by a secretary of state's warrant, and with him went his son Arthur, then a youth. But as nothing appeared like an overt act of treason, both father and son were soon set at liberty, and returned to their own mansion of Knockwinnock to drink healths five fathoms deep and talk of their sufferings in the royal cause. This became so much a matter of habit with Sir Arthur that, even after his father's death, the nonjuring chaplain used to pray regularly for the restoration of the rightful sovereign, for the downfall of the usurper, and for deliverance from their cruel and bloodthirsty enemies; although all idea of serious opposition to the house of Hanover had long mouldered away, and this treasonable liturgy was kept up rather as a matter of form than as conveying any distinct meaning. So much was this the case that, about the year 1770, upon a disputed election occurring in the county, the worthy knight fairly gulped down the oaths of abjuration and allegiance, in order to serve a candidate in whom he was interested; thus renouncing the heir for whose restoration he weekly petitioned Heaven, and acknowledging the usurper, whose dethronement he had never ceased to pray for. And to add to this melancholy instance of human inconsistency, Sir Arthur continued to pray for the house of Stuart even after the family had been extinct, and when, in truth, though in his theoretical loyalty he was pleased to regard them as alive, yet in all actual service and practical exertion he was a most zealous and devoted subject of George III.

In other respects Sir Arthur Wardour lived like most country gentlemen in Scotland—hunted and fished, gave and received dinners, attended races and county meetings, was a deputy-lieutenant and trustee upon turnpike acts. But in his more advanced years, as he became too lazy or unwieldy for field-sports, he supplied them by now and then reading Scottish history; and, having gradually acquired a taste for antiquities, though neither very deep nor very correct, he became a crony of his neighbour, Mr. Oldbuck of Monkbarns, and a joint labourer with him in his antiquarian pursuits.

There were, however, points of difference between these two humourists which sometimes occasioned discord. The faith of Sir Arthur, as an antiquary, was boundless, and Mr. Oldbuck (notwithstanding the affair of the *prœtorium* at the Kaim of Kinprunes) was much more scrupulous in receiving legends as current and authentic coin. Sir Arthur would have deemed himself guilty of the crime of leze-majesty had he doubted the existence of any single individual of that formidable bead-roll of one hundred and four kings of Scotland, received by Boethius, and rendered classical by Buchanan, in virtue of whom James VI. claimed to rule his ancient kingdom, and whose portraits still frown grimly upon the walls of the gallery of Holyrood. Now Oldbuck, a shrewd and suspicious man, and no respecter of divine hereditary right, was apt to cavil at this sacred list, and to affirm that the procession of the posterity of Fergus through the pages of Scottish history was as vain and unsubstantial as the gleamy pageant of the descendants of Banquo through the cavern of Hecate.

Another tender topic was the good fame of Queen Mary, of which the knight was a most chivalrous assertor, while the esquire impugned it, in spite both of her beauty and misfortunes. When, unhappily, their conversation turned on yet later times, motives of discord occurred in almost every page of history. Oldbuck was upon principle a stanch Presbyterian, a ruling elder of the kirk, and a friend to revolution principles and Protestant succession, while Sir Arthur was the very reverse of all this. They agreed, it is true, in dutiful love and allegiance to the sovereign who now fills [1] the throne; but this was their only point of union. It therefore often happened that bickerings hot broke out between them, in which Oldbuck was not always able to suppress his caustic

[1] The reader will understand that this refers to the reign of our late Gracious Sovereign, George the Third.

humour, while it would sometimes occur to the Baronet that
the descendant of a German printer, whose sires had "sought
the base fellowship of paltry burghers," forgot himself, and
took an unlicensed freedom of debate, considering the rank
and ancient descent of his antagonist. This, with the old
feud of the coach-horses, and the seizure of his manor-place
and tower of strength by Mr. Oldbuck's father, would at times
rush upon his mind, and inflame at once his cheeks and his
arguments. And, lastly, as Mr. Oldbuck thought his worthy
friend and compeer was in some respects little better than a
fool, he was apt to come more near communicating to him
that unfavourable opinion than the rules of modern politeness
warrant. In such cases they often parted in deep dudgeon,
and with something like a resolution to forbear each other's
company in future:

> But with the morning calm reflection came;

and as each was sensible that the society of the other had become, through habit, essential to his comfort, the breach was
speedily made up between them. On such occasions Oldbuck, considering that the Baronet's pettishness resembled
that of a child, usually showed his superior sense by compas-
sionately making the first advances to reconciliation. But it
once or twice happened that the aristocratic pride of the far-
descended knight took a flight too offensive to the feelings of
the representative of the typographer. In these cases the
breach between these two originals might have been immortal
but for the kind exertions and interposition of the Baronet's
daughter, Miss Isabella Wardour, who, with a son now absent
upon foreign and military service, formed his whole surviving
family. She was well aware how necessary Mr. Oldbuck was
to her father's amusement and comfort, and seldom failed to
interpose with effect when the office of a mediator between
them was rendered necessary by the satirical shrewdness of
the one or the assumed superiority of the other. Under Isabella's mild influence the wrongs of Queen Mary were forgotten by her father, and Mr. Oldbuck forgave the blasphemy
which reviled the memory of King William. However, as

she used in general to take her father's part playfully in
these disputes, Oldbuck was wont to call Isabella his fair
enemy, though in fact he made more account of her than
any other of her sex, of whom, as we have seen, he was no
admirer.

There existed another connexion betwixt these worthies,
which had alternately a repelling and attractive influence upon
their intimacy. Sir Arthur always wished to borrow; Mr.
Oldbuck was not always willing to lend. Mr. Oldbuck, *per
contra*, always wished to be repaid with regularity; Sir
Arthur was not always, nor indeed often, prepared to gratify
this reasonable desire; and, in accomplishing an arrangement
between tendencies so opposite, little "miffs" would occasionally take place. Still there was a spirit of mutual accommodation upon the whole, and they dragged on like dogs in
couples, with some difficulty and occasional snarling, but
without absolutely coming to a standstill or throttling each
other.

Some little disagreement such as we have mentioned, arising out of business or politics, had divided the houses of
Knockwinnock and Monkbarns when the emissary of the latter
arrived to discharge his errand. In his ancient Gothic
parlour, whose windows on one side looked out upon the rest-
less ocean, and on the other upon the long straight avenue,
was the Baronet seated, now turning over the leaves of a folio,
now casting a weary glance where the sun quivered on the
dark-green foliage and smooth trunks of the large and branching limes with which the avenue was planted. At length,
sight of joy! a moving object is seen, and it gives rise to
the usual inquiries, Who is it? and what can be his errand?
The old whitish-grey coat, the hobbling gait, the hat, half-
slouched, half-cocked, announced the forlorn maker of periwigs, and left for investigation only the second query. This
was soon solved by a servant entering the parlour: "A letter
from Monkbarns, Sir Arthur."

Sir Arthur took the epistle with a due assumption of consequential dignity.

"Take the old man into the kitchen and let him get some

refreshment," said the young lady, whose compassionate eye had remarked his thin grey hair and wearied gait.

"Mr. Oldbuck, my love, invites us to dinner on Tuesday the 17th," said the Baronet, pausing; "he really seems to forget that he has not of late conducted himself so civilly towards me as might have been expected."

"Dear sir, you have so many advantages over poor Mr. Oldbuck that no wonder it should put him a little out of humour; but I know he has much respect for your person and your conversation; nothing would give him more pain than to be wanting in any real attention."

"True, true, Isabella; and one must allow for the original descent: something of the German boorishness still flows in the blood, something of the Whiggish and perverse opposition to established rank and privilege. You may observe that he never has any advantage of me in dispute unless when he avails himself of a sort of pettifogging intimacy with dates, names, and trifling matters of fact, a tiresome and frivolous accuracy of memory which is entirely owing to his mechanical descent."

"He must find it convenient in historical investigation, I should think, sir?" said the young lady.

"It leads to an uncivil and positive mode of disputing; and nothing seems more unreasonable than to hear him impugn even Bellenden's rare translation of Hector Boece, which I have the satisfaction to possess, and which is a black-letter folio of great value, upon the authority of some old scrap of parchment which he has saved from its deserved destiny of being cut up into tailors' measures. And, besides, that habit of minute and troublesome accuracy leads to a mercantile manner of doing business, which ought to be beneath a landed proprietor whose family has stood two or three generations. I question if there's a dealer's clerk in Fairport that can sum an account of interest better than Monkbarns."

"But you'll accept his invitation, sir?"

"Why, ye—yes; we have no other engagement on hand, I think. Who can the young man be he talks of? he seldom picks up new acquaintance; and he has no relation that I ever heard of."

"Probably some relation of his brother-in-law, Captain M'Intyre."

"Very possibly. Yes, we will accept; the M'Intyres are of a very ancient Highland family. You may answer his card in the affirmative, Isabella; I believe I have no leisure to be 'Dear Sirring' myself."

So this important matter being adjusted, Miss Wardour intimated " her own and Sir Arthur's compliments, and that they would have the honour of waiting upon Mr. Oldbuck. Miss Wardour takes this opportunity to renew her hostility with Mr. Oldbuck, on account of his late long absence from Knockwinnock, where his visits give so much pleasure." With this *placebo* she concluded her note, with which old Caxon, now refreshed in limbs and wind, set out on his return to the Antiquary's mansion.

CHAPTER VI.

Moth. By Woden, God of Saxons,
From whence comes Wensday, that is Wodnesday
Truth is a thing that I will ever keep
Unto thylke day in which I creep into
My sepulcre.
CARTWRIGHT'S *Ordinary.*

OUR young friend Lovel, who had received a corresponding invitation, punctual to the hour of appointment, arrived at Monkbarns about five minutes before four o'clock on the 17th of July. The day had been remarkably sultry, and large drops of rain had occasionally fallen, though the threatened showers had as yet passed away.

Mr. Oldbuck received him at the Palmer's Port in his complete brown suit, grey silk stockings, and wig powdered with all the skill of the veteran Caxon, who, having smelt out the dinner, had taken care not to finish his job till the hour of eating approached.

"You are welcome to my symposion, Mr. Lovel; and now let me introduce you to my Clogdogdos, as Tom Otter calls them—my unlucky and good-for-nothing womankind—*malæ bestiæ*, Mr. Lovel."

"I shall be disappointed, sir, if I do not find the ladies very undeserving of your satire."

"Tilley-valley, Mr. Lovel—which, by the way, one commentator derives from *tittivillitium* and another from *talley-ho*—but tilley-valley, I say, a truce with your politeness. You will find them but samples of womankind. But here they be, Mr. Lovel. I present to you, in due order, my most discreet sister Griselda, who disdains the simplicity, as well as patience, annexed to the poor old name of Grizel; and my most exquisite niece Maria, whose mother was called Mary, and sometimes Molly."

The elderly lady rustled in silks and satins, and bore upon her head a structure resembling the fashion in the ladies' memorandum-book for the year 1770, a superb piece of architecture not much less than a modern Gothic castle, of which the curls might represent the turrets, the black pins the *chevaux de frise*, and the lappets the banners.

The face which, like that of the ancient statues of Vesta, was thus crowned with towers, was large and long, and peaked at nose and chin, and bore in other respects such a ludicrous resemblance to the physiognomy of Mr. Jonathan Oldbuck that Lovel, had they not appeared at once, like Sebastian and Viola in the last scene of the "Twelfth Night," might have supposed that the figure before him was his old friend masquerading in female attire. An antique flowered silk gown graced the extraordinary person to whom belonged this unparalleled *tête*, which her brother was wont to say was fitter for a turban for Mahound or Termagant than a headgear for a reasonable creature or Christian gentlewoman. Two long and bony arms were terminated at the elbows by triple blond ruffles, and, being folded saltire-ways in front of her person, and decorated with long gloves of a bright vermilion colour, presented no bad resemblance to a pair of gigantic lobsters. High-heeled shoes, and a short silk cloak, thrown in easy negligence over her shoulders, completed the exterior of Miss Griselda Oldbuck.

Her niece, the same whom Lovel had seen transiently during his first visit, was a pretty young woman, genteelly dressed according to the fashion of the day, with an air of *espièglerie* which became her very well, and which was perhaps derived from the caustic humour peculiar to her uncle's family, though softened by transmission.

Mr. Lovel paid his respects to both ladies, and was answered by the elder with the prolonged courtesy of 1760, drawn from the righteous period

> When folks conceived a grace
> Of half an hour's space,
> And rejoiced in a Friday's capon,

and by the younger with a modern reverence, which, like the festive benediction of a modern divine, was of much shorter duration.

While this salutation was exchanging, Sir Arthur, with his fair daughter hanging upon his arm, having dismissed his chariot, appeared at the garden door, and in all due form paid his respects to the ladies.

"Sir Arthur," said the Antiquary, "and you, my fair foe, let me make known to you my friend Mr. Lovel, a gentleman who, during the scarlet-fever which is epidemic at present in this our island, has the virtue and decency to appear in a coat of a civil complexion. You see, however, that the fashionable colour has mustered in his cheeks which appears not in his garments. Sir Arthur, let me present to you a young gentleman whom your farther knowledge will find grave, wise, courtly, and scholar-like, well seen, deeply read, and thoroughly grounded in all the hidden mysteries of the greenroom and stage, from the days of Davie Lindsay down to those of Dibdin,—he blushes again, which is a sign of grace."

"My brother," said Miss Griselda, addressing Lovel, "has a humorous way of expressing himself, sir, nobody thinks anything of what Monkbarns says; so I beg you will not be so confused for the matter of his nonsense. But you must have had a warm walk beneath this broiling sun; would you take ony thing?—a glass of balm wine?"

Ere Lovel could answer, the Antiquary interposed. "Aroint
5

thee, witch! wouldst thou poison my guests with thy infernal decoctions? Dost thou not remember how it fared with the clergyman whom you seduced to partake of that deceitful beverage?"

"Oh fie, fie, brother! Sir Arthur, did you ever hear the like! He must have everything his ain way, or he will invent such stories. But there goes Jenny to ring the old bell to tell us that the dinner is ready."

Rigid in his economy, Mr. Oldbuck kept no male servant. This he disguised under the pretext that the masculine sex was too noble to be employed in those acts of personal servitude which, in all early periods of society, were uniformly imposed on the female. "Why," would he say, "did the boy Tam Rintherout, whom, at my wise sister's instigation, I, with equal wisdom, took upon trial—why did he pilfer apples, take birds' nests, break glasses, and ultimately steal my spectacles, except that he felt that noble emulation which swells in the bosom of the masculine sex, which has conducted him to Flanders with a musket on his shoulder, and doubtless will promote him to a glorious halbert, or even to the gallows? And why does this girl, his full sister, Jenny Rintherout, move in the same vocation with safe and noiseless step, shod or unshod, soft as the pace of a cat, and docile as a spaniel— why? but because she is in her vocation. Let them minister to us, Sir Arthur—let them minister, I say; it's the only thing they are fit for. All ancient legislators, from Lycurgus to Mahommed, corruptly called Mahomet, agree in putting them in their proper and subordinate rank, and it is only the crazy heads of our old chivalrous ancestors that erected their Dulcineas into despotic princesses."

Miss Wardour protested loudly against this ungallant doctrine; but the bell now rung for dinner.

"Let me do all the offices of fair courtesy to so fair an antagonist," said the old gentleman, offering his arm. "I remember, Miss Wardour, Mahommed (vulgarly Mahomet) had some hesitation about the mode of summoning his Moslemah to prayer. He rejected bells as used by Christians, trumpets as the summons of the Guebres, and finally adopted the human voice. I have had equal doubt concerning my dinner-call. Gongs, now in present use, seemed a newfangled and heathenish invention, and the voice of the female womankind I rejected as equally shrill and dissonant; wherefore, contrary to the said Mahommed, or Mahomet, I have resumed the bell. It has a local propriety, since it was the conventual signal for spreading the repast in their refectory, and it has the advantage over the tongue of my sister's prime minister Jenny, that, though not quite so loud and shrill, it ceases ringing the instant you drop the bell-rope; whereas we know by sad experience that any attempt to silence Jenny only wakes the sympathetic chime of Miss Oldbuck and Mary M'Intyre to join in chorus."

With this discourse he led the way to his dining-parlour, which Lovel had not yet seen; it was wainscotted, and contained some curious paintings. The dining-table was attended by Jenny; but an old superintendent, a sort of female butler, stood by the sideboard, and underwent the burden of bearing several reproofs from Mr. Oldbuck, and innuendos, not so much marked but not less cutting, from his sister.

The dinner was such as suited a professed antiquary, comprehending many savoury specimens of Scottish viands now disused at the tables of those who affect elegance. There was the relishing solan goose, whose smell is so powerful that he is never cooked within doors. Blood-raw he proved to be on this occasion, so that Oldbuck half-threatened to throw the greasy sea-fowl at the head of the negligent housekeeper, who acted as priestess in presenting this odoriferous offering. But, by good hap, she had been most fortunate in the hotchpotch, which was unanimously pronounced to be inimitable. "I knew we should succeed here," said Oldbuck exultingly, · "for Davie Dibble, the gardener—an old bachelor like myself—takes care the rascally women do not dishonour our vegetables. And here is fish and sauce and crappit-heads. I ackowledge our womankind excel in that dish; it procures them the pleasure of scolding, for half an hour at least, twice a week, with auld Maggy Mucklebackit, our fishwife. The chicken-pie, Mr. Lovel, is made after a recipe bequeathed to me by my departed grandmother of happy memory. And if you will venture on a glass of wine you will find it worthy of one who professes the maxim of King Alphonso of Castile: Old wood to burn, old books to read, old wine to drink, and old friends, Sir Arthur—ay, Mr. Lovel, and young friends too—to converse with."

"And what news do you bring us from Edinburgh, Monkbarns?" said Sir Arthur; "how wags the world in Auld Reekie?"

"Mad, Sir Arthur, mad—irretrievably frantic—far beyond dipping in the sea, shaving the crown, or drinking hellebore. The worst sort of frenzy, a military frenzy, hath possessed man, woman, and child."

"And high time, I think," said Miss Wardour, "when we are threatened with invasion from abroad and insurrection at home."

"Oh, I did not doubt you would join the scarlet host against me: women, like turkeys, are always subdued by a red rag. But what says Sir Arthur, whose dreams are of standing armies and German oppression?"

"Why, I say, Mr. Oldbuck," replied the knight, "that, so far as I am capable of judging, we ought to resist *cum toto corpore regni*, as the phrase is, unless I have altogether forgotten my Latin, an enemy who comes to propose to us a Whiggish sort of government, a republican system, and who is aided and abetted by a sort of fanatics of the worst kind in our own bowels. I have taken some measures, I assure you, such as become my rank in the community; for I have directed the constables to take up that old scoundrelly beggar, Edie Ochiltree, for spreading disaffection against church and state through the whole parish. He said plainly to old Caxon that Johnnie Howie's Kilmarnock cowl covered more sense than all the three wigs in the parish. I think it is easy to make out that innuendo. But the rogue shall be taught better manners."

"Oh no, my dear sir," exclaimed Miss Wardour, "not old Edie, that we have known so long. I assure you no constable shall have my good graces that executes such a warrant."

"Ay, there it goes," said the Antiquary; "you, to be a stanch Tory, Sir Arthur, have nourished a fine sprig of Whiggery in your bosom. Why, Miss Wardour is alone sufficient to control a whole quarter-session—a quarter-session? ay, a general assembly or convocation to boot—a Boadicea she, an Amazon, a Zenobia."

"And yet, with all my courage, Mr. Oldbuck, I am glad to hear our people are getting under arms."

"Under arms, Lord love thee! didst thou ever read the history of Sister Margaret, which flowed from a head that, though now old and somedele grey, has more sense and political intelligence than you find nowadays in a whole synod? Dost thou remember the Nurse's dream in that exquisite work, which she recounts in such agony to Hubble Bubble? When she would have taken up a piece of broadcloth in her vision, lo! it exploded like a great iron cannon; when she put out her hand to save a pirn, it perked up in her face in the form of a pistol. My own vision in Edinburgh has been something similar. I called to consult my lawyer; he was clothed in a dragoon's dress, belted and casqued, and about to mount a charger, which his writing-clerk (habited as a sharp-shooter) walked to and fro before his door. I went to scold my agent for having sent me to advise with a madman; he had stuck into his head the plume which in more sober days he wielded between his fingers, and figured as an artillery officer. My mercer had his spontoon in his hand, as if he measured his cloth by that implement instead of a legitimate yard. The banker's clerk, who was directed to sum my cash-account, blundered it three times, being disordered by the recollection of his military 'tellings-off' at the morning drill. I was ill, and sent for a surgeon:

> He came; but valour so had fired his eye,
> And such a falchion glitter'd on his thigh,
> That, by the gods, with such a load of steel,
> I thought he came to murder, not to heal!

I had recourse to a physician, but he also was practising a more wholesale mode of slaughter than that which his profession had been supposed at all times to open to him. And now, since I have returned here, even our wise neighbours of Fair-port have caught the same valiant humour. I hate a gun like a hurt wild duck, I detest a drum like a Quaker; and they thunder and rattle out yonder upon the town's common so that every volley and roll goes to my very heart."

"Dear brother, dinna speak that gate o' the gentlemen volunteers; I am sure they have a most becoming uniform. Weel I wot they have been wet to the very skin twice last week; I met them marching in terribly droukit, an mony a sair hoast was amang them. And the trouble they take, I am sure it claims our gratitude."

"And I am sure," said Miss M'Intyre, "that my uncle sent twenty guineas to help out their equipments."

"It was to buy liquorice and sugar-candy," said the cynic, "to encourage the trade of the place, and to refresh the throats of the officers who had bawled themselves hoarse in the service of their country."

"Take care, Monkbarns! we shall set you down among the black-nebs by and by."

"No, Sir Arthur, a tame grumbler I. I only claim the privilege of croaking in my own corner here, without uniting my throat to the grand chorus of the marsh. *Ni quito rey, ni pongo rey*—I neither make king nor mar king, as Sancho says, but pray heartily for our own sovereign, pay scot and lot, and grumble at the exciseman. But here comes the ewe-milk cheese in good time; it is a better digestive than politics."

When dinner was over and the decanters placed on the table, Mr. Oldbuck proposed the King's health in a bumper, which was readily acceded to both by Lovel and the Baronet, the Jacobitism of the latter being now a sort of speculative opinion merely—the shadow of a shade.

After the ladies had left the apartment, the landlord and Sir Arthur entered into several exquisite discussions, in which the younger guest, either on account of the abstruse erudition which they involved, or for some other reason, took but a slender share, till at length he was suddenly started out of a profound reverie by an unexpected appeal to his judgment

"I will stand by what Mr. Lovel says; he was born in the north of England, and may know the very spot."

Sir Arthur thought it unlikely that so young a gentleman should have paid much attention to matters of that sort.

"I am advised of the contrary," said Oldbuck. "How say you, Mr. Lovel? Speak up for your own credit, man."

Lovel was obliged to confess himself in the ridiculous situation of one alike ignorant of the subject of conversation and controversy which had engaged the company for an hour.

"Lord help the lad, his head has been wool-gathering! I thought how it would be when the womankind were admitted —no getting a word of sense out of a young fellow for six hours after. Why, man, there was once a people called the Piks——"

"More properly Picts," interrupted the Baronet.

"I say the Pikar, Pihar, Piochtar, Piaghter, or Peughtar," vociferated Oldbuck; "they spoke a Gothic dialect——"

"Genuine Celtic," again asseverated the knight.

"Gothic! Gothic, I'll go to death upon it!" counter-asseverated the squire.

"Why, gentlemen," said Lovel, "I conceive that is a dispute which may be easily settled by philologists, if there are any remains of the language."

"There is but one word," said the Baronet, "but, in spite of Mr. Oldbuck's pertinacity, it is decisive of the question."

"Yes, in my favour," said Oldbuck. "Mr. Lovel, you shall be judge. I have the learned Pinkerton on my side."

"I, on mine, the indefatigable and erudite Chalmers."

"Gordon comes into my opinion."

"Sir Robert Sibbald holds mine."

"Innes is with me!" vociferated Oldbuck.

"Ritson has no doubt!" shouted the Baronet.

"Truly, gentlemen," said Lovel, "before you muster your forces and overwhelm me with authorities I should like to know the word in dispute."

"*Benval,*" said both the disputants at once.

"Which signifies *caput valli,*" said Sir Arthur.

"The head of the wall," echoed Oldbuck.

There was a deep pause. "It is rather a narrow foundation to build a hypothesis upon," observed the arbiter.

"Not a whit, not a whit," said Oldbuck; "men fight best in a narrow ring: an inch is as good as a mile for a home-thrust."

"It is decidedly Celtic," said the Baronet; "every hill in the Highlands begins with 'ben.'"

"But what say you to 'val,' Sir Arthur? is it not decidedly the Saxon 'wall'?"

"It is the Roman *vallum*," said Sir Arthur; "the Picts borrowed that part of the word."

"No such thing; if they borrowed anything, it must have been your 'ben,' which they might have from the neighbouring Britons of Strath Cluyd."

"The Piks, or Picts," said Lovel, "must have been singularly poor in dialect, since in the only remaining word of their vocabulary, and that consisting only of two syllables, they have been confessedly obliged to borrow one of them from another language; and, methinks, gentlemen, with submission, the controversy is not unlike that which the two knights fought concerning the shield that had one side white and the other black. Each of you claim one-half of the word, and seem to resign the other. But what strikes me most is the poverty of the language which has left such slight vestiges behind it."

"You are in an error," said Sir Arthur; "it was a copious language, and they were a great and powerful people; built two steeples—one at Brechin, one at Abernethy. The Pictish maidens of the blood royal were kept in Edinburgh Castle, thence called *Castrum Puellarum*."

"A childish legend," said Oldbuck, "invented to give consequence to trumpery womankind. It was called the Maiden Castle, *quasi lucus a non lucendo*, because it resisted every attack, and women never do."

"There is a list of the Pictish kings," persisted Sir Arthur, "well authenticated, from Crentheminachcryme (the date of whose reign is somewhat uncertain) down to Drusterstone, whose death concluded their dynasty. Half of them have the

Celtic patronymic Mac prefixed—Mac, *id est filius;* what do you say to that, Mr. Oldbuck? There is Drust Macmorachin, Trynel Maclachlin (first of that ancient clan, as it may be judged), and Gormach Macdonald, Alpin Macmetegus, Drust Mactallargam (here he was interrupted by a fit of coughing), ugh, ugh, ugh—Golarge Macchan—ugh, ugh—Macchanan—ugh — Macchananail — Kenneth — ugh — ugh — Macferedith, Eachan Macfungus—and twenty more, decidedly Celtic names, which I could repeat if this damned cough would let me."

"Take a glass of wine, Sir Arthur, and drink down that bead-roll of unbaptised jargon, that would choke the devil; why, that last fellow has the only intelligible name you have repeated. They are all of the tribe of Macfungus, mushroom monarchs every one of them, sprung up from the fumes of conceit, folly, and falsehood fermenting in the brains of some mad Highland seannachie."

"I am surprised to hear you, Mr. Oldbuck; you know, or ought to know, that the list of these potentates was copied by Henry Maule of Melgum from the *Chronicles of Loch-Leven* and *Saint Andrews,* and put forth by him in his short but satisfactory *History of the Picts,* printed by Robert Freebairn of Edinburgh, and sold by him at his shop in the Parliament Close, in the year of God seventeen hundred and five, or six, I am not precisely certain which; but I have a copy at home that stands next to my twelvemo copy of the Scots Acts, and ranges on the shelf with them very well. What say you to that, Mr. Oldbuck?"

"Say? Why, I laugh at Harry Maule and his history," answered Oldbuck, "and thereby comply with his request, of giving it entertainment according to its merits."

"Do not laugh at a better man than yourself," said Sir Arthur, somewhat scornfully.

"I do not conceive I do, Sir Arthur, in laughing either at him or his history."

"Henry Maule of Melgum was a gentleman, Mr. Oldbuck."

"I presume he had no advantage of me in *that* particular," replied the Antiquary, somewhat tartly.

"Permit me, Mr. Oldbuck; he was a gentleman of high family and ancient descent, and therefore——"

"The descendant of a Westphalian printer should speak of him with deference? Such may be your opinion, Sir Arthur; it is not mine. I conceive that my descent from that painful and industrious typographer, Wolfbrand Oldenbuck, who, in the month of December, 1493, under the patronage, as the colophon tells us, of Sebaldus Scheyter and Sebastian Kammermaister, accomplished the printing of the great *Chronicle of Nuremberg*—I conceive, I say, that my descent from that great restorer of learning is more creditable to me as a man of letters than if I had numbered in my genealogy all the brawling, bullet-headed, iron-fisted old Gothic barons since the days of Crentheminachcryme, not one of whom, I suppose, could write his own name."

"If you mean the observation as a sneer at my ancestry," said the knight, with an assumption of dignified superiority and composure, "I have the pleasure to inform you that the name of my ancestor Gamelyn de Guardover, *miles*, is written fairly with his own hand in the earliest copy of the Ragman Roll."

"Which only serves to show that he was one of the earliest who set the mean example of submitting to Edward I. What have you to say for the stainless loyalty of your family, Sir Arthur, after such a backsliding as that?"

"It's enough, sir," said Sir Arthur, starting up fiercely and pushing back his chair; "I shall hereafter take care how I honour with my company one who shows himself so ungrateful for my condescension."

"In that you will do as you find most agreeable, Sir Arthur; I hope that, as I was not aware of the extent of the obligation which you have done me by visiting my poor house, I may be excused for not having carried my gratitude to the extent of servility."

"Mighty well—mighty well, Mr. Oldbuck; I wish you a good evening. Mr. a—a—a—Shovel, I wish you a very good evening."

Out of the parlour door flounced the incensed Sir Arthur,

as if the spirit of the whole Round Table inflamed his single bosom, and traversed with long strides the labyrinth of passages which conducted to the drawing-room.

"Did you ever hear such an old tup-headed ass?" said Oldbuck, briefly apostrophising Lovel; "but I must not let him go in this mad-like way neither."

So saying, he pushed off after the retreating Baronet, whom he traced by the clang of several doors which he opened in search of the apartment for tea, and slammed with force behind him at every disappointment. "You'll do yourself a mischief," roared the Antiquary. "*Qui ambulat in tenebris, nescit quo vadit*—you'll tumble down the backstair."

Sir Arthur had now got involved in darkness, of which the sedative effect is well known to nurses and governesses who have to deal with pettish children. It retarded the pace of the irritated Baronet if it did not abate his resentment, and Mr. Oldbuck, better acquainted with the *locale*, got up with him as he had got his grasp upon the handle of the drawing-room door.

"Stay a minute, Sir Arthur," said Oldbuck, opposing his abrupt entrance; "don't be quite so hasty, my good old friend. I was a little too rude with you about Sir Gamelyn. Why, he is an old acquaintance of mine, man, and a favourite; he kept company with Bruce and Wallace, and, I'll be sworn on a black-letter Bible, only subscribed the Ragman Roll with the legitimate and justifiable intention of circumventing the false Southern. 'Twas right Scottish craft, my good knight; hundreds did it. Come, come, forget and forgive; confess we have given the young fellow here a right to think us two testy old fools."

"Speak for yourself, Mr. Jonathan Oldbuck," said Sir Arthur, with much majesty.

"Awell, awell! a wilful man must have his way."

With that the door opened, and into the drawing-room marched the tall gaunt form of Sir Arthur, followed by Lovel and Mr. Oldbuck, the countenances of all three a little discomposed.

"I have been waiting for you, sir," said Miss Wardour, "to

propose we should walk forward to meet the carriage, as the evening is so fine."

Sir Arthur readily assented to this proposal, which suited the angry mood in which he found himself; and having, agreeably to the established custom in cases of pet, refused the refreshment of tea and coffee, he tucked his daughter under his arm, and, after taking a ceremonious leave of the ladies and a very dry one of Oldbuck, off he marched.

"I think Sir Arthur has got the black dog on his back again," said Miss Oldbuck.

"Black dog! black devil! he's more absurd than womankind. What say you, Lovel? Why, the lad's gone too."

"He took his leave, uncle, while Miss Wardour was putting on her things; but I don't think you observed him."

"The devil's in the people! This is all one gets by fussing and bustling and putting one's self out of one's way in order to give dinners, besides all the charges they are put to. O Seged, Emperor of Ethiopia!" said he, taking up a cup of tea in the one hand and a volume of the *Rambler* in the other—for it was his regular custom to read while he was eating or drinking in presence of his sister, being a practice which served at once to evince his contempt for the society of womankind and his resolution to lose no moment of instruction—"O Seged, Emperor of Ethiopia! well hast thou spoken: 'No man should presume to say, This shall be a day of happiness.'"

Oldbuck proceeded in his studies for the best part of an hour, uninterrupted by the ladies, who each in profound silence pursued some female employment. At length a light and modest tap was heard at the parlour door. "Is that you, Caxon? Come in, come in, man."

The old man opened the door, and, thrusting in his meagre face, thatched with thin grey locks, and one sleeve of his white coat, said in a subdued and mysterious tone of voice: "I was wanting to speak to you, sir."

"Come in then, you old fool, and say what you have got to say."

"I'll maybe frighten the ladies," said the ex-friseur.

"Frighten!" answered the Antiquary, "what do you mean?

never mind the ladies. Have you seen another ghaist at the Humlock Knowe?"

"Na, sir; it's no a ghaist this turn," replied Caxon; "but I'm no easy in my mind."

"Did you ever hear of anybody that was?" answered Oldbuck; "what reason has an old battered powder-puff like you to be easy in your mind, more than all the rest of the world besides?"

"It's no for mysell, sir; but it threatens an awfu' night; and Sir Arthur and Miss Wardour, poor thing——"

"Why, man, they must have met the carriage at the head of the loaning or thereabouts; they must be home long ago."

"Na, sir; they didna gang the road by the turnpike to meet the carriage, they gaed by the sands."

The word operated like electricity on Oldbuck. "The sands!" he exclaimed; "impossible!"

"Ou, sir, that's what I said to the gardener; but he says he saw them turn down by the Mussel Craig. 'In troth,' says I to him, 'an that be the case, Davie, I am misdoubting——'"

"An almanack! an almanack!' said Oldbuck, starting up in great alarm; "not that bauble!" flinging away a little pocket almanack which his niece offered him. "Great God! my poor dear Miss Isabella! Fetch me instantly the Fairport Almanack." It was brought, consulted, and added greatly to his agitation. "I'll go myself; call the gardener and ploughman, bid them bring ropes and ladders, bid them raise more help as they come along; keep the top of the cliffs, and halloo down to them; I'll go myself."

"What is the matter?" inquired Miss Oldbuck and Miss M'Intyre.

"The tide! the tide!" answered the alarmed Antiquary.

"Had not Jenny better—but no, I'll run myself," said the younger lady, partaking in all her uncle's terrors—"I'll run myself to Saunders Mucklebackit and make him get out his boat."

"Thank you, my dear, that's the wisest word that has been spoken yet; run! run! To go by the sands!" seizing his hat and cane; "was there ever such madness heard of?"

CHAPTER VII.

Pleased awhile to view
The watery waste, the prospect wild and new;
The now receding waters gave them space
On either side the growing shores to trace;
And then, returning, they contract the scene,
Till small and smaller grows the walk between.

CRABBE.

THE information of Davie Dibble, which had spread such general alarm at Monkbarns, proved to be strictly correct. Sir Arthur and his daughter had set out, according to their first proposal, to return to Knockwinnock by the turnpike road; but, when they reached the head of the loaning, as it was called, or great lane, which on one side made a sort of avenue to the house of Monkbarns, they discerned a little way before them Lovel, who seemed to linger on the way as if to give him an opportunity to join them. Miss Wardour immediately proposed to her father that they should take another direction; and, as the weather was fine, walk home by the sands, which, stretching below a picturesque ridge of rocks, afforded at almost all times a pleasanter passage between Knockwinnock and Monkbarns than the highroad.

Sir Arthur acquiesced willingly. "It would be unpleasant," he said, "to be joined by that young fellow, whom Mr. Old-buck had taken the freedom to introduce them to." And his old-fashioned politeness had none of the ease of the present day, which permits you, if you have a mind, to "cut" the person you have associated with for a week the instant you feel or suppose yourself in a situation which makes it disagreeable to own him. Sir Arthur only stipulated that a little ragged boy, for the guerdon of one penny sterling, should run to meet his coachman and turn his equipage back to Knockwinnock.

When this was arranged, and the emissary despatched, the knight and his daughter left the highroad, and, following a wandering path among sandy hillocks, partly grown over with furze and the long grass called bent, soon attained the side of the ocean.   The tide was by no means so far out as they had computed; but this gave them no alarm : there were seldom ten days in the year when it approached so near the cliffs as not to leave a dry passage.   But, nevertheless, at periods of spring-tide, or even when the ordinary flood was accelerated by high winds, this road was altogether covered by the sea; and tradition had recorded several fatal accidents which had happened on such occasions.   Still, such dangers were considered as remote and improbable; and rather served, with other legends, to amuse the hamlet fireside than to prevent any one from going between Knockwinnock and Monkbarns by the sands.

As Sir Arthur and Miss Wardour paced along, enjoying the pleasant footing afforded by the cool moist hard sand, Miss Wardour could not help observing that the last tide had risen considerably above the usual water-mark.   Sir Arthur made the same observation, but without its occurring to either of them to be alarmed at the circumstance.   The sun was now resting his huge disk upon the edge of the level ocean, and gilded the accumulation of towering clouds through which he had travelled the livelong day, and which now assembled on all sides, like misfortunes and disasters around a sinking empire and falling monarch.   Still, however, his dying splendour gave a sombre magnificance to the massive congregation of vapours, forming out of their unsubstantial gloom the show of pyramids and towers, some touched with gold, some with purple, some with a hue of deep and dark red.   The distant sea, stretched beneath this varied and gorgeous canopy, lay almost portentously still, reflecting back the dazzling and level beams of the descending luminary and the splendid colouring of the clouds amidst which he was setting.   Nearer to the beach, the tide rippled onward in waves of sparkling silver, that imperceptibly, yet rapidly, gained upon the sand.

With a mind employed in admiration of the romantic scene, or perhaps on some more agitating topic, Miss Wardour advanced in silence by her father's side, whose recently offended dignity did not stoop to open any conversation.   Following the windings of the beach, they passed one projecting point or headland of rock after another, and now found themselves under a huge and continued extent of the precipices by which that iron-bound coast is in most places defended. Long projecting reefs of rock, extending under water, and only evincing their existence by here and there a peak entirely bare, or by the breakers which foamed over those that were partially covered, rendered Knockwinnock Bay dreaded by pilots and shipmasters. The crags which rose between the beach and the mainland, to the height of two or three hundred feet, afforded in their crevices shelter for unnumbered sea-fowl, in situations seemingly secured by their dizzy height from the rapacity of man. Many of these wild tribes, with the instinct which sends them to seek the land before a storm arises, were now winging towards their nests with the shrill and dissonant clang which announces disquietude and fear. The disk of the sun became almost totally obscured ere he had altogether sunk below the horizon, and an early and lurid shade of darkness blotted the serene twilight of a summer evening. The wind began next to arise; but its wild and moaning sound was heard for some time, and its effects became visible on the bosom of the sea, before the gale was felt on shore. The mass of waters, now dark and threatening, began to lift itself in larger ridges and sink in deeper furrows, forming waves that rose high in foam upon the breakers, or burst upon the beach with a sound resembling distant thunder.

Appalled by this sudden change of weather, Miss Wardour drew close to her father and held his arm fast. "I wish," at length she said, but almost in a whisper, as if ashamed to express her increasing apprehensions—"I wish we had kept the road we intended, or waited at Monkbarns for the carriage."

Sir Arthur looked round, but did not see, or would not acknowledge, any signs of an immediate storm. They would reach Knockwinnock, he said, long before the tempest began. But the speed with which he walked, and with which Isabella could hardly keep pace, indicated a feeling that some exertion was necessary to accomplish his consolatory prediction.

They were now near the centre of a deep but narrow bay

or recess, formed by two projecting capes of high and inaccessible rock, which shot out into the sea like the horns of a crescent; and neither durst communicate the apprehension which each began to entertain, that, from the unusually rapid advance of the tide, they might be deprived of the power of proceeding by doubling the promontory which lay before them, or of retreating by the road which brought them thither.

As they thus pressed forward, longing doubtless to exchange the easy curving line which the sinuosities of the bay compelled them to adopt for a straighter and more expeditious path, though less conformable to the line of beauty, Sir Arthur observed a human figure on the beach advancing to meet them. "Thank God," he exclaimed, "we shall get round Halket Head! that person must have passed it"; thus giving vent to the feeling of hope, though he had suppressed that of apprehension.

"Thank God indeed!" echoed his daughter, half audibly, half internally, as expressing the gratitude which she strongly felt.

The figure which advanced to meet them made many signs, which the haze of the atmosphere, now disturbed by wind and by a drizzling rain, prevented them from seeing or comprehending distinctly. Some time before they met, Sir Arthur could recognise the old blue-gowned beggar, Edie Ochiltree. It is said that even the brute creation lay aside their animosities and antipathies when pressed by an instant and common danger. The beach under Halket Head, rapidly diminishing in extent by the encroachments of a spring-tide and a northwest wind, was in like manner a neutral field where even a justice of peace and a strolling mendicant might meet upon terms of mutual forbearance.

"Turn back! turn back!" exclaimed the vagrant; "why did ye not turn when I waved to you?"

"We thought," replied Sir Arthur, in great agitation—"we thought we could get round Halket Head."

"Halket Head! The tide will be running on Halket Head by this time like the Fall of Fyers! It was a' I could do to get round it twenty minutes since; it was coming in three

6

feet abreast. We will maybe get back by Ballyburgh Ness Point yet. The Lord help us, it's our only chance. We can but try."

"My God! my child!" "My father, my dear father!" exclaimed the parent and daughter, as, fear lending them strength and speed, they turned to retrace their steps, and endeavoured to double the point, the projection of which formed the southern extremity of the bay.

"I heard ye were here frae the bit callant ye sent to meet your carriage," said the beggar, as he trudged stoutly on a step or two behind Miss Wardour, "and I couldna bide to think o' the dainty young leddy's peril, that has aye been kind to ilka forlorn heart that cam near her. Sae I lookit at the lift and the rin o' the tide, till I settled it that, if I could get down time eneugh to gie you warning, we wad do weel yet. But I doubt, I doubt, I have been beguiled! for what mortal ee ever saw sic a race as the tide is rinning e'en now? See, yonder's the Ratton's Skerry; he aye held his neb abune the water in my day, but he's aneath it now."

Sir Arthur cast a look in the direction in which the old man pointed. A huge rock, which in general, even in spring-tides, displayed a hulk like the keel of a large vessel, was now quite under water, and its place only indicated by the boiling and breaking of the eddying waves which encountered its submarine resistance.

"Mak haste, mak haste, my bonny leddy," continued the old man—"mak haste, and we may do yet! Take haud o' my arm; au auld and frail arm it's now, but it's been in as sair stress as this is yet. Take haud o' my arm, my winsome leddy! D'ye see yon wee black speck amang the wallowing waves yonder? This morning it was as high as the mast o' a brig; it's sma' eneugh now, but, while I see as muckle black about it as the crown o' my hat, I winna believe but we'll get round the Ballyburgh Ness, for a' that's come and gane yet."

Isabella, in silence, accepted from the old man the assistance which Sir Arthur was less able to afford her. The waves had now encroached so much upon the beach that the firm and smooth footing which they had hitherto had on the sand must be exchanged for a rougher path close to the foot of the precipice, and in some places even raised upon its lower ledges. It would have been utterly impossible for Sir Arthur Wardour or his daughter to have found their way along these shelves without the guidance and encouragement of the beggar, who had been there before in high tides, though never, be acknowledged, " in sae awesome a night as this."

It was indeed a dreadful evening. The howling of the storm mingled with the shrieks of the sea-fowl, and sounded like the dirge of the three devoted beings who, pent between two of the most magnificent yet most dreadful objects of nature —a raging tide and an insurmountable precipice—toiled along their painful and dangerous path, often lashed by the spray of some giant billow which threw itself higher on the beach than those that had preceded it. Each minute did their enemy gain ground perceptibly upon them! Still, however, loth to relinquish the last hopes of life, they bent their eyes on the black rock pointed out by Ochiltree. It was yet distinctly visible among the breakers, and continued to be so, until they came to a turn in their precarious path where an intervening projection of rock hid it from their sight. Deprived of the view of the beacon on which they had relied, they now experienced the double agony of terror and suspense. They struggled forward, however; but, when they arrived at the point from which they ought to have seen the crag, it was no longer visible. The signal of safety was lost among a thousand white breakers, which, dashing upon the point of the promontory, rose in prodigious sheets of snowy foam as high as the mast of a first-rate man-of-war against the dark brow of the precipice.

The countenance of the old man fell. Isabella gave a faint shriek, and " God have mercy upon us!" which her guide solemnly uttered, was piteously echoed by Sir Arthur: " My child! my child! to die such a death!"

" My father! my dear father!" his daughter exclaimed, clinging to him; " and you too, who have lost your own life in endeavouring to save ours!"

"That's not worth the counting," said the old man. "I hae lived to be weary o' life; and here or yonder—at the back o' a dyke, in a wreath o' snaw, or in the wame o' a wave, what signifies how the auld gaberlunzie dies?"

"Good man," said Sir Arthur, "can you think of nothing?— of no help? I'll make you rich; I'll give you a farm; I'll——"

"Our riches will be soon equal," said the beggar, looking out upon the strife of the waters; "they are sae already, for I hae nae land, and you would give your fair bounds and barony for a square yard of rock that would be dry for twal hours."

While they exchanged these words they paused upon the highest ledge of rock to which they could attain; for it seemed that any further attempt to move forward could only serve to anticipate their fate. Here, then, they were to await the sure though slow progress of the raging element, something in the situation of the martyrs of the early church, who, exposed by heathen tyrants to be slain by wild beasts, were compelled for a time to witness the impatience and rage by which the animals were agitated, while awaiting the signal for undoing their grates and letting them loose upon the victims.

Yet even this fearful pause gave Isabella time to collect the powers of a mind naturally strong and courageous, and which rallied itself at this terrible juncture. "Must we yield life," she said, "without a struggle? Is there no path, however dreadful, by which we could climb the crag, or at least attain some height above the tide, where we could remain till morning, or till help comes? They must be aware of our situation, and will raise the country to relieve us."

Sir Arthur, who heard but scarcely comprehended his daughter's question, turned, nevertheless, instinctively and eagerly to the old man, as if their lives were in his gift. Ochiltree paused. "I was a bauld craigsman," he said, "ance in my life, and mony a kittywake's and lungie's nest hae I harried up amang thae very black rocks; but it's lang, lang syne, and nae mortal could speel them without a rope; and if I had ane, my ee-sight and my footstep and my hand-grip hae a' failed mony a day sinsyne; and then how could I save *you?* But there was a path here ance, though maybe, if we could see it, ye would rather bide where we are. His name be praised!" he ejaculated suddenly, "there's ane coming down the crag e'en now!" Then, exalting his voice, he halloo'd out to the daring adventurer such instructions as his former practice, and the remembrance of local circumstances, suddenly forced upon his mind: "Ye're right, ye're right! that gate, that gate! Fasten the rope weel round Crummie's Horn, that's the muckle black stane; cast twa plies round it, that's it. Now, weize yoursell a wee easelward, a wee mair yet to that ither stane—we ca'd it the Cat's Lug. There used to be the root o' an aik-tree there. That will do! canny now, lad, canny now; tak tent and tak time, Lord bless ye, tak time. Vera weel! Now ye maun get to Bessy's Apron, that's the muckle braid flat blue stane; and then I think, wi' your help and the tow thegither, I'll win at ye, and then we'll be able to get up the young leddy and Sir Arthur."

The adventurer, following the directions of old Edie, flung him down the end of the rope, which he secured around Miss Wardour, wrapping her previously in his own blue gown, to preserve her as much as possible from injury. Then, availing himself of the rope, which was made fast at the other end, he began to ascend the face of the crag—a most precarious and dizzy undertaking, which, however, after one or two perilous escapes, placed him safe on the broad flat stone beside our friend Lovel. Their joint strength was able to raise Isabella to the place of safety which they had attained. Lovel then descended in order to assist Sir Arthur, around whom he adjusted the rope; and again mounting to their place of refuge, with the assistance of old Ochiltree, and such aid as Sir Arthur himself could afford, he raised himself beyond the reach of the billows.

The sense of reprieve from approaching and apparently inevitable death had its usual effect. The father and daughter threw themselves into each other's arms, kissed and wept for joy, although their escape was connected with the prospect of passing a tempestuous night upon a precipitous ledge of rock, which scarce afforded footing for the four shivering beings who now, like the sea-fowl around them, clung there in hopes of some shelter from the devouring element which raged beneath. The spray of the billows, which attained in fearful succession the foot of the precipice, overflowing the beach on which they so lately stood, flew as high as their place of temporary refuge; and the stunning sound with which they dashed against the rocks beneath seemed as if they still demanded the fugitives in accents of thunder as their destined prey. It was a summer night doubtless; yet the probability was slender that a frame so delicate as that of Miss Wardour should survive till morning the drenching of the spray; and the dashing of the rain, which now burst in full violence, accompanied with deep and heavy gusts of wind, added to the constrained and perilous circumstances of their situation.

"The lassie—the puir sweet lassie," said the old man; "mony such a night have I weathered at hame and abroad; but, God guide us! how can she ever win through it!"

His apprehension was communicated in smothered accents to Lovel; for, with the sort of freemasonry by which bold and ready spirits correspond in moments of danger, and become almost instinctively known to each other, they had established a mutual confidence. "I'll climb up the cliff again," said Lovel, "there's daylight enough left to see my footing—I'll climb up and call for more assistance."

"Do so, do so, for Heaven's sake!" said Sir Arthur, eagerly.

"Are ye mad?" said the mendicant. "Francie o' Fowlsheugh, and he was the best craigsman that ever speel'd heugh (mair by token, he brake his neck upon the Dunbuy of Slaines), wadna hae ventured upon the Halket Head craigs after sundown. It's God's grace, and a great wonder besides, that ye are not in the middle o' that roaring sea wi' what ye hae done already. I didna think there was the man left alive would hae come down the craigs as ye did. I question an I could hae done it mysell, at this hour and in this weather, in the youngest and yauldest of my strength.

But to venture up again—it's a mere and a clear tempting o' Providence."

"I have no fear," answered Lovel; "I marked all the stations perfectly as I came down, and there is still light enough left to see them quite well. I am sure I can do it with perfect safety. Stay here, my good friend, by Sir Arthur and the young lady."

"Deil be in my feet then," answered the bedesman sturdily; "if ye gang, I'll gang too; for between the twa o' us we'll hae mair than wark eneugh to get to the tap o' the heugh."

"No, no; stay you here and attend to Miss Wardour; you see Sir Arthur is quite exhausted."

"Stay yoursell then and I'll gae," said the old man; "let death spare the green corn and take the ripe."

"Stay both of you, I charge you," said Isabella, faintly; "I am well, and can spend the night very well here; I feel quite refreshed." So saying, her voice failed her; she sunk down, and would have fallen from the crag had she not been supported by Lovel and Ochiltree, who placed her in a posture half sitting, half reclining, beside her father, who, exhausted by fatigue of body and mind so extreme and unusual, had already sat down on a stone in a sort of stupor.

"It is impossible to leave them," said Lovel. "What is to be done? Hark! hark! Did I not hear a halloo?"

"The skreigh of a Tammie Norie," answered Ochiltree; "I ken the skirl weel."

"No, by Heaven!" replied Lovel, "it was a human voice."

A distant hail was repeated, the sound plainly distinguishable among the various elemental noises and the clang of the sea-mews by which they were surrounded. The mendicant and Lovel exerted their voices in a loud halloo, the former waving Miss Wardour's handkerchief on the end of his staff to make them conspicuous from above. Though the shouts were repeated, it was some time before they were in exact response to their own, leaving the unfortunate sufferers uncertain whether, in the darkening twilight and increasing storm, they had made the persons who apparently were traversing the verge of the precipice to bring them assistance sensible of the place in which they had found refuge. At length their halloo was regularly and distinctly answered, and their courage confirmed by the assurance that they were within hearing, if not within reach, of friendly assistance.

CHAPTER VIII.

There is a cliff, whose high and bending head
Looks fearfully on the confined deep;
Bring me but to the very brim of it,
And I'll repair the misery thou dost bear.
King Lear.

THE shout of human voices from above was soon augmented, and the gleam of torches mingled with those lights of evening which still remained amidst the darkness of the storm. Some attempt was made to hold communication between the assistants above and the sufferers beneath, who were still clinging to their precarious place of safety; but the howling of the tempest limited their intercourse to cries as inarticulate as those of the winged denizens of the crag, which shrieked in chorus, alarmed by the reiterated sound of human voices where they had seldom been heard.

On the verge of the precipice an anxious group had now assembled. Oldbuck was the foremost and most earnest, pressing forward with unwonted desperation to the very brink of the crag, and extending his head (his hat and wig secured by a handkerchief under his chin) over the dizzy height, with an air of determination which made his more timorous assistants tremble.

"Haud a care, haud a care, Monkbarns!" cried Caxon, clinging to the skirts of his patron, and withholding him from danger as far as his strength permitted. "God's sake, haud a care! Sir Arthur's drowned already, and an ye fa' over the cleugh too, there will be but ae wig left in the parish, and that's the minister's."

"Mind the peak there," cried Mucklebackit, an old fisherman and smuggler—"mind the peak. Steenie, Steenie Wilks, bring up the tackle. I'se warrant we'll sune heave them on board, Monkbarns, wad ye but stand out o' the gate."

"I see them," said Oldbuck—"I see them low down on that flat stone. Hilli-hilloa, hilli-ho-a!"

"I see them mysell weel eneugh," said Mucklebackit; "they are sitting down yonder like hoodiecraws in a mist; but d'ye think ye'll help them wi' skirling that gate like an auld skart before a flaw o' weather? Steenie, lad, bring up the mast. Odd, I'se hae them up as we used to bouse up the kegs o' gin and brandy lang syne. Get up the pickaxe, make a step for the mast, make the chair fast with the rattlin, haul taught and belay!"

The fishers had brought with them the mast of a boat, and as half of the country fellows about had now appeared, either out of zeal or curiosity, it was soon sunk in the ground and sufficiently secured. A yard across the upright mast, and a rope stretched along it, and reeved through a block at each end, formed an extempore crane, which afforded the means of lowering an arm-chair, well secured and fastened, down to the flat shelf on which the sufferers had roosted. Their joy at hearing the preparations going on for their deliverance was considerably qualified when they beheld the precarious vehicle by means of which they were to be conveyed to upper air. It swung about a yard free of the spot which they occupied, obeying each impulse of the tempest, the empty air all around it, and depending upon the security of a rope which in the increasing darkness had dwindled to an almost imperceptible thread. Besides the hazard of committing a human being to the vacant atmosphere in such a slight means of conveyance, there was the fearful danger of the chair and its occupant being dashed, either by the wind or the vibrations of the cord, against the rugged face of the precipice. But, to diminish the risk as much as possible, the experienced seamen had let down with the chair another line, which, being attached to it and held by the persons beneath, might serve by way of "gy," as Mucklebackit expressed it, to render its descent in some measure steady and regular. Still, to commit one's self in such a vehicle, through a howling tempest of wind and rain, with a beetling precipice above and a raging abyss below, required that courage which despair alone can inspire. Yet, wild as the sounds and sights of danger were, both above, beneath, and around, and doubtful and dangerous as the mode of escaping appeared to be, Lovel and the old mendicant agreed, after a moment's consultation, and after the former, by a sudden strong pull, had at his own imminent risk ascertained the security of the rope, that it would be best to secure Miss Wardour in the chair, and trust to the tenderness and care of those above for her being safely craned up to the top of the crag.

"Let my father go first," exclaimed Isabella; "for God's sake, my friends, place him first in safety."

"It cannot be, Miss Wardour," said Lovel; "your life must be first secured; the rope which bears your weight may——"

"I will not listen to a reason so selfish!"

"But ye maun listen to it, my bonny lassie," said Ochiltree, "for a' our lives depend on it; besides, when ye get on the tap o' the heugh yonder, ye can gie them a round guess o' what's ganging on in this Patmos o' ours; and Sir Arthur's far by that, as I am thinking."

Struck with the truth of this reasoning, she exclaimed: "True, most true; I am ready and willing to undertake the first risk! What shall I say to our friends above?"

"Just to look that their tackle does not graze on the face o' the craig, and to let the chair down, and draw it up hooly and fairly; we will halloo when we are ready."

With the sedulous attention of a parent to a child, Lovel bound Miss Wardour with his handkerchief, neckcloth, and the mendicant's leathern belt to the back and arms of the chair, ascertaining accurately the security of each knot, while Ochiltree kept Sir Arthur quiet. "What are ye doing wi' my bairn? What are ye doing? She shall not be separated from me. Isabel, stay with me, I command you."

"Lord sake, Sir Arthur, haud your tongue, and be thankful to God that there's wiser folk than you to manage this job," cried the beggar, worn out by the unreasonable exclamations of the poor Baronet.

"Farewell, my father," murmured Isabella; "farewell,

my—my friends"; and, shutting her eyes, as Edie's experience recommended, she gave the signal to Lovel, and he to those who were above. She rose, while the chair in which she sate was kept steady by the line which Lovel managed beneath. With a beating heart he watched the flutter of her white dress, until the vehicle was on a level with the brink of the precipice.

"Canny now, lads, canny now!" exclaimed old Mucklebackit, who acted as commodore; "swerve the yard a bit. Now—there! there she sits safe on dry land!"

A loud shout announced the successful experiment to her fellow-sufferers beneath, who replied with a ready and cheerful halloo. Monkbarns, in his ecstasy of joy, stripped his greatcoat to wrap up the young lady, and would have pulled off his coat and waistcoat for the same purpose, had he not been withheld by the cautious Caxon. "Haud a care o' us, your honour will be killed wi' the hoast; ye'll no get out o' your night-cowl this fortnight; and that will suit us unco ill. Na, na, there's the chariot down by, let twa o' the folk carry the young leddy there."

"You're right," said the Antiquary, readjusting the sleeves and collar of his coat—"you're right, Caxon; this is a naughty night to swim in. Miss Wardour, let me convey you to the chariot."

"Not for worlds, till I see my father safe."

In a few distinct words, evincing how much her resolution had surmounted even the mortal fear of so agitating a hazard, she explained the nature of the situation beneath, and the wishes of Lovel and Ochiltree.

"Right, right, that's right too; I should like to see the son of Sir Gamelyn de Guardover on dry land myself. I have a notion he would sign the abjuration oath, and the Ragman Roll to boot, and acknowledge Queen Mary to be nothing better than she should be, to get alongside my bottle of old port that he ran away from, and left scarce begun. But he's safe now, and here a' comes—(for the chair was again lowered, and Sir Arthur made fast in it, without much consciousness on his own part)—here a' comes; bowse away, my boys, canny wi' him.

A pedigree of a hundred links is hanging on a tenpenny tow; the whole barony of Knockwinnock depends on three plies of hemp; *respice finem, respice funem*—look to your end, look to a rope's end. Welcome, welcome, my good old friend, to firm land, though I cannot say to warm land or to dry land. A cord for ever against fifty fathom of water, though not in the sense of the base proverb; a fico for the phrase, better *sus. per funem* than *sus. per coll.*"

While Oldbuck ran on in this way, Sir Arthur was safely wrapped in the close embraces of his daughter, who, assuming that authority which the circumstances demanded, ordered some of the assistants to convey him to the chariot, promising to follow in a few minutes. She lingered on the cliff, holding an old countryman's arm, to witness probably the safety of those whose dangers she had shared.

"What have we here?" said Oldbuck, as the vehicle once more ascended. "What patched and weatherbeaten matter is this?" Then, as the torches illumined the rough face and grey hairs of old Ochiltree: "What! is it thou? Come, old mocker, I must needs be friends with thee; but who the devil makes up your party besides?"

"Ane that's weel worth ony twa o' us, Monkbarns: it's the young stranger lad they ca' Lovel; and he's behaved this blessed night as if he had three lives to rely on, and was willing to waste them a' rather than endanger ither folks.' Ca' hooly, sirs, as ye wad win an auld man's blessing! Mind there's naebody below now to haud the gy. Hae a care o' the Cat's Lug corner; bide weel aff Crummie's Horn!"

"Have a care indeed," echoed Oldbuck. "What! is it my *rara avis*, my black swan, my phœnix of companions in a post-chaise? Take care of him, Mucklebackit."

"As muckle care as if he were a greybeard o' brandy; and I canna take mair if his hair were like John Harlowe's. Yo ho, my hearts, bowse away with him!"

Lovel did, in fact, run a much greater risk than any of his precursors. His weight was not sufficient to render his ascent steady amid such a storm of wind, and he swung like an agitated pendulum at the mortal risk of being dashed against the rocks. But he was young, bold, and active, and, with the assistance of the beggar's stout piked staff, which he had retained by advice of the proprietor, contrived to bear himself from the face of the precipice, and the yet more hazardous projecting cliffs which varied its surface. Tossed in empty space like an idle and unsubstantial feather, with a motion that agitated the brain at once with fear and with dizziness, he retained his alertness of exertion and presence of mind; and it was not until he was safely grounded upon the summit of the cliff that he felt temporary and giddy sickness. As he recovered from a sort of half swoon he cast his eyes eagerly around. The object which they would most willingly have sought was already in the act of vanishing. Her white garment was just discernible as she followed on the path which her father had taken. She had lingered till she saw the last of their company rescued from danger, and until she had been assured by the hoarse voice of Mucklebackit that "the callant had come off wi' unbrizzed banes, and that he was but in a kind of dwam." But Lovel was not aware that she had expressed in his fate even this degree of interest, which, though nothing more than was due to a stranger who had assisted her in such an hour of peril, he would have gladly purchased by braving even more imminent danger than he had that evening been exposed to. The beggar she had already commanded to come to Knockwinnock that night. He made an excuse.—"Then to-morrow let me see you."

The old man promised to obey. Oldbuck thrust something into his hand. Ochiltree looked at it by the torchlight and returned it. "Na, na! I never tak gowd; besides, Monkbarns, ye wad aye be rueing it the morn." Then turning to the group of fishermen and peasants: "Now, sirs, wha will gie me a supper and some clean pease-strae?"

"I," "And I," "And I," answered many a ready voice.

"Aweel, since sae it is, and I can only sleep in ae barn at ance, I'll gae down wi' Saunders Mucklebackit; he has aye a soup o' something comfortable about his bigging; and, bairns, I'll maybe live to put ilka ane o' ye in mind some ither night that ye hae promised me quarters and my awmous"; and away he went with the fisherman.

Oldbuck laid the hand of strong possession on Lovel.—" Deil a stride ye's go to Fairport this night, young man; you must go home with me to Monkbarns. Why, man, you have been a hero—a perfect Sir William Wallace by all accounts. Come, my good lad, take hold of my arm; I am not a prime support in such a wind, but Caxon shall help us out. Here, you old idiot, come on the other side of me. And how the deil got you down to that infernal Bessy's Apron, as they call it? Bess, said they—why, curse her, she has spread out that vile pennon or banner of womankind, like all the rest of her sex, to allure her votaries to death and headlong ruin."

"I have been pretty well accustomed to climbing, and I have long observed fowlers practise that pass down the cliff."

"But how, in the name of all that is wonderful, came you to discover the danger of the pettish Baronet and his far more deserving daughter!"

"I saw them from the verge of the precipice."

"From the verge! umph. And what possessed you, *dumosa pendere procul de rupe?* though *dumosa* is not the appropriate epithet—what the deil, man, tempted ye to the verge of the craig?"

"Why, I like to see the gathering and growling of a coming storm; or, in your own classical language, Mr. Oldbuck, *suave est mari magno,* and so forth. But here we reach the turn to Fairport; I must wish you good-night."

"Not a step, not a pace, not an inch, not a shathmont, as I may say; the meaning of which word has puzzled many that think themselves antiquaries. I am clear we should read 'salmon length' for 'shathmont's length.' You are aware that the space allotted for the passage of a salmon through a dam, dike, or wier, by statute, is the length within which a full-grown pig can turn himself round. Now I have a scheme to prove that, as terrestrial objects were thus appealed to for ascertaining submarine measurement, so it must be supposed that the productions of the water were established as gages of the extent of land. Shathmont, salmont—you see the close alliance of the sounds; dropping out two *h's* and a *t*, and assuming an *l*, makes the whole difference. I wish to Heaven no antiquarian derivation had demanded heavier concessions."

"But, my dear sir, I really must go home; I am wet to the skin."

"Shalt have my nightgown, man, and slippers, and catch the antiquarian fever, as men do the plague, by wearing infected garments. Nay, I know what you would be at; you are afraid to put the old bachelor to charges. But is there not the remains of that glorious chicken-pie, which, *meo arbitrio*, is better cold than hot, and that bottle of my oldest port, out of which the silly brain-sick Baronet (whom I cannot pardon, since he has escaped breaking his neck) had just taken one glass when his infirm noddle went a wool-gathering after Gamelyn de Guardover?"

So saying, he dragged Lovel forward, till the Palmer's Port of Monkbarns received them. Never, perhaps, had it admitted two pedestrians more needing rest; for Monkbarns's fatigue had been in a degree very contrary to his usual habits, and his more young and robust companion had that evening undergone agitation of mind which had harassed and wearied him even more than his extraordinary exertions of body.

CHAPTER IX.

> "Be brave," she cried, "you yet may be our guest,
> Our haunted room was ever held the best.
> If, then, your valour can the sight sustain
> Of rustling curtains and the clinking chain;
> If your courageous tongue have powers to talk,
> When round your bed the horrid ghost shall walk;
> If you dare ask it why it leaves its tomb,
> I'll see your sheets well air'd, and show the room."
> *True Story.*

THEY reached the room in which they had dined, and were clamorously welcomed by Miss Oldbuck.

"Where's the younger womankind?" said the Antiquary.

"Indeed, brother, amang a' the steery Maria wadna be

guided by me; she set away to the Halket Craig-head. I
wonder ye didna see her."

"Eh! what—what's that you say, sister? Did the girl go
out in a night like this to the Halket Head? Good God! the
misery of the night is not ended yet!"

"But ye winna wait, Monkbarns; ye are so imperative and
impatient——"

"Tittle-tattle, woman," said the impatient and agitated
Antiquary, "where is my dear Mary?"

"Just where ye suld be yoursell, Monkbarns—upstairs and
in her warm bed."

"I could have sworn it," said Oldbuck, laughing, but obviously much relieved—"I could have sworn it; the lazy monkey
did not care if we were all drowned together. Why did you
say she went out?"

"But ye wadna wait to hear out my tale, Monkbarns. She
gaed out, and she came in again with the gardener sae sune
as she saw that nane o' ye were clodded ower the craig, and
that Miss Wardour was safe in the chariot; she was hame a
quarter of an hour syne, for it's now ganging ten; sair droukit
was she, puir thing, sae I e'en put a glass o' sherry in her
water-gruel."

"Right, Grizel, right; let womankind alone for coddling
each other. But hear ye, my venerable sister. Start not at
the word venerable; it implies many praiseworthy qualities
besides age; though that too is honourable, albeit it is the last
quality for which womankind would wish to be honoured. But
perpend my words; let Lovel and me have forthwith the relics
of the chicken-pie and the reversion of the port."

"The chicken-pie! the port! Ou dear! brother, there was
but a wheen banes and scarce a drap o' the wine."

The Antiquary's countenance became clouded, though he
was too well-bred to give way, in the presence of a stranger,
to his displeased surprise at the disappearance of the viands
on which he had reckoned with absolute certainty. But his
sister understood these looks of ire. "Ou dear! Monkbarns,
what's the use of making a wark?"

"I make no wark, as ye call it, woman."

"But what's the use o' looking sae glum and glunch about a pickle banes? An ye will hae the truth, ye maun ken the minister came in, worthy man; sair distressed he was, nae doubt, about your precarious situation, as he ca'd it (for ye ken how weel he's gifted wi' words), and here he wad bide till he could hear wi' certainty how the matter was likely to gang wi' ye a'. He said fine things on the duty of resignation to Providence's will, worthy man! that did he."

Oldbuck replied, catching the same tone: "Worthy man! he cared not how soon Monkbarns had devolved on an heir female, I've a notion. And while he was occupied in this Christian office of consolation against impending evil, I reckon that the chicken-pie and my good port disappeared?"

"Dear brother, how can you speak of sic frivolities, when you have had sic an escape from the craig?"

"Better than my supper has had from the minister's craig, Grizie; it's all discussed, I suppose?"

"Hout, Monkbarns, ye speak as if there was nae mair meat in the house. Wad ye not have had me offer the honest man some slight refreshment after his walk frae the manse?"

Oldbuck half-whistled, half-hummed, the end of the old Scottish ditty,

> Oh, first they eated the white puddings,
> And then they eated the black, O,
> And thought the gudeman unto himsell,
> The deil clink down wi' that, O!

His sister hastened to silence his murmurs, by proposing some of the relics of the dinner. He spoke of another bottle of wine, but recommended in preference a glass of brandy which was really excellent. As no entreaties could prevail on Lovel to indue the velvet nightcap and branched morning-gown of his host, Oldbuck, who pretended to a little knowledge of the medical art, insisted on his going to bed as soon as possible, and proposed to despatch a messenger (the indefatigable Caxon) to Fairport early in the morning to procure him a change of clothes.

This was the first intimation Miss Oldbuck had received that the young stranger was to be their guest for the night;

7

and such was the surprise with which she was struck by a proposal so uncommon that, had the superincumbent weight of her head-dress, such as we before described, been less preponderant, her grey locks must have started up on end and hurled it from its position.

"Lord haud a care o' us!" exclaimed the astounded maiden.

"What's the matter now, Grizel?"

"Wad ye but just speak a moment, Monkbarns?"

"Speak! What should I speak about? I want to get to my bed; and this poor young fellow—let a bed be made ready for him instantly."

"A bed! The Lord preserve us," again ejaculated Grizel.

"Why, what's the matter now? are there not beds and rooms enough in the house? Was it not an ancient *hospitium*, in which I am warranted to say beds were nightly made down for a score of pilgrims?"

"Oh dear, Monkbarns! wha kens what they might do lang syne? But in our time—beds! ay, troth, there's beds enow sic as they are, and rooms enow too; but ye ken yoursell the beds haena been sleepit in, Lord kens the time, or the rooms aired. If I had kenn'd, Mary and me might hae gane down to the manse. Miss Beckie is aye fond to see us; and sae is the minister, brother. But now, gude save us——!"

"Is there not the Green Room, Grizel?"

"Troth is there, and it is in decent order too, though naebody has sleepit there since Dr. Heavysterne, and——"

"And what?"

"And what! I'm sure ye ken yoursell what a night he had; ye wadna expose the young gentleman to the like o' that, wad ye?"

Lovel interfered upon hearing this altercation, and protested he would far rather walk home than put them to the least inconvenience; that the exercise would be of service to him; that he knew the road perfectly, by night or day, to Fairport; that the storm was abating, and so forth; adding all that civility could suggest as an excuse for escaping from a hospitality which seemed more inconvenient to his host than he could possibly have anticipated. But the howling of the wind and pattering of the rain against the windows, with his knowledge of the preceding fatigues of the evening, must have prohibited Oldbuck, even had he entertained less regard for his young friend than he really felt, from permitting him to depart. Besides, he was piqued in honour to show that he himself was not governed by womankind. "Sit ye down, sit ye down, sit ye down, man," he reiterated; "an ye part so, I would I might never draw a cork again, and here comes out one from a prime bottle of—strong ale, right *anno domini;* none of your wassia quassia decoctions, but brewed of Monkbarns barley. John of the Grinel never drew a better flagon to entertain a wandering minstrel or palmer with the freshest news from Palestine. And to remove from your mind the slightest wish to depart, know, that if you do so your character as a gallant knight is gone for ever. Why, 'tis an adventure, man, to sleep in the Green Room at Monkbarns. Sister, pray see it got ready. And, although the bold adventurer, Heavysterne, dree'd pain and dolour in that charmed apartment, it is no reason why a gallant knight like you, nearly twice as tall, and not half so heavy, should not encounter and break the spell."

"What! a haunted apartment, I suppose?"

"To be sure, to be sure; every mansion in this country of the slightest antiquity has its ghosts and its haunted chamber, and you must not suppose us worse off than our neighbours. They are going, indeed, somewhat out of fashion. I have seen the day when, if you had doubted the reality of the ghost in an old manor-house, you ran the risk of being made a ghost yourself, as Hamlet says. Yes, if you had challenged the existence of Redcowl in the castle of Glenstirym, old Sir Peter Pepperbrand would have had ye out to his courtyard, made you betake yourself to your weapon, and if your trick of fence were not the better, would have sticked you like a paddock on his own baronial middenstead. I once narrowly escaped such an affray; but I humbled myself and apologised to Redcowl; for, even in my younger days, I was no friend to the *monomachia* or duel, and would rather walk with Sir Priest than with Sir Knight; I care not who knows so much of my

valour. Thank God! I am old now, and can indulge my irri-
tabilities without the necessity of supporting them by cold
steel."

Here Miss Oldbuck re-entered with a singularly sage expression of countenance. " Mr. Lovel's bed's ready, brother—
clean sheets, weel aired, a spunk of fire in the chimney. I
am sure, Mr. Lovel (addressing him), it's no for the trouble;
and I hope you will have a good night's rest. But——"

" You are resolved," said the Antiquary, " to do what you
can to prevent it."

" Me? I am sure I have said naething, Monkbarns."

" My dear madam," said Lovel, " allow me to ask you the
meaning of your obliging anxiety on my account."

" Ou, Monkbarns does not like to hear of it; but he kens
himsell that the room has an ill name. It's weel minded that
it was there auld Rab Tull, the town-clerk, was sleeping when
he had that marvellous communication about the grand law-
plea between us and the feuars at the Mussel Craig. It had
cost a hantle siller, Mr. Lovel—for law-pleas were no carried
on without siller lang syne mair than they are now—and the
Monkbarns of that day—our gudesire, Mr. Lovel, as I said
before—was like to be waured afore the Session for want of a
paper. Monkbarns there kens weel what paper it was, but
I'se warrant he'll no help me out wi' my tale,—but it was a
paper of great significance to the plea, and we were to be
waured for want o't. Aweel, the cause was to come on before
the Fifteen—in presence, as they ca't—and auld Rab Tull,
the town-clerk, he cam ower to make a last search for the
paper that was wanting, before our gudesire gaed into Edinburgh to look after his plea; so there was little time to come
and gang on. He was but a doited snuffy body, Rab, as I've
heard; but then he was the town-clerk of Fairport, and the
Monkbarns heritors aye employed him on account of their
connexion wi' the burgh, ye ken."

" Sister Grizel, this is abominable," interrupted Oldbuck;
" I vow to Heaven ye might have raised the ghosts of every
abbot of Trotcosey since the days of Waldimir in the time you
have been detailing the introduction to this single spectre.

Learn to be succinct in your narrative. Imitate the concise style of old Aubrey, an experienced ghost-seer, who entered his memoranda on these subjects in a terse business-like manner; *exempli gratia:* 'At Cirencester, 5th March, 1670, was an apparition. Being demanded whether good spirit or bad, made no answer, but instantly disappeared with a curious perfume and a melodious twang.'—*Vide* his *Miscellanies,* p. 18, as well as I can remember, and near the middle of the page."

"Oh, Monkbarns, man! do ye think everybody is as book-learned as yoursell? But ye like to gar folk look like fools; ye can do that to Sir Arthur, and the minister his very sell."

"Nature has been beforehand with me, Grizel, in both these instances, and in another which shall be nameless; but take a glass of ale, Grizel, and proceed with your story, for it waxes late."

"Jenny's just warming your bed, Monkbarns, and ye maun e'en wait till she's done. Weel, I was at the search that our gudesire, Monkbarns that then was, made wi' auld Rab Tull's assistance; but ne'er-be-licket could they find that was to their purpose. And sae after they had touzled out mony a leather poke-full o' papers, the town-clerk had his drap punch at e'en to wash the dust out of his throat; we never were glass-breakers in this house, Mr. Lovel, but the body had got sic a trick of sippling and tippling wi' the bailies and deacons when they met (which was amaist ilka night) concerning the common gude o' the burgh, that he couldna weel sleep without it. But his punch he gat, and to bed he gaed; and in the middle of the night he gat a fearfu' wakening! He was never just himsell after it, and he was strucken wi' the dead palsy that very day four years. He thought, Mr. Lovel, that he heard the curtains o' his bed fissil, and out he lookit, fancying, puir man, it might hae been the cat. But he saw—God hae a care o' us, it gars my flesh aye creep, though I hae tauld the story twenty times—he saw a weel-fa'ard auld gentleman standing by his bedside in the moonlight, in a queer-fashioned dress, wi' mony a button and band-string about it, and that part o' his garments which it does not become a leddy to particulareeze was baith side and wide, and as mony plies o't as of ony Hamburgh skipper's. He had a beard too, and whiskers turned upwards on his upper-lip, as lang as baudrons'; and mony mair particulars there were that Rab Tull tauld o', but they are forgotten now; it's an auld story. Aweel, Rab was a just-living man for a country writer, and he was less fear'd than maybe might just hae been expected, and he asked in the name o' goodness what the apparition wanted. And the spirit answered in an unknown tongue. Then Rab said he tried him wi' Erse, for he cam in his youth frae the braes of Glenlivat; but it wadna do. Aweel, in this strait he bethought him of the twa or three words o' Latin that he used in making out the town's deeds, and he had nae sooner tried the spirit wi' that than out cam sic a blatter o' Latin about his lugs that poor Rab Tull, wha was nae great scholar, was clean ower-whelmed. Od, but he was a bauld body, and he minded the Latin name for the deed that he was wanting. It was something about a cart I fancy, for the ghaist cried aye, *Carter, carter*——"

"*Carta*, you transformer of languages," cried Oldbuck; "if my ancestor had learned no other language in the other world, at least he would not forget the Latinity for which he was so famous while in this."

"Weel, weel, *carta* be it then, but they ca'd it *carter* that tell'd me the story. It cried aye *carta*, if sae be that it was *carta*, and made a sign to Rab to follow it. Rab Tull keepit a Highland heart, and bang'd out o' bed and till some of his readiest claes; and he did follow the thing upstairs and down-stairs to the place we ca' the high dow-cot (a sort of a little tower in the corner of the auld house, where there was a rickle o' useless boxes and trunks), and there the ghaist gae Rab a kick wi' the tae foot, and a kick wi' the tother, to that very auld east-country tabernacle of a cabinet that my brother has standing beside his library table, and then disappeared like a fuff o' tobacco, leaving Rab in a very pitiful condition."

"*Tenues secessit in auras*," quoth Oldbuck. "Marry, sir, *mansit odor*. But, sure enough, the deed was there found in a drawer of this forgotten repository, which contained many other curious old papers, now properly labelled and arranged, and which seem to have belonged to my ancestor, the first possessor of Monkbarns. The deed thus strangely recovered was the original charter of erection of the abbey, abbey lands, and so forth, of Trotcosey, comprehending Monkbarns and others, into a lordship of regality in favour of the first Earl of Glengibber, a favourite of James the Sixth. It is subscribed by the King at Westminster, the seventeenth day of January, A.D. one thousand six hundred and twelve-thirteen. It's not worth while to repeat the witnesses' names."

"I would rather," said Lovel, with awakened curiosity—"I would rather hear your opinion of the way in which the deed was discovered."

"Why, if I wanted a patron for my legend, I could find no less a one than Saint Augustine, who tells the story of a deceased person appearing to his son, when sued for a debt which had been paid, and directing him where to find the discharge.[1] But I rather opine with Lord Bacon, who says that imagination is much akin to miracle-working faith. There was always some idle story of the room being haunted by the spirit of Aldobrand Oldenbuck, my great-great-great-grandfather,— it's a shame to the English language that we have not a less clumsy way of expressing a relationship of which we have occasion to think and speak so frequently. He was a foreigner, and wore his national dress, of which tradition had preserved an accurate description; and indeed there is a print of him, supposed to be by Reginald Elstracke, pulling the press with his own hand, as it works off the sheets of his scarce edition of the Augsburg Confession. He was a chemist as well as a good mechanic, and either of these qualities in this country was at that time sufficient to constitute a white witch at least. This superstitious old writer had heard all this, and probably believed it, and in his sleep the image and idea cf my ancestor recalled that of his cabinet, which, with the grateful attention to antiquities and the memory of our ancestors not unusually met with, had been pushed into the pigeon-house to be out of the way. Add a *quantum suffficit* of exaggeration, and you have a key to the whole mystery."

[1] See Mr. Rutherford's Dream. Note 2.

"Oh, brother, brother! But Dr. Heavysterne, brother, whose sleep was so sore broken that he declared he wadna pass another night in the Green Room to get all Monkbarns, so that Mary and I were forced to yield our——"

"Why, Grizel, the doctor is a good, honest, pudding-headed German, of much merit in his own way, but fond of the mystical, like many of his countrymen. You and he had a traffic the whole evening, in which you received tales of Mesmer, Schropfer, Cagliostro, and other modern pretenders to the mystery of raising spirits, discovering hidden treasure, and so forth, in exchange for your legends of the green bed-chamber; and considering that the *illustrissimus* ate a pound and a half of Scotch collops to supper, smoked six pipes, and drank ale and brandy in proportion, I am not surprised at his having a fit of the nightmare. But everything is now ready. Permit me to light you to your apartment, Mr. Lovel; I am sure you have need of rest, and I trust my ancestor is too sensible of the duties of hospitality to interfere with the repose which you have so well merited by your manly and gallant behaviour."

So saying, the Antiquary took up a bedroom candlestick of massive silver and antique form, which, he observed, was wrought out of the silver found in the mines of the Harz Mountains, and had been the property of the very personage who had supplied them with a subject for conversation. And having so said, he led the way through many a dusky and winding passage, now ascending and anon descending again, until he came to the apartment destined for his young guest.

CHAPTER X.

When midnight o'er the moonless skies
Her pall of transient death has spread,
When mortals sleep, when spectres rise,
And none are wakeful but the dead ;
No bloodless shape my way pursues,
No sheeted ghost my couch annoys,
Visions more sad my fancy views,—
Visions of long-departed joys.
W. R. SPENSER.

WHEN they reached the Green Room, as it was called, Old-buck placed the candle on the toilet-table, before a huge mirror with a black japanned frame, surrounded by dressing-boxes of the same, and looked around him with something of a disturbed expression of countenance. "I am seldom in this apartment," he said, "and never without yielding to a melancholy feeling; not, of course, on acccount of the childish nonsense that Grizel was telling you, but owing to circumstances of an early and unhappy attachment. It is at such moments as these, Mr. Lovel, that we feel the changes of time. The same objects are before us—those inanimate things which we have gazed on in wayward infancy and impetuous youth, in anxious and scheming manhood—they are permanent and the same; but when we look upon them in cold unfeeling old age, can we, changed in our temper, our pursuits, our feelings— changed in our form, our limbs, and our strength—can we be ourselves called the same? or do we not rather look back with a sort of wonder upon our former selves, as beings separate and distinct from what we now are? The philosopher who appealed from Philip inflamed with wine to Philip in his hours of sobriety did not choose a judge so different as if he had appealed from Philip in his youth 'to Philip in his old age. I cannot but be touched with the feeling so beautifully expressed in a poem which I have heard repeated:[1]

My eyes are dim with childish tears,
My heart is idly stirr'd,
For the same sound is in my ears
Which in those days I heard.

---

[1] Probably Wordsworth's *Lyrical Ballads* had not as yet been published.

> Thus fares it still in our decay ;
>   And yet the wiser mind
> Mourns less for what time takes away
>   Than what he leaves behind.

Well, time cures every wound, and though the scar may remain and occasionally ache, yet the earliest agony of its recent infliction is felt no more." So saying, he shook Lovel cordially by the hand, wished him good-night, and took his leave.

Step after step Lovel could trace his host's retreat along the various passages, and each door which he closed behind him fell with a sound more distant and dead. The guest, thus separated from the living world, took up the candle and surveyed the apartment. The fire blazed cheerfully. Mrs. Grizel's attention had left some fresh wood, should he choose to continue it, and the apartment had a comfortable, though not a lively appearance. It was hung with tapestry, which the looms of Arras had produced in the sixteenth century, and which the learned typographer, so often mentioned, had brought with him as a sample of the arts of the Continent. The subject was a hunting-piece; and as the leafy boughs of the forest-trees, branching over the tapestry, formed the predominant colour, the apartment had thence acquired its name of the Green Chamber. Grim figures, in the old ·Flemish dress, with slashed doublets covered with ribbands, short cloaks, and trunk-hose, were engaged in holding greyhounds or staghounds in the leash, or cheering them upon the objects of their game. Others, with boar-spears, swords, and old-fashioned guns, were attacking stags or boars whom they had brought to bay. The branches of the woven forest were crowded with fowls of various kinds, each depicted with its proper plumage. It seemed as if the prolific and rich invention of old Chaucer had animated the Flemish artist with its profusion, and Oldbuck had accordingly caused the following verses from that ancient and excellent poet to be embroidered in Gothic letters on a sort of border which he had added to the tapestry :

> Lo ! here be oakis grete, streight as a lime,
>   Under the which the grass, so fresh of line,

> Be'th newly sprung—at eight foot or nine.
> Everich tree well from his fellow grew
> With branches broad laden with leaves new,
> That sprongen out against the sonne sheene,
> Some golden red, and some a glad bright green.

And in another canton was the following similar legend:

> And many an hart and many an hind
> Was both before me and behind.
> Of fawns, sownders, bucks, and does
> Was full the wood, aud many roes,
> And many squirrells that ysate
> High on the trees and nuts ate.

The bed was of a dark and faded green, wrought to correspond with the tapestry, but by a more modern and less skilful hand. The large and heavy stuff-bottomed chairs, with black ebony backs, were embroidered after the same pattern, and a lofty mirror over the antique chimney-piece corresponded in its mounting with that on the old-fashioned toilet.

"I have heard," muttered Lovel, as he took a cursory view of the room and its furniture, "that ghosts often chose the best room in the mansion to which they attached themselves; and I cannot disapprove of the taste of the disembodied printer of the Augsburg Confession." But he found it so difficult to fix his mind upon the stories which had been told him, of an apartment with which they seemed so singularly to correspond, that he almost regretted the absence of those agitated feelings, half fear, half curiosity, which sympathise with the old legends of awe and wonder from which the anxious reality of his own hopeless passion at present detached him. For he now only felt emotions like those expressed in the lines—

> Ah! cruel maid, how hast thou changed
> The temper of my mind!
> My heart, by thee from all estranged,
> Becomes like thee unkind.

He endeavoured to conjure up something like the feelings which would at another time have been congenial to his situation, but his heart had no room for these vagaries of imagination. The recollection of Miss Wardour, determined not to acknowledge him when compelled to endure his society, and evincing her purpose to escape from it, would have alone occupied his imagination exclusively. But with this were united recollections more agitating if less painful—her hair-breadth escape, the fortunate assistance which he had been able to render her. Yet, what was his requital? She left the cliff while his fate was yet doubtful, while it was uncertain whether her preserver had not lost the life which he had exposed for her so freely. Surely gratitude, at least, called for some little interest in his fate. But no—she could not be selfish or unjust; it was no part of her nature. She only desired to shut the door against hope, and, even in compassion to him, to extinguish a passion which she could never return.

But this lover-like mode of reasoning was not likely to reconcile him to his fate, since the more amiable his imagination presented Miss Wardour, the more inconsolable he felt he should be rendered by the extinction of his hopes. He was, indeed, conscious of possessing the power of removing her prejudices on some points; but, even in extremity, he determined to keep the original determination which he had formed of ascertaining that she desired an explanation ere he intruded one upon her. And, turn the matter as he would, he could not regard his suit as desperate. There was something of embarrassment as well as of grave surprise in her look when Oldbuck presented him, and, perhaps, upon second thoughts, the one was assumed to cover the other. He would not relinquish a pursuit which had already cost him such pains. Plans, suiting the romantic temper of the brain that entertained them, chased each other through his head, thick and irregular as the motes of the sunbeam, and long after he had laid himself to rest continued to prevent the repose which he greatly needed. Then, wearied by the uncertainty and difficulties with which each scheme appeared to be attended, he bent up his mind to the strong effort of shaking off his love, "Like dew-drops from the lion's mane," and resuming those studies and that career of life which his unrequited affection had so long and so fruitlessly interrupted. In this last resolution he endeavoured to fortify himself by every argument which pride, as well as reason, could suggest.

"She shall not suppose," he said, "that, presuming on an accidental service to her or to her father, I am desirous to intrude myself upon that notice to which, personally, she considered me as having no title. I will see her no more. I will return to the land which, if it affords none fairer, has at least many as fair, and less haughty than Miss Wardour. To-morrow I will bid adieu to these northern shores, and to her who is as cold and relentless as her climate." When he had for some time brooded over this sturdy resolution, exhausted nature at length gave way, and, despite of wrath, doubt, and anxiety, he sunk into slumber.

It is seldom that sleep, after such violent agitation, is either sound or refreshing. Lovel's was disturbed by a thousand baseless and confused visions. He was a bird, he was a fish, or he flew like the one and swam like the other—qualities which would have been very essential to his safety a few hours before. Then Miss Wardour was a syren, or a bird of Paradise; her father a triton, or a sea-gull; and Oldbuck alternately a porpoise and a cormorant. These agreeable imaginations were varied by all the usual vagaries of a feverish dream: the air refused to bear the visionary, the water seemed to burn him; the rocks felt like down pillows as he was dashed against them; whatever he undertook failed in some strange and unexpected manner, and whatever attracted his attention underwent, as he attempted to investigate it, some wild and wonderful metamorphosis, while his mind continued all the while in some degree conscious of the delusion, from which it in vain struggled to free itself by awakening—feverish symptoms all, with which those who are haunted by the night-hag, whom the learned call Ephialtes, are but too well acquainted. At length these crude phantasmata arranged themselves into something more regular, if indeed the imagination of Lovel, after he awoke (for it was by no means the faculty in which his mind was least rich), did not gradually, insensibly, and unintentionally arrange in better order the scene of which his sleep presented, it may be, a less distinct outline. Or it is possible that his feverish agitation may have assisted him in forming the vision.

Leaving this discussion to the learned, we will say that, after a succession of wild images, such as we have above described, our hero, for such we must acknowledge him, so far regained a consciousness of locality as to remember where he was, and the whole furniture of the Green Chamber was depicted to his slumbering eye. And here, once more, let me protest that, if there should be so much old-fashioned faith left among this shrewd and sceptical generation as to suppose that what follows was an impression conveyed rather by the eye than by the imagination, I do not impugn their doctrine. He was then, or imagined himself, broad awake in the Green Chamber, gazing upon the flickering and occasional flame which the unconsumed remnants of the fagots sent forth, as one by one they fell down upon the red embers, into which the principal part of the boughs to which they belonged had crumbled away. Insensibly the legend of Aldobrand Oldenbuck, and his mysterious visits to the inmates of the chamber, awoke in his mind, and with it, as we often feel in dreams, an anxious and fearful expectation, which seldom fails instantly to summon up before our mind's eye the object of our fear. Brighter sparkles of light flashed from the chimney with such intense brilliancy as to enlighten all the room. The tapestry waved wildly on the wall, till its dusky forms seemed to become animated. The hunters blew their horns, the stag seemed to fly, the boar to resist, and the hounds to assail the one and pursue the other; the cry of deer, mangled by throttling dogs, the shouts of men, and the clatter of horses' hoofs, seemed at once to surround him; while every group pursued, with all the fury of the chase, the employment in which the artist had represented them as engaged. Lovel looked on this strange scene devoid of wonder (which seldom intrudes itself upon the sleeping fancy), but with an anxious sensation of awful fear. At length an individual figure among the tissued huntsmen, as he gazed upon them more fixedly, seemed to leave the arras and to approach the bed of the slumberer. As he drew near his figure appeared to alter. His bugle-horn became a brazen clasped volume; his hunting-cap changed to such a furred headgear as graces the burgomasters of Rembrandt; his Flemish garb remained, but his features, no longer agitated with the fury of the chase, were changed to such a state of awful and stern composure as might best pourtray the first proprietor of Monkbarns, such as he had been described to Lovel by his descendants in the course of the preceding evening. As this metamorphosis took place the hubbub among the other personages in the arras disappeared from the imagination of the dreamer, which was now exclusively bent on the single figure before him. Lovel strove to interrogate this awful person in the form of exorcism proper for the occasion; but his tongue, as is usual in frightful dreams, refused its office and clung palsied to the roof of his mouth. Aldobrand held up his finger, as if to impose silence upon the guest who had intruded on his apartment, and began deliberately to unclasp the venerable volume which occupied his left hand. When it was unfolded he turned over the leaves hastily for a short space, and then raising his figure to its full dimensions, and holding the book aloft in his left hand, pointed to a passage in the page which he thus displayed. Although the language was unknown to our dreamer, his eye and attention were both strongly caught by the line which the figure seemed thus to press upon his notice, the words of which appeared to blaze with a supernatural light, and remained riveted upon his memory. As the vision shut his volume a strain of delightful music seemed to fill the apartment. Lovel started and became completely awake. The music, however, was still in his ears, nor ceased till he could distinctly follow the measure of an old Scottish tune.

He sate up in bed, and endeavoured to clear his brain of the phantoms which had disturbed it during this weary night. The beams of the morning sun streamed through the half-closed shutters, and admitted a distinct light into the apartment. He looked round upon the hangings, but the mixed groups of silken and worsted huntsmen were as stationary as tenter-hooks could make them, and only trembled slightly as the early breeze, which found its way through an open crevice of the latticed window, glided along their surface. Lovel leapt out of bed, and, wrapping himself in a morning-gown that had been considerately laid by his bedside, stepped towards the window, which commanded a view of the sea, the roar of whose billows announced it still disquieted by the storm of the preceding evening, although the morning was fair and serene. The window of a turret, which projected at an angle with the wall, and thus came to be very near Lovel's apartment, was half open, and from that quarter he heard again the same music which had probably broken short his dream. With its visionary character it had lost much of its charms; it was now nothing more than an air on the harpsichord, tolerably well performed—such is the caprice of imagination as affecting the fine arts. A female voice sung, with some taste and great simplicity, something between a song and a hymn, in words to the following effect:

> " Why sit'st thou by that ruin'd hall,
>   Thou aged carle so stern and grey?
> Dost thou its former pride recall,
>   Or ponder how it pass'd away?"
>
> " Know'st thou not me!" the Deep Voice cried;
>   " So long enjoy'd, so oft misused,
> Alternate, in thy fickle pride,
>   Desired, neglected and accused?
>
> "Before my breath, like blazing flax,
>   Man and his marvels pass away,
> And changing empires wane and wax,
>   Are founded, flourish, and decay.
>
> " Redeem mine hours—the space is brief—
>   While in my glass the sand-grains shiver,
> And measureless thy joy or grief,
>   When TIME and thou shall part for ever!"

While the verses were yet singing, Lovel had returned to his bed; the train of ideas which they awakened was romantic and pleasing, such as his soul delighted in, and, willingly adjourning till more broad day the doubtful task of determining on his future line of conduct, he abandoned himself to the pleasing languor inspired by the music, and fell into a sound and refreshing sleep, from which he was only awakened at a late hour by old Caxon, who came creeping into the room to render the offices of a *valet-de-chambre*.

"I have brushed your coat, sir," said the old man, when he perceived Lovel was awake; "the callant brought it frae Fairport this morning, for that ye had on yesterday is scantly feasibly dry, though it's been a' night at the kitchen fire; and I hae cleaned your shoon. I doubt ye'll no be wanting me to tie your hair, for (with a gentle sigh) a' the young gentlemen wear crops now, but I hae the curling-tangs here to gie it a bit turn ower the brow, if ye like, before ye gae down to the leddies."

Lovel, who was by this time once more on his legs, declined the old man's professional offices, but accompanied the refusal with such a douceur as completely sweetened Caxon's mortification.

"It's a pity he disna get his hair tied and pouthered," said the ancient frizeur, when he had got once more into the kitchen, in which, on one pretence or other, he spent three-parts of his idle time—that is to say, of his whole time—"it's a great pity, for he's a comely young gentleman."

"Hout awa, ye auld gowk," said Jenny Rintherout, "would ye creesh his bonny brown hair wi' your nasty ulyie, and then moust it like the auld minister's wig? Ye'll be for your breakfast, I'se warrant? Hae, there's a soup o' parritch for ye; it will set ye better to be slaistering at them and the lapper-milk than meddling wi' Mr. Lovel's head; ye wad spoil the maist natural and beautifaest head o' hair in a' Fairport, baith burgh and county."

The poor barber sighed over the disrespect into which his art had so universally fallen, but Jenny was a person too important to offend by contradiction; so, sitting quietly down in the kitchen, he digested at once his humiliation and the contents of a bicker which held a Scotch pint of substantial oatmeal porridge.

8

CHAPTER XI.

Sometimes he thinks that Heaven this pageant sent
And order'd all the pageants as they went;
Sometimes that only 'twas wild Fancy's play,
The loose and scatter'd relics of the day.

WE must now request our readers to adjourn to the break-fast-parlour of Mr. Oldbuck, who, despising the modern slops of tea and coffee, was substantially regaling himself, *more majorum*, with cold roast-beef and a glass of a sort of bever-age called "mum," a species of fat ale brewed from wheat and bitter herbs, of which the present generation only know the name by its occurrence in revenue acts of parliament, coupled with cider, perry, and other excisable commodities. Lovel, who was seduced to taste it, with difficulty refrained from pronouncing it detestable, but *did* refrain, as he saw he should otherwise give great offence to his host, who had the liquor annually prepared with peculiar care, according to the approved recipe bequeathed to him by the so often mentioned Aldobrand Oldenbuck. The hospitality of the ladies offered Lovel a breakfast more suited to modern taste, and while he was engaged in partaking of it he was assailed by indirect in-quiries concerning the manner in which he had passed the night.

"We canna compliment Mr. Lovel on his looks this morn-ing, brother; but he winna condescend on any ground of dis-turbance he has had in the night-time. I am certain he looks very pale, and when he came here he was as fresh as a rose."

"Why, sister, consider this rose of yours has been knocked about by sea and wind all yesterday evening, as if he had been a bunch of kelp or tangle, and how the devil would you have him retain his colour?"

"I certainly do still feel somewhat fatigued," said Lovel, "notwithstanding the excellent accommodations with which your hospitality so amply supplied me."

"Ah, sir!" said Miss Oldbuck, looking at him with a knowing smile, or what was meant to be one, "ye'll not allow of ony inconvenience, out of civility to us."

"Really, madam," replied Lovel, "I had no disturbance; for I cannot term such the music with which some kind fairy favoured me."

"I doubted Mary wad waken you wi' her skreighing; she didna ken I had left open a chink of your window, for, forbye the ghaist, the Green Room disna vent weel in a high wind. But I am judging ye heard mair than Mary's lilts yestreen; weel, men are hardy creatures, they can gae through wi' a' thing. I am sure had I been to undergo ony thing of that nature—that's to say, that's beyond nature—I would hae skreigh'd out at once and raised the house, be the consequence what liket; and I dare say the minister wad hae done as mickle, and sae I hae tauld him. I ken naebody but my brother, Monkbarns himsell, wad gae through the like o't, if, indeed, it binna you, Mr. Lovel."

"A man of Mr. Oldbuck's learning, madam," answered the questioned party, "would not be exposed to the inconvenience sustained by the Highland gentleman you mentioned last night."

"Ay! ay! ye understand now where the difficulty lies—language? He has ways o' his ain wad banish a' thae sort o' worriecows as far as the hindermost parts of Gideon (meaning possibly Midian), as Mr. Blattergowl says; only ane wadna be uncivil to ane's forebear though he be a ghaist. I am sure I will try that receipt of yours, brother, that ye showed me in a book, if ony body is to sleep in that room again, though I think, in Christian charity, ye should rather fit up the matted room; it's a wee damp and dark, to be sure, but then we hae sae seldom occasion for a spare bed."

"No, no, sister; dampness and darkness are worse than spectres, ours are spirits of light; and I would rather have you try the spell."

"I will do that blythely, Monkbarns, an I had the ingredients, as my cookery book ca's them. There was vervain and dill, I mind that—Davie Dibble will ken about them, though maybe he'll gie them Latin names—and peppercorn, we hae walth o' them, for——"

"Hypericon, thou foolish woman!" thundered Oldbuck; "d'ye suppose you're making a haggis; or do you think that a spirit, though he be formed of air, can be expelled by a receipt against wind? This wise Grizel of mine, Mr. Lovel, recollects—with what accuracy you may judge—a charm which I once mentioned to her, and which, happening to hit her superstitious noddle, she remembers better than anything tending to a useful purpose I may chance to have said for this ten years. But many an old woman besides herself——"

"Auld woman! Monkbarns," said Miss Oldbuck, roused something above her usual submissive tone, "ye really are less than civil to me."

"Not less than just, Grizel; however, I include in the same class many a sounding name, from Jamblichus down to Aubrey, who have wasted their time in devising imaginary remedies for non-existing diseases. But I hope, my young friend, that, charmed or uncharmed, secured by the potency of Hypericon,

> With vervain and with dill,
> That hinder witches of their will,

or left disarmed and defenceless to the inroads of the invisible world, you will give another night to the terrors of the haunted apartment, and another day to your faithful and feal friends."

"I heartily wish I could, but——"

"Nay, 'But me no buts'; I have set my heart upon it."

"I am greatly obliged, my dear sir, but——"

"Look ye there now—'but' again! I hate 'but'; I know no form of expression in which he can appear that is amiable excepting as a butt of sack. 'But' is to me a more detestable combination of letters than 'no' itself. 'No' is a surly, honest fellow, speaks his mind rough and round at once. 'But' is a sneaking, evasive, half-bred, exceptious sort of a conjunction, which comes to pull away the cup just when it is at your lips.

> It does allay
> The good precedent; fie upon 'but yet'!
> 'But yet' is as a jailor to bring forth
> Some monstrous malefactor."

"Well, then," answered Lovel, whose motions were really undetermined at the moment, "you shall not connect the recollection of my name with so churlish a particle; I must soon think of leaving Fairport, I am afraid, and I will, since you are good enough to wish it, take this opportunity of spending another day here."

"And you shall be rewarded, my boy. First you shall see John o' the Girnel's grave, and then we'll walk gently along the sands, the state of the tide being first ascertained—for we will have no more Peter Wilkins' adventures, no more Glum and Gawrie work,—as far as Knockwinnock Castle, and inquire after the old knight and my fair foe, which will be but barely civil, and then——"

"I beg pardon, my dear sir; but perhaps you had better adjourn your visit till to-morrow. I am a stranger, you know."

"And are, therefore, the more bound to show civility, I should suppose. But I beg your pardon for mentioning a word that perhaps belongs only to a collector of antiquities. I am one of the old school,

> When courtiers gallop'd o'er four counties
> The ball's fair partner to behold,
> And humbly hope she caught no cold."

"Why, if—if—if you thought it would be expected; but I believe I had better stay."

"Nay, nay, my good friend, I am not so old-fashioned as to press you to what is disagreeable, neither; it is sufficient that I see there is some *remora*, some cause of delay, some mid impediment, which I have no title to inquire into. Or you are still somewhat tired perhaps; I warrant I find means to entertain your intellects without fatiguing your limbs. I am no friend to violent exertion myself—a walk in the garden once a day is exercise enough for any thinking being, none but a fool or a fox-hunter would require more. Well, what shall we set about—my *Essay on Castrametation?* but I have that *in petto* for our afternoon cordial. Or I will show you the controversy upon *Ossian's Poems* between Mac-Cribb and me; I hold with the acute Orcadian, he with the defenders of the authenticity. The controversy began in smooth, oily, lady-like terms, but is now waxing more sour and eager as we get on; it already partakes somewhat of old Scaliger's style. I fear the rogue will get some scent of that story of Ochiltree's; but at worst I have a hard repartee for him on the affair of the abstracted Antigonus. I will show you his last epistle, and the scroll of my answer; egad, it is a trimmer!"

So saying, the Antiquary opened a drawer and began rummaging among a quantity of miscellaneous papers, ancient and modern. But it was the misfortune of this learned gentleman, as it may be that of many learned and unlearned, that he frequently experienced on such occasions what harlequin calls *l'embarras des richesses;* in other words, the abundance of his collection often prevented him from finding the article he sought for. "Curse the papers! I believe," said Oldbuck, as he shuffled them to and fro—"I believe they make themselves wings like grasshoppers and fly away bodily; but here, in the mean while, look at that little treasure." So saying, he put into his hand a case made of oak, fenced at the corner with silver roses and studs. "Pr'ythee undo this button," said he, as he observed Lovel fumbling at the clasp. He did so, the lid opened, and discovered a thin quarto curiously bound in black shagreen: "There, Mr. Lovel, there is the work I mentioned to you last night—the rare quarto of the Augsburg Confession, the foundation at once and the bulwark of the Reformation, drawn up by the learned and venerable Melancthon, defended by the Elector of Saxony and the other valiant hearts who stood up for their faith, even against the front of a powerful and victorious emperor, and imprinted by the scarcely less venerable and praiseworthy Aldobrand Oldenbuck, my happy progenitor, during the yet more tyrannical attempts of Philip II. to suppress at once civil and religious liberty. Yes, sir, for printing this work that eminent man was expelled from his ungrateful country, and driven to establish his household gods even here at Monkbarns, among the ruins of papal superstition and domination. Look upon his venerable effigies, Mr. Lovel, and respect the honourable occupation in which it presents him, as labouring personally at the press for the diffusion of Christian and political knowledge. And see here his favourite motto, expressive of his independence and self-reliance, which scorned to owe anything to patronage that was not earned by desert—expressive also of that firmness of mind and tenacity of purpose recommended by Horace. He was, indeed, a man who would have stood firm had his whole printing-house, presses, founts, forms, great and small pica, been shivered to pieces around him. Read, I say, his motto; for each printer had his motto or device when that illustrious art was first practised. My ancestor's was expressed, as you see, in the Teutonic phrase, *Kunst macht Gunst;* that is, skill or prudence in availing ourselves of our natural talents and advantages will compel favour and patronage, even where it is withheld from prejudice or ignorance."

"And that," said Lovel, after a moment's thoughtful silence —"that then is the meaning of these German words?"

"Unquestionably; you perceive the appropriate application to a consciousness of inward worth, and of eminence in an useful and honourable art. Each printer in those days, as I have already informed you, had his device, his impresa, as I may call it, in the same manner as the doughty chivalry of the age, who frequented tilt and tournament. My ancestor boasted as much in his as if he had displayed it over a conquered field of battle, though it betokened the diffusion of knowledge, not the effusion of blood. And yet there is a family tradition which affirms him to have chosen it from a more romantic circumstance."

"And what is that said to have been, my good sir?" inquired his young friend.

"Why, it rather encroaches on my respected predecessor's fame for prudence and wisdom; *sed semel insanivimus omnes* —everybody has played the fool in their turn. It is said my ancestor, during his apprenticeship with the descendant of old Fust, whom popular tradition hath sent to the devil under the name of Faustus, was attracted by a paltry slip of womankind, his master's daughter, called Bertha. They broke rings, or went through some idiotical ceremony, as is usual on such idle occasions as the plighting of a true-love troth, and Aldo-brand set out on his journey through Germany, as became an honest *handwerker ;* for such was the custom of mechanics at that time, to make a tour through the empire, and work at their trade for a time in each of the most eminent towns, be-fore they finally settled themselves for life. It was a wise custom; for, as such travellers were received like brethren in each town by those of their own handicraft, they were sure in every case to have the means either of gaining or communicat-ing knowledge. When my ancestor returned to Nuremburgh he is said to have found his old master newly dead, and two or three gallant young suitors, some of them half-starved sprigs of nobility forsooth, in pursuit of the Yungfrau Bertha, whose father was understood to have bequeathed her a dowry which might weigh against sixteen armorial quarters. But Bertha, not a bad sample of womankind, had made a vow she would only marry that man who could work her father's press. The skill at that time was as rare as wonderful: be-sides, that the expedient rid her at once of most of her "gentle" suitors, who would have as soon wielded a conjuring wand as a composing stick. Some of the more ordinary typog-raphers made the attempt; but none were sufficiently pos-sessed of the mystery. But I tire you."

"By no means; pray, proceed, Mr. Oldbuck. I listen with uncommon interest."

"Ah! it is all folly. However, Aldobrand arrived in the ordinary dress, as we would say, of a journeyman printer—the same with which he had traversed Germany, and con-versed with Luther, Melancthon, Erasmus, and other learned men, who disdained not his knowledge, and the power he possessed of diffusing it, though hid under a garb so homely. But what appeared respectable in the eyes of wisdom, religion, learning, and philosophy seemed mean, as might readily be supposed, and disgusting, in those of silly and affected womankind, and Bertha refused to acknowledge her former lover in the torn doublet, skin cap, clouted shoes, and leath-ern apron of a travelling handicraftsman or mechanic. He

claimed his privilege, however, of being admitted to a trial;
and when the rest of the suitors had either declined the contest, or made such work as the devil could not read if his
pardon depended on it, all eyes were bent on the stranger.
Aldobrand stepped gracefully forward, arranged the types
without omission of a single letter, hyphen, or comma, imposed them without deranging a single space, and pulled off
the first proof as clear and free from errors as if it had been
a triple revise! All applauded the worthy successor of the
immortal Faustus, the blushing maiden acknowledged her
error in trusting to the eye more than the intellect, and the
elected bridegroom thenceforward chose for his impress or
device the appropriate words, "Skill wins favour." But what
is the matter with you? you are in a brown study? Come,
I told you this was but trumpery conversation for thinking
people; and now I have my hand on the Ossianic controversy."

"I beg your pardon," said Lovel; "I am going to appear
very silly and changeable in your eyes, Mr. Oldbuck, but you
seemed to think Sir Arthur might in civility expect a call
from me?"

"Psha, psha, I can make your apology; and if you must
leave us so soon as you say, what signifies how you stand in
his honour's good graces? And I warn you that the *Essay on
Castrametation* is something prolix, and will occupy the time
we can spare after dinner, so you may lose the Ossianic controversy if we do not dedicate this morning to it. We will
go out to my evergreen bower, my sacred holly tree yonder,
and have it *fronde super viridi.*

> Sing hey-ho! hey-ho! for the green holly,
> Most friendship is feigning, most loving mere folly.

But, egad," continued the old gentleman, "when I look
closer at you I begin to think you may be of a different opinion. Amen, with all my heart; I quarrel with no man's
hobby, if he does not run it a tilt against mine; and if he
does, let him beware his eyes. What say you? in the language of the world and worldlings base, if you can condescend
to so mean a sphere, shall we stay or go?"

"In the language of selfishness then, which is of course the language of the world, let us go by all means."

" 'Amen, amen, quo' the earl marshal,' " answered Oldbuck, as he exchanged his slippers for a pair of stout walking shoes, with "cutikins," as he called them, of black cloth. He only interrupted the walk by a slight deviation to the tomb of John o' the Girnel, remembered as the last bailiff of the abbey who had resided at Monkbarns. Beneath an old oak tree upon a hillock, sloping pleasantly to the south, and catching a distant view of the sea over two or three rich inclosures and the Mussel Crag, lay a moss-grown stone, and, in memory of the departed worthy, it bore an inscription, of which, as Mr. Oldbuck affirmed (though many doubted), the defaced characters could be distinctly traced to the following effect:

> Heir lyeth John o' ye Girnell,
> Erth has ye nit and heuen ye kirnell.
> In hys tyme ilk wyfe's hennis clokit,
> Ilka gud mannis herth wi bairnis was stokit,
> He deled a boll o' bear in firlottis fyve,
> Four for ye halie kirke and ane for pure mennis wyvis.

"You see how modest the author of this sepulchral commendation was: he tells us that honest John could make five firlots, or quarters, as you would say, out of the boll, instead of four; that he gave the fifth to the wives of the parish, and accounted for the other four to the abbot and chapter; that in his time the wives' hens always laid eggs, and devil thank them, if they got one-fifth of the abbey rents; and that honest men's hearths were never unblest with offspring—an addition to the miracle which they, as well as I, must have considered as perfectly unaccountable. But come on; leave we Jock o' the Girnel, and let us jog on to the yellow sands, where the sea, like a repulsed enemy, is now retreating from the ground on which he gave us battle last night."

Thus saying, he led the way to the sands. Upon the links or downs close to them were seen four or five huts inhabited by fishers, whose boats, drawn high upon the beach, lent the odoriferous vapours of pitch melting under a burning sun to contend with those of the offals of fish and other nuisances usually collected round Scottish cottages. Undisturbed by these complicated steams of abomination, a middle-aged woman, with a face which had defied a thousand storms, sat mending a net at the door of one of the cottages. A handkerchief close bound about her head, and a coat which had formerly been that of a man, gave her a masculine air, which was increased by her strength, uncommon stature, and harsh voice. "What are ye for the day, your honour?" she said, or rather screamed, to Oldbuck—"caller haddocks and whitings, a bannock-fluke and a cock-padle?"

"How much for the bannock-fluke and cock-padle?" demanded the Antiquary.

"Four white shillings and saxpence," answered the Naiad.

"Four devils and six of their imps!" retorted the Antiquary; "do ye think I am mad, Maggie?"

"And div ye think," rejoined the virago, setting her arms akimbo, "that my man and my sons are to gae to the sea in weather like yestreen and the day—sic a sea as it's yet outby—and get naething for their fish, and be misca'd into the bargain, Monkbarns? It's no fish ye're buying: it's men's lives."

"Well, Maggie, I'll bid you fair: I'll bid you a shilling for the fluke and the cock-padle, or sixpence separately; and if all your fish are as well paid, I think your man, as you call him, and your sons, will make a good voyage."

"Deil gin their boat were knockit against the Bell Rock rather! it wad be better, and the bonnier voyage o' the twa. A shilling for thae twa bonnie fish! Od, that's ane indeed!"

"Well, well, you old beldam, carry your fish up to Monkbarns and see what my sister will give you for them."

"Na, na, Monkbarns, deil a fit. I'll rather deal wi' yoursell; for, though you're near eneugh, yet Miss Grizel has an unco close grip. I'll gie ye them (in a softened tone) for three-and-saxpence."

"Eighteen-pence, or nothing!"

"Eighteen-pence!!!" in a loud tone of astonishment, which declined into a sort of rueful whine when the dealer turned as if to walk away. "Ye'll no be for the fish then?" Then louder, as she saw him moving off: "I'll gie them—and—and—and a half-a-dozen o' partans to make the sauce, for three shillings and a dram."

"Half-a-crown then, Maggie, and a dram."

"Aweel, your honour maun hae't your ain gate, nae doubt; but a dram's worth siller now, the distilleries is no working."

"And I hope they'll never work again in my time," said Oldbuck.

"Ay, ay; it's easy for your honour and the like o' you gentlefolks to say sae, that hae stouth and routh, and fire and fending, and meat and claith, and sit dry and canny by the fireside; but an ye wanted fire, and meat, and dry claise, and were deeing o' cauld, and had a sair heart, whilk is warst ava', wi' just tippence in your pouch, wadna ye be glad to buy a dram wi't, to be eilding and claise, and a supper and heart's ease into the bargain, till the morn's morning?"

"It's even too true an apology, Maggie. Is your goodman off to sea this morning, after his exertions last night?"

"In troth is he, Monkbarns; he was awa this morning by four o'clock, when the sea was working like barm wi' yestreen's wind, and our bit coble dancing in't like a cork."

"Well, he's an industrious fellow. Carry the fish up to Monkbarns."

"That I will—or I'll send little Jenny, she'll rin faster; but I'll ca' on Miss Grizie for the dram mysell, and say ye sent me."

A nondescript animal, which might have passed for a mermaid, as it was paddling in a pool among the rocks, was summoned ashore by the shrill screams of its dam; and having been made decent, as her mother called it, which was performed by adding a short red cloak to a petticoat, which was at first her sole covering, and which reached scantily below her knee, the child was dismissed with the fish in a basket, and a request on the part of Monkbarns that they might be prepared for dinner. "It would have been long," said Oldbuck, with much self-complacency, "ere my womankind could have made such a reasonable bargain with that old skinflint, though they sometimes wrangle with her for an hour together under my study window, like three sea-gulls screaming and sputtering in a gale of wind. But, come, wend we on our way to Knockwinnock."

CHAPTER XII.

Beggar! The only freeman of your commonwealth;
Free above Scot-free, that observe no laws,
Obey no governor, use no religion
But what they draw from their own ancient custom,
Or constitute themselves, yet they are no rebels.
BROME.

WITH our readers' permission we will outstep the slow though sturdy pace of the Antiquary, whose halts, as he turned round to his companion at every moment to point out something remarkable in the landscape, or to enforce some favourite topic more emphatically than the exercise of walking permitted, delayed their progress considerably.

Notwithstanding the fatigues and dangers of the preceding evening, Miss Wardour was able to rise at her usual hour, and to apply herself to her usual occupations, after she had first satisfied her anxiety concerning her father's state of health. Sir Arthur was no farther indisposed than by the effects of great agitation and unusual fatigue, but these were sufficient to induce him to keep his bedchamber.

To look back on the events of the preceding day was to Isabella a very unpleasing retrospect. She owed her life, and that of her father, to the very person by whom, of all others, she wished least to be obliged, because she could hardly even express common gratitude towards him without encouraging hopes which might be injurious to them both. "Why should it be my fate to receive such benefits, and conferred at so much personal risk, from one whose romantic passion I have so unceasingly laboured to discourage? Why should chance have given him this advantage over me? and why, oh why, should a half-subdued feeling in my own bosom, in spite of my sober reason, almost rejoice that he has attained it!"

While Miss Wardour thus taxed herself with wayward caprice, she beheld advancing down the avenue, not her younger and more dreaded preserver, but the old beggar who had made such a capital figure in the melodrama of the preceding evening.

She rang the bell for her maid-servant. "Bring the old man upstairs."

The servant returned in a minute or two. "He will come up at no rate, madam; he says his clouted shoes never were on a carpet in his life, and that, please God, they never shall. Must I take him into the servants' hall?"

"No; stay, I want to speak with him. Where is he?" for she had lost sight of him as he approached the house.

"Sitting in the sun on the stone-bench in the court, beside the window of the flagged parlour."

"Bid him stay there; I'll come down to the parlour and speak with him at the window."

She came down accordingly, and found the mendicant half-seated, half-reclining upon the bench beside the window. Edie Ochiltree, old man and beggar as he was, had apparently some internal consciousness of the favourable impressions connected with his tall form, commanding features, and long white beard and hair. It used to be remarked of him, that he was seldom seen but in a posture which showed these personal attributes to advantage. At present, as he lay half-reclined, with his wrinkled yet ruddy cheek and keen grey eye turned up towards the sky, his staff and bag laid beside him, and a cast of homely wisdom and sarcastic irony in the expression of his countenance, while he gazed for a moment around the courtyard, and then resumed his former look upward, he might have been taken by an artist as the model of an old philosopher of the Cynic school, musing upon the frivolity of mortal pursuits, and the precarious tenure of human possessions, and looking up to the source from which aught permanently good can alone be derived. The young lady, as she presented her tall and elegant figure at the open window, but divided from the courtyard by a grating, with which, according to the fashion of ancient times, the lower windows of the castle were secured, gave an interest of a different kind, and might be supposed by a romantic imagination an imprisoned damsel communicating a tale of her durance to a palmer, in order that he might call upon the gallantry of every knight whom he should meet in his wanderings to rescue her from her oppressive thraldom.

After Miss Wardour had offered, in the terms she thought would be most acceptable, those thanks which the beggar declined as far beyond his merit, she began to express herself in a manner which she supposed would speak more feelingly to his apprehension. "She did not know," she said, "what her father intended particularly to do for their preserver, but certainly it would be something that would make him easy for life; if he chose to reside at the castle she would give orders——"

The old man smiled and shook his head. "I wad be baith a grievance and a disgrace to your fine servants, my leddy, and I have never been a disgrace to ony body yet, that I ken of."

"Sir Arthur would give strict orders——"

"Ye're very kind, I doubtna, I doubtna; but there are some things a master can command and some he canna. I dare say he wad gar them keep hands aff me—and troth, I think they wad hardly venture on that ony gate—and he wad gar them gie me my soup parritch and bit meat. But trow ye that Sir Arthur's command could forbid the gibe o' the tongue or the blink o' the ee, or gar them gie me my food wi' the look o' kindness that gars it digest sae weel, or that he could make them forbear a' the slights and taunts that hurt ane's spirit mair nor downright misca'ing? Besides, I am the idlest auld carle that ever lived; I downa be bound down to hours o' eating and sleeping; and, to speak the honest truth, I wad be a very bad example in ony weel-regulated family."

"Well then, Edie, what do you think of a neat cottage and a garden, and a daily dole, and nothing to do but to dig a little in your garden when you pleased yourself?"

"An how often wad that be, trow ye, my leddy? maybe no ance atween Candlemas and Yule. And if a' thing were done to my hand as if I was Sir Arthur himsell, I could never bide the staying still in ae place, and just seeing the same joists and couples aboon my head night after night. And then I have a queer humour o' my ain, that sets a strolling beggar weel eneugh, whase word naebody minds; but ye ken Sir Arthur has odd sort o' ways, and I wad be jesting or scorning at them, and ye wad be angry, and then I wad be just fit to hang mysell."

"Oh, you are a licensed man," said Isabella; "we shall give you all reasonable scope. So you had better be ruled, and remember your age."

"But I am no that sair failed yet," replied the mendicant. "Od, ance I gat a wee soupled yestreen I was as yauld as an eel. And then what wad a' the country about do for want o' auld Edie Ochiltree, that brings news and country cracks frae ae farm-steading to anither, and gingerbread to the lasses, and helps the lads to mend their fiddles, and the guidwives to clout their pans, and plaits rush-swords and grenadier caps for the weans, and busks the laird's flees, and has skill o' cow-ills and horse-ills, and kens mair auld sangs and tales than a' the barony besides, and gars ilka body laugh wherever he comes? Troth, my leddy, I canna lay down my vocation: it would be a public loss."

"Well, Edie, if your idea of your importance is so strong as not to be shaken by the prospect of independence——"

"Na, na, Miss; it's because I am mair independent as I am," answered the old man. "I beg nae mair at ony single house than a meal o' meat, or maybe but a mouthfu o't; if it's refused at ae place, I get it at anither, sae I canna be said to depend on ony body in particular, but just on the country at large."

"Well, then, only promise me that you will let me know should you ever wish to settle as you turn old, and more incapable of making your usual rounds; and in the mean time take this."

"Na, na, my leddy; I downa take muckle siller at anes, it's against our rule; and——though it's maybe no civil to be repeating the like o' that——they say that siller's like to be

scarce wi' Sir Arthur himsell, and that he's run himsell out
o' thought wi' his houkings and minings for lead and copper
yonder."

Isabella had some anxious anticipations to the same effect,
but was shocked to hear that her father's embarrassments
were such public talk; as if scandal ever failed to stoop upon
so acceptable a quarry as the failings of the good man, the
decline of the powerful, or the decay of the prosperous. Miss
Wardour sighed deeply. "Well, Edie, we have enough to
pay our debts, let folks say what they will, and requiting you
is one of the foremost; let me press this sum upon you."

"That I might be robbed and murdered some night between
town and town? or, what's as bad, that I might live in constant apprehension o't? I am no (lowering his voice to a
whisper and looking keenly around him)—I am no that clean
unprovided for neither; and though I should die at the back
of a dike, they'll find as muckle quilted in this auld blue
gown as will bury me like a Christian, and gie the lads and
lasses a blythe lykewake too; sae there's the gaberlunzie's
burial provided for, and I need nae mair. Were the like o'
me ever to change a note, wha the deil d'ye think wad be sic
fules as to gie me charity after that? It wad flee through the
country like wild-fire that auld Edie suld hae done siccan a
like thing, and then I'se warrant I might grane my heart out
or ony body wad gie me either a bane or a bodle."

"Is there nothing, then, that I can do for you?"

"Ou ay! I'll aye come for my awmous as usual; and whiles
I wad be fain o' a pickle sneeshin, and ye maun speak to the
constable and ground-officer just to owerlook me, and maybe
ye'll gie a gude word for me to Sandie Netherstanes, the
miller, that he may chain up his muckle dog; I wadna hae
him to hurt the puir beast, for it just does its office in bark-
ing at a gaberlunzie like me. And there's ae thing maybe mair, but ye'll think it's very bauld o' the like o' me to
speak o't."

"What is it, Edie? if it respects you it shall be done, if it
is in my power."

"It respects yoursell, and it is in your power, and I maun

9

come out wi't.   Ye are a bonny young leddy, and a gude ane,
and maybe a weel-tochered ane; but dinna ye sneer awa the
lad Lovel, as ye did a while sinsyne on the walk beneath the
Brierybank, when I saw ye baith, and heard ye too, though
ye saw nae me.   Be canny wi' the lad, for he loes ye weel,
and it's to him, and no to ony thing I could have done for
you, that Sir Arthur and you wan ower yestreen."

He uttered these words in a low but distinct tone of voice;
and, without waiting for an answer, walked towards a low
door which led to the apartments of the servants, and so entered the house.

Miss Wardour remained for a moment or two in the situation in which she had heard the old man's last extraordinary
speech, leaning, namely, against the bars of the window, nor
could she determine upon saying even a single word relative
to a subject so delicate until the beggar was out of sight.   It
was, indeed, difficult to determine what to do.   That her
having had an interview and private conversation with this
young and unknown stranger should be a secret possessed by
a person of the last class in which a young lady would seek a
confidant, and at the mercy of one who was by profession
gossip-general to the whole neighbourhood, gave her acute
agony.   She had no reason, indeed, to suppose that the old
man would wilfully do anything to hurt her feelings, much
less to injure her; but the mere freedom of speaking to her
upon such a subject showed, as might have been expected, a
total absence of delicacy; and what he might take it into his
head to do or say next, *that* she was pretty sure so professed
an admirer of liberty would not hesitate to do or say without
scruple.   This idea so much hurt and vexed her that she half-
wished the officious assistance of Lovel and Ochiltree had been
absent upon the preceding evening.

While she was in this agitation of spirits, she suddenly observed Oldbuck and Lovel entering the court.   She drew instantly so far back from the window that she could, without
being seen, observe how the Antiquary paused in front of the
building, and, pointing to the various scutcheons of its former
owners, seemed in the act of bestowing upon Lovel much

curious and erudite information, which, from the absent look of his auditor, Isabella might shrewdly guess was entirely thrown away. The necessity that she should take some resolution became instant and pressing; she rang, therefore, for a servant, and ordered him to show the visitors to the drawing-room, while she, by another staircase, gained her own apartment, to consider, ere she made her appearance, what line of conduct were fittest for her to pursue. The guests, agreeably to her instructions, were introduced into the room where company was usually received.

CHAPTER XIII.

> The time was that I hated thee,
> And yet it is not that I bear thee love.
> Thy company, which erst was irksome to me,
> I will endure—
> But do not look for further recompense.
>
> *As You Like It.*

MISS ISABELLA WARDOUR'S complexion was considerably heightened when, after the delay necessary to arrange her ideas, she presented herself in the drawing-room.

"I am glad you are come, my fair foe," said the Antiquary, greeting her with much kindness, "for I have had a most refractory, or at least negligent, auditor, in my young friend here, while I endeavoured to make him acquainted with the history of Knockwinnock Castle. I think the danger of last night has mazed the poor lad. But you, Miss Isabel, why, you look as if flying through the night air had been your natural and most congenial occupation. Your colour is even better than when you honoured my *hospitium* yesterday. And Sir Arthur—how fares my good old friend?"

"Indifferently well, Mr. Oldbuck; but, I am afraid, not quite able to receive your congratulations, or to pay—to pay— Mr. Lovel his thanks for his unparalleled exertions."

"I dare say not. A good down pillow for his good white

head were more meet than a couch so churlish as Bessy's Apron, plague on her!"

"I had no thought of intruding," said Lovel, looking upon the ground, and speaking with hesitation and suppressed emotion—"I did not—did not mean to intrude upon Sir Arthur or Miss Wardour the presence of one who—who must necessarily be unwelcome—as associated, I mean, with painful reflections."

"Do not think my father so unjust and ungrateful," said Miss Wardour. "I dare say," she continued, participating in Lovel's embarrassment—"I daresay—I am certain—that my father would be happy to show his gratitude—in any way, that is, which Mr. Lovel could consider it as proper to point out."

"Why, the deuce!" interrupted Oldbuck, "what sort of a qualification is that? On my word, it reminds me of our minister, who, choosing, like a formal old fop as he is, to drink to my sister's inclinations, thought it necessary to add the saving clause, 'Provided, madam, they be virtuous.' Come, let us have no more of this nonsense. I dare say Sir Arthur will bid us welcome on some future day. And what news from the kingdom of subterranean darkness and airy hope? What says the swart spirit of the mine? Has Sir Arthur had any good intelligence of his adventure lately in Glen Withershins?"

Miss Wardour shook her head: "But indifferent, I fear, Mr. Oldbuck; but there lie some specimens which have lately been sent down."

"Ah! my poor dear hundred pounds, which Sir Arthur persuaded me to give for a share in that hopeful scheme, would have bought a porter's load of mineralogy. But let me see them."

And so saying, he sat down at the table in the recess, on which the mineral productions were lying, and proceeded to examine them, grumbling and pshawing at each which he took up and laid aside.

In the mean time Lovel, forced as it were by this secession of Oldbuck into a sort of *tête-à-tête* with Miss Wardour, took an opportunity of addressing her in a low and interrupted tone of voice. "I trust Miss Wardour will impute to circumstances almost irresistible this intrusion of a person who has reason to think himself—so unacceptable a visitor."

"Mr. Lovel," answered Miss Wardour, observing the same tone of caution, "I trust you will not—I am sure you are incapable of abusing the advantages given to you by the services you have rendered us, which, as they affect my father, can never be sufficiently acknowledged or repaid. Could Mr. Lovel see me without his own peace being affected—could he see me as a friend—as a sister—no man will be—and, from all I have ever heard of Mr. Lovel, ought to be—more welcome; but——"

Oldbuck's anathema against the preposition "but" was internally echoed by Lovel.—"Forgive me if I interrupt you, Miss Wardour. You need not fear my intruding upon a subject where I have been already severely repressed; but do not add to the severity of repelling my sentiments the rigour of obliging me to disavow them."

"I am much embarrassed, Mr. Lovel," replied the young lady, "by your—I would not willingly use a strong word— your romantic and hopeless pertinacity. It is for yourself I plead, that you would consider the calls which your country has upon your talents, that you will not waste, in an idle and fanciful indulgence of an ill-placed predilection, time which, well redeemed by active exertion, should lay the foundation of future distinction; let me entreat that you would form a manly resolution——"

"It is enough, Miss Wardour; I see plainly that——"

"Mr. Lovel, you are hurt, and, believe me, I sympathise in the pain which I inflict; but can I, in justice to myself, in fairness to you, do otherwise? Without my father's consent I never will entertain the addresses of any one, and how totally impossible it is that he should countenance the partiality with which you honour me, you are yourself fully aware; and, indeed——"

"No, Miss Wardour," answered Lovel, in a tone of passionate entreaty, "do not go farther—is it not enough to crush every hope in our present relative situation?—do not carry your resolutions farther; why urge what would be your conduct if Sir Arthur's objections could be removed?"

"It is indeed vain, Mr. Lovel," said Miss Wardour, "because their removal is impossible; and I only wish, as your friend, and as one who is obliged to you for her own and her father's life, to entreat you to suppress this unfortunate attachment, to leave a country which affords no scope for your talents, and to resume the honourable line of the profession which you seem to have abandoned."

"Well, Miss Wardour, your wishes shall be obeyed. Have patience with me one little month, and if in the course of that space I cannot show you such reasons for continuing my residence at Fairport as even you shall approve of, I will bid adieu to its vicinity, and with the same breath to all my hopes of happiness."

"Not so, Mr. Lovel; many years of deserved happiness, founded on a more rational basis than your present wishes, are, I trust, before you. But it is full time to finish this conversation. I cannot force you to adopt my advice. I cannot shut the door of my father's house against the preserver of his life and mine; but the sooner Mr. Lovel can teach his mind to submit to the inevitable disappointment of wishes which have been so rashly formed, the more highly he will rise in my esteem; and, in the mean while, for his sake as well as mine, he must excuse my putting an interdict upon conversation on a subject so painful."

A servant at this moment announced that Sir Arthur desired to speak with Mr. Oldbuck in his dressing-room.

"Let me show you the way," said Miss Wardour, who apparently dreaded a continuation of her *tête-à-tête* with Lovel, and she conducted the Antiquary accordingly to her father's apartment.

Sir Arthur, his legs swathed in flannel, was stretched on the couch. "Welcome, Mr. Oldbuck," he said; "I trust you have come better off than I have done from the inclemency of yesterday evening?"

"Truly, Sir Arthur, I was not so much exposed to it: I kept *terra firma;* you fairly committed yourself to the cold night-air in the most literal of all senses. But such adventures become a gallant knight better than a humble esquire—to rise on the wings of the night-wind, to dive into the bowels of the earth. What news from our subterranean Good Hope—the *terra incognita* of Glen Withershins?"

"Nothing good as yet," said the Baronet, turning himself hastily, as if stung by a pang of the gout; "but Dousterswivel does not despair."

"Does he not?" quoth Oldbuck; "I do though, under his favour. Why, old Dr. H——n [1] told me, when I was in Edinburgh, that we should never find copper enough, judging from the specimens I showed him, to make a pair of sixpenny knee-buckles; and I cannot see that those samples on the table below differ much in quality."

"The learned doctor is not infallible, I presume?"

"No; but he is one of our first chemists; and this tramping philosopher of yours, this Dousterswivel, is, I have a notion, one of those learned adventurers described by Kircher, *Artem habent sine arte, partem sine parte, quorum medium est mentiri, vita eorum mendicatum ire ;* that is to say, Miss Wardour——"

"It is unnecessary to translate," said Miss Wardour, "I comprehend your general meaning; but I hope Mr. Dousterswivel will turn out a more trustworthy character."

"I doubt it not a little," said the Antiquary, "and we are a foul way out if we cannot discover this infernal vein that he has prophesied about these two years."

"*You* have no great interest in the matter, Mr. Oldbuck," said the Baronet.

"Too much, too much, Sir Arthur; and yet, for the sake of my fair foe here, I would consent to lose it all so you had no more on the venture."

There was a painful silence of a few moments, for Sir Arthur was too proud to acknowledge the downfall of his golden dreams, though he could no longer disguise to himself that such was likely to be the termination of the adventure. "I understand," he at length said, "that the young gentleman to whose gallantry and presence of mind we were so much in-

[1] Probably Dr. Hutton, the celebrated geologist.

debted last night has favoured me with a visit; I am distressed that I am unable to see him, or indeed any one but an old friend like you, Mr. Oldbuck."

A declination of the Antiquary's stiff backbone acknowledged the preference.

"You made acquaintance with this young gentleman in Edinburgh, I suppose?"

Oldbuck told the circumstances of their becoming known to each other.

"Why, then, my daughter is an older acquaintance of Mr. Lovel than you are," said the Baronet.

"Indeed! I was not aware of that," answered Oldbuck, somewhat surprised.

"I met Mr. Lovel," said Isabella, slightly colouring, "when I resided this last spring with my aunt, Mrs. Wilmot."

"In Yorkshire? and what character did he bear then, or how was he engaged?" said Oldbuck; "and why did not you recognise him when I introduced you?"

Isabella answered the least difficult question, and passed over the other. "He had a commission in the army, and had, I believe, served with reputation; he was much respected as an amiable and promising young man."

"And pray, such being the case," replied the Antiquary, not disposed to take one reply in answer to two distinct questions, "why did you not speak to the lad at once when you met him at my house? I thought you had less of the paltry pride of womankind about you, Miss Wardour."

"There was a reason for it," said Sir Arthur, with dignity; "you know the opinions—prejudices, perhaps you will call them—of our house concerning purity of birth. This young gentleman is, it seems, the illegitimate son of a man of fortune; my daughter did not choose to renew their acquaintance till she should know whether I approved of her holding any intercourse with him."

"If it had been with his mother instead of himself," answered Oldbuck, with his usual dry causticity of humour, "I could see an excellent reason for it. Ah, poor lad! that was the cause then that he seemed so absent and confused while

I explained to him the reason of the bend of bastardy upon the shield yonder under the corner turret!"

"True," said the Baronet with complacency, "it is the shield of Malcolm the Usurper, as he is alled. The tower which he built is termed, after him, Malcolm's Tower, but more frequently Misticot's Tower, which I conceive to be a corruption for 'Misbegot.' He is denominated, in the Latin pedigree of our family, *Milcolumbus Nothus ;* and his temporary seizure of our property, and most unjust attempt to establish his own illegitimate line in the estate of Knockwinnock, gave rise to such family feuds and misfortunes as strongly to found us in that horror and antipathy to defiled blood and illegitimacy which has been handed down to me from my respected ancestry."

"I know the story," said Oldbuck, "and I was telling it to Lovel this moment, with some of the wise maxims and consequences which it has engrafted on your family politics. Poor fellow! he must have been much hurt· I took the wavering of his attention for negligence, and was something piqued at it, and it proves to be only an excess of feeling. I hope, Sir Arthur, you will not think the less of your life because it has been preserved by such assistance?"

"Nor the less of my assistant either," said the Baronet; "my doors and table shall be equally open to him as if he had descended of the most unblemished lineage."

"Come, I am glad of that; he'll know where he can get a dinner, then, if he wants one. But what views can he have in this neighbourhood? I must catechise him; and if I find he wants it—or, indeed, whether he does or not—he shall have my best advice." As the Antiquary made this liberal promise, he took his leave of Miss Wardour and her father, eager to commence operations upon Mr. Lovel. He informed him abruptly that Miss Wardour sent her compliments, and remained in attendance on her father, and then, taking him by the arm, he led him out of the castle.

Knockwinnock still preserved much of the external attributes of a baronial castle. It had its drawbridge, though now never drawn up, and its dry moat, the sides of which had been planted with shrubs, chiefly of the evergreen tribes. Above these rose the old building, partly from a foundation of red rock scarped down to the sea-beach, and partly from the steep green verge of the moat. The trees of the avenue have been already mentioned, and many others rose around of large size, as if to confute the prejudice that timber cannot be raised near to the ocean. Our walkers paused and looked back upon the castle as they attained the height of a small knoll, over which lay their homeward road, for it is to be supposed they did not tempt the risk of the tide by returning along the sands. The building flung its broad shadow upon the tufted foliage of the shrubs beneath it, while the front windows sparkled in the sun. They were viewed by the gazers with very different feelings. Lovel, with the fond eagerness of that passion which derives its food and nourishment from trifles, as the cameleon is said to live on the air, or upon the invisible insects which it contains, endeavoured to conjecture which of the numerous windows belonged to the apartment now graced by Miss Wardour's presence. The speculations of the Antiquary were of a more melancholy cast, and were partly indicated by the ejaculation of "*Cito peritura!*" as he turned away from the prospect. Lovel, roused from his reverie, looked at him as if to inquire the meaning of an exclamation so ominous. The old man shook his head. "Yes, my young friend," said he, "I doubt greatly—and it wrings my heart to say it—this ancient family is going fast to the ground!"

"Indeed!" answered Lovel. "You surprise me greatly!"

"We harden ourselves in vain," continued the Antiquary, pursuing his own train of thought and feeling—"we harden ourselves in vain to treat with the indifference they deserve the changes of this trumpery whirligig world. We strive ineffectually to be the self-sufficing invulnerable being, the *teres atque rotundus* of the poet; the stoical exemption which philosophy affects to give us over the pains and vexations of human life is as imaginary as the state of mystical quietism and perfection aimed at by some crazy enthusiasts."

"And Heaven forbid that it should be otherwise!" said Lovel, warmly—"Heaven forbid that any process of philosophy were capable so to sear and indurate our feelings that nothing should agitate them but what arose instantly and immediately out of our own selfish interests! I would as soon wish my hand to be as callous as horn, that it might escape an occasional cut or scratch, as I would be ambitious of the stoicism which should render my heart like a piece of the nether millstone."

The Antiquary regarded his youthful companion with a look half of pity, half of sympathy, and shrugged up his shoulders as he replied: "Wait, young man—wait till your bark has been battered by the storm of sixty years of mortal vicissitude; you will learn by that time to reef your sails, that she may obey the helm; or, in the language of this world, you will find distresses enough, endured and to endure, to keep your feelings and sympathies in full exercise, without concerning yourself more in the fate of others than you cannot possibly avoid."

"Well, Mr. Oldbuck, it may be so; but as yet I resemble you more in your practice than in your theory, for I cannot help being deeply interested in the fate of the family we have just left."

"And well you may," replied Oldbuck; "Sir Arthur's embarrassments have of late become so many and so pressing that I am surprised you have not heard of them. And then his absurd and expensive operations carried on by this High-German landlouper, Dousterswivel——"

"I think I have seen that person, when by some rare chance I happened to be in the coffee-room at Fairport—a tall, beetle-browed, awkward-built man, who entered upon scientific subjects, as it appeared to my ignorance at least, with more assurance than knowledge, was very arbitrary in laying down and asserting his opinions, and mixed the terms of science with a strange jargon of mysticism; a simple youth whispered me that he was an *Illuminé*, and carried on an intercourse with the invisible world."

"Oh, the same—the same; he has enough of practical knowledge to speak scholarly and wisely to those of whose intelligence he stands in awe; and, to say the truth, this faculty, joined to his matchless impudence, imposed upon me for some time when I first knew him. But I have since understood that, when he is among fools and womankind, he exhibits himself as a perfect charlatan—talks of the *magisterium*, of sympathies and antipathies, of the cabala, of the divining rod, and all the trumpery with which the Rosycrucians cheated a darker age, and which, to our eternal disgrace, has in some degree revived in our own. My friend Heavysterne knew this fellow abroad, and unintentionally—for he, you must know, is, God bless the mark, a sort of believer—let me into a good deal of his real character. Ah! were I caliph for a day, as honest Abou Hassan wished to be, I would scourge me these jugglers out of the commonwealth with rods of scorpions. They debauch the spirit of the ignorant and credulous with mystical trash as effectually as if they had besotted their brains with gin, and then pick their pockets with the same facility. And now has this strolling blackguard and mountebank put the finishing blow to the ruin of an ancient and honourable family!"

"But how could he impose upon Sir Arthur to any ruinous extent?"

"Why, I don't know; Sir Arthur is a good honourable gentleman, but, as you may see from his loose ideas concerning the Pikish language, he is by no means very strong in the understanding. His estate is strictly entailed, and he has been always an embarrassed man. This rapparee promised him mountains of wealth, and an English company was found to advance large sums of money—I fear on Sir Arthur's guarantee. Some gentlemen—I was ass enough to be one—took small shares in the concern, and Sir Arthur himself made great outlay; we were trained on by specious appearances and more specious lies, and now, like John Bunyan, we awake and behold it is a dream."

"I am surprised that you, Mr. Oldbuck, should have encouraged Sir Arthur by your example."

"Why," said Oldbuck, dropping his large grizzled eyebrow, "I am something surprised and ashamed at it myself. It was not the lucre of gain: nobody cares less for money, to be a prudent man, than I do; but I thought I might risk this small sam.   It will be expected, though I am sure I cannot see why, that I should give something to any one who will be kind enough to rid me of that slip of womankind, my niece, Mary M'Intyre; and perhaps it may be thought I should do something to get that jackanapes, her brother, on in the army.   In either case, to treble my venture would have helped me out. And, besides, I had some idea that the Phœnicians had in former times wrought copper in that very spot.   That cunning scoundrel, Dousterswivel, found out my blunt side, and brought strange tales, d—n him! of appearances of old shafts, and vestiges of mining operations, conducted in a manner quite different from those of modern times; and I—in short, I was a fool, and there is an end.   My loss is not much worth speaking about; but Sir Arthur's engagements are, I understand, very deep, and my heart aches for him, and the poor young lady who must share his distress."

Here the conversation paused, until renewed in the next chapter.

CHAPTER XIV.

> It I may trust the flattering eye of sleep,
> My dreams presage some joyful news at hand.
> My bosom's lord sits lightly on his throne,
> And all this day an unaccustom'd spirit
> Lifts me above the ground with cheerful thoughts.
> *Romeo and Juliet.*

THE account of Sir Arthur's unhappy adventure had led Oldbuck somewhat aside from his purpose of catechising Lovel concerning the cause of his residence at Fairport.   He was now, however, resolved to open the subject.   "Miss Wardour was formerly known to you, she tells me, Mr. Lovel?"

"He had had the pleasure," Lovel answered, "to see her at Mrs. Wilmot's, in Yorkshire."

"Indeed! you never mentioned that to me before, and you did not accost her as an old acquaintance."

"I—-I did not know," said Lovel, a good deal embarrassed,

"it was the same lady till we met; and then it was my duty to wait till she should recognise me."

"I am aware of your delicacy; the knight's a punctilious old fool, but I promise you his daughter is above all nonsensical ceremony and prejudice. And now, since you have found a new set of friends here, may I ask if you intend to leave Fairport as soon as you proposed?"

"What if I should answer your question by another," replied Lovel, "and ask you what is your opinion of dreams?"

"Of dreams, you foolish lad! why, what should I think of them but as the deceptions of imagination when reason drops the reins? I know no difference betwixt them and the hallucinations of madness; the unguided horses run away with the carriage in both cases, only in the one the coachman is drunk, and in the other he slumbers. What says our Marcus Tullius: *Si insanorum visis fides non est habenda, cur credatur somnientium visis, quæ multo etiam perturbatiora sunt, non intelligo.*"

"Yes, sir, but Cicero also tells us, that as he who passes the whole day in darting the javelin must sometimes hit the mark, so, amid the cloud of nightly dreams, some may occur consonant to future events."

"Ay—that is to say, *you* have hit the mark in your own sage opinion? Lord! Lord! how this world is given to folly! Well, I will allow for once the oneirocritical science—I will give faith to the exposition of dreams, and say a Daniel hath arisen to interpret them, if you can prove to me that that dream of yours has pointed to a prudent line of conduct."

"Tell me then," answered Lovel, "why, when I was hesitating whether to abandon an enterprise which I have perhaps rashly undertaken, I should last night dream I saw your ancestor pointing to a motto which encouraged me to perseverance? Why should I have thought of those words, which I cannot remember to have heard before, which are in a language unknown to me, and which yet conveyed, when translated, a lesson which I could so plainly apply to my own circumstances?"

The Antiquary burst into a fit of laughing. "Excuse me, my young friend, but it is thus we silly mortals deceive ourselves, and look out of doors for motives which originate in our own wilful will. I think I can help out the cause of your vision. You were so abstracted in your contemplations yesterday after dinner as to pay little attention to the discourse between Sir Arthur and me, until we fell upon the controversy concerning the Piks, which terminated so abruptly; but I remember producing to Sir Arthur a book printed by my ancestor, and making him observe the motto. Your mind was bent elsewhere, but your ear had mechanically received and retained the sounds, and your busy fancy, stirred by Grizel's legend, I presume, had introduced this scrap of German into your dream. As for the waking wisdom which seized on so frivolous a circumstance as an apology for persevering in some course which it could find no better reason to justify, it is exactly one of those juggling tricks which the sagest of us play off now and then to gratify our inclination at the expense of our understanding."

"I own it," said Lovel, blushing deeply; "I believe you are right, Mr. Oldbuck, and I ought to sink in your esteem for attaching a moment's consequence to such a frivolity; but I was tossed by contradictory wishes and resolutions, and you know how slight a line will tow a boat when afloat on the billows, though a cable would hardly move her when pulled up on the bench."

"Right, right," exclaimed the Antiquary; "fall in my opinion! not a whit. I love thee the better, man; why, we have story for story against each other, and I can think with less shame on having exposed myself about that cursed *prætorium*, though I am still convinced Agricola's camp must have been somewhere in this neighbourhood. And now, Lovel, my good lad, be sincere with me. 'What make you from Wittenberg?' Why have you left your own country and professional pursuits for an idle residence in such a place as Fairport? A truant disposition, I fear."

"Even so," replied Lovel, patiently submitting to an interrogatory which he could not well evade; "yet I am so detached from all the world, have so few in whom I am interested, or who are interested in me, that my very state of destitution gives me independence. He whose good or evil fortune affects himself alone has the best right to pursue it according to his own fancy."

"Pardon me, young man," said Oldbuck, laying his hand kindly on his shoulder, and making a full halt; "*sufflamina*— a little patience if you please. I will suppose that you have no friends to share or rejoice in your success in life, that you cannot look back to those to whom you owe gratitude, or forward to those to whom you ought to afford protection; but it is no less incumbent on you to move steadily in the path of duty, for your active exertions are due not only to society, but in humble gratitude to the Being who made you a member of it, with powers to serve yourself and others."

"But I am unconscious of possessing such powers," said Lovel, somewhat impatiently; "I ask nothing of society but the permission of walking innoxiously through the path of life without jostling others, or permitting myself to be jostled. I owe no man anything, I have the means of maintaining myself with complete independence, and so moderate are my wishes in this respect that even these means, however limited, rather exceed than fall short of them."

"Nay, then," said Oldbuck, removing his hand, and turning again to the road, "if you are so true a philosopher as to think you have money enough, there's no more to be said; I cannot pretend to be entitled to advise you: you have attained the acme—the summit of perfection. And how came Fairport to be the selected abode of so much self-denying philosophy? It is as if a worshipper of the true religion had set up his staff by choice among the multifarious idolaters of the land of Egypt. There is not a man in Fairport who is not a devoted worshipper of the Golden Calf—the Mammon of unrighteousness; why, even I, man, am so infected by the bad neighbourhood that I feel inclined occasionally to become an idolater myself."

"My principal amusements being literary," answered Lovel, "and circumstances which I cannot mention having induced me, for a time at least, to relinquish the military service, I have pitched on Fairport as a place where I might follow my pursuits without any of those temptations to society which a more elegant circle might have presented to me."

"Aha!" replied Oldbuck, knowingly, "I begin to understand your application of my ancestor's motto: you are a candidate for public favour, though not in the way I first suspected; you are ambitious to shine as a literary character, and you hope to merit favour by labour and perseverance?"

Lovel, who was rather closely pressed by the inquisitiveness of the old gentleman, concluded it would be best to let him remain in the error which he had gratuitously adopted.

"I have been at times foolish enough," he replied, "to nourish some thoughts of the kind."

"Ah, poor fellow! nothing can be more melancholy; unless, as young men sometimes do, you had fancied yourself in love with some trumpery specimen of womankind, which is, indeed, as Shakspeare truly says, pressing to death, whipping, and hanging all at once."

He then proceeded with inquiries, which he was sometimes kind enough to answer himself. For this good old gentleman had, from his antiquarian researches, acquired a delight in building theories out of premises which were often far from affording sufficient ground for them; and being, as the reader must have remarked, sufficiently opinionative, he did not readily brook being corrected, either in matter of fact or judgment, even by those who were principally interested in the subjects on which he speculated. He went on, therefore, chalking out Lovel's literary career for him.

"And with what do you propose to commence your *début* as a man of letters? But I guess—poetry—poetry, the soft seducer of youth. Yes! there is an acknowledging modesty of confusion in your eye and manner. And where lies your vein? Are you inclined to soar to the higher regions of Parnassus, or to flutter around the base of the hill?"

"I have hitherto attempted only a few lyrical pieces," said Lovel.

"Just as I supposed—pruning your wing and hopping from spray to spray. But I trust you intend a bolder flight. Observe, I would by no means recommend your persevering in

10

this unprofitable pursuit, but you say you are quite independent of the public caprice?"

"Entirely so," replied Lovel.

"And that you are determined not to adopt a more active course of life?"

"For the present such is my resolution," replied the young man.

"Why, then, it only remains for me to give you my best advice and assistance in the object of your pursuit. I have myself published two essays in the *Antiquarian Repository*, and therefore am an author of experience. There was my *Remarks on Hearne's Edition of Robert of Gloucester*, signed 'Scrutator'; and the other signed 'Indagator,' upon a passage in Tacitus. I might add, what attracted considerable notice at the time, and that is my paper in the *Gentleman's Magazine* upon the inscription of Œlia Lelia, which I subscribed 'Œdipus.' So you see I am not an apprentice in the mysteries of author-craft, and must necessarily understand the taste and temper of the times. And now, once more, what do you intend to commence with?"

"I have no instant thoughts of publishing."

"Ah! that will never do; you must have the fear of the public before your eyes in all your undertakings. Let us see now. A collection of fugitive pieces? But no, your fugitive poetry is apt to become stationary with the bookseller. It should be something at once solid and attractive; none of your romances or anomalous novelties; I would have you take high ground at once. Let me see. What think you of a real epic? the grand old-fashioned historical poem which moved through twelve or twenty-four books. We'll have it so; I'll supply you with a subject—the battle between the Caledonians and Romans: *The Caledoniad; or, Invasion Repelled*. Let that be the title; it will suit the present taste, and you may throw in a touch of the times."

"But the invasion of Agricola was *not* repelled."

"No; but you are a poet, free of the corporation, and as little bound down to truth or probability as Virgil himself. You may defeat the Romans in spite of Tacitus."

"And pitch Agricola's camp at the Kaim of—what do you call it," answered Lovel, "in defiance of Edie Ochiltree."

"No more of that, an thou lovest me. And yet I dare say ye may unwittingly speak most correct truth in both instances, in despite of the *toga* of the historian and the blue gown of the mendicant."

"Gallantly counselled. Well, I will do my best; your kindness will assist me with local information."

"Will I not, man? why, I will write the critical and historical notes on each canto, and draw out the plan of the story myself. I pretend to some poetical genius, Mr. Lovel, only I was never able to write verses."

"It is a pity, sir, that you should have failed in a qualification somewhat essential to the art."

"Essential! not a whit: it is the mere mechanical department. A man may be a poet without measuring spondees and dactyls like the ancients, or clashing the ends of lines into rhyme like the moderns, as one may be an architect though unable to labour like a stone-mason. Dost think Palladio or Vitruvius ever carried a hod?"

"In that case there should be two authors to each poem— one to think and plan, another to execute."

"Why, it would not be amiss, at any rate we'll make the experiment—not that I would wish to give my name to the public. Assistance from a learned friend might be acknowledged in the preface after what flourish your nature will; I am a total stranger to authorial vanity."

Lovel was much entertained by a declaration not very consistent with the eagerness wherewith his friend seemed to catch at an opportunity of coming before the public, though in a manner which rather resembled stepping up behind a carriage than getting into one. The Antiquary was, indeed, uncommonly delighted; for, like many other men who spend their lives in obscure literary research, he had a secret ambition to appear in print, which was checked by cold fits of diffidence, fear of criticism, and habits of indolence and procrastination. "But," though he, "I may, like a second Teucer, discharge my shafts from behind the shield of my ally; and, admit that he should not prove to be a first-rate poet, I am in no shape answerable for his deficiencies, and the good notes may very probably help off an indifferent text. But he is—he must be a good poet; he has the real Parnassian abstraction, seldom answers a question till it is twice repeated, drinks his tea scalding, and eats without knowing what he is putting into his mouth. This is the real *œstus*, the *awen* of the Welsh bards, the *divinus afflatus* that transports the poet beyond the limits of sublunary things. His visions, too, are very symptomatical of poetic fury; I must recollect to send Caxon to see he puts out his candle to-night, poets and visionaries are apt to be negligent in that respect." Then, turning to his companion, he expressed himself aloud in continuation:

"Yes, my dear Lovel, you shall have full notes; and, indeed, I think we may introduce the whole of the *Essay on Castrametation* into the appendix; it will give great value to the work. Then we will revive the good old forms so disgracefully neglected in modern times. You shall invoke the Muse; and certainly she ought to be propitious to an author who, in an apostatising age, adheres with the faith of Abdiel to the ancient form of adoration. Then we must have a vision, in which the genius of Caledonia shall appear to Galgacus and show him a procession of the real Scottish monarchs; and in the notes I will have a hit at Boethius—no, I must not touch that topic, now that Sir Arthur is likely to have vexation enough besides; but I'll annihilate Ossian, Macpherson, and Mac-Cribb."

"But we must consider the expense of publication," said Lovel, willing to try whether this hint would fall like cold water on the blazing zeal of his self-elected coadjutor.

"Expense!" said Mr. Oldbuck, pausing and mechanically fumbling in his pocket—"that is true; I would wish to do something, but you would not like to publish by subscription?"

"By no means," answered Lovel.

"No, no!" gladly acquiesced the Antiquary. "It is not respectable. I'll tell you what: I believe I know a bookseller who has a value for my opinion, and will risk print and paper, and I will get as many copies sold for you as I can."

"Oh, I am no mercenary author," answered Lovel, smiling; "I only wish to be out of risk of loss."

"Hush! hush! we'll take care of that; throw it all on the publishers. I do long to see your labours commenced. You will choose blank verse, doubtless? It is more grand and magnificent for an historical subject; and, what concerneth you, my friend, it is, I have an idea, more easily written."

This conversation brought them to Moukbarns, where the Antiquary had to undergo a chiding from his sister, who, though no philosopher, was waiting to deliver a lecture to him in the portico. "Guide us, Monkbarns, are things no dear eneugh already, but ye maun be raising the very fish on us, by giving that randy, Luckie Mucklebackit, just what she likes to ask?"

"Why, Grizel," said the sage, somewhat abashed at this unexpected attack, "I thought I made a very fair bargain."

"A fair bargain! when ye gied the limmer a full half o' what she seekit! An ye will be a wife-carle, and buy fish at your ain hands, ye suld never bid muckle mair than a quarter. And the impudent quean had the assurance to come up and seek a dram. But I trow Jenny and I sorted her!"

"Truly," said Oldbuck (with a sly look to his companion), "I think our estate was gracious that kept us out of hearing of that controversy. Well, well, Grizel, I was wrong for once in my life—*ultra crepidam*, I fairly admit. But hang expenses, care killed a cat; we'll eat the fish, cost what it will. And then, Lovel, you must know I pressed you to stay here to-day the rather because our cheer will be better than usual, yesterday having been a gaudé-day; I love the reversion of a feast better than the feast itself. I delight in the *analecta*, the *collectanea*, as I may call them, of the preceding day's dinner, which appear on such occasions. And see there is Jenny going to ring the dinner-bell."

CHAPTER XV.

Be this letter delivered with haste—haste—post-haste! Ride, villain,
ride, for thy life—for thy life—for thy life!
Ancient Indorsation of Letters of Importance.

LEAVING Mr. Oldbuck and his friend to enjoy their hard
bargain of fish, we beg leave to transport the reader to the
back-parlour of the postmaster's house at Fairport, where his
wife, he himself being absent, was employed in assorting for
delivery the letters which had come by the Edinburgh post.
This is very often in country towns the period of the day
when gossips find it particularly agreeable to call on the
man or woman of letters, in order, from the outside of the
epistles, and, if they are not belied, occasionally from the
inside also, to amuse themselves with gleaning information or
forming conjectures about the correspondence and affairs of
their neighbours. Two females of this description were, at
the time we mention, assisting, or impeding, Mrs. Mailsetter
in her official duty.

"Eh, preserve us, sirs," said the butcher's wife, "there's
ten, eleven, twal letters to Tennant & Co.; thae folk do mair
business than a' the rest o' the burgh."

"Ay; but see, lass," answered the baker's lady, "there's
twa o' them faulded unco square, and sealed at the tae side;
I doubt there will be protested bills in them."

"Is there ony letters come yet for Jenny Caxon?" inquired
the woman of joints and giblets; "the lieutenant's been awa
three weeks."

"Just ane on Tuesday was a week," answered the dame of
letters.

"Was't a ship-letter?" asked the Fornarina.

"In troth was't."

"It wad be frae the lieutenant then," replied the mistress
of the rolls, somewhat disappointed; "I never thought he wad
hae lookit ower his shouther after her."

"Odd, here's another," quoth Mrs. Mailsetter. "A ship-letter, postmark Sunderland." All rushed to seize it. "Na, na, leddies," said Mrs. Mailsetter, interfering, "I hae had eneugh o' that wark. Ken ye that Mr. Mailsetter got an unco rebuke frae the secretary at Edinburgh for a complaint that was made about the letter of Ailie Bisset's that ye opened, Mrs. Shortcake?"

"Me opened!" answered the spouse of the chief baker of Fairport; "ye ken yoursell, madam, it just cam open o' free will in my hand. What could I help it? Folk suld seal wi' better wax."

"Weel I wot that's true, too," said Mrs. Mailsetter, who kept a shop of small wares, "and we have got some that I can honestly recommend, if ye ken ony body wanting it. But the short and the lang o't is, that we'll lose the place gin there's ony mair complaints o' the kind."

"Hout, lass; the provost will take care o' that."

"Na, na; I'll neither trust to provost nor bailie," said the postmistress; "but I wad aye be obliging and neighbourly, and I'm no again your looking at the outside of a letter neither. See, the seal has an anchor on't; he's done't wi' ane o' his buttons, I'm thinking."

"Show me! show me!" quoth the wives of the chief butcher and chief baker, and threw themselves on the supposed love-letter like the weird sisters in Macbeth upon the pilot's thumb, with curiosity as eager and scarcely less malignant. Mrs. Heukbane was a tall woman, she held the precious epistle up between her eyes and the window. Mrs. Shortcake, a little squat personage, strained and stood on tiptoe to have her share of the investigation.

"Ay, it's frae him, sure eneugh," said the butcher's lady. "I can read 'Richard Taffril' on the corner, and it's written, like John Thomson's wallet, frae end to end."

"Haud it lower down, madam," exclaimed Mrs. Shortcake, in a tone above the prudential whisper which their occupation required—"haud it lower down. Div ye think naebody can read hand o' writ but yoursell?"

"Whisht, whisht, sirs, for God's sake!" said Mrs. Mailsetter, "there's somebody in the shop"; then aloud, "Look to the customers, Baby!" Baby answered from without in a shrill tone: "It's naebody but Jenny Caxon, ma'am, to see if there's ony letters to her."

"Tell her," said the faithful postmistress, winking to her compeers, "to come back the morn at ten o'clock, and I'll let her ken, we havena had time to sort the mail letters yet. She's aye in sic a hurry, as if her letters were o' mair consequence than the best merchant's o' the town."

Poor Jenny, a girl of uncommon beauty and modesty, could only draw her cloak about her to hide the sigh of disappointment, and return meekly home to endure for another night the sickness of the heart occasioned by hope delayed.

"There's something about a needle and a pole," said Mrs. Shortcake, to whom her taller rival in gossiping had at length yielded a peep at the subject of their curiosity.

"Now, that's downright shamefu'," said Mrs. Heukbane, "to scorn the puir silly gait of a lassie after he's keepit company wi' her sae lang, and had his will o' her, as I mak nae doubt he has."

"It's but ower muckle to be doubted," echoed Mrs. Shortcake. "To cast up to her that her father's a barber, and has a pole at his door, and that she's but a manty-maker hersell! Hout! fie for shame!"

"Hout, tout, leddies," said Mrs. Mailsetter, "ye're clean wrang. It's a line out o' ane o' his sailors' sangs that I have heard him sing, about being true like the needle to the pole."

"Weel, weel, I wish it may be sae," said the charitable Dame Heukbane, "but it disna look weel for a lassie like her to keep up a correspondence wi' ane o' the king's officers."

"I'm no denying that," said Mrs. Mailsetter; "but it's a great advantage to the revenue of the post-office thae love letters. See, here's five or six letters to Sir Arthur Wardour, maist o' them sealed wi' wafers and no wi' wax; there will be a downcome there, believe me."

"Ay; they will be business letters, and no frae ony o' his grand friends, that seals wi' their coats of arms, as they ca' them," said Mrs. Heukbane. "Pride will hae a fa'. He hasna settled his account wi' my gudeman, the deacon, for this twalmonth; he's but slink, I doubt."

"Nor wi' huz for sax months," echoed Mrs. Shortcake. "He's but a brunt crust."

"There's a letter," interrupted the trusty postmistress, "from his son, the captain, I'm thinking; the seal has the same things wi' the Knockwinnock carriage. He'll be coming hame to see what he can save out o' the fire."

The baronet thus dismissed, they took up the esquire. "Twa letters for Monkbarns; they're frae some o' his learned friends now. See, sae close as they're written, down to the very seal, and a' to save sending a double letter; that's just like Monkbarns himsell. When he gets a frank he fills it up exact to the weight of an unce, that a carvy-seed would sink the scale; but he's ne'er a grain abune it. Weel I wot I wad be broken if I were to gie sic weight to the folk that come to buy our pepper and brimstone, and such like sweet-meats."

"He's a shabby body the Laird o' Monkbarns," said Mrs. Heukbane: "he'll make as muckle about buying a fore quarter o' lamb in August as about a back sey o' beef. Let's taste another drap o' the sinning (perhaps she meant cinnamon) waters, Mrs. Mailsetter, my dear. Ah! lasses, an ye had kend his brother as I did! Mony a time he wad slip in to see me wi' a brace o' wild deukes in his pouch, when my first gudeman was awa at the Falkirk Tryst; weel, weel, we'se no speak o' that e'enow."

"I winna say ony ill o' this Monkbarns," said Mrs. Short-cake; "his brother ne'er brought me ony wild deukes, and this is a douce honest man. We serve the family wi' bread, and he settles wi' huz ilka week; only he was in an unco kippage when we sent him a book instead o' the nicksticks,[1] whiik, he said, were the true ancient way o' counting between tradesmen and customers; and sae they are, nae doubt."

"But look here, lasses," interrupted Mrs. Mailsetter, "here's a sight for sair e'en! What wad ye gie to ken what's in the inside o' this letter? This is new corn: I haena seen

[1] See Note 3.

the like o' this. 'For William Lovel, Esquire, at Mrs. Hadoway's, High Street, Fairport, by Edinburgh, N. B.' This is just the second letter he has had since he was here."

"Lord's sake, let's see, lass! Lord's sake, let's see! That's him that the hale town kens naething about; and a weel-fa'ard lad he is. Let's see—let's see!" Thus ejaculated the two worthy representatives of mother Eve.

"Na, na, sirs," exclaimed Mrs. Mailsetter; "haud awa—bide aff, I tell you; this is nane o' your fourpenny cuts that we might make up the value to the post-office amang ourselves if ony mischance befell it. The postage is five-and-twenty shillings; and here's an order frae the secretary to forward it to the young gentleman by express, if he's no at hame. Na, na, sirs, bide aff; this maunna be roughly guided."

"But just let's look at the outside o't, woman."

Nothing could be gathered from the outside, except remarks on the various properties which philosophers ascribe to matter —length, breadth, depth, and weight. The packet was composed of strong thick paper, imperviable by the curious eyes of the gossips, though they stared as if they would burst from their sockets. The seal was a deep and well-cut impression of arms, which defied all tampering.

"Odd, lass," said Mrs. Shortcake, weighing it in her hand, and wishing, doubtless, that the too, too solid wax would melt and dissolve itself, "I wad like to ken what's in the inside o' this, for that Lovel dings a' that ever set foot on the plainstanes o' Fairport: naebody kens what to make o' him."

"Weel, weel, leddies," said the postmistress, "we'se sit down and crack about it. Baby, bring ben the tea-water. Muckle obliged to ye for your cookies, Mrs. Shortcake; and we'll steek the shop and cry ben Baby, and take a hand at the cartes till the gudeman comes hame; and then we'll try your braw veal sweetbread that ye were so kind as send me, Mrs. Heukbane."

"But winna ye first send awa Mr. Lovel's letter?" said Mrs. Heukbane.

"Troth I kenna wha to send wi't till the gudeman comes hame, for auld Caxon tell'd me that Mr. Lovel stays a' the day at Monkbarns; he's in a high fever wi' pu'ing the Laird and Sir Arthur out o' the sea."

"Silly auld doited carles," said Mrs. Shortcake; "what gar'd them gang to the douking in a night like yestreen?"

"I was gi'en to understand it was auld Edie that saved them," said Mrs. Heukbane—"Edie Ochiltree, the Blue-Gown, ye ken—and that he pu'd the hale three out of the auld fish-pound, for Monkbarns had threepit on them to gang in till't to see the wark o' the monks lang syne."

"Hout, lass, nonsense," answered the postmistress; "I'll tell ye a' about it, as Caxon tell'd it to me. Ye see, Sir Arthur and Miss Wardour and Mr. Lovel suld hae dined at Monkbarns——"

"But, Mrs. Mailsetter," again interrupted Mrs. Heukbane, "will ye no be for sending awa this letter by express? There's our powny and our callant hae gane express for the office or now, and the powny hasna gane abune thirty miles the day. Jock was sorting him up as I came ower by."

"Why, Mrs. Heukbane," said the woman of letters, pursing up her mouth, "ye ken my gudeman likes to ride the expresses himsell: we maun gie our ain fish-guts to our ain sea-maws. It's a red half-guinea to him every time he munts his mear; and I dare say he'll be in sune, or I dare to say it's the same thing whether the gentleman gets the express this night or early next morning."

"Only that Mr. Lovel will be in town before the express gaes aff," said Mrs. Heukbane, "and whare are ye then, lass? But ye ken yere ain ways best."

"Weel, weel, Mrs. Heukbane," answered Mrs. Mailsetter, a little out of humour, and even out of countenance, "I am sure I am never against being neighbour-like, and living and letting live, as they say; and since I hae been sic a fule as to show you the post-office order, ou, nae doubt it maun be obeyed. But I'll no need your callant, mony thanks to ye: I'll send little Davie on your powny, and that will be just five-and-threepence to ilka ane o' us, ye ken."

"Davie! the Lord help ye, the bairn's no ten year auld; and, to be plain wi' ye, our powny reists a bit, and it's dooms sweer to the road, and naebody can manage him but our Jock."

"I'm sorry for that," answered the postmistress, gravely, "it's like we maun wait then till the gudeman comes hame, after a'; for I wadna like to be responsible in trusting the letter to sic a callant as Jock; our Davie belangs in a manner to the office."

"Aweel, aweel, Mrs. Mailsetter, I see what ye wad be at; but an ye like to risk the bairn, I'll risk the beast."

Orders were accordingly given. The unwilling pony was brought out of his bed of straw, and again equipped for service; Davie (a leathern post-bag strapped across his shoulders) was perched upon the saddle, with a tear in his eye and a switch in his hand. Jock good-naturedly led the animal out of the town, and, by the crack of his whip and the whoop and halloo of his too well-known voice, compelled it to take the road towards Monkbarns.

Meanwhile the gossips, like the sibyls after consulting their leaves, arranged and combined the information of the evening, which flew next morning through a hundred channels, and in a hundred varieties, through the world of Fairport. Many, strange, and inconsistent were the rumours to which their communications and conjectures gave rise. Some said Tennant & Co. were broken, and that all their bills had come back protested; others that they had got a great contract from government, and letters from the principal merchants at Glasgow desiring to have shares upon a premium. One report stated that Lieutenant Taffril had acknowledged a private marriage with Jenny Caxon; another, that he had sent her a letter upbraiding her with the lowness of her birth and education, and bidding her an eternal adieu. It was generally rumoured that Sir Arthur Wardour's affairs had fallen into irretrievable confusion, and this report was only doubted by the wise because it was traced to Mrs. Mailsetter's shop, a source more famous for the circulation of news than for their accuracy. But all agreed that a packet from the Secretary of State's office had arrived, directed for Mr. Lovel, and that it had been forwarded by an orderly dragoon, despatched from the headquarters at Edinburgh, who had galloped through Fairport without stopping, except just to inquire the way to Monkbarns. The reason of such an extraordinary mission to a very peaceful and retired individual was variously explained. Some said Lovel was an emigrant noble, summoned to head an insurrection that had broken out in La Vendée, others that he was a spy, others that he was a general officer who was visiting the coast privately, others that he was a prince of the blood who was travelling *incognito*.

Meanwhile the progress of the packet which occasioned so much speculation towards its destined owner at Monkbarns had been perilous and interrupted. The bearer, Davie Mailsetter, as little resembling a bold dragoon as could well be imagined, was carried onwards towards Monkbarns by the pony so long as the animal had in his recollection the crack of his usual instrument of chastisement and the shout of the butcher's boy. But feeling how Davie, whose short legs were unequal to maintain his balance, swung to and fro upon his back, the pony began to disdain further compliance with the intimations he had received. First, then, he slackened his pace to a walk. This was no point of quarrel between him and his rider, who had been considerably discomposed by the rapidity of his former motion, and who now took the opportunity of his abated pace to gnaw a piece of gingerbread which had been thrust into his hand by his mother, in order to reconcile this youthful emissary of the post-office to the discharge of his duty. By and by the crafty pony availed himself of this surcease of discipline to twitch the rein out of Davie's hands, and apply himself to browse on the grass by the side of the lane. Sorely astounded by these symptoms of self-willed rebellion, and afraid alike to sit or to fall, poor Davie lifted up his voice and wept aloud. The pony, hearing this pudder over his head, began apparently to think it would be best both for himself and Davie to return from whence they came, and accordingly commenced a retrograde movement towards Fairport. But, as all retreats are apt to end in utter rout, so the steed, alarmed by the boy's cries and by the flapping of the reins, which dangled about his forefeet, finding also his nose turned homeward, began to set off at a rate which, if Davie kept the saddle (a matter extremely dubious), would soon have presented him at Heukbane's stable-door, when, at a turn of the road, an intervening auxiliary, in the shape of old Edie Ochiltree, caught hold of the rein and stopped his farther proceeding. "Wha's aught ye, callant? whaten a gate's that to ride?"

"I canna help it!" blubbered the express; "they ca' me little Davie."

"And where are ye gaun?"

"I'm gaun to Monkbarns wi' a letter."

"Stirra, this is no the road to Monkbarns."

But Davie could only answer the expostulation with sighs and tears.

Old Edie was easily moved to compassion where childhood was in the case. "I wasna gaun that gate," he thought, "but it's the best o' my way o' life that I canna be weel out o' my road. They'll gie me quarters at Monkbarns readily eneugh, and I'll e'en hirple awa there wi' the wean, for it will knock its harns out, puir thing, if there's no somebody to guide the powny."—"Sae ye hae a letter, hinney? will ye let me see't?"

"I'm no gaun to let naebody see the letter," sobbed the boy, "till I gie't to Mr. Lovel, for I am a faithfu' servant o' the office—if it werena for the powny."

"Very right, my little man," said Ochiltree, turning the reluctant pony's head towards Monkbarns; "but we'll guide him atween us, if he's no a' the sweerer."

Upon the very height of Kinprunes, to which Monkbarns had invited Lovel after their dinner, the Antiquary, again reconciled to the once-degraded spot, was expatiating upon the topics the scenery afforded for a description of Agricola's camp at the dawn of morning, when his eye was caught by the appearance of the mendicant and his *protégé*. "What the devil! here comes old Edie, bag and baggage, I think."

The beggar explained his errand, and Davie, who insisted upon a literal execution of his commission by going on to Monkbarns, was with difficulty prevailed upon to surrender the packet to its proper owner, although he met him a mile nearer than the place he had been directed to. "But my minnie said I maun be sure to get twenty shillings and five shillings for the postage, and ten shillings and sixpence for the express; there's the paper."

"Let me see—let me see," said Oldbuck, putting on his spectacles and examining the crumpled copy of regulations to which Davie appealed. "Express, per man and horse, one day, not to exceed ten shillings and sixpence. One day! why, it's not an hour! Man and horse! why, 'tis a monkey on a starved cat!"

"Father wad hae come himsell," said Davie, "on the muckle red mear, an ye wad hae bidden till the morn's night."

"Four-and-twenty hours after the regular date of delivery! You little cockatrice's egg, do you understand the art of imposition so early?"

"Hout, Monkbarns, dinna set your wit against a bairn," said the beggar; "mind the butcher risked his beast and the wife her wean, and I am sure ten and sixpence isna ower muckle. Ye didna gang sae near wi' Johnnie Howie when——"

Lovel, who, sitting on the supposed *prætorium*, had glanced over the contents of the packet, now put an end to the altercation by paying Davie's demand, and then, turning to Mr. Oldbuck with a look of much agitation, he excused himself from returning with him to Monkbarns that evening. "I must instantly go to Fairport, and perhaps leave it on a moment's notice; your kindness, Mr. Oldbuck, I never can forget."

"No bad news, I hope?" said the Antiquary.

"Of a very chequered complexion," answered his friend. "Farewell; in good or bad fortune I will not forget your regard."

"Nay, nay; stop a moment. If—if—(making an effort)—if there be any pecuniary inconvenience—I have fifty—or a hundred guineas at your service—till—till Whitsunday—or indeed as long as you please."

"I am much obliged, Mr. Oldbuck, but I am amply provid·

ed," said his mysterious young friend. "Excuse me, I really cannot sustain further conversation at present. I will write or see you before I leave Fairport; that is, if I find myself obliged to go." So saying, he shook the Antiquary's hand warmly, turned from him, and walked rapidly towards the town, "staying no longer question."

"Very extraordinary indeed," said Oldbuck; "but there's something about this lad I can never fathom; and yet I cannot for my heart think ill of him neither. I must go home and take off the fire in the Green Room, for none of my woman-kind will venture into it after twilight."

"And how am I to win hame?" blubbered the disconsolate express.

"It's a fine night," said the Blue-Gown, looking up to the skies; "I had as gude gang back to the town and take care o' the wean."

"Do so, do so, Edie"; and, rummaging for some time in his huge waistcoat pocket till he found the object of his search, the Antiquary added, "there's sixpence to ye to buy sneeshin."

———◆———

CHAPTER XVI.

I am bewitched with the rogue's company. If the rascal has not given me
    medicines to make me love him, I'll be hang'd ; it could not be else. I
    have drunk medicines.

Henry IV. Part II.

REGULAR for a fortnight were the inquiries of the Antiquary at the veteran Caxon whether he had heard what Mr. Lovel was about, and as regular were Caxon's answers, "that the town could learn naething about him whatever, except that he had received anither muckle letter or twa frae the south, and that he was never seen on the plainstanes at a'."

"How does he live, Caxon?"

"Ou, Mrs. Hadoway just dresses him a beefsteak or a mutton-chop, or makes him some friar's chicken, or just what she likes hersell, and he eats it in the little red parlour off his bedroom. She canna get him to say that he likes ae thing better than anither; and she makes him tea in a morning, and he settles honourably wi' her every week."

" But does he never stir abroad?"

" He has clean gi'en up walking, and he sits a' day in his room reading or writing; a hantle letters he has written, but he wadna put them into our post-house, though Mrs. Hadoway offered to carry them hersell, but sent them a' under ae cover to the sheriff, and it's Mrs. Mailsetter's belief that the sheriff sent his groom to put them into the post-office at Tannonburgh. It's my puir thought that he jaloused their looking into his letters at Fairport; and weel had he need, for my puir daughter Jenny——"

" Tut, don't plague me with your womankind, Caxon. About this poor young lad, does he write nothing but letters?"

" Ou, ay; hale sheets o' other things, Mrs. Hadoway says. She wishes muckle he could be gotten to take a walk; she thinks he's but looking very puirly, and his appetite's clean gane; but he'll no hear o' ganging ower the door-stane—him that used to walk sae muckle too."

" That's wrong; I have a guess what he's busy about, but he must not work too hard neither. I'll go and see him this very day; he's deep, doubtless, in the *Caledoniad*."

Having formed this manful resolution, Mr. Oldbuck equipped himself for the expedition with his thick walking-shoes and gold-headed cane, muttering the while the words of Falstaff which we have chosen for the motto of this chapter; for the Antiquary was himself rather surprised at the degree of attachment which he could not but acknowledge he entertained for this stranger. The riddle was, notwithstanding, easily solved. Lovel had many attractive qualities, but he won our Antiquary's heart by being on most occasions an excellent listener.

A walk to Fairport had become somewhat of an adventure with Mr. Oldbuck, and one which he did not often care to undertake. He hated greetings in the market-place; and there were generally loiterers in the streets to persecute him either about the news of the day or about some petty pieces of busi-

11

ness. So on this occasion he had no sooner entered the streets of Fairport than it was "Good-morrow, Mr. Oldbuck, a sight o' you's gude for sair een; what d'ye think of the news in the *Sun* the day? they say the great attempt will be made in a fortnight."

"I wish to the Lord it were made and over, that I might hear no more about it."

"Monkbarns, your honour," said the nursery and seedsman, "I hope the plants gied satisfaction? and if ye wanted ony flower roots fresh frae Holland, or (this in a lower key) an anker or twa o' Cologne gin, ane o' our brigs cam in yestreen."

"Thank ye, thank ye, no occasion at present, Mr. Crabtree," said the Antiquary, pushing resolutely onward.

"Mr. Oldbuck," said the town-clerk (a more important person, who came in front and ventured to stop the old gentleman), "the provost, understanding you were in town, begs on no account that you'll quit it without seeing him; he wants to speak to ye about bringing the water frae the Fairwell spring through a part o' your lands."

"What the deuce! have they nobody's land but mine to cut and carve on? I won't consent, tell them."

"And the provost," said the clerk, going on without noticing the rebuff, "and the council wad be agreeable that you should hae the auld stanes at Donagild's chapel, that ye was wussing to hae."

"Eh? what? Oho, that's another story. Well, well, I'll call upon the provost and we'll talk about it."

"But ye maun speak your mind on't forthwith, Monkbarns, if ye want the stanes; for Deacon Harlewalls thinks the carved through-stanes might be put with advantage on the front of the new council-house; that is, the twa cross-legged figures that the callants used to ca' Robin and Bobbin, ane on ilka door cheek; and the other stane, that they ca'd Ailie Dailie, abune the door. It will be very tastefu', the deacon says, and just in the style of modern Gothic."

"Lord deliver me from this Gothic generation!" exclaimed the Antiquary. "A monument of a Knight Templar on each side of a Grecian porch, and a Madonna on the top of it! O *crimini!* Well, tell the provost I wish to have the stones, and we'll not differ about the watercourse. It's lucky I happened to come this way to-day."

They parted mutually satisfied; but the wily clerk had most reason to exult in the dexterity he had displayed, since the whole proposal of an exchange between the monuments (which the council had determined to remove as a nuisance because they encroached three feet upon the public road) and the privilege of conveying the water to the burgh through the estate of Monkbarns was an idea which had originated with himself upon the pressure of the moment.

Through these various entanglements Monkbarns (to use the phrase by which he was distinguished in the country) made his way at length to Mrs. Hadoway's. This good woman was the widow of a late clergyman at Fairport, who had been reduced by her husband's untimely death to that state of straitened and embarrassed circumstances in which the widows of the Scotch clergy are too often found. The tenement which she occupied and the furniture of which she was possessed gave her the means of letting a part of her house, and as Lovel had been a quiet, regular, and profitable lodger, and had qualified the necessary intercourse which they had together with great deal of gentleness and courtesy, Mrs. Hadoway, not perhaps much used to such kindly treatment, had become greatly attached to her lodger, and was profuse in every sort of personal attention which circumstances permitted her to render him. To cook a dish somewhat better than ordinary for "the poor young gentleman's dinner"; to exert her interest with those who remembered her husband, or loved her for her own sake and his, in order to procure scarce vegetables, or something which her simplicity supposed might tempt her lodger's appetite, was a labour in which she delighted, although she anxiously concealed it from the person who was its object. She did not adopt this secrecy of benevolence to avoid the laugh of those who might suppose that an oval face and dark eyes, with a clear brown complexion, though belonging to a woman of five-and-forty, and inclosed within a widow's close-drawn pinners, might possibly still aim at making conquests; for, to say truth, such a ridiculous suspicion having never entered into her own head, she could not anticipate its having birth in that of any one else. But she concealed her attentions solely out of delicacy to her guest, whose power of repaying them she doubted as much as she believed in his inclination to do so, and in his being likely to feel extreme pain at leaving any of her civilities unrequited. She now opened the door to Mr. Oldbuck, and her surprise at seeing him brought tears into her eyes, which she could hardly restrain.

"I am glad to see you, sir—I am very glad to see you. My poor gentleman is, I am afraid, very unwell; and oh, Mr. Oldbuck, he'll see neither doctor nor minister nor writer! And think what it would be if, as my poor Mr. Hadoway used to say, a man was to die without advice of the three learned faculties!"

"Greatly better than with them," grumbled the cynical Antiquary. "I tell you, Mrs. Hadoway, the clergy live by our sins, the medical faculty by our diseases, and the law gentry by our misfortunes."

"Oh fie, Monkbarns, to hear the like o' that frae you! But ye'll walk up and see the poor young lad? Hegh, sirs, sae young and weel-favoured; and day by day he has eat less and less, and now he hardly touches ony thing, only just pits a bit on the plate to make fashion, and his poor cheek has turned every day thinner and paler, sae that he now really looks as auld as me, that might be his mother; no that I might be just that neither, but something very near it."

"Why does he not take some exercise?" said Oldbuck.

"I think we have persuaded him to do that, for he has bought a horse from Gibbie Golightly, the galloping groom. A gude judge o' horse-flesh Gibbie tauld our lass that he was; for he offered him a beast he thought wad answer him weel eneugh, as he was a bookish man, but Mr. Lovel wadna look at it, and bought ane might serve the Master o' Morphie. They keep it at the Græme's Arms, ower the street, and he rode out yesterday morning and this morning before breakfast. But winna ye walk up to his room?"

"Presently, presently; but has he no visitors?"

"Oh dear, Mr. Oldbuck, not ane; if he wadna receive them when he was weel and sprightly, what chance is there of ony body in Fairport looking in upon him now?"

"Ay, ay, very true; I should have been surprised had it been otherwise. Come, show me upstairs, Mrs. Hadoway, lest I make a blunder and go where I should not."

The good landlady showed Mr. Oldbuck up her narrow staircase, warning him of every turn, and lamenting all the while that he was laid under the necessity of mounting up so high. At length she gently tapped at the door of her guest's parlour.

"Come in," said Lovel; and Mrs. Hadoway ushered in the Laird of Monkbarns.

The little apartment was neat and clean, and decently furnished, ornamented too by such relics of her youthful arts of sempstress-ship as Mrs. Hadoway had retained; but it was close, over-heated, and, as it appeared to Oldbuck, an unwholesome situation for a young person in delicate health, an observation which ripened his resolution touching a project that had already occurred to him in Lovel's behalf. With a writing-table before him, on which lay a quantity of books and papers, Lovel was seated on a couch in his nightgown and slippers. Oldbuck was shocked at the change which had taken place in his personal appearance. His cheek and brow had assumed a ghastly white, except where a round bright spot of hectic red formed a strong and painful contrast, totally different from the general cast of hale and hardy complexion which had formerly overspread and somewhat embrowned his countenance. Oldbuck observed that the dress he wore belonged to a deep mourning suit, and a coat of the same colour hung on a chair near to him. As the Antiquary entered, Lovel arose and came forward to welcome him.

"This is very kind," he said, shaking him by the hand and thanking him warmly for his visit—"this is very kind, and has anticipated a visit with which I intended to trouble you; you must know I have become a horseman lately."

"I understand as much from Mrs. Hadoway; I only hope,

my good young friend, you have been fortunate in a quiet horse. I myself inadvertently bought one from the said Gibbie Golightly, which brute ran two miles on end with me after a pack of hounds with which I had no more to do than the last year's snow, and, after affording infinite amusement, I suppose, to the whole hunting field, he was so good as to deposit me in a dry ditch. I hope yours is a more peaceful beast?"

"I hope at least we shall make our excursions on a better plan of mutual understanding."

"That is to say, you think yourself a good horseman?"

"I would not willingly," answered Lovel, "confess myself a very bad one."

"No; all you young fellows think that would be equal to calling yourselves tailors at once. But have you had experience? for, *crede experto*, a horse in a passion is no joker."

"Why, I should be sorry to boast myself as a great horseman, but when I acted as aid-de-camp to Sir —— —— in the cavalry action at ——, last year, I saw many better cavaliers than myself dismounted."

"Ah! you have looked in the face of the grisly god of arms then, you are acquainted with the frowns of Mars armipotent? That experience fills up the measure of your qualifications for the epopea! The Britons, however, you will remember, fought in chariots—*covinarii* is the phrase of Tacitus; you recollect the fine description of their dashing among the Roman infantry, although the historian tells us how ill the rugged face of the ground was calculated for equestrian combat; and truly, upon the whole, what sort of chariots could be driven in Scotland anywhere but on turnpike roads has been to me always matter of amazement. And well now, has the Muse visited you? Have you got anything to show me?"

"My time," said Lovel, with a glance at his black dress, "has been less pleasantly employed."

"The death of a friend?" said the Antiquary.

"Yes, Mr. Oldbuck, of almost the only friend I could ever boast of possessing."

"Indeed! Well, young man," replied his visitor, in a tone of seriousness very different from his affected gravity, "be comforted: to have lost a friend by death while your mutual regard was warm and unchilled, while the tear can drop unembittered by any painful recollection of coldness or distrust or treachery, is perhaps an escape from a more heavy dispensation. Look round you; how few do you see grow old in the affections of those with whom their early friendships were formed! Our sources of common pleasure gradually dry up as we journey on through the vale of Bacha, and we hew out to ourselves other reservoirs, from which the first companions of our pilgrimage are excluded; jealousies, rivalries, envy, intervene to separate others from our side, until none remain but those who are connected with us rather by habit than predilection, or who, allied more in blood than in disposition, only keep the old man company in his life that they may not be forgotten at his death—

Hæc data pœna diu viventibus.

Ah! Mr. Lovel, if it be your lot to reach the chill, cloudy, and comfortless evening of life, you will remember the sorrows of your youth as the light shadowy clouds that intercepted for a moment the beams of the sun when it was rising. But I cram these words into your ears against the stomach of your sense."

"I am sensible of your kindness," answered the youth, "but the wound that is of recent infliction must always smart severely, and I should be little comforted under my present calamity—forgive me for saying so—by the conviction that life has nothing in reserve for me but a train of successive sorrows. And permit me to add, you, Mr. Oldbuck, have least reason of many men to take so gloomy a view of life. You have a competent and easy fortune, are generally respected, may, in your own phrase, *vacare musis*—indulge yourself in the researches to which your taste addicts you; you may form your own society without doors, and within you have the affectionate and sedulous attention of the nearest relatives."

"Why, yes, the womankind; for womankind, are, thanks to my training, very civil and tractable, do not disturb me in my morning studies, creep across the floor with the stealthy pace of a cat when it suits me to take a nap in my easy-chair after dinner or tea. All this is very well, but I want something to exchange ideas with—something to talk to."

"Then why do you not invite your nephew, Captain M'Intyre, who is mentioned by every one as a fine-spirited young fellow, to become a member of your family?"

"Who?" exclaimed Monkbarns, "my nephew Hector! the Hotspur of the North! Why, Heaven love you, I would as soon invite a firebrand into my stackyard. He's an Almanzor, a Chamont, has a Highland pedigree as long as his claymore, and a claymore as long as the High Street of Fairport, which he unsheathed upon the surgeon the last time he was at Fairport. I expect him here one of these days, but I will keep him at staff's end, I promise you. He an inmate of my house! to make my very chairs and tables tremble at his brawls. No, no, I'll none of Hector M'Intyre. But hark ye, Lovel, you are a quiet gentle-tempered lad; had not you better set up your staff at Monkbarns for a month or two, since I conclude you do not immediately intend to leave this country? I will have a door opened out to the garden—it will cost but a trifle, there is the space for an old one which was condemned long ago —by which said door you may pass and repass into the Green Chamber at pleasure, so you will not interfere with the old man, nor he with you. As for your fare, Mrs. Hadoway tells me you are, as she terms it, very moderate of your mouth, so you will not quarrel with my humble table. Your washing——"

"Hold, my dear Mr. Oldbuck," interposed Lovel, unable to repress a smile; "and before your hospitality settles all my accommodations, let me thank you most sincerely for so kind an offer; it is not at present in my power to accept of it, but very likely before I bid adieu to Scotland I shall find an opportunity to pay you a visit of some length."

Mr. Oldbuck's countenance fell. "Why, I thought I had hit on the very arrangement that would suit us both, and who knows what might happen in the long run, and whether we might ever part? Why, I am master of my acres, man; there is the advantage of being descended from a man of more sense than pride; they cannot oblige me to transmit my goods, chattels, and heritages any way but as I please. No string of substitute heirs of entail, as empty and unsubstantial as the morsels of paper strung to the train of a boy's kite, to cumber my flights of inclination and my humours of predilection. Well, I see you won't be tempted at present. But *Caledonia* goes on, I hope?"

"Oh, certainly!" said Lovel, "I cannot think of relinquishing a plan so hopeful."

"It is indeed," said the Antiquary, looking gravely upward, for, though shrewd and acute enough in estimating the variety of plans formed by others, he had a very natural, though rather disproportioned, good opinion of the importance of those which originated with himself—"it is indeed one of those undertakings which, if achieved with spirit equal to that which dictates its conception, may redeem from the charge of frivolity the literature of the present generation."

Here he was interrupted by a knock at the room door, which introduced a letter for Mr. Lovel. The servant waited, Mrs. Hadoway said, for an answer. "You are concerned in this matter, Mr. Oldbuck," said Lovel, after glancing over the billet, and handed it to the Antiquary as he spoke.

It was a letter from Sir Arthur Wardour, couched in extremely civil language, regretting that a fit of the gout had prevented his hitherto showing Mr. Lovel the attentions to which his conduct during a late perilous occasion had so well entitled him, apologising for not paying his respects in person, but hoping Mr. Lovel would dispense with that ceremony and be a member of a small party which proposed to visit the ruins of Saint Ruth's priory on the following day, and afterwards to dine and spend the evening at Knockwinnock Castle. Sir Arthur concluded with saying that he had sent to request the Monkbarns family to join the party of pleasure which he thus proposed. The place of rendezvous was fixed at a turnpike gate, which was about an equal distance from all the points from which the company were to assemble.

"What shall we do?" said Lovel, looking at the Antiquary, but pretty certain of the part he would take.

"Go, man; we'll go by all means.   Let me see—it will cost a post-chaise though, which will hold you and me and Mary M'Intyre very well, and the other womankind may go to the manse; and you can come out in the chaise to Monkbarns, as I will take it for the day."

"Why, I rather think I had better ride."

"True, true, I forgot your Bucephalus.   You are a foolish lad, by the by, for purchasing the brute outright; you should stick to eighteenpence a side, if you will trust any creature's legs in preference to your own."

"Why, as the horses have the advantage of moving considerably faster, and are, besides, two pair to one, I own I incline——"

"Enough said—enough said; do as you please.   Well, then, I'll bring either Grizel or the minister, for I love to have my full pennyworth out of post-horses; and we meet at Tirlingen turnpike on Friday, at twelve o'clock precisely."   And with this agreement the friends separated.

CHAPTER XVII.

Of seats they tell, where priests, 'mid tapers dim,
Breathed the warm prayer or tuned the midnight hymn.
To scenes like these the fainting soul retired,
Revenge and anger in these cells expired,
By Pity soothed, Remorse lost half her fears,
And soften'd Pride dropp'd penitential tears.
                                        CRABBE'S *Borough*.

THE morning of Friday was as serene and beautiful as if no pleasure party had been intended; and that is a rare event, whether in novel-writing or real life.   Lovel, who felt the genial influence of the weather and rejoiced at the prospect of once more meeting with Miss Wardour, trotted forward to the place of rendezvous with better spirits than he had for some time enjoyed.   His prospects seemed in many respects to open and brighten before him, and hope, although breaking like the morning sun through clouds and showers, appeared now about

to illuminate the path before him. He was, as might have
been expected from this state of spirits, first at the place of
meeting, and, as might also have been anticipated, his looks
were so intently directed towards the road from Knockwinnock
Castle that he was only apprised of the arrival of the Monkbarns division by the gee-hupping of the postilion, as the
post-chaise lumbered up behind him. In this vehicle were
pent up, first, the stately figure of Mr. Oldbuck himself;
secondly, the scarce less portly person of the Reverend Mr.
Blattergowl, minister of Trotcosey, the parish in which Monkbarns and Knockwinnock were both situated. The reverend
gentleman was equipped in a buzz wig, upon the top of which
was an equilateral cocked hat. This was the paragon of the
three yet remaining wigs of the parish, which differed, as
Monkbarns used to remark, like the three degrees of comparison—Sir Arthur's ramilies being the positive, his own bob-
wig the comparative, and the overwhelming grizzle of the
worthy clergyman figuring as the superlative. The superintendent of these antique garnitures, deeming, or affecting to
deem, that he could not well be absent on an occasion which
assembled all three together, had seated himself on the board
behind the carriage, "just to be in the way in case they wanted
a touch before the gentlemen sat down to dinner." Between
the two massive figures of Monkbarns and the clergyman was
stuck, by way of bodkin, the slim form of Mary M'Intyre,
her aunt having preferred a visit to the manse and a social
chat with Miss Beckie Blattergowl to investigating the ruins
of the priory of Saint Ruth.

As greetings passed between the members of the Monkbarns
party and Mr. Lovel, the Baronet's carriage, an open barouche,
swept onward to the place of appointment, making, with its
smoking bays, smart drivers, arms, blazoned panels, and a
brace of outriders, a strong contrast with the battered vehicle
and broken-winded hacks which had brought thither the Antiquary and his followers. The principal seat of the carriage
was occupied by Sir Arthur and his daughter. At the first
glance which passed betwixt Miss Wardour and Lovel, her
colour rose considerably; but she had apparently made up her

mind to receive him as a friend, and only as such, and there was equal composure and courtesy in the mode of her reply to his fluttered salutation. Sir Arthur halted the barouche to shake his preserver kindly by the hand, and intimate the pleasure he had on this opportunity of returning him his personal thanks; then mentioned to him, in a tone of slight introduction, "Mr. Dousterswivel, Mr. Lovel."

Lovel took the necessary notice of the German adept, who occupied the front seat of the carriage, which is usually conferred upon dependents or inferiors. The ready grin and supple inclination with which his salutation, though slight, was answered by the foreigner, increased the internal dislike which Lovel had already conceived towards him; and it was plain, from the lour of the Antiquary's shaggy eyebrow, that he too looked with displeasure on this addition to the company. Little more than distant greeting passed among the members of the party, until, having rolled on for about three miles beyond the place at which they met, the carriages at length stopped at the sign of the Four Horseshoes, a small hedge inn, where Caxon humbly opened the door and let down the step of the hack-chaise, while the inmates of the barouche were, by their more courtly attendants, assisted to leave their equipage.

Here renewed greetings passed; the young ladies shook hands; and Oldbuck, completely in his element, placed himself as guide and cicerone at the head of the party, who were now to advance on foot towards the object of their curiosity. He took care to detain Lovel close beside him as the best listener of the party, and occasionally glanced a word of explanation and instruction to Miss Wardour and Mary M'Intyre, who followed next in order. The Baronet and the clergyman he rather avoided, as he was aware both of them conceived they understood such matters as well, or better, than he did; and Dousterswivel, besides that he looked on him as a charlatan, was so nearly connected with his apprehended loss in the stock of the mining company that he could not abide the sight of him. These two latter satellites, therefore, attended upon the orb of Sir Arthur, to whom, moreover, as the most important person of the society, they were naturally induced to attach themselves.

It frequently happens that the most beautiful points of Scottish scenery lie hidden in some sequestered dell, and that you may travel through the country in every direction without being aware of your vicinity to what is well worth seeing, unless intention or accident carry you to the very spot. This is particularly the case in the country around Fairport, which is, generally speaking, open, uninclosed, and bare. But here and there the progress of rills or small rivers has formed dells, glens, or, as they are provincially termed, "dens," on whose high and rocky banks trees and shrubs of all kinds find a shelter, and grow with a luxuriant profusion, which is the more gratifying as it forms an unexpected contrast with the general face of the country. This was eminently the case with the approach to the ruins of Saint Ruth, which was for some time merely a sheep-track along the side of a steep and bare hill. By degrees, however, as this path descended and winded round the hillside, trees began to appear, at first singly, stunted, and blighted, with locks of wool upon their trunks, and their roots hollowed out into recesses, in which the sheep love to repose themselves—a sight much more gratifying to the eye of an admirer of the picturesque than to that of a planter or forester. By and by the trees formed groups, fringed on the edges and filled up in the middle by thorns and hazel bushes; and at length these groups closed so much together that, although a broad glade opened here and there under their boughs, or a small patch of bog or heath occurred which had refused nourishment to the seed which they sprinkled round, and consequently remained open and waste, the scene might on the whole be termed decidedly woodland The sides of the valley began to approach each other more closely; the rush of a brook was heard below, and, between the intervals afforded by openings in the natural wood, its waters were seen hurling clear and rapid under their silvan canopy.

Oldbuck now took upon himself the full authority of cicerone, and anxiously directed the company not to go a foot-breadth off the track which he pointed out to them, if they wished to enjoy in full perfection what they came to see. "You are happy in me for a guide, Miss Wardour," exclaimed the veteran, waving his hand and head in cadence as he repeated with emphasis:

> I know each lane, and every alley green,
> Dingle, or bushy dell, of this wild wood,
> And every bosky bower from side to side.

Ah! deuce take it! that spray of a bramble has demolished all Caxon's labours, and nearly canted my wig into the stream—so much for recitations *hors de propos.*"

"Never mind, my dear sir," said Miss Wardour, "you have your faithful attendant ready to repair such a disaster when it happens, and when you appear with it as restored to its original splendour I will carry on the quotation:

> So sinks the day-star in the ocean bed,
> And yet anon repairs his drooping head,
> And tricks his beams, and with new-spangled ore
> Flames on the forehead——"

"Oh enough, enough!" answered Oldbuck; "I ought to have known what it was to give you advantage over me. But here is what will stop your career of satire, for you are an admirer of nature, I know." In fact, when they had followed him through a breach in a low, ancient, and ruinous wall, they came suddenly upon a scene equally unexpected and interesting.

They stood pretty high upon the side of the glen, which had suddenly opened into a sort of amphitheatre to give room for a pure and profound lake of a few acres extent, and a space of level ground around it. The banks then arose everywhere steeply, and in some places were varied by rocks, in others covered with the copse which run up, feathering their sides lightly and irregularly, and breaking the uniformity of the green pasture-ground. Beneath, the lake discharged itself into the huddling and tumultuous brook which had been their companion since they had entered the glen. At the point at which it issued from "its parent lake" stood the ruins which they had come to visit. They were not of great extent; but the singular beauty, as well as wild and sequestered character, of the spot on which they were situated gave them an interest and importance superior to that which attaches itself to architectural remains of greater consequence, but placed near to ordinary houses, and possessing less romantic accompaniments. The eastern window of the church remained entire, with all its ornaments and tracery work, and the sides upheld by flying buttresses, whose airy support, detached from the wall against which they were placed, and ornamented with pinnacles and carved work, gave a variety and lightness to the building. The roof and western end of the church were completely ruinous, but the latter appeared to have made one side of a square, of which the ruins of the conventual buildings formed other two, and the gardens a fourth. The side of these buildings which overhung the brook was partly founded on a steep and precipitous rock; for the place had been occasionally turned to military purposes, and had been taken with great slaughter during Montrose's wars. The ground formerly occupied by the garden was still marked by a few orchard trees. At a greater distance from the buildings were detached oaks and elms and chestnuts growing singly, which had attained great size. The rest of the space between the ruins and the hill was a close-cropt sward, which the daily pasture of the sheep kept in much finer order than if it had been subjected to the scythe and broom. The whole scene had a repose which was still and affecting without being monotonous. The dark, deep basin in which the clear blue lake reposed, reflecting the water lilies which grew on its surface, and the trees which here and there threw their arms from the banks, was finely contrasted with the haste and tumult of the brook, which broke away from the outlet as if escaping from confinement, and hurried down the glen, wheeling around the base of the rock on which the ruins were situated, and brawling in foam and fury with every shelve and stone which obstructed its passage. A similar contrast was seen between the level green meadow in which the ruins were situated, and the large timber trees which were scattered over it, compared with the precipitous banks which arose at a short distance around, partly fringed with light and feathery underwood, partly rising in steeps clothed with purple heath, and partly more abruptly elevated into fronts of grey rock chequered with lichen, and with those hardy plants which find root even in the most arid crevices of the crags.

"There was the retreat of learning in the days of darkness, Mr. Lovel," said Oldbuck, around whom the company had now grouped themselves while they admired the unexpected opening of a prospect so romantic—"there reposed the sages who were aweary of the world, and devoted either to that which was to come or to the service of the generations who should follow them in this. I will show you presently the library: see that stretch of wall with square-shafted windows—there it existed, stored, as an old manuscript in my possession assures me, with five thousand volumes. And here I might well take up the lamentation of the learned Leland, who, regretting the downfall of the conventual libraries, exclaims, like Rachael weeping for her children, that if the papal laws, decrees, decretals, clementines, and other such drugs of the devil, yea, if Heytesbury's sophisms, Porphyry's universals, Aristotle's logic, and Dunse's divinity, with such other lousy legerdemains (begging your pardon, Miss Wardour) and fruits of the bottomless pit, had leapt out of our libraries, for the accommodation of grocers, candle-makers, soap-sellers, and other worldly occupiers, we might have been therewith contented. But to put our ancient chronicles, our noble histories, our learned commentaries and national muniments, to such offices of contempt and subjection has greatly degraded our nation, and showed ourselves dishonoured in the eyes of posterity to the utmost stretch of time. O negligence most unfriendly to our land!"

"And, O John Knox," said the Baronet, "through whose influence, and under whose auspices, the patriotic task was accomplished!"

The Antiquary, somewhat in the situation of a woodcock caught in his own springe, turned short round and coughed to excuse a slight blush, as he mustered his answer: "As to the Apostle of Scottish Reformation——"

But Miss Wardour broke in to interrupt a conversation so dangerous: "Pray, who was the author you quoted, Mr. Oldbuck?"

"The learned Leland, Miss Wardour, who lost his senses on witnessing the destruction of the conventual libraries in England."

"Now I think," replied the young lady, "his misfortune may have saved the rationality of some modern antiquaries, which would certainly have been drowned if so vast a lake of learning had not been diminished by draining."

"Well, thank Heaven, there is no danger now: they have hardly left us a spoonful in which to perform the dire feat."

So saying, Mr. Oldbuck led the way down the bank by a steep but secure path, which soon placed them on the verdant meadow where the ruins stood. "There they lived," continued the Antiquary, "with nought to do but to spend their time in investigating points of remote antiquity, transcribing manuscripts, and composing new works for the information of posterity."

"And," added the Baronet, "in exercising the rites of devotion with a pomp and ceremonial worthy of the office of the priesthood."

"And if Sir Arthur's excellence will permit," said the German, with a low bow, "the monksh might also make de vary curious experiment in deir laboraties, both in chemistry and *magia naturalis.*"

"I think," said the clergyman, "they would have enough to do in collecting the teinds of the parsonage and vicarage of three good parishes."

"And all," added Miss Wardour, nodding to the Antiquary, "without interruption from womankind."

"True, my fair foe," said Oldbuck; "this was a paradise where no Eve was admitted, and we may wonder the rather by what chance the good fathers came to lose it."

With such criticisms on the occupations of those by whom the ruins had been formerly possessed, they wandered for some time from one moss-grown shrine to another, under the guidance of Oldbuck, who explained with much plausibility the

12

ground-plan of the edifice, and read and expounded to the
company the various mouldering inscriptions which yet were
to be traced upon the tombs of the dead, or under the vacant
niches of the sainted images.   "What is the reason," at length
Miss Wardour asked the Antiquary, "why tradition has preserved to us such meagre accounts of the inmates of these
stately edifices, raised with such expense of labour and taste,
and whose owners were in their times personages of such awful
power and importance?   The meanest tower of a freebooting
baron or squire who lived by his lance and broadsword is consecrated by its appropriate legend, and the shepherd will tell
you with accuracy the names and feats of its inhabitants; but
ask a countryman concerning these beautiful and extensive
remains—these towers, these arches and buttresses and shafted
windows, reared at such cost, three words fill up his answer—
'they were made by the monks lang syne.'"

The question was somewhat puzzling.   Sir Arthur looked
upward, as if hoping to be inspired with an answer; Oldbuck
shoved back his wig; the clergyman was of opinion that his
parishioners were too deeply impressed with the true Presbyterian doctrine to preserve any records concerning the papisti-
cal cumberers of the land, offshoots as they were of the great
overshadowing tree of iniquity, whose roots are in the bowels
of the seven hills of abomination; Lovel thought the question
was best resolved by considering what are the events which
leave the deepest impression on the minds of the common
people.   "These," he contended, "were not such as resemble
the gradual progress of a fertilising river, but the headlong
and precipitous fury of some portentous flood.   The eras by
which the vulgar compute time have always reference to some
period of fear and tribulation, and they date by a tempest, an
earthquake, or burst of civil commotion.   When such are the
facts most alive in the memory of the common people, we cannot wonder," he concluded, "that the ferocious warrior is remembered, and the peaceful abbots are abandoned to forget-
fulness and oblivion."

"If you pleashe, gentlemans and ladies, and ashking pardon
of Sir Arthur and Miss Wardour, and this worthy clergy-

mansh, and my goot friend Mr. Oldenbuck, who is my countrymansh, and of goot young Mr. Lofel also, I think it is all owing to de hand of glory."

"The hand of what?" exclaimed Oldbuck.

"De hand of glory, my goot Master Oldenbuck, which is a vary great and terrible secrets, which de monksh used to conceal their treasures when they were triven from their cloisters by what you call de Reform."

"Ay, indeed! tell us about that," said Oldbuck, "for these are secrets worth knowing."

"Why, my goot Master Oldenbuck, you will only laugh at me. But de hand of glory is vary well known in de countries where your worthy progenitors did live, and it is hand cut off from a dead man as has been hanged for murther, and dried very nice in de shmoke of juniper wood, and if you put a little of what you call yew wid your juniper it will not be any better—that is, it will not be no worse; then you do take something of de fatsh of de bear, and of de badger, and of de great *eber*, as you call de grand boar, and of de little sucking child as has not been christened—for dat is very essentials,—and you do make a candle, and put it into de hand of glory at de proper hour and minute, with de proper ceremonish, and he who seeksh for treasuresh shall never find none at all."

"I dare take my corporal oath of that conclusion," said the Antiquary. "And was it the custom, Mr. Dousterswivel, in Westphalia to make use of this elegant candelabrum?"

"Alwaysh, Mr. Oldenbuck, when you did not want nobody to talk of nothing you wash doing about. And de monksh alwaysh did this when they did hide their church plates, and their great chalices, and de rings, wid very preshious shtones and jewels."

"But, notwithstanding, you knights of the Rosy Cross have means, no doubt, of breaking the spell, and discovering what the poor monks have put themselves to so much trouble to conceal?"

"Ah! goot Mr. Oldenbuck," replied the adept, shaking his head mysteriously, "you was very hard to believe; but if you had seen de great huge pieces of de plate so massive, Sir Arthur, so fine fashion, Miss Wardour, and de silver cross dat we did find—dat was Schroepfer and my ownself—for de Herr Freygraff, as you call de Baron von Blunderhaus, I do believe you would have believed then."

"Seeing *is* believing indeed. But what was your art—what was your mystery, Mr. Dousterswivel?"

"Aha, Mr. Oldenbuck, dat is my little secret, mine goot sir; you sall forgife me that I not tell that. But I will tell you dere are various ways; yes, indeed, dere is de dream dat you dream tree times, dat is a vary goot way."

"I am glad of that," said Oldbuck; "I have a friend (with a side-glance to Lovel) who is peculiarly favoured by the visits of Queen Mab."

"Den dere is de sympathies and de antipathies, and de strange properties and virtues natural of divers herb and of de little divining rod."

"I would gladly rather see some of these wonders than hear of them," said Miss Wardour.

"Ah, but, my much-honoured young lady, this is not de time or de way to do de great wonder of finding all de church's plate and treasure; but to oblige you, and Sir Arthur my patron, and de reverend clergymans, and goot Mr. Oldenbuck, and young Mr. Lofel, who is a very goot young gentleman also, I will show you dat it is possible, a vary possible, to discover de spring of water and de little fountain hidden in de ground, without any mattock or spade or dig at all."

"Umph!" quoth the Antiquary, "I have heard of that conundrum. That will be no very productive art in our country; you should carry that property to Spain or Portugal and turn it to good account."

"Ah! my goot Master Oldenbuck, dere is de Inquisition and de auto-da-fé: they would burn me, who am but a simple philosopher, for one great conjurer."

"They would cast away their coals then," said Oldbuck; "but," continued he, in a whisper to Lovel, "were they to pillory him for one of the most impudent rascals that ever wagged a tongue, they would square the punishment more accurately with his deserts. But let us see, I think he is about to show us some of his legerdemain."

In truth the German was now got to a little copse-thicket at some distance from the ruins, where he affected busily to search for such a wand as should suit the purpose of his mystery; and, after cutting and examining and rejecting several, he at length provided himself with a small twig of hazel terminating in a forked end, which he pronounced to possess the virtue proper for the experiment that he was about to exhibit. Holding the forked ends of the wand each between a finger and thumb, and thus keeping the rod upright, he proceeded to pace the ruined aisles and cloisters, followed by the rest of the company in admiring procession. "I believe dere was no waters here," said the adept, when he had made the round of several of the buildings, without perceiving any of those indications which he pretended to expect—"I believe those Scotch monksh did find de water too cool for de climate, and alwaysh drank de goot comfortable Rhine wine—but, aha! see there." Accordingly, the assistants observed the rod to turn in his fingers, although he pretended to hold it very tight. "Dere is water here about sure enough," and, turning this way and that way, as the agitation of the divining rod seemed to increase or diminish, he at length advanced into the midst of a vacant and roofless inclosure, which had been the kitchen of the priory, when the rod twisted itself so as to point almost straight downwards. "Here is de place," said the adept, "and if you do not find de water here I will give you all leave to call me an impudent knave."

"I shall take that license," whispered the Antiquary to Lovel, "whether the water is discovered or no."

A servant, who had come up with a basket of cold refreshments, was now despatched to a neighbouring forester's hut for a mattock and pick-axe. The loose stones and rubbish being removed from the spot indicated by the German, they soon came to the sides of a regularly built well; and, when a few feet of rubbish were cleared out by the assistance of the forester and his sons, the water began to rise rapidly, to the delight of the philosopher, the astonishment of the ladies, Mr.

Blattergowl, and Sir Arthur, the surprise of Lovel, and the confusion of the incredulous Antiquary. He did not fail, however, to enter his protest in Lovel's ear against the miracle. "This is a mere trick," he said; "the rascal had made himself sure of the existence of this old well, by some means or other, before he played off this mystical piece of jugglery. Mark what he talks of next. I am much mistaken if this is not intended as a prelude to some more serious fraud; see how the rascal assumes consequence, and plumes himself upon the credit of his success, and how poor Sir Arthur takes in the tide of nonsense which he is delivering to him as principles of occult science!"

"You do see, my goot patron, you do see, my goot ladies, you do see, worthy Dr. Bladderhowl, and even Mr. Lofel, and Mr. Oldenbuck may see, if they do will to see, how art has no enemy at all but ignorance. Look at this little slip of hazel nuts, it is fit for nothing at all but to whip de little child" ("I would choose a cat and nine tails for your occasions," whispered Oldbuck apart), "and you put it in the hands of a philosopher, paf! it makes de grand discovery. But this is nothing, Sir Arthur, nothing at all, worthy Dr. Botherhowl, nothing at all, ladies, nothing at all, young Mr. Lofel and goot Mr. Oldenbuck, to what art can do. Ah! if dere was any man that had de spirit and de courage I would show him better things than de well of water, I would show him——"

"And a little money would be necessary also, would it not?" said the Antiquary.

"Bah! one trifle, not worthy talking about, might be necessaries," answered the adept.

"I thought as much," rejoined the Antiquary, drily; "and I, in the mean while, without any divining rod, will show you an excellent venison pasty and a bottle of London particular Madeira, and I think that will match all that Mr. Dousterswivel's art is like to exhibit."

The feast was spread *fronde super viridi*, as Oldbuck expressed himself, under a huge old tree, called the Prior's Oak, and the company sitting down around it did ample honour to the contents of the basket.

CHAPTER XVII.

As when a gryphon through the wilderness,
With winged course, o'er hill and moory dale
Pursues the Arimaspian, who by stealth
Had from his wakeful custody purloin'd
The guarded gold, so eagerly the Fiend——
Paradise Lost.

WHEN their collation was ended, Sir Arthur resumed the account of the mysteries of the divining rod, as a subject on which he had formerly conversed with Dousterswivel. "My friend Mr. Oldbuck will now be prepared, Mr. Dousterswivel, to listen with more respect to the stories you have told us of the late discoveries in Germany by the brethren of your association."

"Ah, Sir Arthur, that was not a thing to speak to those gentlemans, because it is want of credulity—what you call faith—that spoils the great enterprise."

"At least, however, let my daughter read the narrative she has taken down of the story of Martin Waldeck."

"Ah, that was very true story; but Miss Wardour, she is so sly and so witty that she has made it just like one romance, as well as Goethe or Wieland could have done it, by mine honest wort."

"To say the truth, Mr. Dousterswivel," answered Miss Wardour, "the romantic predominated in the legend so much above the probable that it was impossible for a lover of fairyland like me to avoid lending a few touches to make it perfect in its kind. But there it is, and if you do not incline to leave this shade till the heat of the day has somewhat declined, and will have sympathy with my bad composition, perhaps Sir Arthur or Mr. Oldbuck will read it to us."

"Not I," said Sir Arthur; "I was never fond of reading aloud."

"Nor I," said Oldbuck, "for I have forgot my spectacles; but here is Lovel, with sharp eyes and a good voice, for Mr. Blattergowl, I know, never reads anything, lest he should be suspected of reading his sermons."

The task was therefore imposed upon Lovel, who received with some trepidation, as Miss Wardour delivered with a little embarrassment, a paper containing the lines traced by that fair hand, the possession of which he coveted as the highest blessing the earth could offer to him. But there was a necessity of suppressing his emotions; and, after glancing over the manuscript, as if to become acquainted with the character, he collected himself and read the company the following tale:

The Fortunes of Martin Waldeck.[1]

The solitudes of the Harz forest in Germany, but especially the mountains called Blockberg, or rather Brockenberg, are the chosen scene for tales of witches, demons, and apparitions. The occupation of the inhabitants, who are either miners or foresters, is of a kind that renders them peculiarly prone to superstition, and the natural phenomena which they witness in pursuit of their solitary or subterraneous profession are often set down by them to the interference of goblins or the power of magic. Among the various legends current in that wild country, there is a favourite one, which supposes the Harz to be haunted by a sort of tutelar demon, in the shape of a wild man, of huge stature, his head wreathed with oak leaves, and his middle cinctured with the same, bearing in his hand a pine torn up by the roots. It is certain that many persons profess to have seen such a form traversing, with huge strides, in a line parallel to their own course, the opposite ridge of a mountain, when divided from it by a narrow glen; and indeed the fact of the apparition is so generally admitted that modern scepticism has only found refuge by ascribing it to optical deception.[2]

In elder times, the intercourse of the demon with the inhabitants was more familiar, and, according to the traditions of the Harz, he was wont, with the caprice usually ascribed to these earth-born powers, to interfere with the affairs of mortals, sometimes for their weal, sometimes for their woe. But it was observed that even his gifts often turned out in

---

[1] See Note 4.   [2] See Spectre of the Harz. Note 5.

the long run fatal to those on whom they were bestowed, and it was no uncommon thing for the pastors, in their care of their flocks, to compose long sermons, the burden whereof was a warning against having any intercourse, direct or indirect, with the Harz demon. The fortunes of Martin Waldeck have been often quoted by the aged to their giddy children, when they were heard to scoff at a danger which appeared visionary.

A travelling capuchin had possessed himself of the pulpit of the thatched church at a little hamlet called Morgenbrodt, lying in the Harz district, from which he declaimed against the wickedness of the inhabitants, their communication with fiends, witches, and fairies, and, in particular, with the woodland goblin of the Harz. The doctrines of Luther had already begun to spread among the peasantry, for the incident is placed under the reign of Charles V., and they laughed to scorn the zeal with which the venerable man insisted upon his topic. At length, as his vehemence increased with opposition, so their opposition rose in proportion to his vehemence. The inhabitants did not like to hear an accustomed quiet demon, who had inhabited the Brockenberg for so many ages, summarily confounded with Baalpeor, Ashtaroth, and Beelzeoub himself, and condemned without reprieve to the bottomless Tophet. The apprehensions that the spirit might avenge himself on them for listening to such an illiberal sentence added to their national interest in his behalf. A travelling friar, they said, that is here to-day and away to-morrow, may say what he pleases; but it is we, the ancient and constant inhabitants of the country, that are left at the mercy of the insulted demon, and must, of course, pay for all. Under the irritation occasioned by these reflections, the peasants from injurious language betook themselves to stones, and having pebbled the priest pretty handsomely, they drove him out of the parish to preach against demons elsewhere.

Three young men, who had been present and assisting on this occasion, were upon their return to the hut where they carried on the laborious and mean occupation of preparing charcoal for the smelting furnaces. On the way their conversation naturally turned upon the demon of the Harz and the doctrine of the capuchin. Max and George Waldeck, the two elder brothers, although they allowed the language of the capuchin to have been indiscreet and worthy of censure, as presuming to determine upon the precise character and abode of the spirit, yet contended it was dangerous, in the highest degree, to accept of his gifts or hold any communication with him. He was powerful, they allowed, but wayward and capricious, and those who had intercourse with him seldom came to a good end. Did he not give the brave knight, Ecbert of Rabenwald, that famous black steed by means of which he vanquished all the champions at the great tournament at Bremen? and did not the same steed afterwards precipitate itself with its rider into an abyss so steep and fearful that neither horse nor man were ever seen more? Had he not given to Dame Gertrude Trodden a curious spell for making butter come? and was she not burnt for a witch by the grand criminal judge of the Electorate because she availed herself of his gift? But these, and many other instances which they quoted, of mischance and ill-luck ultimately attending on the apparent benefits conferred by the Harz spirit, failed to make any impression upon Martin Waldeck, the youngest of the brothers.

Martin was youthful, rash, and impetuous, excelling in all the exercises which distinguish a mountaineer, and brave and undaunted from his familiar intercourse with the dangers that attend them. He laughed at the timidity of his brothers. "Tell me not of such folly," he said; "the demon is a good demon. He lives among us as if he were a peasant like ourselves, haunts the lonely crags and recesses of the mountains like a huntsman or goatherd; and he who loves the Harz forest and its wild scenes cannot be indifferent to the fate of the hardy children of the soil. But, if the demon were as malicious as you would make him, how should he derive power over mortals who barely avail themselves of his gifts, without binding themselves to submit to his pleasure? When you carry your charcoal to the furnace, is not the money as good that is paid you by blaspheming Blaize, the old reprobate overseer, as if you got it from the pastor himself? It is not the goblin's gifts which can endanger you then, but it is the use you shall make of them that you must account for. And were the demon to appear to me at this moment, and indicate to me a gold or silver mine, I would begin to dig away even before his back were turned, and I would consider myself as under protection of a much Greater than he, while I made a good use of the wealth he pointed out to me."

To this the elder brother replied, that wealth ill won was seldom well spent; while Martin presumptuously declared that the possession of all the treasures of the Harz would not make the slightest alteration on his habits, morals, or character.

His brother entreated Martin to talk less wildly upon this subject, and with some difficulty contrived to withdraw his attention by calling it to the consideration of the approaching boar-chase. This talk brought them to their hut, a wretched wigwam, situated upon one side of a wild, narrow, and romantic dell, in the recesses of the Brockenberg. They released their sister from attending upon the operation of charring the wood, which requires constant attention, and divided among themselves the duty of watching it by night, according to their custom, one always waking while his brothers slept.

Max Waldeck, the eldest, watched during the two first hours of the night, and was considerably alarmed by observing upon the opposite bank of the glen or valley a huge fire, surrounded by some figures that appeared to wheel around it with antic gestures. Max at first bethought him of calling up his brothers; but recollecting the daring character of the youngest, and finding it impossible to wake the elder without also disturbing Martin, conceiving also what he saw to be an illusion of the demon, sent perhaps in consequence of the venturous expressions used by Martin on the preceding evening, he thought it best to betake himself to the safeguard of such prayers as he could murmur over, and to watch in great terror and annoyance this strange and alarming apparition. After blazing for some time, the fire faded gradually away into darkness, and the rest of Max's watch was only disturbed by the remembrance of its terrors.

George now occupied the place of Max, who had retired to

rest.   The phenomenon of a huge blazing fire upon the opposite bank of the glen again presented itself to the eye of the
watchman.   It was surrounded as before by figures, which,
distinguished by their opaque forms being, between the spectator and the red glaring light, moved and fluctuated around it
as if engaged in some mystical ceremony.   George, though
equally cautious, was of a bolder character than his elder
brother.   He resolved to examine more nearly the object of
his wonder; and accordingly, after crossing the rivulet which
divided the glen, he climbed up the opposite bank and approached within an arrow's flight of the fire, which blazed
apparently with the same fury as when he first witnessed it.

The appearance of the assistants who surrounded it resembled those phantoms which are seen in a troubled dream, and
at once confirmed the idea he had entertained from the first,
that they did not belong to the human world.   Amongst these
strange unearthly forms George Waldeck distinguished that of
a giant overgrown with hair, holding an uprooted fir in his
hand, with which from time to time he seemed to stir the
blazing fire, and having no other clothing than a wreath of oak
leaves around his forehead and loins.   George's heart sunk
within him at recognising the well-known apparition of the
Harz demon, as he had been often described to him by the
ancient shepherds and huntsmen who had seen his form traversing the mountains.   He turned and was about to fly; but,
upon second thoughts, blaming his own cowardice, he recited
mentally the verse of the Psalmist, "All good angels, praise
the Lord!" which is in that country supposed powerful as
an exorcism, and turned himself once more towards the
place where he had seen the fire.   But it was no longer
visible.

The pale moon alone enlightened the side of the valley;
and when George, with trembling steps, a moist brow, and
hair bristling upright under his collier's cap, came to the spot
on which the fire had been so lately visible, marked as it was
by a scathed oak-tree, there appeared not on the heath the
slightest vestiges of what he had seen.   The moss and wild
flowers were unscorched, and the branches of the oak-tree,

which had so lately appeared enveloped in wreaths of flame and smoke, were moist with the dews of midnight.

George returned to his hut with trembling steps, and, arguing like his elder brother, resolved to say nothing of what he had seen, lest he should awake in Martin that daring curiosity which he almost deemed to be allied with impiety.

It was now Martin's turn to watch. The household cock had given his first summons, and the night was wellnigh spent. Upon examining the state of the furnace in which the wood was deposited in order to its being coked or charred, he was surprised to find that the fire had not been sufficiently maintained; for in his excursion and its consequences George had forgot the principal object of his watch. Martin's first thought was to call up the slumberers; but observing that both his brothers slept unwontedly deep and heavily, he respected their repose, and set himself to supply the furnace with fuel without requiring their aid. What he heaped upon it was apparently damp and unfit for the purpose, for the fire seemed rather to decay than revive. Martin next went to collect some boughs from a stack which had been carefully cut and dried for this purpose; but when he returned he found the fire totally extinguished. This was a serious evil, and threatened them with loss of their trade for more than one day. The vexed and mortified watchman set about to strike a light in order to rekindle the fire, but the tinder was moist and his labour proved in this respect also ineffectual. He was now about to call up his brothers, for circumstances seemed to be pressing, when flashes of light glimmered not only through the window, but through every crevice of the rudely-built hut, and summoned him to behold the same apparition which had before alarmed the successive watches of his brethren. His first idea was that the Muhllerhaussers, their rivals in trade, and with whom they had had many quarrels, might have encroached upon their bounds for the purpose of pirating their wood, and he resolved to awake his brothers and be revenged on them for their audacity. But a short reflection and observation on the gestures and manner of those who seemed to " work in the fire" induced him to dismiss this belief, and, although rather sceptical in such matters, to conclude that what he saw was a supernatural phenomenon. "But be they men or fiends," said the undaunted forester, "that busy themselves yonder with such fantastical rites and gestures, I will go and demand a light to rekindle our furnace." He relinquished at the same time the idea of awaking his brethren. There was a belief that such adventures as he was about to undertake were accessible only to one person at a time; he feared also that his brothers, in their scrupulous timidity, might interfere to prevent his pursuing the investigation he had resolved to commence; and, therefore, snatching his boar-spear from the wall, the undaunted Martin Waldeck set forth on the adventure alone.

With the same success as his brother George, but with courage far superior, Martin crossed the brook, ascended the hill, and approached so near the ghostly assembly that he could recognise in the presiding figure the attributes of the Harz demon. A cold shuddering assailed him for the first time in his life; but the recollection that he had at a distance dared, and even courted, the intercourse which was now about to take place confirmed his staggering courage, and pride supplying what he wanted in resolution, he advanced with tolerable firmness towards the fire, the figures which surrounded it appearing still more wild, fantastical, and supernatural the more near he approached to the assembly. He was received with a loud shout of discordant and unnatural laughter, which to his stunned ears seemed more alarming than a combination of the most dismal and melancholy sounds that could be imagined. "Who art thou?" said the giant, compressing his savage and exaggerated features into a sort of forced gravity, while they were occasionally agitated by the convulsion of the laughter which he seemed to suppress.

"Martin Waldeck, the forester," answered the hardy youth; "and who are you?"

"The King of the Waste and of the Mine," answered the spectre; "and why hast thou dared to encroach on my mysteries?"

"I came in search of light to rekindle my fire," answered

Martin hardily, and then resolutely asked in his turn: "What mysteries are those that you celebrate here?"

"We celebrate," answered the complaisant demon, "the wedding of Hermes with the Black Dragon. But take thy fire that thou camest to seek and begone; no mortal may long look upon us and live."

The peasant struck his spear point into a large piece of blazing wood, which he heaved up with some difficulty, and then turned round to regain his hut, the shouts of laughter being renewed behind him with treble violence, and ringing far down the narrow valley. When Martin returned to the hut, his first care, however much astonished with what he had seen, was to dispose the kindled coal among the fuel so as might best light the fire of his furnace; but after many efforts, and all exertions of bellows and fire-prong, the coal he had brought from the demon's fire became totally extinct, without kindling any of the others. He turned about and observed the fire still blazing on the hill, although those who had been busied around it had disappeared. As he conceived the spectre had been jesting with him, he gave way to the natural hardihood of his temper, and, determining to see the adventure to an end, resumed the road to the fire, from which, unopposed by the demon, he brought off in the same manner a blazing piece of charcoal, but still without being able to succeed in lighting his fire. Impunity having increased his rashness, he resolved upon a third experiment, and was as successful as before in reaching the fire; but, when he had again appropriated a piece of burning coal and had turned to depart, he heard the harsh and supernatural voice which had before accosted him pronounce these words: "Dare not to return hither a fourth time!"

The attempt to kindle the fire with this last coal having proved as ineffectual as on the former occasions, Martin relinquished the hopeless attempt and flung himself on his bed of leaves, resolving to delay till the next morning the communication of his supernatural adventure to his brothers. He was awakened from a heavy sleep into which he had sunk, from fatigue of body and agitation of mind, by loud exclamations of surprise and joy. His brothers, astonished at finding the fire extinguished when they awoke, had proceeded to arrange the fuel in order to renew it, when they found in the ashes three huge metallic masses, which their skill (for most of the peasants in the Harz are practical mineralogists) immediately ascertained to be pure gold.

It was some damp upon their joyful congratulations when they learned from Martin the mode in which he had obtained this treasure, to which their own experience of the nocturnal vision induced them to give full credit. But they were unable to resist the temptation of sharing in their brother's wealth. Taking now upon him as head of the house, Martin Waldeck bought lands and forests, built a castle, obtained a patent of nobility, and, greatly to the indignation of the ancient aristocracy of the neighbourhood, was invested with all the privileges of a man of family. His courage in public war as well as in private feuds, together with the number of retainers whom he kept in pay, sustained him for some time against the odium which was excited by his sudden elevation and the arrogance of his pretensions.

And now it was seen in the instance of Martin Waldeck, as it has been in that of many others, how little mortals can foresee the effect of sudden prosperity on their own disposition. The evil propensities in his nature, which poverty had checked and repressed, ripened and bore their unhallowed fruit under the influence of temptation and the means of indulgence. As deep calls unto deep, one bad passion awakened another: the fiend of avarice invoked that of pride, and pride was to be supported by cruelty and oppression. Waldeck's character, always bold and daring, but rendered harsh and assuming by prosperity, soon made him odious, not to the nobles only, but likewise to the lower ranks, who saw with double dislike the oppressive rights of the feudal nobility of the empire so remorselessly exercised by one who had risen from the very dregs of the people. His adventure, although carefully concealed, began likewise to be whispered abroad, and the clergy already stigmatised as a wizard and accomplice of fiends the wretch who, having acquired so huge a treasure in so strange a manner, had not sought to sanctify it by dedicating a considerable portion to the use of the church. Surrounded by enemies, public and private, tormented by a thousand feuds, and threatened by the church with excommunication, Martin Waldeck, or, as we must now call him, the Baron von Waldeck, often regretted bitterly the labours and sports of his unenvied poverty. But his courage failed him not under all these difficulties, and seemed rather to augment in proportion to the danger which darkened around him, until an accident precipitated his fall.

A proclamation by the reigning Duke of Brunswick had invited to a solemn tournament all German nobles of free and honourable descent, and Martin Waldeck, splendidly armed, accompanied by his two brothers and a gallantly equipped retinue, had the arrogance to appear among the chivalry of the province and demand permission to enter the lists. This was considered as filling up the measure of his presumption. A thousand voices exclaimed: "We will have no cinder-sifter mingle in our games of chivalry." Irritated to frenzy, Martin drew his sword and hewed down the herald, who, in compliance with the general outcry, opposed his entry into the lists. An hundred swords were unsheathed to avenge what was in those days regarded as a crime only inferior to sacrilege or regicide. Waldeck, after defending himself like a lion, was seized, tried on the spot by the judges of the lists, and condemned, as the appropriate punishment for breaking the peace of his sovereign and violating the sacred person of a herald-at-arms, to have his right hand struck from his body, to be ignominiously deprived of the honour of nobility, of which he was unworthy, and to be expelled from the city. When he had been stripped of his arms, and sustained the mutilation imposed by this severe sentence, the unhappy victim of ambition was abandoned to the rabble, who followed him with threats and outcries levelled alternately against the necromancer and oppressor, which at length ended in violence. His brothers (for his retinue were fled and dispersed) at length succeeded in rescuing him from the hands of the populace, when, satiated with cruelty, they had left him half dead through loss of blood and through the

13

outrages he had sustained. They were not permitted, such was the ingenious cruelty of their enemies, to make use of any other means of removing him, excepting such a collier's cart as they had themselves formerly used, in which they deposited their brother on a truss of straw, scarcely expecting to reach any place of shelter ere death should release him from his misery.

When the Waldecks, journeying in this miserable manner, had approached the verge of their native country, in a hollow way between two mountains they perceived a figure advancing towards them, which at first sight seemed to be an aged man. But as he approached, his limbs and stature increased, the cloak fell from his shoulders, his pilgrim's staff was changed into an uprooted pine-tree, and the gigantic figure of the Harz demon passed before them in his terrors. When he came opposite to the cart which contained the miserable Waldeck, his huge features dilated into a grin of unutterable contempt and malignity, as he asked the sufferer: "How like you the fire MY coals have kindled?" The power of motion, which terror suspended in his two brothers, seemed to be restored to Martin by the energy of his courage. He raised himself on the cart, bent his brows, and, clenching his fist, shook it at the spectre with a ghastly look of hate and defiance. The goblin vanished with his usual tremendous and explosive laugh, and left Waldeck exhausted with this effort of expiring nature.

The terrified brethren turned their vehicle toward the towers of a convent which arose in a wood of pine-trees beside the road. They were charitably received by a barefooted and long-bearded capuchin, and Martin survived only to complete the first confession he had made since the day of his sudden prosperity, and to receive absolution from the very priest whom, precisely on that day three years, he had assisted to pelt out of the hamlet of Morgenbrodt. The three years of precarious prosperity were supposed to have a mysterious correspondence with the number of his visits to the spectral fire upon the hill.

The body of Martin Waldeck was interred in the convent

where he expired, in which his brothers, having assumed the habit of the order, lived and died in the performance of acts of charity and devotion. His lands, to which no one asserted any claim, lay waste until they were reassumed by the emperor as a lapsed fief, and the ruins of the castle, which Waldeck had called by his own name, are still shunned by the miner and forester as haunted by evil spirits. Thus were the miseries attendant upon wealth hastily attained and ill-employed exemplified in the fortunes of Martin Waldeck.

CHAPTER XIX.

> Here has been such a stormy encounter
> Betwixt my cousin captain and this soldier,
> About I know not what! Nothing, indeed—
> Competitions, degrees, and comparatives
> Of soldiership!
>
> *A Fair Quarrel.*

THE attentive audience gave the fair transcriber of the foregoing legend the thanks which politeness required. Oldbuck alone curled up his nose, and observed that Miss Wardour's skill was something like that of the alchemists, for she had contrived to extract a sound and valuable moral out of a very trumpery and ridiculous legend. "It is the fashion, as I am given to understand, to admire those extravagant fictions; for me,

> I bear an English heart,
> Unused at ghosts and rattling bones to start."

"Under your favour, my goot Mr. Oldenbuck," said the German, "Miss Wardour has turned de story, as she does everything as she touches, very pretty indeed; but all the history of de Harz goblin, and how he walks among de desolate mountains wid a great fir-tree for his walking-cane, and wid de great green bush around his head and his waist—that is as true as I am an honest man."

"There is no disputing any proposition so well guaranteed,"

answered the Antiquary, drily. But at this moment the approach of a stranger cut short the conversation.

The new comer was a handsome young man, about five-and-twenty, in a military undress, and bearing in his look and manner a good deal of the martial profession—nay, perhaps a little more than is quite consistent with the ease of a man of perfect good-breeding, in whom no professional habit ought to predominate. He was at once greeted by the greater part of the company. "My dear Hector!" said Miss M'Intyre, as she rose to take his hand——

"Hector, son of Priam, whence comest thou?" said the Antiquary.

"From Fife, my liege," answered the young soldier, and continued, when he had politely saluted the rest of the company, and particularly Sir Arthur and his daughter: "I learned from one of the servants, as I rode towards Monkbarns to pay my respects to you, that I should find the present company in this place, and I willingly embrace the opportunity to pay my respects to so many of my friends at once."

"And to a new one also, my trusty Trojan," said Oldbuck. "Mr. Lovel, this is my nephew, Captain M'Intyre; Hector, I recommend Mr. Lovel to your acquaintance."

The young soldier fixed his keen eye upon Lovel, and paid his compliment with more reserve than cordiality; and, as our acquaintance thought his coldness almost supercilious, he was equally frigid and haughty in making the necessary return to it; and thus a prejudice seemed to arise between them at the very commencement of their acquaintance.

The observations which Lovel made during the remainder of this pleasure party did not tend to reconcile him with this addition to their society. Captain M'Intyre, with the gallantry to be expected from his age and profession, attached himself to the service of Miss Wardour, and offered her on every possible opportunity those marks of attention which Lovel would have given the world to have rendered, and was only deterred from offering by the fear of her displeasure. With forlorn dejection at one moment and with irritated susceptibility at another, he saw this handsome young soldier assume and exercise all the privileges of a *eavaliere servente*. He handed Miss Wardour's gloves, he assisted her in putting on her shawl, he attached himself to her in the walks, had a hand ready to remove every impediment in her path, and an arm to support her where it was rugged or difficult; his conversation was addressed chiefly to her, and, where circumstances permitted, it was exclusively so. All this Lovel well knew might be only that sort of egotistical gallantry which induces some young men of the present day to give themselves the air of engrossing the attention of the prettiest woman in company, as if the others were unworthy of their notice. But he thought he observed in the conduct of Captain M'Intyre something of marked and peculiar tenderness, which was calculated to alarm the jealousy of a lover. Miss Wardour also received his attentions; and, although his candour allowed they were of a kind which could not be repelled without some strain of affectation, yet it galled him to the heart to witness that she did so.

The heart-burning which these reflections occasioned proved very indifferent seasoning to the dry antiquarian discussions with which Oldbuck, who continued to demand his particular attention, was unremittingly persecuting him; and he underwent, with fits of impatience that amounted almost to loathing, a course of lectures upon monastic architecture in all its styles, from the massive Saxon to the florid Gothic, and from that to the mixed and composite architecture of James the First's time, when, according to Oldbuck, all orders were confounded, and columns of various descriptions arose side by side, or were piled above each other, as if symmetry had been forgotten, and the elemental principles of art resolved into their primitive confusion. "What can be more cutting to the heart than the sight of evils," said Oldbuck, in rapturous enthusiasm, "which we are compelled to behold, while we do not possess the power of remedying them?" Lovel answered by an involuntary groan. "I see, my dear young friend and most congenial spirit, that you feel these enormities almost as much as I do. Have you ever approached them or met them without longing to tear, to deface, what is so dishonourable?"

"Dishonourable!" echoed Lovel, "in what respect dis honourable?"

"I mean disgraceful to the arts."

"Where? how?"

"Upon the portico, for example, of the schools of Oxford, where, at immense expense, the barbarous, fantastic, and ignorant architect has chosen to represent the whole five orders of architecture on the front of one building."

By such attacks as these Oldbuck, unconscious of the torture he was giving, compelled Lovel to give him a share of his attention, as a skilful angler by means of his line maintains an influence over the most frantic movements of his agonised prey.

They were now on their return to the spot where they had left the carriages; and it is inconceivable how often in the course of that short walk Lovel, exhausted by the unceasing prosing of his worthy companion, mentally bestowed on the devil, or any one else that would have rid him of hearing more of them, all the orders and disorders of architecture which had been invented or combined from the building of Solomon's temple downwards. A slight incident occurred, however, which sprinkled a little patience on the heat of his distemperature.

Miss Wardour and her self-elected knight-companion rather preceded the others in the narrow path, when the young lady apparently became desirous to unite herself with the rest of the party, and, to break off her *tête-à-tête* with the young officer, fairly made a pause until Mr. Oldbuck came up. "I wished to ask you a question, Mr. Oldbuck, concerning the date of these interesting ruins."

It would be doing injustice to Miss Wardour's *savoir faire* to suppose she was not aware that such a question would lead to an answer of no limited length. The Antiquary, starting like a war-horse at the trumpet sound, plunged at once into the various arguments for and against the date of 1273, which had been assigned to the priory of St. Ruth by a late publication on Scottish architectural antiquities. He raked up the names of all the priors who had ruled the institution, of the nobles who had bestowed lands upon it, and of the monarchs who had slept their last sleep among its roofless courts. As a train which takes fire is sure to light another, if there be such in the vicinity, the Baronet, catching at the name of one of his ancestors which occurred in Oldbuck's disquisition, entered upon an account of his wars, his conquests, and his trophies; and worthy Dr. Blattergowl was induced, from the mention of a grant of lands, *cum decimis inclusis tam vicariis quam garbalibus, et nunquam antea separatis,* to enter into a long explanation concerning the interpretation given by the Teind Court in the consideration of such a clause, which had occurred in a process for localling his last augmentation of stipend. The orators, like three racers, each pressed forward to the goal, without much regarding how each crossed and jostled his competitors. Mr. Oldbuck harangued, the Baronet declaimed, Mr. Blattergowl prosed and laid down the law, while the Latin forms of feudal grants were mingled with the jargon of blazonry and the yet more barbarous phraseology of the Teind Court of Scotland. "He was," exclaimed Oldbuck, speaking of the Prior Adhemar, "indeed an exemplary prelate; and, from his strictness of morals, rigid execution of penance, joined to the charitable disposition of his mind and the infirmities endured by his great age and ascetic habits——"

Here he chanced to cough, and Sir Arthur burst in, or rather continued: "was called popularly Hell-in-Harness; he carried a shield, gules with a sable fess, which we have since disused, and was slain at the battle of Vernoil, in France, after killing six of the English with his own——"

"Decreet of certification," proceeded the clergyman, in that prolonged, steady, prosing tone which, however overpowered at first by the vehemence of competition, promised in the long run to obtain the ascendency in this strife of narrators—"decreet of certification having gone out, and parties being held as confessed, the proof seemed to be held as concluded, when their lawyer moved to have it opened, upon the allegation that they had witnesses to bring forward, that they had been in the habit of carrying the ewes to lamb on the teind-free land, which was a mere evasion, for——"

But here the Baronet and Mr. Oldbuck having recovered their wind and continued their respective harangues, the three strands of the conversation, to speak the language of a rope-work, were again twined together into one undistinguishable string of confusion.

Yet, howsoever uninteresting this piebald jargon might seem, it was obviously Miss Wardour's purpose to give it her attention, in preference to yielding Captain M'Intyre an opportunity of renewing their private conversation. So that, after waiting for a little time with displeasure ill concealed by his haughty features, he left her to enjoy her bad taste, and, taking his sister by the arm, detained her a little behind the rest of the party.

"So I find, Mary, that your neighbourhood has neither become more lively nor less learned during my absence."

"We lacked your patience and wisdom to instruct us, Hector."

"Thank you, my dear sister. But you have got a wiser, if not so lively an addition to your society than your unworthy brother; pray, who is this Mr. Lovel, whom our old uncle has at once placed so high in his good graces? He does not use to be so accessible to strangers."

"Mr. Lovel, Hector, is a very gentleman-like young man."

"Ay, that is to say, he bows when he comes into a room, and wears a coat that is whole at the elbows."

"No, brother; it says a great deal more. It says that his manners and discourse express the feelings and education of the higher class."

"But I desire to know what is his birth and his rank in society, and what is his title to be in the circle in which I find him domesticated?"

"If you mean how he comes to visit at Monkbarns, you must ask my uncle, who will probably reply, that he invites to his own house such company as he pleases; and if you mean to ask Sir Arthur, you must know that Mr. Lovel rendered Miss Wardour and him a service of the most important kind."

"What! that romantic story is true then? And pray, does the valorous knight aspire, as is befitting on such occasions, to the hand of the young lady whom he redeemed from peril? It is quite in the rule of romance, I am aware; and I did think that she was uncommonly dry to me as we walked together, and seemed from time to time as if she watched whether she was not giving offence to her gallant cavalier."

"Dear Hector," said his sister, "if you really continue to nourish any affection for Miss Wardour——"

"If, Mary? What an 'if' was there!"

"—I own I consider your perseverance as hopeless."

"And why hopeless, my sage sister?" asked Captain M'Intyre. "Miss Wardour, in the state of her father's affairs, cannot pretend to much fortune; and as to family, I trust that of M'Intyre is not inferior."

"But, Hector," continued his sister, "Sir Arthur always considers us as members of the Monkbarns family."

"Sir Arthur may consider what he pleases," answered the Highlander, scornfully; "but any one with common sense will consider that the wife takes rank from the husband, and that my father's pedigree of fifteen unblemished descents must have ennobled my mother, if her veins had been filled with printer's ink."

"For God's sake, Hector," replied his anxious sister, "take care of yourself. A single expression of that kind, repeated to my uncle by an indiscreet or interested eavesdropper, would lose you his favour for ever, and destroy all chance of your succeeding to his estate."

"Be it so," answered the heedless young man. "I am one of a profession which the world has never been able to do without, and will far less endure to want for half a century to come; and my good old uncle may tack his good estate and his plebeian name to your apron-string if he pleases, Mary, and you may wed this new favourite of his if you please, and you may both of you live quiet, peaceable, well-regulated lives if it pleases Heaven. My part is taken: I'll fawn on no man for an inheritance which should be mine by birth."

Miss M'Intyre laid her hand on her brother's arm and entreated him to suppress his vehemence. "Who," she said, "injures, or seeks to injure you, but your own hasty temper?

what dangers are you defying but those you have yourself conjured up? Our uncle has hitherto been all that is kind and paternal in his conduct to us, and why should you suppose he will in future be otherwise than what he has ever been since we were left as orphans to his care?"

"He is an excellent old gentleman, I must own," replied M'Intyre, "and I am enraged at myself when I chance to offend him; but then his eternal harangues upon topics not worth the spark of a flint, his investigations about invalided pots and pans and tobacco-stoppers past service—all these things put me out of patience. I have something of Hotspur in me, sister, I must confess."

"Too much, too much, my dear brother. Into how many risks, and, forgive me for saying, some of them little creditable, has this absolute and violent temper led you! Do not let such clouds darken the time you are now to pass in our neighbourhood, but let our old benefactor see his kinsman as he is—generous, kind, and lively, without being rude, head-strong, and impetuous."

"Well," answered Captain M'Intyre, "I am schooled, good manners be my speed! I'll do the civil thing by your new friend: I'll have some talk with this Mr. Lovel."

With this determination, in which he was for the time perfectly sincere, he joined the party who were walking before them. The treble disquisition was by this time ended, and Sir Arthur was speaking on the subject of foreign news and the political and military situation of the country, themes upon which every man thinks himself qualified to give an opinion. An action of the preceding year having come upon the tapis, Lovel, accidentally mingling in the conversation, made some assertion concerning it, of the accuracy of which Captain M'Intyre seemed not to be convinced, although his doubts were politely expressed.

"You must confess yourself in the wrong here, Hector," said his uncle, "although I know no man less willing to give up an argument; but you were in England at the time, and Mr. Lovel was probably concerned in the affair."

"I am speaking to a military man, then," said M'Intyre;

"may I inquire to what regiment Mr. Lovel belongs?" Mr. Lovel gave him the number of the regiment. "It happens strangely that we should never have met before, Mr. Lovel. I know your regiment very well, and have served along with them at different times."

A blush crossed Lovel's countenance. "I have not lately been with my regiment," he replied; "I served the last campaign upon the staff of General Sir —— ——."

"Indeed! that is more wonderful than the other circumstance; for, although I did not serve with General Sir —— ——, yet I had an opportunity of knowing the names of the officers who held situations in his family, and I cannot recollect that of Lovel."

At this observation Lovel again blushed so deeply as to attract the attention of the whole company, while a scornful laugh seemed to indicate Captain M'Intyre's triumph. "There is something strange in this," said Oldbuck to himself, "but I will not readily give up my phœnix of post-chaise companions; all his actions, language, and bearing are those of a gentleman."

Lovel in the mean while had taken out his pocket-book, and selecting a letter, from which he took off the envelope, he handed it to M'Intyre. "You know the general's hand in all probability; I own I ought not to show these exaggerated expressions of his regard and esteem for me." The letter contained a very handsome compliment from the officer in question for some military service lately performed. Captain M'Intyre, as he glanced his eye over it, could not deny that it was written in the general's hand, but drily observed, as he returned it, that the address was wanting. "The address, Captain M'Intyre," answered Lovel in the same tone, "shall be at your service whenever you choose to inquire after it."

"I certainly shall not fail to do so," rejoined the soldier.

"Come, come," exclaimed Oldbuck, "what is the meaning of all this? Have we got Hiren here? We'll have no swaggering, youngsters. Are you come from the wars abroad to stir up domestic strife in our peaceful land? Are you like bull-dog puppies, forsooth, that, when the bull, poor fellow, is removed from the ring, fall to brawl among themselves, worry each other, and bite honest folks' shins that are standing by."

Sir Arthur trusted, he said, that the young gentlemen would not so far forget themselves as to grow warm upon such a trifling subject as the back of a letter.

Both the disputants disclaimed any such intention, and, with high colour and flashing eyes, protested they were never so cool in their lives. But an obvious damp was cast over the party; they talked in future too much by the rule to be sociable, and Lovel, conceiving himself the object of cold and suspicious looks from the rest of the company, and sensible that his indirect replies had given them permission to entertain strange opinions respecting him, made a gallant determination to sacrifice the pleasure he had proposed in spending the day at Knockwinnock.

He affected, therefore, to complain of a violent headache, occasioned by the heat of the day, to which he had not been exposed since his illness, and made a formal apology to Sir Arthur, who, listening more to recent suspicion than to the gratitude due for former services, did not press him to keep his engagement more than good-breeding exactly demanded.

When Lovel took leave of the ladies, Miss Wardour's manner seemed more anxious than he had hitherto remarked it. She indicated by a glance of her eye towards Captain M'Intyre, perceptible only by Lovel, the subject of her alarm, and hoped, in a voice greatly under her usual tone, it was not a less pleasant engagement which deprived them of the pleasure of Mr. Lovel's company. "No engagement had intervened," he assured her; "it was only the return of a complaint by which he had been for some time occasionally attacked."

"The best remedy in such a case is prudence, and I—every friend of Mr. Lovel's—will expect him to employ it."

Lovel bowed low and coloured deeply, and Miss Wardour, as if she felt that she had said too much, turned and got into the carriage. Lovel had next to part with Oldbuck, who during this interval had, with Caxon's assistance, been arranging his disordered periwig and brushing his coat, which exhibited some marks of the rude path they had traversed. "What, man!" said Oldbuck, "you are not going to leave us on account of that foolish Hector's indiscreet curiosity and vehemence? Why, he is a thoughtless boy, a spoiled child from the time he was in the nurse's arms: he threw his coral and bells at my head for refusing him a bit of sugar; and you have too much sense to mind such a shrewish boy; *æquam servare mentem* is the motto of our friend Horace. I'll school Hector by and by, and put it all to rights." But Lovel persisted in his design of returning to Fairport.

The Antiquary then assumed a graver tone. "Take heed, young man, to your present feelings. Your life has been given you for useful and valuable purposes, and should be reserved to illustrate the literature of your country, when you are not called upon to expose it in her defence, or in the rescue of the innocent. Private war, a practice unknown to the civilised ancients, is, of all the absurdities introduced by the Gothic tribes, the most gross, impious, and cruel. Let me hear no more of these absurd quarrels, and I will show you the treatise upon the duello which I composed when the town-clerk and provost Mucklewhame chose to assume the privileges of gentlemen and challenged each other. I thought of printing my essay, which is signed 'Pacificator'; but there was no need, as the matter was taken up by the town-council of the borough."

"But I assure you, my dear sir, there is nothing between Captain M'Intyre and me that can render such respectable interference necessary."

"See it be so, for otherwise I will stand second to both parties."

So saying, the old gentleman got into the chaise, close to which Miss M'Intyre had detained her brother, upon the same principle that the owner of a quarrelsome dog keeps him by his side to prevent his fastening upon another. But Hector contrived to give her precaution the slip, for, as he was on horseback, he lingered behind the carriages until they had fairly turned the corner in the road to Knockwinnock, and then, wheeling his horse's head round, gave him the spur in the opposite direction.

A very few minutes brought him up with Lovel, who, perhaps anticipating his intention, had not put his horse beyond
a slow walk, when the clatter of hoofs behind him announced
Captain M'Intyre. The young soldier, his natural heat of
temper exasperated by the rapidity of motion, reined his horse
up suddenly and violently by Lovel's side, and, touching his
hat slightly, inquired, in a very haughty tone of voice: "What
am I to understand, sir, by your telling me that your address
was at my service?"

"Simply, sir," replied Lovel, "that my name is Lovel, and
that my residence is, for the present, Fairport, as you will see
by this card."

"And this is all the information you are disposed to give
me?"

"I see no right you have to require more."

"I find you, sir, in company with my sister," said the young
soldier, "and I have a right to know who is admitted into Miss
M'Intyre's society."

"I shall take the liberty of disputing that right," replied
Lovel, with a manner as haughty as that of the young soldier;
"you find me in society who are satisfied with the degree of
information on my affairs which I have thought proper to
communicate, and you, a mere stranger, have no right to inquire further."

"Mr. Lovel, if you served as you say you have——"

"If!" interrupted Lovel—"*if* I have served as *I say* I
have?"

"Yes, sir, such is my expression; *if* you have so served,
you must know that you owe me satisfaction either in one
way or other."

"If that be your opinion, I shall be proud to give it to you,
Captain M'Intyre, in the way in which the word is generally
used among gentlemen."

"Very well, sir," rejoined Hector, and, turning his horse
round, galloped off to overtake his party.

His absence had already alarmed them, and his sister, having stopped the carriage, had her neck stretched out of the
window to see where he was.

"What is the matter with you now?" said the Antiquary, "riding to and fro as your neck were upon the wager; why do you not keep up with the carriage?"

"I forgot my glove, sir," said Hector.

"Forgot your glove! I presume you meant to say you went to throw it down; but I will take order with you, my young gentleman: you shall return with me this night to Monkbarns." So saying, he bid the postilion go on.

CHAPTER XX.

If you fail Honour here,
Never presume to serve her any more;
Bid farewell to the integrity of armes,
And the honourable name of soldier
Fall from you, like a shivered wreath of laurel
By thunder struck from a desertlesse forehead.
A Fair Quarrel.

EARLY the next morning a gentleman came to wait upon Mr. Lovel, who was up and ready to receive him. He was a military gentleman, a friend of Captain M'Intyre's, at present in Fairport on the recruiting service. Lovel and he were slightly known to each other. "I presume, sir," said Mr. Lesley (such was the name of the visitor), "that you guess the occasion of my troubling you so early?"

"A message from Captain M'Intyre, I presume?"

"The same; he holds himself injured by the manner in which you declined yesterday to answer certain inquiries which he conceived himself entitled to make respecting a gentleman whom he found in intimate society with his family."

"May I ask if you, Mr. Lesley, would have inclined to satisfy interrogatories so haughtily and unceremoniously put to you?"

"Perhaps not; and therefore, as I know the warmth of my friend M'Intyre on such occasions, I feel very desirous of acting as peacemaker. From Mr. Lovel's very gentleman-like manners every one must strongly wish to see him repel all that sort of dubious calumny which will attach itself to one whose situation is not fully explained. If he will permit me, in friendly conciliation, to inform Captain M'Intyre of his real name, for we are led to conclude that of Lovel is assumed——"

"I beg your pardon, sir, but I cannot admit that inference."

"Or at least," said Lesley, proceeding, "that it is not the name by which Mr. Lovel has been at all times distinguished; if Mr. Lovel will have the goodness to explain this circumstance, which, in my opinion, he should do in justice to his own character, I will answer for the amicable arrangement of this unpleasant business."

"Which is to say, Mr. Lesley, that if I condescend to answer questions which no man has a right to ask, and which are now put to me under penalty of Captain M'Intyre's resentment, Captain M'Intyre will condescend to rest satisfied? Mr. Lesley, I have just one word to say on this subject. I have no doubt my secret, if I had one, might be safely entrusted to your honour, but I do not feel called upon to satisfy the curiosity of any one. Captain M'Intyre met me in society which of itself was a warrant to all the world, and particularly ought to be such to him, that I was a gentleman. He has, in my opinion, no right to go any further, or to inquire the pedigree, rank, or circumstances of a stranger who, without seeking any intimate connexion with him or his, chances to dine with his uncle or walk in company with his sister."

"In that case, Captain M'Intyre requests you to be informed that your farther visits at Monkbarns, and all connexion with Miss M'Intyre, must be dropt, as disagreeable to him."

"I shall certainly," said Lovel, "visit Mr. Oldbuck when it suits me, without paying the least respect to his nephew's threats or irritable feelings. I respect the young lady's name too much—though nothing can be slighter than our acquaintance—to introduce it into such a discussion."

"Since that is your resolution, sir," answered Lesley, "Captain M'Intyre requests that Mr. Lovel, unless he wishes to be announced as a very dubious character, will favour him with a meeting this evening at seven at the thorn-tree in the little valley, close by the ruins of St. Ruth."

"Most unquestionably I will wait upon him. There is only one difficulty: I must find a friend to accompany me, and where to seek one on this short notice, as I have no acquaintances in Fairport— I will be on the spot, however, Captain M'Intyre may be assured of that."

Lesley had taken his hat and was as far as the door of the apartment, when, as if moved by the peculiarity of Lovel's situation, he returned and thus addressed him: "Mr. Lovel, there is something so singular in all this that I cannot help again resuming the argument. You must be yourself aware at this moment of the inconvenience of your preserving an incognito for which, I am convinced, there can be no dishonourable reason. Still, this mystery renders it difficult for you to procure the assistance of a friend in a crisis so delicate; nay, let me add, that many persons will even consider it as a piece of Quixotry in M'Intyre to give you a meeting while your character and circumstances are involved in such obscurity."

"I understand your innuendo, Mr. Lesley," rejoined Lovel, "and though I might be offended at its severity, I am not so, because it is meant kindly. But, in my opinion, he is entitled to all the privileges of a gentleman to whose charge, during the time he has been known in the society where he happens to move, nothing can be laid that is unhandsome or unbecoming. For a friend, I dare say I shall find some one or other who will do me that good turn; and if his experience be less than I could wish, I am certain not to suffer through that circumstance when you are in the field for my antagonist."

"I trust you will not," said Lesley; "but as I must, for my own sake, be anxious to divide so heavy a responsibility with a capable assistant, allow me to say, that Lieutenant Taffril's gun-brig is come into the roadstead, and he himself is now at old Caxon's, where he lodges. I think you have the same degree of acquaintance with him as with me, and, as I am sure I should willingly have rendered you such a service were I not engaged on the other side, I am convinced he will do so at your first request."

"At the thorn-tree, then, Mr. Lesley, at seven this evening. The arms, I presume, are pistols?"

14

"Exactly. M'Intyre has chosen the hour at which he can best escape from Monkbarns; he was with me this morning by five in order to return and present himself before his uncle was up. Good-morning to you, Mr. Lovel." And Lesley left the apartment.

Lovel was as brave as most men; but none can internally regard such a crisis as now approached without deep feelings of awe and uncertainty. In a few hours he might be in another world to answer for an action which his calmer thought told him was unjustifiable in a religious point of view, or he might be wandering about in the present like Cain, with the blood of his brother on his head. And all this might be saved by speaking a single word. Yet pride whispered, that to speak that word now would be ascribed to a motive which would degrade him more low than even the most injurious reasons that could be assigned for his silence. Every one, Miss Wardour included, must then, he thought, account him a mean, dishonoured poltroon, who gave to the fear of meeting Captain M'Intyre the explanation he had refused to the calm and handsome expostulations of Mr. Lesley. M'Intyre's insolent behaviour to himself personally, the air of pretension which he assumed towards Miss Wardour, and the extreme injustice, arrogance, and incivility of his demands upon a perfect stranger, seemed to justify him in repelling his rude investigation. In short, he formed the resolution, which might have been expected from so young a man, to shut the eyes, namely, of his calmer reason, and follow the dictates of his offended pride. With this purpose he sought Lieutenant Taffril.

The Lieutenant received him with the good-breeding of a gentleman and the frankness of a sailor, and listened with no small surprise to the detail which preceded his request that he might be favoured with his company at his meeting with Captain M'Intyre. When he had finished, Taffril rose up and walked through his apartment once or twice.

"This is a most singular circumstance," he said, "and really——"

"I am conscious, Mr. Taffril, how little I am entitled to

make my present request, but the urgency of circumstances hardly leaves me an alternative."

"Permit me to ask you one question," asked the sailor; "is there anything of which you are ashamed in the circumstances which you have declined to communicate?"

"Upon my honour, no; there is nothing but what, in a very short time, I trust I may publish to the whole world."

"I hope the mystery arises from no false shame at the lowness of your friends perhaps, or connexions?"

"No, on my word," replied Lovel.

"I have little sympathy for that folly," said Taffril; "indeed, I cannot be supposed to have any; for, speaking of my relations, I may be said to have come myself from before the mast, and I believe I shall very soon form a connexion which the world will think low enough with a very amiable girl, to whom I have been attached since we were next-door neighbours, at a time when I little thought of the good fortune which has brought me forward in the service."

"I assure you, Mr. Taffril," replied Lovel, "whatever were the rank of my parents, I should never think of concealing it from a spirit of petty pride. But I am so situated at present that I cannot enter on the subject of my family with any propriety."

"It is quite enough," said the honest sailor; "give me your hand; I'll see you as well through this business as I can, though it is but an unpleasant one after all. But what of that? our own honour has the next call on us after our country. You are a lad of spirit, and I own I think Mr. Hector M'Intyre, with his long pedigree and his airs of family, very much of a jackanapes. His father was a soldier of fortune as I am a sailor; he himself, I suppose, is little better, unless just as his uncle pleases; and whether one pursues fortune by land or sea makes no great difference, I should fancy."

"None in the universe, certainly," answered Lovel.

"Well," said his new ally, "we will dine together and arrange matters for this rencounter. I hope you understand the use of the weapon?"

"Not particularly," Lovel replied.

"I am sorry for that; M'Intyre is said to be a marksman."

"I am sorry for it also," said Lovel; "both for his sake and my own. I must then, in self-defence, take my aim as well as I can."

"Well," added Taffril, "I will have our surgeon's mate on the field—a good clever young fellow at caulking a shot-hole. I will let Lesley, who is an honest fellow for a landsman, know that he attends for the benefit of either party. Is there anything I can do for you in case of an accident?"

"I have but little occasion to trouble you," said Lovel; "this small billet contains the key of my escritoir and my very brief secret. There is one letter in the escritoir" (digesting a temporary swelling of the heart as he spoke) "which I beg the favour of you to deliver with your own hand."

"I understand," said the sailor; "nay, my friend, never be ashamed for the matter; an affectionate heart may overflow for an instant at the eyes, if the ship were clearing for action; and, depend on it, whatever your injunctions are, Dan Taffril will regard them like the bequest of a dying brother. But this is all stuff! We must get our things in fighting order, and you will dine with me and my little surgeon's mate at the Græme's Arms, over the way, at four o'clock."

"Agreed," said Lovel.

"Agreed," said Taffril; and the whole affair was arranged.

It was a beautiful summer evening, and the shadow of the solitary thorn-tree was lengthening upon the short green sward of the narrow valley, which was skirted by the woods that closed around the ruins of St. Ruth.[1]

Lovel and Lieutenant Taffril, with the surgeon, came upon the ground with a purpose of a nature very uncongenial to the soft, mild, and pacific character of the hour and scene. The sheep, which, during the ardent heat of the day, had sheltered in the breaches and hollows of the gravelly bank, or under the roots of the aged and stunted trees, had now spread themselves upon the face of the hill to enjoy their evening's pasture, and

[1] Supposed to have been suggested by the old abbey of Arbroath in Forfarshire (*Laing*).

bleated to each other with that melancholy sound which at once gives life to a landscape and marks its solitude. Taffril and Lovel came on in deep conference, having, for fear of discovery, sent their horses back to the town by the Lieutenant's servant. The opposite party had not yet appeared on the field. But, when they came upon the ground, there sat upon the roots of the old thorn a figure as vigorous in his decay as the moss-grown but strong and contorted boughs which served him for a canopy. It was old Ochiltree. "This is embarrassing enough," said Lovel; "how shall we get rid of this old fellow?"

"Here, father Adam," cried Taffril, who knew the mendicant of yore—"here's half-a-crown for you; you must go to the Four Horseshoes yonder—the little inn, you know—and inquire for a servant with blue and yellow livery. If he is not come, you'll wait for him, and tell him we shall be with his master in about an hour's time. At any rate wait there till we come back, and—get off with you—come, come, weigh anchor."

"I thank ye for your awmous," said Ochiltree, pocketing the piece of money; "but I beg your pardon, Mr. Taffril, I canna gang your errand e'en now."

"Why not, man? what can hinder you?"

"I wad speak a word wi' young Mr. Lovel."

"With me?" answered Lovel; "what would you say with me? Come, say on, and be brief."

The mendicant led him a few paces aside. "Are ye indebted ony thing to the Laird o' Monkbarns?"

"Indebted! no, not I. What of that? what makes you think so?"

"Ye maun ken I was at the shirra's the day; for, God help me, I gang about a' gates like the troubled spirit, and wha suld come whirling there in a post-chaise but Monkbarns i an unco carfuffle. Now it's no a little thing that will make his honour take a chaise and post-horse twa days rinnin'."

"Well, well; but what is all this to me?"

"Ou, ye'se hear, ye'se hear. Weel, Monkbarns is closeted wi' the shirra whatever puir folk may be left thereout, ye needna doubt that; the gentlemen are aye unco civil amang themsells."

"For Heaven's sake, my old friend——"

"Canna ye bid me gang to the deevil at ance, Mr. Lovel? it wad be mair purpose fa'ard than to speak o' heaven in that impatient gate."

"But I have private business with Lieutenant Taffril here."

"Weel, weel, a' in gude time," said the beggar. "I can use a little wee bit freedom wi' Mr. Daniel Taffril; mony's the peery and the tap I worked for him lang syne, for I was a worker in wood as weel as a tinkler."

"You are either mad, Adam, or have a mind to drive me mad."

"Nane o' the twa," said Edie, suddenly changing his manner from the protracted drawl of the mendicant to a brief and decided tone. "The shirra sent for his clerk, and, as the lad is rather light o' the tongue, I fand it was for drawing a warrant to apprehend you; I thought it had been on a 'fugie' warrant for debt, for a' body kens the Laird likes naebody to pit his hand in his pouch. But now I may haud my tongue, for I see the M'Intyre lad and Mr. Lesley coming up, and I guess that Monkbarns's purpose was very kind, and that yours is muckle waur than it should be."

The antagonists now approached, and saluted with the stern civility which befitted the occasion. "What has this old fellow to do here?" said M'Intyre.

"I am an auld fallow," said Edie, "but I am also an auld soldier o' your father's, for I served wi' him in the 42d."

"Serve where you please, you have no title to intrude on us," said M'Intyre, "or"—and he lifted his cane *in terrorem*, though without the idea of touching the old man. But Ochiltree's courage was roused by the insult. "Haud down your switch, Captain M'Intyre! I am an auld soldier, as I said before, and I'll take muckle frae your father's son; but no a touch o' the wand while my pike-staff will haud thegither."

"Well, well, I was wrong—I was wrong," said M'Intyre. "Here's a crown for you; go your ways. What's the matter now?"

The old man drew himself up to the full advantage of his uncommon height, and in despite of his dress, which indeed had more of the pilgrim than the ordinary beggar, looked, from height, manner, and emphasis of voice and gesture, rather like a grey palmer or eremite preacher, the ghostly counsellor of the young men who were around him, than the object of their charity. His speech, indeed, was as homely as his habit, but as bold and unceremonious as his erect and dignified demeanour. "What are ye come here for, young men?" he said, addressing himself to the surprised audience; "are ye come amongst the most lovely works of God to break His laws? Have ye left the works of man, the houses and the cities that are but clay and dust, like those that built them; and are ye come here among the peaceful hills, and by the quiet waters, that will last whiles aught earthly shall endure, to destroy each other's lives, that will have but an unco short time, by the course of nature, to make up a lang account at the close o't? Oh sirs! hae ye brothers, sisters, fathers, that hae tended ye, and mothers that hae travailed for ye, friends that hae ca'd ye like a piece o' their ain heart? And is this the way ye tak to make them childless and brotherless and friendless? Ohon! it's an ill feight whar he that wins has the warst o't. Think on't, bairns. I'm a puir man, but I'm an auld man too; and what my poverty takes awa frae the weight o' my counsel, grey hairs and a truthfu' heart should add it twenty times. Gang hame, gang hame, like gude lads; the French will be ower to harry us ane o' thae days, and ye'll hae feighting eneugh, and maybe auld Edie will hirple out himself if he can get a feal-dike to lay his gun ower, and may live to tell you whilk o' ye does the best where there's a good cause afore ye."

There was something in the undaunted and independent manner, hardy sentiment, and manly, rude elocution of the old man that had its effect upon the party, and particularly on the seconds, whose pride was uninterested in bringing the dispute to a bloody arbitrement, and who, on the contrary, eagerly watched for an opportunity to recommend reconciliation.

"Upon my word, Mr. Lesley," said Taffril, "old Adam speaks like an oracle. Our friends here were very angry yesterday, and of course very foolish. To-day they should be cool, or at least we must be so in their behalf. I think the word should be forget and forgive on both sides, that we should all shake hands, fire these foolish crackers in the air, and go home to sup in a body at the Græme's Arms."

"I would heartily recommend it," said Lesley; "for, amidst a great deal of heat and irritation on both sides, I confess myself unable to discover any rational ground of quarrel."

"Gentlemen," said M'Intyre, very coldly, "all this should have been thought of before. In my opinion, persons that have carried this matter so far as we have done, and who should part without carrying it any farther, might go to supper at the Græme's Arms very joyously, but would rise the next morning with reputations as ragged as our friend here, who has obliged us with a rather unnecessary display of his oratory. I speak for myself, that I find myself bound to call upon you to proceed without more delay."

"And I," said Lovel, "as I never desired any, have also to request these gentlemen to arrange preliminaries as fast as possible."

"Bairns, bairns!" cried old Ochiltree; but, perceiving he was no longer attended to: "Madmen, I should say; but your blood be on your heads!" And the old man drew off from the ground, which was now measured out by the seconds, and continued muttering and talking to himself in sullen indignation, mixed with anxiety, and with a strong feeling of painful curiosity. Without paying further attention to his presence or remonstrances, Mr. Lesley and the Lieutenant made the necessary arrangements for the duel, and it was agreed that both parties should fire when Mr. Lesley dropped his handkerchief.

The fatal sign was given, and both fired almost in the same moment. Captain M'Intyre's ball grazed the side of his opponent, but did not draw blood. That of Lovel was more true to the aim: M'Intyre reeled and fell. Raising himself on his arm, his first exclamation was: "It is nothing—it is nothing;

give us the other pistols." But in an instant he said in a lower tone: "I believe I have enough, and what's worse, I fear I deserve it. Mr. Lovel, or whatever your name is, fly and save yourself. Bear all witness, I provoked this matter." Then, raising himself again on his arm, he added: "Shake hands, Lovel. I believe you to be a gentleman; forgive my rudeness, and I forgive you my death. My poor sister!"

The surgeon came up to perform his part of the tragedy, and Lovel stood gazing on the evil of which he had been the active, though unwilling, cause with a dizzy and bewildered eye. He was roused from his trance by the grasp of the mendicant: "Why stand you gazing on your deed? What's doomed is doomed, what's done is past recalling. But awa, awa, if ye wad save your blood from a shamefu' death. I see the men out by yonder that are come ower late to part ye; but out and alack! sune eneugh and ower sune to drag ye to prison."

"He is right—he is right," exclaimed Taffril, "you must not attempt to get on the highroad; get into the wood till night. My brig will be under sail by that time, and at three in the morning, when the tide will serve, I shall have the boat waiting for you at the Mussel Crag. Away, away, for Heaven's sake!"

"Oh yes, fly, fly!" repeated the wounded man, his words faltering with convulsive sobs.

"Come with me," said the mendicant, almost dragging him off, "the Captain's plan is the best; I'll carry ye to a place where ye might be concealed in the mean time, were they to seek ye wi' sleuth-hounds."

"Go, go," again urged Lieutenant Taffril; "to stay here is mere madness."

"It was worse madness to have come hither," said Lovel, pressing his hand. "But farewell!" and he followed Ochiltree into the recesses of the wood.

CHAPTER XXI.

The Lord Abbot had a soul
Subtile and quick and searching as the fire.
By magic stairs ne went as deep as hell,
And if in devils' possession gold be kept,
He brought some sure from thence ; 'tis hid in caves,
Known, save to me, to none.

The Wonder of a Kingdome.

Lovel almost mechanically followed the beggar, who led
the way with a hasty and steady pace, through bush and
bramble, avoiding the beaten path, and often turning to listen
whether there were any sounds of pursuit behind them.   They
sometimes descended into the very bed of the torrent, sometimes kept a narrow and precarious path, that the sheep
(which, with the sluttish negligence towards property of that
sort universal in Scotland, were allowed to stray in the copse)
had made along the very verge of its overhanging banks.
From time to time Lovel had a glance of the path which he
had traversed the day before in company with Sir Arthur, the
Antiquary, and the young ladies.   Dejected, embarrassed, and
occupied by a thousand inquietudes as he then was, what
would he now have given to regain the sense of innocence
which alone can counterbalance a thousand evils!   " Yet,
then," such was his hasty and involuntary reflection—" even
then, guiltless and valued by all around me, I thought myself
unhappy.   What am I now, with this young man's blood upon
my hands?   The feeling of pride which urged me to the deed
has now deserted me, as the actual fiend himself is said to do
those whom he has tempted to guilt."   Even his affection for
Miss Wardour sunk for the time before the first pangs of remorse, and he thought he could have encountered every agony
of slighted love to have had the conscious freedom from blood-
guiltiness which he possessed in the morning.

These painful reflections were not interrupted by any conversation on the part of his guide, who threaded the thicket
before him, now holding back the sprays to make his path

easy, now exhorting him to make haste, now muttering to himself, after the custom of solitary and neglected old age, words which might have escaped Lovel's ear even had he listened to them, or which, apprehended and retained, were too isolated to convey any connected meaning—a habit which may be often observed among people of the old man's age and calling.

At length, as Lovel, exhausted by his late indisposition, the harrowing feelings by which he was agitated, and the exertion necessary to keep up with his guide in a path so rugged, began to flag and fall behind, two or three very precarious steps placed him on the front of a precipice overhung with brushwood and copse. Here a cave, as narrow in its entrance as a fox-earth, was indicated by a small fissure in the rock, screened by the boughs of an aged oak, which, anchored by its thick and twisted roots in the upper part of the cleft, flung its branches almost straight outward from the cliff, concealing it effectually from all observation. It might indeed have escaped the attention even of those who had stood at its very opening, so uninviting was the portal at which the beggar entered. But within, the cavern was higher and more roomy, cut into two separate branches, which, intersecting each other at right angles, formed an emblem of the cross, and indicated the abode of an anchoret of former times. There are many caves of the same kind in different parts of Scotland. I need only instance those of Gorton, near Roslyn, in a scene well known to the admirers of romantic nature.

The light within the cave was a dusky twilight at the entrance, which failed altogether in the inner recesses. "Few folks ken o' this place," said the old man; "to the best o' my knowledge, there's just twa living by mysell, and that's Jingling Jock and the Lang Linker. I have had mony a thought, that when I faund mysell auld and forfairn, and no able to enjoy God's blessed air ony langer, I wad drag mysell here wi' a pickle aitmeal—and see, there's a bit bonny drapping well that popples that selfsame gate simmer and winter—and I wad e'en streek mysell out here, and abide my removal, like an auld dog that trails its useless ugsome carcass into some

bush or bracken, no to gie living things a sconner wi' the
sight o't when it's dead. Ay, and then, when the dogs barked
at the lone farmstead, the gudewife wad cry, 'Whisht, stirra,
that'll be auld Edie,' and the bits o' weans wad up, puir
things, and toddle to the door, to pu' in the auld Blue-Gown
that mends a' their bonny dies; but there wad be nae mair
word o' Edie, I trow."

He then led Lovel, who followed him unresistingly, into one
of the interior branches of the cave. "Here," he said, "is a
bit turnpike stair that gaes up to the auld kirk above. Some
folks say this place was howkit out by the monks lang syne
to hide their treasure in, and some said that they used to bring
things into the abbey this gate by night, that they durstna
sae weel hae brought in by the main port and in open day.
And some said that ane o' them turned a saint—or aiblins
wad hae had folk think sae—and settled him down in this
Saint Ruth's cell, as the auld folks aye ca'd it, and garr'd big
the stair, that he might gang up to the kirk when they were
at the divine service. The Laird o' Monkbarns wad hae a
hantle to say about it, as he has about maist things, if he
kend only about the place. But whether it was made for
man's devices or God's service, I have seen ower muckle sin
done in it in my day, and far ower muckle have I been partaker of; ay, even here in this dark cove. Mony a gudewife's
been wondering what for the red cock didna craw her up in
the morning, when he's been roasting, puir fallow, in this
dark hole. And, ohon! I wish that and the like o' that had
been the warst o't! Whiles they wad hae heard the din we
were making in the very bowels o' the earth, when Sanders
Aikwood, that was forester in thae days, the father o' Ringan
that now is, was gaun daundering about the wood at e'en to
see after the Laird's game; and whiles he wad hae seen a
glance o' the light frae the door o' the cave, flaughtering
against the hazels on the other bank, and then siccan stories
as Sanders had about the worriecows and gyre-carlins that
haunted about the auld wa's at e'en, and the lights that he
had seen, and the cries that he had heard, when there was
nae mortal ee open but his ain; and eh! as he wad thrum

them ower and ower to the like o' me ayont the ingle at e'en, and as I wad gie the auld silly carle grane for grane, and tale for tale, though I kend muckle better about it than ever he did. Ay, ay, they were daft days thae; but they were a' vanity and waur, and it's fitting that thae wha hae led a light and evil life, and abused charity when they were young, suld aiblins come to lack it when they are auld."

While Ochiltree was thus recounting the exploits and tricks of his earlier life, with a tone in which glee and compunction alternately predominated, his unfortunate auditor had sat down upon the hermit's seat, hewn out of the solid rock, and abandoned himself to that lassitude both of mind and body which generally follows a course of events that have agitated both. The effect of his late indisposition, which had much weakened his system, contributed to this lethargic despondency. "The puir bairn," said auld Edie, "an he sleeps in this damp hole he'll maybe wauken nae mair, or catch some sair disease; it's no the same to him as to the like o' us, that can sleep ony gate an anes our wames are fu'. Sit up, Maister Lovel, lad; after a's come and gane, I dare say the captain lad will do weel eneugh; and, after a', ye are no the first that has had this misfortune. I hae seen mony a man killed, and helped to kill them mysell, though there was nae quarrel between us; and if it isna wrang to kill folk we have nae quarrel wi', just because they wear another sort of a cockade and speak a foreign language, I canna see but a man may have excuse for killing his ain mortal foe, that comes armed to the fair field to kill him. I dinna say it's right—God forbid—or that it isna sinfu' to take away what ye canna restore, and that's the breath of man, whilk is in his nostrils; but I say it is a sin to be forgiven if it's repented of. Sinfu' men are we a'; but if ye wad believe an auld grey sinner that has seen the evil o' his ways, there is as much promise atween the twa boards o' the Testament as wad save the warst o' us, could we but think sae."

With such scraps of comfort and of divinity as he possessed, the mendicant thus continued to solicit and compel the attention of Lovel until the twilight began to fade into night.

"Now," said Ochiltree, "I will carry ye to a mair convenient place, where I hae sat mony a time to hear the howlit crying out of the ivy tod, and to see the moonlight come through the auld windows o' the ruins. There can be naebody come here after this time o' night; and if they hae made ony search, thae blackguard shirra'-officers and constables, it will hae been ower lang syne. Odd, they are as great cowards as ither folk, wi' a' their warrants and king's keys. I hae gien some o' them a gliff in my day, when they were coming rather ower near me. But, lauded be grace for it! they canna stir me now for ony waur than an auld man and a beggar, and my badge is a gude protection; and then Miss Isabella Wardour is a tower o' strength, ye ken (Lovel sighed). Aweel, dinna be cast down: bowls may a' row right yet; gie the lassie time to ken her mind. She's the wale o' the country for beauty, and a gude friend o' mine: I gang by the bridewell as safe as by the kirk on a sabbath; deil ony o' them daur hurt a hair o' auld Edie's head now. I keep the crown o' the causey when I gae to the borough, and rub shouthers wi' a bailie wi' as little concern as an he were a brock."

While the mendicant spoke thus, he was busied in removing a few loose stones in one angle of the cave, which obscured the entrance of the staircase of which he had spoken, and led the way into it, followed by Lovel in passive silence.

"The air's free eneugh," said the old man; "the monks took care o' that, for they werena a lang-breathed generation, I reckon; they hae contrived queer tirlie-wirlie holes, that gang out to the open air and keep the stair as caller as a kail-blade."

Lovel accordingly found the staircase well aired, and, though narrow, it was neither ruinous nor long, but speedily admitted them into a narrow gallery contrived to run within the side wall of the chancel, from which it received air and light through apertures ingeniously hidden amid the florid ornaments of the Gothic architecture.

"This secret passage anes gaed round great part o' the biggin," said the beggar, "and through the wa' o' the place I've heard Monkbarns ca' the refractory (meaning probably refectory), and so awa to the prior's ain house. It's like he could use it to listen what the monks were saying at meal-time, and then he might come ben here and see that they were busy skreighing awa wi' the psalms doun below there; and then, when he saw a' was right and tight, he might step awa and fetch in a bonnie lass at the cove yonder, for they were queer hands the monks, unless mony lees is made on them. But our folk were at great pains lang syne to big up the passage in some parts, and pu' it down in others, for fear o' some uncanny body getting into it, and finding their way down to the cove. It wad hae been a fashious job that; by my certie, some o' our necks wad hae been ewking."

They now came to a place where the gallery was enlarged into a small circle, sufficient to contain a stone seat. A niche, constructed exactly before it, projected forward into the chancel, and as its sides were latticed, as it were, with perforated stonework, it commanded a full view of the chancel in every direction, and was probably constructed, as Edie intimated, to be a convenient watch-tower from which the superior priest, himself unseen, might watch the behaviour of his monks, and ascertain by personal inspection their punctual attendance upon those rites of devotion which his rank exempted him from sharing with them. As this niche made one of a regular series which stretched along the wall of the chancel, and in no respect differed from the rest when seen from below, the secret station, screened as it was by the stone figure of St. Michael and the Dragon and the open tracery around the niche, was completely hid from observation. The private passage, confined to its pristine breadth, had originally continued beyond this seat; but the jealous precautions of the vagabonds who frequented the cave of St. Ruth had caused them to build it carefully up with hewn stones from the ruin.

"We shall be better here," said Edie, seating himself on the stone bench and stretching the lappet of his blue gown upon the spot, when he motioned Lovel to sit down beside him—"we shall be better here than doun below; the air's free and mild, and the savour of the wallflowers and siccan shrubs as grow on thae ruined wa's is far mair refreshing than the damp smell doun below yonder. They smell sweetest by night-time thae flowers, and they're maist aye seen about ruined buildings. Now, Maister Lovel, can ony o' your scholars gie a gude reason for that?"

Lovel replied in the negative.

"I am thinking," resumed the beggar, "that they'll be like mony folks' gude gifts, that often seem maist gracious in adversity; or maybe it's a parable, to teach us no to slight them that are in the darkness of sin and the decay of tribulation, since God sends odours to refresh the mirkest hour, and flowers and pleasant bushes to clothe the ruined buildings. And now I wad like a wise man to tell me whether Heaven is maist pleased wi' the sight we are looking upon—thae pleasant and quiet lang streaks o' moonlight that are lying sae still on the floor o' this auld kirk, and glancing through the great pillars and stanchions o' the carved windows, and just dancing like on the leaves o' the dark ivy as the breath o' wind shakes it—I wonder whether this is mair pleasing to Heaven than when it was lighted up wi' lamps, and candles nae doubt, and roughies, and wi' the mirth and the frankincent that they speak of in the Holy Scripture, and wi' organs assuredly, and men and women singers, and sackbuts, and dulcimers, and a' instruments o' music—I wonder if that was acceptable, or whether it is of these grand parafle o' ceremonies that Holy Writ says, 'it is an abomination to Me.' I am thinking, Maister Lovel, if twa puir contrite spirits like yours and mine fand grace to make our petition——"

Here Lovel laid his hand eagerly on the mendicant's arm, saying: "Hush! I heard some one speak."

"I am dull o' hearing," answered Edie in a whisper, "but we're surely safe here; where was the sound?"

Lovel pointed to the door of the chancel, which, highly ornamented, occupied the west end of the building, surmounted by the carved window, which let in a flood of moonlight over it.

"They can be nane o' our folk," said Edie in the same low and cautious tone; "there's but twa o' them kens o' the place, and they're mony a mile off, if they are still bound on their weary pilgrimage. I'll never think it's the officers here at this time o' night. I am nae believer in auld wives' stories about ghaists, though this is gey like a place for them. But, mortal or of the other world, here they come! twa men and a light."

And in very truth, while the mendicant spoke, two human figures darkened with their shadows the entrance of the chancel which had before opened to the moonlight meadow beyond, and the small lantern which one of them displayed glimmered pale in the clear and strong beams of the moon, as the evening star does among the lights of the departing day. The first and most obvious idea was that, despite the asseverations of Edie Ochiltree, the persons who approached the ruins at an hour so uncommon must be the officers of justice in quest of Lovel. But no part of their conduct confirmed the suspicion. A touch and a whisper from the old man warned Lovel that his best course was to remain quiet and watch their motions from their present place of concealment. Should anything appear to render retreat necessary, they had behind them the private staircase and cavern, by means of which they could escape into the wood long before any danger of close pursuit. They kept themselves, therefore, as still as possible, and observed with eager and anxious curiosity every accent and motion of these nocturnal wanderers.

After conversing together some time in whispers, the two figures advanced into the middle of the chancel, and a voice, which Lovel at once recognised from its tone and dialect to be that of Dousterswivel, pronounced in a louder but still a smothered tone: "Indeed, mine goot sir, dere cannot be one finer hour nor season for dis great purpose. You shall see, mine goot sir, dat it is all one bibble-babble dat Mr. Oldenbuck says, and dat he knows no more of what he speaks than one little shild. Mine soul! he expects to get as rich as one Jew for his poor dirty one hundred pounds, which I care no more about, by mine honest wort, than I care for an hundred stivers. But to you, my most munificent and reverend patron, I will show all de secrets dat art can show; ay, de secret of de great Pymander."

15

"That other ane," whispered Edie, "maun be, according to a' likelihood, Sir Arthur Wardour. I ken naebody but himsell wad come here at this time at e'en wi' that German blackguard. Ane wad think he's bewitched him; he gars him e'en trow that chalk is cheese. Let's see what they can be doing."

This interruption, and the low tone in which Sir Arthur spoke, made Lovel lose all Sir Arthur's answer to the adept, excepting the three last emphatic words, "Very great expense"; to which Dousterswivel at once replied: "Expenses! To be sure, dere must be de great expenses; you do not expect to reap before you do sow de seed: de expense is de seed, de riches and de mine of goot metal, and now de great big chests of plate, they are de crop, vary goot crop too, on mine wort. Now, Sir Arthur, you have sowed this night one little seed of ten guineas like one pinch of snuff, or so big, and if you do not reap de great harvest—dat is, de great harvest for de little pinch of seed, for it must be proportions, you must know —then never call one honest man Herman Dousterswivel. Now you see, mine patron—for I will not conceal mine secret from you at all—you see this little plate of silver, you know de moon measureth de whole zodiack in de space of twentyeight day; every shild knows dat. Well, I take a silver plate when she is in her fifteenth mansion, which mansion is in de head of *Libra*, and I engrave upon one side de worts, Shebbarschemoth Schartachan—dat is, de emblems of de intelligence of de moon—and I make his picture like a flying serpent with a turkey-cock's head—vary well. Then upon this side I make de table of de moon, which is a square of nine, multiplied into itself, with eighty-one numbers on every side, and diameter nine—dere it is done very proper. Now I will make dis avail me at de change of every quarter-moon dat I shall find by de same proportions of expenses I lay out in de suffumigations, as nine to de product of nine multiplied into itself. But I shall find no more to-night as may be two or dree times nine, because dere is a thwarting power in de house of ascendency."

"But, Dousterswivel," said the simple Baronet, "does not

this look like magic? I am a true though unworthy son of the Episcopal Church, and I will have nothing to do with the foul fiend."

"Bah! bah! not a bit magic in it at all, not a bit. It is all founded on de planetary influence, and de sympathy and force of numbers. I will show you much finer dan dis. I do not say dere is not de spirit in it, because of de suffumigation; but, if you are not afraid, he shall not be invisible."

"I have no curiosity to see him at all," said the Baronet, whose courage seemed, from a certain quaver in his accent, to have taken a fit of the ague.

"Dat is great pity," said Dousterswivel; "I should have liked to show you de spirit dat guard dis treasure like one fierce watch-dog; but I know how to manage him. You would not care to see him?"

"Not at all," answered the Baronet, in a tone of feigned indifference; "I think we have but little time."

"You shall pardon me, my patron, it is not yet twelve, and twelve precise is just our planetary hours; and I could show you de spirit vary well in de mean while, just for pleasure. You see I would draw a pentagon within a circle, which is no trouble at all, and make my suffumigation within it, and dere we would be like in one strong castle, and you would hold de sword while I did say de needful worts. Den you should see de solid wall open like de gate of ane city, and den—let me see—ay, you should see first one stag pursued by three black greyhounds, and they should pull him down as they do at de Elector's great hunting-match, and den one ugly, little, nasty black negro should appear and take de stag from them, and paf, all should be gone; den you should hear horns winded dat all de ruins should ring—mine wort, they should play fine hunting-piece, as goot as him you call'd Fischer with his oboi; vary well, den comes one herald, as we call Erenhold, winding his horn, and den come de great Peolphan, called the Mighty Hunter of de North, mounted on hims black steed. But you would not care to see all this?" [1]

"Why, I am not afraid," answered the poor Baronet, "if—

[1] See Dousterswivel's Legends. Note 6.

that is—does anything—any great mischiefs—happen on such occasions?"

"Bah, mischiefs! no! Sometimes, if de circle be no quite just, or de beholder be de frightened coward, and not hold de sword firm and straight towards him, de Great Hunter will take his advantage, and drag him exorcist out of de circle and throttle him. Dat does happens."

"Well then, Dousterswivel, with every confidence in my courage and your skill, we will dispense with this apparition and go on to the business of the night."

"With all mine heart, it is just one thing to me, and now it is de time; hold you de sword till I kindle de little what you call chip."

Dousterswivel accordingly set fire to a little pile of chips, touched and prepared with some bituminous substance to make them burn fiercely; and when the flame was at the highest, and lightened with its short-lived glare all the ruins around, the German flung in a handful of perfumes, which produced a strong and pungent odour. The exorcist and his pupil both were so much affected as to cough and sneeze heartily; and, as the vapour floated around the pillars of the building and penetrated every crevice, it produced the same effect on the beggar and Lovel.

"Was that an echo?" said the Baronet, astonished at the sternutation which resounded from above; "or," drawing close to the adept, "can it be the spirit you talked of, ridiculing our attempt upon his hidden treasures?"

"N—n—no," muttered the German, who began to partake of his pupil's terrors, "I hope not."

Here a violent explosion of sneezing, which the mendicant was unable to suppress, and which could not be considered by any means as the dying fall of an echo, accompanied by a grunting, half-smothered cough, confounded the two treasure-seekers. "Lord have mercy on us!" said the Baronet.

"*Alle guten Geister, loben den Herrn!*" ejaculated the terrified adept. "I was begun to think," he continued, after a moment's silence, "that this would be de bestermost done in de daylight; we was bestermost to go away just now."

"You juggling villain," said the Baronet, in whom these expressions awakened a suspicion that overcame his terrors, connected as it was with the sense of desperation arising from the apprehension of impending ruin—"you juggling mountebank, this is some legerdemain trick of yours to get off from the performance of your promise as you have so often done before. But, before Heaven, I will this night know what I have trusted to when I suffered you to fool me on to my ruin! Go on, then; come fairy, come fiend, you shall show me that treasure, or confess yourself a knave and an impostor; or, by the faith of a desperate and ruined man, I'll send you where you shall see spirits enough."

The treasure-finder, trembling between his terror for the supernatural beings by whom he supposed himself to be surrounded, and for his life, which seemed to be at the mercy of a desperate man, could only bring out: "Mine patron, this is not the allerbestmost usage. Consider, mine honoured sir, that de spirits——"

Here Edie, who began to enter into the humour of the scene, uttered an extraordinary howl, being an exaltation and a prolongation of the most deplorable whine in which he was accustomed to solicit charity. Dousterswivel flung himself on his knees: "Dear Sir Arthurs, let us go, or let me go!"

"No, you cheating scoundrel," said the knight, unsheathing the sword which he had brought for the purposes of the exorcism, "that shift shall not serve you. Monkbarns warned me long since of your juggling pranks; I will see this treasure before you leave this place, or I will have you confess yourself an impostor; or, by Heaven, I'll run this sword through you, though all the spirits of the dead should rise around us!"

"For de lofe of Heaven be patient, mine honoured patron, and you shall hafe all de treasure as I knows of—yes, you shall indeed; but do not speak about de spirits, it makes dem angry."

Edie Ochiltree here prepared himself to throw in another groan, but was restrained by Lovel, who began to take a more serious interest as he observed the earnest and almost desperate demeanour of Sir Arthur. Dousterswivel, having at once before his eyes the fear of the foul fiend and the violence of Sir Arthur, played his part of a conjuror extremely ill, hesitating to assume the degree of confidence necessary to deceive the latter, lest it should give offence to the invisible cause of his alarm. However, after rolling his eyes, muttering and sputtering German exorcisms, with contortions of his face and person, rather flowing from the impulse of terror than of meditated fraud, he at length proceeded to a corner of the building where a flat stone lay upon the ground, bearing upon its surface the effigy of an armed warrior in a recumbent posture carved in bas-relief. He muttered to Sir Arthur: "Mine patrons, it is here. Got save us all!"

Sir Arthur, who, after the first moment of his superstitious fear was over, seemed to have bent up all his faculties to the pitch of resolution necessary to carry on the adventure, lent the adept his assistance to turn over the stone, which, by means of a lever that the adept had provided, their joint force with difficulty effected. No supernatural light burst forth from below to indicate the subterranean treasury, nor was there any apparition of spirits, earthly or infernal. But when Dousterswivel had, with great trepidation, struck a few strokes with a mattock, and as hastily thrown out a shovelful or two of earth (for they came provided with the tools necessary for digging), something was heard to ring like the sound of a falling piece of metal, and Dousterswivel, hastily catching up the substance which produced it, and which his shovel had thrown out along with the earth, exclaimed: "On mine dear wort, mine patrons, dis is all, it is indeed; I mean all we can do to-night," and he gazed round him with a cowering and fearful glance, as if to see from what corner the avenger of his imposture was to start forth.

"Let me see it," said Sir Arthur; and then repeated still more sternly: "I will be satisfied, I will judge by mine own eyes." He accordingly held the object to the light of the lantern. It was a small case or casket, for Lovel could not at the distance exactly discern its shape, which, from the Baronet's exclamation as he opened it, he concluded was filled with coin. "Ay," said the Baronet, "this is being indeed in good luck! and if it omens proportional success upon a larger venture, the venture shall be made. That six hundred of Goldieword's, added to the other incumbent claims, must have been ruin indeed. If you think we can parry it by repeating this experiment—suppose when the moon next changes—I will hazard the necessary advance, come by it how I may."

"Oh, mine goot patrons, do not speak about all dat," said Dousterswivel, "as just now, but help me to put de shtone to de rights, and let us begone our own ways." And accordingly, so soon as the stone was replaced, he hurried Sir Arthur, who was now resigned once more to his guidance, away from a spot where the German's guilty conscience and superstitious fears represented goblins as lurking behind each pillar with the purpose of punishing his treachery.

"Saw ony body e'er the like o' that!" said Edie, when they had disappeared like shadows through the gate by which they had entered—"saw ony creature living e'er the like o' that! But what can we do for that puir doited deevil of a knight-baronet? Odd, he showed muckle mair spunk, too, than I thought had been in him. I thought he wad hae sent cauld iron through the vagabond. Sir Arthur wasna half sae bauld at Bessie's Apron yon night; but then his blood was up even now, and that makes an unco difference. I hae seen mony a man wad hae felled another an' anger him that wadna muckle hae liked a clink against Crummie's Harn yon time. But what's to be done?"

"I suppose," said Lovel, "his faith in this fellow is entirely restored by this deception, which, unquestionably, he had arranged beforehand."

"What! the siller? Ay, ay, trust him for that: they that hide ken best where to find. He wants to wile him out o' his last guinea, and then escape to his ain country, the landlouper. I wad like it weel just to hae come in at the clipping-time and gien him a lounder wi' my pike-staff; he wad hae taen it for a bennison frae some o' the auld dead abbots. But it's best no to be rash: sticking disna gang by strength, but by the guiding o' the gully. I'se be upsides wi' him ae day."

"What if you should inform Mr. Oldbuck?" said Lovel.

"Ou, I dinna ken. Monkbarns and Sir Arthur are like, and yet they're no like neither. Monkbarns has whiles influence wi' him, and whiles Sir Arthur cares as little about him as about the like o' me. Monkbarns is no that ower wise himsell in some things; he wad believe a bodle to be an auld Roman coin, as he ca's it, or a ditch to be a camp, upon ony leasing that idle folk made about it. I hae garr'd him trow mony a queer tale mysell, Gude forgie me. But wi' a' that he has unco little sympathy wi' ither folks; and he's snell and dure eneugh in casting up their nonsense to them, as if he had nane o' his ain. He'll listen the hale day, an ye'll tell him about tales o' Wallace and Blind Harry and Davie Lindsay; but ye maunna speak to him about ghaists or fairies, or spirits walking the earth, or the like o' that; he had amaist flung auld Caxon out o' the window—and he might just as weel hae flung awa his best wig after him—for threeping he had seen a ghaist at the Humlock Knowe. Now, if he was taking it up in this way, he wad set up the tother's birse; and maybe do mair ill nor gude; he's done that twice or thrice about thae mine-warks; ye wad thought Sir Arthur had a pleasure in gaun on wi' them the deeper, the mair he was warn'd against it by Monkbarns."

"What say you then," said Lovel, "to letting Miss Wardour know the circumstance?"

"Ou, puir thing, how could she stop her father doing his pleasure? And, besides, what wad it help? There's a sough in the country about that six hundred pounds, and there's a writer chield in Edinburgh has been driving the spur-rowels o' the law up to the head into Sir Arthur's sides to gar him pay it, and if he canna he maun gang to jail or flee the country. He's like a desperate man, and just catches at this chance as a' he has left to escape utter perdition; so what signifies plaguing the puir lassie about what canna be helped? And besides, to say the truth, I wadna like to tell the secret o' this place. It's unco convenient, ye see yoursell, to hae a hiding-hole o' ane's ain, and though I be out o' the line o' needing ane e'en now, and trust in the power o' grace that I'll ne'er do ony thing to need ane again, yet naebody kens what temp-

tation ane may be gien ower to; and, to be brief, I downa
bide the thought of ony body kennin about the place. They
say: 'Keep a thing seven year, an' ye'll aye find a use for't';
and maybe I may need the cove, either for mysell or for some
ither body."

This argument, in which Edie Ochiltree, notwithstanding
his scraps of mortality and of divinity, seemed to take, perhaps from old habit, a personal interest, could not be handsomely controverted by Lovel, who was at that moment reaping the benefit of the secret of which the old man appeared to
be so jealous.

This incident, however, was of great service to Lovel, as
diverting his mind from the unhappy occurrence of the evening, and considerably rousing the energies which had been
stupified by the first view of his calamity. He reflected that
it by no means necessarily followed that a dangerous wound
must be a fatal one; that he had been hurried from the spot
even before the surgeon had expressed any opinion of Captain
M'Intyre's situation; and that he had duties on earth to perform even should the very worst be true, which, if they could
not restore his peace of mind or sense of innocence, would furnish a motive for enduring existence, and at the same time
render it a course of active benevolence.

Such were Lovel's feelings when the hour arrived when,
according to Edie's calculation, who, by some train of process
of his own in observing the heavenly bodies, stood independent of the assistance of a watch or timekeeper, it was fitting
they should leave their hiding-place and betake themselves to
the sea-shore, in order to meet Lieutenant Taffril's boat according to appointment.

They retreated by the same passage which had admitted
them to the prior's secret seat of observation, and when they
issued from the grotto into the wood, the birds, which began
to chirp and even to sing, announced that the dawn was advanced. This was confirmed by the light and amber clouds
that appeared over the sea as soon as their exit from the
copse permitted them to view the horizon. Morning, said to
be friendly to the muses, has probably obtained this character

from its effect upon the fancy and feelings of mankind. Even to those who, like Lovel, have spent a sleepless and anxious night, the breeze of the dawn brings strength and quickening both of mind and body. It was therefore with renewed health and vigour that Lovel, guided by the trusty mendicant, brushed away the dew as he traversed the downs which divided the Den of St. Ruth, as the woods surrounding the ruins were popularly called, from the sea-shore.

The first level beam of the sun, as his brilliant disk began to emerge from the ocean, shot full upon the little gun-brig which was lying-to in the offing. Close to the shore the boat was already waiting, Taffril himself, with his naval cloak wrapped about him, seated in the stern. He jumped ashore when he saw the mendicant and Lovel approach, and, shaking the latter heartily by the hand, begged him not to be cast down. "M'Intyre's wound," he said, "was doubtful, but far from desperate." His attention had got Lovel's baggage privately sent on board the brig; "and," he said, "he trusted that, if Lovel chose to stay with the vessel, the penalty of a short cruise would be the only disagreeable consequence of his *rencontre*. As for himself, his time and motions were a good deal at his own disposal," he said, "excepting the necessary obligation of remaining on his station."

"We will talk of our farther motions," said Lovel, "as we go on board."

Then turning to Edie, he endeavoured to put money into his hand. "I think," said Edie, as he tendered it back again, "the hale folk here have either gane daft, or they hae made a vow to ruin my trade, as they say ower muckle water drowns the miller. I hae had mair gowd offered me within this twa or three weeks than I ever saw in my life afore. Keep the siller, lad, ye'll hae need o't, I'se warrant ye, and I hae nane. My claes is nae great things, and I get a blue gown every year, and as mony siller groats as the king, God bless him, is years auld—you and I serve the same master, ye ken, Captain Taffril—there's rigging provided for; and my meat and drink I get for the asking in my rounds, or at an orra time I can gang a day without it, for I make it a rule never to

pay for nane.   So that a' the siller I need is just to buy
tobacco and sneeshin, and maybe a dram at a time in a cauld
day, though I am nae dram-drinker to be a gaberlunzie.   Sae
take back your gowd and just gie me a lily-white shilling."

Upon these whims, which he imagined intimately connected
with the honour of his vagabond profession, Edie was flint
and adamant, not to be moved by rhetoric or entreaty; and
therefore Lovel was under the necessity of again pocketing his
intended bounty, and taking a friendly leave of the mendicant
by shaking him by the hand, and assuring him of his cordial
gratitude for the very important services which he had rendered him, recommending at the same time secrecy as to what
they had that night witnessed.   " Ye needna doubt that," said
Ochiltree; " I never tell'd tales out o' yon cove in my life,
though mony a queer thing I hae seen in't."

The boat now put off.   The old man remained looking after
it as it made rapidly towards the brig under the impulse of six
stout rowers, and Lovel beheld him again wave his blue bonnet as a token of farewell ere he turned from his fixed posture
and began to move slowly along the sands as if resuming his
customary perambulations.

------◆------

CHAPTER XXII.

> Wiser Raymond, as in his closet pent,
> Laughs at such danger and adventurement,
> When half his lands are spent in golden smoke,
> And now his second hopeful glasse is broke;
> But yet, if haply his third furnace hold,
> Devoteth all his pots and pans to gold.[1]

About a week after the adventures commemorated in our
last chapter, Mr. Oldbuck, descending to his breakfast-par-
lour, found that his womankind were not upon duty, his toast
not made, and the silver jug which wont to receive his liba-
tions of mum not duly aired for its reception.

" This confounded hot-brained boy," he said to himself,

---

[1] The author cannot remember where these lines are to be found ; perhaps in Bishop Hall's *Satires*.—They occur in Book iv. Satire iii. (*Laing*).

"now that he begins to get out of danger, I can tolerate this
life no longer. All goes to sixes and sevens; an universal
saturnalia seems to be proclaimed in my peaceful and orderly
family. I ask for my sister; no answer. I call, I shout, I
invoke my inmates by more names than the Romans gave to
their deities; at length Jenny, whose shrill voice I have heard
this half hour lilting in the Tartarean regions of the kitchen,
condescends to hear me and reply, but without coming upstairs, so the conversation must be continued at the top of my
lungs." Here he again began to holloo aloud: "Jenny, where's
Miss Oldbuck?"

"Miss Grizie's in the Captain's room."

"Umph, I thought so; and where's my niece?"

"Miss Mary's making the Captain's tea."

"Umph, I supposed as much again; and where's Caxon?"

"Awa to the town about the Captain's fowling-gun and his
setting-dog."

"And who the devil's to dress my periwig, you silly jade?
When you knew that Miss Wardour and Sir Arthur were coming here early after breakfast, how could you let Caxon go on
such a Tom Fool's errand?"

"Me! what could I hinder him? Your honour wadna hae
us contradict the Captain e'en now, and he maybe deeing?"

"Dying!" said the alarmed Antiquary, "eh! what? has he
been worse?"

"Na, he's no nae waur that I ken of." [1]

"Then he must be better; and what good is a dog and a
gun to do here, but the one to destroy all my furniture, steal
from my larder, and perhaps worry the cat, and the other to
shoot somebody through the head; he has had gunning and
pistolling enough to serve him one while, I should think."

Here Miss Oldbuck entered the parlour, at the door of which
Oldbuck was carrying on this conversation, he bellowing downward to Jenny, and she again screaming upward in reply.

"Dear brother," said the old lady, "ye'll cry yoursell as
hoarse as a corbie; is that the way to skreigh when there's a
sick person in the house?"

[1] See Nae Waur. Note 7.

"Upon my word, the sick person's like to have all the house to himself. I have gone without my breakfast, and am like to go without my wig; and I must not, I suppose, presume to say I feel either hunger or cold, for fear of disturbing the sick gentleman who lies six rooms off, and who feels himself well enough to send for his dog and gun, though he knows I detest such implements ever since our elder brother, poor Williewald, marched out of the world on a pair of damp feet caught in the Kittlefitting Moss. But that signifies nothing. I suppose I shall be expected by and by to lend a hand to carry Squire Hector out upon his litter, while he indulges his sportsman-like propensities by shooting my pigeons or my turkeys. I think any of the *feræ naturæ* are safe from him for one while."

Miss M'Intyre now entered, and began to her usual morning's task of arranging her uncle's breakfast with the alertness of one who is too late in setting about a task, and is anxious to make up for lost time. But this did not avail her. "Take care, you silly womankind, that mum's too near the fire, the bottle will burst; and I suppose you intend to reduce the toast to a cinder as a burnt-offering for Juno, or what do you call her—the female dog there, with some such Pantheon kind of a name, that your wise brother has, in his first moments of mature reflection, ordered up as a fitting inmate of my house—I thank him—and meet company to aid the rest of the womankind of my household in their daily conversation and intercourse with him."

"Dear uncle, don't be angry about the poor spaniel. She's been tied up at my brother's lodgings at Fairport, and she's broke her chain twice, and come running down here to him; and you would not have us beat the faithful beast away from the door; it moans as if it had some sense of poor Hector's misfortune, and will hardly stir from the door of his room."

"Why," said his uncle, "they said Caxon had gone to Fairport after his dog and gun."

"Oh dear sir, no," answered Miss M'Intyre, "it was to fetch some dressings that were wanted, and Hector only wished him to bring out his gun, as he was going to Fairport at any rate."

"Well, then, it is not altogether so foolish a business, considering what a mess of womankind have been about it. Dressing, quotha! and who is to dress my wig? But I suppose Jenny will undertake," continued the old bachelor, looking at himself in the glass, "to make it somewhat decent. And now let us set to breakfast, with what appetite we may. Well may I say to Hector, as Sir Isaac Newton did to his dog Diamond, when the animal—I detest dogs—flung down the taper among calculations which had occupied the philosopher for twenty years, and consumed the whole mass of materials: 'Diamond, Diamond, thou little knowest the mischief thou hast done!'"

"I assure you, sir," replied his niece, "my brother is quite sensible of the rashness of his own behaviour, and allows that Mr. Lovel behaved very handsomely."

"And much good that will do, when he has frightened the lad out of the country! I tell thee, Mary, Hector's understanding, and far more that of feminity, is inadequate to comprehend the extent of the loss which he has occasioned to the present age and to posterity—*aureum quidem opus*—a poem on such a subject, with notes illustrative of all that is clear, and all that is dark, and all that is neither dark nor clear, but hovers in dusky twilight in the region of Caledonian antiquities. I would have made the Celtic panegyrists look about them. Fingal, as they conceitedly term Fin MacCoul, should have disappeared before my search, rolling himself in his cloud like the spirit of Loda. Such an opportunity can hardly again occur to an ancient and grey-haired man; and to see it lost by the madcap spleen of a hot-headed boy! But I submit, Heaven's will be done!"

Thus continued the Antiquary to "maunder," as his sister expressed it, during the whole time of breakfast, while, despite of sugar and honey and all the comforts of a Scottish morning tea-table, his reflections rendered the meal bitter to all who heard them. But they knew the nature of the man. "Monkbarns's bark," said Miss Griselda Oldbuck in confidential intercourse with Miss Rebecca Blattergowl, "is muckle waur than his bite."

In fact, Mr. Oldbuck had suffered in mind extremely while

his nephew was in actual danger, and now felt himself at liberty, upon his returning health, to indulge in complaints respecting the trouble he had been put to and the interruption of his antiquarian labours. Listened to, therefore, in respectful silence by his niece and sister, he unloaded his discontent in such grumblings as we have rehearsed, venting many a sarcasm against womankind, soldiers, dogs, and guns, all which implements of noise, discord, and tumult, as he called them, he professed to hold in utter abomination.

This expectoration of spleen was suddenly interrupted by the noise of a carriage without, when, shaking off all sullenness at the sound, Oldbuck ran nimbly upstairs and downstairs, for both operations were necessary ere he could receive Miss Wardour and her father at the door of his mansion.

A cordial greeting passed on both sides. And Sir Arthur, referring to his previous inquiries by letter and message, requested to be particularly informed of Captain M'Intyre's health.

"Better than he deserves," was the answer—"better than he deserves, for disturbing us with his vixen brawls, and breaking God's peace and the king's."

"The young gentleman," Sir Arthur said, "had been imprudent; but he understood they were indebted to him for the detection of a suspicious character in the young man Lovel."

"No more suspicious than his own," answered the Antiquary, eager in his favourite's defence; "the young gentleman was a little foolish and headstrong, and refused to answer Hector's impertinent interrogatories—that is all. Lovel, Sir Arthur, knows how to choose his confidants better; ay, Miss Wardour, you may look at me, but it is very true: it was in my bosom that he deposited the secret cause of his residence at Fairport, and no stone should have been left unturned on my part to assist him in the pursuit to which he had dedicated himself."

On hearing this magnanimous declaration on the part of the old Antiquary, Miss Wardour changed colour more than once, and could hardly trust her own ears. For of all confidants to be selected as the depositary of love affairs—and such she naturally supposed must have been the subject of communication—next to Edie Ochiltree, Oldbuck seemed the most uncouth and extraordinary; nor could she sufficiently admire or fret at the extraordinary combination of circumstances which thus threw a secret of such a delicate nature into the possession of persons so unfitted to be entrusted with it. She had next to fear the mode of Oldbuck's entering upon the affair with her father, for such, she doubted not, was his intention. She well knew that the honest gentleman, however vehement in his prejudices, had no great sympathy with those of others, and she had to fear a most unpleasant explosion upon an *éclaircissement* taking place between them. It was therefore with great anxiety that she heard her father request a private interview, and observed Oldbuck readily arise and show the way to his library. She remained behind, attempting to converse with the ladies of Monkbarns, but with the distracted feelings of Macbeth, when compelled to disguise his evil conscience by listening and replying to the observations of the attendant thanes upon the storm of the preceding night, while his whole soul is upon the stretch to listen for the alarm of murder, which he knows must be instantly raised by those who have entered the sleeping apartment of Duncan. But the conversation of the two *virtuosi* turned on a subject very different from that which Miss Wardour apprehended.

"Mr. Oldbuck," said Sir Arthur, when they had, after a due exchange of ceremonies, fairly seated themselves in the *sanctum sanctorum* of the Antiquary, "you who know so much of my family matters, may probably be surprised at the question I am about to put to you."

"Why, Sir Arthur, if it relates to money, I am very sorry, but——"

"It does relate to money matters, Mr. Oldbuck."

"Really then, Sir Arthur," continued the Antiquary, "in the present state of the money-market, and stocks being so low——"

"You mistake my meaning, Mr. Oldbuck," said the Baronet; "I wished to ask your advice about laying out a large sum of money to advantage."

"The devil!" exclaimed the Antiquary; and, sensible that

his involuntary ejaculation of wonder was not over and above civil, he proceeded to qualify it by expressing his joy that Sir Arthur should have a sum of money to lay out when the commodity was so scarce. "And as for the mode of employing it," said he, pausing, "the funds are low at present, as I said before, and there are good bargains of land to be had. But had you not better begin by clearing off encumbrances, Sir Authur? There is the sum in the personal bond, and the three notes of hand," continued he, taking out of the right-hand drawer of his cabinet a certain red memorandum-book, of which Sir Arthur, from the experience of former frequent appeals to it, abhorred the very sight, "with the interest thereon, amounting altogether to—let me see——"

"To about a thousand pounds," said Sir Arthur, hastily; "you told me the amount the other day."

"But there's another term's interest due since that, Sir Arthur, and it amounts—errors excepted—to eleven hundred and thirteen pounds, seven shillings, five pennies, and three-fourths of a penny sterling; but look over the summation yourself."

"I dare say you are quite right, my dear sir," said the Baronet, putting away the book with his hand, as one rejects the old-fashioned civility that presses food upon you after you have eaten till you nauseate—"perfectly right, I dare to say, and in the course of three days or less you shall have the full value; that is, if you choose to accept it in bullion."

"Bullion! I suppose you mean lead. What the deuce! have we hit on the vein then at last? But what could I do with a thousand pounds worth, and upwards, of lead? The former abbots of Trotcosey might have roofed their church and monastery with it indeed, but for me——"

"By bullion," said the Baronet, "I mean the precious metals—gold and silver."

"Ay! indeed? And from what Eldorado is this treasure to be imported?"

"Not far from hence," said Sir Arthur, significantly; "and now I think of it, you shall see the whole process on one small condition."

16

"And what is that?" craved the Antiquary.

"Why, it will be necessary for you to give me your friendly assistance by advancing one hundred pounds or thereabouts."

Mr. Oldbuck, who had already been grasping in idea the sum, principal and interest, of a debt which he had long regarded as wellnigh desperate, was so much astounded at the tables being so unexpectedly turned upon him, that he could only re-echo in an accent of woe and surprise the words, "Advance one hundred pounds!"

"Yes, my good sir," continued Sir Arthur; "but upon the best possible security of being repaid in the course of two or three days."

There was a pause: either Oldbuck's nether-jaw had not recovered its position, so as to enable him to utter a negative, or his curiosity kept him silent.

"I would not propose to you," continued Sir Arthur, "to oblige me thus far, if I did not possess actual proofs of the reality of those expectations which I now hold out to you. And I assure you, Mr. Oldbuck, that, in entering fully upon this topic, it is my purpose to show my confidence in you, and my sense of your kindness on many former occasions."

Mr. Oldbuck professed his sense of obligation, but carefully avoided committing himself by any promise of farther assistance.

"Mr. Dousterswivel," said Sir Arthur, "having discovered——"

Here Oldbuck broke in, his eyes sparkling with indignation: "Sir Arthur, I have so often warned you of the knavery of that rascally quack, that I really wonder you should quote him to me."

"But listen—listen," interrupted Sir Arthur in his turn, "it will do you no harm. In short, Dousterswivel persuaded me to witness an experiment which he had made in the ruins of St. Ruth, and what do you think we found?"

"Another spring of water, I suppose, of which the rogue had beforehand taken care to ascertain the situation and source."

"No, indeed—a casket of gold and silver coins; here they are."

With that Sir Arthur drew from his pocket a large ram's-horn with a copper cover, containing a considerable quantity of coins, chiefly silver, but with a few gold pieces intermixed. The Antiquary's eyes glistened as he eagerly spread them out on the table.

"Upon my word, Scotch, English, and foreign coins, of the fifteenth and sixteenth centuries, and some of them *rari, et rariores, etiam rarissimi!* Here is the bonnet-piece of James V., the unicorn of James II., ay, and the gold testoon of Queen Mary, with her head and the Dauphin's. And these were really found in the ruins of St. Ruth?"

"Most assuredly; my own eyes witnessed it."

"Well," replied Oldbuck, "but you must tell me the when, the where, the how."

"The when," answered Sir Arthur, "was at midnight the last full moon; the where, as I have told you, in the ruins of St. Ruth's priory; the how, was by a nocturnal experiment of Dousterswivel, accompanied only by myself."

"Indeed!" said Oldbuck, "and what means of discovery did you employ?"

"Only a simple suffumigation," said the Baronet, "accompanied by availing ourselves of the suitable planetary hour."

"Simple suffumigation! simple nonsensification; planetary hour! planetary fiddlestick. *Sapiens dominabitur astris.* My dear Sir Arthur, that fellow has made a gull of you above ground and under ground, and he would have made a gull of you in the air too, if he had been by when you was craned up the devil's turnpike yonder at Halket Head; to be sure, the transformation would have been then peculiarly *apropos.*"

"Well, Mr. Oldbuck, I am obliged to you for your indifferent opinion of my discernment; but I think you will give me credit for having seen what I *say* I saw."

"Certainly, Sir Arthur," said the Antiquary, "to this extent at least, that I know Sir Arthur Wardour will not say he saw anything but what he *thought* he saw."

"Well then," replied the Baronet, "as there is a heaven above us, Mr. Oldbuck, I saw with my own eyes these coins dug out of the chancel of St. Ruth at midnight. And as to

Dousterswivel, although the discovery be owing to his science, yet, to tell the truth, I do not think he would have had firmness of mind to have gone through with it if I had not been beside him."

"Ay! indeed?" said Oldbuck, in the tone used when one wishes to hear the end of a story before making any comment.

"Yes, truly," continued Sir Arthur, "I assure you I was upon my guard; we did hear some very uncommon sounds, that is certain, proceeding from among the ruins."

"Oh, you did?" said Oldbuck. "An accomplice hid among them, I suppose?"

"Not a jot," said the Baronet. "The sounds, though of a hideous and preternatural character, rather resembled those of a man who sneezes violently than any other; one deep groan I certainly heard besides; and Dousterswivel assures me that he beheld the spirit Peolphan, the Great Hunter of the North— look for him in your Nicolaus Remigius or Petrus Thyraeus, Mr. Oldbuck—who mimicked the motion of snuff-taking and its effects."

"These indications, however singular as proceeding from such a personage, seem to have been *apropos* to the matter," said the Antiquary; "for you see the case which includes these coins has all the appearance of being an old-fashioned Scottish snuff-mill. But you persevered in spirit of the terrors of this sneezing goblin?"

"Why, I think it probable that a man of inferior sense or consequence might have given way; but I was jealous of an imposture, conscious of the duty I owed to my family in maintaining my courage under every contingency, and therefore I compelled Dousterswivel, by actual and violent threats, to proceed with what he was about to do; and, sir, the proof of his skill and honesty is this parcel of gold and silver pieces, out of which I beg you to select such coins or medals as will best suit your collection."

"Why, Sir Arthur, since you are so good, and on condition you will permit me to mark the value, according to Pinkerton's catalogue and appreciation, against your account in my red book, I will with pleasure select——"

"Nay," said Sir Arthur Wardour, "I do not mean you should consider them as anything but a gift of friendship, and least of all would I stand by the valuation of your friend Pinkerton, who has impugned the ancient and trustworthy authorities upon which, as upon venerable and moss-grown pillars, the credit of Scottish antiquities reposed."

"Ay, ay," rejoined Oldbuck, "you mean, I suppose, Mair and Boece, the Jachin and Boaz, not of history, but of falsification and forgery. And, notwithstanding of all you have told me, I look on your friend Dousterswivel to be as apocryphal as any of them."

"Why, then, Mr. Oldbuck," said Sir Arthur, "not to awaken old disputes, I suppose you think that, because I believe in the ancient history of my country, I have neither eyes nor ears to ascertain what modern events pass before me?"

"Pardon me, Sir Arthur," rejoined the Antiquary, "but I consider all the affectation of terror which this worthy gentleman, your coadjutor, chose to play off as being merely one part of his trick or mystery. And, with respect to the gold or silver coins, they are so mixed and mingled in country and date that I cannot suppose they could be any genuine hoard, and rather suppose them to be, like the purses upon the table of Hudibras's lawyer—

> Money placed for show,
> Like nest-eggs, to make clients lay,
> And for his false opinions pay.

It is the trick of all professions, my dear Sir Arthur. Pray, may I ask you how much this discovery cost you?"

"About ten guineas."

"And you have gained what is equivalent to twenty in actual bullion, and what may be perhaps worth as much more to such fools as ourselves, who are willing to pay for curiosity. This was allowing you a tempting profit on the first hazard, I must needs admit. And what is the next venture he proposes?"

"An hundred and fifty pounds; I have given him one-third part of the money, and I thought it likely you might assist me with the balance."

"I should think that this cannot be meant as a parting blow, it is not of weight and importance sufficient; he will probably let us win this hand also, as sharpers manage a raw gamester. Sir Arthur, I hope you believe I would serve you?"

"Certainly, Mr. Oldbuck; I think my confidence in you on these occasions leaves no room to doubt that."

"Well, then, allow me to speak to Dousterswivel. If the money can be advanced usefully and advantageously for you, why, for old neighbourhood's sake, you shall not want it; but if, as I think, I can recover the treasure for you without making such an advance, you will, I presume, have no objection?"

"Unquestionably, I can have none whatsoever."

"Then where is Dousterswivel?" continued the Antiquary.

"To tell you the truth, he is in my carriage below; but knowing your prejudice against him——"

"I thank Heaven, I am not prejudiced against any man, Sir Arthur: it is systems not individuals that incur my reprobation." He rang the bell. "Jenny, Sir Arthur and I offer our compliments to Mr. Dousterswivel, the gentleman in Sir Arthur's carriage, and beg to have the pleasure of speaking with him here."

Jenny departed and delivered her message. It had been by no means a part of the project of Dousterswivel to let Mr. Oldbuck into his supposed mystery. He had relied upon Sir Arthur's obtaining the necessary accommodation without any discussion as to the nature of the application, and only waited below for the purpose of possessing himself of the deposit as soon as possible, for he foresaw that his career was drawing to a close. But when summoned to the presence of Sir Arthur and Mr. Oldbuck, he resolved gallantly to put confidence in his powers of impudence, of which, the reader may have observed, his natural share was very liberal.

CHAPTER XXIII.

And this doctor,
Your sooty smoky-bearded compeer, he
Will close you so much gold in a bolt's head,
And, on a turn, convey in the stead another
With sublimed mercury, that shall burst i' the heat,
And all fly out *in fumo.*

The Alchemist.

"How do you do, goot Mr. Oldenbuck? and I do hope your young gentleman, Captain M'Intyre, is getting better again? Ach! it is a bat business when young gentlemens will put lead balls into each other's body."

"Lead adventures of all kinds are very precarious, Mr. Dousterswivel; but I am happy to learn," continued the Antiquary, "from my friend Sir Arthur that you have taken up a better trade, and become a discoverer of gold."

"Ach, Mr. Oldenbuck, mine goot and honoured patron should not have told a word about dat little matter; for, though I have all reliance—yes, indeed—on goot Mr. Oldenbuck's prudence and discretion, and his great friendship for Sir Arthur Wardour, yet, my Heavens! it is an great ponderous secret."

"More ponderous than any of the metal we shall make by it, I fear," answered Oldbuck.

"Dat is just as you shall have de faith and de patience for de grand experiment. If you join wid Sir Arthur, as he is put one hundred and fifty—see, here is one fifty in your dirty Fairport bank-note—you put one other hundred and fifty in de dirty notes, and you shall have de pure gold and silver, I cannot tell how much."

"Nor any one for you, I believe," said the Antiquary. "But hark you, Mr. Dousterswivel; suppose, without troubling this same sneezing spirit with any farther fumigations, we should go in a body, and, having fair daylight and our good consciences to befriend us, using no other conjuring implements than good substantial pickaxes and shovels, fairly trench the area of the chancel in the ruins of St. Ruth from one end to the other, and so ascertain the existence of this supposed treasure, without putting ourselves to any farther expense. The ruins belong to Sir Arthur himself, so there can be no objection. Do you think we shall succeed in this way of managing the matter?"

"Bah! you will not find one copper thimble. But Sir Arthur will do his pleasure. I have showed him how it is possible, very possible, to have de great sum of money for his occasions; I have showed him de real experiment. If he likes not to believe, goot Mr. Oldbuck, it is nothing to Herman Dousterswivel; he only loses de money and de gold and de silvers, dat is all."

Sir Arthur Wardour cast an intimidated glance at Oldbuck, who, especially when present, held, notwithstanding their frequent difference of opinion, no ordinary influence over his sentiments. In truth, the Baronet felt, what he would not willingly have acknowledged, that his genius stood rebuked before that of the Antiquary. He respected him as a shrewd, penetrating, sarcastic character, feared his satire, and had some confidence in the general soundness of his opinions. He therefore looked at him as if desiring his leave before indulging his credulity. Dousterswivel saw he was in danger of losing his dupe, unless he could make some favourable impression on the adviser.

"I know, my goot Mr. Oldenbuck, it is one vanity to speak to you about de spirit and de goblin. But look at this curious horn; I know you know de curiosity of all de countries, and how de great Oldenburgh horn, as they keep still in the museum at Copenhagen, was given to de Duke of Oldenburgh by one female spirit of de wood. Now I could not put one trick on you if I were willing, you who know all de curiosity so well, and dere it is, de horn full of coins; if it had been a box or case I would have said nothing."

"Being a horn," said Oldbuck, "does indeed strengthen your argument. It was an implement of nature's fashioning, and therefore much used among rude nations, although it may be the metaphorical horn is more frequent in proportion to the progress of civilisation. And this present horn," he continued, rubbing it upon his sleeve, "is a curious and venerable relic, and no doubt was intended to prove a cornucopia, or horn of plenty, to some one or other; but whether to the adept or his patron may be justly doubted."

"Well, Mr. Oldenbuck, I find you still hard of belief; but let me assure you de monks understood de *magisterium*."

"Let us leave talking of the *magisterium*, Mr. Dousterswivel, and think a little about the magistrate. Are you aware that this occupation of yours is against the law of Scotland, and that both Sir Arthur and myself are in the commission of the peace?"

"Mine Heaven! and what is dat to de purpose when I am doing you all de goot I can?"

"Why, you must know, that when the legislature abolished the cruel laws against witchcraft, they had no hope of destroying the superstitious feelings of humanity on which such chimeras had been founded, and to prevent those feelings from being tampered with by artful and designing persons, it is enacted by the Ninth of George the Second, chap. 5, that whosoever shall pretend, by his alleged skill in any occult or crafty science, to discover such goods as are lost, stolen, or concealed, he shall suffer punishment by pillory and imprisonment, as a common cheat and impostor."

"And is dat de laws?" asked Dousterswivel, with some agitation.

"Thyself shalt see the act," replied the Antiquary.

"Den, gentlemens, I shall take my leave of you, dat is all; I do not like to stand on your what you call pillory, it is very bad way to take de air, I think; and I do not like your prisons no more, where one cannot take de air at all."

"If such be your taste, Mr. Dousterswivel," said the Antiquary, "I advise you to stay where you are, for I cannot let you go, unless it be in the society of a constable; and, moreover, I expect you will attend us just now to the ruins of St. Ruth, and point out the place where you propose to find this treasure."

"Mine Heaven, Mr. Oldenbuck! what usage is this to your old friend, when I tell you so plain as I can speak dat if you go now you will get not so much treasure as one poor shabby sixpence?"

"I will try the experiment, however, and you shall be dealt with according to its success—always with Sir Arthur's permission."

Sir Arthur, during this investigation, had looked extremely embarrassed, and, to use a vulgar but expressive phrase, chop-fallen. Oldbuck's obstinate disbelief led him strongly to suspect the imposture of Dousterswivel, and the adept's mode of keeping his ground was less resolute than he had expected. Yet he did not entirely give him up.

"Mr. Oldbuck," said the Baronet, "you do Mr. Dousterswivel less than justice. He has undertaken to make this discovery by the use of his art, and by applying characters descriptive of the intelligences presiding over the planetary hour in which the experiment is to be made; and you require him to proceed, under pain of punishment, without allowing him the use of any of the preliminaries which he considers as the means of procuring success."

"I did not say that exactly: I only required him to be present when we make the search, and not to leave us during the interval. I fear he may have some intelligence with the intelligences you talk of, and that whatever may be now hidden at St. Ruth may disappear before we get there."

"Well, gentlemens," said Dousterswivel, sullenly, "I will make no objections to go along with you; but I tell you beforehand, you shall not find so much of anything as shall be worth your going twenty yard from your own gate."

"We will put that to a fair trial," said the Antiquary. And the Baronet's equipage being ordered, Miss Wardour received an intimation from her father that she was to remain at Monkbarns until his return from an airing. The young lady was somewhat at a loss to reconcile this direction with the communication which she supposed must have passed between Sir Arthur and the Antiquary; but she was compelled for the present to remain in a most unpleasant state of suspense.

The journey of the treasure-seekers was melancholy enough.

Dousterswivel maintained a sulky silence, brooding at once over disappointed expectation and the risk of punishment; Sir Arthur, whose golden dreams had been gradually fading away, surveyed in gloomy prospect the impending difficulties of his situation; and Oldbuck, who perceived that his having so far interfered in his neighbour's affairs gave the Baronet a right to expect some actual and efficient assistance, sadly pondered to what extent it would be necessary to draw open the strings of his purse. Thus, each being wrapped in his own unpleasant ruminations, there was hardly a word said on either side until they reached the Four Horseshoes, by which sign the little inn was distinguished. They procured at this place the necessary assistance and implements for digging, and while they were busy about these preparations were suddenly joined by the old beggar, Edie Ochiltree.

"The Lord bless your honour," began the Blue-Gown, with the genuine mendicant whine, "and long life to you; weel pleased am I to hear that young Captain McIntyre is like to be on his legs again sune. Think on your poor bedesman the day."

"Aha, old trupenny!" replied the Antiquary. "Why, thou hast never come to Monkbarns since thy perils by rock and flood; here's something for thee to buy snuff," and, fumbling for his purse, he pulled out at the same time the horn which inclosed the coins.

"Ay, and there's something to pit it in," said the mendicant, eyeing the ram's horn; "that loom's an auld acquaintance o' mine. I could take my aith to that sneeshing-mull amang a thousand; I carried it for mony a year, till I niffered it for this tin ane wi' auld George Glen, the dammer and sinker, when he took a fancy till't doun at Glen Withershins yonder."

"Ay! indeed?" said Oldbuck; "so you exchanged it with a miner? But I presume you never saw it so well filled before?" and, opening it, he showed the coins.

"Troth, ye may swear that, Monkbarns; when it was mine it ne'er had abune the like o' saxpenny worth o' black rappee in't at ance. But I reckon ye'll be gaun to make an antic o't, as ye hae dune wi' mony an orra thing besides. Odd, I wish ony body wad make an antic o' me; but mony ane will find worth in rousted bits o' capper and horn and airn, that care unco little about an auld carle o' their ain country and kind."

"You may now guess," said Oldbuck, turning to Sir Arthur, "to whose good offices you were indebted the other night. To trace this cornucopia of yours to a miner is bringing it pretty near a friend of ours. I hope we shall be as successful this morning without paying for it."

"And whare is your honours gaun the day," said the mendicant, "wi' a' your picks and shules? Odd, this will be some o' your tricks, Monkbarns; ye'll be for whirling some o' the auld monks down by yonder out o' their graves afore they hear the last call; but, wi' your leave, I'se follow ye at ony rate and see what ye make o't."

The party soon arrived at the ruins of the priory, and, having gained the chancel, stood still to consider what course they were to pursue next.

The Antiquary, meantime, addressed the adept: "Pray, Mr. Dousterswivel, what is your advice in this matter? Shall we have most likelihood of success if we dig from east to west, or from west to east? or will you assist us with your triangular vial of May-dew, or with your divining-rod of witches-hazel? Or will you have the goodness to supply us with a few thumping, blustering terms of art, which, if they fail in our present service, may at least be useful to those who have not the happiness to be bachelors, to still their brawling children withal?"

"Mr. Oldenbuck," said Dousterswivel, doggedly, "I have told you already, you will make no good work at all, and I will find some way of mine own to thank you for your civilities to me; yes, indeed."

"If your honours are thinking of tirling the floor," said old Edie, "and wad but take a puir body's advice, I would begin below that muckle stane that has the man there streekit out upon his back in the midst o't."

"I have some reason for thinking favourably of that plan myself," said the Baronet.

"And I have nothing to say against it," said Oldbuck. "It was not unusual to hide treasure in the tombs of the deceased; many instances might be quoted of that from Bartholinus and others."

The tombstone, the same beneath which the coins had been found by Sir Arthur and the German, was once more forced aside, and the earth gave easy way to the spade.

"It's travell'd earth that," said Edie, "it howks sae eithly. I ken it weel, for ance I wrought a simmer wi' auld Will Winnet, the bedral, and howkit mair graves than ane in my day. But I left him in winter, for it was unco cald wark; and then it cam a green Yule, and the folk died thick and fast, for ye ken a green Yule makes a fat kirk-yard; and I never dowed to bide a hard turn o' wark in my life, sae aff I gaed, and left Will to delve his last dwellings by himsell for Edie."

The diggers were now so far advanced in their labours as to discover that the sides of the grave which they were clearing out had been originally secured by four walls of freestone, forming a parallelogram, for the reception, probably, of the coffin.

"It is worth while proceeding in our labours," said the Antiquary to Sir Arthur, "were it but for curiosity's sake. I wonder on whose sepulchre they have bestowed such uncommon pains."

"The arms on the shield," said Sir Arthur, and sighed as he spoke it, "are the same with those on Misticot's Tower, supposed to have been built by Malcolm the Usurper. No man knew where he was buried, and there is an old prophecy in our family that bodes us no good when his grave shall be discovered."

"I wot," said the beggar, "I have often heard that when I was a bairn,

> If Malcolm the Misticot's grave were fun',
> The lands of Knockwinnock are lost and won."

Oldbuck, with his spectacles on his nose, had already knelt down on the monument, and was tracing, partly with his eye, partly with his finger, the mouldered devices upon the effigy of the deceased warrior. "It is the Knockwinnock arms sure enough," he exclaimed, "quarterly with the coat of Wardour."

"Richard, called the Red-handed Wardour, married Sybil Knockwinnock, the heiress of the Saxon family, and by that alliance," said Sir Arthur, "brought the castle and estate into the name of Wardour, in the year of God 1150."

"Very true, Sir Arthur, and here is the baton-sinister, the mark of illegitimacy, extended diagonally through both coats upon the shield. Where can our eyes have been that they did not see this curious monument before?"

"Na, whare was the through-stane that it didna come before our een till e'now?" said Ochiltree; "for I hae kend this auld kirk, man and bairn, for saxty lang years, and I ne'er noticed it afore, and it's nae sic mote neither but what ane might see it in their parritch."

All were now induced to tax their memory as to the former state of the ruins in that corner of the chancel, and all agreed in recollecting a considerable pile of rubbish which must have been removed and spread abroad in order to make the tomb visible. Sir Arthur might, indeed, have remembered seeing the monument on the former occasion, but his mind was too much agitated to attend to the circumstance as a novelty.

While the assistants were engaged in these recollections and discussions, the workmen proceeded with their labour. They had already dug to the depth of nearly five feet, and as the flinging out the soil became more and more difficult, they began at length to tire of the job.

"We're down to the till now," said one of them, "and the ne'er a coffin or ony thing else is here; some cunninger chiel's been afore us, I reckon"; and the labourer scrambled out of the grave.

"Hout, lad," said Edie, getting down in his room, "let me try my hand for an auld bedral; ye're gude seekers but ill finders."

So soon as he got into the grave, he struck his pike-staff forcibly down: it encountered resistance in its descent, and the beggar exclaimed, like a Scotch schoolboy when he finds anything: "Nae halvers and quarters! hale o' mine ain and nane o' my neighbour's."

Everybody, from the dejected Baronet to the sullen adept, now caught the spirit of curiosity, crowded round the grave, and would have jumped into it could its space have contained them. The labourers, who had begun to flag in their monotonous and apparently hopeless task, now resumed their tools and plied them with all the ardour of expectation. Their shovels soon grated upon a hard wooden surface, which, as the earth was cleared away, assumed the distinct form of a chest, but greatly smaller than that of a coffin. Now all hands were at work to heave it out of the grave, and all voices, as it was raised, proclaimed its weight and augured its value. They were not mistaken.

When the chest or box was placed on the surface, and the lid forced up by a pickaxe, there was displayed first a coarse canvas cover, then a quantity of oakum, and beneath that a number of ingots of silver. A general exclamation hailed a discovery so surprising and unexpected. The Baronet threw his hands and eyes up to heaven, with the silent rapture of one who is delivered from inexpressible distress of mind. Oldbuck, almost unable to credit his eyes, lifted one piece of silver after another. There was neither inscription nor stamp upon them, excepting one, which seemed to be Spanish. He could have no doubt of the purity and great value of the treasure before him. Still, however, removing piece by piece, he examined row by row, expecting to discover that the lower layers were of inferior value; but he could perceive no difference in this respect, and found himself compelled to admit that Sir Arthur had possessed himself of bullion to the value perhaps of a thousand pounds sterling. Sir Arthur now promised the assistants a handsome recompense for their trouble, and began to busy himself about the mode of conveying this rich windfall to the Castle of Knockwinnock, when the adept, recovering from his surprise, which had equalled that exhibited by any other individual of the party, twitched his sleeve, and, having offered his humble congratulations, turned next to Oldbuck with an air of triumph.

"I did tell you, my goot friend Mr. Oldenbuck, dat I was to seek opportunity to thank you for your civility; now do you not think I have found out vary goot way to return thank?"

"Why, Mr. Dousterswivel, do you pretend to have had any hand in our good success? You forget you refused us all aid of your science, man. And you are here without your weapons that should have fought the battle which you pretend to have gained in our behalf. You have used neither charm, lamen, sigil, talisman, spell, crystal, pentacle, magic mirror, nor geomantic figure. Where be your periapts and your abracadabras, man? your May-fern, your vervain,

> Your toad, your crow, your dragon, and your panther,
> Your sun, your moon, your firmament, your adrop,
> Your lato, azoch, zernich, chibrit, heautarit,
> With all your broths, your menstrues, your materials,
> Would burst a man to name?

Ah! rare Ben Jonson! long peace to thy ashes for a scourge of the quacks of thy day! Who expected to see them revive in our own?"

The answer of the adept to the Antiquary's tirade we must defer to our next chapter.

CHAPTER XXIV.

Clause. You now shall know the king o' the beggars' treasure.
Yes, ere to-morrow you shall find your harbour
Here; fail me not, for if I live I'll fit you.
The Beggar's Bush.

THE German, determined, it would seem, to assert the vantage-ground on which the discovery had placed him, replied with great pomp and statelinesss to the attack of the Antiquary: "Maister Oldenbuck, all dis may be very witty and comedy, but I have nothing to say—nothing at all—to people dat will not believe deir own eyesights. It is vary true dat I ave not any of de things of de art, and it makes de more wonder what I has done dis day. But I would ask of you, mine honoured and goot and generous patron, to put your hand into your right-hand waistcoat pocket and show me what you shall find dere."

Sir Arthur obeyed his direction, and pulled out the small plate of silver which he had used under the adept's auspices upon the former occasion. "It is very true," said Sir Arthur, looking gravely at the Antiquary; "this is the graduated and calculated sigil by which Mr. Dousterswivel and I regulated our first discovery."

"Pshaw! pshaw! my dear friend," said Oldbuck, "you are too wise to believe in the influence of a trumpery crown-piece beat out thin, and a parcel of scratches upon it. I tell thee, Sir Arthur, that if Dousterswivel had known where to get this treasure himself, you would not have been lord of the least share of it."

"In troth, please your honour," said Edie, who put in his word on all occasions, "I think, since Mr. Dunkerswivel has had sae muckle merit in discovering a' the gear, the least ye can do is to gie him that o't that's left behind for his labour, for doubtless he that kend where to find sae muckle will hae nae difficulty to find mair."

Dousterswivel's brow grew very dark at this proposal of leaving him to his "ain purchase," as Ochiltree expressed it; but the beggar, drawing him aside, whispered a word or two in his ear, to which he seemed to give serious attention.

Meanwhile Sir Arthur, his heart warm with his good fortune, said aloud: "Never mind our friend Monkbarns, Mr. Dousterswivel, but come to the Castle to-morrow and I'll convince you that I am not ungrateful for the hints you have given me about this matter, and the fifty Fairport dirty notes, as you call them, are heartily at your service. Come, my lads, get the cover of this precious chest fastened up again."

But the cover had in the confusion fallen aside among the rubbish or the loose earth which had been removed from the grave; in short, it was not to be seen.

"Never mind, my good lads, tie the tarpaulin over it and get it away to the carriage. Monkbarns, will you walk? I must go back your way to take up Miss Wardour."

"And, I hope, to take up your dinner also, Sir Arthur, and

17

drink a glass of wine for joy of our happy adventure. Besides, you should write about the business to the Exchequer, in case of any interference on the part of the Crown. As you are lord of the manor, it will be easy to get a deed of gift should they make any claim. We must talk about it though."

"And I particularly recommend silence to all who are present," said Sir Arthur, looking round. All bowed and professed themselves dumb.

"Why, as to that," said Monkbarns, "recommending secrecy where a dozen of people are acquainted with the circumstance to be concealed is only putting the truth in masquerade, for the story will be circulated under twenty different shapes. But never mind; we will state the true one to the Barons, and that is all that is necessary."

"I incline to send off an express to-night," said the Baronet.

"I can recommend your honour to a sure hand," said Ochiltree, "little Davie Mailsetter and the butcher's reisting powny."

"We will talk over the matter as we go to Monkbarns," said Sir Arthur. "My lads (to the work-people), come with me to the Four Horseshoes, that I may take down all your names. Dousterswivel, I won't ask you to go down to Monkbarns, as the Laird and you differ so widely in opinion; but do not fail to come to see me to-morrow."

Dousterswivel growled out an answer, in which the words, "duty," "mine honoured patron," and "wait upon Sir Arthurs," were alone distinguishable; and after the Baronet and his friend had left the ruins, followed by the servants and workmen, who, in hope of reward and whisky, joyfully attended their leader, the adept remained in a brown study by the side of the open grave.

"Who was it as could have thought this?" he ejaculated unconsciously. "Mine *Heiligkeit!* I have heard of such things, and often spoken of such things; but, sapperment! I never thought to see them! And if I had gone but two or dree feet deeper down in the earth, *mein Himmel!* it had been all mine own; so much more as I have been muddling about to get from this fool's man."

Here the German ceased his soliloquy, for, raising his eyes, he encountered those of Edie Ochiltree, who had not followed the rest of the company, but, resting as usual on his pike-staff, had planted himself on the other side of the grave. The features of the old man, naturally shrewd and expressive almost to an appearance of knavery, seemed in this instant so keenly knowing that even the assurance of Dousterswivel, though a professed adventurer, sunk beneath their glances. But he saw the necessity of an *éclaircissement*, and, rallying his spirits, instantly began to sound the mendicant on the occurrences of the day. "Goot Maister Edies Ochiltrees——"

"Edie Ochiltree, nae maister; your puir bedesman and the king's," answered the Blue-Gown.

"Awell den, goot Edie, what do you think of all dis?"

"I was just thinking it was very kind—for I darena say very simple—o' your honour to gie thae twa rich gentles, wha hae lands and lairdships, and siller without end, this grand pose o' silver and treasure—three times tried in the fire, as the Scripture expresses it—that might hae made yoursell, and ony twa or three honest bodies beside, as happy and content as the day was lang."

"Indeed, Edie, mine honest friends, dat is very true; only I did not know—dat is, I was not sure—where to find de gelt myself."

"What! was it not by your honour's advice and counsel that Monkbarns and the Knight of Knockwinnock came here then?"

"Aha, yes, but it was by another circumstance; I did not know dat dey would have found de treasure, mein friend; though I did guess, by such a tintamarre, and cough, and sneeze, and groan among de spirit one other night here, dat there might be treasure and bullion hereabout. *Ach, mein Himmel!* the spirit will hone and groan over his gelt as if he were a Dutch burgomaster counting his dollars after a great dinner at the *stadthaus.*"

"And do you really believe the like o' that, Mr. Dusterdeevil? a skeelfu' man like you; hout fie!"

"Mein friend," answered the adept, forced by circumstances

to speak something nearer the truth than he generally used to do, "I believed it no more than you and no man at all, till I did hear them hone and moan and groan myself on de oder night, and till I did this day see de cause, which was an great chest all full of de pure silver from Mexico; and what would you ave me think den?"

"And what wad ye gie to ony ane," said Edie, "that wad help ye to sic another kistfu' o' silver?"

"Give? *mein Himmel!* one great big quarter of it."

"Now, if the secret were mine," said the mendicant, "I wad stand out for half; for you see, though I am but a puir ragged body, and couldna carry silver or gowd to sell for fear o' being taen up, yet I could find mony folk would pass it awa for me at unco muckle easier profit than ye're thinking on."

"*Ach, Himmel!* Mein goot friend, what was it I said? I did mean to say you should have de tree-quarter for your half, and de one quarter to be my fair half."

"No, no, Mr. Dusterdeevil, we will divide equally what we find, like brother and brother. Now look at this board that I just flung into the dark aisle out o' the way, while Monkbarns was glowering ower a' the silver yonder. He's a sharp chiel Monkbarns. I was glad to keep the like o' this out o' his sight. Ye'll maybe can read the character better than me; I am nae that book-learned, at least I'm no that muckle in practice."

With this modest declaration of ignorance, Ochiltree brought forth from behind a pillar the cover of the box or chest of treasure, which, when forced from its hinges, had been carelessly flung aside during the ardour of curiosity to ascertain the contents which it concealed, and had been afterwards, as it seems, secreted by the mendicant. There was a word and a number upon the plank, and the beggar made them more distinct by spitting upon his ragged blue handkerchief and rubbing off the clay by which the inscription was obscured. It was in the ordinary black letter.

"Can ye mak ought o't?" said Edie to the adept.

"S," said the philosopher, like a child getting his lesson in the primer—"S, T, A, R, C, H—starch; dat is what the women-washers put in to de neckerchers and de shirt collar."

"Starch!" echoed Ochiltree; "na, na, Mr. Dusterdeevil, ye are mair of a conjuror than a clerk; it's 'search,' man, 'search.' See, there's the 'Ye' clear and distinct."

"Aha! I see it now; it is 'search, number one.' *Mein Himmel!* then there must be a 'number two,' mein goot friend; for 'search' is what you call to seek and dig, and this is but 'number one!' Mine wort, there is one great big prize in de wheel for us, goot Maister Ochiltree."

"Aweel, it may be sae; but we canna howk for't enow. We hae nae shules, for they hae taen them a' awa; and it's like some o' them, will be sent back to fling the earth into the hole, and mak a' things trig again. But an ye'll sit down wi' me a while in the wood, I'se satisfy your honour that ye hae just lighted on the only man in the country that could hae tauld about Malcolm Misticot and his hidden treasure. But first we'll rub out the letters on this board for fear it tell tales."

And, by the assistance of his knife, the beggar erased and defaced the characters so as to make them quite unintelligible, and then daubed the board with clay so as to obliterate all traces of the erasure.

Dousterswivel stared at him in ambiguous silence. There was an intelligence and alacrity about all the old man's movements which indicated a person that could not be easily over-reached, and yet (for even rogues acknowledge in some degree the spirit of precedence) our adept felt the disgrace of playing a secondary part, and dividing winnings with so mean an associate. His appetite for gain, however, was sufficiently sharp to overpower his offended pride, and, though far more an impostor than a dupe, he was not without a certain degree of personal faith even in the gross superstitions by means of which he imposed upon others. Still, being accustomed to act as a leader on such occasions, he felt humiliated at feeling himself in the situation of a vulture marshalled to his prey by a carrion-crow. "Let me, however, hear his story to an end," thought Dousterswivel, "and it will be hard if I do not make mine account in it better, as Maister Edie Ochiltrees makes proposes."

The adept, thus transformed into a pupil from a teacher of the mystic art, followed Ochiltree in passive acquiescence to the Prior's Oak—a spot, as the reader may remember, at a short distance from the ruins—where the German sat down and in silence waited the old man's communication.

"Maister Dustandsnivel," said the narrator, "it's an unco while since I heard this business treated anent; for the Lairds of Knockwinnock, neither Sir Arthur, nor his father, nor his grandfather—and I mind a wee bit about them a'—liked to hear it spoken about; nor they dinna like it yet. But nae matter: ye may be sure it was clattered about in the kitchen, like ony thing else in a great house, though it were forbidden in the ha', and sae I hae heard the circumstance rehearsed by auld servants in the family; and in thir present days, when things o' that auld-warld sort arena keepit in mind round winter firesides as they used to be, I question if there's ony body in the country can tell the tale but mysell; aye out-taken the Laird though, for there's a parchment book about it, as I have heard, in the charter-room at Knockwinnock Castle."

"Well, all dat is vary well; but get you on with your stories, mine goot friend," said Dousterswivel.

"Aweel, ye see," continued the mendicant, "this was a job in the auld times o' rugging and riving through the hale country, when it was ilka ane for himsell, and God for us a'; when nae man wanted property if he had strength to take it, or had it langer than he had power to keep it. It was just he ower her and she ower him, whichever could win upmost, a' through the east country here, and nae doubt through the rest o' Scotland in the self and same manner.

"Sae, in these days Sir Richard Wardour came into the land, and that was the first o' the name ever was in this country. There's been mony of them sin' syne; and the maist, like him they ca'd Hell-in-Harness, and the rest o' them, are sleeping down in yon ruins. They were a proud dour set o' men, but unco brave, and aye stood up for the weel o' the country, God sain them a'—there's no muckle popery in that wish. They ca'd them the Norman Wardours, though they cam frae the south to this country. So this Sir Richard, that they ca'd

Red-hand, drew up wi' the auld Knockwinnock o' that day, for then they were Knockwinnocks of that Ilk, and wad fain marry his only daughter, that was to have the castle and the land. Laith, laith was the lass—Sybil Knockwinnock they ca'd her that tauld me the tale—laith, laith was she to gae into the match, for she had fa'en a wee ower thick wi' a cousin o' her ain that her father had some ill-will to; and sae it was that after she had been married to Sir Richard jimp four months—for marry him she maun it's like—ye'll no hinder her gieing them a present o' a bonny knave bairn. Then there was siccan a ca' thro' as the like was never seen; and she's be burnt and he's be slain was the best words o' their mouths. But it was a' sowdered up again some gait, and the bairn was sent awa, and bred up near the Highlands, and grew up to be a fine wanle fallow, like mony ane that comes o' the wrang side o' the blanket; and Sir Richard wi' the Red hand, he had a fair offspring o' his ain, and a' was lound and quiet till his head was laid in the ground. But then down came Malcolm Misticot—Sir Arthur says it should be Misbegot, but they aye ca'd him Misticot that spoke o't lang syne—down came this Malcolm, the love-begot, frae Glen Isla, wi' a string o' lang-legged Highlanders at his heels, that's aye ready for ony body's mischief, and he threeps the castle and lands are his ain as his mother's eldest son, and turns a' the Wardours out to the hill. There was a sort o' fighting and bludespilling about it, for the gentles took different sides; but Malcolm had the uppermost for a lang time, and keepit the Castle of Knockwinnock, and strengthened it, and built that muckle tower that they ca' Misticot's Tower to this day."

"Mine goot friend, old Mr. Edie Ochiltree," interrupted the German, "this is all as one like de long histories of a baron of sixteen quarters in mine countries; but I would as rather hear of de silver and gold."

"Why, ye see," continued the mendicant, "this Malcolm was weel helped by an uncle, a brother o' his father's, that was prior o' St. Ruth here, and muckle treasure they gathered between them, to secure the succession of their house in the lands of Knockwinnock. Folk said that the monks in thae days had the art of multiplying metals; at ony rate they were very rich. At last it came to this, that the young Wardour, that was Red-hand's son, challenged Misticot to fight with him in the lists, as they ca'd them; that's no lists or tailor's runds and selvedges o' claith, but a palin'-thing they set up for them to fight in like game-cocks. Aweel, Misticot was beaten, and at his brother's mercy; but he wadna touch his life, for the blood of Knockwinnock that was in baith their veins. So Malcolm was compelled to turn a monk, and he died soon after in the priory, of pure despite and vexation. Naebody ever kend whare his uncle the prior earded him, or what he did wi' his gowd and silver, for he stood on the right o' halie kirk, and wad gie nae account to ony body. But the prophecy gat abroad in the country, that whenever Misticot's grave was fund out the estate of Knockwinnock should be lost and won."

"Ach, mine good old friend, Maister Edie, and dat is not so very unlikely, if Sir Arthurs will quarrel wit his goot friends to please Mr. Oldenbuck. And so you do tink dat dis golds and silvers belonged to goot Mr. Malcolm Mishdigoat?"

"Troth do I, Mr. Dousterdeevil."

"And you do believe dat dere is more of dat sorts behind?"

"By my certie do I. How can it be otherwise? 'Search. No. 1'; that is as muckle as to say, search and ye'll find number twa; besides, yon kist is only silver, and I aye heard that Misticot's pose had muckle yellow gowd in't."

"Den, mine goot friends," said the adept, jumping up hastily, "why do we not set about our little job directly?"

"For twa gude reasons," answered the beggar, who quietly kept his sitting posture; "first, because, as I said before, we have naething to dig wi', for they hae taen awa the picks and shules; and, secondly, because there will be a wheen idle gowks coming to glower at the hole as lang as it is daylight, and maybe the Laird may send somebody to fill it up; and ony way we wad be catched. But if you will meet me on this place at twal o'clock wi' a dark lantern, I'll hae tools ready, and we'll gang quietly about our job our twa sells, and naebody the wiser for't."

"Be—be—but, mine goot friend," said Dousterswivel, from whose recollection his former nocturnal adventure was not to be altogether erased, even by the splendid hopes which Edie's narrative held forth, "it is not so goot or so safe to be about goot Maister Mishdigoat's grave at dat time of night; you have forgot how I told you de spirits did hone and mone dere. I do assure you dere is disturbance dere."

"If ye're afraid of ghaists," answered the mendicant, coolly, "I'll do the job mysell, and bring your share o' the siller to ony place ye like to appoint."

"No—no, mine excellent old Mr. Edie, too much trouble for you; I will not have dat; I will come myself, and it will be bettermost; for, mine old friend, it was I, Herman Douster-swivel, discovered Maister Mishdigoat's grave when I was look-ing for a place as to put away some little trumpery coins, just to play one little trick on my dear friend Sir Arthur, for a little sport and pleasures; yes, I did take some what you call rubbish, and did discover Maister Mishdigoat's own monu-mentsh. It is like dat he meant I should be his heirs, so it would not be civility in me not to come mineself for mine inheritance."

"At twal o'clock, then," said the mendicant, "we meet under this tree. I'll watch for a while, and see that naebody meddles wi' the grave—it's only saying the Laird's forbade it—then get my bit supper frae Ringan the poinder up by, and leave to sleep in his barn, and I'll slip out at night and ne'er be mist."

"Do so, mine goot Maister Edie, and I will meet you here on this very place, though all de spirits should moan and sneeze deir very brains out."

So saying, he shook hands with the old man, and, with this mutual pledge of fidelity to their appointment, they separated for the present.

CHAPTER XXV.

See thou shake the bags
Of hoarding abbots; angels imprisoned
Set thou at liberty.
Bell, book, and candle shall not drive me back,
If gold and silver beckon to come on.

King John.

THE night set in stormy, with wind and occasional showers of rain. "Eh, sirs," said the old mendicant, as he took his place on the sheltered side of the large oak-tree to wait for his associate—"eh, sirs, but human nature's a wilful and wilyard thing! Is it not an unco lucre o' gain wad bring this Dousterdivel out in a blast o' wind like this, at twal o'clock at night, to thir wild gousty wa's? and amna I a bigger fule than himsell to bide here waiting for him?"

Having made these sage reflections, he wrapped himself close in his cloak and fixed his eye on the moon as she waded amid the stormy and dusky clouds, which the wind from time to time drove across her surface. The melancholy and uncertain gleams that she shot from between the passing shadows fell full upon the rifted arches and shafted windows of the old building, which were thus for an instant made distinctly visible in their ruinous state, and anon became again a dark, undistinguished, and shadowy mass. The little lake had its share of these transient beams of light, and showed its waters broken, whitened, and agitated under the passing storm, which, when the clouds swept over the moon, were only distinguished by their sullen and murmuring plash against the beach. The wooded glen repeated, to every successive gust that hurried through its narrow trough, the deep and various groan with which the trees replied to the whirlwind, and the sound sunk again, as the blast passed away, into a faint and passing murmur, resembling the sighs of an exhausted criminal after the first pangs of his torture are over. In these sounds superstition might have found ample gratification for that state of excited terror which she fears and yet loves. But such feelings made no part of Ochiltree's composition. His mind wandered back to the scenes of his youth.

"I have kept guard on the outposts baith in Germany and America," he said to himself, "in mony a waur night than this, and when I kend there was maybe a dozen o' their riflemen in the thicket before me. But I was aye gleg at my duty: naebody ever catched Edie sleeping."

As he muttered thus to himself, he instinctively shouldered his trusty pike-staff, assumed the port of a sentinel on duty, and, as a step advanced towards the tree, called, with a tone assorting better with his military reminiscences than his present state: "Stand; who goes there?"

"De devil, goot Edie," answered Douterswivel, "why does you speak so loud as a baarenhauter, or what you call a factionary—I mean a sentinel?"

"Just because I thought I was a sentinel at that moment," answered the mendicant. "Here's an awsome night; hae ye brought the lantern and a pock for the siller?"

"Ay, ay, mine goot friend," said the German, "here it is: my pair of what you call saddlebag; one side will be for you, one side for me. I will put dem on my horse to save you de trouble, as you are old man."

"Have you a horse here, then?" asked Edie Ochiltree.

"Oh yes, mine friend, tied yonder by de stile," responded the adept.

"Weel, I hae just ae word to the bargain: there sall nane o' my gear gang on your beast's back."

"What was it as you would be afraid of?" said the foreigner.

"Only of losing sight of horse, man, and money," again replied the gaberlunzie.

"Does you know dat you make one gentlemans out to be one great rogue?"

"Mony gentlemen," replied Ochiltree, "can make that out for themselves; but what's the sense of quarrelling? If ye want to gang on, gang on. If no, I'll gae back to the gude ait-straw in Ringan Aikwood's barn that I left wi' right ill-will e'now, and I'll pit back the pick and shule whar I got them."

Dousterswivel deliberated a moment whether, by suffering Edie to depart, he might not secure the whole of the expected wealth for his own exclusive use. But the want of digging implements, the uncertainty whether, if he had them, he could clear out the grave to a sufficient depth without assistance, and, above all, the reluctance which he felt, owing to the experience of the former night, to venture alone on the terrors of Misticot's grave, satisfied him the attempt would be hazardous. Endeavouring, therefore, to assume his usual cajoling tone, though internally incensed, he begged "his goot friend Maister Edie Ochiltrees would lead the way, and assured him of his acquiescence in all such an excellent friend could propose."

"Aweel, aweel, then," said Edie, "tak gude care o' your feet amang the lang grass and the loose stanes. I wish we may get the light keepit in neist, wi' this fearsome wind; but there's a blink o' moonlight at times."

Thus saying, old Edie, closely accompanied by the adept, led the way towards the ruins, but presently made a full halt in front of them.

"Ye're a learned man, Mr. Dousterdeevil, and ken muckle o' the marvellous works o' nature; now, will ye tell me ae thing? D'ye believe in ghaists and spirits that walk the earth? d'ye believe in them, ay or no?"

"Now, goot Mr. Edie," whispered Dousterswivel, in an expostulatory tone of voice, "is this a times or a places for such a questions?"

"Indeed is it, baith the tane and the tother, Mr. Dustanshovel; for I maun fairly tell ye there's reports that auld Misticot walks. Now this wad be an uncanny night to meet him in, and wha kens if he wad be ower weel pleased wi' our purpose of visiting his pose?"

"*Alle guten Geister*," muttered the adept, the rest of the conjuration being lost in a tremulous warble of his voice. "I do desires you not to speak so, Mr. Edie, for, from all I heard dat one other night, I do much believes——"

"Now I," said Ochiltree, entering the chancel, and flinging abroad his arm with an air of defiance—"I wadna gie the crack o' my thumb for him were he to appear at this moment; he's but a disembodied spirit as we are embodied anes."

"For the lofe of heavens," said Dousterswivel, "say nothing at all neither about somebodies or nobodies!"

' Aweel," said the beggar, expanding the shade of the lantern, "here's the stane, and, spirit or no spirit, I'se be a wee bit deeper in the grave"; and he jumped into the place from which the precious chest had that morning been removed. After striking a few strokes he tired, or affected to tire, and said to his companion: "I'm auld and failed now, and canna keep at it. Time about's fair play, neighbour; ye maun get in and tak the shule a bit, and shule out the loose earth, and then I'll tak turn about wi' you."

Dousterswivel accordingly took the place which the beggar had evacuated, and toiled with all the zeal that awakened avarice, mingled with the anxious wish to finish the undertaking and leave the place as soon as possible, could inspire in a mind at once greedy, suspicious, and timorous.

Edie, standing much at his ease by the side of the hole, contented himself with exhorting his associate to labour hard. "My certie! few ever wrought for siccan a day's wage; an it be but—say the tenth part o' the size o' the kist No. 1, it will double its value, being filled wi' gowd instead of silver. Odd, ye work as if ye had been bred to pick and shule; ye could win your round half-crown ilka day. Tak care o' your taes wi' that stane!" giving a kick to a large one which the adept had heaved out with difficulty, and which Edie pushed back again, to the great annoyance of his associate's shins.

Thus exhorted by the mendicant, Dousterswivel struggled and laboured among the stones and stiff clay, toiling like a horse, and internally blaspheming in German. When such an unhallowed syllable escaped his lips, Edie changed his battery upon him.

"Oh dinna swear, dinna swear! wha kens wha's listening! Eh! Gude guide us, what's yon! Hout, it's just a branch of ivy flightering awa frae the wa'; when the moon was in it lookit unco like a dead man's arm wi' a taper in't; I thought it was Misticot himsell. But never mind, work you away,

fling the earth weel up bye out o' the gate; odd, if ye're no as
clean a worker at a grave as Will Winnet himsell! What
gars ye stop now? ye're just at the very bit for a chance."

"Stop!" said the German, in a tone of anger and disappointment, "why, I am down at de rocks dat de cursed ruins—God
forgife me!—is founded upon."

"Weel," said the beggar, "that's the likeliest bit of ony: it
will be but a muckle through-stane laid doun to kiver the
gowd; tak the pick till't, and pit mair strength, man; ae
gude downright devvel will split it, I'se warrant ye. Ay,
that will do. Odd, he comes on wi' Wallace's straiks!"

In fact, the adept, moved by Edie's exhortations, fetched
two or three desperate blows, and succeeded in breaking, not
indeed that against which he struck, which, as he had already
conjectured, was the solid rock, but the implement which he
wielded, jarring at the same time his arms up to the shoulder-
blades.

"Hurra, boys! there goes Ringan's pickaxe!" cried Edie;
"it's a shame o' the Fairport folk to sell siccan frail gear.
Try the shule; at it again, Mr. Dusterdeevil."

The adept, without reply, scrambled out of the pit, which
was now about six feet deep, and addressed his associate in a
voice that trembled with anger. "Does you know, Mr. Edies
Ochiltrees, who it is you put off your gibes and your jests
upon?"

"Brawly, Mr. Dusterdeevil—brawly do I ken ye, and has
done mony a day; but there's nae jesting in the case, for I
am wearying to see a' our treasures; we should hae had baith
ends o' the pockmanky filled by this time. I hope it's bowk
eneugh to haud a' the gear?"

"Look you, you base old person," said the incensed philosopher, "if you do put another jest upon me, I will cleave your
skull-piece with this shovels!"

"And whare wad my hands and my pike-staff be a' the
time?" replied Edie, in a tone that indicated no apprehension.
"Hout, tout, Maister Dusterdeevil, I haena lived sae lang in
the warld neither, to be shuled out o't that gate. What ails
ye to be cankered, man, wi' your friends? I'll wager I'll

find out the treasure in a minute"; and he jumped into the pit and took up the spade.

"I do swear to you," said the adept, whose suspicions were now fully awake, "that if you have played me one big trick I will give you one big beating, Mr. Edies."

"Hear till him now," said Ochiltree; "he kens how to gar folk find out the gear. Odd, I'm thinking he's been drilled that way himsell some day."

At this insinuation, which alluded obviously to the former scene betwixt himself and Sir Arthur, the philosopher lost the slender remnant of patience he had left, and, being of violent passions, heaved up the truncheon of the broken mattock to discharge it upon the old man's head. The blow would in all probability have been fatal had not he at whom it was aimed exclaimed in a stern and firm voice: "Shame to ye, man! Do ye think Heaven or earth will suffer ye to murder an auld man that might be your father? Look behind ye, man."

Dousterswivel turned instinctively, and beheld, to his utter astonishment, a tall dark figure standing close behind him. The apparition gave him no time to proceed by exorcism or otherwise, but, having instantly recourse to the *voie de fait*, took measure of the adept's shoulders three or four times with blows so substantial that he fell under the weight of them, and remained senseless for some minutes between fear and stupefaction. When he came to himself he was alone in the ruined chancel, lying upon the soft and damp earth which had been thrown out of Misticot's grave. He raised himself with a confused sensation of anger, pain, and terror, and it was not until he had sat upright for some minutes that he could arrange his ideas sufficiently to recollect how he came there, or with what purpose. As his recollection returned, he could have little doubt that the bait held out to him by Ochiltree to bring him to that solitary spot, the sarcasms by which he had provoked him into a quarrel, and the ready assistance which he had at hand for terminating it in the manner in which it had ended, were all parts of a concerted plan to bring disgrace and damage on Herman Dousterswivel. He could hardly suppose that he was indebted for the fatigue, anxiety, and beating which he had undergone purely to the malice of Edie Ochiltree singly, but concluded that the mendicant had acted a part assigned to him by some person of greater importance. His suspicions hesitated between Oldbuck and Sir Arthur Wardour. The former had been at no pains to conceal a marked dislike of him, but the latter he had deeply injured; and although he judged that Sir Arthur did not know the extent of his wrongs towards him, yet it was easy to suppose he had gathered enough of the truth to make him desirous of revenge. Ochiltree had alluded to at least one circumstance which the adept had every reason to suppose was private between Sir Arthur and himself, and therefore must have been learned from the former. The language of Oldbuck also intimated a conviction of his knavery, which Sir Arthur heard without making any animated defence. Lastly, the way in which Dousterswivel supposed the Baronet to have exercised his revenge was not inconsistent with the practice of other countries with which the adept was better acquainted than with those of North Britain. With him, as with many bad men, to suspect an injury and to nourish the purpose of revenge was one and the same movement. And before Dousterswivel had fairly recovered his legs he had mentally sworn the ruin of his benefactor, which, unfortunately, he possessed too much the power of accelerating.

But, although a purpose of revenge floated through his brain, it was no time to indulge such speculations. The hour, the place, his own situation, and perhaps the presence or near neighbourhood of his assailants, made self-preservation the adept's first object. The lantern had been thrown down and extinguished in the scuffle. The wind, which formerly howled so loudly through the aisles of the ruin, had now greatly fallen, lulled by the rain, which was descending very fast. The moon, from the same cause, was totally obscured, and though Dousterswivel had some experience of the ruins, and knew that he must endeavour to regain the eastern door of the chancel, yet the confusion of his ideas was such that he hesitated for some time ere he could ascertain in what direction he was to seek it. In this perplexity the suggestions of superstition, taking the advantage of darkness and his evil conscience, began again to present themselves to his disturbed imagination. "But bah!" quoth he valiantly to himself, "it is all nonsense—all one part of de damn big trick and imposture. Devil! that one thick-skulled Scotch Baronet, as I have led by the nose for five year, should cheat Herman Dousterswivel!"

As he had come to this conclusion an incident occurred which tended greatly to shake the grounds on which he had adopted it. Amid the melancholy sough of the dying wind and the plash of the raindrops on leaves and stones, arose, and apparently at no great distance from the listener, a strain of vocal music, so sad and solemn as if the departed spirits of the churchmen, who had once inhabited these deserted ruins, were mourning the solitude and desolation to which their hallowed precincts had been abandoned. Dousterswivel, who had now got upon his feet and was groping around the wall of the chancel, stood rooted to the ground on the occurrence of this new phenomenon. Each faculty of his soul seemed for the moment concentred in the sense of hearing, and all rushed back with the unanimous information that the deep, wild, and prolonged chant which he now heard was the appropriate music of one of the most solemn dirges of the Church of Rome. Why performed in such a solitude, and by what class of choristers, were questions which the terrified imagination of the adept, stirred with all the German superstitions of nixies, oak-kings, werwolves, hobgoblins, black spirits and white, blue spirits and grey, durst not even attempt to solve.

Another of his senses was soon engaged in the investigation. At the extremity of one of the transepts of the church, at the bottom of a few descending steps, was a small iron-grated door, opening, as far as he recollected, to a sort of low vault or sacristy. As he cast his eye in the direction of the sound, he observed a strong reflection of red light glimmering through these bars, and against the steps which descended to them. Dousterswivel stood a moment uncertain what to do; then, suddenly forming a desperate resolution, he moved down the aisle to the place from which the light proceeded.

Fortified with the sign of the cross and as many exorcisms as his memory could recover, he advanced to the grate, from which, unseen, he could see what passed in the interior of the vault. As he approached with timid and uncertain steps, the chant, after one or two wild and prolonged cadences, died away into profound silence. The grate, when he reached it, presented a singular spectacle in the interior of the sacristy. An open grave, with four tall flambeaus, each about six feet high, placed at the four corners; a bier, having a corpse in its shroud, the arms folded upon the breast, rested upon tressels at one side of the grave, as if ready to be interred. A priest, dressed in his cope and stole, held open the service-book; another churchman in his vestments bore a holy-water sprinkler; and two boys in white surplices held censers with incense; a man, of a figure once tall and commanding, but now bent with age or infirmity, stood alone and nearest to the coffin, attired in deep mourning—such were the most prominent figures of the group. At a little distance were two or three persons of both sexes, attired in long mourning hoods and cloaks; and five or six others in the same lugubrious dress, still farther removed from the body, around the walls of the vault stood ranged in motionless order, each bearing in his hand a huge torch of black wax. The smoky light from so many flambeaus, by the red and indistinct atmosphere which it spread around, gave a hazy, dubious, and, as it were, phantom-like appearance to the outlines of this singular apparition. The voice of the priest—loud, clear, and sonorous— now recited, from the breviary which he held in his hand, those solemn words which the ritual of the Catholic Church has consecrated to the rendering of dust to dust. Meanwhile Dousterswivel, the place, the hour, and the surprise considered, still remained uncertain whether what he saw was substantial, or an unearthly representation of the rites to which in former times these walls were familiar, but which are now rarely practised in Protestant countries, and almost never in Scotland. He was uncertain whether to abide the conclusion of the ceremony or to endeavour to regain the chancel, when a change in his position made him visible through the grate to one of the at-

tendant mourners. The person who first espied him indicated
his discovery to the individual who stood apart and nearest to
the coffin by a sign, and, upon his making a sign in reply, two
of the group detached themselves, and, gliding along with noiseless steps, as if fearing to disturb the service, unlocked and
opened the grate which separated them from the adept. Each
took him by an arm, and, exerting a degree of force which he
would have been incapable of resisting had his fear permitted
him to attempt opposition, they placed him on the ground in
the chancel and sat down, one on each side of him, as if to
detain him. Satisfied he was in the power of mortals like
himself, the adept would have put some questions to them;
but while one pointed to the vault, from which the sound of
the priest's voice was distinctly heard, the other placed his
finger upon his lips in token of silence, a hint which the German thought it most prudent to obey. And thus they detained
him until a loud Alleluia, pealing through the deserted arches
of St. Ruth, closed the singular ceremony which it had been
his fortune to witness.

When the hymn had died away with all its echoes, the voice
of one of the sable personages under whose guard the adept
had remained, said, in a familiar tone and dialect: "Dear sirs,
Mr. Dousterswivel, is this you? could not ye have let us ken
an ye had wussed till hae been present at the ceremony? My
lord couldna tak it weel your coming blinking and jinking in,
in that fashion."

"In de name of all dat is gootness, tell me what you are?"
interrupted the German in his turn.

"What I am? why, wha should I be but Ringan Aikwood,
the Knockwinnock poinder? And what are ye doing here at
this time o' night, unless ye were come to attend the leddy's
burial?"

"I do declare to you, mine goot Poinder Aikwood," said
the German, raising himself up, "that I have been this vary
night murdered, robbed, and put in fears of my life."

"Robbed! wha wad do sic a deed here? Murdered! odd,
ye speak pretty blythe for a murdered man. Put in fear!
what put you in fear, Mr. Dousterswivel?"

"I will tell you, Maister Poindèr Aikwood Ringan, just dat old miscreant dog villain Blue-Gown as you call Edie Ochiltrees."

"I'll ne'er believe that," answered Ringan; "Edie was kend to me, and my father before me, for a true, loyal, and soothfast man; and, mair by token, he's sleeping up yonder in our barn, and has been since ten at e'en. Sae touch ye wha liket, Mr. Dousterswivel, and whether ony body touched ye or no, I'm sure Edie's sackless."

"Maister Ringan Aikwood Poinders, I do not know what you call sackless, but let alone all de oils and de soot dat you say he has, and I will tell you I was dis night robbed of fifty pounds by your oil and sooty friend, Edies Ochiltree; and he is no more in your barn even now dan I ever shall be in de kingdom of heafen."

"Weel, sir, if ye will gae up wi' me, as the burial company has dispersed, we'se mak ye down a bed at the lodge, and we'se see if Edie's at the barn. There were twa wild-looking chaps left the auld kirk when we were coming up wi' the corpse, that's certain; and the priest, wha likes ill that ony heretics should look on at our church ceremonies, sent twa o' the riding saulies after them; sae we'll hear a' about it frae them."

Thus speaking, the kindly apparition, with the assistance of the mute personage, who was his son, disemcumbered himself of his cloak, and prepared to escort Dousterswivel to the place of that rest which the adept so much needed.

"I will apply to the magistrates to-morrow," said the adept; "*oder*, I will have de law put in force against all the peoples."

While he thus muttered vengeance against the cause of his injury, he tottered from among the ruins, supporting himself on Ringan and his son, whose assistance his state of weakness rendered very necessary.

When they were clear of the priory, and had gained the little meadow in which it stands, Dousterswivel could perceive the torches which had caused him so much alarm issuing in irregular procession from the ruins, and glancing their light, like that of the *ignis fatuus*, on the banks of the lake. After moving along the path for some short space with a fluctuating and irregular motion, the lights were at once extinguished.

"We aye put out the torches at the Halie Cross Well on sic occasions," said the forester to his guest; and accordingly no farther visible sign of the procession offered itself to Douster-swivel, although his ear could catch the distant and decreasing echo of horses' hoofs in the direction towards which the mourners had bent their course.

CHAPTER XXVI.

O weel may the boatie row,
 And better may she speed,
And weel may the boatie row
 That earns the bairnies' bread !
The boatie rows, the boatie rows,
 The boatie rows weel,
And lightsome be their life that bear
 The merlin and the creel !

Old Ballad.

WE must now introduce our reader to the interior of the fisher's cottage mentioned in chapter eleventh of this edifying history. I wish I could say that its inside was well arranged, decently furnished, or tolerably clean. On the contrary, I am compelled to admit, there was confusion, there was dilapidation, there was dirt good store. Yet, with all this, there was about the inmates, Luckie Mucklebackit and her family, an appearance of ease, plenty, and comfort that seemed to warrant their old sluttish proverb, "The clartier the cosier." A huge fire, though the season was summer, occupied the hearth, and served at once for affording light, heat, and the means of preparing food. The fishing had been successful, and the family, with customary improvidence, had, since unlading the cargo, continued an unremitting operation of broiling and frying that part of the produce reserved for home consumption, and the bones and fragments lay on the wooden trenchers, mingled with morsels of broken bannocks and shattered mugs of half-drunk beer. The stout and athletic form of Maggie herself, bustling here and there among a pack of half-grown girls and younger children, of whom she chucked one now here and another now there, with an exclamation of "Get out o' the gate, ye little sorrow!" was strongly contrasted with the passive and half-stupefied look and manner of her husband's mother, a woman advanced to the last stage of human life, who was seated in her wonted chair close by the fire, the warmth of which she coveted, yet hardly seemed to be sensible of, now muttering to herself, now smiling vacantly to the children as they pulled the strings of her "toy" or close cap, or twitched her blue-checked apron. With her distaff in her bosom and her spindle in her hand, she plied lazily and mechanically the old-fashioned Scottish thrift, according to the old-fashioned Scottish manner. The younger children, crawling among the feet of the elder, watched the progress of grannie's spindle as it twisted, and now and then ventured to interrupt its progress as it danced upon the floor in those vagaries which the more regulated spinning-wheel has now so universally superseded that even the fated Princess of the fairy tale might roam through all Scotland without the risk of piercing her hand with a spindle and dying of the wound. Late as the hour was (and it was long past midnight), the whole family were still on foot, and far from proposing to go to bed; the dame was still busy broiling car-cakes on the girdle, and the elder girl, the half-naked mermaid elsewhere commemorated, was preparing a pile of Findhorn haddocks (that is, haddocks smoked with green wood), to be eaten along with these relishing provisions.

While they were thus employed, a slight tap at the door, accompanied with the question, "Are ye up yet, sirs?" announced a visitor. The answer, "Ay, ay, come your ways ben, hinny," occasioned the lifting of the latch, and Jenny Rintherout, the female domestic of our Antiquary, made her appearance.

"Ay, ay," exclaimed the mistress of the family. "Hegh, sirs! can this be you, Jenny? a sight o' you's gude for sair een, lass."

"Oh, woman, we've been sae taen up wi' Captain Hector's

wound up bye that I havena had my fit out ower the door this fortnight; but he's better now, and auld Caxon sleeps in his room in case he wanted ony thing. Sae, as soon as our auld folk gaed to bed, I e'en snooded my head up a bit, and left the house-door on the latch, in case ony body should be wanting in or out while I was awa, and just cam down the gate to see an there was ony cracks amang ye."

"Ay, ay," answered Luckie Mucklebackit, "I see ye hae gotten a' your braws on. Ye're looking about for Steenie now; but he's no at hame the night, and ye'll no do for Steenie, lass: a feckless thing like you's no fit to mainteen a man."

"Steenie will no do for me," retorted Jenny, with a toss of her head that might have become a higher-born damsel; "I maun hae a man that can mainteen his wife."

"Ou ay, hinny, thae's your landward and burrows-town notions. My certie! fisher-wives ken better; they keep the man, and keep the house, and keep the siller too, lass."

"A wheen poor drudges ye are," answered the nymph of the land to the nymph of the sea. "As sune as the keel o' the coble touches the sand, deil a bit mair will the lazy fisher loons work, but the wives maun kilt their coats, and wade into the surf to tak the fish ashore. And then the man casts aff the wat and puts on the dry, and sits down wi' his pipe and his gill-stoup ahint the ingle, like ony auld houdie, and ne'er a turn will he do till the coble's afloat again! And the wife, she maun get the scull on her back and awa wi' the fish to the next burrows-town, and scauld and ban wi' ilka wife that will scauld and ban wi' her till it's sauld; and that's the gait fisher-wives live, puir slaving bodies."

"Slaves! gae wa', lass! Ca' the head o' the house slaves? little ye ken about it, lass. Show me a word my Saunders daur speak, or a turn he daur do about the house, without it be just to tak his meat and his drink and his diversion, like ony o' the weans. He has mair sense than to ca' onything about the bigging his ain, frae the roof-tree down to a crackit trencher on the bink. He kens weel eneugh wha feeds him and cleeds him, and keeps a' tight, thack and rape, when his coble is jowing awa in the Firth, puir fallow. Na, na, lass; them that sell the goods guide the purse; them that guide the purse rule the house. Show me ane o' your bits o' farmer-bodies that wad let their wife drive the stock to the market and ca' in the debts. Na, na." [1]

"Aweel, aweel, Maggie, ilka land has its ain lauch. But where's Steenie the night, when a's come and gane? And where's the gudeman?"

"I hae puttin' the gudeman to his bed, for he was e'en sair forfairn; and Steenie's awa out about some barns-breaking wi' the auld gaberlunzie, Edie Ochiltree; they'll be in sune, and ye can sit doun."

"Troth, gudewife (taking a seat), I haena that muckle time to stop; but I maun tell ye about the news. Ye'll hae heard o' the muckle kist o' gowd that Sir Arthur has fund down bye at St. Ruth? He'll be grander than ever now; he'll no can haud down his head to sneeze, for fear o' seeing his shoon."

"Ou, ay, a' the country's heard o' that; but auld Edie says they ca' it ten times mair than ever was o't, and he saw them howk it up. Odd, it would be lang or a puir body that needed it got sic a windfa'."

"Na, that's sure eneugh. And ye'll hae heard o' the Countess o' Glenallan being dead and lying in state, and how she's to be buried at St. Ruth's as this night fa's, wi' torchlight; and a' the papist servants, and Ringan Aikwood, that's a papist too, are to be there, and it be will be the grandest show ever was seen."

"Troth, hinny," answered the Nereid, "if they let naebody but papists come there it'll no be muckle o' a show in this country; for the auld harlot, as honest Mr. Blattergowl ca's her, has few that drink o' her cup of enchantments in this corner of our chosen lands. But what can ail them to bury the auld carlin—a rudas wife she was—in the night time? I dare say our gudemither will ken."

Here she exalted her voice and exclaimed twice or thrice, "Gudemither! gudemither!" but, lost in the apathy of age

[1] See Scottish Fisher-Women. Note 8.

and deafness, the aged sibyl she addressed continued plying her spindle without understanding the appeal made to her.

"Speak to your grandmither, Jenny; odd, I wad rather hail the coble half a mile aff, and the norwast wind whistling again in my teeth."

"Grannie," said the little mermaid, in a voice to which the old woman was better accustomed, "minnie wants to ken what for the Glenallan folk aye bury by candle-light in the ruins of St. Ruth?"

The old woman paused in the act of twirling the spindle, turned round to the rest of the party, lifted her withered, trembling, and clay-coloured hand, raised up her ashen-hued and wrinkled face, which the quick motion of two light-blue eyes chiefly distinguished from the visage of a corpse, and, as if catching at any touch of association with the living world, answered: "What gars the Glenallan family inter their dead by torchlight, said the lassie? Is there a Glenallan dead e'en now?"

"We might be a' dead and buried too," said Maggie, "for ony thing ye wad ken about it"; and then, raising her voice to the stretch of her mother-in-law's comprehension, she added: "It's the auld Countess, gudemither."

"And is she ca'd hame then at last?" said the old woman, in a voice that seemed to be agitated with much more feeling than belonged to her extreme old age, and the general indifference and apathy of her manner—"is she then called to her last account after her lang race o' pride and power? Oh God forgie her!"

"But minnie was asking ye," resumed the lesser querist, 'what for the Glenallan family aye bury their dead by torchlight?"

"They hae aye dune sae," said the grandmother, "since the time the Great Earl fell in the sair battle o' the Harlaw, when they say the coronach was cried in ae day from the mouth o' the Tay to the Buck of the Cabrach, that ye wad hae heard nae other sound but that of lamentation for the great folks that had fa'en fighting against Donald of the Isles. But the Great Earl's mither was living—they were a doughty

and a dour race the women o' the house o' Glenallan—and she
wad hae nae coronach cried for her son, but had him laid in
the silence o' midnight in his place o' rest, without either
drinking the dirge or crying the lament. She said he had
killed enow that day he died for the widows and daughters o'
the Highlanders he had slain to cry the coronach for them
they had lost and for her son too; and sae she laid him in his
grave wi' dry eyes, and without a groan or a wail. And it
was thought a proud word o' the family, and they aye stickit
by it; and the mair in the latter times, because in the night-
time they had mair freedom to perform their popish ceremonies
by darkness and in secrecy than in the daylight; at least that
was the case in my time. They wad hae been disturbed in
the day-time baith by the law and the commons of Fairport.
They may be owerlooked now, as I have heard; the warld's
changed; I whiles hardly ken whether I am standing or sitting,
or dead or living."

And looking round the fire, as if in the state of unconscious
uncertainty of which she complained, old Elspeth relapsed
into her habitual and mechanical occupation of twirling the
spindle. "Eh, sirs!" said Jenny Rintherout, under her
breath to her gossip, "it's awsome to hear your gudemither
break out in that gait; it's like the dead speaking to the
living."

"Ye're no that far wrang, lass; she minds naething o' what
passes the day, but set her on auld tales, and she can speak
like a prent buke. She kens mair about the Glenallan family
than maist folk; the gudeman's father was their fisher mony
a day. Ye maun ken the papists make a great point o' eating
fish; it's nae bad part o' their religion that, whatever the rest
is. I could aye sell the best o' fish at the best o' prices for
the Countess's ain table, grace be wi' her! especially on a
Friday. But see as our gudemither's hands and lips are
ganging; now it's working in her head like barm. She'll
speak eneugh the night; whiles she'll no speak a word in a
week, unless it be to the bits o' bairns."

"Hegh, Mrs. Mucklebackit, she's an awsome wife!" said
Jenny in reply. "D'ye think she's a'thegither right? Folk

says she downa gang to the kirk or speak to the minister, and that she was ance a papist; but since her gudeman's been dead naebody kens what she is. D'ye think yoursell that she's no uncanny?"

"Canny, ye silly tawpie! think ye ae auld wife's less canny than anither? unless it be Ailison Breck; I really couldna in conscience swear for her; I have kent the boxes she set fill'd wi' partans, when——"

"Whisht, whisht, Maggie," whispered Jenny, "your gude-mither's gaun to speak again."

"Wasna there some ane o' ye said," asked the old sibyl, "or did I dream, or was it revealed to me, that Joscelind, Lady Glenallan, is dead, an buried this night?"

"Yes, gudemither," screamed the daughter-in-law, "it's e'en sae."

"And e'en sae let it be," said old Elspeth; "she's made mony a sair heart in her day; ay, e'en her ain son's. Is he living yet?"

"Ay, he's living yet, but how lang he'll live—however, dinna ye mind his coming and asking after you in the spring, and leaving siller?"

"It may be sae, Maggie, I dinna mind it; but a handsome gentleman he was, and his father before him. Eh! if his father had lived they might hae been happy folk! But he was gane, and the lady carried it in-ower and out-ower wi' her son, and garr'd him trow the thing he never suld hae trowed, and do the thing he has repented a' his life, and will repent still, were his life as lang as this lang and wearisome ane o' mine."

"Oh what was it, grannie?" and "What was it, gude-mither?" and "What was it, Luckie Elspeth?" asked the children, the mother, and the visitor in one breath.

"Never ask what it was," answered the old sibyl, "but pray to God that ye arena left to the pride and wilfu'ness o' your ain hearts. They may be as powerful in a cabin as in a castle; I can bear a sad witness to that. Oh that weary and fearfu' night! will it never gang out o' my auld head? Eh! to see her lying on the floor wi' her lang hair dreeping wi' the salt water! Heaven will avenge on a' that had to do wi't. Sirs! is my son out wi' the coble this windy e'en?"

"Na, na, mither; nae coble can keep the sea this wind; he's sleeping in his bed out-ower yonder ahint the hallan."

"Is Steenie out at sea then?"

"Na, grannie, Steenie's out awa wi' auld Edie Ochiltree, the gaberlunzie; maybe they'll be gaun to see the burial."

"That canna be," said the mother of the family. "We kent naething o't till Jock Rand cam in, and tauld us the Aikwoods had warning to attend; they keep thae things unco private, and they were to bring the corpse a' the way frae the castle, ten miles off, under cloud o' night. She has lain in state this ten days at Glenallan House, in a grand chamber, a' hung wi' black and lighted wi' wax cannle."

"God assoilzie her!" ejaculated old Elspeth, her head apparently still occupied by the event of the Countess's death; "she was a hard-hearted woman, but she's gaen to account for it a', and His mercy is infinite. God grant she may find it sae!" And she relapsed into silence, which she did not break again during the rest of the evening.

"I wonder what that auld daft beggar-carle and our son Steenie can be doing out in sic a night as this," said Maggie Mucklebackit, and her expression of surprise was echoed by her visitor. "Gang awa, ane o' ye, hinnies, up to the heugh head, and gie them a cry in case they're within hearing; the car-cakes will be burnt to a cinder."

The little emissary departed, but in a few minutes came running back with the loud exclamation. "Eh, minnie! eh, grannie! there's a white bogle chasing twa black anes down the heugh."

A noise of footsteps followed this singular annunciation, and young Steenie Mucklebackit, closely followed by Edie Ochiltree, bounced into the hunt. They were panting and out of breath. The first thing Steenie did was to look for the bar of the door, which his mother reminded him had been broken up for firewood in the hard winter three years ago; "for what use," she said, "had the like o' them for bars?"

"There's naebody chasing us," said the beggar, after he had

taken his breath; "we're e'en like the wicked, that flee when no one pursueth."

"Troth, but we were chased," said Steenie, "by a spirit, or something little better."

"It was a man in white on horseback," said Edie, "for the saft grund, that wadna bear the beast, flung him about, I wot that weel; but I didna think my auld legs could have brought me aff as fast; I ran amaist as fast as if I had been at Prestonpans." [1]

"Hout, ye daft gowks," said Luckie Mucklebackit, "it will hae been some o' the riders at the Countess's burial."

"What!" said Edie, "is the auld Countess buried the night at St. Ruth's? Ou, that wad be the lights and the noise that scarr'd us awa. I wish I had kend, I wad hae stude them, and no left the man yonder; but they'll take care o' him. Ye strake ower hard, Steenie; I doubt ye foundered the chield."

"Ne'er a bit," said Steenie, laughing; "he has braw broad shouthers, and I just took the measure o' them wi' the stang. Odd, if I hadna been something short wi' him he wad hae knockit your auld harns out, lad."

"Weel, an I win clear o' this scrape," said Edie, "I'se tempt Providence nae mair. But I canna thinkit an unlawfu' thing to pit a bit trick on sic a landlouping scoundrel that just lives by tricking honester folk."

"But what are we to do with this?" said Steenie, producing a pocket-book.

"Odd guide us, man," said Edie, in great alarm, "what gar'd ye touch the gear? a very leaf o' that pocket-book wad be eneugh to hang us baith."

"I dinna ken," said Steenie; "the book had fa'en out o' his pocket, I fancy, for I fand it amang my feet when I was graping about to set him on his legs again, and I just pat it in my pouch to keep it safe; and then came the tramp of horse, and you cried, 'Rin, rin,' and I had nae mair thought o' the book."

---

[1] Referring to the flight of the Government forces at the battle of Prestonpans, 1745 (*Laing*).

"We maun get it back to the loon some gait or other; ye had better take it yoursell, I think, wi' peep o' light, up to Ringan Aikwood's. I wadna for a hundred pounds it was fund in our hands."

Steenie undertook to do as he was directed.

"A bonny night ye hae made o't, Mr. Steenie," said Jenny Rintherout, who, impatient of remaining so long unnoticed, now presented herself to the young fisherman—"a bonny night ye hae made o't, tramping about wi' gaberlunzies, and getting yoursell hunted wi' worriecows, when ye suld be sleeping in your bed like your father, honest man."

This attack called forth a suitable response of rustic raillery from the young fisherman. An attack was now commenced upon the car-cakes and smoked fish, and sustained with great perseverance by assistance of a bicker or two of twopenny ale and a bottle of gin. The mendicant then retired to the straw of an out-house adjoining; the children had one by one crept into their nests; the old grandmother was deposited in her flock-bed; Steenie, notwithstanding his preceding fatigue, had the gallantry to accompany Miss Rintherout to her own mansion, and at what hour he returned the story saith not; and the matron of the family, having laid the gathering-coal upon the fire and put things in some sort of order, retired to rest the last of the family.

CHAPTER XXVII.

Many great ones
Would part with half their states to have the plan
And credit to beg in the first style.
                                        Beggar's Bush.

OLD Edie was stirring with the lark, and his first inquiry was after Steenie and the pocket-book. The young fisherman had been under the necessity of attending his father before daybreak to avail themselves of the tide, but he had promised that, immediately on his return, the pocket-book, with all its contents, carefully wrapped up in a piece of sail-cloth should be delivered by him to Ringan Aikwood, for Dousterswivel, the owner.

The matron had prepared the morning meal for the family, and, shouldering her basket of fish, tramped sturdily away towards Fairport. The children were idling round the door, for the day was fair and sunshiney. The ancient grandame, again seated on her wicker-chair by the fire, had resumed her eternal spindle, wholly unmoved by the yelling and screaming of the children, and the scolding of the mother, which had preceded the dispersion of the family. Edie had arranged his various bags, and was bound for the renewal of his wandering life, but first advanced with due courtesy to take his leave of the ancient crone.

"Gude day to ye, cummer, and mony ane o' them. I will be back about the fore-end o' har'st, and I trust to find ye baith haill and fere."

"Pray that ye may find me in my quiet grave," said the old woman, in a hollow and sepulchral voice, but without the agitation of a single feature.

"Ye're auld, cummer, and sae am I mysell; but we maun abide His will; we'll no be forgotten in His good time."

"Nor our deeds neither," said the crone; "what's dune in the body maun be answered in the spirit."

"I wot that's true; and I may weel tak the tale hame to mysell, that hae led a misruled and roving life. But ye were aye a canny wife. We're a' frail, but ye canna hae sae muckle to bow ye down."

"Less than I might have had; but mair, oh far mair, than wad sink the stoutest brig e'er sailed out o' Fairport harbour! Didna somebody say yestreen—at least sae it is borne in on my mind, but auld folk hae weak fancies—did not somebody say that Joscelind, Countess of Glenallan, was departed frae life?"

"They said the truth whaever said it," answered old Edie; "she was buried yestreen by torchlight at St. Ruth's, and I, like a fule, gat a gliff wi' seeing the lights and the riders."

"It was their fashion since the days of the Great Earl that

was killed at Harlaw. They did it to show scorn that they should die and be buried like other mortals. The wives o' the house of Glenallan wailed nae wail for the husband, nor the sister for the brother. But is she e'en ca'd to the lang account?"

"As sure," answered Edie, "as we maun a' abide it."

"Then I'll unlade my mind, come o't what will."

This she spoke with more alacrity than usually attended her expressions, and accompanied her words with an attitude of the hand, as if throwing something from her. She then raised up her form, once tall, and still retaining the appearance of having been so, though bent with age and rheumatism, and stood before the beggar like a mummy animated by some wandering spirit into a temporary resurrection. Her light-blue eyes wandered to and fro, as if she occasionally forgot and again remembered the purpose for which her long and withered hand was searching among the miscellaneous contents of an ample old-fashioned pocket. At length she pulled out a small chip-box, and, opening it, took out a handsome ring, in which was set a braid of hair, composed of two different colours, black and light brown, twined together, encircled with brilliants of considerable value.

"Gudeman," she said to Ochiltree, "as ye wad e'er deserve mercy, ye maun gang my errand to the house of Glenallan and ask for the Earl."

"The Earl of Glenallan, cummer! ou, he winna see ony o' the gentles o' the country, and what likelihood is there that he wad see the like o' an auld gaberlunzie?"

"Gang your ways and try, and tell him that Elspeth o' the Craigburnfoot—he'll mind me best by that name—maun see him or she be relieved frae her lang pilgrimage, and that she sends him that ring in token of the business she wad speak o'."

Ochiltree looked on the ring with some admiration of its apparent value, and then carefully replacing it in the box, and wrapping it in an old ragged handkerchief, he deposited the token in his bosom.

"Weel, gudewife," he said, "I'se do your bidding, or it's no be my fault. But surely there was never sic a braw propine as this sent to a yerl by an auld fish-wife, and through the hands of a gaberlunzie beggar."

With this reflection Edie took up his pike-staff, put on his broad-brimmed bonnet, and set forth upon his pilgrimage. The old woman remained for some time standing in a fixed posture, her eyes directed to the door through which her ambassador had departed. The appearance of excitation which the conversation had occasioned gradually left her features, she sunk down upon her accustomed seat, and resumed her mechanical labour of the distaff and spindle with her wonted air of apathy.

Edie Ochiltree meanwhile advanced on his journey. The distance to Glenallan was ten miles, a march which the old soldier accomplished in about four hours. With the curiosity belonging to his idle trade and animated character, he tortured himself the whole way to consider what could be the meaning of this mysterious errand with which he was intrusted, or what connexion the proud, wealthy, and powerful Earl of Glenallan could have with the crimes or penitence of an old doting woman, whose rank in life did not greatly exceed that of her messenger. He endeavoured to call to memory all that he had ever known or heard of the Glenallan family, yet, having done so, remained altogether unable to form a conjecture on the subject. He knew that the whole extensive estate of this ancient and powerful family had descended to the Countess lately deceased, who inherited in a most remarkable degree the stern, fierce, and unbending character which had distinguished the house of Glenallan since they first figured in Scottish annals. Like the rest of her ancestors, she adhered zealously to the Roman Catholic faith, and was married to an English gentleman of the same communion, and of large fortune, who did not survive their union two years. The Countess was therefore left an early widow, with the uncontrolled management of the large estates of her two sons. The elder, Lord Geraldin, who was to succeed to the title and fortune of Glenallan, was totally dependent on his mother during her life. The second, when he came of age, assumed the name and arms of his father, and took possession of his

19

estate, according to the provisions of the Countess's marriage settlement. After this period he chiefly resided in England, and paid very few and brief visits to his mother and brother; and these at length were altogether dispensed with, in consequence of his becoming a convert to the reformed religion.

But even before this mortal offence was given to its mistress, his residence at Glenallan offered few inducements to a gay young man like Edward Geraldin Neville, though its gloom and seclusion seemed to suit the retired and melancholy habits of his elder brother. Lord Geraldin in the outset of life had been a young man of accomplishment and hopes. Those who knew him upon his travels entertained the highest expectations of his future career. But such fair dawns are often strangely overcast. The young nobleman returned to Scotland, and, after living about a year in his mother's society at Glenallan House, he seemed to have adopted all the stern gloom and melancholy of her character. Excluded from politics by the incapacities attached to those of his religion, and from all lighter avocations by choice, Lord Geraldin led a life of the strictest retirement. His ordinary society was composed of the clergymen of his communion, who occasionally visited his mansion; and very rarely, upon stated occasions of high festival, one or two families who still professed the Catholic religion were formally entertained at Glenallan House. But this was all. Their heretic neighbours knew nothing of the family whatever; and even the Catholics saw little more than the sumptuous entertainment and solemn parade which was exhibited on those formal occasions, from which all returned without knowing whether most to wonder at the stern and stately demeanour of the Countess, or the deep and gloomy dejection which never ceased for a moment to cloud the features of her son. The late event had put him in possession of his fortune and title, and the neighbourhood had already begun to conjecture whether gaiety would revive with independence, when those who had some occasional acquaintance with the interior of the family spread abroad a report that the Earl's constitution was undermined by religious austerities, and that in all probability he would soon follow his mother to the grave. This event was the most probable, as his brother had died of a lingering complaint, which in the latter years of his life had affected at once his frame and his spirits; so that heralds and genealogists were already looking back into their records to discover the heir of this ill-fated family, and lawyers were talking with gleesome anticipation of the probability of a "great Glenallan cause."

As Edie Ochiltree approached the front of Glenallan House,[1] an ancient building of great extent, the most modern part of which had been designed by the celebrated Inigo Jones, he began to consider in what way he should be most likely to gain access for delivery of his message; and, after much consideration, resolved to send the token to the Earl by one of the domestics. With this purpose he stopped at a cottage, where he obtained the means of making up the ring in a sealed packet like a petition, addressed, *Forr his Hounor the Yerl of Glenallan—These.* But, being aware that missives delivered at the doors of great houses by such persons as himself do not always make their way according to address, Edie determined, like an old soldier, to reconnoitre the ground before he made his final attack. As he approached the porter's lodge he discovered, by the number of poor ranked before it—some of them being indigent persons in the vicinity, and others itinerants of his own begging profession—that there was about to be a general dole or distribution of charity.

"A good turn," said Edie to himself, "never goes unrewarded; I'll maybe get a good awmous that I wad hae missed but for trotting on this auld wife's errand."

Accordingly, he ranked up with the rest of this ragged regiment, assuming a station as near the front as possible—a distinction due, as he conceived, to his blue gown and badge, no less than to his years and experience; but he soon found there was another principle of precedence in this assembly to which he had not adverted.

"Are ye a triple man, friend, that ye press forward sae bauldly? I'm thinking no, for there's nae Catholics wear that badge."

[1] Supposed to represent Glamis Castle in Forfarshire (*Laing*).

"Na, na, I am no a Roman," said Edie.

"Then shank yoursell awa to the double folk, or single folk, that's the Episcopals or Presbyterians yonder; it's a shame to see a heretic hae sic a lang white beard, that would do credit to a hermit."

Ochiltree, thus rejected from the society of the Catholic mendicants, or those who called themselves such, went to station himself with the paupers of the communion of the Church of England, to whom the noble donor allotted a double portion of his charity. But never was a poor occasional conformist more roughly rejected by a High Church congregation, even when that matter was furiously agitated in the days of good Queen Anne.

"See to him wi' his badge!" they said; "he hears ane o' the king's Presbyterian chaplains sough out a sermon on the morning of every birthday, and now he would pass himsell for ane o' the Episcopal Church! Na, na! we'll take care o' that."

Edie, thus rejected by Rome and prelacy, was fain to shelter himself from the laughter of his brethren among the thin group of Presbyterians, who had either disdained to disguise their religious opinions for the sake of an augmented dole, or perhaps knew they could not attempt the imposition without a certainty of detection.

The same degree of precedence was observed in the mode of distributing the charity, which consisted in bread, beef, and a piece of money to each individual of all the three classes. The almoner, an ecclesiastic of grave appearance and demeanour, superintended in person the accommodation of the Catholic mendicants, asking a question or two of each as he delivered the charity, and recommending to their prayers the soul of Joscelind, late Countess of Glenallan, mother of their benefactor. The porter, distinguished by his long staff headed with silver, and by the black gown tufted with lace of the same colour, which he had assumed upon the general mourning in the family, overlooked the distribution of the dole among the prelatists. The less-favoured kirk-folk were committed to the charge of an aged domestic.

As this last discussed some disputed point with the porter, his name, as it chanced to be occasionally mentioned, and then his features, struck Ochiltree, and awakened recollections of former times. The rest of the assembly were now retiring, when the domestic, again approaching the place where Edie still lingered, said, in a strong Aberdeenshire accent: "Fat is the auld feel-body deeing that he canna gang avay, now that he's gotten baith meat and siller?"

"Francie Macraw," answered Edie Ochiltree, "d'ye no mind Fontenoy, and 'Keep thegither, front and rear!'"

"Ohon, ohon!" cried Francie, with a true north country yell of recognition, "naebody could hae said that word but my auld front-rank man, Edie Ochiltree! But I'm sorry to see ye in sic a peer state, man."

"No sae ill aff as ye may think, Francie. But I'm laith to leave this place without a crack wi' you, and I kenna when I may see you again, for your folk dinna mak Protestants welcome, and that's ae reason that I hae never been here before."

"Fusht, fusht," said Francie, "let that flee stick i' the wa' —when the dirt's dry it will rub out—and come you awa wi' me, and I'll gie ye something better than that beef bane, man."

Having then spoke a confidential word with the porter (probably to request his connivance), and having waited until the almoner had returned into the house with slow and solemn steps, Francie Macraw introduced his old comrade into the court of Glenallan House, the gloomy gateway of which was surmounted by a huge scutcheon, in which the herald and undertaker had mingled, as usual, the emblems of human pride and of human nothingness: the Countess's hereditary coat-of-arms, with all its numerous quarterings, disposed in a lozenge, and surrounded by the separate shields of her paternal and maternal ancestry, intermingled with scythes, hour-glasses, skulls, and other symbols of that mortality which levels all distinctions. Conducting his friend as speedily as possible along the large paved court, Macraw led the way through a side-door to a small apartment near the servants'-hall, which, in virtue of his personal attendance upon the Earl of Glenallan, he was entitled to call his own. To produce cold meat of various kinds, strong beer, and even a glass of spirits, was no difficulty to a person of Francie's importance, who had not lost, in his sense of conscious dignity, the keen northern prudence which recommended a good understanding with the butler. Our mendicant envoy drank ale and talked over old stories with his comrade, until, no other topic of conversation occurring, he resolved to take up the theme of his embassy, which had for some time escaped his memory.

"He had a petition to present to the Earl," he said; for he judged it prudent to say nothing of the ring, not knowing, as he afterwards observed, how far the manners of a single soldier might have been corrupted by service in a great house.

"Hout, tout, man," said Francie, "the Earl will look at nae petitions; but I can gie't to the almoner."

"But it relates to some secret, that maybe my lord wad like best to see't himsell."

"I'm jeedging that's the very reason that the almoner will be for seeing it the first and foremost."

"But I hae come a' this way on purpose to deliver it, Francie, and ye really maun help me at a pinch."

"Ne'er speed then if I dinna," answered the Aberdeenshire man; "let them be as cankered as they like, they can but turn me awa, and I was just thinking to ask my discharge and gang down to end my days at Inverurie."

With this doughty resolution of serving his friend at all ventures, since none was to be encountered which could much inconvenience himself, Francie Macraw left the apartment. It was long before he returned, and when he did his manner indicated wonder and agitation.

"I am nae seere gin ye be Edie Ochiltree o' Carrick's company in the Forty-twa, or gin ye be the deil in his likeness!"

"And what makes ye speak in that gait?" demanded the astonished mendicant.

"Because my lord has been in sic a distress and seerpreese as I ne'er saw a man in my life. But he'll see you; I got that job cookit. He was like a man awa frae himsell for mony minutes, and I thought he wad hae swarv't a'thegither; and fan he cam' to himsell he asked fae brought the packet, and fat trow ye I said?"

"An auld soger," says Edie; "that does likeliest at a gentle's door; at a farmer's it's best to say ye're an auld tinkler, if ye need ony quarters, for maybe the gudewife will hae something to souther."

"But I said ne'er ane o' the twa," answered Francie; "my lord cares as little about the tane as the tother, for he's best to them than can souther up our sins. Sae I e'en said the bit paper was brought by an auld man wi' a lang fite beard; he might be a capeechin freer for fat I kend, for he was dressed like an auld palmer. Sae ye'll be sent for up fanever he can find mettle to face ye."

"I wish I was weel through this business," thought Edie to himsell; "mony folk surmise that the Earl's no very right in the judgment, and wha can say how far he may be offended wi' me for taking upon me sae muckle?"

But there was now no room for retreat: a bell sounded from a distant part of the mansion, and Macraw said, with a smothered accent, as if already in his master's presence: "That's my lord's bell! follow me, and step lightly and cannily, Edie."

Edie followed his guide, who seemed to tread as if afraid of being overheard, through a long passage and up a back-stair, which admitted them into the family apartments. They were ample and extensive, furnished at such cost as showed the ancient importance and splendour of the family. But all the ornaments were in the taste of a former and distant period, and one would have almost supposed himself travers-ing the halls of a Scottish nobleman before the union of the crowns. The late Countess, partly from a haughty contempt of the times in which she lived, partly from her sense of family pride, had not permitted the furniture to be altered or modernised during her residence at Glenallan House. The most magnificent part of the decorations was a valuable collec-tion of pictures by the best masters, whose massive frames were somewhat tarnished by time. In this particular also the gloomy taste of the family seemed to predominate. There

were some fine family portraits by Vandyke and other masters of eminence; but the collection was richest in the Saints
and Martyrdoms of Domenichino, Velasquez, and Murillo,
and other subjects of the same kind, which had been selected
in preference to landscapes or historical pieces. The manner
in which these awful, and sometimes disgusting, subjects were
represented harmonised with the gloomy state of the apartments; a circumstance which was not altogether lost on the
old man, as he traversed them under the guidance of his
quondam fellow-soldier. He was about to express some sentiment of this kind, but Francie imposed silence on him by
signs, and, opening a door at the end of the long picture-
gallery, ushered him into a small antechamber hung with
black. Here they found the almoner, with his ear turned to
a door opposite that by which they entered, in the attitude of
one who listens with attention, but is at the same time afraid
of being detected in the act.

The old domestic and churchman started when they perceived each other. But the almoner first recovered his recollection, and, advancing towards Macraw, said under his breath,
but with an authoritative tone: "How dare you approach the
Earl's apartment without knocking? and who is this stranger,
or what has he to do here? Retire to the gallery, and wait
for me there."

"It's impossible just now to attend your reverence," answered Macraw, raising his voice so as to be heard in the next
room, being conscious that the priest would not maintain the
altercation within hearing of his patron; "the Earl's bell has
rung."

He had scarce uttered the words when it was rung again
with greater violence than before; and the ecclesiastic, perceiving further expostulation impossible, lifted his finger at
Macraw with a menacing attitude, as he left the apartment.

"I tell'd ye sae," said the Aberdeen man in a whisper to
Edie, and then proceeded to open the door near which they
had observed the chaplain stationed.

CHAPTER XXVIII.

This ring—
This little ring, with necromantic force,
Has raised the ghost of Pleasure to my fears,
Conjured the sense of honour and of love
Into such shapes, they fright me from myself.
The Fatal Marriage.

THE ancient forms of mourning were observed in Glenallan House, notwithstanding the obduracy with which the members of the family were popularly supposed to refuse to the dead the usual tribute of lamentation. It was remarked, that when she received the fatal letter announcing the death of her second, and, as was once believed, her favourite son, the hand of the Countess did not shake nor her eyelid twinkle, any more than upon perusal of a letter of ordinary business. Heaven only knows whether the suppression of maternal sorrow which her pride commanded might not have some effect in hastening her own death. It was at least generally supposed that the apoplectic stroke which so soon afterwards terminated her existence was, as it were, the vengeance of outraged nature for the restraint to which her feelings had been subjected. But, although Lady Glenallan forbore the usual external signs of grief, she had caused many of the apartments, amongst others her own and that of the Earl, to be hung with the exterior trappings of woe.

The Earl of Glenallan was therefore seated in an apartment hung with black cloth, which waved in dusky folds along its lofty walls. A screen, also covered with black baize, placed towards the high and narrow window, intercepted much of the broken light which found its way through the stained glass, that represented, with such skill as the fourteenth century possessed, the life and sorrows of the prophet Jeremiah. The table at which the Earl was seated was lighted with two lamps wrought in silver, shedding that unpleasant and doubtful light which arises from the mingling of artificial lustre with that of general daylight. The same table displayed a silver crucifix and one or two clasped parchment books. A large picture, exquisitely painted by Spagnoletto, represented the martyrdom of St. Stephen, and was the only ornament of the apartment.

The inhabitant and lord of this disconsolate chamber was a man not past the prime of life, yet so broken down with disease and mental misery, so gaunt and ghastly, that he appeared but a wreck of manhood; and when he hastily arose and advanced towards his visitor the exertion seemed almost to overpower his emaciated frame. As they met in the midst of the apartment, the contrast they exhibited was very striking. The hale cheek, firm step, erect stature, and undaunted presence and bearing of the old mendicant, indicated patience and content in the extremity of age, and in the lowest condition to which humanity can sink; while the sunken eye, pallid cheek, and tottering form of the nobleman with whom he was confronted, showed how little wealth, power, and even the advantages of youth, have to do with that which gives repose to the mind and firmness to the frame.

The Earl met the old man in the middle of the room, and, having commanded his attendant to withdraw into the gallery, and suffer no one to enter the antechamber till he rung the bell, awaited, with hurried yet fearful impatience, until he heard first the door of his apartment and then that of the antechamber shut and fastened by the spring-bolt. When he was satisfied with this security against being overheard, Lord Glenallan came close up to the mendicant, whom he probably mistook for some person of a religious order in disguise, and said, in a hasty yet faltering tone: "In the name of all our religion holds most holy, tell me, reverend father, what I am to expect from a communication opened by a token connected with such horrible recollections?"

The old man, appalled by a manner so different from what he had expected from the proud and powerful nobleman, was at a loss how to answer, and in what manner to undeceive him. "Tell me," continued the Earl, in a tone of increasing trepidation and agony—"tell me, do you come to say that all that has been done to expiate guilt so horrible has been too little and too trivial for the offence, and to point out new and more efficacious modes of severe penance? I will not blench from it, father; let me suffer the pains of my crime here in the body, rather than hereafter in the spirit!"

Edie had now recollection enough to perceive that, if he did not interrupt the frankness of Lord Glenallan's admissions, he was likely to become the confidant of more than might be safe for him to know. He therefore uttered with a hasty and trembling voice: "Your lordship's honour is mistaken: I am not of your persuasion nor a clergyman, but, with all reverence, only puir Edie Ochiltree, the king's bedesman and your honour's."

This explanation he accompanied by a profound bow after his manner, and then, drawing himself up erect, rested his arm on his staff, threw back his long white hair, and fixed his eyes upon the Earl, as he waited for an answer.

"And you are not, then," said Lord Glenallan, after a pause of surprise—"you are not then a Catholic priest?"

"God forbid!" said Edie, forgetting in his confusion to whom he was speaking; "I am only the king's bedesman and your honour's, as I said before."

The Earl turned hastily away and paced the room twice or thrice, as if to recover the effects of his mistake, and then, coming close up to the mendicant, he demanded, in a stern and commanding tone, what he meant by intruding himself on his privacy, and from whence he had got the ring which he had thought proper to send him. Edie, a man of much spirit, was less daunted at this mode of interrogation than he had been confused by the tone of confidence in which the Earl had opened their conversation. To the reiterated question from whom he had obtained the ring, he answered composedly, "From one who was better known to the Earl than to him."

"Better known to me, fellow?" said Lord Glenallan; "what is your meaning? Explain yourself instantly, or you shall experience the consequence of breaking in upon the hours of family distress."

"It was auld Elspeth Mucklebackit that sent me here," said the beggar, "in order to say——"

"You dote, old man!" said the Earl; "I never heard the name; but this dreadful token reminds me——"

"I mind now, my lord," said Ochiltree; "she tauld me your lordship would be mair familiar wi' her if I ca'd her Elspeth o' the Craigburnfoot. She had that name when she lived on your honour's land, that is, your honour's worshipful mother's that was then. Grace be wi' her!"

"Ay," said the appalled nobleman, as his countenance sunk, and his cheek assumed a hue yet more cadaverous, "that name is indeed written in the most tragic page of a deplorable history. But what can she desire of me? Is she dead or living?"

"Living, my lord; and entreats to see your lordship before she dies, for she has something to communicate that hangs upon her very soul, and she says she canna flit in peace until she sees you."

"Not until she sees me! what can that mean? but she is doting with age and infirmity. I tell thee, friend, I called at her cottage myself, not a twelvemonth since, from a report that she was in distress, and she did not even know my face or voice."

"If your honour wad permit me," said Edie, to whom the length of the conference restored a part of his professional audacity and native talkativeness—"if your honour wad but permit me, I wad say, under correction of your lordship's better judgment, that auld Elspeth's like some of the ancient ruined strengths and castles that ane sees amang the hills. There are mony parts of her mind that appear, as I may say, laid waste and decayed, but then there's parts that look the steever and the stronger and the grander because they are rising just like to fragments amang the ruins o' the rest. She's an awful woman."

"She always was so," said the Earl, almost unconsciously echoing the observation of the mendicant—"she always was different from other women, likest perhaps to her who is now no more in her temper and turn of mind. She wishes to see me, then?"

"Before she dies," said Edie, "she earnestly entreats that pleasure."

"It will be a pleasure to neither of us," said the Earl, sternly, "yet she shall be gratified. She lives, I think, on the seashore to the southward of Fairport?"

"Just between Monkbarns and Knockwinnock Castle, but nearer to Monkbarns. Your lordship's honour will ken the Laird and Sir Arthur, doubtless?"

A stare, as if he did not comprehend the question, was Lord Glenallan's answer. Edie saw his mind was elsewhere, and did not venture to repeat a query which was so little germain to the matter.

"Are you a Catholic, old man?" demanded the Earl.

"No, my lord," said Ochiltree, stoutly, for the remembrance of the unequal division of the dole rose in his mind at the moment; "I thank Heaven I am a good Protestant."

"He who can conscientiously call himself *good* has indeed reason to thank Heaven, be his form of Christianity what it will. But who is he that shall dare to do so?"

"Not I," said Edie; "I trust to beware of the sin of presumption."

"What was your trade in your youth?" continued the Earl.

"A soldier, my lord; and mony a sair day's kemping I've seen. I was to have been made a sergeant, but——"

"A soldier! then you have slain and burnt, and sacked and spoiled?"

"I winna say," replied Edie, "that I have been better than my neighbours: it's a rough trade; war's sweet to them that never tried it."

"And you are now old and miserable, asking from precarious charity the food which in your youth you tore from the hand of the poor peasant?"

"I am a beggar, it is true, my lord; but I am nae just sae miserable neither. For my sins, I hae had grace to repent of them, if I might say sae, and to lay them where they may be better borne than by me; and for my food, naebody grudges an auld man a bit and a drink. Sae I live as I can, and am contented to die when I am ca'd upon."

"And thus, then, with little to look back upon that is pleasant or praiseworthy in your past life, with less to look forward to on this side of eternity, you are contented to drag out the rest of your existence. Go, begone; and, in your age and poverty and weariness, never envy the lord of such a mansion as this, either in his sleeping or waking moments. Here is something for thee."

The Earl put into the old man's hand five or six guineas. Edie would, perhaps, have stated his scruples, as upon other occasions, to the amount of the benefaction, but the tone of Lord Glenallan was too absolute to admit of either answer or dispute. The Earl then called his servant: "See this old man safe from the castle, let no one ask him any questions; and you, friend, begone, and forget the road that leads to my house."

"That would be difficult for me," said Edie, looking at the gold which he still held · in his hand—"that would be e'en difficult, since your honour has gien me such gude cause to remember it."

Lord Glenallan stared, as hardly comprehending the old man's boldness in daring to bandy words with him, and with his hand made him another signal of departure, which the mendicant instantly obeyed.

CHAPTER XXIX.

For he was one in all their idle sport,
And, like a monarch, ruled their little court;
The pliant bow he form'd, the flying ball,
The bat, the wicket, were his labours all.
CRABBE'S *Village.*

FRANCIS MACRAW, agreeably to the commands of his master, attended the mendicant, in order to see him fairly out of the estate without permitting him to have conversation or intercourse with any of the Earl's dependents or domestics. But, judiciously considering that the restriction did not extend to himself, who was the person entrusted with the convoy, he used every measure in his power to extort from Edie the nature of his confidential and secret interview with Lord

Glenallan. But Edie had been in his time accustomed to cross-examinations, and easily evaded those of his quondam comrade. "The secrets of grit folk," said Ochiltree within himself, "are just like the wild beasts that are shut up in cages. Keep them hard and fast snecked up, and it's a' very weel or better; but anes let them out, they will turn and rend you. I mind how ill Dugald Gunn cam aff for letting loose his tongue about the Major's leddy and Captain Bandilier."

Francie was therefore foiled in his assaults upon the fidelity of the mendicant, and, like an indifferent chess-player, became at every unsuccessful movement more liable to the counter-checks of his opponent.

"Sae ye uphauld ye had nae particulars to say to my lord but about your ain matters?"

"Ay, and about the wee bits o' things I had brought frae abroad," said Edie. "I kend you papist folk are unco set on the relics that are fetched frae far—kirks and sae forth."

"Troth, my lord maun be turned feel outright," said the domestic, "an he puts himsell into sic a curfuffle for ony thing ye could bring him, Edie."

"I doubtna ye may say true in the main, neighbour," replied the beggar; "but maybe he's had some hard play in his younger days, Francie, and that whiles unsettles folk sair."

"Troth, Edie, and ye may say that; and since it's like ye'll ne'er come back to the estate, or, if ye dee, that ye'll no find me there, I'se e'en tell you he had a heart in his young time sae wrecked and rent that it's a wonder it hasna broken out-right lang afore this day."

"Ay, say ye sae?" said Ochiltree; "that maun hae been about a woman, I reckon?"

"Troth, and ye hae guessed it," said Francie, "jeest a cusin o' his nain, Miss Eveline Neville, as they suld hae ca'd her; there was a sough in the country about it, but it was hushed up, as the grandees were concerned. It's mair than twenty years syne; ay, it will be three-and-twenty."

"Ay, I was in America then," said the mendicant, "and no in the way to hear the country clashes."

"There was little clash about it, man," replied Macraw;

"he liked this young leddy, and suld hae married her, but his mother fand it out, and then the deil gaed o'er Jock Wabster. At last the peer lass clodded hersell o'er the scaur at the Craigburnfoot into the sea, and there was an end o't."

"An end o't wi' the puir leddy," said the mendicant, "but, as I rackon, nae end o't wi' the yerl."

"Nae end o't till his life makes an end," answered the Aberdonian.

"But what for did the auld Countess forbid the marriage?" continued the persevering querist.

"Fat for? she maybe didna weel ken for fat hersell, for she gar'd a' bow to her bidding, right or wrang. But it was kend the young leddy was inclined to some o' the heresies of the country; mair by token, she was sib to him nearer than our Church's rule admits of. Sae the leddy was driven to the desperate act, and the yerl has never since held his head up like a man."

"Weel, away!" replied Ochiltree; "it's e'en queer I ne'er heard this tale afore."

"It's e'en queer that ʒe hear it now, for deil ane o' the servants durst hae spoken o't had the auld Countess been living. Eh! man, Edie, but she was a trimmer, it wad hae taen a skeely man to hae squared wi' her! But she's in her grave, and we may loose our tongues a bit fan we meet a friend. But fare ye weel, Edie, I maun be back to the evening service. An ye come to Inverurie maybe sax months awa, dinna forget to ask after Francie Macraw."

What one kindly pressed the other as firmly promised; and the friends having thus parted with every testimony of mutual regard, the domestic of Lord Glenallan took his road back to the seat of his master, leaving Ochiltree to trace onward his habitual pilgrimage.

It was a fine summer evening, and the world, that is, the little circle which was all in all to the individual by whom it was trodden, lay before Edie Ochiltree, for the choosing of his night's quarters. When he had passed the less hospitable domains of Glenallan, he had in his option so many places of refuge for the evening that he was nice and even fastidious in the choice. Ailie Sim's public was on the roadside about a mile before him; but there would be a parcel of young fellows there on the Saturday night, and that was a bar to civil conversation. Other "gudemen" and "gudewives," as the farmers and their dames are termed in Scotland, successively presented themselves to his imagination. But one was deaf, and could not hear him; another toothless, and could not make him hear; a third had a cross temper; and a fourth an ill-natured house-dog. At Monkbarns or Knockwinnock he was sure of a favourable and hospitable reception; but they lay too distant to be conveniently reached that night.

"I dinna ken how it is," said the old man, "but I am nicer about my quarters this night than ever I mind having been in my life. I think having seen a' the braws yonder, and finding out ane may be happier without them, has made me proud o' my ain lot; but I wuss it bode me gude, for pride goeth before destruction. At ony rate, the warst barn e'er man lay in wad be a pleasanter abode than Glenallan House, wi' a' the pictures and black velvet and silver bonnie wawlies belanging to it. Sae I'll e'en settle at ance and put in for Ailie Sim's."

As the old man descended the hill above the little hamlet to which he was bending his course, the setting sun had relieved its inmates from their labour, and the young men, availing themselves of the fine evening, were engaged in the sport of long-bowls on a patch of common, while the women and elders looked on. The shout, the laugh, the exclamations of winners and losers came in blended chorus up the path which Ochiltree was descending, and awakened in his recollection the days when he himself had been a keen competitor, and frequently victor, in games of strength and agility. These remembrances seldom fail to excite a sigh, even when the evening of life is cheered by brighter prospects than those of our poor mendicant. "At that time of day," was his natural reflection, "I would have thought as little about ony auld palmering body that was coming down the edge of Kinblythemont as ony o' thae stalwart young chiels does e'enow about auld Edie Ochiltree."

20

He was, however, presently cheered by finding that more importance was attached to his arrival than his modesty had anticipated. A disputed cast had occurred between the bands of players, and, as the gauger favoured the one party and the schoolmaster the other, the matter might be said to be taken up by the higher powers. The miller and smith also had espoused different sides, and, considering the vivacity of two such disputants, there was reason to doubt whether the strife might be amicably terminated. But the first person who caught a sight of the mendicant exclaimed: "Ah! here comes auld Edie, that kens the rules of a' country games better than ony man that ever drave a bowl or threw an axle-tree, or putted a stane either. Let's hae nae quarrelling, callants; we'll stand by auld Edie's judgment."

Edie was accordingly welcomed and installed as umpire with a general shout of gratulation. With all the modesty of a bishop to whom the mitre is proffered, or of a new Speaker called to the chair, the old man declined the high trust and responsibility with which it was proposed to invest him, and in requital for his self-denial and humility had the pleasure of receiving the reiterated assurances of young, old, and middle-aged that he was simply the best qualified person for the office of arbiter "in the haill country-side." Thus encouraged, he proceeded gravely to the execution of his duty, and, strictly forbidding all aggravating expressions on either side, he heard the smith and gauger on one side, the miller and schoolmaster on the other, as junior and senior counsel. Edie's mind, however, was fully made up on the subject before the pleading began, like that of many a judge, who must nevertheless go through all the forms, and endure in its full extent the eloquence and argumentation of the bar. For when all had been said on both sides, and much of it said over oftener than once, our senior, being well and ripely advised, pronounced the moderate and healing judgment that the disputed cast was a drawn one, and should therefore count to neither party. This judicious decision restored concord to the field of players; they began anew to arrange their match and their bets, with the clamorous mirth usual on such occasions of village sport, and the more eager were already stripping their jackets and committing them, with their coloured handkerchiefs, to the care of wives, sisters, and mistresses. But their mirth was singularly interrupted.

On the outside of the group of players began to arise sounds of a description very different from those of sport; that sort of suppressed sigh and exclamation with which the first news of calamity is received by the hearers began to be heard indistinctly. A buzz went about among the women of "Eh, sirs! sae young and sae suddenly summoned!" It then extended itself among the men, and silenced the sounds of sportive mirth. All understood at once that some disaster had happened in the country, and each inquired the cause at his neighbour, who knew as little as the querist. At length the rumour reached in a distinct shape the ears of Edie Ochiltree, who was in the very centre of the assembly. The boat of Mucklebackit, the fisherman whom we have so often mentioned, had been swamped at sea, and four men had perished, it was affirmed, including Mucklebackit and his son. Rumour had in this, however, as in other cases, gone beyond the truth. The boat had indeed been overset; but Stephen, or, as he was called, Steenie Mucklebackit, was the only man who had been drowned. Although the place of his residence and his mode of life removed the young man from the society of the country folks, yet they failed not to pause in their rustic mirth to pay that tribute to sudden calamity which it seldom fails to receive in cases of infrequent occurrence. To Ochiltree, in particular, the news came like a knell, the rather that he had so lately engaged this young man's assistance in an affair of sportive mischief; and, though neither loss nor injury was designed to the German adept, yet the work was not precisely one in which the latter hours of life ought to be occupied.

Misfortunes never come alone. While Ochiltree, pensively leaning upon his staff, added his regrets to those of the hamlet which bewailed the young man's sudden death, and internally blamed himself for the transaction in which he had so lately engaged him, the old man's collar was seized by a peace-officer, who displayed his baton in his right hand and exclaimed: "In the king's name."

The gauger and schoolmaster united their rhetoric to prove to the constable and his assistant that he had no right to arrest the king's bedesman as a vagrant; and the mute eloquence of the miller and smith, which was vested in their clenched fists, was prepared to give Highland bail for their arbiter; "his blue gown," they said, "was his warrant for travelling the country."

"But his blue gown," answered the officer, "is nae protection for assault, robbery, and murder; and my warrant is against him for these crimes."

"Murder!" said Edie—"murder! wha did I e'er murder?"

"Mr. German Doustercivil, the agent at Glen Withershins mining-works."

"Murder Dustersnivel! hout, he's living and life-like, man."

"Nae thanks to you if he be; he had a sair struggle for his life, if a' be true he tells, and ye maun answer for't at the bidding of the law."

The defenders of the mendicant shrunk back at hearing the atrocity of the charges against him, but more than one kind hand thrust meat and bread and pence upon Edie, to maintain him in the prison to which the officers were about to conduct him.

"Thanks to ye, God bless ye a', bairns! I've gotten out o' mony a snare when I was waur deserving o' deliverance; I shall escape like a bird from the fowler. Play out your play and never mind me. I am mair grieved for the puir lad that's gane than for aught they can do to me."

Accordingly, the unresisting prisoner was led off, while he mechanically accepted and stored in his wallets the alms which poured in on every hand, and ere he left the hamlet was as deep-laden as a government victualler. The labour of bearing this accumulating burden was, however, abridged by the officer procuring a cart and horse to convey the old man to a magistrate, in order to his examination and committal.

The disaster of Steenie and the arrest of Edie put a stop to the sports of the village, the pensive inhabitants of which began to speculate upon the vicissitudes of human affairs, which had so suddenly consigned one of their comrades to the grave and placed their master of the revels in some danger of being hanged. The character of Dousterswivel being pretty generally known, which was in his case equivalent to being pretty generally detested, there were many speculations upon the probability of the accusation being malicious. But all agreed that, if Edie Ochiltree behoved in all events to suffer upon this occasion, it was a great pity he had not better merited his fate by killing Dousterswivel outright.

CHAPTER XXX.

> Who is he? One that for the lack of land
> Shall fight upon the water : he hath challenged
> Formerly the grand whale; and by his titles
> Of Leviathan, Behemoth, and so forth,
> He tilted with a sword-fish. Marry, sir,
> Th' aquatic had the best: the argument
> Still galls our champion's breech.
>
> *Old Play.*

"And the poor young fellow, Steenie Mucklebackit, is to be buried this morning," said our old friend the Antiquary, as he exchanged his quilted nightgown for an old-fashioned black coat in lieu of the snuff-coloured vestment which he ordinarily wore; "and I presume it is expected that I should attend the funeral?"

"Ou ay," answered the faithful Caxon, officiously brushing the white threads and specks from his patron's habit; "the body, God help us, was sae broken against the rocks that they're fain to hurry the burial. The sea's a kittle cast, as I tell my daughter, puir thing, when I want her to get up her spirits: 'The sea,' says I, 'Jenny, is as uncertain a calling——'

"As the calling of an old periwig-maker, that's robbed of his business by crops and the powder-tax. Caxon, thy topics of consolation are as ill chosen as they are foreign to the present purpose. *Quid mihi cum fœmina?* What have I to do with thy womankind, who have enough and to spare of mine own? I pray of you again, am I expected by these poor people to attend the funeral of their son?"

"Ou, doubtless your honour is expected," answered Caxon; "weel I wot ye are expected. Ye ken in this country ilka gentleman is wussed to be sae civil as to see the corpse aff his grounds. Ye needna gang higher than the loan head; it's no expected your honour suld leave the land; it's just a Kelso convoy, a step and a half ower the door-stane."

"A Kelso convoy!" echoed the inquisitive Antiquary; "and why a Kelso convoy more than any other?"

"Dear sir," answered Caxon, "how should I ken? it's just a bye-word."

"Caxon," answered Oldbuck, "thou art a mere periwig-maker. Had I asked Ochiltree the question, he would have had a legend ready made to my hand."

"My business," replied Caxon, with more animation than he commonly displayed, "is with the outside of your honour's head, as ye are accustomed to say."

"True, Caxon, true; and it is no reproach to a thatcher that he is not an upholsterer."

He then took out his memorandum-book and wrote down: "Kelso convoy, said to be a step and a half ower the threshold. Authority, Caxon. *Quære*, Whence derived? *Mem.* To write to Dr. Graysteel upon the subject."

Having made this entry, he resumed: "And truly, as to this custom of the landlord attending the body of the peasant, I approve it, Caxon. It comes from ancient times, and was founded deep in the notions of mutual aid and dependence between the lord and cultivator of the soil. And herein, I must say, the feudal system—as also in its courtesy towards womankind, in which it exceeded—herein, I say, the feudal usages mitigated and softened the sternness of classical times. No man, Caxon, ever heard of a Spartan attending the funeral of a helot; yet I dare be sworn that John of the Girnell—ye have heard of him, Caxon?"

"Ay, ay, sir," answered Caxon; "naebody can hae been

lang in your honour's company without hearing of that gentleman."

"Well," continued the Antiquary, "I would bet a trifle there was not a *kolb kerl*, or bondsman, or peasant, *ascriptus glebæ*, died upon the monks' territories down here but John of the Girnell saw them fairly and decently interred."

"Ay, but if it like your honour, they say he had mair to do wi' the births than the burials. Ha! ha! ha!" with a gleeful chuckle.

"Good, Caxon! very good! Why, you shine this morning."

"And besides," added Caxon, slily, encouraged by his patron's approbation, "they say too that the Catholic priests in thae times gat something for ganging about to burials."

"Right, Caxon, right as my glove—by the by, I fancy that phrase comes from the custom of pledging a glove as the signal of irrefragable faith—right, I say, as my glove, Caxon; but we of the Protestant ascendency have the more merit in doing that duty for nothing which cost money in the reign of that empress of superstition whom Spenser, Caxon, terms in his allegorical phrase,

> The daughter of that woman blind,
> Abessa, daughter of Corecca slow.

But why talk I of these things to thee? My poor Lovel has spoiled me, and taught me to speak aloud when it is much the same as speaking to myself. Where's my nephew, Hector M'Intyre?"

"He's in the parlour, sir, wi' the leddies."

"Very well," said the Antiquary, "I will betake me thither."

"Now, Monkbarns," said his sister, on his entering the parlour, "ye maunna be angry."

"My dear uncle!" began Miss M'Intyre.

"What's the meaning of all this?" said Oldbuck, in alarm of some impending bad news, and arguing upon the supplicating tone of the ladies, as a fortress apprehends an attack from the very first flourish of the trumpet which announces the summons— "what's all this? What do you bespeak my patience for?"

"No particular matter, I should hope, sir," said Hector, who, with his arm in a sling, was seated at the breakfast-table; "however, whatever it may amount to, I am answerable for it, as I am for much more trouble that I have occasioned, and for which I have little more than thanks to offer."

"No, no! heartily welcome, heartily welcome; only let it be a warning to you," said the Antiquary, "against your fits of anger, which is a short madness—*Ira furor brevis*. But what is this new disaster?"

"My dog, sir, has unfortunately thrown down——"

"If it please Heaven, not the lachrymatory from Clochnaben!" interjected Oldbuck.

"Indeed, uncle," said the young lady, "I am afraid—it was that which stood upon the sideboard; the poor thing only meant to eat the pat of fresh butter."

"In which she has fully succeeded, I presume, for I see that on the table is salted. But that is nothing; my lachrymatory, the main pillar of my theory, on which I rested to show, in despite of the ignorant obstinacy of Mac-Cribb, that the Romans had passed the defiles of these mountains, and left behind them traces of their arts and arms, is gone—annihilated—reduced to such fragments as might be the shreds of a broken—flowerpot!

> Hector, I love thee,
> But never more be officer of mine."

"Why, really, sir, I am afraid I should make a bad figure in a regiment of your raising."

"At least, Hector, I would have you despatch your camp train, and travel *expeditus* or *relictis impedimentis*. You cannot conceive how I am annoyed by this beast. She commits burglary, I believe, for I heard her charged with breaking into the kitchen after all the doors were locked, and eating up a shoulder of mutton." (Our readers, if they chance to remember Jenny Rintherout's precaution of leaving the door open when she went down to the fisher's cottage, will probably acquit poor Juno of that aggravation of guilt which the lawyers call a *claustrum fregit,* and which makes the distinction between burglary and privately stealing.)

"I am truly sorry, sir," said Hector, "that Juno has committed so much disorder; but Jack Muirhead, the breaker, was never able to bring her under command. She has more travel than any bitch I ever knew, but——"

"Then, Hector, I wish the bitch would travel herself out of my grounds."

"We will both of us retreat to-morrow, or to-day, but I would not willingly part from my mother's brother in unkindness about a paltry pipkin."

"O brother, brother!" ejaculated Miss M'Intyre, in utter despair at this vituperative epithet.

"Why, what would you have me call it?" continued Hector; "it was just such a thing as they use in Egypt to cool wine or sherbet or water. I brought home a pair of them; I might have brought home twenty."

"What!" said Oldbuck, "shaped such as that your dog threw down?"

"Yes, sir, much such a sort of earthern jar as that which was on the sideboard. They are in my lodgings at Fairport; we brought a parcel of them to cool our wine on the passage; they answer wonderfully well. If I could think they would in any degree repay your loss, or rather that they could afford you pleasure, I am sure I should be much honoured by your accepting them."

"Indeed, my dear boy, I should be highly gratified by possessing them. To trace the connexion of nations by their usages, and the similarity of the implements which they employ, has been long my favourite study. Everything that can illustrate such connexions is most valuable to me."

"Well, sir, I shall be much gratified by your acceptance of them, and a few trifles of the same kind. And now, am I to hope you have forgiven me?"

"Oh, my dear boy, you are only thoughtless and foolish."

"But Juno, she is only thoughtless too, I assure you; the breaker tells me she has no vice or stubbornness."

"Well, I grant Juno also a free pardon—conditioned, that you will imitate her in avoiding vice and stubbornness, and that henceforward she banish herself forth of Monkbarns parlour."

"Then, uncle," said the soldier, "I should have been very sorry and ashamed to propose to you anything in the way of expiation of my own sins, or those of my follower, that I thought *worth* your acceptance; but now, as all is forgiven, will you permit the orphan nephew, to whom you have been a father, to offer you a trifle, which I have been assured is really curious, and which only the cross accident of my wound has prevented my delivering to you before? I got it from a French savant, to whom I rendered some service after the Alexandria affair."

The captain put a small ring-case into the Antiquary's hands, which, when opened, was found to contain an antique ring of massive gold, with a cameo, most beautifully executed, bearing a head of Cleopatra. The Antiquary broke forth into unrepressed ecstasy, shook his nephew cordially by the hand, thanked him an hundred times, and showed the ring to his sister and niece, the latter of whom had the tact to give it sufficient admiration; but Miss Griselda (though she had the same affection for her nephew) had not address enough to follow the lead.

"It's a bonny thing," she said, "Monkbarns, and, I dare say, a valuable; but it's out o' my way. Ye ken I am nae judge o' sic matters."

"There spoke all Fairport in one voice!" exclaimed Oldbuck; "it is the very spirit of the borough has infected us all: I think I have smelled the smoke these two days that the wind has stuck, like a *remora*, in the northeast, and its prejudices fly farther than its vapours. Believe me, my dear Hector, were I to walk up the High Street of Fairport, displaying this inestimable gem in the eyes of each one I met, no human creature, from the provost to the town-crier, would stop to ask me its history. But if I carried a bale of linen cloth under my arm, I could not penetrate to the Horsemarket ere I should be overwhelmed with queries about its precise

texture and price. Oh, one might parody their brutal ignorance in the words of Gray:

> Weave the warp and weave the woof,
> The winding-sheet of wit and sense,
> Dull garment of defensive proof
> 'Gainst all that doth not gather pence."

The most remarkable proof of this peace-offering being
quite acceptable was that, while the Antiquary was in full
declamation, Juno, who held him in awe, according to the
remarkable instinct by which dogs instantly discover those
who like or dislike them, had peeped several times into the
room, and, encountering nothing very forbidding in his aspect,
had at length presumed to introduce her full person, and
finally, becoming bold by impunity, she actually ate up Mr.
Oldbuck's toast, as, looking first at one then at another of his
audience, he repeated with self-complacency,

" Weave the warp and weave the woof.—

You remember the passage in the *Fatal Sisters*, which, by
the way, is not so fine as in the original. But, hey-day! my
toast has vanished! I see which way. Ah, thou type of
womankind, no wonder they take offence at thy generic appellation!" (So saying, he shook his fist at Juno, who scoured
out of the parlour.) "However, as Jupiter, according to
Homer, could not rule Juno in heaven, and as Jack Muirhead,
according to Hector M'Intyre, has been equally unsuccessful
on earth, I suppose she must have her own way." And this
mild censure the brother and sister justly accounted a full
pardon for Juno's offences, and sate down well pleased to the
morning meal.

When breakfast was over the Antiquary proposed to his
nephew to go down with him to attend the funeral. The
soldier pleaded the want of a mourning habit.

"Oh, that does not signify; your presence is all that is re-
quisite. I assure you, you will see something that will entertain—no, that's an improper phrase—but that will interest
you, from the resemblances which I will point out betwixt popular customs on such occasions and those of the ancients."

"Heaven forgive me!" thought M'Intyre; "I shall certainly misbel ave, and lose all the credit I have so lately and accidentally gained."

When they set out, schooled as he was by the warning and entreating looks of his sister, the soldier made his resolution strong to give no offence by evincing inattention or impatience. But our best resolutions are frail when opposed to our predominant inclinations. Our Antiquary, to leave nothing unexplained, had commenced with the funeral rites of the ancient Scandinavians, when his nephew interrupted him in a discussion upon the "age of hills," to remark that a large sea-gull which flitted around them had come twice within shot. This error being acknowledged and pardoned, Oldbuck resumed his disquisition.

"These are circumstances you ought to attend to and be familiar with, my dear Hector; for, in the strange contingencies of the present war which agitates every corner of Europe, there is no knowing where you may be called upon to serve. If in Norway, for example, or Denmark, or any part of the ancient Scania, or Scandinavia, as we term it, what could be more convenient than to have at your fingers' ends the history and antiquities of that ancient country, the *officina gentium*, the mother of modern Europe, the nursery of those heroes,

> Stern to inflict and stubborn to endure,
> Who smiled in death?

How animating, for example, at the conclusion of a weary march, to find yourself in the vicinity of a Runic monument, and discover that you had pitched your tent beside the tomb of a hero!"

"I am afraid, sir, our mess would be better supplied if it chanced to be in the neighbourhood of a good poultry-yard."

"Alas, that you should say so! No wonder the days of Cressy and Agincourt are no more, when respect for ancient valour has died away in the breasts of the British soldiery."

"By no means, sir—by no manner of means. I dare say that Edward and Henry, and the rest of these heroes, thought of their dinner, however, before they thought of examining an old tombstone. But I assure you we are by no means insensible to the memory of our fathers' fame; I used often of an evening to get old Rory M'Alpin to sing us songs out of Ossian about the battles of Fingal and Lamon Mor, and Magnus and the spirit of Muirartach."

"And did you believe," asked the aroused Antiquary—"did you absolutely believe that stuff of Macpherson's to be really ancient, you simple boy?"

"Believe it, sir? how could I but believe it, when I have heard the songs sung from my infancy?"

"But not the same as Macpherson's English Ossian; you're not absurd enough to say that, I hope?" said the Antiquary, his brow darkening with wrath.

But Hector stoutly abode the storm; like many a sturdy Celt, he imagined the honour of his country and native language connected with the authenticity of these popular poems, and would have fought knee-deep, or forfeited life and land, rather than have given up a line of them. He therefore undauntedly maintained that Rory M'Alpin could repeat the whole book from one end to another; and it was only upon cross-examination that he explained an assertion so general by adding: "At least, if he was allowed whisky enough, he could repeat as long as anybody would hearken to him."

"Ay, ay," said the Antiquary; "and that, I suppose, was not very long."

"Why, we had our duty, sir, to attend to, and could not sit listening all night to a piper."

"But do you recollect, now," said Oldbuck, setting his teeth firmly together, and speaking without opening them, which was his custom when contradicted—"do you recollect, now, any of these verses you thought so beautiful and interesting, being a capital judge, no doubt, of such things?"

"I don't pretend to much skill, uncle; but it's not very reasonable to be angry with me for admiring the antiquities of my own country more than those of the Harolds, Harfagers, and Hacos you are so fond of."

"Why, these, sir—these mighty and unconquered Goths— *were* your ancestors! The bare-breeched Celts whom they subdued, and suffered only to exist, like a fearful people, in the crevices of the rocks, were but their *mancipia* and serfs!"

Hector's brow now grew red in his turn. "Sir," he said, "I don't understand the meaning of *mancipia* and serfs, but I conceive such names are very improperly applied to Scotch Highlanders. No man but my mother's brother dared to have used such language in my presence; and I pray you will observe that I consider it as neither hospitable, handsome, kind, nor generous usage towards your guest and your kinsman. My ancestors, Mr. Oldbuck——"

"Were great and gallant chiefs, I dare say, Hector; and really I did not mean to give you such immense offence in treating a point of remote antiquity, a subject on which I always am myself cool, deliberate, and unimpassioned. But you are as hot and hasty as if you were Hector and Achilles and Agamemnon to boot."

"I am sorry I expressed myself so hastily, uncle, especially to you, who have been so generous and good. But my ancestors——"

"No more about it, lad; I meant them no affront, none."

"I am glad of it, sir; for the house of M'Intyre——"

"Peace be with them all, every man of them," said the Antiquary. "But to return to our subject. Do you recollect, I say, any of those poems which afforded you such amusement?"

"Very hard this," thought M'Intyre, "that he will speak with such glee of everything which is ancient excepting my family." Then, after some efforts at recollection, he added aloud: "Yes, sir, I think I do remember some lines; but you do not understand the Gaelic language."

"And will readily excuse hearing it. But you can give me some idea of the sense in our own vernacular idiom?"

"I shall prove a wretched interpreter," said M'Intyre, running over the originals, well garnished with "aghes," "aughs," and "oughs," and similar gutturals, and then coughing and hawking as if the translation stuck in his throat. At length, having premised that the poem was a dialogue between the poet Oisin, or Ossian, and Patrick, the tutelar saint of Ireland, and that it was difficult, if not impossible, to render the exquisite felicity of the first two or three lines, he said the sense was to this purpose:

> " Patrick the psalm-singer,
> Since you will not listen to one of my stories,
> Though you never heard it before,
> I am sorry to tell you
> You are little better than an ass——

"Good! good!" exclaimed the Antiquary; "but go on. Why, this is, after all, the most admirable fooling; I dare say the poet was very right. What says the saint?"

"He replies in character," said M'Intyre; "but you should hear M'Alpin sing the original. The speeches of Ossian come in upon a strong deep bass; those of Patrick are upon a tenor key."

"Like M'Alpin's drone and small pipes, I suppose," said Oldbuck. "Well? Pray, go on."

"Well then, Patrick replies to Ossian:

> Upon my word, son of Fingal,
> While I am warbling the psalms,
> The clamour of your old women's tales
> Disturbs my devotional exercises."

"Excellent! why, this is better and better. I hope Saint Patrick sung better than Blattergowl's precentor, or it would be hang-choice between the poet and psalmist. But what I admire is the courtesy of these two eminent persons towards each other. It is a pity there should not be a word of this in Macpherson's translation."

"If you are sure of that," said M'Intyre, gravely, "he must have taken very unwarrantable liberties with his original."

"It will go near to be thought so shortly; but pray proceed."

"Then," said M'Intyre, "this is the answer of Ossian:

> Dare you compare your psalms,
> You son of a——"

"Son of a what!" exclaimed Oldbuck.

"It means, I think," said the young soldier, with some reluctance, "son of a female dog:

> Do you compare your psalms,
> To the tales of the bare-arm'd Fenians?"

"Are you sure you are translating that last epithet correctly, Hector?"

"Quite sure, sir," answered Hector, doggedly.

"Because I should have thought the nudity might have been quoted as existing in a different part of the body."

Disdaining to reply to this insinuation, Hector proceeded in his recitation:

> "I shall think it no great harm
> To wring your bald head from your shoulders——

But what is that yonder?" exclaimed Hector, interrupting himself.

"One of the herd of Proteus," said the Antiquary, "a *phoca* or seal lying asleep on the beach."

Upon which M'Intyre, with the eagerness of a young sportsman, totally forgot both Ossian, Patrick, his uncle, and his wound, and exclaiming, "I shall have her! I shall have her!" snatched the walking-stick out of the hand of the astonished Antiquary, at some risk of throwing him down, and set off at full speed to get between the animal and the sea, to which element, having caught the alarm, she was rapidly retreating.

Not Sancho, when his master interrupted his account of the combatants of Pentapolin with the naked arm to advance in person to the flock of sheep, stood more confounded than Oldbuck at this sudden escapade of his nephew.

"Is the devil in him," was his first exclamation, "to go to disturb the brute that was never thinking of him?" Then elevating his voice: "Hector, nephew, fool, let alone the *phoca* —let alone the *phoca ;* they bite, I tell you, like furies. He minds me no more than a post; there—there they are at it. Gad, the *phoca* has the best of it! I am glad to see it," said he, in the bitterness of his heart, though really alarmed for his nephew's safety—"I am glad to see it, with all my heart and spirit."

In truth the seal, finding her retreat intercepted by the light-footed soldier, confronted him manfully, and having sustained a heavy blow without injury, she knitted her brows, as is the fashion of the animal when incensed, and, making use at once of her fore paws and her unwieldy strength, wrenched the weapon out of the assailant's hand, overturned him on the sands, and scuttled away into the sea without doing him any farther injury. Captain M'Intyre, a good deal out of countenance at the issue of his exploit, just rose in time to receive the ironical congratulations of his uncle upon a single combat worthy to be commemorated by Ossian himself, "since" said the Antiquary, "your magnanimous opponent hath fled, though not upon eagle's wings, from the foe that was low. Egad, she walloped away with all the grace of triumph, and has carried my stick off also, by way of *spolia opima*."

M'Intyre had little to answer for himself, except that a Highlander could never pass a deer, a seal, or a salmon where there was a possibility of having a trial of skill with them, and that he had forgot one of his arms was in a sling. He also made his fall an apology for returning back to Monk-barns, and thus escaped the farther raillery of his uncle, as well as his lamentations for his walking-stick.

"I cut it," he said, "in the classic woods of Hawthornden, when I did not expect always to have been a bachelor. I would not have given it for an ocean of seals. O Hector, Hector! thy namesake was born to be the prop of Troy, and thou to be the plague of Monkbarns!"

CHAPTER XXXI.

Tell me not of it, friend. When the young weep,
Their tears are lukewarm brine ; from our old eyes
Sorrow falls down like hail-drops of the North,
Chilling the furrows of our wither'd cheeks,
Cold as our hopes, and harden'd as our feeling.
Theirs, as they fall, sink sightless ; ours recoil,
Heap the fair plain, and bleaken all before us.
										Old Play.

THE Antiquary, being now alone, hastened his pace, which had been retarded by these various discussions and the *ren-*

21

contre which had closed them, and soon arrived before the half-dozen cottages at Mussel Crag. They now had, in addition to their usual squalid and uncomfortable appearance, the melancholy attributes of the house of mourning. The boats were all drawn up on the beach; and, though the day was fine and the season favourable, the chant which is used by the fishers when at sea was silent, as well as the prattle of the children, and the shrill song of the mother, as she sits mending her nets by the door. A few of the neighbours, some in their antique and well-saved suits of black, others in their ordinary clothes, but all bearing an expression of mournful sympathy with distress so sudden and unexpected, stood gathered around the door of Mucklebackit's cottage, waiting till "the body was lifted." As the Laird of Monkbarns approached they made way for him to enter, doffing their hats and bonnets as he passed with an air of melancholy courtesy, and he returned their salutes in the same manner.

In the inside of the cottage was a scene which our Wilkie alone could have painted, with that exquisite feeling of nature that characterises his enchanting productions.

The body was laid in its coffin within the wooden bedstead which the young fisher had occupied while alive. At a little distance stood the father, whose rugged, weatherbeaten countenance, shaded by his grizzled hair, had faced many a stormy night and night-like day. He was apparently revolving his loss in his mind with that strong feeling of painful grief peculiar to harsh and rough characters, which almost breaks forth into hatred against the world and all that remain in it after the beloved object is withdrawn. The old man had made the most desperate efforts to save his son, and had only been withheld by main force from renewing them at a moment when, without the possibility of assisting the sufferer, he must himself have perished. All this apparently was boiling in his recollection. His glance was directed sidelong towards the coffin, as to an object on which he could not steadfastly look, and yet from which he could not withdraw his eyes. His answers to the necessary questions which were occasionally put to him were brief, harsh, and almost fierce. His family had not yet dared to address to him a word, either of sympathy or consolation. His masculine wife, virago as she was, and absolute mistress of the family, as she justly boasted herself, on all ordinary occasions, was by this great loss terrified into silence and submission, and compelled to hide from her husband's observation the bursts of her female sorrow. As he had rejected food ever since the disaster had happened, not daring herself to approach him, she had that morning, with affectionate artifice, employed the youngest and favourite child to present her husband with some nourishment. His first action was to push it from him with an angry violence that frightened the child; his next to snatch up the boy and devour him with kisses. " Ye'll be a bra' fallow, an ye be spared, Patie; but ye'll never—never can be—what he was to me! He has sailed the coble wi' me since he was ten years auld, and there wasna the like o' him drew a net betwixt this and Buchan Ness. They say folks maun submit; I will try."

And he had been silent from that moment until compelled to answer the necessary questions we have already noticed. Such was the disconsolate state of the father.

In another corner of the cottage, her face covered by her apron, which was flung over it, sat the mother, the nature of her grief sufficiently indicated by the wringing of her hands and the convulsive agitation of the bosom which the covering could not conceal. Two of her gossips, officiously whispering into her ear the commonplace topic of resignation under irremediable misfortune, seemed as if they were endeavouring to stun the grief which they could not console.

The sorrow of the children was mingled with wonder at the preparations they beheld around them, and at the unusual display of wheaten bread and wine, which the poorest peasant or fisher offers to the guests on these mournful occasions; and thus their grief for their brother's death was almost already lost in admiration of the splendour of his funeral.

But the figure of the old grandmother was the most remarkable of the sorrowing group. Seated on her accustomed chair, with her usual air of apathy and want of interest in what surrounded her, she seemed every now and then mechanically to resume the motion of twirling her spindle, then to look towards her bosom for the distaff, although both had been laid aside. She would then cast her eyes about as if surprised at missing the usual implements of her industry, and appear struck by the black colour of the gown in which they had dressed her, and embarrassed by the number of persons by whom she was surrounded; then, finally, she would raise her head with a ghastly look and fix her eyes upon the bed which contained the coffin of her grandson, as if she had at once, and for the first time, acquired sense to comprehend her inexpressible calamity. These alternate feelings of embarrassment, wonder, and grief seemed to succeed each other more than once upon her torpid features. But she spoke not a word, neither had she shed a tear; nor did one of the family understand, either from look or expression, to what extent she comprehended the uncommon bustle around her. Thus she sat among the funeral assembly like a connecting link between the surviving mourners and the dead corpse which they bewailed—a being in whom the light of existence was already obscured by the encroaching shadows of death.

When Oldbuck entered this house of mourning he was received by a general and silent inclination of the head, and, according to the fashion of Scotland on such occasions, wine and spirits and bread were offered round to the guests. Elspeth, as these refreshments were presented, surprised and startled the whole company by motioning to the person who bore them to stop; then, taking a glass in her hand, she rose up, and, as the smile of dotage played upon her shrivelled features, she pronounced, with a hollow and tremulous voice: "Wishing a' your healths, sirs, and often may we hae such merry meetings!"

All shrunk from the ominous pledge, and set down the untasted liquor with a degree of shuddering horror which will not surprise those who know how many superstitions are still common on such occasions among the Scottish vulgar. But as the old woman tasted the liquor she suddenly exclaimed with a sort of shriek: "What's this? this is wine; how should there be wine in my son's house? Ay," she continued with a suppressed groan, "I mind the sorrowful cause now," and, dropping the glass from her hand, she stood a moment gazing fixedly on the bed in which the coffin of her grandson was deposited, and then, sinking gradually into her seat, she covered her eyes and forehead with her withered and pallid hand.

At this moment the clergyman entered the cottage. Mr. Blattergowl, though a dreadful proser, particularly on the subject of augmentations, localities, teinds, and overtures in that session of the General Assembly to which, unfortunately for his auditors, he chanced one year to act as moderator, was nevertheless a good man, in the old Scottish Presbyterian phrase, God-ward and man-ward. No divine was more attentive in visiting the sick and afflicted, in catechising the youth, in instructing the ignorant, and in reproving the erring. And hence, notwithstanding impatience of his prolixity and prejudices, personal or professional, and notwithstanding, moreover, a certain habitual contempt for his understanding, especially on affairs of genius and taste, on which Blattergowl was apt to be diffuse, from his hope of one day fighting his way to a chair of rhetoric or *belles lettres*—notwithstanding, I say, all the prejudices excited against him by these circumstances, our friend the Antiquary looked with great regard and respect on the said Blattergowl, though I own he could seldom, even by his sense of decency and the remonstrances of his womankind, be "hounded out," as he called it, to hear him preach. But he regularly took shame to himself for his absence when Blattergowl came to Monkbarns to dinner, to which he was always invited of a Sunday, a mode of testifying his respect which the proprietor thought fully as agreeable to the clergyman, and rather more congenial to his own habits.

To return from a digression which can only serve to introduce the honest clergyman more particularly to our readers, Mr. Blattergowl had no sooner entered the hut and received the mute and melancholy salutations of the company whom it contained, than he edged himself towards the unfortunate father, and seemed to endeavour to slide in a few words of condolence or of consolation. But the old man was incapable as yet of receiving either; he nodded, however, gruffly, and shook the clergyman's hand in acknowledgment of his good intentions, but was either unable or unwilling to make any verbal reply.

The minister next passed to the mother, moving along the floor as slowly, silently, and gradually as if he had been afraid that the ground would, like unsafe ice, break beneath his feet, or that the first echo of a footstep was to dissolve some magic spell and plunge the hut, with all its inmates, into a subterranean abyss. The tenor of what he had said to the poor woman could only be judged by her answers, as, half-stifled by sobs ill-repressed, and by the covering which she still kept over her countenance, she faintly answered at each pause in his speech: "Yes, sir, yes! Ye're very gude! ye're very gude! Nae doubt, nae doubt! It's our duty to submit! But, oh dear, my poor Steenie, the pride o' my very heart, that was sae handsome and comely, and a help to his family, and a comfort to us a', and a pleasure to a' that lookit on him! O my bairn, my bairn, my bairn! what for is thou lying there, and eh! what for am I left to greet for ye?"

There was no contending with this burst of sorrow and natural affection. Oldbuck had repeated recourse to his snuff-box to conceal the tears which, despite his shrewd and caustic temper, were apt to start on such occasions. The female assistants whimpered, the men held their bonnets to their faces, and spoke apart with each other. The clergyman meantime addressed his ghostly consolation to the aged grandmother. At first she listened, or seemed to listen, to what he said with the apathy of her usual unconsciousness. But as, in pressing this theme, he approached so near to her ear that the sense of his words became distinctly intelligible to her, though unheard by those who stood more distant, her countenance at once assumed that stern and expressive cast which characterised her intervals of intelligence. She drew up her head and body, shook her head in a manner that showed at least impatience, if not scorn, of his counsel, and waved her hand slightly, but with a gesture so expressive as to indicate to all who witnessed it a marked and disdainful rejection of the ghostly consolation proffered to her. The minister stepped back as if repulsed, and, by lifting gently and dropping his hand, seemed to show at once wonder, sorrow, and compassion for her dreadful state of mind. The rest of the company sympathised, and a stifled whisper went through them, indicating how much her desperate and determined manner impressed them with awe and even horror.

In the mean time the funeral company was completed by the arrival of one or two persons who had been expected from Fairport. The wine and spirits again circulated, and the dumb show of greeting was anew interchanged. The grandame a second time took a glass in her hand, drank its contents, and exclaimed, with a sort of laugh: " Ha! ha! I hae tasted wine twice in ae day. Whan did I that before, think ye, cummers? Never since——" And the transient glow vanishing from her countenance, she set the glass down and sunk upon the settle from whence she had risen to snatch at it.

As the general amazement subsided, Mr. Oldbuck, whose heart bled to witness what he considered as the errings of the enfeebled intellect struggling with the torpid chill of age and of sorrow, observed to the clergyman that it was time to proceed with the ceremony. The father was incapable of giving directions, but the nearest relation of the family made a sign to the carpenter, who in such cases goes through the duty of the undertaker, to proceed in his office. The creak of the screw-nails presently announced that the lid of the last mansion of mortality was in the act of being secured above its tenant. The last act which separates us for ever, even from the mortal relics of the person we assemble to mourn, has usually its effect upon the most indifferent, selfish, and hardhearted. With a spirit of contradiction which we may be pardoned for esteeming narrow-minded, the fathers of the Scottish Kirk rejected, even on this most solemn occasion, the form of an address to the Divinity, lest they should be thought to give countenance to the rituals of Rome or of England. With much better and more liberal judgment, it is the present practice of most of the Scottish clergymen to seize this opportunity of offering a prayer and exhortation suitable to make an impression upon the living, while they are yet in the very presence of the relics of him whom they have but lately seen such as they themselves, and who now is such as they must in their time become. But this decent and praise-worthy practice was not adopted at the time of which I am treating, or at least Mr. Blattergowl did not act upon it, and the ceremony proceeded without any devotional exercise.

The coffin, covered with a pall and supported upon hand-spikes by the nearest relatives, now only waited the father to support the head, as is customary. Two or three of these privileged persons spoke to him, but he only answered by shaking his hand and his head in token of refusal. With better intention than judgment, the friends, who considered this as an act of duty on the part of the living and of decency towards the deceased, would have proceeded to enforce their request had not Oldbuck interfered between the distressed father and his well-meaning tormentors, and informed them that he himself, as landlord and master to the deceased, "would carry his head to the grave." In spite of the sor-rowful occasion, the hearts of the relatives swelled within them at so marked a distinction on the part of the Laird; and old Ailison Breck, who was present among other fish-women, swore almost aloud: "His honour Monkbarns should never want sax warp of oysters in the season (of which fish he was understood to be fond), if she should gang to sea and dredge for them hersell in the foulest wind that ever blew." And such is the temper of the Scottish common people, that, by this instance of compliance with their customs and respect of their persons, Mr. Oldbuck gained more popularity than by all the sums which he had yearly distributed in the parish for purposes of private or general charity.

The sad procession now moved slowly forward, preceded by the beadles, or saulies, with their batons—miserable-look-ing old men tottering as if on the edge of that grave to which they were marshalling another, and clad, according to Scottish guise, with threadbare black coats and hunting-caps decorated with rusty crape. Monkbarns would probably have remon-strated against this superfluous expense had he been consulted; but in doing so he would have given more offence than he gained popularity by condescending to perform the office of chief mourner. Of this he was quite aware, and wisely withheld rebuke where rebuke and advice would have been equally unavailing. In truth, the Scottish peasantry are still infected with that rage for funeral ceremonial which once distinguished the grandees of the kingdom, so much that a sumptuary law was made by the Parliament of Scotland for the purpose of restraining it; and I have known many in the lowest stations who have denied themselves not merely the comforts, but almost the necessaries of life, in order to save such a sum of money as might enable their surviving friends to bury them like Christians, as they termed it; nor could their faithful executors be prevailed upon, though equally necessitous, to turn to the use and maintenance of the living the money vainly wasted upon the interment of the dead.

The procession to the churchyard, at about half a mile's distance, was made with the mournful solemnity usual on these occasions, the body was consigned to its parent earth, and when the labour of the gravediggers had filled up the trench and covered it with fresh sod, Mr. Oldbuck, taking his hat off, saluted the assistants, who had stood by in melancholy silence, and with that adieu dispersed the mourners.

The clergyman offered our Antiquary his company to walk homeward; but Mr. Oldbuck had been so much struck with the deportment of the fisherman and his mother that, moved by compassion, and perhaps also, in some degree, by that curiosity which induces us to seek out even what gives us pain to witness, he preferred a solitary walk by the coast, for the purpose of again visiting the cottage as he passed.

CHAPTER XXXII.

What is this secret sin, this untold tale,
That art cannot extract, nor penance cleanse?
. . . Her muscles hold their place,
Nor discomposed, nor form'd to steadiness,
No sudden flushing, and no faltering lip.
Mysterious Mother.

THE coffin had been borne from the place where it rested. The mourners, in regular gradation, according to their rank or their relationship to the deceased, had filed from the cottage, while the younger male children were led along to totter after the bier of their brother, and to view with wonder a ceremonial which they could hardly comprehend. The female gossips next rose to depart, and, with consideration for the situation of the parents, carried along with them the girls of the family, to give the unhappy pair time and opportunity to open their hearts to each other, and soften their grief by communicating it. But their kind intention was without effect. The last of them had darkened the entrance of the cottage as she went out, and drawn the door softly behind her, when the father, first ascertaining by a hasty glance that no stranger remained, started up, clasped his hands wildly above his head, uttered a cry of the despair which he had hitherto repressed, and, in all the impotent impatience of grief, half rushed, half staggered forward to the bed on which the coffin had been deposited, threw himself down upon it, and, smothering, as it were, his head among the bed-clothes, gave vent to the full passion of his sorrow. It was in vain that the wretched mother, terrified by the vehemence of her husband's affliction—affliction still more fearful as agitating a man of hardened manners and a robust frame—suppressed her own sobs and tears, and, pulling him by the skirts of his coat, implored him to rise and remember that, though one was removed, he had still a wife and children to comfort and support. The appeal came at too early a period of his anguish, and was totally unattended to; he continued to remain prostrate, indicating, by sobs so bitter and violent that they shook the bed and partition against which it rested, by clenched hands which grasped the bed-clothes, and by the vehement and convulsive motions of his legs, how deep and how terrible was the agony of a father's sorrow.

"Oh, what a day is this! what a day is this!" said the poor mother, her womanish affliction already exhausted by sobs and tears, and now almost lost in terror for the state in which she beheld her husband—"Oh, what an hour is this! and naebody to help a poor lone woman. Oh, gudemither, could ye but speak a word to him! wad ye but bid him be comforted!"

To her astonishment, and even to the increase of her fear, her husband's mother heard and answered the appeal. She rose and walked across the floor without support, and without much apparent feebleness, and, standing by the bed on which her son had extended himself, she said: "Rise up, my son, and sorrow not for him that is beyond sin and sorrow and temptation. Sorrow is for those that remain in this vale of sorrow and darkness. I, wha dinna sorrow, and wha canna sorrow for ony ane, hae maist need that ye should a' sorrow for me."

The voice of his mother, not heard for years as taking part in the active duties of life, or offering advice or consolation, produced its effect upon her son. He assumed a sitting posture on the side of the bed, and his appearance, attitude, and gestures changed from those of angry despair to deep grief and dejection. The grandmother retired to her nook, the mother mechanically took in her hand her tattered Bible, and seemed to read, though her eyes were drowned with tears.

They were thus occupied when a loud knock was heard at the door.

"Hegh, sirs!" said the poor mother, "wha is it that can be coming in that gait e'enow? They canna hae heard o' our misfortune, I'm sure."

The knock being repeated, she rose and opened the door, saying querulously: "Whatna gait's that to disturb a sorrowfu' house?"

A tall man in black stood before her, whom she instantly recognised to be Lord Glenallan.

"Is there not," he said, "an old woman lodging in this or one of the neighbouring cottages, called Elspeth, who was long resident at Craigburnfoot of Glenallan?"

"It's my gudemither, my lord," said Margaret; "but she canna see ony body e'enow. Ohon! we're dreeing a sair weird; we hae had a heavy dispensation!"

"God forbid," said Lord Glenallan, "that I should on light occasion disturb your sorrow; but my days are numbered, your mother-in-law is in the extremity of age, and, if I see her not to-day, we may never meet on this side of time."

"And what," answered the desolate mother, "wad ye see at an auld woman, broken down wi' age and sorrow and heart-break? Gentle or semple shall not darken my doors the day my bairn's been carried out a corpse."

While she spoke thus, indulging the natural irritability of disposition and profession, which began to mingle itself in some degree with her grief when its first uncontrolled bursts were gone by, she held the door about one-third part open, and placed herself in the gap, as if to render the visitor's entrance impossible. But the voice of her husband was heard from within: "Wha's that, Maggie? what for are ye steeking them out? Let them come in; it doesna signify an auld rope's end wha comes in or wha gaes out o' this house frae this time forward."

The woman stood aside at her husband's command, and permitted Lord Glenallan to enter the hut. The dejection exhibited in his broken frame and emaciated countenance formed a strong contrast with the effects of grief as they were displayed in the rude and weatherbeaten visage of the fisherman and the masculine features of his wife. He approached the old woman as she was seated on her usual settle, and asked her, in a tone as audible as his voice could make it: "Are you Elspeth of the Craigburnfoot of Glenallan?"

"Wha is it that asks about the unhallowed residence of that evil woman?" was the answer returned to his query.

"The unhappy Earl of Glenallan."

"Earl—Earl of Glenallan!"

"He who was called William Lord Geraldin," said the Earl,

"and whom his mother's death has made Earl of Glen-allan."

"Open the bole," said the old woman firmly and hastily to her daughter-in-law—"open the bole wi' speed, that I may see if this be the right Lord Geraldin, the son of my mistress, him that I received in my arms within the hour after he was born, him that has reason to curse me that I didna smother him before the hour was past!"

The window, which had been shut in order that a gloomy twilight might add to the solemnity of the funeral meeting, was opened as she commanded, and threw a sudden and strong light through the smoky and misty atmosphere of the stifling cabin. Falling in a stream upon the chimney, the rays illuminated, in the way that Rembrandt would have chosen, the features of the unfortunate nobleman and those of the old sibyl, who, now, standing upon her feet and holding him by one hand, peered anxiously in his features with her light blue eyes, and, holding her long and withered forefinger within a small distance of his face, moved it slowly as if to trace the outlines, and reconcile what she recollected with that she now beheld. As she finished her scrutiny, she said, with a deep sigh: "It's a sair, sair change; and wha's fault is it? but that's written down where it will be remembered—it's written on tablets of brass with a pen of steel, where all is recorded that is done in the flesh. And what," she said, after a pause—"what is Lord Geraldin seeking from a puir auld creature like me, that's dead already, and only belangs sae far to the living that she isna yet laid in the moulds?"

"Nay," answered Lord Glenallan, "in the name of Heaven, why was it that you requested so urgently to see me? and why did you back your request by sending a token which you knew well I dared not refuse?"

As he spoke thus, he took from his purse the ring which Edie Ochiltree had delivered to him at Glenallan House. The sight of this token produced a strange and instantaneous effect upon the old woman. The palsy of fear was immediately added to that of age, and she began instantly to search her pockets with the tremulous and hasty agitation of one who becomes first apprehensive of having lost something of great importance; then, as if convinced of the reality of her fears, she turned to the Earl, and demanded: "And how came ye by it then? how came ye by it? I thought I had kept it sae securely. What will the Countess say?"

"You know," said the Earl—"at least you must have heard, that my mother is dead."

"Dead! are ye no imposing upon me? Has she left a' at last—lands and lordship and lineages?"

"All, all," said the Earl, "as mortals must leave all human vanities."

"I mind now," answered Elspeth, "I heard of it before; but there has been sic distress in our house since, and my memory is sae muckle impaired. But ye are sure your mother, the Lady Countess, is gane hame?"

The Earl again assured her that her former mistress was no more.

"Then," said Elspeth, "it shall burden my mind nae langer! When she lived, wha dared to speak what it would hae displeased her to hae had noised abroad? But she's gane, and I will confess all."

Then, turning to her son and daughter-in-law, she commanded them imperatively to quit the house, and leave Lord Geraldin (for so she still called him) alone with her. But Maggie Mucklebackit, her first burst of grief being over, was by no means disposed in her own house to pay passive obedience to the commands of her mother-in-law, an authority which is peculiarly obnoxious to persons in her rank of life, and which she was the more astonished at hearing revived, when it seemed to have been so long relinquished and forgotten.

"It was an unco thing," she said, in a grumbling tone of voice, for the rank of Lord Glenallan was somewhat imposing —"it was an unco thing to bid a mother leave her ain house wi' the tear in her ee, the moment her eldest son had carried a corpse out at the door o't."

The fisherman, in a stubborn and sullen tone, added to the same purpose: "This is nae day for your auld-warld stories, mother. My lord, if he be a lord, may ca' some other day,

or he may speak out what he has gotten to say if he likes it.
There's nane here will think it worth their while to listen to
him or you either. But neither for laird or loon, gentle or
semple, will I leave my ain house to pleasure ony body on the
very day my poor——"

Here his voice choked and he could proceed no farther; but
as he had risen when Lord Glenallan came in, and had since
remained standing, he now threw himself doggedly upon a
seat, and remained in the sullen posture of one who was determined to keep his word.

. But the old woman, whom this crisis seemed to repossess in
all those powers of mental superiority with which she had
once been eminently gifted, arose, and, advancing towards
him, said with a solemn voice: "My son, as ye wad shun
hearing of your mother's shame, as ye wad not willingly be a
witness of her guilt, as ye wad deserve her blessing and avoid
her curse, I charge ye, by the body that bore and that nursed
ye, to leave me at freedom to speak with Lord Geraldin what
nae mortal ears but his ain maun listen to. Obey my words,
that when ye lay the moulds on my head—and oh, that the
day were come!—ye may remember this hour without the reproach of having disobeyed the last earthly command that
ever your mother wared on you."

The terms of this solemn charge revived in the fisherman's
heart the habit of instinctive obedience in which his mother
had trained him up, and to which he had submitted implicitly
while her powers of exacting it remained entire. The recollection mingled also with the prevailing passion of the moment; for, glancing his eye at the bed on which the dead body
had been laid, he muttered to himself: "*He* never disobeyed
me, in reason or out o' reason, and what for should I vex *her?*"
Then taking his reluctant spouse by the arm, he led her
gently out of the cottage and latched the door behind them
as he left it.

As the unhappy parents withdrew, Lord Glenallan, to prevent the old woman from relapsing into her lethargy, again
pressed her on the subject of the communication which she
proposed to make to him.

"Ye will have it sune eneugh," she replied; "my mind's clear eneugh now, and there is not—I think there is not—a chance of my forgetting what I have to say. My dwelling at Craigburnfoot is before my een, as it were present in reality —the green bank, with its selvidge, just where the burn met wi' the sea; the twa little barks, wi' their sails furled, lying in the natural cove which it formed; the high cliff that joined it with the pleasure-grounds of the house of Glenallan, and hung right ower the stream. Ah! yes, I may forget that I had a husband and have lost him, that I hae but ane alive of our four fair sons, that misfortune upon misfortune has de-voured our ill-gotten wealth, that they carried the corpse of my son's eldest-born frae the house this morning; but I never can forget the days I spent at bonny Craigburnfoot!"

"You were a favourite of my mother," said Lord Glenallan, desirous to bring her back to the point, from which she was wandering.

"I was—I was; ye needna mind me o' that. She brought me up abune my station, and wi' knowledge mair than my fellows; but, like the tempter of auld, wi' the knowledge of gude she taught me the knowledge of evil."

"For God's sake, Elspeth," said the astonished Earl, "pro-ceed, if you can, to explain the dreadful hints you have thrown out! I well know you are confidant to one dreadful secret, which should split this roof even to hear it named; but speak on farther."

"I will," she said—"I will; just bear wi' me for a little"; and again she seemed lost in recollection, but it was no longer tinged with imbecility or apathy. She was now entering upon the topic which had long loaded her mind, and which doubt-less often occupied her whole soul at times when she seemed dead to all around her. And I may add as a remarkable fact, that such was the intense operation of mental energy upon her physical powers and nervous system, that, notwithstand-ing her infirmity of deafness, each word that Lord Glenallan spoke during this remarkable conference, although in the lowest tone of horror or agony, fell as full and distinct upon Elspeth's ear as it could have done at any period of her life.

She spoke also herself clearly, distinctly, and slowly, as if anxious that the intelligence she communicated should be fully understood—concisely at the same time, and with none of the verbiage or circumlocutory additions natural to those of her sex and condition. In short, her language bespoke a better education, as well as an uncommonly firm and resolved mind, and a character of that sort from which great virtues or great crimes may be naturally expected. The tenor of her communication is disclosed in the following chapter.

CHAPTER XXXIII.

Remorse—she never forsakes us.
A bloodhound stanch, she tracks our rapid step
Through the wild labyrinth of youthful frenzy,
Unheard, perchance, until old age hath tamed us;
Then in our lair, when Time hath chill'd our joints,
And maim'd our hope of combat, or of flight,
We hear her deep-mouth'd bay, announcing all
Of wrath and woe and punishment that bides us.
Old Play.

"I NEED not tell you," said the old woman, addressing the Earl of Glenallan, "that I was the favourite and confidential attendant of Joscelind, Countess of Glenallan, whom God assoilzie (here she crossed herself), and I think, farther, ye may not have forgotten that I shared her regard for mony years. I returned it by the maist sincere attachment, but I fell into disgrace frae a trifling act of disobedience, reported to your mother by ane that thought—and she wasna wrang—that I was a spy upon her actions and yours."

"I charge thee, woman," said the Earl, in a voice trembling with passion, "name not her name in my hearing!"

"I MUST," returned the penitent firmly and calmly, "or how can you understand me?"

The Earl leaned upon one of the wooden chairs of the hut, drew his hat over his face, clenched his hands together, set his teeth like one who summons up courage to undergo a painful operation, and made a signal to her to proceed.

22

"I say then," she resumed, "that my disgrace with my mistress was chiefly owing to Miss Eveline Neville, then bred up in Glenallan House as the daughter of a cousin-german and intimate friend of your father that was gane. There was muckle mystery in her history, but wha dared to inquire farther than the Countess liked to tell? All in Glenallan House loved Miss Neville—all but twa, your mother and mysell: we baith hated her."

"God! for what reason, since a creature so mild, so gentle, so formed to inspire affection never walked on this wretched world?"

"It may hae been sae," rejoined Elspeth, "but your mother hated a' that cam of your father's family—a' but himsell. Her reasons related to strife which fell between them soon after her marriage; the particulars are naething to this purpose. But oh, doubly did she hate Eveline Neville when she perceived that there was a growing kindness atween you and that unfortunate young leddy! Ye may mind that the Countess's dislike didna gang farther at first than just showing o' the cauld shouther—at least it wasna seen farther; but at the lang run it brak out into such downright violence that Miss Neville was even fain to seek refuge at Knockwinnock Castle with Sir Arthur's leddy, wha—God sain her!—was then wi' the living."

"You rend my heart by recalling these particulars. But go on, and may my present agony be accepted as additional penance for the involuntary crime!"

"She had been absent some months," continued Elspeth, "when I was ae night watching in my hut the return of my husband from fishing, and shedding in private those bitter tears that my proud spirit wrung frae me whenever I thought on my disgrace. The sneck was drawn, and the Countess, your mother, entered my dwelling. I thought I had seen a spectre, for, even in the height of my favour, this was an honour she had never done me, and she looked as pale and ghastly as if she had risen from the grave. She sate down and wrung the draps from her hair and cloak, for the night was drizzling, and her walk had been through the plantations, that were a' loaded with dew. I only mention these things that you may understand how weel that night lives in my memory,—and weel it may. I was surprised to see her, but I durstna speak first, mair than if I had seen a phantom. Na, I durst not, my lord, I that hae seen mony sights of terror, and never shook at them. Sae, after a silence, she said: 'Elspeth Cheyne'—for she always gave me my maiden name—'are not ye the daughter of that Reginald Cheyne who died to save his master, Lord Glenallan, on the field of Sherriffmuir?' And I answered her as proudly as hersell nearly: 'As sure as you are the daughter of that Earl of Glenallan whom my father saved that day by his own death.'"

Here she made a deep pause.

"And what followed? what followed? For Heaven's sake, good woman— But why should I use that word! Yet, good or bad, I command you to tell me."

"And little I should value earthly command," answered Elspeth, "were there not a voice that has spoken to me sleeping and waking, that drives me forward to tell this sad tale. Aweel, my lord, the Countess said to me: 'My son loves Eveline Neville; they are agreed, they are plighted. Should they have a son my right over Glenallan merges: I sink from that moment from a Countess into a miserable stipendiary dowager; I, who brought lands and vassals, and high blood and ancient fame to my husband, I must cease to be mistress when my son has an heir-male. But I care not for that; had he married any but one of the hated Nevilles, I had been patient. But for them—that they and their descendants should enjoy the right and honours of my ancestors goes through my heart like a two-edged dirk. And this girl—I detest her!' And I answered, for my heart kindled at her words, that her hate was equalled by mine."

"Wretch!" exclaimed the Earl, in spite of his determination to preserve silence—"wretched woman! what cause of hate could have arisen from a being so innocent and gentle?"

"I hated what my mistress hated, as was the use with the liege vassals of the house of Glenallan; for though, my lord, I married under my degree, yet an ancestor of yours never

went to the field of battle but an ancestor of the frail, demented, auld, useless wretch wha now speaks with you carried
his shield before him. But that was not a'," continued the
beldam, her earthly and evil passions rekindling as she became
heated in her narration—"that was not a'; I hated Miss Eveline Neville for her ain sake. I brought her frae England,
and during our whole journey she gecked and scorned at my
northern speech and habit, as her southland leddies and
kimmers had done at the boarding-school, as they ca'd it"
(and, strange as it may seem, she spoke of an affront offered
by a heedless school-girl without intention with a degree of
inveteracy which, at such a distance of time, a mortal offence
would neither have authorised or excited in any well-consti-
tuted mind). "Yes, she scorned and jested at me; but let
them that scorn the tartan fear the dirk!"

She paused, and then went on. "But I deny not that I
hated her mair than she deserved. My mistress, the Countess,
persevered and said: 'Elspeth Cheyne, this unruly boy will
marry with the false English blood. Were days as they have
been, I could throw her into the massymore of Glenallan, and
fetter him in the keep of Strathbonnel. But these times are
past, and the authority which the nobles of the land should
exercise is delegated to quibbling lawyers and their baser dependents. Hear me, Elspeth Cheyne! If you are your father's daughter as I am mine, I will find means that they shall
not marry. She walks often to that cliff that overhangs your
dwelling to look for her lover's boat'—ye may remember the
pleasure ye then took on the sea, my lord—'let him find her
forty fathom lower than he expects!' Yes! ye may stare and
frown and clench your hand, but, as sure as I am to face the
only Being I ever feared—and oh that I had feared Him
mair!—these were your mother's words. What avails it to
me to lie to you? But I wadna consent to stain my hand
with blood. Then she said: 'By the religion of our holy
Church they are ower sib thegither. But I expect nothing
but that both will become heretics as well as disobedient rep-
robates,'" that was her addition to that argument. And then,
as the fiend is ever ower busy wi' brains like mine, that are

subtle beyond their use and station, I was unhappily permitted to add: 'But they might be brought to think themselves sae sib as no Christian law will permit their wedlock.'"

Here the Earl of Glenallan echoed her words with a shriek so piercing as almost to rend the roof of the cottage: "Ah! then Eveline Neville was not the—the——"

"The daughter, ye would say, of your father?" continued Elspeth. "No, be it a torment or be it a comfort to you, ken the truth, she was nae mair a daughter of your father's house than I am."

"Woman, deceive me not; make me not curse the memory of the parent I have so lately laid in the grave, for sharing in a plot the most cruel, the most infernal——"

"Bethink ye, my Lord Geraldin, ere ye curse the memory of a parent that's gane, is there none of the blood of Glenallan living whose faults have led to this dreadfu' catastrophe?"

"Mean you my brother? he too is gone," said the Earl.

"No," replied the sibyl, "I mean yoursell, Lord Geraldin. Had you not transgressed the obedience of a son by wedding Eveline Neville in secret while a guest at Knockwinnock, our plot might have separated you for a time, but would have left at least your sorrows without remorse to canker them. But your ain conduct had put poison in the weapon that we threw, and it pierced you with the mair force because ye cam rushing to meet it. Had your marriage been a proclaimed and acknowledged action, our stratagem to throw an obstacle into your way that couldna be got ower neither wad nor could hae been practised against ye."

"Great Heaven!" said the unfortunate nobleman, "it is as if a film fell from my obscured eyes! Yes, I now well understand the doubtful hints of consolation thrown out by my wretched mother, tending indirectly to impeach the evidence of the horrors of which her arts had led me to believe myself guilty."

"She could not speak mair plainly," answered Elspeth, "without confessing her ain fraud, and she would have submitted to be torn by wild horses rather than unfold what she had done; and, if she had still lived, so would I for her sake.

They were stout hearts the race of Glenallan, male and female, and sae were a' that in auld times cried their gathering-word of 'Clochnaben'; they stood shouther to shouther. Nae man parted frae his chief for love of gold or of gain, or of right or of wrang. The times are changed, I hear, now."

The unfortunate nobleman was too much wrapped up in his own confused and distracting reflections to notice the rude expressions of savage fidelity, in which, even in the latest ebb of life, the unhappy author of his misfortunes seemed to find a stern and stubborn source of consolation.

"Great Heaven!" he exclaimed, "I am then free from a guilt the most horrible with which man can be stained, and the sense of which, however involuntary, has wrecked my peace, destroyed my health, and bowed me down to an untimely grave. Accept," he fervently uttered, lifting his eyes upwards—"accept my humble thanks! If I live miserable, at least I shall not die stained with that unnatural guilt! And thou, proceed, if thou hast more to tell—proceed, while thou hast voice to speak it and I have powers to listen."

"Yes," answered the beldam, "the hour when you shall hear and I shall speak is indeed passing rapidly away. Death has crossed your brow with his finger, and I find his grasp turning every day caulder at my heart. Interrupt me nae mair with exclamations and groans and accusations, but hear my tale to an end! And then—if ye be indeed sic a Lord of Glenallan as I hae heard of in *my* day—make your merrymen gather the thorn, and the brier, and the green hollin, till they heap them as high as the house-riggin', and burn—burn—burn the auld witch Elspeth, and a' that can put ye in mind that sic a creature ever crawled upon the land!"

"Go on," said the Earl—"go on; I will not again interrupt you."

He spoke in a half-suffocated yet determined voice, resolved that no irritability on his part should deprive him of this opportunity of acquiring proofs of the wonderful tale he then heard. But Elspeth had become exhausted by a continuous narration of such unusual length; the subsequent part of her story was more broken, and, though still distinctly intelligible in most parts, had no longer the lucid conciseness which the first part of her narrative had displayed to such an astonishing degree. Lord Glenallan found it necessary, when she had made some attempts to continue her narrative without success, to prompt her memory, by demanding what proofs she could propose to bring of the truth of a narrative so different from that which she had originally told.

"The evidence," she replied, "of Eveline Neville's real birth was in the Countess's possession, with reasons for its being for some time kept private. They may yet be found, if she has not destroyed them, in the left-hand drawer of the ebony cabinet that stood in the dressing-room; these she meant to suppress for the time, until you went abroad again, when she trusted, before your return, to send Miss Neville back to her ain country or to get her settled in marriage."

"But did you not show me letters of my father's which seemed to me, unless my senses altogether failed me in that horrible moment, to avow his relationship to—to the unhappy——"

"We did; and, with my testimony, how could you doubt the fact, or her either? But we suppressed the true explanation of these letters, and that was, that your father thought it right the young leddy should pass for his daughter for a while, on account o' some family reasons that were amang them."

"But wherefore, when you learned our union, was this dreadful artifice persisted in?"

"It wasna," she replied, "till Lady Glenallan had communicated this fause tale that she suspected ye had actually made a marriage; nor even then did you avow it sae as to satisfy her whether the ceremony had in verity passed atween ye or no. But ye remember—Oh ye canna but remember—weel what passed in that awfu' meeting!"

"Woman! you swore upon the Gospels to the fact which you now disavow."

"I did, and I wad hae taen a yet mair holy pledge on it, if there had been ane; I wad not hae spared the blood of my body or the guilt of my soul to serve the house of Glenallan."

"Wretch! do you call that horrid perjury, attended with consequences yet more dreadful—do you esteem that a service to the house of your benefactors?"

"I served her wha was then the head of Glenallan as she required me to serve her. The cause was between God and her conscience, the manner between God and mine. She is gane to her account, and I maun follow. Have I tauld ye a'?"

"No," answered Lord Glenallan; "you have yet more to tell: you have to tell me of the death of the angel whom your perjury drove to despair, stained, as she thought herself, with a crime so horrible. Speak truth: was that dreadful—was that horrible incident," he could scarcely articulate the words—"was it as reported? or was it an act of yet further, though not more atrocious, cruelty, inflicted by others?"

"I understand you," said Elspeth; "but report spoke truth: our false witness was indeed the cause, but the deed was her ain distracted act. On that fearfu' disclosure, when ye rushed frae the Countess's presence and saddled your horse and left the castle like a fire-flaught, the Countess hadna yet discovered your private marriage; she hadna found out that the union, which she had framed this awfu' tale to prevent, had e'en taen place. Ye fled from the house as if the fire o' Heaven was about to fa' upon it, and Miss Neville, atween reason and the want o't, was put under sure ward. But the ward sleep't, and the prisoner waked, the window was open, the way was before her, there was the cliff, and there was the sea! Oh, when will I forget that!"

"And thus died," said the Earl, "even so as was reported?"

"No, my lord. I had gane out to the cove; the tide was in, and it flowed, as ye'll remember, to the foot of that cliff; it was a great convenience that for my husband's trade. Where am I wandering? I saw a white object dart frae the tap o' the cliff like a sea-maw through the mist, and then a heavy flash and sparkle of the waters showed me it was a human creature that had fa'en into the waves. I was bold and strong, and familiar with the tide. I rushed in and grasped her gown, and drew her out and carried her on my shouthers—I could hae carried twa sic then—carried her to my hut, and laid her on my bed. Neighbours cam and brought help; but the words she uttered in her ravings, when she got back the use of speech, were such that I was fain to send them awa, and get up word to Glenallan House. The Countess sent down her Spanish servant Teresa—if ever there was a fiend on earth in human form that woman was ane. She and I were to watch the unhappy leddy, and let no other person approach. God knows what Teresa's part was to hae been: she tauld it not to me; but Heaven took the conclusion in its ain hand. The poor leddy! she took the pangs of travail before her time, bore a male child, and died in the arms of me—of her mortal enemy! Ay, ye may weep! She was a sightly creature to see to; but think ye, if I didna mourn her then, that I can mourn her now? Na, na! I left Teresa wi' the dead corpse and new-born babe till I gaed up to take the Countess's commands what was to be done. Late as it was, I ca'd her up, and she gar'd me ca' up your brother——"

"My brother?"

"Yes, Lord Geraldin, e'en your brother, that some said she aye wished to be her heir. At ony rate, he was the person maist concerned in the succession and heritance of the house of Glenallan."

"And is it possible to believe, then, that my brother, out of avarice to grasp at my inheritance, would lend himself to such a base and dreadful stratagem?"

"Your mother believed it," said the old beldam with a fiendish laugh; "it was nae plot of my making, but what they did or said I will not say, because I did not hear. Lang and sair they consulted in the black wainscot dressing-room; and when your brother passed through the room where I was waiting it seemed to me—and I have often thought sae since syne—that the fire of hell was in his cheek and een. But he had left some of it with his mother at ony rate. She entered the room like a woman demented, and the first words she spoke were: 'Elspeth Cheyne, did ye ever pull a new-budded flower?' I answered, as ye may believe, that I often had. 'Then,' said she, 'ye will ken the better how to blight the spurious and heretical blossom that has sprung forth this night to disgrace my father's noble house. See here—and she gave me a golden bodkin—nothing but gold must shed the blood of Glenallan. This child is already as one of the dead, and since thou and Teresa alone ken that it lives, let it be dealt upon as ye will answer to me!' and she turned away in her fury, and left me with the bodkin in my hand. Here it is: that and the ring of Miss Neville are a' I hae preserved of my ill-gotten gear, for muckle was the gear I got. And weel hae I keepit the secret, but no for the gowd or gear either."

Her long and bony hand held out to Lord Glenallan a gold bodkin, down which in fancy he saw the blood of his infant trickling.

"Wretch! had you the heart?"

"I kenna if I could hae had it or no. I returned to my cottage without feeling the ground that I trode on; but Teresa and the child were gane, a' that was alive was gane—naething left but the lifeless corpse."

"And did you never learn my infant's fate?"

"I could but guess. I have tauld ye your mother's purpose, and I ken Teresa was a fiend. She was never mair seen in Scotland, and I have heard that she returned to her ain land. A dark curtain has fa'en ower the past, and the few that witnessed ony part of it could only surmise something of seduction and suicide. You yoursell——"

"I know—I know it all," answered the Earl.

"You indeed know all that I can say. And now, heir of Glenallan, can you forgive me?"

"Ask forgiveness of God, and not of man," said the Earl, turning away.

"And how shall I ask of the pure and unstained what is denied to me by a sinner like mysell? If I hae sinned, hae I not suffered? Hae I had a day's peace or an hour's rest since these lang wet locks of hair first lay upon my pillow at Craigburnfoot? Has not my house been burned, wi' my bairn in the cradle? Have not my boats been wrecked, when a' others weathered the gale? Have not a' that were near and dear to me dree'd penance for my sin? Has not the fire had its share o' them, the winds had their part, the sea had her part? And oh!" she added, with a lengthened groan, looking first upwards towards heaven, and then bending her eyes on the floor—"oh! that the earth would take her part that's been lang, lang wearying to be joined to it!"

Lord Glenallan had reached the door of the cottage, but the generosity of his nature did not permit him to leave the unhappy woman in this state of desperate reprobation. "May God forgive thee, wretched woman," he said, "as sincerely as I do! Turn for mercy to Him who can alone grant mercy, and may your prayers be heard as if they were mine own! I will send a religious man."

"Na, na, nae priest! nae priest!" she ejaculated; and the door of the cottage opening as she spoke prevented her from proceeding.

CHAPTER XXXIV.

> Still in his dead hand clench'd remain the strings
> That thrill his father's heart, e'en as the limb,
> Lopp'd off and laid in grave, retains, they tell us,
> Strange commerce with the mutilated stump,
> Whose nerves are twinging still in maim'd existence.
> *Old Play.*

THE Antiquary, as we informed the reader in the end of the thirty-first chapter, had shaken off the company of worthy Mr. Blattergowl, although he offered to entertain him with a abstract of the ablest speech he had ever known in the teind court, delivered by the procurator for the church in the remarkable case of the parish of Gatherem. Resisting this temptation, our senior preferred a solitary path, which again conducted him to the cottage of Mucklebackit. When he came in front of the fisherman's hut, he observed a man working intently, as if to repair a shattered boat which lay upon the beach, and, going up to him, was surprised to find it was Mucklebackit himself. "I am glad," he said, in a tone of sympathy—"I am glad, Saunders, that you feel yourself able to make this exertion."

"And what would ye have me to do," answered the fisher, gruffly, "unless I wanted to see four children starve, because ane is drowned? It's weel wi' you gentles, that can sit in the house wi' handkerchers at your een when ye lose a friend; but the like o' us maun to our wark again, if our hearts were beating as hard as my hammer."

Without taking more notice of Oldbuck, he proceeded in his labour; and the Antiquary, to whom the display of human nature under the influence of agitating passions was never indifferent, stood beside him in silent attention, as if watching the progress of the work. He observed more than once the man's hard features, as if by the force of association, prepare to accompany the sound of the saw and hammer with his usual symphony of a rude tune hummed or whistled, and as often a slight twitch of convulsive expression showed that ere the sound was uttered a cause for suppressing it rushed upon his mind. At length, when he had patched a considerable rent and was beginning to mend another, his feelings appeared altogether to derange the power of attention necessary for his work. The piece of wood which he was about to nail on was at first too long; then he sawed it off too short; then chose another equally ill adapted for the purpose. At length, throwing it down in anger, after wiping his dim eye with his quivering hand, he exclaimed: "There is a curse either on me or on this auld black bitch of a boat, that I have hauled up high and dry, and patched and clouted sae mony years, that she might down my poor Steenie at the end of them, an' be d—d to her!" and he flung his hammer against the boat, as if she had been the intentional cause of his misfortune. Then recollecting himself, he added: "Yet what needs ane be angry at her, that has neither soul nor sense? though I am no that muckle better mysell. She's but a rickle o' auld rotten deals nailed thegither, and warped wi' the wind and the sea; and I am a dour carle, battered by foul weather at sea and land till I am maist as senseless as hersell. She maun be mended though again' the morning tide; that's a thing o' necessity."

Thus speaking, he went to gather together his instruments

and attempt to resume his labour, but Oldbuck took him kindly by the arm. "Came, come," he said, "Saunders, there is
no work for you this day; I'll send down Shavings, the carpenter, to mend the boat, and he may put the day's work into
my account; and you had better not come out to-morrow, but
stay to comfort your family under this dispensation, and the
gardener will bring you some vegetables and meal from Monkbarns."

"I thank ye, Monkbarns," answered the poor fisher; "I
am a plain-spoken man, and hae little to say for mysell; I
might hae learned fairer fashions frae my mither lang syne, but
I never saw muckle gude they did her; however, I thank ye.
Ye were aye kind and neighbourly, whatever folk says o' your
being near and close; and I hae often said in thae times when
they were ganging to raise up the puir folk against the gentles—I hae often said, ne'er a man should steer a hair touching to Monkbarns while Steenie and I could wag a finger; and
so said Steenie too. And, Monkbarns, when ye laid his head
in the grave—and mony thanks for the respect—ye saw the
mouls laid on an honest lad that likit you weel, though he
made little phrase about it."

Oldbuck, beaten from the pride of his affected cynicism,
would not willingly have had any one by upon that occasion
to quote to him his favourite maxims of the Stoic philosophy.
The large drops fell fast from his own eyes as he begged the
father, who was now melted at recollecting the bravery and
generous sentiments of his son, to forbear useless sorrow, and
led him by the arm towards his own home, where another
scene awaited our Antiquary. As he entered, the first person
whom he beheld was Lord Glenallan.

Mutual surprise was in their countenances as they saluted
each other, with haughty reserve on the part of Mr. Oldbuck
and embarrassment on that of the Earl.

"My Lord Glenallan, I think?" said Mr. Oldbuck.

"Yes, much changed from what he was when he knew Mr.
Oldbuck."

"I do not mean," said the Antiquary, "to intrude upon
your lordship; I only came to see this distressed family."

"And you have found one, sir, who has still greater claims on your compassion."

"My compassion! Lord Glenallan cannot need *my* compassion; if Lord Glenallan could need it, I think he would hardly ask it."

"Our former acquaintance," said the Earl——

"Is of such ancient date, my lord, was of such short duration, and was connected with circumstances so exquisitely painful, that I think we may dispense with renewing it."

So saying, the Antiquary turned away and left the hut; but Lord Glenallan followed him into the open air, and, in spite of a hasty "Good morning, my lord," requested a few minutes' conversation, and the favour of his advice in an important matter.

"Your lordship will find many more capable to advise you, my lord, and by whom your intercourse will be deemed an honour. For me, I am a man retired from business and the world, and not very fond of raking up the past events of my useless life; and forgive me if I say I have particular pain in reverting to that period of it when I acted like a fool, and your lordship like——" He stopped short.

"Like a villain, you would say," said Lord Glenallan; "for such I must have appeared to you."

"My lord, my lord, I have no desire to hear your shrift," said the Antiquary.

"But, sir, if I can show you that I am more sinned against than sinning, that I have been a man miserable beyond the power of description, and who looks forward at this moment to an untimely grave as to a haven of rest, you will not refuse the confidence which, accepting your appearance at this critical moment as a hint from Heaven, I venture thus to press on you."

"Assuredly, my lord, I shall shun no longer the continuation of this extraordinary interview."

"I must then recall to you our occasional meetings upwards of twenty years since at Knockwinnock Castle, and I need not remind you of a lady who was then a member of that family."

"The unfortunate Miss Eveline Neville, my lord, I remember it well."

"Towards whom you entertained sentiments——"

"Very different from those with which I before and since have regarded her sex; her gentleness, her docility, her pleasure in the studies which I pointed out to her, attached my affections more than became my age—though that was not then much advanced—or the solidity of my character. But I need not remind your lordship of the various modes in which you indulged your gaiety at the expense of an awkward and retired student, embarrassed by the expression of feelings so new to him, and I have no doubt that the young lady joined you in the well-deserved ridicule. It is the way of womankind. I have spoken at once to the painful circumstances of my addresses and their rejection, that your lordship may be satisfied everything is full in my memory, and may, so far as I am concerned, tell your story without scruple or needless delicacy."

"I will," said Lord Glenallan; "but first let me say, you do injustice to the memory of the gentlest and kindest, as well as to the most unhappy, of women to suppose she could make a jest of the honest affection of a man like you. Frequently did she blame me, Mr. Oldbuck, for indulging my levity at your expense. May I now presume you will excuse the gay freedoms which then offended you? My state of mind has never since laid me under the necessity of apologising for the inadvertencies of a light and happy temper."

"My lord, you are fully pardoned," said Mr. Oldbuck. "You should be aware that, like all others, I was ignorant at the time that I placed myself in competition with your lordship, and understood that Miss Neville was in a state of dependence which might make her prefer a competent independence and the hand of an honest man. But I am wasting time; I would I could believe that the views entertained towards her by others were as fair and honest as mine!"

"Mr. Oldbuck, you judge harshly."

"Not without cause, my lord. When I only, of all the magistrates of this county, having neither, like some of them, the honour to be connected with your powerful family, nor like others, the meanness to fear it—when I made some inquiry into the manner of Miss Neville's death—I shake you, my lord, but I must be plain—I do own I had every reason to believe that she had met most unfair dealing, and had either been imposed upon by a counterfeit marriage, or that very strong measures had been adopted to stifle and destroy the evidence of a real union. And I cannot doubt in my own mind that this cruelty on your lordship's part, whether coming of your own free will or proceeding from the influence of the late Countess, hurried the unfortunate young lady to the desperate act by which her life was terminated."

"You are deceived, Mr. Oldbuck, into conclusions which are not just, however naturally they flow from the circumstances. Believe me, I respected you even when I was most embarrassed by your active attempts to investigate our family misfortunes. You showed yourself more worthy of Miss Neville than I by the spirit with which you persisted in vindicating her reputation even after her death. But the firm belief, that your well-meant efforts could only serve to bring to light a story too horrible to be detailed, induced me to join my unhappy mother in schemes to remove or destroy all evidence of the legal union which had taken place between Eveline and myself. And now let us sit down on this bank, for I feel unable to remain longer standing, and have the goodness to listen to the extraordinary discovery which I have this day made."

They sate down accordingly; and Lord Glenallan briefly narrated his unhappy family history, his concealed marriage; the horrible invention by which his mother had designed to render impossible that union which had already taken place. He detailed the arts by which the Countess, having all the documents relative to Miss Neville's birth in her hands, had produced those only relating to a period during which, for family reasons, his father had consented to own that young lady as his natural daughter, and showed how impossible it was that he could either suspect or detect the fraud put upon him by his mother, and vouched by the oaths of her attendants, Teresa and Elspeth. "I left my paternal mansion," he concluded, "as if the furies of hell had driven me forth, and travelled with frantic velocity I knew not whither. Nor have I the slightest recollection of what I did or whither I went, until I was discovered by my brother. I will not trouble you with an account of my sick-bed and recovery, or how, long afterwards, I ventured to inquire after the sharer of my misfortunes, and heard that her despair had found a dreadful remedy for all the ills of life. The first thing that roused me to thought was hearing of your inquiries into this cruel business; and you will hardly wonder that, believing what I did believe, I should join in those expedients to stop your investigation which my brother and mother had actively commenced. The information which I gave them concerning the circumstances and witnesses of our private marriage enabled them to baffle your zeal. The clergyman, therefore, and witnesses, as persons who had acted in the matter only to please the powerful heir of Glenallan, were accessible to his promises and threats, and were so provided for that they had no objections to leave this country for another. For myself, Mr. Oldbuck," pursued this unhappy man, "from that moment I considered myself as blotted out of the book of the living, and as having nothing left to do with this world. My mother tried to reconcile me to life by every art, even by intimations which I can now interpret as calculated to produce a doubt of the horrible tale she herself had fabricated. But I construed all she said as the fictions of maternal affection. I will forbear all reproach; she is no more, and, as her wretched associate said, she knew not how the dart was poisoned, or how deep it must sink, when she threw it from her hand. But, Mr. Oldbuck, if ever during these twenty years there crawled upon earth a living being deserving of your pity, I have been that man. My food has not nourished me, my sleep has not refreshed me, my devotions have not comforted me, all that is cheering and necessary to man has been to me converted into poison. The rare and limited intercourse which I have held with others has been most odious to me. I felt as if I were bringing the contamination of unnatural and inexpressible guilt among the gay and the innocent. There have been moments when I had

23

thoughts of another description—to plunge into the adventures of war, or to brave the dangers of the traveller in foreign and barbarous climates, to mingle in political intrigue, or to retire to the stern seclusion of the anchorites of our religion. All these are thoughts which have alternately passed through my mind, but each required an energy which was mine no longer after the withering stroke I had received. I vegetated on as I could in the same spot, fancy, feeling, judgment, and health gradually decaying, like a tree whose bark has been destroyed, when first the blossoms fade, then the boughs, until its state resembles the decayed and dying trunk that is now before you. Do you now pity and forgive me?"

"My lord," answered the Antiquary, much affected, "my pity, my forgiveness, you have not to ask, for your dismal story is of itself not only an ample excuse for whatever appeared mysterious in your conduct, but a narrative that might move your worst enemies—and I, my lord, was never of the number—to tears and to sympathy. But permit me to ask what you now mean to do, and why you have honoured me, whose opinion can be of little consequence, with your confidence on this occasion?"

"Mr. Oldbuck," answered the Earl, "as I could never have foreseen the nature of that confession which I have heard this day, I need not say that I had no formed plan of consulting you or any one upon affairs the tendency of which I could not even have suspected. But I am without friends, unused to business, and by long retirement unacquainted alike with the laws of the land and the habits of the living generation; and when, most unexpectedly, I find myself immersed in the matters of which I know least, I catch, like a drowning man, at the first support that offers. You are that support, Mr. Oldbuck. I have always heard you mentioned as a man of wisdom and intelligence, I have known you myself as a man of a resolute and independent spirit, and there is one circumstance," said he, "which ought to combine us in some degree—our having paid tribute to the same excellence of character in poor Eveline. You offered yourself to me in my need, and you were already acquainted with the beginning of my misfortunes.

To you, therefore, I have recourse for advice, for sympathy, for support."

"You shall seek none of them in vain, my lord," said Oldbuck, "so far as my slender ability extends; and I am honoured by the preference, whether it arises from choice or is prompted by chance. But this is a matter to be ripely considered. May I ask what are your principal views at present?"

"To ascertain the fate of my child," said the Earl, "be the consequences what they may, and to do justice to the honour of Eveline, which I have only permitted to be suspected to avoid discovery of the yet more horrible taint to which I was made to believe it liable."

"And the memory of your mother?"

"Must bear its own burden," answered the Earl with a sigh; "better that she were justly convicted of deceit, should that be found necessary, than that others should be unjustly accused of crimes so much more dreadful."

"Then, my lord," said Oldbuck, "our first business must be to put the information of the old woman, Elspeth, into a regular and authenticated form."

"That," said Lord Glenallan, "will be at present, I fear, impossible. She is exhausted herself, and surrounded by her distressed family. To-morrow, perhaps, when she is alone— and yet I doubt, from her imperfect sense of right and wrong, whether she would speak out in any one's presence but my own. I too am sorely fatigued."

"Then, my lord," said the Antiquary, whom the interest of the moment elevated above points of expense and convenience, which had generally more than enough of weight with him, "I would propose to your lordship, instead of returning, fatigued as you are, so far as to Glenallan House, or taking the more uncomfortable alternative of going to a bad inn at Fairport, to alarm all the busybodies of the town—I would propose, I say, that you should be my guest at Monkbarns for this night. By to-morrow these poor people will have renewed their out-of-doors vocation, for sorrow with them affords no respite from labour; and we will visit the old woman, Elspeth, alone and take down her examination."

After a formal apology for the encroachment, Lord Glenallan agreed to go with him, and underwent with patience in their return home the whole history of John of the Girnell, a legend which Mr. Oldbuck was never known to spare any one who crossed his threshold.

The arrival of a stranger of such note, with two saddle horses and a servant in black, which servant had holsters on his saddle-bow and a coronet upon the holsters, created a general commotion in the house of Monkbarns. Jenny Rintherout, scarce recovered from the hysterics which she had taken on hearing of poor Steenie's misfortune, chased about the turkeys and poultry, cackled and screamed louder than they did, and ended by killing one-half too many. Miss Griselda made many wise reflections on the hot-headed wilfulness of her brother, who had occasioned such a devastation by suddenly bringing in upon them a papist nobleman. And she ventured to transmit to Mr. Blattergowl some hint of the unusual slaughter which had taken place in the *basse-cour*, which brought the honest clergyman to inquire how his friend Monkbarns had got home, and whether he was not the worse of being at the funeral, at a period so near the ringing of the bell for dinner that the Antiquary had no choice left but to invite him to stay and bless the meat. Miss M'Intyre had on her part some curiosity to see this mighty peer, of whom all had heard, as an Eastern caliph or sultan is heard of by his subjects, and felt some degree of timidity at the idea of encountering a person of whose unsocial habits and stern manners so many stories were told that her fear kept at least pace with her curiosity. The aged housekeeper was no less flustered and hurried in obeying the numerous and contradictory commands of here mistress concerning preserves, pastry, and fruit, the mode of marshalling and dishing the dinner, the necessity of not permitting the melted butter to run to oil, and the danger of allowing Juno—who, though formally banished from the parlour, failed not to maraud about the out-settlements of the family—to enter the kitchen.

The only inmate of Monkbarns who remained entirely indifferent on this momentous occasion was Hector M'Intyre, who cared no more for an earl than he did for a commoner, and who was only interested in the unexpected visit as it might afford some protection against his uncle's displeasure, if he harboured any, for his not attending the funeral, and still more against his satire upon the subject of his gallant but unsuccessful single combat with the *phoca* or seal.

To these, the inmates of his household, Oldbuck presented the Earl of Glenallan, who underwent with meek and subdued civility the prosing speeches of the honest divine and the lengthened apologies of Miss Griselda Oldbuck, which her brother in vain endeavoured to abridge. Before the dinner hour Lord Glenallan requested permission to retire a while to his chamber. Mr. Oldbuck accompanied his guest to the Green Room, which had been hastily prepared for his reception. He looked around with an air of painful recollection.

"I think," at length he observed—"I think, Mr. Oldbuck, that I have been in this apartment before."

"Yes, my lord," answered Oldbuck, "upon occasion of an excursion hither from Knockwinnock; and since we are upon a subject so melancholy, you may perhaps remember whose taste supplied these lines from Chaucer which now form the motto of the tapestry?"

"I guess," said the Earl, "though I cannot recollect. She excelled me, indeed, in literary taste and information, as in everything else, and it is one of the mysterious dispensations of Providence, Mr. Oldbuck, that a creature so excellent in mind and body should have been cut off in so miserable a manner, merely from her having formed a fatal attachment to such a wretch as I am."

Mr. Oldbuck did not attempt an answer to this burst of the grief which lay ever nearest to the heart of his guest, but, pressing Lord Glenallan's hand with one of his own and drawing the other across his shaggy eyelashes, as if to brush away a mist that intercepted his sight, he left the Earl at liberty to arrange himself previous to dinner.

CHAPTER XXXV.

                    Life, with you,
Glows in the brain and dances in the arteries :
'Tis like the wine some joyous guest hath quaff'd,
That glads the heart and elevates the fancy.
Mine is the poor residuum of the cup,
Vapid, and dull, and tasteless, only soiling,
With its base dregs, the vessel that contains it.
                                   Old Play.

"Now only think what a man my brother is, Mr. Blattergowl, for a wise man and a learned man, to bring this Yerl
into our house without speaking a single word to a body!
And there's the distress of thae Mucklebackits—we canna
get a fin o' fish; and we hae nae time to send ower to Fairport for beef, and the mutton's but new killed; and that silly
fliskmahoy, Jenny Rintherout, has taen the exies, and done
naething but laugh and greet, the skirl at the tail o' the guffa,
for twa days successfully; and now we maun ask that strange
man, that's as grand and as grave as the Yerl himsell, to stand
at the sideboard! And I canna gang into the kitchen to direct
ony thing, for he's hovering there making some pousowdie
for my lord, for he doesna eat like ither folk neither. And
how to sort the strange servant man at dinner-time—I am
sure, Mr. Blattergowl, a'thegither it passes my judgment."

"Truly, Miss Griselda," replied the divine, "Monkbarns
was inconsiderate. He should have taen a day to see the
invitation, as they do wi' the titular's condescendence in the
process of valuation and sale. But the great man could not
have come on a sudden to ony house in this parish where he
could have been better served with 'vivers'—that I must say,
and also that the steam from the kitchen is very gratifying
to my nostrils, and if ye have ony household affairs to attend
to, Mrs. Griselda, never make a stranger of me; I can amuse
myself very weel with the larger copy of Erskine's *Institutes*."

And, taking down from the window seat that amusing folio
(the Scottish Coke upon Littleton), he opened it, as if instinctively, at the tenth title of Book Second, "Of Teinds or

Tythes," and was presently deeply wrapped up in an abstruse discussion concerning the temporality of benefices.

The entertainment, about which Miss Oldbuck expressed so much anxiety, was at length placed upon the table; and the Earl of Glenallan, for the first time since the date of his calamity, sat at a stranger's board surrounded by strangers. He seemed to himself like a man in a dream, or one whose brain was not fully recovered from the effects of an intoxicating potion. Relieved, as he had that morning been, from the image of guilt which had so long haunted his imagination, he felt his sorrows as a lighter and more tolerable load, but was still unable to take any share in the conversation that passed around him. It was, indeed, of a cast very different from that which he had been accustomed to. The bluntness of Oldbuck, the tiresome apologetic harangues of his sister, the pedantry of the divine, and the vivacity of the young soldier, which savored much more of the camp than of the court, were all new to a nobleman who had lived in a retired and melancholy state for so many years that the manners of the world seemed to him equally strange and unpleasing. Miss M'Intyre alone, from the natural politeness and unpretending simplicity of her manners, appeared to belong to that class of society to which he had been accustomed in his earlier and better days.

Nor did Lord Glenallan's deportment less surprise the company. Though a plain but excellent family dinner was provided (for, as Mr. Blattergowl had justly said, it was impossible to surprise Miss Griselda when her larder was empty), and though the Antiquary boasted his best port, and assimilated it to the Falernian of Horace, Lord Glenallan was proof to the allurements of both. His servant placed before him a small mess of vegetables—that very dish the cooking of which had alarmed Miss Griselda—arranged with the most minute and scrupulous neatness. He eat sparingly of these provisions; and a glass of pure water, sparkling from the fountain-head, completed his repast. "Such," his servant said, "had been his lordship's diet for very many years, unless upon the high festivals of the Church, or when company of the first rank were entertained at Glenallan House, when he relaxed a little in the austerity of his diet, and permitted himself a glass or two of wine." But at Monkbarns no anchoret could have made a more simple and scanty meal.

The Antiquary was a gentleman, as we have seen, in feeling, but blunt and careless in expression, from the habit of living with those before whom he had nothing to suppress. He attacked his noble guest without scruple on the severity of his regimen.

"A few half-cold greens and potatoes, a glass of ice-cold water to wash them down—antiquity gives no warrant for it, my lord. This house used to be accounted a *hospitium*, a place of retreat for Christians; but your lordship's diet is that of a heathen Pythagorean or Indian Bramin; nay, more severe than either, if you refuse these fine apples."

"I am a Catholic, you are aware," said Lord Glenallan, wishing to escape from the discussion, "and you know that our church——"

"Lays down many rules of mortification," proceeded the dauntless Antiquary; "but I never heard that they were quite so rigorously practised. Bear witness my predecessor, John of the Girnell, or the jolly abbot who gave his name to this apple, my lord."

And as he pared the fruit, in spite of his sister's "Oh fie, Monkbarns," and the prolonged cough of the minister, accompanied by a shake of his huge wig, the Antiquary proceeded to detail the intrigue which had given rise to the fame of the abbot's apple with more slyness and circumstantiality than was at all necessary. His jest, as may readily be conceived, missed fire, for this anecdote of conventual gallantry failed to produce the slightest smile on the visage of the Earl. Oldbuck then took up the subject of Ossian, Macpherson, and MacCribb; but Lord Glenallan had never so much as heard of any of the three, so little conversant had he been with modern literature. The conversation was now in some danger of flagging, or of falling into the hands of Mr. Blattergowl, who had just pronounced the formidable word, "teind-free," when the subject of the French Revolution was started; a political event on which Lord Glenallan looked with all the prejudiced horror of a bigoted Catholic and zealous aristocrat. Oldbuck was far from carrying his detestation of its principles to such a length.

"There were many men in the first Constituent Assembly," he said, "who held sound Whiggish doctrines, and were for settling the constitution with a proper provision for the liberties of the people. And if a set of furious madmen were now in possession of the government, it was," he continued, "what often happened in great revolutions, where extreme measures are adopted in the fury of the moment, and the state resembles an agitated pendulum which swings from side to side for some time ere it can acquire its due and perpendicular station. Or it might be likened to a storm or hurricane, which, passing over a region, does great damage in its passage, yet sweeps away stagnant and unwholesome vapours, and repays, in future health and fertility, its immediate desolation and ravage."

The Earl shook his head; but, having neither spirit nor inclination for debate, he suffered the argument to pass uncontested.

This discussion served to introduce the young soldier's experiences; and he spoke of the actions in which he had been engaged with modesty, and at the same time with an air of spirit and zeal which delighted the Earl, who had been bred up, like others of his house, in the opinion that the trade of arms was the first duty of man, and believed that to employ them against the French was a sort of holy warfare.

"What would I give," said he apart to Oldbuck, as they rose to join the ladies in the drawing-room—"what would I give to have a son of such spirit as that young gentleman! He wants something of address and manner, something of polish, which mixing in good society would soon give him; but with what zeal and animation he expresses himself, how fond of his profession, how loud in the praise of others, how modest when speaking of himself!"

"Hector is much obliged to you, my lord," replied his uncle, gratified, yet not so much so as to suppress his consciousness of his own mental superiority over the young soldier; "I believe in my heart nobody ever spoke half so much good of him before, except perhaps the sergeant of his company, when he was wheedling a Highland recruit to enlist with him. He is a good lad notwithstanding, although he be not quite the hero your lordship supposes him, and although my commendations rather attest the kindness than the vivacity of his character. In fact, his high spirit is a sort of constitutional vehemence which attends him in everything he sets about, and is often very inconvenient to his friends. I saw him to-day engage in an animated contest with a *phoca* or seal—'sealgh,' our poeple more properly call them, retaining the Gothic guttural *gh*—with as much vehemence as if he had fought against Dumourier. Marry, my lord, the *phoca* had the better, as the said Dumourier had of some other folks. And he'll talk with equal if not superior rapture of the good behaviour of a pointer bitch as of the plan of a campaign."

" He shall have full permission to sport over my grounds," said the Earl, " if he is so fond of that exercise."

" You will bind him to you, my lord," said Monkbarns, " body and soul; give him leave to crack off his birding-piece at a poor covey of partridges or moor-fowl, and he's yours for ever. I will enchant him by the intelligence. But Oh, my lord, that you could have seen my phœnix Lovel! the very prince and chieftain of the youth of this age, and not destitute of spirit neither: I promise you he gave my termagant kinsman a *quid pro quo*—a Rowland for his Oliver, as the vulgar say, alluding to the two celebrated Paladins of Charlemagne."

After coffee, Lord Glenallan requested a private interview with the Antiquary, and was ushered to his library.

" I must withdraw you from your own amiable family," he said, " to involve you in the perplexities of an unhappy man. You are acquainted with the world, from which I have long been banished; for Glenallan House has been to me rather a prison than a dwelling, although a prison which I had neither fortitude nor spirit to break from."

" Let me first ask your lordship," said the Antiquary, " what are your own wishes and designs in this matter?"

" I wish most especially," answered Lord Glenallan, " to declare my luckless marriage and to vindicate the reputation of the unhappy Eveline; that is, if you see a possibility of doing so without making public the conduct of my mother."

"*Suum cuique tribuito*," said the Antiquary, "do right to every one. The memory of that unhappy young lady has too long suffered, and I think it might be cleared without further impeaching that of your mother than by letting it be understood in general that she greatly disapproved and bitterly opposed the match. All—forgive me, my lord—all who ever heard of the late Countess of Glenallan will learn that without much surprise."

"But you forget one horrible circumstance, Mr. Oldbuck," said the Earl, in an agitated voice.

"I am not aware of it," replied the Antiquary.

"The fate of the infant—its disappearance with the confidential attendant of my mother, and the dreadful surmises which may be drawn from my conversation with Elspeth."

"If you would have my free opinion, my lord," answered Mr. Oldbuck, "and will not catch too rapidly at it as matter of hope, I would say that it is very possible the child yet lives. For thus much I ascertained by my former inquiries concerning the event of that deplorable evening, that a child and woman were carried that night from the cottage at the Craigburnfoot in a carriage and four by your brother, Edward Geraldin Neville, whose journey towards England with these companions I traced for several stages. I believed then it was a part of the family compact to carry a child whom you meant to stigmatise with illegitimacy out of that country where chance might have raised protectors and proofs of its rights. But I now think that your brother, having reason, like yourself, to believe the child stained with shame yet more indelible, had nevertheless withdrawn it, partly from regard to the honour of his house, partly from the risk to which it might have been exposed in the neighbourhood of the Lady Glenallan."

As he spoke, the Earl of Glenallan grew extremely pale, and had nearly fallen from his chair. The alarmed Antiquary ran hither and thither looking for remedies; but his museum, though sufficiently well filled with a vast variety of useless matters, contained nothing that could be serviceable on the

present or any other occasion.   As he posted out of the room
to borrow his sister's salts, he could not help giving a constitutional growl of chagrin and wonder at the various incidents
which had converted his mansion, first into an hospital for a
wounded duellist and now into the sick-chamber of a dying
nobleman.   "And yet," said he, "I have always kept aloof
from the soldiery and the peerage.   My *cœnobitium* has only
next to be made a lying-in hospital, and then I trow the
transformation will be complete."

When he returned with the remedy Lord Glenallan was
much better.   The new and unexpected light which Mr. Oldbuck had thrown upon the melancholy history of his family
had almost overpowered him.   "You think, then, Mr. Oldbuck—for you are capable of thinking, which I am not—you
think, then, that it is possible—that is, not impossible—my
child may yet live?"

"I think," said the Antiquary, "it is impossible that it
could come to any violent harm through your brother's means.
He was known to be a gay and dissipated man, but not cruel
nor dishonourable; nor is it possible that, if he had intended
any foul play, he would have placed himself so forward in the
charge of the infant as I will prove to your lordship he did."

So saying, Mr. Oldbuck opened a drawer of the cabinet of
his ancestor, Aldobrand, and produced a bundle of papers tied
with a black ribband and labelled, "Examinations, etc., taken
by Jonathan Oldbuck, J. P., upon the 18th of February 17—."
A little under was written in a small hand *Eheu Evelina!*
The tears dropped fast from the Earl's eyes as he endeavoured
in vain to unfasten the knot which secured these documents.

"Your lordship," said Mr. Oldbuck, "had better not read
these at present.   Agitated as you are, and having much business before you, you must not exhaust your strength.   Your
brother's succession is now, I presume, your own, and it will
be easy for you to make inquiry among his servants and retainers, so as to hear where the child is, if, fortunately, it
shall be still alive."

"I dare hardly hope it," said the Earl, with a deep sigh;
"why should my brother have been silent to me?"

"Nay, my lord! why should he have communicated to your lordship the existence of a being whom you must have supposed the offspring of——"

"Most true; there is an obvious and a kind reason for his being silent. If anything, indeed, could have added to the horror of the ghastly dream that has poisoned my whole existence, it must have been the knowledge that such a child of misery existed."

"Then," continued the Antiquary, "although it would be rash to conclude, at the distance of more than twenty years, that your son must needs be still alive because he was not destroyed in infancy, I own I think you should instantly set on foot inquiries."

"It shall be done," replied Lord Glenallan, catching eagerly at the hope held out to him, the first he had nourished for many years; "I will write to a faithful steward of my father, who acted in the same capacity under my brother Neville; but, Mr. Oldbuck, I am not my brother's heir."

"Indeed! I am sorry for that, my lord: it is a noble estate, and the ruins of the old castle of Neville's Burgh alone, which are the most superb relics of Anglo-Norman architecture in that part of the country, are a possession much to be coveted. I thought your father had no other son or near relative."

"He had not, Mr. Oldbuck," replied Lord Glenallan; "but my brother adopted views in politics and a form of religion alien from those which had been always held by our house. Our tempers had long differed, nor did my unhappy mother always think him sufficiently observant to her. In short, there was a family quarrel, and my brother, whose property was at his own free disposal, availed himself of the power vested in him to choose a stranger for his heir. It is a matter which never struck me as being of the least consequence; for, if worldly possessions could alleviate misery, I have enough and to spare. But now I shall regret it if it throws any difficulty in the way of our inquiries; and I bethink me that it may, for, in case of my having a lawful son of my body and my brother dying without issue, my father's possessions stood entailed upon my son. It is not, therefore, likely that this heir, be he who he may, will afford us assistance in making a discovery which may turn out so much to his own prejudice."

"And in all probability the steward your lordship mentions is also in his service," said the Antiquary.

"It is most likely; and the man being a Protestant, how far it is safe to entrust him——"

"I should hope, my lord," said Oldbuck, gravely, "that a Protestant may be as trustworthy as a Catholic. I am doubly interested in the Protestant faith, my lord. My ancestor, Aldobrand Oldenbuck, printed the celebrated Confession of Augsburg, as I can show by the original edition now in this house."

"I have not the least doubt of what you say, Mr. Oldbuck," replied the Earl, "nor do I speak out of bigotry or intolerance; but probably the Protestant steward will favour the Protestant heir rather than the Catholic—if, indeed, my son has been bred in his father's faith, or alas! if indeed he yet lives."

"We must look close into this," said Oldbuck, "before committing ourselves. I have a literary friend at York, with whom I have long corresponded on the subject of the Saxon horn that is preserved in the minster there; we interchanged letters for six years, and have only as yet been able to settle the first line of the inscription. I will write forthwith to this gentleman, Dr. Dryasdust, and be particular in my inquiries concerning the character, etc., of your brother's heir, of the gentleman employed in his affairs, and what else may be likely to further your lordship's inquiries. In the mean time your lordship will collect the evidence of the marriage, which I hope can still be recovered?"

"Unquestionably," replied the Earl; "the witnesses who were formerly withdrawn from your research are still living. My tutor, who solemnised the marriage, was provided for by a living in France, and has lately returned to this country as an emigrant, a victim of his zeal for loyalty, legitimacy, and religion."

"That's one lucky consequence of the French Revolution, my lord, you must allow that at least," said Oldbuck; "but no offence, I will act as warmly in your affairs as if I were of your own faith in politics and religion. And take my advice: if you want an affair of consequence properly managed, put it into the hands of an antiquary; for, as they are eternally exercising their genius and research upon trifles, it is impossible they can be baffled in affairs of importance. Use makes perfect, and the corps that is most frequently drilled upon the parade will be most prompt in its exercise upon the day of battle. And, talking upon that subject, I would willingly read to your lordship in order to pass away the time betwixt this and supper——"

"I beg I may not interfere with family arrangements," said Lord Glenallan, "but I never taste anything after sunset."

"Nor I either, my lord," answered his host, "notwithstanding it is said to have been the custom of the ancients; but then I dine differently from your lordship, and therefore am better enabled to dispense with those elaborate entertainments which my womankind (that is, my sister and niece, my lord) are apt to place on the table, for the display rather of their own housewifery than the accommodation of our wants. However, a broiled bone, or a smoked haddock, or an oyster, or a slice of bacon of our own curing, with a toast and a tankard, or something or other of that sort, to close the orifice of the stomach before going to bed, does not fall under my restriction, nor, I hope, under your lordship's."

"My 'no supper' is literal, Mr. Oldbuck; but I will attend you at your meal with pleasure."

"Well, my lord," replied the Antiquary, "I will endeavour to entertain your ears at least, since I cannot banquet your palate. What I am about to read to your lordship relates to the upland glens."

Lord Glenallan, though he would rather have recurred to the subject of his own uncertainties, was compelled to make a sign of rueful civility and acquiescence.

The Antiquary, therefore, took out his portfolio of loose sheets, and, after premising that the topographical details here laid down were designed to illustrate a slight *Essay upon Castrametation*, which had been read with indulgence at several societies of antiquaries, he commenced as follows:

"The subject, my lord, is the hill-fort of Quickens Bog, with the site of which your lordship is doubtless familiar. It is upon your store-farm of Mantanner, in the barony of Clochnaben."

"I think I have heard the names of these places," said the Earl, in answer to the Antiquary's appeal.

"Heard the name! and the farm brings him six hundred a year. O Lord!"

Such was the scarce subdued ejaculation of the Antiquary. But his hospitality got the better of his surprise, and he proceeded to read his essay with an audible voice, in great glee at having secured a patient, and, as he fondly hoped, an interested hearer.

"Quickens Bog may at first seem to derive its name from the plant quicken, by which, *Scotticé*, we understand couch-grass, dog-grass, or the *Triticum repens* of Linnæus; and the common English monosyllable 'bog,' by which we mean, in popular language, a marsh or morass, in Latin *palus*. But it may confound the rash adopters of the more obvious etymological derivations to learn that the couch-grass or dog-grass, or, to speak scientifically, the *Triticum repens* of Linnæus, does not grow within a quarter of a mile of this *castrum* or hill-fort, whose ramparts are uniformly clothed with short verdant turf, and that we must seek a bog or *palus* at a still greater distance, the nearest being that of Gird-the-mear, a full half-mile distant. The last syllable, 'bog,' is obviously, therefore, a mere corruption of the Saxon *burgh*, which we find in the various transmutations of *burgh, burrow, brough, bruff, buff,* and *boff,* which last approaches very near the sound in question; since, supposing the word to have been originally *borgh,* which is the genuine Saxon spelling, a slight change, such as modern organs too often make upon ancient sounds, will produce first *bogh,* and then, *elisa h,* or compromising and sinking the guttural, agreeable to the common vernacular practice, you have either *boff* or *bog,* as it happens. The word 'quickens' requires in like manner to be altered—decomposed, as it were—and reduced to its original and genuine sound, ere we can discern its real meaning. By the ordinary exchange of the *qu* into *wh*, familiar to the rudest tyro who has opened a book of old Scottish poetry, we gain either Whilkens or Whichensborgh—put, we may suppose, by way of question, as if those who imposed the name, struck with the extreme antiquity of the place, had expressed in it an interrogation, 'To whom did this fortress belong?' Or, it might be Whackensburgh, from the Saxon *whacken*, to strike with the hand, as doubtless the skirmishes near a place of such apparent consequence must have legitimated such a derivation," etc. etc. etc.

I will be more merciful to my readers than Oldbuck was to his guest; for, considering his opportunities of gaining patient attention from a person of such consequence as Lord Glenallan were not many, he used, or rather abused, the present to the uttermost.

CHAPTER XXXVI.

Crabbed age and youth
  Cannot live together.
Youth is full of pleasance,
  Age is full of care ;
Youth like summer morn,
  Age like winter weather,
Youth like summer brave.
  Age like winter bare.
          SHAKSPEARE.

IN the morning of the following day the Antiquary, who was something of a sluggard, was summoned from his bed a full hour earlier than his custom by Caxon.

"What's the matter now?" he exclaimed, yawning and stretching forth his hand to the huge gold repeater, which, bedded upon his India silk handkerchief, was laid safe by his pillow—"what's the matter now, Caxon? it can't be eight o'clock yet."

"Na, sir, but my lord's man sought me out, for he fancies me your honour's valley-de-sham; and sae I am, there's nae doubt o't, baith your honour's and the minister's, at least ye hae nae other that I ken o'; and I gie a

24

help to Sir Arthur too, but that's mair in the way o' my profession."

"Well, well, never mind that," said the Antiquary, "happy is he that is his own valley-de-sham, as you call it; but why disturb my morning's rest?"

"Ou, sir, the great man's been up since peep o' day, and he's steered the town to get awa an express to fetch his carriage, and it will be here briefly, and he wad like to see your honour afore he gaes awa."

"Gadso!" ejaculated Oldbuck, "these great men use one's house and time as if they were their own property. Well, it's once and away. Has Jenny come to her senses yet, Caxon?"

"Troth, sir, but just middling," replied the barber; "she's been in a swither about the jocolate this morning, and was like to hae toomed it a' out into the slap-basin, and drank it hersell in her ecstasies; but she's won ower wi't, wi' the help o' Miss M'Intyre."

"Then all my womankind are on foot and scrambling, and I must enjoy my quiet bed no longer, if I would have a well-regulated house. Lend me my gown. And what are the news at Fairport?"

"Ou, sir, what can they be about but this grand news o' my lord," answered the old man, "that hasna been ower the doorstane, they threep to me, for this twenty years—this grand news of his coming to visit your honour!"

"Aha!" said Monkbarns, "and what do they say of that, Caxon?"

"'Deed, sir, they hae various opinions. Thae fallows that are the democraws, as they ca' them, that are again' the king and the law, and hair powder and dressing o' gentlemen's wigs—a wheen blackguards!—they say he's come doun to speak wi' your honour about bringing doun his hill lads and Highland tenantry to break up the meetings of the Friends o' the People; and when I said your honour never meddled wi' the like o' sic things where there was like to be straiks and bloodshed, they said, if ye didna, your nevoy did, and that he was weel kend to be a king's-man that wad fight knee-deep, and that ye were the head and he was the hand, and that the Yerl was to bring out the men and the siller."

"Come," said the Antiquary, laughing, "I am glad the war is to cost me nothing but counsel."

"Na, na," said Caxon, "naebody thinks your honour wad either fight yoursell or gie ony feck o' siller to ony side o' the question."

"Umph! well, that's the opinion of the democraws, as you call them. What say the rest of Fairport?"

"In troth," said the candid reporter, "I canna say it's muckle better. Captain Coquet, of the volunteers—that's him that's to be the new collector—and some of the other gentlemen of the Blue and a' Blue Club, are just saying it's no right to let papists that hae sae mony French friends as the Yerl of Glenallan gang through the country, and—but your honour will maybe be angry?"

"Not I, Caxon," said Oldbuck; "fire away as if you were Captain Coquet's whole platoon, I can stand it."

"Weel, then, they say, sir, that as ye didna encourage the petition about the peace, and wadna petition in favour of the new tax, and as ye were again' bringing in the yeomanry at the meal mob, but just for settling the folk wi' the constables —they say ye're no a gude friend to government; and that thae sort o' meetings between sic a powerfu' man as the Yerl and sic a wise man as you—odd, they think they suld be lookit after, and some say ye should baith be shankit aff till Edinburgh Castle."

"On my word," said the Antiquary, "I am infinitely obliged to my neighbours for their good opinion of me! And so I, that have never interfered with their bickerings but to recommend quiet and moderate measures, am given up on both sides as a man very likely to commit high treason, either against king or people? Give me my coat, Caxon—give me my coat. It's lucky I live not in their report. Have you heard anything of Taffril and his vessel?"

Caxon's countenance fell. "Na, sir, and the winds hae been high, and this is a fearfu' coast to cruise on in thae eastern gales: the headlands rin sae far out that a veshell's embayed afore I could sharp a razor; and then there's nae harbour or city of refuge on our coast, a' craigs and breakers. A veshell that rins ashore wi' us flees asunder like the powther when I shake the pluff, and it's as ill to gather ony o't again. I aye tell my daughter thae things when she grows wearied for a letter frae Lieutenant Taffril. It's aye an apology for him. 'Ye suldna blame him,' says I, 'hinny, for ye little ken what may hae happened.'"

"Ay, ay, Caxon, thou art as good a comforter as a *valet-de-chambre*. Give me a white stock, man; d'ye think I can go down with a handkerchief about my neck when I have company?"

"Dear sir, the Captain says a three-nookit hankercher is the maist fashionable overlay, and that stocks belang to your honour and me that are auld-warld folk. I beg pardon for mentioning us twa thegither, but it was what he said."

"The Captain's a puppy and you are a goose, Caxon."

"It's very like it may be sae," replied the acquiescent barber; "I am sure your honour kens best."

Before breakfast Lord Glenallan, who appeared in better spirits than he had evinced in the former evening, went particularly through the various circumstances of evidence which the exertions of Oldbuck had formerly collected; and, pointing out the means which he possessed of completing the proof of his marriage, expressed his resolution instantly to go through the painful task of collecting and restoring the evidence concerning the birth of Eveline Neville which Elspeth had stated to be in his mother's possession.

"And yet, Mr. Oldbuck," he said, "I feel like a man who receives important tidings ere he is yet fully awake, and doubt whether they refer to actual life or are not rather a continuation of his dream. This woman—this Elspeth—she is in the extremity of age, and approaching in many respects to dotage. Have I not—it is a hideous question—have I not been hasty in the admission of her present evidence, against that which she formerly gave me to a very—very different purpose?"

Mr. Oldbuck paused a moment, and then answered with

firmness: "No, my lord, I cannot think you have any reason to suspect the truth of what she has told you last, from no apparent impulse but the urgency of conscience. Her confession was voluntary, disinterested, distinct, consistent with itself, and with all the other known circumstances of the case. I would lose no time, however, in examining and arranging the other documents to which she has referred, and I also think her own statement should be taken down, if possible, in a formal manner. We thought of setting about this together. But it will be a relief to your lordship, and, moreover, have a more impartial appearance, were I to attempt the investigation alone, in the capacity of a magistrate. I will do this—at least I will attempt it—so soon as I shall see her in a favourable state of mind to undergo an examination."

Lord Glenallan wrung the Antiquary's hand in token of grateful acquiescence. "I cannot express to you," he said, "Mr. Oldbuck, how much your countenance and cooperation in this dark and most melancholy business gives me relief and confidence. I cannot enough applaud myself for yielding to the sudden impulse which impelled me, as it were, to drag you into my confidence, and which arose from the experience I had formerly of your firmness in discharge of your duty as a magistrate and as friend to the memory of the unfortunate. Whatever the issue of these matters may prove—and I would fain hope there is a dawn breaking on the fortunes of my house, though I shall not live to enjoy its light—but whatsoever be the issue, you have laid my family and me under the most lasting obligation."

"My lord," answered the Antiquary, "I must necessarily have the greatest respect for your lordship's family, which I am well aware is one of the most ancient in Scotland, being certainly derived from Aymer de Geraldin, who sat in parliament at Perth, in the reign of Alexander II., and who, by the less vouched yet plausible tradition of the country, is said to have been descended from the Marmor of Clochnaben. Yet, with all my veneration for your ancient descent, I must acknowledge that I find myself still more bound to give your lordship what assistance is in my limited power, from sincere sympathy with your sorrows and detestation at the frauds which have so long been practised upon you. But, my lord, the matin meal is, I see, now prepared. Permit me to show your lordship the way through the intricacies of my *cœnobi-tium*, which is rather a combination of cells, jostled oddly together, and piled one upon the top of the other, than a regular house. I trust you will make yourself some amends for the spare diet of yesterday."

But this was no part of Lord Glenallan's system. Having saluted the company with the grave and melancholy politeness which distinguished his manners, his servant placed before him a slice of toasted bread, with a glass of fair water, being the fare on which he usually broke his fast. While the morning's meal of the young soldier and the old Antiquary was despatched in a much more substantial manner, the noise of wheels was heard.

"Your lordship's carriage, I believe," said Oldbuck, stepping to the window. "On my word, a handsome *quadriga*, for such, according to the best *scholium*, was the *vox signata* of the Romans for a chariot which, like that of your lordship, was drawn by four horses."

"And I will venture to say," cried Hector, eagerly gazing from the window, "that four handsomer or better-matched bays never were put in harness. What fine forehands! What capital chargers they would make! Might I ask if they are of your lordship's own breeding?"

"I—I rather believe so," said Lord Glenallan; "but I have been so negligent of my domestic matters that I am ashamed to say I must apply to Calvert" (looking at the domestic).

"They are of your lordship's own breeding," said Calvert, "got by Mad Tom out of Jemima and Yarico, your lordship's brood mares."

"Are there more of the set?" said Lord Glenallan.

"Two, my lord—one rising four, the other five off this grass, both very handsome."

"Then let Dawkins bring them down to Monkbarns to-morrow," said the Earl. "I hope Captain M'Intyre will accept them, if they are at all fit for service."

Captain M'Intyre's eyes sparkled, and he was profuse in grateful acknowledgments; while Oldbuck, on the other hand, seizing the Earl's sleeve, endeavoured to intercept a present which boded no good to his corn-chest and hay-loft.

"My lord—my lord—much obliged—much obliged. But Hector is a pedestrian, and never mounts on horseback in battle. He is a Highland soldier, moreover, and his dress ill adapted for cavalry service. Even Macpherson never mounted his ancestors on horseback, though he has the impudence to talk of their being car-borne; and that, my lord, is what is running in Hector's head: it is the vehicular, not the equestrian exercise, which he envies—

> Sunt quos curriculo pulverem Olympicum
> Collegisse juvat.

His noddle is running on a curricle, which he has neither money to buy nor skill to drive if he had it; and I assure your lordship that the possession of two such quadrupeds would prove a greater scrape than any of his duels, whether with human foe or with my friend the *phoca*."

"You must command us all at present, Mr. Oldbuck," said the Earl, politely, "but I trust you will not ultimately prevent my gratifying my young friend in some way that may afford him pleasure?"

"Anything useful, my lord," said Oldbuck, "but no *curriculum:* I protest he might as rationally propose to keep a *quadriga* at once. And, now I think of it, what is that old post-chaise from Fairport come jingling here for? I did not send for it."

"*I* did, sir," said Hector, rather sulkily, for he was not much gratified by his uncle's interference to prevent the Earl's intended generosity, nor particularly inclined to relish either the disparagement which he cast upon his skill as a charioteer or the mortifying allusion to his bad success in the adventures of the duel and the seal.

"You did, sir?" echoed the Antiquary, in answer to his

concise information. "And pray, what may be your business with a post-chaise? Is this splendid equipage—this *biga*, as I may call it—to serve for an introduction to a *quadriga* or a *curriculum?*"

"Really, sir," replied the young soldier, "if it be necessary to give you such a specific explanation, I am going to Fairport on a little business."

"Will you permit me to inquire into the nature of that business, Hector?" answered his uncle, who loved the exercise of a little brief authority over his relative. "I should suppose any regimental affairs might be transacted by your worthy deputy the sergeant—an honest gentleman, who is so good as to make Monkbarns his home since his arrival among us—I should, I say, suppose that he may transact any business of yours, without your spending a day's pay on two dog-horses and such a combination of rotten wood, cracked glass, and leather—such a skeleton of a post-chaise, as that before the door."

"It is not regimental business, sir, that calls me; and, since you insist upon knowing, I must inform you, Caxon has brought word this morning that old Ochiltree, the beggar, is to be brought up for examination to-day, previous to his being committed for trial; and I am going to see that the poor old fellow gets fair play—that's all."

"Ay? I heard something of this, but could not think it serious. And pray, Captain Hector, who are so ready to be every man's second on all occasions of strife, civil or military, by land, by water, or on the sea-beach, what is your especial concern with old Edie Ochiltree?"

"He was a soldier in my father's company, sir," replied Hector; "and besides, when I was about to do a very foolish thing one day, he interfered to prevent me, and gave me almost as much good advice, sir, as you could have done yourself."

"And with the same good effect, I dare be sworn for it—eh, Hector? Come, confess it was thrown away."

"Indeed it was, sir; but I see no reason that my folly should make me less grateful for his intended kindness."

" Bravo, Hector! that's the most sensible thing I ever heard you say; but always tell me your plans without reserve. Why, I will go with you myself, man; I am sure the old fellow is not guilty, and I will assist him in such a scrape much more effectually than you can do. Besides, it will save thee half-a-guinea, my lad, a consideration which I heartily pray you to have more frequently before your eyes."

Lord Glenallan's politeness had induced him to turn away and talk with the ladies when the dispute between the uncle and nephew appeared to grow rather too animated to be fit for the ear of a stranger, but the Earl mingled again in the conversation when the placable tone of the Antiquary expressed amity. Having received a brief account of the mendicant, and of the accusation brought against him, which Oldbuck did not hesitate to ascribe to the malice of Dousterswivel, Lord Glenallan asked whether the individual in question had not been a soldier formerly. He was answered in the affirmative.

" Had he not," continued his lordship, " a coarse blue coat or gown, with a badge? Was he not a tall, striking-looking old man, with grey beard and hair, who kept his body remarkably erect, and talked with an air of ease and independence which formed a strong contrast to his profession?"

" All this is an exact picture of the man," returned Oldbuck.

" Why, then," continued Lord Glenallan, " although I fear I can be of no use to him in his present condition, yet I owe him a debt of gratitude for being the first person who brought me some tidings of the utmost importance. I would willingly offer him a place of comfortable retirement when he is extricated from his present situation."

" I fear, my lord," said Oldbuck, " he would have difficulty in reconciling his vagrant habits to the acceptance of your bounty—at least I know the experiment has been tried without effect. To beg from the public at large he considers as independence, in comparison to drawing his whole support from the bounty of an individual. He is so far a true philosopher as to be a contemner of all ordinary rules of hours and times. When he is hungry he eats, when thirsty he drinks,

when weary he sleeps, and with such indifference with respect
to the means and appliances about which we make a fuss, that
I suppose he was never ill-dined or ill-lodged in his life.
Then he is, to a certain extent, the oracle of the district
through which he travels—their genealogist, their newsman,
their master of the revels, their doctor at a pinch, or their
divine; I promise you he has too many duties, and is too zealous in performing them, to be easily bribed to abandon his
calling. But I should be truly sorry if they sent the poor
light-hearted old man to lie for weeks in a jail. I am convinced the confinement would break his heart."

Thus finished the conference. Lord Glenallan, having
taken leave of the ladies, renewed his offer to Captain M'Intyre
of the freedom of his manors for sporting, which was joyously
accepted.

"I can only add," he said, "that, if your spirits are not
liable to be damped by dull company, Glenallan House is at
all times open to you. On two days of the week, Friday and
Saturday, I keep my apartment, which will be rather a relief
to you, as you will be left to enjoy the society of my almoner,
Mr. Gladsmoor, who is a scholar and a man of the world."

Hector, his heart exulting at the thoughts of ranging
through the preserves of Glenallan House, and over the well-
protected moors of Clochnaben—nay, joy of joys, the deer-
forest of Strathbonnel, made many acknowledgments of the
honour and gratitude he felt. Mr. Oldbuck was sensible of
the Earl's attention to his nephew; Miss M'Intyre was pleased
because her brother was gratified; and Miss Griselda Oldbuck
looked forward with glee to the potting of whole bags of
moor-fowl and black-game, of which Mr. Blattergowl was
a professed admirer. Thus—which is always the case when
a man of rank leaves a private family where he has studied to
appear obliging—all were ready to open in praise of the Earl
as soon as he had taken his leave, and was wheeled off in his
chariot by the four admired bays. But the panegyric was
cut short, for Oldbuck and his nephew deposited themselves
in the Fairport hack, which, with one horse trotting and the
other urged to a canter, creaked, jingled, and hobbled towards

that celebrated seaport, in a manner that formed a strong contrast to the rapidity and smoothness with which Lord Glenallan's equipage had seemed to vanish from their eyes.

--------◆--------

CHAPTER XXXVII.

Yes! I love justice well, as well as you do;
But since the good dame's blind, she shall excuse me,
If, time and reason fitting, I prove dumb.
The breath I utter now shall be no means
To take away from me my breath in future.

Old Play.

By dint of charity from the town's people in aid of the load of provisions he had brought with him into durance, Edie Ochiltree had passed a day or two's confinement without much impatience, regretting his want of freedom the less as the weather proved broken and rainy.

"The prison," he said, "wasna sae dooms bad a place as it was ca'd. Ye had aye a good roof ower your head to fend aff the weather, and, if the windows werena glazed, it was the mair airy and pleasant for the summer season. And there were folk enow to crack wi', and he had bread eneugh to eat, and what need he fash himsell about the rest o't?"

The courage of our philosophical mendicant began, however, to abate when the sunbeams shone fair on the rusty bars of his grated dungeon, and a miserable linnet, whose cage some poor debtor had obtained permission to attach to the window, began to greet them with his whistle.

"Ye're in better spirits than I am," said Edie, addressing the bird, "for I can neither whistle nor sing for thinking o' the bonnie burnsides and green shaws that I should hae been dandering beside in weather like this. But hae, there's some crumbs t'ye, an ye are sae merry; and troth ye hae some reason to sing an ye kent it, for your cage comes by nae faut o' your ain, and I may thank mysell that I am closed up in this weary place."

Ochiltree's soliloquy was disturbed by a peace-officer, who

came to summon him to attend the magistrate. So he set forth in awful procession between two poor creatures, neither of them so stout as he was himself, to be conducted into the presence of inquisitorial justice. The people, as the aged prisoner was led along by his decrepit guards, exclaimed to each other: "Eh! see sic a grey-haired man as that is, to have committed a highway robbery wi' ae fit in the grave!" And the children congratulated the officers, objects of their alternate dread and sport, Puggie Orrock and Jock Ormston, on having a prisoner as old as themselves.

Thus marshalled forward, Edie was presented (by no means for the first time) before the worshipful Bailie Littlejohn, who, contrary to what his name expressed, was a tall portly magistrate, on whom corporation crusts had not been conferred in vain. He was a zealous loyalist of that zealous time, somewhat rigorous and peremptory in the execution of his duty, and a good deal inflated with the sense of his own power and importance, otherwise an honest, well-meaning, and useful citizen.

"Bring him in, bring him in!" he exclaimed. "Upon my word, these are awful and unnatural times: the very bedesmen and retainers of his Majesty are the first to break his laws. Here has been an old Blue-Gown committing robbery! I suppose the next will reward the royal charity, which supplies him with his garb, pension, and begging license, by engaging in high treason or sedition at least. But bring him in."

Edie made his obeisance, and then stood, as usual, firm and erect, with the side of his face turned a little upward, as if to catch every word which the magistrate might address to him. To the first general questions, which respected only his name and calling, the mendicant answered with readiness and accuracy; but when the magistrate, having caused his clerk to take down these particulars, began to inquire whereabout the mendicant was on the night when Dousterswivel met with his misfortune, Edie demurred to the motion. "Can ye tell me now, Bailie, you that understands the law, what gude will it do me to answer ony o' your questions?"

"Good? no good certainly, my friend, except that giving a

true account of yourself, if you are innocent, may entitle me to set you at liberty."

"But it seems mair reasonable to me, now, that you, Bailie, or ony body that has ony thing to say against me, should prove my guilt, and no to be bidding me prove my innocence."

"I don't sit here," answered the magistrate, "to dispute points of law with you. I ask you, if you choose to answer my question, whether you were at Ringan Aikwood the forester's upon the day I have specified?"

"Really, sir, I dinna feel myself called on to remember," replied the cautious bedesman.

"Or whether, in the course of that day or night," continued the magistrate, "you saw Steven, or Steenie, Mucklebackit? You knew him, I suppose?"

"Oh brawlie did I ken Steenie, puir fallow," replied the prisoner; "but I canna condeshend on ony particular time I have seen him lately."

"Were you at the ruins of St. Ruth any time in the course of that evening?"

"Bailie Littlejohn," said the mendicant, "if it be your honour's pleasure, we'll cut a lang tale short, and I'll just tell ye I am no minded to answer ony o' thae questions. I'm ower auld a traveller to let my tongue bring me into trouble."

"Write down," said the magistrate, "that he declines to answer all interrogatories, in respect that by telling the truth he might be brought to trouble."

"Na, na," said Ochiltree, "I'll no hae that set down as ony part o' my answer; but I just meant to say, that in a' my memory and practice I never saw ony gude come o' answering idle questions."

"Write down," said the Bailie, "that, being acquainted with judicial interrogatories by long practice, and having sustained injury by answering questions put to him on such occasions, the declarant refuses——"

"Na, na, Bailie," reiterated Edie, "ye are no to come in on me that gait neither."

"Dictate the answer yourself then, friend," said the magistrate, "and the clerk will take it down from your own mouth."

"Ay, ay," said Edie, "that's what I ca' fair play; I'se do that without loss o' time. Sae, neighbour, ye may just write down that Edie Ochiltree, the declarant, stands up for the liberty—na, I maunna say that neither, I am nae Liberty Boy; I hae fought again' them in the riots in Dublin; besides, I have ate the king's bread mony a day. Stay, let me see. Ay, write that Edie Ochiltree, the Blue-Gown, stands up for the prerogative—see that ye spell that word right, it's a lang ane—for the prerogative of the subjects of the land, and winna answer a single word that sall be asked at him this day, unless he sees a reason for't. Put down that, young man."

"Then, Edie," said the magistrate, "since you will give me no information on the subject, I must send you back to prison till you shall be delivered in due course of law."

"Aweel, sir, if it's Heaven's will and man's will, nae doubt I maun submit," replied the mendicant. "I hae nae great objection to the prison, only that a body canna win out o't; and if it wad please you as weel, Bailie, I wad gie you my word to appear afore the Lords at the Circuit, or in ony other court ye like, on ony day ye are pleased to appoint."

"I rather think, my good friend," answered Bailie Littlejohn, "your word might be a slender security where your neck may be in some danger. I am apt to think you would suffer the pledge to be forfeited. If you could give me sufficient security, indeed——"

At this moment the Antiquary and Captain M'Intyre entered the apartment. "Good morning to you, gentlemen," said the magistrate; "you find me toiling in my usual vocation, looking after the iniquities of the people; labouring for the *respublica*, Mr. Oldbuck; serving the king our master, Captain M'Intyre, for I suppose you know I have taken up the sword?"

"It is one of the emblems of justice, doubtless," answered the Antiquary; "but I should have thought the scales would have suited you better, Bailie, especially as you have them ready in the warehouse."

"Very good, Monkbarns, excellent. But I do not take the sword up as justice, but as a soldier; indeed, I should rather say the musket and bayonet; there they stand at the elbow of my gouty chair, for I am scarce fit for drill yet. A slight touch of our old acquaintance podagra. I can keep my feet, however, while our sergeant puts me through the manual. I should like to know, Captain M'Intyre, if he follows the regulations correctly; he brings us but awkwardly to the 'present.'" And he hobbled towards his weapon to illustrate his doubts and display his proficiency.

"I rejoice we have such zealous defenders, Bailie," replied Mr. Oldbuck; "and I dare say Hector will gratify you by communicating his opinion on your progress in this new calling. Why, you rival the Hecate of the ancients, my good sir —a merchant on the mart, a magistrate in the town-house, a soldier on the links; *quid non pro patria?* But my business is with the justice; so let commerce and war go slumber."

"Well, my good sir," said the Bailie, "and what commands have you for me?"

"Why, here's an old acquaintance of mine, called Edie Ochiltree, whom some of your myrmidons have mewed up in jail on account of an alleged assault on that fellow Dousterswivel, of whose accusation I do not believe one word."

The magistrate here assumed a very grave countenance. "You ought to have been informed that he is accused of robbery as well as assault—a very serious matter indeed; it is not often such criminals come under my cognizance."

"And," replied Oldbuck, "you are tenacious of the opportunity of making the very most of such as occur. But is this poor old man's case really so very bad?"

"It is rather out of rule," said the Bailie, "but, as you are in the commission, Monkbarns, I have no hesitation to show you Dousterswivel's declaration and the rest of the precognition." And he put the papers into the Antiquary's hands, who assumed his spectacles and sat down in a corner to peruse them.

The officers in the mean time had directions to remove their prisoner into another apartment; but before they could do so

M'Intyre took an opportunity to greet old Edie and to slip a guinea into his hand.

"Lord bless your honour," said the old man; "it's a young soldier's gift, and it should surely thrive wi' an auld ane. I'se no refuse it, though it's beyond my rules; for, if they steek me up here, my friends are like eneugh to forget me: 'Out o' sight out o' mind' is a true proverb. And it wadna be creditable for me, that am the king's bedesman, and entitled to beg by word of mouth, to be fishing for bawbees out at the jail window wi' the fit o' a stocking and a string." As he made this observation he was conducted out of the apartment.

Mr. Dousterswivel's declaration contained an exaggerated account of the violence he had sustained and also of his loss.

"But what I should have liked to have asked him," said Monkbarns, "would have been his purpose in frequenting the ruins of St. Ruth, so lonely a place, at such an hour, and with such a companion as Edie Ochiltree. There is no road lies that way, and I do not conceive a mere passion for the picturesque would carry the German thither in such a night of storm and wind. Depend upon it, he has been about some roguery, and in all probability hath been caught in a trap of his own setting; *nec lex justitior ulla.*"

The magistrate allowed there was something mysterious in that circumstance, and apologised for not pressing Dousterswivel, as his declaration was voluntarily emitted. But for the support of the main charge he showed the declaration of the Aikwoods concerning the state in which Dousterswivel was found, and establishing the important fact that the mendicant had left the barn in which he was quartered, and did not return to it again. Two people belonging to the Fairport undertaker, who had that night been employed in attending the funeral of Lady Glenallan, had also given declarations that, being sent to pursue two suspicious persons who left the ruins of St. Ruth as the funeral approached, and who, it was supposed, might have been pillaging some of the ornaments prepared for the ceremony, they had lost and regained sight of them more than once, owing to the nature of the ground, which was unfavourable for riding, but had at length fairly lodged them both in Mucklebackit's cottage. And one of the men added, that "he, the declarant, having dismounted from his horse and gone close up to the window of the hut, he saw the old Blue-Gown and young Steenie Mucklebackit, with others, eating and drinking in the inside, and also observed the said Steenie Mucklebackit show a pocket-book to the others; and declarant has no doubt that Ochiltree and Steenie Mucklebackit were the persons whom he and his comrade had pursued, as above mentioned." And being interrogated why he did not enter the said cottage, declares, "he had no warrant so to do; and that, as Mucklebackit and his family were understood to be rough-handed folk, he, the declarant, had no desire to meddle or make with their affairs. *Causa scientiæ patet.* All which he declares to be truth," etc.

"What do you say to that body of evidence against your friend?" said the magistrate, when he had observed the Antiquary had turned the last leaf.

"Why, were it in the case of any other person, I own I should say it looked *prima facie* a little ugly; but I cannot allow anybody to be in the wrong for beating Dousterswivel. Had I been an hour younger, or had but one single flash of your warlike genius, Bailie, I should have done it myself long ago. He is *nebulo nebulonum,* an impudent, fraudulent, mendacious quack, that has cost me a hundred pounds by his roguery; and my neighbour, Sir Arthur, God knows how much. And besides, Bailie, I do not hold him to be a sound friend to government."

"Indeed?" said Bailie Littlejohn; "if I thought that it would alter the question considerably."

"Right; for in beating him," observed Oldbuck, "the bedesman must have shown his gratitude to the king by thumping his enemy; and in robbing him he would only have plundered an Egyptian, whose wealth it is lawful to spoil. Now, suppose this interview in the ruins of St. Ruth had relation to politics, and this story of hidden treasure and so forth was a bribe from the other side of the water for some great man, or the funds destined to maintain a seditious club?"

25

"My dear sir," said the magistrate, catching at the idea, "you hit my very thoughts! How fortunate should I be if I could become the humble means of sifting such a matter to the bottom! Don't you think we had better call out the volunteers and put them on duty?"

"Not just yet, while podagra deprives them of an essential member of their body. But will you let me examine Ochiltree?"

"Certainly; but you'll make nothing of him. He gave me distinctly to understand he knew the danger of a judicial declaration on the part of an accused person, which, to say the truth, has hanged many an honester man than he is."

"Well, but, Bailie," continued Oldbuck, "you have no objection to let me try him?"

"None in the world, Monkbarns. I hear the sergeant below, I'll rehearse the manual in the mean while. Baby, carry my gun and bayonet down to the room below; it makes less noise there when we ground arms." And so exit the martial magistrate, with his maid behind him bearing his weapons.

"A good squire that wench for a gouty champion," observed Oldbuck. "Hector, my lad, hook on, hook on. Go with him, boy; keep him employed, man, for half an hour or so; butter him with some warlike terms; praise his dress and address."

Captain M'Intyre, who, like many of his profession, looked down with infinite scorn on those citizen soldiers who had assumed arms without any professional title to bear them, rose with great reluctance, observing that he should not know what to say to Mr. Littlejohn, and that to see an old gouty shopkeeper attempting the exercise and duties of a private soldier was really too ridiculous.

"It may be so, Hector," said the Antiquary, who seldom agreed with any person in the immediate proposition which was laid down—"it may possibly be so in this and some other instances; but at present the country resembles the suitors in a small-debt court, where parties plead in person for lack of cash to retain the professed heroes of the bar. I am sure in the one case we never regret the want of the acuteness and eloquence of the lawyers; and so, I hope, in the other we may manage to make shift with our hearts and muskets, though we shall lack some of the discipline of you martinets."

"I have no objection, I am sure, sir, that the whole world should fight if they please, if they will but allow me to be quiet," said Hector, rising with dogged reluctance.

"Yes, you are a very quiet personage indeed," said his uncle, "whose ardour for quarrelling cannot pass so much as a poor *phoca* sleeping upon the beach!"

But Hector, who saw which way the conversation was tending, and hated all allusions to the foil he had sustained from the fish, made his escape before the Antiquary concluded the sentence.

CHAPTER XXXVIII.

Well, well, at worst, 'tis neither theft nor coinage,
Granting I knew all that you charged me with.
What, tho' the tomb hath borne a second birth,
And given the wealth to one that knew not on't,
Yet fair exchange was never robbery,
Far less pure bounty.

Old Play.

THE Antiquary, in order to avail himself of the permission given him to question the accused party, chose rather to go to the apartment in which Ochiltree was detained than to make the examination appear formal by bringing him again into the magistrate's office. He found the old man seated by a window which looked out on the sea; and as he gazed on that prospect large tears found their way, as if unconsciously, to his eye, and from thence trickled down his cheeks and white beard. His features were, nevertheless, calm and composed, and his whole posture and mien indicated patience and resignation. Oldbuck had approached him without being observed, and roused him out of his musing by saying kindly: "I am sorry, Edie, to see you so much cast down about this matter."

The mendicant started, dried his eyes very hastily with the sleeve of his gown, and, endeavouring to recover his usual tone of indifference and jocularity, answered, but with a voice more tremulous than usual: "I might weel hae judged, Monkbarns, it was you, or the like o' you, was coming in to disturb me; for it's ae great advantage o' prisons and courts o' justice, that ye may greet your een out an ye like, and nane o' the folk that's concerned about them will ever ask you what it's for."

"Well, Edie," replied Oldbuck, "I hope your present cause of distress is not so bad but it may be removed."

"And I had hoped, Monkbarns," answered the mendicant in a tone of reproach, "that ye had kend me better than to think that this bit trifling trouble o' my ain wad bring tears into my auld een, that hae seen far different kind o' distress. Na, na! But here's been the puir lass, Caxon's daughter, seeking comfort, and has gotten unco little. There's been nae speerings o' Taffril's gun-brig since the last gale; and folk report on the key that a king's ship had struck on the Reef of Rattray, and a' hands lost. God forbid! for as sure as you live, Monkbarns, the puir lad Lovel, that ye liked sae weel, must have perished."

"God forbid, indeed!" echoed the Antiquary, turning pale; "I would rather Monkbarns House were on fire. My poor dear friend and coadjutor! I will down to the quay instantly."

"I'm sure ye'll learn naething mair than I hae tauld ye, sir," said Ochiltree, "for the officer-folk here were very civil— that is, for the like o' them—and lookit up a' their letters and authorities, and could thraw nae light on't either ae way or another."

"It can't be true, it shall not be true," said the Antiquary, "and I won't believe it if it were. Taffril's an excellent seaman, and Lovel— my poor Lovel!—has all the qualities of a safe and pleasant companion by land or by sea—one, Edie, whom, from the ingenuousness of his disposition, I would choose, did I ever go a sea voyage—which I never do, unless across the ferry—*fragilem mecum solvere phaselum*, to be the companion of my risk, as one against whom the elements could nourish no vengeance. No, Edie, it is not and cannot be true: it is a fiction of the idle jade Rumour, whom I wish hanged with her trumpet about her neck, that serves only with its screech-owl tones to fright honest folks out of their senses. Let me know how you got into this scrape of your own."

"Are ye axing me as a magistrate, Monkbarns, or is it just for your ain satisfaction?"

"For my own satisfaction solely," replied the Antiquary.

"Put up your pocket-book and your keelyvine pen then, for I downa speak out an ye hae writing materials in your hands; they're a scaur to unlearned folk like me. Odd, ane o' the clerks in the neist room will clink down in black and white as muckle as wad hang a man before ane kens what he's saying."

Monkbarns complied with the old man's humour, and put up his memorandum-book.

Edie then went with great frankness through the part of the story already known to the reader, informing the Antiquary of the scene which he had witnessed between Dousterswivel and his patron in the ruins of St. Ruth, and frankly confessing that he could not resist the opportunity of decoying the adept once more to visit the tomb of Misticot, with the purpose of taking a comic revenge upon him for his quackery. He had easily persuaded Steenie, who was a bold thoughtless young fellow, to engage in the frolic along with him, and the jest had been inadvertently carried a great deal farther than was designed. Concerning the pocket-book, he explained that he had expressed his surprise and sorrow as soon as he found it had been inadvertently brought off; and that publicly, before all the inmates of the cottage, Steenie had undertaken to return it the next day, and had only been prevented by his untimely fate.

The Antiquary pondered a moment, and then said: "Your account seems very probable, Edie, and I believe it from what I know of the parties; but I think it likely that you know a great deal more than you have thought it proper to tell me about this matter of the treasure-trove. I suspect you have acted the part of the Lar Familiaris in Plautus—a sort of brownie, Edie, to speak to your comprehension, who watched over hidden treasures. I do bethink me you were the first person we met when Sir Arthur made his successful attack upon Misticot's grave, and also that, when the labourers began to flag, you, Edie, were again the first to leap into the trench and to make the discovery of the treasure. Now you must explain all this to me, unless you would have me use you as ill as Euclio does Staphyla in the *Aulularia.*"

"Lordsake, sir," replied the mendicant, "what do I ken about your Howlowlaria? it's mair like a dog's language than a man's."

"You knew, however, of the box of treasure being there?" continued Oldbuck.

"Dear sir," answered Edie, assuming a countenance of great simplicity, "what likelihood is there o' that? D'ye think sae puir an auld creature as me wad hae kend o' sic a like thing without getting some gude out o't? And ye wot weel I sought nane and gat nane, like Michael Scott's man. What concern could I hae wi't?"

"That's just what I want you to explain to me," said Oldbuck; "for I am positive you knew it was there."

"Your honour's a positive man, Monkbarns; and, for a positive man, I must needs allow ye're often in the right."

"You allow then, Edie, that my belief is well founded?"

Edie nodded acquiescence.

"Then please to explain to me the whole affair from beginning to end," said the Antiquary.

"If it were a secret o' mine, Monkbarns," replied the beggar, "ye suldna ask twice; for I hae aye said ahint your back that, for a' the nonsense maggots that ye whiles take into your head, ye are the maist wise and discreet o' a' our country gentles. But I'se e'en be open-hearted wi' you and tell you that this is a friend's secret, and that they suld draw me wi' wild horses, or saw me asunder, as they did the children of Ammon, sooner than I would speak a word mair about the matter, excepting this, that there was nae ill intended, but muckle gude, and that the purpose was to serve them that are worth twenty hundred o' me. But there's nae law, I trow, that makes it a sin to ken where ither folks' siller is, if we dinna pit hand till't oursell?"

Oldbuck walked once or twice up and down the room in profound thought, endeavouring to find some plausible reason for transactions of a nature so mysterious, but his ingenuity was totally at fault. He then placed himself before the prisoner.

"This story of yours, friend Edie, is an absolute enigma, and would require a second Œdipus to solve it. Who Œdipus was I will tell you some other time, if you remind me. However, whether it be owing to the wisdom or to the maggots with which you compliment me, I am strongly disposed to believe that you have spoken the truth, the rather that you have not made any of those obtestations of the superior powers which I observe you and your comrades always make use of when you mean to deceive folks. (Here Edie could not suppress a smile.) If, therefore, you will answer me one question, I will endeavour to procure your liberation."

"If ye'll let me hear the question," said Edie, with the caution of a canny Scotchman, "I'll tell you whether I'll answer it or no."

"It is simply," said the Antiquary, "Did Dousterswivel know anything about the concealment of the chest of bullion?"

"He, the ill-fa'ard loon!" answered Edie, with much frankness of manner, "there wad hae been little speerings o't had Dustansnivel kend it was there; it wad hae been butter in the black dog's hause."

"I thought as much," said Oldbuck. "Well, Edie, if I procure your freedom, you must keep your day and appear to clear me of the bail-bond, for these are not times for prudent men to incur forfeitures, unless you can point out another *aulam auri plenam quadrilibrem*—another 'Search No. I.'"

"Ah!" said the beggar, shaking his head, "I doubt the bird's flown that laid thae golden eggs; for I winna ca' her goose, though that's the gait it stands in the story-buick. But I'll keep my day, Monkbarns; ye'se no loss a penny by me. And troth I wad fain be out again, now the weather's fine; and then I hae the best chance o' hearing the first news o' my friends."

"Well, Edie, as the bouncing and thumping beneath has somewhat ceased, I presume Bailie Littlejohn has dismissed his military preceptor, and has retired from the labours of Mars to those of Themis: I will have some conversation with him. But I cannot and will not believe any of those wretched news you were telling me."

"God send your honour may be right!" said the mendicant, as Oldbuck left the room.

The Antiquary found the magistrate, exhausted with the fatigues of the drill, reposing in his gouty chair, humming the air, "How merrily we live that soldiers be!" and between each bar comforting himself with a spoonful of mock-turtle soup. He ordered a similar refreshment for Oldbuck, who declined it, observing that, not being a military man, he did not feel inclined to break his habit of keeping regular hours for meals. "Soldiers like you, Bailie, must snatch their food as they find means and time. But I am sorry to hear ill news of young Taffril's brig."

"Ah, poor fellow!" said the Bailie, "he was a credit to the town, much distinguished on the first of June."

"But," said Oldbuck, "I am shocked to hear you talk of him in the preterite tense."

"Troth, I fear there may be too much reason for it, Monkbarns; and yet let us hope the best. The accident is said to have happened in the Rattray reef of rocks, about twenty miles to the northward, near Dirtenalan Bay. I have sent to inquire about it; and your nephew run out himself as if he had been flying to get the gazette of a victory."

Here Hector entered, exclaiming as he came in: "I believe it's all a damned lie; I can't find the least authority for it but general rumour."

"And pray, Mr. Hector," said his uncle, "if it had been true, whose fault would it have been that Lovel was on board?"

"Not mine, I am sure," answered Hector; "it would have been only my misfortune."

"Indeed!" said his uncle; "I should not have thought of that."

"Why, sir, with all your inclination to find me in the wrong," replied the young soldier, "I suppose you will own my intention was not to blame in this case. I did my best to hit Lovel, and if I had been successful, 'tis clear my scrape would have been his and his scrape would have been mine."

"And whom or what do you intend to hit now, that you are lugging with you that leathern magazine there, marked 'gunpowder'?"

"I must be prepared for Lord Glenallan's moors on the twelfth, sir," said M'Intyre.

"Ah, Hector! thy great *chasse*, as the French call it, would take place best—

> Omne cum Proteus pecus agitaret
> Visere montes——

Could you meet but with a martial *phoca*, instead of an unwarlike heath-bird."

"The devil take the seal, sir, or *phoca*, if you choose to call it so: it's rather hard one can never hear the end of a little piece of folly like that."

"Well, well," said Oldbuck, "I am glad you have the grace to be ashamed of it.   As I detest the whole race of Nimrods, I wish them all as well matched.   Nay, never start off at a jest, man; I have done with the *phoca*, though I dare say the Bailie could tell us the value of sealskins just now."

"They are up," said the magistrate—"they are well up; the fishing has been unsuccessful lately."

"We can bear witness to that," said the tormenting Antiquary, who was delighted with the hank this incident had given him over the young sportsman.   "One word more, Hector, and

> We'll hang a sealskin on thy recreant limbs.

Aha, my boy!   Come, never mind it, I must go to business. Bailie, a word with you; you must take bail—moderate bail, you understand—for old Ochiltree's appearance."

"You don't consider what you ask," said the Bailie; "the offence is assault and robbery."

"Hush! not a word about it," said the Antiquary.   "I gave you a hint before; I will possess you more fully hereafter; I promise you there is a secret."

"But, Mr. Oldbuck, if the state is concerned, I, who do the

whole drudgery business here, really have a title to be consulted, and until I am——"

"Hush! hush!" said the Antiquary, winking and putting his finger to his nose; "you shall have the full credit, the entire management, whenever matters are ripe. But this is an obstinate old fellow, who will not hear of two people being as yet let into his mystery, and he has not fully acquainted me with the clue to Dousterswivel's devices."

"Aha! so we must tip that fellow the alien act, I suppose?"

"To say truth, I wish you would."

"Say no more," said the magistrate, "it shall forthwith be done; he shall be removed *tanquam suspect*—I think that's one of your own phrases, Monkbarns?"

"It is classical, Bailie; you improve."

"Why, public business has of late pressed upon me so much that I have been obliged to take my foreman into partnership. I have had two several correspondences with the Under Secretary of State—one on the proposed tax on Riga hemp-seed and the other on putting down political societies. So you might as well communicate to me as much as you know of this old fellow's discovery of a plot against the state."

"I will instantly when I am master of it," replied Oldbuck; "I hate the trouble of managing such matters myself. Remember, however, I did not say decidedly a plot against the state; I only say, I hope to discover, by this man's means, a foul plot."

"If it be a plot at all, there must be treason in it, or sedition at least," said the Bailie. "Will you bail him for four hundred merks?"

"Four hundred merks for an old Blue-Gown! Think on the act 1701 regulating bail-bonds! Strike off a cipher from the sum; I am content to bail him for forty merks."

"Well, Mr. Oldbuck, everybody in Fairport is always willing to oblige you; and besides, I know that you are a prudent man, and one that would be as unwilling to lose forty as four hundred merks. So I will accept your bail *meo periculo*; what say you to that law phrase again? I had it from a learned counsel: 'I will vouch it, my lord,' he said, ' *meo periculo*.'"

"And I will vouch for Edie Ochiltree *meo periculo*, in like manner," said Oldbuck. "So let your clerk draw out the bail-bond and I will sign it."

When this ceremony had been performed the Antiquary communicated to Edie the joyful tidings that he was once more at liberty, and directed him to make the best of his way to Monkbarns House, to which he himself returned with his nephew, after having perfected their good work.

CHAPTER XXXIX.

Full of wise saws and modern instances.
As You Like It.

"I WISH to Heaven, Hector," said the Antiquary, next morning after breakfast, "you would spare our nerves, and not be keeping snapping that arquebuss of yours."

"Well, sir, I'm sure I'm sorry to disturb you," said his nephew, still handling his fowling-piece; "but it's a capital gun: it's a Joe Manton, that cost forty guineas."

"A fool and his money are soon parted, nephew: there is a Joe Miller for your Joe Manton," answered the Antiquary. "I am glad you have so many guineas to throw away."

"Every one has their fancy, uncle: you are fond of books."

"Ay, Hector," said the uncle, "and if my collection were yours, you would make it fly to the gunsmith, the horse-market, the dog-breaker: *coemptos undique nobiles libros mutare loricis Iberis.*"

"I could not use your books, my dear uncle," said the young soldier, "that's true; and you will do well to provide for their being in better hands; but don't let the faults of my head fall on my heart: I would not part with a Cordery that belonged to an old friend to get a set of horses like Lord Glenallan's."

"I don't think you would, lad—I don't think you would," said his softening relative. "I love to tease you a little sometimes; it keeps up the spirit of discipline and habit of subordination. You will pass your time happily here having me to command you, instead of captain, or colonel, or 'knight in arms,' as Milton has it; and instead of the French," he continued, relapsing into his ironical humour, "you have the *gens humida ponti;* for, as Virgil says,

Sternunt se somno diversæ in littore phocæ,

which might be rendered,

Here *phocæ* slumber on the beach,
Within our Highland Hector's reach.

Nay, if you grow angry I have done.   Besides, I see old Edie in the courtyard, with whom I have business.   Good-bye, Hector.   Do you remember how she splashed into the sea like her master Proteus, *et se jactu dedit æquor in altum?*"

M'Intyre—waiting, however, till the door was shut—then gave way to the natural impatience of his temper.

"My uncle is the best man in the world, and in his way the kindest; but rather than hear any more about that cursed *phoca*, as he is pleased to call it, I would exchange for the West Indies and never see his face again."

Miss M'Intyre, gratefully attached to her uncle and passionately fond of her brother, was on such occasions the usual envoy of reconciliation.   She hastened to meet her uncle on his return before he entered the parlour.

"Well, now, Miss Womankind, what is the meaning of that imploring countenance?   Has Juno done any more mischief?"

"No, uncle; but Juno's master is in such fear of your joking him about the seal.   I assure you, he feels it much more than you would wish; it's very silly of him, to be sure; but then you can turn everybody so sharply into ridicule——"

"Well, my dear," answered Oldbuck, propitiated by the compliment, "I will rein in my satire, and, if possible, speak no more of the *phoca*; I will not even speak of sealing a letter, but say, 'umph,' and give a nod to you when I want the waxlight.   I am not *monitoribus asper*, but, Heaven knows, the most mild, quiet, and easy of human beings, whom sister, niece, and nephew guide just as best pleases them."

With this little panegyric on his own docility, Mr. Oldbuck

entered the parlour, and proposed to his nephew a walk to the Mussel Crag. "I have some questions to ask of a woman at Mucklebackit's cottage," he observed, "and I would willingly have a sensible witness with me; so, for fault of a better, Hector, I must be contented with you."

"There is old Edie, sir, or Caxon; could not they do better than me?" answered M'Intyre, feeling somewhat alarmed at the prospect of a long *tête-à-tête* with his uncle.

"Upon my word, young man, you turn me over to pretty companions, and I am quite sensible of your politeness," replied Mr. Oldbuck. "No, sir, I intend the old Blue-Gown shall go with me, not as a competent witness, for he is at present, as our friend Bailie Littlejohn says—blessings on his learning!—*tanquam suspectus*, and you are *suspicione major*, as our law has it."

"I wish I were a major, sir," said Hector, catching only the last, and, to a soldier's ear, the most impressive word in the sentence; "but, without money or interest, there is little chance of getting the step."

"Well, well, most doughty son of Priam," said the Antiquary, "be ruled by your friends, and there's no saying what may happen. Come away with me, and you shall see what may be useful to you should you ever sit upon a court-martial, sir."

"I have been on many a regimental court-martial, sir," answered Captain M'Intyre. "But here's a new cane for you."

"Much obliged, much obliged."

"I bought it from our drum-major," added M'Inytre, "who came into our regiment from the Bengal army when it came down the Red Sea. It was cut on the banks of the Indus, I assure you."

"Upon my word,' 'tis a fine ratan, and well replaces that which the *ph*——Bah! what was I going to say?"

The party, consisting of the Antiquary, his nephew, and the old beggar, now took the sands towards Mussel Crag—the former in the very highest mood of communicating information, and the others, under a sense of former obligation and some hope for future favours, decently attentive to receive it. The uncle and nephew walked together, the mendicant about a step and a half behind, just near enough for his patron to speak to him by a slight inclination of his neck, and without the trouble of turning round. Petrie, in his essay on *Good-breeding*, dedicated to the magistrates of Edinburgh, recommends, upon his own experience as tutor in a family of distinction, this attitude to all led captains, tutors, dependents, and bottle-holders of every description. Thus escorted, the Antiquary moved along full of his learning, like a lordly man of war, and every now and then yawing to starboard and larboard to discharge a broadside upon his followers.

"And so it is your opinion," said he to the mendicant, "that this windfall—this *arca auri*, as Plautus has it—will not greatly avail Sir Arthur in his necessities?"

"Unless he could find ten times as much," said the beggar, "and that I am sair doubtful of. I heard Puggie Orrock and the tother thief of a sheriff-officer or messenger speaking about it, and things are ill aff when the like o' them can speak crousely about ony gentleman's affairs. I doubt Sir Arthur will be in stane wa's for debt unless there's swift help and certain."

"You speak like a fool," said the Antiquary. "Nephew, it is a remarkable thing that in this happy country no man can be legally imprisoned for debt."

"Indeed, sir?" said M'Intyre. "I never knew that before; that part of our law would suit some of our mess well."

"And if they arena confined for debt," said Ochiltree, "what is't that tempts sae mony puir creatures to bide in the tolbooth o' Fairport yonder? They a' say they were put there by their creditors. Odd! they maun like it better than I do if they're there o' free will."

"A very natural observation, Edie, and many of your betters would make the same; but it is founded entirely upon ignorance of the feudal system. Hector, be so good as to attend, unless you are looking out for another——Ahem! (Hector compelled himself to give attention at this hint.) And you, Edie, it may be useful to you, *rerum cognoscere causas*. The nature and origin of warrant for caption is a thing *haud alienum a Scœvolœ studiis.* You must know then, once more, that nobody can be arrested in Scotland for debt."

"I haena muckle concern wi' that, Monkbarns," said the old man, "for naebody wad trust a bodle to a gaberlunzie."

"I pr'ythee peace, man. As a compulsitor, therefore, of payment—that being a thing to which no debtor is naturally inclined, as I have too much reason to warrant from the experience I have had with my own—we had first the letters of four forms, a sort of gentle invitation, by which our sovereign lord the king, interesting himself, as a monarch should, in the regulation of his subjects' private affairs, at first by mild exhortation and afterwards by letters of more strict enjoinment and more hard compulsion—— What do you see extraordinary about thet bird, Hector? it's but a sea-maw."

"It's a pictarnie, sir," said Edie.

"Well, what an if it were—what does that signify at present? But I see you're impatient; so I will waive the letters of four forms, and come to the modern process of diligence. You suppose, now, a man's committed to prison because he cannot pay his debt? Quite otherwise; the truth is, the king is so good as to interfere at the request of the creditor, and to send the debtor his royal command to do him justice within a certain time—fifteen days, or six, as the case may be. Well, the man resists and disobeys; what follows? Why, that he be lawfully and rightfully declared a rebel to our gracious sovereign, whose command he has disobeyed, and that by three blasts of a horn at the market-place of Edinburgh, the metropolis of Scotland. And he is then legally imprisoned, not on account of any civil debt, but because of his ungrateful contempt of the royal mandate. What say you to that, Hector? there's something you never knew before." [1]

"No, uncle; but I own, if I wanted money to pay my debts, I would rather thank the king to send me some than to declare me a rebel for not doing what I could not do."

"Your education has not led you to consider these things," replied his uncle; "you are incapable of estimating the ele-

[1] See Imprisonment for Debt in Scotland. Note 9.

gance of the legal fiction, and the manner in which it recon-
ciles that duress which, for the protection of commerce, it has
been found necessary to extend towards refractory debtors with
the most scrupulous attention to the liberty of the subject."

"I don't know, sir," answered the unenlightened Hector;
"but if a man must pay his debt or go to jail, it signifies but
little whether he goes as a debtor or a rebel, I should think.
But you say this command of the king's gives a license of
so many days; now, egad, were I in the scrape, I would beat
a march and leave the king and the creditor to settle it among
themselves before they came to extremities."

"So wad I," said Edie; "I wad gie them leg-bail to a
certainty."

"True," replied Monkbarns; "but those whom the law sus-
pects of being unwilling to abide her formal visit, she proceeds
with by means of a shorter and more unceremonious call, as
dealing with persons on whom patience and favour would be
utterly thrown away."

"Ay," said Ochiltree, "that will be what they ca' the 'fugie'
warrants; I hae some skeel in them. There's Border warrants
too in the south country, unco rash uncanny things. I was
taen upon ane at Saint James's Fair, and keepit in the auld
kirk at Kelso the haill day and night; and a cauld goustie
place it was, I'se assure ye. But whatna wife's this, wi' her
creel on her back? It's puir Maggie hersell, I'm thinking."

It was so. The poor woman's sense of her loss, if not diminished, was become at least mitigated by the inevitable necessity of attending to the means of supporting her family; and
her salutation to Oldbuck was made in an odd mixture between
the usual language of solicitation with which she plied her
customers and the tone of lamentation for her recent calamity.

"How's a' wi' ye the day, Monkbarns? I havena had the
grace yet to come down to thank your honour for the credit ye
did puir Steenie, wi' laying his head in a rath grave, puir
fallow." Here she whimpered and wiped her eyes with the
corner of her blue apron. "But the fishing comes on no that
ill, though the gudeman hasna had the heart to gang to sea
himsell. Atweel I wad fain tell him it wad do him gude to

put hand to wark, but I'm maist fear'd to speak to him, and it's an unco thing to hear ane o' us speak that gate o' a man. However, I hae some dainty caller haddies, and they sall be but three shillings the dozen, for I hae nae pith to drive a bargain e'ennow, and maun just take what ony Christian body will gie, wi' few words and nae flyting."

"What shall we do, Hector?" asid Oldbuck, pausing; "I got into disgrace with my womankind for making a bad bargain with her before. These maritime animals, Hector, are unlucky to our family."

"Pooh, sir, what would you do? Give poor Maggie what she asks, or allow me to send a dish of fish up to Monkbarns."

And he held out the money to her; but Maggie drew back her hand. "Na, na, Captain; ye're ower young and ower free o' your siller. Ye should never tak a fish-wife's first bode; and troth I think maybe a flyte wi' the auld housekeeper at Monkbarns or Miss Grizel would do me some gude. And I want to see what that hellicate quean Jenny Rintherout's doing; folk said she wasna weel. She'll be vexing hersell about Steenie, the silly tawpie, as if he wad ever hae lookit ower his shouther at the like o' her! Weel, Monkbarns, they're braw caller haddies, and they'll bid me unco little indeed at the house if ye want crappit-heads the day."

And so on she paced with her burden—grief, gratitude for the sympathy of her betters, and the habitual love of traffic and of gain chasing each other through her thoughts.

"And now that we are before the door of their hut," said Ochiltree, "I wad fain ken, Monkbarns, what has gar'd ye plague yoursell wi' me a' this length? I tell ye sincerely I hae nae pleasure in ganging in there. I downa bide to think how the young hae fa'en on a' sides o' me, and left me an useless auld stump wi' hardly a green leaf on't."

"This old woman," said Oldbuck, "sent you on a message to the Earl of Glenallan, did she not?"

"Ay!" said the surprised mendicant; "how ken ye that sae weel?"

"Lord Glenallan told me himself," answered the Antiquary; "so there is no delation—no breach of trust on your part; and

26

as he wishes me to take her evidence down on some important
family matters, I chose to bring you with me, because in her
situation, hovering between dotage and consciousness, it is
possible that your voice and appearance may awaken trains of
recollection which I should otherwise have no means of exciting. The human mind—— What are you about, Hector?"

"I was only whistling for the dog, sir," replied the Captain; "she always roves too wide. I knew I should be
troublesome to you."

"Not at all, not at all," said Oldbuck, resuming the subject
of his disquisition—"The human mind is to be treated like a
skein of ravelled silk, where you must cautiously secure one
free end before you can make any progress in disentan-
gling it."

"I ken naething about that," said the gaberlunzie; "but an
my auld acquaintance be hersell, or ony thing like hersell, she
may come to wind us a pirn. It's fearsome baith to see and
hear her when she wampishes about her arms, and gets to
her English, and speaks as if she were a prent book, let a-be
an auld fisher's wife. But, indeed, she had a grand education, and was muckle taen out afore she married an unco bit
beneath hersell. She's aulder than me by half a score years;
but I mind weel eneugh they made as muckle wark about her
making a half-merk marriage wi' Simon Mucklebackit, this
Saunders's father, as if she had been ane o' the gentry. But
she got into favour again, and then she lost it again, as I hae
heard her son say, when he was a muckle chield; and then
they got muckle siller, and left the Countess's land and settled
here. But things never throve wi' them. Howsomever, she's
a weel-educate woman, and an she win to her English, as I
hae heard her do at an orra time, she may come to fickle
us a'."

CHAPTER XL.

Life ebbs from such old age, unmark'd and silent,
As the slow neap-tide leaves yon stranded galley.
Late she rock'd merrily at the least impulse
That wind or wave could give; but now her keel
Is settling on the sand, her mast has ta'en
An angle with the sky, from which it shifts not.
Each wave receding shakes her less and less,
Till, bedded on the strand, she shall remain
Useless as motionless.

Old Play.

As the Antiquary lifted the latch of the hut, he was surprised to hear the shrill tremulous voice of Elspeth chanting forth an old ballad in a wild and doleful recitative.

" The herring loves the merry moonlight,
    The mackerel loves the wind,
But the oyster loves the dredging sang,
    For they come of a gentle kind."

A diligent collector of these legendary scraps of ancient poetry, his foot refused to cross the threshold when his ear was thus arrested, and his hand instinctively took pencil and memorandum-book. From time to time the old woman spoke as if to the children: " Oh ay, hinnies, whisht, whisht! and I'll begin a bonnier ane than that—

Now haud your tongue, baith wife and carle,
    And listen, great and sma',
And I will sing of Glenallan's Earl
    That fought on the red Harlaw.

The cronach's cried on Bennachie,
    And doun the Don an a',
And Hieland and Lawland may mournfu' be
    For the sair field of Harlaw.

I dinna mind the neist verse weel; my memory's failed, and there's unco thoughts come ower me. God keep us frae temptation!"

Here her voice sunk in indistinct muttering.

" It's a historical ballad," said Oldbuck, eagerly—" a genuine and undoubted fragment of minstrelsy! Percy would admire its simplicity; Ritson could not impugn its authenticity."

"Ay, but it's a sad thing," said Ochiltree, "to see human nature sae far owertaen as to be skirling at auld sangs on the back of a loss like hers."

"Hush, hush!" said the Antiquary; "she has gotten the thread of the story again"; and as he spoke she sung:

> " They saddled a hundred milk-white steeds,
>   They hae bridled a hundred black,
>   With a chafron of steel on each horse's head,
>   And a good knight upon his back."

"Chafron!" exclaimed the Antiquary, "equivalent, perhaps, to *cheveron*, the word's worth a dollar"; and down it went in his red book.

> " They hadna ridden a mile, a mile,
>   A mile, but barely ten,
>   When Donald came branking down the brae
>   Wi' twenty thousand men.
>
> Their tartans they were waving wide,
>   Their glaives were glancing clear,
>   The pibrochs rung frae side to side,
>   Would deafen ye to hear.
>
> The great Earl in his stirrups stood
>   That Highland host to see:
> ' Now here a knight that's stout and good
>   May prove a jeopardie.
>
> ' What wouldst thou do, my squire so gay,
>   That rides beside my reyne,
>   Were ye Glenallan's Earl the day,
>   And I were Roland Cheyne?
>
> ' To turn the rein were sin and shame,
>   To fight were wondrous peril,
>   What would ye do now, Roland Cheyne,
>   Were ye Glenallan's Earl?'

Ye maun ken, hinnies, that this Roland Cheyne, for as poor and auld as I sit in the chimney-neuk, was my forebear, and an awfu' man he was that day in the fight, but specially after the Earl had fa'en; for he blamed himsell for the counsel he gave, to fight before Mar came up wi' Mearns and Aberdeen and Angus."

Her voice rose and became more animated as she recited the warlike counsel of her ancestor:

> " 'Were I Glenallan's Earl this tide,
>   And ye were Roland Cheyne,
> The spur should be in my horse's side,
>   And the bridle upon his mane.
>
> 'If they hae twenty thousand blades,
>   And we twice ten times ten,
> Yet they hae but their tartan plaids,
>   And we are mail-clad men.
>
> 'My horse shall ride through ranks sae rude
>   As through the moorland fern,
> Then ne'er let the gentle Norman blude
>   Grow cauld for Highland kerne.' "

"Do you hear that, nephew?" said Oldbuck; "you observe your Gaelic ancestors were not held in high repute formerly by the Lowland warriors."

"I hear," said Hector, "a silly old woman sing a silly old song. I am surprised, sir, that you, who will not listen to Ossian's 'Songs of Selma,' can be pleased with such trash. I vow, I have not seen or heard a worse halfpenny ballad; I don't believe you could match it in any pedlar's pack in the country. I should be ashamed to think that the honour of the Highlands could be affected by such doggrel." And, tossing up his head, he snuffed the air indignantly.

Apparently the old woman heard the sound of their voices; for, ceasing her song, she called out: "Come in, sirs, come in; good-will never halted at the door-stane."

They entered, and found to their surprise Elspeth alone, sitting "ghastly on the hearth," like the personification of Old Age in the *Hunter's Song of the Owl*,[1] "wrinkled, tattered, vile, dim-eyed, discoloured, torpid."

"They're a' out," she said, as they entered; "but, an ye will sit a blink, somebody will be in. If ye hae business wi' my gude-daughter or my son, they'll be in belyve: I never speak on business mysell. Bairns, gie them seats. The bairns are a' gane out, I trow (looking around her). I was

---

[1] See Mrs. Grant on the *Highland Superstitions*, vol. ii. p. 260, for this fine translation from the Gaelic.

crooning to keep them quiet a wee while since; but they hae cruppin out some gate. Sit down, sirs, they'll be in belyve"; and she dismissed her spindle from her hand to twirl upon the floor, and soon seemed exclusively occupied in regulating its motion, as unconscious of the presence of the strangers as she appeared indifferent to their rank or business there.

"I wish," said Oldbuck, "she would resume that canticle or legendary fragment: I always suspected there was a skirmish of cavalry before the main battle of the Harlaw." [1]

"If your honour pleases," said Edie, "had ye not better proceed to the business that brought us a' here? I'se engage to get ye the sang ony time."

"I believe you are right, Edie. *Do manus*—I submit. But how shall we manage? She sits there, the very image of dotage. Speak to her, Edie; try if you can make her recollect having sent you to Glenallan House."

Edie rose accordingly, and, crossing the floor, placed himself in the same position which he had occupied during his former conversation with her. "I'm fain to see ye looking sae weel, cummer; the mair, that the black ox has tramped on ye since I was aneath your roof-tree."

"Ay," said Elspeth, but rather from a general idea of misfortune than any exact recollection of what had happened, "there has been distress amang us of late. I wonder how younger folk bide it; I bide it ill. I canna hear the wind whistle and the sea roar, but I think I see the coble whombled keel up, and some o' them struggling in the waves! Eh, sirs, sic weary dreams as folk hae between sleeping and waking, before they win to the lang sleep and the sound! I could amaist think whiles my son, or else Steenie, my oe, was dead, and that I had seen the burial. Isna that a queer dream for a daft auld carline? What for should ony o' them dee before me? it's out o' the course o' nature, ye ken."

"I think you'll make very little of this stupid old woman," said Hector, who still nourished, perhaps, some feelings of the dislike excited by the disparaging mention of his countrymen in her lay—"I think you'll make but little of her, sir;

and it's wasting our time to sit here and listen to her dotage."

"Hector," said the Antiquary, indignantly, "if you do not respect her misfortunes, respect at least her old age and grey hairs. This is the last stage of existence, so finely treated by the Latin poet:

> Omni
> Membrorum damno major dementia, quæ nec
> Nomina servorum, nec vultus agnoscit amici,
> Cum queis preterita cœnavit nocte, nec illos
> Quos genuit, quos eduxit."

"That's Latin!" said Elspeth, rousing herself as if she attended to the lines which the Antiquary recited with great pomp of diction—"that's Latin!" and she cast a wild glance around her. "Has there a priest fund me out at last?"

"You see, nephew, her comprehension is almost equal to your own of that fine passage."

"I hope you think, sir, that I knew it to be Latin as well as she did?"

"Why, as to that—— But stay, she is about to speak."

"I will have no priest, none," said the beldam, with impotent vehemence; "as I have lived I will die: none shall say that I betrayed my mistress, though it were to save my soul!"

"That bespoke a foul conscience," said the mendicant; "I wuss she wad mak a clean breast, an it were but for her ain sake," and he again assailed her.

"Weel, gudewife, I did your errand to the Yerl."

"To what Earl! I ken nae Earl. I kend a Countess ance, I wish to Heaven I had never kend her! for by that acquaintance, neighbour, there cam (and she counted her withered fingers as she spoke) first Pride, then Malice, then Revenge, then False Witness; and Murder tirl'd at the doorpin, if he camna ben. And werena thae pleasant guests, think ye, to take up their quarters in ae woman's heart? I trow there was routh o' company."

"But, cummer," continued the beggar, "it wasna the Countess of Glenallan I meant, but her son, him that was Lord Geraldin."

"I mind it now," she said; "I saw him no that lang syne,

and we had a heavy speech thegither. Eh, sirs, the comely young lord is turned as auld and frail as I am: it's muckle that sorrow and heartbreak and crossing of true love will do wi' young blood. But suldna his mither hae lookit to that hersell? We were but to do her bidding, ye ken. I am sure there's naebody can blame me: he wasna my son, and she was my mistress. Ye ken how the rhyme says—I hae maist forgotten how to sing, or else the tune's left my auld head:

> He turn'd him right and round again,
>   Said, Scorn na at my mither;
> Light loves I may get mony a ane,
>   But minnie ne'er anither.

Then he was but of the half blude, ye ken, and hers was the right Glenallan after a'. Na, na, I maun never maen doing and suffering for the Countess Joscelin. Never will I maen for that."

Then drawing her flax from the distaff, with the dogged air of one who is resolved to confess nothing, she resumed her interrupted occupation.

"I hae heard," said the mendicant, taking his cue from what Oldbuck had told him of the family history—"I hae heard, cummer, that some ill tongue suld hae come between the Earl, that's Lord Geraldin, and his young bride."

"Ill tongue!" she said, in hasty alarm; "and what had she to fear frae an ill tongue? She was gude and fair eneugh, at least a' body said sae. But had she keepit her ain tongue aff ither folk she might hae been living like a leddy for a' that's come and gane yet."

"But I hae heard say, gudewife," continued Ochiltree, "there was a clatter in the country, that her husband and her were ower sib when they married."

"Wha durst speak o' that?" said the old woman, hastily—"wha durst say they were married? Wha kend o' that? Not the Countess, not I; if they wedded in secret they were severed in secret. They drank of the fountains of their ain deceit."

"No, wretched beldam," exclaimed Oldbuck, who could

keep silence no longer, "they drank the poison that you and your wicked mistress prepared for them."

"Ha, ha!" she replied, "I aye thought it would come to this: it's but sitting silent when they examine me. There's nae torture in our days; and if there is, let them rend me! It's ill o' the vassal's mouth that betrays the bread it eats."

"Speak to her, Edie," said the Antiquary; "she knows your voice, and answers to it most readily."

"We shall mak naething mair out o' her," said Ochiltree. "When she has clinkit hersell down that way, and faulded her arms, she winna speak a word, they say, for weeks thegither. And besides, to my thinking, her face is sair changed since we cam in. However, I'se try her ance mair to satisfy your honour.—So you canna keep in mind, cummer, that your auld mistress, the Countess Joscelin, has been removed?"

"Removed!" she exclaimed, for that name never failed to produce its usual effect upon her; "then we maun a' follow. A' maun ride when she is in the saddle. Tell them to let Lord Geraldin ken we're on before them; bring my hood and scarf—ye wadna hae me gang in the carriage wi' my leddy and my hair in this fashion?"

She raised her shrivelled arms, and seemed busied like a woman who puts on her cloak to go abroad, then dropped them slowly and stiffly; and the same idea of a journey still floating apparently through her head, she proceeded in a hurried and interrupted manner: "Call Miss Neville. What do you mean by Lady Geraldin? I said Eveline Neville, not Lady Geraldin; there's no Lady Geraldin; tell her that, and bid her change her wet gown, and no' look sae pale. Bairn! what should she do wi' a bairn? maidens hae nane, I trow. Teresa, Teresa, my lady calls us! Bring a candle, the grand staircase is as mirk as a Yule midnight! We are coming, my lady!" With these words she sunk back on the settle, and from thence sidelong to the floor.[1]

Edie ran to support her, but hardly got her in his arms before he said: "It's a' ower, she has passed away even with that last word."

[1] See Elspeth's Death. Note 11.

"Impossible," said Oldbuck, hastily advancing, as did his nephew. But nothing was more certain. She had expired with the last hurried word that left her lips; and all that remained before them were the mortal relics of the creature who had so long struggled with an internal sense of concealed guilt, joined to all the distresses of age and poverty.

"God grant that she be gane to a better place!" said Edie, as he looked on the lifeless body; "but, oh! there was something lying hard and heavy at her heart. I have seen mony a ane dee, baith in the field o' battle and a fair-strae death at hame; but I wad rather see them a' ower again as sic a fearfu' flitting as hers!"

"We must call in the neighbours," said Oldbuck, when he had somewhat recovered his horror and astonishment, "and give warning of this additional calamity. I wish she could have been brought to a confession. And, though of far less consequence, I could have wished to transcribe that metrical fragment. But Heaven's will must be done!"

They left the hut accordingly and gave the alarm in the hamlet, whose matrons instantly assembled to compose the limbs and arrange the body of her who might be considered as the mother of their settlement. Oldbuck promised his assistance for the funeral.

"Your honour," said Ailison Breck, who was next in age to the deceased, "suld send doun something to us for keeping up our hearts at the lyke-wake, for a' Saunders's gin, puir man, was drucken out at the burial o' Steenie, and we'll no get mony to sit dry-lipped aside the corpse. Elspeth was unco clever in her young days, as I can mind right weel, but there was aye a word o' her no being that chancy. Ane suldna speak ill o' the dead—mair by token, o' ane's cummer and neighbour—but there was queer things said about a leddy and a bairn or she left the Craigburnfoot. And sae, in gude troth, it will be a puir lyke-wake unless your honour sends us something to keep us cracking."

"You shall have some whisky," answered Oldbuck, "the rather that you have preserved the proper word for that ancient custom of watching the dead. You observe, Hector, this is genuine Teutonic, from the Gothic *Leichnam*, a corpse. It is quite erroneously called *Late-wake*, though Brand favours that modern corruption and derivation."

"I believe," said Hector to himself, "my uncle would give away Monkbarns to any one who would come to ask it in genuine Teutonic! Not a drop of whisky would the old creatures have got had their president asked it for the use of the *Late-wake*."

While Oldbuck was giving some farther directions and promising assistance, a servant of Sir Arthur's came riding very hard along the sands, and stopped his horse when he saw the Antiquary. "There had something," he said, "very particular happened at the Castle (he could not, or would not, explain what), and Miss Wardour had sent him off express to Monkbarns, to beg that Mr. Oldbuck would come to them without a moment's delay."

"I am afraid," said the Antiquary, "his course also is drawing to a close. What can I do?"

"Do, sir!" exclaimed Hector, with his characteristic impatience. "Get on the horse and turn his head homeward; you will be at Knockwinnock Castle in ten minutes."

"He is quite a free goer," said the servant, dismounting to adjust the girths and stirrups; "he only pulls a little if he feels a dead weight on him."

"I should soon be a dead weight *off* him, my friend," said the Antiquary. "What the devil, nephew, are you weary of me? or do you suppose me weary of my life, that I should get on the back of such a Bucephalus as that? No, no, my friend, if I am to be at Knockwinnock to-day, it must be by walking quietly forward on my own feet, which I will do with as little delay as possible. Captain M'Intyre may ride that animal himself, if he pleases."

"I have little hope I could be of any use, uncle, but I cannot think of their distress without wishing to show sympathy at least, so I will ride on before and announce to them that you are coming. I'll trouble you for your spurs, my friend."

"You will scarce need them, sir," said the man, taking

them off at the same time and buckling them upon Captain M'Intyre's heels, "he's very frank to the road."

Oldbuck stood astonished at this last act of temerity. "Are you mad, Hector?" he cried, "or have you forgotten what is said by Quintus Curtius, with whom, as a soldier, you must needs be familiar, *Nobilis equus umbra quidem virgæ regitur; ignavus ne calcari quidem excitari potest;* which plainly shows that spurs are useless in every case, and, I may add, dangerous in most?"

But Hector, who cared little for the opinion of either Quintus Curtius or of the Antiquary upon such a topic, only answered with a heedless "Never fear, never fear, sir."

> With that he gave his able horse the head,
> And, bending forward, struck his armed heels
> Against the panting sides of his poor jade,
> Up to the rowel-head ; and starting so,
> He seem'd in running to devour the way,
> Staying no longer question.

"There they go, well matched," said Oldbuck, looking after them as they started—"a mad horse and a wild boy, the two most unruly creatures in Christendom! and all to get half an hour sooner to a place where nobody wants him; for I doubt Sir Arthur's griefs are beyond the cure of our light horseman. It must be the villainy of Dousterswivel, for whom Sir Arthur has done so much; for I cannot help observing that with some natures Tacitus's maxim holdeth good: *Beneficia eo usque læta sunt dum videntur exsolvi posse ; ubi multum antevenere, pro gratia odium redditur*, from which a wise man might take a caution not to oblige any man beyond the degree ir which he may expect to be requited, lest he should make his debtor a bankrupt in gratitude."

Murmuring to himself such scraps of cynical philosophy, our Antiquary paced the sands towards Knockwinnock; but it is necessary we should outstrip him for the purpose of explaining the reasons of his being so anxiously summoned thither.

CHAPTER XLI.

So, while the goose, of whom the fable told,
Incumbent, brooded o'er her eggs of gold,
With hand outstretch'd, impatient to destroy,
Stole on her secret nest the cruel boy,
Whose gripe rapacious changed her splendid dream
For wings vain fluttering and for dying scream.
The Loves of the Sea-weeds.

FROM the time that Sir Arthur Wardour had become possessor of the treasure found in Misticot's grave, he had been
in a state of mind more resembling ecstasy than sober sense.
Indeed, at one time his daughter had become seriously apprehensive for his intellect; for, as he had no doubt that he had
the secret of possessing himself of wealth to an unbounded
extent, his language and carriage were those of a man who
had acquired the philosopher's stone. He talked of buying
contiguous estates that would have led him from one side of
the island to the other, as if he were determined to brook no
neighbour save the sea. He corresponded with an architect
of eminence upon a plan of renovating the castle of his forefathers on a style of extended magnificence that might have
rivalled that of Wisdsor, and laying out the grounds on a suitable scale. Troops of liveried menials were already in fancy
marshalled in his halls, and—for what may not unbounded
wealth authorise its possessor to aspire to?—the coronet of
a marquis, perhaps of a duke, was glittering before his imagination. His daughter—to what matches might she not look
forward? Even an alliance with the blood-royal was not beyond the sphere of his hopes. His son was already a general,
and he himself whatever ambition could dream of in its wildest
visions.

In this mood, if any one endeavoured to bring Sir Arthur
down to the regions of common life, his replies were in the
vein of Ancient Pistol:

A fico for the world and worldlings base!
I speak of Africa and golden joys!

The reader may conceive the amazement of Miss Wardour when, instead of undergoing an investigation concerning the addresses of Lovel, as she had expected from the long conference of her father with Mr. Oldbuck upon the morning of the fated day when the treasure was discovered, the conversation of Sir Arthur announced an imagination heated with the hopes of possessing the most unbounded wealth. But she was seriously alarmed when Dousterswivel was sent for to the Castle, and was closeted with her father, his mishap condoled with, his part taken, and his loss compensated. All the suspicions which she had long entertained respecting this man became strengthened by observing his pains to keep up the golden dreams of her father, and to secure for himself, under various pretexts, as much as possible out of the windfall which had so strangely fallen to Sir Arthur's share.

Other evil symptoms began to appear, following on each other. Letters arrived every post, which Sir Arthur, as soon as he had looked at the directions, flung into the fire without taking the trouble to open them. Miss Wardour could not help suspecting that these epistles, the contents of which seemed to be known to her father by a sort of intuition, came from pressing creditors. In the mean while the temporary aid which he had received from the treasure dwindled fast away. By far the greater part had been swallowed up by the necessity of paying the bill of six hundred pounds which had threatened Sir Arthur with instant distress. Of the rest, some part was given to the adept, some wasted upon extravagances which seemed to the poor knight fully authorised by his full-blown hopes, and some went to stop for a time the mouths of such claimants who, being weary of fair promises, had become of opinion with Harpagon that it was necessary to touch something substantial. At length circumstances announced but too plainly that it was all expended within two or three days after its discovery; and there appeared no prospect of a supply. Sir Arthur, naturally impatient, now taxed Dousterswivel anew with breach of those promises through which he had hoped to convert all his lead into gold. But that worthy gentleman's turn was now served; and, as he had grace enough to wish to avoid witnessing the fall of the house which he had undermined, he was at the trouble of bestowing a few learned terms of art upon Sir Arthur, that at least he might not be tormented before his time. He took leave of him with assurances that he would return to Knockwinnock the next morning with such information as would not fail to relieve Sir Arthur from all his distresses.

"For, since I have consulted in such matters, I have never," said Mr. Herman Dousterwivel, "approached so near de *arcanum*, what you call de great mystery—de Panchresta, de Polychresta; I do know as much of it as Pelaso de Taranta or Basilius, and either I will bring you in two and three days de No. II. of Mr. Mishdigoat, or you shall call me one knave myself, and never look me in de face again no more at all."

The adept departed with this assurance, in the firm resolution of making good the latter part of the proposition, and never again appearing before his injured patron. Sir Arthur remained in a doubtful and anxious state of mind. The positive assurances of the philosopher, with the hard words Panchresta, Basilius, and so forth, produced some effect on his mind. But he had been too often deluded by such jargon to be absolutely relieved of his doubt, and he retired for the evening into his library in the fearful state of one who, hanging over a precipice, and without the means of retreat, perceives the stone on which he rests gradually parting from the rest of the crag and about to give way with him.

The visions of hope decayed, and there increased in proportion that feverish agony of anticipation with which a man, educated in a sense of consequence, and possessed of opulence, the supporter of an ancient name, and the father of two promising children, foresaw the hour approaching which should deprive him of all the splendour which time had made familiarly necessary to him, and send him forth into the world to struggle with poverty, with rapacity, and with scorn. Under these dire forebodings his temper, exhausted by the sickness of delayed hope, became peevish and fretful, and his words and actions sometimes expressed a reckless desperation which alarmed Miss Wardour extremely. We have seen on a

former occasion that Sir Arthur was a man of passions lively
and quick, in proportion to the weakness of his character in
other respects; he was unused to contradiction, and if he had
been hitherto, in general, good-humoured and cheerful, it was
probably because the course of his life had afforded no such
frequent provocation as to render his irritability habitual.

On the third morning after Dousterswivel's departure, the
servant, as usual, laid on the breakfast table the newspaper
and letters of the day. Miss Wardour took up the former to
avoid the continued ill-humour of her father, who had wrought
himself into a violent passion because the toast was over-
browned.

"I perceive how it is," was his concluding speech on this
interesting subject: "my servants, who have had their share
of my fortune, begin to think there is little to be made of me
in future. But while I *am* the scoundrels' master I will be
so, and permit no neglect—no, nor endure a hair's-breadth
diminution of the respect I am entitled to exact from
them."

"I am ready to leave your honour's service this instant,"
said the domestic upon whom the fault had been charged, "as
soon as you order payment of my wages."

Sir Arthur, as if stung by a serpent, thrust his hand into
his pocket and instantly drew out the money which it contained, but which was short of the man's claim. "What
money have you got, Miss Wardour?" he said, in a tone of
affected calmness, but which concealed violent agitation.

Miss Wardour gave him her purse; he attempted to count
the bank notes which it contained, but could not reckon them.
After twice miscounting the sum, he threw the whole to his
daughter, and saying in a stern voice: "Pay the rascal, and
let him leave the house instantly!" he strode out of the room.

The mistress and servant stood alike astonished at the
agitation and vehemence of his manner.

"I am sure, ma'am, if I had thought I was particularly
wrang I wadna hae made ony answer when Sir Arthur challenged me. I hae been lang in his service, and he has been
a kind master, and you a kind mistress, and I wad like ill ye

should think I wad start for a hasty word. I am sure it was very wrang o' me to speak about wages to his honour, when maybe he has something to vex him. I had nae thoughts o' leaving the family in this way."

"Go downstairs, Robert," said his mistress; "something has happened to fret my father—go downstairs, and let Alick answer the bell."

When the man left the room, Sir Arthur re-entered, as if he had been watching his departure. "What's the meaning of this?" he said, hastily, as he observed the notes lying still on the table. "Is he not gone? Am I neither to be obeyed as a master or a father?"

"He is gone to give up his charge to the housekeeper, sir; I thought there was not such instant haste."

"There *is* haste, Miss Wardour," asnwered her father, interrupting her. "What I do henceforth in the house of my forefathers must be done speedily or never."

He then sate down and took up with a trembling hand the basin of tea prepared for him, protracting the swallowing of it, as if to delay the necessity of opening the post-letters which lay on the table, and which he eyed from time to time, as if they had been a nest of adders ready to start into life and spring upon him.

"You will be happy to hear," said Miss Wardour, willing to withdraw her father's mind from the gloomy reflections in which he appeared to be plunged—"you will be happy to hear, sir, that Lieutenant Taffril's gun-brig has got safe into Leith Roads. I observe there had been apprehensions for his safety; I am glad we did not hear them till they were contradicted."

"And what is Taffril and his gun-brig to me?"

"Sir!" said Miss Wardour in astonishment; for Sir Arthur, in his ordinary state of mind, took a fidgety sort of interest in all the gossip of the day and country.

"I say," he repeated, in a higher and still more impatient key, "what do I care who is saved or lost? It's nothing to me, I suppose?"

"I did not know you were busy, Sir Arthur; and thought,

27

as Mr. Taffril is a brave man, and from our own country, you would be happy to hear——"

"Oh, I am happy, as happy as possible; and, to make you happy too, you shall have some of my good news in return."

And he caught up a letter. "It does not signify which I open first, they are all to the same tune."

He broke the seal hastily, run the letter over, and then threw it to his daughter. "Ay; I could not have lighted more happily! this places the copestone."

Miss Wardour, in silent terror, took up the letter. "Read it—read it aloud!" said her father. "It cannot be read too often; it will serve to break you in for other good news of the same kind."

She began to read with a faltering voice, "Dear Sir."

"He 'dears' me too, you see—this impudent drudge of a writer's office, who a twelvemonth since was not fit company for my second table. I suppose I shall be 'dear Knight' with him by and by."

"Dear Sir," resumed Miss Wardour; but, interrupting herself, "I see the contents are unpleasant, sir; it will only vex you my reading them aloud."

"If you will allow me to know my own pleasure, Miss Wardour, I entreat you to go on; I presume, if it were unnecessary, I should not ask you to take the trouble."

"Having been of late taken into copartnery," continued Miss Wardour, reading the letter, "by Mr. Gilbert Greenhorn, son of your late correspondent and man of business, Girnigo Greenhorn, Esq., writer to the signet, whose business I conducted as parliament-house clerk for many years, which business will in future be carried on under the firm of Greenhorn and Grinderson—which I memorandum for the sake of accuracy in addressing your future letters—and having had of late favours of yours, directed to my aforesaid partner, Gilbert Greenhorn, in consequence of his absence at the Lamberton races, have the honour to reply to your said favours."

"You see my friend is methodical, and commences by explaining the causes which have procured me so modest and elegant a correspondent. Go on, I can bear it."

And he laughed that bitter laugh which is perhaps the most fearful expression of mental misery. Trembling to proceed, and yet afraid to disobey, Miss Wardour continued to read: "I am, for myself and partner, sorry we cannot oblige you by looking out for the sums you mention, or applying for a suspension in the case of Goldiebirds' bond, which would be more inconsistent as we have been employed to act as the said Goldiebirds' procurators and attorneys, in which capacity we have taken out a charge of horning against you, as you must be aware by the schedule left by the messenger, for the sum of four thousand seven hundred and fifty-six pounds five shillings and sixpence one-fourth of a penny Sterling, which, with annual rent and expenses effeiring, we presume will be settled during the currency of the charge, to prevent further trouble. Same time, I am under the necessity to observe our own account, amounting to seven hundred and sixty-nine pounds ten shillings and sixpence, is also due, and settlement would be agreeable; but, as we hold your rights, title-deeds, and documents in hypothec, shall have no objection to give reasonable time—say till the next money term. I am, for myself and partner, concerned to add that Messrs. Goldiebirds' instructions to us are, to proceed *peremptorie* and *sine mora*, of which I have the pleasure to advise you to prevent future mistakes, reserving to ourselves otherwise to *agé* as accords. I am, for self and partner, dear sir, your obliged humble servant, Gabriel Grinderson, for Greenhorn and Grinderson."

"Ungrateful villain!" said Miss Wardour.

"Why, no; it's in the usual rule, I suppose. The blow could not have been perfect if dealt by another hand; it's all just as it should be," answered the poor Baronet, his affected composure sorely belied by his quivering lip and rolling eye. "But here's a postscript I did not notice; come, finish the epistle."

"I have to add—not for self but partner—that Mr. Greenhorn will accommodate you by taking your service of plate, or the bay horses, if sound in wind and limb, at a fair appreciation, in part payment of your accompt."

"G—d confound him!" said Sir Arthur, losing all command

of himself at this condescending proposal; "his grandfather shod my father's horses, and this descendant of a scoundrelly blacksmith proposes to swindle me out of mine! But I will write him a proper answer."

And he sate down and began to write with great vehemence, then stopped and read aloud: "Mr. Gilbert Greenhorn, In answer to two letters of a late date, I received a letter from a person calling himself Grinderson, and designing himself as your partner. When I address any one I do not usually expect to be answered by deputy. I think I have been useful to your father, and friendly and civil to yourself, and therefore am now surprised—— And yet," said he, stopping short, "why should I be surprised at that or anything else, or why should I take up my time in writing to such a scoundrel? I shan't be always kept in prison, I suppose, and to break that puppy's bones when I get out shall be my first employment."

"In prison, sir?" said Miss Wardour, faintly.

"Ay, in prison, to be sure. Do you make any question about that? Why, Mr. what's-his-name's fine letter for self and partner seems to be thrown away on you, or else you have got four thousand so many hundred pounds, with the due proportion of shillings, pence, and half-pence, to pay that aforesaid demand, as he calls it."

"I, sir? Oh, if I had the means! But where's my brother? Why does he not come, and so long in Scotland? He might do something to assist us."

"Who, Reginald? I suppose he's gone with Mr. Gilbert Greenhorn, or some such respectable person, to the Lamberton races. I have expected him this week past; but I cannot wonder that my children should neglect me as well as every other person. But I should beg your pardon, my love, who never either neglected or offended me in your life."

And, kissing her cheek as she threw her arms round his neck, he experienced that consolation which a parent feels, even in the most distressed state, in the assurance that he possesses the affection of a child.

Miss Wardour took the advantage of this revulsion of feeling to endeavour to soothe her father's mind to composure. She reminded him that he had many friends.

"I *had* many once," said Sir Arthur; "but of some I have exhausted their kindness with my frantic projects, others are unable to assist me, others are unwilling; it is all over with me. I only hope Reginald will take example by my folly."

"Should I not send to Monkbarns, sir?" said his daughter.

"To what purpose? He cannot lend me such a sum, and would not if he could, for he knows I am otherwise drowned in debt; and he would only give me scraps of misanthropy and quaint ends of Latin."

"But he is shrewd and sensible, and was bred to business, and, I am sure, always loved this family."

"Yes, I believe he did: it is a fine pass we are come to when the affection of an Oldbuck is of consequence to a Wardour! But when matters come to extremity, as I suppose they presently will, it may be as well to send for him. And now go take your walk, my dear; my mind is more composed than when I had this cursed disclosure to make. You know the worst, and may daily or hourly expect it. Go take your walk; I would willingly be alone for a little while."

When Miss Wardour left the apartment her first occupation was to avail herself of the half permission granted by her father, by despatching to Monkbarns the messenger, who, as we have already seen, met the Antiquary and his nephew on the sea-beach.

Little recking, and indeed scarce knowing, where she was wandering, chance directed her into the walk beneath the Briery Bank, as it was called. A brook, which in former days had supplied the castle moat with water, here descended through a narrow dell, up which Miss Wardour's taste had directed a natural path, which was rendered neat and easy of ascent, without the air of being formally made and preserved. It suited well the character of the little glen, which was overhung with thickets and underwood, chiefly of larch and hazel, intermixed with the usual varieties of the thorn and brier. In this walk had passed that scene of explanation between Miss Wardour and Lovel which was overheard by old Edie Ochiltree. With a heart softened by the distress which approached her family, Miss Wardour now recalled every word and argument which Lovel had urged in support of his suit, and could not help confessing to herself it was no small subject of pride to have inspired a young man of his talents with a passion so strong and disinterested. That he should have left the pursuit of a profession in which he was said to be rapidly rising to bury himself in a disagreeable place like Fairport, and brood over an unrequited passion, might be ridiculed by others as romantic, but was naturally forgiven as an excess of affection by the person who was the object of his attachment. Had he possessed an independence, however moderate, or ascertained a clear and undisputed claim to the rank in society he was well qualified to adorn, she might now have had it in her power to offer her father, during his misfortunes, an asylum in an establishment of her own. These thoughts, so favourable to the absent lover, crowded in, one after the other, with such a minute recapitulation of his words, looks, and actions as plainly intimated that his former repulse had been dictated rather by duty than inclination. Isabella was musing alternately upon this subject and upon that of her father's misfortunes when, as the path winded round a little hillock covered with brushwood, the old Blue-Gown suddenly met her.

With an air as if he had something important and mysterious to communicate he doffed his bonnet, and assumed the cautious step and voice of one who would not willingly be overheard. "I hae been wishing muckle to meet wi' your leddyship; for ye ken I darena come to the house for Dousterswivel."

"I heard indeed," said Miss Wardour, dropping an alms into the bonnet—"I heard that you had done a very foolish, if not a very bad thing, Edie, and I am sorry to hear it."

"Hout, my bonny leddy—fulish! A' the warld's fules, and how should auld Edie Ochiltree be aye wise? and for the evil, let them wha deal wi' Dousterswivel tell whether he gat a grain mair than his deserts."

"That may be true, Edie, and yet," said Miss Wardour, "you may have been very wrong."

"Weel, weel, we'se no dispute that e'enow; it's about yoursell I'm gaun to speak. Did ye ken what's hanging ower the house of Knockwinnock?"

"Great distress, I fear, Edie," answered Miss Wardour; "but I am surprised it is already so public."

"Public! Sweepclean, the messenger, will be there the day wi' a' his tackle. I ken it frae ane o' his concurrents, as they ca' them, that's warned to meet him; and they'll be about their wark belyve. Whare they clip there needs nae kame: they sheer close eneugh."

"Are you sure this bad hour, Edie, is so very near? come I know it will."

"It's e'en as I tell you, leddy! but dinna be cast down; there's a heaven ower your head here, as weel as in that fearful night atween the Ballyburgh Ness and the Halket Head. D'ye think He wha rebuked the waters canna protect you against the wrath of men, though they be armed with human authority?"

"It is, indeed, all we have to trust to."

"Ye dinna ken—ye dinna ken; when the night's darkest the dawn's nearest. If I had a gude horse, or could ride him when I had him, I reckon there wad be help yet. I trusted to hae gotten a cast wi' the Royal Charlotte, but she's coupit yonder, it's like, at Kittlebrig. There was a young gentleman on the box, and he behuved to drive; and Tam Sang, that suld hae mair sense, he behuved to let him, and the daft callant couldna tak the turn at the corner o' the brig, and odd! he took the curb-stane, and he's whomled her as I wad whomle a toom bicker—it was a luck I hadna gotten on the tap o' her. Sae I came down atween hope and despair to see if ye wad send me on."

"And, Edie, where would ye go?" said the young lady.

"To Tannonburgh, my leddy" (which was the first stage from Fairport, but a good deal nearer to Knockwinnock), "and that without delay; it's a' on your ain business."

"Our business, Edie? Alas! I give you all credit for your good meaning, but——"

"There's nae 'buts' about it, my leddy, for gang I maun," said the persevering Blue-Gown.

"But what is it that you would do at Tannonburgh? or how can your going there benefit my father's affairs?"

"Indeed, my sweet leddy," said the gaberlunzie, "ye maun just trust that bit secret to auld Edie's grey pow, and ask nae questions about it. Certainly if I wad hae wared my life for you yon night, I can hae nae reason to play an ill pliskie t'ye in the day o' your distress."

"Well, Edie, follow me then," said Miss Wardour, "and I will try to get you sent to Tannonburgh."

"Mak haste then, my bonny leddy, mak haste, for the love o' goodness!" and he continued to exhort her to expedition until they reached the Castle.

CHAPTER XLII.

Let those go see who will; I like it not.
For, say he was a slave to rank and pomp,
And all the nothings he is now divorced from
By the hard doom of stern necessity;
Yet it is sad to mark his alter'd brow,
Where Vanity adjusts her flimsy veil
O'er the deep wrinkles of repentant anguish.

Old Play.

WHEN Miss Wardour arrived in the court of the Castle, she was apprised by the first glance that the visit of the officers of the law had already taken place. There was confusion, and gloom, and sorrow, and curiosity among the domestics, while the retainers of the law went from place to place, making an inventory of the goods and chattels falling under their warrant of distress, or poinding, as it is called in the law of Scotland. Captain M'Intyre flew to her, as, struck dumb with the melancholy conviction of her father's ruin, she paused upon the threshold of the gateway.

"Dear Miss Wardour," he said, "do not make yourself uneasy; my uncle is coming immediately, and I am sure he will find some way to clear the house of these rascals."

"Alas! Captain M'Intyre, I fear it will be too late."

"No," answered Edie, impatiently, "could I but get to Tannonburgh. In the name of Heaven, Captain! contrive some way to get me on, and ye'll do this poor ruined family the best day's doing that has been done them since Red-hand's days; for as sure as e'er an auld saw came true, Knockwinnock house and land will be lost and won this day."

"Why, what good can you do, old man?" said Hector.

But Robert, the domestic with whom Sir Arthur had been so much displeased in the morning, as if he had been watching for an opportunity to display his zeal, stepped hastily forward and said to his mistress: "If you please, ma'am, this auld man, Ochiltree, is very skeely and auld-farrant about mony things, as the diseases of cows, and horse, and sic like, and I am sure he disna want to be at Tannonburgh the day for naething, since he insists on't this gate; and, if your leddyship pleases, I'll drive him there in the taxed cart in an hour's time. I wad fain be of some use; I could bite my very tongue out when I think on this morning."

"I am obliged to you, Robert," said Miss Wardour; "and if you really think it has the least chance of being useful——"

"In the name of God," said the old man, "yoke the cart, Robie, and if I am no o' some use, less or mair, I'll gie ye leave to fling me ower Kittlebrig as ye come back again. But, O man, haste ye, for time's precious this day."

Robert looked at his mistress as she retired into the house, and, seeing he was not prohibited, flew to the stable-yard, which was adjacent to the court, in order to yoke the carriage; for, though an old beggar was the personage least likely to render effectual assistance in a case of pecuniary distress, yet there was among the common people of Edie's circle a general idea of his prudence and sagacity which authorised Robert's conclusion, that he would not so earnestly have urged the necessity of this expedition had he not been convinced of its utility. But so soon as the servant took hold of a horse to harness him for the tax-cart, an officer touched him on the shoulder: "My friend, you must let that beast alone, he's down in the schedule."

"What," said Robert, "am I not to take my master's horse to go my young leddy's errand."

"You must remove nothing here," said the man of office, "or you will be liable for all consequences?"

"What the devil, sir," said Hector, who, having followed to examine Ochiltree more closely on the nature of his hopes and expectations, already began to bristle like one of the terriers of his own native mountains, and sought but a decent pretext for venting his displeasure, "have you the impudence to prevent the young lady's servant from obeying her orders?"

There was something in the air and tone of the young soldier which seemed to argue that his interference was not likely to be confined to mere expostulation, and which, if it promised finally the advantages of a process of battery and deforcement, would certainly commence with the unpleasant circumstances necessary for founding such a complaint. The legal officer, confronted with him of the military, grasped with one doubtful hand the greasy bludgeon which was to enforce his authority, and with the other produced his short official baton, tipped with silver, and having a movable ring upon it: "Captain M'Intyre, sir, I have no quarrel with you, but if you interrupt me in my duty, I will break the wand of peace, and declare myself deforced."

"And who the devil cares," said Hector, totally ignorant of the words of judicial action, "whether you declare yourself divorced or married? And as to breaking your wand, or breaking the peace, or whatever you call it, all I know is, that I will break your bones if you prevent the lad from harnessing the horses to obey his mistress's orders."

"I take all who stand here to witness," said the messenger, "that I showed him my blazon and explained my character. 'He that will to Cupar maun to Cupar,' " and he slid his enigmatical ring from one end of the baton to the other, being the appropriate symbol of his having been forcibly interrupted in the discharge of his duty.

Honest Hector, better accustomed to the artillery of the field than to that of the law, saw this mystical ceremony with great indifference, and with like unconcern beheld the mes-

senger sit down to write out an execution of deforcement.
But at this moment, to prevent the well-meaning hot-headed
Highlander from running the risk of a severe penalty, the
Antiquary arrived puffing and blowing, with his handkerchief
crammed under his hat and his wig upon the end of his stick.

"What the deuce is the matter here?" he exclaimed, hastily
adjusting his headgear; "I have been following you in fear of
finding your idle loggerhead knocked against one rock or other,
and here I find you parted with your Bucephalus and quarrelling with Sweepclean. A messenger, Hector, is a worse foe
than a *phoca*, whether it be the *phoca barbata* or the *phoca
vitulina* of your late conflict."

"D——n the *phoca*, sir," said Hector, "whether it be the one
or the other—I say d——n them both particularly! I think you
would not have me stand quietly by and see a scoundrel like
this, because he calls himself a king's messenger, forsooth—
I hope the king has many better for his meanest errands—insult a young lady of family and fashion like Miss Wardour?"

"Rightly argued, Hector," said the Antiquary; "but the
king, like other people, has now and then shabby errands,
and, in your ear, must have shabby fellows to do them. But
even supposing you unacquainted with the statutes of William
the Lion in which, *capite quarto, versu quinto*, this crime of
deforcement is termed, *despectus domini regis*, a contempt, to
wit, of the king himself, in whose name all legal diligence
issues, could you not have inferred, from the information I
took so much pains to give you to-day, that those who interrupt officers who come to execute letters of caption, are *tanquam participes criminis rebellionis?* seeing that he who aids
a rebel is himself, *quodammodo*, an accessory to rebellion.
But I'll bring you out of the scrape."

He then spoke to the messenger, who, upon his arrival, had
laid aside all thoughts of making a good bye-job out of the
deforcement, and accepted Mr. Oldbuck's assurances that the
horse and taxed cart should be safely returned in the course
of two or three hours.

"Very well, sir," said the Antiquary, "since you are disposed to be so civil, you shall have another job in your own

best way—a little cast of state politics—a crime punishable *per Legem Juliam,* Mr. Sweepclean. Hark thee hither."

And, after a whisper of five minutes, he gave him a slip of paper, on receiving which the messenger mounted his horse, and, with one of his assistants, rode away pretty sharply. The fellow who remained seemed to delay his operations purposely, proceeded in the rest of his duty very slowly, and with the caution and precision of one who feels himself overlooked by a skilful and severe inspector.

In the mean time Oldbuck, taking his nephew by the arm, led him into the house, and they were ushered into the presence of Sir Arthur Wardour, who, in a flutter between wounded pride, agonised apprehension, and vain attempts to disguise both under a show of indifference, exhibited a spectacle of painful interest.

"Happy to see you, Mr. Oldbuck, always happy to see my friends in fair weather or foul," said the poor Baronet, struggling not for composure, but for gaiety, an affectation which was strongly contrasted by the nervous and protracted grasp of his hand, and the agitation of his whole demeanour—"I am happy to see you. You are riding, I see; I hope in this confusion your horses are taken good care of: I always like to have my friends' horses looked after. Egad, they will have all my care now, for you see they are like to leave me none of my own, he! he! he!—eh, Mr. Oldbuck?"

This attempt at a jest was attended by a hysterical giggle, which poor Sir Arthur intended should sound as an indifferent laugh.

"You know I never ride, Sir Arthur," said the Antiquary.

"I beg your pardon; but sure I saw your nephew arrive on horseback a short time since. We must look after officers' horses, and his was a handsome grey charger, as I have seen."

Sir Arthur was about to ring the bell, when Mr. Oldbuck said: "My nephew came on your own grey horse, Sir Arthur."

"Mine!" said the poor Baronet—"mine, was it? then the sun had been in my eyes. Well, I'm not worthy having a horse any longer, since I don't know my own when I see him."

" Good Heaven," thought Oldbuck, "how is this man altered from the formal stolidity of his usual manner! he grows wanton under adversity; *sed pereunti mille figuræ*." He then proceeded aloud: "Sir Arthur, we must necessarily speak a little on business."

" To be sure," said Sir Arthur; "but it was so good that I should not know the horse I have ridden these five years, ha! ha! ha!"

" Sir Arthur," said the Antiquary, "don't let us waste time which is precious; we shall have, I hope, many better seasons for jesting; *desipere in loco* is the maxim of Horace. I more than suspect this has been brought on by the villainy of Dousterswivel."

" Don't mention his name, sir!" said Sir Arthur; and his manner entirely changed from a fluttered affectation of gaiety to all the agitation of fury: his eyes sparkled, his mouth foamed, his hands were clenched—"don't mention his name, sir," he vociferated, "unless you would see me go mad in your presence! That I should have been such a miserable dolt, such an infatuated idiot, such a beast endowed with thrice a beast's stupidity, to be led and driven and spur-galled by such a rascal, and under such ridiculous pretences. Mr. Oldbuck, I could tear myself when I think of it."

" I only meant to say," answered the Antiquary, "that this fellow is like to meet his reward; and I cannot but think we shall frighten something out of him that may be of service to you. He has certainly had some unlawful correspondence on the other side of the water."

" Has he? has he? has he, indeed? Then d—n the household goods, horses, and so forth: I will go to prison a happy man, Mr. Oldbuck. I hope in Heaven there's a reasonable chance of his being hanged?"

" Why, pretty fair," said Oldbuck, willing to encourage this diversion, in hopes it might mitigate the feelings which seemed like to overset the poor man's understanding; "honester men have stretched a rope, or the law has been sadly cheated. But this unhappy business of yours—can nothing be done? Let me see the charge."

He took the papers; and as he read them his countenance grew hopelessly dark and disconsolate. Miss Wardour had by this time entered the apartment, and fixing her eyes on Mr. Oldbuck, as if she meant to read her fate in his looks, easily perceived, from the change in his eye and the dropping of his nether jaw, how little was to be hoped.

"We are then irremediably ruined, Mr. Oldbuck?" said the young lady.

"Irremediably! I hope not; but the instant demand is very large, and others will doubtless pour in."

"Ay, never doubt that, Monkbarns," said Sir Arthur; "where the slaughter is, the eagles will be gathered together. I am like a sheep which I have seen fall down a precipice, or drop down from sickness: if you had not seen a single raven or hooded crow for a fortnight before, he will not lie on the heather ten minutes before half a dozen will be picking out his eyes (and he drew his hand over his own), and tearing at his heart-strings before the poor devil has time to die. But that d—d long-scented vulture that dogged me so long—you have got him fast, I hope?"

"Fast enough," said the Antiquary; "the gentleman wished to take the wings of the morning and bolt in the what d'ye call it—the coach and four there. But he would have found twigs limed for him at Edinburgh. As it is, he never got so far, for the coach being overturned—as how could it go safe with such a Jonah?—he has had an infernal tumble, is carried into a cottage near Kittlebrig, and, to prevent all possibility of escape, I have sent your friend, Sweepclean, to bring him back to Fairport *in nomine regis*, or to act as his sick nurse at Kittlebrig, as is most fitting. And now, Sir Arthur, permit me to have some conversation with you on the present unpleasant state of your affairs, that we may see what can be done for their extrication"; and the Antiquary led the way into the library, followed by the unfortunate gentleman.

They had been shut up together for about two hours, when Miss Wardour interrupted them, with her cloak on as if prepared for a journey. Her countenance was very pale, yet expressive of the composure which characterised her disposition.

"The messenger is returned, Mr. Oldbuck."

"Returned! What the devil! he has not let the fellow go?"

"No; I understand he has carried him to confinement; and now he is returned to attend my father, and says he can wait no longer."

A loud wrangling was now heard on the staircase, in which the voice of Hector predominated. "You an officer, sir, and these ragamuffins a party! a parcel of beggarly tailor fellows! tell yourselves off by nine, and we shall know your effective strength."

The grumbling voice of the man of law was then heard indistinctly muttering a reply, to which Hector retorted: "Come, come, sir, this won't do; march your party, as you call them, out of this house directly, or I'll send you and them to the right about presently."

"The devil take Hector," said the Antiquary, hastening to the scene of action; "his Highland blood is up again, and we shall have him fighting a duel with the bailiff. Come, Mr. Sweepclean, you must give us a little time; I know you would not wish to hurry Sir Arthur."

"By no means, sir," said the messenger, putting his hat off, which he had thrown on to testify defiance of Captain M'Intyre's threats; "but your nephew, sir, holds very uncivil language, and I have borne too much of it already; and I am not justified in leaving my prisoner any longer after the instructions I received, unless I am to get payment of the sums contained in my diligence." And he held out the caption, pointing with the awful truncheon which he held in his right hand to the formidable lines of figures jotted upon the back thereof.

Hector, on the other hand, though silent from respect to his uncle, answered this gesture by shaking his clenched fist at the messenger with a frown of Highland wrath.

"Foolish boy, be quiet," said Oldbuck, "and come with me into the room; the man is doing his miserable duty, and you will only make matters worse by opposing him. I fear, Sir Arthur, you must accompany this man to Fairport; there is no help for it in the first instance. I will accompany you to consult what farther can be done. My nephew will escort Miss Wardour to Monkbarns, which I hope she will make her residence until these unpleasant matters are settled."

"I go with my father, Mr. Oldbuck," said Miss Wardour, firmly; "I have prepared his clothes and my own. I suppose we shall have the use of the carriage?"

"Anything in reason, madam," said the messenger; "I have ordered it out, and it's at the door. I will go on the box with the coachman, I have no desire to intrude; but two of the concurrents must attend on horseback."

"I will attend too," said Hector, and he ran down to secure a horse for himself.

"We must go then," said the Antiquary.

"To jail," said the Baronet, sighing involuntarily. "And what of that?" he resumed, in a tone affectedly cheerful; "it is only a house we can't get out of, after all. Suppose a fit of the gout, and Knockwinnock would be the same. Ay, ay, Monkbarns, we'll call it a fit of the gout without the d—d pain."

But his eyes swelled with tears as he spoke, and his faltering accent marked how much this assumed gaiety cost him. The Antiquary wrung his hand, and, like the Indian Banians, who drive the real terms on an important bargain by signs, while they are apparently talking of indifferent matters, the hand of Sir Arthur, by its convulsive return of the grasp, expressed his sense of gratitude to his friend, and the real state of his internal agony. They stepped slowly down the magnificent staircase, every well-known object seeming to the unfortunate father and daughter to assume a more prominent and distinct appearance than usual, as if to press themselves on their notice for the last time.

At the first landing-place Sir Arthur made an agonised pause; and as he observed the Antiquary look at him anxiously, he said with assumed dignity: "Yes, Mr. Oldbuck, the descendant of an ancient line—the representative of Richard Red-hand and Gamelyn de Guardover—may be pardoned a sigh when he leaves the castle of his fathers thus poorly escorted. When I was sent to the Tower with my late father, in the year 1745, it was upon a charge becoming our birth—upon an accusation of high treason, Mr. Oldbuck. We were escorted from Highgate by a troop of life-guards, and committed upon a secretary of state's warrant; and now, here I am, in my old age, dragged from my household by a miserable creature like that (pointing to the messenger), and for a paltry concern of pounds, shillings, and pence."

"At least," said Oldbuck, "you have now the company of a dutiful daughter and a sincere friend, if you will permit me to say so, and that may be some consolation, even without the certainty that there can be no hanging, drawing, or quartering on the present occasion. But I hear that choleric boy as loud as ever. I hope to God he has got into no new broil! It was an accursed chance that brought him here at all."

In fact, a sudden clamour, in which the loud voice and somewhat northern accent of Hector were again pre-eminently distinguished, broke off this conversation. The cause we must refer to the next chapter.

———◆———

CHAPTER XLIII.

> Fortune, you say, flies from us. She but circles
> Like the fleet sea-bird round the fowler's skiff,
> Lost in the mist one moment, and the next
> Brushing the white sail with her whiter wing,
> As if to court the aim. Experience watches,
> And has her on the wheel.
> *Old Play.*

THE shout of triumph in Hector's warlike tones was not easily distinguished from that of battle. But as he rushed upstairs with a packet in his hand, exclaiming, "Long life to an old soldier! here comes Edie with a whole budget of good news!" it became obvious that his present cause of clamour was of an agreeable nature. He delivered the letter to Oldbuck, shook Sir Arthur heartily by the hand, and wished Miss Wardour joy, with all the frankness of Highland congratulation. The messenger, who had a kind of instinctive

28

terror for Captain M'Intyre, drew towards his prisoner, keeping an eye of caution on the soldier's motions.

"Don't suppose I shall trouble myself about you, you dirty fellow," said the soldier. "There's a guinea for the fright I have given you; and here comes an old Forty-Two man, who is a fitter match for you than I am."

The messenger, (one of those dogs who are not too scornful to eat dirty puddings), caught in his hand the guinea which Hector chucked at his face, and abode warily and carefully the turn which matters were now to take. All voices meanwhile were loud in inquiries, which no one was in a hurry to answer.

"What is the matter, Captain M'Intyre?" said Sir Arthur.

"Ask old Edie," said Hector; "I only know all's safe and well."

"What is all this, Edie?" said Miss Wardour to the mendicant.

"Your leddyship maun ask Monkbarns, for he has gotten the yepistolary correspondensh."

"God save the king!" exclaimed the Antiquary, at the first glance of the contents of his packet, and, surprised at once out of decorum, philosophy, and phlegm, he skimmed his cocked hat in the air, from which it descended not again, being caught in its fall by a branch of the chandelier. He next, looking joyously round, laid a grasp on his wig, which he perhaps would have sent after the beaver, had not Edie stopped his hand, exclaiming: "Lordsake! he's gaun gyte; mind Caxon's no here to repair the damage."

Every person now assailed the Antiquary, clamouring to know the cause of so sudden a transport, when, somewhat ashamed of his rapture, he fairly turned tail, like a fox at the cry of a pack of hounds, and, ascending the stair by two steps at a time, gained the upper landing-place, where, turning round, he addressed the astonished audience as follows:

"My good friends, *favete linguis*. To give you information, I must first, according to logicians, be possessed of it myself; and therefore, with your leaves, I will retire into the library to examine these papers. Sir Arthur and Miss War-

dour will have the goodness to step into the parlour; Mr.
Sweepclean, *secede paulisper*, or, in your own language, grant
us a supersedere of diligence for five minutes. Hector, draw
off your forces and make your bear-garden flourish elsewhere;
and, finally, be all of good cheer till my return, which will
be *instanter*."

The contents of the packet were indeed so little expected
that the Antiquary might be pardoned, first his ecstasy, and
next his desire of delaying to communicate the intelligence
they conveyed, until it was arranged and digested in his own
mind.

Within the envelope was a letter addressed to Jonathan
Oldbuck, Esq., of Monkbarns, of the following purport:

"DEAR SIR—To you, as my father's proved and valued
friend, I venture to address myself, being detained here by
military duty of a very pressing nature. You must by this
time be acquainted with the entangled state of our affairs;
and I know it will give you great pleasure to learn that I am
as fortunately as unexpectedly placed in a situation to give
effectual assistance for extricating them. I understand Sir
Arthur is threatened with severe measures by persons who
acted formerly as his agents; and, by advice of a creditable
man of business here, I have procured the inclosed writing,
which I understand will stop their proceedings until their
claim shall be legally discussed and brought down to its
proper amount. I also inclose bills to the amount of one
thousand pounds to pay any other pressing demands, and request of your friendship to apply them according to your
discretion. You will be surprised I give you this trouble,
when it would seem more natural to address my father directly in his own affairs. But I have yet had no assurance
that his eyes are opened to the character of a person against
whom you have often, I know, warned him, and whose baneful influence has been the occasion of these distresses. And
as I owe the means of relieving Sir Arthur to the generosity
of a matchless friend, it is my duty to take the most certain
measures for the supplies being devoted to the purpose for

which they were destined, and I know your wisdom and kind·
ness will see that it is done. My friend, as he claims an interest in your regard, will explain some views of his own in the
inclosed letter. The state of the post-office at Fairport being
rather notorious, I must send this letter to Tannonburgh; but
the old man Ochiltree, whom particular circumstances have recommended as trustworthy, has information when the packet is
likely to reach that place, and will take care to forward it.
I expect to have soon an opportunity to apologise in person
for the trouble I now give, and have the honour to be, your
very faithful servant,

"REGINALD GAMELYN WARDOUR."

"EDINBURGH, 6th August 179—."

The Antiquary hastily broke the seal of the inclosure, the
contents of which gave him equal surprise and pleasure.
When he had in some measure composed himself after such
unexpected tidings, he inspected the other papers carefully,
which all related to business; put the bills into his pocket-
book, and wrote a short acknowledgment to be despatched by
that day's post, for he was extremely methodical in money
matters; and, lastly, fraught with all the importance of disclosure, he descended to the parlour.

"Sweepclean," said he, as he entered, to the officer, who
stood respectfully at the door, "you must sweep yourself
clean out of Knockwinnock Castle with all your followers,
tag-rag and bob-tail. See'st thou this paper, man?"

"A sist on a bill o' suspension," said the messenger, with
a disappointed look; "I thought it would be a queer thing if
ultimate diligence was to be done against sic a gentleman as
Sir Arthur. Weel, sir, I'se go my ways with my party.
And who's to pay my charges?"

"They who employed thee," replied Oldbuck, "as thou full
well dost know. But here comes another express: this is a
day of news, I think."

This was Mr. Mailsetter on his mare from Fairport, with
a letter for Sir Arthur, another to the messenger, both of
which, he said, he was directed to forward instantly. The

messenger opened his, observing that Greenhorn and Grinderson were good enough men for his expenses, and here was a letter from them desiring him to stop the diligence. Accordingly, he immediately left the apartment, and, staying no longer than to gather his posse together, he did then, in the phrase of Hector, who watched his departure as a jealous mastiff eyes the retreat of a repulsed beggar, evacuate Flanders.

Sir Arthur's letter was from Mr. Greenhorn, and a curiosity in its way. We give it, with the worthy Baronet's comments:

"SIR—[Oh! I am *dear* sir no longer; folks are only dear to Messrs. Greenhorn and Grinderson when they are in adversity]—Sir, I am much concerned to learn, on my return from the country, where I was called on particular business [a bet on the sweepstakes, I suppose], that my partner had the impropriety, in my absence, to undertake the concerns of Messrs. Goldiebirds in preference to yours, and had written to you in an unbecoming manner. I beg to make my most humble apology, as well as Mr. Grinderson's [come, I see he can write for himself and partner too], and trust it is impossible you can think me forgetful of, or ungrateful for, the constant patronage which my family [*his* family! curse him for a puppy!] have uniformly experienced from that of Knockwinnock. I am sorry to find, from an interview I had this day with Mr. Wardour, that he is much irritated, and, I must own, with apparent reason. But, in order to remedy as much as in me lies the mistake of which he complains [pretty mistake, indeed! to clap his patron into jail], I have sent this express to discharge all proceedings against your person or property; and at the same time to transmit my respectful apology. I have only to add, that Mr. Grinderson is of opinion that, if restored to your confidence, he could point out circumstances connected with Messrs. Goldiebirds' present claim which would greatly reduce its amount [so, so, willing to play the rogue on either side]; and that there is not the slightest hurry in settling the balance of your accompt with us; and that I am, for Mr G. as well as myself, Dear

Sir [Oh, ay, he has written himself into an approach to famil
iarity], your much obliged and most humble servant,

"GILBERT GREENHORN."

"Well said, Mr. Gilbert Greenhorn," said Monkbarns.
"I see now there is some use in having two attorneys in one
firm. Their movements resemble those of the man and woman in a Dutch baby-house. When it is fair weather with
the client, out comes the gentleman partner to fawn like a
spaniel; when it is foul, forth bolts the operative brother to
pin like a bull-dog. Well, I thank God that my man of business still wears an equilateral cocked hat, has a house in the
Old Town, is as much afraid of a horse as I am myself, plays
at golf of a Saturday, goes to the kirk of a Sunday, and, in
respect he has no partner, hath only his own folly to apologise for."

"There are some writers very honest fellows," said Hector;
"I should like to hear any one say that my cousin, Donald
M'Intyre, Strathtudlem's seventh son—the other six are in
the army—is not as honest a fellow——"

"No doubt, no doubt, Hector; all the M'Intyres are so;
they have it by patent, man. But, I was going to say that
in a profession where unbounded trust is necessarily reposed,
there is nothing surprising that fools should neglect it in their
idleness and tricksters abuse it in their knavery. But it is
the more to the honour of those—and I will vouch for many
—who unite integrity with skill and attention, and walk honourably upright where there are so many pitfalls and stum-
bling-blocks for those of a different character. To such men
their fellow-citizens may safely entrust the care of protecting
their patrimonial rights, and their country the more sacred
charge of her laws and privileges."

"They are best off, however, that hae least to do with
them," said Ochiltree, who had stretched his neck into the
parlour door; for the general confusion of the family not having yet subsided, the domestics, like waves after the fall of a
hurricane, had not yet exactly regained their due limits, but
were roaming wildly through the house.

"'Aha, old truepenny, art thou there?" said the Antiquary. "Sir Arthur, let me bring in the messenger of good luck, though he is but a lame one. You talked of the raven that scented out the slaughter from afar; but here's a blue pigeon—somewhat of the oldest and toughest, I grant—who smelled the good news six or seven miles off, flew thither in the taxed cart, and returned with the olive branch."

"Ye owe it a' to puir Robie that drave me; puir fallow," said the beggar, "he doubts he's in disgrace wi' my leddy and Sir Arthur."

Robert's repentant and bashful face was seen over the mendicant's shoulder.

"In disgrace with me!" said Sir Arthur, "how so?" for the irritation into which he had worked himself on occasion of the toast had been long forgotten. "Oh, I recollect. Robert, I was angry, and you were wrong; go about your work, and never answer a master that speaks to you in a passion."

"Nor any one else," said the Antiquary; "for 'A soft answer turneth away wrath.'"

"And tell your mother, who is so ill with the rheumatism, to come down to the housekeeper to-morrow," said Miss Wardour, "and we will see what can be of service to her."

"God bless your leddyship," said poor Robert, "and his honour Sir Arthur, and the young laird, and the house of Knockwinnock in a' its branches, far and near; it's been a kind and a gude house to the puir this mony hundred years."

"There," said the Antiquary to Sir Arthur, "we won't dispute; but there you see the gratitude of the poor people naturally turns to the civil virtues of your family. You don't hear them talk of Red-hand, or Hell-in-Harness. For me I must say, *Odi accipitrem qui semper vivit in armis;* so let us eat and drink in peace, and be joyful, Sir Knight."

A table was quickly covered in the parlour, where the party sat joyously down to some refreshment. At the request of Oldbuck, Edie Ochiltree was permitted to sit by the sideboard in a great leather chair, which was placed in some measure behind a screen.

"I accede to this the more readily," said Sir Arthur, "because I remember in my father's days that chair was occupied by Ailshie Gourlay, who, for aught I know, was the last privileged fool or jester maintained by any family of distinction in Scotland."

"Aweel, Sir Arthur," replied the beggar, who never hesitated an instant between his friend and his jest, "mony a wise man sits in a fule's seat, and mony a fule in a wise man's, especially in families o' distinction."

Miss Wardour, fearing the effect of this speech (however worthy of Ailshie Gourlay or any other privileged jester) upon the nerves of her father, hastened to inquire whether ale and beef should not be distributed to the servants and people whom the news had assembled around the Castle.

"Surely, my love," said her father; "when was it ever otherwise in our families when a siege had been raised?"

"Ay, a siege laid by Saunders Sweepclean, the bailiff, and raised by Edie Ochiltree, the gaberlunzie, *par nobile fratrum*," said Oldbuck, "and well pitted against each other in respectability. But never mind, Sir Arthur, these are such sieges and such reliefs as our time of day admits of, and our escape is not less worth commemorating in a glass of this excellent wine. Upon my credit, it is Burgundy I think."

"Were there anything better in the cellar," said Miss Wardour, "it would be all too little to regale you after your friendly exertions."

"Say you so?" said the Antiquary; "why, then, a cup of thanks to you, my fair enemy, and soon may you be besieged as ladies love best to be, and sign terms of capitulation in the chapel of Saint Winnox."

Miss Wardour blushed; Hector coloured and then grew pale.

Sir Arthur answered: "My daughter is much obliged to you, Monkbarns; but, unless you'll accept of her yourself, I really do not know where a poor knight's daughter is to seek for an alliance in these mercenary times."

"Me, mean ye, Sir Arthur? No, not I; I will claim the privilege of the duello, and, as being unable to encounter my fair enemy myself, I will appear by my champion. But of this matter hereafter. What do you find in the papers there, Hector, that you hold your head down over them as if your nose were bleeding?"

"Nothing particular, sir; but only that, as my arm is now almost quite well, I think I shall relieve you of my company in a day or two, and go to Edinburgh. I see Major Neville is arrived there. I should like to see him."

"Major whom?" said his uncle.

"Major Neville, sir," answered the young soldier.

"And who the devil is Major Neville?"" demanded the Antiquary.

"Oh, Mr. Oldbuck," said Sir Arthur, "you must remember his name frequently in the newspapers, a very distinguished young officer indeed. But I am happy to say that Mr. M'Intyre need not leave Monkbarns to see him, for my son writes that the Major is to come with him to Knockwinnock, and I need not say how happy I shall be to make the young gentlemen acquainted—unless, indeed, they are known to each other already."

"No, not personally," answered Hector; "but I have had occasion to hear a good deal of him, and we have several mutual friends, your son being one of them. But I must go to Edinburgh, for I see my uncle is beginning to grow tired of me, and I am afraid——"

"That you will grow tired of him?" interrupted Oldbuck. "I fear that's past praying for. But you have forgotten that the ecstatic twelfth of August approaches, and that you are engaged to meet one of Lord Glenallan's gamekeepers, God knows where, to persecute the peaceful feathered creation."

"True, true, uncle, I had forgot that," exclaimed the volatile Hector; "but you said something just now that put everything out of my head."

"An it like your honours," said old Edie, thrusting his white head from behind the screen, where he had been plentifully regaling himself with ale and cold meat—" an it like your honours, I can tell ye something that will keep the Captain wi' us amaist as weel as the pouting. Hear ye na the French are coming?"

"The French, you blockhead!" answered Oldbuck. "Bah!"

"I have not had time," said Sir Arthur Wardour, "to look over my lieutenancy correspondence for the week—indeed, I generally make a rule to read it only on Wednesdays, except in pressing cases, for I do everything by method; but from the glance I took of my letters I observed some alarm was entertained."

"Alarm!" said Edie; "troth there's alarm; for the provost's gar'd the beacon light on the Halket Head be sorted up—that suld hae been sorted half a year syne—in an unco hurry, and the council hae named nae less a man than auld Caxon himsell to watch the light. Some say it was out o' compliment to Lieutenant Taffril, for it's neist to certain that he'll marry Jenny Caxon; some say it's to please your honour and Monkbarns, that wear wigs; and some say there's some auld story about a periwig that ane o' the bailies got and ne'er paid for. Ony way, there he is, sitting cockit up like a skart upon the tap o' the craig, to skirl when foul weather comes."

"On mine honour, a pretty warder," said Monkbarns; "and what's my wig to do all the while?"

"I asked Caxon that very question," answered Ochiltree, "and he said he could look in ilka morning and gie't a touch afore he gaed to his bed, for there's another man to watch in the daytime, and Caxon says he'll frizz your honour's wig as weel sleeping as wauking."

This news gave a different turn to the conversation, which ran upon national defence, and the duty of fighting for the land we live in, until it was time to part. The Antiquary and his nephew resumed their walk homeward, after parting from Knockwinnock with the warmest expressions of mutual regard, and an agreement to meet again as soon as possible.

CHAPTER XLIV.

Nay, if she love me not, I care not for her:
Shall I look pale because the maiden blooms?
Or sigh because she smiles, and smiles on others?
Not I, by Heaven! I hold my peace too dear,
To let it, like the plume upon her cap,
Shake at each nod that her caprice shall dictate.

Old Play.

"HECTOR," said his uncle to Captain M'Intyre, in the course of their walk homeward, "I am sometimes inclined to suspect that in one respect you are a fool."

"If you only think me so in *one* respect, sir, I am sure you do me more grace than I expected or deserve."

"I mean in one particular *par excellence*," answered the Antiquary. "I have sometimes thought that you have cast your eyes upon Miss Wardour."

"Well, sir," said M'Intyre, with much composure.

"Well, sir!" echoed his uncle. "Deuce take the fellow, he answers me as if it were the most reasonable thing in the world that he, a captain in the army, and nothing at all besides, should marry the daughter of a baronet."

"I presume to think, sir," said the young Highlander, "there would be no degradation on Miss Wardour's part in point of family."

"Oh, Heaven forbid we should come on that topic! No, no, equal both, both on the table-land of gentility, and qualified to look down on every *roturier* in Scotland."

"And in point of fortune we are pretty even, since neither of us have got any," continued Hector. "There may be an error, but I cannot plead guilty to presumption."

"But here lies the error, then, if you call it so," replied his uncle; "she won't have you, Hector."

"Indeed, sir?"

"It is very sure, Hector; and to make it double sure I must inform you that she likes another man. She misunderstood some words I once said to her, and I have since been able to guess at the interpretation she put on them. At the time I was unable to account for her hesitation and blushing; but, my poor Hector, I now understand them as a death-signal to your hopes and pretensions. So I advise you to beat your retreat and draw off your forces as well as you can, for the fort is too well garrisoned for you to storm it."

"I have no occasion to beat any retreat, uncle," said Hector, holding himself very upright, and marching with a sort of dogged and offended solemnity; "no man needs to retreat that has never advanced. There are women in Scotland besides Miss Wardour, of as good family——"

"And better taste," said his uncle. "Doubtless there are, Hector; and, though I cannot say but that she is one of the most accomplished as well as sensible girls I have seen, yet I doubt much of her merit would be cast away on you. A showy figure, now, with two cross feathers above her noddle —one green, one blue; who would wear a riding-habit of the regimental complexion, drive a gig one day, and the next review the regiment on the grey trotting pony which dragged that vehicle, *hoc erat in votis*—these are the qualities that would subdue you, especially if she had a taste for natural history, and loved a specimen of a *phoca*."

"It's a little hard, sir," said Hector, "I must have that cursed seal thrown into my face on all occasions; but I care little about it, and I shall not break my heart for Miss Wardour. She is free to choose for herself, and I wish her all happiness."

"Magnanimously resolved, thou prop of Troy! Why, Hector, I was afraid of a scene. Your sister told me you were desperately in love with Miss Wardour."

"Sir," answered the young man, "you would not have me desperately in love with a woman that does not care about me?"

"Well, nephew," said the Antiquary, more seriously, "there is doubtless much sense in what you say; yet I would have given a great deal, some twenty or twenty-five years since, to have been able to think as you do."

"Anybody, I suppose, may think as they please on such subjects," said Hector.

"Not according to the old school," said Oldbuck; "but, as I said before, the practice of the modern seems in this case the most prudential, though I think scarcely the most interesting. But tell me your ideas now on this prevailing subject of an invasion. The cry is still, They come."

Hector, swallowing his mortification, which he was peculiarly anxious to conceal from his uncle's satirical observation, readily entered into a conversation which was to turn the Antiquary's thoughts from Miss Wardour and the seal. When they reached Monkbarns, the communicating to the ladies the events which had taken place at the Castle, with the counter-information of how long dinner had waited before the womankind had ventured to eat it in the Antiquary's absence, averted these delicate topics of discussion.

The next morning the Antiquary arose early, and, as Caxon had not yet made his appearance, he began mentally to feel the absence of the petty news and small talk, of which the ex-peruquier was a faithful reporter, and which habit had made as necessary to the Antiquary as his occasional pinch of snuff, although he held, or affected to hold, both to be of the same intrinsic value. The feeling of vacuity peculiar to such a deprivation was alleviated by the appearance of old Ochiltree sauntering beside the clipped yew and holly hedges, with the air of a person quite at home. Indeed, so familiar had he been of late, that even Juno did not bark at him, but contented herself with watching him with a close and vigilant eye. Our Antiquary stepped out in his nightgown, and instantly received and returned his greeting.

"They are coming now in good earnest, Monkbarns. I just cam frae Fairport to bring ye the news, and then I'll step away back again; the 'Search' has just come into the bay, and they say she's been chased by a French fleet."

"The 'Search'?" said Oldbuck, reflecting a moment. "Oho!"

"Ay, ay, Captain Taffril's gun-brig, the 'Search.'"

"What! any relation to 'Search No. II.'?" said Oldbuck, catching at the light which the name of the vessel seemed to throw on the mysterious chest of treasure.

The mendicant, like a man detected in a frolic, put his bonnet before his face, yet could not help laughing heartily. "The deil's in you, Monkbarns, for garring odds and evens meet. Wha thought ye wad hae laid that and that thegither? Odd, I am clean catch'd now."

"I see it all," said Oldbuck, "as plain as the legend on a medal of high preservation: the box in which the bullion was found belonged to the gun-brig and the treasure to my phœnix?" (Edie nodded assent.) "And was buried there that Sir Arthur might receive relief in his difficulties?"

"By me," said Edie, "and twa o' the brig's men; but they didna ken its contents, and thought it some bit smuggling concern o' the Captain's. I watched day and night till I saw it in the right hand; and then, when that German deevil was glowering at the lid o' the kist—they liked mutton weel that licket where the yowe lay—I think some Scottish deevil put it into my head to play him yon ither cantrip. Now, ye see, if I had said mair or less to Bailie Littlejohn, I behoved till hae come out wi' a' this story; and vexed would Mr. Lovel hae been to have it brought to light; sae I thought I would stand to ony thing rather than that."

"I must say he has chosen his confidant well," said Oldbuck, "though somewhat strangely."

"I'll say this for mysell, Monkbarns," answered the mendicant, "that I am the fittest man in the haill country to trust wi' siller, for I neither want it nor wish for it, nor could use it if I had it. But the lad hadna muckle choice in the matter, for he thought he was leaving the country for ever—I trust he's mistaen in that though—and the night was set in when we learned, by a strange chance, Sir Arthur's sair distress, and Lovel was obliged to be on board as the day dawned. But five nights afterwards the brig stood into the bay, and I met the boat by appointment, and we buried the treasure where ye fand it."

"This was a very romantic, foolish exploit," said Oldbuck; "why not trust me, or any other friend?"

"The blood o' your sister's son," replied Edie, "was on his hands, and him maybe dead outright; what time had he to take counsel? or how could he ask it of you, by ony body?"

"You are right. But what if Dousterswivel had come before you?"

"There was little fear o' his coming there without Sir Arthur; he had gotten a sair gliff the night afore, and never intended to look near the place again, unless he had been brought there sting and ling. He kend weel the first pose was o' his ain hiding, and how could he expect a second? He just havered on about it to make the mair o' Sir Arthur."

"Then how," said Oldbuck, "should Sir Arthur have come there unless the German had brought him?"

"Umph!" answered Edie, drily, "I had a story about Misticot wad hae brought him forty miles, or you either. Besides, it was to be thought he would be for visiting the place he fand the first siller in: he kend na the secret o' that job. In short, the siller being in this shape, Sir Arthur in utter difficulties, and Lovel determined he should never ken the hand that helped him—for that was what he insisted maist upon—we couldna think o' a better way to fling the gear in his gate, though we simmered it and wintered it e'er sae lang. And if by ony queer mischance Doustercivil had got his claws on't, I was instantly to hae informed you or the sheriff o' the haill story."

"Well, notwithstanding all these wise precautions, I think your contrivance succeeded better than such a clumsy one deserved, Edie. But how the deuce came Lovel by such a mass of silver ingots?"

"That's just what I canna tell ye. But they were put on board wi' his things at Fairport, it's like, and we stowed them into ane o' the ammunition-boxes o' the brig, baith for concealment and convenience of carriage."

"Lord!" said Oldbuck, his recollection recurring to the earlier part of his acquaintance with Lovel; "and this young fellow, who was putting hundreds on so strange a hazard—I must be recommending a subscription to him, and paying his bill at the Ferry! I never will pay any person's bill again, that's certain. And you kept up a constant correspondence with Lovel, I suppose?"

"I just gat ae bit scrape o' a pen frae him, to say tnere wad, as yesterday fell, be a packet at Tannonburgh, wi' letters o' great consequence to the Knockwinnock folk; for they jaloused the opening of our letters at Fairport. And that's as true, I hear Mrs. Mailsetter is to lose her office for looking after ither folks' business and neglecting her ain."

"And what do you expect, now, Edie, for being the adviser, and messenger, and guard, and confidential person in all these matters?"

"Deil haet do I expect, excepting that a' the gentles will come to the gaberlunzie's burial; and maybe ye'll carry the head yoursell, as ye did puir Steenie Mucklebackit's. What trouble was't to me? I was ganging about at ony rate. Oh but I was blythe when I got out of prison, though; for, I thought, what if that weary letter should come when I am closed up here like an oyster, and a' should gang wrang for want o't? And whiles I thought I maun make a clean breast and tell you a' about it; but then I couldna weel do that without contravening Mr. Lovel's positive orders, and I reckon he had to see somebody at Edinburgh afore he could do what he wussed to do for Sir Arthur and his family."

"Well, and to your public news, Edie. So they are still coming, are they?"

"Troth, they say sae, sir; and there's come down strict orders for the forces and volunteers to be alert; and there's a clever young officer to come here forthwith to look at our means o' defence. I saw the Bailie's lass cleaning his belts and white breeks; I gae her a hand, for ye maun think she wasna ower clever at it, and sae I gat a' the news for my pains."

"And what think you, as an old soldier?"

"Troth, I kenna; an they come sae mony as they speak o', they'll be odds against us. But there's mony auld chields amang thae volunteers; and I mauna say muckle about them that's no weel and no very able, because I am something that gate mysell. But we'se do our best."

"What! so your martial spirit is rising again, Edie?

Even in our ashes glow their wonted fires !

I would not have thought you, Edie, had so much to fight for?"

"*Me* no muckle to fight for, sir? Isna there the country to fight for, and the burnsides that I gang daundering beside, and the hearths o' the gudewives that gie me my bit bread, and the bits o' weans that come toddling to play wi' me when I come about a landward town? Deil!" he continued, grasping his pikestaff with great emphasis, "an I had as gude pith as I hae gude-will and a gude cause, I should gie some o' them a day's kemping."

"Bravo, bravo, Edie! The country's in little ultimate danger when the beggar's as ready to fight for his dish as the laird for his land."

Their further conversation reverted to the particulars of the night passed by the mendicant and Lovel in the ruins of St. Ruth, by the details of which the Antiquary was highly amused.

"I would have given a guinea," he said, "to have seen the scoundrelly German under the agonies of those terrors which it is part of his own quackery to inspire into others, and trembling alternately for the fury of his patron and the apparition of some hobgoblin."

"Troth," said the beggar, "there was time for him to be cowed; for ye wad hae thought the very spirit of Hell-in-Harness had taken possession o' the body o' Sir Arthur. But what will come o' the landlouper?"

"I have had a letter this morning, from which I understand he has acquitted you of the charge he brought against you, and offers to make such discoveries as will render the settlement of Sir Arthur's affairs a more easy task than we apprehended. So writes the sheriff; and adds, that he has given some private information of importance to government, in consideration of which I understand he will be sent back to play the knave in his own country."

"And a' the bonny engines and wheels, and the coves and sheughs, doun at Glen Withershins yonder, what's to come o' them?" said Edie.

29

"I hope the men, before they are dispersed, will make a bonfire of their gimcracks, as an army destroy their artillery when forced to raise a siege. And as for the holes, Edie, I abandon them as rat-traps, for the benefit of the next wise men who may choose to drop the substance to snatch at a shadow."

"Hech, sirs! guide us a'! to burn the engines? that's a great waste. Had ye na better try to get back part o' your hundred pounds wi' the sale o' the materials?" he continued, with a tone of affected condolence.

"Not a farthing," said the Antiquary, peevishly, taking a turn from him, and making a step or two away. Then returning, half-smiling at his own pettishness, he said: "Get thee into the house, Edie, and remember my counsel: never speak to me about a mine, or to my nephew Hector about a *phoca*, that is a sealgh, as you call it."

"I maun be ganging my ways back to Fairport," said the wanderer; "I want to see what they're saying there about the invasion; but I'll mind what your honour says, no to speak to you about a sealgh, or to the Captain about the hundred pounds that you gied to Douster——"

"Confound thee! I desire thee not to mention that to me."

"Dear me!" said Edie, with affected surprise; "weel, I thought there was naething but what your honour could hae studden in the way o' agreeable conversation, unless it was about the prætorian yonder, or the bodle that the packman sauld to ye for an auld coin."

"Pshaw, pshaw," said the Antiquary, turning from him hastily, and retreating into the house.

The mendicant looked after him a moment, and with a chuckling laugh, such as that with which a magpie or parrot applauds a successful exploit of mischief, he resumed once more the road to Fairport. His habits had given him a sort of restlessness, much increased by the pleasure he took in gathering news; and in a short time he had regained the town which he left in the morning, for no reason that he knew himself, unless just to "hae a bit crack wi' Monkbarns."

CHAPTER XLV.

Red glared the beacon on Pownell,
On Skiddaw there were three ;
The bugle-horn on moor and fell
Was heard continually.

JAMES HOGG.

THE watch who kept his watch on the hill and looked towards Birnam probably conceived himself dreaming when he first beheld the fated grove put itself into motion for its march to Dunsinane. Even so old Caxon, as, perched in his hut, he qualified his thoughts upon the approaching marriage of his daughter, and the dignity of being father-in-law to Lieutenant Taffril, with an occasional peep towards the signal-post with which his own corresponded, was not a little surprised by observing a light in that direction. He rubbed his eyes, looked again, adjusting his observation by a cross-staff which had been placed so as to bear upon the point. And behold the light increased, like a comet to the eye of the astronomer, "with fear of change perplexing nations."

"The Lord preserve us!" said Caxon, "what's to be done now? But there will be wiser heads than mine to look to that, sae I'se e'en fire the beacon."

And he lighted the beacon accordingly, which threw up to the sky a long wavering train of light, startling the sea-fowl from their nests, and reflected far beneath by the reddening billows of the sea. The brother warders of Caxon, being equally diligent, caught and repeated his signal. The lights glanced on headlands and capes and inland hills, and the whole district was alarmed by the signal of invasion.[1]

Our Antiquary, his head wrapped warm in two double night-caps, was quietly enjoying his repose, when it was suddenly broken by the screams of his sister, his niece, and two maid-servants.

"What the devil is the matter?" said he, starting up in his

[1] See Note 12.

ted; "womankind in my room at this hour of night! are ye all mad?"

"The beacon, uncle!" said Miss M'Intyre.

"The French coming to murder us!" screamed Miss Griselda.

"The beacon, the beacon! the French, the French! murder, murder! and waur than murder!" cried the two hand-maidens, like the chorus of an opera.

"The French!" said Oldbuck, starting up. "Get out of the room, womankind that you are, till I get my things on. And, hark ye, bring me my sword."

"Whilk o' them, Monkbarns?" cried his sister, offering a Roman falchion of brass with the one hand, with the other an Andrea Ferrara without a handle.

"The langest, the langest," cried Jenny Rintherout, dragging in a two-handed sword of the twelfth century.

"Womankind," said Oldbuck, in great agitation, "be composed, and do not give way to vain terror. Are you sure they are come?"

"Sure! sure!" exclaimed Jenny—"ower sure! a' the sea fencibles and the land fencibles, and the volunteers and yeomanry, are on fit, and driving to Fairport as hard as horse and man can gang; and auld Mucklebackit's gane wi' the lave—muckle good he'll do. Hech, sirs! he'll be missed the morn wha wad hae served king and country weel!"

"Give me," said Oldbuck, "the sword which my father wore in the year forty-five; it hath no belt or baldrick, but we'll make shift."

So saying, he thrust the weapon through the cover of his breeches pocket. At this moment Hector entered, who had been to a neighbouring height to ascertain whether the alarm was actual.

"Where are your arms, nephew?" exclaimed Oldbuck; "where is your double-barrelled gun, that was never out of your hand when there was no occasion for such vanities?"

"Pooh! pooh! sir," said Hector, "who ever took a fowling-piece on action? I have got my uniform on, you see: I hope I shall be of more use if they will give me a command than

I could be with ten double-barrels. And you, sir, must get to Fairport, to give directions for the quartering and maintaining the men and horses, and preventing confusion."

"You are right, Hector: I believe I shall do as much with my head as my hand too. But here comes Sir Arthur Wardour, who, between ourselves, is not fit to accomplish much either one way or other."

Sir Arthur was probably of a different opinion; for, dressed in his lieutenancy uniform, he was also on the road to Fairport, and called in his way to take Mr. Oldbuck with him, having had his original opinion of his sagacity much confirmed by late events. And, in spite of all the entreaties of the womankind that the Antiquary would stay to garrison Monkbarns, Mr. Oldbuck, with his nephew, instantly accepted Sir Arthur's offer.

Those who have witnessed such a scene can alone conceive the state of bustle in Fairport. The windows were glancing with a hundred lights, which, appearing and disappearing rapidly, indicated the confusion within doors. The women of lower rank assembled and clamoured in the market-place. The yeomanry, pouring from their different glens, galloped through the streets, some individually, some in parties of five or six, as they had met on the road. The drums and fifes of the volunteers beating to arms were blended with the voice of the officers, the sound of the bugles, and the tolling of the bells from the steeple. The ships in the harbour were lit up, and boats from the armed vessels added to the bustle by landing men and guns destined to assist in the defence of the place. This part of the preparations was superintended by Taffril with much activity. Two or three light vessels had already slipped their cables and stood out to sea, in order to discover the supposed enemy.

Such was the scene of general confusion when Sir Arthur Wardour, Oldbuck, and Hector made their way with difficulty into the principal square, where the town-house is situated. It was lighted up, and the magistracy, with many of the neighbouring gentlemen, were assembled. And here, as upon other occasions of the like kind in Scotland, it was remarkable how the good sense and firmness of the people supplied almost all the deficiencies of inexperience.

The magistrates were beset by the quartermasters of the different corps for billets for men and horses. "Let us, ' said Bailie Littlejohn, "take the horses into our warehouses and the men into our parlours, share our supper with the one and our forage with the other. We have made ourselves wealthy under a free and paternal government, and now is the time to show we know its value."

A loud and cheerful acquiescence was given by all present, and the substance of the wealthy, with the persons of those of all ranks, were unanimously devoted to the defence of the country.

Captain M'Intyre acted on this occasion as military adviser and aid-de-camp to the principal magistrate, and displayed a degree of presence of mind and knowledge of his profession totally unexpected by his uncle, who, recollecting his usual *insouciance* and impetuosity, gazed at him with astonishment from time to time, as he remarked the calm and steady manner in which he explained the various measures of precaution that his experience suggested, and gave directions for executing them. He found the different corps in good order, considering the irregular materials of which they were composed, in great force of numbers, and high confidence and spirits. And so much did military experience at that moment overbalance all other claims to consequence that even old Edie, instead of being left, like Diogenes at Sinope, to roll his tub when all around were preparing for defence, had the duty assigned him of superintending the serving out of the ammunition, which he executed with much discretion.

Two things were still anxiously expected—the presence of the Glenallan volunteers, who, in consideration of the importance of that family, had been formed into a separate corps, and the arrival of the officer before announced, to whom the measures of defence on that coast had been committed by the commander-in-chief, and whose commission would entitle him to take upon himself the full disposal of the military force.

At length the bugles of the Glenallan yeomanry were

heard, and the Earl himself, to the surprise of all who knew
his habits and state of health, appeared at their head in uniform. They formed a very handsome and well-mounted
squadron, formed entirely out of the Earl's Lowland tenants,
and were followed by a regiment of five hundred men, completely equipped in the Highland dress, whom he had brought
down from the upland glens, with their pipes playing in the
van. The clean and serviceable appearance of this band of
feudal dependents called forth the admiration of Captain
M'Intyre; but his uncle was still more struck by the manner
in which, upon this crisis, the ancient military spirit of his
house seemed to animate and invigorate the decayed frame of
the Earl, their leader. He claimed and obtained for himself
and his followers the post most likely to be that of danger,
displayed great alacrity in making the necessary dispositions,
and showed equal acuteness in discussing their propriety.
Morning broke in upon the military councils of Fairport while
all concerned were still eagerly engaged in taking precautions
for their defence.

At length a cry among the people announced, "There's the
brave Major Neville come at last, with another officer"; and
their post-chaise and four drove into the square, amidst the
huzzas of the volunteers and inhabitants. The magistrates,
with their assessors of the lieutenancy, hastened to the door
of their town-house to receive him; but what was the surprise of all present, but most especially that of the Antiquary,
when they became aware that the handsome uniform and
military cap disclosed the person and features of the pacific
Lovel! A warm embrace and a hearty shake of the hand
were necessary to assure him that his eyes were doing him
justice. Sir Arthur was no less surprised to recognise his
son, Captain Wardour, in Lovel's, or rather Major Neville's
company. The first words of the young officers were a positive assurance to all present that the courage and zeal which
they had displayed were entirely thrown away, unless in so
far as they afforded an acceptable proof of their spirit and
promptitude.

"The watchman at Halket Head," said Major Neville, "as

we discovered by an investigation which we made in our route hither, was most naturally misled by a bonfire which some idle people had made on the hill above Glen Withershins, just in the line of the beacon with which his corresponded."

Oldbuck gave a conscious look to Sir Arthur, who returned it with one equally sheepish and a shrug of the shoulders.

"It must have been the machinery which we condemned to the flames in our wrath," said the Antiquary, plucking up heart, though not a little ashamed of having been the cause of so much disturbance. "The devil take Dousterswivel with all my heart! I think he has bequeathed us a legacy of blunders and mischief, as if he had lighted some train of fireworks at his departure. I wonder what cracker will go off next among our shins. But yonder comes the prudent Caxon. Hold up your head, you ass; your betters must bear the blame for you. And here, take this what-d'ye-call-it (giving him his sword). I wonder what I would have said yesterday to any man that would have told me I was to stick such an appendage to my tail."

Here he found his arm gently pressed by Lord Glenallan, who dragged him into a separate apartment. "For God's sake, who is that young gentleman who is so strikingly like——"

"Like the unfortunate Eveline," interrupted Oldbuck. "I felt my heart warm to him from the first, and your lordship has suggested the very cause."

"But who—who is he?" continued Lord Glenallan, holding the Antiquary with a convulsive grasp.

"Formerly I would have called him Lovel, but now he turns out to be Major Neville."

"Whom my brother brought up as his natural son, whom he made his heir. Gracious Heaven! the child of my Eveline!"

"Hold, my lord—hold!" said Oldbuck; "do not give too hasty way to such a presumption; what probability is there?"

"Probability! none. There is certainty—absolute certainty. The agent I mentioned to you wrote me the whole story. I received it yesterday, not sooner. Bring him, for

God's sake, that a father's eyes may bless him before he departs."

"I will; but, for your own sake and his, give him a few moments for preparation."

And, determined to make still farther investigation before yielding his entire conviction to so strange a tale, he sought out Major Neville, and found him expediting the necessary measures for dispersing the force which had been assembled.

"Pray, Major Neville, leave this business for a moment to Captain Wardour and to Hector, with whom, I hope, you are thoroughly reconciled (Neville laughed, and shook hands with Hector across the table), and grant me a moment's audience."

"You have a claim on me, Mr. Oldbuck, were my business more urgent," said Neville, "for having passed myself upon you under a false name, and rewarding your hospitality by injuring your nephew."

"You served him as he deserved," said Oldbuck; "though, by the way, he showed as much good sense as spirit to-day. Egad, if he would rub up his learning, and read Cæsar and Polybius and the *Stratagemata Polyæni*, I think he would rise in the army, and I will certainly lend him a lift."

"He is heartily deserving of it," said Neville; "and I am glad you excuse me, which you may do the more frankly when you know that I am so unfortunate as to have no better right to the name of Neville, by which I have been generally distinguished, than to that of Lovel, under which you knew me."

"Indeed! then I trust we shall find out one for you to which you shall have a firm and legal title."

"Sir! I trust you do not think the misfortune of my birth a fit subject——"

"By no means, young man," answered the Antiquary, interrupting him; "I believe I know more of your birth than you do yourself; and, to convince you of it, you were educated and known as a natural son of Geraldin Neville of Neville's Burgh, in Yorkshire, and, I presume, as his destined heir?"

"Pardon me; no such views were held out to me. I was

liberally educated, and pushed forward in the army by money and interest; but I believe my supposed father long entertained some ideas of marriage, though he never carried them into effect."

"You say your *supposed* father? What leads you to suppose Mr. Geraldin Neville was not your real father?"

"I know, Mr. Oldbuck, that you would not ask these questions on a point of such delicacy for the gratification of idle curiosity. I will, therefore, tell you candidly that last year, while we occupied a small town in French Flanders, I found in a convent near which I was quartered a woman who spoke remarkably good English. She was a Spaniard, her name Teresa D'Acunha. In the process of our acquaintance she discovered who I was, and made herself known to me as the person who had charge of my infancy. She dropped more than one hint of rank to which I was entitled, and of injustice done to me, promising a more full disclosure in case of the death of a lady in Scotland, during whose lifetime she was determined to keep the secret. She also intimated that Mr. Geraldin Neville was not my father. We were attacked by the enemy and driven from the town, which was pillaged with savage ferocity by the republicans. The religious orders were the particular objects of their hate and cruelty. The convent was burned, and several nuns perished, among others Teresa, and with her all chance of knowing the story of my birth: tragic by all accounts it must have been."

"*Raro antecedentem scelestum*, or, as I may here say, *scelestam*," said Oldbuck, "*deseruit pœna*, even Epicureans admitted that; and what did you do upon this?"

"I remonstrated with Mr. Neville by letter, and to no purpose. I then obtained leave of absence, and threw myself at his feet, conjuring him to complete the disclosure which Teresa had begun. He refused, and, on my importunity, indignantly upbraided me with the favours he had already conferred; I thought he abused the power of a benefactor, as he was compelled to admit he had no title to that of a father, and we parted in mutual displeasure. I renounced the name of Neville, and assumed that under which you knew me. It was at this time, when residing with a friend in the north of England who favoured my disguise, that I became acquainted with Miss Wardour, and was romantic enough to follow her to Scotland. My mind wavered on various plans of life, when I resolved to apply once more to Mr. Neville for an explanation of the mystery of my birth. It was long ere I received an answer; you were present when it was put into my hands. He informed me of his bad state of health, and conjured me, for my own sake, to inquire no farther into the nature of his connexion with me, but to rest satisfied with his declaring it to be such and so intimate that he designed to constitute me his heir. When I was preparing to leave Fairport to join him, a second express brought me word that he was no more. The possession of great wealth was unable to suppress the remorseful feelings with which I now regarded my conduct to my benefactor, and some hints in his letters appearing to intimate that there was on my birth a deeper stain than that of ordinary illegitimacy, I remembered certain prejudices of Sir Arthur."

"And you brooded over these melancholy ideas until you were ill, instead of coming to me for advice, and telling me the whole story?" said Oldbuck.

"Exactly; then came my quarrel with Captain M'Intyre, and my compelled departure from Fairport and its vicinity."

"From love and from poetry—Miss Wardour and the *Caledoniad?*"

"Most true."

"And since that time you have been occupied, I suppose, with plans for Sir Arthur's relief?"

"Yes, sir; with the assistance of Captain Wardour at Edinburgh."

"And Edie Ochiltree here; you see I know the whole story. But how came you by the treasure?"

"It was a quantity of plate which had belonged to my uncle, and was left in the custody of a person at Fairport. Some time before his death he had sent orders that it should be melted down. He perhaps did not wish me to see the Glenallan arms upon it."

"Well, Major Neville, or let me say Lovel, being the name in which I rather delight, you must, I believe, exchange both of your *alias's* for the style and title of the Honourable William Geraldin, commonly called Lord Geraldin."

The Antiquary then went through the strange and melancholy circumstances concerning his mother's death.

"I have no doubt," he said, "that your uncle wished the report to be believed that the child of this unhappy marriage was no more; perhaps he might himself have an eye to the inheritance of his brother—he was then a gay wild young man. But of all intentions against your person, however much the evil conscience of Elspeth might lead her to suspect him from the agitation in which he appeared, Teresa's story and your own fully acquit him. And now, my dear sir, let me have the pleasure of introducing a son to a father."

We will not attempt to describe such a meeting. The proofs on all sides were found to be complete, for Mr. Neville had left a distinct account of the whole transaction with his confidential steward in a sealed packet, which was not to be opened until the death of the old Countess; his motive for preserving secrecy so long appearing to have been an apprehension of the effect which the discovery, fraught with so much disgrace, must necessarily produce upon her haughty and violent temper.

In the evening of that day the yeomanry and volunteers of Glenallan drank prosperity to their young master. In a month afterwards Lord Geraldin was married to Miss Wardour, the Antiquary making the lady a present of the wedding ring, a massy circle of antique chasing, bearing the motto of Aldobrand Oldenbuck, *Kunst macht Gunst.*

Old Edie, the most important man that ever wore a bluegown, bowls away easily from one friend's house to another, and boasts that he never travels unless on a sunny day. Latterly, indeed, he has given some symptoms of becoming stationary, being frequently found in the corner of a snug cottage between Monkbarns and Knockwinnock, to which Caxon retreated upon his daughter's marriage, in order to be in the neighbourhood of the three parochial wigs, which he continues to keep in repair, though only for amusement. Edie has been heard to say: "This is a gey bein place, and it's a comfort to hae sic a corner to sit in in a bad day." It is thought, as he grows stiffer in the joints, he will finally settle there.

The bounty of such wealthy patrons as Lord and Lady Geraldin flowed copiously upon Mrs. Hadoway and upon the Mucklebackits. By the former it was well employed, by the latter wasted. They continue, however, to receive it, but under the administration of Edie Ochiltree; and they do not accept it without grumbling at the channel through which it is conveyed.

Hector is rising rapidly in the army, and has been more than once mentioned in the *Gazette*, and rises proportionally high in his uncle's favour. And, what scarcely pleases the young soldier less, he has also shot two seals, and thus put an end to the Antiquary's perpetual harping upon the story of the *phoca*. People talk of a marriage between Miss M'Intyre and Captain Wardour; but this wants confirmation.

The Antiquary is a frequent visitor at Knockwinnock and Glenallan House, ostensibly for the sake of completing two essays, one on the mail-shirt of the Great Earl and the other on the left-hand gauntlet of Hell-in-Harness. He regularly inquires whether Lord Geraldin has commenced the *Caledoniad*, and shakes his head at the answers he receives. *En attendant*, however, he has completed his notes, which, we believe, will be at the service of any one who chooses to make them public, without risk or expense to THE ANTIQUARY.

NOTES TO THE ANTIQUARY.

NOTE 1.—PRÆTORIUM, p. 48.

It may be worth while to mention that the incident of the supposed *prætorium* actually happened to an antiquary of great learning and acuteness, Sir John Clerk of Penicuik, one of the Barons of the Scottish Court of Exchequer, and a parliamentary commissioner for arrangement of the Union between England and Scotland. As many of his writings show, Sir John was much attached to the study of Scottish antiquities. He had a small property in Dumfries-shire, near the Roman station on the hill called Birrenswark. Here he received the distinguished English antiquarian Roger Gale, and of course conducted him to see this remarkable spot, where the lords of the world have left such decisive marks of their martial labours.

An aged shepherd whom they had used as a guide, or who had approached them from curiosity, listened with mouth agape to the dissertations on foss and vellum, ports *dextra*, *sinistra*, and *decumana* which Sir John Clerk delivered *ex cathedrâ*, and his learned visitor listened with the deference due to the dignity of a connoisseur on his own ground. But when the cicerone proceeded to point out a small hillock near the centre of the inclosure as the *prætorium*, Corydon's patience could hold no longer, and, like Edie Ochiltree, he forgot all reverence, and broke in with nearly the same words : " Prætorium here, prætorium there, I made the bourock mysell with a flaughter-spade." The effect of this undeniable evidence on the two lettered sages may be left to the reader's imagination.

The late excellent and venerable John Clerk of Eldin, the celebrated author of *Naval Tactics*, used to tell this story with glee, and, being a younger son of Sir John's, was perhaps present on the occasion.

NOTE 2.—MR. RUTHERFORD'S DREAM, p. 103.

The legend of Mrs. Grizel Oldbuck was partly taken from an extraordinary story which happened about seventy years since in the south of Scotland, so peculiar in its circumstances that it merits being mentioned in this place. Mr. Rutherford of Bowland, a gentleman of landed property in the vale of Gala, was prosecuted for a very considerable sum, the accumulated arrears of teind (or tithe) for which he was said to be indebted to a noble family, the titulars (lay impropriators of the tithes). Mr. Rutherford was strongly impressed with the belief that his father had, by a form of process peculiar to the law of Scotland, purchased these lands from the titular, and therefore that the present prosecution was groundless. But, after an industrious search among his father's papers, an investigation of the public records, and a careful inquiry among all persons who had transacted law business for his father, no evidence could be recovered to support his defence. The period was now near at hand when he conceived the loss of his lawsuit to be inevitable, and he had formed his determination to ride to Edinburgh next day, and make the best bargain he could in the way of compromise. He went to bed with this resolution, and, with all the circumstances of the case floating upon his mind, had a dream to the following purpose: His father, who had been many years dead, appeared to him, he thought, and asked him why he was disturbed in his mind. In dreams men are not surprised at such apparitions. Mr. Rutherford thought that he informed his father of the cause of his distress, adding that the payment of a considerable sum of money was the more unpleasant to him because he had a strong consciousness that it was not due, though he was unable to recover any evidence in support of his belief. "You are right, my son," replied the paternal shade; "I did acquire right to these teinds, for payment of which you are now prosecuted. The papers relating to the transaction are in the hands of Mr. ——, a writer (or attorney), who is now retired from professional business, and resides at Inveresk, near Edinburgh. He was a person whom I employed on that occasion for a particular reason, but who never on any other occasion transacted business on my account. It is very possible," pursued the vision, "that Mr. —— may have forgotten a matter which is now of a very old date; but you may call it to his recollection by this token, that when I came to pay his account there was difficulty in getting change for a Portugal piece of gold, and that we were forced to drink out the balance at a tavern."

Mr. Rutherford awaked in the morning with all the words of the vision imprinted on his mind, and thought it worth while to ride across the country to Inveresk instead of going straight to Edinburgh. When he came there he waited on the gentleman mentioned in the dream, a very old man; without saying anything of the vision, he inquired whether he remembered having conducted such a matter for his deceased father. The old gentleman could not at first bring the circumstance to his recollection, but, on mention of the Portugal piece of gold, the whole returned upon his memory; he made an immediate search for the papers, and recovered them; so that Mr. Rutherford carried to Edinburgh the documents necessary to gain the cause which he was on the verge of losing.

The author has often heard this story told by persons who had the best access to know the facts, who were not likely themselves to be deceived, and were certainly incapable of deception. He cannot therefore refuse to give it credit, however extraordinary the circumstances may appear. The circumstantial character of the information given in the dream takes it out of the general class of impressions of the kind which are occasioned by the fortuitous coincidence of actual events with our sleeping thoughts. On the other hand, few will suppose that the laws of nature were suspended, and a special communication from the dead to the living permitted, for the purpose of saving Mr. Rutherford a certain number of hundred pounds. The author's theory is, that the dream was only a recapitulation of information which Mr. Rutherford had really received from his father while in life, but which at first he merely recalled as a general impression that the claim was settled. It is not uncommon for persons to recover, during sleep, the thread of ideas which they have lost during their waking hours.

It may be added, that this remarkable circumstance was attended with bad consequences to Mr. Rutherford, whose health and spirits were afterwards impaired by the attention which he thought himself obliged to pay to the visions of the night.

NOTE 3.—NICKSTICKS, p. 153.

A sort of tally generally used by bakers of the olden time in settling with their customers. Each family had its own nickstick, and for each loaf as delivered a notch was made on the stick. Accompts in Exchequer, kept by the same kind of check, may have occasioned the Antiquary's partiality. In Prior's time the English bakers had the same sort of reckoning.

> Have you not seen a baker's maid
> Between two equal panniers sway'd?
> Her tallies useless lie and idle,
> If placed exactly in the middle.

NOTE 4.—MARTIN WALDECK, p. 184.

The outline of this story is taken from the German, though the author is at present unable to say in which of the various collections of the popular legends in that language the original is to be found.

NOTE 5.—SPECTRE OF THE HARZ, p. 184.

The shadow of the person who sees the phantom being reflected upon a cloud of mist, like the image of the magic lantern upon a white sheet, is supposed to have formed the apparition.

NOTE 6.—DOUSTERSWIVEL'S LEGENDS, p. 227.

A great deal of stuff to the same purpose with that placed in the mouth of the German adept may be found in Reginald Scot's *Discovery of Witchcraft*, Third Edition, folio, London, 1665. The appendix is entitled, " An Excellent Discourse of the Nature and Substance of Devils and Spirits, in two Books ; the First by the aforesaid author (Reginald Scot), the Second now added in this Third Edition as succedaneous to the former, and conducing to the completing of the whole work." This Second Book, though stated as succedaneous to the first, is, in fact, entirely at variance with it ; for the work of Reginald Scot is a compilation of the absurd and superstitious ideas concerning witches so generally entertained at the time, and the pretended conclusion is a serious treatise on the various means of conjuring astral spirits.

NOTE 7.—NAE WAUR, p. 236.

It is, I believe, a piece of freemasonry, or a point of conscience, among the Scottish lower orders never to admit that a patient is doing better. The closest approach to recovery which they can be brought to allow is, that the party inquired after is " Nae waur."

NOTE 8.—SCOTTISH FISHER-WOMEN, p. 280.

In the fishing villages on the Firths of Forth and Tay, as well as elsewhere in Scotland, the government is gynocracy, as described in the text. In the course of the late war, and during the alarm of invasion, a fleet of transports entered the Firth of Forth, under the convoy of some ships of war which would reply to no signals. A general alarm was excited, in

30

consequence of which all the fishers who were enrolled as sea-fencibles got on board the gun-boats, which they were to man as occasion should require, and sailed to oppose the supposed enemy. The foreigners proved to be Russians, with whom we were then at peace. The county gentlemen of Mid-Lothian, pleased with the zeal displayed by the sea-fencibles at a critical moment, passed a vote for presenting the community of fishers with a silver punch-bowl, to be used on occasions of festivity. But the fisher-women, on hearing what was intended, put in their claim to have some separate share in the intended honorary reward. The men, they said, were their husbands it was they who would have been sufferers if their husbands had been killed, and it was by their permission and injunctions that they embarked on board the gun-boats for the public service. They therefore claimed to share the reward in some manner which should distinguish the female patriotism which they had shown on the occasion. The gentlemen of the county willingly admitted the claim; and, without diminishing the value of their compliment to the men, they made the females a present of a valuable brooch, to fasten the plaid of the queen of the fisher-women for the time.

It may be farther remarked, that these Nereids are punctilious among themselves, and observe different ranks according to the commodities they deal in. One experienced dame was heard to characterise a younger damsel as "a puir silly thing, who had no ambition, and would never," she prophesied, "rise above the *mussell line* of business."

NOTE 9.—IMPRISONMENT FOR DEBT IN SCOTLAND, p. 399.

The doctrine of Monkbarns on the origin of imprisonment for civil debt in Scotland may appear somewhat whimsical, but was referred to, and admitted to be correct, by the Bench of the Supreme Scottish Court on 5th December 1828, in the case of Thom v. Black. In fact, the Scottish law is in this particular more jealous of the personal liberty of the subject than any other code in Europe.

NOTE 10.—BATTLE OF HARLAW, p. 406.

The great battle of Harlaw, here and formerly referred to, might be said to determine whether the Gaelic or the Saxon race should be predominant in Scotland. Donald, Lord of the Isles, who had at that period the power of an independent sovereign, laid claim to the Earldom of Ross during the Regency of Robert, Duke of Albany. To enforce his supposed right, he ravaged the north with a large army of Highlanders and Islesmen. He was encountered at Harlaw, in the Garioch, by Alexander, Earl of Mar, at the head of the northern nobility and gentry of Saxon and Norman descent. The battle was bloody and indecisive; but the invader was obliged to retire in consequence of the loss he sustained, and afterwards was compelled to make submission to the Regent, and renounce his pretensions to Ross; so that all the advantages of the field were gained by the Saxons. The battle of Harlaw was fought July 24th, 1411.

NOTE 11.—ELSPETH'S DEATH, p. 409.

The concluding circumstance of Elspeth's death is taken from an incident said to have happened at the funeral of John, Duke of Roxburghe. All who were acquainted with that accomplished nobleman must remember that he was not more remarkable for creating and possessing a most curious and splendid library than for his acquaintance with the literary treasures it contained. In arranging his books, fetching and replacing the volumes which he wanted, and carrying on all the necessary intercourse which a man of letters holds with his library, it was the Duke's custom to employ, not a secretary or librarian, but a livery servant, called Archie, whom habit had made so perfectly acquainted with the library that he knew every book, as a shepherd does the individuals of his flock, by what is called head-mark, and could bring his master whatever volume he wanted, and afford all the mechanical aid the Duke required in his literary researches. To secure the attendance of Archie, there was a bell hung in his room, which was used on no occasion except to call him individually to the Duke's study.

His Grace died in Saint James's Square, London, in the year 1804; the body was to be conveyed to Scotland, to lie in state at his mansion of Fleurs, and to be removed from thence to the family burial-place at Bowden.

At this time Archie, who had been long attacked by a liver-complaint, was in the very last stage of that disease. Yet he prepared himself to accompany the body of the master whom he had so long and so faithfully waited upon. The medical persons assured him he could not survive the journey. It signified nothing, he said, whether he died in England or Scotland; he was resolved to assist in rendering the last honours to the kind master from whom he had been inseparable for so many years, even if he should expire in the attempt. The poor invalid was permitted to attend the Duke's body to Scotland; but when they reached Fleurs he was totally exhausted, and obliged to keep his bed, in a sort of stupor which announced speedy dissolution. On the morning of the day fixed for removing the dead body of the Duke to the place of burial, the private bell by which he was wont to summon his attendant to his study was rung violently. This might easily happen in the confusion of such a scene, although the people of the neighbourhood prefer believing that the bell sounded of its own accord. Ring, however, it did; but Archie, roused by the well-known summons, rose up in his bed, and faltered, in broken accents, "Yes, my Lord Duke—yes; I will wait on your Grace instantly"; and with these words on his lips he is said to have fallen back and expired.

Note 12.—Alarm of Invasion, p. 451.

The story of the false alarm at Fairport, and the consequences, are taken from a real incident. Those who witnessed the state of Britain, and of Scotland in particular, from the period that succeeded the war which commenced in 1803 to the battle of Trafalgar must recollect those times with feelings which we can hardly hope to make the rising generation comprehend. Almost every individual was enrolled either in a military or civil capacity, for the purpose of contributing to resist the long-suspended threats of invasion which were echoed from every quarter. Beacons were erected along the coast and all through the country, to give the signal for every one to repair to the post where his peculiar duty called him, and men of every description fit to serve held themselves in readiness on the shortest summons. During this agitating period, and on the evening of the 2d February 1804, the person who kept watch on the commanding station of Home Castle, being deceived by some accidental fire in the county of Northumberland, which he took for the corresponding signal-light in that county with which his orders were to communicate, lighted up his own beacon. The signal was immediately repeated through all the valleys on the English Border. If the beacon at Saint Abb's Head had been fired, the alarm would have run northward and roused all Scotland. But the watch at this important point judiciously considered that, if there had been an actual or threatened descent on our eastern sea-coast, the alarm would have come along the coast, and not from the interior of the country.

Through the Border counties the alarm spread with rapidity, and on no occasion when that country was the scene of perpetual and unceasing war was the summons to arms more readily obeyed. In Berwickshire, Roxburghshire, and Selkirkshire the volunteers and militia got under arms with a degree of rapidity and alacrity which, considering the distance individuals lived from each other, had something in it very surprising; they poured to the alarm-posts on the sea-coast in a state so well armed and so completely appointed, with baggage, provisions, etc., as was accounted by the best military judges to render them fit for instant and effectual service.

There were some particulars in the general alarm which are curious and interesting. The men of Liddesdale, the most remote point to the westward which the alarm reached, were so much afraid of being late in the field that they put in requisition all the horses they could find, and when they had thus made a forced march out of their own country, they turned their borrowed steeds loose to find their way back through the hills, and they all got back safe to their own stables. Another remarkable circumstance was the general cry of the inhabitants of the smaller towns for arms, that they might go along with their companions. The Selkirkshire Yeomanry made a remarkable march, for, although some of the individuals lived at twenty and thirty miles' distance from the place where they mustered, they were nevertheless embodied and in order in so short a period that they were at Dalkeith, which was their alarm-post, about one o'clock on the day succeeding the first signal, with men and horses in good order, though the roads were in a bad state, and many of the troopers must have ridden forty or fifty miles without drawing bridle. Two members of the corps chanced to be absent from their homes, and in Edinburgh on private business. The lately married wife of one of these gentlemen, and the widowed mother of the other, sent the arms, uniforms, and charges of the two troopers, that they might join their companions at Dalkeith. The Author was very much struck by the answer made to him by the last-mentioned lady, when he paid her some compliment on the readiness which she showed in equipping her son with the means of meeting danger, when she might have left him a fair excuse for remaining absent. "Sir," she replied, with the spirit of a Roman matron, "none can know better than you that my son is the only prop by which, since his father's death, our family is supported. But I would rather see him dead on that hearth than hear that he had been a horse's length behind his companions in the defence of his king and country." The Author mentions what was immediately under his own eye and within his own knowledge; but the spirit was universal, wherever the alarm reached, both in Scotland and England.

The account of the ready patriotism displayed by the country on this occasion warmed the hearts of Scottishmen in every corner of the world

It reached the ears of the well-known Dr. Leyden, whose enthusiastic love of Scotland, and of his own district of Teviotdale, formed a distinguished part of his character. The account, which was read to him when on a sick-bed, stated (very truly) that the different corps, on arriving at their alarm-posts, announced themselves by their music playing the tunes peculiar to their own districts, many of which have been gathering-signals for centuries. It was particularly remembered that the Liddesdale men before mentioned entered Kelso playing the lively tune:

> Oh wha dare meddle wi me,
> And wha dare meddle wi' me!
> My name it is little Jock Elliot,
> And wha dare meddle wi' me!

The patient was so delighted with this display of ancient Border spirit that he sprung up in his bed and began to sing the old song with such vehemence of action and voice that his attendants, ignorant of the cause of excitation, concluded that the fever had taken possession of his brain ; and it was only the entry of another Borderer, Sir John Malcolm, and the explanation which he was well qualified to give, that prevented them from resorting to means of medical coercion.

The circumstances of this false alarm, and its consequences, may be now held of too little importance even for a note upon a work of fiction; but at the period when it happened it was hailed by the country as a propitious omen that the national force, to which much must naturally have been trusted, had the spirit to look in the face the danger which they had taken arms to repel : and every one was convinced that, on whichever side God might bestow the victory, the invaders would meet with the most determined opposition from the children of the soil.

GLOSSARY

OF

WORDS, PHRASES, AND ALLUSIONS.

ABDIEL, a seraph who withstands Satan when he counsels revolt, in *Paradise Lost*, bk. v.

ABOU HASSAN, an allusion to *The Arabian Nights*, "The Sleeper Awakened"

ABRACADABRA, a cabalistic word used as a charm

ABUNE, above

AE, one

ÆQUAM SERVARE MENTEM, to preserve equanimity

AGAIN E'EN, by or towards evening

AGÉ, to act as may be necessary and legal, a Scottish law term

AGGER, a mound, rampart

AGRICOLA DICAVIT, etc. (p. 47), Agricola dedicated [this] willingly, heartily

AIBLINS, perhaps

AIK, oak

AIRN, iron

AITMEAL, oatmeal

ALEXANDRIA AFFAIR, in all probability the battle is meant in which Sir Ralph Abercrombie fell, or the evacuation of Alexandria by the French immediately afterwards, though the date (1801) does not quite agree

ALIUNDE, from some other authority, quarter

ALLE GUTEN GEISTER, etc. (p. 228), all ye good spirits, praise the Lord

ALLERBESTMOST, a mongrel English-German compound word, meaning "the very, very best"

ALMANZOR, a character in Dryden's tragedy, *Conquest of Granada*

ANALECTA, excerpts, scraps, selections

AN ANES OUR WAMES ARE FU', if once our bellies are filled

ANE ON TUESDAY WAS A WEEK, one on Tuesday week

ANES, ANCE, once

ARCA AURI, chest of gold

AROINT THEE, get thee gone

ARTEM HABENT SINE ARTE, etc. (p. 135), they have an art of their own, and a part where right they have none, their element is lying, and beggary their vocation

ATWEEL, well

AUGHT, own; WHA'S AUGHT YE? whose are you?

AULAM AURI PLENAM QUADRILIBREM, a four-pound-weight jar full of gold

AULD-FARRANT, sagacious

AULULARIA, one of the plays of Plautus

AUREUM QUIDEM OPUS, a work of great value

AUTOMEDON, the charioteer of Achilles, a coachman

AWMOUS, alms

AYE OUT-TAKEN, always excepting

AZOCH, LATO, ZERNICH, etc., alchemical terms, quoted from Ben Jonson's *Alchemist*, Act. ii. Sc. 1

BAARENHAUTER, or BÄRENHÄUTER, a nickname for a German mercenary soldier

BACHA, or BACA, an allusion of Psalms lxxxiv. 6

BACK-SEY, sirloin

BAIN, BANE, bone

BAN, curse

BANNOCK-FLUKE, turbot

BARNS-BREAKING, larking, playing tricks

BARTHOLINUS, THOMAS, author of *Antiquitates Danicæ* (1689)

BASILIUS (-VALENTINE), a celebrated Saxon alchemist of the 15th (or later) century, who believed that he had found a universal panacea in antimony

BASSE-COUR, poultry-yard

BAUDRONS, a pet word for a cat

BEDRAL, sexton

BEIN, comfortable

BELYVE, directly, immediately

BEN, in, within

BICKER, a wooden bowl or dish

BIELD, shelter

BIG, to build

BIGGING, BIGGIN', building

BINK, wall plate-rack

BIRSE, bristle, temper

BIRTH, an obsolete form of *berth*, a situation, office, post

BLACK-NEB, one suspected of sympathising with the French Revolutionists

BLINK, a moment, short space of time

BODE, offer, bid

BODLE, copper coin=½d of English halfpenny

BOGLE, bogie, scarecrow

BOLE, window aperture

BONNET-LAIRD, a petty proprietor, who had the same dress and the same habits as a yeoman

BONNIE WAWLIES, gew-gaws

BOURD, jest

BOUROCK, small heap of stones

BOUSE, haul with tackle

BOWK, bulk

BRANKING, prancing

BRAW, brave ; BRAWLY, excellently well ; BRAWS, fine clothes

BROCK, badger

BRUNT, burnt

BUCK OF THE CABRACH, a mountain near the western boundary of Aberdeenshire

BURROWSTOWN, or BORROWSTOUN, belonging to a borough

BUSK THE LAIRD'S FLEES, dress the squire's flies (for fishing)

BUTTER IN THE BLACK DOG'S HAUSE (throat), something irrecoverable

BUZZ WIG, a large bushy wig

BY, besides ; BYE, beyond

CAIUS CALIGULA, etc. (p. 47), Caius Caligula built this lighthouse

CALLANT, lad

CALLER, fresh

CANKERED, crabbed, in ill-temper with

CANNY, cautious, quiet, sensible

CANTON, a division of a shield in heraldry

CANTRIP, frolic, trick

CAPTION, arrest by judicial process

CAR-CAKE, small cake eaten on Shrove Tuesday

CARFUFFLE, or CURFUFFLE, excitement, agitation

CARLE, fellow

CARLIN, CARLINE, witch, old woman

CARTES, cards

CARVY-SEED, caraway seed

CAST, lot, fate

CASTRA ÆSTIVA, summer camp

CASTRAMETATION, the art of laying out a camp

CASTRA STATIVA, permanent camp

CA'-THRO', an ado

CAUSA SCIENTIÆ PATET, the reason is sufficiently obvious

CAUSEY, causeway

CHAFRON, war-horse's head-piece

CHAMONT, a character in Otway's *Orphan*

CHANCY, lucky, favoured by good fortune

CHIEL, CHIELD, fellow

CITO PERITURA, soon to go to ruin

CLAES, CLAITH, clothes

CLARTIER, dirtier

CLASHES, gossip, scandal

CLEEDS, clothes

CLEUGH, rugged precipice

CLINKIT DOUN, sit down energetically, forcibly

CLIPPING-TIME, the nick of time

CLOD, to dash, hurl

CLOGDOGDO, a nonsense word for a woman. *See* Ben Jonson's *Silent Woman*, Act iv. Sc. 1

CLOUTED SHOES, shoes the soles of which were protected with large nails

COBLE, a small boat

COCK-PÀDLE, lump-fish

COEMPTOS UNDIQUE, etc. (p. 395), barter your hoard of books for Spanish arms

COLLOPS, minced meat

COLOPHON, in old books, the inscription on the last page, giving place and date of publication

COMPLAYNT OF SCOTLAND, a verse broadside, of date 1547, relating to the murder of Darnley

COMPLETE SYREN. a collection of songs, published at London in 1739

CONCURRENT, an assistant to a sheriff's officer

COPPER OTHO, a coin so rare that its authenticity has been doubted. Otho, emperor of Rome, reigned only three months

CORBIE, crow, raven

CORDERY. Maturin Corderius, teacher of Calvin, an author of a book of Latin dialogues (*Colloquiorum Centuria Selecta*, edited by John Clarke), formerly much used in schools

CORONACH, the Highland lament for the dead

COUPIT, upset, overturned

COVES, caves, mining-pits

CRACK, gossip, chat

CRAIG, a crag; the neck or throat

CRAIGSMAN, a fowler or cragsman

CRAPPIT-HEADS, haddocks' heads stuffed with oatmeal, suet, onions, and pepper

CREESH, to grease

CROUSELY, with confidence, boldly

CRUPPEN, crept

CUM DECIMIS INCLUSIS, etc. (p. 199), with tithes included, compounded as well as collected, and not yet allocated

CUMMER, gossip, neighbour

CUM TOTO CORPORE REGNI, with the whole strength of the kingdom

CUTIKINS, leggings, gaiters

DAMMER AND SINKER, a miner

DAUNDER, DANDER, saunter, roam

DEIL GAED O'ER JOCK WABSTER, everything went to the mischief

DESIPERE IN LOCO, to jest in season

DEVVEL, stunning blow

DIE, toy

DING, force, beat, overcome

DIRGE, or DIRGIE, dirge-ale or soul-ale, consumed at a funeral

DIV, do

DOITED, confused, stupid,

DONNARD, grossly stupid, stolid

DOOMS, confoundedly

DOUKING, ducking, plunging into water, bathing

DOUP, end, bottom

DOUR, stubborn, obstinate

DOW, be able; DOWNA BIDE, cannot bear

DOW-COT, dove-cote

DREEING A SAIR WEIRD, enduring a sore misfortune

DROUKIT, drenched

DRUDGING-BOX, DREDGING-BOX, flour-box

DUMOSA PENDERE PROCUL DE RUPE, hang far over the bushy crag

DUNSE, *i.e.* Duns Scotus, the theologian and schoolman

DWAM, swoon

EARDED, or ERDED, buried

EASELWARD, eastward

EEN, eyes; EE, eye

EFFEIR, belong to, become

EILDING, fuel

EITHLY, easily

ESPIÈGLERIE, arch humour

ET SE JACTU, etc. (p. 396), and flung herself into the deep sea

EWKING, itching

EXIES, hysterics

EXPEDITUS, RELICTIS IMPEDIMENTIS, speedily, without encumbrance

FA'ARD, favoured; WEEL-FA'ARD, well-favoured, good-looking

FAE, who

FAIRPORT, this is supposed to be Arbroath in Forfarshire

FAIR-STRAE DEATH, natural death in peace and quietness

FAN, when

FASH, trouble; FASHIOUS, troublesome

FAVETE LINGUIS, be silent

FEAL-DIKE, turf dike or wall

FECK, quantity, part

FECKLESS, feeble, spiritless

FEE AND BOUNTITH, wages, perquisites included

FEEL, fool

FENDING, provisions

FERÆ NATURÆ, wild animals, game

FEUAR, landholder paying ground-rent to a superior

FICKLE, puzzle

FIFTEEN, THE, the supreme law-court of Scotland, presided over by fifteen judges

FIRE-FLAUGHT, flash of fire, lightning

FISCHER, J. C., a celebrated oboist, played at the Vauxhall concerts in London from 1768, and in the Queen's band

FISSIL, rustle (like a mouse)

FIT, foot

FLAUGHTER, flicker

FLAUGHTER-SPADE, turf-spade

FLAW, a blast of wind

FLEE, a fly

FLIGHTERING, quivering, fluttering

FLISKMAHOY, a flirt, giddy girl

FLYTING, scolding, badgering

FORBYE, besides

FOREBEAR, ancestor

FORFAIRN, destitute, worn out

FORNARINA, a baker's wife

FOUNDER, stun

FRAGILEM MECUM, etc. (p. 388) to unmoor with me the fragile boat

FRIAR'S CHICKEN, chicken broth, with eggs beaten up and dropped into it

FRONDE SUPER VIRIDI, under the green leaves

FUGIE WARRANT, warrant to prevent flight

FUST, or FAUST, JOHANN, an associate of Gutenberg, the reputed inventor of printing; he is sometimes confounded with Dr. Faust, the hero of the well-known legend

GABERLUNZIE, or BLUE-GOWN, a beggar carrying a wallet, *see* p. 9

GAE-DOWN, drinking bout

GAIT, or GATE, way, manner, direction

GAR, make, force

GAUDÉ-DAY, festive day

GAWRIE. *See* PETER WILKINS below

GEAR, property

GECK, mock, gibe, taunt

GELT, money

GENS HUMIDA PONTI, moist race of the sea, fish, etc.

GEY, considerably, pretty

GIB, start backward

GIE OUR AIN FISH-GUTS TO OUR AIN SEA-MAWS, keep our own good things for our own people

GILL-STOUP, a flagon

GIN, if

GLEG, sharp, quick, keen

GLIFF, fright

GLOWER, gaze, stare

GLUM. *See* PETER WILKINS below

GLUM AND GLUNCH, sulky and sour-looking

GOOD-NATURED MAN, a play by Goldsmith

GOUSTY, GOUSTIE, ghostly, vacant and dreary

GOWK, fool

GRANE, groan

GREET, cry, weep

GREYBEARD, an old-fashioned stone ware Flemish liquor-jar

GUDEMITHER, mother-in-law

GUDESIRE, grandfather

GUDEWIFE, wife

GUEBRES, the ancient fire-worshippers or Zoroastrians of Persia, the modern Parsis of Bombay

GUFFA, guffaw ; THE SKIRL AT THE TAIL O' THE GUFFA, a wild scream following close upon a loud laugh

GULLY, large knife

GY, a guide rope

GYRE-CARLIN, ogre, hobgoblin

GYTE, beside oneself, delirious

HADDIE, haddock

HÆC DATA, etc. (p. 167), this is the penalty for length of days

HAET, the smallest thing conceivable

HAGGIS, a Scotch pudding, consisting of minced meat, with oatmeal, beef-suet, onions, etc., boiled in a skin bag

HAILL AND FERE, vigorous and well

HALF-MERK (or clandestine) MARRIAGE, probably so called from the price of the ceremony

HALLAN, cottage partition

HALLENSHAKER, or HALLANSHAKER, sturdy beggar, a shabbily-dressed fellow

HALSE, HAUSE, the throat

HANG-CHOICE, the position of one who has to choose between two evils

HANK (A) OVER, advantage, ground for teasing

HANTLE, a good deal; HANTLE SILLER, a good sum of money

HARNS, brains

HARPAGON, the miser in Molière's *L'Avare*

HAUD ALIENUM A SCÆVOLÆ STUDIIS, not foreign to the pursuits of Scævola (a lawyer)

HAUSE, HALSE, the throat

HAVERED, talked nonsense, jargon, at random

HAWTHORNDEN, the seat of the poet Drummond, about 8 miles south of Edinburgh

HEILIGKEIT. holiness

HELLICATE, giddy

HERD, man in charge of the cattle on a Scotch farm

HEUGH, a crag

HEYTESBURY, WILLIAM, an Oxford logician of the 14th century

HINNEY, honey, an affectionate form of address

HIREN, a female swaggerer in Peele's *The Turkish Mahomet. See* also *Henry IV.,* Part II. Act ii. Sc. 4

HIRPLE, hobble

HOAST, cough

HOC ERAT IN VOTIS, this is how your wishes run

HOLLIN, or HOLYN, holly

HOODIECRAW, hooded crow

HOOLY, softly, slowly

HORNING, CHARGE OF, the royal letter calling upon a debtor to pay his debt under pain of being declared a rebel. *See* Imprisonment for Debt in Scotland (pp. 398, 466)

HORS DE PROPOS, ill-timed, unseasonable

HOUDIE, midwife

HOUK, or HOWK, dig

HOWLIT, owl

HURLING, rushing, whirling (of water)

ILLE CALEDONIIS, etc. (p. 47), he who pitched his camp among Caledonian snows

ILLUMINÉ, a member of the Illuminati, a society founded at Ingoldstadt in Bavaria in 1776 for the promotion of rational enlightenment, and the combating of ignorance and the tyranny of the Jesuits

INGLE, the fire, fireplace

IN-OWER AND OUT-OWER, within and without

IN PETTO, in reserve, readiness for

JALOUSED, suspected

JIMP, scarcely

JOE MANTON, a London gunsmith, died in 1835, aged 69, who improved the flint-lock and other sporting-guns

JOHN THOMSON'S WALLET, equivalent to "anybody's" wallet

JOWING, rolling

KAIL-BLADE, leaf of colewort or cabbage

KAIM, camp, hillock

KALE-SUPPER O' FIFE, a term applied to Fifeshire people, who were great consumers of "kale" or broth

KAME, comb

KEELYVINE, black-lead pencil

KEEP ON THIS SIDE. The real words on a stone found in Northumberland, which, on being sent to a learned society, was variously interpreted by its members as being an abbreviated Latin inscription. See *Town and Country Magazine*, 1771, p. 595

KEMP, strive

KILT, to tuck up

KIMMER, neighbour or gossip

KING'S KEYS, the crowbars and hammers used to force doors and locks in execution of the king's warrant

KIPPAGE, fluster, rage

KIRCHER, ATHANASIUS, a German philosopher and antiquary of the 17th century

KIST, chest

KITTLE, ticklish

LAIGH, low, low-lying

LAITH, loth, unwilling

LANDLOUPER, adventurer

LANDWARD TOWN, country house or farm with adjoining cottages

LAPPER MILK, soured, curdled milk

LATO. *See* AZOCH

LAUCH, law

LAUDATOR TEMPORIS ACTI, one who praises the "good old times."

LAVE, remainder

LEASING, lies, falsehood; LEASING-MAKING, high treason

LEZE-MAJESTY, treason

LIBERTY BOYS, a body of Irish volunteers levied originally on the Earl of Meath's "liberties." It embraced (1784) many Roman Catholics of the lowest class, and became a democratic society

LIFT, the sky, firmament

LILT, a cheerful tune; to sing or hum such

LIMMER, a jade, scoundrel

LOANING, lane, meadow

LOOM, or LOME, utensil, vessel

LOON, a fellow, low person

LOUND, tranquil, calm

LOUNDER, heavy stroke

LOVEL OUR DOG, formerly a common name for a dog. Wm. Collingborne was executed in the reign of Richard III. (in 1484) for writing the couplet—

> The rat, the cat, and Lovel our dog
> Rule all England under the hog—

the rat being Ratcliffe, the cat Catesby, Lovel Lord Lovel, and the hog of course Richard the king

LUCKIE, a title given to old ladies, landladies of inns, nurses, etc.

LUCUS A NON LUCENDO, a grove (is so named) from its not giving light. Generally used to denote any self-contradictory etymology

LUNGIE, guillemot bird

LYKE-WAKE, a watch over the dead, a wake

MAEN, or MENE, to complain, utter lamentations

MAGISTERIUM, the authoritative doctrines of magic

MAHOUND OR TERMAGANT, names of opprobrium, applied in the mediæval mystery-plays to Mohammed, who was represented as a devil

MAILING, a rented farm

MAIR PURPOSE-FA'ARD, more becoming

MANSE, the parsonage

MANTY-MAKER, dressmaker

MARMOR, or MAORMOR, a royal steward appointed formerly in Scotland to govern a province; an earl

MASSYMORE, or MASSAMORA, an ancient name for a dungeon, derived from the Moorish language, perhaps as far back as the time of the Crusades

MASTER O' MORPHIE, presumably Robert Grahame of Morphie in Kincardineshire, a gentleman of extravagant habits and member of a family noted for their love of good horses

MAUNDER, talk incoherently, ramble

MEAR, mare

MEIN HIMMEL, Heaven !

MEO ARBITRIO, in my judgment

MERK, Scotch silver coin, value 1s. 1½d.

MIDDEN, dunghill

MIFF, a fit of pettish temper

MINNIE, mother

MIRK, dark

MISCA', abuse

MONITORIBUS ASPER, churlish to advise

MORPION, a crab-louse

MOUL, moulds, a sod

MOUST, or MUST, to powder the hair

MUCKLE, much, large

MUNTS HIS MEAR, mounts his mare

MUTCHKIN, a liquid measure equal to an English pint

NAIN, own

NAPIER'S BONES, small rods of bone used in calculations, invented by Napier of Merchiston

NEBULO NEBULONUM, an arrant rascal

NEC LEX JUSTITIOR ULLA, nor could any law be more just

NE'ER-BE-LICKIT, not a vestige, not a scrap

NEIST, next

NIFFER, barter, higgle

NOBILIS EQUUS UMBRA, etc. (p. 412), the shadow of the switch is enough for a good horse, but the spur can't make a bad one go.

ODER, or

ODI ACCIPITREM, etc. (p. 439), I hate the sparrow-hawk that always has its feathers plumed for fight

OE, grandson

OMNE CUM PROTEUS, etc. (p. 393), when Proteus drove all his flock to view the high mountains

OMNI MEMBRORUM DAMNO, etc. (p. 407), that loss of mental power, worse than all bodily decay, which deprives us of the recollection of our very servants' names, the features of last night's guests, or even our children and nurslings

ORKBORNE, DR., a scholar of the Rev. Josiah Cargill type, in Frances Burney's novel Camilla

ORRA, odd ; ORRA TIME, on occasion

OUTBY, abroad, some distance away

OWER-HEAD, each, per head

OVERLOOK, to overlook, not to heed

OWZEL, a blackbird

PANCHRESTA, a sort of cure-all, panacea

PARAFLE, ostentatious display

PAR NOBILE FRATRUM, a noble pair of brothers

PARTAN, crab

PATERÆ, shallow saucer-like vessels of the ancient Romans

PEERY, peg-top

PELASO DE TARANTA, presumably Filippo Pelazio, an Italian medical writer of the 18th century

PENTACLE, a geometrical figure used in magical incantations

PENTAPOLIN, an allusion to *Don Quixote*

PERIAPT, a charm, amulet

PETER WILKINS, the hero of a fictitious book of travel by R. Pultock, published in 1750. Glum and Gawrie were races of flying creatures met with by Wilkins

PETRIE, ADAM, wrote *Rules of Good Deportment or of Good Breeding*, Edinburgh, 1720

PETRUS THYRÆUS, author of *Loca Infesta* (1598), a work on localities haunted by demons and spirits of the departed, and similar books

PICKLE, a very little, small quantity, few

PICTARNIE, great tern or sea-swallow

PINNERS, lappets of a woman's cap

PIRN, reel

PLACEBO, make-peace

PLAINSTANES, pavement

PLISKIE, trick

PLUFF, an instrument for powdering a wig

POCKMANKY, portmanteau

POIND, to distrain

POKE, POCK, bag, sack

POLYCHRESTA, a sort of cure-all, panacea

POPPLE, trickle, gurgles

POSE, a secret hoard

POUND SCOTS, worth 1s. 8d.

POUSOWDIE, a mess of miscellaneous foods

POUTING, potting, shooting partridges or grouse

POW, head

PRENT BUKE, printed book

PROPINE, gift

PUNAISE, a bug

PUND SCOTS, worth one-twelfth of an English pound

QUAM PRIMUM, as soon as possible

QUI AMBULAT, etc. (p. 75), he who walks in darkness knows not whither he is going

QUID NON PRO PATRIA? what will you not do for your country?

RAGMAN ROLL, list of Scots nobles, gentry, clergy, and burgesses who swore fealty to Edward I. in 1296

RAMILIES, a wig with a long, tapering tail, a large bow at top and a small one at bottom

RANDY, a scold

RARI, ET RARIORES, ETIAM RARISSIMI! rare, rarer, yet most rare!

RARO ANTECEDENTEM, etc. (p. 458), punishment has seldom failed to overtake crime

RATH, early, sudden

RATTON, rat

REIST, to refuse to go forward

REI SUÆ PRODIGUS, lavish of his means

REMIGIUS, NICOLAUS, Nicholas of Remy, author of *Dæmonolatreiæ* (1595), treating of wizards and witches

REMORA, delay

RERUM COGNOSCERE CAUSAS, to know the causes of things

RICKLE, heap

ROTURIER, a commoner

ROUGHIES, links or torches, made of dry twigs or sticks

ROUST, rust

ROUTH, plenty

ROW, to roll

RUDAS, stubborn, masculine

RUGGING AND RIVING, or RYVING robbing and plundering

SACKLESS, innocent

SAIN, to bless

SAINT JAMES'S FAIR, at Kelso, held on 5th August, was one of the most important of those formerly important gatherings in the south of Scotland

SAPIENS DOMINABITUR ASTRIS, a wise man will rule the stars

SAULIES, hired mourners, mutes

SAXON HORN at York. *See Ivanhoe*, Dedicatory Epistle

SCAUR, crag or bluff; scare, cause of alarm

SCHRÖPFER or SCHREPFER, J. G., a Leipzig innkeeper who made himself notorious throughout Saxony as an exorciser of spirits

SCONNER, or SCUNNER, loathing, abhorrence, disgust

SCOT AND LOT, parish taxes

SCULL, shallow basket for fish

SEANNACHIE, Highland bard or genealogist

SECEDE PAULISPER, retire a little

SED PEREUNTI, etc. (p. 429), but he

who is passing away sees a thousand shapes

SHANKIT AFF, hurried away

SHATHMONT, a measure of six inches

SHAW, wood

SHEUGH, ditch, furrow

SHIRRA, sheriff

SHULE, shovel

SIB, related by blood

SIC, SICCAN, such

SIDE AND WIDE, long and wide

SIGIL, an occult sign or mark in magic

SIGNATUM ATQUE SIGILLATUM, signed and sealed

SI INSANORUM VISIS, etc. (p. 142), if we should not put faith in madmen's visions, I know not why we should credit those of dreamers, which are much more disordered

SIMMER AND WINTER, to ponder over, spend much time in forming a plan

SINE MORA, without delay

SINGLE SOLDIER, a private soldier

SINSYNE, since

SIST, a warrant to stay legal proceedings

SISTER MARGARET. The book alluded to is *The History of the Proceedings in the Case of Margaret, commonly called Peg, only lawful Sister to John Bull, Esq.* (1761), attributed to Dr. Adam Ferguson

SKART, cormorant

SKEEL, skill, experience; SKEELY, skilful

SKIRL, scream

SKREIGH, a shrill cry; to shriek, scream

SLAISTER, to bedaub, make a mess of

SLINK, a cheat, deceiver

SNEESHIN, snuff; SNEESHIN-MULL, snuff-box

SNELL AND DURE, severe and stubborn

SNOOD, fillet for binding up the hair

SOMEDELE, somewhat, something

SONSY, plump, jolly

SOUGH, whisper, vague rumour; to murmur, mumble

SOUTER, shoemaker

SOWDER, solder

SOWNDER, or SOUNDER, a boar of two years old

SPEEL, or SPELE, climb

SPEERINGS, tidings

SPOLIA OPIMA, arms taken from a defeated and slain enemy

SPONTOON, a half-pike formerly carried by officers of infantry

STADTHAUS, town-house, town-hall

STANG, a long pole

STEEK, shut

STEER, to touch, meddle with, disturb

STEERY, bustle, tumult

STEEVER, firmer

STING AND LING, entirely, wholly

STIRRA, sturdy, active boy; a corruption of sirrah

STOUP, flagon, pitcher, mug

STOUTH AND ROUTH, plenty, abundance

STRAKE, struck

STREEK, stretch, lay out for burial

STUDE, stood, withstood

SUAVE EST MARI MAGNO, 'tis pleasant on the great sea

SUFFLAMINA, stay a little

SUNT QUOS CURRICULO, etc. (p. 375) there are some who rejoice in having stirred up the Olympic dust (in the games) with their racing chariot

SUPERSEDERE, equivalent to Sist, above

SUS. PER FUNEM THAN SUS. PER COLL., rather hanging by the rope than hung by the neck

SUSPICIONE MAJOR, above suspicion

SWEER, unwilling

SWITHER, confusion, perplexity

TAE, the one

TALE-PYET, tell-tale

TAMMIE NORIE, a puffin

TANQUAM PARTICIPES CRIMINIS REBELLIONIS, virtually participators in rebellion

TANQUAM SUSPECT, under suspicion

TAWPIE, awkward slovenly girl

TEINDS, tithes

TENT, care

TENUES SECESSIT IN AURAS . . . MANSIT ODOR, vanished into thin air . . . the odour remained

TERES ATQUE ROTUNDUS, the comfortable-looking man

THACK (thatch) AND RAPE (rope), a thorough covering

THREEP, persist, insist

THROUGH-STANE, or THRUCH-STANE, a flat gravestone

THRUM, tell, prose over

TILL, a stiff clay

TINTAMARRE, an uproar, confused noise

TIRL, to uncover; TIRL'D AT THE DOORPIN, twirled the latch

TIRLIE-WIRLIE, twisting about, intricate

TITTIVILLITIUM, small trifle

TOCHER, dowry; WEEL-TOCHERED, having a large dowry, well provided for

TOD, a bush; a fox

TOLBOOTH, prison, house of detention

TOOM, empty

TOPIARIAN, relating to landscape gardening. ARS TOPIARIA, the art of clipping yew hedges into fantastic figures

TOUZLE OUT, to search out, turn out confusedly

TOW, a rope

TRIG, neat, trim, shipshape

TRIMMER, vixen

TROKE, traffic

TURNPIKE STAIR, a spiral or v. nding staircase

TWAL, twelve

UGSOME, noisome, exciting abomination

ULTRA CREPIDAM, meddling in others' business

ULYIE, oil

UNBRIZZED, unbruised

UNCO, uncommonly

VILE SABINUM, poor Sabine wine

VIVERS, victuals, sustenance

VOIE DE FAIT, assault, main force

VOLE, at cards winning all the tricks of a hand

VOX SIGNATA, correct term

WALE, the pick, choice

WALLACE'S STRAIKS, strokes as powerful as Sir Wallace's

WAME, belly; WAME O' A WAVE, trough of a wave

WAMPISH, to throw about

WANLE, strong, active

WARE, to spend

WARP, four, the unit of sale applied to oysters

WASSIA QUASSIA, a poor thin liquid, drunk by the peasantry

WAUR, worse; WAURED, worsted

WEAN, child

WEARY, vexatious, troublesome

WEIZE, guide, incline

WHA'S AUGHT YE? whose are you?

WHATEN A GATE? what way? what sort of a way?

WHEEN, a few

WHITE WITCH, a wizard or witch benevolently disposed

WHOMLE, or WHUMMIL, turn over

WILYARD, wayward, unmanageable

WIND A PIRN, work mischief

WIN OUT, get out; WIN THROUGH, get through

WORRIECOW, hobgoblin

WUSSING, wishing

YAULD, active

YERL, earl

YESTREEN, yesternight

YOWE, ewe

ZERNICH. *See* Azoch

INDEX.

31

END OF THE ANTIQUARY.

CLEVELAND, THE PIRATE.

THE PIRATE.

By SIR WALTER SCOTT, BART.

Nothing in him—
But doth suffer a sea-change.
—Tempest.

A. L. BURT COMPANY, PUBLISHERS,
52-58 DUANE STREET, NEW YORK.

INTRODUCTION TO THE PIRATE.

Quoth he, there was a ship.

THIS brief preface may begin like the tale of the *Ancient Mariner*, since it was on shipboard that the Author acquired the very moderate degree of local knowledge and information, both of people and scenery, which he has endeavoured to embody in the romance of the *Pirate*.

In the summer and autumn of 1814, the Author was invited to join a party of Commissioners for the Northern Lighthouse Service, who proposed making a voyage round the coast of Scotland, and through its various groups of islands, chiefly for the purpose of seeing the condition of the many lighthouses under their direction—edifices so important whether regarding them as benevolent or political institutions. Among the commissioners who manage this important public concern, the sheriff of each county of Scotland which borders on the sea holds *ex-officio* a place at the Board. These gentlemen act in every respect gratuitously, but have the use of an armed yacht, well found and fitted up, when they choose to visit the lighthouses. An excellent engineer, Mr. Robert Stevenson, is attached to the Board, to afford the benefit of his professional advice. The Author accompanied this expedition as a guest; for Selkirkshire, though it calls him sheriff, has not, like the kingdom of Bohemia in Corporal Trim's story, a seaport in its circuit, nor its magistrate, of course, any place at the Board of Commissioners—a circumstance of little consequence where all were old and intimate friends, bred to the same profession, and disposed to accommodate each other in every possible manner.

The nature of the important business which was the principal purpose of the voyage was connected with the amusement of visiting the leading objects of a traveller's curiosity; for the wild cape or formidable shelve which requires to be marked out by a lighthouse is generally at no great distance from the most magnificent scenery of rocks, caves, and billows. Our time, too, was at our own disposal, and, as most of us were fresh-water sailors, we could at any time make a fair wind out of a foul one, and run before the gale in quest of some object of curiosity which lay under our lee.

With these purposes of public utility, and some personal amusement, in view, we left the port of Leith on the 26th July, 1814, ran along the east coast of Scotland, viewing its different curiosities, stood over to Zetland and Orkney, where we were some time detained by the wonders of a country which displayed so much that was new to us; and having seen what was curious in the Ultima Thule of the ancients, where the sun hardly thought it worth while to go to bed, since its rising was at this season so early, we doubled the extreme northern termination of Scotland, and took a rapid survey of the Hebrides, where we found many kind friends. There, that our little expedition might not want the dignity of danger, we were favoured with a distant glimpse of what was said to be an American cruiser, and had opportunity to consider what a pretty figure we should have made had the voyage ended in our being carried captive to the United States. After visiting the romantic shores of Morven and the vicinity of Oban, we made a run to the coast of Ireland and visited the Giant's Causeway, that we might compare it with Staffa, which we had surveyed in our course. At length, about the middle of September, we ended our voyage in the Clyde, at the port of Greenock.[1]

And thus terminated our pleasant tour, to which our equipment gave unusual facilities, as the ship's company could form a strong boat's crew, independent of those who might be left on board the vessel, which permitted us the freedom to land wherever our curiosity carried us. Let me add,

[1] [See Lockhart's *Life*, vol. iv. pp. 180–370.]

while reviewing for a moment a sunny portion of my life, that among the six or seven friends who performed this voyage together, some of them doubtless of different tastes and pursuits, and remaining for several weeks on board a small vessel, there never occurred the slightest dispute or disagreement, each seeming anxious to submit his own particular wishes to those of his friends. By this mutual accommodation all the purposes of our little expedition were attained, while for a time we might have adopted the lines of Allan Cunningham's fine sea-song,

> The world of waters was our home,
> And merry men were we!

But sorrow mixes her memorials with the purest remembrances of pleasure. On returning from the voyage which had proved so satisfactory, I found that fate had deprived her country most unexpectedly of a lady qualified to adorn the high rank which she held, and who had long admitted me to a share of her friendship.[1] The subsequent loss of one of those comrades who made up the party, and he the most intimate friend I had in the world,[2] casts also its shade on recollections which, but for these embitterments, would be otherwise so pleasing.

[1] Harriet Katherine, Duchess of Buccleuch, died 24th August 1814 (*Laing*).

[2] William Erskine of Kinedder, son of an Episcopal minister in Perthshire, was educated for the legal profession, and passed advocate 3d July 1790. He was appointed Sheriff-Depute of Orkney 6th June 1809, and in that capacity was accompanied by Scott in the Lighthouse voyage round the coast. He was raised to the bench, and took his seat as Lord Kinedder 29th January 1822. Unfortunately, he did not long enjoy this honour, as he died unexpectedly on the 14th of August following, to the great grief of Sir Walter, who at this very time was wholly occupied with the arrangements connected with George IV.'s visit to Edinburgh. Lord Kinedder, to whom Scott had from boyhood been deeply attached, was a most amiable and accomplished man.

In 1788, when the *Ode on the Popular Superstitions of the Highlands* was first published (which the Wartons thought superior to the other works of Collins, but which Dr. Johnson says, " no search has yet found "), Mr. Erskine wrote several supplementary stanzas, intended to commemorate some Scottish superstitions omitted by Collins. These verses first appeared in the *Edinburgh Magazine* for April 1788 (*Laing*).

I may here briefly observe, that my business in this voyage, so far as I could be said to have any, was to endeavour to discover some localities which might be useful in the *Lord of the Isles*, a poem with which I was then threatening the public, and [which] was afterwards printed without attaining remarkable success. But as at the time the anonymous novel of *Waverley* was making its way to popularity, I already augured the possibility of a second effort in this department of literature, and I saw much in the wild islands of the Orkneys and Zetland which I judged might be made in the highest degree interesting, should these isles ever become the scene of a narrative of fictitious events. I learned the history of Gow the pirate from an old sibyl (see Note 14, p. 454), whose principal subsistence was by a trade in favourable winds, which she sold to mariners at Stromness. Nothing could be more interesting than the kindness and hospitality of the gentlemen of Zetland, which was to me the more affecting as several of them had been friends and correspondents of my father.

I was induced to go a generation or two farther back to find materials from which I might trace the features of the old Norwegian udaller, the Scottish gentry having in general occupied the place of that primitive race, and their language and peculiarities of manner having entirely disappeared. The only difference now to be observed betwixt the gentry of these islands and those of Scotland in general is, that the wealth and property is more equally divided among our more northern countrymen, and that there exists among the resident proprietors no men of very great wealth, whose display of its luxuries might render the others discontented with their own lot. From the same cause of general equality of fortunes, and the cheapness of living which is its natural consequence, I found the officers of a veteran regiment who had maintained the garrison at Fort Charlotte, in Lerwick, discomposed at the idea of being recalled from a country where their pay, however inadequate to the expenses of a capital, was fully adequate to their wants, and it was singular to hear natives of merry England herself regretting their approaching departure from the melancholy isles of the Ultima Thule.

Such are the trivial particulars attending the origin of that publication, which took place several years later than the agreeable journey from which it took its rise.

The state of manners which I have introduced in the romance was necessarily in a great degree imaginary, though founded in some measure on slight hints, which, showing what was, seemed to give reasonable indication of what must once have been, the tone of the society in these sequestered but interesting islands.

In one respect I was judged somewhat hastily, perhaps, when the character of Norna was pronounced by the critics a mere copy of Meg Merrilies. That I had fallen short of what I wished and desired to express is unquestionable, otherwise my object could not have been so widely mistaken; nor can I yet think that any person who will take the trouble of reading the *Pirate* with some attention can fail to trace in Norna—the victim of remorse and insanity, and the dupe of her own imposture, her mind, too, flooded with all the wild literature and extravagant superstitions of the North—something distinct from the Dumfriesshire gipsy, whose pretensions to supernatural powers are not beyond those of a Norwood prophetess. The foundations of such a character may be perhaps traced, though it be too true that the necessary superstructure cannot have been raised upon them, otherwise these remarks would have been unnecessary. There is also great improbability in the statement of Norna's possessing power and opportunity to impress on others that belief in her supernatural gifts which distracted her own mind. Yet, amid a very credulous and ignorant population, it is astonishing what success may be attained by an impostor who is, at the same time, an enthusiast. It is such as to remind us of the couplet which assures us that

> The pleasure is as great
> In being cheated as to cheat.

Indeed, as I have observed elsewhere, the professed explanation of a tale, where appearances or incidents of a supernatural character are referred to natural causes, has often, in the winding up of the story, a degree of improbability almost equal to an absolute goblin narrative. Even the genius of Mrs. Radcliffe could not always surmount this difficulty.

ABBOTSFORD, *1st May 1831.*

ADVERTISEMENT.

THE purpose of the following narrative is to give a detailed and accurate account of certain remarkable incidents which took place in the Orkney Islands, concerning which the more imperfect traditions and mutilated records of the country only tell us the following erroneous particulars:

In the month of January, 1724-25, a vessel, called the "Revenge," bearing twenty large guns and six smaller, commanded by John Gow, or Goffe, or Smith, came to the Orkney Islands, and was discovered to be a pirate by various acts of insolence and villainy committed by the crew. These were for some time submitted to, the inhabitants of these remote islands not possessing arms nor means of resistance; and so bold was the captain of these banditti, that he not only came ashore and gave dancing-parties in the village of Stromness, but, before his real character was discovered, engaged the affections, and received the troth-plight, of a young lady possessed of some property. A patriotic individual, James Fea, younger of Clestron, formed the plan of securing the buccanier, which he effected by a mixture of courage and address, in consequence chiefly of Gow's vessel having gone on shore near the harbour of Calfsound, on the Island of Eda, not far distant from a house then inhabited by Mr. Fea. In the various stratagems by which Mr. Fea contrived finally, at the peril of his life (they being well armed and desperate), to make the whole pirates his prisoners, he was much aided by Mr. James Laing, the grandfather of the late Malcolm Laing, Esq.,[1] the acute and ingenious historian of Scotland during the 17th century.

[1] This gentleman was called to the Scotch Bar in the year 1784, but the

Gow and others of his crew suffered, by sentence of the High Court of Admiralty, the punishment their crimes had long deserved. He conducted himself with great audacity when before the court; and, from an account of the matter by an eye-witness, seems to have been subjected to some unusual severities in order to compel him to plead. The words are these: "John Gow would not plead, for which he was brought to the bar, and the Judge ordered that his thumbs should be squeezed by two men, with a whip-cord, till it did break; and then it should be doubled, till it did again break, and then laid threefold, and that the executioners should pull with their whole strength; which sentence Gow endured with a great deal of boldness." The next morning (27th May, 1725), when he had seen the terrible preparations for pressing him to death, his courage gave way, and he told the marshal of court that he would not have given so much trouble had he been assured of not being hanged in chains. He was then tried, condemned, and executed, with others of his crew.

It is said that the lady whose affections Gow had engaged went up to London to see him before his death, and that, arriving too late, she had the courage to request a sight of his dead body; and then, touching the hand of the corpse, she formally resumed the troth-plight which she had bestowed. Without going through this ceremony, she could not, according to the superstition of the country, have escaped a visit from the ghost of her departed lover, in the event of her bestowing upon any living suitor the faith which she had plighted to the dead. This part of the legend may serve aas a curious commentary on the fine Scottish ballad [1] which begins:

There came a ghost to Margaret's door, etc.

The common account of this incident farther bears, that

infirm state of his health induced him, in 1810, to leave the profession, and to reside on his paternal property near Kirkwall, devoting himself to agricultural pursuits. He died in November 1818, aged fifty-five, and was interred in the nave of St. Magnus's Cathedral (*Laing*).

[1] This ballad of "Willie's Ghost" is printed in Herd's *Collection*, vol. i. p. 76. It is not so well known as Mallet's version, "Willie and Margaret," which begins: "'Twas at the fearful midnight hour" (*Laing*).

Mr. Fea, the spirited individual by whose exertions Gow's career of iniquity was cut short, was so far from receiving any reward from Government, that he could not obtain even countenance enough to protect him against a variety of sham suits, raised against him by Newgate solicitors, who acted in the name of Gow and others of the pirate crew; and the various expenses, vexatious prosecutions, and other legal consequences, in which his gallant exploit involved him, utterly ruined his fortune and his family; making his memory a notable example to all who shall in future take pirates on their own authority.

It is to be supposed, for the honour of George the First's Government, that the last circumstance, as well as the dates, and other particulars of the commonly received story, are inaccurate, since they will be found totally irreconcilable with the following veracious narrative, compiled from materials to which he himself alone has had access, by

THE AUTHOR OF "WAVERLEY."

THE PIRATE.

CHAPTER I.

The storm had ceased its wintry roar,
  Hoarse dash the billows of the sea;
But who on Thule's desert shore
  Cries, Have I burnt my harp for thee?
                              MACNIEL.

THAT long, narrow, and irregular island, usually called the Mainland of Zetland, because it is by far the largest of that archipelago, terminates, as is well known to the mariners who navigate the stormy seas which surround the Thule of the ancients, in a cliff of immense height, entitled Sumburgh Head, which presents its bare scalp and naked sides to the weight of a tremendous surge, forming the extreme point of the isle to the southeast. This lofty promontory is constantly exposed to the current of a strong and furious tide, which, setting in betwixt the Orkney and Zetland Islands, and running with force only inferior to that of the Pentland Firth, takes its name from the headland we have mentioned. and is called the Roost of Sumburgh—"roost" being the phrase assigned in those isles to currents of this description.

On the land side, the promontory is covered with short grass, and slopes steeply down to a little isthmus, upon which the sea has encroached in creeks, which, advancing from either side of the island, gradually work their way forward, and seem as if in a short time they would form a junction and altogether insulate Sumburgh Head, when what is now a cape will become a lonely mountain islet, severed from the Mainland, of which it is at present the terminating extremity.

Man, however, had in former days considered this as a remote or unlikely event; for a Norwegian chief of other times, or, as other accounts said, and as the name of Jarlshof seemed to imply, an ancient Earl of the Orkneys, had selected this neck of land as the place for establishing a mansion-house. It has been long entirely deserted, and the vestiges only can be discerned with difficulty; for the loose sand, borne on the tempestuous gales of those stormy regions, has overblown and almost buried the ruins of the buildings; but in the end of the 17th century a part of the earl's mansion was still entire and habitable. It was a rude building of rough stone, with nothing about it to gratify the eye or to excite the imagination; a large old-fashioned narrow house, with a very steep roof, covered with flags composed of grey sandstone, would perhaps convey the best idea of the place to a modern reader. The windows were few, very small in size, and distributed up and down the building with utter contempt of regularity. Against the main structure had rested, in former times, certain smaller copartments of the mansion-house, containing offices, or subordinate apartments, necessary for the accommodation of the earl's retainers and menials. But these had become ruinous; and the rafters had been taken down for firewood or for other purposes; the walls had given way in many places; and, to complete the devastation, the sand had already drifted amongst the ruins, and filled up what had been once the chambers they contained, to the depth of two or three feet.

Amid this desolation, the inhabitants of Jarlshof had contrived, by constant labour and attention, to keep in order a few roods of land, which had been inclosed as a garden, and which, sheltered by the walls of the house itself from the relentless sea-blast, produced such vegetables as the climate could bring forth, or rather as the sea-gale would permit to grow; for these islands experience even less of the rigour of cold than is encountered on the mainland of Scotland; but, unsheltered by a wall of some sort or other, it is scarce possible to raise even the most ordinary culinary vegetables; and as for shrubs or trees, they are entirely out of the question, such is the force of the sweeping sea-blast.

At a short distance from the mansion, and near to the seaoeach, just where the creek forms a sort of imperfect harbour, in which lay three or four fishing-boats, there were a few most wretched cottages for the inhabitants and tenants of the township of Jarlshof, who held the whole district of the landlord upon such terms as were in those days usually granted to persons of this description, and which, of course, were hard enough. The landlord himself resided upon an estate which he possessed in a more eligible situation in a different part of the island, and seldom visited his possessions at Sumburgh Head. He was an honest, plain Zetland gentleman, somewhat passionate, the necessary result of being surrounded by dependants; and somewhat over-convivial in his habits, the consequence, perhaps, of having too much time at his disposal; but frank-tempered and generous to his people, and kind and hospitable to strangers. He was descended also of an old and noble Norwegian family—a circumstance which rendered him dearer to the lower orders, most of whom are of the same race; while the lairds, or proprietors, are generally of Scottish extraction, who, at that early period, were still considered as strangers and intruders. Magnus Troil, who deduced his descent from the very earl who was supposed to have founded Jarlshof, was peculiarly of this opinion.

The present inhabitants of Jarlshof had experienced, on several occasions, the kindness and good-will of the proprietor of the territory. When Mr. Mertoun—such was the name of the present inhabitant of the old mansion—first arrived in Zetland, some years before the story commences, he had been received at the house of Mr. Troil with that warm and cordial hospitality for which the islands are distinguished. No one asked him whence he came, where he was going, what was his purpose in visiting so remote a corner of the empire, or what was likely to be the term of his stay. He arrived a perfect stranger, yet was instantly overpowered by a succession of invitations; and in each house which he visited he found a home as long as he chose to accept it, and lived as one of the family, unnoticed and unnoticing, until he thought proper to remove to some other dwelling. This apparent indifference to the rank, character, and qualities of their guest did not arise from apathy on the part of his kind hosts, for the islanders had their full share of natural curiosity; but their delicacy deemed it would be an infringement upon the laws of hospitality to ask questions which their guest might have found it difficult or unpleasing to answer; and instead of endeavouring, as is usual in other countries, to wring out of Mr. Mertoun such communications as he might find it agreeable to withhold, the considerate Zetlanders contented themselves with eagerly gathering up such scraps of information as could be collected in the course of conversation.

But the rock in an Arabian desert is not more reluctant to afford water than Mr. Basil Mertoun was niggard in imparting his confidence, even incidentally; and certainly the politeness of the gentry of Thule was never put to a more severe test than when they felt that good-breeding enjoined them to abstain from inquiring into the situation of so mysterious a personage.

All that was actually known of him was easily summed up. Mr. Mertoun had come to Lerwick, then rising into some importance, but not yet acknowledged as the principal town of the island, in a Dutch vessel, accompanied only by his son, a handsome boy of about fourteen years old. His own age might exceed forty. The Dutch skipper introduced him to some of the very good friends with whom he used to barter gin and gingerbread for little Zetland bullocks, smoked geese. and stockings of lambs' wool; and although Meinherr could only say that, "Meinherr Mertoun hab bay his bassage like one gentlemans, and hab given a kreitz-dollar beside to the crew," this introduction served to establish the Dutchman's passenger in a respectable circle of acquaintances, which gradually enlarged, as it appeared that the stranger was a man of considerable acquirements.

This discovery was made almost *per force;* for Mertoun was as unwilling to speak upon general subjects as upon his own affairs. But he was sometimes led into discussions, which showed, as it were in spite of himself, the scholar and the man of the world; and at other times, as if in requital of the hospitality which he experienced, he seemed to compel himself, against his fixed nature, to enter into the society of those around him, especially when it assumed the grave, melancholy, or satirical cast which best suited the temper of his own mind. Upon such occasions, the Zetlarders were universally of opinion that he must have had an excellent education, neglected only in one striking particular, namely, that Mr. Mertoun scarce knew the stem of a ship from the stern; and in the management of a boat a cow could not be more ignorant. It seemed astonishing, such gross ignorance of the most necessary art of life, in the Zetland Isles, at least, should subsist along with his accomplishments in other respects; but so it was.

Unless called forth in the manner we have mentioned, the habits of Basil Mertoun were retired and gloomy. From loud mirth he instantly fled; and even the moderated cheerfulness of a friendly party had the invariable effect of throwing him into deeper dejection than even his usual demeanour indicated.

Women are always particularly desirous of investigating mystery and of alleviating melancholy, especially when these circumstances are united in a handsome man about the prime of life. It is possible, therefore, that amongst the fair-haired and blue-eyed daughters of Thule this mysterious and pensive stranger might have found some one to take upon herself the task of consolation, had he shown any willingness to accept such kindly offices; but, far from doing so, he seemed even to shun the presence of the sex to which in our distresses, whether of mind or body, we generally apply for pity and comfort.

To these peculiarities Mr. Mertoun added another, which was particularly disagreeable to his host and principal patron, Magnus Troil. This magnate of Zetland, descended by the father's side, as we have already said, from an ancient Norwegian family, by the marriage of its representative with a Danish lady, held the devout opinion that a cup of Geneva or Nantz was specific against all cares and afflictions whatever. These were remedies to which Mr. Mertoun never applied: his drink was water, and water alone, and no persuasion or

2

entreaties could induce him to taste any stronger beverage than was afforded by the pure spring. Now this Magnus Troil could not tolerate; it was a defiance to the ancient Northern laws of conviviality, which, for his own part, he had so rigidly observed that, although he was wont to assert that he had never in his life gone to bed drunk (that is, in his own sense of the word), it would have been impossible to prove that he had ever resigned himself to slumber in a state of actual and absolute sobriety. It may be therefore asked, What did this stranger bring into society to compensate the displeasure given by his austere and abstemious habits? He had, in the first place, that manner and self-importance which mark a person of some consequence; and although it was conjectured that he could not be rich, yet it was certainly known by his expenditure that neither was he absolutely poor. He had, besides, some powers of conversation, when, as we have already hinted, he chose to exert them, and his misanthropy or aversion to the business and intercourse of ordinary life was often expressed in an antithetical manner, which passed for wit, when better was not to be had. Above all, Mr. Mertoun's secret seemed impenetrable, and his presence had all the interest of a riddle, which men love to read over and over, because they cannot find out the meaning of it.

Notwithstanding these recommendations, Mertoun differed in so many material points from his host, that, after he had been for some time a guest at his principal residence, Magnus Troil was agreeably surprised when, one evening, after they had sat two hours in absolute silence, drinking brandy and water—that is, Magnus drinking the alcohol and Mertoun the element—the guest asked his host's permission to occupy, as his tenant, this deserted mansion of Jarlshof, at the extremity of the territory called Dunrossness, and situated just beneath Sumburgh Head. "I shall be handsomely rid of him," quoth Magnus to himself, "and his kill-joy visage will never again stop the bottle in its round. His departure will ruin me in lemons, however, for his mere look was quite sufficient to sour a whole ocean of punch."

Yet the kind-hearted Zetlander generously and disinterestedly remonstrated with Mr. Mertoun on the solitude and inconveniences to which he was about to subject himself. "There were scarcely," he said, "even the most necessary articles of furniture in the old house; there was no society within many miles; for provisions, the principal article of food would be sour sillocks, and his only company gulls and gannets."

"My good friend," replied Mertoun, "if you could have named a circumstance which would render the residence more eligible to me than any other, it is that there would be neither human luxury nor human society near the place of my retreat: a shelter from the weather for my own head and for the boy's is all I seek for. So name your rent, Mr. Troil, and let me be your tenant at Jarlshof."

"Rent!" answered the Zetlander; "why, no great rent for an old house which no one has lived in since my mother's time—God rest her!—and as for shelter, the old walls are thick enough, and will bear many a bang yet. But, Heaven love you, Mr. Mertoun, think what you are purposing. For one of us to live at Jarlshof were a wild scheme enough; but you, who are from another country, whether English, Scotch, or Irish, no one can tell——"

"Nor does it greatly matter," said Mertoun, somewhat abruptly.

"Not a herring's scale," answered the laird; "only, that I like you the better for being no Scot, as I trust you are not one. Hither they have come like the clack-geese: every chamberlain has brought over a flock of his own name, and his own hatching, for what I know, and here they roost for ever; catch them returing to their own barren Highlands or Lowlands, when once they have tasted our Zetland beef and seen our bonny voes and lochs. No, sir,"—here Magnus proceeded with great animation, sipping from time to time the half-diluted spirit, which at the same time animated his resentment against the intruders and enabled him to endure the mortifying reflection which it suggested—"no, sir, the ancient days and the genuine manners of these islands are no more; for our ancient possessors—our Patersons, our Feas, our

Schlagbrenners, our Thorbiorns—have given place to Giffords, Scotts, Mouats, men whose names bespeak them or their ancestors strangers to the soil which we the Troils have inhabited long before the days of Turf-Einar, who first taught these isles the mystery of burning peat for fuel, and who has been handed down to a grateful posterity by a name which records the discovery."

This was a subject upon which the potentate of Jarlshof was usually very diffuse, and Mertoun saw him enter upon it with pleasure, because he knew he should not be called upon to contribute any aid to the conversation, and might therefore indulge his own saturnine humour while the Norwegian Zetlander declaimed on the change of times and inhabitants. But just as Magnus had arrived at the melancholy conclusion, "How probable it was that, in another century, scarce a 'merk,' scarce even an 'ure,' of land would be in the possession of the Norse inhabitants, the true udallers [1] of Zetland," he recollected the circumstances of his guest, and stopped suddenly short. "I do not say all this," he added, interrupting himself, "as if I were unwilling that you should settle on my estate, Mr. Mertoun. But for Jarlshof—the place is a wild one. Come from where you will, I warrant you will say, like other travellers, you came from a better climate than ours, for so say you all. And yet you think of a retreat which the very natives run away from. Will you not take your glass?—(This was to be considered as interjectional)—Then here's to you."

"My good sir," answered Mertoun, "I am indifferent to climate: if there is but air enough to fill my lungs, I care not if it be the breath of Arabia or of Lapland."

"Air enough you may have," answered Magnus, "no lack of that; somewhat damp, strangers allege it to be, but we know a corrective for that. Here's to you, Mr. Mertoun. You must learn to *do so,* and to smoke a pipe; and then, as you say, you will find the air of Zetland equal to that of Arabia. But have you seen Jarlshof?"

The stranger intimated that he had not.

[1] See Note 1.

"Then," replied Magnus, "you have no idea of your undertaking. If you think it a comfortable roadstead like this, with the house situated on the side of an inland voe, that brings the herrings up to your door, you are mistaken, my heart. At Jarlshof you will see nought but the wild waves tumbling on the bare rocks, and the Roost of Sumburgh running at the rate of fifteen knots an hour."

"I shall see nothing at least of the current of human passions," replied Mertoun.

"You will hear nothing but the clanging and screaming of scarts, sheerwaters, and sea-gulls from daybreak till sunset."

"I will compound, my friend," replied the stranger, "so that I do not hear the chattering of women's tongues."

"Ah," said the Norman, "that is because you hear just now my little Minna and Brenda singing in the garden with your Mordaunt. Now, I would rather listen to their little voices than the skylark which I once heard in Caithness, or the nightingale that I have read of. What will the girls do for want of their playmate Mordaunt?"

"They will shift for themselves," answered Mertoun: "younger or elder, they will find playmates or dupes. But the question is, Mr. Troil, will you let to me, as your tenant, this old mansion of Jarlshof?"

"Gladly, since you make it your option to live in a spot so desolate."

"And as for the rent?" continued Mertoun.

"The rent!" replied Magnus; "hum—why, you must have the bit of 'plantie cruive,' [1] which they once called a garden, and a right in the 'scathold,' and a sixpenny merk of land, that the tenants may fish for you; eight 'lispunds' of butter and eight shillings sterling yearly is not too much?"

Mr. Mertoun agreed to terms so moderate, and from thenceforward resided chiefly at the solitary mansion which we have described in the beginning of this chapter, conforming not only without complaint, but, as it seemed, with a sullen pleasure, to all the privations which so wild and desolate a situation necessarily imposed on its inhabitant.

[1] See Note 2.

CHAPTER II.

Tis not alone the scene; the man, Anselmo,
The man finds sympathies in these wild wastes
And roughly tumbling seas, which fairer views
And smoother waves deny him.
                                        Ancient Drama.

THE few inhabitants of the township of Jarlshof had at first heard with alarm that a person of rank superior to their own was come to reside in the ruinous tenement which they still called the castle. In those days (for the present times are greatly altered for the better) the presence of a superior, in such a situation, was almost certain to be attended with additional burdens and exactions, for which, under one pretext or another, feudal customs furnished a thousand apologies. By each of these, a part of the tenants' hard-won and precarious profits was diverted for the use of their powerful neighbour and superior, the tacksman, as he was called. But the subtenants speedily found that no oppression of this kind was to be apprehended at the hands of Basil Mertoun. His own means, whether large or small, were at least fully adequate to his expenses, which, so far as regarded his habits of life, were of the most frugal description. The luxuries of a few books, and some philosophical instruments, with which he was supplied from London as occasion offered, seemed to indicate a degree of wealth unusual in those islands; but, on the other hand, the table and the accommodations at Jarlshof did not exceed what was maintained by a Zetland proprietor of the most inferior description.

The tenants of the hamlet troubled themselves very little about the quality of their superior, as soon as they found that their situation was rather to be mended than rendered worse by his presence; and, once relieved from the apprehension of his tyrannising over them, they laid their heads together to make the most of him by various petty tricks of overcharge and extortion, which for a while the stranger submitted to with the most philosophic indifference. An incident, however, occurred which put his character in a new light, and effectually checked all future efforts at extravagant imposition.

A dispute arose in the kitchen of the castle betwixt an old governante, who acted as housekeeper to Mr. Mertoun, and Sweyn Erickson, as good a Zetlander as ever rowed a boat to the "haaf fishing"; which dispute, as is usual in such cases, was maintained with such increasing heat and vociferation as to reach the ears of the master (as he was called), who, secluded in a solitary turret, was deeply employed in examining the contents of a new package of books from London, which, after long expectation, had found its way to Hull, from thence by a whaling vessel to Lerwick, and so to Jarlshof. With more than the usual thrill of indignation which indolent people always feel when roused into action on some unpleasant occasion, Mertoun descended to the scene of contest, and so suddenly, peremptorily, and strictly inquired into the cause of dispute, that the parties, notwithstanding every evasion which they attempted, became unable to disguise from him that their difference respected the several interests to which the honest governante and no less honest fisherman were respectively entitled in an overcharge of about one hundred per cent. on a bargain of rock-cod, purchased by the former from the latter, for the use of the family at Jarlshof.

When this was fairly ascertained and confessed, Mr. Mertoun stood looking upon the culprits with eyes in which the utmost scorn seemed to contend with awakening passion. "Hark you, ye old hag," said he at length to the housekeeper, "avoid my house this instant! and know that I dismiss you, not for being a liar, a thief, and an ungrateful quean—for these are qualities as proper to you as your name of woman—but for daring, in my house, to scold above your breath. And for you, you rascal, who suppose you may cheat a stranger as you would flinch a whale, know that I am well acquainted with the rights which, by delegation from your master, Magnus Troil, I can exercise over you, if I will. Provoke me to a certain pitch, and you shall learn, to your cost, I can break your rest as easily as you can interrupt my leisure. I know the meaning of 'scat,' and 'wattle,' and 'hawkhen,' and 'hagalef,' and every other exaction by which your lords, in ancient and modern days, have wrung your withers; nor is there one of you that shall not rue the day that you could not be content with robbing me of my money, but must also break in on my leisure with your atrocious Northern clamour, that rivals in discord the screaming of a flight of Arctic gulls."

Nothing better occurred to Sweyn, in answer to this objurgation, than the preferring a humble request that his honour would be pleased to keep the cod-fish without payment, and say no more about the matter; but by this time Mr. Mertoun had worked up his passions into an ungovernable rage, and with one hand he threw the money at the fisherman's head, while with the other he pelted him out of the apartment with his own fish, which he finally flung out of doors after him.

There was so much of appalling and tyrannic fury in the stranger's manner on this occasion, that Sweyn neither stopped to collect the money nor take back his commodity, but fled at a precipitate rate to the small hamlet, to tell his comrades that, if they provoked Master Mertoun any farther, he would turn an absolute Pate Stewart [1] on their hand, and head and hang without either judgment or mercy.

Hither also came the discarded housekeeper, to consult with her neighbours and kindred (for she too was a native of the village) what she should do to regain the desirable situation from which she had been so suddenly expelled. The old Ranzellaar of the village, who had the voice most potential in the deliberations of the township, after hearing what had happened, pronounced that Sweyn Erickson had gone too far in raising the market upon Mr. Mertoun; and that, whatever pretext the tacksman might assume for thus giving way to his anger, the real grievance must have been the charging the rock cod-fish at a penny instead of a half-penny a pound; he therefore exhorted all the community never to raise their exactions in future beyond the proportion of threepence upon the shil-

---

[1] Meaning, probably, Patrick Stewart, Earl of Orkney, executed for tyranny and oppression, practised on the inhabitants of those remote islands, in the beginning of the 17th century.—His father, Lord Robert Stuart, was a natural son of James V. (*Laing*).

ling, at which rate their master at the castle could not reasonably be expected to grumble, since, as he was disposed to do them no harm, it was reasonable to think that, in a moderate way, he had no objection to do them good. "And three upon twelve," said the experienced Ranzellaar, "is a decent and moderate profit, and will bring with it God's blessing and St. Ronald's."

Proceeding upon the tariff thus judiciously recommended to them, the inhabitants of Jarlshof cheated Mertoun in future only to the moderate extent of twenty-five per cent—a rate to which all nabobs, army-contractors, speculators in the funds, and others, whom recent and rapid success has enabled to settle in the country upon a great scale, ought to submit as very reasonable treatment at the hand of their rustic neighbours. Mertoun at least seemed of that opinion, for he gave himself no farther trouble upon the subject of his household expenses.

The conscript fathers of Jarlshof, having settled their own matters, took next under their consideration the case of Swertha, the banished matron who had been expelled from the castle, whom, as an experienced and useful ally, they were highly desirous to restore to her office of housekeeper, should that be found possible. But as their wisdom here failed them, Swertha, in despair, had recourse to the good offices of Mordaunt Mertoun, with whom she had acquired some favour by her knowledge in old Norwegian ballads, and dismal tales concerning the Trows, or Drows (the dwarfs of the Scalds), with whom superstitious eld had peopled many a lonely cavern and brown dale in Dunrossness, as in every other district of Zetland. "Swertha," said the youth, "I can do but little for you, but you may do something for yourself. My father's passion resembles the fury of those ancient champions—those Berserkars,[1] you sing songs about."

"Ay—ay, fish of my heart," replied the old woman, with a pathetic whine; "the Berserkars were champions who lived before the blessed days of St. Olave, and who used to run like madmen on swords, and spears, and harpoons, and muskets,

See Note 3.

and snap them all into pieces, as a finner would go through a herring-net, and then, when the fury went off, they were as weak and unstable as water."

"That's the very thing, Swertha," said Mordaunt. "Now, my father never likes to think of his passion after it is over, and is so much of a Berserkar that, let him be desperate as he will to-day, he will not care about it to-morrow. Therefore, he has not filled up your place in the household at the castle, and not a mouthful of warm food has been dressed there since you went away, and not a morsel of bread baked, but we have lived just upon whatever cold thing came to hand. Now, Swertha, I will be your warrant that, if you go boldly up to the castle, and enter upon the discharge of your duties as usual, you will never hear a single word from him."

Swertha hesitated at first to obey this bold counsel. She said: "To her thinking, Mr. Mertoun, when he was angry, looked more like a fiend than any Berserkar of them all: that the fire flashed from his eyes, and the foam flew from his lips; and that it would be a plain tempting of Providence to put herself again in such a venture."

But, on the encouragement which she received from the son, she determined at length once more to face the parent; and, dressing herself in her ordinary household attire, for so Mordaunt particularly recommended, she slipped into the castle, and presently resuming the various and numerous occupations which devolved on her, seemed as deeply engaged in household cares as if she had never been out of office.

The first day of her return to her duty, Swertha made no appearance in presence of her master, but trusted that after his three days' diet on cold meat, a hot dish, dressed with the best of her simple skill, might introduce her favourably to his recollection. When Mordaunt had reported that his father had taken no notice of this change of diet, and when she herself observed that, in passing and repassing him occasionally, her appearance produced no effect upon her singular master, she began to imagine that the whole affair had escaped Mr. Mertoun's memory, and was active in her duty as usual. Neither was she convinced of the contrary until one day when, happening somewhat to elevate her tone in a dispute with the other maid-servant, her master, who at that time passed the place of contest, eyed her with a strong glance, and pronounced the single word, "Remember!" in a tone which taught Swertha the government of her tongue for many weeks after.

If Mertoun was whimsical in his mode of governing his household, he seemed no less so in his plan of educating his son. He showed the youth but few symptoms of parental affection; yet, in his ordinary state of mind, the improvement of Mordaunt's education seemed to be the utmost object of his life. He had both books and information sufficient to discharge the task of tutor in the ordinary branches of knowledge; and in this capacity was regular, calm, and strict, not to say severe, in exacting from his pupil the attention necessary for his profiting. But in the perusal of history, to which their attention was frequently turned, as, well as in the study of classic authors, there often occurred facts or sentiments which produced an instant effect upon Mertoun's mind, and brought on him suddenly what Swertha, Sweyn, and even Mordaunt, came to distinguish by the name of his dark hour. He was aware, in the usual case, of its approach, and retreated to an inner apartment, into which he never permitted even Mordaunt to enter. Here he would abide in seclusion for days, and even weeks, only coming out at uncertain times, to take such food as they had taken care to leave within his reach, which he used in wonderfully small quantities. At other times, and especially during the winter solstice, when almost every person spends the gloomy time within doors in feasting and merriment, this unhappy man would wrap himself in a dark-coloured sea-cloak, and wander out along the stormy beach, or upon the desolate heath, indulging his own gloomy and wayward reveries under the inclement sky, the rather that he was then most sure to wander unencountered and unobserved.

As Mordaunt grew older, he learned to note the particular signs which preceded these fits of gloomy despondency, and to direct such precautions as might ensure his unfortunate parent from ill-timed interruption (which had always the effect of driving him to fury), while, at the same time, full provision was made for his subsistence. Mordaunt perceived that at such periods the melancholy fit of his father was greatly prolonged if he chanced to present himself to his eyes while the dark hour was upon him. Out of respect, therefore, to his parent, as well as to indulge the love of active exercise and of amusement natural to his period of life, Mordaunt used often to absent himself altogether from the mansion of Jarlshof, and even from the district, secure that his father, if the dark hour passed away in his absence, would be little inclined to inquire how his son had disposed of his leisure, so that he was sure he had not watched his own weak moments, that being the subject on which he entertained the utmost jealousy.

At such times, therefore, all the sources of amusement which the country afforded were open to the younger Mertoun, who, in these intervals of his education, had an opportunity to give full scope to the energies of a bold, active, and daring character. He was often engaged with the youth of the hamlet in those desperate sports to which the " dreadful trade of the samphire-gatherer " is like a walk upon level ground— often joined those midnight excursions upon the face of the giddy cliffs, to secure the eggs or the young of the sea-fowl; and in these daring adventures displayed an address, presence of mind, and activity which, in one so young and not a native of the country, astonished the oldest fowlers. [1]

At other times, Mordaunt accompanied Sweyn and other fishermen in their long and perilous expeditions to the distant and deep sea, learning under their direction the management of the boat, in which they equal, or exceed, perhaps, any natives of the British empire. This exercise had charms for Mordaunt independently of the fishing alone.

At this time, the old Norwegian sagas were much remembered, and often rehearsed, by the fishermen, who still preserved among themselves the ancient Norse tongue, which was the speech of their forefathers. In the dark romance of those

---

[1] See Accidents to Fowlers. Note 4.

Scandinavian tales lay much that was captivating to a youthful ear; and the classic fables of antiquity were rivalled at least, if not excelled, in Mordaunt's opinion by the strange legends of Berserkars, of sea-kings, of dwarfs, giants, and sorcerers, which he heard from the native Zetlanders. Often the scenes around him were assigned as the localities of the wild poems, which, half-recited, half-chanted by voices as hoarse, if not so loud, as the waves over which they floated, pointed out the very bay on which they sailed as the scene of a bloody sea-fight; the scarce-seen heap of stones that bristled over the projecting cape as the dun, or castle, of some potent earl or noted pirate; the distant and solitary grey stone on the lonely moor as marking the grave of a hero; the wild cavern, up which the sea rolled in heavy, broad, and unbroken billows, as the dwelling of some noted sorceress.[1]

The ocean also had its mysteries, the effect of which was aided by the dim twilight, through which it was imperfectly seen for more than half the year. Its bottomless depths and secret caves contained, according to the account of Sweyn and others skilled in legendary lore, such wonders as modern navigators reject with disdain. In the quiet moonlight bay, where the waves came rippling to the shore, upon a bed of smooth sand intermingled with shells, the mermaid was still seen to glide along the waters, and mingling her voice with the sighing breeze, was often heard to sing of subterranean wonders, or to chant prophecies of future events. The Kraken, that hugest of living things, was still supposed to cumber the recesses of the Northern Ocean; and often, when some fog-bank covered the sea at a distance, the eye of the experienced boatman saw the horns of the monstrous leviathan welking and waving amidst the wreaths of mist, and bore away with all press of oar and sail, lest the sudden suction, occasioned by the sinking of the monstrous mass to the bottom, should drag within the grasp of its multifarious feelers his own frail skiff. The sea-snake was also known, which, arising out of the depths of ocean, stretches to the skies his enormous neck, covered with a mane like that of a war-horse, and with its

[1] See Norse Fragments. Note 5.

broad, glittering eyes raised mast-head high, looks out, as it seems, for plunder or for victims.

Many prodigious stories of these marine monsters, and of many others less known, were then universally received among the Zetlanders, whose descendants have not as yet by any means abandoned faith in them.[1]

Such legends are, indeed, everywhere current amongst the vulgar; but the imagination is far more powerfully affected by them on the deep and dangerous seas of the North, amidst precipices and headlands, many hundred feet in height; amid perilous straits, and currents, and eddies; long sunken reefs of rock, over which the vivid ocean foams and boils; dark caverns, to whose extremities neither man nor skiff has ever ventured; lonely, and often uninhabited, isles; and occasion-ally the ruins of ancient Northern fastnesses, dimly seen by the feeble light of the Arctic winter.   To Mordaunt, who had much of romance in his disposition, these superstitions formed a pleasing and interesting exercise of the imagination, while, half-doubting, half-inclined to believe, he listened to the tales chanted concerning these wonders of nature and creatures of credulous belief, told in the rude but energetic language of the ancient Scalds.

But there wanted not softer and lighter amusement, that might seem better suited to Mordaunt's age than the wild tales and rude exercises which we have already mentioned. The season of winter, when, from the shortness of the day-light, labour becomes impossible, is in Zetland the time of revel, feasting, and merriment.   Whatever the fisherman has been able to acquire during summer was expended, and often wasted, in maintaining the mirth and hospitality of his hearth during this period; while the landholders and gentlemen of the island gave double loose to their convivial and hospitable dispositions, thronged their houses with guests, and drove away the rigour of the season with jest, glee, and song, the dance, and the wine-cup.

Amid the revels of this merry, though rigorous, season no youth added more spirit to the dance or glee to the revel than

[1] See Sea Monsters.   Note 6.

the young stranger, Mordaunt Mertoun. When his father's state of mind permitted, or indeed required, his absence, he wandered from house to house, a welcome guest wherever he came, and lent his willing voice to the song and his foot to the dance. A boat, or, if the weather, as was often the case, permitted not that convenience, one of the numerous ponies, which, straying in hordes about the extensive moors, may be said to be at any man's command who can catch them, conveyed him from the mansion of one hospitable Zetlander to that of another. None excelled him in performing the warlike sword-dance, a species of amusement which had been derived from the habits of the ancient Norsemen. He could play upon the "gue," and upon the common violin, the melancholy and pathetic tunes peculiar to the country; and with great spirit and execution could relieve their monotony with the livelier airs of the North of Scotland. When a party set forth as maskers, or, as they are called in Scotland, "guizards," to visit some neighbouring laird or rich udaller, it augured well of the expedition if Mordaunt Mertoun could be prevailed upon to undertake the office of "skudler," or leader of the band. Upon these occasions, full of fun and frolic, he led his retinue from house to house, bringing mirth where he went, and leaving regret when he departed. Mordaunt became thus generally known, and beloved as generally, through most of the houses composing the patriarchial community of the Main Isle; but his visits were most frequently and most willingly paid at the mansion of his father's landlord and protector, Magnus Troil.

It was not entirely the hearty and sincere welcome of the worthy old magnate, nor the sense that he was in effect his father's patron, which occasioned these frequent visits. The hand of welcome was indeed received as eagerly as it was sincerely given, while the ancient Udaller, raising himself in his huge chair, whereof the inside was lined with well-dressed sealskins, and the outside composed of massive oak, carved by the rude graving-tool of some Hamburgh carpenter, shouted forth his welcome in a tone which might, in ancient times, have hailed the return of Ioul, the highest festival of the

Goths. There was metal yet more attractive, and younger hearts, whose welcome, if less loud, was as sincere as that of the jolly Udaller. But this is matter which ought not to be discussed at the conclusion of a chapter.

CHAPTER III.

Oh, Bessy Bell and Mary Gray,
   They were twa bonnie lasses;
They biggit a house on yon burn-brae,
   And theekit it ower wi' rashes.

Fair Bessy Bell I looed yestreen,
   And thought I ne'er could alter;
But Mary Gray's twa pawky een
   Have garr'd my fancy falter.
          Scots Song.

WE have already mentioned Minna and Brenda, the daughters of Magnus Troil. Their mother had been dead for many years, and they were now two beautiful girls, the eldest only eighteen, which might be a year or two younger than Mordaunt Mertoun, the second about seventeen. They were the joy of their father's heart and the light of his old eyes; and although indulged to a degree which might have endangered his comfort and their own, they repaid his affection with a love into which even blind indulgence had not introduced slight regard or feminine caprice. The difference of their tempers and of their complexions was singularly striking, although combined, as is usual, with a certain degree of family resemblance.

The mother of these maidens had been a Scottish lady from the Highlands of Sutherland, the orphan of a noble chief, who, driven from his own country during the feuds of the 17th century, had found shelter in those peaceful islands, which, amidst poverty and seclusion, were thus far happy, that they remained unvexed by discord and unstained by civil broil. The father (his name was St. Clair) pined for his native glen, his feudal tower, his clansmen, and his fallen authority, and died not long after his arrival in Zetland. The beauty of his orphan daughter, despite her Scottish lineage, melted the stout heart of Magnus Troil. He sued and was listened to, and she became his bride; but dying in the fifth year of their union, left him to mourn his brief period of domestic happiness.

From her mother, Minna inherited the stately form and dark eyes, the raven locks and finely-pencilled brows, which showed she was, on one side at least, a stranger to the blood of Thule. Her cheek—

O call it fair, not pale !

was so slightly and delicately tinged with the rose that many thought the lily had an undue proportion in her complexion. But in that predominance of the paler flower there was nothing sickly or languid: it was the true, natural colour of health, and corresponded in a peculiar degree with features which seemed calculated to express a contemplative and high-minded character. When Minna Troil heard a tale of woe or of injustice, it was then her blood rushed to her cheeks, and showed plainly how warm it beat, notwithstanding the generally serious, composed, and retiring disposition which her countenance and demeanour seemed to exhibit. If strangers sometimes conceived that these fine features were clouded by melancholy, for which her age and situation could scarce have given occasion, they were soon satisfied, upon further acquaintance, that the placid, mild quietude of her disposition, and the mental energy of a character which was but little interested in ordinary and trivial occurrences, were the real cause of her gravity; and most men, when they knew that her melancholy had no ground in real sorrow, and was only the aspiration of a soul bent on more important objects than those by which she was surrounded, might have wished her whatever could add to her happiness, but could scarce have desired that, graceful as she was in her natural and unaffected seriousness, she should change that deportment for one more gay. In short, notwithstanding our wish to have avoided that hackneyed simile of an angel, we cannot avoid saying there was something in the serious beauty of her aspect, in 'he meas-

3

ured yet graceful ease of her motions, in the music of her voice, and the serene purity of her eye, that seemed as if Minna Troil belonged naturally to some higher and better sphere, and was only the chance visitant of a world that was not worthy of her.

The scarcely less beautiful, equally lovely, and equally innocent Brenda was of a complexion as different from her sister as they differed in character, taste, and expression. Her profuse locks were of that paly brown which receives from the passing sunbeam a tinge of gold, but darkens again when the ray has passed from it. Her eye, her mouth, the beautiful row of teeth, which in her innocent vivacity were frequently disclosed; the fresh, yet not too bright, glow of a healthy complexion, tinging a skin like the drifted snow, spoke her genuine Scandinavian descent. A fairy form, less tall than that of Minna, but still more finely moulded into symmetry; a careless, and almost childish, lightness of step; an eye that seemed to look on every object with pleasure, from a natural and serene cheerfulness of disposition, attracted even more general admiration than the charms of her sister, though perhaps that which Minna did excite might be of a more intense as well as more reverential character.

The dispositions of these lovely sisters were not less different than their complexions. In the kindly affections, neither could be said to excel the other, so much were they attached to their father and to each other. But the cheerfulness of Brenda mixed itself with the every-day business of life, and seemed inexhaustible in its profusion. The less buoyant spirit of her sister appeared to bring to society a contented wish to be interested and pleased with what was going forward, but was rather placidly carried along with the stream of mirth and pleasure than disposed to aid its progress by any efforts of her own. She endured mirth rather than enjoyed it; and the pleasures in which she most delighted were those of a graver and more solitary cast. The knowledge which is derived from books was beyond her reach. Zetland afforded few opportunities in those days of studying the lessons bequeathed

By dead men to their kind ;

and Magnus Troil, such as we have described him, was not a
person within whose mansion the means of such knowledge
were to be acquired. But the book of nature was before
Minna, that noblest of volumes, where we are ever called to
wonder and to admire, even when we cannot understand.
The plants of those wild regions, the shells on the shores, and
the long list of feathered clans which haunt their cliffs and
eyries, were as well known to Minna Troil as to the most
experienced fowler. Her powers of observation were wonderful, and little interrupted by other tones of feeling. The information which she acquired by habits of patient attention
was indelibly riveted in a naturally powerful memory. She
had also a high feeling for the solitary and melancholy grandeur of the scenes in which she was placed. The ocean, in
all its varied forms of sublimity and terror; the tremendous
cliffs, that resound to the ceaseless roar of the billows and
the clang of the sea-fowl, had for Minna a charm in almost
every state in which the changing seasons exhibited them.
With the enthusiastic feelings proper to the romantic race
from which her mother descended, the love of natural objects
was to her a passion capable not only of occupying, but at
times of agitating, her mind. Scenes upon which her sister
looked with a sense of transient awe or emotion, which vanished on her return from witnessing them, continued long to
fill Minna's imagination, not only in solitude and in the silence of the night, but in the hours of society. So that sometimes when she sat like a beautiful statue, a present member
of the domestic circle, her thoughts were far absent, wandering on the wild sea-shore, and among the yet wilder mountains of her native isles. And yet, when recalled to conversation, and mingling in it with interest, there were few to
whom her friends were more indebted for enhancing its enjoy-
ments; and although something in her manners claimed deference (notwithstanding her early youth) as well as affection,
even her gay, lovely, and amiable sister was not more generally beloved than the more retired and pensive Minna.

Indeed, the two lovely sisters were not only the delight of
their friends, but the pride of those islands, where the inhabi-

tants of a certain rank were blended, by the remoteness of
their situation and the general hospitality of their habits,
into one friendly community. A wandering poet and parcel-
musician, who, after going through various fortunes, had returned to end his days as he could in his native islands, had
celebrated the daughters of Magnus in a poem, which he entitled "Night and Day"; and in his description of Minna
might almost be thought to have anticipated, though only in
a rude outline, the exquisite lines of Lord Byron,—

> She walks in beauty, like the night
> Of cloudless climes and starry skies;
> And all that's best of dark and bright
> Meet in her aspect and her eyes:
> Thus mellow'd to that tender light
> Which heaven to gaudy day denies.

Their father loved the maidens both so well that it might
be difficult to say which he loved best; saving that, perchance,
he liked his graver damsel better in the walk without doors,
and his merry maiden better by the fireside; that he more
desired the society of Minna when he was sad, and that of
Brenda when he was mirthful; and, what was nearly the same
thing, preferred Minna before noon, and Brenda after the glass
had circulated in the evening.

But it was still more extraordinary that the affections of
Mordaunt Mertoun seemed to hover with the same impartiality as those of their father betwixt the two lovely sisters.
From his boyhood, as we have noticed, he had been a frequent inmate of the residence of Magnus at Burgh-Westra,
although it lay nearly twenty miles distant from Jarlshof.
The impassable character of the country betwixt these places,
extending over hills covered with loose and quaking bog, and
frequently intersected by the creeks or arms of the sea, which
indent the island on either side, as well as by fresh-water
streams and lakes, rendered the journey difficult, and even
dangerous, in the dark season; yet, as soon as the state of his
father's mind warned him to absent himself, Mordaunt, at
every risk and under every difficulty, was pretty sure to be
found the next day at Burgh-Westra, having achieved his

journey in less time than would have been employed perhaps by the most active native.

He was, of course, set down as a wooer of one of the daughters of Magnus by the public of Zetland; and when the old Udaller's great partiality to the youth was considered, nobody doubted that he might aspire to the hand of either of those distinguished beauties, with as large a share of islets, rocky moorland, and shore fishings as might be the fitting portion of a favoured child, and with the presumptive prospect of possessing half the domains of the ancient house of Troil, when their present owner should be no more. This seemed all a reasonable speculation, and, in theory at least, better constructed than many that are current through the world as unquestionable facts. But, alas! all that sharpness of observation which could be applied to the conduct of the parties failed to determine the main point, to which of the young persons, namely, the attentions of Mordaunt were peculiarly devoted. He seemed, in general, to treat them as an affectionate and attached brother might have treated two sisters, so equally dear to him that a breath would have turned the scale of affection. Or if at any time, which often happened, the one maiden appeared the more especial object of his attention, it seemed only to be because circumstances called her peculiar talents and disposition into more particular and immediate exercise.

Both the sisters were accomplished in the simple music of the North, and Mordaunt, who was their assistant, and sometimes their preceptor, when they were practising this delightful art, might be now seen assisting Minna in the acquisition of those wild, solemn, and simple airs to which Scalds and harpers sung of old the deeds of heroes, and presently found equally active in teaching Brenda the more lively and complicated music which their father's affection caused to be brought from the English or Scottish capital for the use of his daughters. And while conversing with them, Mordaunt, who mingled a strain of deep and ardent enthusiasm with the gay and ungovernable spirits of youth, was equally ready to enter into the wild and poetical visions of Minna or into the lively and often humorous chat of her gayer sister. In short, so little did he seem to attach himself to either damsel exclusively, that he was sometimes heard to say that Minna never looked so lovely as when her light-hearted sister had induced her, for the time, to forget her habitual gravity; or Brenda so interesting as when she sat listening, a subdued and affected partaker of the deep pathos of her sister Minna.

The public of the Mainland were, therefore, to use the hunter's phrase, at fault in their farther conclusions, and could but determine, after long vacillating betwixt the maidens, that the young man was positively to marry one of them, but which of the two could only be determined when his approaching manhood, or the interference of stout old Magnus, the father, should teach Master Mordaunt Mertoun to know his own mind. "It was a pretty thing, indeed," they usually concluded, "that he, no native born, and possessed of no visible means of subsistence that is known to any one, should presume to hesitate, or affect to have the power of selection and choice, betwixt the two most distinguished beauties of Zetland. If they were Magnus Troil, they would soon be at the bottom of the matter," and so forth; all which remarks were only whispered, for the hasty disposition of the Udaller had too much of the old Norse fire about it to render it safe for any one to become an unauthorised intermeddler with his family affairs. And thus stood the relation of Mordaunt Mertoun to the family of Mr. Troil of Burgh-Westra when the following incidents took place.

CHAPTER IV.

This is no pilgrim's morning : yon grey mist
Lies upon hill, and dale, and field, and forest,
Like the dun wimple of a new-made widow ;
And, by my faith, althou·h my heart be soft,
I'd rather hear tha' widow weep and sigh,
And tell the virtues of the dear departed,
Than, when the tempest sends his voice abroad,
Be subject to its fury.

The Double Nuptials.

THE spring was far advanced when, after a week spent in sport and festivity at Burgh-Westra, Mordaunt Mertoun bade adieu to the family, pleading the necessity of his return to Jarlshof. The proposal was combated by the maidens, and more decidedly by Magnus himself : he saw no occasion whatever for Mordaunt returning to Jarlshof. If his father desired to see him, which, by the way, Magnus did not believe, Mr. Mertoun had only to throw himself into the stern of Sweyn's boat, or betake himself to a pony, if he liked a land journey better, and he would see not only his son, but twenty folk besides, who would be most happy to find that he had not lost the use of his tongue entirely during his long solitude, "Although I must own," added the worthy Udaller, "that, when he lived among us, nobody ever made less use of it."

Mordaunt acquiesced both in what respected his father's taciturnity and his dislike to general society; but suggested, at the same time, that the first circumstance rendered his own immediate return more necessary, as he was the usual channel of communication betwixt his father and others; and that the second corroborated the same necessity, since Mr. Mertoun's having no other society whatever seemed a weighty reason why his son's should be restored to him without loss of time. As to his father's coming to Burgh-Westra, "They might as well," he said, "expect to see Sumburgh Cape come thither."

"And that would be a cumbrous guest," said Magnus. "But you will stop for our dinner to-day? There are the families of Muness, Quendale, Thorslivoe, and I know not who else, are expected; and, besides the thirty that were in the house this blessed night, we shall have as many more as chamber and bower, and barn and boat-house, can furnish with beds or with barley-straw; and you will leave all this behind you!"

"And the blythe dance at night," added Brenda, in a tone betwixt reproach and vexation; "and the young men from the Isle of Paba that are to dance the sword-dance, whom shall we find to match them, for the honour of the Main?"

"There is many a merry dancer on the Mainland, Brenda," replied Mordaunt, "even if I should never rise on tiptoe again. And where good dancers are found, Brenda Troil will always find the best partner. I must trip it to-night through the wastes of Dunrossness."

"Do not say so, Mordaunt," said Minna, who, during this conversation, had been looking from the window something anxiously; "go not, to-day at least, through the wastes of Dunrossness."

"And why not to-day, Minna," said Mordaunt, laughing, "any more than to-morrow?"

"Oh, the morning mist lies heavy upon yonder chain of isles, nor has it permitted us since daybreak even a single glimpse of Fitful Head, the lofty cape that concludes yon splendid range of mountains. The fowl are winging their way to the shore, and the shelldrake seems, through the mist, as large as the scart.[1] See, the very sheerwaters and bonxies are making to the cliffs for shelter."

"And they will ride out a gale against a king's frigate," said her father: "there is foul weather when they cut and run."

"Stay, then, with us," said Minna to her friend; "the storm will be dreadful, yet it will be grand to see it from Burgh-Westra, if we have no friend exposed to its fury. See, the air is close and sultry, though the season is yet so early, and the day so calm that not a windlestraw moves on the heath. Stay with us, Mordaunt; the storm which these signs announce will be a dreadful one."

[1] See Note 7.

"I must be gone the sooner," was the conclusion of Mordaunt, who could not deny the signs, which had not escaped his own quick observation. "If the storm be too fierce, I will abide for the night at Stourburgh."

"What!" said Magnus; "will you leave us for the new chamberlain's new Scotch tacksman, who is to teach all us Zetland savages new ways? Take your own gate, my lad, if that is the song you sing."

"Nay," said Mordaunt; "I had only some curiosity to see the new implements he has brought."

"Ay—ay, ferlies make fools fain. I would like to know if his new plough will bear against a Zetland rock?" answered Magnus.

"I must not pass Stourburgh on the journey," said the youth, deferring to his patron's prejudice against innovation, "if this boding weather bring on tempest; but if it only break in rain, as is most probable, I am not likely to be melted in the wetting."

"It will not soften into rain alone," said Minna; "see how much heavier the clouds fall every moment, and see these weather-gaws that streak the lead-coloured mass with partial gleams of faded red and purple."

"I see them all," said Mordaunt; "but they only tell me I have no time to tarry here. Adieu, Minna; I will send you the eagle's feathers, if an eagle can be found on Fair Isle or Foulah. And fare thee well, my pretty Brenda, and keep a thought for me, should the Paba men dance ever so well."

"Take care of yourself, since go you will," said both sisters together.

Old Magnus scolded them formally for supposing there was any danger to an active young fellow from a spring gale, whether by sea or land; yet ended by giving his own caution also to Mordaunt, advising him seriously to delay his journey, or at least to stop at Stourburgh. "For," said he, "second thoughts are best; and as this Scottishman's howf lies right under your lee, why, take any port in a storm. But do not be assured to find the door on latch, let the storm blow ever so hard; there are such matters as bolts and bars in Scotland, though, thanks to St. Ronald, they are unknown here, save that great lock on the old Castle of Scalloway, that all men run to see; maybe they make part of this man's improvements. But go, Mordaunt, since go you will. You should drink a stirrup-cup now, were you three years older; but boys should never drink, excepting after dinner. I will drink it for you, that good customs may not be broken, or bad luck come of it. Here is your bonally, my lad." And so saying, he quaffed a rummer glass of brandy with as much impunity as if it had been spring-water.

Thus regretted and cautioned on all hands, Mordaunt took leave of the hospitable household, and looking back at the comforts with which it was surrounded, and the dense smoke that rolled upwards from its chimneys, he first recollected the guestless and solitary desolation of Jarlshof, then compared with the sullen and moody melancholy of his father's temper the warm kindness of those whom he was leaving, and could not refrain from a sigh at the thoughts which forced themselves on his imagination.

The signs of the tempest did not dishonour the predictions of Minna. Mordaunt had not advanced three hours on his journey before the wind, which had been so deadly still in the morning, began at first to wail and sigh, as if bemoaning beforehand the evils which it might perpetrate in its fury, like a madman in the gloomy state of dejection which precedes his fit of violence; then gradually increasing, the gale howled, raged, and roared with the full fury of a northern storm. It was accompanied by showers of rain mixed with hail, that dashed with the most unrelenting rage against the hills and rocks with which the traveller was surrounded, distracting his attention, in spite of his utmost exertions, and rendering it very difficult for him to keep the direction of his journey in a country where there is neither road nor even the slightest track to direct the steps of the wanderer, and where he is often interrupted by brooks as well as large pools of water, lakes, and lagoons. All these inland waters were now lashed into sheets of tumbling foam, much of which, carried off by the fury of the whirlwind, was mingled with the gale, and transported far from the waves of which it had lately made a part; while the salt relish of the drift which was pelted against his face showed Mordaunt that the spray of the more distant ocean, disturbed to frenzy by the storm, was mingled with that of the inland lakes and streams.

Amidst this hideous combustion of the elements, Mordaunt Mertoun struggled forward as one to whom such elemental war was familiar, and who regarded the exertions which it required to withstand its fury but as a mark of resolution and manhood. He felt even, as happens usually to those who endure great hardships, that the exertion necessary to subdue them is in itself a kind of elevating triumph. To see and distinguish his path when the cattle were driven from the hill, and the very fowls from the firmament, was but the stronger proof of his own superiority. "They shall not hear of me at Burgh-Westra," said he to himself, "as they heard of old doited Ringan Ewenson's boat, that foundered betwixt roadstead and key. I am more of a cragsman than to mind fire or water, wave by sea, or quagmire by land." Thus he struggled on, buffeting with the storm, supplying the want of the usual signs by which travellers directed their progress (for rock, mountain, and headland were shrouded in mist and darkness) by the instinctive sagacity with which long acquaintance with these wilds had taught him to mark every minute object which could serve in such circumstances to regulate his course. Thus, we repeat, he struggled onward, occasionally standing still, or even lying down, when the gust was most impetuous; making way against it when it was somewhat lulled, by a rapid and bold advance even in its very current; or, when this was impossible, by a movement resembling that of a vessel working to windward by short tacks, but never yielding one inch of the way which he had fought so hard to gain.

Yet, notwithstanding Mordaunt's experience and resolution, his situation was sufficiently uncomfortable, and even precarious; not because his sailor's jacket and trowsers, the common dress of young men through these isles when on a journey, were thoroughly wet, for that might have taken place

within the same brief time in any ordinary day in this watery climate; but the real danger was that, notwithstanding
his utmost exertions, he made very slow way through brooks
that were sending their waters all abroad, through morass-
es drowned in double deluges of moisture, which rendered
all the ordinary passes more than usually dangerous, and
repeatedly obliged the traveller to perform a considerable
circuit, which in the usual case was unnecessary.   Thus
repeatedly baffled, notwithstanding his youth and strength,
Mordaunt, after maintaining a dogged conflict with wind,
rain, and the fatigue of a prolonged journey, was truly happy
when, not without having been more than once mistaken in
his road, he at length found himself within sight of the house
of Stourburgh, or Harfra; for the names were indifferently
given to the residence of Mr. Triptolemus Yellowley, who
was the chosen missionary of the chamberlain of Orkney and
Zetland, a speculative person, who designed, through the medium of Triptolemus, to introduce into the Ultima Thule of
the Romans a spirit of improvement which at that early period was scarce known to exist in Scotland itself.

  At length, and with much difficulty, Mordaunt reached the
house of this worthy agriculturist, the only refuge from the
relentless storm which he could hope to meet with for several
miles; and going straight to the door, with the most undoubting confidence of instant admission, he was not a little surprised to find it not merely latched, which the weather might
excuse, but even bolted, a thing which, as Magnus Troil has
already intimated, was almost unknown in the archipelago.
To knock, to call, and finally to batter the door with staff
and stones, were the natural resources of the youth, who was
rendered alike impatient by the pelting of the storm and by
encountering such most unexpected and unusual obstacles to
instant admission.   As he was suffered, however, for many
minutes to exhaust his impatience in noise and clamour, without receiving any reply, we will employ them in informing
the reader who Triptolemus Yellowley was, and how he came
by a name so singular.

  Old Jasper Yellowley, the father of Triptolemus, though

born at the foot of Roseberry Topping, had been "come over" by a certain noble Scottish earl, who, proving too far north for canny Yorkshire, had persuaded him to accept of a farm in the Mearns, where, it is unnecessary to add, he found matters very different from what he had expected. It was in vain that the stout farmer set manfully to work to counterbalance, by superior skill, the inconveniences arising from a cold soil and a weeping climate. These might have been probably overcome; but his neighbourhood to the Grampians exposed him eternally to that species of visitation from the plaided gentry who dwelt within their skirts which made young Norval a warrior and a hero, but only converted Jasper Yellowley into a poor man. This was, indeed, balanced in some sort by the impression which his ruddy cheek and robust form had the fortune to make upon Miss Barbara Clinkscale, daughter to the umquwhile, and sister to the then existing, Clinkscale of that ilk.

This was thought a horrid and unnatural union in the neighbourhood, considering that the house of Clinkscale had at least as great a share of Scottish pride as of Scottish parsimony, and was amply endowed with both. But Miss Baby had her handsome fortune of two thousand merks at her own disposal, was a woman of spirit, who had been *major* and *sui juris* (as the writer who drew the contract assured her) for full twenty years; so she set consequences and commentaries alike at defiance, and wedded the hearty Yorkshire yeoman. Her brother and her more wealthy kinsmen drew off in disgust, and almost disowned their degraded relative. But the house of Clinkscale was allied, like every other family in Scotland at the time, to a set of relations who were not so nice—tenth and sixteenth cousins, who not only acknowledged their kinswoman Baby after her marriage with Yellowley, but even condescended to eat beans and bacon [1]—though the latter was then the abomination of the Scotch as much as of the Jews—with her husband, and would willingly have cemented the friendship by borrowing a little cash from him, had not his good lady, who understood trap as well as any woman in the

[1] [See *Waverley*, Note 22.]

Mearns, put a negative on this advance to intimacy. Indeed, she knew how to make young Deilbelicket, old Dougald Baresword, the Laird of Bandybrawl, and others pay for the hospitality which she did not think proper to deny them, by rendering them useful in her negotiations with the light-handed lads beyond the Cairn, who, finding their late object of plunder was now allied to "kenn'd folks, and owned by them at kirk and market," became satisfied, on a moderate yearly composition, to desist from their depredations.

This eminent success reconciled Jasper to the dominion which his wife began to assume over him; and which was much confirmed by her proving to be—let me see, what is the prettiest mode of expressing it?—in the family way. On this occasion, Mrs. Yellowley had a remarkable dream, as is the usual practice of teeming mothers previous to the birth of an illustrious offspring. She "was a-dreamed," as her husband expressed it, that she was safely delivered of a plough, drawn by three yoke of Angus-shire oxen; and being a mighty investigator into such portents, she sat herself down with her gossips to consider what the thing might mean. Honest Jasper ventured, with much hesitation, to intimate his own opinion that the vision had reference rather to things past than things future, and might have been occasioned by his wife's nerves having been a little startled by meeting in the loan above the house his own great plough with the six oxen, which were the pride of his heart. But the good cummers raised such a hue and cry against this exposition, that Jasper was fain to put his fingers in his ears and to run out of the apartment.

"Hear to him," said an old Whigamore carline—"hear to him, wi' his owsen, that are as an idol to him, even as the calf of Bethel! Na—na, it's nae pleugh of the flesh that the bonny lad-bairn—for a lad it sall be—sall e'er striddle between the stilts o'; it's the pleugh of the Spirit; and I trust mysell to see him wag the head o' him in a pu'pit; or, what's better, on a hillside."

"Now, the deil's in your Whiggery," said the old Lady Glenprosing; "wad ye hae our cummer's bonny lad-bairn wag the head aff his shouthers like your godly Mess James Guthrie,[1] that ye hald such a clavering about? Na—na, he sall walk a mair siccar path, and be a dainty curate; and say he should live to be a bishop, what the waur wad he be?"

The gauntlet thus fairly flung down by one sibyl was caught up by another, and the controversy between Presbytery and Episcopacy raged, roared, or rather screamed, a round of cinnamon-water serving only like oil to the flame, till Jasper entered with the plough-staff; and by the awe of his presence, and the shame of misbehaving "before the stranger man," imposed some conditions of silence upon the disputants.

I do not know whether it was impatience to give to the light a being destined to such high and doubtful fates, or whether poor Dame Yellowley was rather frightened at the hurly-burly which had taken place in her presence, but she was taken suddenly ill; and, contrary to the formula in such cases used and provided, was soon reported to be "a good deal worse than was to be expected." She took the opportunity, having still all her wits about her, to extract from her sympathetic husband two promises—first, that he would christen the child, whose birth was like to cost her so dear, by a name indicative of the vision with which she had been favoured; and next, that he would educate him for the ministry. The canny Yorkshireman, thinking she had a good title at present to dictate in such matters, subscribed to all she required. A man-child was accordingly born under these conditions, but the state of the mother did not permit her for many days to inquire how far they had been complied with. When she was in some degree convalescent, she was informed that, as it was thought fit the child should be immediately christened, it had received the name of Triptolemus; the curate, who was a man of some classical skill, conceiving that this epithet contained a handsome and classical allusion to the visionary plough, with its triple yoke of oxen. Mrs. Yellowley was not much delighted with the manner in which her request had been

---

[1] Mr. James Guthrie, minister of Stirling, and author of the *Causes of the Lord's Wrath*, 1653, was executed at Edinburgh in 1661, and his head affixed on the Netherbow Port or Gate (*Laing*).

complied with; but grumbling being to as little purpose as in the celebrated case of Tristram Shandy, she e'en sat down contented with the heathenish name, and endeavoured to counteract the effects it might produce upon the taste and feelings of the nominee by such an education as might put him above the slightest thought of socks, coulters, stilts, mould-boards, or anything connected with the servile drudgery of the plough.

Jasper, sage Yorkshireman, smiled slyly in his sleeve, conceiving that young Trippie was likely to prove a chip of the old block, and would rather take after the jolly Yorkshire yeoman than the gentle but somewhat *aigre* blood of the house of Clinkscale. He remarked, with suppressed glee, that the tune which best answered the purpose of a lullaby was the "Ploughman's Whistle," and the first words the infant learned to stammer were the names of the oxen; moreover, that the "bern" preferred home-brewed ale to Scotch twopenny, and never quitted hold of the tankard with so much reluctance as when there had been, by some manœuvre of Jasper's own device, a double "straik" of malt allowed to the brewing, above that which was sanctioned by the most liberal recipe of which his dame's household thrift admitted. Besides this, when no other means could be fallen upon to divert an occasional fit of squalling, his father observed that Trip could be always silenced by jingling a bridle at his ear. From all which symptoms he used to swear in private that the boy would prove true Yorkshire, and mother and mother's kin would have small share of him.

Meanwhile, and within a year after the birth of Triptolemus, Mrs. Yellowley bore a daughter, named after herself, Barbara, who, even in earliest infancy, exhibited the pinched nose and thin lips by which the Clinkscale family were distinguished amongst the inhabitants of the Mearns; and as her childhood advanced, the readiness with which she seized, and the tenacity wherewith she detained, the playthings of Triptolemus, besides a desire to bite, pinch, and scratch, on slight or no provocation, were all considered by attentive observers as proofs that Miss Baby would prove "her mother over

again." Malicious people did not stick to say, that the acrimony of the Clinkscale blood had not on this occasion been
cooled and sweetened by that of Old England; that young
Deilbelicket was much about the house, and they could not
but think it odd that Mrs. Yellowley, who, as the whole
world knew, gave nothing for nothing, should be so uncommonly attentive to heap the trencher and to fill the caup of
an idle blackguard ne'er-do-weel. But when folk had once
looked upon the austere and awfully virtuous countenance of
Mrs. Yellowley, they did full justice to her propriety of conduct and Deilbelicket's delicacy of taste.

Meantime, young Triptolemus, having received such instruction as the curate could give him (for, though Dame Yellowley
adhered to the persecuted remnant, her jolly husband, edified
by the black gown and prayer-book, still conformed to the
church as by law established), was, in due process of time, sent
to St. Andrews to prosecute his studies. He went, it is true,
but with an eye turned back with sad remembrances on his
father's plough, his father's pancakes, and his father's ale,
for which the small-beer of the college, commonly there termed
"thorough-go-nimble," furnished a poor substitute. Yet he
advanced in his learning, being found, however, to show a
particular favour to such authors of antiquity as had made
the improvement of the soil the object of their researches.
He endured the *Bucolics* of Virgil; the *Georgics* he had by
heart; but the *Æneid* he could not away with; and he was
particularly severe upon the celebrated line expressing a charge
of cavalry, because, as he understood the word *putrem*,[1] he
opined that the combatants, in their inconsiderate ardour,
galloped over a new-manured ploughed field. Cato, the Roman Censor, was his favourite among classical heroes and
philosophers, not on account of the strictness of his morals,
but because of his treatise, *De Re Rustica*. He had ever in
his mouth the phrase of Cicero, *Jam neminem antepones Catoni*. He thought well of Palladius and of Terentius Varro;
but Columella was his pocket-companion. To these ancient
worthies he added the more modern Tusser, Hartlib, and

---

[1] Quadrupedumque putrem sonitu quatit ungula campum.

4

other writers on rural economics, not forgetting the lucubrations of the *Shepherd of Salisbury Plain*, and such of the bet-
ter-informed philomaths who, instead of loading their alma-
nacks with vain predictions of political events, pretended to
see what seeds would grow and what would not, and direct
the attention of their readers to that course of cultivation
from which the production of good crops may be safely predicted; modest sages, in fine, who, careless of the rise and
downfall of empires, content themselves with pointing out
the fit seasons to reap and sow, with a fair guess at the weather
which each month will be likely to present; as, for example,
that, if Heaven pleases, we shall have snow in January, and
the author will stake his reputation that July proves, on the
whole, a month of sunshine. Now, although the rector of St.
Leonard's was greatly pleased in general with the quiet, laborious, and studious bent of Triptolemus Yellowley, and deemed
him, in so far, worthy of a name of four syllables having a Latin
termination, yet he relished not, by any means, his exclusive
attention to his favourite authors. It savoured of the earth,
he said, if not of something worse, to have a man's mind always grovelling in mould, stercorated or unstercorated; and
he pointed out, but in vain, history, and poetry, and divinity as more elevating subjects of occupation. Triptolemus
Yellowley was obstinate in his own course. Of the battle of
Pharsalia, he thought not as it affected the freedom of the
world, but dwelt on the rich crop which the Emathian fields
were likely to produce the next season. In vernacular poetry,
Triptolemus could scarce be prevailed upon to read a single
couplet, excepting old Tusser, as aforesaid, whose *Hundred
Points of Good Husbandry* he had got by heart; and excepting also *Piers Ploughman's Vision*, which, charmed with the
title, he bought with avidity from a packman, but, after reading the two first pages, flung it into the fire as an impudent
and misnamed political libel. As to divinity, he summed
that matter up by reminding his instructors that to labour the
earth and win his bread with the toil of his body and sweat
of his brow was the lot imposed upon fallen man; and, for his
part, he was resolved to discharge, to the best of his abilities,

a task so obviously necessary to existence, leaving others to speculate as much as they would upon the more recondite mysteries of theology.

With a spirit so much narrowed and limited to the concerns of rural life, it may be doubted whether the proficiency of Triptolemus in learning, or the use he was like to make of his acquisitions, would have much gratified the ambitious hope of his affectionate mother. It is true, he expressed no reluctance to embrace the profession of a clergyman, which suited well enough with the habitual personal indolence which sometimes attaches to speculative dispositions. He had views, to speak plainly (I wish they were peculiar to himself), of cultivating the glebe six days in the week, preaching on the seventh with due regularity, and dining with some fat franklin or country laird, with whom he could smoke a pipe and drink a tankard after dinner, and mix in secret conference on the exhaustless subject,

Quid feciat lætas segetes.

Now this plan, besides that it indicated nothing of what was then called the root of the matter, implied necessarily the possession of a manse; and the possession of a manse inferred compliance with the doctrines of prelacy and other enormities of the time. There was some question how far manse and glebe, stipend, both victual and money, might have outbalanced the good lady's predisposition towards Presbytery; but her zeal was not put to so severe a trial. She died before her son had completed his studies, leaving her afflicted spouse just as disconsolate as was to be expected. The first act of old Jasper's undivided administration was to recall his son from St. Andrews, in order to obtain his assistance in his domestic labours. And here it might have been supposed that our Triptolemus, summoned to carry into practice what he had so fondly studied in theory, must have been, to use a simile which *he* would have thought lively, like a cow entering upon a clover park. Alas, mistaken thoughts and deceitful hopes of mankind!

A laughing philosopher, the Democritus of our day, once,

in a moral lecture, compared human life to a table pierced
with a number of holes, each of which has a pin made exactly
to fit it, but which pins being stuck in hastily, and without
selection, chance leads inevitably to the most awkward mistakes. "For how often do we see," the orator pathetically
concluded—"how often, I say, do we see the round man
stuck into the three-cornered hole!" This new illustration
of the vagaries of fortune set every one present into convulsions of laughter, excepting one fat alderman, who seemed
to make the case his own, and insisted that it was no jesting
matter. To take up the simile, however, which is an excellent one, it is plain that Triptolemus Yellowley had been
shaken out of the bag at least a hundred years too soon. If
he had come on the stage in our own time, that is, if he had
flourished at any time within these thirty or forty years, he
could not have missed to have held the office of vice-president
of some eminent agricultural society, and to have transacted
all the business thereof under the auspices of some noble duke
or lord, who, as the matter might happen, either knew, or
did not know, the difference betwixt a horse and a cart and
a cart-horse. He could not have missed such preferment, for
he was exceedingly learned in all those particulars which,
being of no consequence in actual practice, go, of course, a
great way to constitute the character of a connoisseur in any
art, and especially in agriculture. But, alas! Triptolemus
Yellowley had, as we already have hinted, come into the
world at least a century too soon; for, instead of sitting in
an arm-chair, with a hammer in his hand and a bumper of
port before him, giving forth the toast, "To breeding, in all
its branches," his father planted him betwixt the stilts of a
plough, and invited him to guide the oxen, on whose beauties
he would, in our day, have descanted, and whose rumps he
would not have goaded, but have carved. Old Jasper complained that although no one talked so well of common and
several, wheat and rape, fallow and lea, as his learned son
(whom he always called Tolimus), yet, "dang it," added the
Seneca, "nought thrives wi' un—nought thrives wi' un!" It
was still worse when Jasper, becoming frail and ancient, was

obliged, as happened in the course of a few years, gradually
to yield up the reins of government to the academical neo-
phyte.

As if nature had meant him a spite, he had got one of the
dourest and most intractable farms in the Mearns to try conclusions withal, a place which seemed to yield everything but
what the agriculturist wanted; for there were plenty of this-
tles, which indicates dry land; and store of fern, which is
said to intimate deep land; and nettles, which show where
lime hath been applied; and deep furrows in the most unlikely spots, which intimated that it had been cultivated in former
days by the Peghts, as popular tradition bore. There was
also enough of stones to keep the ground warm, according to
the creed of some farmers, and great abundance of springs
to render it cool and sappy, according to the theory of others.
It was in vain that, acting alternately on these opinions, poor
Triptolemus endeavoured to avail himself of the supposed capabilities of the soil. No kind of butter that might be churned
could be made to stick upon his own bread, any more than on
that of poor Tusser, whose *Hundred Points of Good Husbandry,*
so useful to others of his day, were never to himself worth as
many pennies.[1]

In fact, excepting an hundred acres of infield, to which old
Jasper had early seen the necessity of limiting his labours,
there was not a corner of the farm fit for anything but to
break plough-graith and kill cattle. And then, as for the part
which was really tilled with some profit, the expense of the
farming establishment of Triptolemus, and his disposition to
experiment, soon got rid of any good arising from the cultivation of it. " The carles and the cart-avers," he confessed,
with a sigh, speaking of his farm-servants and horses, " make
it all, and the carles and cart-avers eat it all"—a conclusion
which might sum up the year-book of many a gentleman
farmer.

Matters would have soon been brought to a close with
Triptolemus in the present day. He would have got a bank-
credit, manœuvred with wind-bills, dashed out upon a large

[1] See Tusser's Poverty. Note 8.

scale, and soon have seen his crop and stock sequestered by the sheriff; but in those days a man could not ruin himself so easily. The whole Scottish tenantry stood upon the same level flat of poverty, so that it was extremely difficult to find any vantage ground by climbing up to which a man might have an opportunity of actually breaking his neck with some *éclat*. They were pretty much in the situation of people who, being totally without credit, may indeed suffer from indigence, but cannot possibly become bankrupt. Besides, notwithstanding the failure of Triptolemus's projects, there was to be balanced against the expenditure which they occasioned all the savings which the extreme economy of his sister Barbara could effect; and in truth her exertions were wonderful. She might have realised, if any one could, the idea of the learned philosopher, who pronounced that sleeping was a fancy, and eating but a habit, and who appeared to the world to have renounced both, until it was unhappily discovered that he had an intrigue with the cook-maid of the family, who indemnified him for his privations by giving him private entrée to the pantry and to a share of her own couch. But no such deceptions were practised by Barbara Yellowley. She was up early and down late, and seemed, to her over-watched and over-tasked maidens, to be as "wakerife" as the cat herself. Then, for eating, it appeared that the air was a banquet to her, and she would fain have made it so to her retinue. Her brother, who, besides being lazy in his person, was somewhat luxurious in his appetite, would willingly now and then have tasted a mouthful of animal food, were it but to know how his sheep were fed off. But a proposal to eat a child could not have startled Mistress Barbara more; and, being of a compliant and easy disposition, Triptolemus reconciled himself to the necessity of a perpetual Lent, too happy when he could get a scrap of butter to his oaten cake, or (as they lived on the banks of the Esk) escape the daily necessity of eating salmon, whether in or out of season, six days out of the seven.

But although Mrs. Barbara brought faithfully to the joint stock all savings which her awful powers of economy accomplished to scrape together, and although the dower of their mother was by degrees expended, or nearly so, in aiding them upon extreme occasions, the term at length approached when it seemed impossible that they could sustain the conflict any longer against the evil star of Triptolemus, as he called it himself, or the natural result of his absurd speculations, as it was termed by others. Luckily, at this sad crisis, a god jumped down to their relief out of a machine. In plain English, the noble lord who owned their farm arrived at his mansion-house in their neighbourhood, with his coach and six and his running footmen,[1] in the full spendour of the 17th century.

This person of quality was the son of the nobleman who had brought the ancient Jasper into the country from Yorkshire, and he was, like his father, a fanciful and scheming man. He had schemed well for himself, however, amid the mutations of the time, having obtained, for a certain period of years, the administration of the remote islands of Orkney and Zetland,[2] for payment of a certain rent, with the right of making the most of whatever was the property or revenue of the crown in these districts, under the title of Lord Chamberlain. Now, his lordship had become possessed with a notion, in itself a very true one, that much might be done to render this grant available, by improving the culture of the crown lands, both in Orkney and Zetland; and then having some acquaintance with our friend Triptolemus, he thought (rather less happily) that he might prove a person capable of furthering his schemes. He sent for him to the great hall-house, and was so much edified by the way in which our friend laid down the law upon every given subject relating to rural economy that he lost no time in securing the co-operation of so valuable an assistant, the first step being to release him from his present unprofitable farm.

The terms were arranged much to the mind of Triptolemus, who had already been taught, by many years' experience, a dark sort of notion that, without undervaluing or doubting for a moment his own skill, it would be quite as well that almost

[1] [See *Bride of Lammermoor*, Note 9.]
[2] See Administration of Zetland. Note 9.

all the trouble and risk should be at the expense of his employer. Indeed, the hopes of advantage which he held out to his patron were so considerable, that the Lord Chamberlain dropped every idea of admitting his dependant into any share of the expected profits; for, rude as the arts of agriculture were in Scotland, they were far superior to those known and practised in the regions of Thule, and Triptolemus Yellowley conceived himself to be possessed of a degree of insight into these mysteries far superior to what was possessed or practised even in the Mearns. The improvement, therefore, which was to be expected would bear a double proportion, and the Lord Chamberlain was to reap all the profit, deducting a handsome salary for his steward Yellowley, together with the accommodation of a house and domestic farm, for the support of his family. Joy seized the heart of Mistress Barbara at hearing this happy termination of what threatened to be so very bad an affair as the lease of Cauldacres.

"If we cannot," she said, "provide for our own house when all is coming in and nothing going out, surely we must be worse than infidels!"

Triptolemus was a busy man for some time, huffing and puffing, and eating and drinking in every change-house, while he ordered and collected together proper implements of agriculture, to be used by the natives of these devoted islands whose destinies were menaced with this formidable change. Singular tools these would seem if presented before a modern agricultural society; but everything is relative, nor could the heavy cart-load of timber, called the old Scots plough, seem less strange to a Scottish farmer of this present day than the corslets and casques of the soldiers of Cortes might seem to a regiment of our own army. Yet the latter conquered Mexico, and undoubtedly the former would have been a splendid improvement on the state of agriculture in Thule.

We have never been able to learn why Triptolemus preferred fixing his residence in Zetland to becoming an inhabitant of the Orkneys. Perhaps he thought the inhabitants of the latter archipelago the more simple and docile of the two kindred tribes; or perhaps he considered the situation of the house and farm he himself was to occupy (which was indeed a tolerable one) as preferable to that which he had it in his power to have obtained upon Pomona (so the main island of the Orkneys is entitled). At Harfra, or, as it was sometimes called, Stourburgh, from the remains of a Pictish fort which was almost close to the mansion-house, the factor settled himself in the plenitude of his authority, determined to honour the name he bore by his exertions, in precept and example, to civilise the Zetlanders, and improve their very confined knowledge in the primary arts of human life.

CHAPTER V.

The wind blew keen frae north and east;
  It blew upon the floor.
Quo' our goodman to our goodwife,
  " Get up and bar the door."

" My hand is in my housewifeskep,
  Goodman, as ye may see;
If it shouldna be barr'd this hundred years,
  It's no be barr'd for me ! "

Old Song.

WE can only hope that the gentle reader has not found the latter part of the last chapter extremely tedious; but, at any rate, his impatience will scarce equal that of young Mordaunt Mertoun, who, while the lightning came flash after flash, while the wind, veering and shifting from point to point, blew with all the fury of a hurricane, and while the rain was dashed against him in deluges, stood hammering, calling, and roaring at the door of the old Place of Harfra, impatient for admittance, and at a loss to conceive any position of existing circumstances which could occasion the exclusion of a stranger, especially during such horrible weather. At length, finding his noise and vociferation were equally in vain, he fell back so far from the front of the house as was necessary to enable him to reconnoitre the chimneys; and, amidst "storm and shade," could discover, to the increase of his dismay, that though noon, then the dinner-hour of these islands, was now

nearly arrived, there was no smoke proceeding from the tun-
nels of the vents to give any note of preparation within.

Mordaunt's wrathful impatience was now changed into sympathy and alarm; for, so long accustomed to the exuberant
hospitality of the Zetland Islands, he was immediately induced to suppose some strange and unaccountable disaster had
befallen the family; and forthwith set himself to discover
some place at which he could make forcible entry, in order
to ascertain the situation of the inmates, as much as to obtain
shelter from the still increasing storm. His present anxiety
was, however, as much thrown away as his late clamorous im-
portunities for admittance had been. Triptolemus and his
sister had heard the whole alarm without, and had already
had a sharp dispute on the propriety of opening the door.

Mrs. Baby, as we have described her, was no willing ren-
derer of the rites of hospitality. In their farm of Cauldacres,
in the Mearns, she had been the dread and abhorrence of all
gaberlunzie men, and travelling packmen, gipsies, long remembered beggars, and so forth; nor was there one of them
so wily, as she used to boast, as could ever say they had heard
the clink of her sneck. In Zetland, where the new settlers
were yet strangers to the extreme honesty and simplicity of
all classes, suspicion and fear joined with frugality in her desire to exclude all wandering guests of uncertain character;
and the second of these motives had its effect on Triptolemus
himself, who, though neither suspicious nor penurious, knew
good people were scarce, good farmers scarcer, and had a reasonable share of that wisdom which looks towards self-preservation as the first law of nature. These hints may serve as
a commentary on the following dialogue which took place betwixt the brother and sister.

"Now, good be gracious to us," said Triptolemus, as he
sat thumbing his old school-copy of Virgil, "here is a pure
day for the bear seed! Well spoke the wise Mantuan—*ventis
surgentibus*—and then the groans of the mountains, and the
long-resounding shores; but where's the woods, Baby?—tell
me, I say, where we shall find the *nemorum murmur*, sister
Baby, in these new seats of ours?"

"What's your foolish will?" said Baby, popping her head from out of a dark recess in the kitchen, where she was busy about some nameless deed of housewifery.

Her brother, who had addressed himself to her more from habit than intention, no sooner saw her bleak red nose, keen grey eyes, with the sharp features thereunto conforming, shaded by the flaps of the loose "toy" which depended on each side of her eager face, than he bethought himself that his query was likely to find little acceptation from her, and therefore stood another volley before he would resume the topic.

"I say, Mr. Yellowley," said sister Baby, coming into the middle of the room, "what for are ye crying on me, and me in the midst of my housewifeskep?"

"Nay, for nothing at all, Baby," answered Triptolemus, "saving that I was saying to myself, that here we had the sea, and the wind, and the rain, sufficient enough, but where's the wood?—where's the wood, Baby, answer me that?"

"The wood!" replied Baby. "Were I no to take better care of the wood than you, brother, there would soon be no more wood about the town than the barber's block that's on your own shoulders, Triptolemus. If ye be thinking of the wreckwood that the callants brought in yesterday, there was six ounces of it gaed to boil your parritch this morning; though, I trow, a carefu' man wad have ta'en drammock, if breakfast he behoved to have, rather than waste baith meltith and fuel in the same morning."

"That is to say, Baby," replied Triptolemus, who was somewhat of a dry joker in his way, "that when we have fire we are not to have food, and when we have food we are not to have fire, these being too great blessings to enjoy both in the same day! Good luck, you do not propose we should starve with cold and starve with hunger *unico contextu?* But, to tell you the truth, I could never away with raw oatmeal, slockened with water, in all my life. Call it drammock, or crowdie, or just what ye list, my vivers must thole fire and water."

"The mair gowk you," said Baby; "can ye not make your

brose on the Sunday, and sup them cauld on the Monday, since
ye're sae dainty? Mony is the fairer face than yours that has
licked the lip after such a cogfu'."

"Mercy on us, sister!" said Triptolemus; "at this rate it's
a finished field with me: I must unyoke the pleugh and lie
down to wait for the dead-thraw. Here is that in this house
wad hold all Zetland in meal for a twelvemonth, and ye grudge
a cogfu' of warm parritch to me, that has sic a charge!"

"Whisht! haud your silly clavering tongue!" said Baby,
looking round with apprehension; "ye are a wise man to
speak of what is in the house, and a fitting man to have the
charge of it! Hark, as I live by bread, I hear a tapping at
the outer yett!"

"Go and open it then, Baby," said her brother, glad at
anything that promised to interrupt the dispute.

"Go and open it, said he!" echoed Baby, half-angry, half-
frightened, and half-triumphant at the superiority of her understanding over that of her brother. "Go and open it, said
he, indeed! is it to lend robbers a chance to take all that is
in the house?"

"Robbers!" echoed Triptolemus, in his turn; "there are
no more robbers in this country than there are lambs at Yule.
I tell you, as I have told you an hundred times, there are no
Highlandmen to harry us here. This is a land of quiet and
honesty. *O fortunati nimium !*"

"And what good is St. Ninian to do ye, Tolimus?" said
his sister, mistaking the quotation for a Catholic invocation.
"Besides, if there be no Highlandmen, there may be as bad.
I saw sax or seven as ill-looking chields gang past the Place
yesterday as ever came frae beyont Clochna-ben; ill-faur'd
tools they had in their hands, whaaling-knives they ca'ed
them, but they looked as like dirks and whingers as ae bit
airn can look like anither. There is nae honest men carry siccan tools."

Here the knocking and shouts of Mordaunt were very audible betwixt every swell of the horrible blast which was ca-
reering without. The brother and sister looked at each other
in real perplexity and fear. "If they have heard of the sil-

ler," said Baby, her very nose changing with terror from red to blue, "we are but gane folk!"

"Who speaks now, when they should hold their tongue?" said Triptolemus. "Go to the shot-window instantly, and see how many there are of them, while I load the old Spanish-barrelled duck-gun; go as if you were stepping on new-laid eggs."

Baby crept to the window, and reported that she saw only "one young chield, clattering and roaring as gin he were daft. How many there might be out of sight, she could not say."

"Out of sight! nonsense," said Triptolemus, laying aside the ramrod with which he was loading the piece with a trembling hand. "I will warrant them out of sight and hearing both; this is some poor fellow catched in the tempest, wants the shelter of our roof, and a little refreshment. Open the door, Baby, it's a Christian deed."

"But is it a Christian deed of him to come in at the window, then?" said Baby, setting up a most doleful shriek, as Mordaunt Mertoun, who had forced open one of the windows, leaped down into the apartment, dripping with water like a river god. Triptolemus, in great tribulation, presented the gun which he had not yet loaded, while the intruder exclaimed: "Hold—hold; what the devil mean you by keeping your doors bolted in weather like this, and levelling your gun at folks' heads as you would at a sealgh's?"

"And who are you, friend, and what want you?" said Triptolemus, lowering the butt of his gun to the floor as he spoke, and so recovering his arms.

"What do I want?" said Mordaunt; "I want everything. I want meat, drink, and fire, a bed for the night, and a sheltie for to-morrow morning to carry me to Jarlshof."

"And ye said there were nae caterans or sorners here?" said Baby to the agriculturist, reproachfully. "Heard ye ever a breekless loon frae Lochaber tell his mind and his errand mair deftly? Come—come, friend," she added, addressing herself to Mordaunt, "put up your pipes and gang your gate; this is the house of his lordship's factor, and no place of reset for thiggers or sorners."

Mordaunt laughed in her face at the simplicity of the request. "Leave built walls," he said, "and in such a tempest as this? What take you me for?—a gannet or a scart do you think I am, that your clapping your hands and skirling at me like a madwoman should drive me from the shelter into the storm?"

"And so you propose, young man," said Triptolemus, gravely, "to stay in my house, *volens nolens*—that is, whether we will or no?"

"Will!" said Mordaunt; "what right have you to will anything about it? Do you not hear the thunder? Do you not hear the rain? Do you not see the lightning? And do you not know this is the only house within I wot not how many miles? Come, my good master and dame, this may be Scottish jesting, but it sounds strange in Zetland ears. You have let out the fire, too, and my teeth are dancing a jig in my head with cold; but I'll soon put that to rights."

He seized the fire-tongs, raked together the embers upon the hearth, broke up into life the gathering-peat, which the hostess had calculated should have preserved the seeds of fire, without giving them forth, for many hours; then casting his eye round, saw in a corner the stock of drift-wood, which Mistress Baby had served forth by ounces, and transferred two or three logs of it at once to the hearth, which, conscious of such unwonted supply, began to transmit to the chimney such a smoke as had not issued from the Place of Harfra for many a day.

While their uninvited guest was thus making himself at home, Baby kept edging and jogging the factor to turn out the intruder. But for this undertaking Triptolemus Yellowley felt neither courage nor zeal, nor did circumstances seem at all to warrant the favourable conclusion of any fray into which he might enter with the young stranger. The sinewy limbs and graceful form of Mordaunt Mertoun were seen to great advantage in his simple sea-dress; and with his dark sparkling eye, finely formed head, animated features, close curled dark hair, and bold, free looks, the stranger formed a very strong contrast with the host on whom he had intruded

himself. Triptolemus was a short, clumsy, duck-legged dis-
ciple of Ceres, whose bottle-nose, turned up and handsomely
coppered at the extremity, seemed to intimate something of
an occasional treaty with Bacchus. It was like to be no equal
mellay betwixt persons of such unequal form and strength;
and the difference betwixt twenty and fifty years was nothing
in favour of the weaker party. Besides, the factor was an
honest, good-natured fellow at bottom, and being soon satisfied that his guest had no other views than those of obtaining
refuge from the storm, it would, despite his sister's instiga-
tions, have been his last act to deny a boon so reasonable and
necessary to a youth whose exterior was so prepossessing. He
stood, therefore, considering how he could most gracefully
glide into the character of the hospitable landlord out of that
of the churlish defender of his domestic castle against an unauthorised intrusion, when Baby, who had stood appalled at
the extreme familiarity of the stranger's address and demeanour, now spoke up for herself.

"My troth, lad," said she to Mordaunt, "ye are no blate, to
light on at that rate, and the best of wood, too: nane of your
sharney peats, but good aik timber, nae less maun serve ye!"

"You come lightly by it, dame," said Mordaunt, carelessly;
"and you should not grudge to the fire what the sea gives you
for nothing. These good ribs of oak did their last duty upon
earth and ocean when they could hold no longer together under
the brave hearts that manned the bark."

"And that's true, too," said the old woman, softening;
"this maun be awesome weather by sea. Sit down and warm
ye, since the sticks are alow."

"Ay—ay," said Triptolemus, "it is a pleasure to see siccan
a bonny bleeze. I havena seen the like o't since I left Cauldacres."

"And shallna see the like o't again in a hurry," said Baby,
"unless the house take fire, or there suld be a coal-heugh
found out."

"And wherefore should not there be a coal-heugh found
out?" said the factor, triumphantly—"I say, wherefore should
not a coal-heugh be found out in Zetland as well as in Fife,

now that the chamberlain has a far-sighted and discreet man upon the spot to make the necessary perquisitions? They are baith fishing-stations, I trow!"

"I tell you what it is, Tolimus Yellowley," answered his sister, who had practical reasons to fear her brother's opening upon any false scent, "if you promise my lord sae mony of these bonnie-wallies, we'll no be weel hafted here before we are found out and set a-trotting again. If ane was to speak to ye about a gold mine, I ken weel wha would promise he suld have Portugal pieces clinking in his pouch before the year gaed by."

"And why suld I not?" said Triptolemus. "Maybe your head does not know there is a land in Orkney called Ophir, or something very like it; and wherefore might not Solomon, the wise king of the Jews, have sent thither his ships and his servants for four hundred and fifty talents? I trow he knew best where to go or send, and I hope you believe in your Bible, Baby?"

Baby was silenced by an appeal to Scripture, however *mal à propos*, and only answered by an inarticulate "humph" of incredulity or scorn, while her brother went on addressing Mordaunt. "Yes, you shall all of you see what a change shall coin introduce even into such an unpropitious country as yours. Ye have not heard of copper, I warrant, nor of ironstone, in these islands, neither?" Mordaunt said he had head there was copper near the Cliffs of Konigsburgh. "Ay, and a copper scum is found on the Loch of Swana, too, young man. But the youngest of you, doubtless, thinks himself a match for such as I am!"

Baby, who during all this while had been closely and accurately reconnoitring the youth's person, now interposed in a manner by her brother totally unexpected. "Ye had mair need, Mr. Yellowley, to give the young man some dry clothes, and to see about getting something for him to eat, than to sit there bleezing away with your lang tales, as if the weather were not windy enow without your help; and maybe the lad would drink some 'bland,' or sic-like, if ye had the grace to ask him."

While Triptolemus looked astonished at such a proposal, considering the quarter it came from, Mordaunt answered, he "should be very glad to have dry clothes, but begged to be excused from drinking until he had eaten somewhat."

Triptolemus accordingly conducted him into another apartment, and accommodating him with a change of dress, left him to his arrangements, while he himself returned to the kitchen, much puzzled to account for his sister's unusual fit of hospitality. "She must be fey," [1] he said, "and in that case has not long to live, and though I fall heir to her tocher-good, I am sorry for it; for she has held the house-gear well together: drawn the girth over tight it may be now and then, but the saddle sits the better."

When Triptolemus returned to the kitchen, he found his suspicions confirmed; for his sister was in the desperate act of consigning to the pot a smoked goose, which, with others of the same tribe, had long hung in the large chimney, muttering to herself at the same time: "It maun be eaten sune or syne, and what for no by the puir callant?"

"What is this of it, sister?" said Triptolemus. "You have on the girdle and the pot at ance. What day is this wi' you?"

"E'en such a day as the Israelites had beside the flesh-pots of Egypt, billie Triptolemus; but ye little ken wha ye have in your house this blessed day."

"Troth and little do I ken," said Triptolemus, "as little as I would ken the naig I never saw before. I would take the lad for a jagger, but he has rather ower good havings, and he has no pack."

"Ye ken as little as ane of your ain bits o' nowt, man," retorted sister Baby; "if ye ken na him, do ye ken Tronda Dronsdaughter?"

"Tronda Dronsdaughter!" echoed Triptolemus; "how should I but ken her, when I pay her twal pennies Scots by the day for working in the house here? I trow she works as if the things burned her fingers. I had better give a Scots lass a groat of English siller."

"And that's the maist sensible word ye have said this

[1] See Note 10.

blessed morning.   Weel, but Tronda kens this lad weel, and
she has often spoke to me about him.   They call his father
the Silent Man of Sumburgh, and they say he's uncanny."

"Hout, hout—nonsense, nonsense; they are aye at sic trash
as that," said the brother, "when you want a day's wark out
of them: they have stepped ower the tangs, or they have met
an uncanny body, or they have turned about the boat against
the sun, and then there's nought to be done that day."

"Weel—weel, brother, ye are so wise," said Baby, "because ye knapped Latin at St. Andrews; and can your lair tell
me, then, what the lad has round his halse?"

"A Barcelona napkin, as wet as a dishclout, and I have
just lent him one of my own overlays," said Triptolemus.

"A Barcelona napkin!" said Baby, elevating her voice, and
then suddenly lowering it, as from apprehension of being overheard.   "I say a gold chain."

"A gold chain!" said Triptolemus.

"In troth is it, hinny; and how like you that?   The folk
say here, as Tronda tells me, that the king of the Drows gave
it to his father, the Silent Man of Sumburgh."

"I wish you would speak sense, or be the silent woman,"
said Triptolemus.   "The upshot of it all is, then, that this
lad is the rich stranger's son, and that you are giving him
the goose you were to keep till Michaelmas!"

"Troth, brother, we maun do something for God's sake,
and to make friends; and the lad," added Baby, for even she
was not altogether above the prejudices of her sex in favour
of outward form—"the lad has a fair face of his ain."

"Ye would have let mony a fair face," said Triptolemus,
"pass the door pining, if it had not been for the gold
chain."

"Nae doubt—nae doubt," replied Barbara; "ye wadna
have me waste our substance on every thigger or sorner that
has the luck to come by the door in a wet day?   But this lad
has a fair and a wide name in the country, and Tronda says
he is to be married to a daughter of the rich Udaller, Magnus
Troil, and the marriage-day is to be fixed whenever he makes
choice, set him up! between the twa lasses; and so it wad be

as much as our good name is worth, and our quiet forbye, to let him sit unserved, although he does come unsent for."

"The best reason in life," said Triptolemus, "for letting a man into a house is, that you dare not bid him go by. However, since there is a man of quality amongst them, I will let him know whom he has to do with, in my person." Then advancing to the door, he exclaimed: "*Heus tibi, Dave!*"

"*Adsum,*" answered the youth, entering the apartment.

"Hem!" said the erudite Triptolemus, "not altogether deficient in his humanities, I see. I will try him further. Canst thou aught of husbandry, young gentleman?"

"Troth, sir, not I," answered Mordaunt; "I have been trained to plough upon the sea and to reap upon the crag."

"Plough the sea!" said Triptolemus; "that's a furrow requires small harrowing; and for your harvest on the crag, I suppose you mean these 'scowries,' or whatever you call them. It is a sort of ingathering which the Ranzelman should stop by the law; nothing more likely to break an honest man's bones. I profess I cannot see the pleasure men propose by dangling in a rope's-end betwixt earth and heaven. In my case, I had as lief the other end of the rope were fastened to the gibbet; I should be sure of not falling, at least."

"Now, I would only advise you to try it," replied Mordaunt. "Trust me, the world has few grander sensations than when one is perched in mid-air between a high-browed cliff and a roaring ocean, the rope by which you are sustained seeming scarce stronger than a silken thread, and the stone on which you have one foot steadied affording such a breadth as the kittiwake might rest upon—to feel and know all this, with the full confidence that your own agility of limb and strength of head can bring you as safe off as if you had the wing of the gosshawk—this is indeed being almost independent of the earth you tread on!"

Triptolemus stared at this enthusiastic description of an amusement which had so few charms for him; and his sister, looking at the glancing eye and elevated bearing of the young adventurer, answered by ejaculating: "My certie, lad, but ye are a brave chield!"

"A brave chield!" returned Yellowley; "I say a brave goose, to be flichtering and fleeing in the wind when he might abide upon *terra firma!* But come, here's a goose that is more to the purpose, when once it is well boiled. Get us trenchers and salt, Baby; but in truth it will prove salt enough—a tasty morsel it is. But I think the Zetlanders be the only folk in the world that think of running such risks to catch geese, and then boiling them when they have done."

"To be sure," replied his sister (it was the only word they had agreed in that day), "it would be an unco thing to bid ony gudewife in Angus or a' the Mearns boil a goose, while there was sic things as spits in the warld. But wha's this neist?" she added, looking towards the entrance with great indignation. "My certie, open doors and dogs come in; and wha opened the door to him?"

"I did, to be sure," replied Mordaunt; "you would not have a poor devil stand beating your deaf door-cheeks in weather like this? Here goes something, though, to help the fire," he added, drawing out the sliding bar of oak with which the door had been secured, and throwing it on the hearth, whence it was snatched by Dame Baby in great wrath, she exclaiming at the same time:

"It's sea-borne timber, as there's little else here, and he dings it about as if it were a fir-clog! And who be you, an it please you?" she added, turning to the stranger—"a very hallanshaker loon, as ever crossed my twa een!"

"I am a jagger, if it like your ladyship," replied the uninvited guest, a stout, vulgar, little man, who had indeed the humble appearance of a pedlar, called "jagger" in these islands; "never travelled in a waur day, or was more willing to get to harbourage. Heaven be praised for fire and house-room!"

So saying, he drew a stool to the fire, and sat down without further ceremony. Dame Baby stared "wild as grey goss-hawk," and was meditating how to express her indignation in something warmer than words, for which the boiling pot seemed to offer a convenient hint, when an old half-starved serving-woman—the Tronda already mentioned—the sharer of Barbara's domestic cares, who had been as yet in some remote corner of the mansion, now hobbled into the room, and broke out into exclamations which indicated some cause of alarm.

"O master!" and "O mistress!" were the only sounds she could for some time articulate, and then followed them up with: "The best in the house—the best in the house; set a' on the board, and a' will be little aneugh. There is auld Norna of Fitful Head, the most fearful woman in all the isles!"

"Where can she have been wandering?" said Mordaunt, not without some apparent sympathy with the surprise, if not with the alarm, of the old domestic; "but it is needless to ask—the worse the weather, the more likely is she to be a traveller."

"What new tramper is this?" echoed the distracted Baby, whom the quick succession of guests had driven wellnigh crazy with vexation. "I'll soon settle her wandering, I sall warrant, if my brother has but the saul of a man in him, or if there be a pair of jougs at Scalloway!"

"The iron was never forged on stithy that would hauld her," said the old maid-servant. "She comes—she comes. God's sake, speak her fair and canny, or we will have a ravelled hasp on the yarn-windles!"

As she spoke, a woman, tall enough almost to touch the top of the door with her cap, stepped into the room, signing the cross as she entered, and pronouncing, with a solemn voice: "The blessing of God and St. Ronald on the open door, and their broad malison and mine upon close-handed churls!"

"And wha are ye, that are sae bauld wi' your blessing and banning in other folks' houses? What kind of country is this that folk cannot sit quiet for an hour, and serve Heaven, and keep their bit gear thegither, without gangrel men and women coming thigging and sorning ane after another, like a string of wild geese?"

This speech the understanding reader will easily saddle on Mistress Baby; and what effects it might have produced on the last stranger can only be matter of conjecture, for the old

servant and Mordaunt applied themselves at once to the party
addressed, in order to deprecate her resentment; the former
speaking to her some words of Norse, in a tone of intercession,
and Mordaunt saying in English: "They are strangers, Norna,
and know not your name or qualities; they are unacquainted,
too, with the ways of this country, and therefore we must
hold them excused for their lack of hospitality."

"I lack no hospitality, young man," said Triptolemus,
"*miseris succurrere disco:* the goose that was destined to roost
in the chimney till Michaelmas is boiling in the pot for you;
but if we had twenty geese, I see we are like to find mouths
to eat them every feather. This must be amended."

"What must be amended, sordid slave?" said the stranger
Norna, turning at once upon him with an emphasis that made
him start—"*what* must be amended? Bring hither, if thou
wilt, thy newfangled coulters, spades, and harrows, alter the
implements of our fathers from the ploughshare to the mouse-
trap; but know thou art in the land that was won of old by
the flaxen-haired 'kempions' of the North, and leave us their
hospitality at least, to show we come of what was once noble
and generous. I say to you, beware; while Norna looks forth
at the measureless waters from the crest of Fitful Head, something is yet left that resembles power of defence. If the men
of Thule have ceased to be champions, and to spread the banquet for the raven, the women have not forgotten the arts that
lifted them of yore into queens and prophetesses."

The woman who pronounced this singular tirade was as
striking in appearance as extravagantly lofty in her pretensions and in her language. She might well have represented
on the stage, so far as features, voice, and stature were concerned, the Bonduca or Boadicea of the Britons, or the sage
Velleda, Aurinia, or any other fated pythoness who ever led
to battle a tribe of the ancient Goths. Her features were
high and well formed, and would have been handsome but for
the ravages of time and the effects of exposure to the severe
weather of her country. Age, and perhaps sorrow, had
quenched, in some degree, the fire of a dark blue eye, whose
hue almost approached to black, and had sprinkled snow on

such parts of her tresses as had escaped from under her cap, and were dishevelled by the rigour of the storm. Her upper garment, which dropped with water, was of a coarse, dark-coloured stuff, called wadmaal, then much used in the Zetland Islands, as also in Iceland and Norway. But as she threw this cloak back from her shoulders, a short jacket, of dark-blue velvet, stamped with figures, became visible, and the vest, which corresponded to it, was of crimson colour, and embroidered with tarnished silver. Her girdle was plated with silver ornaments, cut into the shape of planetary signs; her blue apron was embroidered with similar devices, and covered a petticoat of crimson cloth. Strong, thick, enduring shoes, of the half-dressed leather of the country, were tied with straps, like those of the Roman buskins, over her scarlet stockings. She wore in her belt an ambiguous-looking weapon, which might pass for a sacrificing knife or dagger, as the imagination of the spectator chose to assign to the wearer the character of a priestess or of a sorceress. In her hand she held a staff, squared on all sides, and engraved with Runic characters and figures, forming one of those portable and perpetual calendars which were used among the ancient natives of Scandinavia, and which, to a superstitious eye, might have passed for a divining-rod.

Such were the appearance, features, and attire of Norna of the Fitful Head, upon whom many of the inhabitants of the island looked with observance, many with fear, and almost all with a sort of veneration. Less pregnant circumstances of suspicion would, in any other part of Scotland, have exposed her to the investigation of those cruel inquisitors who were then often invested with the delegated authority of the privy council, for the purpose of persecuting, torturing, and finally consigning to the flames, those who were accused of witchcraft or sorcery. But superstitions of this nature pass through two stages ere they become entirely obsolete. Those supposed to be possessed of supernatural powers are venerated in the earlier stages of society. As religion and knowledge increase, they are first held in hatred and horror, and are finally regarded as impostors. Scotland was in the second state: the

fear of witchcraft was great, and the hatred against those suspected of it intense.   Zetland was as yet a little world by itself, where, among the lower and ruder classes, so much of the
ancient Northern superstition remained as cherished the original veneration for those affecting supernatural knowledge and
power over the elements, which made a constituent part of the
ancient Scandinavian creed.   At least, if the natives of Thule
admitted that one class of magicians performed their feats by
their alliance with Satan, they devoutly believed that others
dealt with spirits of a different and less odious class—the
ancient dwarfs, called in Zetland Trows, or Drows, the modern fairies, and so forth.

Among those who were supposed to be in league with disembodied spirits, this Norna, descended from, and representative of, a family which had long pretended to such gifts, was so
eminent, that the name assigned to her, which signifies one of
those fatal sisters who weave the web of human fate, had been
conferred in honour of her supernatural powers.   The name
by which she had been actually christened was carefully concealed by herself and her parents; for to its discovery they
superstitiously annexed some fatal consequences.   In those
times, the doubt only occurred, whether her supposed powers
were acquired by lawful means.   In our days, it would have
been questioned whether she was an impostor, or whether her
imagination was so deeply impressed with the mysteries of
her supposed art that she might be in some degree a believer
in her own pretensions to supernatural knowledge.   Certain
it is, that she performed her part with such undoubting confidence, and such striking dignity of look and action, and
evinced, at the same time, such strength of language and
energy of purpose, that it would have been difficult for the
greatest sceptic to have doubted the reality of her enthusiasm,
though he might smile at the pretensions to which it gave rise.

CHAPTER VI.

If, by your art, you have
Put the wild waters in this roar, allay them.
Tempest.

THE storm had somewhat relaxed its rigour just before the entrance of Norna, otherwise she must have found it impossible to travel during the extremity of its fury. But she had hardly added herself so unexpectedly to the party whom chance had assembled at the dwelling of Triptolemus Yellowley, when the tempest suddenly resumed its former vehemence, and raged around the building with a fury which made the inmates insensible to anything except the risk that the old mansion was about to fall above their heads.

Mistress Baby gave vent to her fears in loud exclamations of "The Lord guide us—this is surely the last day; what kind of a country of guizards and gyre-carlines is this? And you, ye fool carle," she added, turning on her brother, for all her passions had a touch of acidity in them, "to quit the bonny Mearns land to come here, where there is naething but sturdy beggars and gaberlunzies within ane's house, and Heaven's anger on the outside on't!"

"I tell you, sister Baby," answered the insulted agriculturist, "that all shall be reformed and amended—excepting," he added, betwixt his teeth, "the scaulding humours of an ill-natured jaud, that can add bitterness to the very storm!"

The old domestic and the pedlar meanwhile exhausted themselves in entreaties to Norna, of which, as they were couched in the Norse language, the master of the house understood nothing.

She listened to them with a haughty and unmoved air, and replied at length aloud, and in English: "I will not. What if this house be strewed in ruins before morning—where would be the world's want in the crazed projector and the niggardly pinch-commons by which it is inhabited? They will needs come to reform Zetland customs, let them try how they like a Zetland storm. You that would not perish, quit this house!"

The pedlar seized on his little knapsack, and began hastily to brace it on his back, the old maid-servant cast her cloak about her shoulders, and both seemed to be in the act of leaving the house as fast as they could.

Triptolemus Yellowley, somewhat commoved by these appearances, asked Mordaunt, with a voice which faltered with apprehension, whether he thought there was any, that is, so very much danger.

"I cannot tell," answered the youth, "I have scarce ever seen such a storm. Norna can tell us better than any one when it will abate; for no one in these islands can judge of the weather like her."

"And is that all thou thinkest Norna can do?" said the sibyl; "thou shalt know her powers are not bounded within such a narrow space. Hear me, Mordaunt, youth of a foreign land, but of a friendly heart. Dost thou quit this doomed mansion with those who now prepare to leave it?"

"I do not—I will not, Norna," replied Mordaunt; "I know not your motive for desiring me to remove, and I will not leave, upon these dark threats, the house in which I have been kindly received in such a tempest as this. If the owners are unaccustomed to our practice of unlimited hospitality, I am the more obliged to them that they have relaxed their usages and opened their doors in my behalf."

"He is a brave lad," said Mistress Baby, whose superstitious feelings had been daunted by the threats of the supposed sorceress, and who, amidst her eager, narrow, and repining disposition, had, like all who possess marked character, some sparks of higher feeling, which made her sympathise with generous sentiments, though she thought it too expensive to entertain them at her own cost—"he is a brave lad," she again repeated, "and worthy of ten geese, if I had them to boil for him, or roast either. I'll warrant him a gentleman's son, and no churl's blood."

"Hear me, young Mordaunt," said Norna, "and depart from

this house. Fate has high views on you; you shall not remain in this hovel to be crushed amid its worthless ruins, with the relics of its more worthless inhabitants, whose life is as little to the world as the vegetation of the house-leek which now grows on their thatch, and which shall soon be crushed amongst their mangled limbs."

"I—I—I will go forth," said Yellowley, who, despite of his bearing himself scholarly and wisely, was beginning to be terrified for the issue of the adventure; for the house was old, and the walls rocked formidably to the blast.

"To what purpose?" said his sister. "I trust the Prince of the power of the air has not yet such-like power over those that are made in God's image that a good house should fall about our heads because a randy quean (here she darted a fierce glance at the pythoness) should boast us with her glamour, as if we were sae mony dogs to crouch at her bidding!"

"I was only wanting," said Triptolemus, ashamed of his motion, "to look at the bear-braird, which must be sair laid wi' this tempest; but if this honest woman like to bide wi' us, I think it were best to let us a' sit doun canny thegither, till it's working weather again."

"Honest woman!" echoed Baby. "Foul warlock thief! Aroint ye, ye limmer!" she added, addressing Norna directly; "out of an honest house, or, shame fa' me, but I'll take the bittle [1] to you!"

Norna cast on her a look of supreme contempt; then, stepping to the window, seemed engaged in deep contemplation of the heavens, while the old maid-servant, Tronda, drawing close to her mistress, implored, for the sake of all that was dear to man or woman: "Do not provoke Norna of Fitful Head! You have no sic woman on the mainland of Scotland: she can ride on one of these clouds as easily as man ever rode on a sheltie."

"I shall live to see her ride on the reek of a fat tar-barrel," said Mistress Baby; "and that will be a fit pacing palfrey for her."

Again Norna regarded the enraged Mrs. Baby Yellowley

[1] See Note 11.

with a look of that unutterable scorn which her haughty features could so well express, and moving to the window which looked to the northwest, from which quarter the gale seemed at present to blow, she stood for some time with her arms crossed, looking out upon the leaden-coloured sky, obscured as it was by the thick drift, which, coming on in successive gusts of tempest, left ever and anon sad and dreary intervals of expectation betwixt the dying and the reviving blast.

Norna regarded this war of the elements as one to whom their strife was familiar; yet the stern serenity of her features had in it a cast of awe, and at the same time of authority, as the cabalist may be supposed to look upon the spirit he has evoked, and which, though he knows how to subject him to his spell, bears still an aspect appalling to flesh and blood. The attendants stood by in different attitudes, expressive of their various feelings. Mordaunt, though not indifferent to the risk in which they stood, was more curious than alarmed. He had heard of Norna's alleged power over the elements, and now expected an opportunity of judging for himself of its reality. Triptolemus Yellowley was confounded at what seemed to be far beyond the bounds of his philosophy; and, if the truth must be spoken, the worthy agriculturist was greatly more frightened than inquisitive. His sister was not in the least curious on the subject; but it was difficult to say whether anger or fear predominated in her sharp eyes and thin, compressed lips. The pedlar and old Tronda, confident that the house would never fall while the redoubted Norna was beneath its roof, held themselves ready for a start the instant she should take her departure.

Having looked on the sky for some time in a fixed attitude, and with the most profound silence, Norna at once, yet with a slow and elevated gesture, extended her staff of black oak towards that part of the heavens from which the blast came hardest, and in the midst of its fury chanted a Norwegian invocation, still preserved in the Island of Uist [Unst?], under the name of the "Song of the Reim-kennar," though some call it the "Song of the Tempest." The following is a free translation, it being impossible to render literally many of the elliptical and metaphorical terms of expression, peculiar to the ancient Northern poetry:

Song of the Reim=kennar

Stern eagle of the far northwest,
Thou that bearest in thy grasp the thunderbolt,
Thou whose rushing pinions stir ocean to madness,
Thou the destroyer of herds, thou the scatterer of navies,
Thou the breaker down of towers,
Amidst the scream of thy rage,
Amidst the rushing of thy onward wings,
Though thy scream be loud as the cry of a perishing nation,
Though the rushing of thy wings be like the roar of ten thousand waves,
Yet hear, in thine ire and thy haste,
Hear thou the voice of the Reim-kennar.

Thou hast met the pine-trees of Drontheim,
Their dark-green heads lie prostrate beside their uprooted stems,
Thou has met the rider of the ocean,
The tall, the strong bark of the fearless rover,
And she has struck to thee the topsail
That she had not veiled to a royal armada;
Thou hast met the tower that bears its crest among the clouds
The battled massive tower of the jarl of former days,
And the copestone of the turret
Is lying upon its hospitable hearth;
But thou too shalt stoop, proud compeller of clouds,
When thou hearest the voice of the Reim-kennar.

There are verses that can stop the stag in the forest,
Ay, and when the dark-coloured dog is opening on his track
There are verses can make the wild hawk pause on the wing,
Like the falcon that wears the hood and the jesses,
And who knows the shrill whistle of the fowler.
Thou who canst mock at the scream of the drowning mariner,
And the crash of the ravaged forest,
And the groan of the overwhelmed crowds,
When the church hath fallen in the moment of prayer,
There are sounds which thou also must list,
When they are chanted by the voice of the Reim-kennar.

Enough of woe hast thou wrought on the ocean:
The widows wring their hands on the beach.
Enough of woe hast thou wrought on the land:
The husbandman folds his arms in despair.
Cease thou the waving of thy pinions,
Let the ocean repose in her dark strength;
Cease thou the flashing of thine eye:
Let the thunderbolt sleep in the armoury of Odin.
Be thou still at my bidding, viewless racer of the northwestern heaven,
Sleep thou at the voice of Norna the Reim-kennar!

We have said that Mordaunt was naturally fond of romantic poetry and romantic situation; it is not therefore surprising that he listened with interest to the wild address thus uttered to the wildest wind of the compass, in a tone of such dauntless enthusiasm. But though he had heard so much of the Runic rhyme and of the Northern spell, in the country where he had so long dwelt, he was not on this occasion so credulous as to believe that the tempest, which had raged so lately, and which was now beginning to decline, was subdued before the charmed verse of Norna. Certain it was, that the blast seemed passing away, and the apprehended danger was already over; but it was not improbable that this issue had been for some time foreseen by the pythoness, through signs of the weather imperceptible to those who had not dwelt long in the country, or had not bestowed on the meteorological phenomena the attention of a strict and close observer. Of Norna's experience he had no doubt, and that went a far way to explain what seemed supernatural in her demeanour. Yet still the noble countenance, half-shaded by dishevelled tresses, the air of majesty with which, in a tone of menace as well as of command, she addressed the viewless spirit of the tempest, gave him a strong inclination to believe in the ascendency of the occult arts over the powers of nature; for, if a woman ever moved on earth to whom such authority over the ordinary laws of the universe could belong, Norna of Fitful Head, judging from bearing, figure, and face, was born to that high destiny.

The rest of the company were less slow in receiving conviction. To Tronda and the jagger none was necessary: they had long believed in the full extent of Norna's authority over the elements. But Triptolemus and his sister gazed at each other with wondering and alarmed looks, especially when the wind began perceptibly to decline, as was remarkably visible during the pauses which Norna made betwixt the strophes of her incantation. A long silence followed the last verse, until Norna resumed her chant, but with a changed and more soothing modulation of voice and tune:

" Eagle of the far northwestern waters.
Thou hast heard the voice of the Reim-kennar,

Thou hast closed thy wide sails at her bidding,
And folded them in peace by thy side.
My blessing be on thy retiring path!
When thou stoopest from thy place on high,
Soft be thy slumbers in the caverns of the unknown ocean,
Rest till destiny shall again awaken thee;
Eagle of the northwest, thou has heard the voice of the Reim-kennar!"

"A pretty sang that would be to keep the corn from shaking in har'st," whispered the agriculturist to his sister; "we must speak her fair, Baby: she will maybe part with the secret for a hundred pund Scots."

"An hundred fules' heads!" replied Baby; "bid her five merks of ready siller. I never knew a witch in my life but she was as poor as Job."

Norna turned towards them as if she had guessed their thoughts; it may be that she did so. She passed them with a look of the most sovereign contempt, and walking to the table on which the preparations for Mrs. Barbara's frugal meal were already disposed, she filled a small wooden quaigh from an earthern pitcher which contained bland, a subacid liquor made out of the serous part of the milk; she broke a single morsel from a barley-cake, and having eaten and drunk, returned towards the churlish hosts. "I give you no thanks," she said, "for my refreshment, for you bid me not welcome to it; and thanks bestowed on a churl are like the dew of heaven on the cliffs of Foulah, where it finds nought that can be refreshed by its influences. I give you no thanks," she said again, but drawing from her pocket a leathern purse that seemed large and heavy, she added: "I pay you with what you will value more than the gratitude of the whole inhabitants of Hialtland. Say not that Norna of Fitful Head hath eaten of your bread and drunk of your cup, and left you sorrowing for the charge to which she hath put your house." So saying, she laid on the table a small piece of antique gold coin. bearing the rude and half-defaced effigies of some ancient Northern king.

Tripotolemus and his sister exclaimed against this liberality with vehemence; the first protesting that he kept no public, and the other exclaiming: "Is the carline mad?

Heard ye ever of ony of the gentle house of Clinkscale that gave meat for siller?"

"Or for love either?" muttered her brother; "haud to that, tittie."

"What are ye whittie-whattieing about, ye gowk?" said his gentle sister, who suspected the tenor of his murmurs. "Gie the lady back her bonny die there, and be blythe to be sae rid on't: it will be a sclate-stane the morn, if not something worse."

The honest factor lifted the money to return it, yet could not help being struck when he saw the impression, and his hand trembled as he handed it to his sister.

"Yes," said the pythoness again, as if she read the thoughts of the astonished pair, "you have seen that coin before; beware how you use it! It thrives not with the sordid or the mean-souled; it was won with honourable danger, and must be expended with honourable liberality. The treasure which lies under a cold hearth will one day, like the hidden talent, bear witness against its avaricious possessors."

The last obscure intimation seemed to raise the alarm and the wonder of Mrs. Baby and her brother to the uttermost. The latter tried to stammer out something like an invitation to Norna to tarry with them all night, or at least to take share of the "dinner," so he at first called it; but looking at the company, and remembering the limited contents of the pot, he corrected the phrase, and hoped she would take some part of the "snack, which would be on the table ere a man could loose a pleugh."

"I eat not here—I sleep not here," replied Norna; "nay, I relieve you not only of my own presence, but I will dismiss your unwelcome guests. Mordaunt," she added, addressing young Mertoun, "the dark fit is past, and your father looks for you this evening."

"Do you return in that direction?" said Mordaunt. "I will but eat a morsel, and give you my aid, good mother, on the road. The brooks must be out, and the journey perilous."

"Our roads lie different," answered the sibyl, "and Norna needs not mortal arm to aid her on the way. I am summoned far to the east, by those who know well how to smooth my passage. For thee, Bryce Snailsfoot," she continued, speaking to the pedlar, "speed thee on to Sumburgh: the Roost will afford thee a gallant harvest, and worthy the gathering in. Much goodly ware will ere now be seeking a new owner, and the careful skipper will sleep still enough in the deep *haaf*, and care not that bale and chest are dashing against the shores."

"Na—na, good mother," answered Snailsfoot, "I desire no man's life for my private advantage, and am just grateful for the blessing of Providence on my sma' trade. But, doubtless, one man's loss is another's gain; and as these storms destroy a thing on land, it is but fair they suld send us something by sea. Sae, taking the freedom, like yoursell, mother, to borrow a lump of barley-bread and a draught of bland, I will bid good-day and thank you to this good gentleman and lady, and e'en go on my way to Jarlshof, as you advise."

"Ay," replied the pythoness, "where the slaughter is, the eagles will be gathered; and where the wreck is on the shore, the jagger is as busy to purchase spoil as the shark to gorge upon the dead."

This rebuke, if it was intended for such, seemed above the comprehension of the travelling-merchant, who, bent upon gain, assumed the knapsack and ell-wand, and asked Mordaunt, with the familiarity permitted in a wild country, whether he would not take company along with him?

"I wait to eat some dinner with Mr. Yellowley and Mrs. Baby," answered the youth, "and will set forward in half an hour."

"Then I'll just take my piece in my hand," said the pedlar. Accordingly, he muttered a benediction, and, without more ceremony, helped himself to what, in Mrs. Baby's covetous eyes, appeared to be two-thirds of the bread, took a long pull at the jug of bland, seized on a handful of the small fish called sillocks, which the domestic was just placing on the board, and left the room without farther ceremony.

"My certie," said the despoiled Mrs. Baby, "there is the chapman's drouth [1] and his hunger baith, as folk say! If the

See Note 12.

laws against vagrants be executed this gate—— It's no that
I wad shut the door against decent folk," she said, looking to
Mordaunt, "more especially in such judgment-weather. But
I see the goose is dished, poor thing."

This she spoke in a tone of affection for the smoked goose,
which, though it had long been an inanimate inhabitant of
her chimney, was far more interesting to Mrs. Baby in that
state than when it screamed amongst the clouds. Mordaunt
laughed and took his seat, then turned to look for Norna; but
she had glided from the apartment during the discussion with
the pedlar.

"I am glad she is gane, the dour carline," said Mrs. Baby,
"though she has left that piece of gowd to be an everlasting
shame to us."

"Whisht, mistress, for the love of Heaven!" said Tronda
Dronsdaughter; "wha kens where she may be this moment?
We are no sure but she may hear us, though we cannot see her."

Mistress Baby cast a startled eye around, and instantly recovering herself, for she was naturally courageous as well as
violent, said: "I bade her aroint before, and I bid her aroint
again, whether she sees me or hears me, whether she's ower
the cairn and awa'. And you, ye silly sumph," she said to
poor Yellowley, "what do ye stand glowering there for? *You*
a Saunt Andrew's student!—*you* studied lair and Latin humanities, as ye ca' them, and daunted wi' the clavers of an auld
randy wife. Say your best college grace, man, and witch or
nae witch, we'll eat our dinner, and defy her. And for the
value of the gowden piece, it shall never be said I pouched
her siller. I will gie it to some poor body—that is, I will
test [1] upon it at my death, and keep it for a purse-penny till
that day comes, and that's no using it in the way of spending
siller. Say your best college grace, man, and let us eat and
drink in the mean time."

"Ye had muckle better say an *oraamus* to St. Ronald, [2] and
fling a saxpence ower your left shouther, master," said Tronda.

---

[1] Test upon it, *i.e.* leave it in my will—a mode of bestowing charity to
which many are partial as well as the good dame in the text.
[2] See Note 13.

"That ye may pick it up, ye jaud," said the implacable Mistress Baby; "it will be lang or ye win the worth of it ony other gate. Sit down, Triptolemus, and mindna the words of a daft wife."

"Daft or wise," replied Yellowley, very much disconcerted, "she kens more than I would wish she kenn'd. It was awfu' to see sic a wind fa' at the voice of flesh and blood like oursells; and then yon about the hearth-stane. I cannot but think——"

"If ye cannot but think," said Mrs. Baby, very sharply, "at least ye can haud your tongue."

The agriculturist made no reply, but sate down to their scanty meal, and did the honours of it with unusual heartiness to his new guest, the first of the intruders who had arrived, and the last who left them. The sillocks speedily disappeared, and the smoked goose, with its appendages, took wing so effectually that Tronda, to whom the polishing of the bones had been destined, found the task accomplished, or nearly so, to her hand. After dinner, the host produced his bottle of brandy; but Mordaunt, whose general habits were as abstinent almost as those of his father, laid a very light tax upon this unusual exertion of hospitality.

During the meal, they learned so much of young Mordaunt and of his father that even Baby resisted his wish to reassume his wet garments, and pressed him (at the risk of an expensive supper being added to the charges of the day) to tarry with them till the next morning. But what Norna had said excited the youth's wish to reach home, nor, however far the hospitality of Stourburgh was extended in his behalf, did the house present any particular temptations to induce him to remain there longer. He therefore accepted the loan of the factor's clothes, promising to return them and send for his own; and took a civil leave of his host and Mistress Baby, the latter of whom, however affected by the loss of her goose, could not but think the cost well bestowed (since it was to be expended at all) upon so handsome and cheerful a youth.

CHAPTER VII.

She does no work by halves, yon raving ocean;
Engulfing those she strangles, her wild womb
Affords the mariners whom she hath dealt on,
Their death at once, and sepulchre.

Old Play.

THERE were ten "lang Scots miles" betwixt Stourburgh and Jarlshof; and though the pedestrian did not number all the impediments which crossed Tam o' Shanter's path—for in a country where there are neither hedges nor stone inclosures, there can be neither "slaps nor stiles"—yet the number and nature of the "mosses and waters" which he had to cross in his peregrination was fully sufficient to balance the account, and to render his journey as toilsome and dangerous as Tam o' Shanter's celebrated retreat from Ayr. Neither witch nor warlock crossed Mordaunt's path, however. The length of the day was already considerable, and he arrived safe at Jarlshof by eleven o'clock at night. All was still and dark round the mansion, and it was not till he had whistled twice or thrice beneath Swertha's window that she replied to the signal.

At the first sound, Swertha fell into an agreeable dream of a young whale-fisher who some forty years before used to make such a signal beneath the window of her hut; at the second, she waked to remember that Johnnie Fea had slept sound among the frozen waves of Greenland for this many a year, and that she was Mr. Mertoun's governante at Jarlshof; at the third, she arose and opened the window.

"Whae is that," she demanded, "at sic an hour of the night?"

"It is I," said the youth.

"And what for comena ye in? The door's on the latch, and there is a gathering-peat on the kitchen fire, and a spunk beside it; ye can light your ain candle."

"All well," replied Mordaunt; "but I want to know how my father is."

"Just in his ordinary, gude gentleman; asking for you,

Maister Mordaunt; ye are ower far and ower late in your walks, young gentleman."

"Then the dark hour has passed, Swertha?"

"In troth has it, Maister Mordaunt," answered the gouvernante; "and your father is very reasonably good-natured for him, poor gentleman. I spake to him twice yesterday without his speaking first; and the first time he answered me as civil as you could do, and the neist time he bade me no plague him; and then, thought I, three times were aye canny, so I spake to him again for luck's sake, and he called me a chattering old devil; but it was quite and clean in a civil sort of way."

"Enough—enough, Swertha," answered Mordaunt; "and now get up and find me something to eat, for I have dined but poorly."

"Then you have been at the new folks' at Stourburgh; for there is no another house in a' the isles but they wad hae gi'en ye the best share of the best they had. Saw ye aught of Norna of the Fitful Head? She went to Stourburgh this morning, and returned to the town at night."

"Returned! then she is here? How could she travel three leagues and better in so short a time?"

"Wha kens how she travels?" replied Swertha; "but I heard her tell the Ranzelman wi' my ain lugs that she intended that day to have gone on to Burgh-Westra, to speak with Minna Troil, but she had seen that at Stourburgh—indeed, she said at Harfra, for she never calls it by the other name of Stourburgh—that sent her back to our town. But gang your ways round, and ye shall have plenty of supper: ours is nae toom pantry, and still less a locked ane, though my master be a stranger, and no just that tight in the upper rigging, as the Ranzelman says."

Mordaunt walked round to the kitchen accordingly, where Swertha's care speedily accommodated him with a plentiful though coarse meal, which indemnified him for the scanty hospitality he had experienced at Stourburgh.

In the morning, some feelings of fatigue made young Mertoun later than usual in leaving his bed; so that, contrary to

what was the ordinary case, he found his father in the apartment where they eat, and which served them indeed for
every common purpose, save that of a bedchamber or of a
kitchen. The son greeted the father in mute reverence, and
waited until he should address him.

"You were absent yesterday, Mordaunt?" said his father.
Mordaunt's absence had lasted a week and more; but he had
often observed that his father never seemed to notice how time
passed during the period when he was affected with his sullen
vapours. He assented to what the elder Mr. Mertoun had
said.

"And you were at Burgh-Westra, as I think?" continued
his father.

"Yes, sir," replied Mordaunt.

The elder Mertoun was then silent for some time, and paced
the floor in deep silence, with an air of sombre reflection, which
seemed as if he were about to relapse into his moody fit. Suddenly turning to his son, however, he observed, in the tone of
a query: "Magnus Troil has two daughters—they must be now
young women; they are thought handsome, of course?"

"Very generally, sir," answered Mordaunt, rather surprised
to hear his father making any inquiries about the individuals
of a sex which he usually thought so light of—a surprise
which was much increased by the next question, put as
abruptly as the former.

"Which think you the handsomest?"

"I, sir?" replied his son with some wonder, but without
embarrassment, "I really am no judge. I never considered
which was absolutely the handsomest. They are both very
pretty young women."

"You evade my question, Mordaunt; perhaps I have some
very particular reason for my wish to be acquainted with your
taste in this matter. I am not used to waste words for no
purpose. I ask you again, which of Magnus Troil's daughters you think most handsome?"

"Really, sir," replied Mordaunt—"but you only jest in
asking me such a question."

"Young man," replied Mertoun, with eyes which began to

roll and sparkle with impatience, "I *never* jest. I desire an answer to my question."

"Then, upon my word, sir," said Mordaunt, "it is not in my power to form a judgment betwixt the young ladies; they are both very pretty, but by no means like each other. Minna is dark-haired, and more grave than her sister—more serious, but by no means either dull or sullen."

"Um," replied his father; "you have been gravely brought up, and this Minna, I suppose, pleases you most?"

"No, sir, really I can give her no preference over her sister Brenda, who is as gay as a lamb in a spring morning; less tall than her sister, but so well formed and so excellent a dancer——"

"That she is best qualified to amuse the young man who has a dull home and a moody father?" said Mr. Mertoun.

Nothing in his father's conduct had ever surprised Mordaunt so much as the obstinacy with which he seemed to pursue a theme so foreign to his general train of thought and habits of conversation; but he contented himself with answering once more: "That both the young ladies were highly admirable, but he had never thought of them with the wish to do either injustice by ranking her lower than her sister; that others would probably decide between them, as they happened to be partial to a grave or a gay disposition, or to a dark or fair complexion; but that he could see no excellent quality in the one that was not balanced by something equally captivating in the other."

It is possible that even the coolness with which Mordaunt made this explanation might not have satisfied his father concerning the subject of investigation; but Swertha at this moment entered with breakfast, and the youth, notwithstanding his late supper, engaged in that meal with an air which satisfied Mertoun that he held it matter of more grave importance than the conversation which they had just had, and that he had nothing more to say upon the subject explanatory of the answers he had already given. He shaded his brow with his hand, and looked on fixedly upon the young man as he was busied with his morning meal. There was neither abstraction nor a sense of being observed in any of his motions: all was frank, natural, and open.

"He is fancy free," muttered Mertoun to himself, "so young, so lively, and so imaginative, so handsome and so attractive in face and person, strange that at his age, and in his circumstances, he should have avoided the meshes which catch all the world beside!"

When the breakfast was over, the elder Mertoun, instead of proposing, as usual, that his son, who awaited his commands, should betake himself to one branch or other of his studies, assumed his hat and staff, and desired that Mordaunt should accompany him to the top of the cliff, called Sumburgh Head, and from thence look out upon the state of the ocean, agitated as it must still be by the tempest of the preceding day. Mordaunt was at the age when young men willingly exchange sedentary pursuits for active exercise, and started up with alacrity to comply with his father's desire; and in the course of a few minutes they were mounting together the hill, which, ascending from the land side in a long, steep, and grassy slope, sinks at once from the summit to the sea in an abrupt and tremendous precipice.

The day was delightful; there was just so much motion in the air as to disturb the little fleecy clouds which were scattered on the horizon, and by floating them occasionally over the sun, to chequer the landscape with that variety of light and shade which often gives to a bare and uninclosed scene, for the time at least, a species of charm approaching to the varieties of a cultivated and planted country. A thousand flitting hues of light and shade played over the expanse of wild moor, rocks, and inlets, which, as they climbed higher and higher, spread in wide and wider circuit around them.

The elder Mertoun often paused and looked round upon the scene, and for some time his son supposed that he halted to enjoy its beauties; but as they ascended still higher up the hill, he remarked his shortened breath and his uncertain and toilsome step, and became assured, with some feelings of alarm, that his father's strength was, for the moment, exhausted, and that he found the ascent more toilsome and fatiguing than usual. To draw close to his side, and offer him in silence the assistance of his arm, was an act of youthful deference to advanced age, as well as of filial reverence; and Mertoun seemed at first so to receive it, for he took in silence the advantage of the aid thus afforded him.

It was but for two or three minutes, however, that the father availed himself of his son's support. They had not ascended fifty yards farther ere he pushed Mordaunt suddenly, if not rudely, from him; and, as if stung into exertion by some sudden recollection, began to mount the acclivity with such long and quick steps that Mordaunt, in his turn, was obliged to exert himself to keep pace with him. He knew his father's peculiarity of disposition; he was aware, from many slight circumstances, that he loved him not even while he took much pains with his education, and while he seemed to be the sole object of his care upon earth. But the conviction had never been more strongly or more powerfully forced upon him than by the hasty churlishness with which Mertoun rejected from a son that assistance which most elderly men are willing to receive from youths with whom they are but slightly connected, as a tribute which it is alike graceful to yield and pleasing to receive. Mertoun, however, did not seem to perceive the effect which his unkindness had produced upon his son's feelings. He paused upon a sort of level terrace which they had now attained, and addressed his son with an indifferent tone, which seemed in some degree affected.

"Since you have so few inducements, Mordaunt, to remain in these wild islands, I suppose you sometimes wish to look a little more abroad into the world?"

"By my word, sir," replied Mordaunt, "I cannot say I ever have a thought on such a subject."

"And why not, young man?" demanded his father; "it were but natural, I think, at your age. At your age, the fair and varied breadth of Britain could not gratify me, much less the compass of a sea-girdled peat-moss."

"I have never thought of leaving Zetland, sir," replied the son. "I am happy here, and have friends. You yourself, sir, would miss me, unless indeed——"

"Why, thou wouldst not persuade me," said his father, somewhat hastily, "that you stay here, or desire to stay here, for the love of me?

"Why should I not, sir?" answered Mordaunt, mildly; "it is my duty, and I hope I have hitherto performed it."

"Oh ay," repeated Mertoun, in the same tone, "your duty— your duty. "So it is the duty of the dog to follow the groom that feeds him."

"And does he not do so, sir?" said Mordaunt.

"Ay," said his father, turning his head aside; "but he fawns only on those who caress him."

"I hope, sir," replied Mordaunt, "I have not been found deficient?"

"Say no more on't—say no more on't," said Mertoun, abruptly; "we have both done enough by each other; we must soon part. Let that be our comfort, if our separation should require comfort."

"I shall be ready to obey your wishes," said Mordaunt, not altogether displeased at what promised him an opportunity of looking farther abroad into the world. "I presume it will be your pleasure that I commence my travels with a season at the whale-fishing."

"Whale-fishing!" replied Mertoun; "that were a mode indeed of seeing the world! but thou speakest but as thou hast learned. Enough of this for the present. Tell me where you had shelter from the storm yesterday?"

"At Stourburgh, the house of the new factor from Scotland."

"A pedantic, fantastic, visionary schemer," said Mertoun; "and whom saw you there?"

"His sister, sir," replied Mordaunt, "and old Norna of the Fitful Head."

"What! the mistress of the potent spell," answered Mertoun, with a sneer—"she who can change the wind by pulling her curch on one side, as King Erick used to do by turning his cap? The dame journeys far from home; how fares she? Does she get rich by selling favourable winds[1] to those who are port-bound?"

"I really do not know, sir," said Mordaunt, whom certain recollections prevented from freely entering into his father's humour.

"You think the matter too serious to be jested with, or perhaps esteem her merchandise too light to be cared after?" continued Mertoun, in the same sarcastic tone, which was the nearest approach he ever made to cheerfulness; "but consider it more deeply. Everything in the universe is bought and sold, and why not wind, if the merchant can find purchasers? The earth is rented, from its surface down to its most central mines; the fire, and the means of feeding it, are currently bought and sold; the wretches that sweep the boisterous ocean with their nets pay ransom for the privilege of being drowned in it. What title has the air to be exempted from the universal course of traffic? All above the earth, under the earth, and around the earth has its price, its sellers, and its purchasers. In many countries the priests will sell you a portion of Heaven; in all countries men are willing to buy, in exchange for health, wealth, and peace of conscience, a full allowance of Hell. Why should not Norna pursue her traffic?"

"Nay I know no reason against it," replied Mordaunt; "only I wish she would part with the commodity in smaller quantities. Yesterday she was a wholesale dealer; whoever treated with her had too good a pennyworth."

"It is even so," said his father, pausing on the verge of the wild promontory which they had attained, where the huge precipice sinks abruptly down on the wide and tempestuous ocean, "and the effects are still visible."

The face of that lofty cape is composed of the soft and crumbling stone called sand-flag, which gradually becomes decomposed, and yields to the action of the atmosphere, and is split into large masses, that hang loose upon the verge of the precipice, and, detached from it by the violence of the tempests, often descend with great fury into the vexed abyss which lashes the foot of the rock. Numbers of these huge fragments lie strewed beneath the rocks from which they have fallen, and amongst these the tide foams and rages with a fury peculiar to those latitudes.

At the period when Mertoun and his son looked from the verge of the precipice, the wide sea still heaved and swelled with the agitation of yesterday's storm, which had been far too violent in its effects on the ocean to subside speedily. The tide therefore poured on the headland with a fury deafening to the ear and dizzying to the eye, threatening instant destruction to whatever might be at the time involved in its current. The sight of nature, in her magnificence, or in her beauty, or in her terrors, has at all times an overpowering interest, which even habit cannot greatly weaken; and both father and son sat themselves down on the cliff to look out upon that unbounded war of waters which rolled in their wrath to the foot of the precipice.

At once Mordaunt, whose eyes were sharper, and probably his attention more alert, than that of his father, started up and exclaimed: " God in Heaven! there is a vessel in the Roost!"

Mertoun looked to the northwestward, and an object was visible amid the rolling tide. " She shows no sail," he observed; and immediately added, after looking at the object through his spy-glass: " She is dismasted, and lies a sheer hulk upon the water."

" And is drifting on the Sumburgh Head," exclaimed Mordaunt, struck with horror, " without the slightest means of weathering the cape!"

" She makes no effort," answered his father; " she is probably deserted by her crew."

" And in such a day as yesterday," replied Mordaunt, " when no open boat could live were she manned with the best men ever handled an oar: all must have perished."

" It is most probable," said his father, with stern composure; " and one day, sooner or later, all must have perished. What signifies whether the fowler, whom nothing escapes, caught them up at one swoop from yonder shattered deck, or whether he clutched them individually, as chance gave them to his grasp! What signifies it? The deck, the battlefield are scarce more fatal to us than our table and our bed; and we are saved from the one, merely to drag out a heartless and wearisome existence till we perish at the other. Would the hour were come—that hour which reason would teach us to wish for, were it not that nature has implanted the fear of it so strongly within us! You wonder at such a reflection, because life is yet new to you. Ere you have attained my age, it will be the familiar companion of your thoughts."

"Surely, sir," replied Mordaunt, "such distaste to life is not the necessary consequence of advanced age?"

"To all who have sense to estimate that which it is really worth," said Mertoun. "Those who, like Magnus Troil, possess so much of the animal impulses about them as to derive pleasure from sensual gratification may, perhaps, like the animals, feel pleasure in mere existence."

Mordaunt liked neither the doctrine nor the example. He thought a man who discharged his duties towards others as well as the good old Udaller had a better right to have the sun shine fair on his setting than that which he might derive from mere insensibility. But he let the subject drop, for to dispute with his father had always the effect of irritating him, and again he adverted to the condition of the wreck.

The hulk, for it was little better, was now in the very midst of the current, and drifting at a great rate towards the foot of the precipice, upon whose verge they were placed. Yet it was a long while ere they had a distinct view of the object which they had at first seen as a black speck amongst the waters, and then, at a nearer distance, like a whale, which now scarce shows its back-fin above the waves, now throws to view its large black side. Now, however, they could more distinctly observe the appearance of the ship, for the huge swelling waves which bore her forward to the shore heaved her alternately high upon the surface, and then plunged her into the trough or furrow of the sea. She seemed a vessel of two or three hundred tons, fitted up for defence, for they could see her port-holes. She had been dismasted probably in the gale of the preceding day, and lay water-logged on the waves, a prey to their violence. It appeared certain that the crew, finding themselves unable either to direct the vessel's course or to relieve her by pumping, had taken to their boats and left her to her fate. All apprehensions were therefore unnecessary, so far as the immediate loss of human lives was concerned; and yet it was not without a feeling of breathless awe that Mordaunt and his father beheld the vessel—that rare masterpiece by which human genius aspires to surmount the waves and contend with the winds—upon the point of falling a prey to them.

Onward she came, the large black hulk seeming larger at every fathom's length. She came nearer, until she bestrode the summit of one tremendous billow, which rolled on with her unbroken, till the wave and its burden were precipitated against the rock, and then the triumph of the elements over the work of human hands was at once completed. One wave, we have said, made the wrecked vessel completely manifest in her whole bulk, as it raised her and bore her onward against the face of the precipice. But when that wave receded from the foot of the rock, the ship had ceased to exist; and the retiring billow only bore back a quantity of beams, planks, casks, and similar objects, which swept out to the offing, to be brought in again by the next wave, and again precipitated upon the face of the rock.

It was at this moment that Mordaunt conceived he saw a man floating on a plank or water-cask, which, drifting away from the main current, seemed about to go ashore upon a small spot of sand, where the water was shallow and the waves broke more smoothly. To see the danger and to exclaim, "He lives, and may yet be saved!" was the first impulse of the fearless Mordaunt. The next was, after one rapid glance at the front of the cliff, to precipitate himself—such seemed the rapidity of his movement—from the verge, and to commence, by means of slight fissures, projections, and crevices in the rock, a descent which, to a spectator, appeared little else than an act of absolute insanity.

"Stop, I command you, rash boy!" said his father; "the attempt is death. Stop, and take the safer path to the left." But Mordaunt was already completely engaged in his perilous enterprise.

"Why should I prevent him?" said his father, checking his

anxiety with the stern and unfeeling philosophy whose principles he had adopted. "Should he die now, full of generous and high feeling, eager in the cause of humanity, happy in the exertion of his own conscious activity and youthful strength—should he die now, will he not escape misanthropy, and remorse, and age, and the consciousness of decaying powers, both of body and mind? I will not look upon it, however. I will not—I cannot behold his young light so suddenly quenched."

He turned from the precipice accordingly, and hastening to the left for more than a quarter of a mile, he proceeded towards a "riva," or cleft in the rock, containing a path, called Erick's Steps, neither safe, indeed, nor easy, but the only one by which the inhabitants of Jarlshof were wont, for any purpose, to seek access to the foot of the precipice.

But, long ere Mertoun had reached even the upper end of the pass, his adventurous and active son had accomplished his more desperate enterprise. He had been in vain turned aside from the direct line of descent by the intervention of difficulties which he had not seen from above: his route became only more circuitous, but could not be interrupted. More than once, large fragments to which he was about to entrust his weight gave way before him, and thundered down into the tormented ocean; and in one or two instances such detached pieces of rock rushed after him, as if to bear him headlong in their course. A courageous heart, a steady eye, a tenacious hand, and a firm foot carried him through his desperate attempt; and in the space of seven minutes he stood at the bottom of the cliff from the verge of which he had achieved his perilous descent.

The place which he now occupied was the small projecting spot of stones, sand, and gravel that extended a little way into the sea, which on the right hand lashed the very bottom of the precipice, and on the left was scarce divided from it by a small wave-worn portion of beach that extended as far as the foot of the rent in the rocks called Erick's Steps, by which Mordaunt's father proposed to descend.

When the vessel split and went to pieces, all was swallowed

up in the ocean which had, after the first shock, been seen to float upon the waves, excepting only a few pieces of wreck, casks, chests, and the like, which a strong eddy, formed by the reflux of the waves, had landed, or at least grounded, upon the shallow where Mordaunt now stood. Amongst these, his eager eye discovered the object that had at first engaged his attention, and which now, seen at nigher distance, proved to be in truth a man, and in a most precarious state. His arms were still wrapt with a close and convulsive grasp round the plank to which he had clung in the moment of the shock, but sense and the power of motion were fled; and, from the situation in which the plank lay, partly grounded upon the beach, partly floating in the sea, there was every chance that it might be again washed off shore, in which case death was inevitable. Just as he had made himself aware of these circumstances, Mordaunt beheld a huge wave advancing, and hastened to interpose his aid ere it burst, aware that the reflux might probably sweep away the sufferer.

He rushed into the surf, and fastened on the body with the same tenacity, though under a different impulse, with that wherewith the hound seizes his prey. The strength of the retiring wave proved even greater than he had expected, and it was not without a struggle for his own life, as well as for that of the stranger, that Mordaunt resisted being swept off with the receding billow, when, though an adroit swimmer, the strength of the tide must either have dashed him against the rocks or hurried him out to sea. He stood his ground, however, and ere another such billow had returned, he drew up, upon the small slip of dry sand, both the body of the stranger and the plank to which he continued firmly attached. But how to save and to recall the means of ebbing life and strength, and how to remove into a place of greater safety the sufferer, who was incapable of giving any assistance towards his own preservation, were questions which Mordaunt asked himself eagerly, but in vain.

He looked to the summit of the cliff on which he had left his father, and shouted to him for his assistance; but his eye could not distinguish his form, and his voice was only answered by the scream of the sea-birds. He gazed again on the sufferer. A dress richly laced, according to the fashion of the times, fine linen, and rings upon his fingers, evinced he was a man of superior rank; and his features showed youth and comeliness, notwithstanding they were pallid and disfigured. He still breathed, but so feebly that his respiration was almost imperceptible, and life seemed to keep such slight hold of his frame that there was every reason to fear it would become altogether extinguished, unless it were speedily reinforced. To loosen the handkerchief from his neck, to raise him with his face towards the breeze, to support him with his arms, was all that Mordaunt could do for his assistance, whilst he anxiously looked for some one who might lend his aid in dragging the unfortunate to a more safe situation.

At this moment he beheld a man advancing slowly and cautiously along the beach. He was in hopes, at first, it was his father, but instantly recollected that he had not had time to come round by the circuitous descent to which he must necessarily have recourse, and besides, he saw that the man who approached him was shorter in stature.

As he came nearer, Mordaunt was at no loss to recognise the pedlar whom the day before he had met with at Harfra, and who was known to him before upon many occasions. He shouted as loud as he could, "Bryce, halloo!—Bryce, come hither!" But the merchant, intent upon picking up some of the spoils of the wreck, and upon dragging them out of reach of the tide, paid for some time little attention to his shouts.

When he did at length approach Mordaunt, it was not to lend him his aid, but to remonstrate with him on his rashness in undertaking the charitable office. "Are you mad?" said he; "you that have lived sae lang in Zetland, to risk the saving of a drowning man? Wot ye not, if you bring him to life again, he will be sure to do you some capital injury? [1] Come, Master Mordaunt, bear a hand to what's mair to the purpose. Help me to get ane or twa of these kists ashore before anybody else comes, and we shall share, like good Christians, what God sends us, and be thankful."

[1] See Reluctance to save Drowning Men. Note 15.

7

Mordaunt was indeed no stranger to this inhuman superstition, current at a former period among the lower orders of the Zetlanders, and the more generally adopted, perhaps, that it served as an apology for refusing assistance to the unfortunate victims of shipwreck, while they made plunder of their goods. At any rate, the opinion, that to save a drowning man was to run the risk of future injury from him, formed a strange contradiction in the character of these islanders, who, hospitable, generous, and disinterested on all other occasions, were sometimes, nevertheless, induced by this superstition to refuse their aid in those mortal emergencies which were so common upon their rocky and stormy coasts. We are happy to add, that the exhortation and example of the proprietors have eradicated even the traces of this inhuman belief, of which there might be some observed within the memory of those now alive. It is strange that the minds of men should have ever been hardened towards those involved in a distress to which they themselves were so constantly exposed; but perhaps the frequent sight and consciousness of such danger tends to blunt the feelings to its consequences, whether affecting ourselves or others.

Bryce was remarkably tenacious of this ancient belief; the more so, perhaps, that the mounting of his pack depended less upon the warehouses of Lerwick or Kirkwall than on the consequences of such a northwestern gale as that of the day preceding; for which (being a man who, in his own way, professed great devotion) he seldom failed to express his grateful thanks to Heaven. It was indeed said of him, that, if he had spent the same time in assisting the wrecked seamen which he had employed in rifling their bales and boxes, he would have saved many lives, and lost much linen. He paid no sort of attention to the repeated entreaties of Mordaunt, although he was now upon the same slip of sand with him. It was well known to Bryce as a place on which the eddy was likely to land such spoils as the ocean disgorged; and, to improve the favourable moment, he occupied himself exclusively in securing and appropriating whatever seemed most portable and of greatest value. At length, Mordaunt saw the honest pedlar

fix his views upon a strong sea-chest, framed of some Indian
wood, well secured by brass plates, and seeming to be of a
foreign construction. The stout lock resisted all Bryce's
efforts to open it, until, with great composure, he plucked
from his pocket a very neat hammer and chisel, and began
forcing the hinges.

Incensed beyond patience at his assurance, Mordaunt caught
up a wooden stretcher which lay near him, and laying his
charge softly on the sand, approached Bryce with a menacing
gesture, and exclaimed: "You cold-blooded, inhuman rascal!
either get up instantly and lend me your assistance to recover
this man, and bear him out of danger from the surf, or I will
not only beat you to a mummy on the spot, but inform Magnus Troil of your thievery, that he may have you flogged till
your bones are bare, and then banish you from the Mainland!"

The lid of the chest had just sprung open as this rough address saluted Bryce's ears, and the inside presented a tempting
view of wearing-apparel for sea and land, shirts, plain and with
lace ruffles, a silver compass, a silver-hilted sword, and other
valuable articles, which the pedlar well knew to be such as stir
in the trade. He was half-disposed to start up, draw the
sword, which was a cut-and-thrust, and "darraign battaile,"
as Spenser says, rather than quit his prize or brook interruption. Being, though short, a stout, square-made personage,
and not much past the prime of life, having besides the better
weapon, he might have given Mordaunt more trouble than his
benevolent knight-errantry deserved.

Already, as with vehemence he repeated his injunctions that
Bryce should forbear his plunder and come to the assistance
of the dying man, the pedlar retorted with a voice of defiance:
"Dinna swear, sir—dinna swear, sir: I will endure no swearing in my presence; and if you lay a finger on me, that am
taking the lawful spoil of the Egyptians, I will give ye a lesson ye shall remember from this day to Yule!"

Mordaunt would speedily have put the pedlar's courage to
the test, but a voice behind him suddenly said, "Forbear!"
It was the voice of Norna of the Fitful Head, who, during the
heat of their altercation, had approached them unobserved.

"Forbear!" she repeated; "and, Bryce, do thou render Mordaunt the assistance he requires. It shall avail thee more,
and it is I who say the word, than all that you could earn
to-day besides."

"It is se'enteen hundred linen," said the pedlar, giving a
tweak to one of the shirts, in that knowing manner with which
matrons and judges ascertain the texture of the loom—"it's
se'enteen hundred linen, and as strong as an it were dowlas.
Nevertheless, mother, your bidding is to be done; and I would
have done Mr. Mordaunt's bidding too," he added, relaxing
from his note of defiance into the deferential whining tone
with which he cajoled his customers, "if he hadna made use
of profane oaths, which made my very flesh grew, and caused
me, in some sort, to forget myself." He then took a flask
from his pocket, and approached the shipwrecked man. "It's
the best of brandy," he said; "and if that doesna cure him, I
ken nought that will." So saying, he took a preliminary gulp
himself, as if to show the quality of the liquor, and was about
to put it to the man's mouth, when, suddenly withholding his
hand, he looked at Norna: "You ensure me against all risk of
evil from him, if I am to render him my help? Ye ken yoursell what folk say, mother."

For all other answer, Norna took the bottle from the pedlar's hand, and began to chafe the temples and throat of the
shipwrecked man; directing Mordaunt how to hold his head,
so as to afford him the means of disgorging the sea-water
which he had swallowed during his immersion.

The pedlar looked on inactive for a moment, and then said:
"To be sure, there is not the same risk in helping him, now
he is out of the water, and lying high and dry on the beach;
and, to be sure, the principal danger is to those that first
touch him; and, to be sure, it is a world's pity to see how
these rings are pinching the puir creature's swalled fingers:
they make his hand as blue as a partan's back before boiling."
So saying, he seized one of the man's cold hands, which had
just, by a tremulous motion, indicated the return of life, and
began his charitable work of removing the rings, which seemed
to be of some value.

"As you love your life, forbear," said Norna, sternly, "or I will lay that on you which shall spoil your travels through the isles."

"Now, for mercy's sake, mother, say nae mair about it," said the pedlar, "and I'll e'en do your pleasure in your ain way! I *did* feel a rheumatise in my back-spauld yestreen; and it wad be a sair thing for the like of me to be debarred my quiet walk round the country, in the way of trade—making the honest penny, and helping myself with what Providence sends on our coasts."

"Peace, then," said the woman—"peace, as thou wouldst not rue it; and take this man on thy broad shoulders. His life is of value, and you will be rewarded."

"I had muckle need," said the pedlar, pensively looking at the lidless chest and the other matters which strewed the sand; "for he has come between me and as muckle spreacherie as wad hae made a man of me for the rest of my life; and now it maun lie here till the next tide sweep it a' doun the Roost, after them that aught it yesterday morning."

"Fear not," said Norna, "it will come to man's use. See, there come carrion-crows of scent as keen as thine own."

She spoke truly; for several of the people from the hamlet of Jarlshof were now hastening along the beach, to have their share in the spoil. The pedlar beheld them approach with a deep groan. "Ay—ay," he said, "the folk of Jarlshof, they will make clean wark; they ae kenn'd for that far and wide; they winna leave the value of a rotten ratlin; and what's waur, there isna ane o' them has mense or sense eneugh to give thanks for the mercies when they have gotten them. There is the auld Ranzelman, Neil Ronaldson, that canna walk a mile to hear the minister, but he will hirple ten if he hears of a ship embayed."

Norna, however, seemed to possess over him so complete an ascendency, that he no longer hesitated to take the man, who now gave strong symptoms of reviving existence, upon his shoulders; and, assisted by Mordaunt, trudged along the sea-beach with his burden, without farther remonstrance. Ere he was borne off, the stranger pointed to the chest, and attempted to mutter something, to which Norna replied, "Enough. It shall be secured."

Advancing towards the passage called Erick's Steps, by which they were to ascend the cliffs, they met the people from Jarlshof hastening in the opposite direction. Man and woman, as they passed, reverently made room for Norna, and saluted her, not without an expression of fear upon some of their faces. She passed them a few paces, and then turning back, called aloud to the Ranzelman, who (though the practice was more common than legal) was attending the rest of the hamlet upon this plundering expedition. "Neil Ronaldson," she said, "mark my words. There stands yonder a chest, from which the lid has been just prized off. Look it be brought down to your own house at Jarlshof, just as it now is. Beware of moving or touching the slightest article. He were better in his grave, that so much as looks at the contents. I speak not for nought, nor in aught will I be disobeyed."

"Your pleasure shall be done, mother," said Ronaldson. "I warrant we will not break bulk, since sic is your bidding."

Far behind the rest of the villagers followed an old woman, talking to herself, and cursing her own decrepitude, which kept her the last of the party, yet pressing forward with all her might to get her share of the spoil.

When they met her, Mordaunt was astonished to recognise his father's old housekeeper. "How now," he said "Swertha, what make you so far from home?"

"Just e'en daikering out to look after my auld master and your honour," replied Swertha, who felt like a criminal caught in the manner; for, on more occasions than one, Mr. Mertoun had intimated his high disapprobation of such excursions as she was at present engaged in.

But Mordaunt was too much engaged with his own thoughts to take much notice of her delinquency. "Have you seen my father?" he said.

"And that I have," replied Swertha. "The gude gentleman was ganging to hirsel himsell doun Erick's Steps, whilk would have been the ending of him, that is in no way a cragsman. Sae I e'en gat him wiled away hame; and I was just seeking you that you may gang after him to the hall-house, for to my thought he is far frae weel."

"My father unwell?" said Mordaunt, remembering the faintness he had exhibited at the commencement of that morning's walk.

"Far frae weel—far frae weel," groaned out Swertha, with a piteous shake of the head; "white o' the gills—white o' the gills; and him to think of coming down the riva!"

"Return home, Mordaunt," said Norna, who was listening to what had passed. "I will see all that is necessary done for this man's relief, and you will find him at the Ranzelman's when you list to inquire. You cannot help him more than you already have done."

Mordaunt felt this was true, and, commanding Swertha to follow him instantly, betook himself to the path homeward.

Swertha hobbled reluctantly after her young master in the same direction, until she lost sight of him on his entering the cleft of the rock; then instantly turned about, muttering to herself: "Haste home, in good sooth!—haste home, and lose the best chance of getting a new rokelay and owerlay that I have had these ten years! By my certie, na. It's seldom sic rich godsends come on our shore: no since the 'Jenny and James' came ashore in King Charlie's time."

So saying, she mended her pace as well as she could, and, a willing mind making amends for frail limbs, posted on with wonderful despatch to put in for her share of the spoil. She soon reached the beach, where the Ranzelman, stuffing his own pouches all the while, was exhorting the rest "to part things fair and be neighbourly, and to give to the auld and helpless a share of what was going, which," he charitably remarked, "would bring a blessing on the shore, and send them mair wrecks ere winter.'"[1]

[1] See Note 16.

CHAPTER VIII.

He was a lovely youth, I guess;
The panther in the wilderness
　　Was not so fair as he;
And when he chose to sport and play,
No dolphin ever was so gay
　　Upon the tropic sea.
　　　　　　　　　　WORDSWORTH.

THE light foot of Mordaunt Mertoun was not long of bearing him to Jarlshof. He entered the house hastily, for what he himself had observed that morning corresponded in some degree with the ideas which Swertha's tale was calculated to excite. He found his father, however, in the inner apartment, reposing himself after his fatigue; and his first question satisfied him that the good dame had practised a little imposition to get rid of them both.

"Where is this dying man, whom you have so wisely ventured your own neck to relieve?" said the elder Mertoun to the younger.

"Norna, sir," replied Mordaunt, "has taken him under her charge; she understands such matters."

"And is quack as well as witch?" said the elder Mertoun. "With all my heart; it is a trouble saved. But I hastened home, on Swertha's hint, to look out for lint and bandages; for her speech was of broken bones."

Mordaunt kept silence, well knowing his father would not persevere in his inquiries upon such a matter, and not willing either to prejudice the old governante or to excite his father to one of those excesses of passion into which he was apt to burst when, contrary to his wont, he thought proper to correct the conduct of his domestic.

It was late in the day ere old Swertha returned from her expedition, heartily fatigued, and bearing with her a bundle of some bulk, containing, it would seem, her share of the spoil. Mordaunt instantly sought her out, to charge her with the deceits she had practised on both his father and himself; but the accused matron lacked not her reply.

"By her troth," she said, "she thought it was time to bid Mr. Mertoun gang hame and get bandages, when she had seen, with her ain twa een, Mordaunt ganging down the cliff like a wild-cat; it was to be thought broken bones would be the end, and lucky if bandages wad do any good; and, by her troth, she might weel tell Mordaunt his father was puirly, and him looking sae white in the gills, whilk, she wad die upon it, was the very word she used, and it was a thing that couldna be denied by man at this very moment."

"But, Swertha," said Mordaunt, as soon as her clamorous defence gave him time to speak in reply, "how came you, that should have been busy with your housewifery and your spinning, to be out this morning at Erick's Steps, in order to take all this unnecessary care of my father and me? And what is in that bundle, Swertha? for I fear, Swertha, you have been transgressing the law, and have been out upon the wrecking system."

"Fair fa' your sonsy face, and the blessing of St. Ronald upon you!" said Swertha, in a tone betwixt coaxing and jesting; "would you keep a puir body frae mending hersell, and sae muckle gear lying on the loose sand for the lifting? Hout, Maister Mordaunt, a ship ashore is a sight to wile the minister out of his very pu'pit in the middle of his preaching, muckle mair a puir auld ignorant wife frae her rock and her tow. And little did I get for my day's wark: just some rags o' cambric things, and a bit or twa of coorse claith, and siclike; the strong and the hearty get a' thing in this warld."

"Yes, Swertha," replied Mordaunt, "and that is rather hard, as you must have your share of punishment in this world and the next for robbing the poor mariners."

"Hout, callant, wha wad punish an auld wife like me for a wheen duds? Folk speak muckle black ill of Earl Patrick; but he was a freend to the shore, and made wise laws against ony body helping vessels that were like to gang on the breakers.[1] And the mariners, I have heard Bryce Jagger say, lose their right frae the time keel touches sand; and, moreover, they are dead and gane, poor souls—dead and gane, and

---

[1] This was literally true.

care little about warld's wealth now. Nay, nae mair than the great jarls and sea-kings, in the Norse days, did about the treasures that they buried in the tombs and sepulchres auld langsyne. Did I ever tell you the sang, Maister Mordaunt, how Olaf Tryguarson garr'd hide five gold crowns in the same grave with him?"

"No, Swertha," said Mordaunt, who took pleasure in tormenting the cunning old plunderer, "you never told me that; but I tell you, that the stranger whom Norna has taken down to the town will be well enough to-morrow to ask where you have hidden the goods that you have stolen from the wreck."

"But wha will tell him a word about it, hinnie?" said Swertha, looking slyly up in her young master's face. "The mair by token, since I maun tell ye, that I have a bonny remnant of silk amang the lave, that will make a dainty waistcoat to yoursell, the first merry-making ye gang to."

Mordaunt could no longer forbear laughing at the cunning with which the old dame proposed to bribe off his evidence by imparting a portion of her plunder; and, desiring her to get ready what provision she had made for dinner, he returned to his father, whom he found still sitting in the same place, and nearly in the same posture, in which he had left him.

When their hasty and frugal meal was finished, Mordaunt announced to his father his purpose of going down to the town, or hamlet, to look after the shipwrecked sailor.

The elder Mertoun assented with a nod.

"He must be ill accommodated there, sir," added his son—a hint which only produced another nod of assent. "He seemed, from his appearance," pursued Mordaunt, "to be of very good rank; and admitting these poor people do their best to receive him, in his present weak state, yet——"

"I know what you would say," said his father, interrupting him; "we, you think, ought to do something towards assisting him. Go to him, then; if he lacks money, let him name the sum, and he shall have it; but, for lodging the stranger here, and holding intercourse with him, I neither can nor will do so. I have retired to this farthest extremity of the

British Isles to avoid new friends and new faces, and none such shall intrude on me either their happiness or their misery. When you have known the world half a score of years longer, your early friends will have given you reason to remember them, and to avoid new ones for the rest of your life. Go, then—why do you stop?—rid the country of the man: let me see no one about me but those vulgar countenances, the extent and character of whose petty knavery I know, and can submit to, as to an evil too trifling to cause irritation." He then threw his purse to his son, and signed to him to depart with all speed.

Mordaunt was not long before he reached the village. In the dark abode of Neil Ronaldson, the Ranzelman, he found the stranger seated by the peat-fire, upon the very chest which had excited the cupidity of the devout Bryce Snailsfoot, the pedlar. The Ranzelman himself was absent, dividing, with all due impartiality, the spoils of the wrecked vessel amongst the natives of the community; listening to and redressing their complaints of inequality, and (if the matter in hand had not been, from beginning to end, utterly unjust and indefensible) discharging the part of a wise and prudent magistrate in all the details. For at this time, and probably until a much later period, the lower orders of the islanders entertained an opinion, common to barbarians also in the same situation, that whatever was cast on their shores became their indisputable property.

Margery Bimbister, the worthy spouse of the Ranzelman, was in the charge of the house, and introduced Mordaunt to her guest, saying, with no great ceremony: "This is the young tacksman. You will maybe tell him your name, though you will not tell it to us. If it had not been for his four quarters, it's but little you would have said to anybody, sae lang as life lasted."

The stranger arose and shook Mordaunt by the hand; observing, he understood that he had been the means of saving his life and his chest. "The rest of the property," he said, "is, I see, walking the plank; for they are as busy as the devil in a gale of wind."

"And what was the use of your seamanship, then," said Margery, "that you couldna keep off the Sumburgh Head? It would have been lang ere Sumburgh Head had come to you."

"Leave us for a moment, good Margery Bimbister," said Mordaunt; "I wish to have some private conversation with this gentleman."

"Gentleman!" said Margery, with an emphasis; "not but the man is well enough to look at," she added, again surveying him, "but I doubt if there is muckle of the gentleman about him."

Mordaunt looked at the stranger, and was of a different opinion. He was rather above the middle size, and formed handsomely as well as strongly. Mordaunt's intercourse with society was not extensive; but he thought his new acquaintance, to a bold, sunburnt, handsome countenance, which seemed to have faced various climates, added the frank and open manners of a sailor. He answered cheerfully the inquiries which Mordaunt made after his health; and maintained that one night's rest would relieve him from all the effects of the disaster he had sustained. But he spoke with bitterness of the avarice and curiosity of the Ranzelman and his spouse.

"That chattering old woman," said the stranger, "has persecuted me the whole day for the name of the ship. I think she might be contented with the share she has had of it. I was the principal owner of the vessel that was lost yonder, and they have left me nothing but my wearing apparel. Is there no magistrate, or justice of the peace, in this wild country, that would lend a hand to help one when he is among the breakers?"

Mordaunt mentioned Magnus Troil, the principal proprietor, as well as the "fowd," or provincial judge, of the district, as the person from whom he was most likely to obtain redress; and regretted that his own youth, and his father's situation as a retired stranger, should put it out of their power to afford him the protection he required.

"Nay, for your part, you have done enough," said the sailor; "but if I had five out of the forty brave fellows that are fishes' food by this time, the devil a man would I ask to do me the right that I could do for myself!"

"Forty hands!" said Mordaunt; "you were well manned for the size of the ship."

"Not so well as we needed to be. We mounted ten guns, besides chasers; but our cruise on the main had thinned us of men, and lumbered us up with goods. Six of our guns were in ballast. Hands! if I had enough of hands, we would never have miscarried so infernally. The people were knocked up with working the pumps, and so took to their boats, and left me with the vessel, to sink or swim. But the dogs had their pay, and I can afford to pardon them. The boats swamped in the current—all were lost—and here am I."

"You had come north about then, from the West Indies?" said Mordaunt.

"Ay—ay, the vessel was the "Good Hope" of Bristol, a letter of marque. She had fine luck down on the Spanish Main, both with commerce and privateering; but the luck's ended with her now. My name is Clement Cleveland, captain, and part owner, as I said before. I am a Bristol man born; my father was well known on the tollsell—old Clem Cleveland of the College Green."

Mordaunt had no right to inquire farther, and yet it seemed to him as if his own mind was but half satisfied. There was an affectation of bluntness, a sort of defiance, in the manner of the stranger, for which circumstances afforded no occasion. Captain Cleveland had suffered injustice from the islanders, but from Mordaunt he had only received kindness and protection; yet he seemed as if he involved all the neighbourhood in the wrongs he complained of. Mordaunt looked down and was silent, doubting whether it would be better to take his leave or to proceed farther in his offers of assistance. Cleveland seemed to guess at his thoughts, for he immediately added, in a conciliating manner: "I am a plain man, Master Mertoun, for that I understand is your name; and I am a ruined man to boot, and that does not mend one's good manners. But you have done a kind and friendly part by me, and it may be I think as much of it as if I thanked you more.

And so before I leave this place I'll give you my fowling-piece; she will put a hundred swan-shot through a Dutchman's cap at eighty paces; she will carry ball too: I have hit a wild bull within a hundred and fifty yards; but I have two pieces that are as good or better, so you may keep this for my sake."

"That would be to take my share of the wreck," answered Mordaunt, laughing.

"No such matter," said Cleveland, undoing a case which contained several guns and pistols; "you see I have saved my private arm-chest as well as my clothes—*that* the tall old woman in the dark rigging managed for me. And, between ourselves, it is worth all I have lost; for," he added, lowering his voice and looking round, "when I speak of being ruined in the hearing of these land-sharks, I do not mean ruined stock and block. No, here is something will do more than shoot sea-fowl." So saying, he pulled out a great ammunition-pouch marked swan-shot, and showed Mordaunt, hastily, that it was full of Spanish pistoles and Portagues, as the broad Portugal pieces were then called. "No—no," he added, with a smile, "I have ballast enough to trim the vessel again; and now, will you take the piece?"

"Since you are willing to give it me," said Mordaunt, laughing, "with all my heart. I was just going to ask you, in my father's name," he added, showing his purse, "whether you wanted any of that same ballast."

"Thanks, but you see I am provided. Take my old acquaintance, and may she serve you as well as she has served me; but you will never make so good a voyage with her. You can shoot, I suppose?"

"Tolerably well," said Mordaunt, admiring the piece, which was a beautiful Spanish-barrelled gun, inlaid with gold, small in the bore, and of unusual length, such as is chiefly used for shooting sea-fowl and for ball-practice.

"With slugs," continued the donor, "never gun shot closer; and with single ball you may kill a seal two hundred yards at sea from the top of the highest peak of this iron-bound coast of yours. But I tell you again, that the old rattler will never do you the service she has done me."

"I shall not use her so dexterously, perhaps?" said Mordaunt.

"Umph! perhaps not," replied Cleveland; "but that is not the question. What say you to shooting the man at the wheel, just as we run aboard of a Spaniard? So the Don was taken aback, and we laid him athwart the hawse, and carried her cutlass in hand; and worth the while she was—stout brigantine—'El Santo Francisco'—bound for Porto Bello, with gold and negroes. That little bit of lead was worth twenty thousand pistoles."

"I have shot at no such game as yet," said Mordaunt.

"Well, all in good time; we cannot weigh till the tide makes. But you are a tight, handsome, active young man. What is to ail you to take a trip after some of this stuff?" laying his hand on the bag of gold.

"My father talks of my travelling soon," replied Mordaunt, who, born to hold men-of-war's-men in great respect, felt flattered by this invitation from one who appeared a thorough-bred seaman.

"I respect him for the thought," said the captain, "and I will visit him before I weigh anchor. I have a consort off these islands, and be cursed to her. She'll find me out somewhere, though she parted company in the bit of a squall, unless she is gone to Davy Jones too. Well, she was better found than we, and not so deep loaded: she must have weathered it. We'll have a hammock slung for you aboard, and make a sailor and a man of you in the same trip."

"I should like it well enough," said Mordaunt, who eagerly longed to see more of the world than his lonely situation had hitherto permitted; "but then my father must decide."

"Your father! pooh!" said Captain Cleveland; "but you are very right," he added, checking himself. "Gad, I have lived so long at sea that I cannot imagine anybody has a right to think except the captain and the master. But you are very right. I will go up to the old gentleman this instant and speak to him myself. He lives in that handsome, modern-looking building, I suppose, that I see a quarter of a mile off?"

"In that old half-ruined house," said Mordaunt, "he does indeed live; but he will see no visitors."

"Then you must drive the point yourself, for I can't stay in this latitude. Since your father is no magistrate, I must go to see this same Magnus—how call you him?—who is not justice of peace, but something else that will do the turn as well. These fellows have got two or three things that I must and will have back; let them keep the rest, and be d—d to them. Will you give me a letter to him, just by way of commission?"

"It is scarce needful," said Mordaunt. "It is enough that you are shipwrecked and need his help; but yet I may as well furnish you with a letter of introduction."

"There," said the sailor, producing a writing-case from his chest, "are your writing-tools. Meantime, since bulk has been broken, I will nail down the hatches and make sure of the cargo."

While Mordaunt, accordingly, was engaged in writing to Magnus Troil a letter, setting forth the circumstances in which Captain Cleveland had been thrown upon their coast, the captain, having first selected and laid aside some wearing apparel and necessaries enough to fill a knapsack, took in hand hammer and nails, employed himself in securing the lid of his sea-chest by fastening it down in a workmanlike manner, and then added the corroborating security of a cord, twisted and knotted with nautical dexterity. "I leave this in your charge," he said, "all except this," showing the bag of gold, "and these," pointing to a cutlass and pistols, "which may prevent all further risk of my parting company with my Portagues."

"You will find no occasion for weapons in this country, Captain Cleveland," replied Mordaunt: "a child might travel with a purse of gold from Sumburgh Head to the Scaw of Unst, and no soul would injure him."

"And that's pretty boldly said, young gentleman, considering what is going on without doors at this moment."

"Oh," replied Mordaunt, a little confused, "what comes on land with the tide they reckon their lawful property. One would think they had studied under Sir Arthegal, who pronounces—

For equal right in equal things doth stand,
And what the mighty sea hath once possess'd,

And plucked quite from all possessors' hands,
    Or else by wrecks that wretches have distress'd,
He may dispose, by his resistless might,
    As things at random left, to whom he list."

"I shall think the better of plays and ballads as long as I live for these very words," said Captain Cleveland; "and yet I have loved them well enough in my day. But this is good doctrine, and more men than one may trim their sails to such a breeze. What the sea sends is ours, that's sure enough. However, in case that your good folks should think the land as well as the sea may present them with waifs and strays, I will make bold to take my cutlass and pistols. Will you cause my chest to be secured in your own house till you hear from me, and use your influence to procure me a guide to show me the way, and to carry my kit?"

"Will you go by sea or land?" said Mordaunt, in reply.

"By sea!" exclaimed Cleveland. "What, in one of these cockle-shells, and a cracked cockle-shell to boot? No—no; land—land, unless I knew my crew, my vessel, and my voyage."

They parted accordingly, Captain Cleveland being supplied with a guide to conduct him to Burgh-Westra, and his chest being carefully removed to the mansion-house at Jarlshof.

------♦------

CHAPTER IX.

This is a gentle trader, and a prudent.
He's no Autolycus, to blear your eye
With quips of worldly gauds and ganesomeness;
But seasons all his glittering merchandise
With wholesome doctrines, suited to the use,
As men sauce goose with sage and rosemary.
                    Old Play.

On the subsequent morning, Mordaunt, in answer to his father's inquiries, began to give him some account of the shipwrecked mariner whom he had rescued from the waves. But he had not proceeded far in recapitulating the particulars which Cleveland had communicated, when Mr. Mertoun's looks

8

became disturbed; he arose hastily, and, after pacing twice or thrice across the room, he retired into the inner chamber, to which he usually confined himself while under the influence of his mental malady. In the evening he reappeared, without any traces of his disorder; but it may be easily supposed that his son avoided recurring to the subject which had affected him.

Mordaunt Mertoun was thus left without assistance to form at his leisure his own opinion respecting the new acquaintance which the sea had sent him; and, upon the whole, he was himself surprised to find the result less favourable to the stranger than he could well account for. There seemed to Mordaunt to be a sort of repelling influence about the man. True, he was a handsome man, of a frank and prepossessing manner, but there was an assumption of superiority about him which Mordaunt did not quite so much like. Although he was so keen a sportsman as to be delighted with his acquisition of the Spanish-barrelled gun, and accordingly mounted and dismounted it with great interest, paying the utmost attention to the most minute parts about the lock and ornaments, yet he was, upon the whole, inclined to have some scruples about the mode in which he had acquired it.

"I should not have accepted it," he thought; "perhaps Captain Cleveland might give it me as a sort of payment for the trifling service I did him; and yet it would have been churlish to refuse it in the way it was offered. I wish he had looked more like a man whom one would have chosen to be obliged to."

But a successful day's shooting reconciled him to his gun, and he became assured, like most young sportsmen in similar circumstances, that all other pieces were but pop-guns in comparison. But then, to be doomed to shoot gulls and seals, when there were Frenchmen and Spaniards to be come at, when there were ships to be boarded, and steersmen to be marked off, seemed but a dull and contemptible destiny. His father had mentioned his leaving these islands, and no other mode of occupation occurred to his inexperience save that of the sea, with which he had been conversant from his infancy. His ambition had formerly aimed no higher than at sharing the fatigues and dangers of a Greenland fishing expedition; for it was in that scene that the Zetlanders laid most of their perilous adventures. But war was again raging, the history of Sir Francis Drake, Captain Morgan, and other bold adventurers, an account of whose exploits he had purchased from Bryce Snailsfoot, had made much impression on his mind, and the offer of Captain Cleveland to take him to sea frequently recurred to him, although the pleasure of such a project was somewhat damped by a doubt whether, in the long run, he should not find many objections to his proposed commander. Thus much he already saw, that he was opinionative, and might probably prove arbitrary; and that, since even his kindness was mingled with an assumption of superiority, his occasional displeasure might contain a great deal more of that disagreeable ingredient than could be palatable to those who sailed under him. And yet, after counting all risks, could his father's consent but be obtained, with what pleasure, he thought, would he embark in quest of new scenes and strange adventures, in which he proposed to himself to achieve such deeds as should be the theme of many a tale to the lovely sisters of Burgh-Westra—tales at which Minna should weep and Brenda should smile, and both should marvel! And this was to be the reward of his labours and his dangers; for the hearth of Magnus Troil had a magnetic influence over his thoughts, and however they might traverse amid his daydreams, it was the point where they finally settled.

There were times when Mordaunt thought of mentioning to his father the conversation he had held with Captain Cleveland, and the seaman's proposal to him; but the very short and general account which he had given of that person's history, upon the morning after his departure from the hamlet, had produced a sinister effect on Mr. Mertoun's mind, and discouraged him from speaking farther on any subject connected with it. It would be time enough, he thought, to mention Captain Cleveland's proposal when his consort should arrive, and when he should repeat his offer in a more formal manner; and these he supposed events likely very soon to happen.

But days grew to weeks, and weeks were numbered into
months, and he heard nothing from Cleveland; and only
learned by an occasional visit from Bryce Snailsfoot that the
captain was residing at Burgh-Westra as one of the family.
Mordaunt was somewhat surprised at this, although the unlimited hospitality of the islands, which Magnus Troil, both
from fortune and disposition, carried to the utmost extent,
made it almost a matter of course that he should remain in
the family until he disposed of himself otherwise.   Still it
seemed strange he had not gone to some of the northern isles
to inquire after his consort; or that he did not rather choose
to make Lerwick his residence, where fishing-vessels often
brought news from the coasts and ports of Scotland and Holland.   Again, why did he not send for the chest he had deposited at Jarlshof? and still farther, Mordaunt thought it
would have been but polite if the stranger had sent him some
sort of message in token of remembrance.

These subjects of reflection were connected with another
still more unpleasant, and more difficult to account for.   Until the arrival of this person, scarce a week had passed without
bringing him some kind greeting or token of recollection from
Burgh-Westra; and pretences were scarce ever wanting for
maintaining a constant intercourse.   Minna wanted the words
of a Norse ballad; or desired to have, for her various collections, feathers, or eggs, or shells, or specimens of the rarer
sea-weeds; or Brenda sent a riddle to be resolved, or a song to
be learned; or the honest old Udaller—in a rude manuscript,
which might have passed for an ancient Runic inscription—
sent his hearty greetings to his good young friend, with a
present of something to make good cheer, and an earnest request he would come to Burgh-Westra as soon, and stay there
as long, as possible.   These kindly tokens of remembrance
were often sent by special message; besides which, there was
never a passenger or a traveller who crossed from the one
mansion to the other who did not bring to Mordaunt some
friendly greeting from the Udaller and his family.   Of late,
this intercourse had become more and more infrequent; and
no messenger from Burgh-Westra had visited Jarlshof for sev-

eral weeks. Mordaunt both observed and felt this alteration, and it dwelt on his mind, while he questioned Bryce as closely as pride and prudence would permit, to ascertain, if possible, the cause of the change. Yet he endeavoured to assume an indifferent air while he asked the jagger whether there were no news in the country.

"Great news," the jagger replied; "and a gay mony of them. That crack-brained carle, the new factor, is for making a change in the 'bismars' and the 'lispunds'; and our worthy fowd, Magnus Troil, has sworn that, sooner than change them for the still-yard or aught else, he'll fling Factor Yellowley from Brassa Craig."

"Is that all?" said Mordaunt, very little interested.

"All! and eneugh, I think," replied the pedlar. "How are folks to buy and sell, if the weights are changed on them?"

"Very true," replied Mordaunt; "but have you heard of no strange vessels on the coast?"

"Six Dutch doggers off Brassa; and, as I hear, a high-quartered galliot thing, with a gaff mainsail, lying in Scalloway Bay. She will be from Norway."

"No ships of war, or sloops?"

"None," replied the pedlar, "since the 'Kite' tender sailed with the impress men. If it was His will, and our men were out of her, I wish the deep sea had her!"

"Were there no news at Burgh-Westra? Were the family all well?"

"A' weel, and weel to do, out-taken, it may be, something ower muckle daffing and laughing: dancing ilk night, they say, wi' the stranger captain that's living there—him that was ashore on Sumburgh Head the tother day; less daffing served him then."

"Daffing! dancing every night!" said Mordaunt, not particularly well satisfied. "Whom does Captain Cleveland dance with?"

"Ony body he likes, I fancy," said the jagger; "at ony rate, he gars a' body yonder dance after his fiddle. But I ken little about it, for I am no free in conscience to look upon thae flinging fancies. Folk should mind that life is made but of rotten yarn."

"I fancy that it is to keep them in mind of that wholesome truth that you deal in such tender wares, Bryce," replied Mordaunt, dissatisfied as well with the tenor of the reply as with the affected scruples of the respondent.

"That's as muckle as to say, that I suld hae minded you was a flinger and a fiddler yoursell, Maister Mordaunt; but I am an auld man, and maun unburden my conscience. But ye will be for the dance, I sall warrant, that's to be at Burgh-Westra on John's Even—*Saunt* John's, as the blinded creatures ca' him—and nae doubt ye will be for some warldly braws—hose, waistcoats, or sic-like? I hae pieces frae Flanders." With that he placed his movable warehouse on the table, and began to unlock it.

"Dance!" repeated Mordaunt—"dance on St. John's Even? Were you desired to bid me to it, Bryce?"

"Na; but ye ken weel eneugh ye wad be welcome, bidden or no bidden. This captain—how ca' ye him?—is to be skudler, as they ca't—the first of the gang, like."

"The devil take him!" said Mordaunt, in impatient surprise.

"A' in gude time," replied the jagger: "hurry no man's cattle; the devil will hae his due, I warrant ye, or it winna be for lack of seeking. But it's true I'm telling you, for a' ye stare like a wild cat; and this same captain—I watna his name—bought ane of the very waistcoats that I am ganging to show ye—purple, wi' a gowd binding, and bonnily broidered; and I have a piece for you, the neighbour of it, wi' a green grund; and if ye mean to streek yoursell up beside him, ye maun e'en buy it, for it's gowd that glances in the lasses' een nowadays. See—look till't," he added, displaying the pattern in various points of view—"look till *it* through the light and till the light through *it, wi* the grain and *against* the grain: it shows ony gate; cam frae Antwerp a' the gate. Four dollars is the price; and yon captain was sae weel pleased that he flang down a twenty shilling Jacobus, and bade me keep the change and be d—d! Poor silly profane creature, I pity him."

Without inquiring whether the pedlar bestowed his compassion on the worldly imprudence or the religious deficiencies of Captain Cleveland, Mordaunt turned from him, folded his arms, and paced the apartment, muttering to himself, "Not asked. A stranger to be king of the feast!" Words which he repeated so earnestly that Bryce caught a part of their import.

"As for asking, I am almaist bauld to say that ye will be asked, Maister Mordaunt."

"Did they mention my name, then?" said Mordaunt.

"I canna preceesely say that," said Bryce Snailsfoot; "but ye needna turn away your head sae sourly, like a sealgh when he leaves the shore; for, do you see, I heard distinctly that a' the revellers about are to be there; and is't to be thought they would leave out you, an auld kenn'd freend, and the lightest foot at sic frolics—Heaven send you a better praise in His ain gude time!—that ever flang at a fiddle-squeak, between this and Unst? Sae I consider ye altogether the same as invited; and ye had best provide yourself wi' a waistcoat, for brave and brisk will every man be that's there—the Lord pity them!"

He thus continued to follow with his green glazen eyes the motions of young Mordaunt Mertoun, who was pacing the room in a very pensive manner, which the jagger probably misinterpreted, as he thought, like Claudio, that, if a man is sad, it must needs be because he lacks money. Bryce, therefore, after another pause, thus accosted him: "Ye needna be sad about the matter, Maister Mordaunt; for although I got the just price of the article from the captain-man, yet I maun deal freendly wi' you, as a kenn'd freend and customer, and bring the price, as they say, within your purse-mouth; or it's the same to me to let it lie ower till Martinmas, or e'en to Candlemas. I am decent in the warld, Maister Mordaunt; forbid that I should hurry ony body, far mair a freend that has paid me siller afore now. Or I wad be content to swap the garment for the value in feathers or sea-otters' skins, or ony kind of peltrie; nane kens better than yoursell how to come by sic ware, and I am sure I hae furnished you wi' the primest o' powder. I dinna ken if I tell'd ye it was out o' the kist of Captain Plunket, that perished on the Scaw of Unst, wi' the armed brig 'Mary,' sax years syne. He was a prime fowler himself, and luck it was that the kist came ashore dry. I sell that to nane but gude marksmen. And so, I was saying, if ye had ony wares ye liked to coup for the waist-coat, I wad be ready to trock wi' you, for assuredly ye will be wanted at Burgh-Westra on St. John's Even; and ye wadna like to look waur 'than the captain—that wadna be setting."

"I will be there at least, whether wanted or not," said Mordaunt, stopping short in his walk, and taking the waist-coat-piece hastily out of the pedlar's hand; "and, as you say, will not disgrace them."

"Haud a care—haud a care, Maister Mordaunt," exclaimed the pedlar; "ye handle it as it were a bale of coarse wadmaal: ye'll fray't to bits; ye might weel say my ware is tender; and ye'll mind the price is four dollars. Sall I put ye in my book for it?"

"No," said Mordaunt, hastily; and, taking out his purse, he flung down the money.

"Grace to ye to wear the garment," said the joyous pedlar, "and to me to guide the siller; and protect us from earthly vanities and earthly covetousness; and send you the white linen raiment, whilk is mair to be desired than the muslins, and cambrics, and lawns, and silks of this world; and send me the talents which avail more than much fine Spanish gold, or Dutch dollars either; and—but God guide the callant, what for is he wrapping the silk up that gate, like a wisp of hay?"

At this moment, old Swertha, the housekeeper, entered, to whom, as if eager to get rid of the subject, Mordaunt threw his purchase, with something like careless disdain; and, telling her to put it aside, snatched his gun, which stood in the corner, threw his shooting accoutrements about him, and, without noticing Bryce's attempt to enter into conversation upon the "braw seal-skin, as saft as doe-leather," which made the sling and cover of his fowling-piece, he left the apartment abruptly.

The jagger, with those green, goggling, and gain-descrying

kind of optics which we have already described, continued gazing for an instant after the customer who treated his wares with such irreverence.

Swertha also looked after him with some surprise. " The callant's in a creel," quoth she.

"In a creel!" echoed the pedlar; "he will be as wowf as ever his father was. To guide in that gate a bargain that cost him four dollars!—very, very fifish, as the east-country fisher-folk say."

"Four dollars for that green rag!" said Swertha, catching at the words which the jagger had unwarily suffered to escape: "that was a bargain indeed! I wonder whether he is the greater fule or you the mair rogue, Bryce Snailsfoot."

"I didna say it cost him preceesely four dollars," said Snailsfoot; "but if it had, the lad's siller's his ain, I hope; and he is auld eneugh to make his ain bargains. Mair by token, the gudes are weel worth the money and mair."

"Mair by token," said Swertha, coolly, "I will see what his father thinks about it."

"Ye'll no be sae ill-natured, Mrs. Swertha," said the jagger; "that will be but cauld thanks for the bonny owerlay that I hae brought you a' the way frae Lerwick."

"And a bonny price ye'll be setting on't," said Swertha; "for that's the gate your good deeds end."

"Ye sall hae the fixing of the price yoursell; or it may lie ower till ye're buying something for the house or for your master, and it can make a' ae count."

"Troth, and that's true, Bryce Snailsfoot; I am thinking we'll want some napery sune; for it's no to be thought we can spin, and the like, as if there was a mistress in the house; and sae we make nane at hame."

"And that's what I ca' walking by the Word," said the jagger. " 'Go unto those that buy and sell'; there's muckle profit in that text."

"There is a pleasure in dealing wi' a discreet man, that can make profit of ony thing," said Swertha; "and now that I take another look at that daft callant's waistcoat-piece, I think it *is* honestly worth four dollars."

CHAPTER X.

I have possessed the regulation of the weather and the distribution of the
seasons. The sun has listened to my dictates, and passed from tropic
to tropic by my direction ; the clouds, at my command, have poured
forth their waters.   *Rasselas.*

ANY sudden cause for anxious and mortifying reflection,
which, in advanced age, occasions sullen and pensive inactivity, stimulates youth to eager and active exertion; as if, like
the hurt deer, they endeavoured to drown the pain of the shaft
by the rapidity of motion.   When Mordaunt caught up his
gun and rushed out of the house of Jarlshof, he walked on
with great activity over waste and wild, without any determined purpose, except that of escaping, if possible, from the
smart of his own irritation.   His pride was effectually mortified by the report of the jagger, which coincided exactly with
some doubts he had been led to entertain, by the long and
unkind silence of his friends at Burgh-Westra.

If the fortunes of Cæsar had doomed him, as the poet sug-
gests, to have been

But the best wrestler on the green,

it is, nevertheless, to be presumed that a foil from a rival in
that rustic exercise would have mortified him as much as a
defeat from a competitor when he was struggling for the em-
pery of the world.   And even so Mordaunt Mertoun, degraded
in his own eyes from the height which he had occupied as the
chief amongst the youth of the island, felt vexed and irritated,
as well as humbled.   The two beautiful sisters, also, whose
smiles all were so desirous of acquiring, with whom he had
lived on terms of such familiar affection that, with the same
ease and innocence, there was unconsciously mixed a shade of
deeper though undefined tenderness than characterises frater-
nal love—they also seemed to have forgotten him.   He could
not be ignorant that, in the universal opinion of all Dunrossness, nay, of the whole Mainland, he might have had every

chance of being the favoured lover of either; and now at once, and without any failure on his part, he was become so little to them that he had lost even the consequence of an ordinary acquaintance. The old Udaller, too, whose hearty and sincere character should have made him more constant in his friendships, seemed to have been as fickle as his daughters, and poor Mordaunt had at once lost the smiles of the fair and the favour of the powerful. These were uncomfortable reflections, and he doubled his pace, that he might outstrip them if possible.

Without exactly reflecting upon the route which he pursued, Mordaunt walked briskly on through a country where neither hedge, wall, nor inclosure of any kind interrupts the steps of the wanderer, until he reached a very solitary spot, where, embosomed among steep heathy hills, which sunk suddenly down on the verge of the water, lay one of those small fresh-water lakes which are common in the Zetland Isles, whose outlets form the sources of the small brooks and rivulets by which the country is watered, and serve to drive the little mills which manufacture their grain.

It was a mild summer day; the beams of the sun, as is not uncommon in Zetland, were moderated and shaded by a silvery haze, which filled the atmosphere, and, destroying the strong contrast of light and shade, gave even to noon the sober livery of the evening twilight. The little lake, not three-quarters of a mile in circuit, lay in profound quiet; its surface undimpled, save when one of the numerous water-fowl which glided on its surface dived for an instant under it. The depth of the water gave the whole that cerulean tint of bluish green which occasioned its being called the Green Loch; and at present it formed so perfect a mirror to the bleak hills by which it was surrounded, and which lay reflected on its bosom, that it was difficult to distinguish the water from the land; nay, in the shadowy uncertainty occasioned by the thin haze, a stranger could scarce have been sensible that a sheet of water lay before him. A scene of more complete solitude, having all its peculiarities heightened by the extreme serenity of the weather, the quiet, grey, composed tone of the atmosphere, and the perfect silence of the elements, could hardly be imagined. The very aquatic birds, who frequented the spot in great numbers, forbore their usual flight and screams, and floated in profound tranquillity upon the silent water.

Without taking any determined aim, without having any determined purpose, without almost thinking what he was about, Mordaunt presented his fowling-piece and fired across the lake. The large swan-shot dimpled its surface like a partial shower of hail; the hills took up the noise of the report, and repeated it again, and again, and again, to all their echoes; the water-fowl took to wing in eddying and confused wheel, answering the echoes with a thousand varying screams, from the deep note of the swabie, or swartback, to the querulous cry of the tirracke and kittiwake.

Mordaunt looked for a moment on the clamorous crowd with a feeling of resentment, which he felt disposed at the moment to apply to all nature, and all her objects, animate or inanimate, however little concerned with the cause of his internal mortification.

"Ay—ay," he said, "wheel, dive, scream, and clamour as you will, and all because you have seen a strange sight and heard an unusual sound. There is many a one like you in this round world. But you, at least, shall learn," he added, as he reloaded his gun, "that strange sights and strange sounds, ay, and strange acquaintances to boot, have sometimes a little shade of danger connected with them. But why should I wreak my own vexation on these harmless sea-gulls?" he subjoined, after a moment's pause; "they have nothing to do with the friends that have forgotten me. I loved them all so well,—and to be so soon given up for the first stranger whom chance threw on the coast!"

As he stood resting upon his gun, and abandoning his mind to the course of these unpleasant reflections, his meditations were unexpectedly interrupted by some one touching his shoulder. He looked around, and saw Norna of the Fitful Head, wrapped in her dark and ample mantle. She had seen him from the brow of the hill, and had descended to the lake through a small ravine which concealed her, until she came with noiseless step so close to him that he turned round at her touch.

Mordaunt Mertoun was by nature neither timorous nor credulous, and a course of reading more extensive than usual had, in some degree, fortified his mind against the attacks of superstition; but he would have been an actual prodigy if, living in Zetland in the end of the 17th century, he had possessed the philosophy which did not exist in Scotland generally until at least two generations later. He doubted in his own mind the extent, nay, the very existence, of Norna's supernatural attributes, which was a high flight of incredulity in the country where they were universally received; but still his incredulity went no farther than doubts. She was unquestionably an extraordinary woman, gifted with an energy above others, acting upon motives peculiar to herself, and apparently independent of mere earthly considerations. Impressed with these ideas, which he had imbibed from his youth, it was not without something like alarm that he beheld this mysterious female standing on a sudden so close beside him, and looking upon him with such sad and severe eyes, as those with which the Fatal Virgins, who, according to Northern mythology, were called the Valkyriur, or "Choosers of the Slain," were supposed to regard the young champions whom they selected to share the banquet of Odin.

It was, indeed, reckoned unlucky, to say the least, to meet with Norna suddenly alone, and in a place remote from witnesses; and she was supposed, on such occasions, to have been usually a prophetess of evil, as well as an omen of misfortune, to those who had such a rencontre. There were few or none of the islanders, however familiarised with her occasional appearance in society, that would not have trembled to meet her on the solitary banks of the Green Loch.

"I bring you no evil, Mordaunt Mertoun," she said, reading perhaps something of this superstitious feeling in the looks of the young man. "Evil from me you never felt, and never will."

"Nor do I fear any," said Mordaunt, exerting himself to

throw aside an apprehension which he felt to be unmanly. "Why should I, mother? You have been ever my friend."

"Yet, Mordaunt, thou art not of our region; but to none of Zetland blood, no, not even to those who sit around the hearth-stone of Magnus Troil, the noble descendants of the ancient jarls of Orkney, am I more a well-wisher than I am to thee, thou kind and brave-hearted boy. When I hung around thy neck that gifted chain, which all in our isles know was wrought by no earthly artist, but by the Drows,[1] in the secret recesses of their caverns, thou wert then but fifteen years old; yet thy foot had been on the Maiden Skerry of North-maven, known before but to the webbed sole of the swartback, and thy skiff had been in the deepest cavern of Brinnastir, where the 'haaf-fish'[2] had before slumbered in dark obscurity. Therefore I gave thee that noble gift; and well thou knowest that, since that day, every eye in these isles has looked on thee as a son or as a brother, endowed beyond other youths, and the favoured of those whose hour of power is when the night meets with the day."

"Alas! mother," said Mordaunt, "your kind gift may have given me favour, but it has not been able to keep it for me, or I have not been able to keep it for myself. What matters it? I shall learn to set as little by others as they do by me. My father says that I shall soon leave these islands, and therefore, Mother Norna, I will return to you your fairy gift, that it may bring more lasting luck to some other than it has done to me."

"Despise not the gift of the nameless race," said Norna, frowning; then suddenly changing her tone of displeasure to that of mournful solemnity, she added: "Despise them not; but, O Mordaunt, court them not! Sit down on that grey stone; thou art the son of my adoption, and I will doff, as far as I may, those attributes that sever me from the common mass of humanity, and speak with you as a parent with a child."

There was a tremulous tone of grief which mingled with

---

[1] See Note 17.

[2] The larger seal, or sea-calf, which seeks the most solitary recesses for its abode. See Dr. Edmonstone's *Zetland*, vol. ii. p. 294.

the loftiness of her language and carriage, and was calculated
to excite sympathy, as well as to attract attention.   Mordaunt
sat down on the rock which she pointed out—a fragment
which, with many others that lay scattered around, had been
torn by some winter storm from the precipice at the foot of
which it lay, upon the very verge of the water.   Norna took
her own seat on a stone at about three feet distance, adjusted
her mantle so that little more than her forehead, her eyes, and
a single lock of her grey hair were seen from beneath the
shade of her dark wadmaal cloak, and then proceeded in a
tone in which the imaginary consequence and importance so
often assumed by lunacy seemed to contend against the deep
workings of some extraordinary and deeply-rooted mental
affliction.

"I was not always," she said, "that which I now am.   I
was not always the wise, the powerful, the commanding, before whom the young stand abashed and the old uncover their
grey heads.   There was a time when my appearance did not
silence mirth, when I sympathised with human passion, and
had my own share in human joy or sorrow.   It was a time of
helplessness—it was a time of folly—it was a time of idle and
unfruitful laughter—it was a time of causeless and senseless
tears; and yet, with its follies, and its sorrows, and its weak-
nesses, what would Norna of Fitful Head give to be again the
unmarked and happy maiden that she was in her early days!
Hear me, Mordaunt, and bear with me; for you hear me utter
complaints which have never sounded in mortal ears, and
which in mortal ears shall never sound again.   I will be what
I ought," she continued, starting up and extending her lean
and withered arm, "the queen and protectress of these wild
and neglected isles; I will be her whose foot the wave wets
not, save by her permission, ay, even though its rage be at its
wildest madness : whose robe the whirlwind respects, when it
rends the house-rigging from the roof-tree.   Bear me witness,
Mordaunt Mertoun : you heard my words at Harfra—you saw
the tempest sink before them!   Speak, bear me witness!"

To have contradicted her in this strain of high-toned enthusiasm would have been cruel and unavailing, even had Mor-

daunt been more decidedly convinced than he was that an insane woman, not one of supernatural power, stood before him.

"I heard you sing," he replied, "and I saw the tempest abate."

"Abate!" exclaimed Norna, striking the ground impatiently with her staff of black oak; "thou speakest it but half: it sunk at once—sunk in shorter space than the child that is hushed to silence by the nurse. Enough, you know my power; but you know not—mortal man knows not, and never shall know—the price which I paid to attain it. No, Mordaunt, never for the widest sway that the ancient Norsemen boasted, when their banners waved victorious from Bergen to Palestine—never, for all that the round world contains, do thou barter thy peace of mind for such greatness as Norna's." She resumed her seat upon the rock, drew the mantle over her face, rested her head upon her hands, and, by the convulsive motion which agitated her bosom, appeared to be weeping bitterly.

"Good Norna," said Mordaunt, and paused, scarce knowing what to say that might console the unhappy woman— "good Norna," he again resumed, "if there be aught in your mind that troubles it, were you not best to go to the worthy minister at Dunrossness? Men say you have not for many years been in a Christian congregation: that cannot be well, or right. You are yourself well known as a healer of bodily disease; but when the mind is sick, we should draw to the Physician of our souls."

Norna had raised her person slowly from the stooping posture in which she sat; but at length she started up on her feet, threw back her mantle, extended her arm, and while her lip foamed and her eye sparkled, exclaimed in a tone resembling a scream: "Me did you speak—me did you bid seek out a priest! Would you kill the good man with horror? Me in a Christian congregation! Would you have the roof to fall on the sackless assembly, and mingle their blood with their worship? I—I seek to the good Physician! Would you have the fiend claim his prey openly before God and man?"

The extreme agitation of the unhappy speaker naturally led Mordaunt to the conclusion which was generally adopted and accredited in that superstitious country and period. "Wretched woman," he said, "if indeed thou hast leagued thyself with the Powers of Evil, why should you not seek even yet for repentance? But do as thou wilt, I cannot, dare not, as a Christian, abide longer with you; and take again your gift," he said, offering back the chain. "Good can never come of it, if indeed evil hath not come already."

"Be still and hear me, thou foolish boy," said Norna, calmly, as if she had been restored to reason by the alarm and horror which she perceived in Mordaunt's countenance— "hear me, I say. I am not of those who have leagued themselves with the Enemy of Mankind, or derive skill or power from his ministry. And although the unearthly powers *were* propitiated by a sacrifice which human tongue can never utter, yet, God knows, my guilt in that offering was no more than that of the blind man who falls from the precipice which he could neither see nor shun. Oh, leave me not—shun me not— in this hour of weakness! Remain with me till the temptation be passed, or I will plunge myself into that lake, and rid myself at once of my power and my wretchedness!"

Mordaunt, who had always looked up to this singular woman with a sort of affection, occasioned no doubt by the early kindness and distinction which she had shown to him, was readily induced to reassume his seat and listen to what she had further to say, in hopes that she would gradually overcome the violence of her agitation. It was not long ere she seemed to have gained the victory her companion expected, for she addressed him in her usual steady and authoritative manner.

"It was not of myself, Mordaunt, that I purposed to speak, when I beheld you from the summit of yonder grey rock, and came down the path to meet with you. My fortunes are fixed beyond change, be it for weal or for woe. For myself I have ceased to feel much; but for those whom she loves Norna of the Fitful Head has still those feelings which link her to her kind. Mark me. There is an eagle, the noblest that builds

9

in these airy precipices, and into that eagle's nest there has crept an adder; wilt thou lend thy aid to crush the reptile, and to save the noble brood of the lord of the north sky?"

"You must speak more plainly, Norna," said Mordaunt, "if you would have me understand or answer you. I am no guesser of riddles."

"In plain language, then, you know well the family of Burgh-Westra—the lovely daughters of the generous old Udaller, Magnus Troil—Minna and Brenda, I mean? You know them, and you love them?"

"I have known them, mother," replied Mordaunt, "and I have loved them—none knows it better than yourself."

"To know them once," said Norna, emphatically, "is to know them always. To love them once is to love them for ever."

"To have loved them once is to wish them well for ever," replied the youth; "but it is nothing more. To be plain with you, Norna, the family at Burgh-Westra have of late totally neglected me. But show me the means of serving them, I will convince you how much I have remembered old kindness, how little I resent late coldness."

"It is well spoken, and I will put your purpose to the proof," replied Norna. "Magnus Troil has taken a serpent into his bosom: his lovely daughters are delivered up to the machinations of a villain."

"You mean the stranger, Cleveland?" said Mordaunt.

"The stranger who so calls himself," replied Norna—"the same whom we found flung ashore, like a waste heap of seaweed, at the foot of the Sumburgh Cape. I felt that within me that would have prompted me to let him lie till the tide floated him off, as it had floated him on shore. I repent me I gave not way to it."

"But," said Mordaunt, "I cannot repent that I did my duty as a Christian man. And what right have I to wish otherwise? If Minna, Brenda, Magnus, and the rest like that stranger better than me, I have no title to be offended; nay, I might well be laughed at for bringing myself into comparison."

"It is well, and I trust they merit thy unselfish friendship."

"But I cannot perceive," said Mordaunt, "in what you can propose that I should serve them. I have but just learned by Bryce, the jagger, that this Captain Cleveland is all in all with the ladies at Burgh-Westra and with the Kdaller himself. I would like ill to intrude myself where I am not welcome, or to place my home-bred merit in comparison with Captain Cleveland's. He can tell them of battles, when I can only speak of birds' nests; can speak of shooting Frenchmen, when I can only tell of shooting seals; he wears gay clothes and bears a brave countenance, I am plainly dressed and plainly nurtured. Such gay gallants as he can noose the hearts of those he lives with, as the fowler nooses the guillemot with his rod and line."

"You do wrong to yourself," replied Norna—"wrong to yourself, and greater wrong to Minna and Brenda. And trust not the reports of Bryce: he is like the greedy chaffer-whale, that will change his course and dive for the most petty coin which a fisher can cast at him. Certain it is that, if you have been lessened in the opinion of Magnus Troil, that sordid fellow hath had some share in it. But let him count his vantage, for my eye is upon him."

"And why, mother," said Mordaunt, "do you not tell to Magnus what you have told to me?"

"Because," replied Norna, "they who wax wise in their own conceit must be taught a bitter lesson by experience. It was but yesterday that I spoke with Magnus, and what was his reply?—'Good Norna, you grow old.' And this was spoken by one bounden to me by so many and such close ties —by the descendant of the ancient Norse earls—this was from Magnus Troil to me; and it was said in behalf of one whom the sea flung forth as wreck-weed! Since he despises the counsel of the aged, he shall be taught by that of the young; and well that he is not left to his own folly. Go, therefore, to Burgh-Westra, as usual, upon the Baptist's festival."

"I have had no invitation," said Mordaunt: "I am not wanted, not wished for, not thought of—perhaps I shall not be acknowledged if I go thither; and yet, mother, to confess the truth, thither I had thought to go."

"It was a good thought, and to be cherished," replied Norna; "we seek our friends when they are sick in health, why not when they are sick in mind and surfeited with prosperity? Do not fail to go; it may be, we shall meet there. Meanwhile our roads lie different. Farewell, and speak not of this meeting."

They parted, and Mordaunt remained standing by the lake, with his eyes fixed on Norna, until her tall dark form became invisible among the windings of the valley down which she wandered, and Mordaunt returned to his father's mansion, determined to follow counsel which coincided so well with his own wishes.

CHAPTER XI.

All your ancient customs
And long-descended usages I'll change.
Ye shall not eat, nor drink, nor speak, nor move,
Think, look, or walk, as ye were wont to do.
Even your marriage-beds shall know mutation:
The bride shall have the stock, the groom the wall;
For all old practice will I turn and change,
And call it reformation—marry will I!
                    ' Tis Even that we're at Odds.

THE festal day approached, and still no invitation arrived for that guest without whom, but a little space since, no feast could have been held in the island; while, on the other hand, such reports as reached them on every side spoke highly of the favour which Captain Cleveland enjoyed in the good graces of the old Udaller of Burgh-Westra. Swertha and the Ranzelman shook their heads at these mutations, and reminded Mordaunt, by many a half-hint and innuendo, that he had incurred this eclipse by being so imprudently active to secure the safety of the stranger, when he lay at the mercy of the next wave beneath the cliffs of Sumburgh Head. "It is best to let saut water take its gate," said Swertha: "luck never came of crossing it."

"In troth," said the Ranzelman, "they are wise folks that let wave and withy haud their ain : luck never came of a half-drowned man, or a half-hanged ane either. Who was't shot Will Paterson off the Noss?[1] The Dutchman that he saved from sinking, I trow. To fling a drowning man a plank or a tow may be the part of a Christian; but I say, keep hands aff him, if ye wad live and thrive free frae his danger."

"Ye are a wise man, Ranzelman, and a worthy," echoed Swertha, with a groan, "and ken how and when to help a neighbour as weel as ony man that ever drew a net."

"In troth, I have seen length of days," answered the Ranzelman, "and I have heard what the auld folk said to each other anent sic matters; and nae man in Zetland shall go farther than I will in any Christian service to a man on firm land; but if he cry 'Help!' out of the saut waves, that's another story."

"And yet, to think of this lad Cleveland standing in our Maister Mordaunt's light," said Swertha, "and with Magnus Troil, that thought him the flower of the island but on Whit-sunday last; and Magnus, too, that's both held—when he's fresh, honest man!—the wisest and wealthiest of Zetland!"

"He canna win by it," said the Ranzelman, with a look of the deepest sagacity. "There's whiles, Swertha, that the wisest of us, as I am sure I humbly confess mysell not to be, may be little better than gulls, and can no more win by doing deeds of folly than I can step over Sumburgh Head. It has been my own case once or twice in my life. But we shall see soon what ill is to come of all this, for good there cannot come."

And Swertha answered, with the same tone of prophetic wisdom : "Na—na, gude can never come on it, and that is ower truly said."

These doleful predictions, repeated from time to time, had some effect upon Mordaunt. He did not indeed suppose that the charitable action of relieving a drowning man had subjected him, as a necessary and fatal consequence, to the unpleasant circumstances in which he was placed; yet he felt

[1] [See Lockhart's *Life of Scott*, vol. iv. p. 202.]

as if a sort of spell were drawn around him, of which he neither understood the nature nor the extent; that some power, in short, beyond his own control was acting upon his destiny, and, as it seemed, with no friendly influence. His curiosity, as well as his anxiety, was highly excited, and he continued determined, at all events, to make his appearance at the approaching festival, when he was impressed with the belief that something uncommon was necessarily to take place, which should determine his future views and prospects in life.

As the elder Mertoun was at this time in his ordinary state of health, it became necessary that his son should intimate to him his intended visit to Burgh-Westra. He did so; and his father desired to know the especial reason of his going thither at this particular time.

"It is a time of merry-making," replied the youth, "and all the country are assembled."

"And you are doubtless impatient to add another fool to the number. Go; but beware how you walk in the path which you are about to tread: a fall from the cliffs of Foulah were not more fatal."

"May I ask the reason of your caution, sir?" replied Mordaunt, breaking through the reserve which ordinarily subsisted betwixt him and his singular parent.

"Magnus Troil," said the elder Mertoun, "has two daughters; you are of the age when men look upon such gauds with eyes of affection, that they may afterwards learn to curse the day that first opened their eyes upon heaven! I bid you beware of them; for, as sure as that death and sin came into the world by woman, so sure are their soft words and softer looks the utter destruction and ruin of all who put faith in them."

Mordaunt had sometimes observed his father's marked dislike to the female sex, but had never before heard him give vent to it in terms so determined and precise. He replied, that the daughters of Magnus Troil were no more to him than any other females in the islands. "They were even of less importance," he said, "for they had broken off their friendship with him, without assigning any cause."

"And you go to seek the renewal of it?" answered his father. "Silly moth, that hast once escaped the taper without singeing thy wings, are you not contented with the safe obscurity of these wilds, but must hasten back to the flame, which is sure at length to consume thee? But why should I waste arguments in deterring thee from thy inevitable fate? Go where thy destiny calls thee."

On the succeeding day, which was the eve of the great festival, Mordaunt set forth on his road to Burgh-Westra, pondering alternately on the injunctions of Norna, on the ominous words of his father, on the inauspicious auguries of Swertha and the Ranzelman of Jarlshof; and not without experiencing that gloom with which so many concurring circumstances of ill omen combined to oppress his mind.

"It bodes me but a cold reception at Burgh-Westra," said he; "but my stay shall be the shorter. I will but find out whether they have been deceived by this seafaring stranger, or whether they have acted out of pure caprice of temper and love of change of company. If the first be the case, I will vindicate my character, and let Captain Cleveland look to himself; if the latter, why, then, good-night to Burgh-Westra and all its inmates."

As he mentally meditated this last alternative, hurt pride, and a return of fondness for those to whom he supposed he was bidding farewell for ever, brought a tear into his eye, which he dashed off hastily and indignantly, as, mending his pace, he continued on his journey.

The weather being now serene and undisturbed, Mordaunt made his way with an ease that formed a striking contrast to the difficulties which he had encountered when he last travelled the same route; yet there was a less pleasing subject for comparison within his own mind.

"My breast," he said to himself, "was then against the wind, but my heart within was serene and happy. I would I had now the same careless feelings, were they to be bought by battling with the severest storm that ever blew across these lonely hills!"

With such thoughts he arrived about noon at Harfra, the

habitation, as the reader may remember, of the ingenious Mr. Yellowley. Our traveller had, upon the present occasion, taken care to be quite independent of the niggardly hospitality of this mansion, which was now become infamous on that account through the whole island, by bringing with him, in his small knapsack, such provisions as might have sufficed for a longer journey. In courtesy, however, or rather, perhaps, to get rid of his own disquieting thoughts, Mordaunt did not fail to call at the mansion, which he found in singular commotion. Triptolemus himself, invested with a pair of large jack-boots, went clattering up and down stairs, screaming out questions to his sister and his serving-woman Tronda, who replied with shriller and more complicated screeches. At length, Mrs. Baby herself made her appearance, her venerable person endued with what was then called a joseph—an ample garment, which had once been green, but now, betwixt stains and patches, had become, like the vesture of the patriarch whose name it bore, a garment of divers colours. A steeple-crowned hat, the purchase of some long-past moment, in which vanity had got the better of avarice, with a feather which had stood as much wind and rain as if it had been part of a seamew's wing, made up her equipment, save that in her hand she held a silver-mounted whip of antique fashion. This attire, as well as an air of determined bustle in the gait and appearance of Mrs. Barbara Yellowley, seemed to bespeak that she was prepared to take a journey, and cared not, as the saying goes, who knew that such was her determination.

She was the first that observed Mordaunt on his arrival, and she greeted him with a degree of mingled emotion. "Be good to us!" she exclaimed, "if here is not the canty callant that wears yon thing about his neck, and that snapped up our goose as light as if it had been a sandie-lavrock!" The admiration of the gold chain, which had formerly made so deep an impression on her mind, was marked in the first part of her speech, the recollection of the untimely fate of the smoked goose was commemorated in the second clause. "I will lay the burden of my life," she instantly added, "that he is ganging our gate."

"I am bound for Burgh-Westra, Mrs. Yellowley," said Mordaunt.

"And blythe will we be of your company," she added. "It's early day to eat, but if you liked a barley scone and a drink of bland—natheless, it is ill travelling on a full stomach, besides quelling your appetite for the feast that is biding you this day; for all sort of prodigality there will doubtless be."

Mordaunt produced his own stores, and, explaining that he did not love to be burdensome to them on this second occasion, invited them to partake of the provisions he had offered. Poor Triptolemus, who seldom saw half so good a dinner as his guest's luncheon, threw himself upon the good cheer, like Sancho on the scum of Camacho's kettle, and even the lady herself could not resist the temptation, though she gave way to it with more moderation, and with something like a sense of shame. "She had let the fire out," she said, "for it was a pity wasting fuel in so cold a country, and so she had not thought of getting anything ready, as they were to set out so soon; and so she could not but say that the young gentleman's 'nacket' look_d very good; and, besides, she had some curiosity to see whether the folks in that country cured their beef in the same way they did in the north of Scotland"; under which combined considerations, Dame Baby made a hearty experiment on the refreshments which thus unexpectedly presented themselves.

When their extemporary repast was finished, the factor became solicitous to take the road; and now Mordaunt discovered that the alacrity with which he had been received by Mistress Baby was not altogether disinterested. Neither she nor the learned Triptolemus felt much disposed to commit themselves to the wilds of Zetland without the assistance of a guide; and although they could have commanded the aid of one of their own labouring folks, yet the cautious agriculturist observed, that it would be losing at least one day's work; and his sister multiplied his apprehensions by echoing back: "One day's work! ye may weel say twenty; for, set ane of their noses within the smell of a kail-pot, and their lugs within the sound of a fiddle, and whistle them back if ye can!"

Now the fortunate arrival of Mordaunt, in the very nick of time, not to mention the good cheer which he brought with him. made him as welcome as any one could possibly be to a threshold which, on all ordinary occasions, abhorred the passage of a guest; nor was Mr. Yellowley altogether insensible of the pleasure he promised himself in detailing his plans of improvement to his young companion, and enjoying what his fate seldom assigned him—the company of a patient and admiring listener.

As the factor and his sister were to prosecute their journey on horseback, it only remained to mount their guide and companion—a thing easily accomplished where there are such numbers of shaggy, long-backed, short-legged ponies running wild upon the extensive moors, which are the common pasturage for the cattle of every township, where shelties, geese, swine, goats, sheep, and little Zetland cows are turned out promiscuously, and often in numbers which can obtain but precarious subsistence from the niggard vegetation. There is, indeed, a right of individual property in all these animals, which are branded or tattooed by each owner with his own peculiar mark; but when any passenger has occasional use for a pony, he never scruples to lay hold of the first which he can catch, puts on a halter, and, having rode him as far as he finds convenient, turns the animal loose to find his way back again as he best can—a matter in which the ponies are sufficiently sagacious.

Although this general exercise of property was one of the enormities which in due time the factor intended to abolish, yet, like a wise man, he scrupled not, in the mean time, to avail himself of so general a practice, which, he condescended to allow, was particularly convenient for those who, as chanced to be his own present case, had no ponies of their own on which their neighbours could retaliate. Three shelties, therefore, were procured from the hill—little shagged animals, more resembling wild bears than anything of the horse tribe, yet possessed of no small degree of strength and spirit, and able to endure as much fatigue and indifferent usage as any creatures in the world.

Two of these horses were already provided and fully ac-
coutred for the journey. One of them, destined to bear the
fair person of Mistress Baby, was decorated with a huge side-
saddle of venerable antiquity—a mass, as it were, of cushion
and padding, from which depended, on all sides, a housing of
ancient tapestry, which, having been originally intended for
a horse of ordinary size, covered up the diminutive palfrey
over which it was spread, from the ears to the tail, and from
the shoulder to the fetlock, leaving nothing visible but its
head, which looked fiercely out from these enfoldments, like
the heraldic representation of a lion looking out of a bush.
Mordaunt gallantly lifted up the fair Mistress Yellowley, and
at the expense of very slight exertion placed her upon the
summit of her mountainous saddle. It is probable that, on
feeling herself thus squired and attended upon, and experiencing the long unwonted consciousness that she was attired in
her best array, some thoughts dawned upon Mistress Baby's
mind which checkered for an instant those habitual ideas about
thrift that formed the daily and all-engrossing occupation of
her soul. She glanced her eye upon her faded joseph, and on
the long housings of her saddle, as she observed, with a smile,
to Mordaunt, that "travelling was a pleasant thing in fine
weather and agreeable company, if," she added, glancing a
look at a place where the embroidery was somewhat frayed and
tattered, " it was not sae wasteful to ane's horse-furniture."

Meanwhile, her brother stepped stoutly to his steed; and
as he chose, notwithstanding the serenity of the weather, to
throw a long red cloak over his other garments, his pony was
even more completely enveloped in drapery than that of his sister. It happened, moreover, to be an animal of an high and
contumacious spirit, bouncing and curvetting occasionally
under the weight of Triptolemus, with a vivacity which, notwithstanding his Yorkshire descent, rather deranged him in the
saddle; gambols which, as the palfrey itself was not visible,
except upon the strictest inspection, had, at a little distance,
an effect as if they were the voluntary movements of the
cloaked cavalier, without the assistance of any other legs than
those with which nature had provided him; and, to any who

had viewed Triptolemus under such a persuasion, the gravity, and even distress, announced in his countenance must have made a ridiculous contrast to the vivacious caprioles with which he piaffed along the moor.

Mordaunt kept up with this worthy couple, mounted, according to the simplicity of the time and country, on the first and readiest pony which they had been able to press into the service, with no other accoutrement of any kind than the halter which served to guide him; while Mr. Yellowley, seeing with pleasure his guide thus readily provided with a steed, privately resolved that this rude custom of helping travellers to horses, without leave of the proprietor, should not be abated in Zetland until he came to possess a herd of ponies belonging in property to himself, and exposed to suffer in the way of retaliation.

But to other uses or abuses of the country Triptolemus Yellowley showed himself less tolerant. Long and wearisome were the discourses he held with Mordaunt, or (to speak much more correctly) the harangues which he inflicted upon him, concerning the changes which his own advent in these isles was about to occasion. Unskilled as he was in the modern arts by which an estate may be improved to such a high degree that it shall altogether slip through the proprietor's fingers, Triptolemus had at least the zeal, if not the knowledge, of a whole agricultural society in his own person; nor was he surpassed by any who has followed him in that noble spirit which scorns to balance profit against outlay, but holds the glory of effecting a great change on the face of the land to be, like virtue, in a great degree its own reward.

No part of the wild and mountainous region over which Mordaunt guided him but what suggested to his active imagination some scheme of improvement and alteration. He would make a road through yon scarce passable glen, where at present nothing but the sure-footed creatures on which they were mounted could tread with any safety. He would substitute better houses for the skeos, or sheds built of dry stones, in which the inhabitants cured or manufactured their fish; they should brew good ale instead of bland; they should plant forests where tree never grew; and find mines of treasure where a Danish skilling was accounted a coin of a most respectable denomination. All these mutations, with many others, did the worthy factor resolve upon, speaking at the same time with the utmost confidence of the countenance and assistance which he was to receive from the higher classes, and especially from Magnus Troil.

"I will impart some of my ideas to the poor man," he said, "before we are both many hours older; and you will mark how grateful he will be to the instructor who brings him knowledge, which is better than wealth."

"I would not have you build too strongly on that," said Mordaunt, by way of caution. "Magnus Troil's boat is kittle to trim; he likes his own ways, and his country ways, and you will as soon teach your sheltie to dive like a sealgh as bring Magnus to take a Scottish fashion in the place of a Norse one; and yet, if he is steady to his old customs, he may perhaps be as changeable as another in his old friendships."

"Heus, tu inepte!" said the scholar of St. Andrews, "steady or unsteady, what can it matter? Am not I here in point of trust and in point of power? and shall a fowd, by which barbarous appellative this Magnus Troil still calls himself, presume to measure judgment and weigh reasons with me, who represent the full dignity of the chamberlain of the islands of Orkney and Zetland?"

"Still," said Mordaunt, "I would advise you not to advance too rashly upon his prejudices. Magnus Troil, from the hour of his birth to this day, never saw a greater man than himself, and it is difficult to bridle an old horse for the first time. Besides, he has at no time in his life been a patient listener to long explanations, so it is possible that he may quarrel with your proposed reformation before you can convince him of its advantages."

"How mean you, young man!" said the factor. "Is there one who dwells in these islands who is so wretchedly blind as not to be sensible of their deplorable defects? Can a man," he added, rising into enthusiasm as he spoke, "or even a beast, look at that thing there, which they have the impudence to call a corn-mill,[1] without trembling to think that corn should be entrusted to such a miserable molendinary? The wretches are obliged to have at least fifty in each parish, each trundling away upon its paltry millstone, under the thatch of a roof no bigger than a bee-skep, instead of a noble and seemly baron's mill, of which you would hear the clack through the haill country, and that casts the meal through the mill-eye by forpits at a time!"

"Ay—ay, brother," said his sister, "that's spoken like your wise sell. The mair cost the mair honour—that's your word ever mair. Can it no creep into your wise head, man, that ilka body grinds their ain nievefu' of meal in this country, without plaguing themsells about barons' mills, and thirls, and sucken, and the like trade? How mony a time have I heard you bell-the-cat with auld Edie Netherstane, the miller at Grindleburn, and wi' his very knave too, about in-town and out-town multures, lock, gowpen, and knaveship,[2] and a' the lave o't; and now naething less will serve you than to bring in the very same fashery on a wheen puir bodies, that big ilk ane a mill for themselves, sic as it is?"

"Dinna tell me of gowpen and knaveship!" exclaimed the indignant agriculturist; "better pay the half of the grist to the miller, to have the rest grund in a Christian manner, than put good grain into a bairn's whirligig. Look at it for a moment, Baby. Bide still, ye cursed imp!" This interjection was applied to his pony, which began to be extremely impatient, while its rider interrupted his journey to point out all the weak points of the Zetland mill. "Look at it, I say— it's just one degree better than a hand-quern: it has neither wheel nor trindle, neither cog nor happer. Bide still, there's a canny beast. It canna grind a bickerfu' of meal in a quarter of an hour, and that will be mair like a mash for horse than a meltith for man's use. Wherefore—Bide still, I say!— wherefore—wherefore—— The deil's in the beast, and nae good, I think!"

As he uttered the last words, the shelty, which had pranced

and curvetted for some time with much impatience, at length got its head betwixt its legs, and at once canted its rider into the little rivulet which served to drive the depreciated engine he was surveying; then emancipating itself from the folds of the cloak, fled back towards its own wilderness, neighing in scorn, and flinging out its heels at every five yards.

Laughing heartily at his disaster, Mordaunt helped the old man to arise; while his sister sarcastically congratulated him on having fallen rather into the shallows of a Zetland rivulet than the depths of a Scottish mill-pond. Disdaining to reply to this sarcasm, Triptolemus, so soon as he had recovered his legs, shaken his ears, and found that the folds of his cloak had saved him from being much wet in the scanty streamlet, exclaimed aloud: "I will have cussers from Lanarkshire, brood mares from Ayrshire: I will not have one of these cursed abortions left on the islands, to break honest folks' necks. I say, Baby, I will rid the land of them."

"Ye had better wring your ain cloak, Triptolemus," answered Baby.

Mordaunt meanwhile was employed in catching another pony from a herd which strayed at some distance; and, having made a halter out of twisted rushes, he seated the dismayed agriculturist in safety upon a more quiet, though less active, steed than that which he had at first bestrode.

But Mr. Yellowley's fall had operated as a considerable sedative upon his spirits, and, for the full space of five miles' travel, he said scarce a word, leaving full course to the melancholy aspirations and lamentations which his sister Baby bestowed on the old bridle, which the pony had carried off in its flight, and which, she observed, after having lasted for eighteen years come Martinmas, might now be considered as a castaway thing. Finding she had thus the field to herself, the old lady launched forth into a lecture upon economy, according to her own idea of that virtue, which seemed to include a system of privations which, though observed with the sole purpose of saving money, might, if undertaken upon other principles, have ranked high in the history of a religious ascetic. She was but little interrupted by Mordaunt, who, conscious he was now on the eve of approaching Burgh-Westra, employed himself rather in the task of anticipating the nature of the reception he was about to meet with there from two beautiful young women than with the prosing of an old one, however wisely she might prove that small-beer was more wholesome than strong ale, and that, if her brother had bruised his ankle-bone in his tumble, cumfrey and butter was better to bring him round again than all the doctors' drugs in the world.

But now the dreary moorlands, over which their path had hitherto lain, were exchanged for a more pleasant prospect, opening on a salt-water lake, or arm of the sea, which ran up far inland, and was surrounded by flat and fertile ground, producing crops better than the experienced eye of Triptolemus Yellowley had as yet witnessed in Zetland. In the midst of this Goshen stood the mansion of Burgh-Westra, screened from the north and east by a ridge of heathy hills which lay behind it, and commanding an interesting prospect of the lake and its parent ocean, as well as the islands and more distant mountains. From the mansion itself, as well as from almost every cottage in the adjacent hamlet, arose such a rich cloud of vapoury smoke as showed that the preparations for the festival were not confined to the principal residence of Magnus himself, but extended through the whole vicinage.

"My certie," said Mrs. Baby Yellowley, "ane wad think the haill town was on fire! The very hillside smells of their wastefulness, and a hungry heart wad scarce seek better kitchen to a barley scone than just to waft it in the reek that's rising out of yon lums."

CHAPTER XII.

Thou hast described
A hot friend cooling. Ever note, Lucilius,
When love begins to sicken and decay,
It useth an enforced ceremony.
There are no tricks in plain and simple faith.
Julius Cæsar.

IF the smell which was wafted from the chimneys of Burgh-Westra up to the barren hills by which the mansion was surrounded could, as Mistress Barbara opined, have refreshed the hungry, the noise which proceeded from thence might have given hearing to the deaf. It was a medley of all sounds, and all connected with jollity and kind welcome. Nor were the sights associated with them less animating.

Troops of friends were seen in the act of arriving—their dispersed ponies flying to the moors in every direction, to recover their own pastures in the best way they could; such, as we have already said, being the usual mode of discharging the cavalry which had been levied for a day's service. At a small but commodious harbour, connected with the house and hamlet, those visitors were landing from their boats who, living in distant islands and along the coast, had preferred making their journey by sea. Mordaunt and his companions might see each party pausing frequently to greet each other, and strolling on successively to the house, whose ever open gate received them alternately in such numbers that it seemed the extent of the mansion, though suited to the opulence and hospitality of the owner, was scarce, on this occasion, sufficient for the guests.

Among the confused sounds of mirth and welcome which arose at the entrance of each new company, Mordaunt thought he could distinguish the loud laugh and hearty salutation of the sire of the mansion, and began to feel more deeply than before the anxious doubt whether that cordial reception, which was distributed so freely to all others, would be on this occasion extended to him. As they came on, they heard the

10

voluntary scrapings and bravura effusions of the gallant fiddlers, who impatiently flung already from their bows those sounds with which they were to animate the evening. The clamour of the cook's assistants, and the loud scolding tones of the cook himself, were also to be heard—sounds of dissonance at any other time, but which, subdued with others, and by certain happy associations, form no disagreeable part of the full chorus which always precedes a rural feast.

Meanwhile, the guests advanced, each full of their own thoughts. Mordaunt's we have already noticed. Baby was wrapt up in the melancholy grief and surprise excited by the positive conviction that so much victuals had been cooked at once as were necessary to feed all the mouths which were clamouring around her—an enormity of expense which, though she was no way concerned in bearing it, affected her nerves, as the beholding a massacre would touch those of the most indifferent spectator, however well assured of his own personal safety. She sickened, in short, at the sight of so much extravagance, like Abyssinian Bruce, when he saw the luckless minstrels of Gondar hacked to pieces by the order of Ras Michael. As for her brother, they being now arrived where the rude and antique instruments of Zetland agriculture lay scattered in the usual confusion of a Scottish barn-yard, his thoughts were at once engrossed in the deficiencies of the one-stilted plough; of the "twiscar," with which they dig peats; of the sledges, on which they transport commodities; of all and everything, in short, in which the usages of the islands differed from those of the mainland of Scotland. The sight of these imperfect instruments stirred the blood of Triptolemus Yellowley, as that of the bold warrior rises at seeing the arms and insignia of the enemy he is about to combat; and, faithful to his high emprise, he thought less of the hunger which his journey had occasioned, although about to be satisfied by such a dinner as rarely fell to his lot, than upon the task which he had undertaken of civilising the manners, and improving the cultivation, of Zetland.

"*Jacta est alea*," he muttered to himself; "this very day shall prove whether the Zetlanders are worthy of our labours, or whether their minds are as incapable of cultivation as their peat-mosses. Yet, let us be cautious, and watch the soft time of speech. I feel, by my own experience, that it were best to let the body, in its present state, take the place of the mind. A mouthful of that same roast-beef, which smells so delicately, will form an apt introduction to my grand plan for improving the breed of stock."

By this time the visitors had reached the low but ample front of Magnus Troil's residence, which seemed of various dates, with large and ill-imagined additions, hastily adapted to the original building, as the increasing estate, or enlarged family, of successive proprietors appeared to each to demand. Beneath a low, broad, and large porch, supported by two huge carved posts, once the head-ornaments of vessels which had found shipwreck upon the coast, stood Magnus himself, intent on the hospitable toil of receiving and welcoming the numerous guests who successively approached. His strong, portly figure was well adapted to the dress which he wore—a blue coat of an antique cut, lined with scarlet, and laced and looped with gold down the seams and button-holes, and along the ample cuffs. Strong and masculine features, rendered ruddy and brown by frequent exposure to severe weather; a quantity of most venerable silver hair, which fell in unshorn profusion from under his gold-laced hat, and was carelessly tied with a ribbon behind, expressed at once his advanced age, his hasty, yet well-conditioned temper, and his robust constitution. As our travellers approached him, a shade of displeasure seemed to cross his brow, and to interrupt for an instant the honest and hearty burst of hilarity with which he had been in the act of greeting all prior arrivals. When he approached Triptolemus Yellowley, he drew himself up, so as to mix, as it were, some share of the stately importance of the opulent Udaller with the welcome afforded by the frank and hospitable landlord.

"You are welcome, Mr. Yellowley," was his address to the factor—"you are welcome to Westra; the wind has blown you on a rough coast, and we that are the natives must be kind to you as we can. This, I believe, is your sister. Mistress Barbara Yellowley, permit me the honour of a neighbourly salute." And so saying, with a daring and self-devoted courtesy which would find no equal in our degenerate days, he acutally ventured to salute the withered cheek of the spinster, who relaxed so much of her usual peevishness of expression as to receive the courtesy with something which approached to a smile. He then looked full at Mordaunt Mertoun, and, without offering his hand, said, in a tone somewhat broken by suppressed agitation: "You, too, are welcome, Master Mordaunt."

"Did I not think so," said Mordaunt, naturally offended by the coldness of his host's manner, "I had not been here; and it is not yet too late to turn back."

"Young man," replied Magnus, "you know better than most that from these doors no man can turn without an offence to their owner. I pray you, disturb not my guests by your ill-timed scruples. When Magnus Troil says welcome, all are welcome who are within hearing of his voice, and it is an indifferent loud one. Walk on, my worthy guests, and let us see what cheer my lasses can make you within doors."

So saying, and taking care to make his manner so general to the whole party that Mordaunt should not be able to appropriate any particular portion of the welcome to himself, nor yet to complain of being excluded from all share in it, the Udaller ushered the guests into his house, where two large outer rooms, which, on the present occasion, served the purpose of a modern saloon, were already crowded with guests of every description.

The furniture was sufficiently simple, and had a character peculiar to the situation of those stormy islands. Magnus Troil was, indeed, like most of the higher class of Zetland proprietors, a friend to the distressed traveller, whether by sea or land, and had repeatedly exerted his whole authority in protecting the property and persons of shipwrecked mariners; yet so frequent were wrecks upon that tremendous coast, and so many unappropriated articles were constantly flung ashore, that the interior of the house bore sufficient witness to the ravages of the ocean, and to the exercise of those rights which the lawyers term "flotsome and jetsome." The chairs, which were arranged around the walls, were such as are used in cabins, and many of them were of foreign construction; the mirrors and cabinets, which were placed against the walls for ornament or convenience, had, it was plain from their form, been constructed for shipboard, and one or two of the latter were of strange and unknown wood. Even the partition which separated the two apartments seemed constructed out of the bulkhead of some large vessel, clumsily adapted to the service which it at present performed by the labour of some native joiner. To a stranger these evident marks and tokens of human misery might, at the first glance, form a contrast with the scene of mirth with which they were now associated; but the association was so familiar to the natives that it did not for a moment interrupt the course of their glee.

To the younger part of these revellers the presence of Mordaunt was like a fresh charm of enjoyment. All came around him to marvel at his absence, and all, by their repeated inquiries, plainly showed that they conceived it had been entirely voluntary on his side. The youth felt that this general acceptation relieved his anxiety on one painful point. Whatever prejudice the family of Burgh-Westra might have adopted respecting him, it must be of a private nature; and at least he had not the additional pain of finding that he was depreciated in the eyes of society at large; and his vindication, when he found opportunity to make one, would not require to be extended beyond the circle of a single family. This was consoling; though his heart still throbbed with anxiety at the thought of meeting with his estranged but still beloved friends. Laying the excuse of his absence on his father's state of health, he made his way through the various groups of friends and guests, each of whom seemed willing to detain him as long as possible, and having, by presenting them to one or two families of consequence, got rid of his travelling-companions, who at first stuck fast as burrs, he reached at length the door of a small apartment, which, opening from one of the large exterior rooms we have mentioned, Minna and Brenda had been permitted to fit up after their own taste, and to call their peculiar property.

Mordaunt had contributed no small share of the invention and mechanical execution employed in fitting up this favourite apartment, and in disposing its ornaments. It was, indeed, during his last residence at Burgh-Westra, as free to his entrance and occupation as to its proper mistresses. But now, so much were times altered that he remained with his finger on the latch, uncertain whether he should take the freedom to draw it, until Brenda's voice pronounced the words, "Come in, then," in the tone of one who is interrupted by an unwelcome disturber, who is to be heard and despatched with all the speed possible.

At this signal, Mertoun entered the fanciful cabinet of the sisters, which, by the addition of many ornaments, including some articles of considerable value, had been fitted up for the approaching festival. The daughters of Magnus, at the moment of Mordaunt's entrance, were seated in deep consultation with the stranger Cleveland and with a little, slight-made old man, whose eye retained all the vivacity of spirit which had supported him under the thousand vicissitudes of a changeful and precarious life, and which, accompanying him in his old age, rendered his grey hairs less awfully reverend perhaps, but not less beloved, than would a more grave and less imaginative expression of countenance and character. There was even a penetrating shrewdness mingled in the look of curiosity with which, as he stepped for an instant aside, he seemed to watch the meeting of Mordaunt with the two lovely sisters.

The reception the youth met with resembled, in general character, that which he had experienced from Magnus himself; but the maidens could not so well cover their sense of the change of circumstances under which they met. Both blushed, as, rising, and without extending the hand, far less offering the cheek, as the fashion of the times permitted, and almost exacted, they paid to Mordaunt the salutation due to an ordinary acquaintance. But the blush of the elder was one of those transient evidences of flitting emotion that vanish as fast as the passing thought which excites them. In an instant she stood before the youth calm and cold, returning, with guarded and cautious courtesy, the usual civilities, which, with a faltering voice, Mordaunt endeavoured to present to her. The emotion of Brenda bore, externally at least, a deeper and more agitating character. Her blush extended over every part of her beautiful skin which her dress permitted to be visible, including her slender neck and the upper region of a finely-formed bosom. Neither did she even attempt to reply to what share of his confused compliment Mordaunt addressed to her in particular, but regarded him with eyes in which displeasure was evidently mingled with feelings of regret and recollections of former times. Mordaunt felt, as it were, assured upon the instant that the regard of Minna was extinguished, but that it might be yet possible to recover that of the milder Brenda; and such is the waywardness of human fancy, that, though he had never hitherto made any distinct difference betwixt these two beautiful and interesting girls, the favour of her which seemed most absolutely withdrawn became at the moment the most interesting in his eyes.

He was disturbed in these hasty reflections by Cleveland, who advanced, with military frankness, to pay his compliments to his preserver, having only delayed long enough to permit the exchange of the ordinary salutation betwixt the visitor and the ladies of the family. He made his approach with so good a grace, that it was impossible for Mordaunt, although he dated his loss of favour at Burgh-Westra from this stranger's appearance on the coast and domestication in the family, to do less than return his advances as courtesy demanded, accept his thanks with an appearance of satisfaction, and hope that his time had past pleasantly since their last meeting.

Cleveland was about to answer, when he was anticipated by the little old man, formerly noticed, who, now thrusting himself forward and seizing Mordaunt's hand, kissed him on the forehead; and then at the same time echoed and answered his question. "How passes time at Burgh-Westra? Was it you that asked it, my prince of the cliff and of the scaur? How should it pass, but with all the wings that beauty and joy can add to help its flight!"

"And wit and song, too, my good old friend," said Mordaunt, half-serious, half-jesting, as he shook the old man cordially by the hand. "These cannot be wanting where Claud Halcro comes!"

"Jeer me not, Mordaunt, my good lad," replied the old man. "When your foot is as slow as mine, your wit frozen, and your song out of tune——"

"How can you belie yourself, my good master?" answered Mordaunt, who was not unwilling to avail himself of his old friend's peculiarities to introduce something like conversation, break the awkwardness of this singular meeting, and gain time for observation, ere requiring an explanation of the change of conduct which the family seemed to have adopted towards him. "Say not so," he continued. "Time, my old friend, lays his hand lightly on the bard. Have I not heard you say, the poet partakes the immortality of his song? and surely the great English poet you used to tell us of was elder than yourself when he pulled the bow-oar among all the wits of London."

This alluded to a story which was, as the French term it, Halcro's *cheval de bataille*, and any allusion to which was certain at once to place him in the saddle and to push his hobbyhorse into full career.

His laughing eye kindled with a sort of enthusiasm, which the ordinary folk of this world might have called crazed, while he dashed into the subject which he best loved to talk upon. "Alas, alas, my dear Mordaunt Mertoun, silver is silver, and waxes not dim by use; and pewter is pewter, and grows the longer the duller. It is not for poor Claud Halcro to name himself in the same twelvemonth with the immortal John Dryden. True it is, as I may have told you before, that I have seen that great man, nay, I have been in the Wits' Coffee-house, as it was then called, and had once a pinch out of his own very snuff-box. I must have told you all how it happened, but here is Captain Cleveland who never heard it. I lodged, you must know, in Russel Street—I question not but you know Russel Street, Covent Garden, Captain Cleveland?"

"I should know its latitude pretty well, Mr. Halcro," said the captain, smiling; "but I believe you mentioned the circumstance yesterday, and, besides, we have the day's duty in hand: you must play us this song which we are to study."

"It will not serve the turn now," said Halcro: "we must think of something that will take in our dear Mordaunt, the first voice in the island, whether for a part or solo. I will never be he will touch a string to you unless Mordaunt Mertoun is to help us out. What say you, my fairest Night? What think you, my sweet Dawn of Day?" he added, addressing the young women, upon whom, as we have said elsewhere, he had long before bestowed these allegorical names.

"Mr. Mordaunt Mertoun," said Minna, "has come too late to be of our band on this occasion: it is our misfortune, but it cannot be helped."

"How? what?" said Halcro, hastily—"too late—and you have practised together all your lives? Take my word, my bonny lasses, that old tunes are sweetest, and old friends surest. Mr. Cleveland has a fine bass, that must be allowed; but I would have you trust for the first effect to one of the twenty fine airs you can sing where Mordaunt's tenor joins so well with your own witchery. Here is my lovely Day approves of the change in her heart."

"You were never in your life more mistaken, father Halcro," said Brenda, her cheeks again reddening, more with displeasure, it seemed, than with shame.

"Nay, but how is this?" said the old man, pausing and looking at them alternately. "What have we got here? A cloudy night and a red morning? That betokens rough weather. What means all this, young women?—where lies the offence? In me, I fear; for the blame is always laid upon the oldest when young folk like you go by the ears."

"The blame is not with you, father Halcro," said Minna, rising and taking her sister by the arm, "if indeed there be blame anywhere."

"I should fear then, Minna," said Mordaunt, endeavouring to soften his tone into one of indifferent pleasantry, "that the new-comer has brought the offence along with him."

"When no offence is taken," replied Minna, with her usual gravity, "it matters not by whom such may have been offered."

"Is it possible, Minna!" exclaimed Mordaunt, "and is it you who speak thus to me! And you too, Brenda, can you too judge so hardly of me, yet without permitting me one moment of honest and frank explanation?"

"Those who should know best," answered Brenda, in a low but decisive tone of voice, "have told us their pleasure, and it must be done. Sister, I think we have staid too long here, and shall be wanted elsewhere. Mr. Mertoun will excuse us on so busy a day."

The sisters linked their arms together. Halcro in vain endeavoured to stop them, making, at the same time, a theatrical gesture, and exclaiming:

"Now, Day and Night, but this is wondrous strange!"

Then turned to Mordaunt Mertoun, and added: "The girls are possessed with the spirit of mutability, showing, as our master Spenser well saith, that

> Among all living creatures, more or lesse,
> Change still doth reign, and keep the greater sway.

Captain Cleveland," he continued, "know you anything that has happened to put these two juvenile Graces out of tune?"

"He will lose his reckoning," answered Cleveland, "that spends time in inquiring why the wind shifts a point or why a woman changes her mind. Were I Mr. Mordaunt, I would not ask the proud wenches another question on such a subject."

"It is a friendly advice, Captain Cleveland," replied Mordaunt, "and I will not hold it the less so that it has been given unasked. Allow me to inquire if you are yourself as indifferent to the opinion of your female friends as it seems you would have me to be?"

"Who, I?" said the captain, with an air of frank indifference, "I never thought twice upon such a subject. I never saw a woman worth thinking twice about after the anchor was a-peak; on shore it is another thing, and I will laugh, sing, dance, and make love, if they like it, with twenty girls, were they but half so pretty as those who have left us, and make them heartily welcome to change their course in the sound of a boatswain's whistle.   It will be odds but I wear as fast as they can."

A patient is seldom pleased with that sort of consolation which is founded on holding light the malady of which he complains; and Mordaunt felt disposed to be offended with Captain Cleveland both for taking notice of his embarrassment and intruding upon him his own opinion; and he replied, therefore, somewhat sharply: "That Captain Cleveland's sentiments were only suited to such as had the art to become universal favourites wherever chance happened to throw them, and who could not lose in one place more than their merit was sure to gain for them in another."

This was spoken ironically; but there was, to confess the truth, a superior knowledge of the world, and a consciousness of external merit at least, about the man which rendered his interference doubly disagreeable.   As Sir Lucius O'Trigger says, there was an air of success about Captain Cleveland which was mighty provoking.   Young, handsome, and well assured, his air of nautical bluntness sat naturally and easily upon him, and was perhaps particularly well fitted to the simple manners of the remote country in which he found himself; and where, even in the best families, a greater degree of refinement might have rendered his conversation rather less acceptable.   He was contented, in the present instance, to smile good-humouredly at the obvious discontent of Mordaunt Mertoun, and replied: "You are angry with me, my good friend, but you cannot make me angry with you.   The fair hands of all the pretty women I ever saw in my life would never have fished me up out of the Roost of Sumburgh.   So, pray, do not quarrel with me; for here is Mr. Halcro witness that I have struck both jack and topsail, and should you fire a broadside into me, cannot return a single shot."

"Ay—ay," said Halcro, "you must be friends with Captain Cleveland, Mordaunt.   Never quarrel with your friend because a woman is whimsical.   Why, man, if they kept one humour, how the devil could we make so many songs on them as we do?

Even old Dryden himself, glorious old John, could have said little about a girl that was always of one mind: as well write verses upon a mill-pond. It is your tides and your roosts, and your currents and eddies, that come and go, and ebb and flow—by Heaven! I run into rhyme when I so much as think upon them—that smile one day, rage the next, flatter and devour, delight and ruin us, and so forth—it is these that give the real soul of poetry. Did you never hear my 'Adieu to the Lass of Northmaven'? That was poor Bet Stimbister, whom I call Mary for the sound's sake, as I call myself Hacon, after my great ancestor Hacon Goldemund, or Haco with the Golden Mouth, who came to the island with Harold Harfager, and was his chief Scald? Well, but where was I? Oh ay; poor Bet Stimbister, she—and partly some debt—was the cause of my leaving the isles of Hialtland—better so called than Shetland, or Zetland even—and taking to the broad world. I have had a tramp of it since that time. I have battled my way through the world, captain, as a man of mold may, that has a light head, a light purse, and a heart as light as them both; fought my way, and paid my way, that is, either with money or wit; have seen kings changed and deposed as you would turn a tenant out of a scat-hold; knew all the wits of the age, and especially the glorious John Dryden; what man in the islands can say as much, barring lying? I had a pinch out of his own snuff-box; I will tell you how I came by such promotion."

"But the song, Mr. Halcro," said Captain Cleveland.

"The song!" answered Halcro, seizing the captain by the button—for he was too much accustomed to have his audience escape from him during recitation, not to put in practice all the usual means of prevention—"the song! Why, I gave a copy of it, with fifteen others, to the immortal John. You shall hear it—you shall hear them all, if you will but stand still a moment; and you too, my dear boy, Mordaunt Mertoun, I have scarce heard a word from your mouth these six months, and now you are running away from me." So saying, he secured him with his other hand.

"Nay, now he has got us both in tow," said the seaman,

"there is nothing for it but hearing him out, though he spins as tough a yarn as ever an old man-of-war's-man twisted on the watch at midnight."

"Nay, now, be silent—be silent, and let one of us speak at once," said the poet, imperatively; while Cleveland and Mordaunt, looking at each other with a ludicrous expression of resignation to their fate, waited in submission for the well-known and inevitable tale. "I will tell you all about it," continued Halcro. "I was knocked about the world like other young fellows, doing this, that, and t'other for a livelihood; for, thank God, I could turn my hand to anything; but loving still the Muses as much as if the ungrateful jades had found me, like so many blockheads, in my own coach and six. However, I held out till my cousin, old Laurence Linkletter, died, and left me the bit of an island yonder; although, by the way, Cultmalindie was as near to him as I was; but Laurence loved wit, though he had little of his own. Well, he left me the wee bit island—it is as barren as Parnassus itself. What then? I have a penny to spend, a penny to keep my purse, a penny to give to the poor—ay, and a bed and a bottle for a friend, as you shall know, boys, if you will go back with me when this merriment is over. But where was I in my story?"

"Near port, I hope," answered Cleveland; but Halcro was too determined a narrator to be interrupted by the broadest hint.

"Oh ay," he resumed, with the self-satisfied air of one who has recovered the thread of a story, "I was in my old lodgings in Russel Street, with old Timothy Thimblethwaite, the master fashioner, then the best-known man about town. He made for all the wits, and for the dull boobies of fortune besides, and made the one pay for the other. He never denied a wit credit save in jest, or for the sake of getting a repartee; and he was in correspondence with all that was worth knowing about town. He had letters from Crowne, and Tate, and Prior, and Tom Brown, and all the famous fellows of the time, with such pellets of wit, that there was no reading them without laughing ready to die, and all ending with craving a further term for payment."

"I should have thought the tailor would have found that jest rather serious," said Mordaunt.

"Not a bit—not a bit," replied his eulogist, "Tim Thimblethwaite—he was a Cumberland man by birth—had the soul of a prince—ay, and died with the fortune of one; for woe betide the custard-gorged alderman that came under Tim's goose, after he had got one of those letters—egad, he was sure to pay the kain! Why, Thimblethwaite was thought to be the original of little Tom Bibber, in glorious John's comedy of the *Wild Gallant;* and I know that he has trusted, ay, and lent John money to boot out of his own pocket, at a time when all his fine court friends blew cold enough. He trusted me too, and I have been two months on the score at a time for my upper room. To be sure, I was obliging in his way—not that I exactly could shape or sew, nor would that have been decorous for a gentleman of good descent; but I—eh, eh—I drew bills—summed up the books——"

"Carried home the clothes of the wits and aldermen, and got lodging for your labour?" interrupted Cleveland.

"No, no—damn it, no," replied Halcro; "no such thing; you put me out in my story—where was I?"

"Nay, the devil help you to the latitude," said the captain, extricating his button from the gripe of the unmerciful bard's finger and thumb, "for I have no time to take an observation." So saying, he bolted from the room.

"A silly, ill-bred, conceited fool," said Halcro, looking after him; "with as little manners as wit in his empty coxcomb. I wonder what Magnus and these silly wenches can see in him. He tells such damnable long-winded stories, too, about his adventures and sea-fights—every second word a lie, I doubt not. Mordaunt, my dear boy, take example by that man—that is, take warning by him—never tell long stories about yourself. You are sometimes given to talk too much about your own exploits on crags and skerries, and the like, which only breaks conversation, and prevents other folk from being heard. Now, I see you are impatient to hear out what I was saying. Stop, whereabouts was I?"

"I fear we must put it off, Mr. Halcro, until after dinner," said Mordaunt, who also meditated his escape, though desirous of effecting it with more delicacy towards his old acquaintance than Captain Cleveland had thought it necessary to use.

"Nay, my dear boy," said Halcro, seeing himself about to be utterly deserted, "do not you leave me too: never take so bad an example as to set light by old acquaintance, Mordaunt. I have wandered many a weary step in my day; but they were always lightened when I could get hold of the arm of an old friend like yourself."

So saying, he quitted the youth's coat, and sliding his hand gently under his arm, grappled him more effectually; to which Mordaunt submitted, a little moved by the poet's observation upon the unkindness of old acquaintances, under which he himself was an immediate sufferer. But when Halcro renewed his formidable question, "Whereabouts was I?" Mordaunt, preferring his poetry to his prose, reminded him of the song which he said he had written upon his first leaving Zetland—a song to which, indeed, the inquirer was no stranger, but which, as it must be new to the reader, we shall here insert as a favourable specimen of the poetical powers of this tuneful descendant of Haco the Golden-mouthed; for, in the opinion of many tolerable judges, he held a respectable rank among the inditers of madrigals of the period, and was as well qualified to give immortality to his Nancies of the hills or dales as many a gentle sonnetteer of wit and pleasure about town. He was something of a musician also, and on the present occasion seized upon a sort of lute, and, quitting his victim, prepared the instrument for an accompaniment, speaking all the while, that he might lose no time.

"I learned the lute," he said, "from the same man who taught honest Shadwell—plump Tom, as they used to call him—somewhat roughly treated by the glorious John, you remember—Mordaunt, you remember—

> Methinks I see the new Arion sail,
> The lute still trembling underneath thy nail;
> At thy well-sharpen'd thumb, from shore to shore,
> The trebles squeak for fear, the basses roar.

Come, I am indifferently in tune now. What was it to be?

Ay, I remember—nay, 'The Lass of Northmaven' is the ditty
—poor Bet Stimbister!   I have called her Mary in the verses.
Betsy does well for an English song; but Mary is more natural
here."   So saying, after a short prelude, he sung, with a tolerable voice and some taste, the following verses:

Mary.

Farewell to Northmaven,
  Grey Hillswicke, farewell!
To the calms of thy haven,
  The storms on thy fell,
To each breeze that can vary
  The mood of thy main,
And to thee, bonny Mary!
  We meet not again.

Farewell the wild ferry,
  Which Hacon could brave,
When the peaks of the skerry
  Were white in the wave.
There's a maid may look over
  These wild waves in vain
For the skiff of her lover:
  He comes not again.

The vows thou hast broke,
  On the wild currents fling them;
On the quicksand and rock
  Let the mermaidens sing them.
New sweetness they'll give her
  Bewildering strain;
But there's one who will never
  Believe them again.

Oh were there an island,
  Though ever so wild,
Where woman could smile, and
  No man be beguiled;
Too tempting a snare
  To poor mortals were given,
And the hope would fix there,
  That should anchor on heaven!

"I see you are softened, my young friend," said Halcro,
when he had finished his song; "so are most who hear that
same ditty.   Words and music both mine own; and, without
saying much of the wit of it, there is a sort of eh--eh—simplicity and truth about it which gets its way to most folks'

heart. Even your father cannot resist it; and he has a heart as impenetrable to poetry and song as Apollo himself could draw an arrow against. But then he has had some ill luck in his time with the women-folk, as is plain from his owing them such a grudge. Ay—ay, there the charm lies; none of us but has felt the same sore in our day. But come, my dear boy, they are mustering in the hall, men and women both—plagues as they are, we should get on ill without them; but before we go, only mark the last turn—

> And the hope would fix there,—

that is, in the supposed island—a place which neither was nor will be,—

> That should anchor on heaven.

Now you see, my good young man, there are here none of your heathenish rants, which Rochester, Etherege, and these wild fellows used to string together. A parson might sing the song, and his clerk bear the burden; but there is the con-founded bell—we must go now; but never mind, we'll get into a quiet corner at night, and I'll tell you all about it."

CHAPTER XIII.

> Full in the midst the polish'd table shines,
> And the bright goblets, rich with generous wines;
> Now each partakes the feast, the wine prepares,
> Portions the food, and each the portion shares;
> Nor till the rage of thirst and hunger ceased,
> To the high host approach'd the sagacious guest.
> *Odyssey.*

THE hospitable profusion of Magnus Troil's board, the number of guests who feasted in the hall, the much greater number of retainers, attendants, humble friends, and domestics of every possible description, who revelled without, with the multitude of the still poorer and less honoured assistants, who came from every hamlet or township within twenty miles round, to share the bounty of the munificent Udaller, were

11

such as altogether astonished Triptolemus Yellowley, and made him internally doubt whether it would be prudent in him at this time, and amid the full glow of his hospitality, to propose to the host who presided over such a splendid banquet a radical change in the whole customs and usages of his country.

True, the sagacious Triptolemus felt conscious that he possessed in his own person wisdom far superior to that of all the assembled feasters, to say nothing of the landlord, against whose prudence the very extent of his hospitality formed, in Yellowley's opinion, sufficient evidence. But yet the Amphitryon with whom one dines holds, for the time at least, an influence over the minds of his most distinguished guests; and if the dinner be in good style and the wines of the right quality, it is humbling to see that neither art nor wisdom, scarce external rank itself, can assume their natural and wonted superiority over the distributor of these good things, until coffee has been brought in. Triptolemus felt the full weight of this temporary superiority, yet he was desirous to do something that might vindicate the vaunts he had made to his sister and his fellow-traveller, and he stole a look at them from time to time, to mark whether he was not sinking in their esteem from postponing his promised lecture on the enormities of Zetland.

But Mrs. Barbara was busily engaged in noting and registering the waste incurred in such an entertainment as she had probably never before looked upon, and in admiring the host's indifference to, and the guests' absolute negligence of, those rules of civility in which her youth had been brought up. The feasters desired to be helped from a dish which was unbroken, and might have figured at supper, with as much freedom as if it had undergone the ravages of half a dozen guests; and no one seemed to care—the landlord himself least of all—whether those dishes only were consumed which, from their nature, were incapable of reappearance, or whether the assault was extended to the substantial rounds of beef, pasties, and so forth, which, by the rules of good housewifery, were destined to stand two attacks, and which, therefore, according to Mrs. Barbara's ideas of politeness, ought not to have been annihilated by the guests upon the first onset, but spared, like Outis in the cave of Polyphemus, to be devoured the last. Lost in the meditations to which these breaches of convivial discipline gave rise, and in the contemplation of an ideal larder of cold meat which she could have saved out of the wreck of roast, boiled, and baked, sufficient to have supplied her cupboard for at least a twelvemonth, Mrs. Barbara cared very little whether or not her brother supported in its extent the character which he had calculated upon assuming.

Mordaunt Mertoun also was conversant with far other thoughts than those which regarded the proposed reformer of Zetland enormities. His seat was betwixt two blythe maidens of Thule, who, not taking scorn that he had upon other occasions given preference to the daughters of the Udaller, were glad of the chance which assigned to them the attentions of so distinguished a gallant, who, as being their squire at the feast, might in all probability become their partner in the subsequent dance. But, whilst rendering to his fair neighbours all the usual attentions which society required, Mordaunt kept up a covert, but accurate and close, observation upon his estranged friends, Minna and Brenda. The Udaller himself had a share of his attention; but in him he could remark nothing, except the usual tone of hearty and somewhat boisterous hospitality with which he was accustomed to animate the banquet upon all such occasions of general festivity. But in the differing mien of the two maidens there was much more room for painful remark.

Captain Cleveland sat betwixt the sisters, was sedulous in his attentions to both, and Mordaunt was so placed that he could observe all, and hear a great deal, of what passed between them. But Cleveland's peculiar regard seemed devoted to the elder sister. Of this the younger was perhaps conscious, for more than once her eye glanced towards Mordaunt, and, as he thought, with something in it which resembled regret for the interruption of their intercourse, and a sad remembrance of former and more friendly times; while Minna was exclusively engrossed by the attentions of her neighbour; and that it should be so, filled Mordaunt with surprise and resentment.

Minna, the serious, the prudent, the reserved, whose countenance and manners indicated so much elevation of character —Minna, the lover of solitude, and of those paths of knowledge in which men walk best without company—the enemy of light mirth, the friend of musing melancholy, and the frequenter of fountain-heads and pathless glens—she whose character seemed, in short, the very reverse of that which might be captivated by the bold, coarse, and daring gallantry of such a man as this Captain Cleveland, gave, nevertheless, her eye and ear to him, as he sat beside her at table, with an interest and a graciousness of attention which, to Mordaunt, who well knew how to judge of her feelings by her manner, intimated a degree of the highest favour. He observed this, and his heart rose against the favourite by whom he had been thus superseded, as well as against Minna's indiscrete departure from her own character.

"What is there about the man," he said within himself, "more than the bold and daring assumption of importance which is derived from success in petty enterprises, and the exercise of petty despotism over a ship's crew? His very language is more professional than is used by the superior officers of the British navy; and the wit which has excited so many smiles seems to me such as Minna would not formerly have endured for an instant. Even Brenda seems less taken with his gallantry than Minna, whom it should have suited so little."

Mordaunt was doubly mistaken in these his angry speculations. In the first place, with an eye which was, in some respects, that of a rival, he criticised far too severely the manners and behaviour of Captain Cleveland. They were unpolished, certainly; which was of the less consequence in a country inhabited by so plain and simple a race as the ancient Zetlanders. On the other hand, there was an open, naval frankness in Cleveland's bearing, much natural shrewdness, some appropriate humour, an undoubting confidence in himself, and that enterprising hardihood of disposition which, without any other recommendable quality, very often leads to success with the fair sex. But Mordaunt was farther mistaken in supposing that Cleveland was likely to be disagreeable to

Minna Troil, on account of the opposition of their characters in so many material particulars. Had his knowledge of the world been a little more extensive, he might have observed that, as unions are often formed betwixt couples differing in complexion and stature, they take place still more frequently betwixt persons totally differing in feelings, in taste, in pursuits, and in understanding; and it would not be saying, perhaps, too much, to aver that two-thirds of the marriages around us have been contracted betwixt persons who, judging *a priori*, we should have thought had scarce any charms for each other.

A moral and primary cause might be easily assigned for these anomalies, in the wise dispensations of Providence, that the general balance of wit, wisdom, and amiable qualities of all kinds should be kept up through society at large. For, what a world were it if the wise were to intermarry only with the wise, the learned with the learned, the amiable with the amiable, nay, even the handsome with the handsome? and, is it not evident, that the degraded castes of the foolish, the ignorant, the brutal, and the deformed (comprehending, by the way, far the greater portion of mankind), must, when condemned to exclusive intercourse with each other, become gradually as much brutalised in person and disposition as so many ourang-outangs? When, therefore, we see the "gentle joined to the rude," we may lament the fate of the suffering individual, but we must not the less admire the mysterious disposition of that wise Providence which thus balances the moral good and evil of life; which secures for a family, unhappy in the dispositions of one parent, a share of better and sweeter blood, transmitted from the other, and preserves to the offspring the affectionate care and protection of at least one of those from whom it is naturally due. Without the frequent occurrence of such alliances and unions, mis-sorted as they seem at first sight, the world could not be that for which Eternal Wisdom has designed it—a place of mixed good and evil, a place of trial at once and of suffering, where even the worst ills are checkered with something that renders them tolerable to humble and patient minds, and where the best blessings carry with them a necessary alloy of embittering depreciation.

When, indeed, we looked a little closer on the causes of those unexpected and ill-suited attachments, we have occasion to acknowledge that the means by which they are produced do not infer that complete departure from, or inconsistency with, the character of the parties which we might expect when the result alone is contemplated. The wise purposes which Providence appears to have had in view, by permitting such intermixture of dispositions, tempers, and understandings in the married state, are not accomplished by any mysterious impulse by which, in contradiction to the ordinary laws of nature, men or women are urged to an union with those whom the world see to be unsuitable to them. The freedom of will is permitted to us in the occurrences of ordinary life, as in our moral conduct; and in the former as well as the latter case is often the means of misguiding those who possess it. Thus it usually happens, more especially to the enthusiastic and imaginative, that, having formed a picture of admiration in their own mind, they too often deceive themselves by some faint resemblance in some existing being, whom their fancy, as speedily as gratuitously, invests with all the attributes necessary to complete the *beau ideal* of mental perfection. No one, perhaps, even in the happiest marriage, with an object really beloved, ever discovered by experience all the qualities he expected to possess; but in far too many cases he finds he has practised a much higher degree of mental deception, and has erected his airy castle of felicity upon some rainbow, which owed its very existence only to the peculiar state of the atmosphere.

Thus Mordaunt, if better acquainted with life and with the course of human things, would have been little surprised that such a man as Cleveland, handsome, bold, and animated—a man who had obviously lived in danger, and who spoke of it as sport, should have been invested, by a girl of Minna's fanciful disposition, with an extensive share of those qualities which, in her active imagination, were held to fill up the accomplishments of a heroic character. The plain bluntness of his manner, if remote from courtesy, appeared at least as widely different from deceit; and, unfashioned as he seemed by forms, he had enough both of natural sense and natural good-breeding to support the delusion he had created, at least as far as externals were concerned. It is scarce necessary to add, that these observations apply exclusively to what are called love-matches; for when either party fix their attachment upon the substantial comforts of a rental or a jointure, they cannot be disappointed in the acquisition, although they may be cruelly so in their over-estimation of the happiness it was to afford, or in having too slightly anticipated the disadvantages with which it was to be attended.

Having a certain partiality for the dark beauty whom we have described, we have willingly dedicated this digression, in order to account for a line of conduct which we allow to seem absolutely unnatural in such a narrative as the present, though the most common event in ordinary life; namely, in Minna's appearing to have over-estimated the taste, talent, and ability of a handsome young man, who was dedicating to her his whole time and attention, and whose homage rendered her the envy of almost all the other young women of that numerous party. Perhaps, if our fair readers will take the trouble to consult their own bosoms, they will be disposed to allow that the distinguished good taste exhibited by any individual who, when his attentions would be agreeable to a whole circle of rivals, selects *one* as their individual object, entitles him, on the footing of reciprocity, if on no other, to a large share of that individual's favourable, and even partial, esteem. At any rate, if the character shall, after all, be deemed inconsistent and unnatural, it concerns not us, who record the facts as we find them, and pretend no privilege for bringing closer to nature those incidents which may seem to diverge from it, or for reducing to consistence that most inconsistent of all created things—the heart of a beautiful and admired female.

Necessity, which teaches all the liberal arts, can render us also adepts in dissimulation; and Mordaunt, though a novice, failed not to profit in her school. It was manifest that, in order to observe the demeanour of those on whom his attention was fixed, he must needs put constraint on his own, and appear, at least, so much engaged with the damsels betwixt whom he sat that Minna and Brenda should suppose him indifferent to what was passing around him. The ready cheerfulness of Maddie and Clara Groatsettar, who were esteemed considerable fortunes in the island, and were at this moment too happy in feeling themselves seated somewhat beyond the sphere of vigilance influenced by their aunt, the good old Lady Glowrowrum, met and requited the attempts which Mordaunt made to be lively and entertaining; and they were soon engaged in a gay conversation, to which, as usual on such occasions, the gentleman contributed wit, or what passes for such, and the ladies their prompt laughter and liberal applause. But, amidst this seeming mirth, Mordaunt failed not, from time to time, as covertly as he might, to observe the conduct of the two daughters of Magnus; and still it appeared as if the elder, wrapt up in the conversation of Cleveland, did not cast away a thought on the rest of the company; and as if Brenda, more openly as she conceived his attention withdrawn from her, looked with an expression both anxious and melancholy towards the group of which he himself formed a part. He was much moved by the diffidence, as well as the trouble, which her looks seemed to convey, and tacitly formed the resolution of seeking a more full explanation with her in the course of the evening. Norna, he remembered, had stated that these two amiable young women were in danger, the nature of which she left unexplained, but which he suspected to arise out of their mistaking the character of this daring and all-engrossing stranger; and he secretly resolved that, if possible, he would be the means of detecting Cleveland and of saving his early friends.

As he revolved these thoughts, his attention to the Miss Groatsettars gradually diminished, and perhaps he might altogether have forgotten the necessity of his appearing an uninterested spectator of what was passing, had not the signal been given for the ladies retiring from table. Minna, with a native grace, and somewhat of stateliness in her manner, bent her head to the company in general, with a kinder and more particular expression as her eye reached Cleveland. Brenda, with the blush which attended her slightest personal exertion when exposed to the eyes of others, hurried through the same departing salutation with an embarrassment which almost amounted to awkwardness, but which her youth and timidity rendered at once natural and interesting. Again Mordaunt thought that her eye distinguished him amidst the numerous company. For the first time he ventured to encounter and to return the glance; and the consciouness that he had done so doubled the glow of Brenda's countenance, while something resembling displeasure was blended with her emotion.

When the ladies had retired, the men betook themselves to the deep and serious drinking which, according to the fashion of the times, preceded the evening exercise of the dance. Old Magnus himself, by precept and example, exhorted them "to make the best use of their time, since the ladies would soon summon them to shake their feet." At the same time giving the signal to a grey-headed domestic, who stood behind him in the dress of a Dantzic skipper, and who added to many other occupations that of butler, "Eric Scambester," he said, "has the good ship the 'Jolly Mariner of Canton' got her cargo on board?"

"Chokeful loaded," answered the Ganymede of Burgh-Westra, "with good Nantz, Jamaica sugar, Portugal lemons, not to mention nutmeg and toast, and water taken in from the Shellicoat spring."

Loud and long laughed the guests at this stated and regular jest betwixt the Udaller and his butler, which always served as a preface to the introduction of a punch-bowl of enormous size, the gift of the captain of one of the Honourable East India Company's vessels, which, bound from China homeward, had been driven north about by stress of weather into Lerwick Bay, and had there contrived to get rid of part of the cargo, without very scrupulously reckoning for the king's duties.

Magnus Troil, having been a large customer, besides otherwise obliging Captain Coolie, had been remunerated, on the departure of the ship, with this splendid vehicle of convivial·

ity, at the very sight of which, as old Eric Scambester bent
under its weight, a murmur of applause ran through the company.   The good old toasts dedicated to the prosperity of Zetland were then honoured with flowing bumpers.   "Death to
the head that never wears hair!" was a sentiment quaffed to
the success of the fishing, as proposed by the sonorous voice
of the Udaller.   Claud Halcro proposed, with general applause, "The health of their worthy landmaster, the sweet
sister meat-mistresses; health to man, death to fish, and
growth to the produce of the ground."   The same recurring
sentiment was proposed more concisely by a white-headed
compeer of Magnus Troil, in the words: "God open the mouth
of the grey fish, and keep his hand about the corn!" [1]

Full opportunity was afforded to all to honour these interesting toasts.   Those nearest the capacious Mediterranean of
punch were accommodated by the Udaller with their portions,
dispensed in huge rummer glasses by his own hospitable hand,
whilst they who sat at a greater distance replenished their cups
by means of a rich silver flagon, facetiously called the pinnace;
which, filled occasionally at the bowl, served to dispense its
liquid treasures to the more remote parts of the table, and occasioned many right merry jests on its frequent voyages.
The commerce of the Zetlanders .with foreign vessels and
homeward-bound West Indiamen had early served to introduce among them the general use of the generous beverage
with which the "Jolly Mariner of Canton" was loaded; nor
was there a man in the archipelago of Thule more skilled in
combining its rich ingredients than old Eric Scambester, who,
indeed, was known far and wide through the isles by the name
of the Punch-maker, after the fashion of the ancient Norwegians, who conferred on Rollo the Walker, and other heroes
of their strain, epithets expressive of the feats of strength or
dexterity in which they excelled all other men.

The good liquor was not slow in performing its office of ex-
hilaration, and, as the revel advanced, some ancient Norse
drinking-songs were sung with great effect by the guests,
tending to show that if, from want of exercise, the martial

[1] See Hibbert's *Description of the Zetland Islands*, p. 470.

virtues of their ancestors had decayed among the Zetlanders,
they could still actively and intensely enjoy so much of the
pleasures of Valhalla as consisted in quaffing the oceans of
mead and brown ale which were promised by Odin to those
who should share his Scandinavian paradise. At length, excited by the cup and song, the diffident grew bold and the
modest loquacious; all became desirous of talking, and none
were willing to listen; each man mounted his own special
hobby-horse, and began eagerly to call on his neighbours to
witness his agility. Amongst others, the little bard, who had
now got next to our friend Mordaunt Mertoun, evinced a positive determination to commence and conclude, in all its longi-
tude and latitude, the story of his introduction to glorious John
Dryden; and Triptolemus Yellowley, as his spirits arose, shaking off a feeling of involuntary awe with which he was impressed by the opulence indicated in all he saw around him, as
well as by the respect paid to Magnus Troil by the assembled
guests, began to broach to the astonished and somewhat offended Udaller some of those projects for ameliorating the
islands which he had boasted of to his fellow-travellers upon
their journey of the morning.

But the innovations which he suggested, and the reception
which they met with at the hand of Magnus Troil, must be told
in the next chapter.

CHAPTER XIV.

> We'll keep our customs; what is law itself,
> But old established custom? What religion
> (I mean, with one-half of the men that use it),
> Save the good use and wont that carries them
> To worship how and where their fathers worshipp'd?
> All things resolve in custom; we'll keep ours.
>
> *Old Play.*

WE left the company of Magnus Troil engaged in high wassail and revelry. Mordaunt, who, like his father, shunned
the festive cup, did not partake in the cheerfulness which the
ship diffused among the guests as they unloaded it, and the

pinnace, as it circumnavigated the table.   But, in low spirits
as he seemed, he was the more meet prey for the story-telling
Halcro, who had fixed upon him as in a favourable state to
play the part of listener, with something of the same instinct
that directs the hooded crow to the sick sheep among the flock,
which will most patiently suffer itself to be made a prey of.
Joyfully did the poet avail himself of the advantages afforded
by Mordaunt's absence of mind and unwillingness to exert
himself in measures of active defence.   With the unfailing
dexterity peculiar to prosers, he contrived to dribble out his
tale to double its usual length, by the exercise of the privilege
of unlimited digressions; so that the story, like a horse on
the *grand pas*, seemed to be advancing with rapidity, while,
in reality, it scarce was progressive at the rate of a yard in
the quarter of an hour.   At length, however, he had discussed, in all its various bearings and relations, the history
of his friendly landlord, the master fashioner in Russel Street,
including a short sketch of five of his relations, and anecdotes
of three of his principal rivals, together with some general
observations upon the dress and fashion of the period; and
having marched thus far through the environs and outworks
of his story, he arrived at the body of the place, for so the
Wits' Coffee-house might be termed.   He paused on the
threshold, however, to explain the nature of his landlord's
right occasionally to intrude himself into this well-known
temple of the Muses.

"It consisted," said Halcro, "in the two principal points
of bearing and forbearing; for my friend Thimblethwaite
was a person of wit himself, and never quarrelled with any
jest which the wags who frequented that house were flinging
about, like squibs and crackers on a rejoicing-night; and then,
though some of the wits—ay, and I dare say the greater number, might have had some dealings with him in the way of
trade, he never was the person to put any man of genius in
unpleasant remembrance of such trifles.   And though, my
dear young Master Mordaunt, you may think this is but ordinary civility, because in this country it happens seldom that
there is either much borrowing or lending, and because, praised

be Heaven, there are neither bailiffs nor sheriff-officers to take a poor fellow by the neck, and because there are no prisons to put him into when they have done so, yet, let me tell you, that such a lamblike forbearance as that of my poor, dear, deceased landlord, Thimblethwaite, is truly uncommon within the London bills of mortality. I could tell you of such things that have happened even to myself, as well as others, with these cursed London tradesmen, as would make your hair stand on end. But what the devil has put old Magnus into such note? He shouts as if he were trying his voice against a northwest gale of wind."

Loud indeed was the roar of the old Udaller, as, worn out of patience by the schemes of improvement which the factor was now undauntedly pressing upon his consideration, he answered him (to use an Ossianic phrase) like a wave upon a rock.

"Trees, sir factor—talk not to me of trees! I care not though there never be one on the island tall enough to hang a coxcomb upon. We will have no trees but those that rise in our havens—the good trees that have yards for boughs and standing rigging for leaves."

"But touching the draining of the lake of Braebaster, whereof I spoke to you, Master Magnus Troil," said the persevering agriculturist, "whilk I opine would be of so much consequence, there are two ways—down the Linklater glen, or by the Scalmester burn. Now, having taken the level of both——"

"There is a third way, Master Yellowley," answered the landlord.

"I profess I can see none," replied Triptolemus, with as much good faith as a joker could desire in the subject of his wit, "in respect that the hill called Braebaster on the south, and ane high bank on the north, of whilk I cannot carry the name rightly in my head——"

"Do not tell us of hills and banks, Master Yellowley; there is a third way of draining the loch, and it is the only way that shall be tried in my day. You say my Lord Chamberlain and I are the joint proprietors; so be it. Let each of us start an equal proportion of brandy, lime-juice, and sugar

into the loch—a ship's cargo or two will do the job—let us
assemble all the jolly udallers of the country, and in twenty-
four hours you shall see dry ground where the loch of Braebaster now is."

A loud laugh of applause, which for a time actually silenced
Triptolemus, attended a jest so very well suited to time and
place—a jolly toast was given—a merry song was sung—the
ship unloaded her sweets—the pinnace made its genial rounds
—the duet betwixt Magnus and Triptolemus, which had attracted the attention of the whole company from its superior
vehemence, now once more sunk, and merged into the general
hum of the convivial table, and the poet Halcro again resumed
his usurped possession of the ear of Mordaunt Mertoun.

"Whereabouts was I?" he said, with a tone which expressed
to his weary listener more plainly than words could how much
of his desultory tale yet remained to be told. "Oh, I remember—we were just at the door of the Wits' Coffee-house; it
was set up by one——"

"Nay, but, my dear Master Halcro," said his hearer, somewhat impatiently, "I am desirous to hear of your meeting
with Dryden."

"What, with glorious John?—true—ay—where was I? At
the Wits' Coffee-house. Well, in at the door we got—the
waiters, and so forth, staring at me; for as to Thimblethwaite,
honest fellow, his was a well-known face. I can tell you a
story about that——"

"Nay, but John Dryden?" said Mordaunt, in a tone which
deprecated further digression.

"Ay—ay, glorious John—where was I? Well, as we stood
close by the bar, where one fellow sat grinding of coffee, and
another putting up tobacco into penny parcels—a pipe and a
dish cost just a penny—then and there it was that I had the
first peep of him. One Dennis sat near him, who——"

"Nay, but John Dryden—what like was he?" demanded
Mordaunt.

"Like a little fat old man, with his own grey hair, and in
a full-trimmed black suit, that sat close as a glove. Honest
Thimblethwaite let no one but himself shape for glorious

John, and he had a slashing hand at a sleeve, I promise you. But there is no getting a mouthful of common sense spoken here: d—n that Scotchman, he and old Magnus are at it again!"

It was very true; and although the interruption did not resemble a thunder-clap to which the former stentorian exclamation of the Udaller might have been likened, it was a close and clamorous dispute, maintained by question, answer, retort, and repartee, as closely huddled upon each other as the sounds which announce from a distance a close and sustained fire of musketry.

"Hear reason, sir?" said the Udaller; "we will hear reason, and speak reason too; and if reason fall short, you shall have rhyme to boot. Ha, my little friend Halcro!"

Though cut off in the middle of his best story, if that could be said to have a middle which had neither beginning nor end, the bard bristled up at the summons, like a corps of light infantry when ordered up to the support of the grenadiers, looked smart, slapped the table with his hand, and denoted his becoming readiness to back his hospitable landlord, as becomes a well-entertained guest. Triptolemus was a little daunted at this reinforcement of his adversary; he paused, like a cautious general, in the sweeping attack which he had commenced on the peculiar usages of Zetland, and spoke not again until the Udaller poked him with the insulting query: "Where is your reason, now, Master Yellowley, that you were deafening me with a moment since?"

"Be but patient, worthy sir," replied the agriculturist. "What on earth can you or any other man say in defence of that thing you call a plough, in this blinded country? Why, even the savage Highlandmen, in Caithness and Sutherland, can make more work, and better, with their gascromh, or whatever they call it."

"But what ails you at it, sir?" said the Udaller: "let me hear your objections to it. It tills our land, and what would ye more?"

"It hath but one handle or stilt," replied Triptolemus.

"And who the devil," said the poet, aiming at something

smart, "would wish to need a pair of stilts if he can manage to walk with a single one?"

"Or tell me," said Magnus Troil, "how it were possible for Neil of Lupness, that lost one arm by his fall from the crag of Nekbreckan, to manage a plough with two handles?"

"The harness is of raw seal-skin," said Triptolemus.

"It will save dressed leather," answered Magnus Troil.

"It is drawn by four wretched bullocks," said the agriculturist, "that are yoked breast-fashion; and two women must follow this unhappy instrument, and complete the furrows with a couple of shovels."

"Drink about, Master Yellowley," said the Udaller; "and, as you say in Scotland, 'never fash your thumb.' Our cattle are too high-spirited to let one go before the other; our men are too gentle and well-nurtured to take the working-field without the women's company; our ploughs till our land, our land bears us barley; we brew our ale, eat our bread, and make strangers welcome to their share of it. Here's to you, Master Yellowley."

This was said in a tone meant to be decisive of the question; and, accordingly, Halcro whispered to Mordaunt: "That has settled the matter, and now we will get on with glorious John. There he sat in his suit of full-trimmed black—two years due was the bill, as mine honest landlord afterwards told me—and such an eye in his head! None of your burning, blighting, falcon eyes, which we poets are apt to make a rout about, but a soft, full, thoughtful, yet penetrating glance—never saw the like of it in my life, unless it were little Stephen Kleancogg's, the fiddler, at Papastow, who——"

"Nay, but John Dryden?" said Mordaunt, who, for want of better amusement, had begun to take a sort of pleasure in keeping the old gentleman to his narrative, as men herd in a restiff sheep, when they wish to catch him. He returned to his theme, with his usual phrase of "Ay, true—glorious John. Well, sir, he cast his eye, such as I have described it, on mine landlord, and 'Honest Tim,' said he, 'what hast thou got here?' and all the wits, and lords, and gentlemen that used to crowd round him, like the wenches round a pedlar at a fair, they made way for us, and up we came to the fire-side, where he had his own established chair—I have heard it was carried to the balcony in summer, but it was by the fireside when I saw it—so up came Tim Thimblethwaite, through the midst of them, as bold as a lion, and I followed with a small parcel under my arm, which I had taken up partly to oblige my landlord, as the shop porter was not in the way, and partly that I might be thought to have some-thing to do there, for you are to think there was no admit-tance at the Wits' for strangers who had no business there. I have heard that Sir Charles Sedley said a good thing about that——"

"Nay, but you forget glorious John," said Mordaunt.

"Ay, glorious you may well call him. They talk of their Blackmore, and Shadwell, and such-like—not fit to tie the latchets of John's shoes. 'Well,' he said to my landlord, 'what have you got there?' and he, bowing, I warrant, lower than he would to a duke, said he had made bold to come and show him the stuff which Lady Elizabeth had chose for her nightgown. 'And which of your geese is that, Tim, who has got it tucked under his wing?' 'He is an Orkney goose, if it please you, Mr. Dryden,' said Tim, who had wit at will, 'and he hath brought you a copy of verses for your honour to look at.' 'Is he amphibious?' said glorious John, taking the paper, and methought I could rather have faced a battery of cannon than the crackle it gave as it opened, though he did not speak in a way to dash one neither; and then he looked at the verses, and he was pleased to say, in a very encourag-ing way indeed, with a sort of good-humoured smile on his face, and certainly for a fat elderly gentleman—for I would not compare it to Minna's smile or Brenda's—he had the pleasantest smile I ever saw—'Why, Tim,' he said, 'this goose of yours will prove a swan on your hands.' With that he smiled a little, and they all laughed, and none louder than those who stood too far off to hear the jest; for every one knew when he smiled there was something worth laughing at, and so took it upon trust; and the word passed through among the young Templars, and the wits, and the smarts, and there

was nothing but question on question who we were; and one
French fellow was trying to tell them it was only Monsieur
Tim Thimblethwaite; but he made such work with his Dum-
bletate and Timbletate that I thought his explanation would
have lasted——"

"As long as your own story," thought Mordaunt; but the
narrative was at length finally cut short by the strong and
decided voice of the Udaller.

"I will hear no more on it, Mr. Factor!" he exclaimed.

"At least let me say something about the breed of horses,"
said Yellowley, in rather a cry-mercy tone of voice.   "Your
horses, my dear sir, resemble cats in size and tigers in devilry!"

"For their size," said Magnus, "they are the easier for us
to get off and on them ("As Triptolemus experienced this
morning," thought Mordaunt to himself), and as for their
devilry, let no one mount them that cannot manage them."

A twinge of self-conviction on the part of the agriculturist
prevented him from reply.   He darted a deprecatory glance
at Mordaunt, as if for the purpose of imploring secrecy respecting his tumble; and the Udaller, who saw his advantage, although he was not aware of the cause, pursued it with
the high and stern tone proper to one who had all his life
been unaccustomed to meet with, and unapt to endure, opposition.

"By the blood of St. Magnus the Martyr," he said, "but
you are a fine fellow, Master Factor Yellowley!   You come
to us from a strange land, understanding neither our laws,
nor our manners, nor our language, and you propose to become governor of the country, and that we should all be your
slaves!"

"My pupils, worthy sir—my pupils!" said Yellowley,
"and that only for your own proper advantage."

"We are too old to go to school," said the Zetlander.   "I
tell you once more, we will sow and reap our grain as as our
fathers did; we will eat what God sends us, with our doors
open to the stranger, even as theirs were open.   If there is
aught imperfect in our practice, we will amend it in time and

season; but the blessed Baptist's holyday was made for light hearts and quick heels. He that speaks a word more of reason, as you call it, or anything that looks like it, shall swallow a pint of sea-water—he shall, by this hand! And so fill up the good ship, the 'Jolly Mariner of Canton,' once more, for the benefit of those that will stick by her; and let the rest have a fling with the fiddlers, who have been summoning us this hour. I will warrant every wench is on tiptoe by this time. Come, Mr. Yellowley, no unkindness, man; why, man, thou feelest the rolling of the 'Jolly Mariner' still (for, in truth, honest Triptolemus showed a little unsteadiness of motion as he rose to attend his host); but never mind, we shall have thee find thy land-legs to reel it with yonder bonny belles. Come along, Triptolemus; let me grapple thee fast, lest thou *trip*, old Triptolemus—ha, ha, ha!"

So saying, the portly though weather-beaten hulk of the Udaller sailed off like a man-of-war that had braved a hundred gales, having his guest in tow like a recent prize. The greater part of the revellers followed their leader with loud jubilee, although there were several stanch topers who, taking the option left them by the Udaller, remained behind to relieve the "Jolly Mariner" of a fresh cargo, amidst many a pledge to the health of their absent landlord, and to the prosperity of his roof-tree, with whatsoever other wishes of kindness could be devised as an apology for another pint-bumper of noble punch.

The rest soon thronged the dancing-room, an apartment which partook of the simplicity of the time and of the country. Drawing-rooms and saloons were then unknown in Scotland, save in the houses of the nobility, and of course absolutely so in Zetland; but a long, low, anomalous store-room, sometimes used for the deposition of merchandise, sometimes for putting aside lumber, and a thousand other purposes, was well known to all the youth of Dunrossness, and of many a district besides, as the scene of the merry dance, which was sustained with so much glee when Magnus Troil gave his frequent feasts.

The first appearance of this ball room might have shocked

a fashionable party assembled for the quadrille or the waltz. Low as we have stated the apartment to be, it was but imperfectly illuminated by lamps, candles, ship-lanterns, and a variety of other candelabra, which served to throw a dusky light upon the floor, and upon the heaps of merchandise and miscellaneous articles which were piled around; some of them stores for the winter; some, goods destined for exportation; some, the tribute of Neptune, paid at the expense of shipwrecked vessels, whose owners were unknown; some, articles of barter received by the proprietor, who, like most others at the period, was somewhat of a merchant as well as a landholder, in exchange for the fish and other articles, the produce of his estate. All these, with the chests, boxes, casks, etc., which contained them, had been drawn aside, and piled one above the other, in order to give room for the dancers, who, light and lively as if they had occupied the most splendid saloon in the parish of St. James's, executed their national dances with equal grace and activity.

The group of old men who looked on bore no inconsiderable resemblance to a party of aged tritons, engaged in beholding the sports of the sea-nymphs; so hard a look had most of them acquired by contending with the elements, and so much did the shaggy hair and beards, which many of them cultivated after the ancient Norwegian fashion, give their heads the character of these supposed natives of the deep. The young people, on the other hand, were uncommonly handsome, tall, well-made, and shapely: the men with long fair hair, and, until broken by the weather, a fresh, ruddy complexion, which, in the females, was softened into a bloom of infinite delicacy. Their natural good ear for music qualified them to second to the utmost the exertions of a band whose strains were by no means contemptible; while the elders, who stood around or sat quiet upon the old sea-chests which served for chairs, criticised the dancers, as they compared their execution with their own exertions in former days; or, warmed by the cup and flagon, which continued to circulate among them, snapped their fingers and beat time with their feet to the music.

Mordaunt looked upon this scene of universal mirth with the painful recollection that he, thrust aside from his pre-eminence, no longer exercised the important duties of chief of the dancers, or office of leader of the revels, which had been assigned to the stranger Cleveland. Anxious, however, to suppress the feelings of his own disappointment, which he felt it was neither wise to entertain nor manly to display, he approached his fair neighbours to whom he had been so acceptable at table, with the purpose of inviting one of them to become his partner in the dance. But the awfully ancient old lady, even the Lady Glowrowrum, who had only tolerated the exuberance of her nieces' mirth during the time of dinner because her situation rendered it then impossible for her to interfere, was not disposed to permit the apprehended renewal of the intimacy implied in Mertoun's invitation. She therefore took upon herself, in the name of her two nieces, who sat pouting beside her in displeased silence, to inform Mordaunt, after thanking him for his civility, that the hands of her nieces were engaged for that evening; and, as he continued to watch the party at a little distance, he had an opportunity of being convinced that the alleged engagement was a mere apology to get rid of him, when he saw the two good-humoured sisters join the dance under the auspices of the next young men who asked their hands. Incensed at so marked a slight, and unwilling to expose himself to another, Mordaunt Mertoun drew back from the circle of dancers, shrouded himself amongst the mass of inferior persons who crowded into the bottom of the room as spectators, and there, concealed from the observation of others, digested his own mortification as well as he could—that is to say, very ill—and with all the philosophy of his age—that is to say, with none at all.

CHAPTER XV.

A torch for me; let wantons, light of heart,
Tickle the useless rushes with their heels ;
For I am proverb'd with a grandsire phrase—
I'll be a candle-holder, and look on.
                              Romeo and Juliet.

THE youth, says the moralist Johnson, cares not for the
boy's hobby-horse, nor the man for the youth's mistress; and
therefore the distress of Mordaunt Mertoun, when excluded
from the merry dance, may seem trifling to many of my readers, who would, nevertheless, think they did well to be angry
if deposed from their usual place in an assembly of a different
kind.   There lacked not amusement, however, for these whom
the dance did not suit, or who were not happy enough to find
partners to their liking.   Halcro, now completely in his element, had assembled round him an audience, to whom he was
declaiming his poetry with all the enthusiasm of glorious John
himself, and receiving in return the usual degree of applause
allowed to minstrels who recite their own rhymes—so long at
least as the author is within hearing of the criticism.   Halcro's poetry might indeed have interested the antiquary as
well as the admirer of the Muses, for several of his pieces
were translations or imitations from the Scaldic sagas, which
continued to be sung by the fishermen of those islands even
until a very late period; insomuch that, when Gray's poems
first found their way to Orkney, the old people recognised at
once, in the ode of the *Fatal Sisters*, the Runic rhymes which
had amused or terrified their infancy under the title of the
Magicians, and which the fishers of North Ronaldsha and
other remote isles used still to sing when asked for a Norse
ditty.

Half-listening, half-lost in his own reflections, Mordaunt
Mertoun stood near the door of the apartment, and in the
outer ring of the little circle formed around old Halcro, while
the bard chanted to a low, wild, monotonous air, varied only
by the efforts of the singer to give interest and emphasis to

particular passages, the following imitation of a Northern
war song:

The Song of Harold Harfager.

The sun is rising dimly red,
The wind is wailing low and dread;
From his cliff the eagle sallies,
Leaves the wolf his darksome valleys;
In the midst the ravens hover,
Peep the wild-dogs from the cover,
Screaming, croaking, baying, yelling,
Each in his wild accents telling,
"Soon we feast on dead and dying,
Fair-hair'd Harold's flag is flying."

Many a crest in air is streaming,
Many a helmet darkly gleaming,
Many an arm the axe uprears,
Doom'd to hew the wood of spears.
All along the crowded ranks,
Horses neigh and armour clanks;
Chiefs are shouting, clarions ringing,
Louder still the bard is singing,
"Gather, footmen—gather, horsemen,
To the field, ye valiant Norsemen!

"Halt ye not for food or slumber,
View not vantage, count not number;
Jolly reapers, forward still;
Grow the crop on vale or hill,
Thick or scatter'd, stiff or lithe,
It shall down before the scythe.
Forward with your sickles bright,
Reap the harvest of the fight.
Onward, footmen—onward, horsemen,
To the charge, ye gallant Norsemen!

"Fatal Choosers of the Slaughter,
O'er you hovers Odin's daughter;
Hear the voice she spreads before ye-
Victory, and wealth, and glory;
Or old Valhalla's roaring hail,
Her ever-circling mead and ale,
Where for eternity unite
The joys of wassail and of fight.
Headlong forward, foot and horsemen,
Charge the fight, and die like Norsemen!"

"The poor, unhappy, blinded heathens!" said Triptolemus,
with a sigh deep enough for a groan; "they speak of their

eternal cups of ale, and I question if they kenn'd how to manage a croft land of grain!"

"The cleverer fellows they, neighbour Yellowley," answered the poet, "if they made ale without barley."

"Barley! alack-a-day!" replied the more accurate agriculturist, "who ever heard of barley in these parts? Bear, my dearest friend—bear is all they have, and wonderment it is to me that they ever see an awn of it. Ye scart the land with a bit thing ye ca' a pleugh; ye might as weel give it a ritt with the teeth of a redding-kame. Oh, to see the sock, and the heel, and the sole-clout of a real steady Scottish pleugh, with a chield like a Samson between the stilts, laying a weight on them would keep down a mountain; twa stately owsen, and as many broad-breasted horse in the traces, going through soil and till, and leaving a fur in the ground would carry off water like a causeyed syver! They that have seen a sight like that have seen something to crack about in another sort than those unhappy auld-warld stories of war and slaughter, of which the land has seen even but too mickle, for a' your singing and soughing awa' in praise of such bloodthirsty doings, Master Claud Halcro."

"It is a heresy," said the animated little poet, bridling and drawing himself up, as if the whole defence of the Orcadian Archipelago rested on his single arm——"it is a heresy so much as to name one's native country if a man is not prepared when and how to defend himself—ay, and to annoy another. The time has been that, if we made not good ale and aquavitæ, we knew well enough where to find that which was ready made to our hand; but now the descendants of sea-kings, and champions, and Berserkars are become as incapable of using their swords as if they were so many women. Ye may praise them for a strong pull on an oar or a sure foot on a skerry; but what else could glorious John himself say of ye, my good Hialtlanders, that any man would listen to?"

"Spoken like an angel, most noble poet," said Cleveland, who, during an interval of the dance, stood near the party in which this conversation was held. "The old champions you talked to us about yesternight were the men to make a harp ring—gallant fellows, that were friends to the sea and enemies to all that sailed on it. Their ships, I suppose, were clumsy enough; but if it is true that they went upon the account as far as the Levant, I scarce believe that ever better fellows unloosed a topsail."

"Ay," replied Halcro, "there you spoke them right. In those days none could call their life and means of living their own, unless they dwelt twenty miles out of sight of the blue sea. Why, they had public prayers put up in every church in Europe for deliverance from the ire of the Northmen. In France and England, ay, and in Scotland too, for as high as they hold their head nowadays, there was not a bay or a haven but it was freer to our forefathers than to the poor devils of natives; and now we cannot, forsooth, so much as grow our own barley without Scottish help (here he darted a sarcastic glance at the factor). I would I saw the time we were to measure arms with them again!"

"Spoke like a hero once more," said Cleveland.

"Ah!" continued the little bard, "I would it were possible to see our barks, once the water-dragons of the world, swimming with the black raven standard waving at the topmast, and their decks glimmering with arms, instead of being heaped up with stock-fish; winning with our fearless hands what the niggard soil denies; paying back all old scorn and modern injury; reaping where we never sowed, and felling what we never planted; living and laughing through the world, and smiling when we were summoned to quit it!"

So spoke Claud Halcro, in no serious, or at least most certainly in no sober mood, his brain (never the most stable) whizzing under the influence of fifty well-remembered sagas, besides five bumpers of usquebaugh and brandy; and Cleveland, between jest and earnest, clapped him on the shoulder and again repeated: "Spoken like a hero!"

"Spoken like a fool, I think," said Magnus Troil, whose attention had been also attracted by the vehemence of the little bard. "Where would you cruise upon, or against whom? We are all subjects of one realm, I trow, and I would have you to remember that your voyage may bring up at execution dock. I like not the Scots—no offence, Mr. Yellowley—that is, I would like them well enough if they would stay quiet in their own land, and leave us at peace with our own people, and manners, and fashions; and if they would but abide there till I went to harry them like a mad old Berserkar, I would leave them in peace till the day of judgment. With what the sea sends us, and the land lends us, as the proverb says, and a set of honest neighbourly folks to help us to consume it, so help me St. Magnus, as I think we are even but too happy!"

"I know what war is," said an old man, "and I would as soon sail through Sumburgh Roost in a cockle-shell, or in a worse loom, as I would venture there again."

"And, pray, what wars knew your valour?" said Halcro, who, though forbearing to contradict his landlord from a sense of respect, was not a whit inclined to abandon his argument to any meaner authority.

"I was pressed," answered the old triton, "to serve under Montrose,[1] when he came here about the sixteen hundred and fifty-one, and carried a sort of us off, will ye nill ye, to get our throats cut in the wilds of Strathnavern. I shall never forget it. We had been hard put to it for victuals: what would I have given for a luncheon of Burgh-Westra beef—ay, or a mess of sour sillocks? When our Highlandmen brought in a dainty drove of kyloes, much ceremony there was not, for we shot and felled, and flayed, and roasted, and broiled, as it came to every man's hand; till, just as our beards were at the greasiest, we heard—God preserve us—a tramp of horse, then twa or three drapping shots—then came a full salvo—and then, when the officers were crying on us to stand, and maist of us looking which way we might run away, down they broke, horse and foot, with old John Urry, or Hurry,[2] or whatever they called him—he hurried us that day, and worried us to boot—and we began to fall as thick as the stots that we were felling five minutes before."

"And Montrose," said the soft voice of the graceful Minna —"what became of Montrose, or how looked he?"

"Like a lion with the hunters before him," answered the

old gentleman; "but I looked not twice his way, for my own lay right over the hill."

"And so you left him?" said Minna, in a tone of the deepest contempt.

"It was no fault of mine, Mistress Minna," answered the old man, somewhat out of countenance; "but I was there with no choice of my own; and, besides, what good could I have done? all the rest were running like sheep, and why should I have staid?"

"You might have died with him," said Minna.

"And lived with him to all eternity, in immortal verse!" added Claud Halcro.

"I thank you, Mistress Minna," replied the plain-dealing Zetlander, "and I thank you, my old friend Claud; but I would rather drink both your healths in this good bicker of ale, like a living man as I am, than that you should be making songs in my honour, for having died forty or fifty years agone. But what signified it? Run or fight, 'twas all one: they took Montrose, poor fellow, for all his doughty deeds, and they took me that did no doughty deeds at all; and they hanged him, poor man, and as for me——"

"I trust in Heaven they flogged and pickled you," said Cleveland, worn out of patience with the dull narrative of the peaceful Zetlander's poltroonery, of which he seemed so wondrous little ashamed.

"Flog horses and pickle beef," said Magnus. "Why, you have not the vanity to think that, with all your quarter-deck airs, you will make poor old neighbour Haagaen ashamed that he was not killed some scores of years since? You have looked on death yourself, my doughty young friend, but it was with the eyes of a young man who wishes to be thought of; but we are a peaceful people—peaceful, that is, as long as any one should be peaceful, and that is till some one has the imprudence to wrong us or our neighbours; and then, perhaps, they may not find our Northern blood much cooler in our veins than was that of the old Scandinavians that gave us our names and lineage. Get ye along—get ye along to the sword-dance,[1] that

See Note 21.

the strangers that are amongst us may see that our hands and
our weapons are not altogether unacquainted even yet."

A dozen cutlasses, selected hastily from an old arm-chest,
and whose rusted hue bespoke how seldom they left the sheath,
armed the same number of young Zetlanders, with whom mingled six maidens, led by Minna Troil; and the minstrelsy instantly commenced a tune appropriate to the ancient Norwegian war-dance, the evolutions of which are perhaps still
practised in those remote islands.

The first movement was graceful and majestic, the youths
holding their swords erect, and without much gesture; but the
tune, and the corresponding motions of the dancers, became
gradually more and more rapid; they clashed their swords
together, in measured time, with a spirit which gave the exercise a dangerous appearance in the eye of the spectator,
though the firmness, justice, and accuracy with which the
dancers kept time with the stroke of their weapons did, in
truth, ensure its safety. The most singular part of the exhibition was the courage exhibited by the female performers,
who, now surrounded by the swordsmen, seemed like the Sabine maidens in the hands of their Roman lovers; now, moving under the arch of steel which the young men had formed
by crossing their weapons over the heads of their fair partners, resembled the band of Amazons when they first joined
in the Pyrrhic dance with the followers of Theseus. But by
far the most striking and appropriate figure was that of Minna
Troil, whom Halcro had long since entitled the Queen of
Swords, and who, indeed, moved amidst the swordsmen with
an air which seemed to hold all the drawn blades as the proper accompaniments of her person and the implements of her
pleasure. And when the mazes of the dance became more intricate, when the close and continuous clash of the weapons
made some of her companions shrink and show signs of fear,
her cheek, her lip, and her eye seemed rather to announce
that, at the moment when the weapons flashed fastest and rung
sharpest around her, she was most completely self-possessed
and in her own element. Last of all, when the music had
ceased, and she remained for an instant upon the floor by her-

self, as the rule of the dance required, the swordsmen and maidens who departed from around her seemed the guards and the train of some princess, who, dismissed by her signal, were leaving her for a time to solitude. Her own look and attitude, wrapped, as she probably was, in some vision of the imagination, corresponded admirably with the ideal dignity which the spectators ascribed to her; but, almost immediately recollecting herself, she blushed, as if conscious she had been, though but for an instant, the object of undivided attention, and gave her hand gracefully to Cleveland, who, though he had not joined in the dance, assumed the duty of conducting her to her seat.

As they passed, Mordaunt Mertoun might observe that Cleveland whispered into Minna's ear, and that her brief reply was accompanied with even more discomposure of countenance than she had manifested when encountering the gaze of the whole assembly. Mordaunt's suspicions were strongly awakened by what he observed, for he knew Minna's character well, and with what equanimity and indifference she was in the custom of receiving the usual compliments and gallantries with which her beauty and her situation rendered her sufficiently familiar.

"Can it be possible she really loves this stranger?" was the unpleasant thought that instantly shot across Mordaunt's mind. "And if she does, what is my interest in the matter?" was the second; and which was quickly followed by the reflection that, though he claimed no interest at any time but as a friend, and though that interest was now withdrawn, he was still, in consideration of their former intimacy, entitled both to be sorry and angry at her for throwing away her affections on one he judged unworthy of her. In this process of reasoning, it is probable that a little mortified vanity, or some indescribable shade of selfish regret, might be endeavouring to assume the disguise of disinterested generosity; but there is so much of base alloy in our very best (unassisted) thoughts, that it is melancholy work to criticise too closely the motives of our most worthy actions; at least we would recommend to every one to let those of his neighbours pass current, however narrowly he may examine the purity of his own.

The sword-dance was succeeded by various other specimens of the same exercise, and by songs, to which the singers lent their whole soul, while the audience were sure, as occasion offered, to unite in some favourite chorus. It is upon such occasions that music, though of a simple and even rude character, finds its natural empire over the generous bosom, and produces that strong excitement which cannot be attained by the most learned compositions of the first masters, which are caviare to the common ear, although, doubtless, they afford a delight, exquisite in its kind, to those whose natural capacity and education have enabled them to comprehend and relish those difficult and complicated combinations of harmony.

It was about midnight when a knocking at the door of the mansion, with the sound of the "gue" and the "langspiel," announced, by their tinkling chime, the arrival of fresh revellers, to whom, according to the hospitable custom of the country, the apartments were instantly thrown open.

CHAPTER XVI.

My mind misgives,
Some consequence, yet hanging in the stars,
Shall bitterly begin his fearful date
With this night's revels.

Romeo and Juliet.

THE new-comers were, according to the frequent custom of such frolickers all over the world, disguised in a sort of masquing habits, and designed to represent the tritons and mermaids with whom ancient tradition and popular belief have peopled the northern seas. The former, called by Zetlanders of that time "shoupeltins," were represented by young men grotesquely habited, with false hair, and beards made of flax, and chaplets composed of sea-ware interwoven with shells and other marine productions, with which also were decorated their light-blue or greenish mantles of wadmaal, repeatedly before-mentioned. They had fish-spears and other emblems of their assumed quality, amongst which the classical taste of Claud Halcro, by whom the masque was arranged, had not forgotten the conch-shells, which were stoutly and hoarsely winded from time to time by one or two of the aquatic deities, to the great annoyance of all who stood near them.

The nereids and water-nymphs who attended on this occasion displayed, as usual, a little more taste and ornament than was to be seen amongst their male attendants. Fantastic garments of green silk, and other materials of superior cost and fashion, had been contrived so as to imitate their idea of the inhabitants of the waters, and, at the same time, to show the shape and features of the fair wearers to the best advantage. The bracelets and shells which adorned the neck, arms, and ankles of the pretty mermaidens were, in some cases, intermixed with real pearls; and the appearance, upon the whole, was such as might have done no discredit to the court of Amphitrite, especially when the long bright locks, blue eyes, fair complexions, and pleasing features of the maidens of Thule were taken into consideration. We do not indeed pretend to aver that any of these seeming mermaids had so accurately imitated the real siren as commentators have supposed those attendant on Cleopatra did, who, adopting the fish's train of their original, were able, nevertheless, to make their "bends," or "ends" (said commentators cannot tell which), "adornings."[1] Indeed, had they not left their extremities in their natural state, it would have been impossible for the Zetland sirens to have executed the very pretty dance with which they rewarded the company for the ready admission which had been granted to them.

It was soon discovered that these masquers were no strangers, but a part of the guests, who, stealing out a little time before, had thus disguised themselves, in order to give variety to the mirth of the evening. The muse of Claud Halcro, always active on such occasions, had supplied them with an appropriate song, of which we may give the following speci-

[1] See some admirable discussion on this passage in the Variorum Shakspeare.

men. The song was alternate betwixt a nereid or mermaid and a merman or triton—the males and females on either part forming a semi-chorus, which accompanied and bore burden to the principal singer.

MERMAID.

Fathoms deep beneath the wave,
  Stringing beads of glistering pearl,
Singing the achievements brave
  Of many an old Norwegian earl;
Dwelling where the tempest's raving
  Falls as light upon our ear
As the sigh of lover craving
  Pity from his lady dear,
Children of wild Thule, we,
From the deep caves of the sea,
As the lark springs from the lea,
Hither come, to share your glee.

MERMAN.

From reining of the water-horse,
  That bounded till the waves were foaming,
Watching the infant tempest's course,
  Chasing the sea-snake in his roaming;
From winding charge-notes on the shell,
  When the huge whale and sword-fish duel,
Or tolling shroudless seamen's knell,
  When the winds and waves are cruel,
Children of wild Thule, we
Have plough'd such furrows on the sea
As the steer draws on the lea,
And hither we come to share your glee.

MERMAIDS AND MERMEN.

We heard you in our twilight caves,
  A hundred fathom deep below,
For notes of joy can pierce the waves,
  That drown each sound of war and woe.
Those who dwell beneath the sea
  Love the sons of Thule well;
Thus, to aid your mirth, bring we
  Dance, and song, and sounding shell.
Children of dark Thule, know,
Those who dwell by haaf and voe,
Where your daring shallops row,
Come to share the festal show.

The final chorus was borne by the whole voices, excepting those carrying the conch-shells, who had been trained to blow them in a sort of rude accompaniment, which had a good effect. The poetry, as well as the performance, of the masquers received great applause from all who pretended to be judges of such matters; but above all from Triptolemus Yellowley, who, his ear having caught the agricultural sounds of plough and furrow, and his brain being so well drenched that it could only construe the words in their most literal acceptation, declared roundly, and called Mordaunt to bear witness, that, though it was a shame to waste so much good lint as went to form the tritons' beards and periwigs, the song contained the only words of common sense which he had heard all that long day.

But Mordaunt had no time to answer the appeal, being engaged in attending with the utmost vigilance to the motions of one of the female masquers, who had given him a private signal as they entered, which induced him, though uncertain who she might prove to be, to expect some communication from her of importance. The siren who had so boldly touched his arm, and had accompanied the gesture with an expression of eye which bespoke his attention, was disguised with a good deal more care than her sister-masquers, her mantle being loose, and wide enough to conceal her shape completely and her face hidden beneath a silk masque. He observed that she gradually detached herself from the rest of the masquers, and at length placed herself, as if for the advantage of the air, near the door of a chamber which remained open, looked earnestly at him again, and then taking an opportunity, when the attention of the company was fixed upon the rest of her party, she left the apartment.

Mordaunt did not hesitate instantly to follow his mysterious guide, for such we may term the masquer, as she paused to let him see the direction she was about to take, and then walked swiftly towards the shore of the voe, or salt-water lake, now lying full before them, its small summer waves glistening and rippling under the influence of a broad moonlight, which, added to the strong twilight of those regions during the summer solstice, left no reason to regret the absence of the sun, the path of whose setting was still visible on the waves of the west, while the horizon on the east side was already beginning to glimmer with the lights of dawn.

Mordaunt had therefore no difficulty in keeping sight of his disguised guide, as she tripped it over height and hollow to the seaside, and, winding among the rocks, led the way to the spot where his own labours, during the time of his former intimacy at Burgh-Westra, had constructed a sheltered and solitary seat, where the daughters of Magnus were accustomed to spend, when the weather was suitable, a good deal of their time. Here, then, was to be the place of explanation; for the masquer stopped, and, after a moment's hesitation, sat down on the rustic settle. But from the lips of whom was he to receive it? Norna had first occurred to him; but her tall figure and slow, majestic step were entirely different from the size and gait of the more fairy-formed siren, who had preceded him with as light a trip as if she had been a real nereid, who, having remained too late upon the shore, was, under the dread of Amphitrite's displeasure, hastening to regain her native element. Since it was not Norna, it could be only, he thought, Brenda who thus singled him out; and when she had seated herself upon the bench, and taken the mask from her face, Brenda it accordingly proved to be. Mordaunt had certainly done nothing to make him dread her presence; and yet, such is the influence of bashfulness over the ingenuous youth of both sexes, that he experienced all the embarrassment of one who finds himself unexpectedly placed before a person who is justly offended with him. Brenda felt no less embarrassment; but as she had sought this interview, and was sensible it must be a brief one, she was compelled, in spite of herself, to begin the conversation.

"Mordaunt," she said, with a hesitating voice; then correcting herself, she proceeded: "You must be surprised, Mr. Mertoun, that I should have taken this uncommon freedom."

"It was not till this morning, Brenda," replied Mordaunt, "that any mark of friendship or intimacy from you or from your sister could have surprised me. I am far more astonished that you should shun me without reason for so many hours than that you should now allow me an interview. In the name of Heaven, Brenda, in what have I offended you? or why are we on these unusual terms?"

"May it not be enough to say," replied Brenda, looking downward, "that it is my father's pleasure?"

"No, it is not enough," returned Mertoun. "Your father cannot have so suddenly altered his whole thoughts of me, and his whole actions towards me, without acting under the influence of some strong delusion. I ask you but to explain of what nature it is; for I will be contented to be lower in your esteem than the meanest hind in these islands if I cannot show that his change of opinion is only grounded upon some infamous deception or some extraordinary mistake."

"It may be so," said Brenda—"I hope it is so; that I do hope it is so, my desire to see you thus in private may well prove to you. But it is difficult—in short, it is impossible—for me to explain to you the cause of my father's resentment. Norna has spoken with him concerning it boldly, and I fear they parted in displeasure; and you well know no light matter could cause that."

"I have observed," said Mordaunt, "that your father is most attentive to Norna's counsel, and more complaisant to her peculiarities than to those of others; this I have observed, though he is no willing believer in the supernatural qualities to which she lays claim."

"They are related distantly," answered Brenda, "and were friends in youth; nay, as I have heard, it was once supposed they would have been married; but Norna's peculiarities showed themselves immediately on her father's death, and there was an end of that matter, if ever there was anything in it. But it is certain my father regards her with much interest; and it is, I fear, a sign how deeply his prejudices respecting you must be rooted, since they have in some degree quarrelled on your account."

"Now, blessings upon you, Brenda, that you have called them prejudices," said Mertoun, warmly and hastily—"a thousand blessings on you! You were ever gentle-hearted: you could not have maintained even the show of unkindness long."

"It was indeed but a show," said Brenda, softening gradually into the familiar tone in which they had conversed from infancy. "I could never think, Mordaunt—never, that is, seriously believe, that you could say aught unkind of Minna or of me."

"And who dares to say I have?" said Mordaunt, giving way to the natural impetuosity of his disposition—"who dares to say that I have, and ventures at the same time to hope that I will suffer his tongue to remain in safety betwixt his jaws? By St. Magnus the Martyr, I will feed the hawks with it!"

"Nay, now," said Brenda, "your anger only terrifies me, and will force me to leave you."

"Leave me," said he, "without telling me either the calumny or the name of the villainous calumniator!"

"Oh, there are more than one," answered Brenda, "that have possessed my father with an opinion—which I cannot myself tell you—but there are more than one who say——"

"Were they hundreds, Brenda, I will do no less to them than I have said. Sacred Martyr! to accuse me of speaking unkindly of those whom I most respected and valued under Heaven. I will back to the apartment this instant, and your father shall do me right before all the world."

"Do not go, for the love of Heaven!" said Brenda—"do not go, as you would not render me the most unhappy wretch in existence!"

"Tell me then, at least, if I guess aright," said Mordaunt, "when I name this Cleveland for one of those who have slandered me?"

"No—no," said Brenda, vehemently, "you run from one error into another more dangerous. You say you are my friend—I am willing to be yours—be but still for a moment and hear what I have to say; our interview has lasted but too long already, and every additional moment brings additional danger with it."

"Tell me, then," said Mertoun, much softened by the poor girl's extreme apprehension and distress, "what is it that you require of me; and believe me, it is impossible for you to ask aught that I will not do my very uttermost to comply with."

"Well, then, this captain," said Brenda—"this Cleveland——"

"I knew it, by Heaven!" said Mordaunt: "my mind assured me that that fellow was, in one way or other, at the bottom of all this mischief and misunderstanding!"

"If you cannot be silent and patient for an instant," replied Brenda, "I must instantly quit you. What I meant to say had no relation to you, but to another—in one word, to my sister Minna. I have nothing to say concerning her dislike to you, but an anxious tale to tell concerning his attention to her."

"It is obvious, striking, and marked," said Mordaunt; "and, unless my eyes deceive me, it is received as welcome, if, indeed, it is not returned."

"That is the very cause of my fear," said Brenda. "I, too, was struck with the external appearance, frank manners, and romantic conversation of this man."

"His appearance!" said Mordaunt; "he is stout and well-featured enough, to be sure; but, as old Sinclair of Quendale said to the Spanish admiral: 'Farcie on his face! I have seen many a fairer hang on the Borough Moor.' From his manners, he might be captain of a privateer; and, by his conversation, the trumpeter to his own puppet-show: for he speaks of little else than his own exploits."

"You are mistaken," answered Brenda: "he speaks but too well on all that he has seen and learned; besides, he has really been in many distant countries and in many gallant actions, and he can tell them with as much spirit as modesty. You would think you saw the flash and heard the report of the guns. And he has other tones of talking too—about the delightful trees and fruits of distant climates; and how the people wear no dress, through the whole year, half so warm as our summer gowns, and, indeed, put on little except cambric and muslin."

"Upon my word, Brenda, he does seem to understand the business of amusing young ladies," replied Mordaunt.

"He does, indeed," said Brenda, with great simplicity. "I assure you that, at first, I liked him better than Minna did;

and yet, though she is so much cleverer than I am, I know more of the world than she does; for I have . seen more of cities, having been once at Kirkwall; besides that I was thrice at Lerwick, when the Dutch ships were there, and so I should not be very easily deceived in people."

"And pray, Brenda," said Mertoun, "what was it that made you think less favourably of this young fellow, who seems to be so captivating?"

"Why," said Brenda, after a moment's reflection, "at first he was much livelier; and the stories he told were not quite so melancholy or so terrible; and he laughed and danced more."

"And, perhaps, at that time, danced oftener with Brenda than with her sister?" added Mordaunt.

"No—I am not sure of that," said Brenda; "and yet, to speak plain, I could have no suspicion of him at all while he was attending quite equally to us both; for you know that then he could have been no more to us than yourself, Mordaunt Mertoun, or young Swaraster, or any other young man in the islands."

"But why, then," said Mordaunt, "should you not see him, with patience, become acquainted with your sister? He is wealthy, or seems to be so at least. You say he is accomplished and pleasant. What else would you desire in a lover for Minna?"

"Mordaunt, you forget who we are," said the maiden, assuming an air of consequence, which sat as gracefully upon her simplicity as did the different tone in which she had spoken hitherto. "This is a little world of ours, this Zetland, inferior, perhaps, in soil and climate to other parts of the earth, at least so strangers say; but it is our own little world, and we, the daughters of Magnus Troil, hold a first rank in it. It would, I think, little become us, who are descended from seakings and jarls, to throw ourselves away upon a stranger, who comes to our coast, like the eider-duck in spring, from we know not whence, and may leave it in autumn, to go we know not where."

"And who may yet entice a Zetland golden-eye to accompany his migration," said Mertoun.

"I will hear nothing light on such a subject," replied Brenda, indignantly. "Minna, like myself, is the daughter of Magnus Troil, the friend of strangers, but the father of Hialtland. He gives them the hospitality they need; but let not the proudest of them think that they can, at their pleasure, ally with his house."

"She said this in a tone of considerable warmth, which she instantly softened, as she added: "No, Mordaunt, do not suppose that Minna Troil is capable of so far forgetting what she owes to her father and her father's blood as to think of marrying this Cleveland; but she may lend an ear to him so long as to destroy her future happiness. She has that sort of mind into which some feelings sink deeply. You remember how Ulla Storlson used to go, day by day, to the top of Vossdale Head, to look for her lover's ship that was never to return? When I think of her slow step, her pale cheek, her eye, that grew dimmer and dimmer, like the lamp that is half extinguished for lack of oil; when I remember the fluttered look of something like hope with which she ascended the cliff at morning, and the deep, dead despair which sat on her forehead when she returned—when I think on all this, can you wonder that I fear for Minna, whose heart is formed to entertain, with such deep-rooted fidelity, any affection that may be implanted in it?"

"I do not wonder," said Mordaunt, eagerly sympathising with the poor girl; for, besides the tremulous expression of her voice, the light could almost show him the tear which trembled in her eye, as she drew the picture to which her fancy had assimilated her sister—"I do not wonder that you should feel and fear whatever the purest affection can dictate; and if you can but point out to me in what I can serve your sisterly love, you shall find me as ready to venture my life, if necessary, as I have been to go out on the crag to get you the eggs of the guillemot; and, believe me, that whatever has been told to your father or yourself of my entertaining the slightest thoughts of disrespect or unkindness is as false as a fiend could devise."

"I believe it," said Brenda, giving him her hand—"I be-

lieve it, and my bosom is lighter, now I have renewed my
confidence in so old a friend. How you can aid us, I know
not; but it was by the advice, I may say by the commands,
of Norna that I have ventured to make this communication;
and I almost wonder," she added, as she looked around her,
"that I have had courage to carry me through it. At present
you know all that I can tell you of the risk in which my sister
stands. Look after this Cleveland; beware how you quarrel
with him, since you must so surely come by the worst with an
experienced soldier."

"I do not exactly understand," said the youth, "how that
should so surely be. This I know, that, with the good limbs
and good heart that God hath given me, ay, and with a good
cause to boot, I am little afraid of any quarrel which Cleveland can fix upon me."

"Then, if not for your own sake, for Minna's sake," said
Brenda—"for my father's—for mine—for all our sakes, avoid
any strife with him; but be contented to watch him, and, if
possible, to discover who he is, and what are his intentions
towards us. He has talked of going to Orkney to inquire
after the consort with whom he sailed; but day after day and
week after week passes, and he goes not; and while he keeps
my father company over the bottle, and tells Minna romantic
stories of foreign people, and distant wars, in wild and unknown regions, the time glides on, and the stranger, of whom
we know nothing except that he is one, becomes gradually
closer and more inseparably intimate in our society. And
now farewell. Norna hopes to make your peace with my
father, and entreats you not to leave Burgh-Westra to-morrow, however cold he and my sister may appear towards you.
I too," she said, stretching her hand towards him, "must
wear a face of cold friendship as towards an unwelcome visitor, but at heart we are still Brenda and Mordaunt. And
now separate quickly, for we must not be seen together."

She stretched her hand to him, but withdrew it in some
slight confusion, laughing and blushing when by a natural impulse he was about to press it to his lips. He endeavoured
for a moment to detain her, for the interview had for him a

degree of fascination which, as often as he had before been alone with Brenda, he had never experienced. But she extricated herself from him, and again signing an adieu, and pointing out to him a path different from that which she was herself about to take, tripped towards the house, and was soon hidden from his view by the acclivity.

Mordaunt stood gazing after her in a state of mind to which, as yet, he had been a stranger. The dubious neutral ground between love and friendship may be long and safely trodden, until he who stands upon it is suddenly called upon to recognise the authority of the one or the other power; and then it most frequently happens that the party who for years supposed himself only a friend finds himself at once transformed into a lover. That such a change in Mordaunt's feelings should take place from this date, although he himself was unable exactly to distinguish its nature, was to be expected. He found himself at once received, with the most unsuspicious frankness, into the confidence of a beautiful and fascinating young woman, by whom he had, so short a time before, imagined himself despised and disliked; and, if anything could make a change, in itself so surprising and so pleasing, yet more intoxicating, it was the guileless and open-hearted simplicity of Brenda, that cast an enchantment over everything which she did or said. The scene, too, might have had its effect, though there was little occasion for its aid. But a fair face looks yet fairer under the light of the moon, and a sweet voice sounds yet sweeter among the whispering sounds of a summer night. Mordaunt, therefore, who had by this time returned to the house, was disposed to listen with unusual patience and complacency to the enthusiastic declamation pronounced upon moonlight by Claud Halcro, whose ecstasies had been awakened on the subject by a short turn in the open air, undertaken to qualify the vapours of the good liquor, which he had not spared during the festival.

"The sun, my boy," he said, "is every wretched labourer's day-lantern : it comes glaring yonder, out of the east, to summon up a whole world to labour and to misery; whereas the merry moon lights all of us to mirth and to love."

"And to madness, or she is much belied," said Mordaunt, by way of saying something.

"Let it be so," answered Halcro, "so she does not turn us melancholy mad. My dear young friend, the folks of this painstaking world are far too anxious about possessing all their wits, or having them, as they say, about them. At least I know I have been often called half-witted, and I am sure I have gone through the world as well as if I had double the quantity. But stop—where was I? Oh, touching and concerning the moon; why, man, she is the very soul of love and poetry. I question if there was ever a true lover in existence who had not got at least as far as 'O thou,' in a sonnet in her praise."

"The moon," said the factor, who was now beginning to speak very thick, "ripens corn, at least the old folk said so; and she fills nuts also, whilk is of less matter—*sparge nuces, pueri.*"

"A fine—a fine," said the Udaller, who was now in his altitudes; "the factor speaks Greek. By the bones of my holy namesake, St. Magnus, he shall drink off the yawl full of punch, unless he gives us a song on the spot!"

"Too much water drowned the miller," answered Triptolemus. "My brain has more need of draining than of being drenched with more liquor."

"Sing, then," said the despotic landlord, "for no one shall speak any other language here save honest Norse, jolly Dutch, or Danske, or broad Scots, at the least of it. So, Eric Scambester, produce the yawl, and fill it to the brim, as a charge for demurrage."

Ere the vessel could reach the agriculturist, he, seeing it under way and steering towards him by short tacks (for Scambester himself was by this time not over steady in his course), made a desperate effort, and began to sing, or rather to croak forth, a Yorkshire harvest-home ballad, which his father used to sing when he was a little mellow, and which went to the tune of "Hey, Dobbin, away with the waggon." The rueful aspect of the singer, and the desperately discordant tones of his voice, formed so delightful a contrast with the jollity of the words and tune, that honest Triptolemus afforded the same sort of amusement which a reveller might give by appearing on a festival-day in the holyday coat of his grandfather. The jest concluded the evening, for even the mighty and strong-headed Magnus himself had confessed the influence of the sleepy god. The guests went off as they best might, each to his separate crib and resting-place, and in a short time the mansion, which was of late so noisy, was hushed into perfect silence.

CHAPTER XVII.

They man their boats, and all the young men arm
With whatsoever might the monsters harm ;
Pikes, halberds, spits, and darts, that wound afar,
The tools of peace and implements of war.
Now was the time for vigorous lads to show
What love or honour could incite them to ;—
A goodly theatre, where rocks are round
With reverend age and lovely lasses crown'd.
                              Battle of the Summer Islands.

THE morning which succeeds such a feast as that of Magnus Troil usually lacks a little of the zest which seasoned the revels of the preceding day, as the fashionable reader may have observed at a public breakfast during the race-week in a country town; for, in what is called the best society, these lingering moments are usually spent by the company each apart in their own dressing-rooms. At Burgh-Westra, it will readily be believed, no such space for retirement was afforded; and the lasses, with their paler cheeks, the elder dames, with many a wink and yawn, were compelled to meet with their male companions, headaches and all, just three hours after they had parted from each other.

Eric Scambester had done all that man could do to supply the full means of diverting the *ennui* of the morning meal. The board groaned with rounds of hung beef, made after the fashion of Zetland—with pasties—with baked meats—with fish, dressed and cured in every possible manner; nay, with the foreign delicacies of tea, coffee, and chocolate; for, as we

have already had occasion to remark, the situation of these
islands made them early acquainted with various articles of
foreign luxury, which were, as yet, but little known in Scotland, where, at a much later period than that we write of, one
pound of green tea was dressed like cabbage, and another converted into a vegetable sauce for salt beef, by the ignorance
of the good housewives to whom they had been sent as rare
presents.

Besides these preparations, the table exhibited whatever
mighty potions are resorted to by *bons vivans* under the facetious name of a "hair of the dog that bit you." There was
the potent Irish usquebaugh—right Nantz—genuine Schie-
dam—aquavitæ from Caithness—and Golden Wasser from
Hamburgh; there was rum of formidable antiquity, and cor-
dials, from the Leeward Islands. After these details, it were
needless to mention the stout home-brewed ale, the German
mum and schwartz beer; and still more would it be beneath
our dignity to dwell upon the innumerable sorts of pottage
and flummery, together with the bland and various preparations of milk, for those who preferred thinner potations.

No wonder that the sight of so much good cheer awakened
the appetite and raised the spirits of the fatigued revellers.
The young men began immediately to seek out their partners
of the preceding evening, and to renew the small talk which
had driven the night so merrily away; while Magnus, with
his stout old Norse kindred, encouraged, by precept and example, those of elder days and graver mood to a substantial
flirtation with the good things before them. Still, however,
there was a long period to be filled up before dinner; for the
most protracted breakfast cannot well last above an hour; and
it was to be feared that Claud Halcro meditated the occupation
of this vacant morning with a formidable recitation of his own
verses, besides telling, at its full length, the whole history of
his introduction to glorious John Dryden. But fortune relieved the guests of Burgh-Westra from this threatened infliction, by sending them means of amusement peculiarly suited
to their taste and habits.

Most of the guests were using their toothpicks, some were

beginning to talk of what was to be done next, when, with haste in his step, fire in his eye, and a harpoon in his hand, Eric Scambester came to announce to the company that there was a whale on shore, or nearly so, at the throat of the voe! Then you might have seen such a joyous, boisterous, and universal bustle as only the love of sport, so deeply implanted in our nature, can possibly inspire. A set of country squires, about to beat for the first woodcocks of the season, were a comparison as petty in respect to the glee as in regard to the importance of the object. The battue upon a strong cover in Ettrick Forest, for the destruction of the foxes; the insurrection of the sportsmen of the Lennox, when one of the duke's deer gets out from Inch-Mirran; nay, the joyous rally of the fox-chase itself, with all its blythe accompaniments of hound and horn, fall infinitely short of the animation with which the gallant sons of Thule set off to encounter the monster whom the sea had sent for their amusement at so opportune a conjuncture.

The multifarious stores of Burgh-Westra were rummaged hastily for all sorts of arms which could be used on such an occasion. Harpoons, swords, pikes, and halberds fell to the lot of some; others contented themselves with hay-forks, spits, and whatever else could be found, that was at once long and sharp. Thus hastily equipped, one division, under the command of Captain Cleveland, hastened to man the boats which lay in the little haven, while the rest of the party hurried by land to the scene of action.

Poor Triptolemus was interrupted in a plan which he, too, had formed against the patience of the Zetlanders, and which was to have consisted in a lecture upon the agriculture and the capabilities of the country, by this sudden hubbub, which put an end at once to Halcro's poetry and to his no less formidable prose. It may be easily imagined that he took very little interest in the sport which was so suddenly substituted for his lucubrations, and he would not even have deigned to have looked upon the active scene which was about to take place, had he not been stimulated thereunto by the exhortations of Mistress Baby. "Pit yoursell forward, man," said that provi-

dent person—"pit yoursell forward; wha kens whare a blessing may light? They say that a' men share and share equals-
aquals in the creature's ulzie, and a pint o't wad be worth
siller, to light the cruise in the lang dark nights that they
speak of. Pit yoursell forward, man—there's a graip to ye—
faint heart never wan fair lady; wha kens but what, when it's
fresh, it may eat weel eneugh, and spare butter?"

What zeal was added to Triptolemus's motions by the prospect of eating fresh train-oil instead of butter, we know not;
but, as better might not be, he brandished the rural implement (a stable-fork) with which he was armed, and went down
to wage battle with the whale.

The situation in which the enemy's ill fate had placed him
was particularly favourable to the enterprise of the islanders.
A tide of unusual height had carried the animal over a large
bar of sand, into the voe or creek in which he was now lying.
So soon as he found the water ebbing, he became sensible of
his danger, and had made desperate efforts to get over the
shallow water, where the waves broke on the bar; but hitherto he had rather injured than mended his condition, having
got himself partly aground, and lying therefore particularly
exposed to the meditated attack. At this moment the enemy
came down upon him. The front ranks consisted of the young
and hardy, armed in the miscellaneous manner we have described; while, to witness and animate their efforts, the young
women, and the elderly persons of both sexes, took their place
among the rocks which overhung the scene of action.

As the boats had to double a little headland ere they opened
the mouth of the voe, those who came by land to the shores
of the inlet had time to make the necessary reconnoissances
upon the force and situation of the enemy, on whom they were
about to commence a simultaneous attack by land and sea.

This duty the stout-hearted and experienced general, for so
the Udaller might be termed, would entrust to no eyes but his
own; and, indeed, his external appearance and his sage conduct rendered him alike qualified for the command which he
enjoyed. His gold-laced hat was exchanged for a bearskin
eap, his suit of blue broadcloth, with its scarlet lining, and

loops, and frogs of bullion, had given place to a red flannel jacket, with buttons of black horn, over which he wore a seal-skin shirt curiously seamed and plaited on the bosom, such as are used by the Esquimaux, and sometimes by the Greenland whale-fishers. Sea-boots of a formidable size completed his dress, and in his hand he held a large whaling-knife, which he brandished, as if impatient to employ it in the operation of "flinching" the huge animal which lay before them—that is, the act of separating its flesh from its bones. Upon closer examination, however, he was obliged to confess that the sport to which he had conducted his friends, however much it corresponded with the magnificent scale of his hospitality, was likely to be attended with its own peculiar dangers and difficulties.

The animal, upwards of sixty feet in length, was lying perfectly still, in a deep part of the voe into which it had weltered, and where it seemed to await the return of tide, of which it was probably assured by instinct. A council of experienced harpooners was instantly called, and it was agreed that an effort should be made to noose the tail of this torpid leviathan, by casting a cable around it, to be made fast by anchors to the shore, and thus to secure against his escape, in case the tide should make before they were able to despatch him. Three boats were destined to this delicate piece of service, one of which the Udaller himself proposed to command, while Cleveland and Mertoun were to direct the two others. This being decided, they sat down on the strand, waiting with impatience until the naval part of the force should arrive in the voe. It was during this interval that Triptolemus Yellowley, after measuring with his eyes the extraordinary size of the whale, observed that, in his poor mind: "A wain with six owsen, or with sixty owsen either, if they were the owsen of the country, could not drag siccan a huge creature from the water, where it was now lying, to the sea-beach."

Trifling as this remark may seem to the reader, it was connected with a subject which always fired the blood of the old Udaller, who, glancing upon Triptolemus a quick and stern look, asked him what the devil it signified, supposing a hun-

dred oxen could not drag the whale upon the beach? Mr.
Yellowley, though not much liking the tone with which the
question was put, felt that his dignity and his profit compelled him to answer as follows: "Nay, sir, you know yoursell, Master Magnus Troil, and every one knows that knows
anything, that whales of siccan size as may not be masterfully
dragged on shore by the instrumentality of one wain with six
owsen are the right and property of the admiral, who is at
this time the same noble lord who is, moreover, chamberlain
of these isles."

"And I tell you, Mr. Triptolemus Yellowley," said the
Udaller, "as I would tell your master if he were here, that
every man who risks his life to bring that fish ashore shall
have an equal share and partition, according to our ancient
and loveable Norse custom and wont; nay, if there is so much
as a woman looking on, that will but touch the cable, she will
be partner with us; ay, and more than all that, if she will but
say there is a reason for it, we will assign a portion to the babe
that is unborn."

The strict principle of equity which dictated this last arrangement occasioned laughter among the men, and some
slight confusion among the women. The factor, however,
thought it shame to be so easily daunted. "*Suum cuique
tribuito,*" said he: "I will stand for my lord's right and
my own."

"Will you?" replied Magnus; "then, by the Martyr's
bones, you shall have no law of partition but that of God and
St. Olave, which we had before either factor, or treasurer, or
chamberlain were heard of! All shall share that lend a hand,
and never a one else. So you, Master Factor, shall be busy
as well as other folk, and think yourself lucky to share like
other folk. Jump into that boat (for the boats had by this
time pulled round the headland), and you, my lads, make
way for the factor in the stern-sheets: he shall be the first
man this blessed day that shall strike the fish."

The loud, authoritative voice, and the habit of absolute
command inferred in the Udaller's whole manner, together
with the conscious want of favourers and backers amongst the

rest of the company, rendered it difficult for Triptolemus to evade compliance, although he was thus about to be placed in a situation equally novel and perilous. He was still, however, hesitating, and attempting an explanation, with a voice in which anger was qualified by fear, and both thinly disguised under an attempt to be jocular, and to represent the whole as a jest, when he heard the voice of Baby maundering in his ear: "Wad he lose his share of the ulzie, and the lang Zetland winter coming on, when the lightest day in December is not so clear as a moonless night in the Mearns?"

This domestic instigation, in addition to those of fear of the Udaller and shame to seem less courageous than others, so inflamed the agriculturist's spirits that he shook his "graip" aloft, and entered the boat with the air of Neptune himself carrying on high his trident.

The three boats destined for this perilous service now approached the dark mass, which lay like an islet in the deepest part of the voe, and suffered them to approach without showing any sign of animation. Silently, and with such precaution as the extreme delicacy of the operation required, the intrepid adventurers, after the failure of their first attempt, and the expenditure of considerable time, succeeded in casting a cable around the body of the torpid monster, and in carrying the ends of it ashore, when an hundred hands were instantly employed in securing them. But, ere this was accomplished, the tide began to make fast, and the Udaller informed his assistants that either the fish must be killed, or at least greatly wounded, ere the depth of water on the bar was sufficient to float him, or that he was not unlikely to escape from their joint prowess.

"Wherefore," said he, "we must set to work, and the factor shall have the honour to make the first throw."

The valiant Triptolemus caught the word; and it is necessary to say that the patience of the whale, in suffering himself to be noosed without resistance, had abated his terrors, and very much lowered the creature in his opinion. He protested the fish had no more wit, and scarcely more activity, than a black snail; and, influenced by this undue contempt of the

14

adversary, he waited neither for a further signal, nor a better weapon, nor a more suitable position, but, rising in his energy, hurled his graip with all his force against the unfortunate monster. The boats had not yet retreated from him to the distance necessary to ensure safety when this injudicious commencement of the war took place.

Magnus Troil, who had only jested with the factor, and had reserved the launching the first spear against the whale to some much more skilful hand, had just time to exclaim, " Mind yourselves, lads, or we are all swamped!" when the monster, roused at once from inactivity by the blow of the factor's missile, blew, with a noise resembling the explosion of a steam-engine, a huge shower of water into the air, and at the same time began to lash the waves with his tail in every direction. The boat in which Magnus presided received the shower of brine which the animal spouted aloft; and the adventurous Triptolemus, who had a full share of the immersion, was so much astonished and terrified by the consequences of his own valorous deed that he tumbled backwards amongst the feet of the people, who, too busy to attend to him, were actively engaged in getting the boat into shoal water, out of the whale's reach. Here he lay for some minutes, trampled on by the feet of the boatmen, until they lay on their oars to bale, when the Udaller ordered them to pull to shore and land this spare hand, who had commenced the fishing so inauspiciously.

While this was doing, the other boats had also pulled off to safer distance, and now, from these as well as from the shore, the unfortunate native of the deep was overwhelmed by all kinds of missiles: harpoons and spears flew against him on all sides, guns were fired, and each various means of annoyance plied which could excite him to exhaust his strength in useless rage. When the animal found that he was locked in by shallows on all sides, and became sensible, at the same time, of the strain of the cable on his body, the convulsive efforts which he made to escape, accompanied with sounds resembling deep and loud groans, would have moved the compassion of all but a practised whale-fisher. The repeated showers which he spouted into the air began now to be mingled with blood, and the waves which surrounded him assumed the same crimson appearance. Meantime, the attempts of the assailants were redoubled; but Mordaunt Mertoun and Cleveland, in particular, exerted themselves to the uttermost, contending who should display most courage in approaching the monster, so tremendous in its agonies, and should inflict the most deep and deadly wounds upon its huge bulk.

The contest seemed at last pretty well over; for, although the animal continued from time to time to make frantic exertions for liberty, yet its strength appeared so much exhausted, that, even with the assistance of the tide, which had now risen considerably, it was thought it could scarcely extricate itself.

Magnus gave the signal to venture nearer to the whale, calling out at the same time: "Close in, lads, he is not half so mad now. The factor may look for a winter's oil for the two lamps at Harfra. Pull close in, lads."

Ere his orders could be obeyed, the other two boats had anticipated his purpose; and Mordaunt Mertoun, eager to distinguish himself above Cleveland, had, with the whole strength he possessed, plunged a half-pike into the body of the animal. But the leviathan, like a nation whose resources appear totally exhausted by previous losses and calamities, collected his whole remaining force for an effort which proved at once desperate and successful. The wound last received had probably reached through his external defences of blubber, and attained some very sensitive part of the system; for he roared aloud, as he sent to the sky a mingled sheet of brine and blood, and snapping the strong cable like a twig, overset Mertoun's boat with a blow of his tail, shot himself, by a mighty effort, over the bar, upon which the tide had now risen considerably, and made out to sea, carrying with him a whole grove of the implements which had been planted in his body, and leaving behind him, on the waters, a dark red trace of his course.

"There goes to sea your cruise of oil, Master Yellowley," said Magnus, "and you must consume mutton suet or go to bed in the dark."

"*Operam et oleum perdidi,*" muttered Triptolemus; "but if

they catch me whale-fishing again, I will consent that the fish
shall swallow me as he did Jonah."

"But where is Mordaunt Mertoun all this while?" exclaimed
Claud Halcro; and it was instantly perceived that the youth,
who had been stunned when his boat was stove, was unable to
swim to shore as the other sailors did, and now floated senseless upon the waves.

We have noticed the strange and inhuman prejudice which
rendered the Zetlanders of that period unwilling to assist those
whom they saw in the act of drowning, though that is the calamity to which the islanders are most frequently exposed.
Three men, however, soared above this superstition. The
first was Claud Halcro, who threw himself from a small rock
headlong into the waves, forgetting, as he himself afterwards
stated, that he could not swim, and, if possessed of the harp
of Arion, had no dolphins in attendance. The first plunge
which the poet made in deep water reminding him of these
deficiencies, he was fain to cling to the rock from which he
had dived, and was at length glad to regain the shore, at the
expense of a ducking.

Magnus Troil, whose honest heart forgot his late coolness
towards Mordaunt when he saw the youth's danger, would
instantly have brought him more effectual aid, but Eric Scambester held him fast.

"Hout, sir—hout," exclaimed that faithful attendant, "Captain Cleveland has a grip of Mr. Mordaunt; just let the twa
strangers help ilk other, and stand by the upshot. The light
of the country is not to be quenched for the like of them.
Bide still, sir, I say. Bredness Voe is not a bowl of punch,
that a man can be fished out of like a toast with a long spoon."

This sage remonstrance would have been altogether lost
upon Magnus had he not observed that Cleveland had, in fact,
jumped out of the boat and swum to Mertoun's assistance, and
was keeping him afloat till the boat came to the aid of both.
As soon as the immediate danger which called so loudly for
assistance was thus ended, the honest Udaller's desire to
render aid terminated also; and recollecting the cause of offence which he had, or thought he had, against Mordaunt

Mertoun, he shook off his butler's hold, and, turning round scornfully from the beach, called Eric an old fool for supposing that he cared whether the young fellow sank or swam.

Still, however, amid his assumed indifference, Magnus could not help peeping over the heads of the circle which, surrounding Mordaunt as soon as he was brought on shore, were charitably employed in endeavouring to recall him to life; and he was not able to attain the appearance of absolute unconcern until the young man sat up on the beach and showed plainly that the accident had been attended with no material consequences. It was then first that, cursing the assistants for not giving the lad a glass of brandy, he walked sullenly away, as if totally unconcerned in his fate.

The women, always accurate in observing the tell-tale emotions of each other, failed not to remark that, when the sisters of Burgh-Westra saw Mordaunt immersed in the waves, Minna grew as pale as death, while Brenda uttered successive shrieks of terror. But, though there were some nods, winks, and hints that auld acquaintance were not easily forgot, it was, on the whole, candidly admitted that less than such marks of interest could scarce have been expected when they saw the companion of their early youth in the act of perishing before their eyes.

Whatever interest Mordaunt's condition excited while it seemed perilous, began to abate as he recovered himself; and when his senses were fully restored, only Claud Halcro, with two or three others, were standing by him. About ten paces off stood Cleveland—his hair and clothes dropping water, and his features wearing so peculiar an expression as immediately to arrest the attention of Mordaunt. There was a suppressed smile on his cheek, and a look of pride in his eye, that implied liberation from a painful restraint, and something resembling gratified scorn. Claud Halcro hastened to intimate to Mordaunt that he owed his life to Cleveland; and the youth, rising from the ground, and losing all other feelings in those of gratitude, stepped forward with his hand stretched out, to offer his warmest thanks to his preserver. But he stopped short in surprise, as Cleveland, retreating a pace or two, folded his arms on his breast and declined to accept his

proffered hand.   He drew back in turn, and gazed with astonishment at the ungracious manner, and almost insulting look,
with which Cleveland, who had formerly rather expressed a
frank cordiality, or at least openness of bearing, now, after
having thus rendered him a most important service, chose to
receive his thanks.

"It is enough," said Cleveland, observing his surprise, "and
it is unnecessary to say more about it.   I have paid back my
debt, and we are now equal."

"You are more than equal with me, Captain Cleveland,"
answered Mertoun, "because you endangered your life to do
for me what I did for you without the slightest risk; besides,"
he added, trying to give the discourse a more pleasant turn, "I
have your rifle-gun to boot."

"Cowards only count danger for any point of the game,"
said Cleveland.   "Danger has been my consort for life, and
sailed with me on a thousand worse voyages; and for rifles, I
have enough of my own, and you may see, when you will,
which can use them best."

There was something in the tone with which this was said
that struck Mordaunt strongly : it was "miching malicho," as
Hamlet says, "and meant mischief."   Cleveland saw his surprise, came close up to him, and spoke in a low tone of voice :
"Hark ye, my young brother.   There is a custom among us
gentlemen of fortune, that, when we follow the same chase,
and take the wind out of each other's sails, we think sixty
yards of the sea-beach and a brace of rifles are no bad way of
making our odds even."

"I do not understand you, Captain Cleveland," said Mordaunt.

"I do not suppose you do—I did not suppose you would,"
said the captain ; and, turning on his heel, with a smile that
resembled a sneer, Mordaunt saw him mingle with the guests,
and very soon beheld him at the side of Minna, who was talking to him with animated features, that seemed to thank him
for his gallant and generous conduct.

"If it were not for Brenda," thought Mordaunt, "I almost
wish he had left me in the voe, for no one seems to care

whether I am alive or dead. Two rifles and sixty yards of
sea-beach—is that what he points at? It may come; but not
on the day he has saved my life with risk of his own."

While he was thus musing, Eric Scambester was whispering
to Halcro: "If these two lads do not do each other a mischief,
there is no faith in freits. Master Mordaunt saves Cleveland—
well. Cleveland, in requital, has turned all the sunshine of
Burgh-Westra to his own side of the house; and think what
it is to lose favour in such a house as this, where the punch-
kettle is never allowed to cool! Well, now that Cleveland
in his turn has been such a fool as to fish Mordaunt out
of the voe, see if he does not give him sour sillocks for stock-
fish."

"Pshaw—pshaw!" replied the poet, "that is all old women's fancies, my friend Eric; for what says glorious Dryden—sainted John—

> The yellow gall that in your bosom floats
> Engenders all these melancholy thoughts."

"St. John, or St. James either, may be mistaken in the
matter," said Eric; "for I think neither of them lived in Zetland. I only say that, if there is faith in old saws, these
two lads will do each other a mischief; and if they do, I trust
it will light on Mordaunt Mertoun."

"And why, Eric Scambester," said Halcro, hastily and
angrily, "should you wish ill to that poor young man, that is
worth fifty of the other?"

"Let every one roose the ford as he finds it," replied Eric.
"Master Mordaunt is all for wan water, like his old dog-fish
of a father; now Captain Cleveland, d'ye see, takes his glass,
like an honest fellow and a gentleman."

"Rightly reasoned, and in thine own division," said Halcro; and, breaking off their conversation, took his way back
to Burgh-Westra, to which the guests of Magnus were now returning, discussing as they went, with much animation, the
various incidents of their attack upon the whale, and not a
little scandalised that it should have baffled all their exertions.

" I hope Captain Donderdrecht of the 'Eintracht' of Rotterdam will never hear of it," said Magnus; "he would swear, donner and blitzen, we were only fit to fish flounders." [1]

CHAPTER XVIII.

And helter-skelter have I rode to thee,
And tidings do I bring, and lucky joys,
And golden times, and happy news of price.
Ancient Pistol.

FORTUNE, who seems at times to bear a conscience, owed the hospitable Udaller some amends, and accordingly repaid to Burgh-Westra the disappointment occasioned by the unsuccessful whale-fishing by sending thither, on the evening of the day in which that incident happened, no less a person than the jagger, or travelling merchant, as he styled himself, Bryce Snailsfoot, who arrived in great pomp, himself on one pony, and his pack of goods, swelled to nearly double its usual size, forming the burden of another, which was led by a bareheaded, bare-legged boy.

As Bryce announced himself the bearer of important news, he was introduced to the dining-apartment, where (for that primitive age was no respecter of persons) he was permitted to sit down at a side-table, and amply supplied with provisions and good liquor; while the attentive hospitality of Magnus permitted no questions to be put to him, until, his hunger and thirst appeased, he announced, with the sense of importance attached to distant travels, that he had just yesterday arrived at Lerwick from Kirkwall, the capital of Orkney, and would have been here yesterday, but it blew hard off the Fitful Head.

"We had no wind here," said Magnus.

"There is somebody has not been sleeping, then," said the pedlar, "and her name begins with N; but Heaven is above all."

[1] The contest about the whale will remind the poetical reader of Waller's *Battle of the Summer Islands.*

But the news from Orkney, Bryce, instead of croaking about a capful of wind?"

"Such news," replied Bryce, "as has not been heard this thirty years—not since Cromwell's time."

"There is not another Revolution, is there?" said Halcro; "King James has not come back, as blythe as King Charlie did, has he?"

"It's news," replied the pedlar, "that are worth twenty kings, and kingdoms to boot of them; for what good did the revolutions ever do us? and I dare say we have seen a dozen, great and sma'."

"Are any Indiamen come north about?" said Magnus Troil.

"Ye are nearer the mark, fowd," said the jagger; "but it is nae Indiaman, but a gallant armed vessel, chokeful of merchandise, that they part with so easy that a decent man like myself can afford to give the country the best pennyworths you ever saw; and that you will say when I open that pack, for I count to carry it back another sort lighter than when I brought it here."

"Ay—ay, Bryce," said the Udaller, "you must have had good bargains if you sell cheap; but what ship was it?"

"Cannot justly say. I spoke to nobody but the captain, who was a discreet man; but she had been down on the Spanish Main, for she has silks and satins, and tobacco, I warrant you, and wine, and no lack of sugar, and bonnie-wallies baith of silver and gowd, and a bonny dredging of gold dust into the bargain."

"What like was she?" said Cleveland, who seemed to give much attention.

"A stout ship," said the itinerant merchant, "schooner-rigged, sails like a dolphin, they say, carries twelve guns, and is pierced for twenty."

"Did you hear the captain's name?" said Cleveland, speaking rather lower than his usual tone.

"I just ca'd him the captain," replied Bryce Snailsfoot; "for I make it a rule never to ask questions of them I deal with in the way of trade; for there is many an honest captain, begging your pardon, Captain Cleveland, that does not care to have his name tacked to his title; and as lang as we

ken what bargains we are making, what signifies it wha we are
making them wi', ye ken?"

"Bryce Snailsfoot is a cautious man," said the Udaller,
laughing: "he knows a fool may ask more questions than a
wise man cares to answer."

"I have dealt with the fair traders in my day," replied
Snailsfoot, "and I ken nae use, in blurting braid out with a
man's name at every moment; but I will uphold this gentleman to be a gallant commander—ay, and a kind one too; for
every one of his crew is as brave in apparel as himself nearly:
the very foremast-men have their silken scarfs—I have seen
many a lady wear a warse, and think herself nae sma' drink—
and for siller buttons, and buckles, and the lave of sic vanities,
there is nae end of them."

"Idiots!" muttered Cleveland between his teeth; and then
added: "I suppose they are often ashore, to show all their
bravery to the lasses of Kirkwall?"

"Ne'er a bit of that are they. The captain will scarce let
them stir ashore without the boatswain go in the boat—as
rough a tarpaulin as ever swabb'd a deck, and you may as
weel catch a cat without her claws as him without his cutlass
and his double brace of pistols about him; every man stands
as much in awe of him as of the commander himsell."

"That must be Hawkins, or the devil," said Cleveland.

"Aweel, captain," replied the jagger, "be he the tane or
the tither, or a wee bit o' baith, mind it is you that give him
these names, and not I."

"Why, Captain Cleveland," said the Udaller, "this may
prove the very consort you spoke of."

"They must have had some good luck, then," said Cleveland, "to put them in better plight than when I left them.
Did they speak of having lost their consort, pedlar?"

"In troth did they," said Bryce; "that is, they said something about a partner that had gone down to Davie Jones in
these seas."

"And did you tell them what you knew of her?" said the
Udaller.

"And wha the deevil wad hae been the fule, then," said the

pedlar, "that I suld say sae? When they kenn'd what came of the ship, the next question wad have been about the cargo; and ye wad not have had me bring down an armed vessel on the coast to harrie the poor folk about a wheen rags of duds that the sea flung upon their shores?"

"Besides what might have been found in your own pack, you scoundrel!" said Magnus Troil—an observation which produced a loud laugh. The Udaller could not help joining in the hilarity which applauded his jest; but, instantly composing his countenance, he said, in an unusually grave tone: "You may laugh, my friends; but this is a matter which brings both a curse and a shame on the country; and till we learn to regard the rights of them that suffer by the winds and waves, we shall deserve to be oppressed and hag-ridden, as we have been and are, by the superior strength of the strangers who rule us."

The company hung their heads at the rebuke of Magnus Troil. Perhaps some, even of the better class, might be conscience-struck on their own account; and all of them were sensible that the appetite for plunder, on the part of the tenants and inferiors, was not at all times restrained with sufficient strictness. But Cleveland made answer gaily: "If these honest fellows be my comrades, I will answer for them that they will never trouble the country about a parcel of chests, hammocks, and such trumpery that the Roost may have washed ashore out of my poor sloop. What signifies to them whether the trash went to Bryce Snailsfoot, or to the bottom, or to the devil? So unbuckle thy pack, Bryce, and show the ladies thy cargo, and perhaps we may see something that will please them."

"It cannot be his consort," said Brenda, in a whisper to her sister; "he would have shown more joy at her appearance."

"It must be the vessel," answered Minna; "I saw his eye glisten at the thought of being again united to the partner of his dangers."

"Perhaps it glistened," said her sister, still apart, "at the thought of leaving Zetland; it is difficult to guess the thought of the heart from the glance of the eye."

"Judge not, at least, unkindly of a friend's thought," said Minna; "and then, Brenda, if you are mistaken, the fault rests not with you."

During this dialogue, Bryce Snailsfoot was busied in uncoiling the carefully-arranged cordage of his pack, which amounted to six good yards of dressed seal-skin, curiously complicated and secured by all manner of knots and buckles. He was considerably interrupted in the task by the Udaller and others, who pressed him with questions respecting the stranger vessel.

"Were the officers often ashore? and how were they received by the people of Kirkwall?" said Magnus Troil.

"Excellently well," answered Bryce Snailsfoot; "and the captain and one or two of his men had been at some of the vanities and dances which went forward in the town; but there had been some word about customs, or king's duties, or the like, and some of the higher folk, that took upon them as magistrates, or the like, had had words with the captain, and he refused to satisfy them; and then it is like he was more coldly looked on, and he spoke of carrying the ship round to Stromness, or the Langhope, for she lay under the guns of the battery at Kirkwall. But he (Bryce) thought she wad bide at Kirkwall till the summer fair was over, for all that."

"The Orkney gentry," said Magnus Troil, "are always in a hurry to draw the Scotch collar tighter round their own necks. Is it not enough that we must pay "scat" and "wattle," which were all the public dues under our old Norse government; but must they come over us with king's dues and customs besides? It is the part of an honest man to resist these things. I have done so all my life, and will do so to the end of it."

There was a loud jubilee and shout of applause among the guests, who were (some of them at least) better pleased with Magnus Troil's latitudinarian principles with respect to the public revenue (which were extremely natural to those living in so secluded a situation, and subjected to many additional exactions) than they had been with the rigour of his judgment on the subject of wrecked goods. But Minna's inexperienced feelings carried her farther than her father, while she whispered to Brenda, not unheard by Cleveland, that the tame spirit of the Orcadians had missed every chance which late incidents had given them to emancipate these islands from the Scottish yoke.

"Why," she said, "should we not, under so many changes as late times have introduced, have seized the opportunity to shake off an allegiance which is not justly due from us, and to return to the protection of Denmark, our parent country? Why should we yet hesitate to do this, but that the gentry of Orkney have mixed families and friendship so much with our invaders that they have become dead to the throb of the heroic Norse blood which they derived from their ancestors?"

The latter part of this patriotic speech happened to reach the astonished ears of our friend Triptolemus, who, having a sincere devotion for the Protestant succession, and the Revolution as established, was surprised into the ejaculation: "As the old cock crows the young cock learns—hen, I should say, mistress, and I crave your pardon if I say anything amiss in either gender. But it is a happy country where the father declares against the king's customs, and the daughter against the king's crown! and, in my judgment, it can end in naething but trees and tows."

"Trees are scarce among us," said Magnus; "and for ropes, we need them for our rigging, and cannot spare them to be shirt-collars."

"And whoever," said the captain, "takes umbrage at what this young lady says had better keep his ears and tongue for a safer employment than such an adventure."

"Ay—ay," said Triptolemus, "it helps the matter much to speak truths whilk are as unwelcome to a proud stomach as wet clover to a cow's, in a land where lads are ready to draw the whittle if a lassie but looks awry. But what manners are to be expected in a country where folk call a pleugh-sock a markal?"

"Hark ye, Master Yellowley," said the captain, smiling, "I hope my manners are not among those abuses which you come hither to reform; any experiment on them may be dangerous."

"As well as difficult," said Triptolemus, drily; "but fear nothing, Captain Cleveland, from my remonstrances. My labours regard the men and things of the earth, and not the men and things of the sea: you are not of my element."

"Let us be friends, then, old clod-compeller," said the captain.

"Clod-compeller!" said the agriculturist, bethinking himself of the lore of his earlier days. "Clod-compeller *pro* cloud-compeller, νεφεληγερέτα Ζεὺς—*Græcum est ;* in which voyage came you by that phrase?"

"I have travelled books as well as seas in my day," said the captain; "but my last voyages have been of a sort to make me forget my early cruises through classic knowledge. But come here, Bryce; hast cast off the lashing? Come all hands, and let us see if he has aught in his cargo that is worth looking upon."

With a proud, and at the same time a wily, smile did the crafty pedlar display a collection of wares far superior to those which usually filled his packages, and, in particular, some stuffs and embroideries of such beauty and curiosity, fringed, flowered, and worked, with such art and magnificence, upon foreign and arabesque patterns, that the sight might have dazzled a far more brilliant company than the simple race of Thule. All beheld and admired, while Mistress Baby Yellowley, holding up her hands, protested it was a sin even to look upon such extravagance, and worse than murder so much as to ask the price of them.

Others, however, were more courageous; and the prices demanded by the merchant, if they were not, as he himself declared, something just more than nothing, short only of an absolute free gift of his wares, were nevertheless so moderate as to show that he himself must have made an easy acquisition of the goods, judging by the rate at which he offered to part with them. Accordingly, the cheapness of the articles created a rapid sale; for in Zetland, as well as elsewhere, wise folk buy more from the prudential desire to secure a good bargain than from any real occasion for the purchase. The Lady Glowrowrum bought seven petticoats and twelve stomachers on this sole principle, and other matrons present rivalled her in this sagacious species of economy. The Udaller was also a considerable purchaser; but the principal customer for whatever could please the eye of beauty was the gallant Captain Cleveland, who rummaged the jagger's stores in selecting presents for the ladies of the party, in which Minna and Brenda Troil were especially remembered.

"I fear," said Magnus Troil, "that the young women are to consider these pretty presents as keepsakes, and that all this liberality is only a sure sign we are soon to lose you?"

This question seemed to embarrass him to whom it was put.

"I scarce know," he said with some hesitation, "whether this vessel is my consort or no; I must take a trip to Kirkwall to make sure of that matter, and then I hope to return to Dunrossness to bid you all farewell."

"In that case," said the Udaller, after a moment's pause, "I think I may carry you thither. I should be at the Kirkwall fair, to settle with the merchants I have consigned my fish to, and I have often promised Minna and Brenda that they should see the fair. Perhaps also your consort, or these strangers, whoever they be, may have some merchandise that will suit me. I love to see my rigging-loft well stocked with goods, almost as much as to see it full of dancers. We will go to Orkney in my own brig, and I can offer you a hammock, if you will."

The offer seemed so acceptable to Cleveland that, after pouring himself forth in thanks, he seemed determined to mark his joy by exhausting Byrce Snailsfoot's treasures in liberality to the company. The contents of a purse of gold were transferred to the jagger, with a facility and indifference on the part of its former owner which argued either the greatest profusion or consciousness of superior and inexhaustible wealth; so that Baby whispered to her brother that, "If he could afford to fling away money at this rate, the lad had made a better voyage in a broken ship than all the skippers of Dundee had made in their haill anes for a twelvemonth past."

But the angry feeling in which she made this remark was much mollified when Cleveland, whose object it seemed that evening to be to buy golden opinions of all sorts of men, approached her with a garment somewhat resembling in shape the Scottish plaid, but woven of a sort of wool so soft that it felt to the touch as if it were composed of eider-down. "This," he said, "was a part of a Spanish lady's dress, called a *mantilla;* as it would exactly fit the size of Mrs. Baby Yellowley, and was very well suited for the fogs of the climate of Zetland, he entreated her to wear it for his sake." The lady, with as much condescending sweetness as her countenance was able to express, not only consented to receive this mark of gallantry, but permitted the donor to arrange the mantilla upon her projecting and bony shoulder-blades, where, said Claud Halcro, "It hung, for all the world, as if it had been stretched betwixt a couple of cloak-pins."

While the captain was performing this piece of courtesy, much to the entertainment of the company, which, it may be presumed, was his principal object from the beginning, Mordaunt Mertoun made purchase of a small golden chaplet, with the private intention of presenting it to Brenda, when he should find an opportunity. The price was fixed, and the article laid aside. Claud Halcro also showed some desire of possessing a silver box of antique shape, for depositing tobacco, which he was in the habit of using in considerable quantity. But the bard seldom had current coin in promptitude, and, indeed, in his wandering way of life, had little occasion for any; and Bryce, on the other hand, his having been hitherto a ready-money trade, protested that his very moderate profits upon such rare and choice articles would not allow of his affording credit to the purchaser. Mordaunt gathered the import of this conversation from the mode in which they whispered together, while the bard seemed to advance a wishful finger towards the box in question, and the cautious pedlar detained it with the weight of his whole hand, as if he had been afraid it would literally make itself wings and fly into Claud Halcro's pocket. Mordaunt Mertoun at this moment, desirous to gratify an old acquaintance, laid the price of the box on the table, and said he would not permit Master Halcro to purchase that box, as he had settled in his own mind to make him a present of it.

"I cannot think of robbing you, my dear young friend," said the poet; "but the truth is, that that same box does remind me strangely of glorious John's, out of which I had the honour to take a pinch at the Wits' Coffee-house, for which I think more highly of my right-hand finger and thumb than any other part of my body; only you must allow me to pay you back the price when my Urkaster stock-fish come to market."

"Settle that as you like betwixt you," said the jagger, taking up Mordaunt's money; "the box is bought and sold."

"And how dare you sell over again," said Captain Cleveland, suddenly interfering, "what you already have sold to me?"

All were surprised at this interjection, which was hastily made, as Cleveland, having turned from Mistress Baby, had become suddenly, and, as it seemed, not without emotion, aware what articles Bryce Snailsfoot was now disposing of. To this short and fierce question the jagger, afraid to contradict a customer of his description, answered only by stammering, that the "Lord knew he meant nae offence."

"How, sir! no offence!" said the seaman, "and dispose of my property?" extending his hand at the same time to the box and chaplet; "restore the young gentleman's money, and learn to keep your course on the meridian of honesty."

The jagger, confused and reluctant, pulled out his leathern pouch to repay to Mordaunt the money he had just deposited in it; but the youth was not to be so satisfied.

"The articles," he said, "were bought and sold—these were your own words, Bryce Snailsfoot, in Master Halcro's hearing; and I will suffer neither you nor any other to deprive me of my property."

"*Your* property, young man?" said Cleveland. "It is mine: I spoke to Bryce respecting them an instant before I turned from the table."

15

"I—I—I had not just heard distinctly," said Bryce, evidently unwilling to offend either party.

"Come—come," said the Udaller, "we will have no quarrelling about baubles; we shall be summoned presently to the rigging-loft"—so he used to call the apartment used as a ball-room—"and we must all go in good-humour. The things shall remain with Bryce for to-night, and to-morrow I will myself settle whom they shall belong to."

The laws of the Udaller in his own house were absolute as those of the Medes. The two young men, regarding each other with looks of sullen displeasure, drew off in different directions.

It is seldom that the second day of a prolonged festival equals the first. The spirits, as well as the limbs, are jaded, and unequal to the renewed expenditure of animation and exertion; and the dance at Burgh-Westra was sustained with much less mirth than on the preceding evening. It was yet an hour from midnight, when even the reluctant Magnus Troil, after regretting the degeneracy of the times, and wishing he could transfuse into the modern Hialtlanders some of the vigour which still animated his own frame, found himself compelled to give the signal for general retreat.

Just as this took place, Halcro, leading Mordaunt Mertoun a little aside, said he had a message to him from Captain Cleveland.

"A message!" said Mordaunt, his heart beating somewhat thick as he spoke. "A challenge, I suppose?"

"A challenge!" repeated Halcro; "who ever heard of a challenge in our quiet islands? Do you think that I look like a carrier of challenges, and to you of all men living? I am none of those fighting fools, as glorious John calls them; and it was not quite a message I had to deliver—only thus far, this Captain Cleveland, I find, hath set his heart upon having these articles you looked at."

"He shall not have them, I swear to you," replied Mordaunt Mertoun.

"Nay, but hear me," said Halcro; "it seems that, by the marks or arms that are upon them, he knows that they were formerly his property. Now, were you to give me the box, as you promised, I fairly tell you I should give the man back his own."

"And Brenda might do the like," thought Mordaunt to himself, and instantly replied aloud: "I have thought better of it, my friend. Captain Cleveland shall have the toys he sets such store by, but it is on one sole condition."

"Nay, you will spoil all with your conditions," said Halcro; "for, as glorious John says, conditions are but——"

"Hear me, I say, with patience. My condition is, that he keeps the toys in exchange for the rifle-gun I accepted from him, which will leave no obligation between us on either side."

"I see where you would be: this is Sebastian and Dorax all over. Well, you may let the jagger know he is to deliver the things to Cleveland—I think he is mad to have them—and I will let Cleveland know the conditions annexed, otherwise honest Bryce might come by two payments instead of one; and I believe his conscience would not choke upon it."

With these words Halcro went to seek out Cleveland; while Mordaunt, observing Snailsfoot, who, as a sort of privileged person, had thrust himself into the crowd at the bottom of the dancing-room, went up to him, and gave him directions to deliver the disputed articles to Cleveland as soon as he had an opportunity.

"Ye are in the right, Maister Mordaunt," said the jagger; "ye are a prudent and a sensible lad—a calm answer turneth away wrath; and mysell, I sall be willing to please you in ony trifling matters in my sma' way; for, between the Udaller of Burgh-Westra and Captain Cleveland, a man is, as it were, atween the deil and the deep sea; and it was like that the Udaller, in the end, would have taken your part in the dispute, for he is a man that loves justice."

"Which apparently you care very little about, Master Snailsfoot," said Mordaunt, "otherwise there could have been no dispute whatever, the right being so clearly on my side, if you had pleased to bear witness according to the dictates of truth."

"Maister Mordaunt," said the jagger, "I must own there

was, as it were, a colouring or shadow of justice on your side; but then the justice that I meddle with is only justice in the way of trade—to have an ell-wand of due length, if it be not something worn out with leaning on it in my lang and painful journeys, and to buy and sell by just weight and measure, twenty-four merks to the lispund; but I have nothing to do, to do justice betwixt man and man, like a fowd or a lawright-man at a law-ting lang syne."

"No one asked you to do so, but only to give evidence according to your conscience," replied Mordaunt, not greatly pleased either with the part the jagger had acted during the dispute or the construction which he seemed to put on his own motives for yielding up the point.

But Bryce Snailsfoot wanted not his answer. "My conscience," he said, "Maister Mordaunt, is as tender as ony man's in my degree; but she is something of a timorsome nature, cannot abide angry folk, and can never speak above her breath when there is aught of a fray going forward. Indeed, she hath at all times a small and low voice."

"Which you are not much in the habit of listening to," said Mordaunt.

"There is that on your ain breast that proves the contrary," said Bryce, resolutely.

"In my breast!" said Mordaunt, somewhat angrily; "what know I of you?"

"I said *on* your breast, Maister Mordaunt, and not *in* it. I am sure nae eye that looks on that waistcoat upon your own gallant brisket but will say that the merchant who sold such a piece for four dollars had justice and conscience, and a kind heart to a customer to the boot of a' that; sae ye shouldna be sae thrawart wi' me for having spared the breath of my mouth in a fool's quarrel."

"I thrawart!" said Mordaunt; "pooh, you silly man! I have no quarrel with you."

"I am glad of it," said the travelling merchant. "I will quarrel with no man, with my will, least of all with an old customer; and if you will walk by my advice, you will quarrel nane with Captain Cleveland. He is like one of yon cut-

ters and slashers that have come into Kirkwall, that think as
little of slicing a man as we do of flinching a whale: it's their
trade to fight, and they live by it; and they have the advantage of the like of you, that only take it up at your own hand,
and in the way of pastime, when you hae nothing better to do."

The company had now almost all dispersed; and Mordaunt,
laughing at the jagger's caution, bade him good-night, and
went to his own place of repose, which had been assigned to
him by Eric Scambester (who acted the part of chamberlain
as well as butler) in a small room, or rather closet, in one of
the out-houses, furnished for the occasion with the hammock
of a sailor.

CHAPTER XIX.

> I pass like night from land to land,
> I have strange power of speech;
> So soon as e'er his face I see,
> I know the man that must hear me,
> To him my tale I teach.
> COLERIDGE'S *Rime of the Ancient Mariner.*

THE daughters of Magnus Troil shared the same bed, in
a chamber which had been that of their parents before the
death of their mother. Magnus, who suffered grievously under that dispensation of Providence, had become disgusted
with the apartment. The nuptial chamber was abandoned
to the pledges of his bereaved affection, of whom the eldest
was at that period only four years old, or thereabouts; and,
having been their nursery in infancy, continued, though now
tricked and adorned according to the best fashion of the islands and the taste of the lovely sisters themselves, to be their
sleeping-room, or, in the old Norse dialect, their bower.

It had been for many years the scene of the most intimate
confidence, if that could be called confidence where, in truth,
there was nothing to be confided; where neither sister had a
secret; and where every thought that had birth in the bosom
of the one was, without either hesitation or doubt, confided
to the other as spontaneously as it had arisen. But, since

Cleveland abode in the mansion of Burgh-Westra, each of the lovely sisters had entertained thoughts which are not lightly or easily communicated, unless she who listens to them has previously assured herself that the confidence will be kindly received. Minna had noticed what other and less interested observers had been unable to perceive, that Cleveland, namely, held a lower rank in Brenda's opinion than in her own; and Brenda, on her side, thought that Minna had hastily and unjustly joined in the prejudices which had been excited against Mordaunt Mertoun in the mind of their father. Each was sensible that she was no longer the same to her sister; and this conviction was a painful addition to other painful apprehensions which they supposed they had to struggle with. Their manner towards each other was, in outward appearances, and in all the little cares by which affection can be expressed, even more assiduously kind than before, as if both, conscious that their internal reserve was a breach of their sisterly union, strove to atone for it by double assiduity in those external marks of affection which, at other times, when there was nothing to hide, might be omitted without inferring any consequences.

On the night referred to, in particular, the sisters felt more especially the decay of the confidence which used to exist betwixt them. The proposed voyage to Kirkwall, and that at the time of the fair, when persons of every degree in these islands repair thither, either for business or amusement, was likely to be an important incident in lives usually so simple and uniform as theirs; and, a few months ago, Minna and Brenda would have been awake half the night, anticipating, in their talk with each other, all that was likely to happen on so momentous an occasion. But now the subject was just mentioned and suffered to drop, as if the topic was likely to produce a difference betwixt them, or to call forth a more open display of their several opinions than either was willing to make to the other.

Yet such was their natural openness and gentleness of disposition, that each sister imputed to herself the fault that there was aught like estrangement existing between them;

and when, having finished their devotions and betaken themselves to their common couch, they folded each other in their arms, and exchanged a sisterly kiss and a sisterly good-night, they seemed mutually to ask pardon and to exchange forgiveness, although neither said a word of offence, either offered or received; and both were soon plunged in that light and yet profound repose which is only enjoyed when sleep sinks down on the eyes of youth and innocence.

On the night to which the story relates, both sisters were visited by dreams, which, though varied by the moods and habits of the sleepers, bore yet a strange general resemblance to each other.

Minna dreamed that she was in one of the most lonely recesses of the beach, called Swartaster, where the incessant operation of the waves, indenting a calcarious rock, has formed a deep "halier," which, in the language of the island, means a subterranean cavern, into which the tide ebbs and flows. Many of these run to an extraordinary and unascertained depth under ground, and are the secure retreat of cormorants and seals, which it is neither easy nor safe to pursue to their extreme recesses. Amongst these, this halier of Swartaster was accounted peculiarly inaccessible, and shunned both by fowlers and by seamen, on account of sharp angles and turnings in the cave itself, as well as the sunken rocks which rendered it very dangerous for skiffs or boats to advance far into it, especially if there was the usual swell of an island tide. From the dark-browed mouth of this cavern, it seemed to Minna, in her dream, that she beheld a mermaid issue, not in the classical dress of a nereid, as in Claud Halcro's mask of the preceding evening, but with comb and glass in hand, according to popular belief, and lashing the waves with that long scaly train which, in the traditions of the country, forms so frightful a contrast with the fair face, long tresses, and displayed bosom of a human and earthly female of surpassing beauty. She seemed to beckon to Minna, while her wild notes rang sadly in her ear, and denounced, in prophetic sounds, calamity and woe.

The vision of Brenda was of a different description, yet

equally melancholy. She sat, as she thought, in her favourite bower, surrounded by her father and a party of his most
beloved friends, amongst whom Mordaunt Mertoun was not
forgotten. She was required to sing; and she strove to entertain them with a lively ditty, in which she was accounted
eminently successful, and which she sung with such simple
yet natural humour as seldom failed to produce shouts of
laughter and applause, while all who could, or who could not,
sing were irresistibly compelled to lend their voices to the
chorus. But on this occasion it seemed as if her own voice
refused all its usual duty, and as if, while she felt herself unable to express the words of the well-known air, it assumed, in
her own despite, the deep tones and wild and melancholy notes
of Norna of Fitful Head, for the purpose of chanting some
wild Runic rhyme, resembling those sung by the heathen priests
of old, when the victim, too often human, was bound to the
fatal altar of Odin or of Thor.

At length the two sisters at once started from sleep, and,
uttering a low scream of fear, clasped themselves in each other's arms. For their fancy had not altogether played them
false; the sounds which had suggested their dreams were real,
and sung within their apartment. They knew the voice well,
indeed, and yet, knowing to whom it belonged, their surprise
and fear were scarce the less when they saw the well-known
Norna of Fitful Head seated by the chimney of the apartment, which, during the summer season, contained an iron
lamp well trimmed, and in winter a fire of wood or of turf.

She was wrapped in her long and ample garment of wadmaal, and moved her body slowly to and fro over the pale
flame of the lamp, as she sung lines to the following purport,
in a slow, sad, and almost an unearthly accent:

> " For leagues along the watery way,
>   Through gulf and stream my course has been .
> The billows know my Runic lay,
>   And smooth their crests to silent green.
>
> The billows know my Runic lay,—
>   The gulf grows smooth, the stream is still;
> But human hearts, more wild than they,
>   Know but the rule of wayward will.

> One hour is mine, in all the year,
>   To tell my woes, and one alone :
> When gleams this magic lamp, 'tis here ;
>   When dies the mystic light, 'tis gone.
>
> Daughters of northern Magnus, hail !
>   The lamp is lit, the flame is clear,—
> To you I come to tell my tale,
>   Awake, arise, my tale to hear ! "

Norna was well known to the daughters of Troil, but it was not without emotion, although varied by their respective dispositions, that they beheld her so unexpectedly, and at such an hour. Their opinions with respect to the supernatural attributes to which she pretended were extremely different.

Minna, with an unusual intensity of imagination, although superior in talent to her sister, was more apt to listen to, and delight in, every tale of wonder, and was at all times more willing to admit impressions which gave her fancy scope and exercise, without minutely examining their reality. Brenda, on the other hand, had, in her gaiety, a slight propensity to satire, and was often tempted to laugh at the very circumstances upon which Minna founded her imaginative dreams; and, like all who love the ludicrous, she did not readily suffer herself to be imposed upon, or overawed, by pompous pretensions of any kind whatever. But, as her nerves were weaker and more irritable than those of her sister, she often paid involuntary homage, by her fears, to ideas which her reason disowned; and hence Claud Halcro used to say, in reference to many of the traditionary superstitions around Burgh-Westra, that Minna believed them without trembling, and that Brenda trembled without believing them. In our own more enlightened days there are few whose undoubting mind and native courage have not felt Minna's high-wrought tone of enthusiasm; and perhaps still fewer who have not, at one time or other, felt, like Brenda, their nerves confess the influence of terrors which their reason disowned and despised.

Under the power of such different feelings, Minna, when the first moment of surprise was over, prepared to spring from her bed and go to greet Norna, who, she doubted not, had come on some errand fraught with fate; while Brenda, who only beheld in her a woman partially deranged in her under standing, and who yet, from the extravagance of her claims, regarded her as an undefined object of awe, or rather terror, detained her sister by an eager and terrified grasp, while she whispered in her ear an anxious entreaty that she would call for assistance. But the soul of Minna was too highly wrought up by the crisis at which her fate seemed to have arrived to permit her to follow the dictates of her sister's fears; and, extricating herself from Brenda's hold, she hastily threw on a loose nightgown, and, stepping boldly across the apartment, while her heart throbbed rather with high excitement than with fear, she thus addressed her singular visitor:

"Norna, if your mission regards us, as your words seem to express, there is one of us, at least, who will receive its import with reverence, but without fear."

"Norna—dear Norna," said the tremulous voice of Brenda, who, feeling no safety in the bed after Minna quitted it, had followed her, as fugitives crowd into the rear of an advancing army, because they dare not remain behind, and who now stood half concealed by her sister, and holding fast by the skirts of her gown—"Norna—dear Norna," said she, "whatever you are to say, let it be to-morrow. I will call Euphane Fea, the housekeeper, and she will find you a bed for the night."

"No bed for me!" said their nocturnal visitor; "no closing of the eyes for me! They have watched as shelf and stack appeared and disappeared betwixt Burgh-Westra and Orkney; they have seen the Man of Hoy sink into the sea, and the Peak of Hengcliff arise from it, and yet they have not tasted of slumber; nor must they slumber now till my task is ended. Sit down, then, Minna, and thou, silly trembler, sit down, while I trim my lamp. Don your clothes, for the tale is long, and ere 'tis done ye will shiver with worse than cold."

"For Heaven's sake, then, put it off till daylight, dear Norna!" said Brenda; "the dawn cannot be far distant, and if you are to tell us of anything frightful, let it be by day-light, and not by the dim glimmer of that blue lamp!"

"Patience, fool!" said their uninvited guest. "Not by

daylight should Norna tell a tale that might blot the sun out of heaven, and blight the hopes of the hundred boats that will leave this shore ere noon to commence their deep-sea fishing— ay, and of the hundred families that will await their return. The demon, whom the sounds will not fail to awaken, must shake his dark wings over a shipless and a boatless sea, as he rushes from his mountain to drink the accents of horror he loves so well to listen to."

"Have pity on Brenda's fears, good Norna," said the elder sister, "and at least postpone this frightful communication to another place and hour."

"Maiden, no!" replied Norna, sternly; "it must be told while that lamp yet burns. Mine is no daylight tale: by that lamp it must be told, which is framed out of the gibbet-irons of the cruel Lord of Wodensvoe, who murdered his brother; and has for its nourishment—but be that nameless—enough that its food never came either from the fish or from the fruit! See, it waxes dim and dimmer, nor must my tale last longer than its flame endureth. Sit ye down there, while I sit here opposite to you, and place the lamp betwixt us; for within the sphere of its light the demon dares not venture."

The sisters obeyed, Minna casting a slow, awe-struck, yet determined look all round, as if to see the being who, according to the doubtful words of Norna, hovered in their neighbourhood; while Brenda's fears were mingled with some share both of anger and of impatience. Norna paid no attention to either, but began her story in the following words:

"Ye know, my daughters, that your blood is allied to mine, but in what degree ye know not; for there was early hostility betwixt your grandsire and him who had the misfortune to call me daughter. Let me term him by his Christian name of Erland, for that which marks our relation I dare not bestow. Your grandsire Olave was the brother of Erland. But when the wide udal possessions of their father Rolfe Troil, the most rich and well-estated of any who descended from the old Norse stock, were divided betwixt the brothers, the fowd gave to Erland his father's lands in Orkney, and reserved for Olave those of Hialtland. Discord arose between the brethren; for

Erland held that he was wronged; and when the law-ting, with the raddmen and lawright-men, confirmed the division, he went in wrath to Orkney, cursing Hialtland and its inhabitants—cursing his brother and his blood.

"But the love of the rock and of the mountain still wrought on Erland's mind, and he fixed his dwelling not on the soft hills of Orphir or the green plains of Graemsay, but in the wild and mountainous Isle of Hoy,[2] whose summit rises to the sky like the cliffs of Foulah and of Feroe. He knew— that unhappy Erland—whatever of legendary lore Scald and bard had left behind them; and to teach me that knowledge, which was to cost us both so dear, was the chief occupation of his old age. I learned to visit each lonely barrow, each lofty cairn; to tell its appropriate tale, and to soothe with rhymes in his praise the spirit of the stern warrior who dwelt within. I knew where the sacrifices were made of yore to Thor and to Odin; on what stones the blood of the victims flowed; where stood the dark-browed priest; where the crested chiefs, who consulted the will of the idol; where the more distant crowd of inferior worshippers, who looked on in awe or in terror. The places most shunned by the timid peasants had no terrors for me: I dared walk in the fairy circle, and sleep by the magic spring.

"But, for my misfortune, I was chiefly fond to linger about the Dwarfie Stone,[3] as it is called, a relic of antiquity, which strangers look on with curiosity and the natives with awe. It is a huge fragment of rock, which lies in a broken and rude valley, full of stones and precipices, in the recesses of the Ward Hill of Hoy. The inside of the rock has two couches, hewn by no earthly hand, and having a small passage between them. The doorway is now open to the weather; but beside it lies a large stone, which, adapted to grooves still visible in the entrance, once had served to open and to close this extraordinary dwelling, which Trold, a dwarf famous in the Northern sagas, is said to have framed for his own favourite residence. The lonely shepherd avoids the place; for at sunrise, high noon, or sunset the misshapen form of the necro-

[1] See Note 22.   [2] See Note 23.   [3] See Note 24.

mantic owner may sometimes still be seen sitting by the Dwarfie Stone. I feared not the apparition, for, Minna, my heart was as bold and my hand was as innocent as yours. In my childish courage, I was even but too presumptuous, and the thirst after things unattainable led me, like our primitive mother, to desire increase of knowledge even by prohibited means. I longed to possess the power of the voluspæ and divining-women of our ancient race; to wield, like them, command over the elements; and to summon the ghosts of deceased heroes from their caverns, that they might recite their daring deeds and impart to me their hidden treasures. Often, when watching by the Dwarfie Stone, with mine eyes fixed on the Ward Hill, which rises above that gloomy valley, I have distinguished, among the dark rocks, that wonderful carbuncle,[1] which gleams ruddy as a furnace to them who view it from beneath, but has ever become invisible to him whose daring foot has scaled the precipices from which it darts its splendour. My vain and youthful bosom burned to investigate these and an hundred other mysteries, which the sagas that I perused, or learned from Erland, rather indicated than explained; and in my daring mood I called on the lord of the Dwarfie Stone to aid me in attaining knowledge inaccessible to mere mortals."

"And the evil spirit heard your summons?" said Minna, her blood curdling as she listened.

"Hush," said Norna, lowering her voice, "vex him not with reproach; he is with us—he hears us even now."

Brenda started from her seat. "I will to Euphane Fea's chamber, she said, "and leave you, Minna and Norna, to finish your stories of hobgoblins and of dwarfs at your own leisure. I care not for them at any time, but I will not endure them at midnight, and by this pale lamplight."

She was accordingly in the act of leaving the room, when her sister detained her.

"Is this the courage," she said, "of her that disbelieves whatever the history of our fathers tells us of supernatural prodigy? What Norna has to tell concerns the fate, perhaps,

[1] See Note 25.

of our father and his house; if I can listen to it, trusting that God and my innocence will protect me from all that is malignant, you, Brenda, who believe not in such influence, have surely no cause to tremble. Credit me, that for the guiltless there is no fear."

"There may be no danger," said Brenda, unable to suppress her natural turn for humour, "but, as the old jest-book says, there is much fear. However, Minna, I will stay with you; the rather," she added in a whisper, "that I am loth to leave you alone with this frightful woman, and that I have a dark staircase and long passage betwixt [us] and Euphane Fea, else I would have her here ere I were five minutes older."

"Call no one hither, maiden, upon peril of thy life," said Norna, "and interrupt not my tale again; for it cannot and must not be told after that charmed light has ceased to burn."

"And I thank Heaven," said Brenda to herself, "that the oil burns low in the cruise! I am sorely tempted to lend it a puff, but then Norna would be alone with us in the dark, and that would be worse."

So saying, she submitted to her fate, and sat down, determined to listen with all the equanimity which she could command to the remaining part of Norna's tale, which went on as follows:

"It happened on a hot summer day, and just about the hour of noon," continued Norna, "as I sat by the Dwarfie Stone, with my eyes fixed on the Ward Hill, whence the mysterious and ever-burning carbuncle shed its rays more brightly than usual, and repined in my heart at the restricted bounds of human knowledge, that at length I could not help exclaiming, in the words of an ancient saga:

'Dwellers of the mountain, rise,
Trold the powerful, Haims the wise!
Ye who taught weak woman's tongue
Words that sway the wise and strong,—
Ye who taught weak woman's hand
How to wield the magic wand,
And wake the gales on Foulah's steep,
Or lull wild Sumburgh's waves to sleep!
Still are ye yet? Not yours the power
Ye knew in Odin's mightier hour.

What are yé now but empty names,
Powerful Trold, sagacious Haims,
That, lightly spoken, lightly heard,
Float on the air like thistle's beard?"

"I had scarce uttered these words," proceeded Noran, "ere the sky, which had been till then unusually clear, grew so suddenly dark around me that it seemed more like midnight than noon. A single flash of lightning showed me at once the desolate landscape of heath, morass, mountain, and precipice which lay around; a single clap of thunder wakened all the echoes of the Ward Hill, which continued so long to repeat the sound, that it seemed some rock, rent by the thunderbolt from the summit, was rolling over cliff and precipice into the valley. Immediately after fell a gust of rain so violent that I was fain to shun its pelting by creeping into the interior of the mysterious stone.

"I seated myself on the larger stone couch, which is cut at the farther end of the cavity, and, with my eyes fixed on the smaller bed, wearied myself with conjectures respecting the origin and purpose of my singular place of refuge. Had it been really the work of that powerful Trold to whom the poetry of the Scalds referred it? Or was it the tomb of some Scandinavian chief, interred with his arms and his wealth, perhaps also with his immolated wife, that what he loved best in life might not in death be divided from him? Or was it the abode of penance, chosen by some devoted anchorite of later days? Or the idle work of some wandering mechanic, whom chance, and whim, and leisure, had thrust upon such an undertaking? I tell you the thoughts that then floated through my brain, that ye may know that what ensued was not the vision of a prejudiced or prepossessed imagination, but an apparition, as certain as it was awful.

"Sleep had gradually crept on me, amidst my lucubrations, when I was startled from my slumbers by a second clap of thunder; and, when I awoke, I saw, through the dim light which the upper aperture admitted, the unshapely and indistinct form of Trold the dwarf, seated opposite to me on the lesser couch, which his square and misshapen bulk seemed absolutely to fill up. I was startled, but not affrighted; for the blood of the ancient race of Lochlin was warm in my veins. He spoke; and his words were of Norse, so old that few, save my father or I myself, could have comprehended their import —such language as was spoken in these islands ere Olave planted the cross on the ruins of heathenism. His meaning was dark also and obscure, like that which the pagan priests were wont to deliver in the name of their idols, to the tribes that assembled at the Helgafels.[1]   This was the import:

> 'A thousand winters dark have flown,
> Since o'er the threshold of my stone
> A votaress pass'd, my power to own.
> Visitor bold
> Of the mansion of Trold,
> Maiden haughty of heart,
> Who hast hither presumed—
> Ungifted, undoom'd—
> Thou shalt not depart:
> The power thou dost covet
> O'er tempest and wave,
> Shall be thine, thou proud maiden,
> By beach, and by cave,—
> By stack and by skerry, by noup and by voe,
> By air and by wick, and by helyer and gio,
> And by every wild shore which the northern winds know,
> And the northern tides lave.
> But though this shall be given thee, thou desperately brave,
> I doom thee that never the gift thou shalt have,
> Till thou reave thy life's giver
> Of the gift which he gave.'

"I answered him in nearly the same strain; for the spirit of the ancient Scalds of our race was upon me; and, far from fearing the phantom, with whom I sat cooped within so narrow a space, I felt the impulse of that high courage which thrust the ancient champions and Druidesses upon contests with the invisible world, when they thought that the earth no longer contained enemies worthy to be subdued by them. Therefore did I answer him thus:

> 'Dark are thy words, and severe,
> Thou dweller in the stone;

---

[1] Or consecrated mountain, used by the Scandinavian priests for the purposes of their idol-worship.

> But trembling and fear
>   To her are unknown,
> Who hath sought thee here
>   In thy dwelling lone.
> Come what comes soever,
>   The worst I can endure;
> Life is but a short fever,
>   And death is the cure.'

" The demon scowled at me, as if at once incensed and over-awed; and then coiling himself up in a thick and sulphureous vapour, he disappeared from his place. I did not, till that moment, feel the influence of fright, but then it seized me. I rushed into the open air, where the tempest had passed away, and all was pure and serene. After a moment's breath-less pause, I hastened home, musing by the way on the words of the phantom, which I could not, as often happens, recall so distinctly to memory at the time as I have been able to do since.

" It may seem strange that such an apparition should, in time, have glided from my mind like a vision of the night; but so it was. I brought myself to believe it the work of fancy; I thought I had lived too much in solitude, and had given way too much to the feelings inspired by my favourite studies. I abandoned them for a time, and I mixed with the youth of my age. I was upon a visit at Kirkwall when I learned to know your father, whom business had brought thither. He easily found access to the relation with whom I lived, who was anxious to compose, if possible, the feud which divided our families. Your father, maidens, has been rather hardened than changed by years: he had the same manly form, the same old Norse frankness of manner and of heart, the same upright courage and honesty of disposition, with more of the gentle ingenuousness of youth, an eager desire to please, a willingness to be pleased, and a vivacity of spirits which survives not our early years. But though he was thus worthy of love, and though Erland wrote to me authorising his attachment, there was another—a stranger, Minna, a fatal stranger—full of arts unknown to us, and graces which to the plain manners of your father were unknown. Yes, he

16

walked, indeed, among us like a being of another and of a superior race. Ye look on me as if it were strange that I should have had attractions for such a lover; but I present nothing that can remind you that Norna of the Fitful Head was once admired and loved as Ulla Troil: the change betwixt the animated body and the corpse after decease is scarce more awful and absolute than I have sustained while I yet linger on earth. Look on me, maidens—look on me by this glimmering light. Can ye believe that these haggard and weather-wasted features; these eyes, which have been almost converted to stone by looking upon sights of terror; these locks, that, mingled with grey, now stream out, the shattered pennons of a sinking vessel—that these, and she to whom they belong, could once be the objects of fond affection? But the waning lamp sinks fast, and let it sink while I tell my infamy. We loved in secret, we met in secret, till I gave the last proof of fatal and of guilty passion! And now beam out, thou magic glimmer: shine out a little space, thou flame so powerful even in thy feebleness; bid him who hovers near us keep his dark pinions aloof from the circle thou dost illuminate; live but a little till the worst be told, and then sink when thou wilt into darkness as black as my guilt and sorrow!"

While she spoke thus, she drew together the remaining nutriment of the lamp, and trimmed its decaying flame; then again, with a hollow voice and in broken sentences, pursued her narrative.

"I must waste little time in words. My love was discovered, but not my guilt. Erland came to Pomona in anger, and transported me to our solitary dwelling in Hoy. He commanded me to see my lover no more, and to receive Magnus, in whom he was willing to forgive the offences of his father, as my future husband. Alas! I no longer deserved his attachment; my only wish was to escape from my father's dwelling, to conceal my shame in my lover's arms. Let me do him justice: he was faithful—too, too faithful; his perfidy would have bereft me of my senses, but the fatal consequences of his fidelity have done me a tenfold injury."

She paused, and then resumed, with the wild tone of insanity: "It has made me the powerful and the despairing sovereign of the seas and winds!"

She paused a second time after this wild exclamation, and resumed her narrative in a more composed manner.

"My lover came in secret to Hoy, to concert measures for my flight, and I agreed to meet him, that we might fix the time when his vessel should come into the sound. I left the house at midnight."

Here she appeared to gasp with agony, and went on with her tale by broken and interrupted sentences. "I left the house at midnight. I had to pass my father's door, and I perceived it was open. I thought he watched us; and, that the sound of my steps might not break his slumbers, I closed the fatal door—a light and trivial action, but, God in Heaven! what were the consequences! At morn the room was full of suffocating vapour—my father was dead—dead through my act—dead through my disobedience—dead through my infamy! All that follows is mist and darkness—a choking, suffocating, stifling mist envelops all that I said and did, all that was said and done, until I became assured that my doom was accomplished, and walked forth the calm and terrible being you now behold me—the queen of the elements—the sharer in the power of those beings to whom man and his passions give such sport as the tortures of the dog-fish afford the fisherman, when he pierces his eyes with thorns, and turns him once more into his native element, to traverse the waves in blindness and agony.[1] No, maidens, she whom you see before you is impassive to the follies of which your minds are the sport. I am she that have made the offering—I am she that bereaved the giver of the gift of life which he gave me: the dark saying has been interpreted by my deed, and I am taken from humanity to be something pre-eminently powerful, pre-eminently wretched!"

As she spoke thus, the light, which had been long quivering, leaped high for an instant, and seemed about to expire, when Norna, interrupting herself, said hastily: "No more

[1] This cruelty is practised by some fishers, out of a vindictive hatred to these ravenous fishes.

now—he comes—he comes. Enough that ye know me, and the right I have to advise and command you. Approach now, proud spirit! if thou wilt."

So saying, she extinguished the lamp, and passed out of the apartment with her usual loftiness of step, as Minna could observe from its measured cadence.

CHAPTER XX.

Is all the counsel that we two have shared—
The sisters' vows, the hours that we have spent,
When we have chid the hasty-footed time
For parting us—O, and is all forgot?
Midsummer Night's Dream.

THE attention of Minna was powerfully arrested by this tale of terror, which accorded with and explained many broken hints respecting Norna which she had heard from her father and other near relations, and she was for a time so lost in surprise, not unmingled with horror, that she did not even attempt to speak to her sister Brenda. When, at length, she called her by her name, she received no answer, and, on touching her hand, she found it cold as ice. Alarmed to the uttermost, she threw open the lattice and the window-shutters, and admitted at once the free air and the pale glimmer of the hyperborean summer night. She then became sensible that her sister was in a swoon. All thoughts concerning Norna, her frightful tale, and her mysterious connexion with the invisible world, at once vanished from Minna's thoughts, and she hastily ran to the apartment of the old housekeeper, to summon her aid, without reflecting for a moment what sights she might encounter in the long dark passages which she had to traverse.

The old woman hastened to Brenda's assistance, and instantly applied such remedies as her experience suggested; but the poor girl's nervous system had been so much agitated by the horrible tale she had just heard that, when recovered from her swoon, her utmost endeavours to compose her mind could not prevent her falling into a hysterical fit of some duration. This also was subdued by the experience of old Euphane Fea, who was well versed in all the simple pharmacy used by the natives of Zetland, and who, after administering a composing-draught, distilled from simples and wild flowers, at length saw her patient resigned to sleep. Minna stretched herself beside her sister, kissed her cheek, and courted slumber in her turn; but the more she invoked it, the farther it seemed to fly from her eyelids; and if at times she was disposed to sink into repose, the voice of the involuntary parricide seemed again to sound in her ears, and startled her into consciousness.

The early morning hour at which they were accustomed to rise found the state of the sisters different from what might have been expected. A sound sleep had restored the spirit of Brenda's lightsome eye, and the rose on her laughing cheek; the transient indisposition of the preceding night having left as little trouble on her look as the fantastic terrors of Norna's tale had been able to impress on her imagination. The looks of Minna, on the contrary, were melancholy, downcast, and apparently exhausted by watching and anxiety. They said at first little to each other, as if afraid of touching a subject so fraught with emotion as the scene of the preceding night. It was not until they had performed together their devotions, as usual, that Brenda, while lacing Minna's boddice (for they rendered the services of the toilet to each other reciprocally), became aware of the paleness of her sister's looks; and having ascertained, by a glance at the mirror, that her own did not wear the same dejection, she kissed Minna's cheek, and said affectionately: "Claud Halcro was right, my dearest sister, when his poetical folly gave us these names of Night and Day."

"And wherefore should you say so now?" said Minna.

"Because we each are bravest in the season that we take our name from: I was frightened wellnigh to death by hearing those things last night which you endured with courageous firmness; and now, when it is broad light, I can think of them with composure, while you look as pale as a spirit who is surprised by sunrise."

"You are lucky, Brenda," said her sister, gravely, "who can so soon forget such a tale of wonder and horror."

"The horror," said Brenda, "is never to be forgotten, unless one could hope that the unfortunate woman's excited imagination, which shows itself so active in conjuring up apparitions, may have fixed on her an imaginary crime."

"You believe nothing, then," said Minna, "of her interview at the Dwarfie Stone, that wondrous place, of which so many tales are old, and which, for so many centuries, has been reverenced as the work of a demon, and as his abode?"

"I believe," said Brenda, "that our unhappy relative is no impostor; and therefore I believe that she was at the Dwarfie Stone during a thunderstorm, that she sought shelter in it, and that, during a swoon, or during sleep perhaps, some dream visited her, concerned with the popular traditions with which she was so conversant; but I cannot easily believe more."

"And yet the event," said Minna, "corresponded to the dark intimations of the vision."

"Pardon me," said Brenda, "I rather think the dream would never have been put into shape, or perhaps remembered at all, but for the event. She told us herself she had nearly forgot the vision, till after her father's dreadful death; and who shall warrant how much of what she then supposed herself to remember was not the creation of her own fancy, disordered as it naturally was by the horrid accident? Had she really seen and conversed with a necromantic dwarf, she was likely to remember the conversation long enough—at least I am sure I should."

"Brenda," replied Minna, "you have heard the good minister of the Cross kirk say, that human wisdom was worse than folly, when it was applied to mysteries beyond its comprehension; and that, if we believed no more than we could understand, we should resist the evidence of our senses, which presented us, at every turn, circumstances as certain as they were unintelligible."

"You are too learned yourself, sister," answered Brenda, "to need the assistance of the good minister of Cross kirk; but I think his doctrine only related to the mysteries of our religion, which it is our duty to receive without investigation or doubt; but in things occurring in common life, as God has bestowed reason upon us, we cannot act wrong in employing it. But you, my dear Minna, have a warmer fancy than mine, and are willing to receive all those wonderful stories for truth, because you love to think of sorcerers, and dwarfs, and water-spirits, and would like much to have a little trow, or fairy, as the Scotch call them, with a green coat, and a pair of wings as brilliant as the hues of the starling's neck, specially to attend on you."

"It would spare you at least the trouble of lacing my boddice," said Minna, "and of lacing it wrong too; for in the heat of your argument you have missed two eyelet-holes."

"That error shall be presently mended," said Brenda; "and then, as one of our friends might say, I will haul tight and belay—but you draw your breath so deeply, that it will be a difficult matter."

"I only sighed," said Minna, in some confusion, "to think how soon you can trifle with and ridicule the misfortunes of this extraordinary woman."

"I do not ridicule them, God knows!" replied Brenda, somewhat angrily; "it is you, Minna, who turn all I say in truth and kindness to something harsh or wicked. I look on Norna as a woman of very extraordinary abilities, which are very often united with a strong cast of insanity; and I consider her as better skilled in the signs of the weather than any woman in Zetland. But that she has any power over the elements I no more believe than I do in the nursery stories of King Erick, who could make the wind blow from the point he set his cap to."

Minna, somewhat nettled with the obstinate incredulity of her sister, replied sharply: "And yet, Brenda, this woman— half-mad woman, and the veriest impostor—is the person by whom you choose to be advised in the matter next your own heart at this moment!"

"I do not know what you mean," said Brenda, colouring deeply, and shifting to get away from her sister. But as she was now undergoing the ceremony of being laced in her turn, her sister had the means of holding her fast by the silken string with which she was fastening the boddice, and, tapping her on the neck, which expressed, by its sudden writhe and sudden change to a scarlet hue, as much pettish confusion as she had desired to provoke, she added, more mildly: "Is it not strange, Brenda, that, used as we have been by the stranger Mordaunt Mertoun, whose assurance has brought him uninvited to a house where his presence is so unacceptable, you should still look or think of him with favour? Surely, that you do so should be a proof to you that there are such things as spells in the country, and that you yourself labour under them. It is not for nought that Mordaunt wears a chain of elfin gold; look to it, Brenda, and be wise in time."

"I have nothing to do with Mordaunt Mertoun," answered Brenda, hastily, "nor do I know or care what he or any other young man wears about his neck. I could see all the gold chains of all the bailies of Edinburgh, that Lady Glowrowrum speaks so much of, without falling in fancy with one of the wearers." And, having thus complied with the female rule of pleading not guilty in general to such an indictment, she immediately resumed, in a different tone: "But, to say the truth, Minna, I think you, and all of you, have judged far too hastily about this young friend of ours, who has been so long our most intimate companion. Mind, Mordaunt Mertoun is no more to me than he is to you, who best know how little difference he made betwixt us; and that, chain or no chain, he lived with us like a brother with two sisters; and yet you can turn him off at once, because a wandering seaman, of whom we know nothing, and a peddling jagger, whom we do know to be a thief, a cheat, and a liar, speak words and carry tales in his disfavour! I do not believe he ever said he could have his choice of either of us, and only waited to see which was to have Burgh-Westra and Bredness Voe. I do not believe he ever spoke such a word, or harboured such a thought, as that of making a choice between us."

"Perhaps," said Minna, coldly, "you may have had reason to know that his choice was already determined."

"I will not endure this!" said Brenda, giving way to her

natural vivacity, and springing from between her sister's hands; then turning round and facing her, while her glowing cheek was rivalled in the deepness of its crimson by as much of her neck and bosom as the upper part of the half-laced boddice permitted to be visible. "Even from you, Minna," she said, "I will not endure this! You know that all my life I have spoken the truth, and that I love the truth; and I tell you that Mordaunt Mertoun never in his life made distinction betwixt you and me until——"

Here some feeling of consciousness stopped her short, and her sister replied, with a smile: "Until *when*, Brenda? Methinks your love of truth seems choked with the sentence you were bringing out."

"Until you ceased to do him the justice he deserves," said Brenda, firmly, "since I must speak out. I have little doubt that he will not long throw away his friendship on you, who hold it so lightly."

"Be it so," said Minna; "you are secure from my rivalry, either in his friendship or love. But bethink you better, Brenda; this is no scandal of Cleveland's—Cleveland is incapable of slander—no falsehood of Bryce Snailsfoot; not one of our friends or acquaintance but says it has been the common talk of the island, that the daughters of Magnus Troil were patiently awaiting the choice of the nameless and birthless stranger, Mordaunt Mertoun. Is it fitting that this should be said of us, the descendants of a Norwegian jarl, and the daughters of the first udaller in Zetland? or would it be modest or maidenly to submit to it unresented, were we the meanest lasses that ever lifted a milk-pail?"

"The tongues of fools are no reproach," replied Brenda, warmly; "I will never quit my own thoughts of an innocent friend for the gossip of the island, which can put the worst meaning on the most innocent actions."

"Hear but what our friends say," repeated Minna; "hear but the Lady Glowrowrum; hear but Maddie and Clara Groatsettar."

"If I were to hear Lady Glowrowrum," said Brenda, steadily, "I should listen to the worst tongue in Zetland; and as for Maddie and Clara Groatsettar, they were both blythe enough to get Mordaunt to sit betwixt them at dinner the day before yesterday, as you might have observed yourself, but that your ear was better engaged."

"Your eyes, at least, have been but indifferently engaged, Brenda," retorted the elder sister, "since they were fixed on a young man whom all the world but yourself believes to have talked of us with the most insolent presumption; and even if he be innocently charged, Lady Glowrowrum says it is un-maidenly and bold of you even to look in the direction where he sits, knowing it must confirm such reports."

"I will look which way I please," said Brenda, growing still warmer. "Lady Glowrowrum shall neither rule my thoughts, nor my words, nor my eyes. I hold Mordaunt Mer-toun to be innocent—I will look at him as such—I will speak of him as such; and if I did not speak to him also, and be-have to him as usual, it is in obedience to my father, and not for what Lady Glowrowrum and all her nieces, had she twenty instead of two, could think, wink, nod, or tattle about the mat-ter that concerns them not."

"Alas! Brenda," answered Minna, with calmness, "this vivacity is more than is required for the defence of the char-acter of a mere friend! Beware! He who ruined Norna's peace for ever was a stranger, admitted to her affections against the will of her family."

"He was a stranger," replied Brenda, with emphasis, "not only in birth but in manners. She had not been bred up with him from her youth; she had not known the gentleness, the frankness of his disposition by an intimacy of many years. He was indeed a stranger, in character, temper, birth, man-ners, and morals; some wandering adventurer, perhaps, whom chance or tempest had thrown upon the islands, and who knew how to mask a false heart with a frank brow. My good sister, take home your own warning. There are other strangers at Burgh-Westra besides this poor Mordaunt Mer-toun."

Minna seemed for a moment overwhelmed with the rapidity with which her sister retorted her suspicion and her caution.

But her natural loftiness of disposition enabled her to reply with assumed composure.

"Were I to treat you, Brenda, with the want of confidence you show towards me, I might reply that Cleveland is no more to me than Mordaunt was; or than young Swaraster, or Laurence Ericson, or any other favourite guest of my father's, now is. But I scorn to deceive you, or to disguise my thoughts. I love Clement Cleveland."

"Do not say so, my dearest sister," said Brenda, abandoning at once the air of acrimony with which the conversation had been latterly conducted, and throwing her arms round her sister's neck, with looks, and with a tone, of the most earnest affection—"do not say so, I implore you! I will renounce Mordaunt Mertoun, I will swear never to speak to him again; but do not repeat that you love this Cleveland!"

"And why should I not repeat," said Minna, disengaging herself gently from her sister's grasp, "a sentiment in which I glory? The boldness, the strength and energy, of his character, to which command is natural and fear unknown—these very properties, which alarm you for my happiness, are the qualities which ensure it. Remember, Brenda, that when your foot loved the calm, smooth sea-beach of the summer sea, mine ever delighted in the summit of the precipice when the waves are in fury."

"And it is even that which I dread," said Brenda; "it is even that adventurous disposition which now is urging you to the brink of a precipice more dangerous than ever was washed by a spring-tide. This man—do not frown, I will say no slander of him—but is he not, even in your own partial judgment, stern and overbearing? accustomed, as you say, to command; but, for that very reason, commanding where he has no right to do so, and leading whom it would most become him to follow? rushing on danger, rather for its own sake than for any other object? And can you think of being yoked with a spirit so unsettled and stormy, whose life has hitherto been led in scenes of death and peril, and who, even while sitting by your side, cannot disguise his impatience again to engage in them? A lover, methinks, should love his mistress better than his own life; but yours, my dear Minna, loves her less than the pleasure of inflicting death on others."

"And it is even for that I love him," said Minna. "I am a daughter of the old dames of Norway, who could send their lovers to battle with a smile, and slay them with their own hands if they returned with dishonour. My lover must scorn the mockeries by which our degraded race strive for distinction, or must practise them only in sport, and in earnest of nobler dangers. No whale-striking, bird-nesting favourite for me: my lover must be a sea-king, or what else modern times may give that draws near to that lofty character."

"Alas, my sister!" said Brenda, "it is now that I must in earnest begin to believe the force of spells and of charms. You remember the Spanish story which you took from me long since, because I said, in your admiration of the chivalry of the olden times of Scandinavia, you rivalled the extravagance of the hero. Ah, Minna, your colour shows that your conscience checks you, and reminds you of the book I mean; is it more wise, think you, to mistake a windmill for a giant, or the commander of a paltry corsair for a kiempe or a viking?"

Minna did indeed colour with anger at this insinuation, of which, perhaps, she felt in some degree the truth.

"You have a right," she said, "to insult me, because you are possessed of my secret."

Brenda's soft heart could not resist this charge of unkindness; she adjured her sister to pardon her, and the natural gentleness of Minna's feelings could not resist her entreaties.

"We are unhappy," she said, as she dried her sister's tears, "that we cannot see with the same eyes; let us not make each other more so by mutual insult and unkindness. You have my secret; it will not, perhaps, long be one, for my father shall have the confidence to which he is entitled, so soon as certain circumstances will permit me to offer it. Meantime, I repeat, you have my secret, and I more than suspect that I have yours in exchange, though you refuse to own it."

"How, Minna!" said Brenda; "would you have me acknowledge for any one such feelings as you allude to, ere he has said the least word that could justify such a confession?"

"Surely not; but a hidden fire may be distinguished by heat as well as flame."

"You understand these signs, Minna," said Brenda, hanging down her head, and in vain endeavouring to suppress the temptation to repartee which her sister's remark offered; "but I can only say that, if ever I love at all, it shall not be until I have been asked to do so once or twice at least, which has not yet chanced to me. But do not let us renew our quarrel, and rather let us think why Norna should have told us that horrible tale, and to what she expects it should lead."

"It must have been as a caution," replied Minna—"a caution which our situation, and, I will not deny it, which mine in particular, might seem to her to call for; but I am alike strong in my own innocence and in the honour of Cleveland."

Brenda would fain have replied that she did not confide so absolutely in the latter security as in the first; but she was prudent, and, forbearing to awaken the former painful discussion, only replied: "It is strange that Norna should have said nothing more of her lover. Surely he could not desert her in the extremity of misery to which he had reduced her?"

"There may be agonies of distress," said Minna, after a pause, "in which the mind is so much jarred that it ceases to be responsive even to the feelings which have most engrossed it: her sorrow for her lover may have been swallowed up in horror and despair."

"Or he might have fled from the islands in fear of our father's vengeance," replied Brenda.

"If for fear or faintness of heart," said Minna looking upwards, "he was capable of flying from the ruin which he had occasioned, I trust he has long ere this sustained the punishment which Heaven reserves for the most base and dastardly of traitors and of cowards. Come, sister, we are ere this expected at the breakfast board."

And they went thither, arm in arm, with much more of confidence than had lately subsisted between them; the little quarrel which had taken place having served the purpose of a *bourasque*, or sudden squall, which dispels mists and vapours, and leaves fair weather behind it.

On their way to the breakfast apartment, they agreed that it was unnecessary, and might be imprudent, to communicate to their father the circumstance of the nocturnal visit, or to let him observe that they now knew more than formerly of the melancholy history of Norna.

CHAPTER XXI.

> But lost to me, for ever lost those joys,
> Which reason scatters, and which time destroys.
> No more the midnight fairy-train I view,
> All in the merry moonlight tippling dew.
> Even the last lingering fiction of the brain,
> The churchyard ghost, is now at rest again.
>
> *The Library.*

THE moral bard,[1] from whom we borrow the motto of this chapter, has touched a theme with which most readers have some feelings that vibrate unconsciously. Superstition, when not arrayed in her full horrors, but laying a gentle hand only on her suppliant's head, had charms which we fail not to regret, even in those stages of society from which her influence is wellnigh banished by the light of reason and general education. At least, in more ignorant periods, her system of ideal terrors had something in them interesting to minds which had few means of excitement. This is more especially true of those lighter modifications of superstitious feelings and practices which mingle in the amusements of the ruder ages, and are, like the auguries of Hallow-e'en in Scotland, considered partly as matter of merriment, partly as sad and prophetic earnest. And, with similar feelings, people even of tolerable education have, in our times, sought the cell of a fortune-teller, upon a frolic, as it is termed, and yet not always in a disposition absolutely sceptical towards the responses they receive. When the sisters of Burgh-Westra arrived in the apartment destined for a breakfast as ample as that which we have described on the preceding morning, and had undergone a jocular rebuke from the Udaller for their late attendance, they found

[1] Rev. George Crabbe (*Laing*).

the company, most of whom had already breakfasted, engaged in an ancient Norwegian custom of the character which we have just described.

It seems to have been borrowed from those poems of the Scalds in which champions and heroines are so often represented as seeking to know their destiny from some sorceress or prophetess, who, as in the legend called by Gray the *Descent of Odin*, awakens by the force of Runic rhyme the unwilling revealer of the doom of fate, and compels from her answers, often of dubious import, but which were then believed to express some shadow of the events of futurity.

An old sibyl, Euphane Fea, the housekeeper we have already mentioned, was installed in the recess of a large window, studiously darkened by bearskins and other miscellaneous drapery, so as to give it something the appearance of a Laplander's hut, and accommodated, like a confessional chair, with an aperture, which permitted the person within to hear with ease whatever questions should be put, though not to see the querist. Here seated, the voluspa, or sibyl, was to listen to the rhythmical inquiries which should be made to her, and return an extemporaneous answer. The drapery was supposed to prevent her from seeing by what individuals she was consulted, and the intended or accidental reference which the answer given under such circumstances bore to the situation of the person by whom the question was asked often furnished food for laughter, and sometimes, as it happened, for more serious reflection. The sibyl was usually chosen from her possessing the talent of improvisation in the Norse poetry; no unusual accomplishment, where the minds of many were stored with old verses, and where the rules of metrical composition are uncommonly simple. The questions were also put in verse; but as this power of extemporaneous composition, though common, could not be supposed universal, the medium of an interpreter might be used by any querist, which interpreter, holding the consulter of the oracle by the hand, and standing by the place from which the oracles were issued, had the task of rendering into verse the subject of inquiry.[1]

[1] See Fortune-telling Rhymes. Note 26.

On the present occasion, Claude Halcro was summoned, by the universal voice, to perform the part of interpreter; and, after shaking his head and muttering some apology for decay of memory and poetical powers, contradicted at once by his own conscious smile of confidence and by the general shout of the company, the light-hearted old man came forward to play his part in the proposed entertainment.

But, just as it was about to commence, the arrangement of parts was singularly altered. Norna of the Fitful Head, whom every one excepting the two sisters believed to be at the distance of many miles, suddenly, and without greeting, entered the apartment, walked majestically up to the bearskin tabernacle, and signed to the female who was there seated to abdicate her sanctuary. The old woman came forth, shaking her head and looking like one overwhelmed with fear; nor, indeed, were there many in the company who saw with absolute composure the sudden appearance of a person so well known and so generally dreaded as Norna.

She paused a moment at the entrance of the tent; and, as she raised the skin which formed the entrance, she looked up to the north, as if imploring from that quarter a strain of inspiration; then signing to the surprised guests that they might approach in succession the shrine in which she was about to install herself, she entered the tent, and was shrouded from their sight.

But this was a different sport from what the company had meditated, and to most of them seemed to present so much more of earnest than of game that there was no alacrity shown to consult the oracle. The character and pretensions of Norna seemed, to almost all present, too serious for the part which she had assumed; the men whispered to each other, and the women, according to Claud Halcro, realised the description of glorious John Dryden—

With horror shuddering, in a heap they ran.

The pause was interrupted by the loud, manly voice of the Udaller. "Why does the game stand still, my masters? Are you afraid because my kinswoman is to play our voluspa? It is kindly done in her, to do for us what none in the isles can do so well; and we will not baulk our sport for it, but rather go on the merrier."

There was still a pause in the company, and Magnus Troil added: "It shall never be said that my kinswoman sat in her bower unhalsed, as if she were some of the old mountain-giantesses, and all from faint heart. I will speak first myself; but the rhyme comes worse from my tongue than when I was a score of years younger. Claud Halcro, you must stand by me."

Hand in hand they approached the shrine of the supposed sibyl, and after a moment's consultation together, Halcro thus expressed the query of his friend and patron. Now, the Udaller, like many persons of consequence in Zetland, who, as Sir Robert Sibbald has testified[1] for them, had begun thus early to apply both to commerce and navigation, was concerned to some extent in the whale-fishery of the season, and the bard had been directed to put into his halting verse an inquiry concerning its success.

CLAUD HALCRO.

Mother darksome, mother dread,
Dweller on the Fitful Head,
Thou canst see what deeds are done
Under the never-setting sun.
Look through sleet, and look through frost,
Look to Greenland's caves and coast,—
By the iceberg is a sail
Chasing of the swarthy whale:
Mother doubtful, mother dread,
Tell us, has the good ship sped?

The jest seemed to turn to earnest, as all, bending their heads around, listened to the voice of Norna, who, without a moment's hesitation, answered from the recesses of the tent in which she was inclosed:

NORNA.

The thought of the aged is ever on gear,—
On his fishing, his furrow, his flock, and his steer;
But thrive may his fishing, flock, furrow, and herd,
While the aged for anguish shall tear his grey beard.

[1] *The Description of the Isles of Orkney and Zetland* was published by Sir Robert Sibbald, M.D., Edinburgh, 1711, folio (*Laing*).

17

There was a momentary pause, during which Triptolemus had time to whisper: "If ten witches and as many warlocks were to swear it, I will never believe that a decent man will either fash his beard or himself about anything so long as stock and crop goes as it should do."

But the voice from within the tent resumed its low, monotonous tone of recitation, and, interrupting farther commentary, proceeded as follows:

NORNA.

The ship, well-laden as bark need be,
Lies deep in the furrow of the Iceland sea;
The breeze for Zetland blows fair and soft,
And gayly the garland is fluttering aloft;
Seven good fishes have spouted their last,
And their jaw-bones are hanging to yard and mast;
Two are for Lerwick, and two for Kirkwall,
And three for Burgh-Westra, the choicest of all.[2]

"Now the powers above look down and protect us!" said Bryce Snailsfoot; "for it is mair than woman's wit that has spaed out that ferly. I saw them at North Ronaldsha that had seen the good bark, the 'Olave' of Lerwick, that our worthy patron has such a great share in that she may be called his own in a manner, and they had broomed the ship, and, as sure as there are stars in heaven, she answered them for seven fish, exact as Norna has telled us in her rhyme!"

"Umph—seven fish exactly! and you heard it at North Ronaldsha?" said Captain Cleveland, "and I suppose told it as a good piece of news when you came hither?"

"It never crossed my tongue, captain," answered the pedlar. "I have kenn'd mony chapmen, travelling-merchants, and such like, neglect their goods to carry clashes and clavers up and down from one countryside to another; but that is no craffic of mine. I dinna believe I have mentioned the 'Olave's' having made up her cargo to three folks since I crossed to Dunrossness."

"But if one of those three had spoken the news over again, and it is two to one that such a thing happened, the old lady prophesies upon velvet."

¹ See Whaling Customs. Note 27.

Such was the speech of Cleveland, addressed to Magnus Troil, and heard without any applause. The Udaller's respect for his country extended to its superstitions, and so did the interest which he took in his unfortunate kinswoman. If he never rendered a precise assent to her high supernatural pretensions, he was not at least desirous of hearing them disputed by others.

"Norna," he said, "his cousin (an emphasis on the word), held no communication with Bryce Snailsfoot or his acquaintances. He did not pretend to explain how she came by her information; but he had always remarked that Scotsmen, and indeed strangers in general, when they came to Zetland, were ready to find reasons for things which remained sufficiently obscure to those whose ancestors had dwelt there for ages."

Captain Cleveland took the hint, and bowed, without attempting to defend his own scepticism.

"And now forward, my brave hearts," said the Udaller; "and may all have as good tidings as I have! Three whales cannot but yield—let me think how many hogsheads——"

There was an obvious reluctance on the part of the guests to be the next in consulting the oracle of the tent.

"Gude news are welcome to some folks, if they came frae the deil himsell," said Mistress Baby Yellowley, addressing the Lady Glowrowrum—for a similarity of disposition in some respects had made a sort of intimacy betwixt them—"but I think, my leddy, that this has ower mickle of rank witchcraft in it to have the countenance of douce Christian folks like you and me, my leddy."

"There may be something in what you say, my dame," replied the good Lady Glowrowrum; "but we Hialtlanders are no just like other folks; and this woman, if she be a witch, being the Fowd's friend and near kinswoman, it will be ill ta'en if we haena our fortune spaed like a' the rest of them; and sae my nieces may e'en step forward in their turn, and nae harm dune. They will hae time to repent, ye ken, in the course of nature, if there be ony thing wrang in it, Mistress Yellowley."

While others remained under similar uncertainty and apprehension, Halcro, who saw by the knitting of the old Udaller's brows, and by a certain impatient shuffle of his right foot, like the motion of a man who with difficulty refrains from stamping, that his patience began to wax rather thin, gallantly declared that he himself would, in his own person, and not as a procurator for others, put the next query to the pythoness. He paused a minute, collected his rhymes, and thus addressed her:

CLAUD HALCRO.

Mother doubtful, mother dread,
Dweller of the Fitful Head,
Thou hast conn'd full many a rhyme
That lives upon the surge of time:
Tell me, shall my lays be sung,
Like Hacon's of the Golden Tongue,
Long after Halcro's dead and gone?
Or shall Hialtland's minstrel own
One note to rival glorious John?

The voice of the sibyl immediately replied from her sanctuary:

NORNA.

The infant loves the rattle's noise;
Age, double childhood, hath its toys;
But different far the descant rings,
As strikes a different hand the strings.
The eagle mounts the polar sky;
The imber-goose, unskill'd to fly,
Must be content to glide along,
Where seal and sea-dog list his song.

Halcro bit his lip, shrugged his shoulders, and then, instantly recovering his good-humour and the ready, though slovenly, power of extemporaneous composition, with which long habit had invested him, he gallantly rejoined:

CLAUD HALCRO.

Be mine the imber-goose to play,
And haunt lone cave and silent bay;
The archer's aim so shall I shun,
So shall I 'scape the levell'd gun,
Content my verse's tuneless jingle,
With Thule's sounding tides to mingle,
While, to the ear of wondering wight,
Upon the distant headland's height,
Soften'd by murmur of the sea,
The rude sounds seem like harmony!

As the little bard stepped back, with an alert gait and satisfied air, general applause followed the spirited manner in
which he had acquiesced in the doom which levelled him with
an imber-goose. But his resigned and courageous submission
did not even yet encourage any other person to consult the
redoubted Norna.

"The coward fools!" said the Udaller. "Are you, too,
afraid, Captain Cleveland, to speak to an old woman? Ask
her anything—ask her whether the twelve-gun sloop at Kirkwall be your consort or no."

Cleveland looked at Minna, and probably conceiving that
she watched with anxiety his answer to her father's question,
he collected himself, after a moment's hesitation.

"I never was afraid of man or woman. Master Halcro, you
have heard the question which our host desires me to ask; put
it in my name, and in your own way. I pretend to as little
skill in poetry as I do in witchcraft."

Halcro did not wait to be invited twice, but, grasping Captain Cleveland's hand in his, according to the form which the
game prescribed, he put the query which the Udaller had dictated to the stranger, in the following words:

CLAUD HALCRO.

Mother doubtful, mother dread,
Dweller of the Fitful Head,
A gallant bark from far abroad,
St. Magnus hath her in his road,
With guns and firelocks not a few,
A silken and a scarlet crew,
Deep stored with precious merchandise,
Of gold and goods of rare device—
What interest hath our comrade bold
In bark and crew, in goods and gold?

There was a pause of unusual duration ere the oracle would
return any answer; and when she replied, it was in a lower,
though an equally decided, tone with that which she had
hitherto employed:

NORNA.

Gold is ruddy, fair, and free,
Blood is crimson and dark to see!—
I look'd out on St. Magnus Bay,
And I saw a falcon that struck her prey:

> A gobbet of flesh in her beak she bore,
> And talons and singles are dripping with gore;
> Let him that asks after them look on his hand,
> And if there is blood on't, he's one of their band.

Cleveland smiled scornfully, and held out his hand. "Few men have been on the Spanish Main as often as I have without having had to do with the *guarda-costas* once and again; but there never was aught like a stain on my hand that a wet towel would not wipe away."

The Udaller added his voice potential: "There is never peace with Spaniards beyond the line: I have heard Captain Tragendeck and honest old Commodore Rummelaer say so an hundred times, and they have both been down in the Bay of Honduras, and all thereabouts. I hate all Spaniards, since they came here and reft the Fair Isle men of their vivers in 1588.[1] I have heard my grandfather speak of it; and there is an old Dutch history somewhere about the house, that shows what work they made in the Low Countries long since. There is neither mercy nor faith in them."

"True—true, my old friend," said Cleveland: "they are as jealous of their Indian possessions as an old man of his young bride; and if they can catch you at disadvantage, the mines for your life is the word; and so we fight them with our colours nailed to the mast."

"That is the way," shouted the Udaller: "the old British jack should never down! When I think of the wooden walls, I almost think myself an Englishman, only it would be becoming too like my Scottish neighbours; but come, no offence to any here, gentlemen—all are friends, and all are welcome. Come, Brenda, go on with the play: do you speak next, you have Norse rhymes enough, we all know."

"But none that suit the game we play at, father," said Brenda, drawing back.

"Nonsense!" said her father, pushing her onward, while Halcro seized on her reluctant hand; "never let mistimed modesty mar honest mirth. Speak for Brenda, Halcro; it is your trade to interpret maidens' thoughts."

See Armada in Zetland. Note 28.

The poet bowed to the beautiful young woman, with the devotion of a poet and the gallantry of a traveller, and having, in a whisper, reminded her that she was in no way responsible for the nonsense he was about to speak, he paused, looked upward, simpered as if he had caught a sudden idea, and at length set off in the following verses:

CLAUD HALCRO.

Mother doubtful, mother dread,
Dweller of the Fitful Head,
Well thou know'st it is thy task
To tell what beauty will not ask,
Then steep thy words in wine and milk,
And weave a doom of gold and silk;
For we would know, shall Brenda prove
In love, and happy in her love?

The prophetess replied almost immediately from behind her curtain:

NORNA.

Untouch'd by love, the maiden's breast
Is like the snow on Rona's crest,
High seated in the middle sky
In bright and barren purity;
But by the sunbeam gently kiss'd,
Scarce by the gazing eye 'tis miss'd,
Ere down the lonely valley stealing,
Fresh grass and growth its course revealing,
It cheers the flock, revives the flower,
And decks some happy shepherd's bower.

"A comfortable doctrine, and most justly spoken," said the Udaller, seizing the blushing Brenda, as she was endeavouring to escape. "Never think shame for the matter, my girl. To be the mistress of some honest man's house, and the means of maintaining some old Norse name, making neighbours happy, the poor easy, and relieving strangers, is the most creditable lot a young woman can look to, and I heartily wish it to all here. Come, who speaks next? Good husbands are going—Maddie Groatsettar—my pretty Clara, come and have your share."

The Lady Glowrowrum shook her head, and "could not," she said, "altogether approve——"

"Enough said—enough said," replied Magnus; "no com-

pulsion; but the play shall go on till we are tired of it.
Here, Minna, I have got you at command. Stand forth, my
girl; there are plenty of things to be ashamed of besides old-
fashioned and innocent pleasantry. Come, I will speak for
you myself, though I am not sure I can remember rhyme
enough for it."

There was a slight colour which passed rapidly over Minna's face, but she instantly regained her composure, and stood
erect by her father, as one superior to any little jest to which
her situation might give rise.

Her father, after some rubbing of his brow and other mechanical efforts to assist his memory, at length recovered verse
sufficient to put the following query, though in less gallant
strains than those of Halcro:

MAGNUS TROIL.

Mother, speak, and do not tarry,
Here's a maiden fain would marry.
Shall she marry, ay or not?
If she marry, what's her lot?

A deep sigh was uttered within the tabernacle of the soothsayer, as if she compassionated the subject of the doom which
she was obliged to pronounce. She then, as usual, returned
her response:

NORNA.

Untouch'd by love, the maiden's breast
Is like the snow on Rona's crest;
So pure, so free from earthly dye,
It seems, whilst leaning on the sky,
Part of the heaven to which 'tis nigh;
But passion, like the wild March rain,
May soil the wreath with many a stain.
We gaze—the lovely vision's gone—
A torrent fills the bed of stone,
That, hurrying to destruction's shock,
Leaps headlong from the lofty rock.

The Udaller heard this reply with high resentment. "By
the bones of the Martyr," he said, his bold visage becoming
suddenly ruddy, "this is an abuse of courtesy! and, were it
any but yourself that had classed my daughter's name and
the word 'destruction' together, they had better have left the

word unspoken. But come forth of the tent, thou old gal-dragon," he added, with a smile, "I should have known that thou canst not long joy in anything that smacks of mirth, God help thee!" His summons received no answer; and, after waiting a moment, he again addressed her: "Nay, never be sullen with me, kinswoman, though I did speak a hasty word; thou knowest I bear malice to no one, least of all to thee; so come forth, and let us shake hands. Thou mightst have fore-told the wreck of my ship and boats, or a bad herring-fishery, and I should have said never a word; but Minna or Brenda, you know, are things which touch me nearer. But come out, shake hands, and there let there be an end on't."

Norna returned no answer whatever to his repeated invoca-tions, and the company began to look upon each other with some surprise, when the Udaller, raising the skin which cov-ered the entrance of the tent, discovered that the interior was empty. The wonder was now general, and not unmixed with fear; for it seemed impossible that Norna could have, in any manner, escaped from the tabernacle in which she was inclosed, without having been discovered by the company. Gone, however, she was, and the Udaller, after a moment's consideration, dropt the skin-curtain again over the entrance of the tent.

"My friends," he said, with a cheerful countenance, "we have long known my kinswoman, and that her ways are not like those of the ordinary folks of this world. But she means well by Hialtland, and hath the love of a sister for me and for my house; and no guest of mine needs either to fear evil or to take offence at her hand. I have little doubt she will be with us at dinner-time."

"Now, Heaven forbid!" said Mrs. Baby Yellowley; "for, my gude Leddy Glowrowrum, to tell your leddyship the truth, I likena cummers that can come and gae like a glance of the sun or the whisk of a whirlwind."

"Speak lower—speak lower," said the Lady Glowrowrum, "and be thankful that yon carline hasna ta'en the house-side away wi' her. The like of her have played warse pranks, and so has she hersell, unless she is the sairer lied on."

Similar murmurs ran through the rest of the company, until the Udaller uplifted his stentorian and imperative voice to put them to silence, and invited, or rather commanded, the attendance of his guests to behold the boats set off for the haaf or deep-sea fishing.

"The wind has been high since sunrise," he said, "and had kept the boats in the bay; but now it was favourable, and they would sail immediately."

This sudden alteration of the weather occasioned sundry nods and winks amongst the guests, who were not indisposed to connect it with Norna's sudden disappearance; but without giving vent to observations which could not but be disagreeable to their host, they followed his stately step to the shore, as the herd of deer follows the leading stag, with all manner of respectful observance.

CHAPTER XXII.

There was a laughing devil in his sneer,
That raised emotions both of rage and fear;
And where his frown of hatred darkly fell,
Hope withering fled, and Mercy sigh'd farewell.
The Corsair, Canto I.

THE ling or white fishery is the principal employment of the natives of Zetland, and was formerly that upon which the gentry chiefly depended for their income, and the poor for their subsistence. The fishing-season is therefore, like the harvest of an agricultural country, the busiest and most important, as well as the most animating, period of the year.

The fishermen of each district assemble at particular stations, with their boats and crews, and erect upon the shore small huts, composed of shingle and covered with turf, for their temporary lodging, and skeos, or drying-houses, for the fish; so that the lonely beach at once assumes the appearance of an Indian town. The banks to which they repair for the haaf fishing are often many miles distant from the station where the fish is dried; so that they are always twenty or thirty hours absent, frequently longer; and under unfavourable circumstances of wind and tide, they remain at sea, with a very small stock of provisions, and in a boat of a construction which seems extremely slender, for two or three days, and are sometimes heard of no more. The departure of the fishers, therefore, on this occupation has in it a character of danger and of suffering which renders it dignified, and the anxiety of the females who remain on the beach, watching the departure of the lessening boat, or anxiously looking out for its return, gives pathos to the scene.[1]

The scene, therefore, was in busy and anxious animation when the Udaller and his friends appeared on the beach. The various crews of about thirty boats, amounting each to from three to five or six men, were taking leave of their wives and female relatives, and jumping on board their long Norway skiffs, where their lines and tackle lay ready stowed. Magnus was not an idle spectator of the scene: he went from one place to another, inquiring into the state of their provisions for the voyage, and their preparations for the fishing; now and then, with a rough Dutch or Norse oath, abusing them for blockheads for going to sea with their boats indifferently found, but always ending by ordering from his own stores a gallon of gin, a lispund of meal, or some similar essential addition to their sea-stores. The hardy sailors, on receiving such favours, expressed their thanks in the brief, gruff manner which their landlord best approved; but the women were more clamorous in their gratitude, which Magnus was often obliged to silence by cursing all female tongues from Eve's downwards.

At length all were on board and ready, the sails were hoisted, the signal for departure given, the rowers began to pull, and all started from the shore, in strong emulation to get first to the fishing-ground, and to have their lines set before the rest—an exploit to which no little consequence was attached by the boat's crew who should be happy enough to perform it.

While they were yet within hearing of the shore, they

chanted an ancient Norse ditty appropriate to the occasion,
of which Claud Halcro had executed the following literal
translation :

> " Farewell, merry maidens, tossing and to laugh,
> For the brave lads of Westra are bound to the haaf ;
> And we must have labour, and hunger, and pain,
> Ere we dance with the maids of Dunrossness again.
>
> For now, in our trim boats of Norroway deal,
> We must dance on the waves, with the porpoise and seal ;
> The breeze it shall pipe, so it pipe not too high,
> And the gull be our songstress whene'er she flits by.
>
> Sing on, my brave bird, while we follow, like thee,
> By bank, shoal, and quicksand, the swarms of the sea ;
> And when twenty score fishes are straining our line,
> Sing louder, brave bird, for their spoils shall be thine.
>
> We'll sing while we bait, and we'll sing when we haul,
> For the deeps of the haaf have enough for us all :
> There is torsk for the gentle, and skate for the carle,
> And there's wealth for bold Magnus, the son of the earl.
>
> Huzza ! my brave comrades, give way for the haaf,
> We shall sooner come back to the dance and the laugh ;
> For life without mirth is a lamp without oil :
> Then, mirth and long life to the bold Magnus Troil ! "

The rude words of the song were soon drowned in the ripple
of the waves, but the tune continued long to mingle with the
sound of wind and sea, and the boats were like so many black
specks on the surface of the ocean, diminishing by degrees as
they bore far and farther seaward ; while the ear could distinguish touches of the human voice, almost drowned amid that
of the elements.

The fishermen's wives looked their last after the parting
sails, and were now departing slowly, with downcast and anxious looks, towards the huts in which they were to make arrangements for preparing and drying the fish, with which they
hoped to see their husbands and friends return deeply laden.
Here and there an old sibyl displayed the superior importance
of her experience by predicting, from the appearance of the
atmosphere, that the wind would be fair or foul, while others
recommended a vow to the kirk of St. Ninian's for the safety

of their men and boats (an ancient Catholic superstition not
yet wholly abolished), and others, but in a low and timorous
tone, regretted to their companions that Norna of Fitful Head
had been suffered to depart in discontent that morning from
Burgh-Westra, "and, of all days in the year, that they suld
have contrived to give her displeasure on the first day of the
white fishing!"

The gentry, guests of Magnus Troil, having whiled away
as much time as could be so disposed of in viewing the little
armament set sail, and in conversing with the poor women
who had seen their friends embark in it, began now to separate into various groups and parties, which strolled in different directions, as fancy led them, to enjoy what may be called
the clair-obscure of a Zetland summer day, which, though
without the brilliant sunshine that cheers other countries during the fine season, has a mild and pleasing character of its
own, that softens while it saddens landscapes which, in their
own lonely, bare, and monotonous tone, have something in
them stern as well as barren.

In one of the loneliest recesses of the coast, where a deep
indenture of the rocks gave the tide access to the cavern, or,
as it is called, the helyer, of Swartaster, Minna Troil was
walking with Captain Cleveland. They had probably chosen
that walk as being little liable to interruption from others;
for, as the force of the tide rendered the place unfit either for
fishing or sailing, so it was not the ordinary resort of walkers,
on account of its being the supposed habitation of a mermaid,
a race which Norwegian superstition invests with magical as
well as mischievous qualities. Here, therefore, Minna wandered with her lover.

A small spot of milk-white sand, that stretched beneath one
of the precipices which walled in the creek on either side, afforded them space for a dry, firm, and pleasant walk of about
an hundred yards, terminated at one extremity by a dark
stretch of the bay, which, scarce touched by the wind, seemed
almost as smooth as glass, and which was seen from between
two lofty rocks, the jaws of the creek, or indenture, that approached each other above, as if they wished to meet over the

dark tide that separated them. The other end of their promenade was closed by a lofty and almost unscalable precipice,
the abode of hundreds of sea-fowl of different kinds, in the
bottom of which the huge helyer, or sea-cave, itself yawned,
as if for the purpose of swallowing up the advancing tide,
which it seemed to receive into an abyss of immeasurable
depth and extent. The entrance to this dismal cavern consisted not in a single arch, as usual, but was divided into two,
by a huge pillar of natural rock, which, rising out of the sea,
and extending to the top of the cavern, seemed to lend its
support to the roof, and thus formed a double portal to the
helyer, on which the fishermen and peasants had bestowed
the rude name of the Devil's Nostrils. In this wild scene,
lonely and undisturbed but by the clang of the sea-fowl,
Cleveland had already met with Minna Troil more than once;
for with her it was a favourite walk, as the objects which it
presented agreed peculiarly with the love of the wild, the
melancholy, and the wonderful. But now the conversation
in which she was earnestly engaged was such as entirely to
withdraw her attention, as well as that of her companion, from
the scenery around them.

"You cannot deny it," she said, "you have given way to
feelings respecting this young man which indicate prejudice
and violence—the prejudice unmerited, as far as you are concerned at least, and the violence equally imprudent and unjustifiable."

"I should have thought," replied Cleveland, "that the service I rendered him yesterday might have freed me from such
a charge. I do not talk of my own risk, for I have lived in
danger, and love it; it is not every one, however, would have
ventured so near the furious animal to save one with whom
they had no connexion."

"It is not every one, indeed, who could have saved him,"
answered Minna, gravely; "but every one who has courage
and generosity would have attempted it. The giddy-brained
Claud Halcro would have done as much as you had his strength
been equal to his courage; my father would have done as
much, though having such just cause of resentment against

the young man, for his vain and braggart abuse of our hospitality. Do not, therefore, boast of your exploit too much, my good friend, lest you should make me think that it required too great an effort. I know you love not Mordaunt Mertoun, though you exposed your own life to save his."

"Will you allow nothing, then," said Cleveland, "for the long misery I was made to endure from the common and prevailing report that this beardless bird-hunter stood betwixt me and what I on earth coveted most—the affections of Minna Troil?"

He spoke in a tone at once impassioned and insinuating, and his whole language and manner seemed to express a grace and elegance which formed the most striking contrast with the speech and gesture of the unpolished seaman which he usually affected or exhibited. But his apology was unsatisfactory to Minna.

"You have known," she said, "perhaps too soon and too well, how little you had to fear—if you indeed feared—that Mertoun or any other had interest with Minna Troil. Nay, truce to thanks and protestations; I would accept it as the best proof of gratitude that you would be reconciled with this youth, or at least avoid every quarrel with him."

"That we should be friends, Minna, is impossible," replied Cleveland; "even the love I bear you, the most powerful emotion that my heart ever knew, cannot work that miracle."

"And why, I pray you?" said Minna; "there have been no evil offences between you, but rather an exchange of mutual services; why can you not be friends? I have many reasons to wish it."

"And can you, then, forget the slights which he has cast upon Brenda, and on yourself, and on your father's house?"

"I can forgive them all," said Minna; "can you not say so much, who have in truth received no offence?"

Cleveland looked down and paused for an instant; then raised his head and replied: "I might easily deceive you, Minna, and promise you what my soul tells me is an impossibility; but I am forced to use too much deceit with others, and with you I will use none. I cannot be friend to this young man: there is a natural dislike—an instinctive aversion—something like a principle of repulsion, in our mutual nature, which makes us odious to each other. Ask himself—he will tell you he has the same antipathy against me. The obligation he conferred on me was a bridle to my resentment; but I was so galled by the restraint that I could have gnawed the curb till my lips were bloody."

"You have worn what you are wont to call your iron mask so long that your features," replied Minna, "retain the impression of its rigidity even when it is removed."

"You do me injustice, Minna," replied her lover, "and you are angry with me because I deal with you plainly and honestly. Plainly and honestly, however, will I say, that I cannot be Mertoun's friend, but it shall be his own fault, not mine, if I am ever his enemy. I seek not to injure him; but do not ask me to love him. And of this remain satisfied, that it would be vain even if I could do so; for as sure as I attempted any advances towards his confidence, so sure would I be to awaken his disgust and suspicion. Leave us to the exercise of our natural feelings, which, as they will unquestionably keep us as far separate as possible, are most likely to prevent any possible interference with each other. Does this satisfy you?"

"It must," said Minna, "since you tell me there is no remedy. And now tell me why you looked so grave when you heard of your consort's arrival—for that it is her I have no doubt—in the port of Kirkwall?"

"I fear," replied Cleveland, "the consequences of that vessel's arrival with her crew, as comprehending the ruin of my fondest hopes. I had made some progress in your father's favour, and, with time, might have made more, when hither come Hawkins and the rest to blight my prospects for ever. I told you on what terms we parted. I then commanded a vessel braver and better found than their own, with a crew who, at my slightest nod, would have faced fiends armed with their own fiery element; but I now stand alone, a single man, destitute of all means to overawe or to restrain them; and they will soon show so plainly the ungovernable license of their habits and dispositions, that ruin to themselves and to me will in all probability be the consequence."

"Do not fear it," said Minna; "my father can never be so unjust as to hold you liable for the offences of others."

"" But what will Magnus Troil say to my own demerits, fair Minna?" said Cleveland, smiling.

"My father is a Zetlander, or rather a Norwegian," said Minna, "one of an oppressed race, who will not care whether you fought against the Spaniards, who are the tyrants of the New World, or against the Dutch and English, who have succeeded to their usurped dominions. His own ancestors supported and exercised the freedom of the seas in those gallant barks whose pennons were the dread of all Europe."

"I fear, nevertheless," said Cleveland, "that the descendants of an ancient sea-king will scarce acknowledge a fitting acquaintance in a modern rover. I have not disguised from you that I have reason to dread the English laws; and Magnus, though a great enemy to taxes, imposts, scat, wattle, and so forth, has no idea of latitude upon points of a more general character: he would willingly reeve a rope to the yard-arm for the benefit of an unfortunate buccanier."

"Do not suppose so," said Minna; "he himself suffers too much oppression from the tyrannical laws of our proud neighbours of Scotland. I trust he will soon be able to rise in resistance against them. The enemy—such I will call them— are now divided amongst themselves, and every vessel from their coast brings intelligence of fresh commotions—the Highlands against the Lowlands, the Williamites against the Jacobites, the Whigs against the Tories, and, to sum the whole, the kingdom of England against that of Scotland. What is there, as Claud Halcro well hinted, to prevent our availing ourselves of the quarrels of these robbers to assert the independence of which we are deprived?"

"To hoist the raven standard on the Castle of Scalloway," said Cleveland, in imitation of her tone and manner, "and proclaim your father Earl Magnus the First!"

"Earl Magnus the Seventh, if it please you," answered Minna; "for six of his ancestors have worn, or were entitled

18

to wear, the coronet before him. You laugh at my ardour, but what *is* there to prevent all this?"

"Nothing *will* prevent it," replied Cleveland, "because it will never be attempted. Anything *might* prevent it that is equal in strength to the long-boat of a British man-of-war."

"You treat us with scorn, sir," said Minna; "yet yourself should know what a few resolved men may perform."

"But they must be armed, Minna," replied Cleveland, "and willing to place their lives upon each desperate adventure. Think not of such visions. Denmark has been cut down into a second-rate kingdom, incapable of exchanging a single broadside with England; Norway is a starving wilderness; and, in these islands, the love of independence has been suppressed by a long term of subjection, or shows itself but in a few muttered growls over the bowl and bottle. And, were your men as willing warriors as their ancestors, what could the unarmed crews of a few fishing-boats do against the British navy? Think no more of it, sweet Minna; it is a dream, and I must term it so, though it makes your eyes so bright and your step so noble."

"It is indeed a dream!" said Minna, looking down, "and it ill becomes a daughter of Hialtland to look or to move like a freewoman. Our eye should be on the ground, and our step slow and reluctant, as that of one who obeys a taskmaster."

"There are lands," said Cleveland, "in which the eye may look bright upon groves of the palm and the cocoa, and where the foot may move light as a galley under sail, over fields carpeted with flowers, and savannahs surrounded by aromatic thickets, and where subjection is unknown, except that of the brave to the bravest, and of all to the most beautiful."

Minna paused a moment ere she spoke, and then answered: "No, Cleveland. My own rude country has charms for me, even desolate as you think it, and depressed as it surely is, which no other land on earth can offer to me. I endeavour in vain to represent to myself those visions of trees and of groves which my eye never saw; but my imagination can conceive no sight in nature more sublime than these waves when agitated by a storm, or more beautiful than when they come, as they now do, rolling in calm tranquillity to the shore. Not the fairest scene in a foreign land, not the brightest sunbeam that ever shone upon the richest landscape, would win my thoughts for a moment from that lofty rock, misty hill, and wide-rolling ocean. Hialtland is the land of my deceased ancestors and of my living father; and in Hialtland will I live and die."

"Then in Hialtland," answered Cleveland, "will I too live and die. I will not go to Kirkwall: I will not make my existence known to my comrades, from whom it were else hard for me to escape. Your father loves me, Minna; who knows whether long attention, anxious care, might not bring him to receive me into his family? Who would regard the length of a voyage that was certain to terminate in happiness?"

"Dream not of such an issue," said Minna; "it is impossible. While you live in my father's house, while you receive his assistance and share his table, you will find him the generous friend and the hearty host; but touch him on what concerns his name and family, and the frank-hearted Udaller will start up before you the haughty and proud descendant of a Norwegian jarl. See you—a moment's suspicion has fallen on Mordaunt Mertoun, and he has banished from his favour the youth whom he so lately loved as a son. No one must ally with his house that is not of untainted Northern descent."

"And mine may be so for aught that is known to me upon the subject," said Cleveland.

"How!" said Minna; "have you any reason to believe yourself of Norse descent?"

"I have told you before," replied Cleveland, "that my family is totally unknown to me. I spent my earliest days upon a solitary plantation in the little island of Tortuga, under the charge of my father, then a different person from what he afterwards became. We were plundered by the Spaniards, and reduced to such extremity of poverty that my father, in desperation and in thirst of revenge, took up arms, and having become chief of a little band who were in the same circumstances, became a buccanier, as it is called, and cruised against Spain, with various vicissitudes of good and bad fortune, until, while he interfered to check some violence of his companions, he fell by their hands—no uncommon fate among the captains of these rovers. But whence my father came, or what was the place of his birth, I know not, fair Minna, nor have I ever had a curious thought on the subject."

"He was a Briton, at least, your unfortunate father?" said Minna.

"I have no doubt of it," said Cleveland; "his name, which I have rendered too formidable to be openly spoken, is an English one; and his acquaintance with the English language, and even with English literature, together with the pains which he took, in better days, to teach me both, plainly spoke him to be an Englishman. If the rude bearing which I display towards others is not the genuine character of my mind and manners, it is to my father, Minna, that I owe any share of better thoughts and principles, which may render me worthy, in some small degree, of your notice and approbation. And yet it sometimes seems to me that I have two different characters; for I cannot bring myself to believe that I, who now walk this lone beach with the lovely Minna Troil, and am permitted to speak to her of the passion which I have cherished, have ever been the daring leader of the bold band whose name was as terrible as a tornado."

"You had not been permitted," said Minna, "to use that bold language towards the daughter of Magnus Troil had you *not* been the brave and undaunted leader who, with so small means, has made his name so formidable. My heart is like that of a maiden of the ancient days, and is to be won not by fair words but by gallant deeds."

"Alas! that heart," said Cleveland; "and what is it that I may do—what is it that man can do, to win in it the interest which I desire?"

"Rejoin your friends—pursue your fortunes—leave the rest to destiny," said Minna. "Should you return the leader of a gallant fleet, who can tell what may befall?"

"And what shall assure me that, when I return—if return I ever shall—I may not find Minna Troil a bride or a spouse? No, Minna, I will not trust to destiny the only object worth attaining which my stormy voyage in life has yet offered me."

"Hear me," said Minna. "I will bind myself to you, if you dare accept such an engagement, by the promise of Odin,[1] the most sacred of our Northern rites which are yet practised among us, that I will never favour another until you resign the pretensions which I have given to you. Will that satisfy you? for more I cannot, more I will not give."

"Then with that," said Cleveland, after a moment's pause, "I must perforce be satisfied; but remember, it is yourself that throw me back upon a mode of life which the laws of Britain denounce as criminal, and which the violent passions of the daring men by whom it is pursued have rendered infamous."

"But I," said Minna, "am superior to such prejudices. In warring with England, I see their laws in no other light than as if you were engaged with an enemy who, in fulness of pride and power, has declared he will give his antagonist no quarter. A brave man will not fight the worse for this; and, for the manners of your comrades, so that they do not infect your own, why should their evil report attach to you?"

Cleveland gazed at her as he spoke with a degree of wondering admiration, in which, at the same time, there lurked a smile at her simplicity.

"I could not," he said, "have believed that such high courage could have been found united with such ignorance of the world, as the world is now wielded. For my manners, they who best know me will readily allow that I have done my best, at the risk of my popularity and of my life itself, to mitigate the ferocity of my mates; but how can you teach humanity to men burning with vengeance against the world by whom they are proscribed, or teach them temperance and moderation in enjoying the pleasures which chance throws in their way, to vary a life which would be otherwise one constant scene of peril and hardship? But this promise, Minna—this promise, which is all I am to receive in guerdon for my faithful attachment—let me at least lose no time in claiming that."

[1] See Note 30.

"It must not be rendered here, but in Kirkwall. We must invoke, to witness the engagement, the spirit which presides over the ancient Circle of Stennis. But perhaps you fear to name the ancient Father of the Slain, too, the Severe, the Terrible?"

Cleveland smiled. "Do me the justice to think, lovely Minna, that I am little subject to fear real causes of terror; and for those which are visionary I have no sympathy whatever."

"You believe not in them, then?" said Minna, "and are so far better suited to be Brenda's lover than mine."

"I will believe," replied Cleveland, "in whatever you believe. The whole inhabitants of that Valhalla about which you converse so much with that fiddling, rhyming fool, Claud Halcro—all these shall become living and existing things to my credulity. But, Minna, do not ask me to fear any of them."

"Fear! no—not to *fear* them, surely," replied the maiden; "for, not before Thor or Odin, when they approached in the fulness of their terrors, did the heroes of my dauntless race yield one foot in retreat. Nor do I own them as deities; a better faith prevents so foul an error. But, in our own conception, they are powerful spirits for good or evil. And when you boast not to fear them, bethink you that you defy an enemy of a kind you have never yet encountered."

"Not in these northern latitudes," said the lover, with a smile, "where hitherto I have seen but angels; but I have faced, in my time, the demons of the equinoctial line, which we rovers suppose to be as powerful and as malignant as those of the North."

"Have you, then, witnessed those wonders that are beyond the visible world?" said Minna, with some degree of awe.

Cleveland composed his countenance, and replied: "A short while before my father's death, I came, though then very young, into the command of a sloop, manned with thirty as desperate fellows as ever handled a musket. We cruised for a long while with bad success, taking nothing but wretched small craft, which were destined to catch turtle, or otherwise loaded with coarse and worthless trumpery. I had much ado to prevent my comrades from avenging upon the crews of those baubling shallops the disappointment which they had occasioned to us. At length we grew desperate, and made a descent on a village where we were told we should intercept the mules of a certain Spanish governor, laden with treasure. We succeeded in carrying the place; but while I endeavoured to save the inhabitants from the fury of my followers, the muleteers, with their precious cargo, escaped into the neighbouring woods. This filled up the measure of my unpopularity. My people, who had been long discontented, became openly mutinous. I was deposed from my command in solemn council, and condemned, as having too little luck and too much humanity for the profession I had undertaken, to be marooned, as the phrase goes, on one of those little sandy, bushy islets which are called, in the West Indies, keys, and which are frequented only by turtle and by sea-fowl. Many of them are supposed to be haunted—some by the demons worshipped by the old inhabitants; some by the demons worshipped by the old inhabitants; some by caciques and others, whom the Spaniards had put to death by torture, to compel them to discover their hidden treasures; and others by the various spectres in which sailors of all nations have implicit faith. My place of banishment, called Coffin Key,[1] about two leagues and a half to the southeast of Bermudas, was so infamous as the resort of these supernatural inhabitants that I believe the wealth of Mexico would not have persuaded the bravest of the scoundrels who put me ashore there to have spent an hour on the islet alone, even in broad daylight; and when they rowed off, they pulled for the sloop like men that dared not cast their eyes behind them. And there they left me, to subsist as I might on a speck of unproductive sand, surrounded by the boundless Atlantic, and haunted, as they supposed, by malignant demons."

"And what was the consequence?" said Minna, eagerly.

"I supported life," said the adventurer, "at the expense of such sea-fowl, aptly called boobies, as were silly enough to

[1] See Note 31.

let me approach so near as to knock them down with a stick; and by means of turtle-eggs, when these complaisant birds became better acquainted with the mischievous disposition of the human species, and more shy of course of my advances."

"And the demons of whom you spoke?" continued Minna.

"I had my secret apprehensions upon their account," said Cleveland. "In open daylight, or in absolute darkness, I did not greatly apprehend their approach; but in the misty dawn of the morning, or when evening was about to fall, I saw, for the first week of my abode on the key, many a dim and undefined spectre, now resembling a Spaniard, with his *capa* wrapped around him, and his huge *sombrero*, as large as an umbrella, upon his head; now a Dutch sailor, with his rough cap and trunk-hose; and now an Indian cacique, with his feathery crown and long lance of cane."

"Did you not approach and address them?" said Minna.

"I always approached them," replied the seaman; "but—I grieve to disappoint your expectations, my fair friend—whenever I drew near them, the phantom changed into a bush, or a piece of driftwood, or a wreath of mist, or some such cause of deception, until at last I was taught by experience to cheat myself no longer with such visions, and continued a solitary inhabitant of Coffin Key, as little alarmed by visionary terrors as I ever was in the great cabin of a stout vessel, with a score of companions around me."

"You have cheated me into listening to a tale of nothing," said Minna; "but how long did you continue on the island?"

"Four weeks of wretched existence," said Cleveland, "when I was relieved by the crew of a vessel which came thither a-turtling. Yet my miserable seclusion was not entirely useless to me; for on that spot of barren sand I found, or rather forged, the iron mask which has since been my chief security against treason or mutiny of my followers. It was there I formed the resolution to seem no softer-hearted nor better-instructed, no more humane and no more scrupulous, than those with whom fortune had leagued me. I thought over my former story, and saw that seeming more brave, skilful, and enterprising than others had gained me command and respect, and that seeming more gently nurtured and more civilised than they had made them envy and hate me as a being of another species. I bargained with myself then, that, since I could not lay aside my superiority of intellect and education, I would do my best to disguise, and to sink in the rude seaman, all appearance of better feeling and better accomplishments. I foresaw then what has since happened, that, under the appearance of daring obduracy, I should acquire such a habitual command over my followers that I might use it for the insurance of discipline, and for relieving the distresses of the wretches who fell under our power. I saw, in short, that to attain authority I must assume the external semblance, at least, of those over whom it was to be exercised. The tidings of my father's fate, while it excited me to wrath and to revenge, confirmed the resolution I had adopted. He also had fallen a victim to his superiority of mind, morals, and manners above those whom he commanded. They were wont to call him the Gentleman; and, unquestionably, they thought he waited some favourable opportunity to reconcile himself, perhaps at their expense, to those existing forms of society his habits seemed best to suit with, and, even therefore, they murdered him. Nature and justice alike called on me for revenge. I was soon at the head of a new body of the adventurers who are so numerous in those islands. I sought not after those by whom I had been myself marooned, but after the wretches who had betrayed my father; and on them I took a revenge so severe that it was of itself sufficient to stamp me with the character of that inexorable ferocity which I was desirous to be thought to possess, and which, perhaps, was gradually creeping on my natural disposition in actual earnest. My manner, speech, and conduct seemed so totally changed that those who formerly knew me were disposed to ascribe the alteration to my intercourse with the demons who haunted the sands of Coffin Key; nay, there were some superstitious enough to believe that I had actually formed a league with them."

"I tremble to hear the rest!" said Minna; "did you not become the monster of courage and cruelty whose character you assumed?"

"If I have escaped being so, it is to you, Minna," replied
Cleveland, "that the wonder must be ascribed. It is true, I
have always endeavoured to distinguish myself rather by acts
of adventurous valour than by schemes of revenge or of plunder, and that at length I could save lives by a rude jest, and
sometimes, by the excess of the measures which I myself proposed, could induce those under me to intercede in favour of
prisoners; so that the seeming severity of my character has
better served the cause of humanity than had I appeared directly devoted to it."

He ceased, and, as Minna replied not a word, both remained
silent for a little space, when Cleveland again resumed the
discourse.

"You are silent," he said, "Miss Troil, and I have injured
myself in your opinion by the frankness with which I have
laid my character before you. I may truly say that my natural disposition has been controlled, but not altered, by the
untoward circumstances in which I am placed."

"I am uncertain," said Minna, after a moment's consideration, "whether you had been thus candid had you not known
I should soon see your comrades, and discover, from their conversation and their manners, what you would otherwise gladly
have concealed."

"You do me injustice, Minna—cruel injustice. From the
instant that you knew me to be a sailor of fortune, an adventurer, a buccanier, or, if you will have the broad word, a
PIRATE, what had you to expect less than what I have told
you!"

"You speak too truly," said Minna: "all this I might have
anticipated, and I know not how I should have expected it
otherwise. But it seemed to me that a war on the cruel and
superstitious Spaniards had in it something ennobling—something that refined the fierce employment to which you have
just now given its true and dreaded name. I thought that
the independent warriors of the Western Ocean, raised up, as
it were, to punish the wrongs of so many murdered and plundered tribes, must have had something of gallant elevation,
like that of the Sons of North, whose long galleys avenged on

so many coasts the oppressions of degenerate Rome. This I thought and this I dreamed; I grieve that I am awakened and undeceived. Yet I blame you not for the erring of my own fancy. Farewell; we must now part."

"Say at least," said Cleveland, "that you do not hold me in horror for having told you the truth."

"I must have time for reflection," said Minna—"time to weigh what you have said, ere I can fully understand my own feelings. Thus much, however, I can say even now, that he who pursues the wicked purpose of plunder by means of blood and cruelty, and who must veil his remains of natural remorse under an affectation of superior profligacy, is not, and cannot be, the lover whom Minna Troil expected to find in Cleveland; and if she still love him, it must be as a penitent and not as a hero."

So saying, she extricated herself from his grasp (for he still endeavoured to detain her), making an imperative sign to him to forbear from following her. "She is gone," said Cleveland, looking after her; "wild and fanciful as she is, I expected not this. She startled not at the name of my perilous course of life, yet seems totally unprepared for the evil which must necessarily attend it; and so all the merit I have gained by my resemblance to a Norse champion, or king of the sea, is to be lost at once, because a gang of pirates do not prove to be a choir of saints. I would that Rackam, Hawkins, and the rest had been at the bottom of the Race of Portland—I would the Pentland Firth had swept them to hell rather than to Orkney! I will not, however, quit the chase of this angel for all that these fiends can do. I will—I must to Orkney before the Udaller makes his voyage thither; our meeting might alarm even his blunt understanding, although, thank Heaven, in this wild country, men know the nature of our trade only by hearsay, through our honest friends the Dutch, who take care never to speak very ill of those they make money by. Well, if fortune would but stand my friend with this beautiful enthusiast, I would pursue her wheel no farther at sea, but set myself down amongst these rocks, as happy as if they were so many groves of bananas and palmettoes."

With these and such thoughts half rolling in his bosom, half expressed in indistinct hints and murmurs, the pirate Cleveland returned to the mansion of Burgh-Westra.

CHAPTER XXIII.

There was shaking of hands and sorrow of heart,
For the hour was approaching when merry folks must part;
So we call'd for our horses, and ask'd for our way,
While the jolly old landlord said, "Nothing's to pay."
                                        Lilliput, a Poem.

WE do not dwell upon the festivities of the day, which had nothing in them to interest the reader particularly. The table groaned under the usual plenty, which was disposed of by the guests with the usual appetite; the bowl of punch was filled and emptied with the same celerity as usual; the men quaffed, and the women laughed; Claud Halcro rhymed, punned, and praised John Dryden; the Udaller bumpered and sung choruses; and the evening concluded, as usual, in the rigging-loft, as it was Magnus Troil's pleasure to term the dancing-apartment.

It was then and there that Cleveland, approaching Magnus, where he sat betwixt his two daughters, intimated his intention of going to Kirkwall in a small brig which Bryce Snailsfoot, who had disposed of his goods with unprecedented celerity, had freighted thither to procure a supply.

Magnus heard the sudden proposal of his guest with surprise, not unmingled with displeasure, and demanded sharply of Cleveland how long it was since he had learned to prefer Bryce Snailsfoot's company to his own? Cleveland answered, with his usual bluntness of manner, that time and tide tarried for no one, and that he had his own particular reasons for making his trip to Kirkwall sooner than the Udaller proposed to set sail; that he hoped to meet with him and his daughters at the great fair which was now closely approaching, and might perhaps find it possible to return to Zetland along with them.

While he spoke this, Brenda kept her eye as much upon her

sister as it was possible to do without exciting general observation. She remarked, that Minna's pale cheek became yet paler while Cleveland spoke, and that she seemed, by compressing her lips and slightly knitting her brows, to be in the act of repressing the effects of strong interior emotion. But she spoke not; and when Cleveland, having bidden adieu to the Udaller, approached to salute her, as was then the custom, she received his farewell without trusting herself to attempt a reply.

Brenda had her own trial approaching; for Mordaunt Mertoun, once so much loved by her father, was now in the act of making his cold parting from him, without receiving a single look of friendly regard. There was, indeed, sarcasm in the tone with which Magnus wished the youth a good journey, and recommended to him, if he met a bonny lass by the way, not to dream that she was in love because she chanced to jest with him. Mertoun coloured at what he felt as an insult, though it was but half intelligible to him; but he remembered Brenda, and suppressed every feeling of resentment. He proceeded to take his leave of the sisters. Minna, whose heart was considerably softened towards him, received his farewell with some degree of interest; but Brenda's grief was so visible in the kindness of her manner and the moisture which gathered in her eye, that it was noticed even by the Udaller, who exclaimed, half-angrily: "Why, ay, lass, that may be right enough, for he was an old acquaintance; but mind! I have no will that he remain one."

Mertoun, who was slowly leaving the apartment, half overheard this disparaging observation, and half turned round to resent it. But his purpose failed him when he saw that Brenda had been obliged to have recourse to her handkerchief to hide her emotion, and the sense that it was excited by his departure obliterated every thought of her father's unkindness. He retired; the other guests followed his example; and many of them, like Cleveland and himself, took their leave over-night, with the intention of commencing their homeward journey on the succeeding morning.

That night, the mutual sorrow of Minna and Brenda, if it

could not wholly remove the reserve which had estranged the
sisters from each other, at least melted all its frozen and unkindly symptoms. They wept in each other's arms; and
though neither spoke, yet each became dearer to the other;
because they felt that the grief which called forth these drops
had a source common to them both.

It is probable that, though Brenda's tears were most abun-
dant, the grief of Minna was most deeply seated; for, long
after the younger had sobbed herself asleep, like a child, upon
her sister's bosom, Minna lay awake, watching the dubious
twilight, while tear after tear slowly gathered in her eye,
and found a current down her cheek, as soon as it became too
heavy to be supported by her long black silken eyelashes.   As
she lay, bewildered among the sorrowful thoughts which supplied these tears, she was surprised to distinguish, beneath
the window, the sounds of music.   At first she supposed it
was some freak of Claud Halcro, whose fantastic humour
sometimes indulged itself in such serenades.   But it was not
the *gue* of the old minstrel, but the guitar, that she heard—
an instrument which none in the island knew how to touch
except Cleveland, who had learned, in his intercourse with the
South-American Spaniards, to play on it with superior execution.   Perhaps it was in those climates also that he had
learned the song, which, though he now sung it under the
window of a maiden of Thule, had certainly never been composed for the native of a climate so northerly and so severe,
since it spoke of productions of the earth and skies which are
there unknown.

> " Love wakes and weeps
>   While beauty sleeps:
> O for music's softest numbers,
>   To prompt a theme,
>   For beauty's dream,
> Soft as the pillow of her slumbers!
>
>   Through groves of palm
>   Sigh gales of balm,
> Fire-flies on the air are wheeling;
>   While through the gloom
>   Comes soft perfume,
> The distant beds of flowers revealing.

> O wake and live,
> No dream can give
> A shadow'd bliss, the real excelling;
> No longer sleep,
> From lattice peep,
> And list the tale that Love is telling!"

The voice of Cleveland was deep, rich, and manly, and accorded well with the Spanish air, to which the words, probably a translation from the same language, had been adapted. His invocation would not probably have been fruitless, could Minna have arisen without awaking her sister. But that was impossible; for Brenda, who, as we have already mentioned, had wept bitterly before she had sunk into repose, now lay with her face on her sister's neck, and one arm stretched around her, in the attitude of a child which has cried itself to sleep in the arms of its nurse. It was impossible for Minna to extricate herself from her grasp without awaking her; and she could not, therefore, execute her hasty purpose of donning her gown and approaching the window to speak with Cleveland, who, she had no doubt, had resorted to this contrivance to procure an interview. The restraint was sufficiently provoking, for it was more than probable that her lover came to take his last farewell; but that Brenda, inimical as she seemed to be of late towards Cleveland, should awake and witness it was a thought not to be endured.

There was a short pause, in which Minna endeavoured more than once, with as much gentleness as possible, to unclasp Brenda's arm from her neck; but whenever she attempted it, the slumberer muttered some little pettish sound, like a child disturbed in its · sleep, which sufficiently showed that perseverance in the attempt would awaken her fully.

To her great vexation, therefore, Minna was compelled to remain still and silent; when her lover, as if determined upon gaining her ear by music of another strain, sung the following fragment of a sea-ditty:

> " Farewell! farewell! the voice you hear
> Has left its last soft tone with you;
> Its next must join the seaward cheer,
> And shout among the shouting crew.

> The accents which I scarce could form,
>   Beneath your frown's controlling check,
> Must give the word, above the storm,
>   To cut the mast and clear the wreck.
>
> The timid eye I dared not raise,
>   The hand that shook·when press'd to thine,
> Must point the guns upon the chase,
>   Must bid the deadly cutlass shine.
>
> To all I love, or hope, or fear,
>   Honour, or own, a long adieu!
> To all that life has soft and dear,
>   Farewell! save memory of you!" [1]

He was again silent; and again she to whom the serenade was addressed strove in vain to arise without rousing her sister. It was impossible; and she had nothing before her but the unhappy thought that Cleveland was taking leave in his desolation without a single glance or a single word. He, too, whose temper was so fiery, yet who subjected his violent mood with such sedulous attention to her will—could she but have stolen a moment to say adieu, to caution him against new quarrels with Mertoun, to implore him to detach himself from such comrades as he had described—could she but have done this, who could say what effect such parting admonitions might have had upon his character—nay, upon the future events of his life?

Tantalised by such thoughts, Minna was about to make another and decisive effort, when she heard voices beneath the window, and thought she could distinguish that they were those of Cleveland and Mertoun, speaking in a sharp tone, which, at the same time, seemed cautiously suppressed, as if the speakers feared being overheard. Alarm now mingled with her former desire to rise from bed, and she accomplished at once the purpose which she had so often attempted in vain. Brenda's arm was unloosed from her sister's neck without the sleeper receiving more alarm than provoked two or three unintelligible murmurs; while, with equal speed and silence, Minna put on some part of her dress, with the intention to steal to the win-

---

[1] I cannot suppress the pride of saying, that these lines have been beauti fully set to original music by Mrs. Arkwright of Derbyshire.

dow. But, ere she could accomplish this, the sound of the voices without was exchanged for that of blows and struggling, which terminated suddenly by a deep groan.

Terrified at this last signal of mischief, Minna sprung to the window and endeavoured to open it, for the persons were so close under the walls of the house that she could not see them save by putting her head out of the casement. The iron hasp was stiff and rusted, and, as generally happens, the haste with which she laboured to undo it only rendered the task more difficult. When it was accomplished, and Minna had eagerly thrust her body half out at the casement, those who had created the sounds which alarmed her were become invisible, excepting that she saw a shadow cross the moonlight, the substance of which must have been in the act of turning a corner, which concealed it from her sight. The shadow moved slowly, and seemed that of a man who supported another upon his shoulders—an indication which put the climax to Minna's agony of mind. The window was not above eight feet from the ground, and she hesitated not to throw herself from it hastily, and to pursue the object which had excited her terror.

But when she came to the corner of the buildings from which the shadow seemed to have been projected, she discovered nothing which could point out the way that the figure had gone; and, after a moment's consideration, became sensible that all attempts at pursuit would be alike wild and fruitless. Besides all the projections and recesses of the many-angled mansion and its numerous offices—besides the various cellars, store-houses, stables, and so forth, which defied her solitary search, there was a range of low rocks, stretching down to the haven, and which were, in fact, a continuation of the ridge which formed its pier. These rocks had many indentures, hollows, and caverns, into any one of which the figure to which the shadow belonged might have retired with his fatal burden; for fatal, she feared, it was most likely to prove.

A moment's reflection, as we have said, convinced Minna of the folly of further pursuit. Her next thought was to alarm the family; but what tale had she to tell, and of whom was that tale to be told? On the other hand, the wounded

19

man—if indeed he were wounded—alas, if indeed he were not
mortally wounded!—might not be past the reach of assistance;
and, with this idea, she was about to raise her voice, when she
was interrupted by that of Claud Halcro, who was returning
apparently from the haven, and singing, in his manner, a
scrap of an old Norse ditty, which might run thus in English:

> " And you shall deal the funeral dole;
>   Ay, deal it, mother mine,
> To weary body, and to heavy soul,
>   The white bread and the wine.
>
> And you shall deal my horses of pride;
>   Ay, deal them, mother mine;
> And you shall deal my lands so wide,
>   And deal my castles nine.
>
> But deal not vengeance for the deed,
>   And deal not for the crime;
> The body to its place, and the soul to Heaven's grace,
>   And the rest in God's own time."

The singular adaptation of these rhymes to the situation in
which she found herself seemed to Minna like a warning from
Heaven.   We are speaking of a land of omens and superstitions, and perhaps will scarce be understood by those whose
limited imagination cannot conceive how strongly these operate upon the human mind during a certain progress of society.
A line of Virgil, turned up casually, was received in the 17th
century, and in the court of England,[1] as an intimation of future events; and no wonder that a maiden of the distant and
wild isles of Zetland should have considered as an injunction
from Heaven verses which happened to convey a sense anal-
ogous to her present situation.
   " I will be silent," she muttered—" I will seal my lips—

> The body to its place, and the soul to Heaven's grace,
>   And the rest in God's own time."

   "Who speaks there?" said Claud Halcro, in some alarm,

---

[1] The celebrated *sortes Virgilianæ* were resorted to by Charles I. and his
courtiers as a mode of prying into futurity.

for he had not, in his travels in foreign parts, been able by any means to rid himself of his native superstitions. In the condition to which fear and horror had reduced her, Minna was at first unable to reply; and Halcro, fixing his eyes upon the female white figure, which he saw indistinctly (for she stood in the shadow of the house, and the morning was thick and misty), began to conjure her in an ancient rhyme which occurred to him as suited for the occasion, and which had in his gibberish a wild and unearthly sound, which may be lost in the ensuing translation:

> "St. Magnus control thee, that martyr of treason;
> St. Ronan rebuke thee, with rhyme and with reason;
> By the mass of St. Martin, the might of St. Mary,
> Be thou gone, or thy weird shall be worse if thou tarry!
>   If of good, go hence and hallow thee;
>   If of ill, let the earth swallow thee;
>   If thou'rt of air, let the grey mist fold thee;
>   If of earth, let the swart mine hold thee;
>   If a pixie, seek thy ring;
>   If a nixie, seek thy spring;
>   If on middle earth thou'st been
>   Slave of sorrow, shame, and sin,
>   Hast eat the bread of toil and strife,
>   And dree'd the lot which men call life,
> Begone to thy stone! for thy coffin is scant of thee,
> The worm, thy playfellow, wails for the want of thee;
> Hence, houseless ghost! let the earth hide thee,
> Till Michael shall blow the blast, see that there thou bide thee!
> Phantom, fly hence! take the Cross for a token,
> Hence pass till Hallowmass!—my spell is spoken."

"It is I, Halcro," muttered Minna, in a tone so thin and low that it might have passed for the faint reply of the conjured phantom.

"You!—you!" said Halcro, his tone of alarm changing to one of extreme surprise; "by this moonlight, which is waning, and so it is! Who could have thought to find you, my most lovely Night, wandering abroad in your own element! But you saw them, I reckon, as well as I? bold enough in you to follow them, though."

"Saw whom?—follow whom?" said Minna, hoping to gain some information on the subject of her fears and anxiety.

"The corpse-lights which danced at the haven," replied

Halcro; "they bode no good, I promise you: you wot well what the old rhyme says:

> Where corpse-light
> Dances bright,
> Be it day or night,
> Be it by light or dark,
> There shall corpse lie stiff and stark.

I went half as far as the haven to look after them, but they had vanished. I think I saw a boat put off, however; some one bound for the haaf, I suppose. I would we had good news of this fishing. There was Norna left us in anger, and then these corpse-lights! Well, God help the while! I am an old man, and can but wish that all were well over. But how now, my pretty Minna, tears in your eyes! And now that I see you in the fair moonlight, barefooted, too, by St. Magnus! Were there no stockings of Zetland wool soft enough for these pretty feet and ankles, that glance so white in the moonbeam? What, silent!—angry, perhaps," he added, in a more serious tone, "at my nonsense? For shame, silly maiden! Remember I am old enough to be your father, and have always loved you as my child."

"I am not angry," said Minna, constraining herself to speak, "but heard you nothing?—saw you nothing? They must have passed you."

"They!" said Claud Halcro; "what mean you by they? Is it the corpse-lights? No, they did not pass by me, but I think they have passed by you, and blighted you with their influence, for you are as pale as a spectre. Come—come, Minna," he added, opening a side-door of the dwelling, "these moonlight walks are fitter for old poets than for young maidens. And so lightly clad as you are! Maiden, you should take care how you give yourself to the breezes of a Zetland night, for they bring more sleet than odours upon their wings. But, maiden, go in; for, as glorious John says—or, as he does not say, for I cannot remember how his verse chimes—but, as I say myself, in a pretty poem, written when my muse was in her teens:

> Menseful maiden ne'er shall rise,
> Till the first beam tinge the skies;

> Silk-fringed eyelids still should close,
> Till the sun has kiss'd the rose;
> Maiden's foot we should not view,
> Mark'd with tiny print on dew,
> Till the opening flowerets spread
> Carpet meet for beauty's tread——

Stay, what comes next?—let me see."

When the spirit of recitation seized on Claud Halcro, he forgot time and place, and might have kept his companion in the cold air for half an hour, giving poetical reasons why she ought to have been in bed. But she interrupted him by the question, earnestly pronounced, yet in a voice which was scarcely articulate, holding Halcro, at the same time, with a trembling and convulsive grasp, as if to support herself from falling: "Saw you no one in the boat which put to sea but now?"

"Nonsense," replied Halcro; "how could I see any one, when light and distance only enabled me to know that it was a boat, and not a grampus?"

"But there must have been some one in the boat," repeated Minna, scarce conscious of what she said.

"Certainly," answered the poet, "boats seldom work to windward of their own accord. But come, this is all folly; and so, as the queen says in an old play, which was revived for the stage by rare Will D'Avenant, 'To bed—to bed—to bed!'"

They separated, and Minna's limbs conveyed her with difficulty, through several devious passages, to her own chamber, where she stretched herself cautiously beside her still sleeping sister, with a mind harassed with the most agonizing apprehensions. That she had heard Cleveland, she was positive; the tenor of the songs left her no doubt on that subject. If not equally certain that she had heard young Mertoun's voice in hot quarrel with her lover, the impression to that effect was strong on her mind. The groan with which the struggle seemed to terminate, the fearful indication from which it seemed that the conqueror had borne off the lifeless body of his victim—all tended to prove that some fatal event had concluded the contest. And which of the unhappy men had fallen?—which had met a bloody death?—which had achieved a fatal and a bloody victory? These were questions to which the still small voice of interior conviction answered, that her lover Cleveland, from character, temper, and habits, was most likely to have been the survivor of the fray. She received from the reflection an involuntary consolation which she almost detested herself for admitting, when she recollected that it was at once darkened with her lover's guilt and embittered with the destruction of Brenda's happiness for ever.

"Innocent, unhappy sister!" such were her reflections, "thou that art ten times better than I, because so unpretending—so unassuming in thine excellence! How is it possible that I should cease to feel a pang which is only transferred from my bosom to thine?"

As these cruel thoughts crossed her mind, she could not refrain from straining her sister so close to her bosom that, after a heavy sigh, Brenda awoke.

"Sister," she said, "is it you? I dreamed I lay on one of those monuments which Claud Halcro described to us, where the effigy of the inhabitant beneath lies carved in stone upon the sepulchre. I dreamed such a marble form lay by my side, and that it suddenly acquired enough of life and animation to fold me to its cold, moist bosom; and it is yours, Minna, that is indeed so chilly. You are ill, my dearest Minna! for God's sake, let me rise and call Euphane Fea. What ails you? Has Norna been here again?"

"Call no one hither," said Minna, detaining her; "nothing ails me for which any one has a remedy—nothing but apprehensions of evil worse than even Norna could prophesy. But God is above all, my dear Brenda; and let us pray to Him to turn, as He only can, our evil into good."

They did jointly repeat their usual prayer for strength and protection from on high, and again composed themselves to sleep, suffering no word save "God bless you!" to pass betwixt them when their devotions were finished; thus scrupulously dedicating to Heaven their last waking words, if human frailty prevented them from commanding their last waking thoughts. Brenda slept first, and Minna, strongly resisting the dark and evil presentiments which again began to crowd themselves upon her imagination, was at last so fortunate as to slumber also.

The storm which Halcro had expected began about daybreak—a squall, heavy with wind and rain, such as is often felt, even during the finest part of the season, in these latitudes. At the whistle of the wind and the clatter of the rain on the shingle-roofing of the fishers' huts, many a poor woman was awakened, and called on her children to hold up their little hands and join in prayer for the safety of the dear husband and father who was even then at the mercy of the disturbed elements. Around the house of Burgh-Westra, chimneys howled and windows clashed. The props and rafters of the higher parts of the building, most of them formed out of wreck-wood, groaned and quivered, as fearing to be again dispersed by the tempest. But the daughters of Magnus Troil continued to sleep as softly and as sweetly as if the hand of Chantrey had formed them out of statuary marble. The squall had passed away, and the sunbeams, dispersing the clouds which drifted to leeward, shone full through the lattice, when Minna first started from the profound sleep into which fatigue and mental exhaustion had lulled her, and, raising herself on her arm, began to recall events, which, after this interval of profound repose, seemed almost to resemble the baseless visions of the night. She almost doubted if what she recalled of horror, previous to her starting from her bed, was not indeed the fiction of a dream, suggested, perhaps, by some external sounds.

"I will see Claud Halcro instantly," she said; "he may know something of these strange noises, as he was stirring at the time."

With that she sprung from bed, but hardly stood upright on the floor ere her sister exclaimed: "Gracious Heaven! Minna, what ails your foot—your ankle?"

She looked down, and saw with surprise, which amounted to agony, that both her feet, but particularly one of them, was stained with dark crimson, resembling the colour of dried blood.

Without attempting to answer Brenda, she rushed to the window and cast a desperate look on the grass beneath, for there she knew she must have contracted the fatal stain. But the rain, which had fallen there in treble quantity, as well from the heavens as from the eaves of the house, had washed away that guilty witness, if indeed such had ever existed. All was fresh and fair, and the blades of grass, overcharged and bent with raindrops, glittered like diamonds in the bright morning sun.

While Minna stared upon the spangled verdure, with her full dark eyes fixed and enlarged to circles by the intensity of her terror, Brenda was hanging about her, and with many an eager inquiry pressed to know whether or how she had hurt herself?

"A piece of glass cut through my shoe," said Minna, bethinking herself that some excuse was necessary to her sister; "I scarce felt it at the time."

"And yet see how it has bled," said her sister. "Sweet Minna," she added, approaching her with a wetted towel, "let me wipe the blood off—the hurt may be worse than you think of."

But as she approached, Minna, who saw no other way of preventing discovery that the blood with which she was stained had never flowed in her own veins, harshly and hastily repelled the proffered kindness. Poor Brenda, unconscious of any offence which she had given to her sister, drew back two or three paces on finding her service thus unkindly refused, and stood gazing at Minna with looks in which there was more of surprise and mortified affection than of resentment, but which had yet something also of natural displeasure.

"Sister," said she, "I thought we had agreed but last night that, happen to us what might, we would at least love each other."

"Much may happen betwixt night and morning!" answered Minna, in words rather wrenched from her by her situation than flowing forth the voluntary interpreters of her thoughts.

"Much may indeed have happened in a night so stormy," answered Brenda; "for see where the very wall around Eu-

phane's plantie cruive has been blown down; but neither wind
nor rain, nor aught else, can cool our affection, Minna."

"But that may chance," replied Minna, "which may convert it into——"

The rest of the sentence she muttered in a tone so indistinct
that it could not be apprehended; while, at the same time,
she washed the blood-stains from her feet and left ankle.
Brenda, who still remained looking on at some distance, endeavoured in vain to assume some tone which might re-estab-
lish kindness and confidence betwixt them.

"You were right," she said, "Minna, to suffer no one to
help you to dress so simple a scratch; standing where I do,
it is scarce visible."

"The most cruel wounds," replied Minna, "are those which
make no outward show. Are you sure you see it at all?"

"Oh yes!" replied Brenda, framing her answer as she
thought would best please her sister, "I see a very slight
scratch; nay, now you draw on the stocking, I can see nothing."

"You do indeed see nothing," answered Minna, somewhat
wildly; "but the time will soon come that all—ay, all—will
be seen and known."

So saying, she hastily completed her dress, and led the way
to breakfast, where she assumed her place amongst the guests;
but with a countenance so pale and haggard, and manners and
speech so altered and so bewildered, that it excited the attention of the whole company, and the utmost anxiety on the part
of her father Magnus Troil. Many and various were the conjectures of the guests concerning a distemperature which seemed
rather mental than corporeal. Some hinted that the maiden
had been struck with an evil eye, and something they muttered
about Norna of the Fitful Head; some talked of the departure
of Captain Cleveland, and murmured, "It was a shame for a
young lady to take on so after a landlouper of whom no one
knew anything"; and this contemptuous epithet was in particular bestowed on the captain by Mistress Baby Yellowley,
while she was in the act of wrapping round her old skinny
neck the very handsome "owerlay," as she called it, where-

with the said captain had presented her. The old Lady Glowrowrum had a system of her own, which she hinted to Mistress Yellowley, after thanking God that her own connexion with the Burgh-Westra family was by the lass's mother, who was a canny Scotswoman, like herself.

"For, as to these Troils, you see, Dame Yellowley, for as high as they hold their heads, they say that ken (winking sagaciously) that there is a bee in their bonnet. That Norna, as they call her, for it's not her right name neither, is at whiles far beside her right mind; and they that ken the cause say the Fowd was some gate or other linked in with it, for he will never hear an ill word of her. But I was in Scotland then, or I might have kenn'd the real cause as weel as other folk. At ony rate, there is a kind of wildness in the blood. Ye ken very weel daft folk dinna bide to be contradicted; and I'll say that for the Fowd, he likes to be contradicted as ill as ony man in Zetland. But it shall never be said that I said ony ill of the house that I am sae nearly connected wi'. Only ye will mind, dame, it is through the Sinclairs that we are akin, not through the Troils; and the Sinclairs are kenn'd far and wide for a wise generation, dame. But I see there is the stirrup-cup coming round."

"I wonder," said Mistress Baby to her brother, as soon as the Lady Glowrowrum turned from her, "what gars that muckle wife 'dame, dame, dame' that gate at me? She might ken the blude of the Clinkscales is as gude as ony Glowrowrum's amang them."

The guests, meanwhile, were fast taking their departure, scarcely noticed by Magnus, who was so much engrossed with Minna's indisposition that, contrary to his hospitable wont, he suffered them to go away unsaluted. And thus concluded, amidst anxiety and illness, the festival of St. John, as celebrated on that season at the house of Burgh-Westra, adding another caution to that of the Emperor of Ethiopia—with how little security man can reckon upon the days which he destines to happiness.

CHAPTER XXIV.

But this sad evil which doth her infest,
Doth course of natural cause far exceed,
And housed is within her hollow breast,
That either seems some cursed witch's deed,
Or evill spright that in her doth such torment breed.
Faëry Queene, Book III. Canto III.

THE term had now elapsed, by several days, when Mordaunt Mertoun, as he had promised at his departure, should have returned to his father's abode at Jarlshof; but there were no tidings of his arrival. Such delay might, at another time, have excited little curiosity, and no anxiety; for old Swertha, who took upon her the office of thinking and conjecturing for the little household, would have concluded that he had remained behind the other guests upon some party of sport or pleasure. But she knew that Mordaunt had not been lately in favour with Magnus Troil; she knew that he proposed his stay at Burgh-Westra should be a short one, upon account of his father's health, to whom, notwithstanding the little encouragement which his filial piety received, he paid uniform attention. Swertha knew all this, and she became anxious. She watched the looks of her master, the elder Mertoun; but, wrapt in dark and stern uniformity of composure, his countenance, like the surface of a midnight lake, enabled no one to penetrate into what was beneath. His studies, his solitary meals, his lonely walk, succeeded each other in unvaried rotation, and seemed undisturbed by the least thought about Mordaunt's absence.

At length such reports reached Swertha's ear, from various quarters, that she became totally unable to conceal her anxiety, and resolved, at the risk of provoking her master into fury, or perhaps that of losing her place in his household, to force upon his notice the doubts which afflicted her own mind. Mordaunt's good-humour and goodly person must indeed have made no small impression on the withered and selfish heart of the poor old woman, to induce her to take a course so desperate, and from which her friend the Ranzelman endeavoured in vain to deter her. Still, however, conscious that a miscarriage in the matter would, like the loss of Trinculo's bottle in the horse-pool, be attended not only with dishonour but with infinite loss, she determined to proceed on her high emprize with as much caution as was consistent with the attempt.

We have already mentioned, that it seemed a part of the very nature of this reserved and unsocial being, at least since his retreat into the utter solitude of Jarlshof, to endure no one to start a subject of conversation, or to put any question to him, that did not arise out of urgent and pressing emergency. Swertha was sensible, therefore, that, in order to open the discourse favourably which she proposed to hold with her master, she must contrive that it should originate with himself.

To accomplish this purpose, while busied in preparing the table for Mr. Mertoun's simple and solitary dinner-meal, she formally adorned the table with two covers instead of one, and made all her other preparations as if he was to have a guest or companion at dinner.

The artifice succeeded; for Mertoun, on coming from his study, no sooner saw the table thus arranged than he asked Swertha, who, waiting the effect of her stratagem as a fisher watches his ground-baits, was fiddling up and down the room, "Whether Mordaunt was returned from Burgh-Westra?"

This question was the cue for Swertha, and she answered in a voice of sorrowful anxiety, half-real, half-affected: "Na—na! nae sic divot had dunted at their door. It wad be blythe news indeed to ken that young Maister Mordaunt, puir dear bairn, were safe at home."

"And if he be not at home, why should you lay a cover for him, you doting fool?" replied Mertoun, in a tone well calculated to stop the old woman's proceedings. But she replied boldly, "That, indeed, somebody should take thought about Maister Mordaunt; a' that she could do was to have seat and plate ready for him when he came. But she thought the dear bairn had been ower lang awa'; and, if she maun speak out, she had her ain fears when and whether he might ever come hame."

" *Your* fear!" said Mertoun, his eyes flashing as they usually did when his hour of ungovernable passion approached;
" do you speak of your idle fears to me, who know that all of
your sex, that is not fickleness, and folly, and self-conceit,
and self-will, is a bundle of idiotical fears, vapours, and
tremors? What are your fears to me, you foolish old hag?"

It is an admirable quality in womankind that, when a
breach of the laws of natural affection comes under their observation, the whole sex is in arms. Let a rumour arise in
the street of a parent that has misused a child, or a child that
has insulted a parent—I say nothing of the case of husband
and wife, where the interest may be accounted for in sympathy—and all the women within hearing will take animated
and decided part with the sufferer. Swertha, notwithstanding
her greed and avarice, had her share of the generous feeling
which does so much honour to her sex, and was, on this occasion, so much carried on by its impulse that she confronted
her master, and upbraided him with his hard-hearted indifference, with a boldness at which she herself was astonished.

" To be sure, it wasna her that suld be fearing for her young
maister, Maister Mordaunt, even although he was, as she
might weel say, the very sea-calf of her heart; but ony other
father but his honour himsell wad have had speerings made
after the poor lad, and him gane this eight days from Burgh-
Westra, and naebody kenn'd when or where he had gane.
There wasna a bairn in the howff but was maining for him;
for he made all their bits of boats with his knife; there wadna
be a dry eye in the parish if aught worse than weal should
befall him—na, no ane, unless it might be his honour's ain."

Mertoun had been much struck, and even silenced, by the
insolent volubility of his insurgent housekeeper; but, at the
last sarcasm, he imposed on her silence in her turn with an
audible voice, accompanied with one of the most terrific
glances which his dark eye and stern features could express.
But Swertha, who, as she afterwards acquainted the Ranzelman, was wonderfully supported during the whole scene, would
not be controlled by the loud voice and ferocious look of her
master, but proceeded in the same tone as before.

"His honour," she said, "had made an unco wark because a wheen bits of kists and duds, that naebody had use for, had been gathered on the beach by the poor bodies of the township; and here was the bravest lad in the country lost, and cast away, as it were, before his een, and nae ane asking what was come o' him."

"What should come of him but good, you old fool," answered Mr. Mertoun, "as far, at least, as there can be good in any of the follies he spends his time in?"

This was spoken rather in a scornful than an angry tone, and Swertha, who had got into the spirit of the dialogue, was resolved not to let it drop, now that the fire of her opponent seemed to slacken.

"Oh ay, to be sure I am an auld fule; but if Maister Mordaunt should have settled down in the Roost, as mair than ae boat had been lost in that wearifu' squall the other morning—by good luck it was short as it was sharp, or naething could have lived in it; or if he were drowned in a loch coming hame on foot; or if he were killed by miss of footing on a craig—the haill island kenn'd how venturesome he was—who," said Swertha, "will be the auld fule then?" And she added a pathetic ejaculation, that "God would protect the poor motherless bairn! for if he had had a mother, there would have been search made after him before now."

This last sarcasm affected Mertoun powerfully: his jaw quivered, his face grew pale, and he muttered to Swertha to go into his study (where she was scarcely ever permitted to enter) and fetch him a bottle which stood there.

"Oh ho!" quoth Swertha to herself, as she hastened on the commission, "my master knows where to find a cup of comfort to qualify his water with upon fitting occasions."

There was indeed a case of such bottles as were usually employed to hold strong waters, but the dust and cobwebs in which they were enveloped showed that they had not been touched for many years. With some difficulty Swertha extracted the cork of one of them by the help of a fork—for corkscrew was there none at Jarlshof—and having ascertained by smell, and, in case of any mistake, by a moderate mouthful, that it contained wholesome Barbadoes waters, she carried it into the room, where her master still continued to struggle with his faintness. She then began to pour a small quantity into the nearest cup that she could find, wisely judging that, upon a person so much unaccustomed to the use of spirituous liquors, a little might produce a strong effect. But the patient signed to her impatiently to fill the cup, which might hold more than the third of an English pint measure, up to the very brim, and swallowed it down without hesitation.

"Now the saunts above have a care on us!" said Swertha; "he will be drunk as weel as mad, and wha is to guide him then, I wonder?"

But Mertoun's breath and colour returned, without the slightest symptom of intoxication; on the contrary, Swertha afterwards reported that, "Although she had always had a firm opinion in favour of a dram, yet she never saw one work such miracles: he spoke mair like a man of the middle world than she had ever heard him since she had entered his service."

"Swertha," he said, "you are right in this matter, and I was wrong. Go down to the Ranzelman directly, tell him to come and speak with me without an instant's delay, and bring me special word what boats and people he can command; I will employ them all in the search, and they shall be plentifully rewarded."

Stimulated by the spur which maketh the old woman proverbially to trot, Swertha posted down to the hamlet with all the speed of threescore, rejoicing that her sympathetic feelings were likely to achieve their own reward, having given rise to a quest which promised to be so lucrative, and in the profits whereof she was determined to have her share, shouting out as she went, and long before she got within hearing, the names of Neil Ronaldson, Sweyn Erickson, and the other friends and confederates who were interested in her mission. To say the truth, notwithstanding that the good dame really felt a deep interest in Mordaunt Mertoun, and was mentally troubled on account of his absence, perhaps few things would

have disappointed her more than if he had at this moment
started up in her path safe and sound, and rendered unnecessary, by his appearance, the expense and the bustle of searching after him.

Soon did Swertha accomplish her business in the village, and
adjust with the senators of the township her own little share
of percentage upon the profits likely to accrue on her mission;
and speedily did she return to Jarlshof, with Neil Ronaldson
by her side, schooling him to the best of her skill in all the
peculiarities of her master.

"Aboon a' things," she said, "never make him wait for an
answer; and speak loud and distinct, as if you were hailing a
boat, for he downa bide to say the same thing twice over; and
if he asks about distance, ye may make leagues for miles, for
he kens naething about the face of the earth that he lives
upon; and if he speak of siller, ye may ask dollars for shillings, for he minds them nae mair than sclate-stanes."

Thus tutored, Neil Ronaldson was introduced into the presence of Mertoun, but was utterly confounded to find that he
could not act upon the system of deception which had been
projected.   When he attempted, by some exaggeration of distance and peril, to enhance the hire of the boats and of the
men (for the search was to be by sea and land), he found himself at once cut short by Mertoun, who showed not only the
most perfect knowledge of the country, but of distances, tides,
currents, and all belonging to the navigation of those seas, although these were topics with which he had hitherto appeared
to be totally unacquainted.   The Ranzelman, therefore, trembled when they came to speak of the recompense to be afforded
for their exertions in the search; for it was not more unlikely
that Mertoun should be well informed of what was just and
proper upon this head than upon others; and Neil remembered
the storm of his fury when, at an early period after he had
settled at Jarlshof, he drove Swertha and Sweyn Erickson
from his presence.   As, however, he stood hesitating betwixt
the opposite fears of asking too much or too little, Mertoun
stopped his mouth and ended his uncertainty by promising
him a recompense beyond what he dared have ventured to ask,

with an additional gratuity in case they returned with the pleasing intelligence that his son was safe.

When this great point was settled, Neil Ronaldson, like a man of conscience, began to consider earnestly the various places where search should be made after the young man; and having undertaken faithfully that the inquiry should be prose-cuted at all the houses of the gentry, both in this and the neigh-bouring islands, he added that, "After all, if his honour would not be angry, there was ane not far off that, if anybody dared speer her a question, and if she liked to answer it, could tell more about Maister Mordaunt than anybody else could. Ye will ken wha I mean, Swertha? Her that was down at the haven this morning." Thus he concluded, addressing him-self with a mysterious look to the housekeeper, which she answered with a nod and a wink.

"How mean you?" said Mertoun; "speak out, short and open—whom do you speak of?"

"It is Norna of the Fitful Head," said Swertha, "that the Ranzelman is thinking about; for she has gone up to St. Rin-gan's kirk this morning on business of her own."

"And what can this person know of my son?" said Mer-toun; "she is, I believe, a wandering madwoman or impostor."

"If she wanders," said Swertha, "it is for nae lack of means at hame, and that is weel known : plenty of a'thing has she of her ain, forbye that the Fowd himsell would let her want naething."

"But what is that to my son?" said Mertoun, impatiently.

"I dinna ken; she took unco pleasure in Maister Mordaunt from the time she first saw him, and mony a braw thing she gave him at ae time or another, forbye the gowd chain that hangs about his bonny craig. Folk say it is of fairy gold. I kenna what gold it is; but Bryce Snailsfoot says that the value will mount to an hundred pounds English, and that is nae deaf nuts."

"Go, Ronaldson," said Mertoun, "or else send some one, to seek this woman out—if you think there be a chance of her knowing anything of my son."

"She kens a'thing that happens in thae islands," said Neil

20

Ronaldson, "muckle sooner than other folk, and that is Heaven's truth. But as to going to the kirk, or the kirk-yard, to speer after her, there is not a man in Zetland will do it, for meed or for money, and that's Heaven's truth as weel as the other."

"Cowardly, superstitious fools!" said Mertoun. "But give me my cloak, Swertha. This woman has been at Burgh-Westra—she is related to Troil's family—she may know something of Mordaunt's absence and its cause. I will seek her myself. She is at the Cross kirk, you say?"

"No, not at the Cross kirk, but at the auld kirk of St. Ringan's. It's a dowie bit, and far frae being canny; and if your honour," added Swertha, "wad walk by my rule, I wad wait until she came back, and no trouble her when she may be mair busied wi' the dead, for ony thing that we ken, than she is wi' the living. The like of her carena to have other folks' een on them when they are, gude sain us! doing their ain particular turns."

Mertoun made no answer, but throwing his cloak loosely around him (for the day was misty, with passing showers), and leaving the decayed mansion of Jarlshof, he walked at a pace much faster than was usual with him, taking the direction of the ruinous church, which stood, as he well knew, within three or four miles of his dwelling.

The Ranzelman and Swertha stood gazing after him in silence, until he was fairly out of ear-shot, when, looking seriously on each other, and shaking their sagacious heads in the same boding degree of vibration, they uttered their remarks in the same breath.

"Fools are aye fleet and fain," said Swertha.

"Fey folk run fast," added the Ranzelman; "and the thing that we are born to, we cannot win by. I have known them that try to stop folk that were fey. You have heard of Helen Emberson of Camsey, how she stopped all the boles and windows about the house, that her gudeman might not see daylight, and rise to the haaf-fishing, because she feared foul weather; and how the boat he should have sailed in was lost in the Roost; and how she came back, rejoicing in her gude man's safety; but ne'er may care! for there she found him drowned in his own masking-fat, within the wa's of his ain biggin; and moreover——"

But here Swertha reminded the Ranzelman that he must go down to the haven to get off the fishing-boats; "For both that my heart is sair for the bonny lad, and that I am fear'd he cast up of his ain accord before you are at sea; and, as I have often told ye, my master may lead but he winna drive; and if ye do not his bidding and get out to sea, the never a boddle of boat-hire will ye see."

"Weel—weel, good dame," said the Ranzelman, "we will launch as fast as we can; and, by good luck, neither Clawson's boat nor Peter Grot's is out to the haaf this morning, for a rabbit ran across the path as they were going on board, and they came back like wise men, kenning they wad be called to other wark this day. And a marvel it is to think, Swertha, how few real judicious men are left in this land. There is our great Udaller is weel eneugh when he is fresh, but he makes ower mony voyages in his ship and his yawl to be lang sae; and now they say his daughter, Mistress Minna, is sair out of sorts. Then there is Norna kens muckle mair than other folk, but wise woman ye cannot call her. Our tacksman here, Maister Mertoun, his wit is sprung in the bowsprit, I doubt; his son is a daft gowk; and I ken few of consequence hereabouts—excepting always myself, and maybe you, Swertha—but what may, in some sense or other, be called fules."

"That may be, Neil Ronaldson," said the dame; "but if you do not hasten the faster to the shore, you will lose tide; and, as I said to my master some short time syne, wha will be the fule then?"

CHAPTER XXV.

I do love these ancient ruins.
We never tread upon them but we set
Our foot upon some reverend history ;
And, questionless, here, in this open court
(Which now lies naked to the injuries
Of stormy weather), some men lie interr'd,
Loved the church so well, and gave so largely to it,
They thought it should have canopied their bones
Till doomsday ; but all things have their end :
Churches and cities, which have diseases like to men,
Must have like death which we have.

Duchess of Malfy.

THE ruinous church of St. Ninian had, in its time, enjoyed great celebrity ; for that mighty system of Roman superstition which spread its roots over all Europe had not failed to extend them even to this remote archipelago, and Zetland had, in the Catholic times, her saints, her shrines, and her relics, which, though little known elsewhere, attracted the homage, and commanded the observance, of the simple inhabitants of Thule. Their devotion to this church of St. Ninian, or, as he was provincially termed, St. Ringan, situated, as the edifice was, close to the sea-beach, and serving, in many points, as a landmark to their boats, was particularly obstinate, and was connected with so much superstitious ceremonial and credulity that the Reformed clergy thought it best, by an order of the church courts, to prohibit all spiritual service within its walls, as tending to foster the rooted faith of the simple and rude people around in saint-worship and other erroneous doctrines of the Romish Church.

After the church of St. Ninian had been thus denounced as a seat of idolatry, and desecrated of course, the public worship was transferred to another church ; and the roof, with its lead and its rafters, having been stripped from the little rude old Gothic building, it was left in the wilderness to the mercy of the elements. The fury of the uncontrolled winds, which howled along an exposed space resembling that which we have described at Jarlshof, very soon choked up nave and aisle, and on the northwest side, which was chiefly exposed to the wind, hid the outside walls more than half-way up with mounds of drifted sand, over which the gable-ends of the building, with the little belfry, which was built above its eastern angle, arose in ragged and shattered nakedness of ruin.

Yet, deserted as it was, the kirk of St. Ringan still retained some semblance of the ancient homage formerly rendered there. The rude and ignorant fishermen of Dunrossness observed a practice, of which they themselves had wellnigh forgotten the origin, and from which the Protestant clergy in vain endeavoured to deter them. When their boats were in extreme peril, it was common amongst them to propose to vow an "awmous," as they termed it, that is, an alms, to St. Ringan; and when the danger was over, they never failed to absolve themselves of their vow by coming singly and secretly to the old church, and putting off their shoes and stockings at the entrance of the churchyard, walking thrice around the ruins, observing that they did so in the course of the sun. When the circuit was accomplished for the third time, the votary dropped his offering, usually a small silver coin, through the mullions of a lanceolated window, which opened into a side aisle, and then retired, avoiding carefully to look behind him till he was beyond the precincts which had once been hallowed ground; for it was believed that the skeleton of the saint received the offering in his bony hand, and showed his ghastly death's-head at the window into which it was thrown.

Indeed, the scene was rendered more appalling to weak and ignorant minds because the same stormy and eddying winds which, on the one side of the church, threatened to bury the ruins with sand, and had, in fact, heaped it up in huge quantities, so as almost to hide the side wall with its buttresses, seemed in other places bent on uncovering the graves of those who had been laid to their long rest on the southeastern quarter; and, after an unusually hard gale, the coffins, and sometimes the very corpses of those who had been interred without the usual cerements, were discovered, in a ghastly manner, to the eyes of the living.

It was to this desolated place of worship that the elder Mertoun now proceeded, though without any of those religious or superstitious purposes with which the church of St. Ringan was usually approached. He was totally without the superstitious fears of the country—nay, from the sequestered and sullen manner in which he lived, withdrawing himself from human society even when assembled for worship, it was the general opinion that he erred on the more fatal side, and believed rather too little than too much of that which the church receives and enjoins to Christians.

As he entered the little bay, on the shore, and almost on the beach, of which the ruins are situated, he could not help pausing for an instant, and becoming sensible that the scene, as calculated to operate on human feelings, had been selected with much judgment as the site of a religious house. In front lay the sea, into which two headlands, which formed the extremities of the bay, projected their gigantic causeways of dark and sable rocks, on the ledges of which the gulls, scouries, and other sea-fowl appeared like flakes of snow; while, upon the lower ranges of the cliff, stood whole lines of cormorants, drawn up alongside of each other, like soldiers in their battle array, and other living thing was there none to see. The sea, although not in a tempestuous state, was disturbed enough to rush on these capes with a sound like distant thunder, and the billows, which rose in sheets of foam half-way up these sable rocks, formed a contrast of colouring equally striking and awful.

Betwixt the extremities, or capes, of these projecting headlands, there rolled, on the day when Mertoun visited the scene, a deep and dense aggregation of clouds, through which no human eye could penetrate, and which, bounding the vision, and excluding all view of the distant ocean, rendered it no unapt representation of the sea in the *Vision of Mirza*, whose extent was concealed by vapours, and clouds, and storms. The ground rising steeply from the sea-beach, permitting no view into the interior of the country, appeared a scene of irretrievable barrenness, where scrubby and stunted heath, intermixed with the long bent, or coarse grass, which first covers sandy soils, were the only vegetables that could be seen.

Upon a natural elevation, which rose above the beach in the very bottom of the bay, and receded a little from the sea so as to be without reach of the waves, arose the half-buried ruin which we have already described, surrounded by a wasted, half-ruinous, and mouldering wall, which, breached in several places, served still to divide the precincts of the cemetery. The mariners who were driven by accident into this solitary bay pretended that the church was occasionally observed to be full of lights, and, from that circumstance, were used to prophesy shipwrecks and deaths by sea.

As Mertoun approached near to the chapel, he adopted, insensibly, and perhaps without much premeditation, measures to avoid being himself seen until he came close under the walls of the burial-ground, which he approached, as it chanced, on that side where the sand was blowing from the graves in the manner we have described.

Here, looking through one of the gaps in the wall which time had made, he beheld the person whom he sought, occupied in a manner which assorted well with the ideas popularly entertained of her character, but which was otherwise sufficiently extraordinary.

She was employed beside a rude monument, on one side of which was represented the rough outline of a cavalier, or knight, on horseback, while on the other appeared a shield, with the armorial bearings so defaced as not to be intelligible; which escutcheon was suspended by one angle, contrary to the modern custom, which usually places them straight and upright. At the foot of this pillar was believed to repose, as Mertoun had formerly heard, the bones of Ribolt Troil, one of the remote ancestors of Magnus, and a man renowned for deeds of valorous emprize in the 15th century. From the grave of this warrior Norna of the Fitful Head seemed busied in shovelling the sand, an easy task where it was so light and loose; so that it seemed plain that she would shortly complete what the rude winds had begun, and make bare the bones which lay there interred. As she laboured, she muttered her magic song; for without the Runic rhyme no form of Northern superstition was ever performed. We have perhaps pre-

served too many examples of these incantations; but we cannot help attempting to translate that which follows:

> "Champion, famed for warlike toil,
> Art thou silent, Ribolt Troil?
> Sand, and dust, and pebbly stones
> Are leaving bare thy giant bones.
> Who dared touch the wild bear's skin
> Ye slumber'd on while life was in?
> A woman now, or babe, may come,
> And cast the covering from thy tomb.
>
> Yet be not wrathful, chief, nor blight
> Mine eyes or ears with sound or sight!
> I come not, with unhallow'd tread,
> To wake the slumbers of the dead,
> Or lay thy giant relics bare;
> But what I seek thou well canst spare.
> Be it to my hand allow'd
> To shear a merk's weight from thy shroud;
> Yet leave thee sheeted lead enough
> To shield thy bones from weather rough.
>
> See, I draw my magic knife;
> Never while thou wert in life
> Laid'st thou still for sloth or fear,
> When point and edge were glittering near;
> See, the cerements now I sever.
> Waken now, or sleep for ever!
> Thou wilt not wake? the deed is done!—
> The prize I sought is fairly won.
>
> Thanks, Ribolt, thanks; for this the sea
> Shall smooth its ruffled crest for thee,
> And while afar its billows foam,
> Subside to peace near Ribolt's tomb.
> Thanks, Ribolt, thanks; for this the might
> Of wild winds raging at their height,
> When to thy place of slumber nigh,
> Shall soften to a lullaby.
>
> She, the dame of doubt and dread,
> Norna of the Fitful Head,
> Mighty in her own despite,
> Miserable in her might,
> In despair and frenzy great,
> In her greatness desolate
> Wisest, wickedest who lives,
> Well can keep the word she gives."

While Norna chanted the first part of this rhyme, she completed the task of laying bare a part of the leaden coffin of the

ancient warrior, and severed from it, with much caution and apparent awe, a portion of the metal. She then reverentially threw back the sand upon the coffin; and by the time she had finished her song no trace remained that the secrets of the sepulchre had been violated.

Mertoun remained gazing on her from behind the churchyard wall during the whole ceremony, not from any impression of veneration for her or her employment, but because he conceived that to interrupt a madwoman in her act of madness was not the best way to obtain from her such intelligence as she might have to impart. Meanwhile, he had full time to consider her figure, although her face was obscured by her dishevelled hair and by the hood of her dark mantle, which permitted no more to be visible than a Druidess would probably have exhibited at the celebration of her mystical rites. Mertoun had often heard of Norna before; nay, it is most probable that he might have seen her repeatedly, for she had been in the vicinity of Jarlshof more than once since his residence there. But the absurd stories which were in circulation respecting her prevented his paying any attention to a person whom he regarded as either an impostor or a madwoman, or a compound of both. Yet, now that his attention was by circumstances involuntarily fixed upon her person and deportment, he could not help acknowledging to himself that she was either a complete enthusiast or rehearsed her part so admirably that no pythoness of ancient times could have excelled her. The dignity and solemnity of her gesture, the sonorous, yet impressive, tone of voice with which she addressed the departed spirit whose mortal relics she ventured to disturb, were such as failed not to make an impression upon him, careless and indifferent as he generally appeared to all that went on around him. But no sooner was her singular occupation terminated than, entering the churchyard with some difficulty by clambering over the disjointed ruins of the wall, he made Norna aware of his presence. Far from starting or expressing the least surprise at his appearance in a place so solitary, she said, in a tone that seemed to intimate that he had been expected: "So—you have sought me at last?"

"And found you," replied Mertoun, judging he would best introduce the inquiries he had to make by assuming a tone which corresponded to her own.

"Yes!" she replied, "found me you have, and in the place where all men must meet—amid the tabernacles of the dead."

"Here we must, indeed, meet at last," replied Mertoun, glancing his eyes on the desolate scene around, where headstones, half-covered in sand, and others, from which the same wind had stripped the soil on which they rested, covered with inscriptions, and sculptured with the emblems of mortality, were the most conspicuous objects—"here, as in the house of death, all men must meet at length; and happy those that come soonest to the quiet haven."

"He that dares desire this haven," said Norna, "must have steered a steady course in the voyage of life. *I* dare not hope for such quiet harbour. Darest *thou* expect it? or has the course thou hast kept deserved it?"

"It matters not to my present purpose," replied Mertoun; "I have to ask you what tidings you know of my son, Mordaunt Mertoun?"

"A father," replied the sibyl, "asks of a stranger what tidings she has of his son! How should I know aught of him? The cormorant says not to the mallard, 'Where is my brood?'"

"Lay aside this useless affectation of mystery," said Mertoun: "with the vulgar and ignorant it has its effect, but upon me it is thrown away. The people of Jarlshof have told me that you do know, or may know, something of Mordaunt Mertoun, who has not returned home after the festival of St. John's, held in the house of your relative, Magnus Troil. Give me such information, if indeed ye have it to give; and it shall be recompensed, if the means of recompense are in my power."

"The wide round of earth," replied Norna, "holds nothing that I would call a recompense for the slightest word that I throw away upon a living ear. But for thy son, if thou wouldst see him in life, repair to the approaching fair of Kirkwall, in Orkney."

"And wherefore thither?" said Mertoun; "I know he had no purpose in that direction."

"We drive on the stream of fate," answered Norna, "without oar or rudder. You had no purpose this morning of visiting the kirk of St. Ringan, yet you are here; you had no purpose but a minute hence of being at Kirkwall, and yet you will go thither."

"Not unless the cause is more distinctly explained to me. I am no believer, dame, in those who assert your supernatural powers."

"You shall believe in them ere we part," said Norna. "As yet you know but little of me, nor shall you know more. But I know enough of you, and could convince you with one word that I do so."

"Convince me, then," said Mertoun; "for, unless I am so convinced, there is little chance of my following your counsel."

"Mark, then," said Norna, "what I have to say on your son's score, else what I shall say to you on your own will banish every other thought from your memory. You shall go to the approaching fair at Kirkwall; and on the fifth day of the fair you shall walk, at the hour of noon, in the outer aisle of the cathedral of St. Magnus, and there you shall meet a person who will give you tidings of your son."

"You must speak more distinctly, dame," returned Mertoun, scornfully, "if you hope that I should follow your counsel. I have been fooled in my time by women, but never so grossly as you seem willing to gull me."

"Hearken, then!" said the old woman. "The word which I speak shall touch the nearest secret of thy life, and thrill thee through nerve and bone."

So saying, she whispered a word into Mertoun's ear, the effect of which seemed almost magical. He remained fixed and motionless with surprise, as, waving her arm slowly aloft, with an air of superiority and triumph, Norna glided from him, turned round a corner of the ruins, and was soon out of sight.

Mertoun offered not to follow or to trace her. "We fly from our fate in vain!" he said, as he began to recover him-

self; and turning, he left behind him the desolate ruins with
their cemetery. As he looked back from the very last point
at which the church was visible, he saw the figure of Norna,
muffled in her mantle, standing on the very summit of the
ruined tower, and stretching out in the sea-breeze something
which resembled a white pennon, or flag. A feeling of horror, similar to that excited by her last words, again thrilled
through his bosom, and he hastened onwards with unwonted
speed, until he had left the church of St. Ninian, with its
bay of sand, far behind him.

Upon his arrival at Jarlshof, the alteration in his countenance was so great that Swertha conjectured he was about to
fall into one of those fits of deep melancholy which she termed
his dark hour.

"And what better could be expected," thought Swertha,
"when he must needs go visit Norna of the Fitful Head when
she was in the haunted kirk of St. Ringan's?"

But, without testifying any other symptoms of an alienated
mind than that of deep and sullen dejection, her master acquainted her with his intention to go to the fair of Kirkwall—
a thing so contrary to his usual habits that the housekeeper
wellnigh refused to credit her ears. Shortly after he heard,
with apparent indifference, the accounts returned by the different persons who had been sent out in quest of Mordaunt,
by sea and land, who all of them returned without any tidings. The equanimity with which Mertoun heard the report
of their bad success convinced Swertha still more firmly that,
in his interview with Norna, that issue had been predicted to
him by the sibyl whom he had consulted.

The township were yet more surprised when their tacksman, Mr. Mertoun, as if on some sudden resolution, made
preparations to visit Kirkwall during the fair, although he
had hitherto avoided sedulously all such places of public resort. Swertha puzzled herself a good deal, without being able
to penetrate this mystery; and vexed herself still more concerning the fate of her young master. But her concern was
much softened by the deposit of a sum of money, seeming,
however moderate in itself, a treasure in her eyes, which her

master put into her hands, acquainting her at the same time that he had taken his passage for Kirkwall in a small bark belonging to the proprietor of the island of Mousa.

CHAPTER XXVI.

> Nae langer she wept, her tears were a' spent;
> Despair it was come, and she thought it content;
> She thought it content, but her cheek it grew pale,
> And she droop'd, like a lily broke down by the hail.
> *Continuation of Auld Robin Gray.*[1]

THE condition of Minna much resembled that of the village heroine in Lady Ann Lindsay's beautiful ballad. Her natural firmness of mind prevented her from sinking under the pressure of the horrible secret, which haunted her while awake, and was yet more tormenting during her broken and hurried slumbers. There is no grief so dreadful as that which we dare not communicate, and in which we can neither ask nor desire sympathy; and when to this is added the burden of a guilty mystery to an innocent bosom, there is little wonder that Minna's health should have sunk under the burden.

To the friends around, her habits and manners, nay, her temper, seemed altered to such an extraordinary degree that it is no wonder that some should have ascribed the change to witchcraft, and some to incipient madness. She became unable to bear the solitude in which she formerly delighted to spend her time; yet, when she hurried into society, it was without either joining in, or attending to, what passed. Generally she appeared wrapped in sad, and even sullen, abstraction, until her attention was suddenly roused by some casual mention of the name of Cleveland or of Mordaunt Mertoun, at which she started, with the horror of one who sees the lighted match applied to a charged mine, and expects to be instantly involved in the effects of the explosion. And when she observed that the discovery was not yet made, it was so far from being a consolation, that she almost wished the worst

[1] See Motto to Chap. xxvi. Note 32.

were known, rather than endure the continued agonies of suspense.

Her conduct towards her sister was so variable, yet uniformly so painful to the kind-hearted Brenda, that it seemed to all around one of the strongest features of her malady. Sometimes Minna was impelled to seek her sister's company, as if by the consciousness that they were common sufferers, by a misfortune of which she herself alone could grasp the extent; and then suddenly the feeling of the injury which Brenda had received through the supposed agency of Cleveland made her unable to bear her presence, and still less to endure the consolation which her sister, mistaking the nature of her malady, vainly endeavoured to administer. Frequently, also, did it happen that, while Brenda was imploring her sister to take comfort, she incautiously touched upon some subject which thrilled to the very centre of her soul; so that, unable to conceal her agony, Minna would rush hastily from the apartment. All these different moods, though they too much resembled, to one who knew not their real source, the caprices of unkind estrangement, Brenda endured with such prevailing and unruffled gentleness of disposition that Minna was frequently moved to shed floods of tears upon her neck and, perhaps, the moments in which she did so, though embittered by the recollection that her fatal secret concerned the destruction of Brenda's happiness as well as her own, were still, softened as they were by sisterly affection, the most endurable moments of this most miserable period of her life.

The effects of the alternations of moping melancholy, fearful agitation, and bursts of nervous feeling were soon visible on the poor young woman's face and person. She became pale and emaciated; her eye lost the steady, quiet look of happiness and innocence, and was alternately dim and wild, as she was acted upon by a general feeling of her own distressful condition, or by some quicker and more poignant sense of agony. Her very features seemed to change, and become sharp and eager, and her voice, which, in its ordinary tones, was low and placid, now sometimes sunk in indistinct mutterings, and sometimes was raised beyond the natural key, in hasty and abrupt exclamations. When in company with others, she was sullenly silent, and, when she ventured into solitude, was observed (for it was now thought very proper to watch her on such occasions) to speak much to herself.

The pharmacy of the islands was in vain resorted to by Minna's anxious father. Sages of both sexes, who knew the virtues of every herb which drinks the dew, and augmented those virtues by words of might, used while they prepared and applied the medicines, were attended with no benefit; and Magnus, in the utmost anxiety, was at last induced to have recourse to the advice of his kinswoman, Norna of the Fitful Head, although, owing to circumstances noticed in the course of the story, there was at this time some estrangement between them. His first application was in vain. Norna was then at her usual place of residence upon the sea-coast, near the headland from which she usually took her designation; but, although Eric Scambester himself brought the message, she refused positively to see him or to return any answer.

Magnus was angry at the slight put upon his messenger and message; but his anxiety on Minna's account, as well as the respect which he had for Norna's real misfortunes and imputed wisdom and power, prevented him from indulging, on the present occasion, his usual irritability of disposition. On the contrary, he determined to make an application to his kinswoman in his own person. He kept his purpose, however, to himself, and only desired his daughters to be in readiness to attend him upon a visit to a relation whom he had not seen for some time, and directed them, at the same time, to carry some provisions along with them, as the journey was distant, and they might perhaps find their friend unprovided.

Unaccustomed to ask explanations of his pleasure, and hoping that exercise and the amusement of such an excursion might be of service to her sister, Brenda, upon whom all household and family charges now devolved, caused the necessary preparations to be made for the expedition; and, on the next morning, they were engaged in tracing the long and tedious course of beach and of moorland which, only varied by occa-

sional patches of oats and barley, where a little ground had
been selected for cultivation, divided Burgh-Westra from the
northwestern extremity of the Mainland (as the principal
island is called), which terminates in the cape called Fitful Head, as the southwestern point ends in the cape of Sumburgh.

On they went, through wild and over wold, the Udaller
bestriding a strong, square-made, well-barrelled palfrey, of
Norwegian breed, somewhat taller, and yet as stout, as the
ordinary ponies of the country; while Minna and Brenda,
famed, amongst other accomplishments, for their horseman-
ship, rode two of those hardy animals, which, bred and reared
with more pains than is usually bestowed, showed, both by the
neatness of their form and their activity, that the race, so
much and so carelessly neglected, is capable of being improved into beauty without losing anything of its spirit or
vigour.   They were attended by two servants on horseback
and two on foot, secure that the last circumstance would be
no delay to their journey, because a great part of the way
was so rugged, or so marshy, that the horses could only move
at a foot-pace; and that, whenever they met with any considerable tract of hard and even ground, they had only to borrow
from the nearest herd of ponies the use of a couple for the
accommodation of these pedestrians.

The journey was a melancholy one, and little conversation
passed, except when the Udaller, pressed by impatience and
vexation, urged his pony to a quick pace, and again, recollecting Minna's weak state of health, slackened to a walk, and
reiterated inquiries how she felt herself, and whether the fatigue was not too much for her.   At noon the party halted and
partook of some refreshment, for which they had made ample
provision, beside a pleasant spring, the pureness of whose waters, however, did not suit the Udaller's palate, until qualified
by a liberal addition of right Nantz.   After he had a second,
yea, and a third, time filled a large silver travelling-cup, em-
bossed with a German Cupid smoking a pipe and a German
Bacchus emptying his flask down the throat of a bear, he
began to become more talkative than vexation had permitted

him to be during the early part of their journey, and thus addressed his daughters:

"Well, children, we are within a league or two of Norna's dwelling, and we shall soon see how the old spell-mutterer will receive us."

Minna interrupted her father with a faint exclamation, while Brenda, surprised to a great degree, exclaimed: "Is it then to Norna that we are to make this visit? Heaven forbid?"

"And wherefore should Heaven forbid?" said the Udaller, knitting his brows; "wherefore, I would gladly know, should Heaven forbid me to visit my kinswoman, whose skill may be of use to your sister, if any woman in Zetland, or man either, can be of service to her? You are a fool, Brenda; your sister has more sense. Cheer up, Minna! thou wert ever wont to like her songs and stories, and used to hang about her neck, when little Brenda cried and ran from her like a Spanish merchantman from a Dutch caper."

"I wish she may not frighten me as much to-day, father," replied Brenda, desirous of indulging Minna in her taciturnity, and at the same time to amuse her father by sustaining the conversation: "I have heard so much of her dwelling, that I am rather alarmed at the thought of going there uninvited."

"Thou art a fool," said Magnus, "to think that a visit from her kinsfolks can ever come amiss to a kind, hearty, Hialtland heart like my cousin Norna's. And, now I think on't, I will be sworn that is the reason why she would not receive Eric Scambester! It is many a long day since I have seen her chimney smoke, and I have never carried you thither. She hath indeed some right to call me unkind. But I will tell her the truth; and that is, that, though such be the fashion, I do not think it is fair or honest to eat up the substance of lone women-folks, as we do that of our brother udallers, when we roll about from house to house in the winter season, until we gather like a snowball, and eat up all wherever we come."

"There is no fear of our putting Norna to any distress just now," replied Brenda, "for I have ample provision of every-

21

thing that we can possibly need—fish, and bacon, and salted mutton, and dried geese—more than we could eat in a week, besides enough of liquor for you, father."

"Right—right, my girl!" said the Udaller: "a well-found ship makes a merry voyage; so we shall only want the kindness of Norna's roof and a little bedding for you; for, as to myself, my sea-cloak and honest dry boards of Norway deal suit me better than your eider-down cushions and mattresses. So that Norna will have the pleasure of seeing us without having a stiver's worth of trouble."

"I wish she may think it a pleasure, sir," replied Brenda.

"Why, what does the girl mean, in the name of the Martyr?" replied Magnus Troil; "dost thou think my kinswoman is a heathen, who will not rejoice to see her own flesh and blood? I would I were as sure of a good year's fishing! No —no! I only fear we may find her from home at present, for she is often a wanderer, and all with thinking over much on what can never be helped."

Minna sighed deeply as her father spoke, and the Udaller went on:

"Dost thou sigh at that, my girl? Why, 'tis the fault of half the world; let it never be thine own, Minna."

Another suppressed sigh intimated that the caution came too late.

"I believe you are afraid of my cousin as well as Brenda is," said the Udaller, gazing on her pale countenance; "if so, speak the word, and we will return back again as if we had the wind on our quarter, and were running fifteen knots by the line."

"Do, for Heaven's sake, sister, let us return!" said Brenda, imploringly; "you know—you remember—you must be well aware that Norna can do nought to help you."

"It is but too true," said Minna, in a subdued voice; "but I know not—she may answer a question—a question that only the miserable dare ask of the miserable."

"Nay, my kinswoman is no miser," answered the Udaller, who only heard the beginning of the word. "A good income she has both in Orkney and here, and many a fair lispund of butter is paid to her. But the poor have the best share of it, and shame fall the Zetlander who begrudges them; the rest she spends, I wot not how, in her journeys through the islands. But you will laugh to see her house, and Nick Strumpfer, whom she calls Pacolet. Many folks think Nick is the devil; but he is flesh and blood, like any of us—his father lived in Graemsay. I shall be glad to see Nick again."

While the Udaller thus ran on, Brenda, who, in recompense for a less portion of imagination than her sister, was gifted with sound common sense, was debating with herself the probable effect of this visit on her sister's health. She came finally to the resolution of speaking with her father aside, upon the first occasion which their journey should afford. To him she determined to communicate the whole particulars of their nocturnal interview with Norna, to which, among other agitating causes, she attributed the depression of Minna's spirits, and then make himself the judge whether he ought to persist in his visit to a person so singular, and expose his daughter to all the shock which her nerves might possibly receive from the interview.

Just as she had arrived at this conclusion, her father, dashing the crumbs from his laced waistcoat with one hand and receiving with the other a fourth cup of brandy and water, drank devoutly to the success of their voyage, and ordered all to be in readiness to set forward. Whilst they were saddling their ponies, Brenda, with some difficulty, contrived to make her father understand she wished to speak with him in private—no small surprise to the honest Udaller, who, though secret as the grave in the very few things where he considered secrecy as of importance, was so far from practising mystery in general, that his most important affairs were often discussed by him openly in presence of his whole family, servants included.

But far greater was his astonishment when, remaining purposely with his daughter, Brenda, a little in the wake, as he termed it, of the other riders, he heard the whole account of Norna's visit to Burgh-Westra, and of the communication with which she had then astonished his daughters. For a long

time he could utter nothing but interjections, and ended with
a thousand curses on his kinswoman's folly in telling his
daughters such a history of horror.

"I have often heard," said the Udaller, "that she was quite
mad, with all her wisdom and all her knowledge of the seasons; and, by the bones of my namesake the Martyr, I begin
now to believe it most assuredly! I know no more how to
steer than if I had lost my compass. Had I known this before we set out, I think I had remained at home; but now
that we have come so far, and that Norna expects us——"

"Expects us, father!" said Brenda; "how can that be possible?"

"Why, that I know not; but she that can tell how the
wind is to blow can tell which way we are designing to ride.
She must not be provoked; perhaps she has done my family
this ill for the words I had with her about that lad Mordaunt
Mertoun, and if so, she can undo it again; and so she shall,
or I will know the cause wherefore. But I will try fair words
first."

Finding it thus settled that they were to go forward, Brenda
endeavoured next to learn from her father whether Norna's
tale was founded in reality. He shook his head, groaned
bitterly, and, in a few words, acknowledged that the whole,
so far as concerned her intrigue with a stranger and her father's death, of which she became the accidental and most
innocent cause, was a matter of sad and indisputable truth.
"For her infant," he said, "he could never, by any means,
learn what became of it."

"Her infant!" exclaimed Brenda; "she spoke not a word
of her infant!"

"Then I wish my tongue had been blistered," said the
Udaller, "when I told you of it! I see that, young and old,
a man has no better chance of keeping a secret from you women than an eel to keep himself in his hold when he is sniggled with a loop of horse-hair: sooner or later the fisher teazes
him out of his hole, when he has once the noose round his
neck."

"But the infant, my father," said Brenda, still insisting

on the particulars of this extraordinary story, "what became of it?"

"Carried off, I fancy, by the blackguard Vaughan," answered the Udaller, with a gruff accent, which plainly betokened how weary he was of the subject.

"By Vaughan!" said Brenda, "the lover of poor Norna doubtless! What sort of man was he, father?"

"Why, much like other men, I fancy," answered the Udaller. "I never saw him in my life. He kept company with the Scottish families at Kirkwall, and I with the good old Norse folk. Ah! if Norna had dwelt always amongst her own kin, and not kept company with her Scottish acquaintance, she would have known nothing of Vaughan, and things might have been otherwise. But then I should have known nothing of your blessed mother, Brenda; and that," he said, his large blue eyes shining with a tear, "would have saved me a short joy and a long sorrow."

"Norna could but ill have supplied my mother's place to you, father, as a companion and a friend—that is, judging from all I have heard," said Brenda, with some hesitation.

But Magnus, softened by recollections of his beloved wife, answered her with more indulgence than she expected. "I would have been content," he said, "to have wedded Norna at that time. It would have been the soldering of an old quarrel—the healing of an old sore. All our blood relations wished it, and, situated as I was, especially not having seen your blessed mother, I had little will to oppose their counsels. You must not judge of Norna or of me by such an appearance as we now present to you. She was young and beautiful, and I gamesome as a Highland buck, and little caring what haven I made for, having, as I thought, more than one under my lee. But Norna preferred this man Vaughan, and, as I told you before, it was, perhaps, the best kindness she could have done to me."

"Ah, poor kinswoman!" said Brenda. "But believe you, father, in the high powers which she claims—in the mysterious vision of the dwarf—in the——"

She was interrupted in these questions by Magnus, to whom they were obviously displeasing.

"I believe, Brenda," he said, "according to the belief of my forefathers. I pretend not to be a wiser man than they were in their time; and they all believed that, in cases of great worldly distress, Providence opened the eyes of the mind and afforded the sufferers a vision of futurity. It was but a trimming of the boat, with reverence"—here he touched his hat reverentially; "and, after all the shifting of ballast, poor Norna is as heavily loaded in the bows as ever was a Orkneyman's yawl at the dog-fishing: she has more than affliction enough on board to balance whatever gifts she may have had in the midst of her calamity. They are as painful to her, poor soul, as a crown of thorns would be to her brows, though it were the badge of the empire of Denmark. And do not you, Brenda, seek to be wiser than your fathers. Your sister Minna, before she was so ill, had as much reverence for whatever was produced in Norse as if it had been in the Pope's bull, which is all writen in pure Latin."

"Poor Norna!" repeated Brenda; "and her child—was it never recovered?"

"What do I know of her child," said the Udaller, more gruffly than before, "except that she was very ill, both before and after the birth, though we kept her as merry as we could with pipe and harp, and so forth. The child had come before its time into this bustling world, so it is likely it had been long dead. But you know nothing of all these matters, Brenda; so get along for a foolish girl, and ask no more questions about what it does not become you to inquire into."

So saying, the Udaller gave his sturdy little palfrey the spur, and cantering forward over rough and smooth, while the pony's accuracy and firmness of step put all difficultie of the path at secure defiance, he placed himself soon by the side of the melancholy Minna, and permitted her sister to have no farther share in his conversation than as it was addressed to them jointly. She could but comfort herself with the hope that, as Minna's disease appeared to have its sea in the imagination, the remedies recommended by Norn might have some chance of being effectual, since, in all probability, they would be addressed to the same faculty.

Their way had hitherto held chiefly over moss and moor, varied occasionally by the necessity of making a circuit around the heads of those long lagoons, called voes, which run up into and indent the country in such a manner that, though the Mainland of Zetland may be thirty miles or more in length, there is, perhaps, no part of it which is more than three miles distant from the salt water. But they had now approached the northwestern extremity of the isle, and travelled along the top of an immense ridge of rocks, which had for ages withstood the rage of the Northern Ocean, and of all the winds by which it is buffeted.

At length exclaimed Magnus to his daughters: "There is Norna's dwelling! Look up, Minna, my love; for if this does not make you laugh, nothing will. Saw you ever anything but an osprey that would have made such a nest for herself as that is? By my namesake's bones, there is not the like of it that living thing ever dwelt in, having no wings and the use of reason, unless it chanced to be the Frawa Stack [1] off Papa, where the king's daughter of Norway was shut up to keep her from her lovers; and all to little purpose, if the tale be true: for, maidens, I would have you to wot that it is hard to keep flax from the lowe."

CHAPTER XXVII.

Thrice from the cavern's darksome womb
Her groaning voice arose;
And come, my daughter, fearless come,
And fearless tell thy woes!

MEIKLE.

THE dwelling of Norna, though none but a native of Zetland, familiar, during his whole life, with every variety of rock-scenery, could have seen anything ludicrous in this situation, was not unaptly compared by Magnus Troil to the eyrie

[1] See Note 33.

of the osprey, or sea-eagle. It was very small, and had been fabricated out of one of those dens which are called burghs [1] and Picts-houses in Zetland, and duns on the mainland of Scotland and the Hebrides, and which seem to be the first effort at architecture—the connecting-link betwixt a fox's hole in a cairn of loose stones and an attempt to construct a human habitation out of the same materials, without the use of lime or cement of any kind; without any timber, so far as can be seen from their remains; without any knowledge of the arch or of the stair. Such as they are, however, the numerous remains of these dwellings—for there is one found on every headland, islet, or point of vantage which could afford the inhabitants additional means of defence—tend to prove that the remote people by whom these burghs were constructed were a numerous race, and that the islands had then a much greater population than, from other circumstances, we might have been led to anticipate.

The burgh of which we at present speak had been altered and repaired at a later period, probably by some petty despot, or sea-rover, who, tempted by the security of the situation, which occupied the whole of a projecting point of rock, and was divided from the mainland by a rent or chasm of some depth, had built some additions to it in the rudest style of Gothic defensive architecture; had plastered the inside with lime and clay, and broken out windows for the admission of light and air; and, finally, by roofing it over, and dividing it into stories, by means of beams of wreck-wood, had converted the whole into a tower, resembling a pyramidical dovecot, formed by a double wall, still containing within its thickness that set of circular galleries, or concentric rings, which is proper to all the forts of this primitive construction, and which seem to have constituted the only shelter which they were originally qualified to afford to their shivering inhabitants.

This singular habitation, built out of the loose stones which lay scattered around, and exposed for ages to the vicissitudes of the elements, was as grey, weather-beaten, and wasted as the rock on which it was founded, and from which it could

[1] See Note 34.

not easily be distinguished, so completely did it resemble in colour, and so little did it differ in regularity of shape, from a pinnacle or fragment of the cliff.

Minna's habitual indifference to all that of late had passed around her was for a moment suspended by the sight of an abode which, at another and happier period of her life, would have attracted at once her curiosity and her wonder. Even now she seemed to feel interested as she gazed upon this singular retreat, and recollected it was that of certain misery and probable insanity, connected, as its inhabitant asserted, and Minna's faith admitted, with power over the elements and the capacity of intercourse with the invisible world.

"Our kinswoman," she muttered, "has chosen her dwelling well, with no more of earth than a sea-fowl might rest upon, and all around sightless tempests and raging waves. Despair and magical power could not have a fitter residence."

Brenda, on the other hand, shuddered when she looked on the dwelling to which they were advancing, by a difficult, dangerous, and precarious path, which sometimes, to her great terror, approached to the verge of the precipice; so that, Zetlander as she was, and confident, as she had reason to be, in the steadiness and sagacity of the sure-footed pony, she could scarce suppress an inclination to giddiness, especially at one point, when, being foremost of the party, and turning a sharp angle of the rock, her feet, as they projected from the side of the pony, hung for an instant sheer over the ledge of the precipice, so that there was nothing save empty space betwixt the sole of her shoe and the white foam of the vexed ocean, which dashed, howled, and foamed five hundred feet below. What would have driven a maiden of another country into delirium gave her but a momentary uneasiness, which was instantly lost in the hope that the impression which the scene appeared to make on her sister's imagination might be favourable to her cure.

She could not help looking back to see how Minna should pass the point of peril which she herself had just rounded; and could hear the strong voice of the Udaller, though to him such rough paths were familiar as the smooth sea-beach, call, in a tone of some anxiety, "Take heed, jarto," as Minna, with an eager look, dropped her bridle, and stretched forward her arms, and even her body, over the precipice, in the attitude of the wild swan, when, balancing itself and spreading its broad pinions, it prepares to launch from the cliff upon the bosom of the winds. Brenda felt at that instant a pang of unutterable terror, which left a strong impression on her nerves, even when relieved, as it instantly was, by her sister recovering herself and sitting upright on her saddle, the opportunity and temptation (if she felt it) passing away, as the quiet, steady animal which supported her rounded the projecting angle, and turned its patient and firm step from the verge of the precipice.

They now attained a more level and open space of ground, being the flat top of an isthmus of projecting rock, narrowing again towards a point where it was terminated by the chasm which separated the small peak, or "stack," occupied by Norna's habitation, from the main ridge of cliff and precipice. This natural fosse, which seemed to have been the work of some convulsion of nature, was deep, dark, and irregular, narrower towards the bottom, which could not be distinctly seen, and widest at top, having the appearance as if that part of the cliff occupied by the building had been half rent away from the isthmus which it terminated—an idea favoured by the angle at which it seemed to recede from the land and lean towards the sea, with the building which crowned it.

This angle of projection was so considerable, that it required recollection to dispel the idea that the rock, so much removed from the perpendicular, was about to precipitate itself seaward, with its old tower; and a timorous person would have been afraid to put foot upon it, lest an addition of weight so inconsiderable as that of the human body should hasten a catastrophe which seemed at every instant impending.

Without troubling himself about such fantasies, the Udaller rode towards the tower, and there dismounting, along with his daughters, gave the ponies in charge to one of their domestics, with directions to disencumber them of their burdens and turn them out for rest and refreshment upon the nearest heath. This done, they approached the gate, which seemed formerly to have been connected with the land by a rude drawbridge, some of the apparatus of which was still visible. But the rest had been long demolished, and was replaced by a stationary footbridge, formed of barrel-staves covered with turf, very narrow and ledgeless, and supported by a sort of arch, constructed out of the jaw-bones of the whale. Along this "brigg of dread" the Udaller stepped with his usual portly majesty of stride, which threatened its demolition and his own at the same time; his daughters trode more lightly and more safely after him, and the whole party stood before the low and rugged portal of Norna's habitation.

"If she should be abroad after all," said Magnus, as he plied the black oaken door with repeated blows; "but if so, we will at least lie by a day for her return, and make Nick Strumpfer pay the demurrage in bland and brandy."

As he spoke, the door opened and displayed, to the alarm of Brenda, and the surprise of Minna herself, a square-made dwarf, about four feet five inches high, with a head of most portentous size, and features correspondent—namely, a huge mouth, a tremendous nose, with large black nostrils, which seemed to have been slit upwards, blubber lips of an unconscionable size, and huge wall-eyes, with which he leered, sneered, grinned, and goggled on the Udaller as an old acquaintance, without uttering a single word. The young women could hardly persuade themselves that they did not see before their eyes the very demon Trold who made such a distinguished figure in Norna's legend. Their father went on addressing this uncouth apparition in terms of such condescending friendship as the better sort apply to their inferiors when they wish, for any immediate purpose, to conciliate or coax them—a tone, by the by, which generally contains, in its very familiarity, as much offence as the more direct assumption of distance and superiority.

"Ha, Nick!—honest Nick!" said the Udaller, "here you are, lively and lovely as St. Nicholas, your namesake, when he is carved with an axe for the head-piece of a Dutch dogger. How dost thou do, Nick, or Pacolet, if you like that

better?   Nicholas, here are my two daughters, nearly as handsome as thyself, thou seest."

Nick grinned, and did a clumsy obeisance by way of courtesy, but kept his broad, misshapen person firmly placed in
the doorway.

"Daughters," continued the Udaller, who seemed to have
his reasons for speaking this Cerberus fair, at least according
to his own notions of propitiation—"this is Nick Strumpfer,
maidens, whom his mistress calls Pacolet, being a light-limbed
dwarf, as you see, like him that wont to fly about, like a
scourie, on his wooden hobby-horse, in the old story-book of
Valentine and Orson, that you, Minna, used to read whilst
you were a child.   I assure you he can keep his mistress's
counsel, and never told one of her secrets in his life—ha,
ha, ha!"

The ugly dwarf grinned ten times wider than before, and
showed the meaning of the Udaller's jest by opening his immense jaws and throwing back his head, so as to discover
that, in the immense cavity of his mouth, there only remained
the small shrivelled remnant of a tongue, capable, perhaps,
of assisting him in swallowing his food, but unequal to the
formation of articulate sounds.   Whether this organ had been
curtailed by cruelty or injured by disease it was impossible to
guess; but that the unfortunate being had not been originally
dumb was evident from his retaining the sense of hearing.
Having made this horrible exhibition, he repaid the Udaller's
mirth with a loud, horrid, and discordant laugh, which had
something in it the more hideous that his mirth seemed to be
excited by his own misery.   The sisters looked on each other
in silence and fear, and even the Udaller appeared disconcerted.

"And how now?" he proceeded, after a minute's pause.
"When didst thou wash that throat of thine, that is about
the width of the Pentland Firth, with a cup of brandy?   Ha,
Nick! I have that with me which is sound stuff, boy—ha!"

The dwarf bent his beetle brows, shook his misshapen head,
and made a quick, sharp indication, throwing his right hand
up to his shoulder with the thumb pointed backwards.

"What! my kinswoman," said the Udaller, comprehending the signal, "will be angry? Well, shalt have a flask to carouse when she is from home, old acquaintance: lips and throats may swallow through they cannot speak."

Pacolet grinned a grim assent.

"And now," said the Udaller, "stand out of the way, Pacolet, and let me carry my daughters to see their kinswoman. By the bones of St. Magnus, it shall be a good turn in thy way! Nay, never shake thy head, man; for if thy mistress be at home, see her we will."

The dwarf again intimated the impossibility of their being admitted, partly by signs, partly by mumbling some uncouth and most disagreeable sounds, and the Udaller's mood began to arise.

"Tittle tattle, man!" said he; "trouble not me with thy gibberish, but stand out of the way, and the blame, if there be any, shall rest with me."

So saying, Magnus Troil laid his sturdy hand upon the collar of the recusant dwarf's jacket of blue wadmaal, and with a strong, but not a violent, grasp removed him from the doorway, pushed him gently aside, and entered, followed by his two daughters, whom a sense of apprehension, arising out of all which they saw and heard, kept very close to him. A crooked and dusky passage through which Magnus led the way was dimly enlightened by a shot-hole communicating with the interior of the building, and originally intended, doubtless, to command the entrance by a hagbut or culverin. As they approached nearer, for they walked slowly and with hesitation, the light, imperfect as it was, was suddenly obscured; and, on looking upward to discern the cause, Brenda was startled to observe the pale and obscurely-seen countenance of Norna gazing downward upon them, without speaking a word. There was nothing extraordinary in this, as the mistress of the mansion might be naturally enough looking out to see what guests were thus suddenly and unceremoniously intruding themselves on her presence. Still, however, the natural paleness of her features, exaggerated by the light in which they were at present exhibited; the immovable sternness of her look, which showed neither kindness nor courtesy of civil reception; her dead silence; and the singular appearance of everything about her dwelling, augmented the dismay which Brenda had already conceived. Magnus Troil and Minna had walked slowly forward, without observing the apparition of their singular hostess.

CHAPTER XXVIII.

The witch then raised her wither'd arm,
    And waved her wand on high,
And, while she spoke the mutter'd charm,
    Dark lightning fill'd her eye.

                                        MEIKLE.

"THIS should be the stair," said the Udaller, blundering in the dark against some steps of irregular ascent—"this should be the stair, unless my memory greatly fail me; ay, and there she sits," he added, pausing at a half-open door, "with all her tackle about her as usual, and as busy, doubtless, as the devil in a gale of wind."

As he made this irreverent comparison, he entered, followed by his daughters, the darkened apartment in which Norna was seated, amidst a confused collection of books of various languages, parchment scrolls, tablets and stones inscribed with the straight and angular characters of the Runic alphabet, and similar articles, which the vulgar might have connected with the exercise of the forbidden arts. There were also lying in the chamber, or hung over the rude and ill-contrived chimney, an old shirt of mail, with the head-piece, battle-axe, and lance which had once belonged to it; and on a shelf were disposed, in great order, several of those curious stone axes, formed of green granite, which are often found in those islands, where they are called thunderbolts by the common people, who usually preserve them as a charm of security against the effects of lightning. There was, moreover, to be seen amid the strange collection a stone sacrificial knife, used perhaps for immolating human victims, and one or two

of the brazen implements called celts, the purpose of which
has troubled the repose of so many antiquaries. A variety of
other articles, some of which had neither name nor were capable of description, lay in confusion about the apartment; and
in one corner, on a quantity of withered sea-weed, reposed
what seemed, at first view, to be a large, unshapely dog, but,
when seen more closely, proved to be a tame seal, which it
had been Norna's amusement to domesticate.

This uncouth favourite bristled up in its corner, upon the
arrival of so many strangers, with an alertness similar to that
which a terrestrial dog would have displayed on a similar occasion; but Norna remained motionless, seated behind a table
of rough granite, propped up by misshapen feet of the same
material, which, besides the old book with which she seemed
to be busied, sustained a cake of the coarse unleavened bread,
three parts oatmeal and one the sawdust of fir, which is used
by the poor peasants of Norway, beside which stood a jar of
water.

Magnus Troil remained a minute in silence gazing upon his
kinswoman, while the singularity of her mansion inspired
Brenda with much fear, and changed, though but for a moment, the melancholy and abstracted mood of Minna into a
feeling of interest not unmixed with awe. The silence was
interrupted by the Udaller, who, unwilling on the one hand
to give his kinswoman offence, and desirous on the other to
show that he was not daunted by a reception so singular,
opened the conversation thus:

"I give you good e'en, cousin Norna; my daughters and I
have come far to see you."

Norna raised her eyes from her volume, looked full at her
visitors, then let them quietly sink down on the leaf with
which she seemed to be engaged.

"Nay, cousin," said Magnus, "take your own time: our
business with you can wait your leisure. See here, Minna,
what a fair prospect here is of the cape, scarce a quarter of
a mile off; you may see the billows breaking on it topmast
high. Our kinswoman has got a pretty seal, too. Here,
sealchie, my man, whew, whew!"

The seal took no further notice of the Udaller's advances to acquaintance than by uttering a low growl.

"He is not so well trained," continued the Udaller, affecting an air of ease and unconcern, "as Peter MacRaw's,[1] the old piper of Stornoway, who had a seal that flapped its tail to the tune of 'Caberfae,' and acknowledged no other whatever. Well, cousin," he concluded, observing that Norna closed her book, "are you going to give us a welcome at last, or must we go farther than our blood relation's house to seek one, and that when the evening is wearing late apace?"

"Ye dull and hard-hearted generation, as deaf as the adder to the voice of the charmer," answered Norna, addressing them, "why come ye to me? You have slighted every warning I could give of the coming harm, and now that it hath come upon you, ye seek my counsel when it can avail you nothing."

"Look you, kinswoman," said the Udaller, with his usual frankness and boldness of manner and accent, "I must needs tell you that your courtesy is something of the coarsest and the coldest. I cannot say that I ever saw an adder, in regard there are none in these parts; but touching my own thoughts of what such a thing may be, it cannot be termed a suitable comparison to me or to my daughters, and that I would have you to know. For old acquaintance, and certain other reasons, I do not leave your house upon the instant; but as I came hither in all kindness and civility, so I pray you to receive me with the like, otherwise we will depart, and leave shame on your inhospitable threshold."

"How," said Norna, "dare you use such bold language in the house of one from whom all men, from whom you yourself, come to solicit counsel and aid? They who speak to the Reim-kennar must lower their voice to her before whom winds and waves hush both blast and billow."

"Blast and billow may hush themselves if they will," replied the peremptory Udaller, "but that will not I. I speak in the house of my friend as in my own, and strike sail to none."

[1] See Note 35.

"And hope ye," said Norna, "by this rudeness to compel me to answer to your interrogatories?"

"Kinswoman," replied Magnus Troil, "I know not so much as you of the old Norse sagas; but this I know, that when kempies were wont, long since, to seek the habitations of the galdragons and spae-women, they came with their axes on their shoulders and their good swords drawn in their hands, and compelled the power whom they invoked to listen to and to answer them—ay, were it Odin himself."

"Kinsman," said Norna, arising from her seat and coming forward, "thou hast spoken well, and in good time for thyself and thy daughters; for hadst thou turned from my threshold without extorting an answer, morning's sun had never again shone upon you. The spirits who serve me are jealous, and will not be employed in aught that may benefit humanity, unless their service is commanded by the undaunted importunity of the brave and the free. And now speak, what wouldst thou have of me?"

"My daughter's health," replied Magnus, "which no remedies have been able to restore."

"Thy daughter's health?"•answered Norna; "and what is the maiden's ailment?"

"The physician," said Troil, "must name the disease. All that I can tell thee of it is——"

"Be silent," said Norna, interrupting him, "I know all thou canst tell me, and more than thou thyself knowest. Sit down, all of you; and thou, maiden," she said, addressing Minna, "sit thou in that chair," pointing to the place she had just left, "once the seat of Giervada, at whose voice the stars hid their beams and the moon herself grew pale."

Minna moved with slow and tremulous step towards the rude seat thus indicated to her. It was composed of stone, formed into some semblance of a chair by the rough and unskilful hand of some ancient Gothic artist.

Brenda, creeping as close as possible to her father, seated herself along with him upon a bench at some distance from Minna, and kept her eyes, with a mixture of fear, pity, and anxiety, closely fixed upon her. It would be difficult alto-

22

gether to decipher the emotions by which this amiable and affectionate girl was agitated at the moment. Deficient in her sister's predominating quality of high imagination, and little credulous, of course, to the marvellous, she could not but entertain some vague and indefinite fears on her own account, concerning the nature of the scene which was soon to take place. But these were in a manner swallowed up in her apprehensions on the score of her sister, who, with a frame so much weakened, spirits so much exhausted, and a mind so susceptible of the impressions which all around her was calculated to excite, now sat pensively resigned to the agency of one whose treatment might produce the most baneful effects upon such a subject.

Brenda gazed at Minna, who sat in that rude chair of dark stone, her finely-formed shape and limbs making the strongest contrast with its ponderous and irregular angles, her cheeks and lips as pale as clay, and her eyes turned upward, and lighted with the mixture of resignation and excited enthusiasm which belonged to her disease and her character. The younger sister then looked on Norna, who muttered to herself in a low, monotonous manner, as, gliding from one place to another, she collected different articles, which she placed one by one on the table. And, lastly, Brenda looked anxiously to her father, to gather, if possible, from his countenance, whether he entertained any part of her own fears for the consequences of the scene which was to ensue, considering the state of Minna's health and spirits. But Magnus Troil seemed to have no such apprehensions: he viewed with stern composure Norna's preparations, and appeared to wait the event with the composure of one who, confiding in the skill of a medical artist, sees him preparing to enter upon some important and painful operation, in the issue of which he is interested by friendship or by affection.

Norna, meanwhile, went onward with her preparations, until she had placed on the stone table a variety of miscellaneous articles, and among the rest a small chafing-dish full of charcoal, a crucible, and a piece of thin sheet-lead. She then spoke aloud: "It is well that I was aware of your coming hither—ay, long before you yourself had resolved it—how should I else have been prepared for that which is now to be done? Maiden," she contained, addressing Minna, "where lies thy pain?"

The patient answered by pressing her hand to the left side of her bosom.

"Even so," replied Norna—"even so, 'tis the site of weal or woe. And you, her father and her sister, think not this the idle speech of one who talks by guess: if I can tell thee ill, it may be that I shall be able to render that less severe which may not, by any aid, be wholly amended. The heart—ay, the heart! touch that, and the eye grows dim, the pulse fails, the wholesome stream of our blood is choked and troubled, our limbs decay like sapless sea-weed in a summer's sun, our better views of existence are past and gone; what remains is the dream of lost happiness or the fear of inevitable evil. But the Reim-kennar must to her work; well it is that I have prepared the means."

She threw off her long dark-coloured mantle, and stood before them in her short jacket of light blue wadmaal, with its skirt of the same stuff, fancifully embroidered with black velvet, and bound at the waist with a chain or girdle of silver, formed into singular devices. Norna next undid the fillet which bound her grizzled hair, and shaking her head wildly, caused it to fall in dishevelled abundance over her face and around her shoulders, so as almost entirely to hide her features. She then placed a small crucible on the chafing-dish already mentioned, dropped a few drops from a vial on the charcoal below, pointed towards it her wrinkled forefinger, which she had previously moistened with liquid from another small bottle, and said with a deep voice, "Fire, do thy duty"; and the words were no sooner spoken than, probably by some chemical combination of which the spectators were not aware, the charcoal which was under the crucible became slowly ignited; while Norna, as if impatient of the delay, threw hastily back her disordered tresses, and, while her features reflected the sparkles and red light of the fire, and her eyes flashed from amongst her hair like those of a wild animal from its cover, blew fiercely till the whole was in an intense glow. She paused a moment from her toil, and muttering that the elemental spirit must be thanked, recited, in her usual monotonous, yet wild, mode of chanting, the following verses: [1]

> "Thou so needful, yet so dread,
>   With cloudy crest and wing of red—
> Thou, without whose genial breath
> The North would sleep the sleep of death,
> Who deign'st to warm the cottage hearth,
> Yet hurl'st proud palaces to earth,—
> Brightest, keenest of the powers,
> Which form and rule this world of ours,
> With my rhyme of Runic, I
> Thank thee for thy agency."

She then severed a portion from the small mass of sheet-lead which lay upon the table, and, placing it in the crucible, subjected it to the action of the lighted charcoal, and, as it melted, she sung:

> "Old Reim-kennar, to thy art
> Mother Hertha sends her part;
> She, whose gracious bounty gives
> Needful food for all that lives.
> From the deep mine of the North
> Came the mystic metal forth,
> Doom'd, amidst disjointed stones,
> Long to cere a champion's bones,
> Disinhumed my charms to aid—
> Mother Earth, my thanks are paid."

She then poured out some water from the jar into a large cup, or goblet, and sung once more, as she slowly stirred it round with the end of her staff:

> "Girdle of our islands dear,
> Element of water, hear,
> Thou whose power can overwhelm
> Broken mounds and ruin'd realm
>   On the lowly Belgian strand,
> All thy fiercest rage can never
> Of our soil a furlong sever
>   From our rock-defended land;
> Play then gently thou thy part,
> To assist old Norna's art."

---

[1] See Norna's Spells.   Note 36.

She then, with a pair of pincers, removed the crucible from the chafing-dish, and poured the lead, now entirely melted, into the bowl of water, repeating at the same time:

> " Elements, each other greeting,
> Gifts and powers attend your meeting ! "

The melted lead, spattering as it fell into the water, formed, of course, the usual combination of irregular forms which is familiar to all who in childhood have made the experiment, and from which, according to our childish fancy, we may have selected portions bearing some resemblance to domestic articles, the tools of mechanics, or the like. Norna seemed to busy herself in some such researches, for she examined the mass of lead with scrupulous attention, and detached it into different portions, without apparently being able to find a fragment in the form which she desired.

At length she again muttered, rather as speaking to herself than to her guests, " He, the Viewless, will not be omitted: he will have his tribute even in the work to which he gives nothing. Stern compeller of the clouds, thou also shalt hear the voice of the Reim-kennar."

Thus speaking, Norna once more threw the lead into the crucible, where, hissing and spattering as the wet metal touched the sides of the red-hot vessel, it was soon again reduced into a state of fusion. The sibyl meantime turned to a corner of the apartment, and opening suddenly a window which looked to the northwest, let in the fitful radiance of the sun, now lying almost level upon a great mass of red clouds, which, boding future tempest, occupied the edge of the horizon, and seemed to brood over the billows of the boundless sea. Turning to this quarter, from which a low hollow moaning breeze then blew, Norna addressed the Spirit of the Winds, in tones which seemed to resemble his own:

> " Thou, that over billows dark
> Safely send'st the fisher's bark,
> Giving him a path and motion
> Through the wilderness of ocean—
> Thou, that when the billows brave ye,
> O'er the shelves canst drive the navy,

> Did'st thou chafe as one neglected,
> While thy brethren were respected?
> To appease thee, see, I tear
> This full grasp of grizzled hair.
> Oft thy breath hath through it sung,
> Softening to my magic tongue;
> Now, 'tis thine to bid it fly
> Through the wide expanse of sky,
> 'Mid the countless swarms to sail
> Of wild-fowl wheeling on thy gale.
> Take thy portion and rejoice;
> Spirit, thou hast heard my voice!"

Norna accompanied these words with the action which they described, tearing a handful of hair with vehemence from her head, and strewing it upon the wind as she continued her recitation. She then shut the casement, and again involved the chamber in the dubious twilight which best suited her character and occupation. The melted lead was once more emptied into the water, and the various whimsical conformations which it received from the operation were examined with great care by the sibyl, who at length seemed to intimate by voice and gesture that her spell had been successful. She selected from the fused metal a piece about the size of a small nut, bearing in shape a close resemblance to that of the human heart, and approaching Minna, again spoke in song:

> "She who sits by haunted well
> Is subject to the nixie's spell;
> She who walks on lonely beach
> To the mermaid's charmed speech;
> She who walks round ring of green,
> Offends the peevish fairy queen;
> And she who takes rest in the dwarfie's cave,
> A weary weird of woe shall have.
>
> By ring, by spring, by cave, by shore,
> Minna Troil has braved all this and more:
> And yet hath the root of her sorrow and ill
> A source that's more deep and more mystical still."

Minna, whose attention had been latterly something disturbed by reflections on her own secret sorrow, now suddenly recalled it, and looked eagerly on Norna, as if she expected to learn from her rhymes something of deep interest. The Northern sibyl meanwhile proceeded to pierce the piece of lead, which bore the form of a heart, and to fix in it a piece of gold wire, by which it might be attached to a chain or necklace. She then proceeded in her rhyme:

> "Thou art within a demon's hold,
> More wise than Heims, more strong than Trold;
> No siren sings so sweet as he,
> No fay springs lighter on the lea;
> No elfin power hath half the art
> To soothe, to move, to wring the heart,
> Life-blood from the cheek to drain,
> Drench the eye, and dry the vein.
> Maiden, ere we farther go,
> Dost thou note me, ay or no?"

Minna replied in the same rhythmical manner, which, in jest and earnest, was frequently used by the ancient Scandinavians:

> "I mark thee, my mother, both word, look, and sign;
> Speak on with the riddle—to read it be mine."

"Now, Heaven and every saint be praised!" said Magnus; "they are the first words to the purpose which she hath spoken these many days."

"And they are the last which she shall speak for many a month," said Norna, incensed at the interruption, "if you again break the progress of my spell. Turn your faces to the wall, and look not hitherward again, under penalty of my severe displeasure. You, Magnus Troil, from hard-hearted audacity of spirit, and you, Brenda, from wanton and idle disbelief in that which is beyond your bounded comprehension, are unworthy to look on this mystic work; and the glance of your eyes mingles with and weakens the spell; for the powers cannot brook distrust."

Unaccustomed to be addressed in a tone so peremptory, Magnus would have made some angry reply; but reflecting that the health of Minna was at stake, and considering that she who spoke was a woman of many sorrows, he suppressed his anger, bowed his head, shrugged his shoulders, assumed the prescribed posture, averting his head from the table and turning towards the wall. Brenda did the same, on receiving a sign from her father, and both remained profoundly silent.

Norna then addressed Minna once more:

> " Mark me! for the word I speak
> Shall bring the colour to thy cheek.
> This leaden heart, so light of cost,
> The symbol of a treasure lost,
> Thou shalt wear in hope and in peace,
> That the cause of your sickness and sorrow may cease,
> When crimson foot meets crimson hand
> In the Martyr's aisle, and in Orkney-land."

Minna coloured deeply at the last couplet, intimating, as she failed not to interpret it, that Norna was completely acquainted with the secret cause of her sorrow. The same conviction led the maiden to hope in the favourable issue which the sibyl seemed to prophesy; and not venturing to express her feeling in any manner more intelligible, she pressed Norna's withered hand with all the warmth of affection, first to her breast and then to her bosom, bedewing it at the same time with her tears.

With more of human feeling than she usually exhibited, Norna extricated her hand from the grasp of the poor girl, whose tears now flowed freely, and then, with more tenderness of manner than she had yet shown, she knotted the leaden heart to a chain of gold, and hung it around Minna's neck, singing, as she performed that last branch of the spell:

> " Be patient, be patient, for patience hath power
> To ward us in danger, like mantle in shower.
> A fairy gift you best may hold
> In a chain of fairy gold;
> The chain and the gift are each a true token,
> That not without warrant old Norna has spoken;
> But thy nearest and dearest must never behold them,
> Till time shall accomplish the truths I have told them."

The verses being concluded, Norna carefully arranged the chain around her patient's neck so as to hide it in her bosom, and thus ended the spell—a spell which, at the moment I record these incidents, it is known has been lately practised in Zetland, where any decline of health, without apparent cause, is imputed by the lower orders to a demon having stolen the heart from the body of the patient, and where the experiment of supplying the deprivation by a leaden one, prepared in the manner described, has been resorted to within these few years. In a metaphorical sense, the disease may be considered as a general one in all parts of the world; but, as this simple and original remedy is peculiar to the isles of Thule, it were unpardonable not to preserve it at length, in a narrative connected with Scottish antiquities.

A second time Norna reminded her patient that, if she showed, or spoke of, the fairy gifts, their virtue would be lost—a belief so common as to be received into the superstitions of all nations. Lastly, unbuttoning the collar which she had just fastened, she showed her a link of the gold chain, which Minna instantly recognised as that formerly given by Norna to Mordaunt Mertoun. This seemed to intimate he was yet alive, and under Norna's protection; and she gazed on her with the most eager curiosity. But the sibyl imposed her finger on her lips in token of silence, and a second time involved the chain in those folds which modestly and closely veiled one of the most beautiful, as well as one of the kindest, bosoms in the world.

Norna then extinguished the lighted charcoal, and, as the water hissed upon the glowing embers, commanded Magnus and Brenda to look around and behold her task accomplished.

CHAPTER XXIX.

See yonder woman, whom our swains revere,
And dread in secret, while they take her counsel
When sweetheart shall be kind, or when cross dame shall die;
Where lurks the thief who stole the silver tankard,
And how the pestilent murrain may be cured.
This sage adviser's mad, stark mad, my friend;
Yet, in her madness hath the art and cunning
To wring fools' secrets from their inmost bosoms,
And pay inquirers with the coin they gave her.
Old Play.

IT seemed as if Norna had indeed full right to claim the gratitude of the Udaller for the improved condition of his daughter's health. She once more threw open the window, and Minna, drying her eyes and advancing with affectionate confidence, threw herself on her father's neck, and asked his forgiveness for the trouble she had of late occasioned to him. It is unnecessary to add that this was at once granted, with a full, though rough, burst of parental tenderness, and as many close embraces as if his child had been just rescued from the jaws of death. When Magnus had dismissed Minna from his arms, to throw herself into those of her sister, and expressed to her, rather by kisses and tears than in words, the regret she entertained for her late wayward conduct, the Udaller thought proper, in the mean time, to pay his thanks to their hostess, whose skill had proved so efficacious. But scarce had he come out with, "Much respected kinswoman, I am but a plain old Norseman——" when she interrupted him by pressing her finger on her lips.

"There are those around us," she said, "who must hear no mortal voice, witness no sacrifice to mortal feelings: there are times when they mutiny even against me, their sovereign mistress, because I am still shrouded in the flesh of humanity. Fear, therefore, and be silent. I, whose deeds have raised me from the low-sheltered valley of life, where dwell its social wants and common charities—I, who have bereft the giver of the gift which he gave, and stand alone on a cliff of immeasurable height, detached from earth, save from the small portion that supports my miserable tread—I alone am fit to cope with those sullen mates. Fear not, therefore, but yet be not too bold, and let this night to you be one of fasting and of prayer."

If the Udaller had not, before the commencement of the operation, been disposed to dispute the commands of the sibyl, it may be well believed he was less so now that it had terminated to all appearance so fortunately. So he sat down in silence, and seized upon a volume which lay near him as a sort of desperate effort to divert *ennui*, for on no other occasion had Magnus been known to have recourse to a book for that purpose. It chanced to be a book much to his mind, being the well-known work of Olaus Magnus, upon the manners of the ancient Northern nations. The book is unluckily in the Latin language, and the Danske or Dutch were, either of them, much more familiar to the Udaller. But then it was the fine edition published in 1555, which contains representations of the war-chariots, fishing exploits, warlike exercises, and domestic employments of the Scandinavians, executed on copper-plates; and thus the information which the work refused to the understanding was addressed to the eye, which, as is well known both to old and young, answers the purpose of amusement as well, if not better.

Meanwhile the two sisters, pressed as close to each other as two flowers on the same stalk, sat with their arms reciprocally passed over each other's shoulder, as if they feared some new and unforeseen cause of coldness was about to separate them, and interrupt the sister-like harmony which had been but just restored. Norna sat opposite to them, sometimes revolving the large parchment volume with which they had found her employed at their entrance, and sometimes gazing on the sisters with a fixed look, in which an interest of a kind unusually tender seemed occasionally to disturb the stern and rigorous solemnity of her countenance. All was still and silent as death, and the subsiding emotions of Brenda had not yet permitted her to wonder whether the remaining hours of the evening were to be passed in the same manner, when the scene of tranquillity was suddenly interrupted by the entrance of the dwarf Pacolet, or, as the Udaller called him, Nicholas Strumpfer.

Norna darted an angry glance on the intruder, who seemed to deprecate her resentment by holding up his hands and uttering a babbling sound; then, instantly resorting to his usual mode of conversation, he expressed himself by a variety of signs made rapidly upon his fingers, and as rapidly answered by his mistress, so that the young women, who had never heard of such an art, and now saw it practised by two beings so singular, almost conceived their mutual intelligence the work of enchantment. When they had ceased their intercourse, Norna turned to Magnus Troil with much haughtiness and said: " How, my kinsman, have you so far forgot yourself as to bring earthly food into the house of the Reim-kennar,

and make preparations in the dwelling of power and of de·
spair for refection, and wassail, and revelry? Speak not—
answer not," she said; "the duration of the cure which was
wrought even now depends on your silence and obedience:
bandy but a single look or word with me, and the latter condition of that maiden shall be worse than the first!"

This threat was an effectual charm upon the tongue of the
Udaller, though he longed to indulge it in vindication of his
conduct.

"Follow me, all of you," said Norna, striding to the door
of the apartment, "and see that no one looks backwards: we
leave not this apartment empty, though we, the children of
mortality, be removed from it."

She went out, and the Udaller signed to his daughters to
follow and to obey her injunctions. The sibyl moved swifter
than her guests down the rude descent (such it might rather
be termed than a proper staircase) which led to the lower
apartment. Magnus and his daughters, when they entered
the chamber, found their own attendants aghast at the presence and proceedings of Norna of the Fitful Head.

They had been previously employed in arranging the provisions which they had brought along with them, so as to
present a comfortable cold meal as soon as the appetite of the
Udaller, which was as regular as the return of tide, should
induce him to desire some refreshment; and now they stood
staring in fear and surprise, while Norna, seizing upon one
article after another, and well supported by the zealous activity of Pacolet, flung their whole preparations out of the rude
aperture which served for a window, and over the cliff, from
which the ancient burgh arose, into the ocean, which raged
and foamed beneath. "Vifda" (dried beef), hams, and
pickled pork flew after each other into empty space, smoked
geese were restored to the air, and cured fish to the sea, their
native elements indeed, but which they were no longer capable of traversing; and the devastation proceeded so rapidly
that the Udaller could scarce secure from the wreck his silver
drinking-cup; while the large leathern flask of brandy which
was destined to supply his favourite beverage was sent to fol-

low the rest of the supper by the hands of Pacolet, who regarded, at the same time, the disappointed Udaller with a malicious grin, as if, notwithstanding his own natural taste for the liquor, he enjoyed the disappointment and surprise of Magnus Troil still more than he would have relished sharing his enjoyment.

The destruction of the brandy flask exhausted the patience of Magnus, who roared out, in a tone of no small displeasure: " Why, kinswoman, this is wasteful madness: where, and on what, would you have us sup?"

" Where you will," answered Norna, " and on what you will; but not in my dwelling, and not on the food with which you have profaned it. Vex my spirit no more, but begone every one of you! You have been here too long for my good, perhaps for your own."

" How, kinswoman," said Magnus, " would you make outcasts of us at this time of night, when even a Scotchman would not turn a stranger from the door? Bethink you, dame, it is shame on our lineage for ever if this squall of yours should force us to slip cables and go to sea so scantily provided."

" Be silent, and depart," said Norna; " let it suffice you have got that for which you came. I have no harbourage for mortal guests, no provision to relieve human wants. There is beneath the cliff a beach of the finest sand, a stream of water as pure as the well of Kildinguie, and the rocks bear dulse as wholesome as that of Guiodin; and well you wot that the well of Kildinguie and the dulse of Guiodin will cure all maladies save Black Death." [1]

" And well I wot," said the Udaller, " that I would eat corrupted sea-weeds like a starling, or salted seal's flesh like the men of Burraforth, or wilks, buckies, and lampits, like the poor sneaks of Stroma, rather than break wheat bread and drink red wine in a house where it is begrudged me. And yet," he said, checking himself, " I am wrong—very wrong, my cousin, to speak thus to you, and I should rather thank you for what you have done than upbraid you for following your own ways.

[1] So at least says an Orkney proverb.

But I see you are impatient—we will be all under way presently. And you, ye knaves," addressing his servants, "that were in such hurry with your service before it was lacked, get out of doors with you presently, and manage to catch the ponies; for I see we must make for another harbour to-night, if we would not sleep with an empty stomach and on a hard bed."

The domestics of Magnus, already sufficiently alarmed at the violence of Norna's conduct, scarce waited the imperious command of their master to evacuate her dwelling with all despatch; and the Udaller, with a daughter on each arm, was in the act of following them, when Norna said emphatically, "Stop!" They obeyed, and again turned towards her. She held out her hand to Magnus, which the placable Udaller instantly folded in his own ample palm.

"Magnus," she said, "we part by necessity, but, I trust, not in anger?"

"Surely not, cousin," said the warm-hearted Udaller, wellnigh stammering in his hasty disclamation of all unkindness— "most assuredly not. I never bear ill-will to any one, much less to one of my own blood, and who has piloted me with her advice through many a rough tide, as I would pilot a boat betwixt Swona and Stroma, through all the waws, wells, and swelchies of the Pentland Firth."

"Enough," said Norna, "and now farewell, with such a blessing as I dare bestow—not a word more! Maidens," she added, "draw near and let me kiss your brows."

The sibyl was obeyed by Minna with awe, and by Brenda with fear; the one overmastered by the warmth of her imagination, the other by the natural timidity of her constitution. Norna then dismissed them, and in two minutes afterwards they found themselves beyond the bridge, and standing upon the rocky platform in front of the ancient Pictish burgh which it was the pleasure of this sequestered female to inhabit. The night, for it was now fallen, was unusually serene. A bright twilight, which glimmered far over the surface of the sea, supplied the brief absence of the summer's sun; and the waves seemed to sleep under its influence, so faint and slumberous was the sound with which one after another rolled on and burst against the foot of the cliff on which they stood. In front of them stood the rugged fortress, seeming, in the uniform greyness of the atmosphere, as aged, as shapeless, and as massive as the rock on which it was founded. There was neither sight nor sound that indicated human habitation, save that from one rude shot-hole glimmered the flame of the feeble lamp by which the sibyl was probably pursuing her mystical and nocturnal studies, shooting upon the twilight, in which it was soon lost and confounded, a single line of tiny light; bearing the same proportion to that of the atmosphere as the aged woman and her serf, the sole inhabitants of that desert, did to the solitude with which they were surrounded.

For several minutes the party, thus suddenly and unexpectedly expelled from the shelter where they had reckoned upon spending the night, stood in silence, each wrapt in their own separate reflections. Minna, her thoughts fixed on the mystical consolation which she had received, in vain endeavoured to extract from the words of Norna a more distinct and intelligible meaning; and the Udaller had not yet recovered his surprise at the extrusion to which he had been thus whimsically subjected, under circumstances that prohibited him from resenting as an insult treatment which, in all other respects, was so shocking to the genial hospitality of his nature that he still felt like one disposed to be angry, if he but knew how to set about it. Brenda was the first who brought matters to a point by asking whither they were to go, and how they were to spend the night. The question, which was asked in a tone that, amidst its simplicity, had something dolorous in it, entirely changed the train of her father's ideas; and the unexpected perplexity of their situation now striking him in a comic point of view, he laughed till his very eyes ran over, while every rock around him rang, and the sleeping sea-fowl were startled from their repose by the loud, hearty explosions of his obstreperous hilarity.

The Udaller's daughters, eagerly representing to their father the risk of displeasing Norna by this unlimited indulgence of his mirth, united their efforts to drag him to a farther distance from her dwelling. Magnus, yielding to their strength,

which, feeble as it was, his own fit of laughter rendered him
incapable of resisting, suffered himself to be pulled to a considerable distance from the burgh, and then escaping from
their hands, and sitting down, or rather suffering himself to
drop, upon a large stone which lay conveniently by the way-
side, he again laughed so long and lustily that his vexed and
anxious daughters became afraid that there was something
more than natural in these repeated convulsions.

At length his mirth exhausted both itself and the Udaller's
strength. He groaned heavily, wiped his eyes, and said, not
without feeling some desire to renew his obstreperous cachin-
nation: " Now, by the bones of St. Magnus, my ancestor and
namesake, one would imagine that being turned out of doors
at this time of night was nothing short of an absolutely exquisite jest; for I have shaken my sides at it till they ache.
There we sat, made snug for the night, and I made as sure of
a good supper and a can as ever I had been of either; and
here we are all taken aback! and then poor Brenda's doleful
voice, and melancholy question of, 'What is to be done, and
where are we to sleep?' In good faith, unless one of those
knaves, who must needs torment the poor woman by their
trencher-work before it was wanted, can make amends by telling us of some snug port under our lee, we have no other
course for it but to steer through the twilight on the bearing
of Burgh-Westra, and rough it out as well as we can by the
way. I am sorry but for you, girls; for many a cruise have
I been upon when we were on shorter allowance than we are
like to have now; I would I had but secured a morsel for you
and a drop for myself, and then there had been but little to
complain of."

Both sisters hastened to assure the Udaller that they felt
not the least occasion for food.

" Why, that is well," said Magnus, " and so being the case,
I will not complain of my own appetite, though it is sharper
than convenient. And the rascal, Nicholas Strumpfer—what
a leer the villain gave me as he started the good Nantz into
the salt-water! He grinned, the knave, like a seal on a
skerry. Had it not been for vexing my poor kinswoman,

Norna, I would have sent his misbegotten body and mis-shapen jolterhead after my bonny flask, as sure as St. Magnus lies at Kirkwall!"

By this time the servants returned with the ponies, which they had very soon caught; these sensible animals finding nothing so captivating in the pastures where they had been suffered to stray as inclined them to resist the invitation again to subject themselves to saddle and bridle. The prospects of the party were also considerably improved by learning that the contents of their sumpter pony's burden had not been entirely exhausted—a small basket having fortunately escaped the rage of Norna and Pacolet by the rapidity with which one of the servants had caught up and removed it. The same domestic, an alert and ready-witted fellow, had observed upon the beach, not above three miles distant from the burgh, and about a quarter of a mile off their straight path, a deserted "skeo," or fisherman's hut, and suggested that they should occupy it for the rest of the night, in order that the ponies might be refreshed, and the young ladies spend the night under cover from the raw evening air.

When we are delivered from great and serious dangers, our mood is, or ought to be, grave in proportion to the peril we have escaped and the gratitude due to protecting Providence. But few things raise the spirits more naturally or more harmlessly than when means of extrication from any of the lesser embarrassments of life are suddenly presented to us; and such was the case in the present instance. The Udaller, relieved from the apprehensions for his daughters suffering from fatigue, and himself from too much appetite and too little food, carolled Norse ditties, as he spurred Bergen through the twilight, with as much glee and gallantry as if the night-ride had been entirely a matter of his own free choice. Brenda lent her voice to some of his choruses, which were echoed in ruder notes by the servants, who, in that simple state of society, were not considered as guilty of any breach of respect by mingling their voices with the song. Minna, indeed, was as yet unequal to such an effort; but she compelled herself to assume some share in the general hilarity of the meeting; and, contrary to her conduct since the fatal morning which concluded the festival of St. John, she seemed to take her usual interest in what was going on around her, and answered with kindness and readiness the repeated inquiries concerning her health with which the Udaller every now and then interrupted his carol. And thus they proceeded by night, a happier party by far than they had been when they traced the same route on the preceding [that same] morning, making light of the difficulties of the way, and promising themselves shelter and a comfortable night's rest in the deserted hut which they were now about to approach, and which they expected to find in a state of darkness and solitude.

But it was the lot of the Udaller that day to be deceived more than once in his calculations.

"And which way lies this cabin of yours, Laurie?" said the Udaller, addressing the intelligent domestic of whom we just spoke.

"Yonder it should be," said Laurence Scholey, "at the head of the voe; but, by my faith, if it be the place, there are folk there before us. God and St. Ronan send that they be canny company!"

In truth there was a light in the deserted hut, strong enough to glimmer through every chink of the shingles and wreck-wood of which it was constructed, and to give the whole cabin the appearance of a smithy seen by night. The universal superstition of the Zetlanders seized upon Magnus and his escort.

"They are trows," said one voice.

"They are witches," murmured another.

"They are mermaids," muttered a third: "only hear their wild singing!"

All stopped; and, in effect, some notes of music were audible, which Brenda, with a voice that quivered a little, but yet had a turn of arch ridicule in its tone, pronounced to be the sound of a fiddle.

"Fiddle or fiend," said the Udaller, who, if he believed in such nightly apparitions as had struck terror into his retinue, certainly feared them not—"fiddle or fiend, may the devil fetch me if a witch cheats me out of supper to-night for the second time!"

So saying, he dismounted, clenched his trusty truncheon in his hand, and advanced towards the hut, followed by Laurence alone; the rest of his retinue continuing stationary on the beach beside his daughters and the ponies.

CHAPTER XXX.

What ho, my jovial mates! come on! we'll frolic it
Like fairies frisking in the merry moonshine,
Seen by the curtal friar, who, from some christening
Or some blythe bridal, hies belated cell-ward ;
He starts, and changes his bold bottle swagger
To churchman's pace professional, and, ransacking
His treacherous memory for some holy hymn,
Finds but the roundel of the midnight catch.

Old Play.

THE stride of the Udaller relaxed nothing of its length or of its firmness as he approached the glimmering cabin, from which he now heard distinctly the sound of the fiddle. But, if still long and firm, his steps succeeded each other rather more slowly than usual; for, like a cautious, though a brave, general, Magnus was willing to reconnoitre his enemy before assailing him.

The trusty Laurence Scholey, who kept close behind his master, now whispered into his ear: " So help me, sir, as I believe that the ghaist, if ghaist it be, that plays so bravely on the fiddle must be the ghaist of Maister Claud Halcro, or his wraith at least; for never was bow drawn across thairm which brought out the gude auld spring of 'Fair and Lucky' so like his ain."

Magnus was himself much of the same opinion; for he knew the blythe minstrelsy of the spirited little old man, and hailed the hut with a hearty halloo, which was immediately replied to by the cheery note of his ancient messmate, and Halcro himself presently made his appearance on the beach.

The Udaller now signed to his retinue to come up, while he asked his friend, after a kind greeting and much shaking of hands : " How the devil he came to sit there, playing old tunes in so desolate a place, like an owl whooping to the moon?"

"And tell me rather, Fowd," said Claud Halcro, "how you came to be within hearing of me? ay, by my word, and with your bonny daughters, too? Jarto Minna and Jarto Brenda, I bid you welcome to these yellow sands; and there, shake hands, as glorious John, or some other body, says upon the same occasion. And how came you here like two fair swans, making day out of twilight, and turning all you step upon to silver?"

"You shall know all about them presently," answered Magnus; "but what messmates have you got in the hut with you? I think I hear some one speaking."

"None," replied Claud Halcro, "but that poor creature, the factor, and my imp of a boy, Giles. I—but come in—come in; here you will find us starving in comfort—not so much as a mouthful of sour sillocks to be had for love or money."

"That may be in a small part helped," said the Udaller; "for, though the best of our supper is gone over the Fitful Crags to the sealchies and the dog-fish, yet we have got something in the kit still. Here, Laurie, bring up the 'vifda.' "

"*Jokul—jokul!*" was Laurence's joyful answer; and he hastened for the basket.

"By the bicker of St. Magnus,"[1] said Halcro, "and the burliest bishop that ever quaffed it for luck's sake, there is no finding your locker empty, Magnus! I believe sincerely that, ere a friend wanted, you could, like old Luggie,[2] the warlock, fish up boiled and roasted out of the pool of Kibister."

"You are wrong there, Jarto Claud," said Magnus Troil, "for, far from helping me to a supper, the foul fiend, I believe, has carried off great part of mine this blessed evening; but you are welcome to share and share of what is left." This was said while the party entered the hut.

Here, in a cabin which smelled strongly of dried fish, and whose sides and roof were jet-black with smoke, they found the unhappy Triptolemus Yellowley seated beside a fire made of dried sea-weed, mingled with some peats and wreck-wood; his sole companion a barefooted, yellow-haired Zetland boy, who acted occasionally as a kind of page to Claud Halcro, bearing his fiddle on his shoulder, saddling his pony, and rendering him similar duties of kindly observance. The disconsolate agriculturist, for such his visage betokened him, displayed little surprise, and less animation, at the arrival of the Udaller and his companions, until, after the party had drawn close to the fire (a neighbourhood which the dampness of the night air rendered far from disagreeable), the pannier was opened, and a tolerable supply of barley-bread and hung beef, besides a flask of brandy (no doubt smaller than that which the relentless hand of Pacolet had emptied into the ocean), gave assurances of a tolerable supper. Then, indeed, the worthy factor grinned, chuckled, rubbed his hands, and inquired after all friends at Burgh-Westra.

When they had all partaken of this needful refreshment, the Udaller repeated his inquiries of Halcro, and more particularly of the factor, how they came to be nestled in such a remote corner at such an hour of night.

"Master Magnus Troil," said Triptolemus, when a second cup had given him spirits to tell his tale of woe, "I would not have you think that it is a little thing that disturbs me. I came of that grain that takes a sair wind to shake it. I have seen many a Martinmas and many a Whitsunday in my day, whilk are the times peculiarly grievous to those of my craft, and I could aye bide the bang; but I think I am like to be dung ower a'thegither in this damned country of yours. Gude forgie me for swearing; but evil communication corrupteth good manners."

"Now, Heaven guide us," said the Udaller, "what is the matter with the man? Why, man, if you will put your plough into new land, you must look to have it hank on a stone now and then. You must set us an example of patience, seeing you come here for our improvement."

"And the deil was in my feet when I did so," said the factor: "I had better have set myself to improve the cairn on Clochnaben."

"But what is it, after all," said the Udaller, "that has befallen you? what is it that you complain of?"

"Of everything that has chanced to me since I landed on

this island, which I believe was accursed at the very creation," said the agriculturist, "and assigned as a fitting station for sorners, thieves, whores—I beg the ladies' pardon—witches, bitches, and all evil spirits!"

"By my faith, a goodly catalogue!" said Magnus; "and there has been the day that, if I had heard you give out the half of it, I should have turned improver myself, and have tried to amend your manners with a cudgel."

"Bear with me," said the factor, "Maister Fowd, or Maister Udaller, or whatever else they may call you, and as you are strong be pitiful, and consider the luckless lot of any inexperienced person who lights upon this earthly paradise of yours. He asks for drink, they bring him sour whey—no disparagement to your brandy, Fowd, which is excellent. You ask for meat, and they bring you sour sillocks that Satan might choke upon. You call your labourers together, and bid them work; it proves St. Magnus's day, or St. Ronan's day, or some infernal saint or other's; or else, perhaps, they have come out of bed with the wrong foot foremost, or they have seen an owl, or a rabbit has crossed their path, or they have dreamed of a roasted horse—in short, nothing is to be done. Give them a spade, and they work as if it burned their fingers; but set them to dancing, and see when they will tire of funking and flinging!"

"And why should they, poor bodies," said Claud Halcro, "as long as there are good fiddlers to play to them?"

"Ay—ay," said Triptolemus, shaking his head, "you are a proper person to uphold them in such a humour. Well, to proceed. I till a piece of my best ground; down comes a sturdy beggar that wants a kail-yard, or a plantie cruive, as you call it, and he claps down an inclosure in the middle of my bit shot of corn, as lightly as if he was baith laird and tenant; and gainsay him wha likes, there he dibbles in his kail-plants! I sit down to my sorrowful dinner, thinking to have peace and quietness there at least, when in comes one, two, three, four, or half a dozen of skelping long lads, from some foolery or anither; misca' me for barring my ain door against them, and eat up the best half of what my sister's providence—and she is not over bountiful—has allotted for my dinner. Then enters a witch, with an ell-wand in her hand, and she raises the wind or lays it, whichever she likes, majors up and down my house as if she was mistress of it, and I am bounden to thank Heaven if she carries not the broad-side of it away with her!"

" Still," said the Fowd, " this is no answer to my question— how the foul fiend I come to find you at moorings here?"

" Have patience, worthy sir," replied the afflicted factor, "and listen to what I have to say, for I fancy it will be as well to tell you the whole matter. You must know, I once thought that I had gotten a small godsend, that might have made all these matters easier."

" How! a godsend! Do you mean a wreck, Master Factor?" exclaimed Magnus; " shame upon you, that should have set example to others!"

" It was no wreck," said the factor; " but, if you must needs know, it chanced that, as I raised an hearthstane in one of the old chambers at Stourburgh—for my sister is minded that there is little use in mair fireplaces about a house than one, and I wanted the stane to knock bear upon—when what should I light on but a horn full of old coins, silver the maist feck of them, but wi' a bit sprinkling of gold amang them too.[1] Weel, I thought this was a dainty windfa', and so thought Baby, and we were the mair willing to put up with a place where there were siccan braw nest-eggs; and we slade down the stane cannily over the horn, which seemed to me to be the very cornucopia, or horn of abundance; and for further security Baby wad visit the room maybe twenty times in the day, and mysell at an orra time, to the boot of a' that."

" On my word, and a very pretty amusement," said Claud Halcro, " to look over a horn of one's own siller. I question if glorious John Dryden ever enjoyed such a pastime in his life; I am very sure I never did."

" Yes, but you forget, Jarto Claud," said the Udaller, "that the factor was only counting over the money for my lord the chamberlain. As he is so keen for his lordship's

[1] See Antique Coins found in Zetland. Note 39.

rights in whales and wrecks, he would not surely forget him in treasure-trove."

"A-hem! a-hem! a-he—he—hem!" ejaculated Triptolemus, seized at the moment with an awkward fit of coughing; "no doubt, my lord's right in the matter would have been considered, being in the hand of one, though I say it, as just as can be found in Angusshire, let alone the Mearns. But mark what happened of late! One day, as I went up to see that all was safe and snug, and just to count out the share that should have been his lordship's—for surely the labourer, as one may call the finder, is worthy of his hire—nay, some learned men say that, when the finder, in point of trust, and in point of power, representeth the *dominus,* or lord superior, he taketh the whole; but let that pass, as a kittle question *in apicibus juris,* as we wont to say at St. Andrews—well, sir and ladies, when I went to the upper chamber, what should I see but an ugsome, ill-shaped, and most uncouth dwarf, that wanted but hoofs and horns to have made an utter devil of him, counting over the very hornful of siller! I am no timrous man, Master Fowd, but, judging that I should proceed with caution in such a matter—for I had reason to believe that there was devilry in it—I accosted him in Latin—whilk it is maist becoming to speak to aught whilk taketh upon it as a goblin—and conjured him *in nomine,* and so forth, with such words as my poor learning could furnish of a suddenty, whilk, to say truth, were not so many, nor altogether so purely latineezed, as might have been had I not been few years at college and many at the pleugh. Well, sirs, he started at first, as one that heareth that which he expects not; but presently recovering himself, he wawls on me with his grey een, like a wild cat, and opens his mouth, whilk resembled the mouth of an oven, for the deil a tongue he had in it, that I could spy, and took upon his ugly self altogether the air and bearing of a bull-dog, whilk I have seen loosed at a fair upon a mad staig; whereupon I was something daunted, and withdrew myself to call upon sister Baby, who fears neither dog nor devil when there is in question the little penny siller. And truly she raise to the fray as I hae seen the Lindsays and

Ogilives bristle up, when Donald MacDonnoch, or the like, made a start down frae the Highlands on the braes of Islay. But an auld useless carline, called Tronda Dronsdaughter—they might call her Drone the sell of her, without farther addition—flung herself right in my sister's gate, and yelloched and skirled, that you would have thought her a whole generation of hounds; whereupon I judged it best to make ae yoking of it, and stop the pleugh until I got my sister's assistance; whilk when I had done, and we mounted the stair to the apartment in which the said dwarf, devil, or other apparition was to be seen, dwarf, horn, and siller were as clean gane as if the cat had lickit the place where I saw them."

Here Triptolemus paused in his extraordinary narration, while the rest of the party looked upon each other in surprise, and the Udaller muttered to Claud Halcro: " By all tokens, this must have been either the devil or Nicholas Strumpfer; and, if it were him, he is more of a goblin than e'er I gave him credit for, and shall be apt to rate him as such in future." Then addressing the factor, he inquired: " Saw ye nought how this dwarf of yours parted company?"

" As I shall answer it, no," replied Triptolemus, with a cautious look around him, as if daunted by the recollection; "neither I nor Baby, who had her wits more about her, not having seen this unseemly vision, could perceive any way by whilk he made evasion. Only Tronda said she saw him flee forth of the window of the west roundel of the auld house upon a dragon, as she averred. But, as the dragon is held a fabulous animal, I suld pronounce her averment to rest upon *deceptio visus.*"

" But, may we not ask farther," said Brenda, stimulated by curiosity to know as much of her cousin Norna's family as was possible, " how all this operated upon Master Yellowley so as to occasion his being in this place at so unseasonable an hour?"

" Seasonable it must be, Mistress Brenda, since it brought us into your sweet company," answered Claud Halcro, whose mercurial brain far outstripped the slow conceptions of the agriculturist, and who became impatient of being so long silent. "To say the truth, it was I, Mistress Brenda, who recommended to our friend the factor, whose house I chanced to call at just after this mischance—and where, by the way, owing doubtless to the hurry of their spirits, I was but poorly received—to make a visit to our other friend at Fitful Head, well judging from certain points of the story, at which my other and more particular friend than either (looking at Magnus) may chance to form a guess, that they who break a head are the best to find a plaster. And as our friend the factor scrupled travelling on horseback, in respect of some tumbles from our ponies——"

"Which are incarnate devils," said Triptolemus, aloud, muttering under his breath, "like every live thing that I have found in Zetland."

"Well, Fowd," continued Halcro, "I undertook to carry him to Fitful Head in my little boat, which Giles and I can manage as if it were an admiral's barge full manned; and Master Triptolemus Yellowley will tell you how seaman-like I piloted him to the little haven, within a quarter of a mile of Norna's dwelling."

"I wish to Heaven you had brought me as safe back again," said the factor.

"Why, to be sure," replied the minstrel, "I am, as glorious John says—

> A daring pilot in extremity,
> Pleased with the danger when the waves go high.
> I seek the storm; but, for a calm unfit,
> Will steer too near the sands, to show my wit."

"I showed little wit in entrusting myself to your charge," said Triptolemus; "and you still less when you upset the boat at the throat of the voe, as you call it, when even the poor bairn, that was mair than half drowned, told you that you were carrying too much sail; and then ye wad fasten the rape to the bit stick on the boat-side, that ye might have time to play on the fiddle."

"What!" said the Udaller, "make fast the sheets to the thwart? a most unseasonable practice, Claud Halcro."

"And sae came of it," replied the agriculturist; "for the

neist blast—and we are never lang without ane in these parts
—whomled us as a gudewife would whomle a bowie, and
ne'er a thing wad Maister Halcro save but his fiddle. The
puir bairn swam out like a water-spaniel, and I swattered
hard for my life, wi' the help of ane of the oars; and here we
are, comfortless creatures, that, till a good wind blew you
here, had naething to eat but a mouthful of Norway rusk,
that has mair sawdust than rye-meal in it, and tastes liker
turpentine than anything else."

"I thought we heard you very merry," said Brenda, "as we
came along the beach."

"Ye heard a fiddle, Mistress Brenda," said the factor;
"and maybe ye may think there can be nae dearth, miss,
where that is skirling. But then it was Maister Claud Halcro's fiddle, whilk, I am apt to think, wad skirl at his father's
death-bed, or at his ain, sae lang as his fingers could pinch the
thairm. And it was nae sma' aggravation to my misfortune
to have him bumming a' sorts of springs—Norse and Scots,
Highland and Lawland, English and Italian, in my lug, as
if nothing had happened that was amiss, and we all in such
stress and perplexity."

"Why, I told you sorrow would never right the boat, factor," said the thoughtless minstrel, "and I did my best to
make you merry; if I failed, it was neither my fault nor my
fiddle's. I have drawn the bow across it before glorious John
Dryden himself."

"I will hear no stories about glorious John Dryden," answered the Udaller, who dreaded Halcro's narratives as much
as Triptolemus did his music—"I will hear nought of him,
but one story to every three bowls of punch—it is our old pac-
tion, you know. But tell me, instead, what said Norna to
you about your errand?"

"Ay, there was anither fine upshot," said Master Yellowley. "She wadna look at us or listen to us; only she both-
ered our acquaintance, Master Halcro here, who thought he
could have sae much to say wi' her, with about a score of
questions about your family and household estate, Master
Magnus Troil; and when she had gotten a' she wanted out of

him, I thought she wad hae dung him ower the craig, like an empty peacod."

"And for yourself?" said the Udaller.

"She wadna listen to my story, nor hear sae much as a word that I had to say," answered Triptolemus; "and sae much for them that seek to witches and familiar spirits!"

"You needed not to have had recourse to Norna's wisdom, Master Factor," said Minna, not unwilling, perhaps, to stop his railing against the friend who had so lately rendered her service· "the youngest child in Orkney could have told you that fairy treasures, if they are not wisely employed for the good of others, as well as of those to whom they are imparted, do not dwell long with their possessors."

"Your humble servant to command, Mistress Minnie," said Triptolemus; "I thank ye for the hint, and I am blythe that you have gotten your wits—I beg pardon, I meant your health—into the barn-yard again. For the treasure, I neither used nor abused it—they that live in the house with my sister Baby wad find it hard to do either!—and as for speaking of it, whilk they say muckle offends them whom we in Scotland call Good Neighbours, and you call Drows, the face of the auld Norse kings on the coins themselves might have spoken as much about it as ever I did."

"The factor," said Claud Halcro, not unwilling to seize the opportunity of revenging himself on Triptolemus for disgracing his seamanship and disparaging his music—"the factor was so scrupulous as to keep the thing quiet even from his master, the Lord Chamberlain; but, now that the matter has ta'en wind, he is likely to have to account to his master for that which is no longer in his possession; for the Lord Chamberlain will be in no hurry, I think, to believe the story of the dwarf. Neither do I think (winking to the Udaller) that Norna gave credit to a word of so odd a story; and I dare say that was the reason that she received us, I must needs say, in a very dry manner. I rather think she knew that Triptolemus, our friend here, had found some other hiding-hole for the money, and that the story of the goblin was all his own invention. For my part, I will never believe there was such a dwarf to be seen as the creature Master Yellowley describes until I set my own eyes on him."

"Then you may do so at this moment," said the factor; "for, by ——" he muttered a deep asseveration as he sprung on his feet in great horror, "there the creature is!"

All turned their eyes in the direction in which he pointed, and saw the hideous, misshapen figure of Pacolet, with his eyes fixed and glaring at them through the smoke. He had stolen upon their conversation unperceived, until the factor's eye lighted upon him in the manner we have described. There was something so ghastly in his sudden and unexpected appearance that even the Udaller, to whom his form was familiar, could not help starting. Neither pleased with himself for having testified this degree of emotion, however slight, nor with the dwarf who had given cause to it, Magnus asked him sharply what was his business there. Pacolet replied by producing a letter which he gave to the Udaller, uttering a sound resembling the word "shogh."

"That is the Highlandman's language," said the Udaller; "didst thou learn that, Nicholas, when you lost your own?"

Pacolet nodded, and signed to him to read his letter.

"That is no such easy matter by firelight, my good friend," replied the Udaller; "but it may concern Minna, and we must try."

Brenda offered her assistance, but the Udaller answered: "No—no, my girl; Norna's letters must be read by those they are written to. Give the knave, Strumpfer, a drop of brandy the while, though he little deserves it at my hands, considering the grin with which he sent the good Nantz down the crag this morning, as if it had been as much ditch-water."

"Will you be this honest gentleman's cup-bearer—his Ganymede, friend Yellowley, or shall I?" said Claud Halcro aside to the factor; while Magnus Troil, having carefully wiped his spectacles, which he produced from a large copper case, had disposed them on his nose and was studying the epistle of Norna.

"I would not touch him, or go near him, for all the Carse of Gowrie," said the factor, whose fears were by no means entirely removed, though he saw that the dwarf was received as a creature of flesh and blood by the rest of the company; "but I pray you to ask him what he has done with my horn of coins?"

The dwarf, who heard the question, threw back his head and displayed his enormous throat, pointing to it with his finger.

"Nay, if he has swallowed them there is no more to be said," replied the factor; "only I hope he will thrive on them as a cow on wet clover. He is dame Norna's servant, it's like— such man, such mistress! But if theft and witchcraft are to go unpunished in this land, my lord must find another factor; for I have been used to live in a country where men's worldly gear was keepit from infang and outfang thief, as well as their immortal souls from the claws of the deil and his cummers—sain and save us!"

The agriculturist was perhaps the less reserved in expressing his complaints that the Udaller was for the present out of hearing, having drawn Claud Halcro apart into another corner of the hut.

"And tell me," said he, "friend Halcro, what errand took thee to Sumburgh, since I reckon it was scarce the mere pleasure of sailing in partnership with yonder barnacle?"

"In faith, Fowd," said the bard, "and if you will have the truth, I went to speak to Norna on your affairs."

"On my affairs?" replied the Udaller; "on what affairs of mine?"

"Just touching your daughter's health. I heard that Norna refused your message, and would not see Eric Scambester. 'Now,' said I to myself, 'I have scarce joyed in meat, or drink, or music, or aught else, since Jarto Minna has been so ill; and I may say, literally as well as figuratively, that my day and night have been made sorrowful to me.' In short, I thought I might have some more interest with old Norna than another, as Scalds and wise women were always accounted something akin; and I undertook the journey with the hope to be of some use to my old friend and his lovely daughter."

"And it was most kindly done of you, good, warm-hearted

Claud," said the Udaller, shaking him warmly by the hand: "I ever said you showed the good old Norse heart amongst all thy fiddling and thy folly. Tut, man, never wince for the matter, but be blythe that thy heart is better than thy head. Well—and I warrant you got no answer from Norna?"

"None to purpose," replied Claud Halcro; "but she held me close to question about Minna's illness, too; and I told her how I had met her abroad the other morning in no very good weather, and how her sister Brenda said she had hurt her foot—in short, I told her all and everything I knew."

"And something more besides, it would seem," said the Udaller; "for I, at least, never heard before that Minna had hurt herself."

"Oh, a scratch!—a mere scratch!" said the old man; "but I was startled about it—terrified lest it had been the bite of a dog, or some hurt from a venomous thing. I told all to Norna, however."

"And what," answered the Udaller, "did she say, in the way of reply?"

"She bade me begone about my business, and told me that the issue would be known at the Kirkwall fair; and said just the like to this noodle of a factor; it was all that either of us got for our labour," said Halcro.

"That is strange," said Magnus. "My kinswoman writes me in this letter not to fail going thither with my daughters. This fair runs strongly in her head; one would think she intended to lead the market, and yet she has nothing to buy or to sell there that I know of. And so you came away as wise as you went, and swamped your boat at the mouth of the voe?"

"Why, how could I help it?" said the poet. "I had set the boy to steer, and as the flaw came suddenly off shore, I could not let go the tack and play on the fiddle at the same time. But it is all well enough—salt-water never harmed Zetlander, so as he could get out of it, and, as Heaven would have it, we were within man's depth of the shore, and chancing to find this skeo, we should have done well enough, with shelter and fire, and are much better than well with your good

cheer and good company. But it wears late, and Night and
Day must be both as sleepy as old Midnight can make them.
There is an inner crib here, where the fishers slept—somewhat fragrant with the smell of their fish, but that is wholesome. They shall bestow themselves there, with the help of
what cloaks you have, and then we will have one cup of brandy,
and one stave of glorious John, or some little trifle of my own,
and so sleep as sound as cobblers."

"Two glasses of brandy, if you please," said the Udaller,
"if our stores do not run dry; but not a single stave of glorious John, or of any one else to-night."

And this being arranged and executed agreeably to the peremptory pleasure of the Udaller, the whole party consigned
themselves to slumber for the night, and on the next day departed for their several habitations, Claud Halcro having previously arranged with the Udaller that he would accompany
him and his daughters on their proposed visit to Kirkwall.

CHAPTER XXXI.

By this hand, thou think'st me as far in the devil's book as thou and
Falstaff, for obduracy and persistency. Let the end try the man. . . .
Albeit I could tell to thee (as to one it pleases me, for fault of a better,
to call my friend), I could be sad, and sad indeed too.
                                                        Henry IV. Part II.

WE must now change the scene from Zetland to Orkney, and
request our readers to accompany us to the ruins of an elegant,
though ancient, structure called the Earl's Palace. These remains, though much dilapidated, still exist in the neighbourhood of the massive and venerable pile which Norwegian
devotion dedicated to St. Magnus the Martyr, and, being
contiguous to the Bishop's Palace, which is also ruinous, the
place is impressive, as exhibiting vestiges of the mutations
both in church and state which have affected Orkney, as well
as countries more exposed to such convulsions. Several parts
of these ruinous buildings might be selected (under suitable
modifications) as the model of a Gothic mansion, provided

architects would be contented rather to imitate what is really beautiful in that species of building than to make a medley of the caprices of the order, confounding the military, ecclesiastical, and domestic styles of all ages at random, with additional fantasies and combinations of their own device, " all formed out of the builder's brain."

The Earl's Palace forms three sides of an oblong square, and has, even in its ruins, the air of an elegant yet massive structure, uniting, as was usual in the residence of feudal princes, the character of a palace and of a castle. A great banqueting-hall, communicating with several large rounds, or projecting turret-rooms, and having at either end an immense chimney, testifies the ancient Northern hospitality of the Earls of Orkney, and communicates, almost in the modern fashion, with a gallery or withdrawing-room of corresponding dimensions, and having, like the hall, its projecting turrets. The lordly hall itself is lighted by a fine Gothic window of shafted stone at one end, and is entered by a spacious and elegant staircase, consisting of three flights of stone steps. The exterior ornaments and proportions of the ancient building are also very handsome; but, being totally unprotected, this remnant of the pomp and grandeur of earls, who assumed the license as well as the dignity of petty sovereigns, is now fast crumbling to decay, and has suffered considerably since the date of our story.

With folded arms and downcast looks, the pirate Cleveland was pacing slowly the ruined hall which we have just described—a place of retirement which he had probably chosen because it was distant from public resort. His dress was considerably altered from that which he usually wore in Zetland, and seemed a sort of uniform, richly laced, and exhibiting no small quantity of embroidery; a hat with a plume, and a small sword very handsomely mounted, then the constant companion of every one who assumed the rank of a gentleman, showed his pretensions to that character. But if his exterior was so far improved, it seemed to be otherwise with his health and spirits. He was pale, and had lost both the fire of his eye and the vivacity of his step, and his whole appearance

24

indicated melancholy of mind, or suffering of body, or a combination of both evils.

As Cleveland thus paced these ancient ruins, a young man, of a light and slender form, whose showy dress seemed to have been studied with care, yet exhibited more extravagance than judgment or taste, whose manner was a janty affectation of the free and easy rake of the period, and the expression of whose countenance was lively, with a cast of effrontery, tripped up the staircase, entered the hall, and presented himself to Cleveland, who merely nodded to him, and pulling his hat deeper over his brows, resumed his solitary and discontented promenade.

The stranger adjusted his own hat, nodded in return, took snuff, with the air of a *petit maître*, from a richly chased gold box, offered it to Cleveland as he passed, and being repulsed rather coldly, replaced the box in his pocket, folded his arms in his turn, and stood looking with fixed attention on his motions whose solitude he had interrupted. At length Cleveland stopped short, as if impatient of being longer the subject of his observation, and said abruptly, "Why can I not be left alone for half an hour, and what the devil is it that you want?"

"I am glad you spoke first," answered the stranger, carelessly; "I was determined to know whether you were Clement Cleveland or Cleveland's ghost, and they say ghosts never take the first word, so I now set it down for yourself in life and limb; and here is a fine old hurly-house you have found out for an owl to hide himself in at mid-day, or a ghost to revisit the pale glimpses of the moon, as the divine Shakspeare says."

"Well—well," answered Cleveland, abruptly, "your jest is made, and now let us have your earnest."

"In earnest, then, Captain Cleveland," replied his companion, "I think you know me for your friend."

"I am content to suppose so," said Cleveland.

"It is more than supposition," replied the young man: "I have proved it—proved it both here and elsewhere."

"Well—well," answered Cleveland, "I admit you have been always a friendly fellow—and what then?"

"Well, well—and what then!" replied the other; "this is but a brief way of thanking folk. Look you, captain, here is Benson, Barlowe, Dick Fletcher, and a few others of us who wished you well, have kept your old comrade Captain Goffe in these seas upon the lookout for you, when he and Hawkins, and the greater part of the ship's company, would fain have been down on the Spanish Main, and at the old trade."

"And I wish to God that you had all gone about your business," said Cleveland, "and left me to my fate."

"Which would have been to be informed against and hanged, captain, the first time that any of these Dutch or English rascals whom you have lightened of their cargoes came to set their eyes upon you; and no place more likely to meet with seafaring men than in these islands. And here, to screen you from such a risk, we have been wasting our precious time, till folk are grown very peery; and when we have no more goods or money to spend amongst them, the fellows will be for grabbing the ship."

"Well, then, why do you not sail off without me?" said Cleveland. "There has been fair partition, and all have had their share; let all do as they like. I have lost my ship, and having been once a captain, I will not go to sea under command of Goffe or any other man. Besides, you know well enough that both Hawkins and he bear me ill-will for keeping them from sinking the Spanish brig, with the poor devils of negroes on board."

"Why, what the foul fiend is the matter with thee?" said his companion. "Are you Clement Cleveland, our own old true-hearted Clem of the Cleugh, and do you talk of being afraid of Hawkins and Goffe, and a score of such fellows, when you have myself, and Barlowe, and Dick Fletcher at your back? When was it we deserted you, either in council or in fight, that you should be afraid of our flinching now? And as for serving under Goffe, I hope it is no new thing for gentlemen of fortune who are going on the account to change a captain now and then? Let us alone for that—captain you shall be; for death rock me asleep if I serve under that fellow Goffe, who is as very a bloodhound as ever sucked bitch!

No, no, I thank you—my captain must have a little of the gentleman about him, howsoever. Besides, you know, it was you who first dipped my hands in the dirty water, and turned me from a stroller by land to a rover by sea."

"Alas, poor Bunce!" said Cleveland, "you owe me little thanks for that service."

"That is as you take it," replied Bunce; "for my part, I see no harm in levying contributions on the public either one way or t'other. But I wish you would forget that name of Bunce and call me Altamont, as I have often desired you to do. I hope a gentleman of the roving trade has as good a right to have an *alias* as a stroller, and I never stepped on the boards but what I was Altamont at the least."

"Well, then, Jack Altamont," replied Cleveland, "since Altamont is the word——"

"Yes, but, captain, *Jack* is not the word, though Altamont be so. Jack Altamont! why, 'tis a velvet coat with paper lace. Let it be Frederick, captain: Frederick Altamont is all of a piece."

"Frederick be it, then, with all my heart," said Cleveland; "and pray tell me, which of your names will sound best at the head of the 'Last Speech, Confession, and Dying Words of John Bunce, *alias* Frederick Altamont, who was this morning hanged at Execution Dock for the crime of Piracy upon the High Seas'?"

"Faith, I cannot answer that question without another can of grog, captain; so, if you will go down with me to Bet Haldane's on the quay, I will bestow some thought on the matter, with the help of a right pipe of Trinidado. We will have the gallon bowl filled with the best stuff you ever tasted, and I know some smart wenches who will help us to drain it. But you shake your head—you're not i' the vein? Well, then, I will stay with you; for, by this hand, Clem, you shift me not off. Only I will ferret you out of this burrow of old stones, and carry you into sunshine and fair air. Where shall we go?"

"Where you will," said Cleveland, "so that you keep out of the way of our own rascals and all others."

"Why, then," replied Bunce, "you and I will go up to the

Hill of Whitford, which overlooks the town, and walk together as gravely and honestly as a pair of well-employed attorneys."

As they proceeded to leave the ruinous castle, Bunce, turning back to look at it, thus addressed his companion:

"Hark ye, captain, dost thou know who last inhabited this old cockloft?"

"An earl of the Orkneys, they say," replied Cleveland.

"And are you avised what death he died of?" said Bunce; "for I have heard that it was of a tight neck-collar—a hempen fever, or the like."

"The people here do say," replied Cleveland, "that his lordship, some hundred years ago, had the mishap to become acquainted with the nature of a loop and a leap in the air."

"Why, la ye there now!" said Bunce; "there was some credit in being hanged in those days, and in such worshipful company. And what might his lordship have done to deserve such promotion?"

"Plundered the liege subjects, they say," replied Cleveland; "slain and wounded them, fired upon his Majesty's flag, and so forth."

"Near akin to a gentleman rover, then," said Bunce, making a theatrical bow towards the old building; "and, therefore, my most potent, grave, and reverend Signior Earl, I crave leave to call you my loving cousin, and bid you most heartily adieu. I leave you in the good company of rats and mice, and so forth, and I carry with me an honest gentleman, who, having of late had no more heart than a mouse, is now desirous to run away from his profession and friends like a rat, and would therefore be a most fitting denizen of your earlship's palace."

"I would advise you not to speak so loud, my good friend Frederick Altamont, or John Bunce," said Cleveland; "when you were on the stage, you might safely rant as loud as you listed; but, in your present profession, of which you are so fond, every man speaks under correction of the yard-arm and a running nose."

The comrades left the little town of Kirkwall in silence, and ascended the Hill of Whitford, which raises its brow of dark heath, uninterrupted by inclosures or cultivation of any kind, to the northward of the ancient burgh of St. Magnus. The plain at the foot of the hill was already occupied by numbers of persons who were engaged in making preparations for the fair of St. Olla, to be held upon the ensuing day, and which forms a general rendezvous to all the neighbouring islands of Orkney, and is even frequented by many persons from the more distant archipelago of Zetland. It is, in the words of the proclamation, "A free mercat and fair, holden at the good burgh of Kirkwall on the third of August, being St. Olla's day," and continuing for an indefinite space thereafter, extending from three days to a week and upwards. The fair is of great antiquity, and derives its name from Olaus, Olave, Ollaw, the celebrated monarch of Norway, who, rather by the edge of his sword than any milder argument, introduced Christianity into those isles, and was respected as the patron of Kirkwall some time before he shared that honour with St. Magnus the Martyr.

It was no part of Cleveland's purpose to mingle in the busy scene which was here going on; and, turning their route to the left, they soon ascended into undisturbed solitude, save where the grouse,[1] more plentiful in Orkney, perhaps, than in any other part of the British dominions, rose in covey, and went off before them. Having continued to ascend till they had wellnigh reached the summit of the conical hill, both turned round, as with one consent, to look at and admire the prospect beneath.

The lively bustle which extended between the foot of the hill and the town gave life and variety to that part of the scene; then was seen the town itself, out of which arose, like a great mass, superior in proportion as it seemed to the whole burgh, the ancient cathedral of St. Magnus, of the heaviest order of Gothic architecture, but grand, solemn, and stately, the work of a distant age and of a powerful hand. The quay, with the shipping, lent additional vivacity to the scene; and not only the whole beautiful bay, which lies betwixt the promontories of Inganess and Quanterness, at the bottom of which

[1] See Note 40.

Kirkwall is situated, but all the sea, so far as visible, and in particular the whole strait betwixt the island of Shapinsha and that called Pomona, or the Mainland, was covered and enlivened by a variety of boats and small vessels, freighted from distant islands to convey passengers or merchandise to the fair of St. Olla.

Having attained the point by which this fair and busy prospect was most completely commanded, each of the strangers, in seaman fashion, had recourse to his spy-glass, to assist the naked eye in considering the Bay of Kirkwall and the numerous vessels by which it was traversed. But the attention of the two companions seemed to be arrested by different objects. That of Bunce, or Altamont, as he chose to call himself, was riveted to the armed sloop, where, conspicuous by her square rigging and length of beam, with the English jack and pennon, which they had the precaution to keep flying, she lay among the merchant vessels, as distinguished from them by the trim neatness of her appearance as a trained soldier amongst a crowd of clowns.

"Yonder she lies," said Bunce; "I wish to God she was in the Bay of Honduras—you captain, on the quarter-deck, I your lieutenant, and Fletcher quartermaster, and fifty stout fellows under us—I should not wish to see these blasted heaths and rocks again for a while! And captain you shall soon be. The old brute Goffe gets drunk as a lord every day, swaggers, and shoots, and cuts among the crew; and, besides, he has quarrelled with the people here so damnably that they will scarce let water or provisions go on board of us, and we expect an open breach every day."

As Bunce received no answer, he turned short round on his companion, and, perceiving his attention otherwise engaged, exclaimed: "What the devil is the matter with you? or what can you see in all that trumpery small craft, which is only loaded with stock-fish, and ling, and smoked geese, and tubs of butter that is worse than tallow?—the cargoes of the whole lumped together would not be worth the flash of a pistol. No—no, give me such a chase as we might see from the masthead off the island of Trinidado. Your Don, rolling as deep in the water as a grampus, deep-loaden with rum, sugar, and bales of tobacco, and all the rest ingots, moidores, and gold dust; then set all sail, clear the deck, stand to quarters, up with the Jolly Roger;[1] we near her—we make her out to be well manned and armed——"

"Twenty guns on her lower deck," said Cleveland.

"Forty, if you will," retorted Bunce, "and we have but ten mounted—never mind. The Don blazes away—never mind yet, my brave lads—run her alongside, and on board with you—to work, with your grenadoes, your cutlasses, pole-axes, and pistols. The Don cries '*Misericordia,*' and we share the cargo without *co licencio, Seignior!*"

"By my faith," said Cleveland, "thou takest so kindly to the trade that all the world may see that no honest man was spoiled when you were made a pirate. But you shall not prevail on me to go farther in the devil's road with you; for you know yourself that what is got over his back is spent—you wot how. In a week, or a month at most, the rum and the sugar are out, the bales of tobacco have become smoke, the moidores, ingots, and gold dust have got out of our hands into those of the quiet, honest, conscientious folks who dwell at Port Royal and elsewhere, wink hard on our trade as long as we have money, but not a jot beyond. Then we have cold looks, and it may be a hint is given to the judge marshal; for, when our pockets are worth nothing, our honest friends, rather than want, will make money upon our heads. Then comes a high gallows and a short halter, and so dies the gentleman rover. I tell thee, I will leave this trade, and, when I turn my glass from one of these barks and boats to another, there is not the worst of them which I would not row for life rather than continue to be what I have been. These poor men make the sea a means of honest livelihood and friendly communication between shore and shore, for the mutual benefit of the inhabitants; but we have made it a road to the ruin of others and to our own destruction here and in eternity. I am determined to turn honest man and use this life no longer!"

[1] The pirates gave this name to the black flag, which, with **many horri-**ble devices to enhance its terrors, was their favourite ensign.

"And where will your honesty take up its abode, if it please you?" said Bunce. "You have broken the laws of every nation, and the hand of the law will detect and crush you wherever you may take refuge. Cleveland, I speak to you more seriously than I am wont to do. I have had my reflections, too; and they have been bad enough, though they lasted but a few minutes, to spoil me weeks of joviality. But here is the matter—what can we do but go on as we have done, unless we have a direct purpose of adorning the yard-arm?"

"We may claim the benefit of the proclamation of those to our sort who come in and surrender," said Cleveland.

"Umph!" answered his companion, drily; "the date of that day of grace has been for some time over, and they may take the penalty or grant the pardon at their pleasure. Were I you, I would not put my neck in such a venture."

"Why, others have been admitted but lately to favour, and why should not I?" said Cleveland.

"Ay," replied his associate, "Harry Glasby and some others have been spared; but Glasby did what was called good service, in betraying his comrades and retaking the 'Jolly Fortune'; and that I think you would scorn, even to be revenged of the brute Goffe yonder."

"I would die a thousand times sooner," said Cleveland.

"I will be sworn for it," said Bunce; "and the others were forecastle fellows—petty larceny rogues, scarce worth the hemp it would have cost to hang them. But your name has stood too high amongst the gentlemen of fortune for you to get off so easily. You are the prime buck of the herd, and will be marked accordingly."

"And why so, I pray you?" said Cleveland; "you know well enough my aim, Jack."

"Frederick, if you please," said Bunce.

"The devil take your folly! Prithee keep thy wit, and let us be grave for a moment."

"For a moment—be it so," said Bunce; "but I feel the spirit of Altamont coming fast upon me. I have been a grave man for ten minutes already."

"Be so then for a little longer," said Cleveland. "I know,

Jack, that you really love me; and, since we have come thus far in this talk, I will trust you entirely. Now tell me, why should I be refused the benefit of this gracious proclamation? I have borne a rough outside, as thou knowest; but, in time of need, I can show the numbers of lives which I have been the means of saving, the property which I have restored to those who owned it, when, without my intercession, it would have been wantonly destroyed. In short, Bunce, I can show——"

"That you were as gentle a thief as Robin Hood himself," said Bunce; "and, for that reason, I, Fletcher, and the better sort among us, love you, as one who saves the character of us gentlemen rovers from utter reprobation. Well, suppose your pardon made out, what are you to do next?—what class in society will receive you?—with whom will you associate? Old Drake, in Queen Bess's time, could plunder Peru and Mexico without a line of commission to show for it, and, blessed be her memory! he was knighted for it on his return. And there was Hal Morgan, the Welshman, nearer our time, in the days of merry King Charles, brought all his gettings home, had his estate and his country house, and who but he? But that is all ended now: once a pirate, and an outcast for ever. The poor devil may go and live, shunned and despised by every one, in some obscure seaport, with such part of his guilty earnings as courtiers and clerks leave him—for pardons do not pass the seals for nothing—and, when he takes his walk along the pier, if a stranger asks who is the down-looking, swarthy, melancholy man for whom all make way, as if he brought the plague in his person, the answer shall be, that is such a one, the pardoned pirate! No honest man will speak to him, no woman of repute will give him her hand."

"Your picture is too highly coloured, Jack," said Cleveland, suddenly interrupting his friend: "there are women—there is one at least, that would be true to her lover, even if he were what you have described."

Bunce was silent for a space, and looked fixedly at his friend. "By my soul!" he said, at length, "I begin to think myself a conjurer. Unlikely as it all was, I could not help suspecting from the beginning that there was a girl in the ease. Why, this is worse than Prince Volscius in love—ha! ha! ha!"

"Laugh as you will," said Cleveland, "it is true: there is a maiden who is contented to love me, pirate as I am; and I will fairly own to you, Jack, that, though I have often at times detested our roving life, and myself for following it, yet I doubt if I could have found resolution to make the break which I have now resolved on but for her sake."

"Why, then, God-a-mercy!" replied Bunce, "there is no speaking sense to a madman; and love in one of our trade, captain, is little better than lunacy. The girl must be a rare creature, for a wise man to risk hanging for her. But, hark ye, may she not be a little touched, as well as yourself? and is it not sympathy that has done it? She cannot be one of our ordinary cockatrices, but a girl of conduct and character."

"Both are as undoubted as that she is the most beautiful and bewitching creature whom the eye ever opened upon," answered Cleveland.

"And she loves thee, knowing thee, most noble captain, to be a commander among those gentlemen of fortune whom the vulgar call pirates?"

"Even so—I am assured of it," said Cleveland.

"Why, then," answered Bunce, "she is either mad in good earnest, as I said before, or she does not know what a pirate is."

"You are right in the last point," replied Cleveland. "She has been bred in such remote simplicity, and utter ignorance of what is evil, that she compares our occupation with that of the old Norsemen, who swept sea and haven with their victorious galleys, established colonies, conquered countries, and took the name of sea-kings."

"And a better one it is than that of pirate, and comes much to the same purpose, I dare say," said Bunce. "But this must be a mettled wench! Why did you not bring her aboard? Methinks it was pity to baulk her fancy."

"And do you think," said Cleveland, "that I could so utterly play the part of a fallen spirit as to avail myself of her enthusiastic error, and bring an angel of beauty and innocence acquainted with such a hell as exists on board of yonder infernal ship of ours? I tell you, my friend, that, were all my former sins doubled in weight and in dye, such a villainy would have outglared and outweighed them all."

"Why, then, Captain Cleveland," said his confidant, "methinks it was but a fool's part to come hither at all. The news must one day have gone abroad that the celebrated pirate Captain Cleveland, with his good sloop the 'Revenge,' had been lost on the Mainland of Zetland, and all hands perished; so you would have remained hid both from friend and enemy, and might have married your petty Zetlander, and converted your sash and scarf into fishing-nets, and your cutlass into a harpoon, and swept the seas for fish instead of florins."

"And so I had determined," said the captain; "but a jagger, as they call them here, like a meddling, peddling thief as he is, brought down intelligence to Zetland of your lying here, and I was fain to set off, to see if you were the consort of whom I had told them, long before I thought of leaving the roving trade."

"Ay," said Bunce, "and so far you judged well. For, as you had heard of our being at Kirkwall, so we should have soon learned that you were at Zetland; and some of us for friendship, some for hatred, and some for fear of your playing Harry Glasby upon us, would have come down for the purpose of getting you into our company again."

"I suspected as much," said the captain, "and therefore was fain to decline the courteous offer of a friend who proposed to bring me here about this time. Besides, Jack, I recollected that, as you say, my pardon will not pass the seals without money; my own was waxing low—no wonder, thou knowest I was never a churl of it; and so——"

"And so you came for your share of the cobs?" replied his friend. "It was wisely done; and we shared honourably; so far Goffe has acted up to articles, it must be allowed. But keep your purpose of leaving him close in your breast, for I dread his playing you some dog's trick or other; for he certainly thought himself sure of your share, and will hardly forgive your coming alive to disappoint him."

"I fear him not," said Cleveland, "and he knows that well.
I would I were as well clear of the consequences of having
been his comrade as I hold myself to be of all those which
may attend his ill-will. Another unhappy job I may be
troubled with: I hurt a young fellow, who has been my plague
for some time, in an unhappy brawl that chanced the morning
I left Zetland."

"Is he dead?" asked Bunco. "It is a more serious question here than it would be on the Grand Caimains or the Ba-
hama Isles, where a brace or two of fellows may be shot in a
morning, and no more heard of, or asked about, them than if
they were so many wood-pigeons. But here it may be otherwise; so I hope you have not made your friend immortal."

"I hope not," said the captain, "though my anger has been
fatal to those who have given me less provocation. To say
the truth, I was sorry for the lad notwithstanding, and especially as I was forced to leave him in mad keeping."

"In mad keeping!" said Bunce; "why, what means that?"

"You shall hear," replied his friend. "In the first place,
you are to know, this young man came suddenly on me while
I was trying to gain Minna's ear for a private interview before I set sail, that I might explain my purpose to her. Now,
to be broken in on by the accursed rudeness of this young fellow at such a moment——"

"The interruption deserved death," said Bunce, "by all the
laws of love and honour!"

"A truce with your ends of plays, Jack, and listen one moment. The brisk youth thought proper to retort, when I commanded him to be gone. I am not, thou knowest, very patient, and enforced my commands with a blow, which he returned
as roundly. We struggled, till I became desirous that we
should part at any rate, which I could only effect by a stroke
of my poniard, which, according to old use, I have, thou
knowest, always about me. I had scarce done this when I
repented; but there was no time to think of anything save escape and concealment, for, if the house rose on me, I was lost;
as the fiery old man, who is head of the family, would have
done justice on me had I been his brother. I took the body

hastily on my shoulders to carry it down to the sea-shore, with the purpose of throwing it into a riva, as they call them, or chasm of great depth, where it would have been long enough in being discovered. This done, I intended to jump into the boat which I had lying ready, and set sail for Kirkwall. But, as I was walking hastily towards the beach with my burden, the poor young fellow groaned, and so apprised me that the wound had not been instantly fatal. I was by this time well concealed amongst the rocks, and, far from desiring to complete my crime, I laid the young man on the ground, and was doing what I could to stanch the blood, when suddenly an old woman stood before me. She was a person whom I had frequently seen while in Zetland, and to whom they ascribe the character of a sorceress, or, as the negroes say, an Obi woman. She demanded the wounded man of me, and I was too much pressed for time to hesitate in complying with her request. More she was about to say to me, when we heard the voice of a silly old man, belonging to the family, singing at some distance. She then pressed her finger on her lip as a sign of secrecy, whistled very low, and a shapeless, deformed brute of a dwarf coming to her assistance, they carried the wounded man into one of the caverns with which the place abounds, and I got to my boat and to sea with all expedition. If that old hag be, as they say, connected with the King of the Air, she favoured me that morning with a turn of her calling; for not even the West Indian tornadoes, which we have weathered together, made a wilder racket than the squall that drove me so far out of our course that, without a pocket-compass, which I chanced to have about me, I should never have recovered the Fair Isle, for which we run, and where I found a brig which brought me to this place. But, whether the old woman meant me weal or woe, here we came at length in safety from the sea, and here I remain in doubts and difficulties of more kinds than one."

"Oh, the devil take the Sumburgh Head," said Bunce, "or whatever they call the rock that you knocked our clever little 'Revenge' against!"

"Do not say *I* knocked her on the rock," said Cleveland;

"have I not told you fifty times, if the cowards had not taken to their boat, though I showed them the danger, and told them they would all be swamped, which happened the instant they cast off the painter, she would have been afloat at this moment? Had they stood by me and the ship, their lives would have been saved; had I gone with them, mine would have been lost; who can say which is for the best?"

"Well," replied his friend, "I know your case now, and can the better help and advise. I will be true to you, Clement, as the blade to the hilt; but I cannot think that you should leave us. As the old Scottish song says, 'Wae's my heart that we should sunder!' But come, you will aboard with us to-day, at any rate?"

"I have no other place of refuge," said Cleveland, with a sigh.

He then once more ran his eyes over the bay, directing his spy-glass upon several of the vessels which traversed its surface, in hopes, doubtless, of discerning the vessel of Magnus Troil, and then followed his companion down the hill in silence.

CHAPTER XXXII.

I strive like to the vessel in the tide-way,
Which, lacking favouring breeze, hath not the power
To stem the powerful current. Even so,
Resolving daily to forsake my vices,
Habits, strong circumstance, renew'd temptation,
Sweep me to sea again. O heavenly breath,
Fill thou my sails, and aid the feeble vessel,
Which ne'er can reach the blessed port without thee!
              'Tis Odds when Evens meet.

CLEVELAND, with his friend Bunce, descended the hill for a time in silence, until at length the latter renewed their conversation.

"You have taken this fellow's wound more on your conscience than you need, captain: I have known you do more, and think less on't."

"Not on such slight provocation, Jack," replied Cleveland.

"Besides, the lad saved my life; and, say that I requited him the favour, still we should not have met on such evil terms; but I trust that he may receive aid from that woman, who has certainly strange skill in simples."

"And over simpletons, captain," said his friend, "in which class I must e'en put you down, if you think more on this subject. That you should be made a fool of by a young woman, why it is many an honest man's case; but to puzzle your pate about the mummeries of an old one is far too great a folly to indulge a friend in. Talk to me of your Minna, since you so call her, as much as you will; but you have no title to trouble your faithful squire-errant with your old mumping magician. And now here we are once more amongst the booths and tents which these good folk are pitching; let us look, and see whether we may not find some fun and frolic amongst them. In merry England, now, you would have seen, on such an occasion, two or three bands of strollers, as many fire-eaters and conjurers, as many shows of wild beasts; but, amongst these grave folk, there is nothing but what savours of business and of commodity—no, not so much as a single squall from my merry gossip Punch and his rib Joan."

As Bunce thus spoke, Cleveland cast his eyes on some very gay clothes, which, with other articles, hung out upon one of the booths, that had a good deal more of ornament and exterior decoration than the rest. There was in front a small sign of canvas painted, announcing the variety of goods which the owner of the booth, Bryce Snailsfoot, had on sale, and the reasonable prices at which he proposed to offer them to the public. For the further gratification of the spectator, the sign bore on the opposite side an emblematic device, resembling our first parents in their vegetable garments, with this legend:

> " Poor sinners whom the snake deceives
> Are fain to cover them with leaves.
> Zetland hath no leaves, 'tis true,
> Because that trees are none, or few;
> But we have flax and taits of woo',
> For linen cloth and wadmaal blue;
> And we have many of foreign knacks
> Of finer waft than woo' or flax.

> Ye gallanty Lambmas lads,[1] appear,
> And bring your Lambmas sisters here,
> Bryce Snailsfoot spares not cost or care,
> To pleasure every gentle pair."

While Cleveland was perusing these goodly rhymes, which brought to his mind Claud Halcro, to whom, as the poet laureate of the island, ready with his talent alike in the service of the great and small, they probably owed their origin, the worthy proprietor of the booth, having cast his eye upon him, began with hasty and trembling hand to remove some of the garments, which, as the sale did not commence till the ensuing day, he had exposed either for the purpose of airing them or to excite the admiration of the spectators.

"By my word, captain," whispered Bunce to Cleveland, "you must have had that fellow under your clutches one day, and he remembers one gripe of your talons and fears another. See how fast he is packing his wares out of sight, as soon as he set eyes on you!"

"*His* wares!" said Cleveland, on looking more attentively at his proceedings. "By Heaven, they are my clothes which I left in a chest at Jarlshof when the 'Revenge' was lost there. Why, Bryce Snailsfoot, thou thief, dog, and villain, what means this? Have you not made enough of us by cheap buying and dear selling, that you have seized on my trunk and wearing-apparel?"

Bryce Snailsfoot, who probably would otherwise not have been willing to *see* his friend the captain, was now by the vivacity of his attack obliged to pay attention to him. He first whispered to his little foot-page, by whom, as we have already noticed, he was usually attended: "Run to the town-council-house, jarto, and tell the provost and bailies they maun send some of their officers speedily, for here is like to be wild wark in the fair."

So having said, and having seconded his commands by a push on the shoulder of his messenger which sent him spinning out of the shop as fast as heels could carry him, Bryce Snailsfoot turned to his old acquaintance, and, with that am-

[1] See Note 41.

25

plification of words and exaggeration of manner which in Scotland is called "making a phrase," he ejaculated: "The Lord be gude to us! the worthy Captain Cleveland, that we were all sae grieved about, returned to relieve our hearts again! Wat have my cheeks been for you (here Bryce wiped his eyes), and blythe am I now to see you restored to your sorrowing friends!"

"My sorrowing friends, you rascal!" said Cleveland; "I will give you better cause for sorrow than ever you had on my account, if you do not tell me instantly where you stole all my clothes."

"Stole!" ejaculated Bryce, casting up his eyes; "now the Powers be gude to us!—the poor gentleman has lost his reason in that weary gale of wind."

"Why, you insolent rascal!" said Cleveland, grasping the cane which he carried, "do you think to bamboozle me with your impudence? As you would have a whole head on your shoulders, and your bones in a whole skin, one minute longer, tell me where the devil you stole my wearing-apparel?"

Bryce Snailsfoot once more ejaculated a repetition of the word "Stole! Now Heaven be gude to us!" but at the same time, conscious that the captain was likely to be sudden in execution, cast an anxious look to the town, to see the loitering aid of the civil power advance to his rescue.

"I insist on an instant answer," said the captain, with upraised weapon, "or else I will beat you to a mummy, and throw out all your frippery upon the common!"

Meanwhile, Master John Bunce, who considered the whole affair as an excellent good jest, and not the worse one that it made Cleveland very angry, seized hold of the captain's arm, and, without an idea of ultimately preventing him from executing his threats, interfered just so much as was necessary to protract a discussion so amusing.

"Nay, let the honest man speak," he said, "messmate; he has as fine a cozening face as ever stood on a knavish pair of shoulders, and his are the true flourishes of eloquence, in the course of which men snip the cloth an inch too short. Now, I wish you to consider that you are both of a trade: he measures bales by the yard, and you by the sword; and so I will not have him chopped up till he has had a fair chase."

"You are a fool!" said Cleveland, endeavouring to shake his friend off. "Let me go! for, by Heaven, I will be foul of him!"

"Hold him fast," said the pedlar—"good dear merry gentleman, hold him fast!"

"Then say something for yourself," said Bunce: "use your gob-box, man; patter away, or, by my soul, I will let him loose on you!"

"He says I stole these goods," said Bryce, who now saw himself run so close that pleading to the charge became inevitable. "Now, how could I steal them when they are mine by fair and lawful purchase?"

"Purchase! you beggarly vagrant!" said Cleveland; "from whom did you dare to buy my clothes? or who had the impudence to sell them?"

"Just that worthy professor Mrs. Swertha, the housekeeper at Jarlshof, who acted as your executor," said the pedlar; "and a grieved heart she had."

"And so she was resolved to make a heavy pocket of it, I suppose," said the captain; "but how did she dare to sell the things left in her charge?"

"Why, she acted all for the best, good woman!" said the pedlar, anxious to protract the discussion until the arrival of succours; "and, if you will but reason, I am ready to account with you for the chest and all that it holds."

"Speak out, then, and let us have none of thy damnable evasions," said Captain Cleveland; "if you show ever so little purpose of being somewhat honest for once in thy life, I will not beat thee."

"Why, you see, noble captain," said the pedlar, and then muttered to himself, "Plague on Pate Paterson's cripple knee, they will be waiting for him, hirpling, useless body!"—then resumed aloud—"the country, you see, is in great perplexity —great perplexity, indeed—much perplexity, truly. There was your honour missing, that was loved by great and small —clean missing—nowhere to be heard of—a lost man—umquhile—dead—defunct!"

"You shall find me alive to your cost, you scoundrel!" said the irritated captain.

"Weel, but take patience, ye will not hear a body speak," said the jagger. "Then there was the lad Mordaunt Mertoun——"

"Ha!" said the captain, "what of him?"

"Cannot be heard of," said the pedlar; "clean and clear tint—a gone youth—fallen, it is thought, from the craig into the sea: he was aye venturous. I have had dealings with him for furs and feathers, whilk he swapped against powder and shot, and the like; and now he has worn out from among us—clean retired—utterly vanished, like the last puff of an auld wife's tobacco pipe."

"But what is all this to the captain's clothes, my dear friend?" said Bunce. "I must presently beat you myself unless you come to the point·"

"Weel, weel—patience, patience," said Bryce, waving his hand; "you will get all time enough. Weel, there are two folks gane, as I said, forbye the distress at Burgh-Westra about Mistress Minna's sad ailment——"

"Bring not *her* into your buffoonery, sirrah," said Cleveland, in a tone of anger, not so loud, but far deeper and more concentrated than he had hitherto used; "for, if you name her with less than reverence, I will crop the ears out of your head and make you swallow them on the spot!"

"He, he, he!" faintly laughed the jagger; "that were a pleasant jest! you are pleased to be witty. But, to say naething of Burgh-Westra, there is the carle at Jarlshof, he that was the auld Mertoun, Mordaunt's father, whom men thought as fast bound to the place he dwelt in as the Sumburgh Head itsell, naething maun serve him but he is lost as weel as the lave about whom I have spoken. And there's Magnus Troil —wi' favour be he named—taking horse; and there is pleasant Maister Claud Halcro taking boat, whilk he steers worst of any man in Zetland, his head running on rambling rhymes; and the factor body is on the stir—the Scots factor, him that is aye speaking of dikes and delving, and such unprofitable wark, which has naething of merchandise in it, and he is on the lang trot, too; so that ye might say, upon a manner, the tae half of the Mainland of Zetland is lost, and the other is running to and fro seeking it—awfu' times!"

Captain Cleveland had subdued his passion and listened to this tirade of the worthy man of merchandise, with impatience indeed, yet not without the hope of hearing something that might concern him. But his companion was now become impatient in his turn. "The clothes!" he exclaimed—"the clothes—the clothes—the clothes!" accompanying each repetition of the words with a flourish of his cane, the dexterity of which consisted in coming mighty near the jagger's ears without actually touching them.

The jagger, shrinking from each of these demonstrations, continued to exclaim: "Nay, sir—good sir—worthy sir—for the clothes—I found the worthy dame in great distress on account of her old maister, and on account of her young maister, and on account of worthy Captain Cleveland, and because of the distress of the worthy fowd's family, and the trouble of the great fowd himself, and because of the factor, and in respect of Claud Halcro, and on other accounts and respects. Also we mingled our sorrows and our tears with a bottle, as the holy text hath it, and called in the Ranzelman to our council, a worthy man, Neil Ronaldson by name, who hath a good reputation."

Here another flourish of the cane came so very near that it partly touched his ear. The jagger started back, and the truth, or that which he desired should be considered as such, bolted from him without more circumlocution; as a cork, after much unnecessary buzzing and fizzing, springs forth from a bottle of spruce beer.

"In brief, what the deil mair would you have of it? The woman sold me the kist of clothes: they are mine by purchase, and that is what I will live and die upon."

"In other words," said Cleveland, "this greedy old hag had the impudence to sell what was none of hers; and you, honest Bryce Snailsfoot, had the assurance to be the purchaser?"

"Ou dear, captain," said the conscientious pedlar, "what wad ye hae had twa poor folk to do? There was yoursell

gane that aught the things, and Maister Mordaunt was gane
that had them in keeping, and the things were but damply put
up, where they were rotting with moth and mould, and——"

"And so this old thief sold them, and you bought them, I
suppose, just to keep them from spoiling?" said Cleveland.

"Weel then," said the merchant, "I'm thinking, noble
captain, that wad be jest the gate of it."

"Well then, hark ye, you impudent scoundrel," said the
captain, "I do not wish to dirty my fingers with you, or to
make any disturbance in this place——"

"Good reason for that, captain—aha!" said the jagger, slyly.

"I will break your bones if you speak another word," replied Cleveland. "Take notice—I offer you fair terms: give
me back the black leathern pocket-book with the lock upon
it, and the purse with the doubloons, with some few of the
clothes I want, and keep the rest in the devil's name!"

"Doubloons ! ! !" exclaimed the jagger, with an exaltation
of voice intended to indicate the utmost extremity of surprise.
"What do I ken of doubloons? my dealing was for doublets,
and not for doubloons. If there were doubloons in the kist,
doubtless Swertha will have them in safe keeping for your
honour; the damp wouldna harm the gold, ye ken."

"Give me back my pocket-book and my goods, you rascally
thief, said Cleveland, "or without a word more I will beat
your brains out!"

The wily jagger, casting eye around him, saw that succour
was near, in the shape of a party of officers, six in number;
for several rencontres with the crew of the pirate had taught
the magistrates of Kirkwall to strengthen their police parties
when these strangers were in question.

"Ye had better keep the *thief* to suit yoursell, honoured
captain," said the jagger, emboldened by the approach of the
civil power; "for wha kens how a' these fine goods and bonny
dies were come by?"

This was uttered with such provoking slyness of look and
tone, that Cleveland made no further delay, but, seizing upon
the jagger by the collar, dragged him over his temporary coun-
ter, which was, with all the goods displayed thereon, overset

in the scuffle; and, holding him with one hand, inflicted on him with the other a severe beating with his cane. All this was done so suddenly and with such energy that Bryce Snailsfoot, though rather a stout man, was totally surprised by the vivacity of the attack, and made scarce any other effort at extricating himself than by roaring for assistance like a bull-calf. The "loitering aid" having at length come up, the officers made an effort to seize on Cleveland, and by their united exertions succeeded in compelling him to quit hold of the pedlar in order to defend himself from their assault. This he did with infinite strength, resolution, and dexterity, being at the same time well seconded by his friend Jack Bunce, who had seen with glee the drubbing sustained by the pedlar, and now combated tightly to save his companion from the consequences. But, as there had been for some time a growing feud between the townspeople and the crew of the rover, the former, provoked by the insolent deportment of the seamen, had resolved to stand by each other, and to aid the civil power upon such occasions of riot as should occur in future; and so many assistants came up to the rescue of the constables that Cleveland, after fighting most manfully, was at length brought to the ground and made prisoner. His more fortunate companion had escaped by speed of foot, as soon as he saw that the day must needs be determined against them.

The proud heart of Cleveland, which, even in its perversion, had in its feelings something of original nobleness, was like to burst when he felt himself borne down in this unworthy brawl, dragged into the town as a prisoner, and hurried through the streets towards the council-house, where the magistrates of the burgh were then seated in council. The probability of imprisonment, with all its consequences, rushed also upon his mind, and he cursed an hundred times the folly which had not rather submitted to the pedlar's knavery than involved him in so perilous an embarrassment.

But, just as they approached the door of the council-house, which is situated in the middle of the little town, the face of matters was suddenly changed by a new and unexpected incident.

Bunce, who had designed, by his precipitate retreat, to serve as well his friend as himself, had hied him to the haven, where the boat of the rover was then lying, and called the cockswain and boat's crew to the assistance of Cleveland. They now appeared on the scene—fierce desperadoes, as became their calling, with features bronzed by the tropical sun under which they had pursued it. They rushed at once amongst the crowd, laying about them with their stretchers; and, forcing their way up to Cleveland, speedily delivered him from the hands of the officers, who were totally unprepared to resist an attack so furious and so sudden, and carried him off in triumph towards the quay,—two or three of their number facing about from time to time to keep back the crowd, whose efforts to recover the prisoner were the less violent that most of the seamen were armed with pistols and cutlasses, as well as with the less lethal weapons which alone they had as yet made use of.

They gained their boat in safety, and jumped into it, carrying along with them Cleveland, to whom circumstances seemed to offer no other refuge, and pushed off for their vessel, singing in chorus to their oars an old ditty, of which the natives of Kirkwall could only hear the first stanza:

> "Robin Rover
> Said to his crew,
> 'Up with the black flag,
> Down with the blue!
> Fire on the main-top,
> Fire on the bow,
> Fire on the gun-deck,
> Fire down below!'"

The wild chorus of their voices was heard long after the words ceased to be intelligible. And thus was the pirate Cleveland again thrown almost involuntarily amongst those desperate associates from whom he had so often resolved to detach himself.

CHAPTER XXXIII.

Parental love, my friend, has power o'er wisdom,
And is the charm which, like the falconer's lure,
Can bring from heaven the highest soaring spirits.
So, when famed Prosper doff'd his magic robe,
It was Miranda pluck'd it from his shoulders.
                                        Old Play.

OUR wandering narrative must now return to Mordaunt Mertoun. We left him in the perilous condition of one who has received a severe wound, and we now find him in the condition of a convalescent—pale, indeed, and feeble from the loss of much blood and the effects of a fever which had followed the injury, but so far fortunate, that the weapon, having glanced on the ribs, had only occasioned a great effusion of blood, without touching any vital part, and was now wellnigh healed; so efficacious were the vulnerary plants and salves with which it had been treated by the sage Norna of Fitful Head.

The matron and her patient now sat together in a dwelling in a remote island. He had been transported, during his illness, and ere he had perfect consciousness, first to her singular habitation near Fitful Head and thence to her present abode, by one of the fishing-boats on the station of Burgh-Westra. For such was the command possessed by Norna over the superstitious character of her countrymen, that she never failed to find faithful agents to execute her commands, whatever these happened to be; and, as her orders were generally given under injunctions of the strictest secrecy, men reciprocally wondered at occurrences which had in fact been produced by their own agency and that of their neighbours, and in which, had they communicated freely with each other, no shadow of the marvellous would have remained.

Mordaunt was now seated by the fire, in an apartment indifferently well furnished, having a book in his hand, which he looked upon from time to time with signs of *ennui* and impatience—feelings which at length so far overcame him that, flinging the volume on the table, he fixed his eyes on the fire, and assumed the attitude of one who is engaged in unpleasant meditation.

Norna, who sat opposite to him, and appeared busy in the composition of some drug or unguent, anxiously left her seat, and, approaching Mordaunt, felt his pulse, making at the same time the most affectionate inquiries whether he felt any sudden pain, and where it was seated. The manner in which Mordaunt replied to these earnest inquiries, although worded so as to express gratitude for her kindness, while he disclaimed any feeling of indisposition, did not seem to give satisfaction to the pythoness.

"Ungrateful boy!" she said, "for whom I have done so much; you whom I have rescued, by my power and skill, from the very gates of death—are you already so weary of me, that you cannot refrain from showing how desirous you are to spend at a distance from me the very first intelligent days of the life which I have restored you?"

"You do me injustice, my kind preserver," replied Mordaunt: "I am not tired of your society; but I have duties which recall me to ordinary life."

"Duties!" repeated Norna; "and what duties can or ought to interfere with the gratitude which you owe to me? Duties! Your thoughts are on the use of your gun, or on clambering among the rocks in quest of sea-fowl. For these exercises your strength doth not yet fit you; and yet these are the duties to which you are so anxious to return!"

"Not so, my good and kind mistress," said Mordaunt. "To name one duty, out of many, which makes me seek to leave you, now that my strength permits, let me mention that of a son to his father."

"To your father!" said Norna, with a laugh that had something in it almost frantic. "Oh! you know not how we can, in these islands, at once cancel such duties! And, for your father," she added, proceeding more calmly, "what has he done for you, to deserve the regard and duty you speak of? Is he not the same who, as you have long since told me, left you for so many years poorly nourished among strangers, without inquiring whether you were alive or dead, and only sending, from time to time, supplies in such fashion as men relieve the leprous wretch to whom they fling alms from a distance? And, in these later years, when he had made you the companion of his misery, he has been by starts your pedagogue, by starts your tormentor, but never, Mordaunt—never your father."

"Something of truth there is in what you say," replied Mordaunt. "My father is not fond; but he is, and has ever been, effectively kind. Men have not their affections in their power; and it is a child's duty to be grateful for the benefits which he receives, even when coldly bestowed. My father has conferred instruction on me, and I am convinced he loves me. He is unfortunate; and, even if he loved me not——"

"And he does *not* love you," said Norna, hastily; "he never loved anything, or any one, save himself. He is unfortunate, but well are his misfortunes deserved. O Mordaunt, you have one parent only—one parent, who loves you as the drops of the heart-blood!"

"I know I have but one parent," replied Mordaunt: "my mother has been long dead. But your words contradict each other."

"They do not—they do not," said Norna, in a paroxysm of the deepest feeling; "you have but one parent. Your unhappy mother is not dead—I would to God that she were!—but she is not dead. Thy mother is the only parent that loves thee; and I—I, Mordaunt," throwing herself on his neck, "am that most unhappy, yet most happy, mother."

She closed him in a strict and convulsive embrace; and tears, the first, perhaps, which she had shed for many years, burst in torrents as she sobbed on his neck. Astonished at what he heard, felt, and saw, moved by the excess of her agitation, yet disposed to ascribe this burst of passion to insanity, Mordaunt vainly endeavoured to tranquillise the mind of this extraordinary person.

"Ungrateful boy!" she said, "who but a mother would have watched over thee as I have watched? From the instant I saw thy father, when he little thought by whom he was observed, a space now many years back, I knew him well; and, under his charge, I saw you, then a stripling; while nature, speaking loud in my bosom, assured me thou wert blood of my blood and bone of my bone. Think how often you have wondered to see me, when least expected, in your places of pastime and resort! Think how often my eye has watched you on the giddy precipices, and muttered those charms which subdue the evil demons, who show themselves to the climber on the giddiest point of his path, and force him to quit his hold! Did I not hang around thy neck, in pledge of thy safety, that chain of gold, which an elfin king gave to the founder of our race? Would I have given that dear gift to any but to the son of my bosom? Mordaunt, my power has done that for thee that a mere mortal mother would dread to think of. I have conjured the mermaid at midnight, that thy bark might be prosperous on the haaf! I have hushed the winds, and navies have flapped their empty sails against the mast in inactivity, that you might safely indulge your sport upon the crags!"

Mordaunt, perceiving that she was growing yet wilder in her talk, endeavoured to frame an answer which should be at once indulgent, soothing, and calculated to allay the rising warmth of her imagination.

"Dear Norna," he said, "I have indeed many reasons to call you mother, who have bestowed so many benefits upon me; and from me you shall ever receive the affection and duty of a child. But the chain you mentioned—it has vanished from my neck: I have not seen it since the ruffian stabbed me."

"Alas! and can you think of it at this moment?" said Norna, in a sorrowful accent. "But be it so; and know, it was I took it from thy neck, and tied it around the neck of her who is dearest to you; in token that the union betwixt you, which has been the only earthly wish which I have had the power to form, shall yet—even yet, be accomplished—ay, although hell should open to forbid the banns!"

"Alas!" said Mordaunt, with a sigh, "you remember not

the difference betwixt our situation—her father is wealthy, and of ancient birth."

"Not more wealthy than will be the heir of Norna of Fitful Head," answered the pythoness; "not of better or more ancient blood than that which flows in thy veins, derived from thy mother, the descendant of the same jarls and sea-kings from whom Magnus boasts his origin. Or dost thou think, like the pedant and fanatic strangers who have come amongst us, that thy blood is dishonoured because my union with thy father did not receive the sanction of a priest? Know, that we were wedded after the ancient manner of the Norse: our hands were clasped within the circle of Odin, with such deep vows of eternal fidelity as even the laws of these usurping Scots would have sanctioned as equivalent to a blessing before the altar. To the offspring of such a union Magnus has nought to object. It was weak, it was criminal, on my part, but it conveyed no infamy to the birth of my son."

The composed and collected manner in which Norna argued these points began to impose upon Mordaunt an incipient belief in the truth of what she said; and, indeed, she added so many circumstances, satisfactorily and rationally connected with each other, as seemed to confute the notion that her story was altogether the delusion of that insanity which sometimes showed itself in her speech and actions. A thousand confused ideas rushed upon him, when he supposed it possible that the unhappy person before him might actually have a right to claim from him the respect and affection due to a parent from a son. He could only surmount them by turning his mind to a different, and scarce less interesting, topic, resolving within himseilf to take time for farther inquiry and mature consideration ere he either rejected or admitted the claim which Norna preferred upon his affection and duty. His benefactress, at least, she undoubtedly was, and he could not err in paying her, as such, the respect and attention due from a son to a mother; and so far, therefore, he might gratify Norna without otherwise standing committed.

"And do you then really think, my mother—since so you bid me term you," said Mordaunt, "that the proud Magnus

Troil may, by any inducement, be prevailed upon to relinquish the angry feelings which he has of late adopted towards me, and to permit my addresses to his daughter Brenda?"

"Brenda!" repeated Norna—"who talks of Brenda? it was of Minna that I spoke to you."

"But it was of Brenda that I thought," replied Mordaunt, "of her that I now think, and of her alone that I will ever think."

"Impossible, my son!" replied Norna. "You cannot be so dull of heart, so poor of spirit, as to prefer the idle mirth and housewife simplicity of the younger sister to the deep feeling and high mind of the noble-spirited Minna? Who would stoop to gather the lowly violet that might have the rose for stretching out his hand?"

"Some think the lowliest flowers are the sweetest," replied Mordaunt, "and in that faith will I live and die."

"You dare not tell me so!" answered Norna, fiercely; then, instantly changing her tone, and taking his hand in the most affectionate manner, she proceeded: "You must not—you will not tell me so, my dear son: you will not break a mother's heart in the very first hour in which she has embraced her child! Nay, do not answer, but hear me. You must wed Minna; I have bound around her neck a fatal amulet, on which the happiness of both depends. The labours of my life have for years had this direction. Thus it must be, and not otherwise: Minna must be the bride of my son!"

"But is not Brenda equally near, equally dear to you?" replied Mordaunt.

"As near in blood," said Norna, "but not so dear—no, not half so dear, in affection. Minna's mild, yet high and contemplative, spirit renders her a companion meet for one whose ways, like mine, are beyond the ordinary paths of this world. Brenda is a thing of common and ordinary life, an idle laugher and scoffer, who would level art with ignorance, and reduce power to weakness, by disbelieving and turning into ridicule whatever is beyond the grasp of her own shallow intellect."

"She is, indeed," answered Mordaunt, "neither superstitious nor enthusiastic, and I love her the better for it. Remember also, my mother, that she returns my affection, and that Minna, if she loves any one, loves the stranger Cleveland."

"She does not—she dares not," answered Norna, "nor dares he pursue her farther. I told him, when first he came to Burgh-Westra, that I destined her for you."

"And to that rash annunciation," said Mordaunt, "I owe this man's persevering enmity, my wound, and wellnigh the loss of my life. See, my mother, to what point your intrigues have already conducted us, and, in Heaven's name, prosecute them no farther!"

It seemed as if this reproach struck Norna with the force at once and vivacity of lightning; for she struck her forehead with her hand, and seemed about to drop from her seat. Mordaunt, greatly shocked, hastened to catch her in his arms, and, though scarce knowing what to say, attempted to utter some incoherent expressions.

"Spare me, Heaven—spare me!" were the first words which she muttered; "do not let my crime be avenged by his means! Yes, young man," she said, after a pause, "you have dared to tell what I dared not tell myself. You have pressed that upon me which, if it be truth, I cannot believe and yet continue to live!"

Mordaunt in vain endeavoured to interrupt her with protestations of his ignorance how he had offended or grieved her, and of his extreme regret that he had unintentionally done either. She proceeded, while her voice trembled wildly, with vehemence.

"Yes! you have touched on that dark suspicion which poisons the consciousness of my power—the sole boon which was given me in exchange for innocence and for peace of mind! Your voice joins that of the demon which, even while the elements confess me their mistress, whispers to me: 'Norna, this is but delusion: your power rests but in the idle belief of the ignorant, supported by a thousand petty artifices of your own.' This is what Brenda says—this is what you would say; and false, scandalously false, as it is, there are rebellious thoughts in this wild brain of mine (touching her forehead with her finger as she spoke) that, like an insurrection in an invaded country, arise to take part against their distressed sovereign. Spare me, my son!" she continued, in a voice of supplication—"spare me! the sovereignty of which your words would deprive me is no enviable exaltation. Few would covet to rule over gibbering ghosts, and howling winds, and raging currents. My throne is a cloud, my sceptre a meteor, my realm is only peopled with fantasies; but I must either cease to be, or continue to be the mightiest as well as the most miserable of beings!" [1]

"Do not speak thus mournfully, my dear and unhappy benefactress," said Mordaunt, much affected; "I will think of your power whatever you would have me believe. But, for your own sake, view the matter otherwise. Turn your thoughts from such agitating and mystical studies—from such wild subjects of contemplation, into another and a better channel. Life will again have charms, and religion will have comforts, for you."

She listened to him with some composure, as if she weighed his counsel, and desired to be guided by it; but, as he ended, she shook her head and exclaimed:

"It cannot be. I must remain the dreaded—the mystical—the Reim-kennar—the controller of the elements, or I must be no more! I have no alternative, no middle station. My post must be high on yon lofty headland, where never stood human foot save mine, or I must sleep at the bottom of the unfathomable ocean, its white billows booming over my senseless corpse. The parricide shall never also be denounced as the impostor!"

"The parricide!" echoed Mordaunt, stepping back in horror.

"Yes, my son!" answered Norna, with a stern composure even more frightful than her former impetuosity, "within these fatal walls my father met his death by my means. In yonder chamber was he found a livid and lifeless corpse. Beware of filial disobedience, for such are its fruits!"

So saying, she arose and left the apartment, where Mordaunt remained alone to meditate at leisure upon the extraordinary communication which he had received. He himself

[1] See Character of Norna. Note 42.

had been taught by his father a disbelief in the ordinary superstitions of Zetland; and he now saw that Norna, however ingenious in duping others, could not altogether impose on herself. This was a strong circumstance in favour of her sanity of intellect; but, on the other hand, her imputing to herself the guilt of parricide seemed so wild and improbable as, in Mordaunt's opinion, to throw much doubt upon her other assertions.

He had leisure enough to make up his mind on these particulars, for no one approached the solitary dwelling, of which Norna, her dwarf, and he himself were the sole inhabitants. The Hoy Island in which it stood is rude, bold, and lofty, consisting entirely of three hills, or rather one huge mountain divided into three summits, with the chasms, rents, and valleys which descend from its summit to the sea, while its crest, rising to great height, and shivered into rocks which seem almost inaccessible, intercepts the mists as they drive from the Atlantic, and, often obscured from the human eye, forms the dark and unmolested retreat of hawks, eagles, and other birds of prey.[1]

The soil of the island is wet, mossy, cold, and unproductive, presenting a sterile and desolate appearance, excepting where the sides of small rivulets, or mountain ravines, are fringed with dwarf bushes of birch, hazel, and wild currant, some of them so tall as to be denominated trees in that bleak and bare country.

But the view of the sea-beach, which was Mordaunt's favourite walk, when his convalescent state began to permit him to take exercise, had charms which compensated the wild appearance of the interior. A broad and beautiful sound, or strait, divides this lonely and mountainous island from Pomona, and in the centre of that sound lies, like a tablet composed of emerald, the beautiful and verdant little island of Graemsay. On the distant Mainland is seen the town or village of Stromness, the excellence of whose haven is generally evinced by a considerable number of shipping in the roadstead, and, from the bay growing narrower and lessening as

[1] See Note 43.

it recedes, runs inland into Pomona, where its tide fills the fine sheet of water called the Loch of Stennis.

On this beach Mordaunt was wont to wander for hours, with an eye not insensible to the beauties of the view, though his thoughts were agitated with the most embarrassing meditations on his own situation. He was resolved to leave the island as soon as the establishment of his health should permit him to travel; yet gratitude to Norna, of whom he was at least the adopted, if not the real, son, would not allow him to depart without her permission, even if he could obtain means of conveyance, of which he saw little possibility. It was only by importunity that he extorted from his hostess a promise that, if he would consent to regulate his motions according to her directions, she would herself convey him to the capital of the Orkney Islands, when the approaching fair of St. Olla should take place there.

CHAPTER XXXIV.

Hark to the insult loud, the bitter sneer,
The fierce threat answering to the brutal jeer:
Oaths fly like pistol-shots, and vengeful words
Clash with each other like conflicting swords.
The robber's quarrel by such sounds is shown,
And true men have some chance to gain their own.
                              Captivity, a Poem.

WHEN Cleveland, borne off in triumph from his assailants in Kirkwall, found himself once more on board the pirate vessel, his arrival was hailed with hearty cheers by a considerable part of the crew, who rushed to shake hands with him and offer their congratulations on his return; for the situation of a buccanier captain raised him very little above the level of the lowest of his crew, who, in all social intercourse, claimed the privilege of being his equal.

When his faction, for so these clamorous friends might be termed, had expressed their own greetings, they hurried Cleveland forward to the stern, where Goffe, their present commander, was seated on a gun, listening in a sullen and discontented mood to the shout which announced Cleveland's welcome. He was a man betwixt forty and fifty, rather under the middle size, but so very strongly made that his crew used to compare him to a sixty-four cut down. Black-haired, bull-necked, and beetle-browed, his clumsy strength and ferocious countenance contrasted strongly with the manly figure and open countenance of Cleveland, in which even the practice of his atrocious profession had not been able to eradicate a natural grace of motion and generosity of expression. The two piratical captains looked upon each other for some time in silence, while the partizans of each gathered around him. The elder part of the crew were the principal adherents of Goffe, while the young fellows, among whom Jack Bunce was a principal leader and agitator, were in general attached to Cleveland.

At length Goffe broke silence: "You are welcome aboard, Captain Cleveland. Smash my taffrail! I suppose you think yourself commodore yet! but that was over, by G—, when you lost your ship, and be d—d!"

And here, once for all, we may take notice that it was the gracious custom of this commander to mix his words and oaths in nearly equal proportions, which he was wont to call *shotting* his discourse. As we delight not, however, in the discharge of such artillery, we shall only indicate by a space like this —— the places in which these expletives occurred; and thus, if the reader will pardon a very poor pun, we will reduce Captain Goffe's volley of sharp-shot into an explosion of blank cartridges. To his insinuations that he was come on board to assume the chief command, Cleveland replied, that he neither desired nor would accept any such promotion, but would only ask Captain Goffe for a cast of the boat to put him ashore in one of the other islands, as he had no wish either to command Goffe or to remain in a vessel under his orders.

"And why not under my orders, brother?" demanded Goffe, very austerely; "—— —— —— are you too good a man, —— —— —— with your cheese-toaster and your jib there, —— —— to serve under my orders, and be d—d to you, where there are so many gentlemen that are elder and better seamen than yourself?"

"I wonder which of these capital seamen it was," said Cleveland, coolly, "that laid the ship under the fire of yon six-gun battery, that could blow her out of the water, if they had a mind, before you could either cut or slip? Elder and better sailors than I may like to serve under such a lubber, but I beg to be excused for my own share, captain—that's all I have got to tell you."

"By G—, I think you are both mad!" said Hawkins, the boatswain: "a meeting with sword and pistol may be devilish good fun in its way when no better is to be had; but who the devil that had common sense amongst a set of gentlemen in our condition would fall a-quarrelling with each other, to let these duck-winged, web-footed islanders have a chance of knocking us all upon the head?"

"Well said, old Hawkins!" observed Derrick, the quarter-master, who was an officer of very considerable importance among these rovers; "I say, if the two captains won't agree to live together quietly, and club both heart and head to defend the vessel, why, d—n me, depose them both, say I, and choose another in their stead!"

"Meaning yourself, I suppose, Master Quartermaster!" said Jack Bunce; "but that cock won't fight. He that is to command gentlemen should be a gentleman himself, I think; and I give my vote for Captain Cleveland, as spirited and as gentleman-like a man as ever daffed the world aside and bid it pass!"

"What! you call yourself a gentleman, I warrant!" retorted Derrick; "why, —— your eyes! a tailor would make a better out of the worst suit of rags in your strolling wardrobe! It is a shame for men of spirit to have such a Jack-a-dandy scarecrow on board!"

Jack Bunce was so incensed at these base comparisons that, without more ado, he laid his hand on his sword. The carpenter, however, and boatswain interfered, the former brandishing his broad axe, and swearing he would put the skull of the first who should strike a blow past clouting, and the latter reminding them that, by their articles, all quarrelling, striking, or more especially fighting, on board was strictly prohibited; and that, if any gentleman had a quarrel to settle, they were to go ashore and decide it with cutlass and pistol in presence of two of their messmates.

"I have no quarrel with any one, — — —!" said Goffe, sullenly. "Captain Cleveland has wandered about among the islands here, amusing himself, — — —! and we have wasted our time and property in waiting for him, when we might have been adding twenty or thirty thousand dollars to the stock-purse. However, if it pleases the rest of the gentlemen-adventurers, — — —! why, I shall not grumble about it."

"I propose," said the boatswain, "that there should be a general council called in the great cabin, according to our articles, that we may consider what course we are to hold in this matter."

A general assent followed the boatswain's proposal; for every one found his own account in these general councils, in which each of the rovers had a free vote. By far the greater part of the crew only valued this franchise as it allowed them, upon such solemn occasions, an unlimited quantity of liquor— a right which they failed not to exercise to the uttermost—by way of aiding their deliberations. But a few amongst the adventurers, who united some degree of judgment with the daring and profligate character of their profession, were wont, at such periods, to limit themselves within the bounds of comparative sobriety, and by these, under the apparent form of a vote of the general council, all things of moment relating to the voyage and undertakings of the pirates were in fact determined. The rest of the crew, when they recovered from their intoxication, were easily persuaded that the resolution adopted had been the legitimate effort of the combined wisdom of the whole senate.

Upon the present occasion the debauch had proceeded until the greater part of the crew were, as usual, displaying inebriation in all its most brutal and disgraceful shapes: swearing empty and unmeaning oaths; venting the most horrid imprecations in the mere gaiety of their heart; singing songs, the ribaldry of which was only equalled by their profaneness; and, from the middle of this earthly hell, the two captains, together with one or two of their principal adherents, as also the carpenter and boatswain, who always took a lead on such occasions, had drawn together into a pandemonium, or privy council, of their own, to consider what was to be done; for, as the boatswain metaphorically observed, they were in a narrow channel, and behoved to keep sounding the tide-way.

When they began their consultations, the friends of Goffe remarked, to their great displeasure, that he had not observed the wholesome rule to which we have just alluded; but that, in endeavouring to drown his mortification at the sudden appearance of Cleveland, and the reception he met with from the crew, the elder captain had not been able to do so without overflowing his reason at the same time. His natural sullen taciturnity had prevented this from being observed until the council began its deliberations, when it proved impossible to hide it.

The first person who spoke was Cleveland, who said that, so far from wishing the command of the vessel, he desired no favour at any one's hand, except to land him upon some island or holm at a distance from Kirkwall, and leave him to shift for himself.

The boatswain remonstrated strongly against this resolution. "The lads," he said, "all knew Cleveland, and could trust his seamanship, as well as his courage; besides, he never let the grog get quite uppermost, and was always in proper trim, either to sail the ship or to fight the ship, whereby she was never without some one to keep her course when he was on board. And as for the noble Captain Goffe," continued the mediator, "he is as stout a heart as ever broke biscuit, and that I will uphold him; but then, when he has his grog aboard—I speak to his face—he is so d—d funny with his cranks and his jests, that there is no living with him. You all remember how nigh he had run the ship on that cursed Horse of Copinsha, as they call it, just by way of frolic; and then you know how he fired off his pistol under the table when we were at the great council, and shot Jack Jenkins in the knee, and cost the poor devil his leg with his pleasantry."[1]

"Jack Jenkins was not a chip the worse," said the carpen-

See Avery's Pleasantry. Note 44.

ter. "I took the leg off with my saw as well as any loblolly-boy in the land could have done, heated my broad axe, and seared the stump—ay, by ——! and made a jury-leg that he shambles about with as well as ever he did; for Jack could never cut a feather."

"You are a clever fellow, carpenter," replied the boatswain —"a d—d clever fellow! but I had rather you tried your saw and red-hot axe upon the ship's knee-timbers than on mine, sink me! But that here is not the case. The question is, if we shall part with Captain Cleveland here, who is a man of thought and action, whereby it is my belief it would be heaving the pilot overboard when the gale is blowing on a lee-shore. And, I must say, it is not the part of a true heart to leave his mates, who have been here waiting for him till they have missed stays. Our water is wellnigh out, and we have junketed till provisions are low with us. We cannot sail without provisions; we cannot get provisions without the good-will of the Kirkwall folks. If we remain here longer, the 'Halcyon' frigate will be down upon us—she was seen off Peterhead two days since—and we shall hang up at the yard-arm to be sun-dried. Now, Captain Cleveland will get us out of the hobble, if any can. He can play the gentleman with these Kirkwall folks, and knows how to deal with them on fair terms, and foul too, if there be occasion for it."

"And so you would turn honest Captain Goffe a-grazing, would ye?" said an old weatherbeaten pirate, who had but one eye; "what though he has his humours, and made my eye douse the glim in his fancies and frolics, he is as honest a man as ever walked a quarter-deck, for all that; and d—n me but I stand by him so long as t'other lantern is lit!"

"Why, you would not hear me out," said Hawkins: "a man might as well talk to so many negers! I tell you, I propose that Cleveland shall only be captain from one *post meridiem* to five A.M., during which time Goffe is always drunk."

The captain of whom he last spoke gave sufficient proof of the truth of his words by uttering an inarticulate growl, and attempting to present a pistol at the mediator Hawkins.

"Why, look ye now!" said Derrick, "there is all the sense he has, to get drunk on council-day, like one of these poor silly fellows!"

"Ay," said Bunce, "drunk as Davy's sow, in the face of the field, the fray, and the senate!"

"But, nevertheless," continued Derrick, "it will never do to have two captains in the same day. I think week about might suit better; and let Cleveland take the first turn."

"There are as good here as any of them," said Hawkins; "howsomdever, I object nothing to Captain Cleveland, and I think he may help us into deep water as well as another."

"Ay," exclaimed Bunce, "and a better figure he will make at bringing these Kirkwallers to order than his sober predecessor! So Captain Cleveland for ever!"

"Stop, gentlemen," said Cleveland, who had hitherto been silent; "I hope you will not choose me captain without my own consent?"

"Ay, by the blue vault of heaven will we," said Bunce, "if it be *pro bono publico!*"

"But hear me, at least," said Cleveland. "I do consent to take command of the vessel, since you wish it, and because I see you will ill get out of the scrape without me."

"Why, then, I say, Cleveland for ever, again!" shouted Bunce.

"Be quiet, prithee, dear Bunce!—honest Altamont!" said Cleveland. "I undertake the business on this condition— that, when I have got the ship cleared for her voyage, with provisions and so forth, you will be content to restore Captain Goffe to the command, as I said before, and put me ashore somewhere, to shift for myself. You will then be sure it is impossible I can betray you, since I will remain with you to the last moment."

"Ay, and after the last moment, too, by the blue vault! or I mistake the matter," muttered Bunce to himself.

The matter was now put to the vote; and so confident were the crew in Cleveland's superior address and management, that the temporary deposition of Goffe found little resistance even among his own partizans, who reasonably enough observed: "He might at least have kept sober to look after his own business. E'en let him put it to rights again himself next morning, if he will."

But when the next morning came, the drunken part of the crew, being informed of the issue of the deliberations of the council, to which they were virtually held to have assented, showed such a superior sense of Cleveland's merits, that Goffe, sulky and malcontent as he was, judged it wisest for the present to suppress his feelings of resentment, until a safer opportunity for suffering them to explode, and to submit to the degradation which so frequently took place among a piratical crew.

Cleveland, on his part, resolved to take upon him, with spirit and without loss of time, the task of extricating his ship's company from their perilous situation. For this purpose, he ordered the boat, with the purpose of going ashore in person, carrying with him twelve of the stoutest and best men of the crew, all very handsomely appointed (for the success of their nefarious profession had enabled the pirates to assume nearly as gay dresses as their officers), and above all, each man being sufficiently armed with cutlass and pistols, and several having pole-axes and poniards.

Cleveland himself was gallantly attired in a blue coat, lined with crimson silk, and laced with gold very richly, crimson damask waistcoat and breeches, a velvet cap, richly embroidered, with a white feather, white silk stockings, and red-heeled shoes, which were the extremity of finery among the gallants of the day. He had a gold chain several times folded round his neck, which sustained a whistle of the same metal, the ensign of his authority. Above all, he wore a decoration peculiar to those daring depredators, who, besides one, or perhaps two, brace of pistols at their belt, had usually two additional brace, of the finest mounting and workmanship, suspended over their shoulders in a sort of sling or scarf of crimson ribbon. The hilt and mounting of the captain's sword corresponded in value to the rest of his appointments, and his natural good mien was so well adapted to the whole equipment that, when he appeared on deck, he was received with a general shout by the crew, who, as in other popular societies, judged a great deal by the eye.

Cleveland took with him in the boat, amongst others, his predecessor in office, Goffe, who was also very richly dressed, but who, not having the advantage of such an exterior as Cleveland's, looked like a boorish clown in the dress of a courtier, or rather like a vulgar-faced footpad decked in the spoils of some one whom he has murdered, and whose claim to the property of his garments is rendered doubtful in the eyes of all who look upon him by the mixture of awkwardness, remorse, cruelty, and insolence which clouds his countenance. Cleveland probably chose to take Goffe ashore with him to prevent his having any opportunity, during his absence, to debauch the crew from their allegiance. In this guise they left the ship, and, singing to their oars, while the water foamed higher at the chorus, soon reached the quay of Kirkwall.

The command of the vessel was in the mean time entrusted to Bunce, upon whose allegiance Cleveland knew that he might perfectly depend, and, in a private conversation with him of some length, he gave him directions how to act in such emergencies as might occur.

These arrangements being made, and Bunce having been repeatedly charged to stand upon his guard alike against the adherents of Goffe and any attempt from the shore, the boat put off. As she approached the harbour, Cleveland displayed a white flag, and could observe that their appearance seemed to occasion a good deal of bustle and alarm. People were seen running to and fro, and some of them appeared to be getting under arms. The battery was manned hastily, and the English colours displayed. These were alarming symptoms, the rather that Cleveland knew that, though there were no artillerymen in Kirkwall, yet there were many sailors perfectly competent to the management of great guns, and willing enough to undertake such service in case of need.

Noting these hostile preparations with a heedful eye, but suffering nothing like doubt or anxiety to appear on his countenance, Cleveland ran the boat right for the quay, on which several people, armed with muskets, rifles, and fowling-pieces, and others with half-pikes and whaling-knives, were now assembled, as if to oppose his landing. Apparently, however, they had not positively determined what measures they were to pursue; for, when the boat reached the quay, those immediately opposite bore back, and suffered Cleveland and his party to leap ashore without hinderance. They immediately drew up on the quay, except two, who, as their captain had commanded, remained in the boat, which they put off to a little distance—a manœuvre which, while it placed the boat (the only one belonging to the sloop) out of danger of being seized, indicated a sort of careless confidence in Cleveland and his party, which was calculated to intimidate their opponents.

The Kirkwallers, however, showed the old Northern blood, put a manly face upon the matter, and stood upon the quay, with their arms shouldered, directly opposite to the rovers, and blocking up against them the street which leads to the town.

Cleveland was the first who spoke, as the parties stood thus looking upon each other. "How is this, gentlemen burghers?" he said; "are you Orkney folks turned Highlandmen, that you are all under arms so early this morning; or have you manned the quay to give me the honour of a salute, upon taking the command of my ship?"

The burghers looked on each other, and one of them replied to Cleveland: "We do not know who you are; it was that other man," pointing to Goffe, "who used to come ashore as captain."

"That other gentleman is my mate, and commands in my absence," said Cleveland; "but what is that to the purpose? I wish to speak with your lord mayor, or whatever you call him."

"The provost is sitting in council with the magistrates," answered the spokesman.

"So much the better," replied Cleveland. "Where do their worships meet?"

"In the council-house," answered the other.

"Then make way for us, gentlemen, if you please, for my people and I are going there."

There was a whisper among the townspeople; but several

were unresolved upon engaging in a desperate, and perhaps an unnecessary, conflict with desperate men; and the more determined citizens formed the hasty reflection that the strangers might be more easily mastered in the house, or perhaps in the narrow streets which they had to traverse, than when they stood drawn up and prepared for battle upon the quay. They suffered them, therefore, to proceed unmolested; and Cleveland, moving very slowly, keeping his people close together, suffering no one to press upon the flanks of his little detachment, and making four men, who constituted his rear-guard, turn round and face to the rear from time to time, rendered it, by his caution, a very dangerous task to make any attempt upon them.

In this manner they ascended the narrow street, and reached the council-house, where the magistrates were actually sitting, as the citizen had informed Cleveland. Here the inhabitants began to press forward, with the purpose of mingling with the pirates, and availing themselves of the crowd in the narrow entrance to secure as many as they could, without allowing them room for the free use of their weapons. But this also had Cleveland foreseen, and, ere entering the council-room, he caused the entrance to be cleared and secured, commanding four of his men to face down the street, and as many to confront the crowd who were thrusting each other from above. The burghers recoiled back from the ferocious, swarthy, and sunburnt countenances, as well as the levelled arms, of these desperadoes, and Cleveland, with the rest of his party, entered the council-room, where the magistrates were sitting in council, with very little attendance. These gentlemen were thus separated effectually from the citizens, who looked to them for orders, and were perhaps more completely at the mercy of Cleveland than he, with his little handful of men, could be said to be at that of the multitude by whom they were surrounded.

The magistrates seemed sensible of their danger; for they looked upon each other in some confusion, when Cleveland thus addressed them:

"Good morrow, gentlemen; I hope there is no unkindness

betwixt us. I am come to talk with you about getting supplies for my ship yonder in the roadstead; we cannot sail without them."

"Your ship, sir!" said the provost, who was a man of sense and spirit; "how do we know that you are her captain?"

"Look at me," said Cleveland, "and you will, I think, scarce ask the question again."

The magistrate looked at him, and accordingly did not think proper to pursue that part of the inquiry, but proceeded to say: "And if you are her captain, whence comes she, and where is she bound for? You look too much like a man-of-war's-man to be master of a trader, and we know that you do not belong to the British navy."

"There are more men-of-war on the sea than sail under the British flag," replied Cleveland; "but say that I were commander of a free-trader here, willing to exchange tobacco, brandy, gin, and such-like for cured fish and hides, why, I do not think I deserve so very bad usage from the merchants of Kirkwall as to deny me provisions for my money?"

"Look you, captain," said the town-clerk, "it is not that we are so very strait-laced neither; for, when gentlemen of your cloth come this way, it is as weel, as I tauld the provost, just to do as the collier did when he met the devil; and that is, to have naething to say to them, if they have naething to say to us; and there is the gentleman," pointing to Goffe, "that was captain before you, and may be captain after you— ("The cuckold speaks truth in that," muttered Goffe)—he knows well how handsomely we entertained him, till he and his men took upon them to run through the town like hellicat devils. I see one of them there! that was the very fellow that stopped my servant-wench on the street, as she carried the lantern home before me, and insulted her before my face!"

"If it please your noble mayorship's honour and glory," said Derrick, the fellow at whom the town-clerk pointed, "it was not I that brought-to the bit of a tender that carried the lantern in the poop: it was quite a different sort of a person."

"Who was it then, sir?" said the provost.

"Why, please your majesty's worship," said Derrick, making several sea bows, and describing as nearly as he could the exterior of the worthy magistrate himself, "he was an elderly gentleman, Dutch-built, round in the stern, with a white wig and a red nose—very like your majesty, I think"; then, turning to a comrade, he added: "Jack, don't you think the fellow that wanted to kiss the pretty girl with the lantern t'other night was very like his worship?"

"By G—, Tom Derrick," answered the party appealed to, "I believe it is the very man!"

"This is insolence which we can make you repent of, gentlemen!" said the magistrate, justly irritated at their effrontery; "you have behaved in this town as if you were in an Indian village at Madagascar. You yourself, captain, if captain you be, were at the head of another riot no longer since than yesterday. We will give you no provisions till we know better whom we are supplying. And do not think to bully us; when I shake this handkerchief out at the window which is at my elbow, your ship goes to the bottom. Remember she lies under the guns of our battery."

"And how many of these guns are honeycombed, Mr. Mayor?" said Cleveland. He put the question by chance; but instantly perceived, from a sort of confusion which the provost in vain endeavoured to hide, that the artillery of Kirkwall was not in the best order. "Come—come, Mr. Mayor," he said, "bullying will go down with us as little as with you. Your guns yonder will do more harm to the poor old sailors who are to work them than to our sloop; and if we bring a broadside to bear on the town, why, your wives' crockery will be in some danger. And then to talk to us of seamen being a little frolicsome ashore, why, when are they otherwise? You have the Greenland whalers playing the devil among you every now and then; and the very Dutchmen cut capers in the streets of Kirkwall, like porpoises before a gale of wind. I am told you are a man of sense, and I am sure you and I could settle this matter in the course of a five minutes' palaver."

"Well, sir," said the provost, "I will hear what you have to say, if you will walk this way."

Cleveland accordingly followed him into a small interior apartment, and, when there, addressed the provost thus: "I will lay aside my pistols, sir, if you are afraid of them."

"D—n your pistols!" answered the provost; "I have served the king, and fear the smell of powder as little as you do!"

"So much the better," said Cleveland, "for you will hear me the more coolly. Now, sir, let us be what perhaps you suspect us, or let us be anything else, what, in the name of Heaven, can you get by keeping us here but blows and bloodshed? for which, believe me, we are much better provided than you can pretend to be. The point is a plain one: you are desirous to be rid of us, we are desirous to be gone. Let us have the means of departure, and we leave you instantly."

"Look ye, captain," said the provost, "I thirst for no man's blood. You are a pretty fellow, as there were many among the buccaniers in my time; but there is no harm in wishing you a better trade. You should have the stores and welcome, for your money, so you would make these seas clear of you. But then, here lies the rub. The 'Halcyon' frigate is expected here in these parts immediately; when she hears of you she will be at you; for there is nothing the white lapelle loves better than a rover: you are seldom without a cargo of dollars. Well, he comes down, gets you under his stern——"

"Blows us into the air, if you please," said Cleveland.

"Nay, that must be as *you* please, captain," asid the provost; "but then, what is to come of the good town of Kirkwall, that has been packing and peeling with the king's enemies? The burgh will be laid under a round fine, and it may be that the provost may not come off so easily."

"Well, then," said Cleveland, "I see where your pinch lies. Now, suppose that I run round this island of yours, and get into the roadstead at Stromness? We could get what we want put on board there, without Kirkwall or the provost seeming to have any hand in it; or, if it should be ever questioned, your want of force and our superior strength will make a sufficient apology."

"That may be," said the provost; "but, if I suffer you to leave your present station and go elsewhere, I must have some security that you will not do harm to the country."

"And we," said Cleveland, "must have some security, on our side, that you will not detain us, by dribbling out our time, till the 'Halcyon' is on the coast. Now, I am myself perfectly willing to continue on shore as a hostage, on the one side, provided you will give me your word not to betray me, and send some magistrate, or person of consequence, aboard the sloop, where his safety will be a guarantee for mine."

The provost shook his head, and intimated it would be difficult to find a person willing to place himself as hostage in such a perilous condition; but said he would propose the arrangement to such of the council as were fit to be trusted with a matter of such weight.

CHAPTER XXXV.

I left my poor plough to go ploughing the deep!
DIBDIN.

WHEN the provost and Cleveland had returned into the public council-room, the former retired a second time with such of his brethren as he thought proper to advise with; and, while they were engaged in discussing Cleveland's proposal, refreshments were offered to him and his party. These the captain permitted his people to partake of, but with the greatest precaution against surprisal, one party relieving the guard whilst the others were at their food.

He himself, in the mean while, walked up and down the apartment, and conversed upon indifferent subjects with those present, like a person quite at his ease.

Amongst these individuals he saw, somewhat to his surprise, Triptolemus Yellowley, who, chancing to be at Kirkwall, had been summoned by the magistrates, as representative, in a certain degree, of the Lord Chamberlain, to attend council on this occasion. Cleveland immediately renewed the acquaintance which he had formed with the agriculturist at Burgh-Westra, and asked him his present business in Orkney.

"Just to look after some of my little plans, Captain Cleveland. I am weary of fighting with wild beasts at Ephesus yonder, and I just cam ower to see how my orchard was thriving, whilk I had planted four or five miles from Kirkwall, it may be a year bygane, and how the bees were thriving, whereof I had imported nine skeps, for the improvement of the country, and for the turning of the heather-bloom into wax and honey."

"And they thrive, I hope?" said Cleveland, who, however little interested in the matter, sustained the conversation, as if to break the chilly and embarrassed silence which hung upon the company assembled.

"Thrive!" replied Triptolemus; "they thrive like everything else in this country, and that is the backward way."

"Want of care, I suppose?" said Cleveland.

"The contrary, sir—quite and clean the contrary," replied the factor; "they died of ower muckle care, like Lucky Christie's chickens. I asked to see the skeps, and cunning and joyful did the fallow look who was to have taken care of them. 'Had there been ony body in charge but mysell,' he said, 'ye might have seen the skeps, or whatever you ca' them; but there wad hae been as mony solan-geese as flees in them, if it hadna been for my four quarters; for I watched them so closely, that I saw them a' creeping out at the little holes one sunny morning, and if I had not stopped the leak on the instant with a bit clay, the deil a bee, or flee, or whatever they are, would have been left in the skeps, as ye ca' them!' In a word, sir, he had clagged up the hives, as if the puir things had had the pestilence, and my bees were as dead as if they had been smeaked; and so ends my hope *generandi gloria mellis*, as Virgilius hath it."

"There is an end of your mead, then," replied Cleveland; "but what is your chance of cider? How does the orchard thrive?"

"O captain! this same Solomon of the Orcadian Ophir—I am sure no man need to send thither to fetch either talents of

27

gold or talents of sense!—I say, this wise man had watered the young apple-trees, in his great tenderness, with hot water, and they are perished, root and branch! But what avails grieving? And I wish you would tell me, instead, what is all the din that these good folks are making about pirates? and what for all these ill-looking men, that are armed like so mony Highland-men, assembled in the judgment-chamber? for I am just come from the other side of the island, and I have heard nothing distinct about it. And, now I look at you yoursell, captain, I think you have mair of these foolish pistolets about you than should suffice an honest man in quiet times?"

"And so I think, too," said the pacific triton, old Haagen, who had been an unwilling follower of the daring Montrose; "if you had been in the Glen of Edderachyllis, when we were sae sair worried by Sir John Worry——"

"You have forgot the whole matter, neighbour Haagen," said the factor: "Sir John Urry was on your side, and was ta'en with Montrose; by the same token, he lost his head."

"Did he?" said the triton. "I believe you may be right; for he changed sides mair than anes, and wha kens whilk he died for? But always he was there, and so was I; a fight there was, and I never wish to see another!"

The entrance of the provost here interrupted their desultory conversation. "We have determined," he said, "captain, that your ship shall go round to Stromness, or Scalpa Flow, to take in stores, in order that there may be no more quarrels between the fair folks and your seamen. And as you wish to stay on shore to see the fair, we intend to send a respectable gentle-man on board your vessel to pilot her round the Mainland, as the navigation is but ticklish."

"Spoken like a quiet and sensible magistrate, Mr. Mayor," said Cleveland, "and no otherwise than as I expected. And what gentleman is to honour our quarter-deck during my absence?"

"We have fixed that, too, Captain Cleveland," said the pro-vost; "you may be sure we were each more desirous than another to go upon so pleasant a voyage, and in such good company; but, being fair time, most of us have some affairs in hand. I myself, in respect of my office, cannot be well spared—the eldest bailie's wife is lying-in—the treasurer does not agree with the sea—two bailies have the gout—the other two are absent from town—and the other fifteen members of council are all engaged on particular business."

"All that I can tell you, Mr. Mayor," said Cleveland, raising his voice, "is, that I expect——"

"A moment's patience, if you please, captain," said the provost, interrupting him—"So that we have come to the resolution that our worthy Mr. Triptolemus Yellowley, who is factor of the Lord Chamberlain of these islands, shall, in respect of his official situation, be preferred to the honour and pleasure of accompanying you."

"Me!" said the astonished Triptolemus; "what the devil should I do going on your voyages? my business is on dry land."

"The gentlemen want a pilot," said the provost, whispering to him, "and there is no eviting to give them one."

"Do they want to go bump on shore, then?" said the factor, "how the devil should I pilot them, that never touched rudder in my life?"

"Hush!—hush!—be silent!" said the provost; "if the people of this town heard ye say such a word, your utility, and respect, and rank, and everything else, is clean gone! No man is anything with us island folks unless he can hand, reef, and steer. Besides, it is but a mere form; and we will send old Pate Sinclair to help you. You will have nothing to do but to eat, drink, and be merry all day."

"Eat and drink!" said the factor, not able to comprehend exactly why this piece of duty was pressed upon him so hastily, and yet not very capable of resisting or extricating himself from the toils of the more knowing provost—"eat and drink! That is all very well; but, to speak truth, the sea does not agree with me any more than with the treasurer, and I have always a better appetite for eating and drinking ashore."

"Hush! hush! hush!" again said the provost, in an undertone of earnest expostulation; "would you actually ruin your character out and out? A factor of the High Chamberlain of the Isles of Orkney and Zetland, and not like the sea! you might as well say you are a Highlander, and do not like whisky!"

"You must settle it somehow, gentlemen," said Captain Cleveland; "it is time we were under weigh. Mr. Triptolemus Yellowley, are we to be honoured with your company?"

"I am sure, Captain Cleveland," stammered the factor, "I would have no objection to go anywhere with you, only——"

"He has no objection," said the provost, catching at the first limb of the sentence, without awaiting the conclusion.

"He has no objection," cried the treasurer.

"He has no objection," sung out the whole four bailies together; and the fifteen councillors, all catching up the same phrase of assent, repeated it in chorus, with the additions of— "good man"—"public-spirited"—"honourable gentleman"— "burgh eternally obliged"—"where will you find such a worthy factor?" and so forth.

Astonished and confused at the praises with which he was overwhelmed on all sides, and in no shape understanding the nature of the transaction that was going forward, the astounded and overwhelmed agriculturist became incapable of resisting the part of the Kirkwall Curtius thus insidiously forced upon him, and was delivered up by Captain Cleveland to his party, with the strictest injunctions to treat him with honour and attention. Goffe and his companions began now to lead him off, amid the applauses of the whole meeting, after the manner in which the victim of ancient days was garlanded and greeted by shouts, when consigned to the priests, for the purpose of being led to the altar and knocked on the head, a sacrifice for the commonweal. It was while they thus conducted, and in a manner forced, him out of the council-chamber, that poor Triptolemus, much alarmed at finding that Cleveland, in whom he had some confidence, was to remain behind the party, tried, when just going out at the door, the effect of one remonstrating bellow. "Nay, but, provost!—captain!—bailies!—treasurer!—councillors! f Captain Cleveland does not go aboard to protect me, it is nae bargain, and go I will not, unless I am trailed with cart-ropes!"

His protest was, however, drowned in the unanimous chorus of the magistrates and councillors, returning him thanks for his public spirit—wishing him a good voyage—and praying to Heaven for his happy and speedy return. Stunned and overwhelmed, and thinking, if he had any distinct thoughts at all, that remonstrance was vain, where friends and strangers seemed alike determined to carry the point against him, Triptolemus, without farther resistance, suffered himself to be conducted into the street, where the pirate's boat's crew, assembling around him, began to move slowly towards the quay, many of the townsfolk following out of curiosity, but without any attempt at interference or annoyance; for the pacific compromise which the dexterity of the first magistrate had achieved was unanimously approved of as a much better settlement of the disputes betwixt them and the strangers than might have been attained by the dubious issue of an appeal to arms.

Meanwhile, as they went slowly along, Triptolemus had time to study the appearance, countenance, and dress of those into whose hands he had been thus delivered, and began to imagine that he read in their looks not only the general expression of a desperate character, but some sinister intentions directed particularly towards himself. He was alarmed by the truculent looks of Goffe, in particular, who, holding his arm with a gripe which resembled in delicacy of touch the compression of a smith's vice, cast on him from the outer corner of his eye oblique glances, like those which the eagle throws upon the prey which she has clutched, ere yet she proceeds, as it is technically called, to plume it. At length Yellowley's fears got so far the better of his prudence that he fairly asked his terrible conductor, in a sort of crying whisper: "Are you going to murder me, captain, in the face of the laws baith of God and man?"

"Hold your peace, if you are wise," said Goffe, who had his own reasons for desiring to increase the panic of his captive; "we have not murdered a man these three months, and why should you put us in mind of it?"

"You are but joking, I hope, good worthy captain!" replied

Triptolemus. "This is worse than witches, dwarfs, dirking of whales, and couping of cobles, put all together!—this is an away-ganging crop, with a vengeance! What good, in Heaven's name, would murdering me do to you?"

"We might have some pleasure in it, at least," said Goffe. "Look these fellows in the face, and see if you see one among them that would not rather kill a man than let it alone? But we will speak more of that when you have first had a taste of the bilboes—unless, indeed, you come down with a handsome round handful of Chili boards [1] for your ransom."

"As I shall live by bread, captain," answered the factor, "that misbegotten dwarf has carried off the whole hornful of silver!"

"A cat-and-nine-tails will make you find it again," said Goffe, gruffly; "flogging and pickling is an excellent receipt to bring a man's wealth into his mind; twisting a bowstring round his skull till the eyes start a little is a very good remembrancer too."

"Captain," replied Yellowley, stoutly, "I have no money; seldom can improvers have. We turn pasture to tillage, and barley into aits, and heather into greensward, and the poor 'yarpha,' as the benighted creatures here call their peat-bogs, into baittle grass-land; but we seldom make anything of it that comes back to our ain pouch. The carles and the cart-avers make it all, and the carles and the cart-avers eat it all, and the deil clink doun with it!"

"Well—well," said Goffe, "if you be really a poor fellow, as you pretend, I'll stand your friend"; then, inclining his head so as to reach the ear of the factor, who stood on tiptoe with anxiety, he said: "If you love your life, do not enter the boat with us."

"But how am I to get away from you, while you hold me so fast by the arm that I could not get off if the whole year's crop of Scotland depended on it?"

"Hark ye, you gudgeon," said Goffe, "just when you come to the water's edge, and when the fellows are jumping in and taking their oars, slue yourself round suddenly to the

[1] Commonly called by landsmen Spanish dollars.

larboard—I will let go your arm—and then cut and run for your life!"

Triptolemus did as he was desired, Goffe's willing hand relaxed the grasp as he had promised, the agriculturist trundled off like a football that has just received a strong impulse from the foot of one of the players, and, with celerity which surprised himself as well as all beholders, fled through the town of Kirkwall. Nay, such was the impetus of his retreat that, as if the grasp of the pirate was still open to pounce upon him, he never stopped till he had traversed the whole town and attained the open country on the other side. They who had seen him that day—his hat and wig lost in the sudden effort he had made to bolt forward, his cravat awry, and his waistcoat unbuttoned—and who had an opportunity of comparing his round spherical form and short legs with the portentous speed at which he scoured through the street, might well say that, if fury ministers arms, fear confers wings. His very mode of running seemed to be that peculiar to his fleecy care, for, like a ram in the midst of his race, he ever and anon encouraged himself by a great bouncing attempt at a leap, though there were no obstacles in his way.

There was no pursuit after the agriculturist; and though a musket or two were presented, for the purpose of sending a leaden messenger after him, yet Goffe, turning peacemaker for once in his life, so exaggerated the dangers that would attend a breach of the truce with the people of Kirkwall, that he prevailed upon the boat's crew to forbear any active hostilities, and to pull off for their vessel with all despatch.

The burghers, who regarded the escape of Triptolemus as a triumph on their side, gave the boat three cheers by way of an insulting farewell; while the magistrates, on the other hand, entertained great anxiety respecting the probable consequences of this breach of articles between them and the pirates; and, could they have seized upon the fugitive very privately, instead of complimenting him with a civic feast in honour of the agility which he displayed, it is likely they might have delivered the runaway hostage once more into the hands of his foemen. But it was impossible to set their face publicly to such an act of violence, and therefore they contented themselves with closely watching Cleveland, whom they determined to make responsible for any aggression which might be attempted by the pirates. Cleveland, on his part, easily conjectured that the motive which Goffe had for suffering the hostage to escape was to leave him answerable for all consequences, and, relying more on the attachment and intelligence of his friend and adherent, Frederick Altamont, *alias* Jack Bunce, than on anything else, expected the result with considerable anxiety, since the magistrates, though they continued to treat him with civility, plainly intimated they would regulate his treatment by the behaviour of the crew, though he no longer commanded them.

It was not, however, without some reason that he reckoned on the devoted fidelity of Bunce; for no sooner did that trusty adherent receive from Goffe and the boat's crew the news of the escape of Triptolemus, than he immediately concluded it had been favoured by the late captain, in order that, Cleveland being either put to death or consigned to hopeless imprisonment, Goffe might be called upon to resume the command of the vessel.

"But the drunken old boatswain shall miss his mark," said Bunce to his confederate Fletcher; "or else I am contented to quit the name of Altamont, and be called Jack Bunce, or Jack Dunce, if you like it better, to the end of the chapter."

Availing himself accordingly of a sort of nautical eloquence, which his enemies termed slack-jaw, Bunce set before the crew, in a most animated manner, the disgrace which they all sustained by their captain remaining, as he was pleased to term it, in the bilboes, without any hostage to answer for his safety; and succeeded so far that, besides exciting a good deal of discontent against Goffe, he brought the crew to the resolution of seizing the first vessel of a tolerable appearance, and declaring that the ship, crew, and cargo should be dealt with according to the usage which Cleveland should receive on shore. It was judged at the same time proper to try the faith of the Orcadians, by removing from the roadstead of Kirkwall, and going round to that of Stromness, where, ac cording to the treaty betwixt Provost Torfe and Captain Cleveland, they were to victual their sloop. They resolved, in the mean time, to entrust the command of the vessel to a council, consisting of Goffe, the boatswain, and Bunce himself, until Cleveland should be in a situation to resume his command.

These resolutions having been proposed and acceded to, they weighed anchor and got their sloop under sail, without experiencing any opposition or annoyance from the battery, which relieved them of one important apprehension incidental to their situation.

CHAPTER XXXVI.

Clap on more sail, pursue, up with your fights,
Give fire—she is my prize, or ocean whelm them all!
                                        SHAKSPEARE.

A VERY handsome brig, which, with several other vessels, was the property of Magnus Troil, the great Zetland udaller, had received on board that magnate himself, his two lovely daughters, and the facetious Claud Halcro, who, for friendship's sake chiefly, and the love of beauty proper to his poetical calling, attended them on their journey from Zetland to the capital of Orkney, to which Norna had referred them, as the place where her mystical oracles should at length receive a satisfactory explanation.

They passed, at a distance, the tremendous cliffs of the lonely spot of earth called the Fair Isle, which, at an equal distance from either archipelago, lies in the sea which divides Orkney from Zetland; and at length, after some baffling winds, made the Start of Sanda. Off the headland so named, they became involved in a strong current, well known, by those who frequent these seas, as the Roost of the Start, which carried them considerably out of their course, and, joined to an adverse wind, forced them to keep on the east side of the island of Stronsa, and finally compelled them to lie by for the night in Papa Sound, since the navigation in dark or thick weather, amongst so many low islands, is neither pleasant nor safe.

On the ensuing morning they resumed their voyage under more favourable auspices; and, coasting along the island of Stronsa, whose flat, verdant, and comparatively fertile shores formed a strong contrast to the dun hills and dark cliffs of their own islands, they doubled the cape called the Lamb Head, and stood away for Kirkwall.

They had scarce opened the beautiful bay betwixt Pomona and Shapinsha, and the sisters were admiring the massive church of St. Magnus, as it was first seen to rise from amongst the inferior buildings of Kirkwall, when the eyes of Magnus and of Claud Halcro were attracted by an object which they thought more interesting. This was an armed sloop, with her sails set, which had just left the anchorage in the bay, and was running before the wind by which the brig of the Udaller was beating in.

"A tight thing that, by my ancestor's bones!" said the old Udaller; "but I cannot make out of what country, as she shows no colours. Spanish built, I should think her."

"Ay—ay," said Claud Halcro, "she has all the look of it. She runs before the wind that we must battle with, which is the wonted way of the world. As glorious John says:

> With roomy deck, and guns of mighty strength,
>   Whose low-laid mouths each mounting billow laves,
> Deep in her draught, and warlike in her length,
>   She seems a sea-wasp flying on the waves."

Brenda could not help telling Halcro, when he had spouted this stanza with great enthusiasm, "That though the description was more like a first-rate than a sloop, yet the simile of the sea-wasp served but indifferently for either."

"A sea-wasp!" said Magnus, looking with some surprise, as the sloop, shifting her course, suddenly bore down on them. "Egad, I wish she may not show us presently that she has a sting!"

What the Udaller said in jest was fulfilled in earnest; for, without hoisting colours or hailing, two shots were discharged from the sloop, one of which ran dipping and dancing upon the water just ahead of the Zetlander's bows, while the other went through his mainsail.

Magnus caught up a speaking-trumpet and hailed the sloop, to demand what she was and what was the meaning of this unprovoked aggression. He was only answered by the stern command: "Down topsails instantly, and lay your mainsail to the mast; you shall see who we are presently."

There were no means within the reach of possibility by which obedience could be evaded, where it would instantly have been enforced by a broadside; and, with much fear on the part of the sisters and Claud Halcro, mixed with anger and astonishment on that of the Udaller, the brig lay-to to await the commands of the captors.

The sloop immediately lowered a boat, with six armed hands, commanded by Jack Bunce, which rowed directly for their prize. As they approached her, Claud Halcro whispered to the Udaller: "If what we hear of buccaniers be true, these men, with their silk scarfs and vests, have the very cut of them."

"My daughters! my daughters!" muttered Magnus to himself, with such an agony as only a father could feel. "Go down below and hide yourselves, girls, while I——"

He threw down his speaking-trumpet, and seized on a handspike, while his daughters, more afraid of the consequences of his fiery temper to himself than of anything else, hung round him and begged him to make no resistance. Claud Halcro united his entreaties, adding, "It were best pacify the fellows with fair words. They might," he said, "be Dunkirkers, or insolent man-of-war's-men on a frolic."

"No—no," answered Magnus, "it is the sloop which the jagger told us of. But I will take your advice: I will have patience for these girls' sakes; yet——"

He had no time to conclude the sentence, for Bunce jumped on board with his party, and drawing his cutlass, struck it upon the companion-ladder and declared the ship was theirs.

"By what warrant or authority do you stop us on the high seas?" said Magnus.

"Here are half a dozen of warrants," said Bunce, showing the pistols which were hung round him, according to a pirate fashion already mentioned, "choose which you like, old gentleman, and you shall have the perusal of it presently."

"That is to say, you intend to rob us?" said Magnus. "So be it—we have no means to help it—only be civil to the women, and take what you please from the vessel. There is not much, but I will and can make it worth more if you use us well."

"Civil to the women!" said Fletcher, who had also come on board with the gang—" when were we else than civil to them? ay, and kind to boot? Look here, Jack Bunce! what a trim-going little thing here is! By G—, she shall make a cruise with us, come of old Squaretoes what will!"

He seized upon the terrified Brenda with one hand, and insolently pulled back with the other the hood of the mantle in which she had muffled herself.

"Help, father!—help, Minna!" exclaimed the affrighted girl; unconscious, at the moment, that they were unable to render her assistance.

Magnus again uplifted the handspike, but Bunce stopped his hand. "Avast, father!" he said, "or you will make a bad voyage of it presently. And you, Fletcher, let go the girl!"

"And d—n me! why should I let her go?" said Fletcher.

"Because I command you, Dick," said the other, "and because I'll make it a quarrel else. And now let me know, beauties, is there one of you bears that queer heathen name of Minna, for which I have a certain sort of regard?"

"Gallant sir!" said Halcro, "unquestionably it is because you have some poetry in your heart."

"I have had enough of it in my mouth in my time," answered Bunce; "but that day is by, old gentleman; however, I shall soon find out which of these girls is Minna. Throw back your mufflings from your faces, and don't be afraid, my Lindamiras: no one here shall meddle with you to do you wrong. On my soul, two pretty wenches! I wish I were at sea in an egg-shell, and a rock under my lee-bow, if I would wish a better leaguer-lass than the worst of them! Hark you, my girls; which of you would like to swing in a rover's hammock? you should have gold for the gathering!"

The terrified maidens clung close together, and grew pale at the bold and familiar language of the desperate libertine.

"Nay, don't be frightened," said he; "no one shall serve under the noble Altamont but by her own free choice: there is no pressing amongst gentlemen of fortune. And do not look so shy upon me neither, as if I spoke of what you never thought of before. One of you, at least, has heard of Captain Cleveland, the rover."

Brenda grew still paler, but the blood mounted at once in Minna's cheeks, on hearing the name of her lover thus unexpectedly introduced; for the scene was in itself so confounding, that the idea of the vessel's being the consort of which Cleveland had spoken at Burgh-Westra had occurred to no one save the Udaller.

"I see how it is," said Bunce, with a familiar nod, "and I will hold my course accordingly. You need not be afraid of any injury, father," he added, addressing Magnus familiarly; "and though I have made many a pretty girl pay tribute in my time, yet yours shall go ashore without either wrong or ransom."

"If you will assure me of that," said Magnus, "you are as welcome to the brig and cargo as ever I made man welcome to a can of punch."

"And it is no bad thing that same can of punch," said Bunce, "if we had any one here that could mix it well."

"I will do it," said Claud Halcro, "with any man that ever squeezed lemon—Eric Scambester, the punch-maker of Burgh-Westra, being alone excepted."

"And you are within a grapnel's length of him, too," said the Udaller. "Go down below, my girls," he added, "and send up the rare old man and the punch-bowl."

"The punch-bowl!" said Fletcher; "I say, the bucket, d—n me! Talk of bowls in the cabin of a paltry merchantman, but not to gentlemen strollers—rovers, I would say," correcting himself, as he observed that Bunce looked sour at the mistake.

"And I say, these two pretty girls shall stay on deck and fill my can," said Bunce; "I deserve some attendance, at least, for all my generosity."

"And they shall fill mine, too," said Fletcher—"they shall fill it to the brim! and I will have a kiss for every drop they spill—broil me if I won't!"

"Why, then, I tell you, you shan't!" said Bunce; "for I'll be d—d if any one shall kiss Minna but one, and that's neither you nor I; and her other little bit of a consort shall 'scape for company; there are plenty of willing wenches in Orkney. And so, now I think on it, these girls shall go down below and bolt themselves into the cabin; and we shall have the punch up here on deck, *al fresco*, as the old gentleman proposes."

"Why, Jack, I wish you knew your own mind," said Fletcher; "I have been your messmate these two years, and I love you; and yet flay me like a wild bullock, if you have not as many humours as a monkey! And what shall we have to make a little fun of, since you have sent the girls down below?"

"Why, we will have Master Punch-maker here," answered Bunce, "to give us toasts and sing us songs. And, in the mean time, you there, stand by sheets and tacks, and get her under way! and you, steersman, as you would keep your brains in your skull, keep her under the stern of the sloop. If you attempt to play us any trick, I will scuttle your sconce as if it were an old calabash!"

The vessel was accordingly got under way, and moved slowly on in the wake of the sloop, which, as had been previously agreed upon, held her course, not to return to the Bay of Kirkwall, but for an excellent roadstead called Inganess Bay, formed by a promontory which extends to the eastward two or three miles from the Orcadian metropolis, and where the vessels might conveniently lie at anchor, while the rovers maintained any communication with the magistrates which the new state of things seemed to require.

Meantime, Claud Halcro had exerted his utmost talents in compounding a bucketful of punch for the use of the pirates, which they drank out of large cans; the ordinary seamen, as well as Bunce and Fletcher, who acted as officers, dipping them into the bucket with very little ceremony, as they came and went upon their duty. Magnus, who was particularly apprehensive that liquor might awaken the brutal passions of these desperadoes, was yet so much astonished at the quantities which he saw them drink, without producing any visible effect upon their reason, that he could not help expressing his surprise to Bunce himself, who, wild as he was, yet appeared by far the most civil and conversable of his party, and whom he was, perhaps, desirous to conciliate by a compliment of which all boon topers know the value.

"Bones of St. Magnus!" said the Udaller, "I used to think I took off my can like a gentleman; but to see your men swallow, captain, one would think their stomachs were as bottomless as the hole of Laifell in Foula, which I have sounded myself with a line of an hundred fathoms. By my soul, the bicker of St. Magnus were but a sip to them!"

"In our way of life, sir," answered Bunce, "there is no stint till duty calls or the puncheon is drunk out."

"By my word, sir," said Claud Halcro, "I believe there is not one of your people but could drink out the mickle bicker of Scarpa, which was always offered to the Bishop of Orkney brimful of the best bummock that ever was brewed."

"If drinking could make them bishops," said Bunce, "I should have a reverend crew of them; but as they have no other clerical qualities about them, I do not propose that they shall get drunk to-day; so we will cut our drink with a song."

"And I'll sing it, by ——!" said or swore Dick Fletcher, and instantly struck up the old ditty—

> "It was a ship, and a ship of fame,
> Launch'd off the stocks, bound for the main,
> With an hundred and fifty brisk young men,
> All pick'd and chosen every one."

"I would sooner be keel-hauled than hear that song over again," said Bunce; "and confound your lantern jaws, you can squeeze nothing else out of them!"

"By ——," said Fletcher, "I will sing my song, whether

you like it or no"; and again he sung, with the doleful tone of a northeaster whistling through sheet and shrouds:

> "Captain Glen was our captain's name;
> A very gallant and brisk young man,
> As bold a sailor as e'er went to sea ;
> And we were bound for High Barbary."

"I tell you again," said Bunce, "we will have none of your screech-owl music here; and I'll be d—d if you shall sit here and make that infernal noise!"

"Why, then, I'll tell you what," said Fletcher, getting up, "I'll sing when I walk about, and I hope there is no harm in that, Jack Bunce." And so, getting up from his seat, he began to walk up and down the sloop, croaking out his long and disastrous ballad.

"You see how I manage them," said Bunce, with a smile of self-applause. "Allow that fellow two strides on his own way, and you make a mutineer of him for life; but I tie him strict up, and he follows me as kindly as a fowler's spaniel after he has got a good beating. And now your toast and your song, sir," addressing Halcro; "or rather your song without your toast. I have got a toast for myself. Here is success to all roving blades, and confusion to all honest men!"

"I should be sorry to drink that toast, if I could help it," said Magnus Troil.

"What! you reckon yourself one of the honest folks, I warrant?" said Bunce. "Tell me your trade, and I'll tell you what I think of it. As for the punch-maker here, I knew him at first glance to be a tailor, who has, therefore, no more pretensions to be honest than he has not to be mangy. But you are some High-Dutch skipper, I warrant me, that tramples on the cross when he is in Japan, and denies his religion for a day's gain."

"No," replied the Udaller, "I am a gentleman of Zetland."

"Oh, what!" retorted the satirical Mr. Bunce, "you are come from the happy climate where gin is a groat a bottle, and where there is daylight for ever?"

"At your service, captain," said the Udaller, suppressing

with much pain some disposition to resent these jests on his country, although under every risk and at all disadvantage.

"At *my* service!" said Bunce. "Ay, if there was a rope stretched from the wreck to the beach, you would be at my service to cut the hawser, make flotsome and jetsome of ship and cargo, and well if you did not give me a rap on the head with the back of the cutty-axe; and you call yourself honest! But never mind—here goes the aforesaid toast—and do you sing me a song, Mr. Fashioner; and look it be as good as your punch."

Halcro, internally praying for the powers of a new Timotheus, to turn his strain and check his auditor's pride, as glorious John had it, began a heart-soothing ditty with the following lines:

> "Maidens fresh as fairest rose,
> Listen to this lay of mine."

"I will hear nothing of maidens or roses," said Bunce; "it puts me in mind what sort of a cargo we have got on board; and, by ——, I will be true to my messmate and my captain as long as I can! And now I think on't, I'll have no more punch either; that last cup made innovation, and I am not to play Cassio to-night; and if I drink not, nobody else shall."

So saying, he manfully kicked over the bucket, which, notwithstanding the repeated applications made to it, was still half full, got up from his seat, shook himself a little to rights, as he expressed it, cocked his hat, and, walking the quarter-deck with an air of dignity, gave, by word and signal, the orders for bringing the ships to anchor, which were readily obeyed by both, Goffe being then, in all probability, past any rational state of interference.

The Udaller, in the mean time, condoled with Halcro on their situation. "It is bad enough," said the tough old Norseman, "for these are rank rogues; and yet, were it not for the girls, I should not fear them. That young vapouring fellow, who seems to command, is not such a born devil as he might have been."

"He has queer humours, though," said Halcro; "and I wish

28

we were loose from him.   To kick down a bucket half full of
the best punch ever was made, and to cut me short in the
sweetest song I ever wrote—I promise you, I do not know
what he may do next—it is next door to madness."

Meanwhile, the ships being brought to anchor, the valiant
Lieutenant Bunce called upon Fletcher, and, resuming his
seat by his unwilling passengers, he told them they should
see what message he was about to send to the wittols of Kirkwall, as they were something concerned in it.   "It shall run
in Dick's name," he said, "as well as in mine.   I love to give
the poor young fellow a little countenance now and then—
don't I, Dick, you d—d stupid ass?"

"Why, yes, Jack Bunce," said Dick, "I can't say but as
you do, only you are always bullocking one about something
or other, too; but, howsomdever, d'ye see——"

"Enough said—belay your jaw, Dick," said Bunce, and
proceeded to write his epistle, which, being read aloud,
proved to be of the following tenor: "For the Mayor and
Aldermen of Kirkwall—Gentlemen, As, contrary to your good
faith given, you have not sent us on board a hostage for the
safety of our captain, remaining on shore at your request,
these come to tell you, we are not thus to be trifled with.
We have already in our possession a brig, with a family of
distinction, its owners and passengers; and as you deal with
our captain, so will we deal with them in every respect.   And
as this is the first, so assure yourselves it shall not be the last,
damage which we will do to your town and trade, if you do
not send on board our captain, and supply us with stores according to treaty.

"Given on board the brig 'Mergoose' of Burgh-Westra, lying in Inganess Bay.   Witness our hands, commanders of the
'Fortune's Favourite,' and gentlemen adventurers."

He then subscribed himself Frederick Altamont, and handed
the letter to Fletcher, who read the said subscription with much
difficulty; and, admiring the sound of it very much, swore he
would have a new name himself, and the rather that Fletcher
was the most crabbed word to spell and conster, he believed,

in the whole dictionary. He subscribed himself accordingly, Timothy Tugmutton.

"Will you not add a few lines to the coxcombs?" said Bunce, addressing Magnus.

"Not I," returned the Udaller, stubborn in his ideas of right and wrong, even in so formidable an emergency. "The magistrates of Kirkwall know their duty, and were I they——" But here the recollection that his daughters were at the mercy of these ruffians blanked the bold visage of Magnus Troil, and checked the defiance which was just about to issue from his lips.

"D—n me," said Bunce, who easily conjectured what was passing in the mind of his prisoner—"that pause would have told well on the stage: it would have brought down pit, box, and gallery, egad, as Bayes has it."

"I will hear nothing of Bayes," said Claud Halcro, himself a little elevated, "it is an impudent satire on glorious John; but he tickled Buckingham off for it—

> In the first rank of these did Zimri stand,
> A man so various——"

"Hold your peace!" said Bunce, drowning the voice of the admirer of Dryden in louder and more vehement asseveration, "the *Rehearsal* is the best farce ever was written; and I'll make him kiss the gunner's daughter that denies it. D—n me, I was the best Prince Prettyman ever walked the boards—

> Sometimes a fisher's son, sometimes a prince.

But let us to business. Hark ye, old gentleman (to Magnus), you have a sort of sulkiness about you, for which some of my profession would cut your ears out of your head, and broil them for your dinner with red pepper. I have known Goffe do so to a poor devil, for looking sour and dangerous when he saw his sloop go to Davy Jones's locker with his only son on board. But I'm a spirit of another sort; and if you or the ladies are ill-used, it shall be the Kirkwall people's fault, and not mine, and that's fair; and so you had better let them know your condition, and your circumstances, and so forth— and that's fair, too."

Magnus, thus exhorted, took up the pen and attempted to write; but his high spirit so struggled with his paternal anxiety that his hand refused its office. "I cannot help it," he said, after one or two illegible attempts to write—"I cannot form a letter, if all our lives depended upon it."

And he could not, with his utmost efforts, so suppress the convulsive emotions which he experienced, but that they agitated his whole frame. The willow which bends to the tempest often escapes better than the oak which resists it; and so, in great calamities, it sometimes happens that light and frivolous spirits recover their elasticity and presence of mind sooner than those of a loftier character. In the present case, Claud Halcro was fortunately able to perform the task which the deeper feelings of his friend and patron refused. He took the pen, and, in as few words as possible, explained the situation in which they were placed, and the cruel risks to which they were exposed, insinuating at the same time, as delicately as he could express it, that, to the magistrates of the country, the life and honour of its citizens should be a dearer object than even the apprehension or punishment of the guilty; taking care, however, to qualify the last expression as much as possible, for fear of giving umbrage to the pirates.

Bunce read over the letter, which fortunately met his approbation; and, on seeing the name of Claud Halcro at the bottom, he exclaimed, in great surprise, and with more energetic expressions of asseveration than we choose to record: "Why, you are the little fellow that played the fiddle to old Manager Gadabout's company, at Hogs Norton, the first season I came out there! I thought I knew your catchword of glorious John."

At another time this recognition might not have been very grateful to Halcro's minstrel pride; but, as matters stood with him, the discovery of a golden mine could not have made him more happy. He instantly remembered the very hopeful young performer who came out in *Don Sebastian,* and judiciously added, that the muse of glorious John had never received such excellent support during the time that he was first (he might have added, and only) violin to Mr. Gadabout's company.

" Why, yes," said Bunce, " I believe you are right: I think I might have shaken the scene as well as Booth or Betterton either. But I was destined to figure on other boards (striking his foot upon the deck), and I believe I must stick by them till I find no board at all to support me. But now, old acquaintance, I will do something for you; slue yourself this way a bit—I would have you solus." They leaned over the taffrail, while Bunce whispered with more seriousness than he usually showed: " I am sorry for this honest old heart of Norway pine—blight me if I am not—and for the daughters too; besides, I have my own reasons for befriending one of them. I can be a wild fellow with a willing lass of the game; but to such decent and innocent creatures—d—n me, I am Scipio at Numantia, and Alexander in the tent of Darius. You remember how I touch off Alexander? (here he started into heroics)—

> Thus from the grave I rise to save my love;
> All draw your swords with wings of lightning move.
> When I rush on, sure none will dare to stay;
> 'Tis beauty calls, and glory shows the way."

Claud Halcro failed not to bestow the necessary commendations on his declamation, declaring that, in his opinion as an honest man, he had always thought Mr. Altamont's giving that speech far superior in tone and energy to Betterton.

Bunce, or Altamont, wrung his hand tenderly. " Ah, you flatter me, my dear friend," he said; " yet, why had not the public some of your judgment! I should not then have been at this pass. Heaven knows, my dear Mr. Halcro—Heaven knows with what pleasure I could keep you on board with me, just that I might have one friend who loves as much to hear as I do to recite the choicest pieces of our finest dramatic authors. The most of us are beasts; and, for the Kirkwall hostage yonder, he uses me, egad, as I use Fletcher, I think, and huffs me the more, the more I do for him. But how delightful it would be in a tropic night, when the ship was hanging on the breeze, with a broad and steady sail, for me to rehearse *Alexander*, with you for my pit, box, and gallery! Nay—for you are a follower of the Muses, as I remember—who knows but you and I might be the means of inspiring, like Orpheus and Eurydice, a pure taste into our companions, and softening their manners, while we excited their better feelings?"

This was spoken with so much unction, that Claud Halcro began to be afraid he had both made the actual punch over potent and mixed too many bewitching ingredients in the cup of flattery which he had administered; and that, under the influence of both potions, the sentimental pirate might detain him by force, merely to realise the scenes which his imagination presented. The conjuncture was, however, too delicate to admit of any active effort on Halcro's part to redeem his blunder, and therefore he only returned the tender pressure of his friend's hand, and uttered the interjection "alas!" in as pathetic a tone as he could.

Bunce immediately resumed: "You are right, my friend, these are but vain visions of felicity, and it remains but for the unhappy Altamont to serve the friend to whom he is now to bid farewell. I have determined to put you and the two girls ashore, with Fletcher for your protection; and so call up the young women, and let them begone before the devil get aboard of me or of some one else. You will carry my letter to the magistrates, and second it with your own eloquence, and assure them that, if they hurt but one hair of Cleveland's head, there will be the devil to pay, and no pitch hot."

Relieved at heart by this unexpected termination of Bunce's harangue, Halcro descended the companion-ladder two steps at a time, and, knocking at the cabin door, could scarce find intelligible language enough to say his errand. The sisters hearing, with unexpected joy, that they were to be set ashore, muffled themselves in their cloaks, and, when they learned that the boat was hoisted out, came hastily on deck, where they were apprised, for the first time, to their great horror, that their father was still to remain on board of the pirate.

"We will remain with him at every risk," said Minna; "we may be of some assistance to him, were it but for an instant: we will live and die with him!"

"We shall aid him more surely," said Brenda, who com-

prehended the nature of their situation better than Minna,
" by interesting the people of Kirkwall to grant these gentlemen's demands."

"Spoken like an angel of sense and beauty," said Bunce;
"and now away with you; for, d—n me, if this is not like
having a lighted linstock in the powder-room: if you speak
another word more, confound me if I know how I shall bring
myself to part with you!"

"Go, in God's name, my daughters," said Magnus. "I am
in God's hand; and when you are gone I shall care little for
myself; and I shall think and say, as long as I live, that this
good gentleman deserves a better trade. Go—go—away with
you!" for they yet lingered in reluctance to leave him.

"Stay not to kiss," said Bunce, "for fear I be tempted to
ask my share. Into the boat with you—yet stop an instant."
He drew the three captives apart. "Fletcher," said he, "will
answer for the rest of the fellows, and will see you safe off the
sea-beach. But how to answer for Fletcher I know not, except
by trusting Mr. Halcro with this little guarantee."

He offered the minstrel a small double-barrelled pistol,
which, he said, was loaded with a brace of balls. Minna observed Halcro's hand tremble as he stretched it out to take
the weapon. "Give it to me, sir," she said, taking it from
the outlaw; "and trust to me for defending my sister and
myself."

"Bravo—bravo!" shouted Bunce. "There spoke a wench
worthy of Cleveland, the King of Rovers!"

"Cleveland!" repeated Minna, "do you then know that
Cleveland whom you have twice named?"

"Know him! Is there a man alive," said Bunce, "that
knows better than I do the best and stoutest fellow ever
stepped betwixt stem and stern? When he is out of the
bilboes, as, please Heaven, he shall soon be, I reckon to see
you come on board of us and reign the queen of every sea we
sail over. You have got the little guardian; I suppose you
know how to use it? If Fletcher behaves ill to you, you need
only draw up this piece of iron with your thumb, so; and if
he persists, it is but crooking your pretty forefinger thus, and

I shall lose the most dutiful messmate that ever man had, though, d—n the dog, he will deserve his death if he disobeys my orders. And now, into the boat; but stay, one kiss for Cleveland's sake."

Brenda, in deadly terror, endured his courtesy; but Minna, stepping back with disdain, offered her hand. Bunce laughed, but kissed, with a theatrical air, the fair hand which she extended as a ransom for her lips, and at length the sisters and Halcro were placed in the boat, which rowed off under Fletcher's command.

Bunce stood on the quarter-deck, soliloquising after the manner of his original profession. "Were this told at Port-Royal now, or at the Isle of Providence, or in the Petits Guaves, I wonder what they would say of me! Why, that I was a good-natured milksop—a Jack-a-Lent—an ass. Well, let them. I have done enough of bad to think about it; it is worth while doing one good action, if it were but for the rarity of the thing, and to put one in good humour with oneself. Then turning to Magnus Troil, he proceeded: "By —— these are bona-robas, these daughters of yours! The eldest would make her fortune on the London boards. What a dashing attitude the wench had with her, as she seized the pistol! d—n me, that touch would have brought the house down! What a Roxalana the jade would have made!" for, in his oratory, Bunce, like Sancho's gossip, Thomas Cecial, was apt to use the most energetic word which came to hand, without accurately considering its propriety. "I would give my share of the next prize but to hear her spout:

> Away, begone, and give a whirlwind room,
> Or I will blow you up like dust. Avaunt!
> Madness but meanly represents my rage.

And then, again, that little, soft, shy, tearful trembler, for Statira, to hear her recite:

> He speaks the kindest words, and looks such things,
> Vows with such passion, swears with so much grace,
> That 'tis a kind of heaven to be deluded by him.

What a play we might have run up! I was a beast not to think of it before I sent them off—I to be Alexander—Claud Halcro, Lysimachus—this old gentleman might have made a Clytus for a pinch. I was an idiot not to think of it!"

There was much in this effusion which might have displeased the Udaller; but, to speak truth, he paid no attention to it. His eye, and finally his spy-glass, were employed in watching the return of his daughters to the shore. He saw them land on the beach, and, accompanied by Halcro and another man (Fletcher, doubtless), he saw them ascend the acclivity and proceed upon the road to Kirkwall; and he could even distinguish that Minna, as if considering herself as the guardian of the party, walked a little aloof from the rest, on the watch, as it seemed, against surprise, and ready to act as occasion should require. At length, as the Udaller was just about to lose sight of them, he had the exquisite satisfaction to see the party halt, and the pirate leave them, after a space just long enough for a civil farewell, and proceed slowly back, on his return to the beach. Blessing the Great Being who had thus relieved him from the most agonizing fears which a father can feel, the worthy Udaller, from that instant, stood resigned to his own fate, whatever that might be.

CHAPTER XXXVII.

Over the mountains and under the waves,
Over the fountains and under the graves,
   Over floods that are deepest,
      Which Neptune obey,
   Over rocks that are steepest,
      Love will find out the way.
                                    Old Song.

THE parting of Fletcher from Claud Halcro and the sisters of Burgh-Westra, on the spot where it took place, was partly occasioned by a small party of armed men being seen at a distance in the act of advancing from Kirkwall, an apparition hidden from the Udaller's spy-glass by the swell of the ground, but quite visible to the pirate, whom it determined to consult his own safety by a speedy return to his boat. He was just turning away, when Minna occasioned the short delay which her father had observed.

"Stop," she said, "I command you! Tell your leader from me that, whatever the answer may be from Kirkwall, he shall carry his vessel, nevertheless, round to Stromness; and, being anchored there, let him send a boat ashore for Captain Cleveland when he shall see a smoke on the Bridge of Broisgar."

Fletcher had thought, like his messmate Bunce, of asking a kiss, at least, for the trouble of escorting these beautiful young women; and, perhaps, neither the terror of the approaching Kirkwall men nor of Minna's weapon might have prevented his being insolent. But the name of his captain, and, still more, the unappalled, dignified, and commanding manner of Minna Troil, overawed him. He made a sea bow, promised to keep a sharp lookout, and, returning to his boat, went on board with his message.

As Halcro and the sisters advanced towards the party whom they saw on the Kirkwall road, and who, on their part, had halted as if to observe them, Brenda, relieved from the fears of Fletcher's presence, which had hitherto kept her silent, exclaimed: "Merciful Heaven! Minna, in what hands have we left our dear father?"

"In the hands of brave men," said Minna, steadily. "I fear not for him."

"As brave as you please," said Claud Halcro, "but very dangerous rogues for all that. I know that fellow Altamont, as he calls himself, though that is not his right name neither —as deboshed a dog as ever made a barn ring with blood and blank verse. He began with *Barnwell*, and everybody thought he would end with the gallows, like the last scene in *Venice Preserved*."

"It matters not," said Minna—"the wilder the waves, the more powerful is the voice that rules them. The name alone of Cleveland ruled the mood of the fiercest amongst them."

"I am sorry for Cleveland," said Brenda, "if such are his companions; but I care little for him in comparison to my father."

"Reserve your compassion for those who need it," said

Minna, "aud fear nothing for our father. God knows, every silver hair on his head is to me worth the treasure of an un-sunned mine; but I know that he is safe while in yonder vessel, and I know that he will be soon safe on shore."

"I would I could see it," said Claud Halcro; "but I fear the Kirkwall people, supposing Cleveland to be such as I dread, will not dare to exchange him against the Udaller. The Scots have very severe laws against theft-boot, as they call it."

"But who are those on the road before us?" said Brenda; "and why do they halt there so jealously?"

"They are a patrol of the militia," answered Halcro. "Glorious John touches them off a little sharply; but then John was a Jacobite, —

> Mouths without hands, maintain'd at vast expense,
> In peace a charge, in war a weak defence;
> Stout once a month, they march, a blustering band,
> And ever, but in time of need, at hand.

I fancy they halted just now, taking us, as they saw us on the brow of the hill, for a party of the sloop's men; and now they can distinguish that you wear petticoats, they are mov-ing on again."

They came on accordingly, and proved to be, as Claud Halcro had suggested, a patrol sent out to watch the motions of the pirates, and to prevent their attempting descents to damage the country.

They heartily congratulated Claud Halcro, who was well known to more than one of them, upon his escape from cap-tivity; and the commander of the party, while offering every assistance to the ladies, could not help condoling with them on the circumstances in which their father stood, hinting, though in a delicate and doubtful manner, the difficulties which might be in the way of his liberation.

When they arrived at Kirkwall, and obtained an audience of the provost and one or two of the magistrates, these diffi-culties were more plainly insisted upon. "The 'Halcyon' frigate is upon the coast," said the provost: "she was seen

off Duncansbay Head; and, though I have the deepest respect
for Mr. Troil of Burgh-Westra, yet I shall be answerable to
law if I release from prison the captain of this suspicious vessel, on account of the safety of any individual who may be
unhappily endangered by his detention. This man is now
known to be the heart and soul of these buccaniers, and am I
at liberty to send him abroad, that he may plunder the country, or perhaps go fight the king's ship? for he has impudence
enough for anything."

"*Courage* enough for anything, you mean, Mr. Provost,"
said Minna, unable to restrain her displeasure.

"Why, you may call it as you please, Miss Troil," said the
worthy magistrate; "but, in my opinion, that sort of courage which proposes to fight singly against two is little better
than a kind of practical impudence."

"But our father?" said Brenda, in a tone of the most earnest entreaty—"our father—the friend, I may say the father,
of his country—to whom so many look for kindness, and so
many for actual support—whose loss would be the extinction
of a beacon in a storm—will you indeed weigh the risk which
he runs against such a trifling thing as letting an unfortunate
man from prison, to seek his unhappy fate elsewhere?"

"Miss Brenda is right," said Claud Halcro; "I am for let-
a-be for let-a-be, as the boys say; and never fash about a warrant of liberation, provost, but just take a fool's counsel, and
let the goodman of the jail forget to draw his bolt on the
wicket, or leave a chink of a window open, or the like, and
we shall be rid of the rover, and have the one best honest
fellow in Orkney or Zetland on the lee-side of a bowl of punch
with us in five hours."

The provost replied in nearly the same terms as before,
that he had the highest respect for Mr. Magnus Troil of
Burgh-Westra, but that he could not suffer his consideration
for any individual, however respectable, to interfere with the
discharge of his duty.

Minna then addressed her sister in a tone of calm and sarcastic displeasure. "You forget," she said, "Brenda, that
you are talking of the safety of a poor insignificant udaller

of Zetland to no less a person than the chief magistrate of the
metropolis of Orkney—can you expect so great a person to
condescend to such a trifling subject of consideration? It will
be time enough for the provost to think of complying with the
terms sent to him—for comply with them at length he both
must and will—when the church of St. Magnus is beat down
about his ears."

"You may be angry with me, my pretty young lady," said
the good-humoured Provost Torfe, "but I cannot be offended
with you. The church of St. Magnus has stood many a day,
and, I think, will outlive both you and me, much more yonder
pack of unhanged dogs. And besides that your father is half
an Orkney man, and has both estate and friends among us,
I would, I give you my word, do as much for a Zetlander in
distress as I would for any one, excepting one of our own native Kirkwallers, who are doubtless to be preferred. And if
you will take up your lodgings here with my wife and myself,
we will endeavour to show you," continued he, "that you are
as welcome in Kirkwall as ever you could be in Lerwick or
Scalloway."

Minna deigned no reply to this good-humoured invitation;
but Brenda declined it in civil terms, pleading the necessity
of taking up their abode with a wealthy widow of Kirkwall,
a relation, who already expected them.

Halcro made another attempt to move the provost, but
found him inexorable. "The collector of the customs had
already threatened," he said, "to inform against him for entering into treaty, or, as he called it, packing and peeling,
with those strangers, even when it seemed the only means of
preventing a bloody affray in the town; and, should he now
forego the advantage afforded by the imprisonment of Cleveland and the escape of the factor, he might incur something
worse than censure." The burden of the whole was, "That
he was sorry for the Udaller, he was sorry even for the lad
Cleveland, who had some sparks of honour about him; but
his duty was imperious, and must be obeyed." The provost
then precluded farther argument by observing that another
affair from Zetland called for his immediate attention. A

gentleman named Mertoun, residing at Jarlshof, had made complaint against Snailsfoot, the jagger, for having assisted a domestic of his in embezzling some valuable articles which had been deposited in his custody, and he was about to take examinations on the subject, and cause them to be restored to Mr. Mertoun, who was accountable for them to the right owner.

In all this information there was nothing which seemed interesting to the sisters excepting the word "Mertoun," which went like a dagger to the heart of Minna, when she recollected the circumstances under which Mordaunt Mertoun had disappeared, and which, with an emotion less painful, though still of a melancholy nature, called a faint blush into Brenda's cheek, and a slight degree of moisture into her eye. But it was soon evident that the magistrate spoke not of Mordaunt, but of his father; and the daughters of Magnus, little interested in his detail, took leave of the provost to go to their own lodgings.

When they arrived at their relation's, Minna made it her business to learn, by such inquiries as she could make without exciting suspicion, what was the situation of the unfortunate Cleveland, which she soon discovered to be exceedingly precarious. The provost had not, indeed, committed him to close custody, as Claud Halcro had anticipated, recollecting, perhaps, the favourable circumstances under which he had surrendered himself, and loth, till the moment of the last necessity, altogether to break faith with him. But although let apparently at large, he was strictly watched by persons well armed and appointed for the purpose, who had directions to detain him by force, if he attempted to pass certain narrow precincts which were allotted to him. He was quartered in a strong room within what is called the King's Castle, and at night his chamber door was locked on the outside, and a sufficient guard mounted to prevent his escape. He therefore enjoyed only the degree of liberty which the cat, in her cruel sport, is sometimes pleased to permit to the mouse which she has clutched; and yet, such was the terror of the resources, the courage, and ferocity of the pirate captain, that the provost was blamed by the collector and many other sage citizens of Kirkwall for permitting him to be at large upon any conditions.

It may be well believed that, under such circumstances, Cleveland had no desire to seek any place of public resort, conscious that he was the object of a mixed feeling of curiosity and terror. His favourite place of exercise, therefore, was the external aisles of the cathedral of St. Magnus, of which the eastern end alone is fitted up for public worship. This solemn old edifice, having escaped the ravage which attended the first convulsions of the Reformation, still retains some appearance of Episcopal dignity. This place of worship is separated by a screen from the nave and western limb of the cross, and the whole is preserved in a state of cleanliness and decency which might be well proposed as an example to the proud piles of Westminster and St. Paul's.

It was in this exterior part of the cathedral that Cleveland was permitted to walk, the rather that his guards, by watching the single open entrance, had the means, with very little inconvenience to themselves, of preventing any possible attempt at escape. The place itself was well suited to his melancholy circumstances. The lofty and vaulted roof rises upon ranges of Saxon pillars, of massive size, four of which, still larger than the rest, once supported the lofty spire, which, long since destroyed by accident, has been rebuilt upon a disproportioned and truncated plan. The light is admitted at the eastern end through a lofty, well-proportioned, and richly ornamented Gothic window; and the pavement is covered with inscriptions, in different languages, distinguishing the graves of noble Orcadians, who have at different times been deposited within the sacred precincts.

Here walked Cleveland, musing over the events of a misspent life, which, it seemed probable, might be brought to a violent and shameful close, while he was yet in the prime of youth. "With these dead," he said, looking on the pavement, "shall I soon be numbered; but no holy man will speak a blessing, no friendly hand register an inscription, no proud descendant sculpture armorial bearings, over the grave of the pirate Cleveland. My whitening bones will swing in the gibbet-irons, on some wild beach or lonely cape, that will be esteemed fatal and accursed for my sake. The old mariner, as he passes the sound, will shake his head, and tell of my name and actions, as a warning to his younger comrades. But, Minna!—Minna! what will be thy thoughts when the news reaches thee? Would to God the tidings were drowned in the deepest whirlpool betwixt Kirkwall and Burgh-Westra, ere they came to her ear! and oh! would to Heaven that we had never met, since we never can meet again!"

He lifted up his eyes as he spoke, and Minna Troil stood before him. Her face was pale, and her hair dishevelled; but her look was composed and firm, with its usual expression of high-minded melancholy. She was still shrouded in the large mantle which she had assumed on leaving the vessel. Cleveland's first emotion was astonishment; his next was joy, not unmixed with awe. He would have exclaimed—he would have thrown himself at her feet; but she imposed at once silence and composure on him by raising her finger and saying, in a low but commanding accent: "Be cautious—we are observed; there are men without—they let me enter with difficulty. I dare not remain long; they would think—they might believe——Oh, Cleveland! I have hazarded everything to save you!"

"To save me? Alas! poor Minna!" answered Cleveland, "to save me is impossible. Enough that I have seen you once more, were it but to say: 'For ever farewell!'"

"We must indeed say farewell," said Minna; "for fate, and your guilt, have divided us for ever. Cleveland, I have seen your associates; need I tell you more—need I say, that I know now what a pirate is?"

"You have been in the ruffians' power!" said Cleveland, with a start of agony. "Did they presume——"

"Cleveland," replied Minna, "they presumed nothing: your name was a spell over them. By the power of that spell over these ferocious banditti, and by that alone, I was reminded of the qualities I once thought my Cleveland's!"

"Yes," said Cleveland, proudly, "my name has and shall

have power over them, when they are at the wildest; and, had they harmed you by one rude word, they should have found—— Yet what do I rave about? I am a prisoner!"

"You shall be so no longer," said Minna. "Your safety—the safety of my dear father—all demand your instant freedom. I have formed a scheme for your liberty, which, boldly executed, cannot fail. The light is fading without; muffle yourself in my cloak, and you will easily pass the guards. I have given them the means of carousing, and they are deeply engaged. Haste to the Loch of Stennis, and hide yourself till day dawns; then make a smoke on the point, where the land, stretching into the lake on each side, divides it nearly in two at the Bridge of Broisgar. Your vessel, which lies not far distant, will send a boat ashore. Do not hesitate an·instant!"

"But you, Minna! Should this wild scheme succeed," said Cleveland, "what is to become of you?"

"For my share in your escape," answered the maiden, "the honesty of my own intention will vindicate me in the sight of Heaven; and the safety of my father, whose fate depends on yours, will be my excuse to man."

In a few words, she gave him the history of their capture, and its consequences. Cleveland cast up his eyes and raised his hands to Heaven, in thankfulness for the escape of the sisters from his evil companions, and then hastily added: "But you are right, Minna: I must fly at all rates—for your father's sake I must fly. Here, then, we part—yet not, I trust, for ever."

"For ever!" answered a voice, that sounded as from a sepulchral vault.

They started, looked around them, and then gazed on each other. It seemed as if the echoes of the building had returned Cleveland's last words, but the pronunciation was too emphatically accented.

"Yes, for ever!" said Norna of the Fitful Head, stepping forward from behind one of the massive Saxon pillars which support the roof of the cathedral. "Here meet the crimson foot and the crimson hand. Well for both that the wound is

29

healed whence that crimson was derived—well for both, but best for him who shed it. Here, then, you meet, and meet for the last time!"

"Not so," said Cleveland, as if about to take Minna's hand; "to separate me from Minna, while I have life, must be the work of herself alone."

"Away!" said Norna, stepping betwixt them—"away with such idle folly! Nourish no vain dreams of future meetings: you part here, and you part for ever. The hawk pairs not with the dove; guilt matches not with innocence. Minna Troil, you look for the last time on this bold and criminal man. Cleveland, you behold Minna for the last time!"

"And dream you," said Cleveland, indignantly, "that your mummery imposes on me, and that I am among the fools who see more than trick in your pretended art?"

"Forbear, Cleveland—forbear!" said Minna, her hereditary awe of Norna augmented by the circumstance of her sudden appearance. "Oh, forbear! she is powerful—she is but too powerful. And do you, O Norna, remember my father's safety is linked with Cleveland's."

"And it is well for Cleveland that I do remember it," replied the pythoness; "and that, for the sake of one, I am here to aid both. You, with your childish purpose of passing one of his bulk and stature under the disguise of a few paltry folds of wadmaal—what would your device have procured him but instant restraint with bolt and shackle? I will save him—I will place him in security on board his bark. But let him renounce these shores for ever, and carry elsewhere the terrors of his sable flag and his yet blacker name; for if the sun rises twice and finds him still at anchor, his blood be on his own head. Ay, look to each other—look the last look that I permit to frail affection, and say, if ye *can* say it: 'Farewell for ever!'"

"Obey her," stammered Minna—"remonstrate not, but obey her."

Cleveland, grasping her hand and kissing it ardently, said, but so low that she only could hear it: "Farewell, Minna, but *not* for ever."

"And now, maiden, begone," said Norna, "and leave the rest to the Reim-kennar."

"One word more," said Minna, "and I obey you. Tell me but if I have caught aright your meaning. Is Mordaunt Mertoun safe and recovered?"

"Recovered, and safe," said Norna; "else woe to the hand that shed his blood!"

Minna slowly sought the door of the cathedral, and turned back from time to time to look at the shadowy form of Norna, and the stately and military figure of Cleveland, as they stood together in the deepening gloom of the ancient cathedral. When she looked back a second time they were in motion, and Cleveland followed the matron as, with a slow and solemn step, she glided towards one of the side aisles. When Minna looked back a third time, their figures were no longer visible. She collected herself, and walked on to the eastern door by which she had entered, and listened for an instant to the guard, who talked together on the outside.

"The Zetland girl stays a long time with this pirate fellow," said one. "I wish they have not more to speak about than the ransom of her father."

"Ay, truly," answered another, "the wenches will have more sympathy with a handsome young pirate than an old bed-ridden burgher."

Their discourse was here interrupted by her of whom they were speaking; and, as if taken in the manner, they pulled off their hats, made their awkward obeisances, and looked not a little embarrassed and confused.

Minna returned to the house where she lodged, much affected, yet, on the whole, pleased with the result of her expedition, which seemed to put her father out of danger, and assured her at once of the escape of Cleveland and of the safety of young Mordaunt. She hastened to communicate both pieces of intelligence to Brenda, who joined her in thankfulness to Heaven, and was herself wellnigh persuaded to believe in Norna's supernatural pretensions, so much was she pleased with the manner in which they had been employed. Some time was spent in exchanging their mutual congratulations, and mingling tears of hope, mixed with apprehension, when, at a late hour in the evening, they were interrupted by Claud Halcro, who, full of a fidgeting sort of importance, not unmingled with fear, came to acquaint them that the prisoner, Cleveland, had disappeared from the cathedral, in which he had been permitted to walk, and that the provost, having been informed that Minna was accessory to his flight, was coming, in a mighty quandary, to make inquiry into the circumstances.

When the worthy magistrate arrived, Minna did not conceal from him her own wish that Cleveland should make his escape, as the only means which she saw of redeeming her father from imminent danger. But that she had any actual accession to his flight, she positively denied; and stated, "That she had parted from Cleveland in the cathedral, more than two hours since, and then left him in company with a third person, whose name she did not conceive herself obliged to communicate."

"It is not needful, Miss Minna Troil," answered Provost Torfe; "for, although no person but this Captain Cleveland and yourself was seen to enter the kirk of St. Magnus this day, we know well enough that your cousin, old Ulla Troil, whom you Zetlanders call Norna of Fitful Head, has been cruising up and down, upon sea and land, and air, for what I know, in boats and on ponies, and it may be on broomsticks; and there has been her dumb Drow, too, coming and going, and playing the spy on every one; and a good spy he is, for he can hear everything, and tells nothing again, unless to his mistress. And we know, besides, that she can enter the kirk when all the doors are fast, and has been seen there more than once, God save us from the Evil One! and so, without farther questions asked, I conclude it was old Norna whom you left in the kirk with this slashing blade; and if so, they may catch them again that can. I cannot but say, however, pretty Mistress Minna, that you Zetland folks seem to forget both law and Gospel, when you use the help of witchcraft to fetch delinquents out of a legal prison; and the least that you, or your cousin, or your father, can do, is to use influence with

this wild fellow to go away as soon as possible, without hurting the town or trade, and then there will be little harm in
what has chanced; for, Heaven knows, I did not seek the
poor lad's life, so I could get my hands free of him without
blame; and far less did I wish that, through his imprisonment, any harm should come to worthy Magnus Troil of
Burgh-Westra."

"I see where the shoe pinches you, Mr. Provost," said
Claud Halcro, "and I am sure I can answer for my friend
Mr. Troil, as well as for myself, that we will say and do all
in our power with this man, Captain Cleveland, to make him
leave the coast directly."

"And I," said Minna, "am so convinced that what you
recommend is best for all parties, that my sister and I will
set off early to-morrow morning to the House of Stennis, if
Mr. Halcro will give us his escort, to receive my father when
he comes ashore, that we may acquaint him with your wish,
and to use every influence to induce this unhappy man to
leave the country."

Provost Torfe looked upon her with some surprise. "It is
not every young woman," he said, "would wish to move eight
miles nearer to a band of pirates."

"We run no risk," said Claud Halcro, interfering. "The
House of Stennis is strong; and my cousin, whom it belongs
to, has men and arms within it. The young ladies are as
safe there as in Kirkwall; and much good may arise from an
early communication between Magnus Troil and his daughters. And happy am I to see that, in your case, my good old
friend, as glorious John says—

> After much debate,
> The man prevails above the magistrate."

The provost smiled, nodded his head, and indicated, as far
as he thought he could do so with decency, how happy he
should be if the "Fortune's Favourite" and her disorderly
crew would leave Orkney without further interference or violence on either side. He could not authorise their being supplied from the shore, he said; but, either for fear or favour,

they were certain to get provisions at Stromness. This pacific magistrate then took leave of Halcro and the two ladies, who proposed the next morning to transfer their residence to the House of Stennis, situated upon the banks of the salt-water lake of the same name, and about four miles by water from the Road of Stromness, where the rover's vessel was lying.

CHAPTER XXXVIII.

Fly, Fleance, fly! Thou mayst escape.
Macbeth.

It was one branch of the various arts by which Norna endeavoured to maintain her pretensions to supernatural powers, that she made herself familiarly and practically acquainted with all the secret passes and recesses, whether natural or artificial, which she could hear of, whether by tradition or otherwise, and was, by such knowledge, often enabled to perform feats which were otherwise unaccountable. Thus, when she escaped from the tabernacle at Burgh-Westra, it was by a sliding board which covered a secret passage in the wall, known to none but herself and Magnus, who, she was well assured, would not betray her. The profusion, also, with which she lavished a considerable income, otherwise of no use to her, enabled her to procure the earliest intelligence respecting whatever she desired to know, and, at the same time, to secure all other assistance necessary to carry her plans into effect. Cleveland, upon the present occasion, had reason to admire both her sagacity and her resources.

Upon her applying a little forcible pressure, a door, which was concealed under some rich wooden sculpture in the screen which divides the eastern aisle from the rest of the cathedral, opened, and disclosed a dark, narrow, winding passage, into which she entered, telling Cleveland, in a whisper, to follow, and be sure he shut the door behind him. He obeyed, and followed her in darkness and silence, sometimes descending steps, of the number of which she always apprised him, sometimes ascending, and often turning at short angles. The air was more free than he could have expected, the passage being ventilated at different parts by unseen and ingeniously contrived spiracles, which communicated with the open air. At length their long course ended by Norna drawing aside a sliding panel, which, opening behind a wooden, or box-bed, as it is called in Scotland, admitted them into an ancient, but very mean, apartment, having a latticed window and a groined roof. The furniture was much dilapidated; and its only ornaments were, on the one side of the wall, a garland of faded ribbons, such as are used to decorate whale-vessels; and, on the other, an escutcheon, bearing an earl's arms and coronet, surrounded with the usual emblems of mortality. The mattock and spade, which lay in one corner, together with the appearance of an old man, who, in a rusty black coat and slouched hat, sat reading by a table, announced that they were in the habitation of the church beadle, or sexton, and in the presence of that respectable functionary.

When his attention was attracted by the noise of the sliding panel, he arose, and, testifying much respect, but no surprise, took his shadowy hat from his thin grey locks, and stood uncovered in the presence of Norna with an air of profound humility.

"Be faithful," said Norna to the old man, "and beware you show not any living mortal the secret path to the sanctuary."

The old man bowed, in token of obedience and of thanks, for she put money in his hand as she spoke. With a faltering voice, he expressed his hope that she would remember his son, who was on the Greenland voyage, that he might return fortunate and safe, as he had done last year, when he brought back the garland, pointing to that upon the wall.

"My cauldron shall boil, and my rhyme shall be said, in his behalf," answered Norna. "Waits Pacolet without with the horses?"

The old sexton assented, and the pythoness, commanding Cleveland to follow her, went through a back door of the apartment into a small garden, corresponding, in its desolate appearance, to the habitation they had just quitted. The low and broken wall easily permitted them to pass into another and larger garden, though not much better kept, and a gate, which was upon the latch, let them into a long and winding lane, through which, Norna having whispered to her companion that it was the only dangerous place on their road, they walked with a hasty pace. It was now nearly dark, and the inhabitants of the poor dwellings on either hand had taken themselves to their houses. They saw only one woman, who was looking from her door, but blessed herself, and retired into her house with precipitation, when she saw the tall figure of Norna stalk past her with long strides. The lane conducted them into the country, where the dumb dwarf waited with three horses, ensconced behind the wall of a deserted shed. On one of these Norna instantly seated herself, Cleveland mounted another, and, followed by Pacolet on the third, they moved sharply on through the darkness; the active and spirited animals on which they rode being of a breed rather taller than those reared in Zetland.

After more than an hour's smart riding, in which Norna acted as guide, they stopped before a hovel, so utterly desolate in appearance that it resembled rather a cattle-shed than a cottage.

"Here you must remain till dawn, when your signal can be seen from your vessel," said Norna, consigning the horses to the care of Pacolet, and leading the way into the wretched hovel, which she presently illuminated by lighting the small iron lamp which she usually carried along with her. "It is a poor," she said, "but a safe, place of refuge; for, were we pursued hither, the earth would yawn and admit us into its recesses ere you were taken. For know, that this ground is sacred to the gods of old Valhalla. And now say, man of mischief and of blood, are you friend or foe to Norna, the sole priestess of these disowned deities?"

"How is it possible for me to be your enemy?" said Cleveland. "Common gratitude——"

"Common gratitude," said Norna, interrupting him, "is a common word; and words are the common pay which fools accept at the hands of knaves; but Norna must be requited by actions—by sacrifices."

"Well, mother, name your request."

"That you never seek to see Minna Troil again, and that you leave this coast in twenty-four hours," answered Norna.

"It is impossible," said the outlaw: "I cannot be soon enough found in the sea-stores which the sloop must have."

"You can. I will take care you are fully supplied; and Caithness and the Hebrides are not far distant—you can depart if you will."

"And why should I," said Cleveland, "if I will not?"

"Because your stay endangers others," said Norna, "and will prove your own destruction. Hear me with attention. From the first moment I saw you lying senseless on the sand beneath the cliffs of Sumburgh, I read that in your countenance which linked you with me, and those who were dear to me; but whether for good or evil, was hidden from mine eyes. I aided in saving your life, in preserving your property. I aided in doing so the very youth whom you have crossed in his dearest affections—crossed by tale-bearing and slander."

"*I* slander Mertoun!" exclaimed Cleveland. "By Heaven I scarce mentioned his name at Burgh-Westra, if it is that which you mean. The peddling fellow Bryce, meaning, I believe, to be my friend, because he found something could be made by me, did, I have since heard, carry tattle, or truth, I know not which, to the old man, which was confirmed by the report of the whole island. But, for me, I scárce thought of him as a rival; else I had taken a more honourable way to rid myself of him."

"Was the point of your double-edged knife, directed to the bosom of an unarmed man, intended to carve out that more honourable way?" said Norna, sternly.

Cleveland was conscience-struck, and remained silent for an instant, ere he replied: "There, indeed, I was wrong; but he is, I thank Heaven, recovered, and welcome to an honourable satisfaction."

"Cleveland," said the pythoness, "no! The fiend who employs you as his implement is powerful; but with me he shall not strive. You are of that temperament which the dark Influences desire as the tools of their agency—bold, haughty, and undaunted, unrestrained by principle, and having only in its room a wild sense of indomitable pride, which such men call honour. Such you are, and as such your course through life has been—onward and unrestrained, bloody and tempestuous. By me, however, it shall be controlled," she concluded, stretching out her staff, as if in the attitude of determined authority—"ay, even although the demon who presides over it should now arise in his terrors."

Cleveland laughed scornfully. "Good mother," he said, "reserve such language for the rude sailor that implores you to bestow him fair wind, or the poor fisherman that asks success to his nets and lines. I have been long inaccessible both to fear and to superstition. Call forth your demon, if you command one, and place him before me. The man that has spent years in company with incarnate devils can scarce dread the presence of a disembodied fiend."

This was said with a careless and desperate bitterness of spirit which proved too powerfully energetic even for the delusions of Norna's insanity; and it was with a hollow and tremulous voice that she asked Cleveland: "For what, then, do you hold me, if you deny the power I have bought so dearly?"

"You have wisdom, mother," said Cleveland; "at least you have art, and art is power. I hold you for one who knows how to steer upon the current of events, but I deny your power to change its course. Do not, therefore, waste words in quoting terrors for which I have no feeling, but tell me at once wherefore you would have me depart?"

"Because I will have you see Minna no more," answered Norna. "Because Minna is the destined bride of him whom men call Mordaunt Mertoun. Because, if you depart not within twenty-four hours, utter destruction awaits you. In these plain words there is no metaphysical delusion. Answer me as plainly."

"In as plain words, then," answered Cleveland, "I will *not* leave these islands—not, at least, till I have seen Minna Troil; and never shall your Mordaunt possess her while I live."

"Hear him!" said Norna—"hear a mortal man spurn at the means of prolonging his life! Hear a sinful—a most sinful being, refuse the time which fate yet affords repentance, and for the salvation of an immortal soul! Behold him how he stands erect, bold and confident in his youthful strength and courage! My eyes, unused to tears—even my eyes, which have so little cause to weep for him, are blinded with sorrow, to think what so fair a form will be ere the second sun set!"

"Mother," said Cleveland, firmly, yet with some touch of sorrow in his voice, "I in part understand your threats. You know more than we do of the course of the 'Halcyon,' perhaps have the means—for I acknowledge you have shown wonderful skill of combination in such affairs—of directing her cruise our way. Be it so, I will not depart from my purpose for that risk. If the frigate comes hither, we have still our shoal water to trust to; and I think they will scarce cut us out with boats, as if we were a Spanish xebeck. I am therefore resolved I will hoist once more the flag under which I have cruised, avail ourselves of the thousand chances which have helped us in greater odds, and, at the worst, fight the vessel to the very last; and, when mortal man can do no more, it is but snapping a pistol in the powder-room, and, as we have lived, so will we die."

There was a dead pause as Cleveland ended; and it was broken by his resuming, in a softer tone: "You have heard my answer, mother; let us debate it no further, but part in peace. I would willingly leave you a remembrance, that you may not forget a poor fellow to whom your services have been useful, and who parts with you in no unkindness, however unfriendly you are to his dearest interests. Nay, do not shun to accept such a trifle," he said, forcing upon Norna the little silver enchased box which had been once the subject of strife betwixt Mertoun and him; "it is not for the sake of the metal, which I know you value not, but simply as a memorial that you have met him of whom many a strange tale will hereafter be told in the seas which he has traversed."

"I accept your gift," said Norna, "in token that, if I have

in aught been accessory to your fate, it was as the involuntary and grieving agent of other powers. Well did you say we direct not the current of the events which hurry us forward, and render our utmost efforts unavailing; even as the wells [1] of Tuftiloe can wheel the stoutest vessel round and round in despite of either sail or steerage. Pacolet!" she exclaimed in a louder voice—"what, ho! Pacolet!"

A large stone, which lay at the side of the wall of the hovel, fell as she spoke, and to Cleveland's surprise, if not somewhat to his fear, the misshapen form of the dwarf was seen, like some overgrown reptile, extricating himself out of a subterranean passage, the entrance to which the stone had covered.

Norna, as if impressed by what Cleveland had said on the subject of her supernatural pretensions, was so far from endeavouring to avail herself of this opportunity to enforce them, that she hastened to explain the phenomenon he had witnessed.

"Such passages," she said, "to which the entrances are carefully concealed, are frequently found in these islands—the places of retreat of the ancient inhabitants, where they sought refuge from the rage of the Normans, the pirates of that day. It was that you might avail yourself of this, in case of need, that I brought you hither. Should you observe signs of pursuit, you may either lurk in the bowels of the earth until it has passed by, or escape, if you will, through the farther entrance near the lake, by which Pacolet entered but now. And now farewell! Think on what I have said; for as sure as you now move and breathe a living man, so surely is your doom fixed and sealed, unless, within four-and-twenty hours, you have doubled the Burgh Head."

"Farewell, mother!" said Cleveland, as she departed, bending a look upon him, in which, as he could perceive by the lamp, sorrow was mingled with displeasure.

The interview, which thus concluded, left a strong effect even upon the mind of Cleveland, accustomed as he was to imminent dangers and to hairbreadth escapes. He in vain

[1] See Wells and Waves. Note 45.

attempted to shake off the impression left by the words of
Norna, which he felt the more powerful, because they were
in a great measure divested of her wonted mystical tone,
which he contemned. A thousand times he regretted that
he had from time to time delayed the resolution, which he had
long adopted, to quit his dreadful and dangerous trade; and
as often he firmly determined that, could he but see Minna
Troil once more, were it but for a last farewell, he would
leave the sloop as soon as his comrades were extricated from
their perilous situation, endeavour to obtain the benefit of the
king's pardon, and distinguish himself, if possible, in some
more honourable course of warfare.

This resolution, to which he again and again pledged himself, had at length a sedative effect on his mental perturba-
tion, and, wrapt in his cloak, he enjoyed, for a time, that
imperfect repose which exhausted nature demands as her
tribute, even from those who are situated on the verge of the
most imminent danger. But, how far soever the guilty may
satisfy his own mind and stupify the feelings of remorse by
such a conditional repentance, we may well question whether
it is not, in the sight of Heaven, rather a presumptuous aggravation than an expiation of his sins.

When Cleveland awoke, the grey dawn was already mingling with the twilight of an Orcadian night. He found himself on the verge of a beautiful sheet of water, which, close
by the place where he had rested, was nearly divided by two
tongues of land that approach each other from the opposing
sides of the lake, and are in some degree united by the Bridge
of Broisgar, a long causeway, containing openings to permit
the flow and reflux of the tide. Behind him, and fronting to
the bridge, stood that remarkable semicircle of huge upright
stones which has no rival in Britain, excepting the inimitable
monument at Stonehenge. These immense blocks of stone,
all of them above twelve feet, and several being even fourteen
or fifteen feet in height, stood around the pirate in the grey
light of the dawning like the phantom forms of antediluvian
giants, who, shrouded in the habiliments of the dead, came to
revisit, by this pale light, the earth which they had plagued by

their oppression and polluted by their sins, till they brought down upon it the vengeance of long-suffering Heaven.

Cleveland was less interested by this singular monument of antiquity than by the distant view of Stromness, which he could as yet scarce discover. He lost no time in striking a light, by the assistance of one of his pistols, and some wet fern supplied him with fuel sufficient to make the appointed signal. It had been earnestly watched for on board the sloop; for Goffe's incapacity became daily more apparent; and even his most steady adherents agreed it would be best to submit to Cleveland's command till they got back to the West Indies.

Bunce, who came with the boat to bring off his favourite commander, danced, cursed, shouted, and spouted for joy when he saw him once more at freedom. "They had already," he said, "made some progress in victualling the sloop, and they might have made more but for that drunken old swab Goffe, who minded nothing but splicing the mainbrace."

The boat's crew were inspired with the same enthusiasm, and rowed so hard that, although the tide was against them, and the air of wind failed, they soon placed Cleveland once more on the quarter-deck of the vessel which it was his misfortune to command.

The first exercise of the captain's power was to make known to Magnus Troil that he was at full freedom to depart; that he was willing to make him any compensation in his power for the interruption of his voyage to Kirkwall; and that Captain Cleveland was desirous, if agreeable to Mr. Troil, to pay his respects to him on board his brig, thank him for former favours, and apologise for the circumstances attending his detention.

To Bunce, who, as the most civilised of the crew, Cleveland had entrusted this message, the old plain-dealing Udaller made the following answer: "Tell your captain that I should be glad to think he had never stopped any one upon the high sea save such as have suffered as little as I have. Say, too, that, if we are to continue friends, we shall be most so at a

[1] See The Standing Stones of Stennis. Note 46.

distance, for I like the sound of his cannon-balls as little by sea as he would like the whistle of a bullet by land from my rifle-gun. Say, in a word, that I am sorry I was mistaken in him, and that he would have done better to have reserved for the Spaniard the usage he is bestowing on his countrymen."

"And so that is your message, old Snapcholerick?" said Bunce. "Now, stap my vitals if I have not a mind to do your errand for you over the left shoulder, and teach you more respect for gentlemen of fortune! But I won't, and chiefly for the sake of your two pretty wenches, not to mention my old friend Claud Halcro, the very visage of whom brought back all the old days of scene-shifting and candle-snuffing. So good morrow to you, Gaffer Seal's-cap, and all is said that need pass between us."

No sooner did the boat put off with the pirates, who left the brig and now returned to their own vessel, than Magnus, in order to avoid reposing unnecessary confidence in the honour of these gentlemen of fortune, as they called themselves, got his brig under way; and, the wind coming favourably round, and increasing as the sun rose, he crowded all sail for Scalpa Flow, intending there to disembark and go by land to Kirkwall, where he expected to meet his daughters and his friend Claud Halcro.

CHAPTER XXXIX.

Now, Emma, now the last reflection make,
What thou wouldst follow, what thou must forsake.
By our ill-omen'd stars and adverse Heaven,
No middle object to thy choice is given.
Henry and Emma.

THE sun was high in heaven; the boats were busily fetching off from the shore the promised supply of provisions and water, which, as many fishing skiffs were employed in the service, were got on board with unexpected speed, and stowed away by the crew of the sloop with equal despatch. All worked with good will; for all, save Cleveland himself, were weary of a coast where every moment increased their danger, and where, which they esteemed a worse misfortune, there was no booty to be won. Bunce and Derrick took the immediate direction of this duty, while Cleveland, walking the deck alone, and in silence, only interfered from time to time, to give some order which circumstances required, and then relapsed into his own sad reflections.

There are two sorts of men whom situations of guilt, terror, and commotion bring forward as prominent agents. The first are spirits so naturally moulded and fitted for deeds of horror that they stalk forth from their lurking-places like actual demons, to work in their native element, as the hideous apparition of the Bearded Man came forth at Versailles, on the memorable 5th October 1789, the delighted executioner of the victims delivered up to him by a bloodthirsty rabble. But Cleveland belonged to the second class of these unfortunate beings, who are involved in evil rather by the concurrence of external circumstances than by natural inclination, being, indeed, one in whom his first engaging in this lawless mode of life, as the follower of his father, nay, perhaps, even his pursuing it as his father's avenger, carried with it something of mitigation and apology; one also who often considered his guilty situation with horror, and had made repeated, though ineffectual, efforts to escape from it.

Such thoughts of remorse were now rolling in his mind, and he may be forgiven if recollections of Minna mingled with and aided them. He looked around, too, on his mates, and, profligate and hardened as he knew them to be, he could not think of their paying the penalty of his obstinacy. "We shall be ready to sail with the ebb tide," he said to himself; "why should I endanger these men by detaining them till the hour of danger predicted by that singular woman shall arrive? Her intelligence, however acquired, has been always strangely accurate; and her warning was as solemn as if a mother were to apprise an erring son of his crimes and of his approaching punishment. Besides, what chance is there that I can again see Minna? She is at Kirkwall, doubtless, and to hold my course thither would be to steer right upon the rocks. No, I will not endanger these poor fellows: I will sail with the ebb tide. On the desolate Hebrides, or on the northwest coast of Ireland, I will leave the vessel and return hither in some disguise; yet, why should I return, since it will perhaps be only to see Minna the bride of Mordaunt? No; let the vessel sail with this ebb tide without me. I will abide and take my fate."

His meditations were here interrupted by Jack Bunce, who, hailing him noble captain, said they were ready to sail when he pleased.

"When *you* please, Bunce; for I shall leave the command with you, and go ashore at Stromness," said Cleveland.

"You shall do no such matter, by Heaven!" answered Bunce. "The command with me, truly! and how the devil am I to get the crew to obey *me?* Why, even Dick Fletcher rides rusty on me now and then. You know well enough that, without you, we shall be all at each other's throats in half an hour; and, if you desert us, what a rope's end does it signify whether we are destroyed by the king's cruisers or by each other? Come—come, noble captain, there are black-eyed girls enough in the world, but where will you find so tight a sea-boat as the little 'Favourite' here, manned as she is with a set of tearing lads,

> Fit to disturb the peace of all the world,
> And rule it when 'tis wildest?"

"You are a precious fool, Jack Bunce," said Cleveland, half-angry, and, in despite of himself, half-diverted, by the false tones and exaggerated gesture of the stage-struck pirate.

"It may be so, noble captain," answered Bunce; "and it may be that I have my comrades in my folly. Here are you, now, going to play *All for Love and [or] the World well Lost*, and yet you cannot bear a harmless bounce in blank verse. Well, I can talk prose for the matter, for I have news enough to tell—and strange news, too—ay, and stirring news to boot."

"Well, prithee deliver them—to speak thy own cant—like a man of this world."

"The Stromness fishers will accept nothing for their provisions and troubles," said Bunce—"there is a wonder for you!"

30

"And for what reason, I pray?" said Cleveland; "it is the first time I have ever heard of cash being refused at a seaport."

"True! they commonly lay the charges on as thick as if they were caulking. But here is the matter. The owner of the brig yonder, the father of your fair Imoinda, stands paymaster, by way of thanks for the civility with which we treated his daughters, and that we may not meet our due, as he calls it, on these shores."

"It is like the frank-hearted old Udaller!" said Cleveland. "But is he at Stromness? I thought he was to have crossed the island for Kirkwall."

"He did so purpose," said Bunce; "but more folks than King Duncan change the course of their voyage. He was no sooner ashore than he was met with by a meddling old witch of these parts, who has her finger in every man's pie, and by her counsel he changed his purpose of going to Kirkwall, and lies at anchor for the present in yonder white house, that you may see with your glass up the lake yonder. I am told the old woman clubbed also to pay for the sloop's stores. Why she should shell out the boards I cannot conceive an idea, except that she is said to be a witch, and may befriend us as so many devils."

"But who told you all this?" said Cleveland, without using his spy-glass, or seeming so much interested in the news as his comrade had expected.

"Why," replied Bunce, "I made a trip ashore this morning to the village, and had a can with an old acquaintance, who had been sent by Master Troil to look after matters, and I fished it all out of him, and more, too, than I am desirous of telling you, noble captain."

"And who is your intelligencer?" said Cleveland; "has he got no name?"

"Why, he is an old, fiddling, foppish acquaintance of mine called Halcro, if you must know," said Bunce.

"Halcro!" echoed Cleveland, his eyes sparkling with surprise—"Claud Halcro? why, he went ashore at Inganess with Minna and her sister. Where are they?"

"Why, that is just what I did not want to tell you," replied the confidant; "yet hang me if I can help it, for I cannot baulk a fine situation. That start had a fine effect. Oh ay, and the spy-glass is turned on the House of Stennis *now!* Well, yonder they are, it must be confessed—indifferently well guarded, too. Some of the old witch's people are come over from that mountain of an island—Hoy, as they call it; and the old gentleman has got some fellows under arms himself. But what of all that, noble captain! give you but the word, and we snap up the wenches to-night—clap them under hatches—man the capstern by daybreak—up topsails—and sail with the morning tide."

"You sicken me with your villainy," said Cleveland, turning away from him.

"Umph! villainy, and sicken you!" said Bunce. "Now, pray, what have I said but what has been done a thousand times by gentlemen of fortune like ourselves?"

"Mention it not again," said Cleveland; then took a turn along the deck, in deep meditation, and, coming back to Bunce, took him by the hand, and said: "Jack, I will see her once more."

"With all my heart," said Bunce, sullenly.

"Once more will I see her, and it may be to abjure at her feet this cursed trade, and expiate my offences——"

"At the gallows!" said Bunce, completing the sentence. "With all my heart! confess and be hanged is a most reverend proverb."

"Nay—but, dear Jack!" said Cleveland.

"Dear Jack!" answered Bunce, in the same sullen tone, "a dear sight you have been to dear Jack. But hold your own course; I have done with caring for you for ever. I should but sicken you with my villainous counsels."

"Now, must I soothe this silly fellow as if he were a spoiled child," said Cleveland, speaking at Bunce, but not to him; "and yet he has sense enough, and bravery enough, too; and, one would think, kindness enough to know that men don't pick their words during a gale of wind."

"Why, that's true, Clement," said Bunce, "and there is

my hand upon it. And, now I think upon't, you shall have your last interview, for it's out of my line to prevent a parting scene; and what signifies a tide? We can sail by to-morrow's ebb as well as by this."

Cleveland sighed, for Norna's prediction rushed on his mind; but the opportunity of a last meeting with Minna was too tempting to be resigned either for presentiment or prediction.

"I will go presently ashore to the place where they all are," said Bunce; "and the payment of these stores shall serve me for a pretext; and I will carry any letters or message from you to Minna with the dexterity of a *valet-de-chambre*."

"But they have armed men; you may be in danger," said Cleveland.

"Not a whit—not a whit," replied Bunce. "I protected the wenches when they were in my power; I warrant their father will neither wrong me nor see me wronged."

"You say true," said Cleveland, "it is not in his nature. I will instantly write a note to Minna." And he ran down to the cabin for that purpose, where he wasted much paper ere, with a trembling hand and throbbing heart, he achieved such a letter as he hoped might prevail on Minna to permit him a farewell meeting on the succeeding morning.

His adherent, Bunce, in the mean while, sought out Fletcher, of whose support to second any motion whatever he accounted himself perfectly sure; and, followed by this trusty satellite, he intruded himself on the awful presence of Hawkins, the boatswain, and Derrick, the quartermaster, who were regaling themselves with a can of rumbo, after the fatiguing duty of the day.

"Here comes he can tell us," said Derrick. "So, Master Lieutenant, for so we must call you now, I think, let us have a peep into your counsels. When will the anchor be a-trip?"

"When it pleases Heaven, Master Quartermaster," answerd Bunce, "for I know no more than the stern-post."

"Why, d—n my buttons," said Derrick, "do we not weigh this tide?"

"Or to-morrow's tide, at farthest?" said the boatswain.

"Why, what have we been slaving the whole company for, to get all these stores aboard?"

"Gentlemen," said Bunce, "you are to know that Cupid has laid our captain on board, carried the vessel, and nailed down his wits under hatches."

"What sort of play-stuff is all this?" said the boatswain, gruffly. "If you have anything to tell us, say it in a word, like a man."

"Howsomdever," said Fletcher, "I always think Jack Bunce speaks like a man, and acts like a man too; and so, d'ye see——"

"Hold your peace, dear Dick—best of bully-backs, be silent," said Bunce. "Gentlemen, in one word, the captain is in love."

"Why, now, only think of that!" said the boatswain; "not but that I have been in love as often as any man, when the ship was laid up."

"Well, but," continued Bunce, "Captain Cleveland is in love. Yes—Prince Volscius is in love; and, though that's the cue for laughing on the stage, it is no laughing matter here. He expects to meet the girl to-morrow, for the last time; and that, we all know, leads to another meeting, and another, and so on till the 'Halcyon' is down on us, and then we may look for more kicks than halfpence."

"By ——," said the boatswain, with a sounding oath, "we'll have a mutiny, and not allow him to go ashore—eh, Derrick?"

"And the best way too," said Derrick.

'What d'ye think of it, Jack Bunce?' said Fletcher, in whose ears this counsel sounded very sagely, but who still bent a wistful look upon his companion.

"Why, look ye, gentlemen," said Bunce, "I will mutiny none, and stap my vitals if any of you shall!"

"Why, then I won't, for one," said Fletcher; "but what are we to do, since howsomdever——"

"Stopper your jaw, Dick, will you?" said Bunce. "Now, boatswain, I am partly of your mind, that the captain must be brought to reason by a little wholesome force. But you all know he has the spirit of a lion, and will do nothing unless

he is allowed to hold on his own course.   Well, I'll go ashore
and make this appointment.   The girl comes to the rendezvous in the morning, and the captain goes ashore; we take a
good boat's crew with us, to row against tide and current, and
we will be ready at the signal to jump ashore and bring off
the captain and the girl, whether they will or no.   The pet-
child will not quarrel with us, since we bring off his whirligig
along with him; and if he is still fractious, why, we will weigh
anchor without his orders, and let him come to his senses at
leisure, and know his friends another time."

"Why, this has a face with it, Master Derrick," said Hawkins.

"Jack Bunce is always right," said Fletcher; "howsomdever, the captain will shoot some of us, that is certain."

"Hold your jaw, Dick," said Bunce; "pray, who the devil
cares, do you think, whether you are shot or hanged?"

"Why, it don't much argufy for the matter of that," replied Dick; "howsomdever——"

"Be quiet, I tell you," said his inexorable patron, "and
hear me out.   We will take him at unawares, so that he shall
neither have time to use cutlass nor pops; and I myself, for
the dear love I bear him, will be the first to lay him on his
back.   There is a nice tight-going bit of a pinnace that is a
consort of this chase of the captain's; if I have an opportunity, I'll snap her up on my own account."

"Yes—yes," said Derrick, "let you alone for keeping on
the lookout for your own comforts."

"Faith, nay," said Bunce, "I only snatch at them when
they come fairly in my way, or are purchased by dint of my
own wit; and none of you could have fallen on such a plan as
this.   We shall have the captain with us, head, hand, and
heart and all, besides making a scene fit to finish a comedy.
So I will go ashore to make the appointment, and do you possess some of the gentlemen who are still sober, and fit to be
trusted, with the knowledge of our intentions."

Bunce, with his friend Fletcher, departed accordingly, and
the two veteran pirates remained looking at each other in silence, until the boatswain spoke at last.   "Blow me, Derrick,

if I like these two daffadandilly young fellows: they are not the true breed. Why, they are no more like the rovers I have known than this sloop is to a first-rate. Why, there was old Sharpe, that read prayers to his ship's company every Sunday, what would he have said to have heard it proposed to bring two wenches on board?"

"And what would tough old Black Beard have said," answered his companion, "if they had expected to keep them to themselves? They deserve to be made to walk the plank for their impudence; or to be tied back to back and set a-diving, and I care not how soon."

"Ay, but who is to command the ship, then?" said Hawkins.

"Why, what ails you at old Goffe?" answered Derrick.

"Why, he has sucked the monkey so long and so often," said the boatswain, "that the best of him is buffed. He is little better than an old woman when he is sober, and he is roaring mad when he is drunk; we have had enough of Goffe."

"Why, then, what d'ye say to yourself, or to me, boatswain?" demanded the quartermaster. "I am content to toss up for it."

"Rot it, no," answered the boatswain after a moment's consideration; "if we were within reach of the trade winds, we might either of us make a shift; but it will take all Cleveland's navigation to get us there; and so, I think, there is nothing like Bunce's project for the present. Hark, he calls for the boat; I must go on deck and have her lowered for his honour, d—n his eyes."

The boat was lowered accordingly, made its voyage up the lake with safety, and landed Bunce within a few hundred yards of the old mansion-house of Stennis. Upon arriving in front of the house, he found that hasty measures had been taken to put it in a state of defence, the lower windows being barricaded, with places left for use of musketry, and a ship-gun being placed so as to command the entrance, which was besides guarded by two sentinels. Bunce demanded admission at the gate, which was briefly and unceremoniously refused, with an exhortation to him, at the same time, to be gone about his business before worse came of it. As he continued, however, importunately to insist on seeing some one of the family, and stated his business to be of the most urgent nature, Claud Halcro at length appeared, and, with more peevishness than belonged to his usual manner, that admirer of glorious John expostulated with his old acquaintance upon his pertinacious folly.

"You are," he said, "like foolish moths fluttering about a candle, which is sure at last to consume you."

"And you," said Bunce, "are a set of stingless drones, whom we can smoke out of your defences at our pleasure, with half a dozen of hand-grenades."

"Smoke a fool's head!" said Halcro; "take my advice, and mind your own matters, or there will be those upon you will smoke you to purpose. Either begone or tell me in two words what you want; for you are like to receive no welcome here save from a blunderbuss. We are men enough of ourselves; and here is young Mordaunt Mertoun come from Hoy, whom your captain so nearly murdered."

"Tush, man," said Bunce, "he did but let out a little malapert blood."

"We want no such phlebotomy here," said Claud Halcro; "and, besides, your patient turns out to be nearer allied to us than either you or we thought of; so you may think how little welcome the captain or any of his crew are like to be here."

"Well, but what if I bring money for the stores sent on board?"

"Keep it till it is asked of you," said Halcro. "There are two bad paymasters—he that pays too soon, and he that does not pay at all."

"Well, then, let me at least give our thanks to the donor," said Bunce.

"Keep them, too, till they are asked for," answered the poet.

"So this is all the welcome I have of you for old acquaintance' sake?" said Bunce.

"Why, what can I do for you, Master Altamont?" said Halcro, somewhat moved. "If young Mordaunt had had his own will, he would have welcomed you with 'the red Burgundy, No. 1000.' For God's sake begone, else the stage direction will be: 'Enter guard, and seize Altamont.'"

"I will not give you the trouble," said Bunce, "but will make my exit instantly. Stay a moment; I had almost forgot that I have a slip of paper for the tallest of your girls there—Minna, ay, Minna is her name. It is a farewell from Captain Cleveland; you cannot refuse to give it her?"

"Ah, poor fellow!" said Halcro; "I comprehend—I comprehend. Farewell, fair Armida—

> 'Mid pikes and 'mid bullets, 'mid tempests and fire,
> The danger is less than in hopeless desire!

Tell me but this—is there poetry in it?"

"Chokeful to the seal with song, sonnet, and elegy," answered Bunce; "but let her have it cautiously and secretly."

"Tush, man! teach me to deliver a billet-doux!—me, who have been in the Wits' Coffee-house, and have seen all the toasts of the Kit-Cat Club! Minna shall have it, then, for old acquaintance' sake, Mr. Altamont, and for your captain's sake too, who has less of the core of devil about him than his trade requires. There can be no harm in a farewell letter."

"Farewell, then, old boy, for ever and a day!" said Bunce; and seizing the poet's hand, gave it so hearty a gripe that he left him roaring and shaking his fist, like a dog when a hot cinder has fallen on his foot.

Leaving the rover to return on board the vessel, we remain with the family of Magnus Troil, assembled at their kinsman's mansion of Stennis, where they maintained a constant and careful watch against surprise.

Mordaunt Mertoun had been received with much kindness by Magnus Troil, when he came to his assistance, with a small party of Norna's dependants, placed by her under his command. The Udaller was easily satisfied that the reports instilled into his ears by the jagger, zealous to augment his favour towards his more profitable customer, Cleveland, by diminishing that of Mertoun, were without foundation. They had, indeed, been confirmed by the good Lady Glowrowrum and by common fame, both of whom were pleased to represent Mordaunt Mertoun as an arrogant pretender to the favour of the sisters of Burgh-Westra, who only hesitated, sultan-like, on whom he should bestow the handkerchief. But common fame, Magnus considered, was a common liar, and he was sometimes disposed, where scandal was concerned, to regard the good Lady Glowrowrum as rather an uncommon specimen of the same genus. He therefore received Mordaunt once more into full favour, listened with much surprise to the claim which Norna laid to the young man's duty, and with no less interest to her intention of surrendering to him the considerable property which she had inherited from her father. Nay, it is even probable that, though he gave no immediate answer to her hints concerning an union betwixt his eldest daughter and her heir, he might think such an alliance recommended as well by the young man's personal merits as by the chance it gave of reuniting the very large estate which had been divided betwixt his own father and that of Norna. At all events, the Udaller received his young friend with much kindness, and he and the proprietor of the mansion joined in entrusting to him, as the youngest and most active of the party, the charge of commanding the night-watch, and relieving the sentinels around the House of Stennis.

CHAPTER XL.

Of an outlawe, this is the lawe—
That men him take and bind,
Without pitie hang'd to be,
And waive with the wind.
The Ballad of the Nut-Brown Maid.

MORDAUNT had caused the sentinels who had been on duty since midnight to be relieved ere the peep of day, and having given directions that the guard should be again changed at sunrise, he had retired to a small parlour, and, placing his arms beside him, was slumbering in an easy-chair, when he felt himself pulled by the watch-cloak in which he was enveloped.

"Is it sunrise," said he, "already?" as, starting up, he discovered the first beams lying level upon the horizon.

"Mordaunt!" said a voice, every note of which thrilled to his heart.

He turned his eyes on the speaker, and Brenda Troil, to his joyful astonishment, stood before him. As he was about to address her eagerly, he was checked by observing the signs of sorrow and discomposure in her pale cheeks, trembling lips, and brimful eyes.

"Mordaunt," she said, "you must do Minna and me a favour: you must allow us to leave the house quietly, and without alarming any one, in order to go as far as the Standing Stones of Stennis."

"What freak can this be, dearest Brenda?" said Mordaunt, much amazed at the request—"some Orcadian observance of superstition, perhaps; but the time is too dangerous, and my charge from your father too strict, that I should permit you to pass without his consent. Consider, dearest Brenda, I am a soldier on duty, and must obey orders."

"Mordaunt," said Brenda, "this is no jesting matter: Minna's reason—nay, Minna's life, depends on your giving us this permission."

"And for what purpose?" said Mordaunt; "let me at least know that."

"For a wild and a desperate purpose," replied Brenda. "It is that she may meet Cleveland."

"Cleveland!" said Mordaunt. "Should the villain come ashore, he shall be welcomed with a shower of rifle-balls. Let me within a hundred yards of him," he added, grasping his piece, "and all the mischief he has done me shall be balanced with an ounce bullet!"

"His death will drive Minna frantic," said Brenda; "and him who injures Minna, Brenda will never again look upon."

"This is madness—raving madness!" said Mordaunt. "Consider your honour—consider your duty."

"I can consider nothing but Minna's danger," said Brenda, breaking into a flood of tears: "her former illness was nothing to the state she has been in all night. She holds in her hand his letter, written in characters of fire rather than of ink, imploring her to see him, for a last farewell, as she would save a mortal body and an immortal soul; pledging himself for her safety; and declaring no power shall force him from the coast till he has seen her. You *must* let us pass."

"It is impossible!" replied Mordaunt, in great perplexity. "This ruffian has imprecations enough, doubtless, at his fingers' ends; but what better pledge has he to offer? I cannot permit Minna to go."

"I suppose," said Brenda, somewhat reproachfully, while she dried her tears, yet still continuing sobbing, "that there is something in what Norna spoke of betwixt Minna and you; and that you are too jealous of this poor wretch to allow him even to speak with her an instant before his departure."

"You are unjust, "said Mordaunt, hurt, and yet somewhat flattered, by her suspicions—"you are as unjust as you are imprudent. You know—you cannot but know—that Minna is chiefly dear to me as *your* sister. Tell me, Brenda—and tell me truly—if I aid you in this folly, have you no suspicion of the pirate's faith?"

"No, none," said Brenda; "if I had any, do you think I would urge you thus? He is wild and unhappy, but I think we may in this trust him."

"Is the appointed place the Standing Stones, and the time daybreak?" again demanded Mordaunt.

"It is, and the time is come," said Brenda; "for Heaven's sake, let us depart!"

"I will myself," said Mordaunt, "relieve the sentinel at the front door for a few minutes, and suffer you to pass. You will not protract this interview, so full of danger?"

"We will not," said Brenda; "and, you, on your part, will not avail yourself of this unhappy man's venturing hither to harm or to seize him?"

"Rely on my honour," said Mordaunt. "He shall have no harm unless he offers any."

"Then I go to call my sister," said Brenda, and quickly left the apartment.

Mordaunt considered the matter for an instant, and then going to the sentinel at the front door, he desired him to run instantly to the main-guard, and order the whole to turn out with their arms; to see the order obeyed, and to return when they were in readiness. Meantime, he himself, he said, would remain upon the post.

During the interval of the sentinel's absence, the front door was slowly opened, and Minna and Brenda appeared, muffled in their mantles. The former leaned on her sister, and kept her face bent on the ground, as one who felt ashamed of the step she was about to take. Brenda also passed her lover in silence, but threw back upon him a look of gratitude and affection, which doubled, if possible, his anxiety for their safety.

The sisters, in the mean while, passed out of sight of the house; when Minna, whose step till that time had been faint and feeble, began to erect her person and to walk with a pace so firm and so swift that Brenda, who had some difficulty to keep up with her, could not forbear remonstrating on the imprudence of hurrying her spirits and exhausting her force by such unnecessary haste.

"Fear not, my dearest sister," said Minna: "the spirit which I now feel will, and must, sustain me through the dreadful interview. I could not but move with a drooping head and dejected pace while I was in view of one who must necessarily deem me deserving of his pity or his scorn. But you know, my dearest Brenda, and Mordaunt shall also know, that the love I bore to that unhappy man was as pure as the rays of that sun that is now reflected on the waves. And I dare attest that glorious sun and yonder blue heaven to bear me witness that, but to urge him to change his unhappy course of life, I had not, for all the temptations this round world holds, ever consented to see him more."

As she spoke thus, in a tone which afforded much confidence to Brenda, the sisters attained the summit of a rising ground, whence they commanded a full view of the Orcadian

Stonehenge, consisting of a huge circle and semicircle of the Standing Stones, as they are called, which already glimmered a greyish white in the rising sun, and projected far to the westward their long gigantic shadows. At another time, the scene would have operated powerfully on the imaginative mind of Minna, and interested the curiosity at least of her less sensitive sister. But at this moment neither was at leisure to receive the impressions which this stupendous monument of antiquity is so well calculated to impress on the feelings of those who beheld it; for they saw in the lower lake, beneath what is termed the Bridge of Broisgar, a boat well manned and armed, which had disembarked one of its crew, who advanced alone, and wrapped in a naval cloak, towards that monumental circle which they themselves were about to reach from another quarter.

"They are many, and they are armed," said the startled Brenda, in a whisper to her sister.

"It is for precaution's sake," answered Minna, "which, alas! their condition renders but too necessary. Fear no treachery from him; that, at least, is not his vice."

As she spoke, or shortly afterwards, she attained the centre of the circle, on which, in the midst of the tall, erect pillars of rude stone that are raised around, lies one flat and prostrate, supported by short stone pillars, of which some relics are still visible, that had once served, perhaps, the purpose of an altar.

"Here," she said, "in heathen times (if we may believe legends which have cost me but too dear), our ancestors offered sacrifices to heathen deities; and here will I, from my soul, renounce, abjure, and offer up to a better and a more merciful God than was known to them the vain ideas with which my youthful imagination has been seduced."

She stood by the prostrate table of stone, and saw Cleveland advance towards her, with a timid pace and a downcast look, as different from his usual character and bearing as Minna's high air and lofty demeanour, and calm, contemplative posture, were distant from those of the love-lorn and broken-hearted maiden whose weight had almost borne down the support of her sister as she left the House of Stennis. If the belief of those is true who assign these singular monuments exclusively to the Druids, Minna might have seemed the Haxa, or high priestess, of the order from whom some champion of the tribe expected inauguration. Or, if we hold the circles of Gothic and Scandinavian origin, she might have seemed a descended vision of Freya, the spouse of the Thundering Deity, before whom some bold sea-king or champion bent with an awe which no mere mortal terror could have inflicted upon him. Brenda, overwhelmed with inexpressible fear and doubt, remained a pace or two behind, anxiously observing the motions of Cleveland, and attending to nothing around save to him and to her sister.

Cleveland approached within two yards of Minna, and bent his head to the ground. There was a dead pause, until Minna said, in a firm but melancholy tone: "Unhappy man, why didst thou seek this aggravation of our woe? Depart in peace, and may Heaven direct thee to a better course than that which thy life has yet held!"

"Heaven will not aid me," said Cleveland, "excepting by your voice. I came hither rude and wild, scarce knowing that my trade—my desperate trade, was more criminal in the sight of man or of Heaven than that of those privateers whom your law acknowledges. I was bred in it, and, but for the wishes you have encouraged me to form, I should have perhaps died in it, desperate and impenitent. Oh, do not throw me from you! let me do something to redeem what I have done amiss, and do not leave your own work half-finished!"

"Cleveland," said Minna, "I will not reproach you with abusing my inexperience, or with availing yourself of those delusions which the credulity of early youth had flung around me, and which led me to confound your fatal course of life with the deeds of our ancient heroes. Alas, when I saw your followers that illusion was no more! but I do not upbraid you with its having existed. Go, Cleveland; detach yourself from those miserable wretches with whom you are associated, and believe me that, if Heaven yet grants you the means of distinguishing your name by one good or glorious action, there are eyes left in these lonely islands that will weep as much for joy as—as—they must now do for sorrow."

"And is this all?" said Cleveland; "and may I not hope that, if I extricate myself from my present associates; if I can gain my pardon by being as bold in the right as I have been too often in the wrong cause; if, after a term, I care not how long, but still a term which may have an end, I can boast of having redeemed my fame, may I not—may I not hope that Minna may forgive what my God and my country shall have pardoned?"

"Never, Cleveland—never!" said Minna, with the utmost firmness; "on this spot we part, and part for ever, and part without longer indulgence. Think of me as of one dead, if you continue as you now are; but if, which may Heaven grant, you change your fatal course, think of me then as one whose morning and evening prayers will be for your happiness, though she has lost her own. Farewell, Cleveland!"

He kneeled, overpowered by his own bitter feelings, to take the hand which she held out to him, and in that instant his confidant Bunce, starting from behind one of the large upright pillars, his eyes wet with tears, exclaimed:

"Never saw such a parting scene on any stage! But I'll be d—d if you make your exit as you expect!"

And so saying, ere Cleveland could employ either remonstrance or resistance, and indeed before he could get upon his feet, he easily secured him by pulling him down on his back, so that two or three of the boat's crew seized him by the arms and legs, and began to hurry him towards the lake. Minna and Brenda shrieked, and attempted to fly, but Derrick snatched up the former with as much ease as a falcon pounces on a pigeon, while Bunce, with an oath or two which were intended to be of a consolatory nature, seized on Brenda; and the whole party, with two or three of the other pirates, who, stealing from the water-side, had accompanied them on the ambuscade, began hastily to run towards the boat, which was left in charge of two of their number. Their course, however, was unexpectedly interrupted, and their criminal purpose entirely frustrated.

When Mordaunt Mertoun had turned out his guard in arms, it was with the natural purpose of watching over the safety of the two sisters. They had accordingly closely observed the motions of the pirates, and when they saw so many of them leave the boat and steal towards the place of rendezvous assigned to Cleveland, they naturally suspected treachery, and by cover of an old hollow way or trench, which perhaps had anciently been connected with the monumental circle, they had thrown themselves unperceived between the pirates and their boat. At the cries of the sisters, they started up and placed themselves in the way of the ruffians, presenting their pieces, which, notwithstanding, they dared not fire, for fear of hurting the young ladies, secured as they were in the rude grasp of the marauders. Mordaunt, however, advanced with the speed of a wild deer on Bunce, who, loth to quit his prey, yet unable to defend himself otherwise, turned to this side and that alternately, exposing Brenda to the blows which Mordaunt offered at him. This defence, however, proved in vain against a youth possessed of the lightest foot and most active hand ever known in Zetland, and, after a feint or two, Mordaunt brought the pirate to the ground with a stroke from the butt of the carabine, which he dared not use otherwise. At the same time firearms were discharged on either side by those who were liable to no such cause of forbearance, and the pirates who had hold of Cleveland dropped him, naturally enough, to provide for their own defence or retreat. But they only added to the numbers of their enemies; for Cleveland, perceiving Minna in the arms of Derrick, snatched her from the ruffian with one hand, and with the other shot him dead on the spot. Two or three more of the pirates fell or were taken, the rest fled to their boat, pushed off, then turned their broadside to the shore, and fired repeatedly on the Orcadian party, which they returned, with little injury on either side. Meanwhile Mordaunt, having first seen that the sisters were at liberty and in full flight towards the house, advanced on Cleveland with his cutlass drawn. The pirate presented a pistol, and calling out at the same time, "Mordaunt, I never missed my aim," he fired into the air, and threw it into the

31

lake; then drew his cutlass, brandished it round his head, and flung that also as far as his arm could send it, in the same direction. Yet such was the universal belief of his personal strength and resources, that Mordaunt still used precaution, as, advancing on Cleveland, he asked if he surrendered.

"I surrender to no man," said the pirate captain; "but you may see I have thrown away my weapons."

He was immediately seized by some of the Orcadians without his offering any resistance; but the instant interference of Mordaunt prevented his being roughly treated or bound. The victors conducted him to a well-secured upper apartment in the House of Stennis, and placed a sentinel at the door. Bunce and Fletcher, both of whom had been stretched on the field during the skirmish, were lodged in the same chamber; and two prisoners, who appeared of lower rank, were confined in a vault belonging to the mansion.

Without pretending to describe the joy of Magnus Troil, who, when awakened by the noise and firing, found his daughters safe and his enemy a prisoner, we shall only say, it was so great that he forgot, for the time at least, to inquire what circumstances were those which had placed them in danger; that he hugged Mordaunt to his breast a thousand times, as their preserver; and swore as often by the bones of his sainted namesake that, if he had a thousand daughters, so tight a lad and so true a friend should have the choice of them, let Lady Glowrowrum say what she would.

A very different scene was passing in the prison-chamber of the unfortunate Cleveland and his associates. The captain sat by the window, his eyes bent on the prospect of the sea which it presented, and was seemingly so intent on it as to be insensible of the presence of the others. Jack Bunce stood meditating some ends of verse, in order to make his advances towards a reconciliation with Cleveland; for he began to be sensible, from the consequences, that the part he had played towards his captain, however well intended, was neither lucky in its issue nor likely to be well taken. His admirer and adherent, Fletcher, lay half asleep, as it seemed, on a truckle-bed in the room, without the least attempt to interfere in the conversation which ensued.

"Nay, but speak to me, Clement," said the penitent lieutenant, "if it be but to swear at me for my stupidity!

> What! not an oath? Nay, then the world goes hard,
> If Clifford cannot spare his friends an oath."

"I prithee peace, and begone!" said Cleveland; "I have one bosom friend left yet, and you will make me bestow its contents on you or on myself."

"I have it!" said Bunce—"I have it!" and on he went in the vein of Jaffeir—

> "Then, by the hell I merit, I'll not leave thee,
> Till to thyself at least thou'rt reconciled,
> However thy resentment deal with me!'"

"I pray you once more to be silent," said Cleveland. "Is it not enough that you have undone me with your treachery, but you must stun me with your silly buffoonery? I would not have believed *you* would have lifted a finger against me, Jack, of any man or devil in yonder unhappy ship."

"Who, I?" exclaimed Bunce. "I lift a finger against you! and if I did, it was in pure love, and to make you the happiest fellow that ever trode a deck, with your mistress beside you, and fifty fine fellows at your command. Here is Dick Fletcher can bear witness I did all for the best, if he would but speak, instead of lolloping there like a Dutch dogger laid up to be careened. Get up, Dick, and speak for me, won't you?"

"Why, yes, Jack Bunce," answered Fletcher, raising himself with difficulty, and speaking feebly, "I will if I can, and I always knew you spoke and did for the best; but howsomdever, d'ye see, it has turned out for the worst for me this time, for I am bleeding to death, I think."

"You cannot be such an ass!" said Jack Bunce, springing to his assistance, as did Cleveland. But human aid came too late: he sunk back on the bed, and, turning on his face, expired without a groan.

"I always thought him a d—d fool," said Bunce, as he wiped a tear from his eye, "but never such a consummate idiot as to hop the perch so sillily. I have lost the best follower——" and he again wiped his eye.

Cleveland looked on the dead body, the rugged features of which had remained unaltered by the death-pang. "A bulldog," he said, "of the true British breed, and, with a better counsellor, would have been a better man."

"You may say that of some other folks, too, captain, if you are minded to do them justice," said Bunce.

"I may indeed, and especially of yourself," said Cleveland in reply.

"Why then, say, 'Jack, I forgive you,'" said Bunce; "it's but a short word, and soon spoken."

"I forgive you from all my soul, Jack," said Cleveland, who had resumed his situation at the window; "and the rather that your folly is of little consequence: the morning is come that must bring ruin on us all."

"What! you are thinking of the old woman's prophecy you spoke of?" said Bunce.

"It will soon be accomplished," answered Cleveland. "Come hither; what do you take yon large square-rigged vessel for, that you see doubling the headland on the east, and opening the Bay of Stromness?"

"Why, I can't make her well out," said Bunce, "but yonder is old Goffe takes her for a West Indiaman loaded with rum and sugar, I suppose, for d—n me if he does not slip cable and stand out to her!"

"Instead of running into the shoal-water, which was his only safety," said Cleveland. "The fool! the dotard! the drivelling, drunken idiot! he will get his flip hot enough; for yon is the 'Halcyon.' See, she hoists her colours and fires a broadside! and there will soon be an end of the 'Fortune's Favourite!' I only hope they will fight her to the last plank. The boatswain used to be stanch enough, and so is Goffe, though an incarnate demon. Now she shoots away, with all the sail she can spread, and that shows some sense."

"Up goes the Jolly Hodge, the old black flag, with the death's-head and hour-glass, and that shows some spunk," added his comrade.

"The hour-glass is turned for us, Jack, for this bout: our sand is running fast. Fire away yet, my roving lads! The deep sea or the blue sky rather than a rope and a yard-arm!"

There was a moment of anxious and dead silence; the sloop, though hard pressed, maintaining still a running fight, and the frigate continuing in full chase, but scarce returning a shot. At length the vessels neared each other, so as to show that the man-of-war intended to board the sloop, instead of sinking her, probably to secure the plunder which might be in the pirate vessel.

"Now, Goffe—now, boatswain!" exclaimed Cleveland, in an ecstasy of impatience, and as if they could have heard his commands, "stand by sheets and tacks—rake her with a broadside, when you are under her bows, then about ship, and go off on the other tack like a wild goose. The sails shiver—the helm's a-lee. Ah! deep sea sink the lubbers! they miss stays, and the frigate runs them aboard!"

Accordingly, the various manœuvres of the chase had brought them so near that Cleveland, with his spy-glass, could see the man-of-war's-men boarding by the yards and bowsprit, in irresistible numbers, their naked cutlasses flashing in the sun, when, at that critical moment, both ships were enveloped in a cloud of thick black smoke, which suddenly arose on board the captured pirate.

"*Exeunt omnes!*" said Bunce, with clasped hands.

"There went the 'Fortune's Favourite,' ship and crew!" said Cleveland, at the same instant.

But the smoke immediately clearing away, showed that the damage had only been partial, and that, from want of a sufficient quantity of powder, the pirates had failed in their desperate attempt to blow up their vessel with the "Halcyon."

Shortly after the action was over, Captain Weatherport of the "Halcyon" sent an officer and a party of marines to the House of Stennis, to demand from the little garrison the pirate seamen who were their prisoners, and, in particular, Cleveland and Bunce, who acted as captain and lieutenant of the gang.

This was a demand which was not to be resisted, though

Magnus Troil could have wished sincerely that the roof under which he lived had been allowed as an asylum at least to Cleveland. But the officer's orders were peremptory; and he added, it was Captain Weatherport's intention to land the other prisoners, and send the whole, with a sufficient escort, across the island to Kirkwall, in order to undergo an examination there before the civil authorities, previous to their being sent off to London for trial at the High Court of Admiralty. Magnus could therefore only intercede for good usage to Cleveland, and that he might not be stripped or plundered, which the officer, struck by his good mien, and compassionating his situation, readily promised. The honest Udaller would have said something in the way of comfort to Cleveland himself, but he could not find words to express it, and only shook his head.

"Old friend," said Cleveland, "you may have much to complain of, yet you pity instead of exulting over me; for the sake of you and yours, I will never harm human being more. Take this from me—my last hope, but my last temptation also"; he drew from his bosom a pocket-pistol, and gave it to Magnus Troil. "Remember me to—— But no, let every one forget me. I am your prisoner, sir," said he to the officer.

"And I also," said poor Bunce; and putting on a theatrical countenance, he ranted, with no very perceptible faltering in his tone, the words of Pierre:

> "Captain, you should be a gentleman of honour;
> Keep off the rabble, that I may have room
> To entertain my fate, and die with decency."

———◆———

CHAPTER XLI.

Joy, joy, in London now !
SOUTHEY.

THE news of the capture of the rover reached Kirkwall about an hour before noon, and filled all men with wonder and with joy. Little business was that day done at the fair, whilst people of all ages and occupations streamed from the place to see the prisoners as they were marched towards Kirkwall, and to triumph in the different appearance which they now bore from that which they had formerly exhibited when ranting, swaggering, and bullying in the streets of that town. The bayonets of the marines were soon seen to glisten in the sun, and then came on the melancholy troop of captives, handcuffed two and two together. Their finery had been partly torn from them by their captors, partly hung in rags about them; many were wounded and covered with blood, many blackened and scorched with the explosion by which a few of the most desperate had in vain striven to blow up the vessel. Most of them seemed sullen and impenitent, some were more becomingly affected with their condition, and a few braved it out, and sung the same ribald songs to which they had made the streets of Kirkwall ring when they were in their frolics.

The boatswain and Goffe, coupled together, exhausted themselves in threats and imprecations against each other; the former charging Goffe with want of seamanship, and the latter alleging that the boatswain had prevented him from firing the powder that was stowed forward, and so sending them all to the other world together. Last came Cleveland and Bunce, who were permitted to walk unshackled; the decent melancholy, yet resolved manner, of the former contrasting strongly with the stage strut and swagger which poor Jack thought it fitting to assume, in order to conceal some less dignified emotions. The former was looked upon with compassion, the latter with a mixture of scorn and pity; while most of the others inspired horror, and even fear, by their looks and their language.

There was one individual in Kirkwall who was so far from hastening to see the sight which attracted all eyes, that he was not even aware of the event which agitated the town. This was the elder Mertoun, whose residence Kirkwall had been for two or three days, part of which had been spent in attending to some judicial proceedings, undertaken at the instance of the procurator-fiscal, against that grave professor, Bryce Snailsfoot. In consequence of an inquisition into the proceedings of this worthy trader, Cleveland's chest, with his papers and other matters therein contained, had been restored to Mertoun, as the lawful custodier thereof, until the right owner should be in a situation to establish his right to them. Mertoun was at first desirous to throw back upon justice the charge which she was disposed to entrust him with; but, on perusing one or two of the papers, he hastily changed his mind—in broken words, requested the magistrate to let the chest be sent to his lodgings, and, hastening homeward, bolted himself into the room, to consider and digest the singular information which chance had thus conveyed to him, and which increased, in a tenfold degree, his impatience for an interview with the mysterious Norna of the Fitful Head.

It may be remembered that she had required of him, when they met in the churchyard of St. Ninian, to attend in the outer aisle of the cathedral of St. Magnus, at the hour of noon, on the fifth day of the fair of St. Olla, there to meet a person by whom the fate of Mordaunt would be explained to him. "It must be herself," he said; "and that I should see her at this moment is indispensable. How to find her sooner I know not; and better lose a few hours even in this exigence than offend her by a premature attempt to force myself on her presence."

Long, therefore, before noon—long before the town of Kirkwall was agitated by the news of the events on the other side of the island, the elder Mertoun was pacing the deserted aisle of the cathedral, awaiting, with agonizing eagerness, the expected communication from Norna. The bell tolled twelve—no door opened—no one was seen to enter the cathedral; but the last sounds had not ceased to reverberate through the vaulted roof when, gliding from one of the interior side-aisles, Norna stood before him. Mertoun, indifferent to the apparent mystery of her sudden approach (with the secret of which the reader is acquainted), went up to her at once, with the earnest ejaculation: "Ulla—Ulla Troil, aid me to save our unhappy boy."

"To Ulla Troil," said Norna, "I answer not: I gave that name to the winds on the night that cost me a father!"

"Speak not of that night of horror," said Mertoun; "we have need of our reason—let us not think on recollections which may destroy it; but aid me, if thou canst, to save our unfortunate child!"

"Vaughan," answered Norna, "he is already saved—long since saved; think you a mother's hand—and that of such a mother as I am—would await your crawling, tardy, ineffectual assistance? No, Vaughan, I made myself known to you but to show my triumph over you: it is the only revenge which the powerful Norna permits herself to take for the wrongs of Ulla Troil."

"Have you indeed saved him—saved him from the murderous crew?" said Mordaunt [Mertoun], or Vaughan—"speak! and speak truth! I will believe everything—all you would require me to assent to!—prove to me only he is escaped and safe!"

"Escaped and safe, by my means," said Norna—"safe, and in assurance of an honoured and happy alliance. Yes, great unbeliever!—yes, wise and self-opinioned infidel! these were the works of Norna! I knew you many a year since; but never had I made myself known to you save with the triumphant consciousness of having controlled the destiny that threatened my son. All combined against him: planets which threatened drowning—combinations which menaced blood; but my skill was superior to all. I arranged—I combined—I found means—I made them—each disaster has been averted; and what infidel on earth, or stubborn demon beyond the bounds of earth, shall hereafter deny my power?"

The wild ecstasy with which she spoke so much resembled triumphant insanity that Mertoun answered: "Were your pretensions less lofty, and your speech more plain, I should be better assured of my son's safety."

"Doubt on, vain sceptic!" said Norna. "And yet know, that not only is our son safe, but vengeance is mine, though I sought it not—vengeance on the powerful implement of the darker Influences by whom my schemes were so often thwarted, and even the life of my son endangered. Yes, take it as a guarantee of the truth of my speech that Cleveland—the pirate Cleveland—even now enters Kirkwall as a prisoner,

and will soon expiate with his life the having shed blood
which is of kin to Norna's."

"Who didst thou say was prisoner?" exclaimed Mertoun,
with a voice of thunder—"*who*, woman, didst thou say should
expiate his crimes with his life?"

"Cleveland—the pirate Cleveland!" answered Norna; "and
by me, whose counsel he scorned, he has been permitted to
meet his fate."

"Thou most wretched of women!" said Mertoun, speaking
from between his clenched teeth, "thou hast slain thy son as
well as thy father!"

"My son! what son? what mean you? Mordaunt is your
son—your only son!" exclaimed Norna, "is he not?—tell me
quickly, is he not?"

"Mordaunt is indeed *my* son," said Mertoun; "the laws,
at least, gave him to me as such. But, O unhappy Ulla!
Cleveland is your son as well as mine—blood of our blood,
bone of our bone; and if you have given him to death, I will
end my wretched life along with him!"

"Stay—hold—stop, Vaughan!" said Norna; "I am not yet
overcome—prove but to me the truth of what you say, I would
find help, if I should evoke hell! But prove your words, else
believe them I cannot."

"*Thou* help! wretched, overweening woman! In what
have thy combinations and thy stratagems—the legerdemain
of lunacy—the mere quackery of insanity—in what have these
involved thee? And yet I will speak to thee as reasonable—
nay, I will admit thee as powerful. Hear, then, Ulla, the
proofs which you demand, and find a remedy, if thou canst:

"When I fled from Orkney," he continued, after a pause—
"it is now five-and-twenty years since—I bore with me the
unhappy offspring to whom you had given light. It was sent
to me by one of your kinswomen, with an account of your illness, which was soon followed by a generally received belief
of your death. It avails not to tell in what misery I left
Europe. I found refuge in Hispaniola, wherein a fair young
Spaniard undertook the task of comforter. I married her;
she became mother of the youth called Mordaunt Mertoun."

" You married her !" said Norna, in a tone of deep reproach.

" I did, Ulla," answered Mertoun; " but you were avenged. She proved faithless, and her infidelity left me in doubts whether the child she bore had a right to call me father. But I also was avenged."

" You murdered her !" said Norna, with a dreadful shriek.

" I did that," said Mertoun, without a more direct reply, " which made an instant flight from Hispaniola necessary. Your son I carried with me to Tortuga, where we had a small settlement. Mordaunt Vaughan, my son by marriage, about three or four years younger, was residing in Port Royal, for the advantages of an English education. I resolved never to see him again, but I continued to support him. Our settlement was plundered by the Spaniards when Clement was but fifteen. Want came to aid despair and a troubled conscience. I became a corsair, and involved Clement in the same desperate trade. His skill and bravery, though then a mere boy, gained him a separate command; and after a lapse of two or three years, while we were on different cruises, my crew rose on me, and left me for dead on the beach of one of the Bermudas. I recovered, however, and my first inquiries, after a tedious illness, were after Clement. He, I heard, had been also marooned by a rebellious crew, and put ashore on a desert islet, to perish with want. I believed he had so perished."

" And what assures you that he did not?" said Ulla; " or how comes this Cleveland to be identified with Vaughan?"

" To change a name is common with such adventurers," answered Mertoun; " and Clement had apparently found that of Vaughan had become too notorious; and this change, in his case, prevented me from hearing any tidings of him. It was then that remorse seized me, and that, detesting all nature, but especially the sex to which Louisa belonged, I resolved to do penance in the wild islands of Zetland for the rest of my life. To subject myself to fasts and to the scourge was the advice of the holy Catholic priests whom I consulted. But I devised a nobler penance : I determined to bring with me the unhappy boy Mordaunt, and to keep always before me the living memorial of my misery and my guilt. I have done so,

and I have thought over both till reason has often trembled
on her throne. And now, to drive me to utter madness, my
Clement—my own, my undoubted son—revives from the dea
to be consigned to an infamous death by the machinations of
his own mother!"

"Away—away!" said Norna, with a laugh, when she had
heard the story to an end, "this is a legend framed by the old
corsair to interest my aid in favour of a guilty comrade. How
could I mistake Mordaunt for my son, their ages being so
different?"

"The dark complexion and manly stature may have done
much," said Basil Mertoun; "strong imagination must have
done the rest."

"But give me proofs—give me proofs that this Cleveland is
my son, and, believe me, this sun shall sooner sink in the east
than they shall have power to harm a hair of his head."

"These papers—these journals," said Mertoun, offering the
pocket-book.

"I cannot read them," she said, after an effort: "my brain
is dizzy."

"Clement had also tokens which you may remember, but
they must have become the booty of his captors. He had a
silver box with a Runic inscription, with which in far other
days you presented me—a golden chaplet."

"A box!" said Norna, hastily. "Cleveland gave me one
but a day since; I have never looked at it till now."

Eagerly she pulled it out, eagerly examined the legend
around the lid, and as eagerly exclaimed: "They may now
indeed call me Reim-kennar, for by this rhyme I know myself
murderess of my son as well as of my father!"

The conviction of the strong delusion under which she had
laboured was so overwhelming that she sunk down at the foot
of one of the pillars. Mertoun shouted for help, though in
despair of receiving any; the sexton, however, entered, and,
hopeless of all assistance from Norna, the distracted father
rushed out, to learn, if possible, the fate of his son.

CHAPTER XLII.

Go, some of you, cry a reprieve!
Beggar's Opera.

CAPTAIN WEATHERPORT had, before this time, reached
Kirkwall in person, and was received with great joy and
thankfulness by the magistrates, who had assembled in council for the purpose. The provost, in particular, expressed
himself delighted with the providential arrival of the "Halcyon" at the very conjuncture when the pirate could not escape
her. The captain looked a little surprised, and said: "For
that, sir, you may thank the information you yourself supplied."

"That I supplied?" said the provost, somewhat astonished.

"Yes, sir," answered Captain Weatherport, "I understand
you to be George Torfe, chief magistrate of Kirkwall, who
subscribes this letter."

The astonished provost took the letter addressed to Captain
Weatherport of the "Halcyon," stating the arrival, force, etc.,
of the pirates' vessel; but adding, that they had heard of the
"Halcyon" being on the coast, and that they were on their
guard and ready to baffle her, by going among the shoals, and
through the islands and holms, where the frigate could not
easily follow; and, at the worst, they were desperate enough
to propose running the sloop ashore and blowing her up, by
which much booty and treasure would be lost to the captors.
The letter, therefore, suggested that the "Halcyon" should
cruise betwixt Duncansbay Head and Cape Wrath for two or
three days, to relieve the pirates of the alarm her neighbourhood occasioned, and lull them into security, the more especially as the letter-writer knew it to be their intention, if the
frigate left the coast, to go into Stromness Bay, and there put
their guns ashore for some necessary repairs, or even for ca-
reening their vessel, if they could find means. The letter
concluded by assuring Captain Weatherport that, if he could
bring his frigate into Stromness Bay on the morning of the

24th of August, he would have a good bargain of the pirates; if sooner, he was not unlikely to miss them.

"This letter is not of my writing or subscribing, Captain Weatherport," said the provost; "nor would I have ventured to advise any delay in your coming hither."

The captain was surprised in his turn. "All I know is, that it reached me when I was in the Bay of Thurso, and that I gave the boat's crew that brought it five dollars for crossing the Pentland Firth in very rough weather. They had a dumb dwarf as cockswain, the ugliest urchin my eyes ever opened upon. I give you much credit for the accuracy of your intelligence, Mr. Provost."

"It is lucky as it is," said the provost; "yet I question whether the writer of this letter would not rather that you have found the nest cold and the bird flown."

So saying, he handed the letter to Magnus Troil, who returned it with a smile, but without any observation, aware, doubtless, with the sagacious reader, that Norna had her own reasons for calculating with accuracy on the date of the "Halcyon's" arrival.

Without puzzling himself farther concerning a circumstance which seemed inexplicable, the captain requested that the examinations might proceed; and Cleveland and Altamont, as he chose to be called, were brought up the first of the pirate crew, on the charge of having acted as captain and lieutenant. They had just commenced the examination when, after some expostulation with the officers who kept the door, Basil Mertoun burst into the apartment and exclaimed: "Take the old victim for the young one! I am Basil Vaughan, too well known on the Windward station—take my life, and spare my son's!"

All were astonished, and none more than Magnus Troil, who hastily explained to the magistrates and Captain Weatherport that this gentleman had been living peaceably and honestly on the Mainland of Zetland for many years.

"In that case," said the captain, "I wash my hands of the poor man, for he is safe, under two proclamations of mercy; and, by my soul, when I see them, the father and his offspring, hanging on each other's neck, I wish I could say as much for the son."

"But how is it—how can it be?" said the provost; "we always called the old man Mertoun, and the young Cleveland, and now it seems they are both named Vaughan."

"Vaughan," answered Magnus, "is a name which I have some reason to remember; and from what I have lately heard from my cousin Norna, that old man has a right to bear it."

"And, I trust, the young man also," said the captain, who had been looking over a memorandum. "Listen to me a moment," added he, addressing the younger Vaughan, whom we have hitherto called Cleveland. "Hark you, sir, your name is said to be Clement Vaughan—are you the same who, then a mere boy, commanded a party of rovers, who, about eight or nine years ago, pillaged a Spanish village called Quempoa, on the Spanish Main, with the purpose of seizing some treasure?"

"It will avail me nothing to deny it," answered the prisoner.

"No," said Captain Weatherport, "but it may do you service to admit it. Well, the muleteers escaped with the treasure while you were engaged in protecting, at the hazard of your own life, the honour of two Spanish ladies against the brutality of your followers. Do you remember anything of this?"

"I am sure *I* do," said Jack Bunce; "for our captain here was marooned for his gallantry, and I narrowly escaped flogging and pickling for having taken his part."

"When these points are established," said Captain Weatherport, "Vaughan's life is safe: the women he saved were persons of quality, daughters to the governor of the province, and application was long since made by the grateful Spaniard to our government for favour to be shown to their preserver. I had special orders about Clement Vaughan when I had a commission for cruising upon the pirates, in the West Indies, six or seven years since. But Vaughan was gone then as a name amongst them; and I heard enough of Cleveland in his room. However, captain, be you Cleveland or Vaughan, I think that, as the Quempoa hero, I can assure you a free pardon when you arrive in London."

Cleveland bowed, and the blood mounted to his face. Mertoun fell on his knees and exhausted himself in thanksgiving to Heaven. They were removed, amidst the sympathising sobs of the spectators.

"And now, good Master Lieutenant, what have you got to say for yourself?" said Captain Weatherport to the *ci-devant* Roscius.

"Why, little or nothing, please your honour; only that I wish your honour could find my name in that book of mercy you have in your hand; for I stood by Captain Clement Vaughan in the Quempoa business."

"You call yourself Frederick Altamont," said Captain Weatherport. "I can see no such name here; one John Bounce, or Bunce, the lady put on her tablets."

"Why, that is me—that is I myself, captain—I can prove it; and I am determined, though the sound be something plebeian, rather to live Jack Bunce than to hang as Frederick Altamont."

"In that case," said the captain, "I can give you some hopes as John Bunce."

"Thank your noble worship!" shouted Bunce; then changing his tone, he said: "Ah, since an *alias* has such virtue, poor Dick Fletcher might have come off as Timothy Tugmutton; but howsomdever, d'ye see, to use his own phrase——"

"Away with the lieutenant," said the captain, "and bring forward Goffe and the other fellows; there will be ropes reeved for some of them, I think." And this prediction promised to be amply fulfilled, so strong was the proof which was brought against them.

The "Halcyon" was accordingly ordered round to carry the whole prisoners to London, for which she set sail in the course of two days.

During the time that the unfortunate Cleveland remained at Kirkwall, he was treated with civility by the captain of the "Halcyon"; and the kindness of his old acquaintance, Magnus Troil, who knew in secret how closely he was allied to his blood, pressed on him accommodations of every kind, more than he could be prevailed on to accept.

Norna, whose interest in the unhappy prisoner was still more deep, was at this time unable to express it. The sexton had found her lying on the pavement in a swoon, and when she recovered, her mind for the time had totally lost its equipoise, and it became necessary to place her under the restraint of watchful attendants.

Of the sisters of Burgh-Westra, Cleveland only heard that they remained ill, in consequence of the fright to which they had been subjected, until the evening before the "Halcyon" sailed, when he received, by a private conveyance, the following billet: "Farewell, Cleveland; we part for ever, and it is right that we should. Be virtuous and be happy. The delusions which a solitary education and limited acquaintance with the modern world had spread around me are gone and dissipated for ever. But in you, I am sure, I have been thus far free from error, that you are one to whom good is naturally more attractive than evil, and whom only necessity, example, and habit have forced into your late course of life. Think of me as one who no longer exists, unless you should become as much the object of general praise as now of general reproach; and then think of me as one who will rejoice in your reviving fame, though she must never see you more!" The note was signed "M. T."; and Cleveland, with a deep emotion, which he testified even by tears, read it an hundred times over, and then clasped it to his bosom.

Mordaunt Mertoun heard by letter from his father, but in a very different style. Basil bade him farewell for ever, and acquitted him henceforward of the duties of a son, as one on whom he, notwithstanding the exertions of many years, had found himself unable to bestow the affections of a parent. The letter informed him of a recess in the old house of Jarlshof, in which the writer had deposited a considerable quantity of specie and of treasure, which he desired Mordaunt to use as his own. "You need not fear," the letter bore, "either that you lay yourself under obligation to me or that you are sharing the spoils of piracy. What is now given over to you is almost entirely the property of your deceased mother, Louisa Gonzago, and is yours by every right. Let us forgive

32

each other," was the conclusion, "as they who must meet no more." And they never met more; for the elder Mertoun, against whom no charge was ever preferred, disappeared after the fate of Cleveland was determined, and was generally believed to have retired into a foreign convent.

The fate of Cleveland will be most briefly expressed in a letter which Minna received within two months after the "Halcyon" left Kirkwall. The family were then assembled at Burgh-Westra, and Mordaunt was a member of it for the time, the good Udaller thinking he could never sufficiently repay the activity which he had shown in the defence of his daughters. Norna, then beginning to recover from her temporary alienation of mind, was a guest in the family, and Minna, who was sedulous in her attention upon this unfortunate victim of mental delusion, was seated with her, watching each symptom of returning reason, when the letter we allude to was placed in her hands.

"Minna," it said—"dearest Minna! farewell, and for ever! Believe me, I never meant you wrong—never. From the moment I came to know you, I resolved to detach myself from my hateful comrades, and had framed a thousand schemes, which have proved as vain as they deserved to be; for why, or how, should the fate of her that is so lovely, pure, and innocent be involved with that of one so guilty? Of these dreams I will speak no more. The stern reality of my situation is much milder than I either expected or deserved; and the little good I did has outweighed, in the minds of honourable and merciful judges, much that was evil and criminal. I have not only been exempted from the ignominious death to which several of my compeers are sentenced; but Captain Weatherport, about once more to sail for the Spanish Main, under the apprehension of an immediate war with that country, has generously solicited and obtained permission to employ me, and two or three more of my less guilty associates, in the same service—a measure recommended to himself by his own generous compassion, and to others by our knowledge of the coast, and of local circumstances, which, by whatever means acquired, we now hope to use for the service of our country. Minna, you will hear my name pronounced with honour, or you will never hear it again. If virtue can give happiness, I need not wish it to you, for it is yours already.— Farewell, Minna."

Minna wept so bitterly over this letter that it attracted the attention of the convalescent Norna. She snatched it from the hand of her kinswoman, and read it over at first with the confused air of one to whom it conveyed no intelligence, then with a dawn of recollection, then with a burst of mingled joy and grief, in which she dropped it from her hand. Minna snatched it up and retired with her treasure to her own apartment.

From that time Norna appeared to assume a different character. Her dress was changed to one of a more simple and less imposing appearance. Her dwarf was dismissed, with ample provision for his future comfort. She showed no desire of resuming her erratic life; and directed her observatory, as it might be called, on Fitful Head, to be dismantled. She refused the name of Norna, and would only be addressed by her real appellation of Ulla Troil. But the most important change remained behind. Formerly, from the dreadful dictates of spiritual despair arising out of the circumstances of her father's death, she seemed to have considered herself as an outcast from Divine grace; besides that, enveloped in the vain occult sciences which she pretended to practise, her study, like that of Chaucer's physician, had been "but little in the Bible." Now the sacred volume was seldom laid aside; and to the poor ignorant people who came as formerly to invoke her power over the elements she only replied: "The winds are in the hollow of His hand." Her conversion was not, perhaps, altogether rational; for this the state of a mind disordered by such a complication of horrid incidents probably prevented. But it seemed to be sincere, and was certainly useful. She appeared deeply to repent of her former presumptuous attempts to interfere with the course of human events, superintended as they are by far higher powers, and expressed bitter compunction when such her former pretensions were in any manner recalled to her memory. She still showed a partiality to Mordaunt, though, perhaps, arising chiefly from habit; nor was it easy to know how much or how little she remembered of the complicated events in which she had been connected. When she died, which was about four years after the events we have commemorated, it was found that, at the special and earnest request of Minna Troil, she had conveyed her very considerable property to Brenda. A clause in her will specially directed that all the books, implements of her laboratory, and other things connected with her former studies, should be committed to the flames.

About two years before Norna's death, Brenda was wedded to Mordaunt Mertoun. It was some time before old Magnus Troil, with all his affection for his daughter, and all his partiality for Mordaunt, was able frankly to reconcile himself to this match. But Mordaunt's accomplishments were peculiarly to the Udaller's taste, and the old man felt the impossibility of supplying his place in his family so absolutely, that at length his Norse blood gave way to the natural feeling of the heart, and he comforted his pride, while he looked around him, and saw what he considered as the encroachments of the Scottish gentry upon THE COUNTRY (so Zetland is fondly termed by its inhabitants), that as well "his daughter married the son of an English pirate as of a Scottish thief," in scornful allusion to the Highland and Border families, to whom Zetland owes many respectable landholders, but whose ancestors were generally esteemed more renowned for ancient family and high courage than for accurately regarding the trifling distinctions of *meum* and *tuum*. The jovial old man lived to the extremity of human life, with the happy prospect of a numerous succession in the family of his younger daughter; and having his board cheered alternately by the minstrelsy of Claud Halcro and enlightened by the lucubrations of Mr. Triptolemus Yellowley, who, laying aside his high pretensions, was, when he became better acquainted with the manners of the islanders, and remembered the various misadventures which had attended his premature attempts at reformation, an honest and useful representative of his principal, and never so happy as when he could escape from the spare commons of his sister

Barbara to the genial table of the Udaller. Barbara's temper also was much softened by the unexpected restoration of the horn of silver coins, the property of Norna, which she had concealed in the mansion of old Stourburgh, for achieving some of her mysterious plans, but which she now restored to those by whom it had been accidentally discovered, with an intimation, however, that it would again disappear unless a reasonable portion was expended on the sustenance of the family—a precaution to which Tronda Dronsdaughter (probably an agent of Norna's) owed her escape from a slow and wasting death by inanition.

Mordaunt and Brenda were as happy as our mortal condition permits us to be. They admired and loved each other, enjoyed easy circumstances, had duties to discharge which they did not neglect, and, clear in conscience as light of heart, laughed, sung, danced, daffed the world aside, and bid it pass.

But Minna—the high-minded and imaginative Minna—she, gifted with such depth of feeling and enthusiasm, yet doomed to see both blighted in early youth, because, with the inexperience of a disposition equally romantic and ignorant, she had built the fabric of her happiness on a quicksand instead of a rock—was she, could she be happy? Reader, she *was* happy; for, whatever may be alleged to the contrary by the sceptic and the scorner, to each duty performed there is assigned a degree of mental peace and high consciousness of honourable exertion, corresponding to the difficulty of the task accomplished. That rest of the body which succeeds to hard and industrious toil is not to be compared to the repose which the spirit enjoys under similar circumstances. Her resignation, however, and the constant attention which she paid to her father, her sister, the afflicted Norna, and to all who had claims on her, were neither Minna's sole nor her most precious source of comfort. Like Norna, but under a more regulated judgment, she learned to exchange the visions of wild enthusiasm, which had exerted and misled her imagination, for a truer and purer connexion with the world beyond us than could be learned from the sagas of heathen bards or the visions of later rhymers. To this she owed the support by which she was enabled, after various accounts of the honourable and gallant conduct of Cleveland, to read with resignation, and even with a sense of comfort mingled with sorrow, that he had at length fallen, leading the way in a gallant and honourable enterprise, which was successfully accomplished by those companions to whom his determined bravery had opened the road. Bunce, his fantastic follower in good as formerly in evil, transmitted an account to Minna of this melancholy event, in terms which showed that, though his head was weak, his heart had not been utterly corrupted by the lawless life which he had for some time led, or at least that it had been amended by the change; and that he himself had gained credit and promotion in the same action seemed to be of little consequence to him compared with the loss of his old captain and comrade.[1] Minna read the intelligence, and thanked Heaven, even while the eyes which she lifted up were streaming with tears, that the death of Cleveland had been in the bed of honour; nay, she even had the courage to add her gratitude that he had been snatched from a situation of temptation ere circumstances had overcome his new-born virtue; and so strongly did this reflection operate that her life, after the immediate pain of this event had passed away, seemed not only as resigned, but even more cheerful than before. Her thoughts, however, were detached from the world, and only visited it, with an interest like that which guardian spirits take for their charge, in behalf of those friends with whom she lived in love, or of the poor she could serve and comfort. Thus passed her life, enjoying from all who approached her an affection enhanced by reverence; insomuch that, when her friends sorrowed for her death, which arrived at a late period of her existence, they were comforted by the fond reflection that the humanity which she then laid down was the only circumstance which had placed her, in the words of Scripture, "a little lower than the angels!"

<hr>

See Bunce's Fate. Note 47.

NOTES TO THE PIRATE.

NOTE 1.—UDALLERS, p. 20.

THE udallers are the allodial possessors of Zetland, who hold their possessions under the old Norwegian law, instead of the feudal tenures introduced among them from Scotland.

NOTE 2.—" PLANTIE CRUIVE," p. 21.

Patch of ground for vegetables. The liberal custom of the country permits any person, who has occasion for such a convenience, to select out of the uninclosed moorland a small patch, which he surrounds with a drystone wall and cultivates as a kail-yard, till he exhausts the soil with cropping, and then he deserts it and incloses another. This liberty is so far from inferring an invasion of the right of proprietor and tenant, that the last degree of contempt is inferred of an avaricious man when a Zetlander says he would not hold a " plantie cruive" of him.

NOTE 3.—THE BERSERKARS, p. 25.

The sagas of the Scalds are full of descriptions of these champions, and do not permit us to doubt that the Berserkars, so called from fighting without armour, used some physical means of working themselves into a frenzy, during which they possessed the strength and energy of madness. The Indian warriors are well known to do the same by dint of opium and bang.

NOTE 4.—ACCIDENTS TO FOWLERS, p. 28.

Fatal accidents, however, sometimes occur. When I visited the Fair Isle in 1814, a poor lad of fourteen had been killed by a fall from the rocks about a fortnight before our arrival. The accident happened almost within sight of his mother, who was casting peats at no great distance. The body fell into the sea, and was seen no more. But the islanders account this an honourable mode of death ; and as the children begin the practice of climbing very early, fewer accidents occur than might be expected.

NOTE 5.—NORSE FRAGMENTS, p. 29.

Near the conclusion of chapter ii. it is noticed that the old Norwegian sagas were preserved and often repeated by the fishermen of Orkney and Zetland, while that language was not yet quite forgotten. Mr. Baikie of Tankerness, a most respectable inhabitant of Kirkwall, and an Orkney proprietor, assured me of the following curious fact :

A clergyman, who was not long deceased, remembered well when some remnants of the Norse were still spoken in the island called North Ronaldsha. When Gray's ode, entitled the *Fatal Sisters*, was first published, or at least first reached that remote island, the reverend gentleman had the well-judged curiosity to read it to some of the old persons of the isle, as a poem which regarded the history of their own country. They listened with great attention to the preliminary stanzas:

> Now the storm begins to lour,
> Haste the loom of hell prepare,
> Iron sleet of arrowy shower
> Hurtles in the darken'd air.

But when they had heard a verse or two more, they interrupted the reader, telling him they knew the song well in the Norse language, and had often sung it to him when he asked them for an old song. They called it the "Magician's" or the "Enchantresses." It would have been singular news to the elegant translator, when executing his version from the text of Bartholin, to have learned that the Norse original was still preserved by tradition in a remote corner of the British dominions. The circumstances will probably justify what is said in the text concerning the traditions of the inhabitants of those remote isles at the beginning of the 18th century.

Even yet, though the Norse language is entirely disused, except in so far as particular words and phrases are still retained, these fishers of the Ultima Thule are a generation much attached to these ancient legends. Of this the Author learned a singular instance.

About twenty years ago, a missionary clergyman had taken the resolution of traversing those wild islands, where he supposed there might be a lack of religious instruction, which he believed himself capable of supplying. After being some days at sea in an open boat, he arrived at North Ronaldsha, where his appearance excited great speculation. He was a very little man, dark-complexioned, and from the fatigue he had sustained in removing from one island to another, appeared before them ill-dressed and unshaved; so that the inhabitants set him down as one of the ancient Picts, or, as they call them with the usual strong guttural, Peghts. How they might have received the poor preacher in this character was at least dubious; and the schoolmaster of the parish, who had given quarters to the fatigued traveller, set off to consult with Mr. Stevenson, the able and ingenious engineer of the Scottish Lighthouse Service, who chanced to be on the island. As his skill and knowledge were in the highest repute, it was conceived that Mr. Stevenson could decide at once whether the stranger was a Peght, or ought to be treated as such. Mr. Stevenson was so good-natured as to attend the summons, with the view of rendering the preacher some service. The poor missionary, who had watched for three nights, was now fast asleep, little dreaming what odious suspicions were current respecting him. The inhabitants were assembled round the door. Mr. Stevenson, understanding the traveller's condition, declined disturbing him, upon which the islanders produced a pair of very little, uncouth-looking boots, with prodigiously thick soles, and appealed to him whether it was possible such articles of raiment could belong to any one but a Peght. Mr. Stevenson, finding the prejudice of the natives so strong, was induced to enter the sleeping-apartment of the traveller, and was surprised to recognise in the supposed Peght a person whom he had known in his worldly profession of an Edinburgh shopkeeper, before he had assumed his present vocation. Of course he was enabled to refute all suspicions of Peghtism.

NOTE 6.—SEA MONSTERS, p. 30.

I have said, in the text, that the wondrous tales told by Pontoppidan, the Archbishop of Upsal, still find believers in the Northern Archipelago. It is in vain they are cancelled even in the later editions of Guthrie's *Grammar*, of which instructive work they used to form the chapter far most attractive to juvenile readers. But the same causes which probably gave birth to the legends concerning mermaids, sea-snakes, krakens, and other marvellous inhabitants of the Northern Ocean, are still afloat in those climates where they took their rise. They had their origin probably from the eagerness of curiosity manifested by our elegant poetess, Mrs. Hemans :

> What hidest thou in thy treasure-caves and cells,
> Thou ever-sounding and mysterious sea?

The additional mystic gloom which rests on these Northern billows for half the year, joined to the imperfect glance obtained of occasional objects, encourage the timid or the fanciful to give way to imagination, and frequently to shape out a distinct story from some object half-seen and imperfectly examined. Thus, some years since, a large object was observed in the beautiful Bay of Scalloway in Zetland, so much in vulgar opinion resembling the kraken, that though it might be distinguished for several days, if the exchange of darkness to twilight can be termed so, yet the hardy boatmen shunned to approach it, for fear of being drawn down by the suction supposed to attend its sinking. It was probably the hull of some vessel which had foundered at sea.

The belief in mermaids, so fanciful and pleasing in itself, is ever and anon refreshed by a strange tale from the remote shores of some solitary islet.

The Author heard a mariner of some reputation in his class vouch for having seen the celebrated sea-serpent. It appeared, so far as could be guessed, to be about a hundred feet long, with the wild mane and fiery eyes which old writers ascribe to the monster ; but it is not unlikely the spectator might, in the doubtful light, be deceived by the appearance of a good Norway log floating on the waves. I have only to add, that the remains of an animal, supposed to belong to this latter species, were driven on shore in the Zetland Isles within the recollection of man. Part of the bones were sent to London, and pronounced by Sir Joseph Banks to be those of a basking shark ; yet it would seem that an animal so well known ought to have been immediately distinguished by the Northern fishermen

NOTE 7.—THE SCART OR CORMORANT, p. 40.

The scart or cormorant may be seen frequently dashing in wild flight along the roosts and tides of Zetland, and yet more often drawn up in ranks on some ledge of rock, like a body of the Black Brunswickers in 1815.

Note 8.—Tusser's Poverty, p. 53.

This is admitted by the English agriculturist:

> My music since hath been the plough
> Entangled with some care among;
> The gain not great, the pain enough,
> Hath made me sing another song.

Note 9.—Administration of Zetland, p. 55.

At the period supposed, the Earls of Morton held the islands of Orkney and Zetland, originally granted in 1643, confirmed in 1707, and rendered absolute in 1742. This gave the family much property and influence, which they usually exercised by factors, named chamberlains. In 1766 this property was sold by the then Earl of Morton to Sir Lawrence Dundas, by whose son, Lord Dundas, it is now held.—Thomas Lord Dundas of Aske, in Yorkshire, was created Earl of Zetland in 1838 (*Laing*).

Note 10.—" To be Fey," p. 65.

When a person changes his condition suddenly, as when a miser becomes liberal or a churl good-humoured, he is said, in Scotch, to be "fey"; that is, predestined to speedy death, of which such mutations of humour are received as a sure indication. [The same word *fei*, with the same meaning, is current amongst the people of the North Frisian Islands—Sylt, Föhr, etc.]

Note 11.—The Bittle, or Beetle, p. 75.

The beetle with which the Scottish housewives used to perform the office of the modern mangle, by beating newly-washed linen on a smooth stone for the purpose, called the beetling-stone.

Note 12.—Chapman's Drouth, p. 81.

The chapman's drouth—that is, the pedlar's thirst—is proverbial in Scotland, because these pedestrian traders were in the use of modestly asking only for a drink of water, when, in fact, they were desirous of food.

Note 13.—An " Oramus " to St. Ronald, p. 82.

Although the Zetlanders were early reconciled to the Reformed faith, some ancient practices of Catholic superstition survived long among them. In very stormy weather a fisher would vow an *oramus* to St. Ronald, and acquitted himself of the obligation by throwing a small piece of money in at the window of a ruinous chapel.

Note 14.—Sale of Winds, p. 90.

The King of Sweden, the same Erick quoted by Mordaunt [Mertoun], " was," says Olaus Magnus, " in his time held second to none in the magical art; and he was so familiar with the evil spirits whom he worshipped, that what way soever he turned his cap, the wind would presently blow that way. For this he was called Windycap."—*Historia de Gentibus Septentrionalibus; Romæ*, 1555. It is well known that the Laplanders derive a profitable trade in selling *winds;* but it is perhaps less notorious that within these few years such a commodity might be purchased on British ground, where it was likely to be in great request. At the village of Stromness, on the Orkney main island, called Pomona, lived, in 1814, an aged dame called Bessie Millie, who helped out her subsistence by selling favourable winds to mariners. He was a venturous master of a vessel who left the roadstead of Stromness without paying his offering to propitiate Bessie Millie; her fee was extremely moderate, being exactly sixpence, for which, as she explained herself, she boiled her kettle and gave the bark advantage of her prayers, for she disclaimed all unlawful arts. The wind thus petitioned for was sure, she said, to arrive, though occasionally the mariner had to wait some time for it. The woman's dwelling and appearance were not unbecoming her pretensions: her house, which was on the brow of the steep hill on which Stromness is founded, was only accessible by a series of dirty and precipitous lanes, and for exposure might have been the abode of Eolus himself, in whose commodities the inhabitant dealt. She herself was, as she told us, nearly one hundred years old, withered and dried up like a mummy. A clay-coloured kerchief, folded round her head, corresponded in colour to her corpse-like complexion. Two light blue eyes that gleamed with a lustre like that of insanity, an utterance of astonishing rapidity, a nose and chin that almost met together, and a ghastly expression of cunning, gave her the effect of Hecate. She remembered Gow, the pirate, who had been a native of these islands, in which he closed his career, as mentioned in the preface. Such was Bessie Millie, to whom the mariners paid a sort of tribute, with a feeling betwixt jest and earnest.

Note 15.—Reluctance to save Drowning Men, p. 98.

It is remarkable that, in an archipelago where so many persons must be necessarily endangered by the waves, so strange and inhuman a maxim should have ingrafted itself upon the minds of a people otherwise kind, moral, and hospitable. But all with whom I have spoken agree that it was almost general in the beginning of the 18th century, and was with difficulty weeded out by the sedulous instructions of the clergy, and the rigorous injunctions of the proprietors. There is little doubt it had been originally introduced as an excuse for suffering those who attempted to escape from the wreck to perish unassisted, so that, there being no survivor, she might be considered as lawful plunder. A story was told me, I hope an untrue one, that a vessel having got ashore among the breakers on one of the remote Zetland islands, five or six men, the whole or greater part of the unfortunate crew, endeavoured to land by assistance of a hawser, which they had secured to a rock; the inhabitants were assembled, and looked on with some uncertainty, till an old man said: "Sirs, if these men come ashore, the additional mouths will eat all the meal we have in store for winter ; and how are we to get more?" A young fellow, moved with this argument, struck the rope asunder with his axe, and all the poor wretches were immersed among the breakers, and perished.

Note 16.—"Mair Wrecks ere Winter," p. 103.

The ancient Zetlander looked upon the sea as the provider of his living, not only by the plenty produced by the fishings, but by the spoil of wrecks. Some particular islands have fallen off very considerably in their rent since the commissioners of the lighthouses have ordered lights on the

Isle of Sanda and the Pentland skerries. A gentleman, familiar with those seas, expressed surprise at seeing the farmer of one of the isles in a boat with a very old pair of sails. "Had it been His will," said the man, with an affected deference to Providence very inconsistent with the sentiment of his speech—"had it been *His* will that light had not been placed yonder, I would have had enough of new sails last winter."

NOTE 17.—THE DROWS, OR TROWS, p. 126.

The Drows, or Trows, the legitimate successors of the Northern *duergar*, and somewhat allied to the fairies, reside, like them, in the interior of green hills and caverns, and are most powerful at midnight. They are curious artificers in iron, as well as in the precious metals, and are sometimes propitious to mortals, but more frequently capricious and malevolent. Among the common people of Zetland, their existence still forms an article of universal belief. In the neighbouring isles of Feroe they are called Foddenskencand, or subterranean people; and Lucas Jacobson Debes, well acquainted with their nature, assures us that they inhabit those places which are polluted with the effusion of blood or the practice of any crying sin. They have a government, which seems to be monarchical.

NOTE 18.—CORN-MILLS, p. 142.

There is certainly something very extraordinary to a stranger in Zetland corn-mills. They are of the smallest possible size; the wheel which drives them is horizontal, and the cogs are turned diagonally to the water. The beam itself stands upright, and is inserted in a stone quern of the old-fashioned construction, which it turns round, and thus performs its duty. Had Robinson Crusoe ever been in Zetland, he would have had no difficulty in contriving a machine for grinding corn in his desert island. These mills are thatched over in a little hovel, which has much the air of a pig-sty. There may be five hundred such mills on one island, not capable any one of them of grinding above a sackful of corn at a time.—[Mills similar in construction to these, and very little larger in size, may be seen in Norway at the present time, in the year 1893.]

NOTE 19.—MONTROSE IN ZETLAND, p. 186.

Montrose, in his last and ill-advised attempt to invade Scotland, augmented his small army of Danes and Scottish Royalists by some bands of raw troops, hastily levied, or rather pressed into his service, in the Orkney and Zetland Isles, who, having little heart either to the cause or manner of service, behaved but indifferently when they came into action.

NOTE 20.—SIR JOHN URRY, p. 186.

Here, as afterwards remarked in the text, the Zetlander's memory deceived him grossly. Sir John Urry, a brave soldier of fortune, was at that time in Montrose's army, and made prisoner along with him. He had changed so often that the mistake is pardonable. After the action, he was executed by the Covenanters; and

> Wind-changing Warwick then could change no more.

Strachan commanded the body by which Montrose was routed.

Note 21.—The Sword-Dance, p. 187.

The sword-dance is celebrated in general terms by Olaus Magnus. He seems to have considered it as peculiar to the Norwegians, from whom it may have passed to the Orkneymen and Zetlanders, with other Northern customs.

Of their Dancing in Arms.

Moreover, the northern Goths and Swedes had another sport to exercise youth withall, that they will dance and skip amongst naked swords and dangerous weapons; and this they do after the manner of masters of defence, as they are taught from their youth by skilful teachers, that dance before them, and sing to it. And this play is showed especially about Shrovetide, called in Italian *maschararum.* For, before carnivals, all the youth dance for eight days together, holding their swords up, but within the scabbards, for three times turning about; and then they do it with their naked swords lifted up. After this, turning more moderately, taking the points and pummels one of the other, they change ranks, and place themselves in an triagonal figure, and this they call *rosam;* and presently they dissolve it by drawing back their swords and lifting them up, that upon every one's head there may be made a square *rosa,* and then by a most nimbly whisking their swords about collaterally, they quickly leap back, and end the sport, which they guide with pipes or songs, or both together; first by a more heavy, then by a more vehement, and lastly by a most vehement, dancing. But this speculation is scarce to be understood but by those who look on, how comely and decent it is, when at one word, or one commanding, the whole armed multitude is directed to fall to fight, and clergymen may exercise themselves and mingle themselves amongst others at this sport, because it is all guided by most wise reason.

To the Primate's account of the sword-dance, I am able to add the words sung or chanted on occasion of this dance, as it is still performed in Papa Stour, a remote island of Zetland, where alone the custom keeps its ground. It is, it will be observed by antiquaries, a species of play or mystery, in which the Seven Champions of Christendom make their appearance, as in the interlude presented in *All's Well that Ends Well.* This dramatic curiosity was most kindly procured for my use by Dr. Scott of Haslar Hospital, son of my friend Mr. Scott of Mewbie, Zetland. Mr. Hibbert has, in his *Description of the Zetland Islands,* given an account of the sword-dance, but somewhat less full than the following:

Words used as a Prelude to the Sword-Dance, a Danish or Norwegian Ballet, composed some Centuries ago, and preserved in Papa Stour, Zetland.

Personæ Dramatis. [1]

(*Enter* Master *in the character of* St. George.)
Brave gentles all within this boor, [2]
If ye delight in any sport,
Come see me dance upon this floor,
Which to you all shall yield comfort.
Then shall I dance in such a sort,
As possible I may or can;

---

[1] So placed in the old MS.
[2] So spelt to accord with the vulgar pronunciation of the word " bower."

You, minstrel man, play me a porte,[1]
That I on this floor may prove a man.
                (*He bows, and dances in a line.*)
Now have I danced with heart and hand,
Brave gentles all, as you may see,
For I have been tried in many a land,
As yet the truth can testify;
In England, Scotland, Ireland, France, Italy, and Spain
Have I been tried with that good sword of steel.
                (*Draws and flourishes.*)
Yet, I defy that ever a man did make me yield;
For in my body there is strength,
As by my manhood may be seen;
And I, with that good sword of length,
Oft times in perils I have been,
And over champions I was king.
And by the strength of this right hand,
Once on a day I kill'd fifteen,
And left them dead upon the land.
Therefore, brave minstrel, do not care,
But play to me a porte most light,
That I no longer do forbear,
But dance in all these gentles' sight;
Brave gentles all, be not afraid,
Although my strength makes you abased,
For here are six champions, with me, staid,
All by my manhood I have raised.
                (*He dances.*)
Since I have danced, I think it best
To call my brethren in your sight,
That I may have a little rest,
And they may dance with all their might;
With heart and hand as they are knights,
And shake their swords of steel so bright,
And show their main strength on this floor,
For we shall have another bout
Before we pass out of this boor.
Therefore, brave minstrel, do not care
To play to me a porte most light,
That I no longer do forbear,
But dance in all these gentles' sight.
        (*He dances, and then introduces his knights, as under.*)
Stout James of Spain, both tried and stour,
Thine acts are known full well indeed;
And champion Dennis, a French knight,
Who stout and bold is to be seen;
And David, a Welchman born,
Who is come of noble blood;
And Patrick also, who blew the horn,
An Irish knight, amongst the wood;
Of Italy, brave Anthony the good,
And Andrew of Scotland king;
St. George of England, brave indeed,
Who to the Jews wrought muckle tinte.

---

[1] So spelt in the original. The word is known as indicating a piece of music on the bagpipe, to which ancient instrument, which is of Scandinavian origin, the sword-dance may have been originally composed.

Away with this ! Let us come to sport,
Since that ye have a mind to war,
Since that ye have this bargain sought,
Come let us fight and do not fear.
Therefore, brave minstrel, do not care
To play to me a porte most light,
That I no longer do forbear,
But dance in all these gentles' sight.
   (*He dances, and advances to* JAMES OF SPAIN.)
Stout James of Spain, both tried and stour,
Thine acts are known full well indeed,
Present thyself within our sight,
Without either fear or dread.
Count not for favour or for feed,
Since of thy acts thou hast been sure ;
Brave James of Spain, I will thee lead,
To prove thy manhood on this floor.
    (JAMES *dances.*)
Brave champion Dennis, a French knight,
Who stout and bold is to be seen,
Present thyself here in our sight,
Thou brave French knight,
Who bold hast been ;
Since thou such valiant acts hast done,
Come let us see some of them now
With courtesy, thou brave French knight,
Draw out thy sword of noble hue.
   (DENNIS *dances, while the others retire to a side.*)
Brave David a bow must string, and by with awe
Set up a wand upon a stand,
And that brave David will cleave in twa.[1]
    (DAVID *dances solus.*)
Here is, I think, an Irish knight,
Who does not fear, or does not fright,
To prove thyself a valiant man,
As thou hast done full often bright ;
Brave Patrick, dance, if that thou can.
    (*He dances.*)
Thou stout Italian, come thou here ;
Thy name is Anthony, most stout ;
Draw out thy sword that is most clear,
And do thou fight without any doubt ;
Thy leg thou shake, thy neck thou lout,
And show some courtesy on this floor,
For we shall have another bout
Before we pass out of this boor.
Thou kindly Scotsman, come thou here ;
Thy name is Andrew of Fair Scotland ;
Draw out thy sword that is most clear,
Fight for the king with thy right hand ;
And aye as long as thou canst stand,
Fight for thy king with all thy heart ;
And then, for to confirm his band,
Make all his enemies for to smart.
   (*He dances.*) (*Music begins.*)

---

[1] Something is evidently amiss or omitted here. David probably exhibited some feat of archery.

Figure.

The six stand in rank with their swords reclining on their shoulders. The master (St. George) dances, and then strikes the sword of James of Spain, who follows George, then dances, strikes the sword of Dennis, who follows behind James. In like manner the rest—the music playing—swords as before. After the six are brought out of rank, they and the master form a circle, and hold the swords point and hilt. This circle is danced round twice. The whole, headed by the master, pass under the swords held in a vaulted manner. They jump over the swords. This naturally places the swords across, which they disentangle by passing under their right sword. They take up the seven swords and form a circle, in which they dance round,

The master runs under the sword opposite, which he jumps over backwards. The others do the same. He then passes under the right-hand sword, which the others follow, in which position they dance, until commanded by the master, when they form into a circle, and dance round as before. They then jump over the right-hand sword, by which means their backs are to the circle, and their hands across their backs. They dance round in that form until the master calls " Loose," when they pass under the right sword, and are in a perfect circle.

The master lays down his sword, and lays hold of the point of James's sword. He then turns himself, James, and the others, into a clue. When so formed, he passes under out of the midst of the circle ; the others follow ; they vault as before. After several other evolutions, they throw themselves into a circle, with their arms across the breast. They afterwards form such figures as to form a shield of their swords, and the shield is so compact that the master and his knights dance alternately with this shield upon their heads. It is then laid down upon the floor. Each knight lays hold of their former points and hilts with their hands across, which disentangle by figuirs directly contrary to those that formed the shield. This finishes the ballet.

Epilogue.

Mars does rule, he bends his brows,
He makes us all agast ;
After the few hours that we stay here,
Venus will rule at last.

Farewell, farewell, brave gentles all,
That herein do remain,
I wish you health and happiness
Till we return again.　　　　　　　[*Exeunt.*

The manuscript from which the above was copied was transcribed from *a very old one* by Mr. William Henderson, jun., of Papa Stour, in Zetland. Mr. Henderson's copy is not dated, but bears his own signature, and, from various circumstances, it is known to have been written about the year 1788.

Note 22.—The Law-ting, p. 236.

The Law-ting was the comitia, or supreme court, of the country, being retained both in Orkney and Zetland, and presenting, in its constitution, the rude origin of a parliament.

Note 23.—Hill of Hoy, p. 236.

And from which Hill of Hoy, at midsummer, the sun may be seen, it is said, at midnight. So says the geographer Bleau, although according to

Dr. Wallace, it cannot be the true body of the sun which is visible, but only its image refracted through some watery cloud upon the horizon.

NOTE 24.—THE DWARFIE STONE, p. 236.

This is one of the wonders of the Orkney Islands, though it has been rather undervalued by their late historian, Mr. Barry. The Island of Hoy rises abruptly, starting as it were out of the sea, which is contrary to the gentle and flat character of the other isles of Orkney. It consists of a mountain, having different eminences or peaks. It is very steep, furrowed with ravines, and placed so as to catch the mists of the Western Ocean, and has a noble and picturesque effect from all points of view. The highest peak is divided from another eminence called the Ward Hill by a long swampy valley full of peat-bogs. Upon the slope of this last hill, and just where the principal mountain of Hoy opens in a hollow swamp, or corrie, lies what is called the Dwarfie Stone. It is a great fragment of sandstone, composing one solid mass, which has long since been detached from a belt of the same materials, cresting the eminence above the spot where it now lies, and which has slid down till it reached its present situation. The rock is about seven feet high, twenty-two feet long, and seventeen feet broad. The upper end of it is hollowed by iron tools, of which the marks are evident, into a sort of apartment, containing two beds of stone, with a passage between them. The uppermost and largest bed is five feet eight inches long, by two feet broad, which was supposed to be used by the dwarf himself; the lower couch is shorter, and rounded off, instead of being squared at the corners. There is an entrance of about three feet and a half square, and a stone lies before it calculated to fit the opening. A sort of skylight window gives light to the apartment. We can only guess at the purpose of this monument, and different ideas have been suggested. Some have supposed it the work of some travelling mason; but the *cui bono* would remain to be accounted for. The Rev. Mr. Barry conjectures it to be a hermit's cell; but it displays no symbol of Christianity, and the door opens to the westward. The Orcadian traditions allege the work to be that of a dwarf, to whom they ascribe supernatural powers and a malevolent disposition, the attributes of that race in Norse mythology. Whoever inhabited this singular den certainly enjoyed

> Pillow cold, and sheets not warm.

I observed that, commencing just opposite to the Dwarfie Stone, and extending in a line to the sea-beach, there are a number of small barrows, or cairns, which seem to connect the stone with a very large cairn where we landed. This curious monument may therefore have been intended as a temple of some kind to the Northern *Dii Manes*, to which the cairns might direct worshippers.

NOTE 25.—CARBUNCLE ON THE WARD HILL, p. 237.

" At the west end of this stone (*i.e.* the Dwarfie Stone) stands an exceeding high mountain of a steep ascent, called the Ward Hill of Hoy, near the top of which, in the months of May, June, and July, about midday, is seen something that shines and sparkles admirably, and which will be seen a great way off. It hath shined more brightly before than it does now; . . . though many have climbed up the hill and attempted to search

33

for it, yet they could find nothing. The vulgar talk of it as some enchanted carbuncle, but I rather take it to be some water sliding down the face of a smooth rock, which, when the sun, at such a time, shines upon, the reflection causeth that admirable splendour."—Dr. Wallace's *Description of the Islands of Orkney*, 12mo, 1700, p. 52.

NOTE 26.—FORTUNE-TELLING RHYMES, p. 255.

The Author has in chapter xxi. supposed that a very ancient Northern custom, used by those who were accounted soothsaying women, might have survived, though in jest rather than earnest, among the Zetlanders, their descendants. The following original account of such a scene will show the ancient importance and consequence of such a prophetic character as was assumed by Norna:

There lived in the same territory (Greenland) a woman named Thorbiorga, who was a prophetess, and called the little Vola (or fatal sister), the only one of nine sisters who survived. Thorbiorga during the winter used to frequent the festivities of the season, invited by those who were desirous of learning their own fortune and the future events which impended. Torquil being a man of consequence in the country, it fell to his lot to enquire how long the dearth was to endure with which the country was then afflicted; he therefore invited the prophetess to his house, having made liberal preparation, as was the custom, for receiving a guest of such consequence. The seat of the soothsayer was placed in an eminent situation, and covered with pillows filled with the softest eider-down. In the evening she arrived, together with a person who had been sent to meet her and show her the way to Torquil's habitation. She was attired as follows: She had a sky-blue tunick, having the front ornamented with gems from the top to the bottom, and wore around her throat a necklace of glass beads.[1] Her head-gear was of black lambskin, the lining being the fur of a white wild cat. She leant on a staff, having a ball at the top.[2] The staff was ornamented with brass, and the ball or globe with gems or pebbles. She wore a Hunland (or Hungarian) girdle, to which was attached a large pouch, in which she kept her magical implements. Her shoes were of sealskin, dressed with the hair outside, and secured by long and thick straps, fastened by brazen clasps. She wore gloves of the wild cat's skin, with the fur inmost. As this venerable person entered the hall, all saluted her with due respect; but she only returned the compliments of such as were agreeable to her. Torquil conducted her with reverence to the seat prepared for her, and requested she would purify the apartment and company assembled by casting her eyes over them. She was by no means sparing of her words. The table being at length covered, such viands were placed before Thorbiorga as suited her character of a soothsayer. These were, a preparation of goat's milk and a mess composed of the hearts of various animals; the prophetess made use of a brazen spoon and a pointless knife, the handle of which was composed of a whale's tooth, and ornamented with two rings of brass. The table being removed, Torquil addressed Thorbiorga, requesting her opinion of his house and guests, at the same time intimating the subjects on which he and the company were desirous to consult her.

Thorbiorga replied, it was impossible for her to answer their enquiries until she had slept a night under his roof. The next morning, therefore,

---

[1] We may suppose the beads to have been of the potent adder-stone, to which so many virtues were ascribed.

[2] Like those anciently borne by porters at the gates of distinguished persons, as a badge of office.

the magical apparatus necessary for her purpose was prepared, and she then enquired, as a necessary part of the ceremony, whether there was any female present who could sing a magical song called *Vardlokur*. When no songstress such as she desired could be found, Gudrida, the daughter of Torquil, replied, " I am no sorceress or soothsayer ; but my nurse, Haldisa, taught me, when in Iceland, a song called *Vardlokur*." " Then thou knowest more than I was aware of," said Torquil. "But as I am a Christian," continued Gudrida, " I consider these rites as matters which it is unlawful to promote, and the song itself as unlawful." " Nevertheless, " answered the soothsayer, "thou mayst help us in this matter without any harm to thy religion, since the task will remain with Torquil to provide everything necessary for the present purpose." Torquil also earnestly entreated Gudrida, till she consented to grant his request. The females then surrounded Thorbiorga, who took her place on a sort of elevated stage ; Gudrida then sung the magic song, with a voice so sweet and tuneful as to excel anything that had been heard by any present. The soothsayer, delighted with the melody, returned thanks to the singer, and then said : " Much I have now learned of dearth and disease approaching the country, and many things are now clear to me which before were hidden as well from me as others. Our present dearth of substance shall not long endure for the present, and plenty will in the spring succeed to scarcity. The contagious diseases also, with which the country has been for some time afflicted, will in a short time take their departure. To thee, Gudrida, I can, in recompense for thy assistance on this occasion, announce a fortune of higher import than any one could have conjectured. You shall be married to a man of name here in Greenland ; but you shall not long enjoy that union, for your fate recalls you to Iceland, where you shall become the mother of a numerous and honourable family, which shall be enlightened by a luminous ray of good fortune. So, my daughter, wishing thee health, I bid thee farewell." The prophetess, having afterwards given answers to all queries which were put to her, either by Torquil or his guests, departed to show her skill at another festival, to which she had been invited for that purpose. But all which she had presaged, either concerning the public or individuals, came truly to pass.

The above narrative is taken from the Saga of Erick Rauda, as quoted by the learned Bartholin in his curious work. He mentions similar instances, particularly of one Heida, celebrated for her predictions, who attended festivals for the purpose, as a modern Scotsman might say, of "spaeing" fortunes, with a gallant " tail, " or retinue, of thirty male and fifteen female attendants.—See *De Causis Contemptæ a Danis adhuc Gentilibus Mortis*, lib. iii. cap. 4.

Note 27.—Whaling Customs. p, 258.

The garland is an artificial coronet, composed of ribbons by those young women who take an interest in a whaling vessel or her crew; it is always displayed from the rigging, and preserved with great care during the voyage.

The best oil exudes from the jaw-bones of the whale, which, for the purpose of collecting it, are suspended to the masts of the vessel.

There is established among whalers a sort of telegraphic signal, in which a certain number of motions, made with a broom, express to any other vessel the number of fish which they have caught.

Note 28.—Armada in Zetland, p. 262.

The admiral of the Spanish Armada was wrecked on the Fair Isle, half-way betwixt the Orkney and Zetland Archipelago. The Duke of Medina Sidonia landed, with some of his people, and pillaged the islanders of their winter stores. These strangers are remembered as having remained on the island by force, and on bad terms with the inhabitants, till spring returned, when they effected their escape.—[The Spanish admiral who was wrecked on Fair Island was not the Duke of Medina Sidonia, but Don Juan Gomez de Medina. See *Diary of James Melville*, Bannatyne Club ed., 1829.]

NOTE 29.—FISHERMEN'S WIVES, p. 267.

Dr. Edmonston, the ingenious author of a *View of the Ancient and Present State of the Zetland Islands*, has placed this part of the subject in an interesting light :

It is truly painful to witness the anxiety and distress which the wives of these poor men suffer on the approach of a storm. Regardless of fatigue, they leave their homes and fly to the spot where they expect their husbands to land, or ascend the summit of a rock, and look for them on the bosom of the deep. Should they get a glimpse of a sail, they watch with trembling solicitude its alternate rise and disappearance on the waves ; and although often tranquillised by the safe arrival of the objects of their search, yet it is sometimes their lot "to hail the bark that never can return." Subject to the influence of a variable climate, and engaged on a sea naturally tempestuous, with rapid currents, scarcely a season passes over without the occurrence of some fatal accident or hairbreadth escape.— *View, etc., of the Zetland Islands*, vol. i. pp. 238, 239.

Many interesting particulars respecting the fisheries and agriculture of Zetland, as well as its antiquities, may be found in the work we have quoted.

NOTE 30.—PROMISE OF ODIN, p. 277.

Although the father of Scandinavian mythology has been as a deity long forgotten in the archipelago, which was once a very small part of his realm, yet even at this day his name continues to be occasionally attested as security for a promise.

It is curious to observe that the rites with which such attestations are still made in Orkney correspond to those of the ancient Northmen. It appears from several authorities that in the Norse ritual, when an oath was imposed, he by whom it was pledged passed his hand, while pronouncing it, through a massive ring of silver kept for that purpose.[1] In like manner, two persons, generally lovers, desirous to take the promise of Odin, which they considered as peculiarly binding, joined hands through a circular hole in a sacrificial stone which lies in the Orcadian Stonehenge, called the Circle of Stennis, of which we speak more in Note 46, p. 520. The ceremony is now confined to the troth-plighting of the lower classes, but at an earlier period may be supposed to have influenced a character like Minna in the higher ranks.

NOTE 31.—COFFIN KEY, p. 279.

An elder brother, now no more, who was educated in the navy, and had been a midshipman in Rodney's squadron in the West Indies, used to astonish the Author's boyhood with tales of those haunted islets. On one of them, called, I believe, Coffin Key, the seamen positively refused to pass the night, and came off every evening while they were engaged in completing the watering of the vessel, returning the following sunrise.

---

[1] See the *Eyrbyggja Saga.*

NOTE 32.—MOTTO TO CHAP. XXVI., p. 317.

It is worth while saying that this motto, and the ascription of the beautiful ballad from which it is taken to the Right Honourable Lady Ann Lindsay, occasioned the ingenious authoress's acknowledgment of the ballad, of which the Editor, by her permission, published a small impression, inscribed to the Bannatyne Club.

NOTE 33.—FRAWA-STACK, p. 327.

The Frawa-Stack, or Maiden-Rock, an inaccessible cliff, divided by a narrow gulf from the Island of Papa, has on the summit some ruins, concerning which there is a legend similar to that of Danaë.

NOTE 34.—THE PICTISH BURGH, p. 328.

The Pictish burgh, a fort which Norna is supposed to have converted into her dwelling-house, has been fully described in *Ivanhoe* (Note 27, p. 531 of this edition). An account of the celebrated Castle of Mousa is there given, to afford an opportunity of comparing it with the Saxon Castle of Coningsburgh. It should, however, have been mentioned that the Castle of Mousa underwent considerable repairs at a comparatively recent period. Accordingly, Torfæus assures us that even this ancient pigeon-house, composed of dry stones, was fortification enough, not indeed to hold out a ten years' siege, like Troy in similar circumstances, but to wear out the patience of the besiegers. Erland,[1] the son of Harold the Fair-spoken, had carried off a beautiful woman, the mother of a Norwegian earl, also called Harold, the son of Maddadh, and sheltered himself with his fair prize in the Castle of Mousa. Earl Harold followed with an army, and finding the place too strong for assault, endeavoured to reduce it by famine ; but such was the length of the siege, that the offended earl found it necessary to listen to a treaty of accommodation, and agreed that his mother's honour should be restored by marriage. This transaction took place in the beginning of the 13th century, in the reign of William the Lion of Scotland.[2] It is probable that the improvements adopted by Erland on this occasion were those which finished the parapet of the castle, by making it project outwards, so that the Tower of Mousa rather resembles the figure of a dice-box, whereas others of the same kind have the form of a truncated cone. It is easy to see how the projection of the highest parapet would render the defence more easy and effectual.—

In 1859 the Society of Antiquaries exerted themselves in effecting repairs on the tower (*Laing*).—[It is now included among the buildings protected by the Ancient Monument Protection Act, 1882.]

NOTE 35.—THE MACRAWS, p. 336.

The MacRaws were followers of the MacKenzies, whose chief has the name of Caberfae, or Buckshead, from the cognizance borne on his standards. Unquestionably the worthy piper trained the seal on the same principle of respect to the clan term which I have heard has been taught to dogs, who, unused to any other air, dance after their fashion to the tune of " Caberfae."

---

[1] [See Glossary.]　　　　[2] See Torfæi *Orcades*, p. 131.

Note 36.—Norna's Spells, p. 340.

The spells described in chapter xxviii. are not altogether imaginary. By this mode of pouring lead into water, and selecting the part which chances to assume a resemblance to the human heart, which must be worn by the patient around her or his neck, the sage persons of Zetland pretend to cure the fatal disorder called the loss of a heart.

Note 37.—Bicker of St. Magnus, p. 356.

The bicker of St. Magnus, a vessel of enormous dimensions, was preserved at Kirkwall, and presented to each bishop of the Orkneys. If the new incumbent was able to quaff it out at one draught, which was a task for Hercules or Rory Mohr of Dunvegan, the omen boded a crop of unusual fertility.

Note 38.—Luggie, p. 356.

Luggie, a famous conjurer, was wont, when storms prevented him from going to his usual employment of fishing, to angle over a steep rock at the place called, from his name, Luggie's Knoll. At other times he drew up dressed food while they were out at sea, of which his comrades partook boldly from natural courage, without caring who stood cook. The poor man was finally condemned and burnt at Scalloway.

Note 39.—Antique Coins found in Zetland, p. 359.

While these sheets were passing through the press, I received a letter from an honourable and learned friend, containing the following passage relating to a discovery in Zetland: "Within a few weeks the workmen, taking up the foundation of an old wall, came upon a hearthstone, under which they found a horn, surrounded with massive silver rings, like bracelets, and filled with coins of the Heptarchy in perfect preservation. The place of finding is within a very short distance of the [supposed] residence of Norna of the Fitful Head." Thus one of the very improbable fictions of the tale is verified by a singular coincidence.

Note 40.—Grouse in Orkney, p. 374.

It is very curious that the grouse, plenty in Orkney as the text declares, should be totally unknown in the neighbouring archipelago of Zetland, which is only about sixty miles' distance, with the Fair Isle as a step between.

Note 41.—Lambmas Lads, p. 385.

It was anciently a custom at St. Olla's fair at Kirkwall that the young people of the lower class, and of either sex, associated in pairs for the period of the fair, during which the couple were termed Lambmas brother and sister. It is easy to conceive that the exclusive familiarity arising out of this custom was liable to abuse, the rather that it is said little scandal was attached to the indiscretions which it occasioned.

Note 42.—Character of Norna, p. 400.

The character of Norna is meant to be an instance of that singular kind of insanity, during which the patient, while she or he retains much subtlety and address for the power of imposing upon others, is still more ingenious in endeavouring to impose upon themselves. Indeed, maniacs of this kind may be often observed to possess a sort of double character, in one of which they are the being whom their distempered imagination shapes out, and in the other their own natural self as seen to exist by other people. This species of double consciousness makes wild work with the patient's imagination, and, judiciously used, is perhaps a frequent means of restoring sanity of intellect. Exterior circumstances striking the senses often have a powerful effect in undermining or battering the airy castles which the disorder has excited.

A late medical gentleman, my particular friend, told me the case of a lunatic patient confined in the Edinburgh Infirmary. He was so far happy that his mental alienation was of a gay and pleasant character, giving a kind of joyous explanation to all that came in contact with him. He considered the large house, numerous servants, etc., of the hospital as all matters of state and consequence belonging to his own personal establishment, and had no doubt of his own wealth and grandeur. One thing alone puzzled this man of wealth. Although he was provided with a first-rate cook and proper assistants, although his table was regularly supplied with every delicacy of the season, yet he confessed to my friend that, by some uncommon depravity of the palate, everything which he ate *tasted of porridge*. This peculiarity, of course, arose from the poor man being fed upon nothing else, and because his stomach was not so easily deceived as his other senses.

NOTE 43.—BIRDS OF PREY, p. 401.

So favourable a retreat does the Island of Hoy afford for birds of prey, that instances of their ravages, which seldom occur in other parts of the country, are not unusual there. An individual was living in Orkney not long since, whom, while a child in its swaddling-clothes, an eagle actually transported to its nest in the Hill of Hoy. Happily, the eyrie being known and the bird instantly pursued, the child was found uninjured, playing with the young eagles. A story of a more ludicrous transportation was told me by the reverend clergyman who is minister of the island. Hearing one day a strange grunting, he suspected his servants had permitted a sow and pigs, which were tenants of his farm-yard, to get among his barley crop. Having in vain looked for the transgressors upon solid earth, he at length cast his eyes upward, when he discovered one of the litter in the talons of a large eagle, which was soaring away with the unfortunate pig, squeaking all the while with terror, towards her nest in the crest of Hoy.

NOTE 44.—AVERY'S PLEASANTRY, p. 406.

This was really an exploit of the celebrated Avery, the pirate, who suddenly, and without provocation, fired his pistols under the table where he sat drinking with his messmates, wounded one man severely, and thought the matter a good jest. What is still more extraordinary, his crew regarded it in the same light.

NOTE 45.—WELLS AND WAVES, p. 460.

A "well," in the language of those seas, denotes one of the whirlpools, or circular eddies, which wheel and boil with astonishing strength, and are very dangerous. Hence the distinction, in old English, betwixt wells and waves, the latter signifying the direct onward course of the tide, and the former the smooth, glassy, oily-looking whirlpools, whose strength seems to the eye almost irresistible.

NOTE 46.—THE STANDING STONES OF STENNIS, p. 462.

The Standing Stones of Stennis, as by a little pleonasm this remarkable monument is termed, furnishes an irresistible refutation of the opinion of such antiquaries as hold that the circles usually called Druidical were peculiar to that race of priests. There is every reason to believe that the custom was as prevalent in Scandinavia as in Gaul or Britain, and as common to the mythology of Odin as to Druidical superstition. There is even reason to think that the Druids never occupied any part of the Orkneys, and tradition, as well as history, ascribes the Stones of Stennis to the Scandinavians. Two large sheets of water, communicating with the sea, are connected by a causeway, with openings permitting the tide to rise and recede, which is called the Bridge of Broisgar. Upon the eastern tongue of land appear the Standing Stones, arranged in the form of a half circle, or rather a horse-shoe, the height of the pillars being fifteen feet and upwards. Within this circle lies a stone, probably sacrificial. One of the pillars, a little to the westward, is perforated with a circular hole, through which loving couples are wont to join hands when they take the promise of Odin, as has been repeatedly mentioned in the text. The inclosure is surrounded by barrows, and on the opposite isthmus, advancing towards the Bridge of Broisgar, there is another monument of standing stones, which, in this case, is completely circular. They are less in size than those on the eastern side of the lake, their height running only from ten or twelve to fourteen feet. This western circle is surrounded by a deep trench drawn on the outside of the pillars; and I remarked four tumuli, or mounds of earth, regularly disposed around it. Stonehenge excels this Orcadian monument; but that of Stennis is, I conceive, the only one in Britain which can be said to approach it in consequence. All the Northern nations marked by those huge inclosures the places of popular meeting, either for religious worship or the transaction of public business of a temporal nature. The *Northern Popular Antiquities* contain, in an abstract of the *Eyrbyggja Saga*, a particular account of the manner in which the Helga Fels, or Holy Rock, was set apart by the Pontiff Thorolf for solemn occasions.

I need only add that, different from the monument on Salisbury Plain, the stones which were used in the Orcadian circle seem to have been raised from a quarry upon the spot, of which the marks are visible.

NOTE 47.—BUNCE'S FATE, p. 502.

We have been able to learn nothing with certainty of Bunce's fate; but our friend, Dr. Dryasdust, believes he may be identified with an old gentleman who, in the beginning of the reign of George I., attended the Rose Coffee-house regularly, went to the theatre every night, told mercilessly long stories about the Spanish Main, controlled reckonings, bullied waiters, and was generally known by the name of Captain Bunce.

GLOSSARY

OF

WORDS, PHRASES, AND ALLUSIONS.

ABOON, above

ACCOUNT, WENT UPON THE, took part in piratical excursions

ADSUM, here I am

AIGRE, sour, acrimonious

AIK, oak

AILS AT, have objection to, dissatisfaction with

AIN, own

AIR, an open sea-beach

AIRN, iron

AITS, oats

ALEXANDER, the hero of Nathaniel Lee's *Alexander the Great*, one of Betterton's great rôles

ALEXANDER IN THE TENT OF DARIUS, a reference to Alexander's generous treatment of the wife and mother of the Persian king, Darius, when, after his defeat, they were brought prisoners before the conqueror

ALL FOR LOVE, OR THE WORLD WELL LOST, a tragedy by Dryden

ALOW, ablaze

ALTAMONT, the name of the hero of Sir Wm. D'Avenant's *Just Italian* (1630)

"AMONG ALL LIVING CREATURES," etc. (p. 154), adapted from Spenser, *Faërie Queene*, the fragment entitled "Two Cantos of Mutability," canto vii.

AMPHITRYON WITH WHOM ONE DINES, the wealthy and hospitable provider of the feast. Both Plautus and Molière have written a comedy with this title

ANES, once

ANGUSSHIRE, ancient name for Forfarshire

A-PEAK, said of an anchor, when before drawing it up the vessel is brought immediately above it

ARION, a celebrated Greek musician, who, driven into the sea by covetous sailors, was carried safely to land by a dolphin

ARMIDA, a character in Tasso's *Gerusalemme Liberata*, who was smitten with a frantic passion for Rinaldo

AROINT, avaunt, begone

A-TRIP, just raised (an anchor) perpendicularly off the ground when it is being weighed

AUGHT, owned

AURINIA, a prophetess of the ancient Germans, mentioned in Tacitus, *Germ.* ch. viii.

AVER, a cart-horse

"AWAY, BEGONE," etc. (p. 440), from Lee's *Rival Queens*, Act iii. sc. 1

AWAY-GANGING CROP, a crop sown in the last year of tenancy, to be reaped by the incoming tenant

AWMOUS, alms

BABY, affectionate diminutive of Barbara

BACK-SPAULD, the back of the shoulder

BAITTLE, rich with grass

BANG, OR BHANG, the Indian name of the common hemp, from which a strong narcotic is made

BARBADOES WATERS, a cordial flavoured with orange and lemon-peel

BARNWELL, chief character in George Lillo's tragedy, *George Barnwell* (1732)

BAUBLING, contemptible, paltry

BEAR, or BERE, a variety of barley; BEAR-BRAIRD, sprouting bear or barley

BEARDED MAN AT VERSAILLES, Matthieu Jouve Jourdan, who beheaded two of the royal guards in the Marble Court at Versailles, on 6th October 1789

BELL-THE-CAT, beard the lion

BENDS, OR ENDS (of mermaids). *See* the passage in *Antony and Cleopatra*, Act ii. sc. 2

BERN, a bairn, or child

BERSERKAR, Scandinavian warrior, of proved valour and unusual strength, in a martial frenzy

BICKER, a wooden dish, drinking-cup

BIDE, endure, bear; BIDE THE BANG, bear the brunt

BIG, or BIGG, to build; BIGGIN, building, dwelling

BILBOES, an iron bar, with sliding shackles for confining prisoners

BILLIE, a familiar mode of address, brother

BISMAR, a small steelyard

BLACKBEARD, OLD, the buccaneer captain, Edward Teach, or rather Drummond, who terrorised the Spanish Main between 1710 and 1718

BLACK BRUNSWICKERS, a regiment, wearing a black uniform, who fought along with the English in the Peninsular War and at Waterloo

BLACKMORE, SIR RICHARD, a physician and writer of the Restoration and Queen Anne period

BLAND, a drink made from buttermilk

BLATE, modest, shy

BOAST (us with her glamour), threaten

BODLE, or BODDLE, a small Scotch coin $=\frac{1}{6}$ penny

BOLE, a small aperture

BONALLY, or BONAILLIE, a parting drink

BONA-ROBA, a bold wench

BONNIE-WALLIES, good things, gewgaws

BONNY DIE, toy, trinket

BONXIE, the skua-gull

BOROUGH MOOR, stretched between Craigmillar and Merchiston Castles, on the south side of Edinburgh; there criminals were hanged, and usually buried

BOURASQUE, or BOURRASQUE, sudden squall, storm

BOWIE, a wooden dish for milk, pail

BRAID, broad

BRAWS, fine clothes

BREEKLESS, trouserless

BRINNASTIR, presumably Brindister, on the west side of the Mainland

BROSE, oatmeal over which boiling water has been poured

BROWN, TOM, a satirical writer, died in 1704

BUCKIE, the small black whelk

BUFFED, fit for nothing, useless; perhaps from "buff," to puff out, inflate

BULLOCKING, bullying

BULLY-BACK, one bully who backs up another

BUMMING, buzzing, humming, droning

BUMMOCK, ale brewed for a merrymaking

BURRAFORTH, or BURRAFRITH, on the island of Unst, in Shetland

CABALIST, a practiser of magic, spirit-raising, etc.

CACIQUE, a native Indian chief in and around the Caribbean Sea

CAIRN, a mountain; the Grampians, behind which was the country of the predatory Highlanders

CALLANT, lad; CANTY CALLANT, a cheerful, lively lad, a term of affection

CAMACHO'S KETTLE. *See* Sancho

CANNY, propitious, lucky

CANTED, threw with a sudden jerk

CAPA, a Spanish mantle

CAPER, privateer

"CAPTAIN, YOU SHOULD BE," etc. (p. 486), from Otway's *Venice Preserved*, Act v.

CARLE, farm-servant

CARLINE, an old woman, witch

CARSE OF GOWRIE, a very fertile district on the north side of the Firth of Forth, in Perthshire

CART-AVERS, cart-horses

CASTING PEATS, digging turf

CATERAN, a Highland robber

CAUP, or CAP, a wooden bowl for holding food

CECIAL, THOMAS. *See Don Quixote*, Part II. chap. xiv.

CHANGE-HOUSE, inn, country tavern

CHEVAL DE BATAILLE, stock anecdote

CHIELD, a fellow

CHOOSERS OF THE SLAUGHTER, more usually Choosers of the Slain, *i.e.* the Valkyrior, or Maidens of Fate, in Scandinavian mythology

CLACK-GEESE, barnacle geese, probably called clack-geese from the cry they make

CLAGGED, clogged, obstructed, with clay

CLASHES AND CLAVERS, scandal and gossip

CLAUDIO. *See* Shakespeare's *Much Ado about Nothing*, Act iii. sc. 2; but it is Pedro, not Claudio, who gives utterance to the sentiment

CLAVERING, chattering

CLEM, or CLYM, OF THE CLEUGH, a noted outlaw of Englewood Forest, near Carlisle, as famous an archer as Robin Hood. *See* a ballad in Percy's *Reliques*, vol. i.

CLIFFORD, in Shakespeare's *Henry VI.* Part III. Act ii. sc. 6

CLOCHNA-BEN, a hill in Kincardineshire, nearly 2000 feet high

CLOUTING, mending, patching

CLYTUS, a character in Nat. Lee's *Alexander, or Rival Queens*

COAL-HEUGH, coal-pit

COBLE, a small boat

COBS, Spanish dollars or pieces of eight. *See* Portugal pieces

COG, a wooden bowl; COGFU', a wooden bowl full

CO LICENCIO, SEIGNIOR, By your leave, sir

COLLIER AND THE DEVIL, in the old play of *Grim, the Collier of Croydon*

COLUMELLA, a Roman writer on agriculture, of the 1st century A.D.

CONSTER, or CONSTRUE, to interpret, make out

COUP, to exchange, barter

COUPING OF COBLES, overturning of boats

CRACK ABOUT, talk, boast about

CRAIG, neck

CREEL, TO BE IN A, to be temporarily confused, distracted

CROFT LAND, the best quality of land, always in cultivation

CROWDIE, a thick pottage made of oatmeal stirred in water

CROWNE, JOHN, a dramatist of Charles II.'s time

CUMFREY, or COMFREY, a water-plant, used as a "cooler of the blood"

CUMMERS, gossips, old women

CURCH, a woman's kerchief for covering the head

CURTIUS, according to ancient Roman legend, sacrificed himself for his country's good by leaping into a chasm that opened in the city

CUSSER, a stallion

CUT A FEATHER, to move swiftly through the water, so that the ripples stream off from the ship's bow on both sides

CUTTY-AXE, a short axe

DAFFED, put aside

DAFFING, larking, merriment

DAFT, crazy

DAIKERING, sauntering

DANSKE, Danish

DARRAIGN BATTAILE, justify himself by combat

D'AVENANT, WILL, or SIR WILLIAM D'AVENANT, poet and dramatist of the 17th century

DEAD-THRAW, death-throes

DEAF NUT, a nut that has no kernel

DEBES, LUCAS JACOBSON, dean of Thorshaven, in the Faeroe Islands, in the 17th century, wrote in Danish a description of those islands and their inhabitants

DECEPTIO VISUS, an ocular deception

DENMARK, OUR PARENT COUNTRY. Norway, which was the real parent country of Orkney and Shetland, was subject to Denmark from 1397 to 1814. Orkney and Shetland were given up to Scotland in 1468

DENNIS, JOHN, as associate of the coffee-house wits, afterwards a literary critic, died in 1734

DIE, a toy ornament

DII MANES, protecting deities

DING, knock

DIVOT, thin turf used for roofing cottages

DOITED, stupid

DON SEBASTIAN, a tragedy by Dryden (1690)

DOOR-CHEEKS, door-posts

DOUBLOON, a Spanish gold coin equal to the double pistole, and worth about 30s.

DOUCE, respectable

DOUR, stubborn, sullen, hard

DOUSE THE GLIM, put out the light

DOWIE, dark, melancholy

DOWLAS, a strong, coarse, linen cloth, supposed to derive its name from Doullens, in dept. Somme, France

DOWNA, cannot, will not

DRAMMOCK, raw meal and water

DREE'D, endured

DROW. *See* Trow

DRUNK AS DAVY'S SOW. A Welshman, David Lloyd, had a sow with six legs. A visitor whom he brought to see the curiosity found David's wife lying dead drunk beside the animal, and exclaimed, " It's the drunkenest sow I ever saw "

DUDS, clothes

DULSE, a species of sea-weed

DUNG OWER, beaten, mastered

DUNKIRKERS, pirates

DUNT, to knock, bang

EDDERACHYLLIS, or EDDRACHILLIS, GLEN OF, in the west of Sutherlandshire

EEN, eyes

EINTRACHT, means " c o n c o r d," " unity."

ELD, antiquity, old men of olden time

EMATHIAN FIELDS, a part of ancient Thessaly, practically identical with the district of Pharsalia

EMPEROR OF ETHIOPIA, Seged, in Dr. Johnson's *Rambler*, Nos. 204, 205

ERLAND, not Earl Erland, the son of Harold the Fair-spoken, but a minor Orcadian chief called Erland the Younger, who carried off Margaret, mother of Earl Harold and wife of Maddadh, a Scottish chief

ETHEREGE, SIR GEORGE, a witty dramatist of Charles II.'s reign

ETTRICK FOREST, a former royal hunting-ground in Selkirkshire

EVITING, avoiding, escaping from

FAIR TRADERS, smugglers

FARCIE ON HIS FACE, a malediction

FASH, FASHERY, trouble

FEATHER, CUT A. *See* Cut a feather

FECK, MAIST, the greatest part

FERLIES MAKE FOOLS FAIN, wonders astonish fools; FERLY, wonderfully

FEY, fated, or predestined to speedy death

FIFISH, crazy, eccentric

FINNER, a small whale

FIR-CLOG, a log of fir-wood

FLICHTER, to flutter or tremble

FLINCH, or FLENSE, A WHALE, slice the blubber from the bones

FLIP, ale or cider, sweetened, spiced, and made hot, generally by plunging the red-hot poker into the liquid

FORBYE, besides

FORPIT, the fourth part of a peck

FOUR QUARTERS, hands and feet, applied to help

FOWD, or FOGD, district judge or magistrate

FREIT, charm, superstition

FROGS, fastenings for a coat, consisting of ornamental buttons and loops

FUNKING, kicking up the heels

FUR, a furrow

GABERLUNZIE, a beggar or tinker

GALDRAGON, corrupted from the Norse *galdra*, to bewitch, and *kvinde*, or *kvinna*, a woman: a witch, sorceress

GANE, gone; GANGING, going

GANGREL, wandering vagrant

GAR, to oblige, force, make

GASCROMH, an i n s t r u m e n t for trenching ground, shaped like a currier's knife, with a crooked handle

GATE, way, road, manner

GATHERING-PEAT, the piece left to keep the fire alight

GAUDS, flimsy ornaments, gimcracks

GAY MONY, good many

GEAR, property

GENERANDI GLORIA MELLIS, the glory of producing honey

GENEVA, gin

GIERVADA, more correctly GIERRIDA, a sorceress mentioned in the *Eyrbyggja Saga*

GIO, a deep ravine which admits the sea

GIRDLE, an iron frame for cooking cakes on

GLEBE, land belonging to the parish minister in right of his office

GLIM, DOUSE THE. *See* Douse the glim

GLOWER, to gaze fixedly

GOBBET, lump, fragment

GOB-BOX, mouth

GOLDEN-EYE, a species of wild duck

GOLDEN WASSER, or GOLD-WASSER, a liqueur mixed and coloured with gold-leaf ground down fine

GOOSE, a tailor's smoothing-iron

GOVERNANTE, housekeeper

GOWK, fool

GOWRIE, CARSE OF. *See* Carse of Gowrie

GRÆCUM EST, it is Greek

GRAIP, a three-pronged stable-fork

GRAITH, gears, fitting

GRAND CAIMAINS, or CAYMANS, three coral islands in the Caribbean Sea

GREW, or GRUE, to shiver, creep (of the flesh)

GREY FISH, fry of coal-fish, sillocks

GUARDA-COSTA, coastguard vessel, Spanish war-vessel

GUDEMAN AND GUDEWIFE, the heads of the house

GUE, a two-stringed (of horsehair) violin

GUIDE, make (good) use of, treat, behave to

GUIZARDS, or GUISARDS, New Year's maskers or mummers

GYRE-CARLINE, witch, hobgoblin

HAAF, or HAF, the deep sea

HAFT, to fix or settle

HAGALEF, or HOGALIF, payment for liberty to cut peat

HAILL, whole, entire

HAIM, or HEIM, in all probability the giant Hymir, who in the *Hymiskvida* of the *Elder Edda* is called " Huge-wise," or exceedingly wise

HALIER, or HELYER, a cavern into which the tide flows

HALLANSHAKER, a vagabond, sturdy ragamuffin

HALSE, the throat

HANK ON, stick fast on

HAROLD HARFAGER, first king of *all* Norway, conquered the Shetland Islands in 875

HAR'ST, harvest

HARTLIB, SAMUEL, a friend of Milton, and author of numerous pamphlets on husbandry

HAVINGS, behaviour, manners

HAWKHEN, or HALKHEN, hawks exacted by the royal falconer on his visits to the islands, in force till 1839

HAXA, or HEXE, a generic name for a witch or sorceress

HELLICAT, wild, giddy

HELYER. *See* Halier

HERTHA, MOTHER, or NERTHUS, the earth-goddess of the ancient German races

" HE SPEAKS THE KINDEST WORDS," etc. (p. 440), from Lee's *Rival Queens*, Act i.

HEUS TIBI, DAVE! Hallo there, Davus! Davus was a common name for a slave in Rome

HEUS TU, INEPTE! Hallo there, you fool!

HIALTLAND, or HJALTLAND, the old Norse name for Shetland

HIGH-DUTCH, German

HINNY, honey, a term of endearment

HIRPLE, hobble

HIRSEL, to move or slide down

HISPANIOLA, the island of Hayti, in the West Indies

HOUSEWIFESKEP, housewifery

HOWF, a haunt, haven

HURLY-HOUSE, a large house in a bad state of disrepair

ILKA, each

IMBER-GOOSE, or EMBER-GOOSE, a variety of northern diver or loon

IMOINDA, the heroine of Mrs. Aphra Behn's novel, *The History of Oroonoko or the Royal Slave* (1698)

IN APICIBUS JURIS, amongst the knotty points of law

INCH-MIRRAN, or INCH-MURRIN, an island near the south end of Loch Lomond, kept as a deer park by the Duke of Montrose

INFANG AND OUTFANG, the right of trying thieves, whether taken within or outside of the feudal domain

INFIELD, land periodically manured and in regular cultivation

" IN THE FIRST RANK OF THESE DID ZIMRI STAND." *See Absalom and Achitophel*, Part I.

IOUL, JOL, or JUL, Yuletide, Christmas

ISLE OF PROVIDENCE, one of the Bahamas, and a notorious rendezvous for buccaneers

JACK-A-LENT, a puppet at which boys threw sticks in Lent, a blockhead

JACOBUS, TWENTY-SHILLING, gold coin issued by James I. of England

JACTA EST ALEA, the die is cast, the decision is taken

JAFFEIR, one of the conspirators in Otway's *Venice Preserved*

JAGGER, pedlar

JAM NEMINEM ANTEPONES CATONI, no one is to be preferred to Cato

JARL, earl

JARLSHOF, means "the earl's mansion or house"

JARTO, or HJARTE, (my) heart, sweetheart

JAUD, jade

JOKUL, yes, sir

JOSEPH, an old-fashioned riding-coat

JOUGS, pillory

KAIL-YARD, cabbage-garden; KAIL-POT, large pot for boiling broth

KAIN, contribution in kind, as poultry, eggs, etc., paid by the tenant to the landlord

KEMPIONS, champions, warriors

KENN'D FOLKS, well-known, respectable people

KEY, or QUAY, a wharf, landing-stage

KIEMPE, KEMPIE, a Norse champion, warrior

KISS THE GUNNER'S DAUGHTER, be flogged on shipboard, whilst laid along the breech of a gun

KIST, a chest

KIT-CAT CLUB, a literary society of Hanoverian politics, that existed in London between 1700 and 1720

KITCHEN (to), a relish to dry bread, as cheese, dried fish, or the like

KITTLE, difficult, ticklish

KNAPPED LATIN, spoke Latin

KRAKEN, a fabulous sea-monster

KREITZ-DOLLAR, or KREUZ-THALER, the "cross" dollar, called also the "crown" dollar, coined by Austria for her Netherlands possessions

KYLOES, small black Highland cattle

LAIR, learning

LANDLOUPER, adventurer

LANGSPIEL, a kind of harp, formerly in use in the Shetlands

LAPELLE, WHITE, alluding to the white turned-up lappets worn by officers of the Royal Navy

LAVE, rest, residue

LAWRIGHT-MAN, an officer whose chief duty was the regulation of weights and measures

LAW-TING, the supreme court in ancient Shetland and Orkney

LEAGUER-LASS, female camp-follower

LENNOX, a former county of Scotland, embracing Dunbarton and parts of Stirling, Perth, and Lanark

LIMMER, idle hussy

LINDAMIRA, the only lady who, according to Steele in *Spectator*, No. 41, might justifiably paint her face

LISPUND, a weight, in Scandinavian countries = 17.6 lbs. avoirdupois, varied in Shetland from 12 to 36 lbs. avoir., and was divided into 24 merks

LOAN, a lane between stone walls

LOBLOLLY-BOY, a ship-surgeon's boy or attendant

LOCHLIN, RACE OF. The Norsemen are so called in *Ossian*

LOOM, any kind of tub or similar vessel

LOON, lad, fellow

LOUT, to bend or bow down

LOWE, flame

LUM, chimney

LYSIMACHUS, a character in Nat. Lee's *Alexander, or Rival Queens*

MAIN, to moan

MAIR, more; MAIR BY TOKEN, particularly

MAIST FECK. *See* Feck, maist

MALLARD, the male of the common wild duck

MANSE, parsonage

MANTUAN, Virgil, who was born at Mantua in North Italy

MARKAL, or MERCAL, a rude wooden plough-share

MAROONED, abandoned on a desert island

MASKING-FAT, a mashing vat or tub

MAUN, must

MEARNS, old name for Kincardineshire

MEAT-MISTRESSES. In Norway the mistress of the house is now sometimes called in familiar language the meat-mother (*matmor*)

MELLAY, struggle, contest

MELTITH, food; a meal

MENSE AND SENSE, honour, gratitude

MERK, a Scotch coin = 1s. 1½d.; the twenty-fourth part of a lispund (*q.v.*); MERK OF LAND, a measure varying from one to three acres

"METHINKS I SEE THE NEW ARION," etc. (p. 159), from *MacFlecknoe*, Dryden's satire on Shadwell

MICHING MALICHO, skulking villainy

MILE, SCOTS = 9 furlongs

MISCA', abuse

MISERIS SUCCURRERE DISCO, I learn to succour those in distress

MISSED STAYS, failed to go about from one tack to another, lost the opportunity

MOIDORE, a gold coin of Portugal = 27s.

MOLD, MAN OF, a man of character

MOLENDINARY, relating to a mill

MOSSES AND WATERS, boggy places and water-courses

MOULD BOARD, that part of the plough which turns over the ground, the plough-breast

MUCKLE, much

MULTURES, dues paid for grinding grain; IN-TOWN MULTURES, referring to corn grown on cultivated land near the homestead; OUT-TOWN MULTURES, to corn grown on land occasionally cultivated

MUM, strong ale brewed from wheat and bitter herbs

NACKET, a portable luncheon

NANCIES OF THE HILLS OR DALES, an allusion to Shenstone's poem, *Nancy of the Vale*

NANTZ, or NANTES, brandy

NATHELESS, nevertheless

NEIST, next

NEMORUM MURMUR, the murmur of the groves

νεφεληγερέτα Ζεύς, Zeus the cloud-gatherer

NIEVEFU', a handful

NORVAL, a peasant's son in Home's tragedy, *Douglas*

NORWOOD PROPHETESS, Margaret Finch, a gipsy, who told fortunes at Norwood, near London, for ten years before her death in 1740, aged 108

NOUP, a headland, precipitous to the sea and sloping inland

NOWT, black cattle

NUT, DEAF. *See* Deaf nut.

O FORTUNATI NIMIUM, O *too* fortunate !

OLAF TRYGUARSON, or OLAF TRYGG-VESON, old Norse king and hero, threw himself into the waves during a sea-fight in the year 1000

OLAUS MAGNUS, was appointed archbishop of Upsala in the 16th century

OLAVE PLANTED THE CROSS. The Orkney Islands were conquered by Harold Fair-hair in heathen times (875). The Norsemen were christianised by St. Olaf, their king, a century and a half later

OPERAM ET OLEUM PERDIDI, I have lost my labour and my oil

OPHIR. A part of the Mainland (Pomona) of Orkney is called Orphir

ORAAMUS, or ORAMUS, a vow, prayer, and offering. *See* Note 13, p. 506

ORRA TIME, occasionally, every now and then

OUTIS IN THE CAVE OF POLYPHEMUS, *i.e.* Ulysses, when captured by the monster Polyphemus (*Odyss.*, Bk. ix.)

OUT-TAKEN, except

OWERLAY, a neck-cloth

OWSEN, oxen

PALLADIUS, a Roman writer on agriculture, of the 4th century A.D.

PARCEL-MUSICIAN, an indifferent musician

PARRITCH, porridge

PARTAN, a crab

PEERY, inquisitive, prying

PEGHTS, Picts, the ancient inhabitants of Scotland, looked upon by the vulgar as supernatural beings

PELTRIE, or PELTRY, furs

PENNY SCOTS = 1⁄12d. English

PETIT MAÎTRE, dandy

PETITS GUAVES, or PETIT GOAVE, a small harbour on the West Indian island of Hayti

PHARSALIA, in Thessaly, where in 48 B.C. Cæsar gained his great victory over his rival Pompey

PHILOMATH, a lover of learning, almanac-maker

PIAFFED, stepped with a high, slow, showy action—said of a horse

PIERRE, one of the conspirators in Otway's *Venice Preserved*

PISTOLE, a gold coin of Spain, worth about 15s.

PIXIE, a fairy

PLANTIE CRUIVE, a kail-yard

PLAY CASSIO, to get drunk and be made a catspaw of

POMONA, the Mainland, or principal island of Orkney

PONTOPPIDAN, ERIC, the Younger, whose *Forsög til Norges Naturlige Historie* (Eng. trans. 1755) is referred to (p. 505), was bishop of Bergen, not archbishop of Upsala. *See* Olaus Magnus

POPS, pistols

PORTO BELLO, a town on the north side of the Isthmus of Panama

PORTUGAL PIECES, PORTAGUES, pieces of eight (reals) = 4s., silver coins struck in Portugal

PRIMATE (p. 509), Olaus Magnus. *See* Pontoppidan

PRINCE PRETTYMAN, a character, sometimes a fisherman's son, sometimes a prince, in the Duke of Buckingham's farce, *The Rehearsal* (1672)

PRINCE VOLSCIUS, a character in Buckingham's *The Rehearsal*

PRIOR, MATTHEW, poet, died in 1721

PRO BONO PUBLICO, for the public good

PROVIDENCE ISLAND. *See* Isle of Providence

PUND SCOTS, 1s. 8d. sterling

QUADRUPEDUMQUE PUTREM SONITU QUATIT UNGULA CAMPUM, the hoofs of the horses shake the crumbling field

QUAIGH, a small wooden cup or drinking-bowl

QUEAN, a woman, wench; RANDY QUEAN, disorderly, vagrant woman

QUEEN IN THE OLD PLAY. *See Macbeth*, Act v. sc. 1. Shakespeare's play was altered and put on the stage by Sir William D'Avenant in 1674

QUERN, hand-mill

QUID FACIUNT LAETAS SEGETES, how the crops are getting on

RACE OF PORTLAND, a dangerous current south of Portland Bill in Dorset

RADDMAN, or RAADMAN, a councillor

RANZELMAN, or RANCELLOR, a kind of parish constable, one of his chief duties being to "rancel" or search for stolen goods

RAVEN FLAG (of vikings), the raven was sacred to Odin or Woden

REDDING-KAIM, a wide-toothed comb for the hair

REIM-KENNAR, one who knows mystic rhyme

RESET, PLACE OF, resort of beggars and loose characters

RESTIFF, or RESTIVE, stubborn, obstinate

RIDES RUSTY, or TURNS RUSTY, sets at defiance, behaves obstinately

RITT, a scratch or incision

RIVA, a cleft in a rock

ROCHESTER, EARL OF, the witty but dissolute favourite of Charles II.

ROCK, a distaff

ROKELAY, a short cloak

ROLLO THE WALKER, or HROLF THE GANGER, according to traditional history, the ancestor of the Dukes of Normandy and Norman kings of England

RONA'S CREST, the highest hill (1500 ft.) in Shetland, in the north of the Mainland

ROOSE, to praise, commend

ROOST, a strong and boisterous current

RORY MOHR OF DUNVEGAN. *See* Boswell's *Tour to the Hebrides*, under date Sept. 15, and Scott's *Lord of the Isles*, Appendix, Note M

ROSCIUS, a celebrated actor of ancient Rome

ROSEBERRY TOPPING, a conspicuous hill in Cleveland, North Riding of Yorkshire

ROSE TAVERN, in Russell Street, Covent Garden, a celebrated resort of wits and men of fashion

ROXALANA, or ROXANA, a character in Nathaniel Lee's *Rival Queens, or Alexander the Great* (1677)

RUMBO, rum

RUNES, letters of the ancient Norse alphabet; a mystic saying or verse of poetry

SACKLESS, innocent

SAIN, bless

ST. JOHN, FESTIVAL OF, one of the principal festivals of the year in all Scandinavian countries

St. Leonard's, one of the colleges of the University of St. Andrews

St. Magnus, an earl of Orkney, assassinated by his cousin Haco in the island of Egilshay on 16th April 1115

St. Olave, or Olaf, king of Norway, most zealous for the introduction of Christianity into that country in the 11th century

St. Ronald, or Rognvald, a famous jarl or earl of Orkney of the 12th century, built the cathedral of St. Magnus at Kirkwall

Sair, sore, sorry ; sairer, greatly

Samphire, a succulent plant growing amongst rocks and on salt marches near the sea, used for making pickles. *See King Lear*, Act iv. sc. 6

Sancho (on the scum of Camacho's kettle). *See Don Quixote*, Pt. II. chap. xx. The "scum" consisted of "three pullets and a couple of geese"

Sandie-laverock, a lark

Saunt, saint

Saut, salt

Scald, an ancient Scandinavian bard or poet

Scart, a cormorant ; to scratch

Scat, a land-tax paid to the crown ; scathold, a common. On p. 156 we should probably read "scatland," land paying *skat* or tribute, instead of "scathold"

Scaur, a precipitous bank, rock

Schwartz beer, black beer

Scipio at Numantia. Scipio Africanus Minor found amongst the Spanish (Celtiberian) captives, after the surrender of Numantia (134 b.c.), a beautiful maiden, whom he generously restored to her betrothed

Sclate stane, piece of rough slate

Scouries, or scauries, young sea-gulls

Sealgh, sealchie, a seal

Sea-ware, seaweed

Sebastian and Dorax, in Dryden's tragedy *Don Sebastian* (1689), dispute and become reconciled

Sedley, Sir Charles, a wit and poet of Charles II.'s reign

Sell of her, herself

Set him up, forsooth, a term expressive of contempt for an assuming person

Setting, becoming, befitting

Several, an inclosed field as opposed to an open common

Shadwell, a dramatist satirised by Dryden under the name of Og in *Absalom and Achitophel*, and as MacFlecknoe in the poem so called

Sharney peat, fuel made of dried cow's dung

Sharpe, Old, the buccaneer captain, Bartholomew Sharpe, who was active on the Spanish Main about 1680

Sheerwater, or shearwater, a sea-bird of the petrel family, so called from its low flight, skimming close to the water

Sheltie, a Shetland pony

Shepherd of Salisbury Plain, by Hannah More, setting forth the homely wisdom and piety of one David Saunders

Shogh (Gaelic), there

Shot, a field, plot of land

Shot-window, a small projecting window

Shoupeltin, a triton

Sic, such

Siccar, sure, safe

Sillocks, or saithe, the fry of the coal-fish

Sinclair (Malcolm) of Quendale, when asked by the shipwrecked Duke of Medina Sidonia, or rather by his brother, whether he had ever seen such a great man as stood before him, made the reply in the text. *See* Hibbert's *Description of the Zetland Islands*, pp. 92, etc.

Singles, talons of a hawk

Sir Arthegal, the impersonation of Justice in Spenser's *Faërie Queene*, from the fifth book (Canto iv.) of which the passage on p. 112 is taken

Sir Lucius O'Trigger, in Sheridan's *Rivals*

Skelping, nimble-footed

Skeo, a hut for drying fish

Skerry, a bare, rocky islet

Skilling, Danish = one farthing

Skirl, scream

Skudler, the leader of a band of maskers, dancers, etc.

Slap, a gap, breach

Slocken, to cool, drench

Smeaked, killed by smoke

SNACK, a hasty meal

SNECK, the latch of the door

SNIGGLED, caught by dropping bait into the (eel's) lurking-place

SOCK, ploughshare

SOLE-CLOUT, the lowest part of a plough, which runs along the bottom of the furrow

SONSY, stout and handsome, bonny

SORNER, a beggar or vagabond, who extorts money or victuals through intimidation

SOUGH, a sigh; to con over, hum a tune

SPAED, foretold; SPAE-WOMEN, sorceresses, fortune-tellers

SPARGE NUCES, PUERI, scatter the nuts, boys

SPEERINGS, inquiries

SPREACHERIE, or SPRECHERY, insignificant moveables, especially such as have been purloined or gathered in a raid

SPRUCE-BEER, beer made from the young leaves of the spruce-fir

SPUNK, match, torch

STACK, an insulated, precipitous rock

STAIG, a young, unbroken horse

STATIRA, a character in Nathaniel Lee's tragedy, *Rival Queens*

STILTS (of plough), handles

STOCK-FISH, dried cod-fish and ling

STOT, a steer, young bullock

STOUR, stalwart, stout and strong

STOURBURGH may be interpreted "great fort"

STRAIK, strike, a measure of capacity, about two bushels

STRATHNAVERN, a valley leading southwards from the coast of Sutherlandshire. Montrose's last fight took place at Invercarron, on the borders of Ross-shire

STREEK, stretch, measure oneself with

STRIDDLE, straddle

STROMA, an island in the Pentland Firth, north of Scotland

SUCKEN, the jurisdiction attaching to a mill under feudal tenure

SUCK THE MONKEY, to drink rum or other liquor

SUI JURIS, in possession of full legal rights

SUMPH, a lubberly fellow, blockhead

SUNE OR SYNE, sooner or later

SUUM CUIQUE TRIBUITO, give every one his due

SWABIE, SWARTBACK, the great black-backed gull

SWATTER, to swim quickly and awkwardly

SWELCHIE, whirlpool

SWONA, one of the Orkney islands in the Pentland Firth

SYNE, since

SYVER, a sewer, covered drain

TACKSMAN, an intermediate tenant

TA'EN, taken

TAIT OF WOO', a tuft or small piece of wool

TATE, NAHUM, poet - laureate and dramatist, died in 1715

TEMPLARS, law-students of the Temple

TERENTIUS VARRO, Roman writer on agriculture, of the 1st century B.C.

THAIRM, catgut

THEFT-BOOT, hush-money, receiving stolen goods from a thief against pecuniary consideration

"THEN, BY THE HELL I MERIT," etc. (p. 483) from Otway's *Venice Preserved*, Act. iv. sc. 2.

THIGGER, a common beggar

THIRL, the obligation on a tenant to have his flour ground at a certain mill and to pay dues for its maintenance

THOLE, endure, stand

THRAWART, perverse

"THUS FROM THE GRAVE," etc. (p. 437), from Lee's *Rival Queens*, Act iv.

TILL, a stiff cold clay

TIMOTHEUS, an ancient Greek musician, celebrated from the innovations he made in the art he practised. *See also* Pope's *Essay on Criticism*

TINT, lost; TINTE, loss

TIRRACKE, OTTARROCK, the kittiwake gull, a guillemot

TITTIE, little sister

TOCHER-GOOD, dowry, portion

TOLLSELL, or TOLLSEY, the place where merchants usually assemble, exchange

TOOM, empty

TORSK, dried cod-fish

TORTUGA, an island in the West Indies, off the Venezuelan coast

TOW, rope

TOWN, the homestead, farm-house and its buildings

TOY, a woman's linen or woollen head-dress hanging down over the shoulders

TRAP, TO UNDERSTAND, to be knowing, wide-awake

TRINCULO'S BOTTLE. See *Tempest*, Act iv. sc. 1

TRINIDADO, Trinidad tobacco

TRIPTOLEMUS, in ancient Greek mythology, the inventor of the plough and of agriculture

TROCK, or TRUCK, to barter, bargain

TROW, or TROLD, a monster, demon of the mountains and of the sea; in this romance, a fairy

TURF-EINAR, or TORV-EINAR, an illegitimate son of Earl Rognvald of Norway, and the founder of the dynasty of the Earls of Orkney

TUSSER, THOMAS, a famous 16th century writer on husbandry

TWISCAR, TUSHKAR, or TORVSKAR, a spade for cutting peats

UDALLER, or ODALLER, a freehold proprietor

UGSOME, frightful, horrible

ULZIE, oil

UMQUHILE, the late, deceased

UNCANNY, dangerous, not quite sane

UNCO, strange, particularly

UNDERSTAND TRAP. *See* Trap, understand

UNHALSED, unhailed or unsaluted

UNICO CONTEXTU, all of a piece

URE, the eighth part of a merk of land (*q.v.*)

USQUEBAUGH, whisky

VELEDA, a prophetess of the ancient Germans, mentioned in Tacitus, *Germ.*, ch. viii.

VELVET, PROPHESIES UPON, foretells what she certainly knows. Compare the racing phrase "to stand on velvet," to bet in such a way as to win with certainty

VENTIS SURGENTIBUS, with rising winds

VIFDA, or VIVDA, beef dried without salt

VISION OF MIRZA, by Addison, in No. 159 of *Spectator*

VIVERS, victuals

VOE, an inlet of the sea, creek

VOLUSPA, VOLUSPÆ, strictly a part of the *Poetic Edda*; in this romance incorrectly used for prophetess, sybil

WADMAAL, or VADMEL, homespun woollen cloth. The Norwegian peasantry still make their clothes of it at the present day

VAFT, or WEFT, the cross thread or woof of a web

WAKERIFE, wakeful, watchful

WAN (water), filthy, dark-coloured

WARLOCK, wizard

WA'S, walls

WATER-DRAGONS. The ancient Norsemen loved to call their vessels "The Dragon," "Serpent," etc. King Olaf Tryggveson's ship, one of the wonders of the North in ship-building, was called "The Long Serpent"

WATTLE, an assessment for the salary of the fowd (magistrate)

WAUR, worse

WAW, wave. See Note 45, p. 519

WAWLS, looks wildly, rolls (his) eyes

WEATHER-GAWS, the secondary or reflected rainbow

WEIRD, destiny, fate

WELKING, fading, disappearing

WELL, a whirlpool, eddy. *See* Note 45, p. 519

WENT UPON THE ACCOUNT. *See* Account, went upon the

WHEEN, few

WHIGAMORE, Covenanting

WHILES, AT, sometimes, at times

WHINGER, large knife, dirk

WHITTIE-WHATTIEING, muttering, talking frivolously

WHITTLE, a large knife, usually worn at the belt

WHOMLED, turned over

WICK, an open bay

WINDLESTRAW, bent grass

"WITH ROOMY DECK," etc. (p. 426), from Dryden's *Annus Mirabilis*

WITS' COFFEE-HOUSE, in St. James's Street, the resort of the bluest old Tories in Queen Anne's reign. *See also* Rose Tavern

WOO', wool

WOWF, crazy

XEBECK, a small, three-masted vessel, used in the Mediterranean

YARN WINDLE, a yarn-winder

YELLOCHED, yelled, shrieked

YETT, a gate

INDEX.

END OF THE PIRATE.